Dramatis personae

in the year 1459, as this book opens, the main characters stood in relation to each other as the table below shows:

HOUSE OF YORK

Richard Plantagenet, Duke of York
Cecily Neville, Duchess of York, his wife
Edward, Earl of March, their eldest son
Edmund, Earl of Rutland, their second son
George, their third son
Richard, their last-born
Anne, Duchess of Exeter, their eldest daughter
Eliza, Duchess of Suffolk, their second daughter
Margaret, their youngest daughter

HOUSE OF LANCASTER

Henry VI, King of England
Marguerite d'Anjou, his French-born Queen
Edouard, Prince of Wales, their son and heir

HOUSE OF NEVILLE

Richard Neville, Earl of Salisbury, brother to Cecily Neville
Richard Neville, Earl of Warwick, his eldest son
Anne Beauchamp, Countess of Warwick, his wife
Isabel Neville, Warwick's elder daughter
Anne Neville, Warwick's younger daughter
John Neville, Warwick's brother

Isabella Inglethorpe, his wife
George Neville, Bishop of Exeter, Warwick's brother
Thomas Neville, Warwick's brother

HOUSE OF TUDOR

Jasper Tudor, half-brother to Henry VI
Margaret Beaufort, wife to Henry VI's half-brother Edmund Tudor,
  mother of Henry Tudor
Henry Tudor, son of Margaret Beaufort and Edmund Tudor
Harry Stafford, Duke of Buckingham, cousin to Edward and Richard
Plantagenet
Harry Beaufort, Duke of Somerset, cousin to Henry VI
Edmund Beaufort, his younger brother

HOUSE OF WOODVILLE

Richard Woodville
Jacquetta Woodville, his wife
Elizabeth Woodville Grey, their eldest daughter
Anthony Woodville, Elizabeth's favourite brother
Katherine Woodville, Elizabeth's younger sister
Lionel and Edward and Richard and John, Elizabeth's younger brothers
Thomas Grey, Elizabeth's eldest son by Sir John Grey
Dick Grey, her second son by Sir John Grey

The Sunne
in Splendour

Also by Sharon Penman

The Historical Novels

Here Be Dragons
Falls the Shadow
The Reckoning
When Christ and His Saints Slept
Time and Chance
Devil's Brood
Lionheart

The Medieval Mysteries

The Queen's Man
Cruel as the Grave
Dragon's Lair
Prince of Darkness

The Sunne in Splendour

Sharon Penman

Including a new Author's Note

MACMILLAN

First published in the USA 1982 by Holt, Rinehart and Winston, New York
First published in Great Britain 1983 by Macmillan

This edition published in Great Britain 2013 by Macmillan
an imprint of Pan Macmillan, a division of Macmillan Publishers Limited
Pan Macmillan, 20 New Wharf Road, London N1 9RR
Basingstoke and Oxford
Associated companies throughout the world
www.panmacmillan.com

ISBN 978-0-230-76869-7 HB
ISBN 978-1-4472-4783-8 TPB

A CIP catalogue record for this book is available from
the British Library.

Typeset by Ellipsis Digital Limited, Glasgow
Printed and bound by CPI Group (UK) Ltd, Croydon, CR0 4YY

Visit www.panmacmillan.com to read more about all our books
and to buy them. You will also find features, author interviews and
news of any author events, and you can sign up for e-newsletters
so that you're always first to hear about our new releases.

To Julie McCaskey Wolff

Acknowledgments

I owe a debt of gratitude to so many. First and foremost, to my parents, for their support, their faith and their patience. To Julie McCaskey Wolff, for her encouragement, her enthusiasm and her belief in the book. Don McKinney for opening the door and to Carolyn Hammond and Julie Lord for taking so much of the pain out of my research. To two friends who brought medieval York to life before my eyes, Dorothy Mitchell and Chris Arnott. To the Richard III Societies in the United States and England for making their libraries available to me. To the libraries of the University of Pennsylvania, University of Texas, Los Angeles, New York City, York, England, Salisbury, Nottingham, Ludlow, Oxford and London. To my American agent, Molly Friedrich, who was willing to accept an unknown author's twelve-hundred page manuscript, and able to pilot it into a safe harbour; and to my British agent, Mic Cheetham, who was so skilful in navigating the British publishing seas on my behalf. To my editor at Macmillan London, James Hale, whose kindnesses have been too numerous to count. Last, but definitely not least, to my editor at Holt, Rinehart and Winston, Marian Wood, who shapes and polishes words and ideas with the precision and skill of a master diamond-cutter.

BOOK ONE

Edward

I

Ludlow

September 1459

Richard did not become frightened until darkness began to settle over the woods. In the fading light, the trees began to take on unfamiliar and menacing shapes. There was movement in the shadows. Low-hanging branches barred his path; rain-sodden leaves trailed wetly across his cheek. He could hear sounds behind him and kept quickening his pace, until he tripped over the exposed roots of a massive oak and sprawled headlong into the dark. Unknown horrors reached for him, pinning him to the ground. He felt something burn across his neck; his face was pressed into the dampness of the earth. He lay very still but he heard only the unsteady echoes of his own breathing. Opening his eyes, he saw that he had fallen into a thicket, was held captive by nothing more sinister than brambles and branches broken off by the weight of his body.

He was no longer drowning in fear; the wave was receding. In its wake, he felt shame burn his face and was grateful that none had been there to witness his flight. He thought himself to be too old to yield so easily to panic for, in just eight days' time, he would be seven years old. He rolled clear of the bushes and sat up. After a moment's deliberation, he retreated to the shelter of a lightning-scarred beech. Bracing himself against the trunk, he settled down to wait for Ned to find him.

That Ned would come, he did not doubt. He only hoped that Ned would come soon and, while he waited, he tried to keep his mind on daylight thoughts, tried not to think at all about what might be lurking in the dark beyond the beech tree.

He found it hard to understand how so perfect a day would so suddenly sour. The morning had dawned with infinite promise and, when Joan yielded to his coaxing and agreed to take him riding along the wooded trails around Whitcliffe, his spirits had soared skyward. His excitement proved contagious and his pony had responded with unaccustomed élan to his urgings, breaking into a gallop even before they'd passed through the gateway that led from the outer castle bailey.

With Joan trailing him like an indulgent, sedate shadow, he raced the little animal through the village at an exhilarating pace. Circling the market cross twice, he jumped the pony neatly over the ancient dog dozing in the street by Broad Gate and then drew rein just before the small chapel of St Catherine, which stood on Ludford Bridge. As Joan was not yet in sight, he leaned recklessly over the stone arch and tossed a groat down into the currents swirling below. One of the village youths had once assured him that he would gain great good fortune by so doing, and the superstition now became engraved in Richard's faith as Scripture even before the coin sank from sight.

Riders were coming up the road that led south toward Leominster. The leading stallion was white, marked with a queer dark star; the favourite mount of Richard's favourite brother. Richard sent his pony towards them at a breakneck run.

Ned wore no armour and the wind was whipping his sun-streaked tawny hair about like straw. He towered above his companions, as always; Richard had seen few men as tall as Ned, who stood three full fingers above six feet. He was Earl of March, Lord of Wigmore and Clare, eldest of the four sons of the Duke of York. At seventeen, Ned was, in Richard's eyes, a man grown. On this summerlike September morning there was no one he would rather have encountered. Had Ned permitted it, Richard would happily have trailed after him from dawn till dusk.

Richard thought Joan was pleased to see Ned, too. Her face was suddenly the colour of rose petals and she was looking at Ned sideways, filtering laughter through her lashes in the way Richard had seen other girls do with Ned. Richard was glad; he wanted Joan to like his brother. What Joan thought mattered a great deal to him. The nurses he'd had in the past, before he'd come this spring to live at Ludlow Castle, had not been at all like Joan; they'd been dour, thin-lipped, without laps or humour. Joan smelled of sunflowers and had burnished bright hair, as soft and red as fox fur. She laughed at his riddles and had enthralling tales to tell of unicorns and knights and crusades into the Holy Land.

Seeing now how she was smiling at Ned, Richard felt first a warm contentment and then incredulous delight, unable to believe Ned was truly going to come with them. But Ned was dismissing their escort, waving his own companions on, and with the prospect dawning of an entire day in the company of these two people he loved, Richard wondered why he had never thought to throw a coin over the bridge before.

The day seemed likely to surpass all his expectations. Ned was in high spirits; he laughed a great deal and told Richard stories of his own boyhood at Ludlow with their brother Edmund. He offered to show Richard how he had fished for eels in the swift-running waters of the Teme and he promised to take Richard to the faire to be held in Ludlow just four days hence. He coaxed Joan into putting aside the head-dress that covered her hair and, with nimble fingers, he adroitly loosened the upswept braids that gleamed like red-gold rope.

Richard was caught up in wonder, captivated by this sudden cascade of bright hot colour; he knew, of course, that red hair was said to be unlucky but he found it difficult to understand why. Joan had smiled and borrowed Ned's dagger to cut a lock, wrapping it in her own handkerchief and tucking it inside Richard's tunic. Ned claimed a lock, too, but Joan seemed strangely reluctant to give it to him. Richard rooted about in Joan's basket while Ned and Joan debated his demand, a murmured exchange that soon gave way to whispers and laughter. When he turned back to them, Richard saw that Ned had a lock of her hair and Joan was the colour of rose petals again.

When the sun was directly overhead, they unpacked the food in Joan's basket, using Ned's dagger to slice the manchet loaf and cut thick pieces of cheese. Ned ate most of the food, and then shared an apple with Joan, passing the fruit back and forth between them and trading bites until only the core remained.

After that, they lay on Joan's blanket and searched the grass about them for lucky clovers. Richard won and was awarded the last of the sugared comfits as his prize. The sun was warm, the air fragrant with the last flowering of September. Richard rolled over onto his stomach to escape Ned who was bent upon tickling his nose with a strand of Joan's hair. After a while, he fell asleep. When he awoke, the blanket had been tucked around him and he was alone. Sitting up abruptly, he saw his pony and Joan's mare still hitched across the clearing. Ned's white stallion, however, was gone.

Richard was more hurt than alarmed. He didn't think it was quite fair for them to go off and leave him while he slept, but adults were often less than fair with children and there was little to be done about it. He settled down on the blanket to wait for them to come back for him; it never for a moment occurred to him that they wouldn't. He rummaged in the basket, finished what was left of the manchet bread and, lying on his back, watched clouds forming over his head.

Soon, however, he grew bored and decided it was permissible to explore the clearing while he awaited their return. Much to his delight, he discovered a shallow stream, a narrow ribbon of water that wound its way through the grass and off into the surrounding trees. Lying flat on his stomach by the bank, he thought he could detect silvery shadows darting about in the icy ripples but, try as he might, he was unable to capture even one of the ghostly little fish.

It was as he was lying there that he saw the fox; on the other side of the stream, watching him with unblinking golden eyes, so still it might have been a carven image of a fox rather than one of flesh and blood. Richard froze, too. Less than a fortnight ago, he'd found a young fox cub abandoned in the meadows around the village. For more than a week, he'd tried to gentle the wild creature with limited success and, when he'd carelessly let his mother see the teeth marks in the palm of his hand, she'd given him the choice of freeing it or drowning it. Now he felt a throb of excitement, an absolute certainty that this was his former pet. With infinite care he sat up, searched for stepping-stones to cross the stream. The fox faded back into the woods but without apparent alarm. Encouraged, Richard followed after it.

An hour later, he was forced to concede that he'd lost both fox and his way. He'd wandered far from the clearing where the horses were hitched. When he shouted for Ned, he heard only the startled rustling of woodland creatures responding to a human voice. As the afternoon ebbed away, the clouds continued to gather; at last all blue was smothered in grey and, soon after, a light warming rain began to fall. Richard had been attempting to chart his path by the sun, knowing that Ludlow lay to the east. Now he was completely at a loss and felt the first stirrings of fear, until, with the coming of dark, he gave way to panic.

He wasn't sure how long he huddled under the beech. Time seemed to have lost its familiar properties, minutes to have lengthened into unrecognizable proportions. He tried counting backwards from one hundred, but there were queer gaps in his memory, and he found himself fumbling for numbers he should have known without hesitation.

'Dickon! Shout if you can hear me!'

Relief rose in Richard's throat with the intensity of pain. 'Here,

Edmund, I'm here!' he cried and, within moments, he was being lifted up onto his brother's horse.

With one arm holding Richard securely in the saddle, Edmund skilfully turned his mount, gave the animal its head to find its way through the thick tangle of underbrush. Once they emerged into a splash of moonlight, he subjected Richard to a critical appraisal.

'Well, you're bedraggled enough, in truth! But are you hurt, Dickon?'

'No, just hungry.' Richard smiled, somewhat shyly. Edmund, who was sixteen, was not as approachable as Ned, was much more apt to react with impatience or, when provoked, with a quick cuff around the ears.

'You owe me for this, little brother. I assure you I've more pleasant ways to pass my nights than prowling the woods for you! The next time you take it into your head to run away, I rather think I'll wait and let the wolves find you first.'

Richard could not always tell when Edmund was serious. This time, however, he caught a telltale glint, knew Edmund was teasing, and laughed.

'There are no wolves ...' he began, and then the import of Edmund's words struck him.

'I didn't run away, Edmund. I got lost following my fox. ... You remember, the one I tamed. ... Whilst I was waiting for Ned to come back ...' His words trailed off; he looked sharply at Edmund, chewing his lip.

'I should have guessed,' Edmund said softly, and then, 'That damned fool. When he knows how our father feels about taking our pleasures with the women of the household!' He broke off, looked down at Richard with a fleeting smile.

'You do not have any idea what I'm talking about, do you? Just as well, I daresay.'

He shook his head. Richard heard him repeating, 'The damned fool,' under his breath and, after a while, Edmund laughed aloud.

They rode in silence for a time. Richard had understood more than Edmund realized, knew that Ned had somehow done something that would much displease their father.

'Where is he, Edmund?' he asked, sounding so forlorn that Edmund ruffled his hair in a careless gesture of consolation.

'Looking for you, where else? He sent your Joan back to the castle for help when dark came and they still could not find you. We've had half the household scouring the woods for you since dusk.'

Silence fell between them again. When Richard was beginning to recognize landmarks, knew they would soon be in sight of Ludford Bridge, he heard Edmund say thoughtfully, 'No one knows yet what happened this afternoon, Dickon. No one has talked to Ned yet, and the girl was so distraught it was hard to get anything sensible from her. We just assumed you took off on a lark of your own.' He hesitated and then continued, still in the unfamiliar yet intriguing confidential tones of one adult to another.

'You know, Dickon, if our lord father were to think that Ned had left you alone in the meadows, he'd be none too happy about it. He'd be most wroth with Ned, of course. But he'd blame your Joan, too, I fear. He might even send her away.'

'No!' Richard twisted in the saddle to look up at his brother. 'Ned did not leave me alone,' he said breathlessly. 'He did not, Edmund! I ran after the fox, that's all!'

'Well then, if that be true, you need not worry about Ned or Joan. After all, if the fault was yours, none could blame Ned, could they? But you do understand, Dickon, that if the fault was yours, you'll be the one to be punished?'

Richard nodded. 'I know,' he whispered, and turned to gaze into the river currents flowing beneath the bridge, where he'd sacrificed a coin so many eventful hours ago, for luck.

'You know, Dickon, I've been meaning to ask you. . . . Would you like me to make you a wooden sword like the one George has? I cannot promise you when I'll get around to it, mind you, but. . . .'

9

'You do not have to do that, Edmund. I'd not tell on Ned!' Richard interrupted, sounding somewhat offended, and hunched his shoulders forward involuntarily as the walls of the castle materialized from the darkness ahead.

Edmund was distinctly taken aback and then bit back a grin. 'My mistake, sorry!' he said, looking at his brother with the bemused expression of an adult suddenly discovering that children could be more than nuisances to be tolerated until they were old enough to behave as rational beings, could even be distinct individuals in their own right.

As they approached the drawbridge that spanned the moat of lethal pointed stakes, torches flared to signal Richard's safe return, and by the time Edmund passed through the gatehouse that gave entry into the inner bailey, their mother was awaiting them upon the ramp leading up into the great hall. Reining in before her, Edmund swung Richard down and into her upraised arms. As he did, he flashed Richard a grin and Richard was able to derive a flicker of comfort from that, the awareness that he, for once, had won Edmund's unqualified approval.

Richard was sitting on a table in the solar, so close to the east-wall fireplace that the heat from its flames gave his face a sunburnt flush. He winced as his mother swabbed with wine-saturated linen at the scratches upon his face and throat, but submitted without complaint to her ministrations. He was rather pleased, in fact, to command her attention so thoroughly; he could remember few occasions when she had treated his bruises with her own hand. Generally this would have been for Joan to do. But Joan was too shaken to be of assistance. Eyes reddened and swollen, she hovered in the background, from time to time reaching out to touch Richard's hair, as tentatively as if she were daring a liberty that was of a sudden forbidden.

Richard smiled at her with his eyes, quite flattered that she should have been crying so on his behalf, but she seemed little

consoled by his sympathy and when he'd explained, rather haltingly, to his mother that he'd become separated from Ned and
Joan in pursuit of his fox cub, Joan inexplicably began to cry
again.

'I heard you're to be locked in the cellar under the great hall
as your punishment . . . in the dark with the rats!'

His brother George had sidled nearer, awaiting the chance to
speak as soon as their mother moved away from the table. He
was watching Richard now with intent blue-green eyes, and
Richard tried to conceal his involuntary shudder. He had no intention of letting George know he had a morbid horror of rats, aware
that if he did, he was all too likely to find one in his bed.

Edmund came to his rescue, leaning over George to offer
Richard a sip from his own cup of mulled wine.

'Mind your mouth, George,' he said softly. 'Or you might find
yourself taking a tour of the cellar some night.'

George glared at Edmund but did not venture a response, for
he was not all that certain Edmund wouldn't, if sufficiently
provoked, follow through with his threat. Playing it safe, he held
his tongue; although still a month shy of his tenth bithday, George
had already developed a sophisticated sense of self-preservation.

Setting Edmund's cup down so abruptly that wine sloshed over
onto the table, Richard slid hastily to the floor. He had at last
heard the one voice he'd been waiting for.

Edward was dismounting before the round Norman nave that
housed the chapel named for St Mary Magdalene. He saw Richard
as the boy bolted through the doorway of the solar and in three
strides he covered the ground between them, catching Richard
to him in a tight, bone-bruising embrace and then laughing and
swinging the youngster up into the air, high over his head.

'Jesú, but you did give me some bad moments, lad! Are you all
right?'

'He's fine.' Edmund had come through the doorway behind
Richard, and now stood looking down at them as Edward knelt

beside Richard in the dust. His eyes raked Edward with ironic amusement and a message flashed between them that passed, figuratively and literally, over Richard's head.

'He's fine,' Edmund repeated, 'but I daresay he'll be taken severely to task for running off as he did. It seems he became lost chasing after that damned pet fox of his. But then I need not tell you that, need I, Ned? After all, you were there.'

'That's right,' Edward said coolly. 'I was.' His mouth twitched and then, as if on cue, he and Edmund were laughing. Coming lightly to his feet, Edward kept his arm warm around Richard's shoulders as they moved across the bailey, murmuring, 'Fox hunting, were you?'

His voice was noncommittal and Richard nodded shyly, keeping his eyes upon Edward's face.

'Well . . . you might not be too good at keeping put, Dickon, but you're very good indeed at keeping faith!' Edward said softly and, meeting Richard's eyes, he winked and then grinned, and Richard discovered the joyful difference between being a sacrificial lamb and a trusted conspirator.

Much to Richard's surprise, Joan fled the solar as soon as Edward came through the doorway. But he had no time to dwell on her peculiar behaviour, for Edward was lifting him up and depositing him back upon the table, saying, 'Let me have a look at you.' Shaking his head in mock disbelief, he said wryly, 'You look like you've been jousting with a bramble-bush,' and Richard laughed.

'I was,' he confided, and then looked up as his mother laid a hand lightly on his shoulder.

She was studying her eldest son, her eyes speculative. He met her gaze levelly, with a faintly quizzical smile, and at length she said only, 'You were lucky, Edward. Very lucky, indeed.'

'Somehow, he always is, ma mère,' Edmund observed laconically.

'I am, aren't I?' Edward agreed complacently and, stepping back, brought his elbow up, as if by chance, to jostle Edmund's arm and spill his drink. Edmund, just as quick, tilted the cup so that it splashed upon the sleeve of Edward's doublet.

'Edward! Edmund! This is no time to play the fool, tonight of all nights!'

There was such unaccustomed asperity in the rebuke that they stared at her.

'But that is what we do best, ma mère,' Edmund demurred, feeling it advisable to placate his irate parent with charm.

Edward, a shade more perceptive, was frowning. 'Why do you say "tonight of all nights", ma mère? It cannot be Dickon; he came to no harm. What has your nerves so on the raw?'

She didn't respond at once, shifting her gaze between their faces. 'You read people well, Edward,' she said at last. 'I hadn't meant to tell you till the morrow. . . . While you both were out searching for Richard, word reached us from my brother.'

The two boys exchanged glances. Their uncle, the Earl of Salisbury, was expected to reach Ludlow that week, leading an armed force from the North to join with their father's men and those soon to come from Calais under command of their cousin, Salisbury's son, the Earl of Warwick.

'He was ambushed at a place called Blore Heath, to the north of Shrewsbury, by the Queen's army. Your cousins, Thomas and John, were taken captive but my brother and others were able to fight their way free. He sent word ahead to warn us, should reach Ludlow by tomorrow night.'

There was silence, broken at last by Edward, who said matter-of-factly, 'If the Queen is set upon war, she'll not long keep the royal army at Coventry. She'll march on Ludlow, ma mère, and soon.'

The Duchess of York nodded. 'Yes, Edward, you are quite right,' she said slowly. 'She'll move on Ludlow. I very much fear we can count on it.'

2

Ludlow

October 1459

Death waited in the dark. Richard could feel its presence, knew it was there. Death was no stranger to him, for all that he was just ten days past his seventh birthday. Death had always been very much a part of his world, had claimed a baby sister in her cradle, had taken cousins and playmates, and more than once in his earliest years of life, had threatened to take him, too. Now it was back and, like him, awaiting the coming of day. He shivered and pulled the fox-fur coverlet up toward his chin, retreated still further into the refuge of the bed. Beside him, his brother stirred sleepily and jabbed him in the ribs with an elbow.

'Stop squirming, Dickon,' he mumbled and reached over to claim Richard's pillow.

Richard made a halfhearted attempt to regain his stolen property, but once again George's three-year advantage proved to be a telling one and the older boy was soon asleep, both pillows enfolded securely against his chest. Richard cushioned his head on his arm, watching with envy as his brother slept. In all of his seven years, he had never been awake at such an hour. But in all of his seven years, he had never been so afraid.

He thought of the dawning day with dread. On the morrow there was to be a battle. Men were to die for reasons he did not fully understand. But he did understand, with chilling clarity, that when the day was done, his father and Ned and Edmund might be numbered among the dead.

14

His brother's pillow covering had slipped; he could see the tip of a protruding feather. He edged closer and fished it out, eyeing George with caution. But George was snoring softly and soon there was a downy pile between them on the bed. He began to separate them into two camps which he mentally identifed as 'York' and 'Lancaster'. The feathery forces of York were led, of course, by his father, the Duke of York, and those of Lancaster by the King, Harry of Lancaster, and the Frenchwoman who was his Queen.

He continued methodically plucking feathers from George's pillow and aligning them in opposing camps, but it didn't help. He was unable to forget his fear. What if his father were to die? Or Ned? Ned and Edmund were men grown. Old enough to ride into battle tomorrow. Old enough to die.

He began to build up the army of York until it vastly outnum-bered Lancaster. He knew his father did not want to fight the King and he did not think the King truly wanted to fight his father. Again and again he'd heard it said that the King shrank from shedding blood.

But the Queen had no such qualms. Richard knew she hated his father with all the passion the King lacked. She wanted his father dead; Richard had heard his cousin Warwick say so that very day. He wasn't all that sure just why the Queen should hate his father so but he had heard men say that his father had a better claim to the English crown than the King and he suspected this might have something to do with the Queen's unrelenting hostility. It was confusing to Richard, though, for his father repeat-edly vowed that the King was his sovereign and liege lord. He didn't understand why his father could not just assure the Queen of his loyalty to King Harry. If she understood that, perhaps she would not hate his father so much then. Perhaps there need be no battle. . . .

He stiffened suddenly and then jerked upright in the bed, jarring George into wakeful wrath. He emerged from the coverlets with an oath pirated from Edward, irritation giving way to outrage as he inhaled a mouthful of feathers.

'Damn you, Dickon,' he spluttered, grabbing for the younger boy. Richard was generally adroit at evading George's vengeance but now he made no attempt to escape and George soon pinned him down against the mattress, somewhat surprised at the ease of his victory.

'George, listen! Can you not hear? Listen!'

Buffeting him with the pillow, with more exuberance now than anger, George at last heeded Richard's muffled protests and cocked his head, listening.

'Men are shouting,' he said uneasily.

Dressing hastily in the dark, they crept from their bedchamber in the Pendower Tower. All of Ludlow was suddenly deep in unfriendly shadows, had become a sinister refuge for every malignant spirit that could be conjured up by the feverish imaginings of two fearful small boys. By the time they reached the east door of the great hall, they were stumbling over each other in their urgency to gain the security of torchlight and known voices.

The great hall was sixty feet in length, thirty feet in width, and crowded with men, men rudely roused from sleep, men who were fastening hastily donned garments, buckling scabbards at hip and thigh, kicking impatiently at the castle dogs that were circling about in frenzied excitement. At first, Richard saw only the swords, what seemed to him to be a forest of naked blades, each nearly as long as a man's height and capable of shearing a head from its body with one stroke. Gradually he began to pick out familiar faces. His mother's brother, Richard Neville, Earl of Salisbury. Salisbury's grown son and namesake, Richard Neville, Earl of Warwick. William Hastings, a youthful friend of his father's. And by the open stone hearth, Ned and Edmund.

It was some moments, however, before he was able to find his parents. The Duke of York and his Duchess were standing apart from the others in the hall. As Richard watched, his mother reached up and touched her fingers lightly to her husband's lips. He enfolded her hand within his own. Richard caught his breath. He had never seen his mother other than immaculate, never less than perfect in her person and her poise. This white-faced woman with masses of unbound hair enveloping her in bright disarray was a stranger to him.

'Take care, Dickon, lest we be seen,' George was hissing in his ear, but Richard shook off his brother's restraining hand and slipped around the dais into the hall. As desperate as he was for reassurance, he dared not approach his parents. He chose, instead, to wend his way cautiously through the press toward his brothers.

'But why should you go with our uncle Salisbury and cousin Warwick rather than with our lord father and me, Ned?'

As Edward started to answer Edmund, a small shadow materialized unexpectedly at his elbow, so silently and suddenly that his taut nerves betrayed him and he snapped, 'For Christ's sake, Dickon, how came you to be here? Why are you not abed?'

But as he looked into the boy's stricken dark eyes, he relented. Reaching down, he swung Richard up easily into his arms and, with Edmund trailing behind, shoved his way across the hall, toward the screen that extended across the south-west end of the chamber.

As he set Richard back on his feet, footsteps sounded behind them and George dived breathlessly behind the screen. For a long moment nothing was said, and then Richard whispered, 'Tell us, Ned . . . please.'

Edward glanced at Edmund, who shrugged. His eyes flicked back to Richard and George. 'Aye, it's best that you know. We've been betrayed. Look around the hall. There's one face you'll not see here, one we were foolish enough to trust. Andrew Trollope has gone over to Lancaster, and with him, the whole of his Calais garrison. Moreover, he has full knowledge of what our battle captains planned to do on the morrow.'

17

'What will you do?'

Edward shrugged. 'What can we do, George? We do not have the men to fight, not with Trollope's defection. And Ludlow could not withstand a siege. We can only order our army to disperse, to scatter. And then ride like the devil were on our tails.'

They were both staring at him, stunned. George, recovering first, blurted out, 'You mean . . . run away?' And then shrank back before their rage.

'What would you have us do?' Edward flared. 'Keep our pride and lose our heads? Need I tell you what will befall us if we're in Ludlow come the morrow? Every man in this hall would be dead by sunset.'

'No!' Richard gasped. 'No, you must not stay!'

Edmund, no less angry than Edward, was glaring at George. 'Send them back to bed, Ned,' he said curtly.

Edward, though, was belatedly remembering that a ten-year-old boy could not, in justice, be held accountable for all that he said. He felt a pressure against his arm, saw that Richard had moved closer. Until this moment he'd not given much thought to Richard and George beyond assuring himself that none would harm a child, not even Lancaster's vengeful Queen. Thinking now of what the little boy would face on the morrow, he realized, somewhat to his surprise, that he'd have given a great deal to be able to spare Richard what lay ahead when Ludlow fell to the forces of Lancaster.

As if sensitive to his thoughts, Richard asked uncertainly, 'Do we go with you, Ned?' And his heartbeat seemed to speed up, to fill his ears with the sound as Edward shook his head.

'That's not possible, Dickon. Not the way we must ride.'

'You're leaving us to Lancaster?' George demanded incredulously, sounding so horrified that Edward was at once upon the defensive.

'You need not make it sound as if you're being given over to infidels for ritual slaughter, George!' he said, rather more sharply than he intended. He caught himself, marvelling how George had so unerring an instinct for irritating him, and then said, more gently, 'You need not fear, George. Lancaster does not take vengeance upon children. You'll be safe enough; far safer, I warrant, than if we tried to take you with us.'

Edmund had been shifting impatiently, too tense not to begrudge this time being squandered upon children when time was their only lifeline.

'Ned, our cousin Warwick beckons to us.' Edward nodded but continued to linger, reaching out to ruffle first George's fair head and then Richard's dark one. Never had they looked so young to him, so utterly defenceless, as now when they were to be left to face an enemy army. Forcing a smile, he gave George a playful blow on the arm.

'Do not look so woebegone,' he said lightly. 'In truth, there's no need to fear. You'll not be ill-treated by Lancaster.'

'I'm not afraid,' George said quickly and, when Edward said nothing in response, he fancied he could read scepticism in Edward's silence and repeated insistently, 'I'm not afraid, not at all!'

Edward straightened up, said dryly, 'I'm gratified to hear it, George.'

He started to follow after Edmund and then, on impulse, turned back to Richard. Kneeling by the boy, he looked intently into his face, said softly, 'What of you, Dickon? Are you afraid?'

Richard opened his mouth to deny it and then slowly nodded his head. 'Yes,' he confessed, almost inaudibly, flushing as if he'd made the most shameful of admissions.

'I'll share a secret with you, Dickon. . . . So am I,' Edward said, and then laughed outright at the astonished look on the boy's face.

'Truly?' he said dubiously, and Edward nodded.

'Truly. There's not a man alive who does not know fear, Dickon. The brave man is the one who has learned to hide it, that's all. You remember that tomorrow, lad.'

Edmund was back. 'Name of God, Ned, are you going to tarry all night?'

Edward came to his feet. Looking down at Richard, he grinned.

'And think of the tales you'll have to tell me when next I do see you! After all, you'll have been the one to witness the surrender of Ludlow, not I.'

And then he was gone, hastening to join Edmund, leaving the two boys alone behind the screen, trying to come to terms with the incredible reality that, with the coming of dawn, would come, too, the Lancastrian army into the village of Ludlow.

Edmund read his brother without difficulty, had been able to do so since they were small boys, and now he wasn't surprised to find that Edward was no longer following him. Retracing his steps, he located his brother by the dais, deep in discussion with their mother. He hastened toward them, arrived in time to hear the Duchess of York say, 'Edward, I do believe you're mad! To even consider so reckless a scheme. . . . It is out of the question.'

'Wait, ma mère, hear me out. I admit it does sound risky at first hearing, but it has merit. It would work, I know it would.'

Edmund didn't much like the sound of that; it had been his experience that what Edward was apt to consider feasible others would consider the height of imprudence. 'What would work, Ned?'

'I want to take ma mère and the boys from here tonight.'

Edmund so forgot himself as to swear in front of his mother. 'I hope to Christ you're not serious.'

'But I am. I know we did agree that it were best for them to remain in Ludlow, and I know ma mère is convinced no harm will come to them. But I'm not so sure, Edmund. I'm just not that sure.'

'None of us are happy with it, Ned,' Edmund said reasonably. 'But we cannot take them with us. A woman and two small boys . . . The way we must ride? It'd be safer by far for them in Ludlow.

Women and children are not abused. It's not done, even by Lancaster. They'll be taken to the King and, most likely, a steep fine will be levied upon Ludlow. There may be some looting, too, I grant you. But Jesú, Ned, this is no French village for the plundering. Ludlow is still English.'

'Yes, but . . .'

'Besides,' Edmund demanded, 'where could you hope to take them?' He saw that he'd blundered for Edward grinned.

'Wigmore,' he said triumphantly. 'The Augustine abbey close by the castle. I know I could get them safely there in a few hours. It would not be that difficult. No, do not talk, just listen. We could leave now, take back roads. There's not a path in Shropshire I do not know. You'd not deny that, surely?' he challenged, and Edmund shook his head.

'No, I'd not deny that. But once you get them to Wigmore . . . assuming you do . . . what then? Does that not leave you stranded alone out in the Shropshire countryside? In the midst of the Lancastrian army?'

Edward shrugged impatiently. 'Have you forgotten I grew up here in Ludlow? I know this area. I'd not be taken. Once I got them safe to Wigmore, I'd catch up with you and our lord father without difficulty.' He grinned again, said persuasively, 'You do see it could work, do you not? Admit it, Edmund, the plan is a sound one.'

'I think it is madness. On your own whilst the Lancastrians cast a net over the entire countryside? You'd not have a chance, Ned. Not a chance.' Edmund paused, saw the stubborn set of Edward's mouth, and concluded grimly, 'But I see you are bound and determined to follow through with this madness. So we might as well get the horses saddled, fetch the boys. We have not much time.'

Edward laughed softly, showed no surprise. 'I knew I could count on you,' he said approvingly and then shook his head. 'But this is one time when I'll have to forego your company. I think it best I take them myself.'

'Very noble,' Edmund said caustically, 'but not very bright. Do not be stupid, Ned. You know you need me to . . .'

The Duchess of York, who had been listening to her sons in disbelief, now said sharply, 'I cannot credit what I'm hearing! Did you not hear me say I had no intention of leaving Ludlow? What, pray, had you in mind, Edward? Throwing me across your stallion as if I were a saddle blanket?'

They turned startled faces toward her, dismayed and flustered by her fury when they'd have taken their father's more familiar wrath in their stride. At that moment, suddenly looking so young to her, her anger ebbed and a surge of protective pride caught at her heart, threaded through with fear for them. She hesitated, searching for the right words, for that patience peculiar to the mothers of teenage sons, reminding herself that they were citizens now of two countries, passing back and forth across the unmarked borders between manhood and boyhood with such frequency that she never knew with certainty where they'd be found at any given time.

'Your concern does you credit, Edward, does you both credit. Do you think I'm not proud that you're willing to risk your lives for my sake, for your little brothers? But the risk would be taken for no good cause. To spare us discomfort, you might well bring about your own deaths. Do you think I could permit that?'

'The risk would not be that great, ma mère,' Edward began, and she shook her head, reaching up and touching him lightly on the cheek in what was, for her, a surprisingly public gesture of affection.

'I do not agree. I think the risk would be of the greatest magnitude imaginable. And for nothing, Edward, for nothing! We're in no danger here. Do you truly think I'd ever keep George and Richard in Ludlow if I thought any harm might come to them?'

She saw she'd scored a telling point, saw Edward concede it with a grimace.

'No, ma mère, of course you would not. But. . . .'

'And if I were truly to face danger from Lancaster, Edward, it would be no less at Wigmore. The castle there belongs to York. It would not be hard to guess our whereabouts. No, I do mean to stay in Ludlow. I have no fears for myself or your brothers, but I will confess to you that I do fear for the villagers. They are our people; I should be here to speak for them.'

'As you will, ma mère,' Edward said at last. 'I daresay you are right.' But he was still young enough to add in a troubled undertone, 'I do hope to God that you are.'

Deserted streets, shops tightly shuttered, market stalls empty; even Ludlow's dogs were strangely silent. Only the lowing of cattle penned in the market bullring broke the eerie unnatural stillness that enclosed the village as the advance guard of the Lancastrian army rode across Ludford Bridge and into Ludlow.

They'd encountered no resistance; the Yorkist earthworks that had blocked the road to Leominster were unmanned. Advancing up Broad Street, they passed through Broad Gate unchallenged. In unnerving silence they moved north toward High Street. There they drew rein abruptly for a woman and two small boys were awaiting them upon the steps of the high market cross.

The Lancastrian army was surging into Ludlow. The narrow streets were jammed with jubilant soldiers. The Swan and Rose banners of Lancaster caught the wind, fluttered aloft over the heads of the Duchess of York and her two youngest sons.

When the mounted knight first came into view, sunlight striking with blinding brilliance upon polished plate armour, Richard wondered if he might be King Harry. But the face half-shadowed by the upraised vizor was far too young; this man was not all that much older than his brother Ned. Richard risked a whispered query to George and was much impressed by the latter's boldness when George whispered back, 'You're not likely to see Harry here, Dickon. They say he's daft, not able to tell a goose from a gander in the dark.'

Richard had, from time to time, overheard puzzling and cryptic references to the King's health said with such sardonic significance that he comprehended, however imperfectly, that there was something 'not quite right' with the King. But the hints were so clearly not meant for his hearing, were given so guardedly and grudgingly, that he instinctively shrank back from the subject even with Edward. He had never heard the truth put so baldly as now, in the midst of the soldiers of that self-same King, and he looked at George with mingled apprehension and admiration.

George was staring at the young knight, by now approaching the steps of the market cross. Tugging at his mother's sleeve, he murmured, 'Ma mère? Who is he? The man who betrayed us . . . Trollope?'

'No . . . my lord Somerset,' she said quietly, and none could have guessed from the even, matter-of-fact tones that she had just named a man who had more reason than most to hate the House of York, a man whose father had died the loser on a battlefield her husband had won. And, with that, she moved down the steps to meet him.

Henry Beaufort, Duke of Somerset, was just twenty-three years of age, but to him had been entrusted the command of the King's army. Marguerite d'Anjou, Lancaster's French-born Queen, might defy convention by riding with her troops, but there were certain constraints even she was forced to recognize, not the least of which was that there was no Joan of Arc in English folklore.

Somerset had not dismounted. Curbing his restive stallion with a practised hand, he listened impatiently as the Duchess of York made an impassioned and persuasive appeal on behalf of the villagers of Ludlow.

Cecily Neville was, at forty-four, still a strikingly handsome woman, with the lithe slimness of early youth and direct dark

24

grey eyes. Somerset was not altogether indifferent to the attract-ive image she presented standing alone on the market cross, flanked by her young sons. He suspected, however, that her posture was one carefully calculated to appeal to chivalric susceptibilities. He had no liking for this proud woman who was wife to his sworn enemy, and he noted, with gratified if rather grim amusement, that the role of supplicant did not come easily to her.

While he felt compelled to accord her the courtesy due her rank and sex, to let her speak for Ludlow, he had no intention of heeding her plea. Ludlow had long been a Yorkist stronghold; a day of reckoning would have a salutary effect upon other towns wavering in their loyalty to Lancaster.

He interrupted to demand what he already knew. York's Duchess answered readily enough. Her husband? He was gone from Ludlow, as was her brother, the Earl of Salisbury and her nephew, the Earl of Warwick. Her sons, Edward, Earl of March and Edmund, Earl of Rutland? Gone, too, she said coolly.

Somerset rose in his stirrups, gazing down High Street toward the rising stone walls of the outer castle bailey. He knew she spoke the truth; her very presence here was all the proof he needed that the Yorkists had fled. He was remembering, moreover, that there was a bridge behind the castle, spanning the River Teme and linking with the road leading west into Wales.

He gestured abruptly and soldiers moved onto the steps of the cross. The children shrank back and he had the satisfaction of seeing sudden fear upon Cecily Neville's haughty handsome face. She gathered her sons to her and demanded to know if my lord Somerset meant to take vengeance upon innocent children.

'My men are here to see to your safety, Madame.' Her defiance had rankled; she was, after all, only a woman, and York's woman at that. He saw no reason not to remind her of the realities of their respective positions, said bluntly that he'd wager she'd be thankful for the presence of an armed guard before the day was done.

She whitened, hearing in his words the death knell of Ludlow; knowing now that there was only one man who could avert the coming carnage, that strange gentle soul who yearned only for peace of spirit and was wed to the woman the Yorkists saw as Messalina.

'I wish to see His Grace the King,' she said steadily. 'He has no subjects more loyal than the people of Ludlow.'

Her request was impossible, but it could not be acknowledged as such. He swallowed a bitter retort, said tersely, 'It suited the King's Grace to remain at Leominster.'

Cecily, however, was no longer watching Somerset. Richard, who was standing so close to her that he was treading upon the hem of her gown, now felt her body stiffen, in a small indecisive movement, quickly stilled. And then she was sinking down upon the steps in a curtsy, a very precise and controlled gesture that was totally lacking in her customary grace. Richard hastily followed her example, and it was kneeling upon the steps of the market cross that he had his first glimpse of the Lancastrian Queen.

His first impression, quite simply, was one of awe. Marguerite d'Anjou was the most beautiful woman he'd ever seen, as beautiful as the queens of Joan's bedtime tales. All in gold and black, like the swallowtail butterflies he'd chased all summer in such futile fascination. Her eyes were huge and black, blacker even than the rosaries of Whitby jet so favoured by his mother. Her mouth was scarlet, her skin like snow, her dark hair covered by a head-dress of golden gauze, her face framed in floating folds of a glittery shimmering material that seemed to be made from sunlight; he'd never seen anything like it, couldn't keep his eyes from it, or from her.

'Where is your husband, Madame? Surely he'd not abandon you to pay the price for his treason?'

Richard loved the sound of his mother's voice, clear and low-pitched, as musical to him as chapel chimes. The Queen's voice was a disappointment, shrill and sharply edged with mockery, so strongly flavoured with the accent of her native Anjou that he distinguished her words with some difficulty.

'My husband swore an oath of allegiance to His Grace the King and has held true to that oath.'

The Queen laughed. Richard didn't like the sound of it any more than he had her voice. He unobtrusively edged closer to his mother's side, slipped his hand into the sleeve of her gown.

With a sudden shock, he realized those glittering black eyes had come to rest upon him. Frozen under her gaze, he stared up at the Lancastrian Queen, unable to free his eyes from hers. He was accustomed to having adults look at him without seeing, accepted that as a peculiarity of adult vision, that children were so little visible to them. He saw now that this was not true of the Queen, that she saw him very clearly. There was something very cold and queerly measuring in her look; he was frightened by it without exactly knowing why.

The Queen was now looking at his mother. 'Since your husband and your sons, March and Rutland, have so courageously fled the consequences of their treachery, it remains for you, Madame, to stand witness in their stead. Mark you well what price we exact from those disloyal to the Crown.'

Cecily's response was both immediate and unexpected. She stepped in front of Marguerite's glossy ebony mare.

'These people are good people, God-fearing people, loyal to their King. They owe Your Grace no debt of disloyalty, I do assure you.'

'Madame, you bar my path,' Marguerite said softly.

Richard saw her leather riding crop cut the air above his head. The mare lunged forward and, for a moment of heartstopping horror, he thought his mother would fall beneath the animal's hooves. She'd seen enough of Marguerite's face to be forewarned, however, and sprang clear in time, kept on her feet by the most alert of Somerset's soldiers.

Richard brushed past the soldier, pressed against his mother;

George had already reached her. She was trembling and for a moment leaned against George as if he were a man grown.

'Send my sons from the village,' she said huskily. 'I do implore Your Grace. . . . You, too, are a mother.'

Marguerite had turned in the saddle. Now she jerked at the reins, guiding the mare back toward the cross. 'Yes, I am a mother. My son was born six years ago today . . . and almost from the day of his birth, there have been those who would deny his birthright, those who dared say that my Edouard is not the true son of my husband, the King. And you know as well as I, Madame, the man most responsible for such vile slanders . . . Richard Neville, Earl of Warwick. Warwick . . . your nephew, Madame! Your nephew!'

This last came out in a hiss, in a surge of scalding fury, followed by a burst of French, too fast and furious to be decipherable. Pausing for breath, she looked down in silence at the ashen woman and fear-frozen children. Very slowly and deliberately, she removed one of her riding gloves, finely stitched Spanish leather furred with sable. She saw Cecily Neville raise her chin, saw Somerset grin, knew they both expected her to strike Cecily across the face with it. She flung it, instead, in the dust at Cecily's feet.

'I want this town to learn what befalls those who give support to traitors. See to it, my lord Somerset,' she said shortly, and not waiting for his response, brought her riding crop down again upon her mare's flanks, wheeling it about in an eye-catching display of showy horsemanship and then swinging back down Broad Street at a pace to send soldiers scattering from her path.

A girl was screaming. The sound washed over Richard in chilling waves, set him to trembling. There was so much terror in her cries that he felt a sick relief when the screams became muffled, more indistinct and, at last, ceased altogether. He swallowed, kept his eyes averted from the direction of the churchyard where the girl's screams came from.

The wind shifted suddenly, brought to him the acrid odour of burning flesh. More and more houses were being put to the torch, and the flames had spread to an adjoining pigsty, trapping several of the unfortunate animals within. Mercifully, the cries of the dying pigs could no longer be heard, for the agonized squealing of the doomed creatures had sickened him. He'd seen animals butchered for beef, had once even been taken by Edward and Edmund on a September stag hunt. But this was different; this was a world gone mad.

A world in which men were prodded up the streets like cattle, hemp ropes dangling about their necks. A world in which soldiers stripped looted shops for timber to erect a gallows before the guild hall. A world in which the younger son of the town clerk had been clubbed and left for dead in the middle of Broad Street. From the cross Richard could still see the body. He tried not to look at it; the clerk's son had helped him to trap the fox cub he'd discovered that memorable summer morning in Dinham meadow.

Turning his eyes resolutely from the body of the boy he'd known and liked, Richard found himself staring at a queer reddish stain that was spreading into the dust at the base of the cross, rivulets of red seeping off into the gutters. He watched for several moments, and then realization struck him and he recoiled abruptly.

'George, look!' Pointing in fascinated horror. 'Blood!'

George stared and then squatted down and stirred up ripples with an experimental finger.

'No,' he pronounced finally. 'Wine . . . from over there, see?' Gesturing toward the corner, where several huge hogsheads of wine had been dragged from a plundered tavern and spilled open into the centre gutter.

George and Richard turned to watch as a bull galloped past, cheered on by the bored soldiers Somerset had charged to guard them. Richard was ill at ease with his guards; while they had so far acted to keep the Duchess of York and her sons from being molested by the soldiers reeling about the cross, it was apparent that they were none too happy with this duty. They'd been watching glumly as their comrades shared the plunder of the looted town, and Richard felt sure most would have been quite willing to heed his mother's insistent urgings that they be taken to the King's camp. One man remained adamant, however, that they could not act without orders from His Grace the Duke of Somerset and, as the authority was his, none could leave the precarious sanctuary of the cross, neither captives nor their reluctant captors.

The Duchess of York suddenly cried out. A man was limping down High Street, moving slowly, without direction or purpose. Foundering like a ship without a rudder, he seemed oblivious of the soldiers who jostled against him, arms full of booty from the castle, by now stripped to the walls, and rising above the hapless village like the exposed skeletal remains of some past, predatory kill. Now, as he trod upon the heels of a plunderladen soldier, he was roundly cursed, elbowed aside. Other hands, however, reached out to break his fall, even acted to clear his way; men fresh from rape and the makeshift gallows who, nonetheless, scrupled to do violence to a priest.

His habit and cowl proclaimed him to be one of the Carmelite brothers of St Mary White Friars, but the once immaculate white was liberally streaked with soot, even a splattering of blood. As he drew nearer, they saw he wore but one sandal, yet plunged unheedingly into the mud churned up in the street, into the murky wine that now stood ankle-deep in the gutters around the cross. At the sound of his name, he paused, blinking about him blindly. The Duchess of York called out again to him and this time he saw her.

The guards made no attempt to stop him as he clambered up the steps of the cross, looking on indifferently as Cecily moved to grasp his outstretched hand between her own. Her eyes flickered over the stained habit, back to the blanched, begrimed face.

'Are you hurt?'

He shook his head dully. 'No. . . . They slaughtered our live-stock. The milk cows, the ewes. . . . The stables are befouled with blood. . . .'

His voice trailed off, his eyes seemed to cloud over, and only when she repeated his name did he rouse himself, focus once more upon her and the two children staring at him in wonderment. He looked like no friar they had ever seen, as bedraggled and unkempt as the poorest beggar, with the glazed eyes and slack mouth of one deep in his cups.

'Madame. . . . They sacked the friary. They took all, Madame, all. Then they burned the buildings. The buttery, the brewhouse, even the infirmary and the almshouse. They stripped the church. . . . Even the pyx and chalices, Madame, the chalices. . . .'

'Listen to me,' she demanded. 'Listen, for God's sake!'

At last her urgency communicated itself to him and he fell silent, staring at her.

'You must go to the castle. Find the Duke of Somerset. Tell him he must give orders to take my sons to the King's camp.' She glanced down at the children, dropped her voice still lower, said fiercely, 'Before it is too late. Do you understand? Go now, and go quickly! The soldiers will not harm a priest; they'll let you pass. If Somerset is not at the castle, seek him at the guild hall. They are making use of it as a prison and he may be there. But find him. . . .' Her voice was no more now than a whisper. 'For the love of Jesus, the Only-begotten Son, find him.'

The friar nodded, seared by her intensity. 'I will, Madame,' he vowed. 'I'll not fail you.'

George had understood enough of this exchange to feel a thrill of fear, and now he moved closer to his mother as she watched the friar hasten back up High Street, the once white habit soon swallowed up amongst the looting soldiers.

'Do you not trust our guards, ma mère?' he whispered.

She turned toward him. He was the fairest of all her children, as blond as Richard was dark, and now she let her hand linger on the soft sunlit hair that fell across his forehead. After hesitating, she temporized with a half-truth.

'Yes, George, I trust them. But there are evils happening here neither you nor Richard should see. That is why I want you taken to the King at Leominster. You must . . . Richard!'

With a cry, she grabbed for her youngest son, caught him just in time to prevent him from plunging down the steps of the cross. Kneeling, she pulled him to her, to berate him in a voice made rough by fright. He endured her rebuke in silence and, when she released him, slumped down on the steps and locked his arms around his drawn-up knees in a futile attempt to check the tremors that shook the thin little body. Cecily did not know what he had seen to give him such grief, nor did she wait to find out. She spun about, turning upon her guards with such fury that the men recoiled.

'I'll not have my sons kept here to watch Ludlow's death throes! You send a man to Somerset! Now, damn you, now!'

The men wilted under her wrath, shifted about in instinctive unease; she was still of the class they'd been indoctrinated since birth to obey. But George saw at once that she raged in vain; she'd not be heeded. He watched awhile and then lowered himself onto the steps beside Richard.

'Dickon? What did you see?'

Richard raised his head. His eyes were blind, were queerly dark, all blue eclipsed by the shock-dilated pupils.

'Well?' George demanded. 'Tell me what you did see! What could be as bad as all that?'

'I saw the girl,' Richard said at last. 'The girl the soldiers dragged into the churchyard.'

Even now, George could not resist an opportunity to display his worldly understanding. 'The one the soldiers had their way with?' he said knowingly.

His words meant nothing to Richard. He scarcely heard them.

'It was Joan! . . . She was over there. . . .' He gestured off to his right. 'In Butcher's Row. She kept stumbling and then fell down in the street and lay there. Her gown was all torn and there was blood . . .' He shuddered convulsively and continued only under George's insistent prodding.

'A soldier came from the church. He . . . he knotted his hand in her hair and pulled her to her feet. Then he took her back inside.' And with that, he drew a strangled breath that threatened to become a sob, but somehow he fought it back, stared at George.

'George . . . it was Joan!' he repeated, almost as if he expected George to contradict him, to assure him he was wrong, that the girl he'd seen could not possibly have been Joan.

He held his breath, awaiting George's response. He soon saw George was not going to reassure him, not going to make any consoling denials. He had never seen George at a loss for words before, nor had George ever looked at him as he did now. There was unmistakable pity in the older boy's eyes and Richard knew suddenly that whatever had befallen Joan was far worse than the ugliness he'd just witnessed in Butcher's Row.

A soldier ran by, yelling and brandishing a wine flask. It was uncorked and wine was spraying out in his wake, dousing all who came within range. Richard had leaned forward, dropping his head back into his arms. He looked up abruptly, though, as the man passed, hearing enough for alarm.

'George? Are men being hanged?'

George nodded. 'Be thankful, Dickon, that our father is safe away from Ludlow,' he said soberly. 'Had he or our brothers fallen into the Queen's hands, she'd have struck their heads above the town gates and, as likely as not, forced us to watch as it was done.'

Richard looked at him with horror and then jumped to his feet as a woman's scream echoed across the market square. George was on his feet, too, catching Richard roughly by the shoulders.

'It was not Joan, Dickon,' he said hastily. 'That scream did not come from the church. It was not Joan.'

Richard stopped struggling, stared at him. 'Are you sure?' he whispered, but as George nodded, the woman screamed again. That was too much for Richard. He jerked from George's grasp with such violence that he lost his balance and fell forward down the steps of the market cross, into the path of a horse and rider just turning the corner of Broad Street.

Richard wasn't hurt; the ground was too soft for that. But the impact of his fall had driven all the air from his lungs and, suddenly, the sky above his head was filled with flying forelegs and down-plunging hooves. When he dared open his eyes again, his mother was kneeling in the mud by his side and the stallion had been reined in scant feet from where he lay.

Cecily's hands were shaking so badly that she was forced to lace her fingers together to steady herself. Leaning forward, she began to wipe the mud from her child's face with the sleeve of her gown.

'For the love of Jesus! Madame, why are you still here?'

She raised her head sharply, to look up into a face that was young and frowning and vaguely familiar. She fumbled for recognition and then it came. The knight who'd come so close to trampling her son beneath his stallion was Edmund Beaufort, younger brother of the Duke of Somerset.

'In the name of God,' she said desperately, 'see my sons safe from here!'

He stared down at her and then swung from the saddle to stand beside her in the street.

'Why were you not taken at once to the camp of the King at Leominster?' He sounded angry and incredulous. 'My brother will have someone flayed alive for this. Lancaster does not make war on women and children.'

Cecily said nothing, merely looked at him and saw colour burn across his cheekbones. He turned away abruptly and began to give directives to the men who'd ridden into Ludlow under his command. With deep-felt relief, she saw that they all were sober.

'My men will escort you to the royal encampment, Madame.'

She nodded and watched tensely while he dismissed her guards, found horses for them and, with a disgusted oath, swung with the flat of his sword at the more drunken of the soldiers squabbling over spoils of victory. Even now, with deliverance seemingly at hand, she breathed no easier, would not until she saw her sons safely on the road that led from Ludlow. And then, as she led the boys forward to their waiting mounts, Richard suddenly balked. At that, she gave way at last to the strains of the past twenty-four hours and slapped him across the face. He gasped but accepted the punishment without outcry or protest. The objection came from George who moved swiftly to his brother's side.

'Do not blame Dickon, ma mère,' he entreated. 'He saw her, you see. He saw Joan.' Seeing her lack of comprehension, he pointed toward the parish church. 'The girl in the churchyard. It was Joan.'

Cecily looked down at her youngest son and then knelt and drew him gently to her. She saw the tears on his lashes and the imprint of her slap on his cheek.

'Oh, Richard,' she whispered, 'why did you not say so?'

As they'd awaited the coming of the Lancastrian army that morning, she'd taken pains to impress both boys with the urgency of their need for control. Now, however, she no longer cared about pride or honour or any thing but the pain in her child's eyes, pain that should have been forever alien to childhood.

It was then that Edmund Beaufort performed the act of kindness she would never forget, would not have dared expect. As she gazed up at him, framing an appeal she thought to be futile, he said before she could speak, 'I'll send some of my men into the churchyard to see to the girl. I'll have her taken to you at Leominster. Unless she . . .' He hesitated, looking down at the little boy she was cradling, and concluded neutrally, 'Whatever must be done will be, Madame. Now, I would suggest that we not tarry here any longer.'

She nodded numbly. He was holding out his hand. She reached up, let him raise her to her feet. He was, she now saw, very young, no more than four or five years older than her own Edmund. Very young and none too happy about what he'd found in Ludlow, and perceptive enough to realize that she did not want Richard to be present when Joan was found.

'I shall not forget your kindness, my lord,' she said softly and with far more warmth than she would ever have expected to feel for a member of the Beaufort family.

'In war, Madame, there are always . . . excesses,' he said, very low, and then the strange flicker of empathy that had passed between them was gone. He stepped back, issued a few terse commands. Men moved across the square toward the church-yard. Others waited to escort the Duchess of York and her sons to the royal camp at Leominster. Edmund Beaufort nodded, gave the order to move out. Cecily reined her mount in before him.

'Thank you, my lord.'

His eyes were guarded, shadowed by the uneasy suspicions of a man who'd surprised himself by his own candour and now wondered if he'd compromised himself by that candour.

'Do not mistake me, Madame. I have full faith in my brother's judgement. He did what he had to do. It was necessary that a lesson be learned here this day, one not to be soon forgotten.'

Cecily stared down at him. 'You need not fear, my lord,' she said bitterly. 'Ludlow will not be forgotten.'

3

Sandal Castle Yorkshire

December 1460

The Duke of York's second son was sitting cross-legged in the oriel window seat of the West Tower, watching with disbelief as his cousin, Thomas Neville, devoured a heaped plateful of cold roast capon and pompron buried in butter. As Thomas signalled to a page for a third refill of his ale tankard, Edmund could restrain himself no longer.

'Don't stint yourself, Cousin. After all, it's been two full hours since our noonday dinner . . . with four hours yet to go till supper.'

Thomas glanced up with a grin, proving himself once again to be totally impervious to sarcasm, and speared a large piece of capon meat. Edmund suppressed a sigh, yearning for the cut-and-thrust parries that had spiced his conversations with Edward. The problem, as he saw it, was that Thomas was too good-hearted to dislike, yet after ten days with him in the solitude of Sandal Castle, his unfailing cheer and relentless optimism were rubbing raw against Edmund's nerves.

Watching Thomas eat and acknowledging glumly that his boredom would drag him down to new depths if he could think of no better way to pass the time, Edmund found himself marvelling anew how four brothers could be as unlike as his four Neville cousins.

His cousin Warwick was assured, arrogant, audacious, and yet with an undeniable charm about him, withal. Edmund was nowhere near as taken with Warwick as Edward was but even he was not immune to the force of his flamboyant cousin's personality. He had a deeper fondness, however, for Warwick's younger brother Johnny, reserved and gravely deliberate, possessed of a wry Yorkshire wit and a sense of duty that was as unwavering as it was instinctive. He had no liking at all, though, for the third Neville brother named George like Edmund's own eleven-year-old brother. George Neville was a priest but only because it was traditional for one son of a great family to enter the Church. He was the most worldly man Edmund had ever encountered and one of the most ambitious, already Bishop of Exeter although still only in his twenties.

And then there was Thomas, the youngest. Thomas who might have been a changeling, so little did he resemble his siblings. Fair where they were dark, as tall even as Edward, though easily twenty-five pounds the heavier, with milk-blue eyes so serene that Edmund was given to sardonic speculation whether Thomas shared the same world as they did; a stranger to spite and, seemingly, to stress; as utterly courageous as the enormous mastiffs bred for bear-baiting and, in Edmund's considered judgement, with a good deal less imagination.

'Tell me about when you and Johnny were taken captive by Lancaster last year, after the battle of Blore Heath, Tom. Were you ill-treated?'

Thomas broke off a chunk of bread, shook his head. 'No . . . it's too common to take prisoners to risk abusing them. After all, you never know when you might yourself be taken.'

'But surely you must have felt some unease . . . at least at first?' Edmund persisted, and Thomas halted his knife in midair, looked at him in mild surprise.

'No,' he said at last, as if he'd had to give the matter some thought. 'No . . . I do not recall that I did.' He completed his knife's journey to his mouth, and then grinned again, saying with a ponderous playfulness that was as jovial as it was lacking in malice, 'What is the matter, Edmund? Are you fretting about the Lancastrian hordes at our gates?'

Edmund gazed coolly at him. 'Greensick with fear,' he snapped, with heavy sarcasm so that none would doubt he spoke only in jest.

As Thomas turned back to the capon, Edmund shifted his own gaze toward the window behind him, staring out into the bailey of the castle, deep in snow. He didn't doubt that Ned would have answered Thomas quite differently, would have laughed and conceded cheerfully that, Jesus, yes, he was unnerved. Ned never seemed to concern himself with what others thought and generally disarmed even as he surprised with his careless candour. Edmund wished he could do the same and knew it was quite impossible. He cared too much what others thought of him, even those he could not take all that seriously like Thomas. To Ned alone could he have confessed his fears. And Ned was far to the south, back at Ludlow to raise troops for the Yorkist banner. He'd not be coming north to Sandal Castle for days yet.

It was queer, he thought, that he still minded Ned's absence so much. After all, he should be used to it by now; in the four-teen months since their flight from Ludlow, he and Ned had been apart for fully a year's time. They'd been reunited only that past October 10th, when Edmund and his father at last reached London where Ned and their uncle Salisbury awaited them. And then they'd lingered in London two scant months, Ned leaving for Ludlow and the Welsh borders on December 9, the same day that Edmund, his father and uncle Salisbury headed north into Yorkshire.

Edmund was glad there was but one day remaining in this year of grace, 1460. It had been an eventful year for the House of York, but not a happy year for him. For him, it had been a year of waiting, chafing at the isolation and inactivity of his Irish exile. Ned had drawn much the best of the bargain, in Edmund's view, for Ned had been in Calais with Salisbury and Warwick.

When they fled Ludlow into Wales, Edmund would have liked to have gone with his Neville kin, too. The freewheeling port of

39

Calais held far greater allure for him than the staid seclusion of Dublin. But he'd felt honour-bound to accompany his father while envying Ned his freedom to elect otherwise. It was an election that had not pleased their father in the least. Politely reluctant to offend the Nevilles by implying they'd give Ned less than satisfactory supervision, he'd nonetheless managed to make his views known to Ned, who'd listened respectfully and then proceeded to do as he pleased, which was to accompany his Neville kin to Calais.

That was generally the case, Edmund conceded. Ned never argued with their father, he was unfailingly polite and then nonchalantly went his own way; whereas, he, Edmund, deferred dutifully to his father's authority and then found himself resenting both his parent's austere discipline and his own reluctance to rebel.

Edmund had envisioned all too well how Ned was amusing himself in Calais, and his discontent festered into a lingering depression when word reached Dublin in July that Ned and the Nevilles had landed upon English soil. They'd been welcomed into London and acted swiftly to consolidate their position. Eight days later they'd marched north from London to confront the King's forces at the town of Northampton. The Queen was some thirty miles distant at Coventry but the hapless person of the King had fallen into the hands of the victorious Yorkists after the battle. Edmund had yet to ride into battle and it was with ambivalent emotions that he learned Ned had been entrusted with command of one of the Yorkist wings by his cousin Warwick. The day his father would do the same for him, Edmund was convinced, would never come. The King had been conveyed back to London after the battle and, with all due respect, installed in the royal residence at the Tower. For it was the Queen, not His Grace, good King Harry, whom they opposed, Warwick took pains to assure one and all as London awaited the return of the Duke of York from Ireland.

York came in October and stunned Warwick, Salisbury and

his son Edward when he strode into Westminster Hall and laid his hand upon the vacant throne. During his months of Irish exile, he had at last concluded that he must either claim the crown in his own right or be doomed to fight an unending series of bloody and bitter skirmishes with the Queen and her cohorts.

Edmund concurred heartily in his father's decision. To him a puppet King was even more dangerous than a boy King, and Scriptures spoke clearly enough on that subject: 'Woe unto thee, O Land, when thy King is a child!' Harry of Lancaster was no more than a pale icon of authority, a shadow manipulated to give substance to the acts of sovereignty done in his name, first by Marguerite and now by Warwick.

The Duke of York, moreover, had a superior claim to the throne. Sixty years ago the royal succession of England had been torn asunder, brutally disrupted when Harry of Lancaster's grand-father deposed and murdered the man who held rightful title to the English throne. Six decades later the echoes of that violent upheaval were still reverberating. The murdered King was child-less; the crown should, under English law, have passed to the heirs of his uncle, Lionel of Clarence, the third son of Edward III. The man who'd seized the crown was the son of John of Gaunt, the fourth son of the same Edward III, but he showed no in-clination to adhere to the finer points of English inheritance law, and so began the Lancastrian dynasty.

Had Harry of Lancaster not been so unmitigated a disaster as a monarch, it was likely that few would have chosen to challenge the consequences of a coup legitimized, if not legalized, by the passage of sixty years. But Harry was weak and well-meaning and wed to Marguerite d'Anjou, and seven years ago he had, at last, gone quite mad. Suddenly people remembered the dire injustice done the heirs of the long-dead Lionel of Clarence, and Marguerite showed herself willing to go to any lengths to destroy the man who might one day lay claim to the Crown, the Duke of York, who traced his lineage from that same Lionel of Clarence.

Edmund saw this complex dynastic conflict as a very simple issue indeed. In his eyes, it was right and just and pure common-sense self-preservation that his father should act to claim the crown that was his by rights. He soon discovered, however, that right and just though it might be, it was a political blunder. While few disputed the validity of York's claim, all were unexpectedly reluctant to strip the crown from a man who'd been born a King's son, had been acknowledged as England's King since his tenth month of life.

It had taken Marguerite nearly ten years of unrelenting hostility to transform York from a loyal peer of the realm into the royal rival she'd always perceived him to be. But now he'd crossed the Rubicon as he crossed the Irish Sea and he was stubbornly and single-mindedly convinced that he had no choice but to claim the crown; was not to be dissuaded, even when faced with a conspicuous lack of enthusiasm for his claims by his Neville kindred and his own eldest son. It was not that they had any sentimental attachment to the man they referred to among themselves as 'Holy Harry'. But they'd read the mood of the Commons and the country more accurately than York. Mad though Harry might be, he was the man anointed by God to reign, and the fact that he was utterly incompetent to rule seemed suddenly to be of little consequence when it had become a question of dethroning him.

In the end, a compromise of sorts was reached, one that satisfied no one and outraged most. Under the Act of Accord passed on October 24, Richard Plantagenet, Duke of York, was formally recognized as the heir to the English throne but he was compelled to defer his claims during the course of Harry's lifetime. Only upon Harry's death would he ascend the throne as the third Richard to rule England since the Conquest.

As Harry was then thirty-nine years of age, a full ten years younger than the Duke of York, and enjoyed the robust health of one unburdened by the worldly concerns that so aged and encumbered other men, York and his supporters were, not surprisingly, less than thrilled by this Solomonlike solution. And as, under the Act of Accord, Marguerite's seven-year-old son was summarily disinherited, an action of expediency many saw to be confirmation of the suspicions so prevalent as to the boy's paternity, there was never any possibility that Marguerite and her adherents would give consent except at swordpoint. The only one professing satisfaction with the Accord was Harry himself who, in his beclouded eccentric way, clung tenaciously to his crown, yet strangely evidenced little concern that his son was thus rudely uprooted from the line of succession.

After the July battle that had delivered the King into Warwick's power, Marguerite had retreated into Wales and then into Yorkshire, long an enclave of Lancastrian loyalties. There she'd been reunited with the Duke of Somerset and Andrew Trollope, who'd spent several frustrating months attempting to dislodge Warwick and Edward from Calais.

These Lancastrian lords were now securely ensconced in the massive stronghold of Pontefract Castle, just eight miles from York's own Sandal Castle, and they'd recently been joined by two men who'd long nurtured a bitter hatred for the House of York, Lord Clifford and the Earl of Northumberland. Their fathers had died with Somerset's at the battle of St Albans, won by York and Warwick five years past, and they'd neither forgotten nor forgiven. Marguerite herself had ventured up into Scotland in hopes of forging an alliance with the Scots; the bait she dangled was a proposed marriage between her small son and the daughter of the Queen of Scotland.

And so Edmund found himself spending the Christmas season in a region he little liked, finding Yorkshire stark and bleak and unfriendly to the House of York, with the grim prospect ahead of a battle soon to come in the new year, a battle that would decide whether England should be Yorkist or Lancastrian, at a cost of lives too high to contemplate.

It had been one of the bleakest Christmas seasons within his memory. His father and uncle were too preoccupied with the coming confrontation with Lancaster to have either the time or the inclination for holiday cheer. Edmund, acutely sensitive to the disadvantages of being a seventeen-year-old novice to warfare midst seasoned soldiers, had forced himself to shrug off the lack of holiday festivities with what he fancied to be adult indifference. But secretly he'd grieved for the Christmas celebrations of years past, thought with longing of the seasonal merrymaking he was missing in London.

His cousin Warwick had remained in the capital to safeguard custody of the Lancastrian King, and Edmund knew Warwick would keep a princely Christmas at the Herber, his palatial London manor house. From Warwick Castle would come his Countess and Isabel and Anne, his young daughters. Edmund knew his own mother would be sure to join them there, too, with his little brothers, George and Dickon, and Meg, who, at fourteen, was the only one of Edmund's sisters still unmarried. There'd be eggnog and evergreen and the minstrel gallery above the great hall would be echoing from dawn till dusk with music and mirth.

Edmund sighed, staring out at the drifting snow. For ten endless days now they'd been sequestered at Sandal Castle with only one brief excursion into the little village of Wakefield, two miles to the north, to break the monotony. He sighed again, hearing Thomas call for still more bread. The traditional Christmas truce was drawing to an end; by the time it expired, Ned should have ridden up from the Welsh Marches with enough men to give the Yorkists unchallenged military supremacy. Edmund would be very glad to see his brother for any number of reasons, not the least of which was that he could talk to Ned as he could not talk to Thomas. He decided he'd write to Ned tonight. He felt better at that, swung off the window seat.

'I've some dice in my chamber, Tom. If I have them fetched, will you forsake your capon for a game of "hazard"?'

Thomas was predictably and pleasantly agreeable, and Edmund's spirits lifted. He turned, intending to send a servant for the dice, when the door was flung open and Sir Robert Apsall, the young knight who was both his friend and his tutor, entered the chamber. It was a large room, half the size of the great hall, was filled with bored young men, but it was to Edmund and Thomas that he hastened.

Stamping snow from his boots, he said without preamble, 'I've been sent to summon you both to the great hall.'

'What is it, Rob?' Edmund queried, suddenly tense and, as usual, anticipating disaster while Thomas shoved his chair back from the trestle table, came unhurriedly to his feet.

'Trouble, I fear. That foraging party we sent out at dawn is long overdue. They should've reported back hours ago. His Grace the Duke fears Lancaster may have broken the truce, that they may have been ambushed.'

'Why do we tarry, then?' Edmund demanded and had reached the door before the other two could respond.

'Wait, Edmund, get your cloak.' Thomas was reaching for the garment crumpled on the window seat, saw that Edmund was already out the door and, with a shrug, followed his young cousin from the chamber without it.

The Duke of York's suspicions soon proved to have been justified. Ambushed at Wakefield Bridge by a large Lancastrian force, the foraging party had died almost to a man. A few survivors fought their way free, however, and with the Lancastrians in close pursuit, raced for the refuge of Sandal Castle. Between the castle and the banks of the River Calder stretched a wide expanse of marshland, known locally as Wakefield Green. This was the only open ground between Sandal Castle and the village of Wakefield and the fleeing Yorkists knew their one chance of escape lay across this meadow, knew that to enter the thick wooded areas to their left and right would be to mire their mounts down in belly-deep snowdrifts, to flounder helplessly until caught and killed.

Across Wakefield Green they galloped, scant yards before their pursuers. Just when it seemed that capture was inevitable, arrows pierced the sky over their heads. The Lancastrians fell back under this aerial onslaught and the outer drawbridge was hastily lowered onto the stone platform that jutted out into the moat. As the drawbridge linked with the platform, the surviving soldiers raced across the moat, through the gatehouse, and on into the castle bailey. Behind them, the drawbridge was rapidly rising again and, even as they dismounted, they could hear the reassuring sounds of the iron-barred portcullis sliding into place across the gate-house entranceway.

Sleet had been falling intermittently all day, but the clouds over the castle were, for the moment, no longer spilling icy flakes into the sky. Visibility was such that the Yorkists on the castle battle-ments could see the enemy gathering in the meadow below. They seemed to be in a state of some confusion, even at a distance, as if uncertain whether to withdraw or to lay siege to the castle itself.

Within the great hall, a heated argument raged among the Yorkist lords. A sharp and irreconcilable split had developed, between those who favoured engaging the Lancastrians in combat and those who considered it folly to leave the safety of the castle. The spokesman for the latter position was a friend of long standing of the Duke of York, Sir David Hall. He argued with force and conviction that common sense dictated but one course of action, to hold their men within the castle walls and await the coming of His Grace's eldest son, Edward of March, with the men he was gathering along the Welsh Marches.

Others, however, scorned such restraint as if it reflected upon their courage and contended, with equal passion, that the only honourable action open to them was to accept the challenge thrown down by Lancaster.

For a brief time, the decision seemed to hang in the balance but two factors tipped it in favour of assault. The Duke of York himself was most sympathetic to this argument, and the Lancastrians on Wakefield Green had now swelled their ranks. With reinforcements, they were growing progressively bolder and had ventured within provocation distance of the castle, although prudently just beyond arrow range.

Edmund stood in the shadows, listening in silence. Unlike most of his family, he had dark eyes, a striking shade of blue-grey that faithfully mirrored his mercurial shifts of mood. They showed only grey now, moving from face to face in the most searching of appraisals. Even at seventeen, he was not, had never been, a romantic. Common sense was what swayed him, not abstract concepts like 'honour' and 'gallantry'. It seemed stupid to him to risk so much merely for the dubious satisfaction of avenging their foraging party. It was true the risk did not appear to be exces-sive; they commanded a clear numerical superiority over the Lancastrians. But it did appear to him to be unnecessary, to be a self-indulgent exercise in chivalry.

He wondered now if his father was motivated by a desire to seek vengeance for Ludlow. But then he found himself wondering if his own reluctance to engage the Lancastrians was really rooted in common sense. What if it were cowardice? He had, after all, never been in battle, could feel his stomach knotting up even now at the prospect. Ned had always insisted that fear was as common to men as fleas were to dogs and inns, but Edmund had his doubts. He felt sure his father and uncle Salisbury could not possibly know the lurch of a heart suddenly beating up in the vicinity of the throat, could not possibly share the icy sweat that traced a frozen path from armpit to knee. They were old, after all; his father was nigh on fifty, his uncle even older. Edmund could not imagine death holding the same fear for them as it did for him, any more than he could imagine that they were driven by the same sexual hungers.

No, he'd never been able to agree with Ned; Ned, who would speak quite candidly of having been scared pissless and yet seemed to thrive on danger, to deliberately seek out risks Edmund would much rather have bypassed. He'd grimly matched Ned, risk for risk, all during their boyhood, riding along the crumbling edge of cliffs and swimming their mounts through rain-swollen rivers spanned by perfectly adequate bridges. But he could never quite convince himself that Ned ever knew the fear he did, and when others praised him for his daring, he felt a secret shame, as if he'd somehow perpetrated a gigantic hoax upon the world, a hoax that would one day inevitably be unmasked.

Doubting his courage, he now doubted his judgement as well; could no longer be sure why he viewed the planned assault with such disfavour. Yet even had he been sure, it would have been impossible for him to have given any answer other than the one he gave when his father at last turned to him and said, 'Well, Edmund, what say you? Shall we show Lancaster the price to be paid for breaking the truce?'

'I think we've no choice, sir,' he said soberly.

Where the River Calder suddenly snaked into a horseshoe curve toward the west, the ground rose somewhat and afforded a clear view of Sandal Castle and the sloping expanse of Wakefield Green. A small group of horsemen now waited within the trees of this snow-covered hillock. As they watched, the drawbridge of the castle began to lower, slowly settled over the moat. The favoured banners of York, a Falcon within a Fetterlock and a White Rose, took the wind, flared to full length through the swirl of falling snow.

Henry Beaufort, Duke of Somerset, leaned forward intently, permitted himself a small tight smile.

'There they come,' he announced, needlessly, for his companions were watching the castle with equal absorption. It was unlikely York had a more bitter trinity of enemies than these three men: Somerset, Lord Clifford and Henry Percy, Earl of Northumberland. Only Marguerite herself nursed a greater grudge against the man now leading his army against the Lancastrians on Wakefield Green.

The Lancastrians were not standing their ground, were retreating before the Yorkist advance. It was clear to the three watching men that the Lancastrian forces seemed on the verge of catastrophe, on the verge of being trapped between the banks of the River Calder and the oncoming Yorkist army. Yet none of the three evidenced alarm; on the contrary, they watched with grim satisfaction as their own men gave way and the Yorkists bore down upon them in an exultant sweep toward easy victory.

The Lancastrians at last seemed to be making a stand. Men came together with shuddering impact. Steel gleamed, blood spurted over the snow. Horses reared, lost their balance on the ice and plunged backward, crushing their riders beneath them.

Beside Somerset, Lord Clifford forced his breath through clenched teeth. 'Now, God damn you, now!'

Almost as if his imprecation had been heard, from the woods on both sides of Wakefield Green came the hidden left and right wings of the Lancastrian army. Under the Earl of Wiltshire, the cavalry was sweeping around and behind the Yorkists, between them and the distant snow-shadowed walls of Sandal Castle. The foot soldiers of the right wing continued to surge from the woods until all of Wakefield Green seemed to have been engulfed in a sea of struggling humanity. Even to an untrained eye, it was evident that the trapped Yorkists were hopelessly outnumbered. To the practised eyes of Somerset and Clifford, the Yorkists numbered no more than five thousand; facing an army of fifteen thousand.

Clifford had been searching in vain for York's personal standard. Now he abandoned the effort and spurred his stallion down the hill into what was no longer a battle, what was now a slaughter. Somerset and Northumberland also urged their mounts forward, followed after him.

*

Edmund swung his sword as the man grabbed for the reins of his horse. The blade crashed against the upraised shield, sent the soldier reeling to his knees. But Edmund did not follow through on his advantage; his sword thrust had been an instinctive gesture of defence, perfected through years of practice in the tiltyard at Ludlow Castle. Edmund was in a state of shock; he'd just seen his cousin Thomas killed, dragged from his stallion into the bloody snow, held down as his armour was hacked through by a score of blades.

The snow was falling fast and thick now; through the slits of his visor, Edmund saw only a blur of wind-whipped whiteness. All around him, men were running, screaming, dying. He'd long since lost sight of his father and uncle. He now looked around desperately for Rob Apsall, saw only the soldiers of Lancaster and the dead of York.

Someone was reaching again for his reins; there was someone else at his stirrup. He dug his rowels deep into his stallion's side. The animal reared, throwing off the hands at its head, and then plunged forward. There was a startled cry; the stallion stumbled, hooves hitting flesh, and then Edmund had broken away from the encircling men, was free. He gave the horse its head, found himself caught up in the midst of fleeing soldiers floundering awkwardly through the snow, casting aside weapons and shields as they ran, panic-stricken prey for the pursuing Lancastrians.

His stallion shied suddenly to the right, veered off so abruptly that Edmund was nearly unseated. Only then did he see the river looming ahead, see the fate his stallion had spared him. Drowning men clutched with frozen fingers at the floating bodies of Yorkist comrades while, on the bank above them, soldiers of Lancaster probed with lance and pole axe as Edmund had once seen a man at a faire spearing fish in a barrel.

The sight sent Edmund even deeper into shock. He tugged at the reins, an irrational resolve compelling him back toward the battlefield to find his father. As he did, a Lancastrian soldier blocked his way, wielding a chained mace in a wide arc toward Edmund's head. Edmund lashed out with his sword and the man fell back, sought easier quarry.

His attention thus distracted, Edmund did not see the second soldier, not until the man thrust upward with a bloodied blade, gutting Edmund's horse. The stallion screamed, thrashed about wildly in the snow. Edmund had time only to kick his feet free of the stirrups, to fling himself sideways as the animal went down. He hit the ground hard; pain seared up his spine, exploded in his head in a burst of feverish colour. Opening his eyes, he saw queer white light, saw an armoured figure swimming above him. From another world, another lifetime, he remembered his sword, groped for it, found only snow.

'Edmund! Christ, Edmund, it's me!'

The voice was known to him. He blinked, fought his way back to reality, whispered, 'Rob?'

The knight nodded vigorously. 'Thank God Jesus! I feared you were dead!'

Rob was tugging at him. Somehow he willed his body to move but, when he put his weight on his left leg, it doubled up under him and only Rob's supporting arm kept him on his feet.

'My knee . . .' he gasped. 'Rob, I . . . I doubt I can walk. Go on, save yourself. . . .'

'Do not talk like a fool! Do you think it was by chance that I found you? I've been scouring the field for you. I swore oath to your lord father that I'd see to your safety.'

There was an Edmund who'd once have been mortally offended by such embarrassing parental solicitude. That was long ago, part of the lifetime lived before he'd ridden into the horror that was Wakefield Green.

The body of his stallion lay off to his left. Closer at hand was the body of a man, skull battered into a grisly pulp of bone and brain. Edmund looked down at the bloodied battle-axe Rob had dropped on the snow beside them, back up at the face of his friend, grey and haggard in the circle of upraised visor. He opened his mouth to thank Rob for saving his life, but the youthful tutor was in no mood to tarry, was saying urgently, 'Make haste, Edmund!'

'My father . . .'

'If he's alive, he's fled the field by now. If he's not, there's nothing you can do for him here,' Rob said bluntly and pushed Edmund toward his waiting horse.

'We'll have to share my mount. Lean on me, that's it. . . . Hold on, now. . . .'

As he spurred the stallion forward, sending two scavenging Lancastrians diving from his path, Edmund cried out, 'My sword! Rob, wait!'

The wind carried his cry away. Rob turned the horse toward the village of Wakefield.

Pain was savaging Edmund. With each step he took, it flamed through his leg, burned through to bone and marrow, convulsed his lungs in queasy, suffocating spasms. They'd lost Rob's horse; the double burden of two armoured men proved too much for the animal to bear. It had stumbled once too often, laming itself and pitching both youths into a snowbank too glazed with ice to cushion the impact of their fall. Rob had been shaken but Edmund's injured knee struck solid rock and he spiralled down into the dark. He came to consciousness moments later to find Rob desperately rubbing his face with snow.

Discarding what armour they could, they staggered on. Rob was panting, his heart beating in sickening starts and fits. Edmund's arm was leaden about his shoulders; he knew the boy was nearly out on his feet, had long since exhausted all reserves of endurance. Yet each time Edmund swayed, sagged against him, each time Rob felt a fearful certainty that the boy was blacking out again, Edmund somehow found the strength to cling to consciousness, to take another step into the snow that lay knee-deep before them.

Rob at last glimpsed the outlines of Wakefield Bridge. Half dragging and half carrying Edmund, he strained toward it. Beyond the bridge lay the village of Wakefield. Edmund could not go much farther. Each time Rob looked at the boy, he found new cause for concern; saw the blood matting Edmund's hair, saw the glazed sheen that clouded Edmund's eyes. Knowing the castle was ringed by Lancaster, Rob had instinctively headed for the village. Now he dared hope they might be able to reach the parish church at the end of Kirkgate, might be able to claim right of sanctuary. He was grasping at straws, knew it, could do nothing else. He stumbled forward, blinded by snow, and propelled Edmund onto the bridge.

They were in the middle of the bridge when Rob saw the Lancastrians come from the shadows, move without haste onto the far end of the bridge. Rob whirled about, so abruptly that Edmund staggered, grabbed at the stone railing for support. Soldiers now barred their retreat, watched with hard-eyed triumphant grins. Rob closed his eyes for a moment, whispered, 'God forgive me, Edmund. I've taken you into a trap.'

Dusk was still an hour away, but light was already fading from the sky. Edmund had slumped against the bridge railing, staring down into the dark waters below. He'd long since stripped off his gauntlets, and his fingers were now so numb that he spilled most of the snow he meant to bring up to his mouth. Sucking at the snow until his thirst was slaked, he rubbed the rest against his forehead, saw with incurious eyes that it came away red. He'd not realized until then that his head had been gashed open when he was thrown from his horse. He had never been so cold, never been so exhausted, and his mind was beginning to play terrifying tricks upon him. He could no longer trust his senses; voices seemed to come at him from all sides, uncommonly loud and strangely garbled, and then, as suddenly, would fade away to muffled oblivion, into the thinnest, weakest of echoes.

Becoming aware that yet another of his Lancastrian captors was bending over him, he looked up numbly, jerking back in involuntary protest as the man reached for his wrists. Ignoring Edmund's recoil, the soldier swiftly bound his hands tightly together at the wrists and then stepped back to inspect his handiwork.

'This one's no more than a lad,' he remarked idly, looking down at Edmund with a notable lack of antagonism.

'And wearing armour that'd please even the most high-handed of lords. . . . We'll do right well with that one. I warrant you he has kinfolk who'll pay, and pay dear, to see him safe home.'

The soldiers were now turning to watch approaching riders. Edmund listened with indifference to the argument that developed, heard a sharp command given to clear the bridge, the sullen response of the soldiers. Men were grudgingly giving way to let these new arrivals pass. They rode across the bridge in a spray of snow to the muttered curses of the men they'd splashed. Edmund was attempting awkwardly to bring his bound hands up to wipe snow from his eyes when a stallion was reined in directly before him. From a great distance, he heard a voice echoing, 'That boy there! Let me see him!'

Edmund raised his head. The face within the visor was swarthy, almost familiar, but recognition eluded him.

'I thought so . . . Rutland!'

At sound of his own name, Edmund suddenly knew the speaker. Andrew Trollope, York's onetime ally, the man who'd betrayed them at Ludlow. Trollope's treachery had been a bitter initiation into adulthood for Edmund; he'd rather liked Trollope. Now, however, he found himself strangely bereft of rage, even of resentment. He felt nothing, nothing at all.

Pandemonium reigned briefly on the bridge; Edmund's captors could scarcely credit their good luck. The Earl of Rutland! A prince of the blood! No ransom would be too high for such a prize; they suddenly saw themselves to be made men.

'Somerset will want to know of this,' one of Trollope's companions was saying, and the voice triggered a buried memory in Edmund's numbed brain; the man was Henry Percy, Earl of Northumberland. These men were his father's avowed enemies. What, then, was he doing here in their midst, bound and cold and sick and totally at their mercy? And then he heard Northumberland say, 'That leaves only Salisbury unaccounted for.'

Edmund tried to rise, found his knee no longer took commands from his brain. The words were out of his mouth before he even realized he meant to speak. 'Trollope! What of my father?'

Both men had turned in the saddle. 'Dead,' Trollope answered.

They rode on, Northumberland's voice drifting back across the bridge as he regaled his companions with details of their enemy's death. '. . . under those three willow trees east of the castle. Yes, that be the place . . . body stripped of armour . . . hailed as "King without a kingdom"! Or a head, if Clifford does have his way! Of course it's not common to behead the dead after battle, but tell that to Clifford!'

The voices faded from earshot. On the other side of the bridge, Rob Apsall tried to cross to Edmund, was roughly shoved back.

'Edmund. . . . Edmund, I'm sorry.'

Edmund said nothing. He'd turned his head away, toward the expanse of water beyond the bridge; Rob could see only a tangle of dark brown hair.

Other riders were now coming from the direction of the battle-field. Looting of the bodies had begun. There was a commotion at the end of the bridge. A soldier hadn't moved aside with enough alacrity to suit one of the horsemen, and he'd turned his stallion into the offending soldier. Pinioned against the bridge railing, the man yelled in fear and strained futilely against the animal's heaving flanks.

Rob's captors hastily cleared a path, lined up along the railing. Rob did likewise. He was suddenly rigid, felt as if the air had

55

been forcibly squeezed from his lungs. With foreboding, he watched the horseman riding across the bridge toward them. Lord Clifford of Skipton-Craven. Clifford, one of the guiding hands behind the ambush on Wakefield Green. Clifford, whose savage temper had long been a byword, even among his own men; who was known to harbour a remorseless hatred for the Duke of York.

Edmund gradually became conscious of the sudden silence. Turning his head, he saw a mounted knight staring down at him, staring with an unblinking intensity that reminded Edmund, inexplicably, of the eyes of his favourite falcon as it first sighted prey. He returned the stare, swallowed with difficulty; it was queer, but his tongue no longer felt as if it belonged in his mouth. Why he should so suddenly feel such purely physical fear, he didn't know; it was as if his body were reacting to an awareness that had yet to reach his brain.

'Who is he?' The knight had addressed the nearest soldier, without taking his eyes from Edmund. When an answer wasn't forthcoming, he snarled, 'Did you not hear me, you stupid son of a whore? His name, and now! I'd hear it spoken aloud.'

The man looked frightened, mumbled 'Rutland,' as Edmund found his voice, said unsteadily,

'I am Edmund Plantagenet, Earl of Rutland.'

Clifford had known. There was no surprise in his voice as he said, much too softly, 'York's cub.'

He swung from the saddle, let his reins drop to the bridge to anchor his mount. All eyes were upon him. Edmund suddenly recognized him as Clifford, recognized him with a surge of fear that was no longer instinctive, was well grounded in reality. He reached up for the railing, but his bonds were too restrictive, kept him from getting a handhold.

'Help me up.'

A soldier stretched out his hand and then recoiled, eyes cutting quickly to Clifford, who nodded, said, 'Get him on his feet.'

Fear made the man clumsy and Edmund was no help to him at all; his muscles cramped with cold, constricted with pain and fright. The soldier managed to help him rise but, in so doing, knocked them both into the railing. Pain radiated upward from Edmund's torn knee, racked his body with agony. The darkness was shot through with a blood-red haze, swirling colours of hot, hurtful brightness that faded then into blackness.

When he came back to the bridge, he was assailed by sound, rushing at him in waves and then retreating. The soldiers were shouting. Rob was shouting. He heard words but they meant nothing to him. He reeled back against the railing, and the soldier who'd been holding him upright hastily withdrew, so that he stood alone. There was something wrong with his eyesight; the men seemed to be wavering, out of focus. He saw contorted faces, twisted mouths, saw Clifford and then saw the dagger drawn, held in Clifford's hand.

'No,' he said, with the calm of utter disbelief. This wasn't real. This couldn't possibly be happening. Not to him. Prisoners were not put to death. Hadn't Tom said so? Tom, who'd been taken prisoner, too. Tom, who was dead. He began to tremble. This was madness, a delusion of his pain-clouded mind. Less than one hour ago, he'd been standing beside his father in the great hall of Sandal Castle. That was real, but not this. Not this.

'Jesus, my lord, his hands are bound!' a soldier was crying, as if this had somehow escaped Clifford and needed only be called to his notice. Held immobile by men who looked scarcely less horror-struck than he did, Rob jerked wildly at his ropes, shouted at Clifford, 'Think, man, think! He's a prince's son, will do you more good alive than dead!'

Clifford's eyes flicked briefly to Rob. 'He's York's son, and by God, I'll have vengeance!'

With that, he swung around upon the stunned boy. Rob wrenched free, flung himself forward. Someone grabbed for him, missed; other hands caught his leg, jerked with such force that he sprawled heavily upon the ground. Spitting out his own blood, he struggled to rise, and now no one hindered him. He was permitted to crawl the few feet that lay between him and Edmund.

Kneeling by the dying boy, he tried to cradle Edmund against him, tried to staunch Edmund's blood with his own hands, kept on trying long after he knew Edmund was dead.

His anguished sobbing was all that echoed upon the bridge. Clifford was being watched in absolute silence, watched with revulsion. He sensed it, saw it on the faces of the men; soldiers who, nonetheless, made certain distinctions between killings. In their eyes, this had been no battlefield death, had been cold-blooded murder. One, moreover, that had deprived them of a goodly ransom.

'York bore the blame for the death of my father,' Clifford said loudly. 'I had the right to kill the son!'

No one spoke. Rob held Edmund and wept. He looked up at last, to turn upon Clifford so burning a stare that one of the Lancastrian soldiers was moved to lay a restraining hand upon his shoulder.

'Easy, man,' he cautioned softly. 'It was a bloody piece of work, I grant you. But it's done, and you'll not be changing that by throwing your own life away.'

'Done?' Rob echoed, his voice raw, incredulous. 'Done, you say? Jesus God! After today, it is just beginning.'

As Marguerite d'Anjou rode through the Yorkshire countryside toward the city of York, snow-blanketed fields glistened with a crystalline brilliance that blinded the eye and the sky over her head was the deep vivid blue more common to July than January.

Her journey up into the rugged terrain of western Scotland had proven to be a fruitful one. At Lincluden Abbey just north of Dumfries, she'd met with the Scottish Queen-regent and a bargain had been struck, sealed with the intended marriage of their respective children. In return for Marguerite's promise to surrender to Scotland the border fortress of Berwick-upon-Tweed, Marguerite was to be provided with a Scottish army with which to march upon London. She was at Carlisle when word reached her of the slaughter at Sandal Castle and, as she neared the town of Ripon on her way south toward York, she was met by the Duke of Somerset and the Earl of Northumberland, and there given the full and gratifying details of her enemy's destruction.

Ahead rose the white limestone city walls of York. The massive twin-turreted towers and barbican of Micklegate Bar marked the chief gateway into York, guarding the Ermine Way, which led south, led to London. As Marguerite was approaching from the northwest, however, she thought to enter the city by way of Bootham Bar. Somewhat to her surprise, Somerset insisted they bypass Bootham, take the longer route through Micklegate.

She now saw why, saw that a crowd had gathered before the city gate, ready to welcome her into York. The Lord Mayor was clad in his best blue, as were the city aldermen, while the sheriffs wore red. There were certain conspicuous absences, for there were some in the city who'd come under the magnetic influence of the Earl of Warwick whose favourite residence lay some forty-five miles northwest of the city at Middleham. But, all in all, it was an impressive turnout, gave proof once again that the city of York held fast for the House of Lancaster.

The honour of greeting the Queen had been conceded to Lord Clifford who was not a man to be denied much. Marguerite smiled down at him as he knelt before her, smiled again as she gave him her hand to kiss. He was smiling, too, in admiring tribute both to her beauty and her Scots triumph.

'My lord Clifford, I shall not forget the service you've done me and my son. I shall never forget Sandal Castle.'

'Madame, your war is done.' He stepped back, and then gestured upward, toward the city gates high above their heads. 'Here I bring you your King's ransom.'

Marguerite followed the direction of his outflung arm, stared up at Micklegate Bar and saw for the first time that it was crowned with a grisly cluster of human heads set upon pikes.

'York?' she said at last. When Clifford nodded grimly, she looked upward in silence for some moments and then said, 'A pity you didn't face his head cityward, my lord Clifford. Then York could look out over York,' and all within earshot laughed.

'Maman?' The beautiful child who rode his pony at Marguerite's stirrup now drew closer, staring like the adults up at Micklegate Bar. Marguerite turned at once, gazed down fondly at her son and waved a graceful hand in the air.

'They are our enemies, bien-aimé, and now no more. For which we may thank the lords of Somerset and Clifford.'

'All our enemies?' the child asked, already losing interest in the unsightly trophies so far above his own eye level.

'All save one, Edouard,' Marguerite said softly. 'All save Warwick.'

'Edward of March, too, Madame,' Somerset reminded her. 'York's eldest son was not at Sandal Castle, was off at Ludlow.'

'A pity,' she said succinctly and then shrugged. 'But he's no threat in his own right, only eighteen or thereabouts as I recall. Warwick . . . Warwick is the enemy.' The dark eyes glittered. 'I'd give fully half of all I own to see his head, too, on Micklegate Bar.'

'Madame, I left space for two more heads.' Clifford gestured upward again. 'Between York and Rutland . . . for Warwick and York's other son.'

At mention of the name of Edmund of Rutland, a derisive smile twisted Somerset's mouth. 'I was surprised, my lord Clifford, that you chose to mount Rutland's head here in York. I thought, perhaps, you'd want to see it above the gateway of your own Skipton Castle . . . to remind you of a valiant deed well done.'

Clifford flushed a dark, dangerous shade of red and the nervous rustle of laughter that had swept the bystanders was abruptly stilled.

'What of Salisbury?' His voice was thick, roughened with the embittered outrage of a man who feels himself unjustly accused but can find few to champion his cause. 'When he was taken captive hours after the battle, you and Northumberland debated all night whether to accept the extravagant sum he offered up for his life and then sent him to the block the next morning after Northumberland decided he'd rather have his head than his gold. How is Salisbury's death any different from Rutland's, I do ask you?'

'If I need explain it to you, my lord, it is beyond your understanding,' Somerset said with a sneer, and Clifford's hand dropped to the hilt of his sword.

Marguerite spurred her mount forward, between them. 'My lords, that will do! I need you both; I'll not have you falling out amongst yourselves, not whilst Warwick still draws breath. As for this stupid squabbling over Rutland, what matters is that he is dead, not how he happened to die.'

Her son reached up at that, snatched at the reins of her horse, so abruptly that her startled mare shied, careered into Somerset's stallion.

'Maman, can we not go into the city now? I'm hungry.'

Marguerite had some difficulty in soothing her mount, but if she was irritated by her child's inopportune interruption, it showed neither in her face nor her voice.

'Mais oui, Edouard. We shall go at once.' She tilted her head up, took one final look at the heads upon Micklegate Bar.

'York sought a crown; I would see that he has it. Have one made of straw, my lord Clifford, and crown him with it.'

4

London

February 1461

Kneeling alone before the candlelit altar in the Lady Chapel of St Paul's Cathedral, Cecily Neville made the sign of the cross and then she dropped her face into her hands and wept.

Her attendants waited without in the choir to escort her safely back to Baynard's Castle, the Yorkist place just southwest of the cathedral, on the River Thames. She had come to St Paul's from the wharves, where she'd seen her two youngest sons safely aboard a ship bound for the realm of Burgundy. The boys had been bewildered, fresh from their bed at Baynard's Castle, but voiced no protests; in the seven weeks since Sandal Castle the fear had never ceased to haunt both children that one day the Lancastrians would come for them, too. Now, it had happened. They did not need to be told their mother feared for their lives, knew no lesser fear could have compelled her to send them from England.

Cecily had been driven to so desperate a measure by the news that the city council had voted that afternoon to open the city gates to the approaching army of Lancaster. But, in truth, she'd known for four days that it would come to this, to the little boys and a trusted squire sailing with the tide for refuge in Burgundy. She'd known there was no other course of action open to her ever since word reached London of Warwick's defeat at the battle of St Albans just twenty miles north of the city.

The city of London had been plunged into panic. All knew the tales of the brutal deeds done by Marguerite's marauding army of border mercenaries and Scots. She'd promised plunder in lieu of pay and once south of the River Trent, her men had taken her at her word, with a resulting savagery not known within living memory of the English. As her troops advanced southward, they left a trail of devastation fully thirty miles wide and the sacking of Ludlow paled before the fall of Grantham, Stamford, Peterborough, Huntingdon, Royston.

The list of towns taken seemed endless, and always farther south, closer still to London. To the terrified people in the Lancastrian army's path it seemed as if half of England was in flames and all had atrocity stories to share of villages burned, churches looted, women raped and men murdered, stories that were enhanced and embellished upon with each telling until Londoners were convinced they faced a fate not to be equalled in horror since Rome had been threatened by the Huns.

London had not thought Warwick would lose. He'd always commanded a large following in the city and he was, at thirty-two, a soldier of renown, friend to foreign Kings, a man surrounded by splendour even a monarch might envy. The city had sighed with relief as he marched north with an army of nine thousand and the puppet King, Harry of Lancaster.

And then, four days ago, Yorkish fugitives fled back into the city with a garbled tale of a battle fought at St Albans, that unlucky village that had been the site of a Yorkish–Lancastrian clash just five years ago. Warwick, it seemed, had been taken by surprise, had fallen victim to an extraordinary night march and flank attack by Marguerite's army.

From all accounts, Warwick himself had managed to escape, although his present whereabouts were unknown, were cause for the utmost conjecture. His brother, John Neville, had been taken, however, and, given the gory example set at Sandal Castle, few would lay odds on his long surviving the battle.

Harry of Lancaster was now a recovered pawn, had been found sitting under a tree near the battlefield. A chilling story began to be circulated, that the Yorkish knights who'd stayed to safe-guard the King upon his promise of a pardon were then taken to Marguerite and beheaded before the eyes of her seven-year-old son. None could say with certainty if this was true or not but the mood of the city was such that it was widely credited.

With Warwick's defeat, only Edward, Earl of March, and now titled Duke of York, was free to offer a last challenge to Lancaster. Edward was thought to be in Wales; in mid-February, reports had reached London of a battle fought to the west, between the Lancastrian Jasper Tudor, a half brother of King Harry, and the youthful Duke of York. Accounts were still sketchy, but it seemed the victory had gone to Edward. Nothing else was known, how-ever, and all else was then eclipsed by the devastating news of the Shrove Tuesday battle of St Albans.

Now the fear-stricken city awaited the coming of Marguerite d'Anjou and Cecily dared delay no longer. She'd awakened Richard and George, conveyed them to the wharves and now she wept with a desolation she'd not known since that January day when her nephew, the Earl of Warwick, had come to her with word of the battle fought at Sandal Castle, the battle that had taken from her a husband, a son, a brother and a nephew.

In those first stunned days she'd turned to Warwick for support, as her only adult male kinsman, and, for a time, tried to forget the opinion she'd long ago formed of her celebrated nephew, that he reminded her of the trick ebony wood boxes she'd seen sold at faires, glossy and eye-catching boxes painted in dazzling patterns of gold and vermilion, which, upon closer inspection, were found to be sealed shut, never meant to be opened at all.

As great as her need was, she could not long deceive herself. Her nephew gave off all the glittering brilliance of a sky full of stars, and as much warmth and heat. There was no true surprise then, the day she'd stood in the great hall of the Herber, his London manor, and heard him dictate a letter to the Vatican, a letter in praise of the services of a papal legate who'd since become a convert to the Yorkish cause, a letter in which he referred to the destruction of some of his kinsmen at Sandal Castle ten days past. Cecily had stared at him. '. . . the destruction of some of my kinsmen.' His father, brother, uncle and cousin! And then she'd called for her cloak, forgotten her gloves and returned through the snow to Baynard's Castle.

By a twist of irony, that was the day she heard from Edward. That afternoon, in the gathering dusk that foretold still more snow, the letters came. Dispatched by special courier from the city of Gloucester, from Edward. Cecily had, until then, permitted herself the balm of tears only in the privacy of her chamber, alone at night. But as she read her eldest son's letter, she broke down at last and wept without restraint, while Warwick's flustered wife fluttered about her like a moth maimed and yet unable to alight.

Edward's letter was the first flare of light in the dark that had descended upon Cecily with word of the killings at Sandal Castle. It was a beautiful letter, not one she'd have expected to receive from a boy of his years, and Cecily, who was almost totally without sentimentality, found herself performing the most unlikely of acts, folding the letter into a small square and tucking it into the bodice of her gown; keeping it there in the days to come, in a film of thin silk against her skin, counteracting the more familiar chill of her crucifix chain.

She was moved, but not surprised, to find Edward had thought to write to the children as well. Edmund had been the more responsible of the two boys, but it was Edward who'd always found the time for his little brothers and sisters. In that she'd never faulted him, knew how deep his family loyalties ran.

Now, in the anguished aftermath of Sandal Castle, she had only Edward. A boy not yet nineteen confronted with burdens few grown men could have shouldered.

Her fear was not only for Edward, though. She was frantic with fear for her younger sons, when once she'd been serenely sure that none would harm a child. Gone were the comforting certainties of constraints dictated by decency, of limits imposed by honour. She no longer believed what had, until Sandal Castle, been a tenet of absolute faith, that there were acts men would not do. The murder of a dazed and defenceless seventeen-year-old boy. The mutilation of the bodies of men who'd died honourably in battle. She knew now the nature of her enemy, knew she could count on neither rank nor innocence to spare her children, and she was frightened for them as she'd never before been frightened in her life.

She was frightened not only for their physical safety but for their emotional well-being, too. Cecily was haunted at night by the image of her children's stricken eyes. Even her irrepressible George seemed to have been rendered mute. As for her youngest, Richard was beyond reach, retreating into a silence that bore no relationship to childhood. In despair, Cecily found herself almost wishing that Richard could suffer the same terrifying nightmares that had begun to tear George's sleep asunder.

Several times a week now, she found herself sitting on the edge of George's bed, pressing a wet cloth to his sweat-drenched temples and listening to the halting voice speak of bloody snow and headless bodies and horrors beyond imagining. Perhaps, if Richard had been racked with such nightmares, too, she could then have given him the comfort, the solace she was able to give to George. But Richard guarded even his sleep, made no comments upon his brother's nightmares, voiced no complaints at having his own sleep so rudely disrupted night after night, and watched her in silence as she sat on the bed and stroked George's matted blond hair, watched with opaque blue-grey eyes that never failed to tear at her heart, Edmund's eyes.

Day after day, she watched her son withdraw further and further from the world around him, and she didn't know how to help him. She knew only too well the morbid horrors that can inhabit the mind of a child, knew Richard had always been a child with an uncommonly rich imagination. She bitterly regretted that she had not spent more time with her youngest son when he was still young enough for her to have won his confidence, bitterly regretted that he did not seem able to share his grief with her.

If only he were as easy to reach as George! George had always come to her, always ready to confide, to carry tales and, infrequently, to confess. Strange, how very different her sons were in that respect. Richard suffered in silence, Edward didn't appear to suffer at all, George told her more than she truly cared to know, and Edmund . . .

At that, she stumbled to her feet, fled to the prie-dieu in her bedchamber, to drop down on her knees and try to seek respite from pain in prayer. She spent hours praying for her husband and son in those numbing January days. It was all she knew to do. But, for the first time in her life, prayer availed her little.

It was not as if she were unfamiliar with death. She'd borne twelve children, seen five die swaddled in baby linens, stood dry-eyed and grieving as the tiny coffins were lowered into the ground by pitifully sparse tombstones that gave only the dates of their meagre lifespans and their names; names she repeated each day as she repeated her rosary; Henry, William, John, Thomas, Ursula.

No past grief, however, had prepared her for the loss she'd suffered at Sandal Castle. Nothing would ever be the same for her again, not from the moment she stood on the stairway at Baynard's Castle, staring down at her nephew and knowing, even before he spoke, that he brought death into her household. She sought refuge in hate and then in prayer and, at last, recognized that her grief was not going to heal, that it would be an open, gaping wound she'd take to her grave. Once she came to terms with that, she found she could once more take up the burdens of daily living, the numbing duties of motherhood. But she'd lost forever the ability to sympathize with the weaknesses of others, would never again find patience for those who broke under pressure.

If at night she allowed herself those bitter hours till dawn to grieve for her husband and her murdered son, her days now were given over to the living, to the children whose needs must come first. With the arrival of her eldest son's letter, she felt the first flicker of hope. Edward was, for the moment, beyond the reach of Lancaster. He was young, so very young. But, unlike her husband, Cecily had never been deceived by Edward's wildness into underestimating his ability; she knew he had a shrewd, discerning mind, a will of granite and a jaunty confidence in his own destiny that she never completely appreciated but recognized as the strength it was. And his conduct since Sandal Castle had given her only pride, fierce and intense and maternal.

He'd continued to gather troops to his banner with a coolness that the most experienced battle commander might have envied, and rumour had it that he'd already claimed his first victory. Most heartening of all for Cecily, he had somehow raised the money to ransom Rob Apsall, the young knight who'd been with Edmund on Wakefield Bridge. She could not stifle her dismay that she'd not thought to do this herself; she saw her failure as an inexcusable dereliction of duty, a lapse not much mitigated in her own mind by the magnitude of her loss. But Edward hadn't been as remiss as she; he'd recognized their obligation to one who'd loyally served the House of York, served Edmund. Cecily saw more than generosity in her son's actions, saw it as the responsible and honourable gesture of a man grown. She so desperately needed him to prove that now. But, for her, the most meaningful action he took in the wake of the slaughter at Sandal Castle was to write to his little brothers and younger sister. To Cecily the letters came as a godsend, a lifeline thrown to her troubled children at a time when her own efforts seemed to fall short. She understood, comprehended that only a man could stand between them and the unspeakable horrors now bound up for them in the name Lancaster, and Edward seemed instinctively to know what they needed to hear.

Each of her children had responded in characteristic fashion to these letters addressed to their personal pain, their private fears. George read his letter aloud to all who wanted to hear it and to those who didn't, as well, explaining proudly that this, the first letter he'd ever received, was written by his brother, the Earl of March, who was now Duke of York, too. Margaret had come into Cecily's bedchamber that evening to share selected passages with her mother, tears freely streaking her face as she read aloud in a clear unfaltering voice. But what Edward had written to Richard, Cecily was never to know.

The little boy had retreated with it up into the stable loft, to emerge hours later with swollen eyes and set pale face. He made no mention of the letter and Cecily, acting intuitively, forbore to question him about it. But the next day, while attending a Requiem Mass for the dead of Sandal Castle at St Paul's Cathedral, Richard had become violently ill. Cecily had not known of her son's distress until the completion of the Mass when she suddenly realized that both her sons had disappeared and Warwick's wife leaned across her own litle girls to murmur that Richard and George had slipped out midway through the Mass. That was so flagrant an offence that Cecily felt a throb of alarm, sure that only dire necessity could have occasioned such a breach of conduct. She'd hastened down the length of the nave and, on impulse, crossed through the small doorway in the south aisle that led out into the cloisters.

She'd found them there on the lower walk of the cloisters, almost directly across from the towering octagonal Chapter House. Richard was as white as the snow that lay just beyond in the inner garth of the cloisters, slumped against an arched pillar as George searched in vain for a handkerchief inside his doublet. Richard was too sick and George too intent to notice her approach; as she drew near, she heard George give an exasperated cry.

'Jesú, Dickon, if you're going to puke, don't do it in here! Lean over, out into the garth!' And with surprising skill, George, who

could be both the bane of Richard's existence and the most steadfast of allies, supported the younger boy until the spasm passed.
By then Cecily had reached them.

Richard suddenly realized that the soft cushion for his head was
his mother's lap and he started to sit up, unable to believe his elegant, immaculate mother was actually sitting upon the ground of
the walkway, heedless of her velvet skirts bordered in sable.

'Lie still,' she said firmly, and he was too weak to resist, lay
back gratefully.

'I'm sorry I was sick, ma mère.'

'I do feel sick, too, Richard, when I think of what befell your
father and brother.' She saw his face twitch, said softly, 'That was
it, was it not? During the Mass, you were ... remembering.'

'Yes,' he whispered. 'I cannot stop thinking about ... about
what happened at Sandal Castle. I think about it all the time,
ma mère. I do not want to, but I cannot help myself.'

'Are you afraid, Richard?' she asked carefully, scarcely daring
to believe she'd broken through his barriers at last.

'Yes ...'

'You feared it might happen, too, to you and George?'

He nodded. 'Yes. And to Ned. ... To Ned, most of all.' His
face was hot against her fingers; she could see tears escape the
tangled wet lashes, streak unevenly across his cheek.

'But it will not now,' he added, and opened those heartbreaking
dark eyes to regard her confidently.

'Ned promised me,' he said.

Now Cecily's youngest were gone to Burgundy. It was very late
when Cecily at last walked from the Lady Chapel at St Paul's,
was taken by litter the short distance to Baynard's Castle through
city streets bereft of all signs of life. Already London resembled
a city under siege.

On her way to her bedchamber she found herself faltering,
stood for a time alone on the narrow darkened stairway that led

to the upper chambers. And then she turned right rather than left, passed through the door-way that led to the small bedchamber shared by her sons.

The door was ajar; a candle burned, low and sputtering, on the coffer chest by the bed. The bed-curtains were open, the blankets rumpled and, as she leaned over, it seemed as if she could still feel the body warmth of the boys in the indented hollows where they'd lain but hours before. Almost without volition, she sank down on the edge of the bed, staring into the dark.

The sound came from the garde-robe in the far corner of the room. She raised her head abruptly, suddenly alert. It came, again. She didn't pause to reflect, snatched up the candle and swept aside the heavy curtain that blocked the garde-robe doorway.

Far above the garde-robe seat a narrow window glinted, an arrow slit enlarged during the last century, acting as a filter now for the faintest glimmer of moonlight. The walls were hung with russet and amber tapestries to combat the pervasive chill of stone and mortar; it seemed to her that in the darkest corner the material was billowing out from the wall, bunching queerly near the floor. As she watched, it rippled again, as no draught could have done. She reached for the tapestry, jerked it back.

'Anne!'

She wasn't sure what she'd expected to find but not this little face upturned to hers, a delicate little heart as pale and exquisitely drawn as white Spanish lace, the most fragile of frames for the enormous dark smudges that seemed too grave and too fearful, by far, for the eyes of a child still more than three months from her fifth birthday.

'Anne,' she repeated, more gently, and reached down, drew the child from her hiding place. She seemed lighter than air to Cecily, no more substantial than the cobwebs catching the candlelight above their heads.

'Do not scold me,' the little girl whispered, and buried her face in Cecily's neck. 'Please, Aunt Cecily . . . please.'

71

The frail little arms clung with surprising tenacity, and after a moment, Cecily no longer tried to disengage her hold, sat down instead on the bed with Anne on her lap.

Cecily was very fond of Anne, the younger of Warwick's two daughters and so loving, so sweet-tempered a child that there was not an adult heart within the household of York that had long withstood Anne's artless siege. Even Edmund, who'd not been particularly comfortable with children, nonetheless found time to show Anne how to cast shadows on the wall, to help her search for her strayed pets. The memory sent scalding tears to burn Cecily's eyes. Resolutely, she repressed both and rocked the silky head against her breast, wondering what could have driven Anne from her bed and into the silent darkened chambers of the castle at such an hour, for Anne was, she knew, a rather timid child, the least likely candidate for such a rash escapade.

'Whatever were you doing here, Anne, and at such an hour?'

'I was scared. . . .'

Cecily, who had so little patience with adults, could, when the need arose, have all the patience imaginable with very young children, and now she waited without prompting for Anne to speak.

'Bella . . . my sister,' Anne added conscientiously, as if her great-aunt might otherwise confuse the nine-year-old Isabel Neville with any other like-named children possibly residing in Baynard's Castle, and Cecily hid a smile, said encouragingly, 'What of Bella, Anne?'

'She told me . . . she told me Papa was dead. The Queen had taken him . . . had taken him and cut off his head like she did with our grandpapa and Cousin Edmund and Uncle Tom! She told me . . .'

'Your father is not dead, Anne,' Cecily said swiftly, with so much conviction that Anne gulped, swallowed a sob, and stared up at her with mouth open and improbably long wet lashes fringed with tears.

'Truly?'

'Truly. We do not know where your father is right just now but we've no reason to think him dead. Your father, child, is a man who knows how to see to his own welfare. Moreover, had harm come to him, we'd have heard by now. Here . . . take my handkerchief and tell me how you came to be here, in my sons' bedchamber.'

'I wanted to see mama, to ask if Bella spoke true. But her ladies said she was in bed, that her head hurt, and said, crossly, that I was to go back to bed. But I know why her head hurts, Aunt Cecily. She was weeping. All day, she was weeping! Why was she weeping . . . 'cept that papa was dead, like Bella said. . . .'

Anne's voice, muffled against Cecily's breast, now grew more certain. 'So I came to wake up Dickon. But he was gone, Aunt Cecily, he and George were gone! I waited for him to come back and then I heard you and got scared and hid in the garde-robe and, please, Aunt Cecily, do not scold me but why is Dickon not here and why did Bella say papa was dead?'

'Bella is fearful, Anne, and when people are afraid, they often confuse what they dread with what they know to be true. As for your cousins . . . Richard and George have had to go away from here for a while. They did not know they were leaving, had no chance to say farewell to you and Bella. It was sudden, you see. . . .'

'Away? Away where?'

'Far away, Anne. Very far. . . .' She sighed, shaping a simple explanation to enable Anne to understand where Burgundy was, when the little girl made a soft choking sound and then wailed,

'Dead! He's dead, isn't he? Dead like grandpapa!'

Cecily stared at her, appalled. 'Oh, Anne, my dearest child, no! No, Anne, no.'

Anne had begun to squirm; Cecily had unconsciously tightened her embrace. Now she brushed her lips to the child's forehead, said with quiet and compelling force, 'Anne, listen to me. People do go away without dying. You must believe that, dearest.

Your cousin Richard is not dead. He will come back . . . as will your father. I promise you.'

With that, she pulled the coverlets back. 'Would you like to sleep here in Richard's room tonight?' And was both touched and faintly amused when Anne at once brightened at the prospect.

The little girl had proven, that autumn, to be a source of considerable embarrassment to Cecily's youngest son; easily the most sensitive of her children, he was genuinely reluctant to cause hurt to the adoring little cousin who was, from the superior vantage point of his eight years, a mere baby. Cecily suspected, moreover, that Richard was secretly flattered by Anne's unabashed admiration and she'd noticed that he was willing enough to play with Anne if there were no boys available as playmates or if George was elsewhere. But he clearly had no liking for the amused glances of the adults as Anne trailed him in loving pursuit and still less did he care for the merciless teasing he was subjected to by George, who'd infuriated and discomfited Richard only that week by announcing loudly at supper that he meant to name his pet turtledoves Dickon and Anne.

While memories could comfort, they could also rend without pity. This was not the night to dwell upon past remembrances; Cecily knew herself to be too vulnerable. She reached down to pull the blankets over Anne and stopped in midmovement, staring down at a threadbare woollen blanket that looked strangely out of place among the other bedclothes piled upon the bed.

The blanket, once a vivid sun-yellow and now a drab mustard colour, belonged to Richard. In one of his few overt concessions to childhood frailties, Richard insisted upon having that particular blanket on his bed, would not go to sleep without it. How and why it had come to mean so much to him, Cecily did not know, somehow had never found the time to ask, merely trying to see that it was laundered occasionally. Even George, who was too quick, for Cecily's liking, to jeer at the weaknesses of others, no longer baited his brother about that blanket, having once provoked Richard into a wild and uncharacteristic rage when he theatened to cut it up into mock battle standards for his endless games of warfare. Cecily plucked now at the faded gold wool with nerveless fingers, thinking of her youngest alone out in the dark upon the treacherous English Channel without the talisman he seemed so desperately to need.

She was so immobile that Anne became uneasy, slipped a small hand into the sleeve of Cecily's gown in a gesture of uncertain consolation. Cecily smiled at her great-niece and tucked the blanket securely around her, saying steadily, 'There. . . . This is Richard's blanket. He left it for you. Sleep now, Anne.'

With the frayed familiar wool drawn up to her chin Anne was content and, all at once, very sleepy. 'Can I keep it till Dickon comes home?'

'Yes, dearest . . . till he comes home.' As if she were sure that one day her sons would, indeed, be able to come home.

Cecily softly closed the door of Anne's bedchamber, stood irresolute for the space of several deep breaths. Within, Anne's elder sister Isabel slept, curled up in a tangle of bedclothes at the foot of the bed. Cecily's flaring candle had tracked the trail of tears on the girl's face; shone upon the swollen puffy eyelids, upon the thumb, long since freed from its nightly bondage to Isabel's mouth and now suddenly pressed back into its former servitude. Cecily had backed out stealthily, now struggled to control her rage, rage directed at Nan Neville, her niece.

Warwick's wife had never been a favourite of hers. When word reached London of Warwick's rout at St Albans, she'd done her best to console his stricken wife, insisted that Nan and her daughters leave the Herber for Baynard's Castle, but her sympathies were strained through a finely veiled contempt. Nan had no reason to think her husband dead. Yet, for three days now, she'd scarcely ventured from her bed and, when Cecily had ushered her frightened little girls into the chamber, she'd outraged Cecily by drawing her daughers tearfully to her and sobbing so incoherently that both Anne and Isabel at once became hysterical.

Now Cecily thought of Nan sequestered in her bedchamber while Isabel cried herself to sleep and Anne was compelled to seek comfort from her eight-year-old cousin, and she felt a terrible anger. Nan was very much in love with Warwick, she knew that. But she herself had been in love with Richard Plantagenet, the man who'd been her playmate in childhood, then friend, lover, companion and husband during an enduring and eventful marriage, and she had not permitted his children to see her weep for him.

The urge was overwhelming in its intensity to confront her niece in her tear-sodden bed, to accuse her of an unforgivable indifference to the daughters who needed her more than Richard Neville, Earl of Warwick, ever would, to vent upon Nan all of the anguish and rage and frustration of the past seven weeks. She was not a woman, however, to give in to urges. She'd speak to Nan, but tomorrow . . . tomorrow, when the anger had frozen into ice.

She found her daughter Margaret in the solar, wrapped in a fur cover before the fire, blonde head bent over a book. Cecily stood unobserved in the doorway, watching the girl. Margaret was nearly fifteen. Too pretty, by far. It was a thought alien to the world as Cecily had known it before Sandal Castle, a fear she'd never have expected to feel for a daughter of hers.

'Ma mère?' Margaret had looked up at last. 'Did you see George and Dickon safe on board?'

Cecily nodded. Her daughter's eyes were suspiciously circled, her eyelids reddened; it was Margaret who had acted as a surrogate mother to her younger brothers during Cecily's frequent absences.

'Were you weeping, Meg?' she asked softly, and Margaret gave her a startled look, for her mother alone of all the family preferred to address her children by their Christian names. She dropped the book by the hearth, went to Cecily. They were, by tempera-ment and training, a restrained and undemonstrative family; only Margaret and her brother Edward were naturally given to phys-ical expressions of affection. Now she hesitated and then slipped her arm around her mother in a tentative embrace.

'Ma mère, what is to happen to us?'

Cecily was too exhausted to lie, too heartsick to speak the truth as she feared it to be.

'I do not know,' she said and sat down wearily upon the closest seat, an uncomfortable coffer-chest. 'I believe that was the hardest thing I've ever done in my life . . . putting those children on that ship. So young they looked . . . so fearful . . . and trying so hard to hide it. . . .'

She'd startled herself as much as she had Margaret. She'd never been one to share griefs. Least of all, to confide in her own children . . . in a fearful fourteen-year-old girl who wanted so desperately to offer comfort and didn't know how. A measure of the scorn she'd felt for Nan Neville she now spared for herself.

'I'm tired, child. Bone-tired. You must not pay any mind to what I say tonight. It is very late; we'd best be up to bed.'

Margaret was kneeling by the coffer-seat; she was still inclined to fling herself about with coltlike abandon, to sprawl in poses Cecily thought quite unbecoming for her age.

'Ma mère . . . is it wrong to pray to God to punish the Frenchwoman?'

Margaret was very much in earnest and Cecily even more tired than she'd realized, for she almost laughed, caught herself in time.

'Wrong, no . . . presumptuous, mayhap.'

'Oh, ma mère, I am serious!' Margaret's face had hardened, the soft mouth suddenly rigid, and, in the grey eyes that now stared at Cecily, she glimpsed the woman her daughter would one day become; and then the mirror blurred, blurred in the tears that were swelling in the girl's eyes, spilling down her face.

'Ma mère, I do hate her so much,' she whispered. 'When I think of father and Edmund—'

'Do not!' Cecily said sharply. She fought a brief bitter battle of control, won, and repeated, 'Do not, Meg.'

In the silence that followed, there came a familiar reassuring sound. The Gabriel Bell of St Paul's was chiming its nightly salute to the Blessed Mother of God. The echoes had not yet been borne away upon the wind from the river when word came to them in the solar that a boat had just tied up at the dock that gave river entry to the castle. A man with an urgent message for the Duchess of York. A message from her son.

Cecily stared at the man kneeling before her. She prided herself upon her memory; nor did it fail her now. William Hastings of Leicestershire. Eldest son of Sir Leonard Hastings, a trusted friend of her husband. At Ludlow with them last year. Pardoned by Lancaster soon after, only to then offer his services to Edward at Gloucester. After Sandal Castle, when the Yorkist cause could hold little allure for men of ambition. Cecily was not easily impressed, yet she found herself warming toward this man who'd been willing to stand by her son when Edward most needed such support. She was somewhat surprised, too, by his presence here. It was almost unprecedented for a man of his rank to act in the capacity of courier; Edward's message must be urgent.

'We heard there'd been a battle fought south of Ludlow, that my son did prevail. But no other word has reached us till now. Did the reports speak true?'

'Better than true, Madame. Your son did far more than prevail. He had an overwhelming victory.' He grinned. 'I can scarcely credit the fact that he's still some two months shy of his nine-teen bithday, for I've seen no better battle commander, Madame. It may be that he has no equal on the field in all England.'

Cecily heard Margaret give a soft cry, midway between a laugh and a sob. 'Tell us,' she said and they listened in rapt silence as he recounted for them the battle fought on Candlemas, at

Mortimer's Cross, four miles to the south of Wigmore, where Edward once thought to find sanctuary for his mother and little brothers.

'His intent was to march east, to join with my lord of Warwick. Word did reach us, however, that Jasper Tudor, the King's Welsh half brother, and the Earl of Wiltshire were gathering a large force in Wales. Your son thought it best to swing back toward Wales, to check their advance. We took them by surprise, Madame. They'd not expected His Grace of York to take the offensive or to move with such speed. We laid our lines not far from Ludlow and awaited their coming and, when the battle was done, the field was ours.' He paused and then added, with an enigmatic smile, 'It was a victory such as my lord of Warwick could not gain at St Albans.'

'You know, then, such of St Albans! Has Edward had word from Warwick?'

'Yes, Madame. He sent a courier to your son with word of his less than spectacular showing at St Albans.' The malice now was unmistakable. As if in afterthought, he said, 'We do expect to meet with the Earl in the Cotswolds within a day's time.'

'Should we not tell Cousin Nan, ma mère?' Margaret interjected breathlessly, and Cecily shook her head.

'Later,' she said coolly, kept her eyes on Hastings.

He smiled again, said, 'Your son bade me tell you to take heart, that he has ten thousand men at his command and is now less than a week's march from London. He said to tell you, Madame, that by Thursday next he should be at the city gates.'

'Deo gratias,' Cecily murmured. She closed her eyes; her lips moved. Margaret laughed, seemed on the verge of flinging herself into Hastings's arms and then, thinking better of it, threw her arms around her mother instead.

'Ned has always been lucky, ma mère! We should have remembered that!'

Hastings laughed, too, and shook his head. 'Men do make their luck, Lady Margaret, and never have I seen that better proven than at Mortimer's Cross. For ere the battle, there appeared a most fearsome and strange sight in the sky.' He paused. 'Three suns* did we see over us, shining full clear.'

Margaret gasped and crossed herself. Cecily's eyes widened perceptibly; she, too, crossed herself and then said slowly, 'I did hear of such a happening once before, in my girlhood at Raby Castle. It was said men wept in the streets, sure it did foretell the end of the world. Were not Edward's men fearful?'

Hastings nodded. 'In truth! I do not know what would have happened, for many were ready to flee the field, had not your son the wit to shout out that it was a sign of Divine Providence, that the three suns did betoken the Holy Trinity and meant the victory would go to York.'

Cecily caught her breath and then she laughed for the first time in many weeks, as she'd thought she'd never be able to laugh again.

'How like Edward that is!' She smiled at Hastings, and he was struck by the sudden beauty that illuminated her face. 'He never thinks so fast as when he has the most to lose!'

'You'd not credit the stories he could spin on the spur of the moment to explain away sins our father found out!' Margaret confided with the giddiness of hope come so sudden upon the heels of utter despair, and Cecily passed over, with a smile, the indiscretion that would normally have earned her daughter an astringent rebuke.

'My daughter does exaggerate in that. But Edward ever has had a way with words. His brother Edmund did swear he must think with his tongue, so persuasively could he . . .'

Suddenly hearing her own words, she stopped, stricken in midsentence. It was the first time in seven weeks that Edmund's name had slipped so naturally and easily into her speech; the first

---

* Phenomenon known as a parhelion, generally caused by the formation of ice crystals in the upper air.

80

step in the healing process, but one that now seared to the heart with unbearable pain. She turned away abruptly, blindly moved to the hearth.

'What of Jasper Tudor?' Margaret fumbled for words, any words, to cast into the suffocating silence that filled the room. 'Was he taken?'

'I regret not. Both he and Wiltshire were able to flee the field. We did, however, take a fair number of prisoners, including Tudor's father, Owen Tudor, the Welshman who wed secretly with King Harry's mother after she'd been widowed. Not that we held him for long.' A grim smile shadowed his mouth. He said with remembered satisfaction, 'We took him to Hereford and there His Grace of York ordered him beheaded in the marketplace, with nine others he judged to be deserving of death. . . .'

His voice dropped suddenly, the last word from his mouth tumbling down a verbal cliff into uncertain oblivion; a perceptive man, he'd registered the abrupt change in atmosphere, saw they both were staring at him.

'Edward did that?' Cecily said wonderingly.

Hastings nodded. 'Yes, Madame, he did,' he said, in a voice that was now devoid of all expression, was carefully neutral.

'I'm glad,' Margaret said suddenly. The grey eyes so like Cecily's own were defiant, bright with tears. 'I do not fault Ned . . . not at all! He had the right, ma mère. He had the right!'

'You need not defend your brother to me, child,' Cecily said at last, said with an effort. 'I was taken aback, I admit. But I should not have been. I should have expected it.'

She was staring beyond them, into the fire. 'You see,' she said, and her voice was little more than a whisper, low and throbbing, and yet very distinct, 'he did love his brother very much.'

When word spread throughout London that Edward of York was less than fifty miles distant and coming to the aid of the beleaguered city, the citizens overrode their fearful council, rioted in the streets and burned the food carts being loaded to send to the Queen's camp at Barnet, some ten miles north of the city. It was now known what Marguerite's troops had done to the village at St Albans in the wake of Warwick's defeat and the Lord Mayor of London yielded to the turbulent crowds urging defiance, sent word to Marguerite that the city gates would be barred to her.

By now, even Marguerite was becoming alarmed by the excesses of her army, most of whom seemed more intent upon plunder than upon confrontation with the approaching army of York. After consultation with her commanders, Marguerite chose to withdraw her forces northward. She had no way of knowing how long London might hold out under siege and Edward of York was suddenly a military force to be reckoned with; his army was said to be swelling daily and word of his victory at Mortimer's Cross now seemed to be on every tongue. Marguerite elected to make a strategic retreat back into Yorkshire, to celebrate two months of triumph, to regroup and reassert discipline over an army more than twice the number under Edward's command.

As Marguerite's army pulled back, once more sacking those helpless villages and towns that lay along the road north, the reprieved city of London went quite wild with joy and relief. People swarmed into the streets again, this time to give fervent thanks to God and York, to embrace strangers as sudden friends, to spill rivers of wine into the gutters, and to overflow both alehouses and churches.

On Thursday, February 26th, the city gates swung open wide to admit the army led by Richard Neville, Earl of Warwick, and Edward Plantagenet, Duke of York and Earl of March, and the men rode into a welcome such as had not been seen in London within memory of any Londoner then living.

Cecily Neville stood with her daughter, Margaret, and the family of the Earl of Warwick by the north door of St Paul's Cathedral, surrounded by retainers clad in the blue and murrey of York. The churchyard was so crowded with people that she felt as if she were looking out upon an unending sea of faces. The sight made her slightly dizzy; never had she seen so many gathered in one place and she marvelled that, midst the shoving and pushing, none had yet been trampled underfoot. The White Rose of York was everywhere, adorning hats and the flowing hair of little girls, pinned to cloaks and jerkins, as if every hand in London had been turned to fashioning paper flowers to defy the powdering of snow that still clung to the ground. Many, she saw, also flaunted streaming sun emblems to denote her son's triumph under the triple suns at Mortimer's Cross.

Her nephew, George Neville, Bishop of Exeter, turned toward her, smiled; she saw his lips move, could not hear his words. It seemed as if every church bell in London were pealing. Seeing the smoke spiralling into the sky from a dozen different directions, knowing that meant the jubilant Londoners were burning bonfires in the streets as if this were the June Feast Day of St John the Baptist, Cecily breathed a brief prayer that God might mercifully spare the city from fire this noon, for there was no way the fire bells could ever be heard or heeded.

The volume of noise was increasing; she'd not have thought it possible. The shouts were audible now, shouts of 'York' and 'Warwick'. But, overriding all, one name again and again, a hoarse chant that sent shivers of emotion up Cecily's spine . . . Edward! Edward! Until the entire city echoed with the sound, with the name of her son.

Cecily swallowed, saw her daughter was brushing the back of her hand against her cheek. Impulsively, she reached out, squeezed the girl's hand, and Margaret turned a radiant face toward her, leaned up to shout against Cecily's ear, 'They've passed through Newgate by now! Soon, ma mère, soon!'

Incredibly, the noise of the crowd intensified. A wave of cheering broke over the churchyard, sweeping in from the street in a roar so deafening that Cecily knew it could have but one meaning, that Edward and Warwick had reached the cathedral grounds. There was a sudden swirl of movement across the yard; people were grudgingly giving way, retreating in the direction of Paul's Cross. Slowly a path was being cleared before Little Gate, the entrance onto Cheapside; riders were coming through. Soldiers who laughed and bantered with the crowd yielding so reluctantly before them, their faces flushed with this extraordinary acclaim, the manes of their skittish mounts incongruously bedecked with bright hair ribbons given in tribute by giggling girls. People were reaching up to share swallows from flasks of ale, to make extravagant offers of meals and lodgings as if they were welcoming blood kin home from the wars, and now, much to the delight of the crowd, one young soldier leaned recklessly from the saddle, claimed a kiss from a girl with Yorkist paper roses festooned in masses of bright blonde hair.

Cecily couldn't believe it, had never seen anything like this, ever. She watched in disbelief and then Margaret cried out, gestured eagerly, and she saw the Earl of Warwick.

He was at once engulfed by well-wishers. Attempting to manoeuvre his mount through the crush, laughing, shrugging off the hands that reached upward to him, keeping a tight rein under the sudden flurry of scarves waving the Neville red. Cecily swiftly bent down, lifted Anne up so that the child could see. As she did, another outburst of cheering rocked the chuchyard, eclipsing all that had gone before, and she knew even as she straightened up that her son had ridden through the gateway.

He was astride a magnificent white stallion with a silvery tail that trailed almost to the ground and he seemed to be enveloped in light, with the sun directly over his head gilding his armour and tawny hair.

'Oh, ma mère!' Margaret gasped, in a voice that was strangely uncertain, unexpectedly awed. 'He does look like a king!'

'Yes, he does,' Cecily said softly, forgetting that she had to shout to make herself heard. 'He does, indeed.'

He held his helmet in the crook of his arm and, as she watched, he reached into it and scattered a handful of coins into the crowd. In the scramble that ensued, a young girl darted forward and thrust an object upward. From the corner of his eye, Edward saw and reached down. For an instant their fingers touched and then he held her gift aloft, a scarf of bright bold colours upon which had been stitched, with incredible patience and perseverance, a blazing sun on a field of white roses. Edward now brandished the scarf for all to see and, then, to the wild cheering of the crowd, he knotted it about his throat so that it caught the breeze, fluttered out jauntily behind him.

'That was nicely done,' a voice murmured at Cecily's ear and she gave a start; so intent had she been upon Edward's approach that she'd not realized Warwick now stood at her side. Greetings exchanged, he nodded again toward her son who was making little headway through the crowd.

'A pretty gesture, that,' he remarked complacently. 'The sort of thing sure to win favour with the people.' There was in his voice the satisaction of a master for an apt pupil and Cecily turned thoughtful eyes upon him, said nothing.

Unable to extricate his mount from the press of bodies that walled him in on all sides, Edward now rose in his saddle, raised his voice in a command for silence that, rather remarkably, was obeyed.

'Good people, I'm most eager to greet my lady mother and sister! If you'll but clear the way for me?' he queried with a grin, and suddenly, magically, a path had opened before him.

Cecily came forward as he dismounted. She held out her hand and he brought it to his mouth, said, 'Madame', with flawless formality. And then he laughed, and she found herself enfolded within a boyish, exuberant embrace, from which she emerged bruised and breathless. He turned then to Margaret, catching her as she flung her arms aound his neck and swinging her up off the ground in a swirl of silk. As an exercise in crowd satisfaction, it was masterful; the level of noise now reached painful proportions.

Cecily clutched at her composure, smiled at her son. 'Never have I seen such a welcome, Edward . . . never in my lifetime!'

'Welcome, ma mère?' he echoed and kissed her lightly on both cheeks so that his voice reached her ear alone. 'I rather thought it to be a coronation.'

For a moment their eyes held, smoke-grey met the most vivid of blues. And then Cecily nodded slowly and Edward turned back to face the crowds thronging the churchyard, raising his hand in careless salute of the continuing cheers. She watched, the faintest of smiles curving the corners of her mouth.

5

City of York

March 1461

Marguerite d'Anjou tilted her candle at an angle so that no wax might splatter upon her son. Her strained nerves eased somewhat, as always, at sight of the sleep-smudged little profile, feathery golden lashes alighting upon skin as soft to the touch as it was flawless to the eye. She leaned forward, intending to brush her lips to his hair too lightly to disturb the delicate fabric of his sleep. But the lashes stirred, seemed about to take flight, and she reluctantly abandoned the caress. Once awakened, he'd be up and eager to leave the bed; so fiercely did he resist bedtime that, more than once, Marguerite found herself countermanding his nurse, making him a gift of the hours in dispute.

He was strong-willed, her son. Let others whisper of the boy's

lack of discipline, she didn't care. The fools, they did not understand. How could they?

She was thirty-one years old and never in her life had she met
a more patient, pious soul than the man asleep in the adjoining
bedchamber. Even in his worst fits of madness, her husband still
clung to remembered vestiges of bygone courtesies. Nothing
disturbed him more than what he felt to be unseemly displays of
lewdness or public nudity; and yet, when once he'd been mortally
offended by the scanty costumes of a troupe of dancers performing
at their Christmas court, he fled the scene himself rather than
order the women from his presence. That was many years ago
but Marguerite had not forgotten.

Another memory came to her now, one far more recent but
no more pleasant to recall. Upon their triumphant return to York,
the citizenry had turned out again in heartening welcome. A
welcome that had been marred for Marguerite by her husband's
bizarre behaviour at Micklegate Bar. He'd taken great pains not
to glance up, kept his eyes averted from the sight of the Yorkist
heads high above him, and in his haste to enter through the
barbican gate, he'd dropped first his reins and then his hat.

There'd been some snickering among the spectators at that,
and Marguerite had burned with the familiar frustration, the
impotent anger that always seemed to accompany her husband's
public appearances. Henri was, after all, an anointed King; to
mock him was to mock God. But, in her seventeen years in
England, she'd come to expect little better from the English. They
were not her people, would never be her people. But they were
her subjects, hers and Henri's, and she'd never yield them up to
that wretched boy, that swaggering youth who dared now to
proclaim himself as His Sovereign Grace, King Edward, fourth
of that name since the Conquest.

She reached down, smoothed the coverlets over her son. There
was a scattering of crumbs about his mouth and she smiled at
the sight, knowing that, if she touched him, her fingers would

find his cheek sticky with the marzipan he'd insisted upon taking to bed with him. He knew what he wanted, did her Edouard and, even at seven years of age, he understood, as Henri never had, that he must reach out for what he did want. Nothing came to the weak. Not in this world. Let others be content to wait for the rewards of the hereafter. She was not one of them. And, by the grace of God and her own resolve, Edouard would not be one either.

In the bedchamber yielded up to them by Abbot Cottingham, her husband slept. She could hear the gentle, rhythmic snore. As if there were not a battle taking place just twelve miles to the south of York, a battle that meant everything.

Just three months since Sandal Castle. How had York managed to turn fortune's wheel in so brief a time? The day she'd reined in her mare before Micklegate Bar, she'd truly believed that she had, in Clifford's words, won her war. Yet not two months later, Edward of York had contrived to have the crown offered to him by a rebellious London mob and a handful of disloyal nobles, and he was now challenging her army at Towton in what Somerset had called the final throw of the dice. It was not a phrase Marguerite relished; she had never liked to gamble.

She knew now that she'd blundered in yielding London so easily to Edward of York. Her face grew warm every time she thought of the tumultuous welcome he'd been given, for all the world as if he'd just liberated Jerusalem from the infidels. Only Londoners would confuse the entry into London of a nineteen-year-old rake-hell with the Second Coming of the Lord Christ. London canaille! There were times when she thought all her troubles with her English subjects were London-bred.

It was said more than four thousand people gathered in the cold of St John's Field that Sunday. Warwick's glib-tongued brother, the Bishop of Exeter, had incited the crowd with the ease of an accomplished orator; he'd soon had them screaming assent that Lancaster had broken the Act of Accord by the violence done at Sandal Castle, that no man had a better right to the crown than Edward of York, England's true King and the man who'd delivered London from the perils of fire and sword. Marguerite marvelled that he'd overlooked flood and famine, wondered cynically how many Warwick retainers had been strategically positioned throughout the crowd to stir up the audience's enthusiasm.

Two days later, Warwick led a delegation of nobles and clergy to Baynard's Castle to formally entreat Edward of York to accept the crown of England. Within hours, he was being acclaimed in Westminster Hall where, not five months before, his father had stood and advanced a like claim to embarrassing silence.

And that was the dangerous difference between them, Marguerite thought grimly. The reason why the son was proving to be a greater threat than ever the father had. The Duke of York had not been a man to strike passion in his followers, to evoke any emotion more intense than admiration. However upright his nature, or perhaps because of it, he had not the force of personality to captivate a city as his son Edward had captivated London.

How ironic it was that the very factor she'd weighed so heavily against Edward, his youth, should have been turned by him to such telling advantage. She'd seen him, at first, as an appendage of Warwick's body, an arm to be lopped off before it could strike a lucky blow; sure that, if Warwick fell, so too would Edward, no more able to survive independently of Warwick than the arm could exist without the body.

Yet the victory at Mortimer's Cross had gone to Edward, not to Warwick. Theirs was an age in which all men of their class studied the arts of war from early boyhood; it was to be expected that some men would prove to be more apt pupils than others. It was her accursed ill luck that Edward of York had now shown himself to be such a man, one with a natural affinity for command and the ways of war.

But what disturbed Marguerite the most about the young

Yorkist Duke now calling himself King was that he was seducer as well as soldier. He'd won London with his smile as much as with his sword, as his father could never have done.

Somerset conceded that Edward would be a dangerous foe to face across a battlefield. But he remained convinced that, in political matters, Edward was Warwick's dupe and content to be so, the pleasure-seeking puppet of his power-seeking cousin. As he reminded Marguerite more than once, Warwick himself had few peers in the game of crowd seduction. The Nevilles were all infuriatingly adroit at playing upon the emotions of the simple and the trusting, and this Edward of York was half Neville, after all. Why then, should Madame be surprised that he now showed himself to be as skilled as they in the dubious manoeuvres of rabble-rousing?

Recollection of Somerset's scorn brought a smile to Marguerite's mouth; it hovered but did not linger. She was trying to remember the last time she'd met Edward of York face to face. It was, she decided, upon that notorious farce called the 'Love-Day', three years ago, when, at the urging of Henri and the Commons, the Yorkists and Lancastrians had gathered to hear a solemn Mass of reconciliation at St Paul's. Edward had then been – she calculated rapidly – sixteen, already taller than most men grown and very conscious of his own charm. A handsome boy.

Marguerite bit her lip, chewed away the last of her ochre lip rouge. Yes, put him astride a white stallion, in plate armour that shone like polished pier glass and the far more potent armour of youth and health, and she could well understand how he must have dazzled the London multitudes. They were accustomed, after all, to her Henri.

Henri, who insisted upon wearing shapeless long gowns, eschewed the fashionable pointed-toe shoes, wore his hair clipped short like a peasant. What a bitter jest of God, she thought, that the only time in his life when Henri looked like a king had been during those terrifying months, eighteen in all, when he'd lapsed into a trance like one bewitched, unable to speak or feed himself and, therefore, unable, too, to select his own clothing!

Henri who was so poor a horseman he must be provided with mild-tempered geldings and never seemed to feel the humiliation in having such unmanly mounts. Henri who wore hair shirts and forbade profanity in his hearing and once had ridden all the way from the Tower to Westminster with an empty scabbard at his hip because he'd forgotten his sword and none of his attendants had thought to remind him of it.

It had not happened again; Marguerite had seen to that. But she could not blot from mind or memory the laughter of the London rabble, the sly innuendoes of the Yorkist sympathizers, and Jesú knew there were plenty such in London; the jests, that she knew to be swapped in ale house and tavern, about the King's lack of a sword and whether he did feel the lack most on the battlefield or in the bedchamber.

But there was no need to dwell upon Henri's failings. Somerset had more than forty thousand men under his command; numerical superiority lay decidedly with Lancaster. Somerset also had seasoned battle captains in Clifford, Northumberland and Trollope. By this time tomorrow, there'd be new Yorkist heads for Micklegate Bar, and one of the first would be John Neville, she vowed silently.

Warwick's brother was being held within York Castle where he'd been incarcerated since their arrival in York. That Neville still lived, that he had not gone to the block immediately upon his capture at St Albans last month was due entirely to Somerset and the misfortunes of Somerset's younger brother. Edmund Beaufort had recently fallen into Yorkist hands at Calais, a city that had always been staunchly Neville in its loyalties. Somerset feared, quite understandably, that, if he executed John Neville, his own brother Edmund would then be the one to feel the edge of Neville's vengeance. Marguerite had reluctantly agreed with him. The common sense of it could hardly be denied; moreover, she was rather fond of Edmund Beaufort. So John Neville still lived, but she promised herself that, once Warwick's power was broken, the reprieve would come to the most abrupt end possible.

No, she had reason and more for optimism. She had what must surely be the largest army ever gathered in England. She'd made Edward and Warwick come to her, to fight in territory traditionally hostile to the House of York. She had faith in Somerset, in Clifford and in Northumberland. Only . . . only why had she not heard by now? The battle was expected to have been joined at dawn and it was now well past dark. The battle should have been over hours ago. Why had she not heard?

Marguerite did not even try to sleep. She sat, instead, with a book of hours open on her lap, not registering any of the prayers engraved upon the page she was turning with fingers increasingly and infuriatingly clumsy, unable to perform the most simple of tasks. After splashing hot wax upon her hand and wine upon the sleeve of her gown, she swore, first in French and then in English, and, calling for her cloak, escaped the Abbot's lodging, for the abbey garth.

The snow had stopped at last but all about her was evidence of a storm of unseasonal savagery, even for Yorkshire; it was, after all, Palm Sunday, with April but two days hence. An eerie stillness enveloped the monastery, intensified by the heavy drifts of snow that lay between her and the distant gatehouse. She could barely discern the shape of the abbey walls. Although St Mary's was not within the city walls, she had no qualms for her safety for the monastery walls were no less formidable, securely sealing off the religious community from the rest of the world. *Jesus et Marie*, how dark it was! She could almost believe herself alone in the world, a world suddenly bereft of all other people. No sounds of life. No light. No movement beyond the ghostly swirling of the shadows which had always harboured a multitude of demons for her as a fanciful child. Until she'd learned that demons were to be confronted.

To her left lay the great abbey church and some yards beyond, the gatehouse, made invisible by dark and distance. It was the only entrance into the abbey grounds and she briefly considered waiting there to intercept Somerset's messenger. But, to reach it, she'd have to struggle through knee-deep snow. And it was bitterly cold; patches of ice glinted ominously where the light of her torch struck. By morning, a thick crust of ice would have glazed over all open ground within the monastery, would have transformed it into a glacial hell for the sandal-shod monks.

And what sights would morning bring to the fields beyond the village of Towton? Bodies upon bodies in the rigid ungainly sprawl of death, limbs twisted grotesquely in postures no living man could emulate, blood frozen solid beneath layers of discoloured dark ice, to soak the ground with ghastly flow of gore at the first thaw. Marguerite knew what she could expect to find; she'd seen battlefields before. But whose bodies? Whose blood?

She saw that some of the monks had been busy with salt and shovel; a narrow path beckoned through the drifts. Perhaps if she went up into Marygate Tower, she might be able to keep watch.

She was in sight of the abbey walls bordering onto Bootham when she first heard the shout. Stopping so precipitately that she had to grab her servant for support, she listened. The shout came again, seemed to come from the north – from the gatehouse.

Marguerite's heart skipped, took up an uneven rapid rhythm. Panting, cursing herself for attempting this fool's trek into the dark, she hastened to retrace her steps. At last her eyes caught movement, flickering light. Figures were emerging from the Abbot's lodging.

'Signal with your torch,' she told her servant. 'Yes . . . they see us now.'

As they came nearer, she recognized the Abbot. He held a lantern aloft, and had the look of one bringing word of sudden death to unsuspecting kin.

'Madame,' he said.

Marguerite stared past him at the soldier. At the bloody brigandine, leather ripped away to show metal plate beneath. At the portcullis badge worn on his breast, the Beaufort cognizance. At the blood-caked welt that gaped open and ugly from temple to cheekbone. At the left eye, swollen to the merest of slits, surrounded by puffy discoloured tissue that contrasted queasily with the rest of his face, made raw by windburn and the first thawing of frostbite. His uninjured eye was what held her, however, was an uncommonly vivid shade of green, was utterly out of place in so young a face.

'Your Grace . . .' he began, and seemed about to kneel before her. Instead, he slid to the snow at her feet.

It was Marguerite who now knelt, grasping his hand between her own. 'Tell me,' she said harshly. 'Hold nothing back.'

'All is lost. The victory has gone to York.'

It was what she'd known he would say. And yet the impact was no less brutal. She gasped, drew icy air into lungs suddenly constricted, unable to function, and cried, 'How? We had the greater army. . . . How?'

She was as skilled a strategist as any man, knew how to wage war as other women knew how to manage households. She knew battles were not decided by numbers alone. Yet now she found herself repeating numbly, 'How could we lose? Ours was the larger force!'

'That did favour us at first, madame. In the early stages of the battle, the Yorkists did give ground. . . . But York was all over the field, in the thick of the fighting and he held them, madame. All day we fought, hacked at each other like madmen, and the dead . . . Oh, my God, madame, the dead! So many bodies there were that we had to climb over our own dead to reach the Yorkists . . . only to find they too were walled in by the bodies of the dead and dying. Never have I seen—'

'What of Somerset? Does he still live?'

He seemed unnerved by her interruption. 'Yes,' he said doubtfully. 'That is, I do believe so, madame. We were able to escape the field at the last, when we saw all hope had gone . . . when the Yorkist reserves suddenly appeared upon our right flank. The Duke of Norfolk it was, madame; I saw his standard. We fought on, but the battle was lost with his arrival, all did know it. We were pushed back toward the Cocke, into the marsh . . . and then our line broke, then the slaughter truly began!' He shuddered, not from cold, and then said bleakly, 'My lord Somerset charged me to give you word of our defeat, to warn you away from here. My lord Somerset said . . . said you must flee into Scotland, madame. He said you must not let yourself or the King fall into the hands of the Yorkist usurper.'

'What of the other lords? Northumberland? Trollope? Exeter and Clifford? Surely they cannot all be dead!'

'We did hear the Earl of Northumberland was struck down in the fighting. Trollope, I do know to be dead. I know nothing of Exeter. It was a slaughter, madame. Thousands must be dead. . . . We gave the command before the battle that no quarter be shown and York was said to have done the same. For ten hours, madame, the battle did last . . . ten hours! With the wind coming from the south and blowing the snow back into our faces till men found their eyes sealed shut with ice and our arrows were falling short and they gathered them up and used them against us . . . and the river . . . Oh, Lord Jesus, the river! So many men drowned that a bridge of bodies formed for the living and it ran red for miles, like no water I've ever seen. . . .'

He was losing himself in his recital of horrors, reliving it in the retelling, and Marguerite dug her nails sharply into the palm of his hand to staunch the flow of words.

'Enough!' she cried fiercely. 'There's no time! Not now! What of Clifford? Is he dead, too?'

'Clifford?' The green eye widened; so close she was to him that she actually saw the pupil contract. 'Jesú, madame, do you not

95

know? Clifford died yesterday noon, at the Ferrybridge crossing for the River Aire, some nine or ten miles below Towton.'

Marguerite made a small sound. If Somerset was her rock, Clifford had been her sword. 'How?' she said, so stiffly that she was forced to repeat herself.

'The Yorkists sent out a party to repair the Ferrybridge crossing, for we'd burned the bridge behind us. Lord Clifford knew they'd try to mend the bridge; he took them by surprise and many died. Warwick himself was there, madame. But Edward of York had sent a second party to ford the river further upstream. They crossed at Castleford and we knew it not until they hit hard at Lord Clifford's right flank. In the retreat that followed, most of his men were killed; I think but three did escape. Clifford fell prey to a freak arrow shot. It somehow pierced his gorget, lodged in his throat.

'He did choke to death on his own blood,' he added, gratuitously and with so conspicuous a lack of regret that Marguerite stared at him, remembering the name Clifford had won for himself after word spread of the stabbing on Wakefield Bridge. He'd been nearly deranged with fury once he knew; he had gone to Marguerite, his only sympathetic ear, to blister the air with his oaths and his outrage that he, Lord Clifford of Skipton-Craven, should now be branded, even amongst his own men, as the 'Butcher'.

Marguerite was suddenly conscious of the cold again; snow had seeped into her pattens until she could no longer feel her feet. Her skirt and underkirtle were damp, too, clung about her ankles and trapped her in clammy folds as she struggled to rise.

She was already up before the Abbot could offer assistance but, as he shifted the lantern, he inadvertently brought it up to her eyes. Night-blinded, she was caught in its glare, just long enough to step back onto a treacherous icy glaze. She had no hope of preventing her fall, landed with jarring impact upon the base of her spine. The Abbot cried out, dropped the lantern as he reached for her and, when his own balance went, almost tumbled down on top of her. The soldier wisely stayed where he was and coughed to cover the startled laugh that was as involuntary as a sneeze and as devoid of amusement.

Weighed down by her sodden skirt, unable to catch her breath, watching as the Abbot floundered beside her in the snow, while her servant struggled to maintain his own footing and gingerly extended his hand toward her, Marguerite suddenly began to laugh, jagged bursts of strangled mirth, the sound of which nightmares are made.

'Madame, you must not give way!' The Abbot, less timid than her servant at laying hands upon royalty, grabbed her shoulders, shook her vigorously.

'But it is so very amusing; surely you see that? I've a little boy and a sweet helpless fool asleep in your lodging and no money and I've just been told I no longer have an army and look at us, my lord Abbot, sacré Dieu, look at us! If I do not laugh,' she gasped, 'I might believe all this were truly happening, and happening to me!'

'Madame . . .' The Abbot hesitated, and then plunged ahead courageously. 'You need not flee, you know. York would not harm a woman, still less a child. Your lives would be safe with him, I do believe that. Stay here, Madame. Entreat York's mercy, accept him as King. Even if you reach Scotland, what then? Ah, Madame, can you not let it lie?'

The lantern light no longer fell on her face; he could not discern her expression. But he heard her intake of breath, a sibilant hiss of feline intensity. Her hand jerked from his.

'Oui, Monseigneur,' she spat. 'On my deathbed!'

Somehow she'd scrambled to her feet, so swiftly that he sat gaping up at her.

'If I were you, my lord Abbot,' she said venomously, 'I'd be too concerned for my abbey to offer unwanted and unwise political counsel. St Mary's is one of the richest houses of your very rich order, is it not? You'd be better advised to spend some hours on your knees, praying that Edward of York does leave you with two groats to call your own. What do you think will befall this city once he does turn it over to his men for their sport?'

'Madame?' The soldier had regained his feet. 'In truth, I've little interest in what York does or does not do to this city. But I've an overriding interest in your safety and that of the King. I'm the Duke of Somerset's sworn man; he himself did send me to you. It is my thinking that we've no time to tarry. My lord Abbot may be correct in his surmise that York would not do violence to a woman or child. That is not, however, a belief I'd care to put to the test.'

She stared at him and then nodded. 'Come with me,' she said, linking her arm through his before he could move. 'You must lean on me should you feel weak. Do you think you can ride? Good. Now ...' She paused and then concluded, in tautly controlled tones, 'Now I think it time to awaken my son.' Another pause. 'And Henri.' She spoke so softly that he barely heard her, with an emotional inflection he could not identify. 'Yes,' she said, still softly. 'We must not forget my husband, the King.'

He gave her a quick look, saw only the beautiful profile, the wealth of glossy dark hair freed from constraint by her tumble in the snow, saw only what she wanted him to see.

The abbot came painfully to his feet, brushing snow from his habit, shaking it from the folds of the cowled hood that lay across his shoulders, a stark solitary figure clad in the black of the Benedictines, surrounded by drifts of unrelenting white. His lips were moving. He'd taken Marguerite d'Anjou's sardonic suggestion to heart, was praying for the city he loved and the magnificent Abbey of St Mary's that was his life.

The citizens of York awoke to fear on Monday morning. Word swiftly spread throughout the city. Towton, the most savage battle ever fought on English soil; Towton was Edward of York's bloody coronation. There were none now to challenge his sovereignty.

England was his and the people of York had given him no reason to look with favour upon their city.

A pallid sun made hesitant advances and hasty retreats, and windswept snow and debris gave the city streets a look of utter desolation. Occasional apprentices appeared, scouring about for firewood with which to board up their masters' shops. The over-hanging upper storeys of the timber frame houses were tightly shuttered. The major market sites of the city, Thursday Market and Pavement, were virtually deserted; stalls, that should have been heavily laden with Lenten fish, apple butter, and herbs, were barren or had not been set up at all. There were reports of crowds forming on the river quays just below Ouse Bridge where all seagoing ships docked upon arrival in York.

Generally, however, the city was quiet, the mood one of appre-hension rather than panic. Mention might be made of flight but only by the very foolish and the very frightened. York was England's second largest city with a population of fifteen thousand. Fifteen thousand people could not stream off into the frozen country-side leaving the elderly and infirm to their fate. Theirs was the cardinal sin of backing the wrong side in a civil war and now they braced themselves courageously for the consequences of their lapse in judgement. There was an unusually high turnout for Morrow Mass in the forty-one parish churches in and about the city. And then the waiting began.

William Stockton, the Lord Mayor of York, stood with John Kent and Richard Claybruke, sheriffs of York, before Micklegate Bar. Behind them were gathered the city chamberlains, aldermen, and most of the members of the common council. All wore their ceremonial robes of scarlet mantled with fur, to honour the Yorkist King. All looked markedly ill at ease.

A small crowd had collected as the morning wore on, those who'd always held for the House of York and those hoping to curry favour with their new sovereign, the intrepid, the young, the morbidly curious. Little was happening yet, though; they passed the time by fabricating outlandish rumours and staring at the man by the Lord Mayor's side.

John Neville was thirty, looked much older with the weathered face of a soldier and deep-set brown eyes that missed little. Upon learning of the Lancastrian loss at Towton, the city leaders had hastened at once to York Castle to free the man who was brother to the powerful Earl of Warwick, cousin to the King. He'd listened impassively as they implored him to speak on the city's behalf, gave them courtesy but little else, so that they had no solid clue as to either his emotions or his intentions.

Now John Kent, the younger of the sheriffs, edged closer to him, said politely, 'My lord? Is it true that the King's Grace forbade his men to commit robbery, rape or sacrilege, upon pain of death?'

This was the most comforting rumour circulating at the moment and had a certain plausibility in that it had existed before the Yorkist victory at Towton.

John Neville shrugged. 'As to that, Master Kent, I'm not the one to ask. I've been a prisoner of Lancaster for these six weeks past. I fear I'm rather out of touch with the activities of the King's Grace.'

'Do you . . . do you think it likely he would?' Kent persisted, but John Neville had raised his hand against the uneven glare of winter sunlight upon the surrounding sea of snow.

'Riders approach,' he said just as sentries up on the city walls shouted, turning all heads toward the road south.

At sight of his brother, the Earl of Warwick broke into a grin, reined in his stallion. John Neville's sombre face was transformed; shedding years with his smile. He came forward as Warwick dismounted. Their hands clasped, held.

'I never thought you could look so good to me, Johnny!'

'I was lucky,' John said simply, and Warwick laughed.

'Ned and I hoped they'd fear to send you to the block but it was no hope to hold a man's weight. Thank God Jesus that Somerset saw himself as his brother's keeper!'

'She's gone, of course Dick. Sometime last night.'

Warwick nodded, said matter-of-factly, 'We did expect as much.'

'Was the win as great as that, then? What were our losses?'

'Ah, yes, Johnny, it was as great as that! But the losses . . . were unbelievable, like nothing I've ever seen. We'll be digging grave pits for days to come. I'd not be surprised if the dead do number twice ten thousand when all is said and done!'

'My God!'

'I've not seen you for fully six weeks and you've not seen Ned since last December, have you? There's too much to tell, Johnny; I'd not know where to begin.'

'I think it would be a kindness if you'd begin by greeting the Lord Mayor and those doleful-looking souls waiting like sheep for the slaughter,' John suggested with a smile, and his brother laughed, moved forward to be welcomed into York by its troubled Mayor.

Warwick was more receptive than the Mayor dared hope, listened with encouraging attentiveness as they avowed their fealty to the King's Grace, offered congratulations upon his splendid victory at Towton and expressed the heartfelt hope that His Grace the King would look with charity upon past loyalties pledged to Lancaster.

Warwick's response was noncommital but so amiable that they took heart, and it was with renewed confidence that they turned now to watch the approach of their young King.

The Yorkists in the crowd set up a spontaneous cheer and it was prudently taken up by the others. Edward saw smiles upon every face, an impressive flurry of Yorkist white roses, and his own Sunne in Splendour badge, Neville scarlet and the blue and murrey of York. He also saw the Lord Mayor, the aldermen and, with a surge of pleasure, his cousin John. John was grinning, raised his hand in a singular salute. His palm cut the air sideways; it was a gesture from Edward's boyhood, sign language he and Edmund had shared with their Neville cousins, expressing the approval they reserved for only the most audacious of exploits. Edward laughed, touched his spurs lightly to his mount's flanks.

It was then that he saw the heads above him on Micklegate Bar.

He yanked upon his reins so savagely that his startled stallion reared up wildly and, to the appalled audience, it seemed likely that Edward would lose his seat and the stallion its balance. There were sudden screams. The crowd was small enough so that all could see what had happened. There wasn't the usual shoving and pushing but several people moved into the road as if intending to grab for the plunging stallion. Cooler heads prevailed and several soldiers waved them back. Edward now had the horse under control but, as he soothed the frightened animal, it was evident to all that he was acting from instinct, that he had no awareness of what he did. He was still staring up at Micklegate Bar.

The crowd was silent. The Yorkist soldiers were no less silent. Even the horses seemed to have been frozen in place. The moment of petrified immobility did not shatter, seemed to drag on and on, seemed as if it would never end.

Warwick followed Edward's upward gaze. He'd seen the heads, too, as he first drew rein before the gateway; had looked up and then away. The sight was hardly pleasant but recognition was an utter impossibility, not after three months' exposure to the elements of a Yorkshire winter. He'd not expected this reaction. Edward was not easily rattled, from his mid-teens had shown a self-possession rather remarkable for his years. Warwick had occasionally been irked by the boy's easy assurance but he realized now how much he'd come to rely upon it, upon the certainty that Edward could be counted upon to keep calm under pressure, to keep his emotions conveniently curbed. It made him an invaluable ally, an agreeable companion.

Warwick might have been staring at a stranger. Edward had gone very white; the blood had so suddenly drained from his face that he looked ill. He'd not taken his eyes from the grisly spectacle above his head but Warwick noticed that he'd knotted the reins, had wrapped a length around his fist, was methodically pulling it taut and then letting it go slack. Warwick knew Edward's strength, found himself staring expectantly at those jerking reins, saw the leather give way under the pressure, snap off in his cousin's hand.

The stallion shied. Edward seemed equally startled, stared down at his hands as if they'd been engaging in an activity independent of his control. The broken strip of leather flew through the air, landed at the feet of the nearest of the spectators. He flinched as if struck but a youngster darted forward, scooped it up, and then raised it high so others could see, bestowing upon Edward the admiring glance due to one able to manage so impressive a feat and with so little effort.

People could move again; no longer were they stricken dumb. There was stirring in the crowd and uneasy murmurs became audible. Until Edward turned upon the Lord Mayor and the aldermen, demanded to know why the heads of his father and brother had not been taken from Micklegate Bar in a voice raw with rage, unrecognizable as his own even to those who knew him best.

They were unable to speak, seeing York in flames, reduced to ashes and cinders and charred bodies. A few did look despairingly at Warwick but it was John Neville who moved, coming forward to stand at Edward's stirrup.

'There was not time, Ned,' he said, very quietly. 'The Frenchwoman fled the city only hours ago and nothing could be done while she held York. And then . . . Well, fear does not lend itself to clear thinking. In the little time left, I doubt if it occurred to them, so fearful were they that you might exact from York the price paid by Ludlow. And, in fairness, you could as well blame me. I could have given the order; I did not. I fear I have not been thinking all that clearly myself this morning.' He smiled slightly.

'I reckoned today would mark the end of my confinement, one way or the other. But it was that 'other' which gave me pause!'

Edward stared down at him. A muscle jerked in his cheek. He raised a hand to still it. None spoke. All waited.

'I want them taken down now,' Edward said at last, very low. 'See to it for me, Johnny.'

John nodded. For a moment their eyes held, and then Edward turned in the saddle, gazed up at Micklegate Bar, before saying in a hard, carrying voice, 'My lord of Warwick!'

'Your Grace?' Warwick had been mesmerized by this unexpected exposure of an unhealed grief, had been startled to see he did not know his Yorkist cousin as well as he thought he did. Moving toward Edward, he said composedly, 'What is Your Grace's pleasure?'

'The prisoners taken . . .' Edward turned fathomless blue eyes upon Warwick, eyes that now had a brilliant and frightening glitter. 'I see no reason to delay the executions. Have them carried out. Now.'

Warwick nodded. 'The Lord Mayor tells me the Earl of Devon did not flee with Marguerite. He was bed-ridden with fever, is being held now within the castle, awaiting your pleasure. Shall we,' he jested grimly, 'rid him of his fever?'

Warwick's gallows humour did not sit well with his brother; John had too recently been a captive himself not to have a qualm or two at executing a sick prisoner. He opened his mouth to speak, saw that his young cousin was looking up again at the heads upon Micklegate Bar. There was little in Edward's face of youth and nothing of mercy. All watching knew what he would say.

'Take Devon to the marketplace. The one called Pavement. Have him beheaded before the pillory.'

'It shall be done forthwith,' Warwick said agreeably. 'And then?' he prompted, accurately anticipating Edward's next command.

'Then I would see his head where my brother and father now are.'

Warwick nodded again. 'As Your Grace wills it, so shall it be,' he said loudly, and then dropped his voice for Edward's hearing alone.

'Ned? Are you all right? You did look greensick for a moment there. . . .'

'Did I?' Edward said tonelessly and, at that moment, Warwick had no idea what the boy might be thinking; nothing showed on his face, nothing at all.

For an unexpectedly awkward moment nothing was said, and then Edward moved his stallion forward, said over his shoulder, 'Tell me when it has been done. But no prisoners below the rank of knight. I'd not charge a man for a full loaf of bread if he's had but crumbs. See to it, Cousin.'

He reined in his mount before Lord Mayor Stockton and the aldermen. The Mayor rallied, began a courageous if doomed appeal on behalf of his city, but Edward cut him off in midsentence.

'My Lord Mayor, I'm bone-weary. I want nothing so much now as a hot bath, a soft bed and a strong drink. To be very candid, I'm in no mood to hear you explain away your allegiance to Lancaster. So, if I may spare us both a plea that need not be made . . . or heard?'

The Mayor nodded numbly, so bewildered by this unusual response that he found himself assenting as if Edward had actually posed a question that wanted answering.

Edward almost smiled at that and then said very deliberately, 'I've no intention of sacking the city of York. Your fears are groundless, do me no credit. My quarrel is with the House of Lancaster, not the good people of York.'

He looked around at the intent faces upturned to him, saw the dawning joy, and found a smile for them, said, 'You've shown you can give great loyalty to your sovereign. As your sovereign, that can scarcely displease me, can it?'

When he could make himself heard again, he set off another demonstration by suggesting that the Lord Mayor might like to escort them all into the city.

Watching as the crowd thronged forward, squeezing through the barbican, and as church bells began to peal throughout the city, sending men and women out into the streets to verify their reprieve, Warwick glanced at his brother, said softly, 'Not the worst of beginnings, Johnny. There are more than enough Lancastrian malcontents to foment disorder here but there'll be others now, as well, who'll remember the prick of the sword at the throat and that we chose to withdraw it unbloodied.'

John nodded. 'He did give me a bad moment there, though. He so desperately needed a target, needed someone to blame that I feared he might lash out at York. God knows, it was the most visible target.'

'I admit the same thought crossed my mind,' Warwick conceded, and then grinned. 'I should have known better, though. He's a good lad, Johnny. Keeps his head when it counts. His record was well nigh perfect until today! Passing strange . . . I've fought beside Ned on the field, shared exile, got drunk with him, claimed a crown together, and this was the first time I've ever seen him truly shaken. And after all he's seen . . . queer!'

'If you think you can endure two such shocks in one morn, Dick, I'll tell you quite frankly that it was not one of my better days when I rode through that damned gate for the first time, either.'

Warwick gave John a quizzical look. 'It's merely a question of discipline, Johnny. You only see what you let yourself see; that's the secret. Now, if you look up at that gate and imagine you see Tom, or Ned does the same and sees Edmund, Christ, man, of course it'll turn your stomach! Now, I see only . . .'

'I do not think I want to know, Dick,' John said hastily, and managed a sour smile. 'You're most likely right, but if ever my head does end up on Micklegate Bar, I'd rather my loved ones were not quite so philosophical about it!'

Warwick laughed; of all his kin, he was fondest of this brother. 'I'll bear that in mind!'

Looking around, he signalled for his horse. 'Well, I'd best see to those executions for our young cousin, the King. And I expect we'll be going to St Peter's to make an offering and hear Mass. . . .'

Within moments, he'd given the necessary orders and returned to his brother, confident they'd be carried out with dispatch and without mishap. All in Warwick's service were disciplined, dependable, and most were, as well, personally devoted to him; he paid more lavishly than any lord in England and his badge of the Bear and Ragged Staff conferred an enviable social status upon its wearer. Now he resumed the broken threads of conversation, said, 'Ned said he meant to stay with the Franciscans; we'll find quarters for you there, too, Johnny. That was not where the French harlot stayed? I'd not put it past her to have poisoned the drinking well or worse, the wine kegs, as a parting gift to our cousin, the King!'

'I think she was lodged at St Mary's,' John said absently, and then echoed, 'Our cousin, the King.'

'What?'

'Our cousin, the King,' John repeated. 'Were you aware, Dick, that twice in our conversation you made use of that phrase?'

'So?'

'I'm not all that sure. But I think I'd feel more comfortable in my own mind had you said, "The King, our cousin."'

Warwick stared at him and then he laughed. 'Christ, I did miss you, Johnny, these six weeks past! Shall I tell you what I did miss the most about you? That cloud of gloom you drag around like a lap robe!'

Still laughing, he swung easily up into the saddle, sent his mount cantering through Micklegate Bar. He did not look up as he passed through, nor did he look back. John Neville watched, and then he smiled to himself and mounting his own stallion, followed after his brother.

6

Durham

December 1462

On Christmas Day, the northern border castle of Bamburgh fell to the Yorkists. The siege had lasted more than a month and, in the final days, the trapped Lancastrians had been reduced to eating their horses. But they thus only prolonged their own suffering. The end was inevitable. Marguerite was in Scotland; she had not the forces at her command to come to the aid of Bamburgh. With the dawning of Christmas Day, Edward's standard of the Sunne in Splendour gleamed white and gold above the castle battlements and John Neville, now titled as Lord Montagu, formally accepted Bamburgh's surrender in the name of the Yorkist King.

Henry Beaufort, Duke of Somerset, knew himself to be a dead man. He measured his life now in terms of hours, in the time still remaining before they reached Durham. At Durham, Edward of York awaited his arrival. Edward had been taken ill a fortnight ago, unable to assume personal command of the siege of Bamburgh. He'd closely followed its progress from his sickbed but the actual direction of the military operation had fallen to his Neville cousins, Warwick and John. It was John who now conveyed Somerset south to Durham and death.

Somerset had always known what he might expect should he ever fall into Yorkist hands. What there was of mercy or magnanimity in the Yorkist–Lancastrian rivalry had died with Edmund of Rutland on Wakefield Bridge. Somerset knew that, in Yorkist eyes, his sins were legion: Ludlow, Sandal Castle, St Albans,

Towton. And, in the twenty-one months since Edward's bloody victory at Towton, he'd given Edward even more reason to wish him dead. He'd journeyed to France in a futile attempt to win French backing for Marguerite, negotiated with the Scots on her behalf, had taken Bamburgh in her name. Marguerite had no more devoted loyalists than Somerset and his younger brothers, and John Neville had accepted Somerset's surrender with the grim gratificaton of a hunter who'd at long last run his prey to earth after a particularly gruelling and punishing chase.

But Somerset was now discovering the bitter distinction between contemplating death as an eventuality and confronting it as an actuality. He could not, in conscience, fault Edward of York for what he would himself have done had the chance ever arisen. He had never questioned his own courage, nor did he do so now. He'd faced death often enough to feel sure he'd not dishonour his last moments of life. But he was still only twenty-six years of age, had a healthy, disciplined body that served him well and he found much to love in life, even as a hunted rebel under Bill of Attainder. On the road to Durham, he came to understand that the fear of a battlefield death was comparable to the fear of the executioner's axe only in the way that a fear of consumption was comparable to the doomed realization of one who'd begun to cough and bring up blood.

Durham lay sixty-five miles to the south of Bamburgh. It was there, in the Benedictine Priory of St Cuthbert, that Edward had kept Christmas, his second since laying claim to England's crown. With him was his cousin Warwick. With him, too, was his youngest brother, Richard, who'd been permitted a brief escape from his studies in Latin, French, mathematics, law, music, manners and the survival skills of war and weaponry at Warwick's Middleham Castle, some fifty miles distant from Durham.

John Neville had gone at once to his cousin, the King. Somerset expected to be taken to the Lyinge House, the prison cell beneath the master's chamber in the infirmary. Somewhat to his surprise, he was led, instead, to a small chamber next to the Chapter House. It was, he was told, where monks guilty of minor offences were confined and the monk blinked at him in bewilderment when Somerset burst into unsteady laughter.

'Minor offences!' he gasped. 'Shall we call it petty treason, then?'

The joke, if indeed it was one, eluded the monk entirely. He shrugged, edged away. As the door slammed behind him, the draught extinguished the only candle. Somerset was left alone in the dark.

Soon thereafter came the summons Somerset had steeled himself to expect. He followed his guards into the Prior's lodging, into the great hall crowded with Yorkist retainers. The solar, too, was thronged with men. He was jeered and jostled somewhat as his guards steered him through but the atmosphere was more expectant than angry, much like the almost festive mood of a crowd gathering for the public hanging of a notorious highwayman.

He was pushed through the solar doorway, found himself in a large chamber some thirty by twenty feet. He recognized the Prior's privy chamber, recognized, too, the Prior. John Burnaby was a man well known to the Beaufort family; he'd granted Somerset a night's shelter at the priory on Somerset's flight into Scotland after Towton Field. Yet now his eyes slid past Somerset without acknowledgment, with only a trace of embarrassment.

But, before Somerset could fully take in his surroundings, his guards were pulling him across the privy chamber, propelling him through an open doorway none too gently. He stumbled, regained his balance, and looked about him in astonishment.

He was in a torchlit bedchamber, hung with red to banish fever, heated by a huge recessed hearth and several braziers heaped with smouldering coals. Two enormous wolfhounds and a smaller alaunt hound lay by the fire; a tethered peregrine falcon watched unblinkingly from a far corner. Somerset's bonds were suddenly slack, cut cleanly through, falling to the floor at his feet. He rubbed his wrists before he could think better of it and then raised his head high.

The dogs were regarding him with lazy goodwill, the Earl of Warwick and John Neville with chill appraisal. He returned their stare and then sought the Yorkist King. Edward was sprawled, fully dressed, upon the bed, propped up by half a dozen feather pillows. His colour was high but he showed no other effects of his recent illness, watched Somerset with speculative eyes.

No one spoke. Somerset's guards backed away, moving unobtrusively toward the door. Only then did Somerset notice the boy sitting cross-legged on cushions by the bed with yet another alaunt stretched out on the floor beside him. He was a dark-haired youngster of no more than ten or thereabouts and Somerset felt a distinct shock, bitter disbelief that his death sentence was to be passed in Edward of York's bedchamber in the presence of a child.

'You do know my Neville cousins,' Edward said dryly and, as Somerset stared at him, flushing with impotent fury, he gestured toward the boy on the floor. 'My brother Richard, Duke of Gloucester.'

The boy gave Somerset a cool, composed look.

'We met at Ludlow,' he said and Edward laughed, so did the Nevilles. Somerset felt a surge of hatred that, for the moment, overrode any feelings of fear.

'Do you mean to have me beheaded here in your bedchamber before the boy?' he challenged, with a burst of defiant scorn.

John Neville came to his feet. 'Have a care, Somerset,' he said softly. 'Tonight or tomorrow, it is all the same to me.'

Warwick hadn't bothered to move but the dark eyes had narrowed, conveyed an antagonism more implacable and ominous than his brother's dispassionate warning.

Edward, however, was shaking his head, now said impatiently, 'You're no fool, Somerset. Why, then, do you choose to sound like one? For Christ's sake, man, do you truly think I'd have you brought to my private chamber like this if I meant then to strike your head from your shoulders?'

The Nevilles looked no less stunned than Somerset. Only Richard seemed unaffected, twisting aound to look up at his brother with extreme interest.

Warwick spoke first, dismissing what they fancied they'd heard with a brusque, 'You cannot mean to spare his life, Ned. Somerset, of all men? Impossible.'

Undisturbed by his cousin's peremptory tone, Edward reached down, added one of Richard's cushions to the pile already on the bed and then settled back comfortably on his elbows.

'You tell me, Somerset,' he said calmly. 'Is my cousin of Warwick correct? Is it, indeed, impossible?'

Somerset had no answer for him. This sudden suggestion of reprieve overwhelmed his defences, engulfed him in raw emotion. He could think only that this must be some particularly vindictive and vengeful prelude to execution.

'I do not understand,' he said at last and even that admission cost him dear.

'You've been labouring for a cause lost these twenty-one months past. Your Queen can beg in every court of Europe for all it'll avail her. England is mine, man. Can you accept that? Come to terms with a Yorkist monarchy?'

Somerset was silent. He no longer felt certain this was a cruel hoax, York's satisfaction for Sandal Castle. He stared at Edward and then at the disbelieving Nevilles, suddenly seeing that Marguerite was right in her estimation of Edward and he was wrong, that this casual twenty-year-old youth was no man's puppet, was accommodating to his Neville kin only because it suited him to be so.

'And if I could?' he said warily, not yet willing to embrace hope, not yet able to believe Edward's matter-of-fact offer was genuine.

'I'd be willing to give you a full pardon. To welcome you at my court.' Edward paused. 'And to restore to you the titles and lands which were forfeit under the Bill of Attainder passed against you by my first parliament last year.'

'My God,' Somerset breathed, no longer able to dissemble, no

112

longer able to do anything but wonder at the magnitude of his enemy's offer.

Edward glanced over at his speechless cousins and then down at his wide-eyed younger brother before looking back at Somerset.

'Well?' he said. 'What say you?'

'You truly mean it?' Somerset blurted out, so flustered that, for the moment, he looked the younger of the two. But for the first time in many years, pride no longer counted for all. He felt only confusion and a sudden intoxication of the senses, so intense that he was in danger of becoming drunk on air alone.

'Am I right in assuming you accept my offer?' Edward asked and grinned, so infectiously that the dazed Somerset found himself grinning, too.

'I'd be a fool beyond redemption if I did not!' he heard himself confess, saw Edward laugh in genuine amusement. He moved then, crossed the chamber and, as Edward sat up on the bed, he knelt before the young Yorkist King and swore the oath of allegiance pledged to one's sovereign.

Warwick moved toward Richard and smiled down at the boy.

'Dickon, why not take the dogs out to the priory garth for a run? They've been penned up here all night, need the exercise.'

'Yes, sir.' Richard started obediently to rise when Edward caught his arm and, laughing, pulled him onto the bed.

'What our cousin Warwick means, Dickon, is that he plans to quarrel with me and wants you safely away from the field of battle.'

He grinned, shook his head. 'Let the lad stay, Dick. I daresay he'll find it more entertaining than walking those abominable hounds of yours.'

Richard looked uncertainly between the two. He hadn't needed to be told that Warwick's suggestion was a strategem. His cousin's anger was palpable and he'd been much distressed by it. Since joining Warwick's household at Middleham, Richard had become very attached to the cousin whom many had begun to call the

'Kingmaker'. Richard could not help but be impressed by Warwick's expansive good humour, his munificence, his unerring instinct for the dramatic gesture, the eye-catching exploit, and Warwick's periodic visits to Middleham were notable occasions for Richard. His cousin made things happen, livened everyday routine and invariably brought excitement with him as he rode laughing into the castle bailey with a retinue even larger than Edward's riding household. But the truth was simpler; the truth was that Warwick, who had no son of his own, had given Richard more attention and approval in thirteen months than Richard had got from his own father in eight years.

Now the thought that this much admired cousin might quarrel with Edward was deeply disturbing to Richard. Until he looked more closely at Edward, saw that his brother was quite composed, showed no signs of anger. He relaxed somewhat then, decided that if Ned were so little concerned by this looming confrontation, he need not be all that concerned, either. He settled himself as inconspicuously as possible at the foot of the bed, quite happy to be included in these interesting adult happenings, grateful that Edward had seen fit to let him witness so exciting an event as Somerset's capitulation.

Warwick saw Richard wanted to remain, saw no reason to make an issue of the boy's presence. Nor could he contain his anger any longer.

'Ned, you must be mad! Marguerite has had no more stead-fast ally than Somerset. She's always had the backing of the Beauforts and little wonder! It's more than likely Somerset is half brother to that little bastard she dares claim to be Lancaster's son. You remember how blatantly she favoured Somerset's father, do you not?'

'I cannot exactly say I remember . . . I was, after all, only eleven when the brat was born!'

Warwick was not amused and Edward leaned back against the pillows, made no further atempts at levity.

'Your point's well taken, Dick. If Harry of Lancaster himself thinks the Holy Ghost did sire her son, I'd say the late Duke of Somerset is as good a guess as any. But it is the present Duke of Somerset who does concern me. The Beaufort family has been to Lancaster what the Nevilles have been to York – of inestimable value. If I can win the Beauforts to York, I'll have gone far toward reconciling the country to my rule. Surely you'd not deny the truth of that?'

John Neville now spoke for the first time. 'I do not think it possible, Ned.'

'You may well be right, Johnny. But I think it worth the gamble, that the reward to be gained warrants the risk to be taken.'

'I see no risk whatsoever in separating Somerset's head from his body,' Warwick said flatly, and for an instant, impatience shadowed Edward's face.

'You both know I'm not loath to shed blood if that is what must be done. I've done my share. Most from necessity and a few . . .' He paused and then concluded with a bleak twisted smile, 'Well, a few for auld lang syne.'

It was a Scots expression not known to Richard but the allusion was unmistakable. He didn't know how to give comfort, though, only how to share hurt. Edward saw and reached out, pulled the boy to him for a brief wordless hug. He was instinctively inclined to make a physical response to emotional need, especially with children and women; with the former, he found a hug generally to be the most effective form of comfort and, with the latter, it more often than not led to far more pleasant offerings than consolation. Now he smiled at his little brother and then looked up at his cousins, saying coolly, 'I grant you that necessity is as loose a term as a Southwark whore's virtue. But I'm not convinced that I need put Somerset to death. If I'm right, we gain a great deal. If he does prove me wrong . . .' With an expressive shrug.

Warwick stared down at him. It had been on his tongue to

remind Edward of the beheadings he'd ordered after Mortimer's Cross and Towton Field. Now he was glad he had not, disarmed by Edward's candid admission of executions meant only to avenge. He was remembering, too, Edward's uncharacteristic outpouring of emotion before York's Micklegate Bar, remembering that brief glimpse of a bitter grief seeking release in rage. It had been two years since Sandal Castle; time enough, he thought, for all wounds to heal but he saw no reason now to probe for scars. If Ned had the bit between his teeth on this, so be it. Ned would learn the hard way with Somerset, and mayhap that was not all that bad, either.

'All right, Ned. We'll do it your way.' He summoned the resolute smile of a good loser. 'You may be right, after all. . . . Who's to say?'

'Who, indeed?' Edward echoed and although it was said placidly enough, even with a hint of ironic amusement, John Neville moved swiftly to the sideboard and, without waiting to summon a servant, poured the wine himself, passing cups to his brother and cousin.

'Shall we drink, then, to Somerset's conversion to the True Faith?' he said lightly and felt an undefined yet very real sense of relief when both Edward and Warwick laughed.

7

Middleham Castle Yorkshire

May 1464

Middleham Castle, the Yorkshire stronghold of Richard Neville, Earl of Warwick, was situated on the southern slope of Wensleydale, a mile and a half above the crossing of the Ure and Cover rivers. For three hundred years, the castle had dominated the surrounding moors and the limestone Norman keep towered fifty feet into the chill northern sky, encircled by a quadrangular castle bailey, a dark-water moat, massive outer walls, and a grey stone gatehouse that faced north toward the village that thrived in the shadow of the Neville Bear and Ragged Staff.

Francis Lovell hated Middleham from the first moment he laid eyes upon it, eyes that stung from held-back tears and the dust of a six-day journey. With each mile that took him farther from the Lovell manor in Oxfordshire, his heart grew heavier, his mood more oppressive, his self-pity more acute. Francis did not want to leave Minster Lovell, did not want to leave his mother and little sisters. Still less did he want to join the household of the Earl of Warwick. Francis knew a great deal about Warwick, as who in England did not? Warwick was the mightiest of the Yorkist lords. Admiral of England. Captain of Calais. Warden of the West March toward Scotland. The greatest landholder in England, for King Edward had shown himself to be a monarch of lavish generosity and none had benefited more handsomely under his reign than his cousin of Warwick.

It was due to the King's partiality to his Neville kinsman that Francis found himself making his reluctant journey northward that May. Francis was the only son and heir of John, Baron Lovell of Tichmersh, a man who was one of the wealthiest lords of the realm below the rank of Earl. Lord Lovell had died that January, leaving a ten-year-old boy as his sole heir, a boy suddenly very wealthy and, therefore, very important. The wardship of Francis Lovell was a lucrative prize, one that soon passed to Warwick, courtesy of his cousin, the King.

In a dizzying space of time, the world as Francis had known it was forever changed. His father died. He was to be the ward of the Earl of Warwick. And less than a month ago, he'd been wed to Anna Fitz-Hugh, the eight-year-old daughter of Lord Fitz-Hugh and Alice Neville, Warwick's favourite sister. Francis was told he was most fortunate to be able to call the Earl of Warwick his kinsman. Francis was not so young, however, that he didn't understand Warwick had acted to secure a wealthy husband for his little niece. That the marriage had not been of his choosing mattered to no one but Francis.

And so, on a cool morning in mid-May, he arrived at Middleham to take up residence and to take up study of the courtesies and craft of knighthood. As he rode across the drawbridge into the inner bailey of Middleham Castle, he did so with considerable apprehension and a muted degree of antagonism. The Lovells were Lancastrian.

More than three years had passed since Edward's bloody crowning at Towton. Francis's father had fought that March day for Harry of Lancaster, but he was a man able to recognize the realities of power. He'd soon come to terms with the Yorkist King, had taught Francis to do the same.

That had not been difficult for Francis. He'd been only seven when the battle of Towton was fought, had no memories of the exiled Lancastrian King and Queen. Marguerite d'Anjou was something of a mythical figure to him, was one with those beautiful tragic queens of legend. Certainly, there was legend in the making in the tales told of her troubles these three years past. Hazardous Channel crossings back and forth to the Continent in vain attempts to win French or Burgundian backing for her cause. Encounters with highwaymen. A shipwreck off the Yorkshire coast. Debts she could never hope to repay. Yet still she persevered, refused to admit defeat.

The stories were dramatic in the extreme and were so embroidered in the telling that fact and fiction became inextricably entwined. Francis believed all and felt very sorry for the woman who'd once been Queen of England, who'd been forced at last to seek refuge in France. He accepted Edward of York, however, as England's King, the only one he could truly remember. It was one thing, though, to accept the Yorkists. It was quite another to find himself suddenly in their very midst, to find himself in the Yorkist citadel of Middleham, home of His Most Formidable Grace, the Earl of Warwick, and the King's own brother, the Duke of Gloucester.

To his relief, neither Warwick nor Gloucester was at Middleham upon his arrival, both being at York with the King who'd come north that spring to deal with yet another Lancastrian uprising. Francis had been courteously received into the Earl's household and settled down to learn the routines of his new world.

The two weeks that followed were the loneliest of his life. He was woefully homesick, found no friends among the other boys in the Earl's service, like him, sons of the nobility, but with impeccable Yorkist credentials. It wasn't that they tormented Francis for his Lancastrian heritage. Worse, they ignored him.

Determined not to shame himself before these indifferent adversaries, Francis applied himself grimly to his studies, passed the morning hours practising his penmanship, conjugating Latin verbs, pouring over the *Rules of Chivalry* and *The Government of Kings and Princes.* The afternoons he spent in the tiltyard, trying to hold his horse on a straight course toward the quintain, to master the elusive art of hitting the target and then ducking to avoid its bruising backswing, which, more often than not, sent him tumbling to the sawdust that so ineffectively softened his fall.

After supper, he was occasionally ushered into the private solar of the Earl, to make stilted and 'courtly' conversation with his new kinswomen by marriage, the Earl's two daughters, Isabel and Anne. And then he retired to the quarters shared with his fellow knightly apprentices, to struggle silently to swallow the lump of misery that rose relentlessly in his throat each night, that he dared not allow to escape in that most disgraceful of all sounds, a muffled sob. Each night he won his war; each day his battle began anew.

The last day of May dawned with the promise of summer languor, the sky so blue that it dazzled Francis to look up at it and raised his spirits in spite of himself. There was to be no practice at the tiltyard this afternoon; there were to be further executions at Middleham and the Countess of Warwick did not want the boys to witness the beheadings. They were taken, instead, out onto the moors, each with a hooded falcon perched upon a leather-sheathed wrist. Francis alone remained; he'd taken a particularly bruising fall at the quintain the day before, had twisted an ankle too severely for a day on horseback.

He'd been cautioned to keep to his quarters; of course he didn't. He wandered aimlessly for a time in the inner bailey, but as he passed the auditor's kitchen, he saw a large wooden tub of honey sitting just inside the doorway. To his own astonishment, he saw himself reach out, tip the tub over in a sweet sticky flood. There was a startled squawk from one of the cooks, followed by a burst of profanity colourful enough to have impressed Francis had he waited around to hear it. He hadn't. Realizing at once the enormity of his inexplicable sin, he'd taken to his heels, was already sprinting through the gatehouse and into the outer bailey.

He slowed, panting, when he saw he'd either outdistanced pursuit or escaped detection. His ankle was throbbing again. He limped along the outer curtain wall toward the outlying buildings that housed the granary, the stables, the brewery. As he drew near the slaughterhouse, he came to a sudden halt, remembering that for today a block had been set up within, for the execution of the Lancastrian rebels.

In the two weeks since Francis had come to Middleham, there'd been a number of beheadings, all in the wake of the battle of Hexham fought by the banks of the Devilswater River, a battle that ended in defeat and death for the turncoat Duke of Somerset.

Though Lancastrian, Francis had little pity for Somerset. Somerset was twice a Judas. He'd forsaken Marguerite at Durham when offered a pardon by Edward of York, only to repent of his Yorkist allegiance this past December, almost a year to the day since he pledged his loyalty to Edward.

To Francis, this had seemed doubly dishonourable and he'd said as much to his father, who agreed with him but offered an intriguing explanation for Somerset's defection. Lord Lovell was of the opinion that Edward of York appeared so easygoing, so rarely riled and so pleasure-loving that people tended to dwell upon his conquests in the bedchamber whilst forgetting his equally formidable conquests upon the field. There were those, he told Francis, who could not believe a man who so loved his own ease and the company of women was secure upon his throne.

'That is a fatal mistake, Francis,' he'd said soberly and for Henry Beaufort, Duke of Somerset, the grim prediction was to be borne out before five months had passed.

On May 15th, Somerset had confronted John Neville at Hexham. The result had been a resounding Yorkist victory and, for Somerset, there was to be no second reprieve. Wounded in the fighting, he was captured after the battle. John Neville had taken him to the village of Hexham. There in the marketplace, his spurs were struck off, his coat of arms torn from him and he was beheaded before a jeering crowd.

Yorkist justice now proved swift and lethal. Four others were executed that day with Somerset. On May 17th, five more died at Newcastle. The next day, seven Lancastrian rebels were beheaded at Middleham and, on May 26th, fourteen went to the block at York. Today, two more were to die at Middleham and Francis found himself drawn inexorably toward the door of the slaughterhouse.

No soldiers barred the way. He decided he could risk a quick glimpse within, perhaps even get a look at the two doomed prisoners. He sidled closer, taut with the anticipation of reprimand. None came. He gathered up his nerve, slipped silently through the open doorway.

Within, the light was dim and, coming from bright sunlight, he blinked, and at first saw little. A number of men were standing in the shadows. A large wooden block was set up in the centre of the chamber. A man was sprawled across it, in what looked to be an improbably awkward position. Realization hit Francis then but, even as his brain acknowledged what his eyes were registering, the blade above the kneeling man's head was sweeping downward and, suddenly, there was nothing in Francis's world but the horror of that decapitated head hitting the straw and the blood gushing over the block, the straw, the executioner and the twitching thing that but seconds before had been the body of a living man.

Francis choked, stumbled back and then bolted from the slaughterhouse, out into the sunlit bailey. He only made it as far as the stables before his revulsion burst from his constricted throat. Throwing himself down upon the straw, he was violently ill.

Time passed. No one entered the stables; even the grooms seemed to have disappeared. Francis was alone with his misery. Once his stomach no longer heaved, he rose to his knees and crawled over into an empty stall, lay still. After a while, he cried.

He had no idea how long he lay there. He tried not to think, to keep his mind perfectly blank, to concentrate only upon the scratchy feel of the straw against his cheek, the pungent odour of horse dung, the soft nickering of the horses. When he heard stallions being brought into the stable for unsaddling, he kept very still, listening as these new arrivals were led into stalls to be rubbed down, watered. No one came toward his end of the stable and eventually the laughter and banter faded away. It was quiet again.

He was swallowing with difficulty. His mouth tasted vile and the sour smell of vomit seemed to cling to his clothes, his skin. He rolled over, sat up and then came shakily to his feet. But, as he emerged from the stall, he saw that he was not alone.

Another boy stood looking at him in surprise. He was older than Francis but no taller, a thin dark youngster with a bridle in his hand and a quizzical expression on his face.

'Where did you come from?' he asked, sounding curious but not unfriendly.

Francis was mute. There was no way he could make casual conversation with this stranger. He wanted only to escape the stables before the other boy discovered the evidence of his weak stomach and laughed at him, wanted nothing so much as to be a thousand miles from Middleham and all the hateful people it housed. He debated making a dash for the door but his knees felt weak, his ankle ached. It was too late, anyway. He saw the other boy glance down at the soiled straw, see the unmistakable signs of sickness.

He raised his eyes swiftly to Francis, saw how white and shaken Francis was. Before Francis knew what he was about, he stepped forward, caught Francis by the elbow.

'Over here,' he directed and, giving Francis no opportunity to object, he pulled Francis toward a bench near the far wall.

'Sit there,' he said, still in the same peremptory tone, and as Francis sank down upon the bench, he disappeared into one of the stalls, returning with a pail of water. At that, Francis abandoned pride, leaned over to plunge his face into the water. Rinsing his mouth, he spat into the straw and then took the handkerchief the boy was silently holding out to him.

'Thank you,' he mumbled, reluctantly remembering his manners.

The other youngster seated himself beside Francis on the bench.

'Was breakfast as bad as that?'

Francis subjected him to a suspicious stare, but could find no malice in the other's subdued amusement.

'No', he said and then with a touch of bravado, 'I saw the beheadings.'

'I see.' The boy was silent for a moment. 'That was foolish, you know. Such things must be done. But there's little pleasure in the viewing of them.'

He sounded so matter-of-fact that Francis frowned, not sure what reaction he'd expected but vaguely disappointed, nonetheless.

'Did you ever see a man's head struck from his body?' he challenged.

'No,' the boy said tersely, but then he gave Francis a sideways grin, confessed, 'I do not trust my stomach enough!'

Francis liked him for that, grinned back. 'It was ghastly,' he confided. 'Blood all over.' This was the first person who'd been even passably friendly to Francis in a fortnight and he groped now for a conversational topic.

'I've been here since May seventeenth, but I've not seen you before. Are you in the Earl's service, too?'

A nod. 'I've been at Pontefract. We only returned this noon. I knew I had not seen you before either.'

This last was said with a smile and Francis was encouraged to probe further.

'Have you been long at Middleham? Do you like it here?'

'Three years come November. And, yes, I do like it here very much.' Another smile. 'Middleham is home to me.'

Francis felt a pang at that, a wave of longing for Minster Lovell and his own world. One thing he did know for certes, that Middleham would never be home to him.

'I'm the Earl's ward,' he said. 'I was wed last month to his niece.'

The other boy was leaning forward, sorting through the straw for a stalk of unusual length. Finding one, he flipped it deftly through the air, watched it sink below the surface of the bucket.

'That will make us kin one day then,' he remarked casually. 'The Earl means for me to wed with his daughter when we're of an age.'

Francis made no response, struggling with a keen sense of disappointment in his new acquaintance. He knew very well that Warwick's daughter was one of the greatest heiresses in England. The other boy must think him very gullible, indeed, to believe such boasting. His pride was affronted, a sceptical challenge was taking shape. But the other didn't follow through with his bragging, seemed unaware that he'd said anything out of the ordinary. Francis hesitated, and then decided to let it pass. He was finding too much pleasure in the first friendly encounter he'd had since arriving at Middleham to sabotage it willingly.

'If you are the Earl's ward, then your own father must be dead?' the other boy said suddenly and Francis nodded.

'Yes. He died on January ninth.'

'My father is dead, too. Three years last December.'

They looked at one another, recognizing a common kinship of loss.

Francis wanted suddenly to impress his new friend, but didn't know how to best do so. 'I once met the Duke of Somerset,' he said, after some thought. 'He was friend to my father.' Honesty compelling him to amend that to, 'Well, they did know each other.'

The other boy did not look impressed, however, merely shrugged, and Francis tried again.

'I met his brother, too . . . Edmund Beaufort. Does he now become Duke of Somerset?' Answering his own question, he decided, 'He must, I think, since Somerset died without a son.'

'I met Edmund Beaufort once.' Indifferently. 'Or so my lady mother told me. It was years ago and I truly do not remember him. Your family is Lancastrian, then?'

The question was quietly posed, without undue emphasis. Francis was remembering, however, where he was. This was Middleham. He'd win few friends here by boasting of his Lancastrian ties.

'My father fought for Lancaster at Towton. But he then accepted King Edward as his sovereign,' he said carefully.

He saw at once that his answer had been the right one. The other boy studied him for a moment and then smiled.

'What is your name?'

There was no mistaking the friendly intent and Francis smiled, too.

'Francis Lovell . . .' he began, and then broke off abruptly, for a man had appeared in the doorway of the stable. The most magnificently dressed man Francis had ever seen, with thigh-high boots of gleaming Spanish leather, brightly coloured hose and a wide-shouldered doublet studded with gems, a dagger hilt sheathed in gold.

'There you are, Dickon,' he said, at the same time that a voice somewhere behind him shouted, 'My lord of Warwick is at the stables. Have you word for him on the beheadings. . . .'

The rest of the sentence was lost to Francis. In his ears echoed only the words 'my lord of Warwick'. He scrambled to his feet, stared tongue-tied at the Earl of Warwick and then at his new friend, who'd risen, too, was moving toward Warwick with no evidence of unease and every evidence of pleasure.

'My girls are waiting to welcome you home, Dickon. Nan sent me to fetch you!' This last said lightly, with the playful indulgence it amused him to assume toward his wife.

'I'm eager to see them, too, Cousin.' He turned then, gestured toward Francis.

'This is your ward, Cousin. Francis Lovell, who arrived in our absence.'

Francis remembered little of what followed. In a daze, he mumbled something, he never knew what, to Warwick's welcome. Saw the way the Earl rested his arm affectionately around the other boy's shoulders, listened as they exchanged the easy banter of intimates.

At last Warwick had gone, and they were alone again. The other boy reached down, picked up his forgotten bridle, hung it on a hook over his head.

'I have to go,' he said. 'I'll look for you tonight at supper.'

Francis found his tongue then. 'You're the Duke of Gloucester,' he blurted out, so abruptly that he made it sound almost like an accusation.

He saw the older boy arch an eyebrow at his tone. 'Yes, I know,' he said, with what, had he been older, would have been unmistakable as irony.

The Duke of Gloucester did not look at all as Francis had imagined King Edward's brother to be. Nor did he act the way Francis fancied a royal Duke would act. It seemed monstrously unfair to him that this boy he'd begun to like should turn out to be Richard Plantagenet, Duke of Gloucester. The one person who'd been friendly to him a Yorkist Prince, blood kin to the awesome Edward!

He tried to remember what his mother had cautioned about court etiquette, knew he was supposed to kneel, but that seemed crazy here in the middle of a stable, especially when the royal Duke had given him his own handkerchief to wipe the traces of vomit from his face. Was a Duke addressed as 'Your Grace' like the King? Or did 'my lord' suffice? It was hopeless; it had all gone completely from his head.

'What am I to call you?' he asked at length, too unhappy to hide his discomfort, feeling very gauche and lonelier than at any time in this, the loneliest fortnight of his life.

Richard gave him a thoughtful look and then a smile of sudden charm.

'My friends call me Dickon,' he said.

8

Middleham Castle Yorkshire

October 1464

Propping his journal against his drawn-up knees, Francis poised his pen above the parchment, and then began the day's entry, neatly lettering at the top of the page:

Begun this 14th day of October, the 20th Sunday after Holy Trinity, at Middleham Castle, Wensleydale, Yorkshire, in the year of Our Lord 1464, fourth year of the reign of His Sovereign Grace, King Edward.

I write this in the solar of his Grace, the Earl of Warwick. The hearth log has burned fully a quarter since we heard Vespers rung in the village, so we must soon be abed. We have been playing at forfeits with roasted chestnuts as the stakes; Isabel and Anne and Will and Rob Percy and Dickon and me.

Isabel is the Earl's daughter. She is 13 and has very pale hair and green-gold eyes like a cat. She can spit like a cat, too, when vexed.

Her sister Anne is different. Anne rarely gets angry. She has fair braids which Dickon likes to pull and brown eyes like her father, the Earl. Her birthdate is in June. She is 8 years of age, like Anna. . . .

Here his pen faltered, and then he resolutely inked in the words 'my wife'. He hoped repetition would make the idea seem less strange to him. After building himself a cache of chestnuts, he resumed:

Will is Will Parr. He is small for his 13 years, like Dickon, but with a face full of freckles and green eyes. He is unfailingly good-natured and my friend.

Rob Percy is one of the Percys of Northumbria. His family is Yorkist but he is a distant cousin to the Lancastrian Henry Percy, Earl of Northumberland, who died at Towton, and to the Henry Percy, his son and heir, sent to the Tower this spring at King Edward's command. The title should have passed to the son but King Edward bestowed it upon John Neville this May as his reward for the victory at Hexham.

Rob talked too much about how pleased he was that John Neville is now Earl of Northumberland. I think Rob fears people will confuse him with his Lancastrian cousins for he boasts about York more than anyone at Middleham, even Dickon! Like all his kin, Rob has hair like flax and blue eyes. He has a quick temper and is overly fond of jests. He is more Dickon and Will's friend than mine.

Dickon is my most steadfast friend. He has hair as black as ink and dark eyes of a colour midst blue and grey. He has his right arm in a sling of black silk as he took a bad fall tilting at the quintain two days past. Her Grace, the Lady Nan, was much disquieted as he'd broken his shoulder in such a fall a few years ago, soon after he'd become attached to the Earl's household. She berated him soundly for his rashness. I think she suspects he was showing off for his cousins, Isabel and Anne. She is right, he was!

'What are you writing, Lovell?' Rob Percy rose to his knees, leaned closer.

Francis reacted instinctively, jerking the book back, and Rob's curiosity inflamed.

'Let me see,' he demanded, and reached over to claim the journal.

Evading his grasp, Francis said tightly, 'I will not. It's private.'

Rob persisted; the page tore and Francis fell backward. Rob glanced at the fragment clutched in his fist, and his eyes widened.

'Jesú, he's writing of us!'

He lunged for the journal and, as the two boys rolled around on the floor, Richard's wolfhound puppy clambered over their twisting bodies and deposited wet kisses indiscriminately. Managing at last to regain his feet, Francis shoved the larger boy back. Rob stumbled, lost his balance and tripped over the wooden mazer filled with chestnuts. Scrambling to maintain his footing, he reached out for support and caught Richard's sling, sending them both crashing to the floor.

Rob saw at once that the other boy was hurt and Francis was forgotten. 'Dickon . . . Your Grace. I'm sorry, in truth I am!'

Richard's breath was coming back and he pushed Rob's hand away when Rob tried to help him rise. Rob backed away as Will and the Neville girls knelt by Richard, all talking at once.

'Will you cease your hovering?' Richard snapped irritably. Using his free arm to push himself up to a sitting position, he glared at Rob.

'You see what happens when you play the fool?' he accused.

'Sometimes, Rob, you act as if you have not the sense God gave a sheep.'

He winced as Anne tried to adjust the bandage and Rob was assailed by remorse. 'It was Lovell's doing,' he muttered, and Francis, who'd watched transfixed, burst out with a heated denial which threatened to kindle the quarrel all over again. It was Isabel, with the inbred imperious authority of a Neville, who silenced them both.

'Clodhoppers, the pair of you!' She pointed disdainfully at the discarded book, lying smudged and torn by the hearth. 'Take your silly scribblings. As for you, Rob Percy, just be thankful you did not cause Dickon serious hurt!'

She looked back over her shoulder. 'Dickon, mayhap we should summon my mother's physician?'

'Good God, no!' Richard exclaimed, in genuine alarm. He glanced about at the others. 'And I'll not forgive the one who says a word of this to the Lady Nan.'

Satisfied that his warning had penetrated, he let Will help him to his feet while Rob seized the opportunity to retreat and Francis to retrieve his journal.

'Dickon . . . does it pain you much?'

'No, not much, Francis.' Richard elected to sit on the settle, far more sedately than was his wont. 'Were you truly writing about us?'

Francis nodded unwillingly and was relieved when Richard let it drop.

Isabel, growing bored, now departed the solar and the others, settling down with the mazer of chestnuts, resumed a familiar topic of conversation, selecting a name for Richard's wolfhound. The dog, already enormous at four months and as black as proverbial sin, was a birthday gift from his brother, the King, having arrived by special courier only that week.

The puppy had stretched out at Richard's feet and was covertly eyeing the soft leather of his shoe. Watching, Francis grinned.

He'd been very much impressed that the King should have remembered the birthdate of a younger brother, he felt sure this was not a common characteristic of older brothers, at least not the ones he'd known. Of course Edward had confused the dates somewhat, as Richard had actually turned twelve on October 2nd, but Francis knew Edward no longer paid any heed whatsoever to the birthdate of his other brother, George, the fifteen-year-old Duke of Clarence.

Not that he faulted Edward for that. Francis held no high opinion of George, who'd paid an interminable visit to the Earl of Warwick and Richard that summer. Francis was thankful George did not reside in the Earl's household. When provoked, George had a viper's tongue and he had an unsettling way of finding humour in things that would amuse no one else. Francis found it hard to understand why Richard seemed fond of George. But he had no trouble at all in understanding Richard's devotion to his eldest brother.

Edward had remained in York until mid-July, negotiating a truce with the Scots. Before departing Yorkshire, he'd detoured north to accept the Earl of Warwick's hospitality at Middleham. His visit had generated much welcome excitement. Their northern neighbours, the Metcalfes of Nappa Hall and Lord and Lady Scrope of nearby Bolton Castle, flocked to Middleham to honour the King. Francis had noted, with secret surprise, that even the mighty Earl seemed less in Edward's presence.

He'd envied Richard sorely in the days following Edward's visit, for the King had made much of his younger brother, keeping Richard by his side long past the boy's normal bedtime, coming to watch Richard practise with lance and broadsword at the quintain.

Francis now thought Edward's favourite cognizance, the Sunne in Splendour, to be remarkably well chosen. The pale shadow of Marguerite d'Anjou receded, blotted out by the sun of York, and, for the first time, Francis found himself giving credence to the stories Richard told him of the Frenchwoman's cruelties. Perhaps she was not so tragic a heroine after all, he concluded somewhat regretfully.

Nonetheless, he felt a lingering pity for the Lancastrian Queen, now living in straitened circumstances in France with her eleven-year-old son and a few faithful followers like Edmund Beaufort, newly Duke of Somerset, and his younger brother, John Beaufort. He felt some pity, too, for King Harry, reputed to be sheltered by the Scots. But such sympathies Francis did not confide to Richard, or to any others at Middleham. There were certain sacrifices to be made on behalf of his newly forged Yorkist friendships and discretion was not the least of such demands.

Now he opened the journal he'd been holding in his lap, grimly assessing the damage Rob Percy had done. Plague take him for his prying! With Rob sure to bear a grudge, how could he dare keep the journal? Percy would ferret it from the most secret hiding place and Francis would burn each and every page before he'd risk having Rob set eyes upon them. Defiantly, he reached down and picked up his pen. Smoothing the page with his sleeve, he wrote:

Will favours Gawain for Dickon's dog, being much taken with *Gawain and the Grene Knight*. Anne fancies Robin. She has a spaniel which she calls Maid Marian. Dickon says that if the dog were but a bitch, he could name it Marguerite d'Anjou. That amuses Will but is lost on Anne.

Dickon is out of sorts tonight. His arm pains him, I think. Dickon endures pain without complaint, but he accepts inconvenience with poor grace and now he is vexed because he cannot shell the chestnuts with his left hand. Anne offers to share hers.

Will now suggests that Dickon name the dog Somerset after the man the Earl claims to be the true father of Marguerite d'Anjou's son and Dickon laughs. But I fear the puppy will be grey with age ere he decides.

'Francis?'

His pen jerked, smeared the page.

Anne had slipped silently from the settle and was standing before him. 'Francis . . . if you like, I could keep your journal safe for you. I know you've little privacy, sharing quarters with Rob and Dickon and the other pages. I could fetch it for you whenever you wished to write in it.'

When he didn't respond immediately, she coloured. 'I'd take a solemn vow, in the Blessed Lady's name, that I'd not read it, and I'd never profane such an oath, Francis, truly I would not.'

Francis no longer hesitated, held out the journal to her. 'I need no such oath from you, Anne. I would be much beholden to you if you would keep it in your chamber for me.'

'I'll not tell a soul where I store it,' she promised gravely. 'Not even Dickon.'

He had no chance to reply. Isabel was back, breathless and eager to share her news.

'Dickon! Father is here! He has just ridden into the bailey and Uncle Johnny and George are with him.'

Richard looked pleased. 'I thought he was to remain at Reading with Ned till after Martinmas. Have they moved up the date for the York parliament?'

Isabel had no interest in parliaments. She shrugged, shook her head.

'I don't know. But this I can tell you, something is very wrong. I saw Father briefly as he came up the stairs into the keep, and he's in a tearing rage. Never have I seen him so wroth.' She paused; she had an intuitive flair for the dramatic. 'And it is your brother who has riled him so!'

Richard showed little surprise. 'What has George done now?'

'Not George.' Triumphantly. 'Ned!'

'Ned?' Richard echoed incredulously, and she nodded. Her excitement ebbed somewhat and she said earnestly,

'Dickon, I think Ned must have done something truly dreadful.'

They had not long to wait. Within moments, the youthful Duke of Clarence strode into the solar, shouting for Richard even as he came through the doorway that led out into the great hall.

'Dickon! Wait till you hear . . .' He paused, his eyes flickering incuriously over Richard's black silk sling. 'What the devil happened to you? You'll not believe it, God's truth you will not. I tell you, he's gone mad, stark raving mad!'

Richard was frowning. 'What are you saying, George?'

'We were at Reading and the council was meeting. Our cousin Warwick reported that the negotiations were proceeding well for Ned's marriage with the sister-in-law of the French King, when Ned suddenly announced that such a marriage was out of the question, must be dismissed out of hand. And when they pressed him on it, he shrugged and said it so happened that he already had a wife!'

George paused, letting the suspense build to a gratifying pitch before saying with heavy sarcasm, 'It seems Ned made a secret May marriage . . . and then forgot to mention it during all those months that our cousin was labouring on his behalf to conclude the French marriage.'

'A secret marriage?' Richard repeated. He sounded stunned and Francis well understood why. If George was to be believed, Edward had done what no other King of England had dared to do in the four hundred years since the Norman Conquest, chosen a wife for his own pleasure.

George nodded. 'You did hear me, Little Brother. A secret marriage . . . to a wench he found fair to look upon! Little wonder our cousin Warwick is sorely affronted!'

'Who is she?' The question coming in perfect unison from Richard and Isabel.

'He was wed in a clandestine ceremony this past May at Grafton Manor in Northamptonshire . . . to Elizabeth Grey.'

Richard spoke for them all. 'Who,' he asked, 'is Elizabeth Grey?'

135

George turned brilliant blue-green eyes upon Richard, eyes that took the light like turquoise. 'That is the truly incredible part of this charade. She's a Woodville, the widow of Sir John Grey, who died fighting for Lancaster at St Albans! She has two sons by Grey, one nearly as old as you, Dickon! And she's a full five years older than Ned!' He laughed suddenly.

'A twenty-seven-year-old widow with two sons,' he repeated, drawing the words out with evident relish. 'And, if that were not damning enough, she's distant kin to Marguerite d'Anjou! Her aunt was wed to an uncle of Marguerite's! Christ on the Cross, Dickon, do you not see now why I say Ned must be mad?'

'Or bewitched.'

All eyes turned toward Isabel.

'What other explanation could there be, George? Why else would he marry her if she'd not resorted to witchcraft?'

George dutifully crossed himself, but he looked sceptical. 'Knowing Ned,' he said cynically, 'it would take no more to bewitch him than white thighs, a rounded belly, and . . .'

'Hold your tongue, for pity's sake,' Isabel interrupted hastily. 'You know my lady mother frowns upon such bawdy talk in Anne's hearing. Or mine,' she added as an afterthought, and she and George grinned at each other.

'Jesú, but you're quiet of a sudden, Dickon!' George glanced quizzically at the younger boy and, when Richard didn't reply, he laughed.

'You're not often so loath to make known your opinions. What say you of our brother's folly? Bewitched as Bella suspects? Or just overly eager to ride the grey mare?'

He laughed but Richard did not.

'I should like to know,' he said, very low, 'why Ned's falling out with our cousin seems to give you such pleasure.'

No longer laughing, George said curtly, 'You're daft.'

It was then that the Earl of Warwick came into the solar.

Francis was shivering; the north-wall window seat was swept by draughts. But he dared not move, fearful of calling attention to himself. If only he'd taken the chance to slip away with Will! He felt sure he was not meant to be a witness to the Earl's wrath. Richard and George, after all, were Warwick's cousins. But he was not blood kin, and he waited apprehensively for the Earl to notice his obtrusive presence, to order him from the solar for a birching.

Isabel had been right; Warwick was in a tearing rage, awesome even for a man whose tempers were known the breadth and length of England. Ostensibly, his tirade was directed at the Lady Nan, his Countess, and his brother John, newly named Earl of Northumberland. Francis sensed, however, that Warwick was speaking to one man and one man only, his cousin the King, saying all that must, of necessity, have been choked back at Reading. For surely he'd not have dared to say to Edward what he was now saying in the solar of Middleham Castle. At least, Francis didn't think he'd have dared; even from the Kingmaker, such words bordered on the treasonous.

'Woodvilles,' Warwick spat, and in his mouth the name became profanity. 'I tell you, Johnny, it defies belief. Anthony Woodville faced Ned at Towton and now he's to be embraced as a brother-in-law?'

'So it seems,' John said. Rising from the settle, he approached the other man. 'I like it no more than you do, Dick, but it's done. He's wed the woman and whatever we do think of her family, she's to be Queen. . . .'

'Queen? By the Mass, man, how can the very words not choke in your throat? The grand-daughter of a squire, the widow of a Lancastrian knight. . . . A right fine wife Ned has chosen for himself! If she's fit to be Queen of England, I'm bidding fair to supplant His Holiness the Pope!'

John didn't argue, and after a moment, he went quietly from the solar. Francis yearned with all his heart that he might follow.

He wasn't surprised when John yielded; there were few men who would willingly face down the Earl of Warwick in a rage. Francis felt a sudden surge of admiration for King Edward who had dared the Earl's wrath so cavalierly.

The Lady Nan was now at the Earl's side, speaking too softly for Francis to hear, and he took the opportunity to observe how his companions were bearing up under this prolonged exposure to Warwick's wrath. Never had he seen such tense, unhappy faces, with one singular exception. George was following the Earl's words with alert interest, a suggestion of a smile quirking the corner of his mouth, and Francis thought, Dickon was right, he is enjoying Edward's fall from grace. He knew a certain strain had surfaced in Edward's relationship with George, but only now did he see how deep it ran.

Turning his gaze from George, he glanced briefly at Warwick's subdued daughters and then sought the eyes of his friend. But Richard was bending over the wolfhound puppy and all Francis could see was a thatch of dark hair, falling forward to screen his face.

'How in Christ's name do you expect me to react?' Warwick said suddenly, with such violence that Francis flinched. 'He played me for a fool, Nan. Am I to forget that he stood mute all the while I dealt with the French, striving to bring about a marriage for England's good? Am I to allow him to humiliate me before the whole of Europe for the sake of a parvenu trollop? I tell you, Nan, it is not to be borne! He's made me the laughingstock of England and all for a slut shrewd enough to keep her legs closed to him till he was hot enough to wed her!'

Francis was shocked; he'd never heard the Earl speak so crudely in the presence of his daughters. George laughed aloud, a startling sound in the sudden silence. That should have earned him a disapproving rebuke from the Countess, but she didn't even deign to glance in his direction, not taking her eyes from her husband.

There was a stifled sound; Isabel coughed, trying to choke back a nervous giggle and, to Francis's horror, it proved contagious. He found himself struggling against a diabolic urge to laugh, until he saw the expression on Richard's face. He had jerked his head up at Warwick's words and Francis felt his heart begin to pound sickeningly against his ribs. Richard was flushed, taut as a bowstring, and for an appalled instant, Francis thought him to be on the verge of speech. Dickon, no! he willed silently, and sighed deeply when Richard kept still.

'And what am I to tell the French? How do I explain that there's to be no alliance, no French bride . . . because my cousin the King is such a fool that he values a strumpet's white skin and green eyes more than the weal of England!'

'No!'

'Oh, Jesus God, Dickon,' Francis whispered through frozen lips as the Earl spun around.

'Come here, Dickon.'

Richard came slowly to his feet, obediently moving to stand before Warwick.

'You spoke, lad?'

Richard was mute and, after a long, searching look at the boy's tense face, Warwick said, a shade too dispassionately, 'You may speak freely. You are Ned's brother, after all, and his marriage does concern you, too. Say what is on your mind.'

Richard swallowed. Always soft-spoken, he was almost inaudible now as he said, 'I'd . . . I'd rather not, Cousin.'

'Surely you do not approve of this marriage, Dickon? Does this woman sound as if she should grace a throne?'

'No,' Richard admitted, and Francis slumped back in the window seat, weak with a relief that dissipated with Richard's next words.

'But . . . that choice was not mine to make. It was Ned's.'

'I see.' Very softly. 'Are you saying then, that the choice being Ned's, I should forbear to find fault with it?'

'Cousin . . .'

'Christ, Dickon, have you not heard a word I've said? How can you justify Ned's actions? A clandestine marriage to a Lancastrian widow. . . . How does that serve England?'

Richard hesitated and Warwick snapped, 'I'm awaiting your response. Tell me how your brother has served England with this accursed marriage!'

'I do not know,' Richard conceded huskily. 'I know only that Ned would never act dishonourably.'

'Indeed?' Warwick said, and the inflection in his voice chilled all within the room.

Francis was trembling, burning with a bright blasphemous rage; rage directed against the Earl of Warwick, the Kingmaker, who was choosing to vent his anger at King Edward upon Dickon. Anne was crying softly, Isabel on the verge of tears and George, no longer amused, was biting his lower lip, blue-green eyes flickering from his cousin to his brother and back again and, at last, to the Lady Nan.

His silent appeal seemed to work, for she took a step toward her husband. But she went no further. Nor did she speak.

'So Ned could not act dishonourably,' Warwick echoed, savagely sardonic. 'You have a queer concept of honour, by God. He married in secret, married a woman who has no attributes for queenship, married her for no reason save that he desired her body. And then he said nothing whilst I planned a French marriage, knowing full well such plans must come to naught. Tell me the honour in that, Dickon. I should truly like to know!'

Richard was staring at his cousin with the strained, exhausted look of one condemned and no longer even hoping for reprieve.

'I cannot speak for Ned. But you were the one who sought the French marriage, Cousin. Perhaps . . . perhaps you misread Ned. Perhaps you acted without making certain that he did indeed favour the marriage. Ned . . . Ned told me this spring that he thought you to be too fond of your friend, the King of France. . . .'

His voice trailed off, in belated realization of a broken confi-

140

dence. Colour had scorched Warwick's face. He took a step toward the boy and the sound of metal striking wood resounded loudly behind him. A silver tray and wine flagon had been placed on the heavy oaken table. Tray, flagon and wine cups now lay scattered on the floor. The patterned Flemish carpet was darkening with a spreading reddish stain and wine was streaking the polished wood-grained table legs, splashing the lime-green of his daughter's bodice.

'My God, Anne!' He stared at the girl and then at the wreckage-strewn floor. Anne stared, too, at the havoc she'd wrought and burst into tears. It was then that John Neville came back into the solar.

He stood in the doorway, taking in the scene. His tearful little niece, the relief that so suddenly shone upon George's face as George saw him, his brother's fury. But it was at Richard that he looked the longest, saw the boy's despair. He understood, and his normally phlegmatic temperament suddenly caught fire.

Warwick pulled his daughter to him. 'What possessed you, girl? Look what you've done!'

Anne sobbed, stammered what would have been a plea for forgiveness had her words been intelligible. And suddenly the solar was full of sound.

Isabel cried, 'Oh, but it was an accident!'

Nan was shaking her head. 'Really, Anne, such clumsiness!'

It was Richard, however, who drew Warwick's attention back to himself, saying swiftly, 'Do not blame Anne, Cousin. The fault was ours. We distressed her with our quarrel.'

Warwick released his daughter, swung back toward Richard. The expression on his face was such that Richard instinctively took a step backward. Warwick acted instinctively, too, grabbed the boy to forestall what he thought to be flight and jerked Richard roughly toward him. As he did, John moved. In three strides, he'd crossed the solar, clamped his hand down upon Warwick's wrist.

'A word with you . . . brother,' he said tightly, and Warwick, who'd not even noticed his return to the solar, was now further taken aback by the heat in those normally placid brown eyes.

Before Warwick could reply, John's grip tightened on his arm and he quite literally pulled Warwick toward the door. And so rare was his brother's rage that Warwick found himself submitting in surprise.

John slammed the solar door shut behind them. In the empty grandeur of the great hall, they faced each other. Warwick was the first to break the silence.

'Well, Johnny,' he said brusquely, 'what had you to say that was so important it could not wait?'

'What the bloody hell did you think you were doing in there?' John demanded hotly. 'I do understand your anger with Ned. But to hold Dickon accountable for what Ned has done . . . Christ, man, what were you thinking of? He's only a boy, Dick, cannot be blamed for being loyal to his brother. You know he thinks the world of Ned!' He shook his head in disgust. 'You do surprise me, in truth. It did seem to me that you've gone to some pains to win Dickon's affection. Moreover, you always did act as if you were fond of him yourself.'

'Of course I'm fond of Dickon,' Warwick said impatiently. 'He happens to be important to me, to my plans. . . .'

'I'd suggest, then, that you do try to remember that in the future,' John said in tones Warwick would have accepted from no other man. 'Just think on this; what would have happened had Anne not knocked over that tray?'

That gave Warwick pause.

'Perhaps I did lose my temper,' he conceded. He fell silent, began to pace.

'Yes, you've a point, Johnny. I do not want Dickon bearing some fanciful grudge for what was said or done in the heat of anger. That's not the way . . .'

He turned and, not waiting for John, flung the solar door open.

Francis Lovell still sat frozen in the window seat. Under her mother's critical eye, Anne was picking up the scattered wine cups and depositing them back on the table. Isabel watched sympathetically but it didn't seem to have occurred to her to offer assistance. It had occurred to Richard but the Countess said rather coolly that he'd caused enough of a disturbance for one evening and Anne could manage without his help. He'd flushed under the rebuke, moved toward the hearth. There he'd been joined by George who looked as if he weren't sure whether he wanted to offer comfort or box the younger boy's ears. He seemed to be inclining toward consolation but he backed away hastily from Richard when he saw Warwick standing in the doorway.

At sight of her father, Anne abandoned her efforts and ran toward him. He looked down into her imploring dark eyes, and then touched her wet cheek. She slipped her hand into his, raised up on tiptoe to whisper, 'You are not still wroth with Dickon, are you, Papa?'

Warwick had to laugh. For a timid child, she could be surprisingly persistent. But her loyalty to her cousin pleased him; he had, after all, done what he could to foster it. He seized upon the opening she unwittingly provided and said, 'No, Anne, I'm not wroth with Dickon.'

He looked across the room at Richard.

'Come here, Dickon.'

He saw Richard's reluctance, but the boy came.

'When men are angry, Dickon, they are often intemperate. I fear that was true tonight for us all. I want you to understand that I do not blame you for speaking as rashly as you did.'

He paused and dropped his hand on Richard's shoulder. 'You are Ned's brother and it is only right that he should command your loyalties. However, I'll admit to being disappointed in you, Cousin. You see, I would have thought that I, too, laid claim to your loyalties.'

Richard looked stricken. 'You do!'

'I would hope so, Dickon,' Warwick said slowly. 'For I confess, it would be painful to think otherwise.'

Francis and Richard were alone in the solar. Warwick had retired for further discussion with his brother and, much to his delight, George, who'd been flattered beyond words at being included in adult politics. The Countess of Warwick had ushered her daughters toward the door immediately thereafter, with an especially warm hug for Richard now that he'd been restored to favour.

Francis sagged against the window cushions. 'Christ keep us,' he said softly. He wanted to tell Richard he admired him for defending his brother to the Earl but he did not think Richard would be receptive to such a compliment. He'd never seen the other boy look as troubled as he did at that moment. No, he did not think the Earl of Warwick to be a safe topic of discussion.

It never occurred to him to bring up the subject of King Edward's incredible marriage. Francis understood perfectly why Edward had sought to keep the marriage secret as long as possible. But what had possessed him to wed a Lancastrian widow in the first place? Love? Lust? Witchcraft, as Isabel suggested? It would have been great fun to speculate upon the reasons for an action unprecedented in the history of the English monarchy. But Francis knew better, knew that whatever Richard thought of his brother's astonishing behaviour, no one but he would ever know. George of Clarence, however, was another matter.

'Does your brother of Clarence not like His Grace, the King, Dickon?'

Richard made a sudden grab for the wolfhound, rescuing a candlestick that had fallen to the floor with the tray of silver.

'Sometimes, I do wonder, Francis,' he admitted. 'There are times when I think he is jealous. . . .'

He stopped, having said more than he'd intended. The candle was so thoroughly chewed that he felt it best to dispose of the evidence, and was moving toward the hearth when the door opened and Anne rushed back into the solar. Darting to the settle, she knelt and rose clutching Francis's journal.

Giving Francis an apologetic smile, she said softly, 'Goodnight, Francis, Dickon.'

As she passed Richard, he reached out, caught one of her blonde braids.

'If you like, Anne, you may pick the name for my wolfhound.'

She nodded. 'I should like that.' And holding the journal tightly against her, she backed toward the door, keeping her eyes on him all the while. At the door, she paused, gazed thoughtfully at the dog and said, 'Let's call him Gareth . . . like the knight.'

Richard was testing the name on his tongue, and now looked at the dog. 'Gareth! Here, Gareth. Here, boy.'

The puppy yawned and both boys laughed, not because they thought it all that amusing, but because laughter seemed the safest way to release the pent-up tensions of a night neither was likely ever to forget.

Francis slid off the window seat, stiff with cold.

'Dickon . . .' He stopped, realizing there was nothing that could safely be said.

In silence they made their way out onto the covered wooden bridge that spanned the inner bailey and connected the keep with the west-wall chambers. As he snapped his fingers to coax the lagging puppy, Richard's step slowed.

'I wonder . . .'

'What, Dickon?'

He regarded Francis unsmilingly. 'I wonder what she will be like . . . Elizabeth Woodville Grey.'

9

London

June 1467

Elizabeth Woodville may have been the most beautiful woman to ever wear the coronet of an English Queen. Men who saw Elizabeth no longer shared the certainty of their wives that only witchcraft could have beguiled Edward into so shocking a mésalliance. Even John Neville, quite happily wed to a placid, perceptive woman who was attractive only in his eyes, had been struck speechless at his first sight of Edward's Queen.

Warwick, too, had been forced grudgingly to concede her astonishing beauty, and lovely women were no novelty to Warwick. He'd had his share of liaisons and his wife, Nan, whom he'd married when he was six and she eight, was not only one of England's greatest heiresses but a pretty hazel-eyed blonde as well. But he had to admit, if only to himself, that he'd never seen a woman as beautiful as Elizabeth Woodville.

He'd been prepared to dislike her at first sight. It had taken little time, however, for him to learn to hate her, to hate her with the embittered enmity he'd previously reserved for Marguerite d'Anjou. He'd always thought her to be a totally unsuitable Queen for his cousin. Once he came to know her, he thought her to be a bitch as well.

In this, he was not alone. Elizabeth awed with her beauty but alienated with her arrogance. Warwick doubted there had ever been a Queen as little liked as the woman Edward had taken as his wife.

He would have preferred to believe Edward regretted the marriage; unfortunately, he could find no such indications. As much as it irked him to acknowledge it, his cousin seemed quite content with the beautiful haughty wife he'd chosen for himself. He was not faithful to her, but none who knew Edward would have expected fidelity and if Elizabeth objected to her husband's adulteries, only she and Edward ever knew.

As yet, though, she'd not given Edward a son; a daughter had been born the previous year. That pleased Warwick, although he'd never stopped to analyse why it should, for a son was essential to safeguard the Yorkist dynasty. But he didn't doubt that Edward's unpopular Queen would eventually give him a male heir. Edward clearly found enough pleasure in her bed, even after three years of marriage, to spend considerable time there, and she came from an extremely fertile family.

The very thought of that fertile family of Woodvilles was enough to sour Warwick's day. He found it impossible to resign himself to the rapid rise of Elizabeth's relatives. She'd brought no dowry to her marriage, Warwick thought grimly, but by God, she suffered no lack of blood kin!

She had six unwed sisters for whom titled husbands were needed and, in short order, the heirs of the Earls of Arundel, Essex, and Kent had Woodville wives and the twelve-year-old Duke of Buckingham was unwillingly wed to Elizabeth's young sister, Katherine.

Five brothers there were, too, to claim their share of their sister's sudden glory. Her favourite brother, Anthony Woodville, was named Governor of the Isle of Wight. Another brother had been knighted. And citizen and courtier alike had been scandalized by the marriage made between twenty-year-old John Woodville and the wealthy dowager Duchess of Norfolk, who was nearly fifty years his elder.

Elizabeth's father had been titled as Earl Rivers and Warwick was acutely aware of the rumours that Edward meant to name his father-in-law as Lord Constable of England, an office of immense power and prestige. But most galling of all for Warwick was the matter of the Exeter marriage.

The Duke of Exeter was an avowed Lancastrian but he'd consented, nonetheless, to wed Edward's eldest sister Anne in 1447 when he was seventeen and she a child of eight years. The marriage had not won him over to York, however. He'd fought against Edward at Towton and was now in exile in Burgundy. During a rather troubled marriage, he and Anne had produced a daughter who was, as the heiress of the Exeter estates, a much sought-after marital prize. The girl had been promised to John Neville's young son. But that past October, Elizabeth had paid her sister-in-law of Exeter the sum of four thousand marks to secure the young heiress for Thomas Grey, Elizabeth's twelve-year-old son by her first marriage.

Edward professed to be somewhat uncomfortable with this transaction. He had privately apologized to John and promised to see that John's son would be given a bride no less wealthy. But he refused Warwick's demands that he forbid the match, and disclaimed responsibility with the rather disingenuous argument that it was a matter between his wife and sister only. Edward ever preferred to dispose of unpleasantness by evading or ignoring it, and while he was too intelligent not to realize a day of reckoning could be deferred but not denied, it never seemed to trouble him unduly.

John understood this; he saw his cousin Ned with affection but without illusions, and so he accepted the Exeter–Grey marriage with such good grace as he could muster. Only to his wife did he voice his resentment at the way Elizabeth had pirated the Exeter heiress from his own son.

Warwick, not being of so stoic a temperament as John, had raged with a dangerous lack of discretion at what he saw as Woodville perfidy. He never doubted that Elizabeth Woodville had more in mind than gaining a rich wife for her son; he knew

148

she took gleeful satisfaction at taking anything away from the Nevilles.

But on this evening in late June, Warwick's mood was not darkened with any thoughts of the despised Woodvilles. He had just returned from a triumphant tour of France, a tour that had exceeded all expectations and strengthened his conviction that his future, England's future, must lie with France. Surely now, his cousin the King would see he was right.

He'd been gone for a month's time, was now returning with a French embassy headed by no less a personage than the Archbishop of Narbonne. Arriving at the Herber, he left his distinguished guests in the great hall while he went to advise his wife of his return. He was looking forward to her surprise; he knew she hadn't expected him back so soon.

The scene in the solar was very much a family one. Nan had a satin gown spread out on the trestle table and was showing John's wife Isabella how a steeping in verjuice had removed a stain from the skirt. John lounged nearby on the settle, cracking walnuts for his six-year-old son. Across the solar, his cousin George sat with Warwick's daughter Isabel and, by the hearth, Anne, his youngest, was playing chess with Richard.

Warwick stayed motionless and unnoticed for a moment in the doorway. Isabel was two months shy of her sixteenth birthday and, each time Warwick looked at her, he felt a throb of paternal pride. Isabel had flowered in the past year, had begun to turn male heads. And, much to Warwick's satisfaction, none seemed more captivated than George.

He'd always meant, of course, that George should one day wed Isabel and had, without undue difficulty, conditioned them to view such a marriage as quite the most natural thing in the world. That spring, he'd instructed his brother, now the Archbishop of York, to open secret negotiations with the Pope and he was already setting aside the gold it would take to secure the papal dispensation that would enable George and Isabel to wed. Such a dispensation was required by the laws of consanguinity, George and Isabel being first cousins once removed. And the negotiations were being conducted in secrecy to circumvent Edward's anticipated opposition to the marriage; so strained had the relationship between the two men become that Edward now looked with disfavour upon any alliance between his brothers and Warwick's daughters.

Warwick had no intention, however, of having his cherished plans thwarted by his cousin, King or not. He felt quite confident that the papal dispensation would be forthcoming for Edward's own agent in Rome was secretly sworn to act on his behalf, having been won over with lavish offerings of Neville gold.

Isabel was holding George's hand between her own; she now made an elaborate show of tracing his lifeline for him. That was not an activity Warwick's wife would normally have sanctioned for it was too close to soothsaying. But she made no objection, even smiled, knowing full well that it was only an excuse for touching. Warwick smiled, too, and then looked toward Anne.

That winter, Anne had taken it into her head that she wanted to learn to play chess. At last he'd yielded to her importunings and agreed to teach her, but with no expectation of success. Warwick did not think women were capable of the intellectual concentration needed for so demanding a discipline as chess and felt himself vindicated when the second chess lesson ended with Anne in tears and the board on the floor where he'd flung it in disgust. When Richard had then volunteered to teach her, Warwick wryly wished him well. But, secretly, he'd been pleased for he'd sensed a change in Richard; the boy had been drawing away from his Neville kin.

No, that was not strictly true, he conceded. Dickon was still on the best of terms with Johnny. He was as friendly as ever with Isabel. And with Anne nothing had changed; he teased her and kept her secrets and was as protective of her as any brother could have been. No, it was not his Neville kin he'd begun to avoid. As little as Warwick liked to admit it, he was the one Dickon no longer seemed comfortable with.

Warwick knew why, of course, and mentally heaped more curses upon the head of his cousin, the King. The chess lessons pleased him, therefore. While it was true that Dickon's blind loyalty to Ned was proving to be irksome, Warwick was far from ready to give up on the boy. He knew Dickon's heart was at Middleham; knew, too, that Dickon had no liking for his brother's Woodville in-laws. He did not imagine life could be very pleasant for the boy at the Woodville court. For that was how Warwick now saw his cousin's court, as infested by Woodvilles.

Apparently, Richard had proven to be a more adept tutor than Warwick anticipated; both youngsters seemed thoroughly engrossed in the chessboard. Warwick moved into the room, and his wife looked up, cried, 'Dick!' Warwick laughed, came forward into the warmth of their welcome.

The French King had honoured Warwick with a magnificent golden goblet studded with emeralds, rubies, and diamonds, and the family passed it around with murmurs of admiration. But it was the gifts Warwick himself had brought back that elicited real excitement. King Louis had opened the famed textile shops of Rouen to the English. Now Nan and John's Isabella and Warwick's daughters exclaimed with delight over the bolts of crimson velvet, patterned damask and cloth of gold.

George was equally delighted with what Warwick had brought back for him, a small rhesus monkey imported to Rouen from the Holy Land. George had never shown much interest in pets but he found such a novelty to be irresistible and announced at once that he would call his new possession Anthony. As that happened to be the name of Anthony Woodville, best-loved brother of the Woodville Queen, it seemed likely that the monkey would attract more than its share of attention when he flaunted it at Westminster. But George seemed to thrive upon such border-line insolences and here, in the House of Neville, his choice evoked only laughter.

For John, Warwick had a magnificent leather-bound edition of *Froissart's Chronicles*, that renowned work of the fourteenth-century French historian. He knew, of course, that John was far from an avid reader, but the ownership of books was becoming as much a status symbol as was the possession of cut window glass or Flemish carpets.

He deliberately saved his gift for Richard till the last, knowing the boy expected nothing, and then presented his young cousin with proof positive of the superior skill of French craftsmen, a slender-bladed dagger that shone like silver as Richard unwrapped it.

Warwick leaned over to point out the unique carving upon the hilt, the Whyte Boar of Gloucester, a remarkably accurate depiction of the cognizance Richard had in the past year chosen for his own, as an anagram for York. Richard said little, merely mumbled his thanks. But Warwick had been close enough to the boy to see the sudden tears that had blurred his first sight of the Whyte Boar, tears that had been blinked back so hastily no one but Warwick had noticed. That involuntary response told Warwick all he wanted to know, showed him that his young cousin's loyalties were painfully divided, and he was content.

Settling down with some of the Bordeaux wine he'd been given by the King of France, he began to relate a tale of triumph. With that flair for the theatrical which was peculiarly his, he described the lavish welcome he'd been given by King Louis, described his spectacular entry into Rouen, with the citizens bearing flowers and banners of Neville crimson, and the priests holding aloft flaming torches, holy water, and crosses of beaten gold. He told them of the avowals of friendship made by the French King. He told them that Louis had made a most handsome offer for the hand of Ned's sister Meg, a marriage with the son of the Duke of Savoy. Meg was, at twenty-one, overly ripe for marriage; after all, most girls were wed by age fifteen or thereabouts.

He did not tell them, however, of the secret talks conducted in a Dominican friary. He said nothing of the planned destruction of France's hated enemy of Burgundy or that Louis had suggested that the provinces of Holland and Zeeland, now held by the Duke of Burgundy, should then pass to his friend, the Earl of Warwick. Why should not his dear friend hold both an English earldom and a principality in what had once been Burgundy? Warwick agreed. Why not, indeed?

Instead, he related to them a lurid tale told him by King Louis, of the mysterious winter disappearance of a rural woodcutter's family, believed to have been trapped and eaten by a pack of starving wolves.

For the first time since his brother's return, John allowed himself to relax, felt some of his tension ebb, for it now seemed as if the reckoning would be put off until morning. He listened with amusement as his cousins and nieces discussed the killer wolves with considerable animation. No wolves had been seen in England for years; the few surviving animals had long since retreated into the mountains of Wales. But the youngsters at once accepted Warwick's account as true. It was only to be expected, they agreed, that wolves should still roam French roads.

Warwick frowned at that and John hid a smile. The English dislike of the French ran deep. If it surfaced in Warwick's own household, John thought, it must flow like a river through the streets of London. He just did not understand how his brother could so easily discount so ancient a bias. France was England's traditional enemy; since the middle of the last century, the English kings had claimed the French throne. John understood that the English did not want a treaty with France; they wanted another Agincourt. His cousin Ned also understood this very well. John wondered why his brother did not.

He grinned, for Richard was now assuring Anne and Isabel

that their father's cherished alaunt hounds were blood kin to the
wolf, so closely interbred that it was too dangerous to use alaunts
for hunting wolves. Greyhounds and mastiffs had to be used,
instead, Richard explained; the risk was too great that the alaunts
would revert back to the wild and turn upon their masters.

Both girls were now casting suspicious looks at the alaunt bitch
stretched out by the hearth, seeing in her slanted amber eyes and
twitching wolflike ears confirmation of Richard's tale. It was only
when Richard could contain his laughter no longer that they realized they'd been hoodwinked. They were threatening dire recrim-
inations in soft ladylike tones that would escape their mother's
hearing when George said suddenly, 'The wolves have been on
the prowl here, too, Cousin, while you've been away. But here
they do go by the name Woodville.'

Only iron control and the fact that George was not within
range kept John from backhanding his cousin across the mouth.
George saw his anger but it didn't disturb him; he was not that
attached to John. He leaned forward, facing the cousin who did
matter.

'It seems Johnny and Dickon are shy of telling you, Cousin.
But you must know what was done in your absence.'

Warwick glanced over at his brother, back at George. He was
fond of the boy but he wished George did not derive such relish
from bearing bad tidings.

'If you refer to the visit of the Burgundian delegation, I am
well informed on that matter, George. The visit was planned ere
I left England, after all. Moreover, it was my understanding that
the Burgundian envoys have departed back to their country upon
learning of the Duke of Burgundy's death a fortnight ago.'

'Not all of them, Cousin. Louis de la Gruuthuse has remained
behind . . . to resolve the final points of the marriage contract.'

Warwick had been aware, of course, that Charles, Count of
Charolais, son and heir of the recently deceased Duke of Burgundy,
had evinced an interest in a marital alliance with England. Edward

had seemed rather intrigued by the prospect, much to Warwick's annoyance. Quite apart from his political preference for France, Warwick had a personal aversion to the Count of Charolais, now the new Duke of Burgundy; they'd met the year before at Boulogne and had taken an instant and hearty dislike to one another.

But Warwick had not taken the Burgundian proposal that seriously. He knew Charles of Burgundy liked nothing so much as baiting his avowed enemy and nominal liege lord, the King of France. He knew, too, that Charles was sympathetic to the House of Lancaster, was sheltering both Edmund Beaufort, Duke of Somerset, and Edward's Lancastrian brother-in-law, the Duke of Exeter, at his court.

Most importantly, he did not think his cousin Ned would pay so little heed to his counsel. The Woodville marriage ... well, that was an act of lust, inexcusable yet understandable. Politics was quite another matter. He did not think Ned would dare choose an alliance he so firmly opposed.

'Marriage?' he now said slowly. 'You do not mean ...'

George nodded. 'Yes, I do. Ned has agreed to wed my sister Meg to Charles of Burgundy. Nothing has been put to paper as yet, but he has consulted Meg to make sure she is willing.' He paused. 'It seems, Cousin, that she is.'

Warwick was staring at him incredulously. 'He would so dare ...' he said softly, but with such intensity that George found himself hesitating before telling his cousin the rest, the worst.

'There's more, Cousin. Ned invited the Burgundians to attend the opening session of parliament. Your brother George, as Chancellor, was to make the opening address. But at the last moment, he sent word he was ill. Ned ... well, Ned seemed to think our cousin was not ill at all, that he was showing his displeasure that the Burgundian envoys had been accorded so much favour.

'On Monday last, Ned rode himself to your brother's manor in Charing Cross and demanded that he relinquish to him the Great Seal of the chancellorship. He then gave the chancellorship to the Bishop of Bath and Wells, Robert Stillington, Keeper of the Privy Seal. . . .'

George trailed off. Even though his loyalties were undivided, were given gladly to his cousin of Warwick, he was vaguely disturbed by the fury he saw in the Earl's face. Men who looked like that most generally had murder in mind, he thought uneasily.

George did not like his brother, had not liked Edward for years now, not since the early days of Edward's kingship, and perhaps, even before that. He'd always resented the way Edward had favoured Richard, a favouritism that seemed to him to grow more pronounced with the passing years. He resented, too, what he saw as Edward's refusal to take him seriously, resented the way that all seemed to come so easily to Edward, with so little effort, and that Edward would deny him the right to wed Isabel Neville. Above all, he resented the fact that the gold circlet of kingship was Edward's and would never be his, except in the unlikely event that Elizabeth Woodville kept giving Edward only daughters, and George knew better than to count on that.

But as little as he liked Edward and as much as he liked his cousin of Warwick, George was unnerved by Warwick's wrath. He'd expected his cousin to be angry, of course. But not as angry as this.

When Warwick stormed from the solar, John had not at first realized his intent. Warwick had thus gained an invaluable advantage in time and distance, was probably already at Westminster. John forced himself to sit back in his barge, to stare at the passing blackness that hid the houses clustered along the riverbank. And he tried not to think what he might find once he at last reached Westminster.

Westminster Palace was dark. As John scrambled onto the King's dock, he could hear the clock in the outer bailey marking the midnight hour. Guards stepped from the shadows to bar his way and at once moved aside in respectful recognition. Trailed by a handful of retainers, he made his way to the King's chambers and there found his worst fears realized.

The antechamber was ablaze with torches. The door to Edward's bedchamber was blocked by men wearing the Yorkist badge of the Sunne in Splendour. They were very polite to His Grace, the Earl of Warwick, and very adamant. The King's Grace had retired for the night, could not be disturbed, not even by my lord of Warwick. Warwick never travelled without a sizable escort and now his men crowded around their lord, staring defiantly at the king's servants.

'I said I would see my cousin, the King,' Warwick said, in the tones of one accustomed to unquestioning obedience.

Edward's men, however, did not budge, and this time the refusal given was not quite so polite. Warwick's men began to murmur among themselves; the growing ill will between Warwick and Edward had begun to filter down to their followers. Someone must have spread the word, for men were now moving past John into the chamber, men who wore the livery of York.

One of these new arrivals bumped into a Warwick retainer. With what was either incredibly bad luck or the most deliberate provocation, as he stumbled, his hand clutched at the other's sleeve, tore away the Neville badge of the Bear and Ragged Staff. Warwick's man gave an outraged gasp and then lunged at the Yorkist.

John had never moved so fast in his life, would never know how he'd managed to cross the chamber in time to grab the offender. But the tension in the room wanted only a spark to flare into violence, to turn an ugly incident into the unthinkable, a brawl between the men of the King and the Earl of Warwick in the King's own chambers.

'Stay there,' John snarled to the man he'd shoved against the wall, and started toward his brother who'd turned at the sound of the commotion behind him.

Voices were now raised, men had begun to trade insults with

one another, but a path cleared for John without difficulty. He had no idea what he'd say to his brother. In any event, he was not given the chance. Just as he reached Warwick, the bedchamber door was flung open.

The inner chamber was still illuminated by candles. Those closest to the door had a glimpse of a woman retreating toward the curtained bed. She moved too fast for any to see more than an enticing expanse of creamy skin and a swirl of hip-length dark honey hair. But at that particular moment, even the most vicariously curious of the spectators had no time to spare for a royal mistress, however desirable she seemed to be. It was Edward who was the focus of all eyes, Edward alone.

He was partially dressed in hose and an unfastened cambric shirt. The torchlight caught the golden hairs upon his chest, showed the incongruous smear of a woman's lip rouge across his throat. As he surveyed the scene before him, his astonishment gave way swiftly to an anger such as few had ever seen him show.

The room was suddenly still. Men began to back away, to seek more inconspicuous positions in the shadows. Warwick and John stood alone in the centre of the room, but it was Warwick and only Warwick who held Edward's attention.

'As interested as I'd have been to know of your return to England, my lord of Warwick, I hardly think it necessary for you to have broken into my bedchamber in the middle of the night to announce your arrival.'

Edward's voice was hard, and had in it an edge Warwick had never heard from him before. Warwick had expected his cousin to be conciliatory, or perhaps defensive, but he'd not expected derision, so closely akin to contempt. He was thrown off-balance for a moment and then said tightly, 'It was necessary that I have words with you tonight. It could not wait.'

'Necessary for you, perhaps. I see no such need myself.'

Warwick could not believe Edward was daring to refuse him. 'It cannot wait,' he repeated stonily.

'Then you, my lord of Warwick, do have a problem. For I have no intention of speaking with you, or any other, at such an hour.'

Edward had not raised his voice, but each word struck Warwick with the force of a shout. He stared at his cousin in disbelief.

'If you wish an audience, you may return to Westminster at ten tomorrow morn. I'll see you then,' Edward said and then dropped his voice still lower, said for Warwick alone, 'Now get your men out of here, and right fast.'

He didn't wait to see if he'd be obeyed, was turning toward the door as Warwick grabbed his arm.

'Ned!' he began in a strangled voice, so choked with incredulous anger that he had to pause before he could translate his fury into coherent speech.

Edward made no attempt to free himself.

'You're dangerously close to expending the last of your credit, cousin,' he said softly.

And then John stepped between them.

Warwick made a supreme effort, forced himself back from the furthest reaches of a rage that was blind to consequences, to common sense. He loosened his hand from Edward's arm, brought it up to his own face; to his surprise, he found his forehead was damp.

'I shall be back upon the morrow,' he said, very slowly and distinctly. He did not wait for the requisite royal leave before departing the chamber.

John stared bleakly at Edward, but no words came to mind. He was turning to follow his brother from the rapidly clearing chamber when Edward spoke.

'Stay a moment, my lord of Northumberland. There is something I would say to you.'

'My liege?' John hoped he didn't sound sullen, or worse, hostile. At that moment, all he felt was a vast weariness.

'In private,' Edward said and beckoned John into the bedchamber. The girl now swung her legs over the side of the bed, started to rise, saying, 'Is all well now, my love?'

But, at sight of John, she hastily dived back under the covers. John liked her for that; not all of Edward's light o' loves were so modest.

'I want a few words with my cousin, sweetheart.'

Edward was still tense with rage but he managed to find a passable smile for the girl, and strode over to draw the curtains around the bed. Coming back to the table where a wine flagon was always kept to quench night thirsts, he looked questioningly at John who shook his head, and then poured himself a drink.

'You'd best talk to him, Johnny,' he said abruptly. 'My patience is well nigh exhausted.'

John shook his head. 'I fear he will not listen to me, Ned,' he admitted reluctantly.

Edward looked at him. 'For his sake, for all our sakes, I do hope you're wrong, Johnny.'

John said nothing. He knew he was not. After a moment, Edward set the wine cup on the table. John moved toward the door, Edward toward the bed. As he reached for the latch, the bedroom went dark. Edward had just extinguished the last of the candles.

John took pains to be sure to be at Westminster by ten the next morning. But his hopes of serving as a buffer between his brother and cousin came to naught. As he passed through the crowded antechamber, he recognized many faces, mostly Woodville, and stopped briefly to exchange courtesies with Sir John Howard, a steadfast Yorkist and old friend. He then continued on into the adjoining chamber, where he was not surprised to find Lord Hastings and not pleased to find his young cousin, George of Clarence.

He greeted George with perfunctory courtesy; he still bore George a grudge for last night's untimely revelation. He should have expected George to be there, though. George is always in the front row at a bear-baiting, he thought grimly, and turned to acknowledge the salutation by Hastings.

In the six years since Edward had claimed the crown, William Hastings had scaled the pinnacles of success with what seemed to be extraordinary ease. Knighted on the field at Towton by Edward, he'd been created Baron Hastings within a month of Edward's June coronation. In that same month, he'd been given the prestigious position of Lord Chamberlain. No greater proof of his sudden prominence could be evidenced than the fact that in 1462, John Neville and the Earl of Warwick had deemed Hastings to be a worthy husband for their sister Katherine.

John greeted his brother-in-law with polite goodwill, if little real affection. He and Hastings were too unlike for friendship, but he had no objections to the man. Strangely enough, few at court did, save only the Queen, and it occurred to John that Elizabeth must mind Ned's infidelities more than she let on, else why would she dislike Hastings so? For Hastings was more than Edward's Lord Chamberlain. Despite the eleven years in age between the two men, Will Hastings was the closest friend and favourite carousing companion of the twenty-five-year-old King.

There was no one else in the chamber. John frowned, puzzled, and then saw the closed door and understood.

'Are they within?' he asked, and Hastings nodded.

'Ned is right in this, you know,' he said quietly.

'I know, Will. Once a treaty is signed, Charles will restore free trade and lift that damnable embargo they placed on the import of English wool.'

To John's surprise, Will shook his head.

'What do you mean? Surely, Will, you're not denying that Burgundy has always been our best market for the cloth trade.'

'Of course not. The trade considerations weighed heavily with Ned. As much, I think, as his conviction that to seek the friend-ship of Louis of France is to open the barn wide and entice the wolf in to shelter with the sheep. No, that was not what I meant. I meant that even if I thought Ned was mistaken to favour Burgundy over France, I'd still say he was in the right and my brother-in-law of Warwick in the wrong. It is Ned, after all,' he said mildly, 'who is King.'

John happened to agree with all that Will said. But reason and passion may exist quite independently of each other. No matter how enraged he might become with his brother, he could brook no criticism of Warwick from outsiders, and now he said quite coolly, 'Do you mean to suggest that I need such a reminder, my lord Hastings?'

Will looked at him, somewhat sadly. 'No, Johnny. You, of all men, need no such reminder.'

They heard it then, raised voices from within the adjoining chamber. The door opened suddenly with such violence that the ancient hinges shrieked and the heavy metal bolt slipped, slid down the door at a queer drunken angle. Warwick's voice came to them with startling clarity.

'I do not have to listen to this!'

He strode through the doorway, but spun around again as Edward jerked the door back with equal force.

'Oh, but you do! Because you're not dismissed yet, my lord!'

'You dare to speak thus to me? You seem to have forgotten, my liege' – that last said with savage scorn – 'that had it not been for me, your Kingship would never have come into being!'

'Indeed? So speaks the victor of St Albans?'

Warwick had been darkly flushed. Yet now his colour deepened still further as Edward said scathingly, 'I've never denied the aid you gave me and you've been richly rewarded for it. But a kingmaker, cousin, you never were. Yes, you spoke out on my behalf, argued that the crown should be offered to me. But you also came damned near to losing all with that blunder at St Albans. Had I not won Mortimer's Cross, London would've yielded to Lancaster without so much as a whimper of protest. You'd best think on that, cousin, before you make claims that have no more foundation than empty air.'

John felt sick. He could see this was a resentment that had

been gnawing at Edward for years, and justice compelled him to concede there was truth in what his cousin said. But he knew, too, that his brother would never forgive Edward for saying it.

'And a fine king you've made, in truth! What have you done with your kingship, my liege? Precious little beyond filling your bed with harlots and your court with Woodvilles! And lest we forget, giving a full pardon to a man who should have been given no more than five minutes with his confessor! A man who played you for a fool ere the year was out!'

'I need account to no man for what I do. Least of all, to you, my lord of Warwick. But this I will tell you. For three years and more now, you've been throwing Somerset in my teeth, and I'm heartily sick of hearing about it. I think you'd best not speak of it again, Cousin.'

'Do you threaten me?'

'Take it any way you like as long as you do bear it in mind.'

John suddenly realized that the door into the antechamber was open, that the quarrel between his cousin and brother was now audible to the score or more of people clustered without. Almost as appalled by that as he was by what was being said, he turned toward the door, saw that Will had the same idea.

Will grabbed for the door latch, started to slam it in the fascinated faces of their unwanted audience, and then pulled the door open wide, saying in a voice rich with relief, 'Madame!'

For a horrified instant, John feared Will was addressing Edward's Queen; her entry now would be utter disaster. Will stepped back and as the woman came into the chamber, John let his breath escape in a sudden release of tension. For it was the Duchess of York.

She didn't wait for Will, closed the door firmly behind her. Cool grey eyes moved from face to face.

'Well?' she said at last. 'Do you not mean to greet me, Edward?'

Edward rallied, even summoned a taut smile. 'Forgive my manners, ma mère.'

Turning away from her eldest son, she looked not at George but at Warwick, held out a slender hand.

He raised it to his lips but he was far less successful than Edward at masking his rage. If Cecily saw, however, she gave no indication.

'Welcome home. I should be most interested to hear of your time in France. You will dine with me this week, will you not, Dick and tell me of it?'

The familiar family name did as much, perhaps, to defuse some of the tension as did her unruffled demeanour. Warwick nodded. He was rarely rude to a woman; least of all, to this one.

'It will be my pleasure,' he said, the emotion he was expressing at startling variance with what all could read in his eyes.

'Good,' Cecily said calmly.

No one else spoke at all.

George waited a few discreet moments after Warwick's departure before attempting to follow his cousin. He'd never seen Edward as angry as this, was awed in spite of himself, and decided it could not hurt to be somewhat circumspect. However, his mother's voice halted him at the door.

'Your cousin does not need you to escort him safe home, George,' she said tartly, and George flushed. No matter how often he told himself that he was, at seventeen, a man grown, his mother managed to demolish his poise with no trouble whatsoever.

'Actually, ma mère, I was planning to . . . look for Dickon. He asked me to meet him at Westminster this morning.'

He saw she looked sceptical and was about to elaborate upon his alibi, knowing he could count upon Richard to back him up, when Edward intervened.

'Dickon will have to make do without your company,' he said, so impassively that George couldn't tell if Edward believed him or was indulging in sarcasm.

'Why?' he asked uncertainly. He hated the way Ned could make him feel like a raw youth without assurance or social graces. Sometimes, he thought Ned did it deliberately.

'Our cousin of Warwick brought back to England more than the good wishes of the French King. He brought, as well, a French delegation. He told them they were to be welcomed at court this afternoon. I want you to be there to greet them, George, on my behalf.' A pause. 'Do you think you might act on my behalf . . . for a change?'

George swallowed. 'I'm your brother. Why would I not act in your interests?' he challenged, and was relieved when Edward chose to let it pass.

As George exited the chamber, Edward turned to John for the first time, said softly, 'I'm sorry, Johnny. You were not meant to hear what you did.' He jerked his head toward the small chamber. 'It was not meant to go beyond there.'

At that moment, Will Hastings reappeared with a richly dressed man who was thin of face and unimpressive of appearance, his fine garments notwithstanding. Edward smiled at the sight of him, though, smiled with genuine pleasure, and turned to his mother.

'Madame, I do want you to meet the Seigneur de la Gruuthuse, one of our good friends of Burgundy. For certes, one of mine!'

He moved toward the Burgundian envoy with the warmth that was, at one and the same time, the secret of his popularity with his subjects and a source of irritation to his lords, who felt his free and easy ways unseemly for a man who was the anointed of God. When Edward turned back, however, intending to introduce Gruuthuse to John, he found his cousin had gone.

John, who was ordinarily a man little given to squandering time, now found himself wandering aimlessly about Westminster. He did not want to go home. He thought his Isabella to be a perfect wife in all the ways that mattered but it did not occur to him to burden her with his discontent or worse, to alarm her with his forebodings. There were some troubles, he felt, that a man must shoulder alone.

Still less did he want to go to the Herber. The last person he wanted to see at that moment was his brother. Either one of them, he amended. His brother the earl or his brother the archbishop. He did not want to think what they might do now, the brother who'd been stripped of the chancellorship and the brother who'd been denied his dreams of glory. Dreams fed him with a silver spoon by His Most Cunning Grace, the Christian King of France. John cursed under his breath, long and hard. It didn't help.

He found himself before the royal gate that led from the inner bailey into the precincts of the abbey, passed on through. Courtesy compelled him to pause to exchange stilted greetings with Anthony Woodville and the encounter only soured his spirits all the more. But as he neared the Lady Chapel he saw George Norwich, the Lord Abbot, and, with him, the one person he suddenly knew he'd been hoping to find, the only one who could understand how he felt. He paused, waited for Richard to come toward him.

They didn't talk at first; too many others were within earshot. Entering the King's private entrance into the abbey, they paused at the font of holy water and then crossed the south transept, exiting out the east door of the cloisters. To their right lay the carrels, the small alcoves where the monks studied and copied psalms, Gospels and an occasional manuscript. They began to walk down the east walkway, instead, toward the Chapter House. It was only then that Richard turned to John.

'What happened, Johnny? Was it bad?'

'Yes,' John said bluntly. 'Very bad.' He gave Richard a curious look. 'Your brother George was there to hear for himself. You could have been there too, Dickon. Why were not you?'

'I did not want to be,' Richard said simply and, after a moment, John nodded.

'None could blame you for that.' He grimaced, did not even realize he did so. 'It could have been worse than it was, though. Your lady mother happened to make a most fortuitous entrance. If she had not. . . .' He saw it then, saw the truth. He stared at Richard and then began to laugh.

'I should have guessed at once! That was inspiration, Dickon, in truth it was!'

Richard looked pleased, both with the praise and with himself. 'No,' he said. 'That was desperation.'

They stood for several moments looking out into the flowering inner garth.

'It was all I could think to do, Johnny. I cannot say my mother was much pleased to be awakened at midnight but, once she ceased yelling at me, she agreed a visit to Westminster was long overdue.' Richard smiled but sobered almost immediately. 'It was all too easy to learn when my cousin was expected at Westminster this morning. All the court knew,' he said and sighed.

They'd almost reached the Chapter House and both stopped, avoiding it by common accord, for the abbey Chapter House was where the Commons sat when in session and neither the boy nor the man felt in the mood to deal with politicians.

Turning, they began to retrace their path.

'How old are you, Dickon . . . fourteen?'

'Fifteen in October.' Richard hesitated and then blurted out, 'Fourteen is such a wretched age to be, Johnny.'

The outburst was so unlike him that John had to smile.

'As I recall, I did not think much of being fourteen either. You have to endure all those endless lectures from your elders, needed or not.'

He saw Richard grin and added lightly, 'No, fourteen is not much fun, is it? If you're not having your ears bent with unwanted advice, you're getting your backside warmed with a birch switch. Or fretting because you've suddenly discovered the fairer sex and do not know quite what to do about it.'

Richard was still grinning but now he was slightly flushed, as well, and John smiled at him.

'But take heart, Dickon. The first will pass. And the other . . . well, you'll find out soon enough, I daresay,' he said, with such obvious affection in his voice that Richard was warmed by it, was moved to confide.

'Jesú, I do hope so!'

He'd meant to sound wry, sounded wistful instead. He flushed much more noticeably now and then laughed at himself. John laughed, too. The days were long gone, he knew, when Dickon could come to Warwick. Nor did he think the boy was likely to approach Ned. In carnal matters, Ned was too knowing. The mere fact that Ned had no inhibitions to speak of would, in itself, be inhibiting to a youngster, John suspected.

He looked at Richard, and suddenly a dark thought crossed his mind, at the very instant that a billowing cloud blotted out the sun. When his own son reached Dickon's age, would there be anyone for him to turn to for advice or reassurance? He stared up at the cloud hovering above their heads, felt a queer superstitious pang, and resolutely shook it off. As if making idle conversation, he observed, 'I was nigh on sixteen when I lay with a girl for my first time. In a stable loft, of all places. It took me two days to get all the straw from my hair.'

Richard was looking extremely interested; now said, with what he hoped was tact, 'Almost sixteen? Was that not . . . well, late, Johnny?'

'It's not a question of being late or early, Dickon . . . just of being ready. When you are, you'll be the first to know. Of course, the right opportunity must present itself or all the readiness in the world does not help.'

Richard digested this in thoughtful silence, then said, 'Ned was thirteen. . . . He told me once.'

'I do not doubt it,' John said dryly, and then turned toward the boy. 'You know, Dickon,' he said, suddenly so serious that he surprised himself as much as Richard, 'you'd do best not to measure yourself by Ned's standards. Ned is a law unto himself, in more ways than one. You need not look so troubled. I'm not saying Ned's standards are at fault, merely that they're his. And anytime you try to walk around in someone else's boots, you're apt to find them a poor fit.'

Richard was frowning. 'Do I do that?'

'Sometimes. I think Edmund did, too, and it would have been better for him if he had not.'

Richard was not comfortable speaking of his dead brother; he tried not to think at all of those winter months of 1461. Nor did he like what John had just said about Edward, even though he knew it was well meant.

By now, they'd traversed the entire length of the north walkway, past the industrious monks who didn't deign even to glance up at their approach.

'I still do think fourteen is a rotten age,' Richard said, and John gave him a thoughtful, probing look, suddenly seeing what the boy had been referring to all along.

Richard was standing in the sun; it set fire to the jewelled Yorkist collar of roses and suns he wore about his shoulders, gilded the shining dagger he had at his hip, his cousin's gift. John's eyes flickered between them, the Yorkist collar and the dagger, before saying, 'Because you feel helpless, caught between loyalties?'

Richard nodded and John reached out, let his hand rest on Richard's shoulder.

'I regret to tell you, lad, that age has not a damned thing to do with how you feel right now. You see, Dickon, I'm thirty-six and it still hurts, hurts more than I care to admit.

IO

Olney

August 1469

There were times that summer when Richard felt as if the world had gone mad. How else explain the predicament in which he and Ned found themselves, trapped in a sleepy Buckinghamshire village by the enemy army? An army led not by Lancastrians but by their cousin Warwick and their brother George.

The street before him was quiet, the air heavy with August heat, the sun hot on his face. He was deeply tanned after two months in the saddle. Being the dark one in a fair family had its advantages, after all. Edward had suffered far more from the same sun, had spent several uncomfortable days with peeling nose and skin too sensitive to shave.

Queer, he thought, how normal it all looked. As if nothing had changed. As if the inconceivable had not happened. But was it truly inconceivable? Or was it just that he'd refused to face it until now?

Ironically enough, the campaign had begun for him in a flurry of excitement. Two northern rebellions had broken out that spring. John Neville had undertaken to crush the one led by the rebel calling himself Robin of Holderness. He'd dispatched the insurgents with his usual efficiency; in Richard's opinion, Johnny was by far the best soldier in the Neville family.

Marguerite d'Anjou had been suspected, of course, of instigating the revolt but the rebellion was soon revealed to have been fomented on behalf of the Lancastrian Henry Percy, still confined to the Tower, the man whose title John now held. There was much sentiment in Yorkshire for restoring the earldom of Northumberland to the Percy family. Not surprisingly, Richard thought, Johnny took a rather dim view of the advocacy. He'd defeated the rebels at the very gates of York and beheaded Robin of Holderness in the marketplace of the city.

The second insurgency was spearheaded by another Robin, this one styling himself as Robin of Redesdale. Richard had wondered on that, until Edward had explained that ambitious malcontents thought it advantageous to stir up memories of the most renowned of all political rebels, Robin Hood of Sherwood Forest.

Edward had scoffed at such political propaganda but decided to deal with Robin of Redesdale himself. Much to Richard's delight, he'd been able to convince Edward that he was, at sixteen, old enough for his first military campaign. With Elizabeth Woodville's father, Earl Rivers, and her brothers, Anthony and John Woodville, they'd departed London in early June, riding north to the shrine of Our Lady of Walsingham, recruiting men to the Yorkist standard along the way.

It had been an enjoyable journey for Richard, even surrounded as he was by Woodvilles. This was his first full taste of the adult responsibilities he was so eager to assume and he'd taken pride and pleasure in calling men to arms under his own banner of the Whyte Boar. Edward had been in no hurry; they'd moved from Walsingham up into Lincolnshire, pausing for some days at Richard's birthplace, Fotheringhay Castle, and then on to Newark.

It was at Newark that they learned the truth, a truth that exploded with the force of gunpowder in the sheltered centre of Richard's world. Robin of Redesdale had been unmasked as one Sir John Conyers, a cousin by marriage of the Earl of Warwick. And what had seemed to be a minor border rebellion was, in fact, a major military threat; Conyers had massed an army more than three times what Edward commanded.

Edward had at once retreated into the stone-walled security of Nottingham Castle, urgently summoning aid from Lords Herbert and Stafford. He had, at the same time, dispatched a personal letter to his cousin and another to his brother, requesting that they meet with him to discuss their grievances. He soon had his answer, though not in the manner expected. Word reached Nottingham that Warwick and George had slipped across the Channel to Calais. There, on July 11, George Neville, Archbishop of York, had wed George to Isabel Neville in open defiance of Edward's wishes.

Edward had been furious by the marriage, Richard disconcerted. How must it appear to his cousin Anne, that George would dare Ned's wrath for Bella when he would not do the same for her? Richard found the thought of hurting Anne intolerable. Almost as intolerable as the thought of betraying his brother. For he had no illusions now, a betrayal it would be. He was forced to face at last what he'd been trying for five years to deny, that he was confronted with irreconcilable loyalties. Either he stood with Ned or he stood with Warwick. One or the other.

Richard yearned for the chance to try to explain to Anne, to assure her that his loyalty to Ned did not lessen his affection for her. Anne was part of his life; nothing could change that. Had Edward not forbidden a betrothal, he'd have been quite willing to plight troth with Anne as Warwick wanted. But he couldn't bring himself to pay Warwick's price.

He consoled himself as best he could with the thought that Anne was very young yet; by the time she was of marriageable age, perhaps circumstances would be different. He'd made a halting attempt to talk to Edward about it, sought some sort of assurance from his brother that he might reconsider the match at a later date. Edward had been irked, but Richard had persevered and finally won from Edward a grudging concession, an adamant 'No' softened into a 'We'll see.' With that, Richard had been content . . . until he learned of George's marriage and recognized the effect it would have upon Anne.

Not that he had much time to dwell upon the unhappiness of his young cousin. Things had gone from bad to worse for them that July. Warwick and George had not lingered in Calais. Once back in England, they rapidly mustered a large force, ostensibly in the King's name. But they also issued a proclamation that Richard thought to be tantamount to a declaration of war.

The Woodvilles were savagely assailed for their evil influence upon the King. A number of Warwick's personal enemies, among them Lords Herbert and Stafford, were also denounced. But, most ominously of all, the proclamation likened Edward to three monarchs notorious for inept rule, the three English Kings who'd been deposed and dethroned; Edward II, Richard II and the hapless Harry of Lancaster.

Will Hastings had been quick to answer Edward's summons, wasted no time in joining them at Nottingham Castle. The Woodvilles had been just as quick to depart, Anthony Woodville to his estates in Norfolk, Earl Rivers and his son John toward Wales. Richard would have liked to know whether Edward sent them from Nottingham for their own safety, as the true targets of Warwick's proclamation, or whether they'd fled of their own choosing. He did not ask Edward, though; the only way he'd been able to accept Edward's Queen was to refrain from ever discussing the Woodvilles with his brother.

After three anxious weeks of waiting in Nottingham, Edward decided to start south, expecting to join forces with the approaching armies of Lords Herbert and Stafford. They had reached the little village of Olney this morning, had paused for food and drink while Edward sent out scouts to make sure the road ahead was clear. They soon brought back disquieting reports of a large force coming up slowly from the southwest and Edward elected to remain in Olney until these first sketchy reports could be confirmed.

He was upstairs now with Will Hastings in the inn he'd chosen as his headquarters, having his first meal in some eight hours.

Richard was too tense to eat, even though he'd had nothing but manchet bread and ale in a hastily bolted dawn breakfast. He was standing, instead, in the street before the inn, wondering how the scene could be so ordinary as if it were a day like all others. He turned to go back into the inn and then the shouting began.

A rider was coming down the street, whipping his mount with a frenzy that earned him Richard's instinctive disapproval. He stopped to watch. This was not one of their scouts but he knew at once that something was wrong, very wrong.

The horseman was heading for the inn, directed by the shouts of several villagers. He was close enough now for Richard to recognize the badge he wore upon his breast, the cognizance of Lord Herbert. Richard's heart suddenly speeded up; so did his pulse, his breathing. As the rider tumbled from the saddle, Richard darted forward, caught the lathered animal by the reins.

'You come from Lord Herbert? What news have you?'

The courier was not much older than Richard himself. He didn't recognize Richard, but he did recognize the authority in Richard's voice, answered without hesitation.

'The road south is blocked. A large host and well armed. I almost blundered into their ranks.' He was panting, leaned for a moment against his equally laboured mount.

Richard made himself ask, 'Under whose command?'

'The Archbishop of York.'

Richard sucked in his breath. Catching Rob Percy's eye, he said bitterly, 'It seems my cousin has seen fit to exchange his cassock for a cuirass.' With an effort, he brought his attention back to Herbert's man.

'What of my lord Herbert? When does he reach Olney?'

The youth now knew Richard's identity. He hesitated and then said, 'My lord . . . he will not. He's dead. Six days ago, Lord Herbert and Lord Stafford met the armies of Robin of Redesdale and the Earl of Warwick. Near Banbury, at a place called Edgecot. Our forces were butchered, my lord. Lord Herbert and his brother were taken prisoner. Warwick, he . . . he had them beheaded, my lord. For fighting for their lawful king. That was murder, Your Grace. Murder, and no other word for it.'

Richard stared at him. He could not believe what he was hearing. He could not be standing here in the summer sunlight, listening to a stranger pronounce what might be a death sentence for him, for Ned, for them all.

He turned, saw Rob Percy was now beside him, regarding him with wide fearful eyes. He saw other faces then, too; the court-yard was suddenly full of soldiers, shocked into silence, looking to him, all of them.

He swallowed, forced the words up from a throat so tight not even saliva could trickle down it.

'You'd best come with me. The King's Grace will wish to question you.'

With the courier at his heels, he walked toward the entrance-way of the inn; people moved aside to let him pass. But once he was inside, he could hold back no longer. He whirled for the stairs, took them three at a time to burst into his brother's chamber bereft of breath for speech. But one glance at his face was enough to bring Edward to his feet with an oath.

'Ned, you've got to get away from here, and fast!' Will Hastings was ashen. 'Now, with no delay!'

Richard concurred heartily but held his tongue, awaiting his brother's response. Edward had been strangely silent since Richard had first gasped out the news of Edgecot. He'd listened without interruption to the courier's account of the battle which had been a fiasco of leadership for Herbert and Stafford.

According to the courier, their armies had converged by previous arrangement at Banbury but there they'd quarrelled about billeting their troops. Stafford had become so enraged he'd pulled his men out, gone on ahead. Herbert was thus alone when the army of Robin Redesdale fell upon him without warning. He

175

fought valiantly but, by the time Stafford was able to bring his men back to Herbert's aid, it was too late. Redesdale was victorious and Stafford found himself facing not only Redesdale but the Earl of Warwick who arrived in time to complete the destruction of the two Yorkist armies. Hastings had cursed with rare savagery at the tale. Edward, however, had said nothing, had moved to the window, staring down into the courtyard as the precious moments drained away, one by one.

'Ned, you did hear me?'

Edward turned back to face the room. 'Yes, Will, I heard you. But where would you have me go?'

'Back toward Nottingham, north to Fotheringhay. Anywhere, Ned, but here!'

'Do you truly think I'd ever reach either, Will?'

'I do not know. But what other choice have you?' Will moved toward the younger man, said, 'Your Queen has given you only daughters, Ned. If you die, the crown passes to George of Clarence. Warwick's new son-in-law.'

'Tell me something I do not know, Will,' Edward said and, for the first time a roughness crept into his voice.

Richard bit his lip until he tasted blood. He wanted to cry out that Will was wrong, that Warwick was not capable of such an act. He couldn't.

The door was thrown back with such violence that they all jumped. John Howard hastened into the room. He always looked sombre; now, however, his face looked like nothing so much as an alabaster death-mask, ravaged with lines and crevices and hollows.

'Our men are deserting,' he said bluntly. 'By the scores. Word's spread of Herbert and Stafford's defeat and that Neville's approaching Olney with an army thrice the size of ours. Most of them are not willing to wait for him.'

Will swore but Edward only shrugged. 'Who can blame them?' he said dispassionately.

'Name of God, Ned!' Will was staring at him. 'I've never known you to surrender without a struggle. Are you going to put your head in Warwick's noose yourself? We can at least make a run for it! What have we to lose?'

Richard was no less perplexed than Will. He didn't think this was like Ned, either. He crossed to his brother, said in a low voice husky with urgency, 'Will's right, Ned. Let's try for Fotheringhay . . . please.'

Edward looked into the boy's eyes, saw the desperation in their depths. 'Easy, lad. I've no intention of sticking my neck meekly in our cousin's noose, as Will puts it. Do not panic on me now, though. If I'm to keep my head, I need you and Will to keep yours.'

Richard nodded wordlessly and Edward looked toward Will.

'The last time we went hunting in Great Epping, this past May . . . do you remember, Will? The hounds flushed a day-old fawn. Tell Dickon what happened to it.'

Will was bewildered. 'It froze with fear, did not run. Ned, I do not see. . . .'

'Tell him of the dogs, Will. What did they do?'

'Nothing. They began to bark and circle about in confusion.'

Richard felt a glimmer of comprehension. 'Because they expected flight?'

'Exactly, Dickon. Now, tell me what would have happened had the fawn tried to flee.'

Will now saw, too. 'It would've been torn to pieces,' he said slowly. He frowned, leaned across the table. 'Ned, what do you have in mind?'

The corner of Edward's mouth twitched, in what was not a smile. 'Staying alive, Will. Staying alive.'

'I think we'd be better off chancing flight,' Will said, but without conviction.

Richard understood exactly how he felt; a man could hardly be expected to muster any enthusiasm for such a choice. Edward, who had a smattering of Spanish picked up from a Spanish girl in Calais, had taught Richard a proverb that he rather fancied, 'Entre la espada y la pared.' Between the sword and the wall. Richard had liked it, too. Until now.

He bit his lip again, felt a twinge of pain. To him, flight was still the lesser of evils; his instinctive preference would always be for action, even if ill advised.

He opened his mouth and Edward, who read him easily, as always, shook his head.

'No, Dickon. What good would you do me caged in the same cell? Let's just hope our cousin the archbishop sees you as too young to matter and remembers, as well, that Will is his brother-in-law.' With a sudden flash of strained irony, 'I can wish now, Will, that you'd been a more loving husband to your Kate,' he said tightly, and Will grimaced in a game attempt at a smile, one that didn't quite make it.

Richard watched his brother in awe, marvelling at Edward's icy composure, until Edward reached over to claim the wine flagon and, in pouring himself a full cup, spilled wine freely over the table, even onto the floor, with a hand nowhere near as steady as his voice.

George Neville, Archbishop of York, felt his stomach muscles contract as he came in sight of the village of Olney. His vizor was up but the helmet was stifling. Sweat soaked his hair; his padded tunic was sodden, chafed him unbearably. He was not accustomed to armour, felt confined and awkward. Above all, he felt fear, fear for what he might find in Olney.

In his discomfort, he sought release in anger; anger directed at his brother, awaiting him in Coventry. He was no soldier; this should have been undertaken by Warwick, not him. Conveniently forgetting for the moment that the suggestion had been his, that he'd thought he could better persuade Ned to yield without a struggle than Warwick or, God forbid, George of Clarence.

That was what frightened him so, the thought that Ned would offer resistance. What if he refused to submit? What if he were killed in the violence that was bound to follow? The Archbishop was well aware that regicide was a mortal sin in the eyes of the common people. He had no desire to go down in English history as the priest who'd killed a King. Let Warwick have that dubious honour, he thought grimly, if such was his intent. He didn't know what his brother meant to do, was not sure he wanted to know. He did know what Johnny would do, however, if Ned died in his custody. Johnny would never forgive him.

He turned in his saddle, signalled for water; he wondered if men in battle were consumed with thirst like this. He thrust the flask aside, raked his spurs into the side of his mount so that it sprang forward, lengthened stride. He was desperately determined to take Ned prisoner, at any cost. He had no choice. They'd gone this far; they dare not back down. Ned had to be taken.

But there kept flashing before his eyes a truly terrifying image. Ned defiant, having to be seized at swordpoint. He could see it as if it had already happened, see the struggling bodies, the village street dark with blood, the air thick with dust stirred up by panicked horses. Ned was England's King; if men were to see him dragged to his horse like a felon, what would their reaction be? He cursed Ned for his plight, cursed Warwick, too; he was much too agitated to think of prayer.

His inner turmoil was such that he was slightly queasy as they rode into Olney. The narrow streets of the village were packed with people. Confused yet curious faces stared up at him. Soldiers of the White Rose of York mingled among the villagers; they looked neither confused nor curious, merely afraid, and in a few cases, hostile.

Edward stood in the doorway of the inn, flanked by Richard and Will Hastings, watching as the Archbishop rode into the courtyard. Hastings was grim; Richard had the taut stillness of a colt confronting the unknown, rigid when his every instinct was to bolt. Edward, however, was impassive; the Archbishop could read nothing in his face.

He reined in his mount, not in the least assured by the sight of so many people in the courtyard: citizens, soldiers, even the parish priest. Edward had carefully provided an audience for this encounter. With increasing unease, the Archbishop wondered why.

'Welcome to Olney, my lord Archbishop.'

'Your Grace is most kind.'

His response had been an automatic acknowledgment of sovereignty, but he did not know what to say next. This was a situation totally beyond his experience; There are no guidelines, he thought morosely, for capturing a King. It occurred to him that he should ask for Edward's sword, then saw Edward wasn't wearing one. He sat his horse in the courtyard of the inn, under the eyes of wondering townspeople and watchful soldiers, and tried to get a grip upon his raw nerves.

Edward moved forward, came to stand at the Archbishop's stirrup. He reached out, began to stroke the arched neck of the other's mount.

'I assume you wish me to accompany you, cousin?'

The Archbishop knew Edward could see how sweet and sweeping his relief was; he didn't care. 'Yes,' he said quickly, but keeping the presence of mind to pitch his voice as low as Edward's had been. 'I think that would be advisable, Ned.'

Edward stared at him and then raised his hand. One of his men emerged from the stables, leading a fractious white stallion. At the Archbishop's look of surprise, Edward said evenly, 'I saw no reason to delay your journey. I knew you'd not want to tarry in Olney.'

The Archbishop nodded dumbly, unable to believe all was going so smoothly. He watched intently as Edward walked toward his mount, as if expecting his cousin to spring some last-moment treachery.

Edward reached for the reins, pausing in the act of mounting to glance back over his shoulder.

'I see no reason for Lord Hastings and the Duke of Gloucester to accompany us, do you, my lord?' he queried, as all eyes in the crowd turned with his words toward Richard and Hastings

'No, Your Grace, I do not,' the Archbishop agreed hastily. 'Of course Lord Hastings and His Grace of Gloucester may remain in Olney if they choose.'

Once he saw Edward mounted beside him, saw Edward was truly going to ride willingly from Olney with them, he permitted himself an audible escape of breath, began to feel in control of the situation for the first time since riding into the village.

'However, I must insist, my liege, that Earl Rivers and his sons do come with us.'

'That will not be possible.'

All complacency vanished, was supplanted by tension. The archbishop forgot the need to preserve the fiction of civility, said in a voice suddenly shrill, 'You are not now in a position to tell me what is or is not possible, my lord.'

There were murmurings among the villagers at that. They did not think this was the proper tone to take with the King, even if the speaker did happen to be His Eminence, the Archbishop of York, and the King's kinsman. Edward's jaw muscles tightened noticeably but he said only, 'You misunderstand me, my lord Archbishop. What I did mean was that my father-by-marriage and his sons are not in Olney. Otherwise, they'd have been no less willing than I to accept your hospitality.' And, for the first time, he allowed himself an instant of expressive emotion, a tight bitter smile twisted his mouth.

The archbishop stared at him. 'I mean no disrespect, Your Grace, but I feel I must ascertain that for myself.'

Edward shrugged. 'As you wish,' he said, as if it were a matter of indifference, and he watched without expression as the archbishop's men shoved past Richard and Hastings, entered the inn.

Only then did he let his eyes seek those of his brother and the Lord Chamberlain.

The inn suddenly emptied of people. Most were hastening from the courtyard to follow the progress of the archbishop and the King through the village, watching until the last of the soldiers had disappeared down the road that led west, toward Coventry.

Richard and Will Hastings stood in silence in the deserted courtyard. Richard had been grasping the hilt of his dagger, clutching it as if it were a lifeline. Now, as his hold suddenly slackened, his fingers began to tingle with the returning rush of blood. He flexed them absently and then looked down at the dagger as if becoming aware of it for the first time. It slipped smoothly from its sheath, a beautiful lethal weapon, slender of blade and jewelled of hilt, engraven with a tusked boar.

Suddenly he was running, across the courtyard and out to the village well. He didn't pause, leaned over, and dropped the dagger down into the depths of the well. The water closed over it at once, with hardly a ripple. As he watched, the surface smoothed over, so that none could tell it had been disturbed at all.

II

Warwick Castle

August 1469

The night was unbearably hot. Edward sat up, unfastened his shirt. It didn't help. He leaned over, began to rummage through the stack of books piled on the floor by the bed. He selected several at random, settled back against the pillows.

The first one he opened was a slim volume bound in Moroccan leather, a thirteenth-century Latin poem, *The Debate of the Body and the Soul.* He began to read.

> *Thou, that wert ever wont on prancing steed*
> *To ride abroad, by country or by town;*
> *Thou, that wert known for many a shining deed*
> *Of high emprise, a knight of fair renown;*
> *How are thy swelling honours stricken down,*
> *Thy heart of lion-daring lowly bowed!*
> *Where now is thy imperious voice, thy frown*
> *Of withering hate? Thou, that wert so proud,*
> *What dost thou lying here, wrapt in a vulgar shroud?*

Edward laughed, with considerable bitterness. A good question, that last. Why, indeed, was he lying here in a stifling bedchamber in his cousin's castle? Because he'd been a bloody trusting fool, that was why. How could he have been duped by that Robin of Redesdale ruse? How could he have been so gullible?

> *Where is thy arras stiffening with gold,*
> *Thy couches all with gorgeous hangings strewd,*
> *The ambling jennets, and thy destrier bold,*
> *The hawks and hounds, that came to thee for food?*
> *Where now the troops of friends that round thee stood?*

That was another intriguing question. He'd have given a great deal to know the answer, to know the whereabouts of his friends, his supporters. Had the entire country passively acquiesced in his captivity? What of London? He'd always been well liked in London; had the citizens meekly submitted to Warwick's assumption of authority?

183

He slammed the book shut. That was the worst, the not knowing. The utter isolation. For eleven days now, he'd had no contact with the outside world, knew no more of what was happening in his own realm than he did of the goings-on in Cathay.

His own realm. A rare jest, that! At the moment, he had no more control over events than that pitiful fool reading his prayer missals in the Tower. It was four years now since Harry of Lancaster had fallen into Yorkist hands and it was said he seemed more content in confinement than ever he had in the days of his king-ship. Edward wondered if it had occurred to his cousin Warwick that he held no less than two Kings of England in his power. Doubtless, it had. That was just the sort of irony to appeal to Warwick's monumental pride.

Yet had it not been for that very pride, Edward was convinced, he'd have been dead these eleven days past. It was Warwick's vanity, his glorified image of himself, that had stayed his hand, kept him from murder. For the moment.

Edward believed Warwick was no more eager than the Archbishop of York to take upon himself the onus of killing an anointed king. But he knew Warwick, knew he'd have done it had he felt no other choice was open to him. He was alive now because he'd taken his cousin by surprise with his surrender, with his willingness to accede to Warwick's wishes, to sign what he was told to sign, to play the puppet King. All under the guise of flawless courtesy, the gracious host and the grateful guest. It was a deadly little game he and his cousin were playing. How long it could last, he didn't know, doubted that Warwick did, either.

He reached for another book, flipped through it listlessly.

> Winter rouses all my grief;
> Branches strip til they are bare,
> And sighing in sorrow, I despair
> That earthly pleasures come to nothing.

Seed I planted green now withers,
Jesus, your high purpose show;
Stave off Hell, for when I go
From here, and where, I do not know.

That was too much. Edward yielded to impulse, sent the book sailing across the room. It slammed into the door and the voices in the outer chamber ceased at once. He didn't doubt his 'body-guards' were alarmed, wondering how their King was amusing himself. Amusing himself! Christ, he was going mad with sheer boredom. In some ways, that was even worse than the uncertainty of what each dawning day might hold. He'd never experienced a period of forced inactivity before, had never before been denied those pleasures he'd always taken for granted.

He closed his eyes, put off summoning a servant for a while longer. Warwick saw that his needs were well served, had arranged for a man to act as his body squire. Edward did not credit that to Warwick's generosity. He knew that as long as he was cooperating, it was in Warwick's interest to preserve the aura of kingship.

After a few moments, he sat up again, shoved the pillow back into shape. Not that all his needs were being served. Except for rare bouts of illness or during campaigns, this was the longest that he'd gone without a woman in his bed. And now, more than at any other time in his life, he needed the relief, the distraction. He should remind his cousin that it was customary to offer a condemned man one last meal.

Not surprisingly, such thoughts brought Elizabeth to his mind. He wasn't all that worried for her physical safety for he did not think Warwick would harm a woman. She must be frantic, though, must be wild with fear, and with more reason than any others knew. She'd joined him briefly at Fotheringhay last month and had told him then that she thought she might be with child.

She still hadn't been sure and none had been told. Thank God for that! The only one he'd mentioned it to was Dickon and the boy was bright enough to hold his tongue. No, it was best if Warwick did not know Lisbet was breeding again, that she might be carrying the son who would take from George his one dubious distinction, that he stood between Edward's little girls and the throne.

Not that he could be sure that was Warwick's intent, to claim the crown for George. He was damned well sure, though, that it had occurred to them both and frequently. If they thought they could get away with it. . . . If they thought the country would accept George. . . . If Johnny could be persuaded to hold aloof. . . .

He knew he was tormenting himself for naught, that such feverish speculation did him no good, but he couldn't seem to stop. His head was throbbing again, had been paining him for days now. The strain was telling. He awoke at night drenched in sweat, jerked from sleep by the pounding of his own heart.

He found himself recalling a sardonic jest he'd once made when Will had chided him for wandering about London with only a token escort. Who, he'd laughed, would be willing to kill him, knowing that meant George would then be King? Those within earshot had been much amused but Edward now found nothing remotely amusing in the memory.

The door opened. One of his guards stood there, conspicuously ill at ease.

'Your Grace . . . my lord of Warwick has ridden in this night from Coventry. He requests that you join him in the presence chamber.'

Edward didn't move, stared at him. Remembering a summer night two years ago when he'd refused Warwick's demand for a midnight audience. It was, he reckoned, nearly midnight now.

The documents had been spread out on the table for him, awaiting his signature. Edward read rapidly. He was not surprised to find Warwick was claiming for himself the office of Chief Justice and

186

Chamberlain of South Wales, a post that had been held by Lord Herbert, who'd gone to the block at Warwick's command just eighteen days ago. He scribbled his signature, reached for the next document.

This one gave him pause. Warwick was appointing Will Hastings as Chamberlain for North Wales. Edward felt a surge of relief for that meant Warwick had decided Will was worth winning over. Yet, at the same time, he could not deny a certain disquiet. Will was his friend. He trusted Will as much as he trusted any man alive. But his trust was not what it once had been. He'd once trusted Warwick; he truly hadn't believed Warwick would ever resort to armed rebellion, not after all they'd shared.

It occurred to him now that there was no man he could trust without reservations. Not one. Not Johnny. Not Jack Howard. For sure, not Lisbet's Woodville kindred. Not even Will and Dickon, for Dickon was an untried boy and Will . . . Will was Warwick's brother-in-law. It would seem, he thought bleakly, that he'd just discovered yet another unpleasant aspect of confinement, the erosion of trust.

'I assure you it is all in order, Cousin.'

Edward looked up, met Warwick's eyes. 'I've no doubt of that,' he said coolly, 'but I was once told that a man who signs any paper without reading it beforehand is a fool twice over.'

Warwick's mouth quirked as if he'd suppressed a smile. 'As I recall, I was the one who did so caution you.'

'Yes . . . I know. It was during those months we spent in Calais, after we were forced to flee Ludlow.'

This time their eyes held. By the hearth, George watched with displeasure. There was much about his cousin's relationship with Ned that he found hard to comprehend. He thought Warwick had every reason to hate Ned and most of the time acted as though he did. And then suddenly he'd let himself be caught up in some common memory. Once, much to George's exasperation, he'd even found them laughing together over some stupid incident that had happened years ago. It irked him that Warwick seemed unable to sever all ties with the past, that he let memories matter. It was only today that counted. And today, Ned was a threat.

George did not trust Ned in the least, however amiable he was making himself out to be. George knew Ned too well for that and, for the first time, he found himself wondering if Warwick's perception of Ned was not flawed. Unfortunately, he knew Warwick was not likely to heed him. There were times when it seemed to George as if his father-in-law of a month took him no more seriously than did Ned.

It would have been so much easier had Ned offered resistance at Olney, been killed in the fighting. George had been sure that would happen, had been truly shocked when Ned surrendered himself into Warwick's hands without so much as a struggle. George had only recently admitted it to himself, would never have said it aloud, but he would rather his brother were dead. Ned's death would be the solution to all their problems.

He did not want, however, to have a hand in Ned's murder. Not when he thought of his lady mother, thought of Meg and Dickon. He'd never be able to face them if that happened. Never. Not unless Ned gave him no choice.

Well, it might not come to that. Warwick had a scheme, one that gave George a great deal of excitement. There were other ways to depose a king than by death, after all. There was, Warwick had pointed out, that rumour put about years ago by enemies of York that Ned was, in fact, illegitimate, was not the true son of the Duke of York.

George doubted if even the most devout Lancastrian had ever believed it but belief wasn't all that important. It could be used, could give parliament the excuse it must have to act, to confer the crown upon him. He did not permit himself to tarnish his dream by considering his mother's reaction to such an accusation. He'd convinced himself that she'd understand it was Warwick's doing, not his.

Still, though, it was risky. So very risky. His smile faded. No, far better for them if Ned were dead. He studied his brother with cold eyes. What a pity he'd not died at Olney!

Edward reached for the last of the documents put before him. But with the first words, he stiffened, stared down in disbelief.

'The King, to the venerable father in Christ, Thomas, Cardinal and Archbishop of Canterbury, greetings. Because, on the Friday before Michaelmas next to come, We decree to hold a parliament at York, We order you to be present in person on the day and place aforesaid. . . .'

Edward's head came up sharply to find Warwick watching him with a sardonic smile.

'As you can see, Ned, there's to be a parliament in York on the twenty-second of next month. I want you, therefore, to send out writs under the privy seal to the prelates and peers of the realm.'

Edward stared at him. His mind was racing. A parliament . . . why? To confer the crown upon George?

'I see,' he said slowly.

'I rather thought you would, Cousin.' Warwick saw with satisfaction that some of Edward's vaunted control had slipped; there was a tightness about his mouth that hadn't been there moments before.

'George did think you might refuse. Why, I do not know.'

Warwick was enjoying himself. There were times, he admitted, when the unreality of their situation struck him with overwhelming force, when he found it impossible to believe he and Ned had ever come to this. But not now. Now he relished this particular moment, thought it ample payment for what he saw as years of Woodville-inflicted humiliations.

'I told George he was wrong, of course. I said I was sure you'd appreciate . . . the necessities involved, would be quite willing to cooperate.'

Edward's fist had clenched. He gazed down at the whitened knuckles, the ruby-red coronation ring. A moment passed and then another. And then he reached for the pen.

'Why not?' he said briefly, and Warwick looked over to smile at his son-in-law.

'That's a trait I've often admired in you, Ned,' he said pleasantly. 'You've always been a realist.'

He moved to the sideboard, signalled for a servant to pour him wine.

'Now your brother Edmund, as I recall, took a rather pessimistic view of events. And Dickon, God help him, is both an idealist and a moralist. But you've always taken a very clearsighted approach to life, uncluttered by lofty notions of chivalry or high moral principles. That's commendable, Cousin, it truly is.'

Warwick heard George laugh but Edward refused the bait, said only, 'You're slighting your son-in-law, are you not, Dick? What of George?'

'I think he can speak for himself. Tell us, George, how would you describe yourself?'

George was watching Edward, even as he answered Warwick's playful query. 'As a man who knows how to make the most of an opportunity,' he said softly.

The chamber was silent for some moments after that. Both Warwick and George were watching Edward as he wrote. Warwick sipped his wine, savouring both the taste and what was to come.

'There is one more thing, Ned. You'd best prepare yourself for a journey.'

He saw Edward's pen pause and then continue smoothly across the page and he felt a flicker of admiration. He'd seen few men who could equal Ned's coolness in a crisis. With a smile that was almost affectionate, he said, 'Yes, I've decided your interests would best be served by a stay at Middleham.'

Edward betrayed himself at that; his pen jerked involuntarily. Middleham! Two hundred and fifty miles from London. In a region that had long held for Lancaster, had high regard for Warwick. But not for him, not for the House of York. He saw he'd blotted ink upon his signature; the first four letters of 'Edwardus Rex' were unreadable. He crossed it out, wrote above it in a slanting scrawl quite unlike his usual Italic hand, and then looked up.

'It's been five years since I've been north. I'd say a visit is long overdue,' he said calmly, and saw Warwick was amused by his unruffled response, that George was not.

It was queer, Edward thought, that George should have proven to be the most difficult to deal with. He'd never before realized just how much George disliked him. Blood ties did mean so much to him that he'd refused to recognize they could mean so little to George.

Now it was George who said mockingly, 'You know, Ned, I've always wondered how fond you were of your Woodville kin. Clearly enough, you were rather taken by the lady herself for reasons we all do understand well enough. But what of the rest of the Woodville clan? How do you feel about them? Your father-in-law, say?'

'I do not see how that matters, George, or how it concerns you,' Edward said, very evenly, and George smiled lazily at him.

'Oh, but it does, Ned. I'm curious, you see. Indulge me.'

The last of Edward's patience ebbed away in the hot sticky silence that followed.

'Lisbet comes from a large family. It is to be expected that I'd not feel the same degree of affection for them all,' Edward said wearily, and paused only an instant before adding, 'Unfortunately, Brother George, a man cannot choose his relatives as he can his friends.'

Surprisingly enough, George's smile didn't waver. Edward was suddenly alert; his brother was never one to accept insult with amusement.

'Well then, that does put my mind at ease, Ned, about what I have to tell you.'

Edward knew he was expected to probe now for details; he said nothing.

'Did you know . . . no, I expect not; you've been rather out of touch these past eleven days, have you not, Ned? Well, it so happens that your wife's father and brother John were taken the other day near Chepstow.'

Edward was very still, kept his eyes on George. His brother seemed in no hurry to speak, however. He drained his wine-cup, set it down on the floor rushes by his chair, snapped his fingers at one of Warwick's alaunts and at last, glanced up.

'We had them beheaded yesterday noon outside the walls of Coventry,' he said and smiled.

12

Middleham

August 1469

In the five years since Edward had taken Elizabeth Woodville as his wife, Francis Lovell had conscientiously chronicled the fragmenting relationship between the Earl of Warwick and his royal cousin and, on this humid August night, Francis was flipping back through his journal entries as the Earl's household awaited his arrival with his unwilling guest, the captive King of England.

Francis had been no more prepared for the Earl's action than had Edward himself and he was still dazed and disbelieving a month after the King had been taken prisoner at Olney. He didn't know what Warwick meant to do, knew only that the entire incredible episode filled him with apprehension. Apprehension shared by Warwick's wife and daughter Anne who were now awaiting the Earl in the great hall, word having been sent ahead to expect his arrival within the hour. Francis was sure they'd had no advance warning of Warwick's intentions; the news of Olney seemed to stun them as much as it had the country at large. For if rumour were to be credited, England was in turmoil.

Francis eagerly pounced upon every scrap of gossip that came his way and drew some consolation from what he heard. Warwick, it was becoming increasingly apparent, had misread the mood of his countrymen. Even those who were most virulent in their opposition to the Woodvilles had been shocked that Warwick should have moved against Edward himself. Francis knew that was why Warwick had chosen to convey Edward northward to Middleham. Warwick Castle was too close to London and London was still loyal to Edward.

Francis closed his journal; it made disheartening reading. Rising, he returned the journal to the security of his coffer and began to extinguish the candles one by one. As he did, he heard the barking of the castle dogs.

The great hall was aflare with a score or more of torches, keeping the shadows at bay and casting flickering light over the scene being enacted before Francis's astonished eyes. Standing in the glare of torch-fire, Edward bore little resemblance to a man who'd endured a six-day forced march. Still less did he resemble a man held prisoner for nearly a month's time. He was accepting the deferential but uncertain salutations of the earl's retainers as if holding court at Westminster and, as Francis knelt before him, he smiled easily.

'Francis Lovell. . . . Of course I do remember you. Ward of my cousin of Warwick and companion to my brother of Gloucester as I recall.'

His words bore evidence to an uncannily accurate memory.

His tone was friendly. But his eyes were opaque, sealed all secrets in a sea of clearest blue. Francis glanced over at Warwick, who was being greeted by his wife and daughter, and then back at Edward. He is far more clever than Warwick, he thought suddenly, and for the first time since word of Olney reached Middleham, Francis was no longer so fearful for what the future might hold.

Prisoner or not, Edward was well able to take care of himself, Francis decided, and gave the Yorkist King a smile of such unguarded admiration that Edward paused, let his eyes linger on Francis in sudden appraisal.

Much to Francis's secret amusement, Edward greeted Warwick's wife with such warmth that she was visibly flustered, pulled back from his embrace with an abruptness that bordered on rudeness. Edward, appearing oblivious of the unsettling effect he'd had on the mother, now turned toward the daughter, Nan's namesake.

Anne was in the shadows, came forward reluctantly to drop a stiff curtsy before him. He caught her by the elbows, raising her to her feet and drawing her toward him. Tilting her chin up, he stared into her face with an interest that was unfeigned.

Francis, who knew Anne's face as well as his own, found himself studying her with Edward's unfamiliar eyes. Isabel would always overshadow the fragile Anne. But Francis noted now the translucent skin without flaw, the wide-set eyes, a warm deep brown flecked with gold. He saw that there was a bright lustrous shimmer to her hair; it had darkened considerably since childhood and was sun-streaked chestnut to a burnished russet-gold. Saw, as if for the first time, that her full lower lip gave her mouth a provocative pout in unexpected and arresting contrast to the finely drawn cheekbones and narrow straight nose, and thought, in some surprise, Why, she's quite pretty!

It was a startling revelation to Francis for, until tonight, he'd always viewed Anne with the same affectionate unseeing eyes that he turned upon his own sisters. His sudden appreciation went no further than that, however; he was well aware that Anne's heart had been given long ago. He did find himself thinking, though, for the first time in many months, of Anna, his wife, who was Anne's age but far more of a stranger to him than Anne could ever be. Had she, too, been flowering into womanhood? he wondered, suddenly curious.

So caught up was he in these novel speculations that he missed the murmured exchange between Anne and Edward. Edward's comment, rather, for Anne had said nothing. She backed away, bumped into Francis, and he saw her skin was burning with hot colour.

'Whatever did he say to you, Anne?' he whispered.

She hesitated and then said in a very low voice, so that he had to strain to catch her words, 'He said ... he said, "So, you're Dickon's Anne."'

In mid-September, George and Isabel rode with an impressive entourage into Middleham Castle and villagers, long accustomed to the magnificent pageantry that seemed always to surround their lord of Warwick, were, nonetheless, dazzled by the elaborately staged arrival of the Duke of Clarence and his Duchess.

It was only then that Edward learned the scheduled parliament had suddenly and without explanation been cancelled. Learned, too, that he'd been right in his suspicions as to Warwick's true intent.

It was Isabel Neville who unwittingly confirmed his fears; Isabel, who avoided his company whenever possible, who seemed acutely uncomfortable in his presence. He had no trouble guessing why. Isabel knew what her husband and father were planning, to crown George in his stead, and she did not know how to treat the man they meant to dethrone, or worse. He'd amused himself by teasing her at first but soon saw she was genuinely distressed and, after that, took pity on her, made no further attempts to seek out her company.

He continued to feign nonchalance, was so gallantly attentive to Nan that she finally began to thaw under his smiles and was soon acting as if he were, indeed, an honoured guest and no more than that. He'd made a deliberate attempt to charm the unresponsive Anne before realizing that, as with Isabel, the greatest kindness he could do her was to leave her alone.

Only with George did his mask slip; with George, Edward was hard pressed to be civil. It was, in part, a natural reaction to George's intensifying hostility. But, more than that, it was a bitter reaction to what he saw as a betrayal of his own blood. George was his brother and, to Edward, that made his treachery as unnatural as it was unforgivable.

As for his cousin, Edward thought it fortunate that Warwick wasn't much at Middleham that September for he was finding it more and more difficult to deflect the barbs, the sarcasms, with faintly ironic courtesy, to discipline a tongue that had never before known constraints not of his own choosing.

Not only were his nerves fraying under the unrelenting pressure, but Warwick's own affability was souring. Warwick was becoming far more apt deliberately to select words meant to wound, was curt now when he'd been complacent, patronizingly polite, just weeks ago. Edward noted the change with intense interest, understood it meant that his own position was now more hopeful and, paradoxically, more dangerous, than at any time since those first hours at Coventry.

In these weeks since Olney, Edward knew himself to be as close to death as he'd ever been. But, even now, he never quite despaired. From boyhood, he'd done as he pleased, taken what he wanted, and had never found the price too high to pay.

Only once had luck failed him, in the snow before Sandal Castle, and he'd never been able to stifle the conviction that had he been there that December day with his father and Edmund, he'd have somehow been able to keep them from the folly of that fatal assault. He could not believe that he would lose, even though his cousin seemed to hold all the cards and he had only time on his side.

The September sun was slanting through the unshuttered solar windows, touching Edward's hair with coppery glints, setting his rings ablaze as his hand hovered over the chessboard. He claimed a knight and looked up at Francis with a challenging smile, while reaching down to fondle the head pressing against his knee.

Francis watched the alaunt lavish a wet caress upon Edward's hand and laughed aloud.

'It seems even His Grace's hounds have been won over by you, my liege.'

'Do not let my cousin hear you say that, Francis. There's no surer way to gain a man's enmity than to win his dogs away from him. Better you should seduce his wife, instead.'

Francis laughed, dared to say, 'I doubt even you could seduce the Lady Nan, Your Grace. For her, there is but one man in the world . . . my lord of Warwick.'

Edward suppressed the ribald retort that came to mind, in deference to his youthful companion's years. He said instead, 'That may explain then, Francis, why my cousin seems to trust his wife to my keeping and yet does begrudge me the companionship of his daughters.'

Francis had noticed, too, how both Anne and Isabel were so little in Edward's company. His discretion had become somewhat lax after exposure to Edward's easy amiability and now he said boldly, 'It may be your brother of Clarence is jealous, my lord.'

Edward gave a noncommittal smile and a shrug. He'd sensed Francis was sympathetic from that first moment in the great hall and the boy had confirmed it by the eagerness with which he responded to Edward's friendly overtures. But Francis was still Warwick's ward, was wed to Warwick's niece. Moreover, if his memory did serve him, the Lovells held Lancastrian loyalties. He preferred not to commit himself, not until he could be sure he'd securely won the boy's affections.

Now he raised guileless eyes to Francis's dark ones, and detoured the conversation away from the dangerous subject of his brother's jealousies.

'Well, be that as it may, that still does leave the younger girl and she's been as elusive as a wood sprite. I've not laid eyes upon her twice in the past week.'

Francis stared down at the chessboard, experiencing a protective pang for Anne Neville.

'She was much grieved, my liege, when you refused to permit her betrothal to His Grace, the Duke of Gloucester.'

'Not as grieved as my cousin of Warwick, I trust,' Edward said dryly and, when Francis said nothing, he prodded, 'Your move, Francis.' Adding, in careless curiosity, 'I daresay she was even more grieved, then, that Gloucester would not countenance an elopement in defiance of my wishes as did Clarence?'

'No, Your Grace, that's not so,' Francis said, with enough emotion to earn him a quizzical look from Edward. 'She knows him far too well for that.' He shook his head soberly. 'Your brother of Gloucester did love the Earl once. But he made his choice nigh on five years ago. I know, I was there.'

Edward was regarding him with sudden absorption. 'I do remember now. . . . You are a particular friend to Dickon, aren't you?'

Francis caught the subtle shading of the query, nodded.

'I have that privilege, Your Grace.'

He swallowed, kept his gaze upon the ivory chess pieces. He knew Edward was watching him, could feel the man's eyes upon him, with probing intensity that was like a physical touch. He reached tentatively for his endangered pawn and Edward's hand closed on his. The coronation ring shone for Francis with a blinding brilliance. He raised his eyes to meet Edward's, knowing what would be asked and what he would say.

'Just how good a friend to Dickon are you, Francis?'

Francis did not need to consider the consequences of his reply. He already knew, had long ago acknowledged a private truth, that his loyalties were pledged not to the Earl of Warwick or the forgotten Queen of Lancaster, but to the House of York. To Dickon and the man who now gripped his hand across the chessboard.

'There is nothing I would not do for your brother of Gloucester,' he said softly, and then his heart gave a guilty lurch for the incriminating words were no sooner out of his mouth than the solar door opened and the Earl of Warwick entered the chamber.

Warwick frowned at the sight of Francis but forbore to make comment. He could hardly expect to isolate Edward from contact with all in his household, not unless he had him confined to quarters under constant guard. And even that might not be sufficient.

He still remembered the unpleasant shock he'd felt upon entering Edward's chamber at Warwick Castle, soon after he'd taken his cousin into custody, and finding Edward playing cards with the men charged to guard him. He'd taken steps to see Edward would not be able to fraternize so freely with his gaolers in the future, but the memory of the incident lingered, gave him some uneasy moments. As much as it galled him to admit it, his cousin had a winning way when he so chose and that, he thought bitterly, made Ned a very dangerous man, indeed. Too dangerous to be set free.

Yet his choices seemed to be narrowing. It would have been one thing to have put Ned to death at Olney or when he'd been brought before them at Coventry. It was quite another to kill him in cold blood after six weeks of captivity. He looked at his cousin, impersonally weighing what he would risk and what he would gain if he did now what he was beginning to believe he should have done at Coventry. He already knew the answer, though, knew that to kill Ned now was a risk he was not willing to take, not unless forced to it.

199

'You may go, Francis,' he said abruptly, and looked at Edward as if daring him to object to this arbitrary interruption of their game. But Edward gestured casually toward the chessboard, said, 'We'll pursue this further at a more opportune time, Francis.'

Warwick watched as his ward fled the solar and then turned unfriendly eyes upon Edward. There was no reflection of remembered affection in his gaze, only cold, measuring hostility. In the past month, his feelings for Edward had suffered a sea change, had become encrusted with resentment, emptied of all warmth. Somehow, things weren't going as he'd planned. He found himself beset with difficulties, encountering obstacles where he'd least expected them, and he could only attribute his mounting problems to the fact that his cousin still lived.

London remained restive, stubbornly loyal to Edward. The Duke of Burgundy was making threats on his brother-in-law's behalf. There were increasing outbursts of violence and pillaging as opportunists and outlaws alike took advantage of the disruption of authority. Some of Warwick's own supporters were among those swept up in this lawless surge. Suddenly, it was as if the country had been plunged back into those chaotic days when Harry of Lancaster reigned and Marguerite d'Anjou and the Duke of York fought to see who would rule.

Warwick was deeply disturbed by these tales of civil unrest; he was shrewd enough to see that he had to keep the peace if he hoped to exercise authority and, in recent days, both seemed to be slipping away from him. His frustration was all the greater because he didn't understand what had gone wrong.

For several years now, Edward's popularity had been ebbing. The people felt themselves to be burdened with inequitable taxes, blamed Edward because the treaty with Burgundy had not yet brought the anticipated economic benefits, were disgruntled because the Commons had voted Edward a grant of sixty-two thousand pounds last year for war with France but Edward had not as yet got around to doing anything about it. Warwick had not expected there to be significant opposition to deposing Edward, did not think people were likely to care, one way or the other, not after more than ten wearying years of strife between York and Lancaster. He was wrong, was now finding that the country still supported his cousin.

Even his own family was giving him more stress than support. His wife could not hide her fear. His daughter Anne, who had little reason to think kindly of Edward, had come to him deeply distressed by gossip she'd heard among her cousin George's retainers, that he meant to strip Ned of his crown and bestow it upon George. Should he not take measures to punish those who so dared to slander his honour? she'd asked him worriedly.

He'd had an embittered confrontation with his aunt Cecily before he left London, another with his brother at Sheriff Hutton Castle. John had warned him bluntly that if Edward were to die in his custody, he'd never believe it to be anything but murder, even if Warwick could summon a score of physicians and priests to swear Edward died through illness or accident.

Warwick was fond of his brother; it had been a painful interview. Nor could he ignore the political implications of John's stand. As the Earl of Northumberland and a seasoned soldier able to attract a large following to his badge of the Griffin, John was a powerful political figure in his own right. Warwick needed his support; after Sheriff Hutton, he had to face the fact that he didn't have it.

He'd been forced at last to cancel the York parliament; with the country on the brink of anarchy, he'd have no chance of winning acceptance for George's claim to the crown. But as bad as the news had been for him that September, he'd not been prepared for the grim tidings his brother George now brought from London.

Outlaws were not the only ones to turn the unrest to their own advantage. A Lancastrian-kindled revolt had flared up along the Scots border, and Warwick swiftly set about raising troops to quell the rising. The response had been disturbingly slow in coming, though, and this afternoon the Archbishop had ridden into Middleham with truly alarming word from the capital. In the South, none would answer their summons to arms. Not as long as the King remained captive.

'I want you to accompany me into the city of York,' he said bluntly, saw surprise flicker briefly in Edward's eyes, to be quickly replaced by guarded wariness.

'I will be honest with you, Ned. I do need your help in summoning men to arms to put down the Lancastrian revolt.'

He was watching Edward closely but the younger man showed no identifiable emotion, said nothing, merely continued to finger the chess piece he'd been holding as Warwick entered the solar, his face thoughtful. Warwick took the seat Francis had vacated, said evenly, 'I said I'd be honest with you, cousin. That means I'll do whatever is necessary should you decide upon some rash and foolish action whilst in York. You will, I remind you, be riding with my men.'

Edward leaned back in his chair, said with a cold smile, 'You need not worry, Dick. I happen to think it to be very much in my own interest to put a quick end to any rebellion backed by Lancaster.'

Warwick nodded. 'Just so we do understand each other.'

Following Edward's public appearance with Warwick in York, men responded to the call to arms. The rebellion was soon quashed and its leaders beheaded in York on the 29th of September as Edward and the Nevilles watched.

With such pressing concerns, Warwick had no time to spare for the whereabouts of his young ward. Francis prudently waited till the Earl had ridden to Pontefract but he did not anticipate difficulty in finding the courier he sought. Francis had not lived five years in Yorkshire for nothing, knew which men were loyal to York. He slipped away one dawn, took the road south to Scotton, where the family of Rob Percy had long had a manor house. That attempt proved futile, though; he discovered the Percys had been in Scarborough for the past six weeks.

But as he rode home through the village of Masham, his luck suddenly took a dramatic turn for the better. Crossing the bridge that spanned the River Ure, he encountered Thomas Wrangwysh, and Thomas he knew to be one of the few citizens of York who'd always given unwavering support to the Yorkist King. In no time at all, he'd confided to the other what Edward wanted done and was soon galloping north toward Middleham, exultantly sure that Wrangwysh was even then bearing the King's message south.

October that year gave promise of considerable beauty, dawning with harvest skies and foliage splashed with vibrant colour. The noonday sun was directly overhead as the Earl of Warwick and his son-in-law rode into the inner bailey of Middleham Castle after an overnight stay at nearby Bolton Castle.

It had been a fruitful visit. Lord Scrope had agreed to head a commission of oyer and terminer to investigate the continuing disturbances in the South. He'd also bolstered Warwick's flagging spirits by reaffirming both his loyalty and his friendship at a time when Warwick found himself much in need of such assurance. It should have helped; it didn't. Tense and tired, Warwick felt more and more these days as if he were fighting phantoms, that control was ebbing away from him.

Surrendering his mount to a waiting groom, he dismissed their escort and, as George hastened across the bailey toward the Lady Chamber in search of his wife, Warwick rapidly mounted the stairs leading up into the keep. Striding into the great hall, he came to an abrupt halt, staring in disbelief at what he saw before him. Men eating and drinking at long oaken trestle tables, men who wore the badges of England's nobility. He recognized at once the Duke of Suffolk, who was wed to Eliza Plantagenet, the second of Edward's sisters. He recognized, too, the languidly elegant Earl of Arundel. The swarthy Sir John Howard and, by the open hearth, the fifteen-year-old Duke of Buckingham, kneeling to romp with several of Warwick's dogs. He looked up now, to smile at Warwick with a boy's unconcern.

Buckingham alone seemed oblivious of the tension in the hall. The men were watching Warwick with expectant interest; several, like John Howard, were openly challenging. Warwick's eyes moved from face to face until, at last, he found the one he sought. Edward was standing with the Archbishop of York. The latter was resplendent in the jewelled mitre and robes of a prince of the Church but as white of face as one being marched to the gallows. Edward had been laughing as Warwick entered the hall; he was flushed with triumph, looked surprisingly young and suddenly carefree.

For a moment, time seemed to fragment, the intervening eight years seemed to disappear as if they'd never been, and Warwick was seeing again the jubilant nineteen-year-old youth who'd ridden beside him into London to deafening cheers on that long-ago February day that was to lead to the throne. And then the eerie illusion shattered and Warwick was facing a man who watched him with hard mocking eyes and a smile that promised not remembrance, but retribution.

Francis had twisted around on the window seat of the solar, one that faced west, trying to catch a glimpse of the road that led up from the south. He turned quickly as the door opened, staring in dismay as Warwick and Edward came into the chamber, trailed by the Archbishop of York. He shrank back into the window recess but they were far too angry to give him any notice.

'I do not know what you've got in mind, Ned, but I'm telling you now, it will not work. I do not give a damn if you've managed to summon every peer in England to Middleham.'

'As it happens, Cousin, that is just what I have done.'

Warwick drew a laboured breath, said flatly, 'You're lying.'

'Am I?' Edward jeered, and Warwick found he was gripping

204

the hilt of his dagger so tightly that the studding of jewels left deep indentaions in the palm of his hand. He forced his fingers to unclench, let the dagger slide down the sheath.

'Even if you speak true, it matters for naught,' he said at last. 'This is Middleham, not Westminster. I do give the commands here. You seem to have forgotten that.'

'No, I have not. I assure you I'm not likely to forget anything that has happened in the past two months.'

Francis was frightened by the hatred he saw in Warwick's face. He had no doubt that, at this moment, Warwick wanted his cousin dead. Edward saw it, too; there was both bitterness and triumph in the twist of his mouth.

'Damn you,' Warwick said suddenly. 'Do you truly think I'll do nothing whilst . . .'

'No, I'm not suggesting you do nothing, cousin. I would suggest you return to the great hall and stand ready to welcome your guests to Middleham. That is, I believe, called "appreciating the necessities involved", is it not?'

The archbishop said, too eagerly, 'He's right, Dick. What else can we do but put a good face upon it. . . .' He was ignored.

The silence was smothering. Edward leaned back against the trestle table, kept his eyes on Warwick. One of the Earl's ever-present alaunts sidled up to Edward, rubbed affectionately against his legs. The silence dragged on until Francis thought he could endure not another moment of it. The Archbishop seemed to share his sentiments. But Warwick looked murderous and Edward as if he were enjoying himself.

'And what if I do say no?' Warwick said softly. 'What if I say you do not leave here, cousin? Need I remind you that the men of Middleham do answer to me and only to me?'

Edward did not seem at all impressed but the archbishop was appalled.

'My God, Dick, you cannot resort to violence before half the lords of the realm!'

Francis was no less appalled than the Archbishop. He shifted uneasily, and thus brought upon himself what he least desired, the Earl's attention. Warwick turned to stare at the boy.

'What do you here, Lovell? Well, answer me! Get over here, now!'

Francis moved stiffly across the solar. He was very frightened, knew he was to be the sacrificial lamb for Warwick's rage. He could only pray that Warwick was acting out of frustrated fury and not something more ominous. He'd willingly face Warwick's anger if only he could be sure it was free of suspicion.

'My lord . . .' he whispered, and then staggered backward as Warwick struck him across the face. It wasn't a particularly hard blow; he'd been punished more severely for lesser infractions. But one of Warwick's rings happened to catch the corner of his mouth. He gasped, blood beginning to trickle down his chin, and braced himself for whatever Warwick saw fit to inflict upon him.

'You have leave to go, Francis.'

This time Francis's gasp was not of pain, was one of surprise. He spun around. He'd not expected Edward to intervene on his behalf, but he'd not expected Edward to share Warwick's anger at his presence either. Yet Edward was watching him with eyes indifferent to his pain; now said in a voice that had nothing in it of past friendliness, 'Did you not hear me, Francis? I gave you a command. Do not make me repeat it.'

Francis was shaken by Edward's icy dismissal as he'd not been by Warwick's blow. Even though it meant he was spared further exposure to Warwick's wrath, it hurt; it hurt dreadfully. He gave Warwick a nervous glance, saw Warwick was now looking at Edward, not at him.

'Yes, Your Grace,' he said miserably, made an awkard obeisance as Edward moved away from the table, jerked his head toward the door.

'Go on, get out of here,' he said impatiently. But, in turning, his back was to Warwick. As he spoke, he winked at Francis and the boy's spirits soared in less than a heartbeat from despair to elation. He backed hastily toward the door, struggling to maintan a properly chastised appearance.

He heard Warwick say, 'I was not aware you took such an interest in my ward. I find myself wondering why.'

Francis froze at that but was reassured somewhat by Edward's derisive reply.

'I do not give a damn about your ward. But this is not a conversation for other ears. Unless, of course, you want an audience to watch you play the fool, cousin? In that case, I suggest we return to the great hall and continue this discussion there.'

Francis grabbed for the latch, just as the door sprang back in his face. He recoiled as George of Clarence stumbled into the solar.

'Men at arms!' he gasped. 'Approaching from the south, five hundred at the least!'

The Nevilles turned as one toward Edward.

Edward said nothing. He looked at Warwick and laughed.

Warwick didn't move, didn't take his eyes from Edward even as he said to George, 'Look to the standards. Under whose command do they march?'

George had yet to look at his brother. Now he hastened to the window seat where Francis had been keeping vigil. Kneeling on the seat, he straightened almost at once and turned to face his father-in-law.

'Hastings,' he said, in a muffled voice. 'And the Whyte Boar of Gloucester . . . Dickon.'

They were all staring at Edward now but it was to Warwick alone that he said, 'Just so. My brother of Gloucester and my Lord Chamberlain have seen fit to provide a proper escort for my journey back to London.'

For the chilled intake of a breath, their eyes held and then Warwick's shoulders slackened.

'I see,' he said tonelessly.

Edward's gaze flicked suddenly to George and then back to Warwick.

'You should have held them at Olney, Dick.' He sounded almost amused but there was something chilling, as well, in his voice.

Warwick was silent.

Francis, who'd listened spellbound, belatedly became aware of his peril and took several stealthful steps toward the door. Then George moved toward his brother, said in a low strained voice, 'Is it your wish that I accompany you to London, Ned?'

Warwick stiffened, turning to stare at his son-in-law.

So did Edward. 'You may go to Hell and be damned for all I care where you go,' he said, slowly and very deliberately.

George flushed, blood pulsing into his face and throat.

'Ned, you do not see . . .'

'Oh, but I do see . . . brother George. And what I see sickens me, in truth.'

George was rigid, a clenched fist digging bruisingly into his thigh. 'You'd best take heed, my liege. . . . For I'll not come to heel like one of your damned hunting dogs.'

The Archbishop of York gasped. Warwick, however, was impassive, seemed to be focusing on something far beyond the solar, beyond his Yorkist cousins. And Francis found himself hoping that no one would ever look at him as Edward was now looking at his brother.

For a long moment, Edward regarded George and then raised his hand. The snapping fingers jolted Warwick's lounging dogs to their feet and to his side where they waited, obediently expectant of command.

Francis had seen enough. He dived through the doorway and hastened through the great hall onto the covered porch landing, down the stairs into the sunlit bailey.

There, confusion reigned. A lean fair man whom he recognized as Lord Dacre was dismounting by the stairs. A man brushed by Francis, wearing the Stafford Knot, badge of the youthful

Harry Stafford, Duke of Buckingham. Across the bailey, he saw the Earl of Essex, and he felt a surge of partisan pleasure that England's lords had heeded Edward's summons with such alacrity. No matter how they may despise the Woodvilles, Edward still holds their allegiance, he thought, and then turned at the sound of his name.

Anne Neville was hurrying toward him. 'Francis, a large force approaches. They told me at the gatehouse that they do number in the hundreds.'

'I know.'

She caught his arm. 'They're still some distance away so I cannot be sure. ... But, Francis, I think the banner they fly is the *Blancsanglier*. The Whyte Boar.'

He nodded and her hand slipped from his sleeve.

'I knew. ... Even before I saw Richard's standard, I knew,' she whispered and Francis could only nod again.

Within the past year, Anne had begun to make exclusive use of her cousin's given name. Francis had been unable to resist teasing, 'Why do you alone prefer Richard when all others call him Dickon?' And she'd laughed at him, 'Have you so little imagination, Francis? For that very reason, because all others do call him Dickon.'

Francis was remembering that conversation now as she said, 'I cannot see him, Francis.'

'Ah, Anne, that's so unfair. I'd not have thought that you, too, would blame him for his loyalty to his brother. Not knowing him as you do.'

The dark eyes widened. 'Oh, but I do not! God's truth, I do not!'

'If you refuse to see him, Anne, he's bound to believe otherwise.'

She shook her head. 'I cannot, Francis.' Her voice wavered. 'I cannot.' And then she cried out for he'd turned to face her fully for the first time and she saw the blood that welled in the corner of his mouth.

'Francis, you're hurt! What happened?'

'Your father hit me,' he said before he thought, and at once wished he could have called the words back, for she looked as stricken as if she were the one who'd been struck.

'I do think the world's gone mad,' she gasped, and before he could reply, she'd turned, was running across the bailey toward the south-wall quarters. From the way she stumbled, bumped blindly into those who crossed her path, Francis knew she was crying.

Francis had not seen Richard for months and now he edged closer as his friend and Lord Hastings rode toward the stairs of the keep, where Edward awaited them, flanked by the Earl of Warwick and the Archbishop of York. A smile hovered about Will Hastings's mouth as he swung from the saddle to kneel before Edward and as his eyes encountered his brother-in-law, the Earl of Warwick, he laughed outright. But Francis did not note Warwick's reaction for he was watching Richard's approach.

The sun was striking him full on, giving the glossy dark hair the sheen of polished ebony and causing him to raise his hand to shield the glare. Unlike Hastings, his thoughts were masked; only the strain showed. Francis thought he looked exhausted. The skin was stretched tightly across the high, hollowed cheekbones; there were smudges under the deep-set dark eyes, the expressive mouth frozen in a taut curve. To Francis, the most conclusive evidence of Richard's unease was the fact that his friend, a skilled rider, was having some difficulty in handling his horse. The animal, a lathered grey stallion, was shying nervously as if his rider's mood were contagious; as a result, Richard did not reach the stairs until Will Hastings had already dismounted.

But, as he met his brother's eyes over the stallion's tossing mane, Richard's face changed abruptly and he flashed a smile, so radiant with relief that Francis saw at once just what dark thoughts had haunted him during the two months of Edward's captivity.

Edward was grinning, came forward to raise Richard swiftly up as the boy knelt before him. Richard was always shy of public display of emotion; Edward wasn't. Careless of formality, he greeted his brother with laughter and an affectionate embrace.

Francis slanted a quick look toward Warwick but once again he was disappointed; the Earl was watching without expression. Ever since Warwick had emerged from the solar at his royal cousin's side, Francis had been hoping for signs of strain. He yearned for nothing so much as to see the Earl humiliated before the lords of the realm, but he saw that it was not to be.

His feelings for Warwick were far from benevolent at that moment but he grudgingly gave credit where due. It was no small feat to summon smiles and make small talk when you have murder in your heart, he thought, and, if Warwick was not altogether convincing as the gracious lord of the manor, he was at least in control.

That was more than Francis could say for Warwick's fellow conspirators. The Archbishop of York was painfully ill at ease; the more he sought to conceal it, the more apparent it became. As for George of Clarence, he was nowhere in evidence.

Standing by his brother's side as Edward welcomed the lords who continued to ride into the bailey, Richard had seen Francis almost at once and signalled his recognition with a quick warm grin. But the sun had begun its slow slide toward the west before they had the chance to speak together alone.

Meeting in the shadow of the garde-robe turret that extended from the south wall of the keep, they had exchanged only a few words when the Earl of Warwick detached himself from the nobles surrounding the King and crossed the bailey toward them.

'Renewing old friendships, Francis?'

Francis's mouth went dry with sudden certainty that Warwick knew the part he'd played in Edward's stratagem. It was with considerable relief, therefore, that he saw the Earl's eyes had slid past him unheedingly, to Richard.

'My compliments, Dickon. It is a surprise, I admit, but not an unwelcome one. I would far rather it should go to you than to a Woodville.'

Richard had stiffened warily at Warwick's approach. Now, however, he looked confused. So did Francis. Warwick saw and smiled thinly.

'It seems that not only am I to be the first to congratulate you, I'm to be the one to give you the news. Since I had Earl Rivers beheaded at Coventry, the post of Lord Constable has been vacant. It was to pass with Rivers' titles to his eldest son, Anthony Woodville. Your brother has just told me, however, that he does mean to bestow it upon you.'

Francis was stunned. The Lord Constable of England wielded enormous powers, not the least of which was the right to determine treasonable offences and to pass judgment upon the guilty. He looked at his friend; Richard was just five days past his seventeenth birthday.

Richard was startled and it showed. He opened his mouth, abruptly clamped his teeth down upon his lower lip as Warwick smiled at him, said, 'Ned must put great faith in your judgment, to burden you with such responsibilities at so young an age. But I would be the last one to doubt your abilities. It was at Middleham, after all, that they were first tested.'

It was a familiar tactic to Francis; he'd often seen Warwick make claims upon Richard in the guise of Middleham memories. He'd never failed to resent it, on Richard's behalf, knowing how vulnerable his friend was to that particular appeal. Now he was sorry but not surprised to hear Richard say, 'I was well instructed during my years in your household, cousin.'

'I am glad you do remember that, Dickon.'

Richard did not return the other's smile.

'In all save honour,' he said, softly but very distinctly.

Francis felt a surge of hot pleasure. Ah, but you were not expecting that, were you, my lord Kingmaker, he thought gleefully, seeing Warwick's mouth twist, the dark eyes go suddenly cold.

'Have a care, Dickon. That is dangerous talk. You owe me better than that.'

'Any debt I did owe you, cousin, was paid in full at Olney.'

'No, Dickon. You're wrong. There was no payment demanded at Olney. There could have been but there was not. You'd best not count upon that again. And that, my young cousin of Gloucester, you may take as the counsel of a friend or as a warning, whichever you choose.' He smiled then, brief and bitter, said, 'And I do not think I much care which it is.'

When Richard made no response, Warwick turned away, adding as if in afterthought, 'Have you a message you wish conveyed to my daughter?' And he had the ephemeral satisfaction of seeing that Richard's painstakingly devised defences were flawed, after all.

Watching as Warwick walked away, Francis swore softly and spontaneously and Richard said abruptly, 'Let's walk, Francis. We've much to say and little time.'

As Francis fell in step beside him, they crossed the inner bailey, away from the keep and the press of men milling about the stairs where Edward stood laughing in the sun.

Francis was studying England's new Lord Constable, said ruefully, 'It does occur to me, Dickon, that you're apt to end up passing judgment upon some of my own kin. One of Anna's brothers died fighting for Warwick at the battle of Edgecot last July and my father-in-law is hand-in-glove with the Earl.'

Richard shrugged. He had ambivalent feelings about Warwick's revelation, an uneasy blend of excitement and apprehension. He did not want to discuss it before he could speak with his brother; said, instead, 'Rob Percy is with me. Did you see him yet?'

Francis shook his head. His friendship with Rob Percy, which had once rested on no stronger foundation than proximity, had gradually evolved into a genuine affection. But he, nonetheless, was now aware of an unfocused undercurrent of resentment. Rob was free to take part in the most consequential happenings while he, as the Earl's ward, must remain sequestered at Middleham.

After a sideways glance at his friend's pensive profile, Richard said, 'I have a message for you from my brother. He said to tell you that he does not forget wounds got in his service.'

Francis laughed, thinking a split lip a small price to pay for the favour of a King.

'I am the one who should be thanking His Grace. He did save me from the Earl's wrath, yet without stirring suspicion in one notoriously lacking in trust.'

'I cannot say that surprises me. I've known few who can think as fast as he does.' Richard glanced with some sympathy at the younger boy's swollen cheek; already, it gave promise of discolouring into a truly spectacular bruise.

'He also wished me to tell you that he considers me to be most fortunate in my friendships. So do I, Francis.'

They looked at one another and then, suddenly self-conscious, began to walk again.

'Have you seen my brother of Clarence, Francis?'

Taken by surprise, Francis almost blurted out an account of that acrimonious exchange in the Earl's solar. Thinking better of it, he shook his head.

'It's passing strange,' Richard said in the ensuing silence and there were echoes of baffled anger in his voice. 'George is three years my elder and he's no child, not at twenty. Yet he can be as easily led as the greenest stripling.'

Francis made an appropriately neutral reply, ambiguous enough to satisfy his conscience and, at the same time, to encourage further confidences if Richard were so inclined. But, at that moment, Isabel Neville appeared in the doorway leading up to the Lady Chamber.

She faltered and then walked directly toward them, faced Richard with a brittle smile.

'Well, Dickon, I'll grant you this much. . . . Your homecomings are nothing if not spectacular.'

'Not by choice,' he said, enunciating each word with chill precision.

She stared at him bleakly and then sighed, gesturing, palms up, in involuntary appeal.

'Sweet Jesú does know we live in ill-fated times. But I must confess. There's no way on God's earth that I can bring myself to see you as an enemy, Dickon.'

'As a brother-in-law, then?' he suggested softly, and when she took a step toward him, he caught her in his arms. For a heartbeat, they stood in a wordless embrace, and then moved apart to smile at each other.

'Dickon, no one knows yet, not even my father. We were waiting till I was sure. But I want you to know . . . I'm with child.'

Richard caught his breath and she reached up to touch his cheek in soft entreaty, said coaxingly, 'Be happy for us, Dickon. Please be happy.'

'I am, Bella,' he said truthfully, and kissed her lightly. As he did, she gave him a quick, convulsive hug and her voice took on a sudden urgency.

'Dickon, talk to Ned . . . please. He would not listen to George. But he may listen to you. Make him understand that my father and George wanted only to detach him from the Woodvilles . . . God's truth, no more than that. It was the Woodvilles they acted against, not Ned. Make him see that.'

'I'll speak to him on George's behalf, Bella,' Richard agreed, after a prolonged pause, and Francis wondered if Isabel discerned the subtle yet significant difference between what was asked and what was promised.

'Thank you, Dickon. I knew we could rely on you.'

As she hugged him again, Richard lowered his voice, pitched it for her ear alone, and Francis caught only fragments of phrases.

'Tell her . . . the little chapel off the great hall . . . await her there . . .'

Isabel had been listening intently and now she nodded.

'Of course I will, Dickon.' She hestitated and then said, 'But I do not think she will come.'

Francis didn't think so, either, and his belief was borne out within the hour. Richard was once more at his brother's side and as he read Francis's silent query, he slowly shook his head.

Most of the men were mounted now and Edward, astride the blooded white stallion brought by Hastings and Richard, was exchanging sardonic courtesies with the Earl of Warwick, assuring his cousin that he'd remember the Earl's hospitality.

Richard, taking advantage of these spare moments, guided his stallion toward the east-wall servant dorters where Francis stood alone.

Francis was experiencing the inevitable letdown of one who was to be left behind. 'God keep you, Dickon . . . and His Grace, the King,' he said sombrely.

'Take care, Francis.'

'Tell His Grace that I . . .' He never completed the compliment for a blurred flash of colour caught his eye.

'Dickon!' With a meaningful jerk of his head.

Anne was flushed, her breath coming in gasps. Her eyes were swollen and her hair unbound, framing her face in soft swirls and tumbles. Seeing Richard, she slowed to a walk and then came to a complete halt as he turned in the saddle.

He swung his horse about and they met in the centre of the bailey. Francis was not within earshot but they did not appear to be speaking. As he watched, Richard leaned from the saddle and brushed back the chestnut hair from her face. Then he reined his mount in a tight semicircle and cantered across the clearing courtyard. As he passed Francis, he saluted him silently before spurring his stallion over the drawbridge and onto the road that led through the village and then south, away from Middleham.

Two months later, Francis wrote in his journal:

It is reported that King Edward was acclaimed with much fervour upon his entry into London. The Lord Mayor, the aldermen and two hundred city craftsmen clad in blue gathered at Newgate to welcome His Grace into the city. He had with him a thousand horsemen and in his escort were the Dukes of Gloucester, Suffolk and Buckingham; the Earls of Arundel and Essex; and Lords Hastings, Howard and Dacre.

He was accompanied, too, by His Grace, the Earl of Northumberland. John Neville joined the King on his progress south and rode at the King's side as they entered into London. It can be no easy thing to be forced to choose between one's brother and one's sovereign for I doubt not that he does love them both.

The King has ordered the Lancastrian Henry Percy freed from the Tower and he did name Dickon, Lord Constable, just as my lord of Warwick told us he would do. Dickon has now been dispatched to the border to quell a rebellion in Wales and to recapture Carmarthen and Cardigan which were seized by the rebels. It is his first military command.

He hesitated, blotted the page with ink, and then added, as a postscript, all he deemed it safe to say about the power struggle taking place between the King and his cousin, the Kingmaker.

The Earl of Warwick and the Duke of Clarence remain in the North. The King did summon them to London but they have so far refused to obey his summons. It is as if England were split asunder. I do not know what will happen now but I do fear for the future. I see naught but sorrows in what is to come.

13

Westminster

December 1469

'Why, Ned? Name of God, why? How could you?'

'Because I had no choice, Lisbet.'

Elizabeth stared at him. Edward saw her disbelief, saw his words had not registered with her.

'No choice?' she echoed blankly. 'My father and brother died at Warwick's command. And now you tell me you've no choice but to pardon him?'

Her voice rose. He moved toward her but she eluded him, stepped out of reach.

'Yes,' he said quietly. 'That is exactly what I am telling you. I had no choice. If you cannot destroy your enemy, Lisbet, you're compelled to come to terms with him. That's an elemental rule of warfare, my love, however little we may like it.'

'You have the power . . .' she began and he cut her off in mid-sentence.

'No, Lisbet. I regret to say that I do not. I do, of course, have the moral authority of kingship.' A sardonic smile touched his mouth before he added, 'Unfortunately, moral authority has traditionally fared rather poorly upon the battlefield, sweet-heart.'

She was oblivious to his sarcasm, was shaking her head. 'You're the King,' she said stubbornly. 'That does give you the power. . . .'

'The way Harry of Lancaster had the power? Christ, Lisbet, my father feuded with Marguerite d'Anjou for years and there was damned little Lancaster could do about it, even when it turned bloody.'

'Because he was simple.'

'That's true enough but the answer lies as much in my father's strength as in Harry's weakness. Strength enough to defy the crown, even to taking up arms against the King. How many battles were fought in the years before Towton. . . . Four? Five? You spoke of power. Well, my father did have the power to challenge the King. And however much it galls me to admit it, so does my cousin of Warwick. . . . At least, for now.'

She didn't reply and he slid his arm around her waist, drew her to him. Lowering his head, he brushed light kisses against her temples, her eyelids; spoke softly and coaxingly, recognizing the justice of her demand for vengeance but reminding her that the King had no army of his own, was dependent upon the lords to gather men to arms, reminding her that Warwick had his own power base in the North, that he could put a formidable force in the field under his own standard of the Bear and Ragged Staff. She made no response, merely turned her cheek slightly so that his lips just grazed her mouth.

'I do understand your bitterness, sweetheart. Do you think I wanted this? I can assure you that never was a pardon more grudgingly given. My cousin of Warwick does owe me a debt. It is not one I mean to forget. But I am not yet in a position to demand payment. I know it's not easy for you, my love, but. . . .'

She pulled free from his embrace. Never had he seen eyes so green, a glazed glittering emerald, pupils contracted to the merest slits of scalding fury.

'No, you do not know. The truth is that the deaths of my kindred mean little or nothing to you. You talk to me of necessity. Just tell me what necessity could ever have forced you to come to terms with Clifford! Nothing on God's earth could have compelled you to pardon the man who murdered your brother. But it seems my brother's death counts for less.'

He was now angry, too, but he made an attempt to stifle it, said patiently, 'You're not being fair, Lisbet. I told you why I agreed to pardon Warwick. You must know it is not what I wanted to do. . . .'

'No,' she spat. 'No, I do not. I know only that you are giving a pardon to the man who murdered my father and brother, and that is all I need to know.'

Never in their five-year marriage had they quarrelled this seriously; in the end Edward stalked from the bedchamber in disgust while Elizabeth gave vent to her rage by wreaking havoc upon the furnishings of the chamber, sweeping ivory combs and Venetian glass bottles to the floor and heaving the pillow across the room with such force that it ripped open in a flurry of escaping feathers.

Edward's anger was short-lived. He'd spoken the truth; the pardon was no more than a realistic recognition of the power inherent in the earldom of Warwick. But Elizabeth had spoken truth, too, and he knew it. The humiliations he'd been forced to endure at Warwick's hands rankled more with him than the deaths of his wife's kin.

His Woodville in-laws had sorely disillusioned him within months of his marriage. An extraordinarily handsome family, they soon showed themselves to be endowed with little more than good looks, to be grasping and inept at all but making enemies, at which they excelled. Edward was not long in reaching the conclusion that his interests would have been far better served had his wife been an only child and he could only marvel that a family so weak should have produced Lisbet, whose strength of will and ambition rivalled his own.

He regretted the executions of his father-in-law and brother-in-law on Coventry's Gosforth Green but he did not grieve for them and Elizabeth knew it. Knew it and resented it. He did not blame her. Nor did he fault her for vowing to take vengeance upon the man she held responsible.

Edward had long known his beautiful wife would make an implacable enemy. He knew, too, what it was to suffer a loss that demanded to be redeemed in blood. And, knowing that, he was willing to accept from her what he'd have accepted from no one else. He gave no more thought to their quarrel, diplomatically overlooked her icy demeanour in the days that followed and discreetly stayed away from her bed for several nights in order to give her temper time to cool.

It was on the fourth night after their quarrel that he came to her. He'd underestimated the extent of her anger, however. Time had only served to inflame and the grievances she bore him loomed ever larger with the passing days.

Sitting before her dressing table, Elizabeth watched her husband's mirrored movements in the polished pier glass she'd ordered from a master craftsman of Genoa. Her face was without expression; inwardly, she was seething. Her first impulse had been to voice her resentment, to tell him to take his pleasure with one of the harlots he kept about the court, to assail him with stinging words of rejection. She repressed the urge but only with considerable effort.

During the agreeable uneventful years of her marriage to John Grey, she'd never scrupled to withhold sexual favours as a means of winning her own way. It had proven to be a highly effective weapon with the slow-spoken earnest knight who'd never quite lost his awe at the breathtaking beauty of the girl he'd taken to his bed as a virgin bride of fifteen.

It had proven to be otherwise with Edward. Early on in their marriage, Elizabeth had rebuffed his amorous advances after a minor disagreement and thus provoked a quarrel of unexpected and alarming intensity. It was the first time she'd seen her easygoing new husband genuinely angry and she'd stored the memory away for future reference. Elizabeth was selfwilled but she was pragmatic, too. She knew how important it was to please Edward and, in the years to come, she did not make the same mistake again.

Now, as much as she longed to deny him, she hesitated to do so and she had too much pride to feign illness. But by the time her ladies had brushed her hair and perfumed her at throat and wrists, she had the solution to her dilemma.

She rose, came slowly across the room in reluctant response to his summons, stood before him, waiting as he rose from the bed, drew her into his arms. She yielded passively to his embrace, let him stroke her hair, explore her mouth with his tongue, strip away her dressing robe. She submitted silently to his caresses, made no response even when he touched her in places and in ways that he knew gave her the greatest pleasure. Now, however, she felt nothing and rejoiced in her triumph of will over body.

As he lowered her onto the bed, she met his eyes for the first time. He was, she saw, amused by her affectation of indifference, complacent that it was only a pose, that he could soon bring her to an unwilling acknowledgment of arousal.

It had occurred to her, too, that her own body might betray her, that this might be a form of retaliation that was more effective in theory than in practice. The sexual attraction between them was intense in the extreme, had been so from the moment of their first meeting. Even now, after five years and countless infidelities, he could smile at her across a room and suddenly her body would be trembling, would be suffused in heat. She had never tried to repress her desire for him, was not sure she could.

She found, somewhat to her surprise, that it was not difficult at all. She had only to think of Warwick. Warwick, who had ridden to Westminster under her husband's royal safe-conduct. Warwick, who was attending the great council as if the events of Olney had never been, as if he'd not murdered her kinsmen and imprisoned her husband.

With that, she went cold, a coldness that chilled her blood and quenched all flickerings of desire so thoroughly that she could not have reponded to Edward even had she suddenly wanted to do so. She felt numb as if her mind had somehow severed all ties to her body, she lay inert and uncaring under her husband's weight while her brain was filled with images of Warwick and her heart was filled with hate.

Hatred was an emotion that came easily to Elizabeth; even as a child, she'd not been one to forgive a wrong done her. She vowed now that the day would come when she'd see the destruction of Warwick and all who were his. Nor would she forget the part played in her father's murder by George of Clarence. Clarence, too, she owed a blood debt.

She shifted her shoulders; she was pinned against the bed in a position that was none too comfortable and she hoped Ned would soon finish for she was developing a cramp in her leg. Perhaps this time he might get her with child. She fervently hoped so; she was eager, desperate even, to give him a son and it had been months now since her womb was full. Her pregnancy of the past summer had proven to be false. . . . Either that or she'd miscarried late in the second month. That had been August when Ned was taken captive at Olney. Yes, that might well be another debt to be charged to Warwick. It gave her a certain bleak satisfaction to think so, to blame him for her present barrenness.

She belatedly became aware that her husband was suddenly still and his immobility took her by surprise for she knew he had not yet gained satisfaction. She raised herself on her elbow to look up questioningly into his face. With a start, she found that he was staring at her, perhaps had been studying her for some moments. He showed no amusement now; his eyes were very light in colour and sheeted in ice.

'Would you like a book to help you pass the time?' he asked, very softly, and Elizabeth realized that she'd wounded him in a way he'd not expected, was not likely to forgive. And lying there entwined in the most intimate of lovers' embraces, they regarded each other with the accusing eyes of enemies.

*

Elizabeth was not a nervous woman, nor was she one to conjure up spectres or entertain forebodings of unnamed dread. What little imagination she possessed was strictly disciplined, not given to fanciful wanderings beyond the well-defined boundaries she'd long ago set down for herself.

Yet now she found herself unable to sleep at night and, when she did, her sleep was fitful, troubled. She began to flinch at unexpected loud noises and, when a careless page overturned a heavy ceramic pitcher in her bedchamber, she lost her temper completely and slapped the boy repeatedly across the face, with such force that for days afterward he bore the marks of her outburst on his cheek.

By the middle of the second week, her nerves were so frayed that those in her service dreaded to be summoned to her presence. She had been driven to seek a sleeping potion from Dominic de Serego, one of the court physicians, and each night swallowed a vile-tasting mixture of opium, henbane and wine, but she found little relief in sleep so heavy and thick that she felt drugged for hours after awaking. Her appetite was failing her; nothing tasted as it should and, after every meal, her food seemed to lie in her stomach like lead. She forced herself to eat, however, just as she forced herself to attend each and every entertainment of this, their Christmas court.

Elizabeth had always loved to dance, had always delighted in the music of minstrels, in the antics of jugglers and their trained bears and monkeys, in the morality plays given by the guilds and travelling troupes of actors. Now she hated it all, knowing that all eyes were upon her, speculative, prying, unfriendly. For there were few secrets at court. Her husband treated her with irreproachable courtesy when they met in public, but few activities of the King escaped the scrutiny of ever present eyes and all knew by now that he no longer came to Elizabeth's bed.

Elizabeth had long known she was hated but that awareness had only made her all the more imperious, all the more set upon having her own way, Now, however, she found herself watched with an intensity that was somehow different, that was . . . expectant, she decided. It put her in mind of the way a wolf pack would trail a deer for days, waiting for the signs of exhaustion that would bring them in for the kill.

Such a thought was so foreign to Elizabeth that she made a sound of dismay. In a voice suddenly unsteady, she ordered her attendants from her bed chamber and then walked across the room to stare at the woman reflected in her pier glass. And for once she did not see the beauty that even her most virulent enemies never denied. She saw only the haunted, fearful eyes.

After a time, she moved to the bed and lay down upon it, fully clothed. For a fortnight now, she'd been refusing to face it, to face the fact that she was frightened by this estrangement that was deepening daily between her and Ned. First it was her anger and then her pride that kept her from seeing the truth, from admitting which of them had the most to lose.

She was an unloved queen who had failed to give her husband a son and heir. Three daughters she'd given him and it was nigh on nine months since the birth of the last babe. And she had enemies, sweet Jesú, enemies enough for a lifetime with some to spare. Enemies but no friends, none she could trust. Only her family who would fall if she did. What would happen to her if Ned should stop wanting her, stop loving her?

After a while, she rose and returned to the mirror. A powdery perfume lay open before her; she reached for it and began to rub the fragrance into her throat and the hollow between her breasts. And then she began to undress, not bothering to summon her ladies, letting the items of clothing drop to the floor at her feet, until she stood in a circle of discarded silk and satin.

'You need not announce me,' she said to the men posted at the door of her husband's bedchamber, said with all the hauteur she could command, and they made haste to give her entry. She

225

breathed a swift silent prayer that he'd be alone and moved into the chamber.

He wasn't alone, but there was no woman with him tonight and she thanked God for that. The grooms of the chamber were engaged in the elaborate ritual of making the royal bed, were concluding by sprinking holy water upon the turned-back coverlets. Two others were stoking the hearth for the night. Wine and bread had already been set out on the bedside table and, nearby, a chair had been positioned within sight of the bed where, upon a red velvet cushion, the crown of England glittered in the firelight. In the midst of all this activity, her husband was reclining in the window seat, playing at Tables with his brother.

Elizabeth's entrance stopped all conversation. She crossed the chamber, waited as Richard scrambled hastily to his feet. He bent over the hand she extended, dropped to one knee until she nodded, freeing him to rise.

She had no liking for this dark quiet boy so little like Ned or that wretch, Clarence. Her dislike was not personal; she did not know him well enough for that. But she disliked on instinct anyone who laid claim to her husband's affections and she thought Ned to be overly fond of his youngest brother.

The boy had only that morning returned to court; he'd been off in Wales for the past month, doing something or other for Ned. She was not sure what, vaguely recalled fragments of conversation she'd heard that afternoon, that he'd captured a castle or some such act. But she felt a sudden surge of friendliness toward him, for had he not been here now with Ned, she might have found Ned in bed with one of his trollops. With that thought in mind, she gave Richard a dazzling smile, offered her congratulations upon his success.

For an unguarded moment, he looked startled by her unexpected cordiality; she generally accorded him no more than perfunctory courtesy. He did have tact, though; she'd grant him that, for he'd not lingered, swiftly making a discreet departure.

The grooms were quick to follow, so that within moments she was alone with her husband.

'You wished to speak with me, Lisbet?'

Edward was regarding her with a polite disinterest that set her teeth on edge. Swallowing her resentment, she nodded.

'I came to tell you that you've won, Ned. I accept your terms.'

If only she could read him as easily as she knew he read her. His expression told her nothing of his thoughts and, when he spoke, his voice was no more revealing than his face.

'Should you not first be sure you know what my terms are?'

'I know exactly what they are,' she said flatly. 'Unconditional surrender.'

She thought she saw amusement flicker in his eyes and, before he could speak, she stepped forward, moved toward him. She did not want to talk, did not trust herself, knew how little it would take to kindle their quarrel all over again.

She stopped before him and, leaning over, kissed him on the mouth. He didn't rebuff her but he didn't respond either and, as she straightened up, it was with the sudden fear that he might mean to pay her back in her own coin. If he did, she knew she'd never be able to forget the humiliation, nor ever be able to forgive him for that humiliation.

Not daring to wait, she began to fumble with the ivory combs binding up her hair. It fell about her in a swirl of silvery brightness. 'Spun moonlight,' he'd often called it, liked to bury his face in it, feel it against his chest, a silken barrier between them in bed.

These memories of his past passion were strong enough and vivid enough to dispel her present doubts and she unfastened the sash of her dressing robe, let it fall open and then caught it loosely at the waist, so that she stood revealed from ankle to midthigh and from swelling breasts to throat.

He was no longer smiling. The atmosphere between them had changed, was charged with sudden sexual tension.

'Jesú, but you're beautiful,' he said at last, said softly, almost wonderingly.

Elizabeth had no trouble reading him now. Her mouth was suddenly dry and it was not nerves now that quickened her breathing. She knew he'd find no fault with her responsiveness this night. She felt giddy, lightheaded with excitement, with triumph, and, above all, with relief, and she laughed, let go of the robe.

He reached out, drew her down onto his lap. His mouth was hot; she gave herself up gladly to its heat, let him burn kisses along the curving line of her throat into the softness of her shoulder. She'd begun to unfasten his doublet, tugged at the shirt underneath until she was able to slip her hands inside, against his skin. He'd lowered his mouth to her breast, was sending jolts of feeling searing up her nerve ends, stirring sensations almost unbearable in their intensity.

The leather points binding his doublet to hose now came loose in her hand. He gasped as she found his groin, found swelling proof of the urgency of his need for her. She twisted around in his arms so that their mouths met, entangling them both in a cloud of lustrous blonde hair, until the erotic intimacy of his caresses caused her to arch against him, with an indrawn breath that slurred his name beyond recognition. By the time he lifted her in his arms to take her to the waiting bed, she would have found it impossible to say which one was the seducer and which the seduced.

Elizabeth was peeling an orange, her favourite fruit. She never tired of them for she'd never tasted one until she found herself wed to England's King; they had to be shipped from Italy, were outrageously expensive, and she valued them as much for that as for the sweet tangy taste. She leaned over, trailing her hair against Edward's chest, and fed him one of the orange sections, then leaned over still further to lick the juice from his mouth with the tip of her tongue. He opened his eyes, smiled at her.

'Shall I remove all this?' she murmured, gesturing toward the platter beside them in the bed. It was piled with food, cheese and bread and fruit; having satisfied their hunger for each other, they'd both been seized by hunger of another sort and stirred up a commotion in the kitchens with their unexpected demand for a midnight meal.

He nodded and she placed the platter upon the floor; lay back in his arms. From the bed, she could see the glimmer of his crown. She liked the tradition of placing it by his bedside, liked to be able to see the tangible proof of his kingship.

She no longer regretted yielding to him in their war of wills, was irked with herself for not doing so sooner, for not sparing herself so many uneasy days and endless nights. It was true, she mused, that she'd never have been willing to humble her pride for her first husband. But Ned was unlike John in every respect, unlike any man she'd ever met. Her eyes again sought, lingered upon, the muted brilliance of the crown; even in firelight, it still shone with a reassuring radiance.

She was aware of an increasing languor, a delightful free-floating sensation, as if her bones had turned to liquid. She fought the feeling, though; she was not yet ready to sleep. Beside her, Edward stretched, drew her still closer to him. He was holding her within the circle of his left arm; it rested on her, just under her breasts. She could see faint red marks on his skin where her nails had scraped and she reached out, traced their path with her finger.

She was well aware that those who hated her called her harlot and slut, hinted that she'd somehow cast a satanic sexual spell upon Edward to bewitch him into marriage. She was sometimes indifferent to and, at other times, resentful of, such accusations but, had her nature been other than it was, she might have found a certain grim amusement in them, for the truth was that she'd laid with but two men in her life and married them both.

She'd been fifteen when she wed John Grey and was not at all reluctant to learn what he had to teach her in their marriage bed.

She'd been an apt pupil, would have been quite willing to experiment further had he been so inclined. But she soon found that he was disconcerted if she made the first overtures, that he would rather she played a passive role in their lovemaking.

Elizabeth was a poor judge of people, for she was not curious enough to speculate upon the needs and wants that motivated others. But, even to her, it was clear that her husband felt somehow threatened by the realization that her sexual needs existed independently of his own desires. Because she had no basis of comparison, Elizabeth assumed that all men were so and resigned herself to a sexual relationship that was moderately pleasing to her but was, as well, unimaginative and thoroughly predictable.

Her second marriage was unlike her first in all respects; above all, in bed. Edward encouraged her to initiate lovemaking, was delighted when she showed that she wanted him and the more uninhibited she was, the better he liked it. From him, she'd learned undreamed-of ways to give physical pleasure and she came in time to understand that the secret of his ardent passion for her lay not so much in her beauty as in her own eagerness for their couplings. She wanted him as much as he wanted her and it was the intensity of this shared need that had drawn them together from their first meeting, had linked their lives in a marriage that, by every standard of their time, should never have been, and yet endured in the face of universal outrage, his flagrant infidelities and her failure to give him a son.

Elizabeth continued to run her fingers lightly up and down his forearm and then shifted slightly so that his arm was pressing pleasantly against her breasts. She was satisfied but not sated and the sexual comparisons she'd been making between the two men had turned her thoughts in that direction again. She began to play with the bright soft hairs upon his chest, tugging gently; she knew his body as if it were her own, knew how to pleasure and how to tease and how to bring him to sudden arousal.

'Ned?'

He made a wordless reply, a sound of sleepy content, and she slid her hand lower, down his hip and onto his thigh. She confined her caresses there for a time and then moved up, between his legs.

He was not long in shrugging off sleepiness, was quite willing to give himself over to the soft skilled hands that soon had him sighing with pleasure.

Elizabeth leaned over him again, for a lingering kiss.

'Ned?' She was breathing against his ear, waited till he opened an inquiring eye.

'Ned . . . what happens now that Warwick has his pardon?'

'I wait,' he said laconically

'Wait for what?' she whispered.

She was so close that their mouths were but her whisper apart. He saw that she was watching him intently, not breathing, as if the fate of the world hung upon his answer.

'For him to overreach himself, my love,' he said softly and seriously.

'Will he? Are you sure, Ned?'

'I'd wager my life on it,' he said and saw her smile.

'I would rather you wagered his,' she said. Her mouth was on his. Her perfume was elusive, a beguiling sensual fragrance that beckoned him to seek its source, and where her body touched him, she was warm, skin like silk drawn taut, smooth yet firm.

'For me?' she murmured. 'Would you not claim his life for me, Ned?' And she sought his mouth again, only to stop abruptly, for he'd begun to laugh.

'And when Salome danced for King Herod, he promised to give her whatsoever she asked and she did ask for the head of John the Baptist to be brought before her upon a silver platter,' he quoted with a grin, as Elizabeth stared at him, saying nothing.

With an effort, she bit back a sharp retort. He was, at one and the same time, the most exciting man she'd ever known and the most exasperating, too, and nothing exasperated her so much as the sense of humour she found to be perverse, unpredictable and, more often than not, incomprehensible. There was much she did not understand about him, but above all else, she did not understand how he could take so little in life seriously, for there was little that she did not.

'I find it difficult to laugh, Ned, where Warwick is concerned,' she said evenly. 'Can you blame me for that?'

'Of course not, sweetheart.'

He sounded contrite but Elizabeth knew him too well to be disarmed.

'When Warwick does overreach himself, when he falls . . . what then, Ned?' she persisted. 'You told me he did owe you a debt. How do you mean to collect it?'

'Why not come here, Salome, and we'll discuss it?'

He was laughing again and, before she could object, rolled over on top of her. Elizabeth was not deceived, knew that he meant to distract her attention from a question he did not want to answer. She would have persevered, have coaxed or coerced a reply, but his kisses were claiming her breath and his body was hard upon hers, and she found herself tightening her arms around his neck, moving to meet his desire. She did not forget her question, though; nor that he'd not been willing to answer it.

Elizabeth had taken what consolation she could from Edward's assurance that Warwick would soon entangle himself in a web of his own making and she was to discover before the new year was three months old that her husband had a gift for political prophecy.

Tensions flared anew that spring of 1470. A revolt had broken out in Lincolnshire, sparked by the assault of the Lancastrian Lord Welles and his son upon the manor house of a man who was not only a steadfast Yorkist but an officer of Edward's own household. But as was the case with Robin of Redesdale, the Welles rebellion soon showed Neville colours.

Lord Welles was a second cousin of Warwick and, on March

4th, Sir Robert Welles published in all churches of Lincolnshire a summons to arms on behalf of the Earl of Warwick and the man who, it was now claimed, held rightful title to the crown of England, George, Duke of Clarence.

Edward moved into Lincolnshire in early March. Warwick and George were then at Leicester. They strenuously denied any involvement in the Welles rebellion but refused Edward's demand that they appear before him. They did not linger at Leicester, headed north, but at Chesterfield word reached them that an army led by Sir Robert Welles had confronted the forces of the King at the village of Empingham. Whenever Edward commanded his army in person, he did not lose. The battle of Empingham was so overwhelming a Yorkist victory that it became known as Lose-Cote Field for the piles of discarded armour that littered the field in the wake of the fleeing rebels.

Warwick and George had no choice but to take flight. They raced for the South through villages and towns that greeted their call to arms with indifference. The lords who had allied themselves to Warwick scrambled to cover their tracks or hastily submitted to Edward.

It came as no surprise, therefore, when on March 24th, Edward formally proclaimed his cousin of Warwick and his brother of Clarence as traitors and offered one thousand pounds for their capture.

14

Coventry

April 1470

'Johnny!'

Guiding his mount through the gatehouse of St Mary's Priory Richard reined in abruptly at sight of his cousin. He called again and this time caught John's attention.

'It looks as though three months in Wales did agree with you, Dickon.'

Richard laughed, knowing he'd never looked worse than he did at that moment: his boots caked with mud, his cloak stretched with trail dust, his hair windblown and his face windburnt. He'd just put in three weeks of hard riding and it showed, every mile of it. But, for the moment, the familiar bone-weariness had eased; he was too glad to be at Coventry to register fatigue, not yet.

'I'd be hard put to say which is worse, Johnny . . . my appearance or your bad manners in commenting upon it.' He grinned and John laughed but made no comment. Richard swung from the saddle and, giving his stallion over into trustworthy hands, waved his men on toward the stables.

He'd not seen John since early January when Edward had sent him back into Wales, this time to head a commission of oyer and terminer. During these past months, as he explored a terrain far more intimidating than the rugged hill-country of Wales, the unfamiliar reaches of leadership, there'd been many times when he'd yearned for his cousin's counsel. And yet now he found himself fumbling for a topic of conversation . . . with Johnny, of all men.

234

John seemed to be afflicted by the same malady. They walked in silence for some moments. A large shaggy mongrel had begun to trail them, hopeful for a handout, and, glancing at it, John said, 'How's that big wolfhound of yours? You do still have him?'

'Gareth?' Richard nodded. 'When Ned sent me back into Wales, I left him with my sister Eliza for safekeeping.' He smiled slightly. 'I hope I do not regret it. . . . Or rather, that Gareth does not. My nephew Jack is just seven but he's already a hellion.'

How in God's name had he and Johnny been reduced to this? After three months, nothing to talk about but a damned dog! No, not nothing. Too much. For Jesú, there was so much that could not be said between them now. And when Warwick and George were taken what then?

'Lord Constable. Chief Justice of North Wales. And now Chief Justice and Chamberlain of South Wales, too. That's quite an array of titles, Dickon.'

Richard shrugged. Neither chose to mention that the last-named post was the one Edward had been compelled to yield to Warwick under duress eight months ago.

'Ned's asking a lot of you. More, I think, than is fair for your age. Do the burdens never weigh down upon you, Dickon?'

Richard would have accepted that from no one else. But John had earned the right to criticize Edward if any man had. Besides, it was a rare relief to be able to confide, as he did now, 'Well, there are times . . . mostly at night . . . when you've the say over men's lives come morning, and if you do choose wrong . . .' This was more than he'd meant to admit, however, and he caught himself abruptly, gave John a brief smile.

'You're too able a listener for my own good, Johnny. You'll have me confessing to sins I have not even commited if I do not watch myself!'

They'd reached the entrance of the prior's lodging when Thomas Parr, Richard's squire, caught up with them.

'My lord? What of our men?'

Richard was embarrassed. That was something he should've seen to at once but his pleasure at seeing John had put his men momentarily from his mind. He glanced sideways at John, but his cousin was more merciful than Edward would have been, forbore to tease; instead, he suggested casually, 'I doubt there's room enough in the priory, Dickon, and I'd wager, as well, that most of the inns close by are full. You might try the White Rose in Little Parke Street, though.'

Richard nodded gratefully, turned back to Thomas. 'We'll have to billet them wherever we can find rooms, Tom. Try the White Rose and the Angel. Let me know straightaway if problems arise in getting them settled.'

He jerked his head then toward the prior's lodging, said, 'What with the King's Grace lodged here in Prior Deram's chambers, I doubt there's even a pallet to spare, so we'd best plan to quarter in the guest house. Take care of that for me, too, Tom, if you will. And my lord of Northumberland will be supping with me tonight, so see to that, too. . . .' Richard glanced back at John. 'That is acceptable, Johnny?'

'I would suggest you do ask the Earl of Northumberland,' John said evenly, and Richard turned to stare at him.

'I thought I just did,' he said after a moment, with the quizzical uncertain smile of one who misses the humour of a joke but wishes to be polite, nonetheless.

'You truly do not know? No, I see you do not. As it happens, Dickon, that title no longer is mine. Nine days ago Ned restored the earldom of Northumberland to Henry Percy.'

Richard caught his breath. He could think of nothing to say, nothing at all.

Richard originally meant to send word to his brother that he had arrived and then bathe and change his clothes before joining Edward in the prior's lodging. That plan had been formulated, however, before he was told that the Lancastrian Henry Percy was now Earl of Northumberland and his cousin newly named as Marquess of Montagu. Now his need to see Edward was such that he wasted no time in seeking his brother out.

The prior's great hall was illuminated by two oriel windows and several smaller ones, but the light was considerably less than in the sunlit outer garth and Richard paused a moment to adjust his eyesight accordingly. Will Hastings was there, smiled at the sight of him. So did John Howard.

His brother-in-law, the Duke of Suffolk, nodded from across the hall, with no noticeable enthusiasm. Richard was not well acquainted with Suffolk, a Lancastrian who'd been wed to Richard's sister Eliza years ago in hopes of winning him over to York. Suffolk had proven to be more tractable than Richard's other brother-in-law, the exiled Duke of Exeter, but Richard doubted that Suffolk had any genuine affection for the House of York.

A slender youth with lanky fair hair and secretive pale eyes was standing by the nearest window. Richard recognized him as Henry Percy, the twenty-three-year-old Lancastrian lord who had so suddenly been elevated to his family's former earldom. Richard exchanged polite greetings with Percy and started across the hall toward his brother, only to stop abruptly after taking several strides, staring at the man who stood by Edward's chair.

He was of medium height, of stocky build, in his midthirties. The wide-shouldered velvet doublet, silken hose, gem-encrusted rings all vied to proclaim the wearer a man of wealth. But the gaudiness of his dress was eclipsed by the neatly trimmed moustache and pointed brown beard, a carefully groomed and cultivated defiance of current fashion that Richard saw as an affectation. But then, Richard had no charitable thoughts to spare for Thomas, Lord Stanley. None at all.

In the past six months, as Edward began to give Richard ever-increasing responsibilities, Richard had endured more than his share of unpleasant moments, moments of private doubt and inner uncertainties. It could be as sobering as it was exhilarating to have other men looking to him for leadership; he was all too conscious, for his own comfort, of his age and inexperience. But no moment had been as bad as the tense encounter he'd had with Stanley a fortnight ago on the Hereford–Shrewsbury road.

Both forces had been taken by surprise and Richard had suddenly been confronted with the need to make an instantaneous decision, one which might have immediate military consequences for him and long-term political ones for his brother. He knew Stanley, thought him to be as untrustworthy a man as any in England. He wasn't sure why Stanley should be riding toward Manchester with a well-armed force but he didn't like it; he didn't like it at all. Instinct and suspicion and Stanley's kinship to Warwick all merged in his mind and, with an icy assurance that sounded surprisingly convincing, even to himself, he demanded that Stanley clear the road. He'd convinced Stanley, at any rate. The latter had yielded, grudgingly and under protest, but yielded, nonetheless.

Now the sight of Stanley brought it all back to Richard in a rush and, even as he moved to kneel before his brother, he kept his eyes upon Stanley. At the same time, he found himself wishing he'd taken the time for that bath and change of clothes. He felt uncomfortably scruffy, defensive, apprehensive, and defiant, all at once.

'My lord of Gloucester,' his brother was saying, and smiled at him as he touched his lips to the splendour of Edward's coronation ring.

'I need not tell you how pleased I am to have you safely back from Wales. However, my lord Stanley has a grievance to voice against you. He has made the claim that you acted in a lawless and unjustified manner on the Hereford–Shrewsbury road a fortnight ago. He contends'—and here Edward glanced toward Stanley for confirmation—'that you did interfere with his peaceful use of the King's road and insulted him in the bargain. Is that a fair summing up, my lord Stanley?'

Stanley was staring balefully at Richard. 'Quite fair, Your Grace.'

Richard opened his mouth and then shut it stubbornly. He was aware of a hollow sensation in his stomach, an uneasy swelling suspicion that he'd entangled Ned in a sticky political situation, all because he'd been too impulsive, too quick to act. But no . . . no, he had not! He'd been right to suspect Stanley, he knew he had, and he'd be damned if he'd say different, even for Ned. But there was something off-key in Ned's voice, the slightest suggestion of . . . anger? Disappointment? Richard was not sure; the emotion was undefinable but unmistakably there.

Edward was looking expectantly at him, awaiting his response. They all were, Richard saw. Saw, too, with a small shock, that in only one face, that of John Howard, was there any sympathy for his plight. Hastings was amused, Suffolk mildly interested, Percy cautiously neutral. Yet Richard knew not one of them liked Stanley in the least. Strange, but he'd never before realized that he, too, might be a target for jealousy, that there were those who resented him because he was Ned's brother and for no other reason. That would bear thinking about, but now he pulled himself together, said tautly,

'My liege?'

'Do you not want to respond to Lord Stanley's accusations?'

Richard glanced again at Stanley, found anger to be a useful crutch for his faltering assurance, and said, quite steadily, 'Lord Stanley did neglect to make the one charge that must have discomfited him the most. Had it not been for our encounter on the Hereford–Shrewsbury road, he could then have proceeded at his ease to meet with the Earl of Warwick at Manchester.'

'You've no proof of that, my lord of Gloucester. I do deny it most emphatically and you've no evidence to support such an accusation. You know you do not.' Swinging back toward Edward, Stanley said sharply, 'Your Grace, I deeply resent such a slur being cast upon my loyalty.'

'I would expect as much, my lord.' But still there was that

elusive intonation in Edward's voice, one that Richard could not quite identify.

'Have you any such proof, my lord of Gloucester?'

'No, Your Grace,' Richard said unwillingly, and resolutely refused to elaborate upon or explain away that terse admission. But he could not keep from casting at his brother a swift searching glance that had in it a small measure of appeal.

'Well, my lords . . . As I do see it, it sounds rather like an unfortunate misunderstanding. Your avowals of allegiance are, of course, most welcome, Lord Stanley. I am not inclined to question your good faith, yet I do trust my brother of Gloucester's judgment. Under the circumstances, I think the incident should best be forgotten. I daresay you both do agree with me?'

Edward leaned back in his chair, regarding them both over the rim of his wine cup. Richard nodded, almost imperceptibly. Stanley, however, said loudly and with some heat, 'No, Your Grace, I do not. Why should I be held to account for a boy's suspicions? I do not think you do fully comprehend, Your Grace, just how insulting he was. He dared to say . . .'

Edward glanced at Richard, cutting through Stanley's harangue to inquire curiously, 'What exactly did you say, Dickon?'

Richard was more angry now than uncertain and Edward's inadvertent use of 'Dickon' dispelled the last of his doubts. He knew that his brother was going to back him up, at least in public. He still wasn't sure what to expect once they were alone.

'I told him to clear the road. When he refused, I said we could go through his men or over them, that the choice was his,' he said, taking care to enunciate each word quite clearly, and Edward choked on his drink.

He gasped, sputtered and began to cough, and both Richard and Will Hastings started forward before realizing that he was struggling not for breath but to suppress laughter. But it had been too long pent up and he could do nothing but yield to it, laughing until he was blinking back tears of mirth, too convulsed for speech.

Stanley stood very still, staring down at Edward. His face was on fire, had gone a shade of red never meant by nature. He, too, had tears in his eyes, tears of rage; they burned like cinders, blurring his glimpse of the other men. They were all grinning now, he saw: Hastings and Howard and Suffolk, even Percy. And Gloucester – Gloucester was watching him in poorly concealed triumph.

'By Your Grace's leave,' he managed to say, jerking the words through rigidly clenched teeth.

Edward's amusement had subsided somewhat and he started to rise, saying with a grin, 'You're too thin-skinned, Tom. We know each other well enough to overlook an occasional lapse of manners, surely?'

Stanley stared at him. Surprised by the surge of dislike that beat back his anger, cold and measuring and contemptuous. He'd never liked Edward of York but he'd never seen the younger man as clearly and critically as he did at this moment. How very like York this was, he thought bitterly. So cocksure none could resist his charm, that he had only to smile and make a jest. So bloody sure of himself, sure there was no sin he could not be forgiven.

He didn't realize how clearly his thoughts showed in his face until he saw Edward's smile change, chill considerably.

'Once you do think on it, Lord Stanley, I do not doubt you'll agree with me, that this entire incident is best forgotten.' Edward held his hand out for Stanley's submission, saying in a cool ironic voice, 'I would suggest, as well, that you bear in mind that I am well aware of your worth, my lord. I do, you see, know precisely what value to place upon your loyalty.'

Richard's good intentions abruptly went the way of most such resolves. He'd been trying very hard to be a gracious winner, not to gloat openly. But at that he couldn't help himself and laughed aloud. Edward glanced toward him; as their eyes met, he laughed, too. Their laughter followed Stanley from the chamber. He seemed to hear it even after he'd emerged into the warmth of the sunsplashed priory garth.

Thomas Parr was both industrious and efficient; by the time Richard entered his bedchamber, water was already being heated for his bath. Thomas had also sent to the buttery for wine and was glad he'd thought of it when he saw that his young lord was not alone, accompanied by Lord Hastings and His Grace, the King.

'Ned, I know I was right about Stanley. I'll never believe otherwise.'

Richard's voice was muffled, coming as it did from within the folds of his doublet. He hadn't bothered to unfasten all the buttons, impatiently pulled it over his head with some assistance from Thomas. Free again, he resumed.

'He meant to join with Warwick and George at Manchester. I know he did.'

'I do not doubt it, Dickon,' Edward agreed complacently. He'd sprawled out on the bed, was reaching up for the wine cup Thomas held out to him.

'There's little in life that's constant, little brother, but this you can take as true, that you can never go wrong suspecting a Stanley.'

Richard joined in his laughter; so did Will. After a moment, Edward sobered somewhat, said with a grin, 'You did me a service I'll not soon forget, Dickon. But I must tell you, lad, that you're woefully lacking in tact.'

Will gave a hoot of disbelief. 'Tact? Holy Mother Mary!'

He stood gazing down at Edward, with the freedom of long familiarity, now said, 'That's a rare jest, Ned, coming from you. I rather doubt Stanley expected you to take his complaint seriously; as hard as it might be to believe sometimes, he's not an utter fool. But I very much doubt that when he came to you to save face, he did expect you to damned near rupture yourself laughing at him.'

'It was not one of my more diplomatic moments, was it?' Edward conceded, sounding thoroughly unrepentant. 'But Jesus, Will, the man's such an ass!'

'You need not tell me!' Will made a face. 'We are kin of sorts, after all, the both of us having Neville wives.'

'I wish to God Warwick would run out of sisters! He has far too many brothers-in-law for my taste. He's drawn the Earl of Oxford into his net now, too.'

Richard tossed his shirt to Thomas, glancing over at Edward in surprise. 'Oxford? He's Lancastrian, is he not?'

'More or less. But last year he wed Warwick's sister Madge and it seems he's been paying Warwick too much attention ever since. He's somewhat lacking in nerve, though. He bolted as soon as he got word that I'd won Lose-Cote Field, fled to the coast and took ship for France.'

Edward drained his cup, set it down on the floor.

'I wonder if the Most Christian King of France will be quite so enthusiastic about his Neville allies once they start turning up with prices on their heads and no money in their purses,' he said acidly and signalled to Thomas for a refill.

Richard was pleased to see the French King discomfited, to see French foreign policy in such chaos, but Jesus God, at what a price! He could not envision Warwick and George as impoverished exiles at the French court. But if they did not escape, if they fell into Ned's hands . . . what then? He preferred not to thing about that.

The bath was scented with bay leaves and marjoram, was fragrant with mint and delightfully hot. This was a luxury that had been much missed by Richard and he sank down contentedly in the wooden tub, resting his head against the folded towel that had been placed behind his neck. The room was quiet for the moment. Will Hastings had departed and the servants pouring water under Thomas's supervision were too awed by the presence of the King to do more than whisper among themselves.

'Ned, I saw Johnny when I first rode into the priory. He told me you'd restored Northumberland to Percy.'

Richard wasn't accustomed to questioning his brother's judgment; in fact, had never done so before. He hesitated and then said, simply, 'Why, Ned?'

'There's no mystery in it, Dickon. You know the trouble I've been having in the North. The Percy family has long been a power there. It's a popular move, will do much to ease local grievances. It does not hurt, little brother, to show the people you can be responsive to their complaints . . . provided that you do not make a habit of it.'

'I know there's much support for Percy in Yorkshire,' Richard admitted. 'But . . .' He wasn't sure what he wanted to say, though, found himself hesitating again.

'Do you realize, Dickon, that it was nine years ago this Thursday last since I did win Towton? Nine years and still I'm forced to waste my energies in putting down Lancastrian rebellions. I can think of better ways to spend the next nine years, little brother, I do assure you. No, if a restored title can placate the Percy family, that's a cheap price to pay. I need the Percys to keep the North quiet for me . . . and that, Dickon, is the answer to your question.'

'But . . . but is Johnny not the one to pay the price?'

'Did he say that?' Edward was sitting upright now, sounded surprised. It occurred to Richard for the first time that loyalty to Johnny and loyalty to Ned might not be one and the same.

'No, of course not,' he said quickly. 'That was my thought, not his.'

'I hardly think Johnny ill used, Dickon,' Edward said slowly. 'Not only did I name him as Marquess of Montagu but I gave him, as well, the bulk of the estates once held by the Earl of Devon. Moreover, as you do know, I created his son Duke of Bedford and agreed to betroth the boy to my Bess. That could make his son King of England one day. Is the earldom of

Northumberland too high a price to pay for that? I think not, Dickon.'

Richard was inclined to agree. The betrothal of his little niece and John's boy, which had taken place just before he'd left London for Wales, was impressive proof, indeed, of royal favour. Edward had three daughters and, if he died without a son, the crown would now pass to his Bess and John's son, rather than to George.

'As you explain it, Ned, it makes much sense,' Richard conceded. But as he stared down at the wavering bath water, it was not his own reflection that stared back at him; it was the face of his cousin, as he'd last seen him in the courtyard of the priory, tense and drawn and unhappy.

'Johnny said nothing to me about this, Ned,' he said, choosing his words with uncharacteristic care. 'I've been speaking for myself, not for him. It was only . . . only that he did seem so careworn this afternoon, like a man with one wound too many.'

'I do not wonder at that, Dickon,' Edward said, and his voice was suddenly flat. 'You see, I ordered the arrest of the Archbishop of York this morning.'

Richard nodded. 'Poor Johnny,' he said softly. He had only to think of George to understand all too well how Johnny must be feeling. He was suddenly cold, hadn't realized the bath water had been cooling. He didn't bother to call for more hot water; somehow, it didn't seem to be worth the effort. He signalled, instead, for a towel.

'Ned, have you any word on the whereabouts of Warwick's wife, his girls? Are they still at Warwick Castle?'

'I do not know. There were rumours that Isabel has been in Exeter for the past fortnight but whether that is true or not . . .' Edward shrugged.

For the first time, Richard realized that if Warwick and George fled England, they might mean to take their wives with them. And Anne. This was so disquieting a thought that he found reasons to reject it almost at once and shook his head incredulously.

245

'Surely they do not mean to take the women? My God, Ned, Bella's babe is due this month!'

Edward didn't answer. Richard wasn't surprised. What, after all, was there to say?

Word was slow to trickle north and it was on an evening in late May some weeks later that Francis reached for a quill pen and, with deliberation, made the following entry in his journal:

> Done at Middleham on this the day before Ascension, in the year of Our Lord 1470, tenth year of the reign of King Edward.
>
> The Earl of Warwick reached Exeter on the Devonshire coast on April 10th and took ship that same day for France. After a perilous Channel crossing, he was turned away from Calais by his erstwhile ally, Lord Wenlock. He then sought sanctuary at Honfleur in Normandy and was warmly welcomed by the French King. No more is known at present, either as to his whereabouts or his plans. But this I do know, that my lord of Warwick is not a man to tamely accept an exile's lot.

15

York

August 1470

During the last week of July, Edward had word of an uprising in Yorkshire instigated by Lord Fitz-Hugh, ally and brother-in-law of the exiled Earl of Warwick. Edward wasted little time in gathering a force and, with Will Hastings, rode north to rendezvous at York with Richard who had spent the summer recruiting soldiers in the western midlands.

But, by the time Edward reached the ancient market town of Ripon, the rebellion was over. Fitz-Hugh fled across the border into Scotland; his accomplices hastily offered submission to the Yorkist King. Edward returned triumphant to York and there set about restoring order in this, the most troubled and troublesome region of his realm.

The news of Lord Fitz-Hugh's abortive rebellion brought dismay to the beautiful Valley of Windrush, some 185 miles to the south, scenic setting for Minster Lovell Hall. Francis was appalled; Lord Fitz-Hugh was his father-in-law. He was not long in receiving a hysterical letter from Anna, imploring him to intervene with the King on her father's behalf.

Francis needed no such urgings. He did not want Anna to suffer for her father's folly. Still less did he want Fitz-Hugh's treachery to cast a shadow upon the Lovells. For treason he knew to be the most contagious of afflictions and innocence no guarantee of immunity.

Francis mulled over Anna's letter, and dawn the next day found him on the Ermine Way that led north, toward York. Though not yet seventeen, he was acutely aware of his family obligations. His mother had been dead for four years now, after a brief and ill-considered second marriage to Sir William Stanley, younger brother of Thomas, Lord Stanley. His sisters had only what protection he could provide and he was determined that they'd not be tainted in any way by their unwilling association with Anna's foolhardy family.

He was spurred on by apprehension and, by Monday, August 27th, he was in sight of the white limestone city walls of York. There he was welcomed with enthusiasm by Richard and with flattering friendliness by the King. Almost at once, he blurted out the reason for his mission and Richard listened in astonishment and Edward in amusement, as he solemnly assured them that Lovell loyalty was pledged unwaveringly to York, for now and for all time to come.

At that, Edward laughed and said he demanded no avowal of loyalty that extended beyond the length of a man's lifetime and Richard interrupted to ask how Francis could ever imagine his loyalty might be doubted. Francis, happily submitting to the banter of the one and the reproaches of the other, knew that he would never have such fears for his family again. His future was inextricably entwined with that of the House of York and he was more than willing to have it so.

He saw disappointingly little of Richard in the days that followed, for his friend was heading a commission of oyer and terminer in York and his hours, from dawn till well past dusk, were taken up with the duties of this latest responsibility. On the third night following his arrival, Richard at last managed to make time for pleasure and the two boys ventured forth to sample the more disreputable delights York had to offer.

Francis wanted to sup in one of the inns on Conyng Street but Richard was seeking an escape into anonymity, and he prevailed. They purchased baked lamprey pies at a cookshop close by the Augustine friary where Richard was lodged, gagged at the sour-tasting wine they bought to wash down the fish and wandered into first one and then another of the shabby alehouses that stood on the riverside, only to encounter recognition for Richard in even the seediest such tavern.

Much to Francis's amusement, the only ones who failed to recognize Richard that night were the watch, who promptly halted them for hostile questioning, it being an hour when all decent men were settled by their own hearths. But before they could respond to their interrogators, a third man was hurrying toward them, shoving his irked colleagues aside for a whispered conference in which Francis clearly caught one word, repeated and then echoed with growing dismay, the name Gloucester, and suddenly they were free to continue on their way, with apologies profusely scattered about the street in their path.

At that, Richard conceded defeat and, less than half an hour after St Michael's rang curfew, they turned down Conyng Street and back toward the friary that stretched from Ald-Conyng Street to the river. Their progress was slow, for York had no ordinance requiring street lighting as did London and the only light came from a silvered crescent moon and the lamp that hung in the octagonal lantern tower of All Hallows' Church. But Francis suspected that Richard's leisurely pace was due to more than the dark, that his friend was reluctant to take up the adult respon-sibilities awaiting him upon his return to the friary.

As late as it was, there were people still waiting at the Prior's lodging, hoping for an audience, however brief, with Richard. Richard had been compelled to spare some minutes for Robert Anmas, a city sheriff who was bearing a message from Lord Mayor Holbeck, but the others, he said firmly, would have to return on the morrow.

Francis, hovering in the background, had soon grown bored and slipped away to await Richard in the chamber that had been set aside for his use while in York.

The room was orderly, austere even, bearing few traces of the personality of the current occupant. Francis had expected as much, knowing that Richard, of necessity, had long ago learned to travel light. A long trestle table was littered with books, papers, quill pens, a silver inkwell, candles and a large map of the Scots border region which was splattered with wax and covered with cryptic scrawls that meant nothing to Francis. A stack of papers was piled neatly in one corner, awaiting Richard's signature; others, already signed, were ready for dispatch. Francis glanced briefly at the slanting 'R. Gloucestre' on the top letter, noting with interest that it was addressed to John Neville, Marquess of Montagu.

Restlessly, he scanned the titles of the books strategically pos-itioned to anchor the map; *Treatise on War, a Book of Hours, The Art*

249

of Falconry. As he leaned over the table, he felt a sudden pressure against the back of his knee and he reached down to acknowledge the presence of an enormous black wolfhound. The big dog accepted his caress gravely, to Francis's amusement, much as one equal to another, and lay down at his feet as he sat on the bed.

A coffer-chest had been positioned, for convenience, by the bed, and served as a resting place for a large wax candle and a book bound in Moroccan leather. Curious, Francis picked it up. Glancing at the title, he was not surprised to see it was a historical treatise, Froissart's *Chronicles*, for Richard had a disciplined, practical turn of mind, but he was surprised to see it appeared to be well read. He wondered when Dickon ever found the time.

He began to flip idly through the pages, paused at the inscription on the frontispiece, and saw then that the book had been borrowed from John Neville. He was not surprised at this proof of intimacy, knew how deeply Richard cared for the Neville brother who'd stayed loyal to Edward. He found himself wondering when Dickon had seen Johnny last. He wondered, too, and with much pity, what it would be like to be awaiting an invasion of French troops, an army led by one's own brother. He closed the book, thinking he'd not have changed places with Johnny Neville for half the gold in Christendom. Or with Dickon, either. There were times when he almost forgot that Dickon, too, had a brother in French exile.

As he replaced the book on the coffer, a creased paper fell from the pages, fluttered to the floor at his feet. Retrieving it, he saw that it was a letter, unfinished and apparently forgotten, for it was dated, in Richard's own hand, more than a fortnight ago. Francis needed to look no further than the salutation, 'My sweet Kate,' to understand why Richard had chosen not to dictate this particular letter to his scribe.

Francis liked to think he was Richard's most intimate friend, yet he knew little or nothing of Richard's liaisons. Unlike Edward, who troubled not at all to conceal his numerous infidelities, denying neither his paramours nor the bastard-born issue of his philanderings, Richard was discreet in the extreme, displaying a reticence unexpected in a Plantagenet Prince.

Francis was aware there had been a prolonged involvement with a girl whose name he knew only as Kathryn, an attachment that had been formed shortly after Richard's sixteenth birthday and endured into the present. But he knew no more than that, and that only because she had borne Richard a child this past spring, a daughter he'd openly acknowledged, named Kathryn after her mysterious mother.

Francis had no doubts that she was the 'sweet Kate' of Richard's letter and he was sorely tempted to read further. He wavered but Richard's formidable wolfhound was regarding him trustingly and he reluctantly replaced the letter in the book, thus sparing himself considerable embarrassment, for Richard returned within moments of his triumph of conscience over curiosity.

Watching as his friend thumbed rapidly through the waiting correspondence, Francis thought: little wonder Dickon looks wary now even when he laughs. Lord High Constable of England, Chief Justice of North Wales, Chief Steward, Approver and Surveyor of all Wales, Chief Justice and Chamberlain of South Wales . . . and now the wardenship of the West Marches toward Scotland, too, and not one an empty title, but offices heavy with authority and obligations. I'd not want to answer for the lives of other men; not at seventeen, by God's Grace.

'This one letter cannot wait, Francis. I want it to be in the hands of my cousin, Johnny Neville, with no undue delay.'

While Richard gave instructions to his chosen courier, Francis played with the dog, waiting till they were alone to satisfy his curiosity about a matter he'd been puzzling over since first hearing that Edward was going north to quell Fitz-Hugh's rising.

'Dickon, why did His Grace the King feel the need to come himself into Yorkshire? Why was not the rebellion put down by the Earl of Northumberland?'

Richard shrugged. 'Northumberland sent word that the rebel forces far surpassed his own,' he said, in the neutral tones he used whenever he was making a conscious effort to be fair, to pass no judgments. But the fact that he felt the need to make such an effort was, in itself, a judgment of sorts, and Francis knew him well enough to comprehend that.

'It wasn't much of a rebellion as I see it,' he scoffed. 'They fled from the King's Grace like so many spooked horses! If Northumberland had only bestirred himself, he'd have seen what a puny threat was posed.'

'Northumberland tends to err on the side of caution, I think. He puts me in mind, Francis, of a treed cat that's unwilling to leave its perch till it is sure what lies below.' Richard shrugged again, said without conviction, 'But it's been less than a twelve-month since he was freed from the Tower. He may just need time. . . .'

He didn't bother completing the sentence; nor did Francis bother to prod him further. His real curiosity lay not with Northumberland but with the man who'd once held that title, and now he said pensively, 'What of Johnny Neville, Dickon? He, too, was in a position to move against Fitz-Hugh. Why did he not do so?'

Richard was silent for a time. 'I do not know,' he admitted at last. 'My brother appointed Johnny to a commission of oyer and terminer for Lincolnshire in July and I saw him briefly then whilst I was in Lincoln. He went north again after that and we've had no word from him since.'

Francis, who was quite fond of John Neville, now cautiously ventured to probe what he saw to be a sensitive subject.

'Dickon, how did he take it when the King gave the earldom of Northumberland back to Percy?'

Richard rose, moved to the table. With his back still to Francis, he said in a low voice, 'In restoring the earldom of North-umberland to Percy, my brother sought to placate the North. He's not forgotten the violence here in York last year. . . . What began as a protest against paying a tithe for St Léonard's Hospital ended with a mob stoning the city watch while shouting for Percy.

'If that could happen in York, Francis, where they like the Nevilles well. . . . No, I do understand my brother the King's reasons. Moreover, I trust Johnny Neville as much as any man in Christendom.' He hesitated, turning back to face Francis, and then concluded in a rush, 'But I would to God he had not done it, Francis. I would to God he had not.'

Francis wished now that he hadn't asked, decided a new topic of conversation was in order. 'I want to purchase a mare whilst I'm here for my sister Joan. I promised I'd bring her back a fine Yorkshire filly.'

'We could ride out to Jervaulx Abbey to see their stock. Since that's a good day's ride, I'd not be able to get away till Monday next but if you're willing to wait, Francis, you'll not find a better horse anywhere than one of theirs. They breed the best in Wensleydale.'

The idea of such an outing appealed greatly to Francis. 'And Middleham's not four miles further up the road,' he said enthusiastically. 'It's been forfeit to the King, has it not? So we could spend the night there rather than with the monks.'

He saw at once that it'd been a mistake to mention Middleham, saw Richard's eyes darken so that he could not be sure if they were blue or grey, could be sure only of sudden shadowed pain. And then it was gone and Richard was smiling, said lightly, 'Who knows, you might even find a filly at Jervaulx that you'd like to give to Anna.'

Francis had been about to bring up the name he'd not heard Richard speak since Warwick's flight to France, the name of the fourteen-year-old girl who'd been dragged into exile with him. He was distracted now by Richard's jibe and the name that passed his lips was that of Anna Fitz-Hugh rather than Anne Neville.

'It's been decided that Anna is to come to live with me at

Minster Lovell next year, once she's past her fifteenth birthday. It's a queer feeling, Dickon, to have a wife I hardly know. . . . We've nothing to say to each other, nothing at all.'

The door opened suddenly and they both turned, expecting to see Thomas Parr, Richard's squire, or perhaps one of the black-clad Augustine friars. The man before them was unfamiliar, wearing the blue and murrey of York.

'My lord of Gloucester. . . . Begging Your Grace's pardon, but the Hospitaller bade me come direct to you when I told him I came from His Grace, the King. My lord, it is the wish of the King's Grace that you attend upon him at once. He awaits you now at the friary of the Franciscans.'

Richard said nothing, merely nodded. The man withdrew and Thomas came in, hard on his heels. He wasted no time, said tersely, 'I've given orders to saddle your horse, my lord.'

'Dickon . . . I'll wait for you. If that be all right?'

Richard turned toward Francis, nodded again, but Francis did not think he truly heard him. Richard had paled noticeably. His mouth was suddenly taut as if bracing for news he already knew to be bad. Before Francis could repeat his question, Richard was gone and he was alone in the quiet chamber. He sat down on the narrow bed and tried to convince himself that the King might summon Richard at such an hour for mundane matters, for other than catastrophe.

'Come in, Dickon. I've news to share. It seems the most Christian country of France has been given to witness a miracle. . . . And I daresay we'll soon be told the blind did see and the lame leapt like deer.'

'I can think of few places less likely to be so blessed than France,' Richard said uncertainly, for there was a bright hard glaze to his brother's eyes and the mockery rang false. 'What has happened, Ned?'

'The cat is amongst the pigeons for true, little brother. A message has arrived from Westminster, from Lisbet. Meg has sent word from Burgundy. . . . Warwick has come to terms with the French harlot.'

For the first time in his life, Richard knew what it meant to be speechless with shock. 'I do not believe it,' he said at last.

'Believe it, Dickon,' Edward said and smiled grimly. 'Warwick and Marguerite d'Anjou met at Angers on the twenty-second of last month and there discovered that they did share a common interest . . . in my downfall.'

'Yea, and behold, that the wolf and the lamb shall feed together,' Will Hastings murmured, but Richard could see little humour in so unholy an alliance and said, still incredulous, 'If he'd take Marguerite d'Anjou as ally, he'd not have scrupled to make a pact with the very Archfiend of Hell.' Adding in spite of himself, 'God pity him, that he should come to this. . . .'

'"*Facilis descensus Averui,*"' Edward said with a shrug. 'The descent into Hell is easy.'

'Jesú, Ned, his father and brother died with ours at Sandal Castle,' Richard persisted, 'at the hands of Marguerite's men!'

'Aye, and Warwick branded her son a bastard for all the world to hear. But the King of France has a honeyed tongue and enlightened self interest seems to have carried the day,' Edward said, very dryly, and Richard turned smoke-grey eyes upon him in belated comprehension. 'This is a web of the French King's making, is it not?'

'Who else, Dickon? Warwick has not the imagination. . . . For if he had, he could never have backed brother George's claims to the throne. As for the French harlot . . .' Edward laughed, without mirth. 'I verily think she hates Warwick even more than she does me.'

'And exile has not softened her any,' Will volunteered. 'She kept Warwick on his knees for a full quarter-hour ere she'd deign to pardon him.'

'I should have wished to see that,' Richard said bitterly, and Edward gave him a smile of sardonic understanding.

'So would I, lad. . . . So would I.'

'What of George?' Richard asked suddenly, and this time Edward's laughter was not forced.

'What, indeed? Warwick has as much need for George as a man gelded has for a warm-blooded wench, and even George must realize that he's now like a teat on a bull, a curiosity but of no earthly use.'

Will laughed but Richard was frowning, still struggling with disbelief.

'But how can Warwick ever hope to put Harry of Lancaster back on the throne?' he demanded. 'God Almighty, Ned, he's madder than Bedlam and Warwick well knows it.'

'If they dare, they'll bypass the old man and crown the boy,' Will predicted and Edward jibed, 'They've not set foot in England as yet and you have the boy crowned already?'

Catching his error of speech, Will grinned and recovered quickly. 'They would . . . but they will not.'

'No, they will not, Will. But they'll damned well try.'

'I think not, Ned. I'd wager they'll be at swordspoint ere the first frost . . . and our cousin Warwick will have bartered the last of his honour for a handful of cobwebs and smoke.'

'I'd not count on that happening if I were you, Dickon.'

'You cannot believe this accursed alliance will last? It's a pairing as unnatural as Rome and Carthage, or Sparta and Troy.'

'You seem to forget, Dickon, that we are dealing with the Spider King. Louis realized, just as you have, that it would take more to mate dog to cat than a shared lust for the English crown.'

Edward paused, shook his head. 'No, that son of a whore baited his trap with care . . . and then sealed this ungodly mésalliance within the sacrament of marriage. Though I should truly like to know how he ever prevailed upon Marguerite to wed her precious nestling to a daughter of Warwick's.' He shook his head again, wonderingly. 'Now that truly defies belief.'

'I dare say the boy swayed her.' Will turned to Richard,

explaining, 'It seems he was taken with the girl and was not averse to bedding her, not with a crown in the offering, as well.'

Even as Will spoke, there was a sudden commotion across the table from him. A squire of the royal household had been moving inconspicuously among them, filling their winecups from a heavy glass flagon. But, as he paused before Richard, Richard jerked around without warning to stare at his brother, and the hapless attendant suddenly found himself pouring wine for a cup that was no longer there.

The man was looking with dismay at the puddle forming among the floor rushes, saw with even greater dismay that wine had splashed, as well, upon the blue velvet sleeve of the young Duke's doublet, and braced himself for a reprimand he did not deserve but did not expect to escape.

None was forthcoming. There was an abrupt silence, broken at last by Will when it was clear that no one else meant to speak. Will had been startled by Richard's heedless act but was far too well mannered to remark upon it. He chose, instead, to give the squire a discreet signal to withdraw and then resumed, as smoothly as if there'd been no disruption of the conversation.

'But Marguerite is not utterly witless. Although she sanctioned the betrothal, the wedding is not to take place till Warwick holds England.' He laughed at that, before concluding cheerfully, 'And he has as much chance of that as he does of successfully laying siege to the Holy City of Jerusalem.'

He paused for the expected response, soon saw he waited in vain. By now he was becoming aware of tensions above and beyond the natural shock at Warwick's accord with the Lancastrian Queen. He made no further attempts at conversation, looked instead to Edward for his cue. It was not long in coming.

'Will, I would speak with my brother alone,' Edward said abruptly, and as the door closed behind Will, he leaned forward. But Richard pulled away from his touch.

Edward found himself at an uncharacteristic loss for words,

watching in silence as Richard crossed to the window, where he took undue care in unlatching the shutters.

As cool air invaded the chamber, flaring the candles and giving hint of coming rain, Edward swore softly under his breath.

'Dickon, I did not know . . . It never occurred to me that you might still care for Warwick's daughter.'

Richard said nothing and, somewhat to his surprise, Edward heard himself saying defensively, 'After all, you've not seen her for nigh on a twelvemonth. . . . Time enough and more to fancy and then forget fully a score of sweethearts. At your age, I know I would . . . and did.'

Richard turned at that. 'Last year, when you forbade our betrothal, I told you, then, that I cared for Anne . . . and you said that, if my feelings were the same a year or so hence, you might reconsider. You do remember saying that?'

Edward had no liking for accusations, implied or otherwise, and he was provoked into responding with caustic candour.

'I remember. It seemed little enough to promise. You were but sixteen and I felt that for certes the fancy would pass with time.'

It was candour he at once regretted; he'd not realized how callous that would sound till he heard it spoken aloud. He sighed and then swore again, feeling at a loss. He was not accustomed to identifying so closely with the pain of another, did not like the sensation in the least. After some moments, he said slowly, 'Dickon, I do not know what to tell you. If only you'd said something these months past. Had I but known you still had a fondness for the girl, I'd never have let you hear of her betrothal the way you did. For that, I am truly and deeply sorry. But I cannot say that I am sorry I forbade the match. I'll not lie to you about that.'

Richard nodded, almost imperceptibly, a gesture that said nothing and could have meant anything.

'Damnation, Dickon, we're making more of this than it warrants. As Will said, the marriage is not to be until Warwick claims

England. If that be true, your little cousin will never see the day dawn when she must wed Lancaster. That much I can promise you, little brother.'

16

Doncaster

September 1470

Edward was unable to sleep: turning upon his stomach, rolling over onto his back, pounding his pillow into softened submission. After a time, he abandoned the effort and propped himself up on his elbows to survey the darkened room. A solitary white candle burned, for luck and light, the shutters tightly barred against unhealthy night air. He could discern the motionless form of his squire, stretched out on a pallet by the door; the soft steady wheeze bespoke deep, blessed sleep. Irked, Edward briefly considered awakening him to share these accursed idle hours.

Before long, the sky would be streaking with light, and he had to be up with the sun. This day he expected to join his three thousand men with the five thousand under command of his cousin, John Neville, Marquess of Montagu.

It was an uncommon occurrence for Edward, to be wakeful and uneasy of mind while others slept. Most nights, he slept like a cat, easy and light. But not for the past week. Not since he got word of Warwick's landing in the South.

All September an English fleet had cruised the French coast. But, in midmonth, squalls had swept the Channel from Dover to Honfleur. His ships had been scattered in the storm and Warwick seized his chance to bypass the blockade. More than a fortnight had passed now since a French fleet had landed Warwick and George at Dartmouth.

Edward was not normally given to regretting what was done and beyond recall. He knew he had no reason to reproach himself for the defensive measures he'd taken this summer, in anticipation of Warwick's return. He'd done all he could. And yet he could not shake off a nagging suspicion that he'd done what Warwick wanted him to do – go north. Just what role, he wondered, had Fitz-Hugh really played? The penitent maladroit rebel? Or a successful decoy?

He knew such thoughts were hardly conducive to untroubled sleep but he could deny neither the suspicion nor the fact that, when Warwick landed at Dartmouth, he'd been more than three hundred miles to the north.

Warwick had made a shrewd move in heading for Devon; Edward grudgingly conceded him that. Devon had always been partial to the House of Lancaster, and there they'd swelled their ranks with unreconciled Lancastrians and like malcontents. And as he raced south to intercept them, they'd turned east, toward London.

If it came to that, he thought London would hold fast for him. But he felt sure Warwick would forsake even such a prize as London to meet his advance. Warwick was vain, fancied himself to be the most able battle commander since Harry of Monmouth won Agincourt. Edward thought otherwise. He had never lost a battle and he did not fear his cousin. Warwick had been routed at St Albans, faltered at Towton. No, the only soldier worth fearing in the Neville family was Johnny.

Retrieving a pillow from the floor, he shoved it back against the headboard. He had not wanted it this way. But tonight he was tired and bitter and wanted above all else to make an end to it. To do whatever had to be done. It was a pity, he thought, that Marguerite had insisted upon keeping her stripling by her in France, had not let him sail with Warwick. He'd rather have made an end to it all.

Closing his eyes, he thought of his wife, in residence at the Tower of London, awaiting her confinement. Her time was nearing; the midwives said the babe would be born within a fortnight of All Saints' Day. He was concerned, but not unduly so for this would be the fourth child in just six years of marriage. Lisbet birthed easily, had never been touched by the milk fever that claimed so many a woman after her child was born.

Three daughters she'd given him: Bessie, Mary and Cecily, the last named to placate his unyielding lady mother, who'd never accepted Lisbet, never forgiven him for that Maytime marriage at Grafton Manor. Three fair little girls. He'd never shared Lisbet's disappointment in their daughters, never doubted that she'd give him the sons a king must have, and he was sure the child she now carried would be a boy. He'd been sure even as far back as the first time she'd felt the babe quicken within her womb. Four had always been a lucky number for him.

He sat up abruptly for the night's quiet had suddenly been torn asunder. Loud voices were echoing in the antechamber, followed by muffled sounds much like grappling bodies. Edward flung himself from the bed, groping for his sword. His squire was already up, kicking the pallet aside as the door was shoved back with such force that the unlatched bolt tore loose, clattered to the floor.

All at once the room was full of men, shouting, swearing, stumbling against each other, swords drawn. But their quarry was already on his knees before Edward.

'Your Grace . . .' he panted, sobbing for breath, shoulders heaving like one convulsed.

By now the room was ablaze with torches and, as the light fell upon the florid begrimed face, Edward recognized him as Alexander Carlisle, the sergeant of his minstrels. As Edward lowered his sword, Carlisle found his voice.

'Save yourself, Your Grace. . . . Your enemies are coming to take you. . . .'

'You're raving,' Edward said tersely.

The night was chill, yet sweat ran like rain down Carlisle's face; his doublet, torn from shoulder to elbow, was stained with dark wet splotches.

'The enemy . . .' he repeated, like one who knew no other words.

'Who, man?' Edward demanded impatiently. 'Warwick is more than two days' march from Doncaster. What phantom foes did you conjure. . . .'

Carlisle actually dared to interrupt. 'I do not know, my liege . . . but I saw them,' he insisted stubbornly. 'Men at arms, not more than six miles away . . . and they are not for York.'

Edward reached for a torch, held it close to the man's face. Carlisle flinched but kept his eyes on his King and Edward handed the torch back to his squire. The man might be mad but his fear was real enough.

His gaze raked the circle of suddenly silent men, found a face he could trust.

'See to this. If his tale be true, there'll be fugitives aplenty making for Doncaster. Find them and report back to me.'

The man nodded, knelt before him and backed from the room. If possible, the quiet was even more absolute, marred only by Carlisle's laboured breathing.

He was wiping away blood with his sleeve; his cheek had been gashed in the struggle to block his precipitous entry into Edward's bedchamber.

'I swear before Almighty God . . . I've told you true, Your Grace.'

Edward believed him. Instinct stronger than reason told him Carlisle spoke the truth. Glancing about him, he saw his belief reflected in the frightened faces of his attendants. The fear in the room was a tangible thing, would take flame like sun-dried straw, blaze into a panic that might engulf his entire army.

A man sank to his knees, began to babble, 'Oh, Lord, my God, You Who take away the sins of the world, have mercy upon us. . . .'

The others stirred, fearful eyes flicking in contagious communication of this unknown dread, and Edward profaned the prayer with a virulent oath.

Asserting command, he waited until they lapsed into submissive silence. One of his squires was hovering nearby, clutching an armful of clothing; a boot slipped from his uneasy grasp, nearly landed on Edward's bare foot. He grimaced, aware of the incongruous image he presented, stark naked with sword in hand. But for once, his sense of humour failed him.

'Get me Gloucester,' he snapped. 'And Hastings. . . . Awaken the others.'

Edward looked about him at the three men who stood closest to him; his brother Richard, his brother-in-law Anthony Woodville, his Lord Chamberlain, Will Hastings. Three more unlike men he could not imagine, though they now shared a common expression, one of stunned apprehension. Three pairs of eyes, dark blue, pale green and brown, were focused unwaveringly on him, waiting.

Anthony kept running his tongue over dry lips. He was blanched with fear but Edward didn't fault him for that. Only a madman like Harry of Lancaster faced the sword with equanimity. But the fear must be ridden with a curb bit; slacken the reins and all control would be forfeit. He gave Anthony a hard appraising look, concluded that as long as the others kept their heads, Anthony would bear up.

Turning his gaze upon Will and Richard, he found reason for reassurance in their tense expectant faces. Will was too jaded, at thirty-nine, to be truly surprised by any act of man or God; he'd take defeat in his stride if it came to that. And Dickon had the blessed adaptability of the very young, too caught up in the action of the moment to dwell upon the risk of defeat and death within the hour.

'Have you confirmed the man's story, Ned?' Will asked sensibly.

'We wait upon him now.' Taking a step toward the ante-chamber, he said, 'We'd best give orders to have the horses saddled, just in case. . . .'

Richard, tugging at the undersleeve of his hastily donned doublet, looked up at that. 'I did,' he said briefly, and Edward gave him a grimly approving nod.

'Good lad. I need not tell you . . .' He paused, suddenly alert.

Richard reached the door first, jerking it open as Edward's courier stumbled into the chamber. And when he brushed past Richard, Duke of Gloucester and a Plantagenet Prince, without so much as a nod, Edward knew what he would say.

'You are in mortal peril, my liege.'

Edward swallowed, finding his mouth too dry for speech. 'From whom?'

'Montagu,' the man blurted. 'He's declared for his brother, for Warwick . . . and his army is less than two leagues distant, Your Grace.'

It should have come as no surprise. From the moment he'd accepted Carlisle's tale as true, Edward had known there could be but one army within reach of Doncaster. But he'd refused to let himself believe it. There were truths too devastating to be accepted. Johnny. Jesus God, what had he done?

No one spoke. He doubted they even breathed. He compelled himself to turn his head, to look at his companions. Saw that Richard and Will had guessed the truth too; Anthony alone looked startled.

'Montagu?' he echoed incredulously. 'How could he, Ned? After all you've done for him!'

No one heeded him. Will was watching Edward. Richard, too, watched his brother. Edward swung around so he'd not have to meet their eyes, bumped blindly into the bed. Johnny – Johnny, of all men. That accursed earldom. God forgive him, he should have seen, should have realized. Lisbet, what would become of her? And his little girls? The men who'd trusted him? Will; Dickon. Dickon, who was seventeen, like Edmund. And it was his doing. He'd brought them to this, brought them here to die in Doncaster.

He'd never come this close to panic in his life. Never before lost faith in himself, seen himself as beaten, seen them all as dead men.

He lost track of time. The silence seemed to endure forever, had neither beginning nor end to it. In reality, only seconds passed. He felt now a light touch on his arm. His brother had come to stand beside him. He turned to face the boy. Dickon was afraid. It showed in the rigidness of his posture, the way he hunched his shoulders forward, his sudden pallor. Too stunned for pain; that would come later, if he lived long enough. But the eyes didn't waver, looked back at him steadily. Edmund's eyes, full of trust.

Edward drew an uneven breath, found it hurt to breathe, as if he'd taken a jarring blow to the midsection. When he spoke, however, his voice was very much his own, held no hint of panic.

'It's a well-timed trap he's sprung on us. I always said Johnny was the soldier in the Neville family.' He alone was surprised that he could sound so controlled, detached even. To the others, it was no more than they expected of him.

'What do we do, Ned?' The question came from Richard, had in it much of that sobering faith he'd seen in the boy's eyes.

Will, too, was awaiting his response. Anthony, however, had begun to pace, as if movement could somehow forestall the coming catastrophe; unable to contain himself any longer, he burst out with an agitated 'What can we do but fight? If we rally our men. . . .'

Edward turned to stare at his brother-in-law. 'They have us outnumbered by damned near two to one,' he said, not troubling to conceal his scorn. 'More importantly, they're ready to fight and we're not. Long before we could gather our forces, they'd be upon us. You did hear the man say they're less than six miles distant?'

Anthony flushed scarlet. There was another brief silence as they took in the awesome implications of Edward's words.

'Have we time to withdraw, Ned?' Will was watching him intently and looked pained but not surprised when Edward shook his head.

'We'd be butchered,' he said succinctly. 'Whether we try to make a stand here or pull our men back. We do not have the time, we're greatly outmanned and Warwick's army is doubtlessly on the move at this very moment to cut off escape to the south.'

He paused, his eyes moving from face to face. 'My father and brother were slain at Sandal Castle because they engaged a far superior force. It was daring, heroic, foolhardy . . . and fatal. I'll not make the same mistake.

'Give the order to disperse. Tell our men to scatter as they will. Now . . . get me Will Hatteclyffe.'

Within moments, his secretary-physician was standing before him, anticipating his need, numbly offering pen and paper. With a sweep of his arm, Edward cleared the table. The others watched; there was no sound but the rapid scratching of his pen. Straightening, he handed the message, unread, to Hatteclyffe.

'Pick a man you can trust. Have him convey this to the Queen. Tell her to seek sanctuary at St Martin's or Westminster. Better yet, take it yourself, Will.'

'Do not ask that of me, Your Grace.' Hatteclyffe's voice cracked, thickened with emotion. 'I would go with you . . . be it into the very pits of Hell.'

Edward almost smiled at that—almost. 'Not as far as that, Will . . . at least, not yet. For now, it's to be Burgundy.'

Burgundy. Saying it aloud suddenly made it real. He knew time was of the essence, knew Johnny would reach Doncaster within the hour. Yet for a moment he stood immobile. And then, with an effort, he roused himself, looked to see the impact upon his companions. Anthony seemed dazed. Will was pale but composed; thank God for Will, and for Dickon.

'Christ keep you, lad,' he said abruptly, 'this will be the second time you've had to seek refuge in Burgundy.'

266

Richard had moved to the window. Now that the worst was known, he was finding this delay to be intolerable. His nerves were raw, taut with the need for action, to be gone from here. He'd felt as if those few moments Ned had taken to write to Elizabeth had lasted the whole of his lifetime, and with each passing minute he expected to hear the sounds of the approaching enemy force echoing in the courtyard. That the enemy was Johnny and that flight meant foreign exile, he was too numbed truly to take in. Now he wanted only to escape this room, escape this waking nightmare into which he had so suddenly been thrust. The shutters were securely latched, resisting his probing fingers; all at once, it was crucial to him that the window be open and he jerked the bolt until the aged wood splintered, gave way grudgingly.

At Edward's surprising words, he swung around to regard his brother searchingly. After hesitating, he managed a moderately passable grin and a self-conscious shrug.

'Old habits die hard, Ned.'

The reply was unexpected. Edward stared and then he grinned, too, more convincingly than Richard but still leaving much to be desired.

'So do men, little brother,' he said grimly. 'Therefore, I suggest we ride as if our lives depend upon it. . . . For they do.'

The fortified manor house occupied by England's king still flew the Yorkist banner as John Neville entered Doncaster. But the man he sought was miles away, racing east through the night as the sky ahead paled and turned a soft misty grey.

Reaching the northern shore of The Wash, the Yorkist fugitives commandeered what craft they could and headed for Lynn, a fishing village on the Norfolk coast. Edward's legendary luck seemed to have deserted him; their small ships were battered mercilessly in an unseasonal gale and a number of their men drowned, Edward himself barely escaping a like fate.

On September 30th they landed in Lynn, and, with several hundred of their more steadfast followers crammed into small fishing vessels, they abandoned England and sailed for Burgundy. It was a Tuesday, October 2nd, the Feast Day of the Guardian Angels, just twenty days since Warwick had landed at Dartmouth. It was also Richard's eighteenth birthday.

17

London

October 1470

Not until Monday, October 1, did word reach London of John Neville's defection and Edward's midnight flight from the northern village of Doncaster. Sir Geoffrey Gate, a man sworn to the Earl of Warwick, immediately seized his opportunity and led a successful assault upon the Southwark prisons. Scores of political prisoners, men loyal to Lancaster or Warwick, were freed. Freed, too, however, were countless convicted felons and they surged through the streets of Southwark, looting shops and alehouses, terrorizing the sizable community of Flemish merchants and creating panic even in the eighteen bankside bordellos of that area of Southwark commonly known as 'the stews'.

London's Mayor ordered the city gates closed to the mob but throughout the day the air was acrid with the smoke of Southwark fires. At dark, Elizabeth Woodville, in her eighth month of pregnancy, gathered her three small daughters and her two young sons and sought refuge at Westminster in the abbey of St Peter. Robert

Stillington, Edward's Chancellor, fled to sanctuary at St Martin le Grand and, by dawn, the churches were crowded with those Yorkists unwilling or unable to recant their support for the White Rose.

On Friday, October 5th, George Neville, Archbishop of York, rode boldly into London, took command of the Tower of London and released Harry of Lancaster from his long confinement. A bewildered Harry, clutching his prayer missals and the companions of his captivity, a small grey spaniel and a caged starling, was taken from the spartan chamber he'd liked to call his monk's cell. After courtesies that evoked dim memories deep within the troubled brain, he found himself a reluctant resident of the lavishly furnished apartment still fragrant with the perfume of Edward's Queen.

On Saturday afternoon, October 6th, Richard Neville, Earl of Warwick, entered the city through Newgate. Greeted by his brother, the Archbishop, he proceeded in state to the Tower of London, where he knelt and swore fealty to the man who neither comprehended nor cared that he was once more His Sovereign Grace, Henry VI.

The men, women and children of London turned out to watch as the Lancastrian King and the Kingmaker rode slowly through the city streets toward St Paul's Cathedral. Brightly coloured banners fluttered from upper windows. The open-fronted shops and market stalls were closed. Silk streamers painted with the Bear and Ragged Staff were strung the width of cobbled streets. The conduits ran with wine as if it were a Coronation Day and it seemed as if the entire citizenry was waving or wearing Neville crimson.

The Earl of Warwick was mounted on a magnificent destrier, an Arabian war horse as creamy-white as frothed milk; it drew many an admiring glance as it swept by, chafing under its rider's restraining hand.

George, Duke of Clarence, had chosen, too, to ride a white

stallion. Unlike Warwick, however, he wore no armour, and a cloak of crimson velvet caught the breeze and the attention of the crowd. But the more discerning observer noted the thinned line of his mouth, the wary eyes, and found cause for conjecture.

John Neville, Marquess of Montagu, rode beside his ordained brother, as sombre of visage as the archbishop was exultant. The spectators nudged each other and murmured as he passed by, this reserved taciturn man who had brought down a king and looked not at all as if he gloried in his victory.

Lord Stanley, brother-in-law to Warwick, rode in their wake. Next came the Earl of Oxford and Lord Fitz-Hugh, handsomely mounted and well attended. But only Warwick himself drew more stares than the middle-aged man clad in a long gown of blue velvet, a gown that draped him as shapelessly as a shroud, having been made for a much larger man, the deposed Yorkist King.

Warwick had prudently seen that Harry of Lancaster was astride a docile grey gelding and the animal moved obediently along even though the reins trailed loosely through lax fingers. Milky blue eyes blinked repeatedly as though unused to the light. An un-focused smile would shape his mouth from time to time but he seemed not to understand that the tepid cheers of 'God save the King!' were meant for him.

Will Parr watched as Harry of Lancaster rode by. For a moment, the pale eyes looked in his direction; Harry smiled, a smile of singular sweetness, and Will saluted his King, thinking, The poor witless creature, God pity him . . . God pity us all.

'Where do you think they will go after they make offerings at St Paul's?' he asked his companion, low-voiced.

'Warwick will doubtlessly stay at the Bishop's Palace, or perhaps the Herber, and I expect they will take His Grace the King to Bedlam.'

Bedlam was the popular name for St Mary of Bethlehem Hospital, London's asylum for the deranged of mind . . . and Francis had not troubled to drop his voice. Laughter rustled through the crowd and disapproving murmurs as well, motivated, perhaps, more by expediency than loyalty to Lancaster, but dangerous withal.

'For Christ's sake, Francis, guard your tongue!' Grabbing Francis by the arm, Will jerked him back, pulling him hastily toward the nearest cross street.

'This way . . . and hurry! You may not care if your head graces Drawbridge Gate but I've no wish to be carrion for the ravens!'

Francis didn't resist, following as Will roughly shouldered his way through the crowd. Once they moved away from Lombard Street, the path of the procession, the congestion eased considerably and Will slowed to glare at his friend.

'Why not just shout for York on the steps of St Paul's and have done with it?'

Francis had the grace to look contrite. 'You're right, Will. I did not mean to endanger you. But when I saw that poor pious fool with the crown of England on his head . . . I could not bear it,' he concluded simply.

Mollified, Will patted his arm in an awkward gesture of comfort. 'I know. I was at Middleham, too, Francis. But it will not change things if I die a martyr for York . . . and the same holds true for you. Try to bear that in mind.'

Francis nodded. 'Rob Percy was with Dickon; did you know that, Will?' he asked, after they'd walked a full block in silence.

'No, I did not. Are you sure?'

'I left York on September eleventh for the Fitz-Hugh manor at Tanfield, and Rob was still there with no plans to depart.'

'They say Edward ordered his army to scatter. Rob may be back in Scotton even now.'

'You know better than that,' Francis said shortly, and Will frowned.

'Yes, I confess I do. If the tale be true that they have fled to Burgundy, then Rob is in Burgundy, too.'

'I heard today that their ship was sunk in a gale, with the loss of all aboard,' Francis said, in so neutral a tone that Will turned a sharp inquiring look in his direction.

'And I heard that they were taken by the French; would you rather believe that? Jesú, Francis, you know better than to heed idle tavern talk! Not even Warwick knows for certes the whereabouts of Edward of York.'

Francis had no chance to respond. A cascade of greasy water gushed from an upper window of an overhanging second storey. Francis, cat-quick, pulled Will back in time, but two other passersby were not as fortunate and were drenched. Understandably outraged, they directed a stream of sputtering oaths upward, where a woman's face appeared briefly to assess indifferently the damage done and slam the shutters on their tirade.

'The graceless jade!' One of the victims appealed angrily to Will and Francis. 'You saw. . . . Look at my jerkin; I'm soaked through!' Raising his voice to a shout.

'Plague take you, you careless bitch! May your man lay with harlots and bring you back the pox! May you have even as many griefs as the Woodville slut!'

Francis and Will walked on, leaving him to rant under the street-wise eyes of two small boys and an emaciated mongrel dog.

'A week ago, he'd have said that at the risk of his head,' Francis said bitterly. 'God, how quick they are to pick the bones clean!'

Cecily Neville, Duchess of York, had long shown a preference for her rural retreat at Berkhampsted over Baynard's Castle, the London palace of York. But with the approach of All Hallows' Eve, she was once more in residence by the River Thames, and each time she ventured forth to attend Mass at St Paul's or to make charitable offerings to the hospitals of St Bartholomew and St Thomas, Londoners remembered her son, the young Yorkist King.

It was dusk. Earlier in the day a festive procession had thronged the city streets, moving from the guildhall in Aldermenbury Street through Cheapside, Fleet Street and the Strand, toward Westminster where the newly elected Lord Mayor of London would take oath of office. Now, however, the streets were passable once more and Francis had no difficulty in engaging a barge to ferry him from Southwark to Paul's Wharf, within walking distance of Baynard's Castle.

The Presence Chamber oriel window faced south and Francis had an unobstructed view of the Thames where flickering lights marked the passing river traffic. He'd not really expected the Duchess of York to receive him and he was beginning to regret the impulse that, in the common room of a Southwark inn, had seemed inspired, but in the Presence Chamber of Baynard's Castle, seemed audacious in the extreme.

She'd come in so silently that he'd heard neither the door nor the light step, and he spun around, startled, as she spoke his name.

Her first words brought her sons vividly to his mind, for she shared with all of her children an uncommonly pleasing voice, well modulated, melodious, not easily forgotten. She extended her hand to him and he kissed the long tapering fingers, barren of jewelry save an ornate wedding band of heavy gem-encrusted gold.

She held a folded paper in her other hand and, as he straightened, she passed it to him with the faintest glimmer of a smile.

'I would caution you not to commit your indiscretions to print,' she said coolly. 'You'd best burn this.'

Francis crumpled the message which had gained him entry. 'I am proud to be friend to His Grace, the Duke of Gloucester. Nothing which has happened in the past four weeks has changed that, Your Grace.'

'You shall not prosper, I fear, under Lancaster, Francis Lovell.'

'I should not care to, Madame.'

'Why did you wish to speak with me?'

The grey eyes were disconcertingly direct, and he felt compelled to speak the truth.

'London has become a virtual cesspool for rumours and gossip . . . of the vilest sort.' His mouth twisted. 'The scandalmongers and doomsayers delight in the most outlandish tales, each one warranted as gospel truth.'

'Ah . . . I see. You fear the stories are true? That Edward drowned while attempting a Channel crossing?'

'I do not know, Madame,' he conceded quietly. 'And that is what I cannot endure. I truly believe I would rather know the worst than know nothing at all. I thought, perhaps, that you would have word . . . that you might know. . . .'

'Edward came ashore at Texel in Holland nigh on a month ago, the same day that Richard's ship put in safely on the island of Walcheren in Zeeland. They were reunited at The Hague on the eleventh of October.'

'*Deo gratias*,' he breathed, so sincerely that she gave him a smile such as she reserved for very few.

Scorning the cushion he offered, she seated herself in a heavy high-backed chair and, indicating the nearest footstool, bade him do likewise.

'What I am to tell you comes from the pen of my daughter, Duchess of Burgundy, written in her own hand and dispatched by secret courier as soon as she learned of Edward's landing in her husband's realm.

'There is some truth in those grim tales being traded in London alehouses. The Easterlings* were on the alert for the Yorkist ships; the captain who captured Edward of York could have claimed his own reward from the French King. They pursued Edward into the very port of Texel but it was ebb tide and neither ship could dock. The Easterlings dropped anchor, were waiting till the tide would rise enough for them to board Edward's ship.'

Francis gasped. 'What saved him, Madame?'

'His gift for friendship,' she said, and smiled at his surprise.

* English name for the German cities which comprised the Hanseatic League.

'When the Burgundians were negotiating for the marriage of their Duke to my daughter in the summer of 1467, Edward won the admiration and affection of one of their envoys, Louis de Bruges, Seigneur de la Gruuthuse. Most fortuitously, he is now Governor of the province of Holland and, when he heard of my son's plight, he compelled the Easterlings to withdraw and gave Edward safe entry into the harbour.'

'It was a propitious day for York when the Lady Margaret joined her House to that of Burgundy,' Francis said warmly.

The graceful white fingers were suddenly still, linking in her lap. 'I suspect Charles of Burgundy may think otherwise.'

Francis frowned. 'But surely he will give aid to York? He is King Edward's brother-in-law, after all. . . .'

'As George is Edward's brother.'

Francis stared at her. 'Are you saying Charles will not help your sons, Madame?'

'I would say that he . . . lacks enthusiasm for such a venture. He wants no war with England and, if he backs Edward, he gives Warwick reason to join forces with the French King against Burgundy. He can scarcely deny his wife's brother refuge but he refuses to meet with him, and Edward would be hard-pressed, indeed, were it not for Gruuthuse's generosity.'

She gave Francis a sober, searching look. 'They had little more than the clothes they wore when they fled England, after all, and Edward had only a cloak of marten fur to give to the captain of his ship.'

Shaken, Francis could think of nothing to say. His fear had been that Edward and Richard would not reach Burgundy. Once there, he'd taken it for granted that Charles would give them the gold and soldiers they'd need to challenge Warwick. Now his mind was filled with one image and one image only; Edward Plantagenet, King of England and France, Lord of Ireland, paying for passage with a fur-lined cloak.

The Duchess of York did not seem uncomfortable with the

lengthening silence. Rising, she brushed aside his helping hand and crossed to the prie-dieu that faced the hearth. Picking up a coral rosary, she fastened it about a slender wrist and then turned back to the boy who was regarding her with anxious eyes.

'Tell me, did you ever take notice of a pilgrim token worn by my youngest son? A small silver coin graven with a Latin cross?'

Mystified, he nodded. 'Yes, Your Grace, I did. As I recall, he was never without it during our years at Middleham.'

A magnificent arras hanging covered the entire east wall of the chamber, an elaborately detailed depiction of the siege of Jerusalem. She was staring past Francis at the tapestry, tracing the familiar intricately woven patterns of topaz and russet as she said, 'When I was in my fifteenth year, I was stricken with the tertian fever. I was not expected to live ... and my favourite brother vowed that if I did, he would make a pilgrimage to the Blessed Shrine of St Caecilia at Trastevere.'

She gave him a distant smile. 'I did live and he kept his vow and I wore his pilgrim pledge on a silver chain around my neck for nigh on thirty years.'

Francis made a properly pious reply, hoping his face did not betray his bafflement.

'When my husband, my brother and my son Edmund were murdered at Sandal Castle, and my nephew Warwick defeated at St Albans, I feared for the lives of my youngest sons, resolved to send them to safety in Burgundy, beyond the reach of Lancaster.

'That night I removed the pilgrim cross for the first time. I fastened it around Richard's neck and I entrusted my sons to the mercy of the Almighty, not knowing if I'd see them again in this lifetime.'

Francis did not know the response expected of him. It was a vivid, poignant tale, yet told as dispassionately as if she were relating her household accounts.

'I'm sure he wears your cross even now, Madame, and it will safeguard him as once it did before.'

'Richard is no longer eight years old,' she said icily. 'He is quite able to fend for himself.'

Francis blinked. 'Madame?'

'I find your pity presumptuous, as I do your assumption that I am a grieving mother to be indulged and consoled with platitudes. I assure you I had quite a different purpose in mind when I related that story.' Her lip curled. 'I have my failings, Francis, but I am never maudlin.'

'No, Madame, indeed you are not,' he agreed, so fervently that she relented, said with uncharacteristic patience,

'I wanted you to understand how it was here in the city when word reached us that Warwick had been beaten at St Albans. I knew what would happen when London fell to Lancaster. The night that I hastened Richard and George aboard ship for Burgundy, I fully expected the Lancastrians to be in London within hours. The city was in a panic. Shops were boarded up, men were frantic with fear for their wives and daughters, the streets were deserted as if it were a plague town.

'All seemed lost. And then, by the grace of God, came word from Edward. Warwick had reached him with the dire news of St Albans and he rallied a force, was racing hellbent for London.

'On February twenty-sixth, nine days after Warwick lost St Albans, Edward won London. You will never in your lifetime see such a scene as greeted him upon his entry into the city.' A smile came and went so quickly he couldn't track its passage. 'On that day, Londoners made his cause their own.

'Three days later, a deputation of nobles led by Warwick came here to Baynard's Castle and, in this very room, offered him the crown.

'His coronation, however, had to wait. In just eleven days, he mustered a fighting force and marched north. He overtook Marguerite's army at Towton, twelve miles from York. The battle was fought in the worst snowstorm in years and lasted ten hours. When it was over, they say the River Cocke Beck ran pure crimson

277

and twenty thousand men were dead or dying. And Edward had the victory.

'Just three months lay between my husband's death at Sandal Castle and Edward's triumph at Towton. What my husband could not do, what Warwick could not do, Edward did . . . whilst still a month shy of his nineteenth birthday.

'Do you understand me? My son and I have often disagreed. He is a true Plantagenet and given to sins of the flesh and a prideful arrogance which served Warwick all too well. But this I do tell you for a certainty . . . that nothing on God's blessed earth shall keep him from returning to claim what is his. If Charles of Burgundy refuses him aid, he'll seek it from Francis of Brittany or John of Aragon . . . and, if need be, from the Grand Vizier of the Ottoman Empire.

'I know my son. He will return . . . and when he faces Warwick across a battlefield, he will prevail.'

'Yes,' Francis said softly. 'I do believe that.' Honesty compelled him to add, 'I have to believe that.'

Cecily looked at him. 'So do I,' she said evenly.

18

Westminster

November 1470

As October yielded to November, the weather took a nasty turn. Snow had begun to fall at dawn on Friday, All Souls' Day, and, by the time Elizabeth Woodville had been delivered of her child, the city was at a standstill, as a storm of unwonted savagery swept the streets of all signs of life and churned the Thames into an icy froth, spreading fears of flooding in the low-lying bankside and driving all but the most foolhardy boatmen to the shelter of tavern and alehouse.

Alison, Lady Scrope of Bolton Castle, was returning to the Jerusalem Chamber in the Abbot's lodging, which lay within the confines of the Benedictine Abbey of St Peter at Westminster. It was here that Elizabeth had sought sanctuary for herself and her children.

Elizabeth had received a warmer welcome than the grudging admittance accorded those unfortunates of lesser rank who came to claim this ancient right of refuge. Thomas Millyng, the Lord Abbot, had received the wife of the exiled Yorkist King as if she were still the consort of a reigning sovereign, turning over his own private quarters for her use. She was far more comfortable than she would otherwise have been but Alison was willing to concede that this was still quite a come-down for a woman accustomed to the splendours of the royal palaces at Westminster, Eltham, Windsor and Shene.

Alison was balancing on a small wooden tray a steaming mug of raspberry-leaf tea. Not that she expected Elizabeth to need its known therapeutic benefits. Alison had seen few births as easy as this one and Marjory Cobb, Elizabeth's midwife, had concurred.

She paused in the doorway. Alison had no liking for the Yorkist Queen; she had agreed to attend her only to accommodate her husband's friend and northern neighbour, the Earl of Warwick. But she acknowledged now that they presented a fetching tableau, the mother with baby nestled at her breast and her oldest daughter, a pretty precocious child not yet five, perched on the foot of the bed, watching with extreme interest as the infant suckled.

How are the mighty fallen, Alison thought, with malicious satisfaction. The woman who'd once eaten only from plate of gold now maintained herself and her children on half a beef and two muttons delivered to her every week by a butcher with Yorkist sympathies and the baskets sent as a charity by the Duchess of York.

Alison was not moved by Elizabeth's plight. It was her opinion that Elizabeth should consider herself thankful that Warwick was a man of honour who scorned to revenge himself upon a woman. Had he not personally requested that she attend Elizabeth during her lying-in? No, Alison felt Warwick had accorded Elizabeth mercies she did not deserve and would never have returned had their positions been reversed.

All in all, Alison and her husband thought their friend had been most magnanimous in the month that he'd exercised power. He'd claimed no blood debts, sought no settlements of old scores. Of course, he'd wasted no time restoring the Chancellorship to his brother, the Archbishop of York, but he'd pardoned the man who'd held the Chancellorship until Edward's fall, Robert Stillington, Bishop of Bath and Wells. Much to Alison's wonderment, Warwick had even agreed to pardon one of Elizabeth's younger brothers. And when parliament was to meet on November twenty-sixth, Alison and her husband knew that Warwick intended to seek only two Bills of Attainder, for Edward of York and his brother, Richard of Gloucester.

Elizabeth looked up as she entered and Alison thought a woman in childbed had no right to look as beautiful as did this woman; it was uncanny, unnatural. Those who spoke of Elizabeth's gilt hair did not exaggerate. It was luxuriant, lustrous, purest silver-blonde in colour, and even now, hanging in disarray about her breasts and shoulders, made one wish to touch it, to see if it were really as soft, as silken as it seemed. Her skin was perfect enough to bear the most critical examination; Alison, not without envy, doubted whether Elizabeth had ever had to cope with the blemishes and freckles that were the lot of her less fortunate sisters. She had a full mouth, sullenly sensual in repose and the high wide brow so prized by minstrels and poets. Only in eye-colour did she fail to satisfy the fashionable standards of their day; china-blue was the most preferred of hues, and Elizabeth's heavy-lidded eyes were cat-green.

Alison knew Elizabeth was in her early thirties, well past a woman's prime, yet she had a body any man would desire, any woman would envy; and no one who saw those full firm breasts would ever have thought she'd been brought to bed of six children. Not for the first time, it occurred to Alison that there might be truth to those tales which held Elizabeth to be one who practised the black arts.

Alison closed the door softly behind her, moved toward the bed. Elizabeth watched in silence; she never bothered to make polite conversation, never addressed Alison at all unless she had some need she wanted met.

Alison had not been witness to Elizabeth's initial response to the devastating news of Doncaster. Rumour had it that she'd at first refused to believe it, stubbornly rejected all evidence brought before her, and continued to do so until she was confronted with a hastily scribbled warning in her husband's own hand. It was said that she'd then given in to hysterics, an emotional outburst so violent that she'd raised fears for the well-being of the child she carried. Her recovery had been rapid enough, however, for her to have thought to take with her into sanctuary all her jewelry and much of her wardrobe.

It had been a fortnight now since Alison had come into the sanctuary, and she sought in vain for cracks in the aloof composure that sealed off from the world whatever pain or fears tormented Elizabeth's private hours. Alison had to admit that the other woman was bearing up remarkably well under the circumstances. Much as it vexed her pride, Alison knew that, were she in Elizabeth's predicament, she'd not have done half as well as this woman she liked so little.

'How does he?' she made herself ask politely. What a pity this child must be a boy! How much simpler it would have been had she given birth to yet another daughter.

'He sleeps now.' Elizabeth glanced down at the small head pillowed on her breast. The corners of her mouth curved upward, as if in secret satisfaction of a pleasure too sweet to share.

'Tell me, Lady Scrope, do you not think it an omen that my son should be born here . . . in the Jerusalem Chamber?'

Seeing Alison's lack of comprehension, she smiled. 'It was in this very chamber, was it not, that the first of the Lancastrian Kings died? Do you not find the contrast striking, a Lancastrian death and a Yorkist birth?'

Alison had no intention of being trapped in a pointless political discussion. 'I know nothing of omens, Madame,' she said brusquely. 'Nurse Cobb will be back directly she has supped. May I do anything for you?'

'As it happens, you can. I have asked Abbot Thomas to stand as godfather.' Elizabeth was stroking the cheek of the sleeping child, all the while watching Alison. 'Will you act as godmother to my son, Lady Scrope?'

Alison was too surprised to hide it. She knew Elizabeth was well aware of her animosity. She looked from Elizabeth to the small wrinkled bundle Elizabeth held, swathed in folds of white linen. He had a surprisingly thick thatch of hair but so light in colour that at first glance he looked bald. He was awake and kneading with tiny pink fingers the soft warm flesh he found within his grasp.

'Yes . . . yes I will,' Alison said at last, and Elizabeth inclined her head, as if there were nothing extraordinary in either the offer or the acceptance.

'Why cannot I be godmother?' Bess demanded, and pouted when Elizabeth said, 'You're too young, sweet.'

Alison reached down to fondle the child's flaxen hair. She'd grown fond of Bess, for all that she talked incessantly of her father. She'd been his pet and in this strange cramped world she now occupied, it was his absence she found hardest to accept or understand.

Now she leaned closer to peer at her brother, and then asked, with the candour peculiar to very young children, 'Will papa still love me now he has a son?'

Alison was touched, but Elizabeth said composedly, 'Yes, Bess. You are his firstborn and that is special in itself.'

'What will we name him, Mama?'

Elizabeth looked from her son to Alison.

'He shall be christened Edward . . . Prince Edward of England. And in time, Bess, he shall be titled as Prince of Wales, as befitting the heir to England's crown.'

'That is a title which belongs, by rights, to the son of His Grace, King Henry,' Alison said coolly.

But in a darkened corner of her mind, she cried out in protest that she, Lady Scrope of Bolton Castle, should have to proclaim a Frenchwoman's bastard son as England's king-to-be; that for Warwick, whom they did love, she and her John must accept Lancaster, whom they did not.

'The son of the French whore? He's no son to Harry and all do know it. But even if the Lord God Almighty were to declare him a true-born son of Lancaster, it matters little.'

Elizabeth raised the squirming child, held him up as he began to wail. 'Here is the heir of England . . . my son.'

'You take considerable risk in speaking so,' Alison said slowly, as she sought to keep her temper in check. 'The Earl of Warwick will not take punitive measures against you for your rash talk. But I would caution you, Madame. When Marguerite d'Anjou is once more in England, she'll brook no such claims as you make now. Such defiance will cost you dear.'

Elizabeth guided the whimpering child's mouth to her breast. 'You do know my husband, Lady Scrope. Do you truly think he will be content to keep to Burgundy whilst Warwick rules England? My husband?'

She laughed and Alison decided that if her amusement was not genuine, she was a gifted actress.

'And when Edward is once more in England, he'll brook no such claims as you make now,' Elizabeth echoed mockingly, and Alison flushed.

It was only with a conscious effort that she reminded herself this woman had given birth but hours before; reminded herself, too, of the innocent presence of Edward's daughter, rapt at mention of her father's name.

Elizabeth leaned back against the pillow. 'Prince Edward of England,' she said recklessly, and smiled. 'And you may tell Warwick what I said . . . word for word.'

19

Amboise, France

December 1470

Anne Neville and Prince Edouard of Lancaster were distant cousins, as his great-grandfather, Henry IV, and her great-grand-mother, Joan Beaufort, were brother and sister. It was necessary, therefore, to secure a papal dispensation before they could wed. An understanding was reached between Warwick and his friend, Louis of France. As Warwick sailed for England, the French King exercised his renowned powers of persuasion upon a merchant of Tours, who prudently agreed to advance the gold needed for an appeal to the Holy See.

On July 25th, the betrothal of the Houses of Lancaster and Neville had been solemnized in the Cathedral of Angers, sworn on the blessed Cross of St Laud d'Angers. Since then, the Earl's wife and daughters had resided in the household of Marguerite d'Anjou at Amboise, in central France.

At Amboise, they'd learned of Warwick's success in winning over his disgruntled unhappy brother; learned of John's *volte-face*, which had driven their cousins of York into exile; learned, too, of Warwick's triumphal entry into London. And, at Amboise word had reached them that a dispensation for the wedding had been secured from the Patriarch of Jerusalem. On this Thursday, the thirteenth of December, the Grand Vicar of Bayeux was to wed the seventeen-year-old Lancastrian prince to the younger daughter of the Earl of Warwick.

Isabel Neville had risen at dawn to hear Mass in the Queen's Chapel and now she and her ladies were returning to her chambers to dress for the wedding ceremony to be held at noon. Isabel was only three months beyond her nineteenth birthday, yet she leaned heavily upon the arm of a solicitous attendant and she had to pause repeatedly as they mounted the stone stairway.

More than seven months had passed since she'd gone into labour aboard ship in the harbour at Calais but she had yet to recover her health. Always slender, she was thin now, dangerously so, and her pallor was so pronounced that even her future brother-in-law had noticed and suggested she consult a physician. She had no appetite, no energy and, when she rose in the mornings, the hazel eyes were dulled, shadow-smudged.

Lord Wenlock, the Deputy Governor of Calais, was a friend of long standing and Warwick had anticipated cooperation or, at the least, neutrality. But Calais was so honeycombed with Edward's agents that Wenlock dared not give entry to a declared enemy of the crown and, as their ship wallowed sickeningly in heavy swells, Isabel had been brought to birth of her child.

She'd been in labour for fully a day and night, with only her mother and Anne to attend her; with no hot water, no camomile oil or rue plant, not even egg whites. At the last, Wenlock had heeded Warwick's desperate pleas and dispatched two casks of wine for Isabel, but the wine could neither numb her pain nor save her child.

The baby, a son, was stillborn and, when Isabel began to haemorrhage, it seemed certain that she, too, would die. When the bleeding ceased, they could only attribute it to the divine mercy of the Blessed Mother Mary; and, as Isabel lay delirious, her mother and sister washed the infant, wrapped him in a white blanket and prayed as the small body was lowered into the sea.

There'd been a time when Isabel had seen herself as Queen of England. Under her father's tutelage, she was encouraged to entertain visions of a truly dazzling future. Ned had shown himself unworthy to be King. He would be deposed and George would be crowned. She would rule as his consort, would be loved by the people as Elizabeth Woodville never was. Life would once more be sweet, as in the days before her father's quarrel with her cousin shadowed the happiness she'd once so innocently accepted as her birthright.

As beautiful as this dream had been, it had proven to be no more substantial than the soap bubbles Isabel had so delighted in playing with as a small child. Reality was a frantic midnight flight aboard ship at Exeter. Reality was the tiny bundle buried at sea, the baby she'd never even seen. Reality was a sickbed at Honfleur in Normandy, when the French midwife summoned to nurse her bluntly expressed doubts that she would ever carry a child to full term. Reality was the plight-troth of her sister Anne to the heir of Lancaster, an alliance that had transformed her married life into a hell of recrimination and accusation. Her embittered husband had turned upon her the resentment he dare not voice to her father and, by the time his fury was tempered by the realization that her disappointment was as keen as his own, the damage had been done.

She was in extremely low spirits this morning, plagued by fatigue, back pain and a particularly severe headache. She'd slept little that night, thinking of the dismal future she faced at a Lancastrian court, thinking of the marriage that would make Anne Princess of Wales and, one day, Queen of England ... if their father prevailed. And on this icy December day, with Edward of York a penniless fugitive and her father in unchallenged command of England, there was no reason for Isabel to doubt that he would indeed prevail.

'*Madame la Duchesse! Votre soeur, la Princesse Anne* ...'

It was some moments before Isabel was able to understand. Her command of French was fair and improving daily, but the girl was excited, rattling on breathlessly at an incomprehensible speed.

'Sweet Blood of Christ!' she swore when she did understand, and those of her attendants who knew enough of her language to appreciate English oaths exchanged surreptitious smiles of amused speculation. It would be a scandal of delightful proportions if the English girl was truly refusing to wed Prince Edouard.

Isabel briefly considered alerting her mother and then decided against it. Anne was no closer to their mother than she herself was. The confines of the Countess of Warwick's world were circumscribed by the breath and blood of her lord husband. As far back as Isabel could remember, it had been so, and she did not think her lady mother was likely to be of assistance now.

Anne's chamber was cold; neither the Flemish wall arras nor a heated brazier could withstand the chill. Yet Anne was clad only in a kirtle of cream-coloured silk, sitting before the pier glass, surrounded by an impressive array of perfumes, rose water, and cosmetics: kohl and belladonna for the eyes, ceruse to whiten the skin, red ochre lip rouge, marigold balm.

Her sister was not alone; another girl was leaning over her. She looked up quickly as Isabel entered, and Isabel recognized Véronique de Crécy, one of the young Frenchwomen who'd been chosen to attend Anne. This particular girl was only a few years older than Anne, and they seemed to have developed a degree of intimacy during these four months at Amboise.

'Anne? Why are you not dressing? You've less than three hours.'

Anne continued to stare into the pier glass.

'Go away, Isabel,' she said dully.

Isabel waved the French girl aside, stepped closer to her sister. 'I was told you dismissed your ladies. . . . Is that true? Anne, look at me! What nonsense is this?' Seeing she had Anne's unwilling attention, she continued coldly, 'Surely you are not going to give us yet another tearful display of self-pity?'

'I cannot do this, Isabel,' Anne whispered. 'I cannot.'

'You will, though, and we both do know it. We've been over this till there cannot possibly be anything left unsaid. Our father's future depends upon this marriage. He has given his word to the French King. He must have French support . . . and this marriage is the price he must pay for that support. You know that, Anne.'

'The price *he* must pay?' Anne sounded incredulous. 'As I see it, *I* am the one who must pay. I am the one who must wed with Lancaster, wed a man I despise.'

'Watch your tongue,' Isabel cautioned. 'Such things are not safe to say.'

'But true, nonetheless.' Anne turned away from the mirror to look imploringly at Isabel. 'Isabel, all my life I've been taught to hate Lancaster. They killed our grandfather, our uncle Tom, our cousin Edmund. How can I forget that?'

'You have no choice,' Isabel said, so implacably that Anne slammed a small fist down on the cluttered side table, sending phials and jars careening into each other. 'Jesú, Isabel, can you not understand how I feel? Will you not even try?'

Anne shivered and Véronique came forward, draping a dressing robe across her shoulders. Isabel hesitated and then picked up an ivory comb.

'Come, now, and I will help you with your hair.'

Anne jerked her head away, however, and Isabel snapped, 'Must I say it again? You have no choice!'

'So you keep telling me,' Anne said bitterly. 'It seems I gave up all choice when I followed our father into French exile. Well, today, I would to God I had not! I would to God I'd never left England!'

'You talk like such a child, Anne. You know you could not have remained in England. You'd have found few friends willing to aid the daughter of a declared traitor.'

'No?' Anne said stubbornly, and Isabel lost all patience.

'You mean to imply, I suppose, that you could always have appealed to our cousin of Gloucester?' She shook her head in disgust. 'You seem to forget, Sister, that Dickon did not want you.'

Anne's dark eyes were burning like charcoal against the chalk-whiteness of her face. 'Why do you hate me?'

'You know I do not.'

'Yes, you do,' Anne insisted. 'Ever since Father compelled this betrothal, you've been different toward me . . . as if it were my fault, somehow. It's not fair to blame me because he bypassed George. This is none of my choosing. Dear God, you know that! I never wanted to be wife to Lancaster . . . never. I would rather be dead,' she concluded, so passionately that Isabel was moved in spite of herself.

'It is not as bad as that, Anne,' she said with a sigh. 'You must try to remember. . . . As his wife, you'll be Queen of England one day.'

'I do not want to be Queen of England!'

Isabel stared at her. 'You are truly a fool then,' she said at last.

'No,' Anne said, in a tight flat voice that sounded like the voice of a stranger, not Anne's voice at all. 'No, I am a commodity. I was sold to Lancaster for a price, as one would barter a cloak or a gold pendant.'

This was indeed what was being said, even at the jaded French court, and Isabel well knew it.

'You must not say things like that,' she chided, without conviction. She was tired, very tired. She supposed she should feel sorry for her sister but it was hard, so very hard, to summon up pity, to feel any emotion at all. She'd achieved her objective, quenched Anne's last feeble attempt at rebellion, but she could take no pleasure in it. Tears had begun silently to streak Anne's face. Isabel had known it would end like this, end in Anne's tears. It always did.

'I will summon your other ladies so you may dress,' she said.

Anne didn't seem to have heard. The tears were coming faster now. She wrapped her arms around herself, rocked back and forth. In appearance she was still more child than woman; only in the past year had her slender girl's body begun to round and soften, to take on the curves and contours of a woman, and she still had a way to go. Isabel bit her lip. She did not want to think of that, did not want to see her sister's tears. There was nothing she could do. Nothing.

She bent down, brushed her lips against Anne's wet cheek. 'I'll send your ladies to you,' she said softly. She didn't wait for Anne's response. Knew none would be forthcoming. But Anne would allow herself to be dressed in the bridal silk laid out on the bed. She would wed Lancaster. Isabel raised her hand to aching temples; the light blurred and danced before her eyes. Their father, she thought, would be pleased.

As she stepped out into the corridor, however, the door opened behind her, almost at once.

'Why are you not attending to the Lady Anne, Véronique?'

'She is fearful, Madame; can you not see that? Can you not understand?'

'You presume,' Isabel said icily, not at all pleased by the realization that the French girl understood far more English than she'd surmised.

'I care, Madame,' the girl persisted audaciously. 'The Lady Anne is my friend. Could you not be kind to her, this day of all days? She has need of you now. Could you not remember that she is but fourteen years of age, a virgin maid, to be wed to a man she neither likes nor trusts. . . .'

Isabel cut her off with a gesture. 'I cannot help that,' she said drearily, wondering why she was standing there explaining herself to this impertinent French girl.

'Anne is my sister. I take no pleasure in her unhappiness, I assure you. But in this world we must do what is expected of us. Anne is a Neville; she must act as a Neville.'

Véronique had a challenging direct gaze that found no favour with Isabel, which provoked her into snapping cynically, 'Moreover, I see not why Anne is to be pitied. There are worse fates than to be Queen of England.'

Isabel was turning away as Véronique said, very low and very fast, 'But I'd have thought that you, of all women, would have compassion for her plight. You, after all, were fortunate enough to wed the man of your choice, Madame.'

Isabel opened her mouth to deliver a stinging rebuke and heard herself say, 'Yes, it was my choice, was it not? It truly was. . . .'

Astonished by her own words, she was even more astonished when she began to laugh. Sobering with an effort, she met the other girl's eyes. They were hazel like her own and, to her fury, had in them a hint of pity.

'I believe I bade you to attend to my sister, Véronique. Why do you tarry then? Make her fair for Lancaster; he will expect as much.'

20

Bruges Burgundy

December 1470

For the first time in his life, Rob Percy dreaded the coming of Christmas. As a youngster, he'd begun anticipating the Yuletide revelries as early as Martinmas. His family celebrated the holiday in the Yorkshire fashion and the days from St Nicholas Day until Epiphany were bright with banqueting, gift-giving, mummeries and the allegorical morality plays performed in the churches of York in which Virtue triumphed over Vice, but only at the last possible moment.

But there would be scant joy in this Christmas for the English exiles in Bruges. Their credit was well nigh exhausted; their debts were large enough to stir both antagonism and alarm around the merchants of the city. It was true that the Duke of Burgundy was reluctantly providing his brother-in-law of York with a monthly stipend, and may the Almighty bless her Grace the Duchess Margaret for that, Rob thought fervently.

But five hundred crowns a month would only go so far and Rob wondered how long Edward could impose upon the hospitality of the Seigneur de la Gruuthuse. Gruuthuse had proven to be that rarest of men, the friend who sticketh closer than a brother. But Gruuthuse was also a subject of the Duke of Burgundy and, when Charles first heard that Edward had landed at Texel, he snapped, 'I would rather have been told that he was dead.'

Leaving the inn where he and a score of his companions were lodged, Rob sighed with relief at having made it out to the street without encountering their disgruntled landlord. The man's demands for payment were becoming increasingly truculent; Rob knew all that stood between them and eviction was the innkeeper's reluctance to resort to violence during Advent. Rob had been aware for some weeks that time served Warwick, not York.

He took his usual shortcut through the churchyard of Saint Salvator's Cathedral, which led him out onto Groote Herjlig Geest Straete; even after two months in Burgundy, that was still too much of a mouthful for Rob. He envied Richard for his friend's French was fluent enough to bridge that guttural gap between English and Flemish. But Rob had no ear at all for languages. At Middleham, none had learned how to wield a broadsword more lethally than he but he'd never mastered French, was utterly baffled by Latin and, when confronted now with Flemish, felt as if his tongue were tied in knots.

Rob quickened his pace. December was no month to be about in Bruges; the wind was unrelenting and the canals clogged with ice. He clutched his cloak more firmly about his throat; it was much mended, and he shivered as a sudden blast of icy air almost pulled it from his grasp. His fractured French troubled him nowhere near as much as the empty purse that hung from his belt.

Ahead, he saw the soaring spire of Onze Lieve Vrouwkert or, as the French-speaking citizens called it, Eglise Notre-Dame. Rob always thought of it as the Church of Our Lady. It was the tallest church he'd ever seen, loftier even than St Paul's Cathedral, and towered far above all the buildings in its shadow, even the magnificent mansion known as Herenhuis Gruuthuse.

Each time he saw the Gruuthuse palace the irony struck Rob anew, that his Yorkist lords should be so hard-pressed for money whilst dwelling in a manor house as splendid as a ducal residence. Trust King Edward to find himself a friend as rich as Croesus, he thought now, and lucky it was, for had they to live on the largesse of his tight-fisted brother-in-law, they'd be in a tangled coil for certes. And might be yet.

Rob entered the courtyard of Herenhuis Gruuthuse. He was recognized on sight now by the Gruuthuse household and was permitted to pass unchallenged. The entrance hall never failed to impress him, with its high wooden-beamed ceiling, dazzling white marble stairway and brightly patterned tile floor. In spite of himself, Rob thought of the dank airless room he shared with four of his fellow fugitives, a bed stuffed with straw and vermin, with chinks in the wall through which he could pass his hand were he so minded.

He was at once shamed by the thought; it had never before been in his nature to envy others. It was this damnable Christmas season, he decided; it rubbed the nerves raw. Taking the marble stairs two at a time, he was admitted to the chamber of the Duke of Gloucester by Thomas Parr. Richard wasn't there but he was in no hurry, was quite willing to pass the time with the young Yorkshireman who'd served as his friend's squire for as long as he could remember.

He knew Richard had been meeting that afternoon with several English merchants newly come from Calais, in hopes of securing a loan on his brother's behalf, and he now asked Thomas quietly, 'How went things with His Grace today?'

Thomas shook his head but, at that moment, Richard came through the doorway and it was he who answered the question Rob had discreetly directed at Thomas.

'None too well, Rob. . . . Fair words, and those in plenty, but no more than that.'

After an awkward pause, Rob ventured consolingly, 'Well, if they speak so kindly of His Grace, they may yet decide to advance him the gold we need. . . .'

'Aye, and if wishes were horses, beggars would ride,' Richard said tersely. 'Are you ready, Rob? Tom, you need not wait on me. I expect to be quite late.'

*

294

After hearing Vespers in the Gruuthuse pew at Notre-Dame Cathedral, the boys exited onto Den Dijver. December dusk was settling over the city, the air crisp and very cold. Knowing the Gruuthuse stables were at Richard's disposal, but knowing, too, how reluctant his friend was to accept favours he might never be able to repay, Rob suggested none too hopefully, 'Shall we go back for horses, Dickon?'

Richard shook his head. 'No, let's walk, Rob.'

Richard remembered little of those unhappy months he'd spent in Bruges and Utrecht as an eight-year-old fugitive from Lancastrian vengeance. Seeing Bruges now as an adult, he'd fallen at once under the spell of this walled city crisscrossed with canals and arched stone bridges. The streets were cobbled and far cleaner than those of London. Gardens flourished for much of the year, and the houses of the citizenry were substantial structures of brick and stone, with multicoloured slate roofs which shone in the sun in silvery hues of green and blue and bright hot shades of red. Swans vied with small craft for the right-of-way on the canals; scores of windmills, a novelty to Richard, silhouetted the city skyline and, even in his present frame of mind, Richard was able to derive a degree of pleasure from his surroundings.

Rob, who was blind to beauty in all but women, was still wishing Richard had chosen to ride. Unlike London, Bruges had no ordinance requiring street lanterns to be hung and dark was rapidly descending. He dropped his hand to the hilt of his sword as they crossed the bridge spanning the Dijver Rei and turned into Wolle Straete, for several men were staggering from a tavern just ahead and more than a few of the Yorkists had been bloodied in street brawls or in fending off would-be robbers. The men passed them without incident, though, and he relaxed somewhat, for they were entering the torch-lit square, known as the Grote Markt, the site of tournament jousting, market trading, and public executions,

Above the covered market called the Hallen rose the graceful silhouette of the Belfort. It was now chiming the hour, in melodic warning that the nine city gates were closing for the night. Two of the uniformed scadebelleters of the city watch were posted at the belfry doorway; another stood guard over the lone wretched man imprisoned in the wooden pillory, the leather purse dangling from his neck giving evidence to the crime of theft. He moaned as they passed by, mumbling a plea in the guttural Flemish that eluded Rob so completely.

'What does he say, d'you think?' he speculated, and Richard, who'd not even glanced at the prisoner, shrugged.

'Who knows?' he said without interest, and pointed left down Saint Amands Straete, toward a lighted doorway.

'Shall we stop for wine?'

The Gulden Vlies was small and rather shabby, but the innkeeper spoke English and his inn had quickly become a favourite meeting place for the homesick English exiles. Edward himself had, on occasion, forsaken the princely hospitality of the Herenhuis Gruuthuse for the more dubious pleasures of the Gulden Vlies.

Rob acquiesced with enthusiasm and, after exchanging a few pleasantries and a few coins with the innkeeper, they found themselves seated alone at a corner table. The common room was not yet crowded and Rob failed to find a familiar face. He was disappointed for he did not feel comfortable midst so many foreigners.

Bruges was the commercial centre of Europe and merchants from the Italian city-states and Spanish kingdoms mingled freely with traders of the Holy Roman Empire and the Hanseatic League. Tonight, though, Rob would have welcomed even the presence of the English merchants who'd so far kept a prudent distance from their Yorkist countrymen. But for the moment, at least, he and Richard appeared to be the only English-speaking patrons in the inn.

Rob drained his wine cup, far too swiftly for one who hadn't eaten since noon. But Richard was already signalling to the serving maid and this time she left a flagon on their table.

Rob debated telling Richard about the troubles with his landlord, decided against it. Richard had already made one trip to see the man, promised to assume personal responsibility for all the debts his men incurred. Unfortunately, the promise of one under sentence of death in his own land carried less and less weight as the debts mounted.

Rob glanced pensively at his companion. He knew Richard was as unhappy as he was and he would have liked to talk about it but he did not know how. Richard had never been one to share his innermost thoughts and Rob was unaccustomed himself to expressing emotion in words. He'd never before felt the need to confide in others, to confess his fears for the future. But then, he'd never been in exile before, either.

It occurred to him that it made no sense that he and Richard could risk death together and yet not be able to confess to homesickness or fear. . . . But there it was. He drank again, broodingly. With his other companions, pride compelled him to adopt a bravura posture, as if the loss of family and home were well worth the sacrifice if honour be saved. With Richard, though, he should be able to speak the truth and he was frustrated and discontented because he could not.

'Do you think much of home, Rob?'

He looked up quickly. Richard was giving him the chance he wanted. He need only say the words that burned so bitter on his tongue . . . but he found he could not do it. Habit was too strong, his nonchalant pose too familiar. He was silenced above all by a question, a question that was never far from his conscious awareness these cheerless December days. Had he fully realized just what foreign exile would mean, would he still have chosen to sail with Dickon and Edward to Burgundy?

In the chaos that was Doncaster and in the frantic flight that followed, there'd been little time to think clearly. Edward was his sovereign and Dickon his friend. How could he do otherwise than share their fate?

Now, however, he was confronted with the shabby realities of exile, with hostile Flemings and no money and the dawning real-ization that he might never see England again, that he might end up having to sell his sword to one of the princes of the Italian city-states. Now he could no longer be sure what he would have done at Doncaster. But nothing on earth could have induced him to admit that to Richard.

'Oh, at times, I do,' he said carelessly, and grinned. 'But it's not as if we'll not soon be returning. And, till then, there are many ways a man may pleasure himself here in Bruges.'

Richard regarded him with unreadable dark eyes. 'To pleasure, then,' he said and raised his wine cup, touching it to Rob's in mock salute.

Rob scanned the room again, searching in vain for English faces. His eyes flickered over the Flemings and Italians, returned to a girl poised on the stairway that led to the upper chambers. She had hair like wheat, a painted red mouth and a low-cut bodice that barely contained its bounty. Intercepting his stare, she smiled and gestured in a communication that needed no translation.

Rob returned the smile. Her name was Annecke, and he'd not found his lack of Flemish or her lack of English to be more than an inconvenience on the two occasions past when he'd shared her bed above stairs. In London the brothels were licensed and confined to the more disreputable areas of the city, but the pros-titutes of Bruges often kept rooms in those inns where they were most likely to find willing customers, a practice Rob found both convenient and sensible.

He made no move to rise, however, and reluctantly with-drawing his eyes from Annecke's highly visible charms, he saw that Richard, too, had noticed the girl.

'My compliments upon your taste, Rob. . . . It's improving.'

Rob laughed. 'You do not miss much, do you?'

'I'd hope not. But I'd suggest you act before her attentions are otherwise engaged.'

Rob shrugged, saying nothing.

Richard hesitated, as if weighing his words, and then unfastened a leather pouch from his belt, spilling coins out onto the table. Separating them into two approximately equal piles, he shoved half across the table toward Rob.

'It almost slipped my mind. . . . I owe you for our last game of Tables.'

When Rob didn't touch the money, Richard said softly, 'For God's sake, Rob, do not deny me this much, at least.'

Rob needed no further urging, reached for the coins. 'I know of no reason why you should think yourself indebted to me, Dickon. But I am rather short and I'll accept this . . . as a loan. Agreed?'

Richard nodded. 'Now go on with you. She'll not wait on you for long.'

'You're sure? I should not like to leave you alone. . . .'

'Jesú, do I need a nursemaid? Moreover, with luck, I'll not be alone for long.'

Rob grinned and pushed the bench back. 'For God and York!' he said, and Richard laughed.

Richard poured himself a full cup, hoping the wine would warm. He was accustomed to the bitter winters of Yorkshire, but he was not accustomed to being without fur-lined jackets and heavy travelling cloaks. But his pride had so far prevented him from asking Gruuthuse for yet another loan; they were already so deeply indebted to the Lord of Bruges that Richard wondered how they could ever possibly repay him.

Setting the cup down, he slid the candle toward him. Within its faltering light, he withdrew from his doublet a neatly folded linen handkerchief, which he carefully unwrapped to reveal a packet of well-worn letters.

The top paper was smudged and bore the seal of the Duchess of York. His mother's letter was brief, characteristically concise and to the point. She recounted, without comment, that Warwick now styled himself as King's Lieutenant of the Realm, that he was once more Captain of Calais, Lord Admiral and Great Chamberlain. Warwick had as yet taken no reprisals against Yorkist supporters but, when parliament met, both Richard and Edward had been attainted. Edward had been declared a usurper and John Neville had been compelled to make public apology for having stayed loyal to Edward as long as he did.

At that, Richard felt a familiar ache. Are you happy now, Johnny? He very much doubted it.

John, she wrote, had not been restored to the earldom of Northumberland, but Warwick had taken from Henry Percy the office of Warden of the East Marches toward Scotland and given it back to his brother. This, Richard had already known; Edward was in secret correspondence with Percy, doing his best to foster those suspicions that must surely be festering in Percy's mind, asking Percy how long he thought he'd keep his earldom once Warwick had consolidated his power enough to feel secure.

Brother George had been restored to his former post as Lord Lieutenant of Ireland. He had also been named as Lancaster's heir should Prince Edouard and Anne Neville have no children, and he was given the right to lay claim to the duchy of York, as the eldest born legitimate son of the late lord Duke of York. Cecily added laconically that she'd received a message from George in which he'd begged her pardon for the parliamentary act that branded her as an adulteress. George claimed that it was Warwick who thus slurred her name and none of his doing.

Knowing his mother as he did, Richard read volumes into the single slash of black ink which underlined the word *legitimate*. Nor was he surprised that George had not dared to face her after this latest outrage. He was discovering that, as his own troubles mounted, he was less and less inclined to take a charitable view of George's follies.

He resumed reading, even though he knew the words by heart. Edward's infant son was doing well, as were the boy's sisters. Richard grinned at this; not a mention made of the children's mother, her daughter-in-law. London was quiet; waiting, she said, for whatever was to come. But for now, they'd accepted Lancaster.

Only in the last sentence did she permit emotion to surface and, even then, under considerable constraint. 'Our cause is just, Richard, and will prevail. My dear son, you must not despair.'

The opening paragraphs of the letter from Francis were stilted, marred by crossed-out words and the ink blots of a hesitant pen. What does one say, after all, to a friend in exile? Their boyhood lessons in the social graces did not cover that subject, Richard thought, with a flicker of black humour.

But Francis soon found his stride. He described Warwick's entry into London. 'As prideful as a peacock.' A reference to George had been thought better of and was carefully inked out. But, with an acid pen, he brought Harry of Lancaster, whom Richard had never seen, vividly to life in the pages of his letter; the long greying hair lying limply over the collar of Edward's blue robe, the untroubled eyes of a child, his wobbling in the saddle like a sackful of straw.

England's King, Richard thought, with wonderment and a fair measure of bitterness. Warwick must be as mad as Harry.

Francis had reported, too, and here a hint of genuine pity coloured his narrative, that it was said Harry had scribbled on the wall of his Tower chamber, 'Royalty is only care.'

Richard rapidly scanned the rest of the now-familiar letter. He was amused by Francis's mock expression of regret that they had found it necessary to take a sea voyage for their health, and he was touched by Francis's concluding confession, that he was hard put to wait for spring, when the white rose would once more be in season.

Not for the first time since his mother's courier had brought him the letters, Richard thought, Christ keep Francis if this be his notion of discretion. He set the letters down to refill his cup and emptied it again before he picked up the third letter.

This letter was not as creased and frayed as the other two; it had arrived only the day before from Aire, in Artois, where his sister Margaret was in residence. Margaret's letter was stubbornly cheerful, almost fiercely optimistic; just as Margaret herself had been during their brief reunion at Aire soon after he and Edward arrived in Bruges.

Margaret expressed confidence that Charles would soon see fit to give them a more princely sum than the five hundred crowns she'd wangled from him to help defray their expenses. She glossed over the fact that Charles had once again refused to meet with them, and said nothing at all about the continued presence at his court of the Dukes of Somerset and Exeter, men as dedicated to the cause of Lancaster as Marguerite d'Anjou herself.

She told Richard that Saint-Quentin, which had been besieged by the French since December tenth, had finally fallen. She confided that she had received a letter from England, from one whose welfare was dear to them both, from one who was realizing the folly of having heeded Warwick's honeyed words. She would relate more on this subject when next she saw him. But he should not make mention of this to Ned, not yet.

She had no other news to report, other than that Marguerite d'Anjou still tarried in France, delaying departure for England once again. . . . How little she must trust Warwick! She was in Paris now, having left Amboise within the past week, accompanied by her son and his wife, for he'd finally wed Warwick's daughter on December thirteenth. The Countess of Warwick was with them, too, and George's wife, who was said to be ailing.

Richard read no further, replaced the letters in his doublet. He hadn't misled Rob; he'd not minded being left alone. In fact, he'd welcomed the solitude. As Gruuthuse's houseguest, he had to ride his emotions with a tight rein, knowing that an offhand remark made in an unguarded moment might give rise to rumour that could be exploited by Lancaster.

But he was finding that his solitude was illusory. He was surrounded by phantoms who sat at the table with him and shared his wine flagon and mocked him with memories that served no purpose but to inflict pain. And so, when he felt a light touch on his arm and looked up into sea-green eyes that offered to share far more than the companionship being offered so demurely, green eyes to banish the most stubborn spirit, he welcomed the intrusion with genuine relief.

She settled herself beside him with a self-possession that belied her age, which he judged to be close to his own, and, for a time, kept his ghosts at bay with an animated cascade of questions.

He was English, no? He spoke French better than most of his countrymen; had he spent time in France, perhaps? Yes, she would like wine, or ale, if he'd as lief have that. She herself spoke French and Flemish equally well. . . . She was from the capital, Dijon, but had lived here in Bruges since she was fourteen. She spoke some German, too, and even a little Italian. . . . Where had she learned them? Could he not guess? . . . In bed, of course!

Had he been long in Bruges? He had not the look of a merchant. . . . Was he, perhaps, in the service of the exiled prince who was brother to their duchess? Yes, she thought as much! Did he think he would soon be returning to England?

'I would to God I knew,' Richard confessed morosely, and washed his words down with wine. When he raised the cup again, she leaned over, catching his hand. Her fingers slid along his wrist, under the cuff of his doublet, her nails lightly scraping the skin on his forearm.

'Softly, sweet, softly,' she smiled coaxingly. 'If you've a need to forget I can offer you more than wine.'

Her hair was long and straight, a firelight brown shot through with gold and deep glints of copper, and caught the candlelight as he fanned it through his fingers.

'The colour of darkest honey,' he said admiringly. 'All russet and gold like autumn leaves.'

She laughed, moving closer on the bench. 'I thought you English were partial to flaxen hair,' she teased. Blue eyes and golden hair

. . . Was that not the measure of beauty in England? She'd often wished she had sunlit hair like her friend Annecke. . . . But at least she had light eyes; some girls were unfortunate enough to have eyes of brown . . . verily like gypsies.

She'd long ago learned to read the moods of men and she saw at once that she'd somehow blundered. Loosening his hold on her hair, he let it slip through his fingers and reached for the wine flagon.

'Yes, brown eyes are unlucky,' he agreed tonelessly.

'Your thoughts are straying again, Richar',' she chided, reclaiming his hand.

'Richard,' he corrected, giving his name the English pronunciation and then smiling at her appealing attempt to anglicize French vowels,

'What would my name be in your language?'

He hesitated, not remembering, and was reprieved when she entreated, 'Marie-Elise . . . Say it in English?'

'Mary . . . Mary Eliza,' he translated, and she burst out laughing, mouthing the unfamiliar words with infectious amusement.

'How queer that sounds! I much prefer Marie.' She reached under the table to tug at her skirts and her hand brushed his leg, came to rest on his thigh.

'Yes, Marie is kinder to the ear,' he agreed. 'And softer to the touch. . . .'

She moved under his caress and he wrapped her hair around his hand, drawing her toward him until their mouths all but touched. He could feel her breath, warm and shallow, on his neck and, when he kissed her, she responded with practised passion, prolonging the embrace until he grew careless of time and place.

'I have a room above stairs,' she whispered, resting her hands on his chest and toying with a pendant he wore about his neck; on impulse, he drew the chain over his head and fastened it around her throat.

'For me?' Fingering it with amazed delight. 'You are too generous!'

It occurred to him that she was probably right; the way his luck was going lately, he'd have done better to hold on to the pendant. It had no real value but the day might yet be coming when he'd need to pawn it.

He laughed shortly and then shook his head at her questioning look. 'Never mind, sweet. . . . 'Tis a private jest, and like most such jests, sadly lacking in humour.'

'I do not understand, *chéri*,' she confessed, with an uncertain smile.

'I'll explain it to you above stairs.' As he rose, the wine made itself felt. Pleasantly light-headed, he fumbled for coins while she reached for the candle, murmuring,

'Do you wish to bring a flagon with us?'

'No, only you . . . only Marie-Elise and Mary Eliza.'

She giggled and stumbled, swaying against him so provocatively that he turned, took her in his arms, and kissed her again.

As he released her, a voice said, very close at hand, 'I've been scouring the city for you but I wonder if you'll forgive me for having found you!'

Richard spun around. 'Ned?' Incredulously, and then flatly, 'This is a surprise.'

Fighting laughter and losing, Edward glanced at the girl clinging possessively to Richard's arm. 'Yes, I daresay it is!'

The inkeeper was hovering anxiously in the background, so obsequiously eager to please that Richard knew Edward had been recognized. A flustered serving maid was hurrying toward them with a platter of manchet bread and spermyse cheese, far above the usual quality of food served in the tavern, and the innkeeper himself poured their wine, while surreptitiously wiping the dust from the table with his sleeve.

As Edward bantered with his companions, bidding them to 'Debauch yourselves whilst I speak with my brother,' Richard

305

reclaimed his seat, none too happy to be the focus of all eyes of a sudden. Drawing the sulky Marie down beside him, he was mollifying her with murmured promises as Edward finally succeeded in dismissing the inkeeper.

'You've time for a drink, I trust, Dickon,' he queried, with a malicious solicitude that did not improve Richard's humour.

'If you wish,' he agreed ungraciously.

'I gather you had no luck with the Calais merchants?'

Richard's irritation ebbed, to be replaced with a numbing weariness. 'No . . . I'm sorry, Ned.'

Edward shook his head. 'Do not be. I expected as much.'

With an effort, Richard forced animation into his voice.

'I had another letter from Meg yesterday. She seems most hopeful that she can persuade Charles to open his coffers to us.'

'And how many ships can we man with hope, Dickon?' Edward asked pleasantly.

Richard stared at him. This was the closest Edward had yet come to conceding that aid from Charles might not be forthcoming. It chilled him to hear his own fears so unexpectedly expressed aloud, but he rallied and said gamely, 'I've never yet known Meg not to have her way. If Charles dared refuse us, she'd make his life one merry hell and he knows it.'

'You put too much faith in Meg, Dickon. You've yet to learn that women generally play a very small role in the scheme of things.'

'Women seem to play a very large role in your scheme of things.' Richard jibed but his banter rang hollow, even to him, and he abandoned further pretence. 'You know Meg's loyalties are to York, to us. Why, then, do you suddenly discount her influence? Is there something I do not know, Ned?'

Edward didn't respond at once and Richard was quick to draw the darkest conclusions from his silence.

'I'm right. Something has happened. . . .'

'Yes.'

'You've had word from Charles?'

'No. But I did have word from Meg. I do not know if she told you or not and, if not, I'd rather you heard it from me. Last week Warwick's Anne was wed to Edouard of Lancaster.'

That wasn't what Richard was expecting to hear. 'Yes, I know,' he said, very evenly.

Edward looked relieved. 'Do you want to talk about it, Dickon?' he asked, after a pause.

'No.'

'As you wish,' Edward agreed, so readily that a shadowy smile tugged at the corner of Richard's mouth.

'Do not push so, Ned.'

Edward had the grace to laugh. 'I admit it would be an un-familiar role for me, that of father confessor. But if you've a need to talk of the girl, I'm willing to listen.'

Richard shook his head.

Edward now felt compelled to persist. 'You are sure?'

'Ned, I do not want to talk and I doubt that you want to listen. I'd rather you let it lie.'

'As you say,' Edward said equably. Unsheathing his dagger, he cut into the loaf and spread a chunk of the herb-flavored cheese onto the bread.

'Here, help yourselves,' he invited, sliding the platter toward them. Marie complied, welcoming the luxury of sampling bread baked with white flour, but Richard ignored the food. He was playing with a strand of Marie's hair, entwining it around his fingers, but he wasn't looking at the girl. He was watching the candle flare with each draught from the opening door, unaware of Edward's appraising eyes.

'You've been to the races at Smithfield, have you not, Dickon?'

Richard looked up with a quizzical half-smile. 'Yes, why?'

'Were you lucky in your wagers?'

A shrug. 'Sometimes.'

'Surely it has occurred to you that this time you may have wagered on the wrong horse?'

'No,' Richard said, too quickly and too loudly. 'No, by God, it has not!'

Edward disregarded the denial. 'It was different with Will and Anthony. They could expect nothing from Warwick. But you had a choice, Dickon. You mattered to Warwick, both as kinsman and ally. I know how actively he did seek your support; I've always known. Had you heeded him, you'd not be here in Bruges tonight.'

'Ned, I said no!'

'You'd be in England . . . with your cousin Anne.'

Richard came to his feet so abruptly that the table rocked and Marie's startled exclamation turned heads in their direction.

'Damn you, do not!'

Edward didn't move, didn't take his eyes from his brother and, under his level gaze, colour burned into Richard's face and then ebbed, leaving him white and shaken.

'Sit down, Dickon,' Edward said, with so little inflection in his voice that it could have been either a command or a request.

Seconds slid by . . . and then Richard sat down again next to Marie.

Edward shoved the flagon across the table and, when Richard didn't touch it, he poured a generous amount into Richard's cup.

'So, you've never thought of that,' he said, very dryly.

Richard was silent. Beside him, Marie squeezed his arm in uncomprehending, instinctive sympathy but he paid her no heed.

'Yes,' he conceded bitterly. 'You're right. Anne would not have been bartered to Lancaster had I served you as George did. But I would think you'd be the last man to remind me of that.'

Edward leaned across the table. 'Why do you think I did, Dickon? Do you think I was merely amusing myself? That I meant to hurt you? You know better than that.

'I said what I did because it was true. I've always known what Warwick meant to you. I know now what the girl means. And I need no one to tell me where your loyalty has led . . . to Bruges.'

'Ned. . . .'

308

'Do you not think it time we were honest with each other, Dickon?'

Their eyes met, held.

'It does not look good, lad. It does not look good at all. . . . Is it not about time we admitted it?'

Richard nodded. 'I know,' he said bleakly.

They looked at each other in silence, while around them swirled the sounds of a Flemish tavern.

Reaching for the flagon, Edward refilled his cup; Richard's was still untouched.

'No . . . no more game-playing, Dickon,' he said softly. 'I have not the heart for it . . . not tonight. I've a brother-in-law who's bidding fair to embrace the Neville Bear and Ragged Staff, a wife in sanctuary, a son I may never get to see . . . and, the worst of it, Dickon, is that so much of it is my own damned fault.'

Richard made a tentative, indecisive movement; his hand brushed Edward's sleeve.

'I'll concede you George if you'll own up to Johnny,' he said at last, and Edward gave him a look that was at once amused, mocking, and affectionate.

'Poor Johnny. . . . Between us, Warwick and I put him on the rack, in truth.' Edward shook his head slowly. 'Dick Neville was once my friend and there are times, even now, when I do remember that. But my deepest regrets are for Johnny . . . and the choice I forced upon him.'

This was the first time they'd spoken openly and honestly of John's betrayal. But Richard had thought of little else these three months past, thought he could understand why Johnny made the choice he did. He was convinced that it would never have happened had Ned not taken the earldom of Northumberland from Johnny. Yet now, hearing his brother say aloud what he'd so often thought, he was perversely driven to defend Edward against the very conclusions he himself had drawn.

'You did not force a choice on Johnny, Ned. It was his to make and he alone made it. It did not have to be that way.'

'I appreciate your loyalty, Dickon, but we both know better. If a man is in robust health, it's likely he can suffer a sudden river-dousing without taking a chill. But if he were burning with fever when he had such a mishap, it's apt to be the death of him. Johnny's loyalty to me did cost him dear; he loved his brothers. When I took the earldom from him, I asked for one sacrifice too many. I should have seen that. You did. . . . Did you not?'

Richard hesitated and then nodded. 'I had no idea how deep the hurt did go with him. But that he was hurt . . . Yes, that I knew.' He wished that he'd not broken his self-imposed silence on Johnny. Talking about it didn't help, didn't ease the ache at all.

'Francis Lovell wrote me that Johnny looked heartsore upon his entry into London,' he said softly.

'I do not doubt it, Dickon. Johnny's one of the few truly decent men I've known. Betrayal was not in his nature. Yet he must live with the fact that he betrayed his sovereign, betrayed men who trusted him. I suspect he's finding that harder to live with than ever he did with any wrong I may have done him.'

Neither spoke for some minutes after that. Never had Richard felt closer to his brother. Close enough to ask the one question he'd not have thought could be put into words between them.

'Ned. . . . If Charles will not aid us . . . what shall we do, then?'

Edward seemed to have been expecting just that question. 'Ask me that next week, next month, and I might have a different answer for you. But tonight there's only one answer I can give you, little brother—that I do not know.'

Richard would once have insisted he'd wanted an honest answer, no matter how disheartening, and would have believed he meant it. Now he knew better.

Beside him, Marie had been fidgeting with increasing restlessness, and now she seized upon one of the few English words she knew.

'Brother?' she echoed. *'Vous êtes frères?'*

When Richard nodded, she leaned forward to whisper in his ear, laughing at his reply and pressing her body against him, her lips brushing the corner of his mouth.

Richard, meeting Edward's amused eyes, smiled self-consciously. 'She does not believe we are brothers, not with our unlike colouring,' he said, with the wry resignation born of a lifetime of such comments, as the dark one in a fair family.

'I explained, though, that you were a changeling,' he added, and Edward grinned.

'Now that I think of it, that might well account for George! He is Irish-born, after all, and God knows, he's acted as one bewitched from the day he first found his tongue.'

'Not bewitched, Ned,' Richard said, and sighed. 'Just accursedly weak.'

'Well, whatever, be thankful you and brother George are so little alike . . . in any respect!' Edward tilted his head to the side appraisingly. 'Actually, you look rather like Edmund. You have his eyes, and his hair was dark, too, though not as dark as yours.'

He misread Richard's startled look. 'But then, you were only seven when he died. No wonder you do not remember.'

'I was eight,' Richard corrected, 'and I do remember. It was not that. . . . It's that you so rarely speak of Edmund.'

'I know,' Edward acknowledged. 'For longer than I care to recall, it was too painful.'

Richard was at a loss for words. Edward didn't share his griefs; Richard had not thought that the wound left by Edmund's death might still be unhealed even after ten years. He realized suddenly that he was jealous and, shamed by that realization, he made amends by saying, 'My memories of Edmund are all of the two of you together. I remember how intrigued I was at the way you'd converse in half-finished sentences, a code no one else could comprehend . . . as if you did not need words between you.'

Edward laughed. 'Most of the time we did not, Dickon. There

was just a year between us. . . . It was often as if we shared one life, we were that close. Oh, we had our share of squabbles, too. But not when it counted. When he died, I felt as if I'd been split in half.'

Richard was quiet and, after a prolonged pause, Edward said, 'I was at Gloucester when word reached me of the battle fought at Sandal Castle. It was a bloody December day for York. To be told I'd lost father, brother, uncle, and cousin. . . . But it was Edmund's death that I found hardest to accept. I could not believe it. Not Edmund. If he could die, then anyone could . . . even me!'

He grinned unexpectedly, but the blue eyes were dark with memories long repressed. Picking up his cup, he raised it to his mouth and then set it down, untasted.

'Jesú, but I've not thought of this in years,' he confessed. 'I had so little time to grieve. . . . Suddenly all eyes were looking to me and, God above, how fast it all did come, Dickon. . . . I remember being angry more than anything else. Christ, it was so stupid. They should never have ventured from Sandal Castle. It was sheer folly, should never have happened. . . .

'I did know for a certainty, though, that I'd never dare trust another living soul as I did Edmund. That was the worst, I think, even worse than the loss of his companionship. For nigh on eighteen years, the whole of my life, I'd had a constant confidant. . . . and suddenly there was no one.'

'What of Will Hastings? Or Jack Howard. . . .?'

'I'm not talking of friendship, Dickon. I'm talking of trust.'

'But. . . .'

'Ah, you think they're one and the same?'

Richard considered. 'Yes, I do.'

'Not for kings, little brother. Not for kings.' Edward's mouth tightened; for a moment, he permitted the bitterness to show. 'If ever I did think so, our cousin Warwick taught me otherwise.'

Richard was unable to restrain himself any longer. 'Do you not think you can trust me?'

Edward drank to conceal his smile. 'Well . . . I surely trust you more than brother George!'

'Thank you.' But the sarcasm went awry, and Edward saw and relented.

'Trust is a learned response, Dickon. Whilst I've always been unaccountably fond of you, little brother, I cannot say that I trusted you more than . . . well, more than a score of others I could name.' He paused. 'That is, not until you gave me reason to trust you.'

He laughed suddenly. 'And if memory serves me right, you first gave me such reason for trust some eleven years ago, in a meadow not far from Ludlow Castle.'

'Do you mean to tell me that you still remember that? After all those years . . . and all those women.'

'Of course I remember. It was then that I first suspected you might be an ally worth having. And, I confess, time has not proven me wrong in that.'

Richard was pleased but shy to show it. 'And for my part, I think I might safely say as much for you,' he said generously.

Edward grinned. 'Hell, you'd trust me unto death and we both do know it. Face it, Dickon, you've always been a faulty judge of character!'

As Richard laughed, Marie stirred and, yawning, settled herself back against his shoulder. 'Soon, *chéri?*'

'Soon, sweet,' Richard said automatically, but he kept his eyes on his brother. 'Ned, you said you were seeking me tonight. . . . Why? If it was just to tell me of Anne's marriage, I cannot believe you wouldn't have waited till I got back.'

'You're right, I would,' Edward admitted, unabashed. 'Mayhap you're a better judge of character than I thought. No, if you want the truth of it, I did feel the need to talk and the need was such that I cared not if you had . . . more pressing needs of your own.'

Richard glanced at Marie who was amusing herself by polishing the pendant on the hanging sleeve of her gown.

'Now that you do mention it,' he said wryly, 'it is not that I do not enjoy your company, but . . .'

Edward laughed but then he reached across the table and laid his hand on Richard's arm.

'I should have told you at once, Dickon. I did mean to. But there were other things, too, that needed to be said between us.'

Richard's throat was suddenly tight. Jesus God, did all news have to be bad these days? All at once he knew that he did not want to hear it. He did not want to know the worst; even if they were doomed, he wanted Ned to keep it to himself, at least for this one night.

'What has happened now?' he asked dully, and then wondered if his brother had read his mind for Edward seemed reluctant to speak. He drank again and then surprised Richard by saying, 'Do you remember, Dickon, when you rode at the quintain, how you had a twofold concern? . . . First to hit the target full on and then to avoid being struck when the impact of your blow whipped it around behind you.'

'I've good reason to remember,' Richard said bemusedly. 'That was how I broke my shoulder when I was ten. I was hit and unhorsed when the sandbag swung back on me. But what does that have to do with now?'

'It's as good a description as any for the way I feel tonight. I was braced for the first shock. But I was not ready for the sand-bag. . . .'

Reaching into his doublet, Edward tossed a rolled sheet of paper onto the table in front of Richard.

'Read that.'

Richard picked it up. There was no salutation or signature; both had been cut away. The handwriting was unfamiliar to him and written in English. A sentence in the opening paragraph caught his eye: 'I protest that I have always held aloof from the quarrels about the English throne.' He glanced up quickly at Edward and then dropped his gaze to the text of the letter.

'I should be sorely grieved if the ambition of a single man should give occasion for dissension and hostilities between me and a people and kingdom to which I have ever shown myself so strongly attached.'

By now, Richard knew the writer to be his brother-in-law. The bombastic style was unmistakable. He threw it down with an oath.

'I see Charles's fine hand in this,' he said sarcastically. 'But to whom was it written?'

'To John Wenlock, at Calais.'

'How did you get hold of it, Ned?'

'Wenlock is playing a high-risk game. He holds Calais for Warwick, as once he did for me. But he knows fortune may yet show herself to be a fickle bitch and so he keeps a weather eye to the future.'

'So you had it from Wenlock himself. . . .' Richard grimaced. 'I could pity Warwick his friends . . . almost.' Picking up the letter again, he skimmed the remaining paragraphs rapidly.

'"Descended from the blood of Lancaster,"' he quoted caustically. 'How convenient for Charles that he now recollects his mother can claim kinship to Lancaster! And he stands ready to recognize the English King, whomsoever he might be!'

He swore again and then pulled the candle toward him, held the letter to the flame as Edward and Marie watched.

'He's a fool, Ned, if he thinks he'll prosper once he comes to terms with Warwick.'

'Charles likes Warwick no better than he does me. But Warwick holds England, and . . .'

'And he'd pledge the whole of Northumbria to keep you in Burgundy,' Richard finished grimly, and Edward nodded.

'Dickon . . . there's more. The sandbag, remember?' Edward leaned forward, said quietly, 'Meg sent a courier to me tonight. To warn us that Charles intends to issue a proclamation forbidding his subjects to give any aid or assistance to York.'

Richard caught his breath and then slammed his fist down on

the table. Wine sloshed from their cups and the candle holder skidded across the wet wood till it teetered on the very edge of space. Marie alone noticed and reached out to steady it.

'Christ, Ned, how can Charles be so shortsighted? Louis has already declared war on Burgundy; there are French troops in Picardy even now. Whatever Warwick might promise Charles, he's bound to France both by choice and necessity. With Warwick and Lancaster ruling England, war with Burgundy is inevitable.'

'As you said, Dickon, our brother-in-law of Burgundy is a fool,' Edward said acidly. He drained his wine cup, set it down.

'You'd best plan to meet with me and Will in the morning. It seems as good a time as any to dispatch another letter to Francis of Brittany. An exercise in futility, I do not doubt, but our options are narrowing.'

'Ned, we've got to talk to Meg again. Somehow we must persuade Charles to see you. If you could just talk to him. . . .'

'I think your confidence is misplaced, Dickon . . . if rather flattering. We are in agreement, though, on what must be done. We've but one chance; to make Charles see that his only security lies in a Yorkist England.'

He pushed the bench back, rising abruptly to his feet.

'But if we fail in that . . . then you'd best resign youself to the ways of Burgundy, for you'll be here for some time to come.'

Richard started to speak, hesitated, and then said in a rush, 'Ned, you said I'd had a choice. If it were mine to make again, I'd do it no differently.'

Edward stood looking down at him. His expression was sombre, fatigued and, for once, free of mockery. 'I know, Dickon . . . and in the past year, I've come to depend upon that loyalty, to trust you as I've trusted no one else. . . . Not even Edmund.'

Richard was speechless and, after a moment, Edward laughed. 'But for God's sake, do not let it go to your head!'

'That might be difficult,' Richard said huskily, and gestured about the now crowded common room, strident with foreign tongues and hazy with smoke, '. . . given all that I've gained for my loyalty.'

Edward's eyes lightened with silent, sardonic laughter. 'You'll do, damn you, you'll do.'

He bent down, retrieved his cloak from the bench. It was in far better condition than Richard's; he didn't share the boy's qualms about accepting Gruuthuse's bounty.

'And now, take this patient and pretty wanton to bed and, for a few hours, try to forget Warwick and Brother George and the little cousin you should have wed.'

Richard realized that an oblique apology had just been tendered, an unspoken regret implied. He smiled.

'Go with God, my liege.'

21

Aire, Burgundy

January 1471

Philippe de Commynes, Lord Chamberlain of Burgundy, was only twenty-five years of age, but no one stood higher than he in the esteem and confidence of the man known to intimates and enemies alike as Charles the Bold. Philippe was valued as a trusted confidant, astute adviser, skilled diplomat, and when, in late December, he reversed himself and urged Charles to meet with his brother-in-law of York, Charles listened and reconsidered. On December 26th, he summoned Edward to meet with him in early January at Aire, in Artois.

Neither Charles nor Philippe had ever met Edward of York before Aire, although they both had preconceived expectations as to what he would be like, this pleasure-loving Plantagenet who was as renowned for his exploits in the bedchamber as for those on the battlefield. Charles, a man who'd scandalized his court with the quaint belief that a husband should be faithful to his wife, was prepared to dislike the English exile on sight. Philippe, who admired discipline above all other qualities, was equally certain that he'd find little to like in this self-indulgent, arrogant prince who'd forfeited his throne for lack of care.

As his master and the Yorkist King exchanged wary courtesies, Philippe took the opportunity to appraise the adversary. Edward Plantagenet had been called the handsomest man to ever grace the English throne and Philippe tended to agree with that assessment. Edward of York had a resonant voice, remarkably even features, eyes of a blue rarely seen beyond Dublin and the yellow-gold hair common to Plantagenet princes since the first of their line, Henry Fitz-Empress, had claimed the crown in 1154. But while the physical description fitted the man, the reputation did not and Philippe found himself watching the Englishman closely, searching for clues to the character of this man who was not what Philippe had expected him to be.

Philippe cared little about the fortunes of the English royal House; he had no personal stake in the dynastic duel between York and Lancaster. Harry of Lancaster he knew to be a fool and, until now, he'd had little reason to think much more highly of Edward of York. When Edward sought refuge in Burgundy, Philippe had shared his sovereign's disgust at the unexpected turn of events. At Charles's bidding, he had journeyed to Calais in October, in an attempt to counteract the damage being done by Edward's continuing presence in his country. The visit had been a revelation to him.

Philippe prided himself upon his pragmatic, objective approach to statecraft; he'd often wished that his stubborn, tempestuous duke had more in common with their deadliest foe, the calculating King of France. Nonetheless, he'd been taken aback by the cynical speed with which Calais embraced the Bear and Ragged Staff.

Dining with Lord Wenlock and the English lords of Calais, he'd listened, bemused, as Edward of York was reviled by all present in the most scathing terms imaginable. Philippe decided he was not quite the supreme realist he'd thought himself to be. He'd been genuinely shocked by Warwick's willingness to sacrifice his daughter for political gain and now he found himself disconcerted by, and disdainful of, these English lords who were so quick to jettison York for Lancaster. His sense of moral superiority did not deter him, however, from earnestly assuring Wenlock and company that the troublesome Edward of York was dead.

He'd thus bought time for his lord and for his land, but he knew the reprieve would be fleeting. Sooner or later, he and his duke must deal with France. Philippe knew war to be inevitable. The question as yet unanswered was whether it was possible to prevent a French-English alliance directed against Burgundy and Philippe was growing increasingly pessimistic about that prospect.

Since mid-December, French envoys had been consulting with Warwick in London. There were unsettling rumours, as yet unconfirmed, that the French King was tempting Warwick with the promise of Flemish territory as the Kingmaker's share of the spoils of war against Burgundy. With these ominous portents in the wind, Philippe had deemed it time to reconsider all their options, one of which was most certainly the man sitting across the table from him.

'I've heard much of my brother-in-law of Burgundy's Lord Chamberlain, more than enough to bestir my curiosity, Monsieur de Commynes,' Philippe's option was saying, and Philippe acknowledged the compliment, if indeed it was meant to be one, with an innocuous pleasantry.

The English jarred his ear and he felt a momentary irritation with his duke for insisting that the conference be conducted in their guest's mother tongue. Edward spoke French, as did all well-born Englishmen, and they could as easily have conversed in that language, one far more familiar to Philippe. But Charles, who spoke French, Flemish, English, Latin and some Italian, was proud of his fluency in English and could never resist an opportunity to display his linguistic skills.

Charles now leaned forward; he scorned subtlety as other men might deplore sloth or greed. 'Tell me, my Yorkist friend, why should I help you? Why should I risk incurring the hostility of the man who rules England for the sake of a man who has not a sou or a soldier to his name?'

Philippe winced; when would his lord learn to tread that fine line between audacity and outrage? Edward did not look insulted, however. He seemed more amused than anything else.

'Because, my lord, you cannot afford not to help me,' he said with a smile, and Philippe noted with interest how unhesitatingly he'd abandoned courtesy for candour.

'Indeed? Perhaps you'd be good enough to explain?' Charles said coolly. 'I should be most interested in your reply.'

So was Philippe, and he kept his eyes on the Englishman as Edward said, 'Burgundy is a state of immense wealth and power. But even Burgundy would be hard-pressed to fight a war on two fronts. Your Grace can, in all likelihood, prevail against Louis of France. I doubt, however, that you can withstand a concerted two-pronged attack by both France and England.

'We both know Louis would barter his very soul to see the fleur-de-lis flying over Burgundy. If I were you, I'd not sleep well nights knowing that England is to be ruled by a French-woman and a seasoned soldier who is far too fond of the French king.'

'Granted,' Charles said without hesitation. 'But you are making a supposition, my lord, which has yet to be proven; that Warwick will, in fact, go to war for the King of France. However much he may like Louis, I rather doubt that their friendship is worth that much to Warwick.'

'So do I,' Edward agreed at once, and Charles frowned.

'Well, then?' he asked impatiently.

'Men do not wage war for friendship; you are right in that. They fight for more tangible aims; to hold on to a needed alliance, to eliminate a potential threat. And often, my lord and esteemed brother-in-law, they fight for personal gain.'

Philippe straightened; the Englishman was speaking like one holding a trump card. He wanted to know what it was.

'Personal gain, Your Grace?' he queried politely.

'Holland and Zeeland, Monsieur de Commynes. I would surely count the acquisition of such rich provinces as gain, would you not?'

'What are you saying?' Charles demanded. 'That Louis has promised Burgundian territory to Warwick in return for English support?'

'"The counties and lordships of Holland and Zeeland,"' Edward said, as if quoting from memory, and when he did not elaborate further, Philippe reluctantly awarded him points, thinking that, even if this were no more than a high-stakes bluff, Edward played his hand very well.

'If I may seek clarification, my lord. . . . My English is not all it should be. . . . Monseigneur de Warwick is to take our lands of Holland and Zeeland as his reward for joining in a war upon Burgundy? Is this your meaning?'

'Precisely my meaning, sir.'

Charles and Philippe exchanged glances. Charles nodded almost imperceptibly and Philippe smiled, with a regretful shake of his head.

'Forgive me, my lord, if I appear to doubt your word. . . . It is only that you do amaze me so with such news. May I ask how you came by this information?'

'From one who is closer than a friend to my cousin of Warwick.'

'A son-in-law, perhaps?' Philippe suggested, and Edward shrugged.

'Perhaps.'

Charles lost patience; there were times when his Lord Chamberlain could be tiresomely French in his preference for the oblique, the circular approach.

'Is your brother Clarence contemplating a second betrayal?' he asked bluntly.

Edward grinned. 'I prefer to think of it as a heretic returning to the True Faith.'

'I'd say the Duke of Clarence changes faiths as other men change clothing,' Charles said after a brief silence, but the sarcasm was offered almost absently, without rancour. He was, Philippe saw, absorbed in contemplative consideration of the plot suddenly suggested to them; Clarence as the Trojan Horse in the Warwick camp. It did, Philippe admitted, alter the odds somewhat.

Charles shoved his chair back, subjecting his Yorkist brother-in-law to a challenging critical scrutiny. 'Let us assume, for the sake of argument, that what Clarence told you is true, that Warwick has been given ample reason for war with Burgundy. Even so, it does not necessarily follow that I can resolve all my problems by backing you.' He paused.

'To be frank, my lord of York, I like not your chances of defeating Warwick. And others do share my view. Perhaps you've heard what the Milanese Ambassador said of your chances? "It is difficult to go back through the window after leaving by the door."' Charles smiled at Edward, said with a touch of malice, 'He wagers that if you attempt a return to England, you'll leave your skin there.'

Edward laughed and, even to the suspicious ears of his audience, it sounded genuine enough.

'I'll take that wager,' he said easily. 'Will you? What say you, Charles le Téméraire? My skin against a Yorkist England unfriendly to France. . . . How could you possibly lose?'

Philippe grinned, bringing his hand up belatedly to hide it, and after a pause Charles laughed grudgingly.

'I admit I like you better than I thought I would,' he conceded. 'But I doubt that I like you well enough to finance an expedition doomed to failure.'

Edward was still smiling. 'My sister told me you do speak your mind. If I might do likewise. . . . You can lose only by doing nothing. If you back me, I can assure you that I'll keep my cousin Warwick too busy to concern himself with wars of conquest. If you do not, you're sure to face an Anglo-French force before the spring thaw.'

'You truly think you can win?' Charles sounded more curious than sceptical, and both Edward and Philippe noted the change in tone.

'I think I might best answer that by putting a question to you, brother-in-law. Tell me this; have you ever heard it said that the Earl of Warwick could defeat Edward of York in the field?'

'You are persuasive, my lord of York,' Charles said at last. 'But you forget my fondness for the House of Lancaster. Am I not a great-grandson of John of Gaunt, the first Duke of Lancaster? Although I wed your sister, and glad I am for it, the fact is that I have always befriended Lancaster. As you doubtlessly do know, for several years now two of the mightiest Lancastrian lords, the Dukes of Somerset and Exeter, have resided at my court.'

Edward nodded. 'Brave men, both,' he said coolly. 'And true to Lancaster unto death. If I were in your place, do you know what I would do with those noble lords?'

'I can guess,' Charles said, with a grim smile. 'You'd send them to God.'

'No . . . I'd send them to England.'

Charles was too startled to hide his surprise. 'But they are pledged heart and soul to Lancaster.'

Edward smiled, said nothing.

Philippe was impassive, but it took an effort of will. He was careful not to meet the eyes of the Englishman, sure that if he did, he'd reveal that he'd recognized a kindred spirit in Edward of York. He turned, instead, to Charles.

'Indeed, they are, Your Grace,' he agreed. 'But I think His Grace of York is more interested in their enmities than their loyalties. Neither man bears any love for the Earl of Warwick.' With a courteously questioning look at Edward. 'Do they, my lord?'

'No, Monsieur de Commynes, I would think not,' Edward said composedly. 'There has ever been bad blood between the Beauforts and the Nevilles. As for Exeter, he has feuded with the Nevilles for years. He blames Warwick for his years in exile. . . . Or so I've been told.'

Charles glanced from his brother-in-law to his Lord Chamberlain. 'And they call Louis the Spider King,' he said dryly.

The portrait was of a man in his thirties. His hair was thick and as black as pitch; the eyes were of a startlingly vivid shade of blue; the face was rounded, the features well formed; while the swarthy complexion attested to the blood of his Portuguese mother and the protruding jaw to a stubborn, inflexible nature.

Stepping back to study the painting from another angle, Richard exclaimed admiringly, 'Jesú, but this is well done, Meg! Who's the artist?'

Margaret joined her brother before the elegantly framed portrait of her husband.

'Rogier van der Weyden. A remarkable talent, is he not? This one was done while Charles was still Count of Charolais and is my favourite, without question. It is as if Charles were here in the room with us.'

'I wish he were. At least the waiting would be over.'

Margaret smiled and reached out to ruffle his hair. 'Do not fret so, Dickon. As I told you, I do truly believe Charles will back

324

Ned. Now come and sit down. To pass the time, I'll show you how we play Primero, which is even more popular at our court than Trump or All Fours.'

Richard complied, with a marked lack of enthusiasm, and Margaret began to expertly deal the playing cards onto the marble-top table.

'Remember, each card is worth three times its face value and the knave of hearts is the "quinona" card, which counts as any card of any suite you desire to. . . . Dickon, pay attention!'

Richard threw his cards down on the table.

'Meg, there's no way on God's earth that I can concentrate on a game of cards, not whilst so much hangs in the balance.'

'All right, Dickon,' she said indulgently. 'I do not wonder that your nerves are on the raw. What should you like to talk about, then, while we wait for Ned?'

'You. We've had so little time together and we've done nothing but speak of politics. I want to know about you. Are you happy, Meg? No regrets?'

Margaret was only eight months into her twenty-fifth year but the smile she gave Richard was unmistakably maternal.

'No regrets, dearest. I like my life well as Duchess of Burgundy. But I do thank you for your concern on my behalf; you can be very sweet at times.'

'And every October I have yet another birthday,' he reminded her mildly. 'I'm not still fifteen, Meg.'

'*Mea culpa,*' she acknowledged with a laugh. 'It is difficult, I confess, to think of you as a man grown. But I will endeavour to try.'

They smiled at each other, sharing unspoken memories of Fotheringhay Castle, their birthplace, where they and George had passed the early years of childhood.

'These two years we've been apart have been eventful for you, have they not, Dickon? Ned says he thinks you've the makings of a right able battle commander.'

'Did he?' Richard grinned, and Margaret nodded. She had lovely grey eyes, very like her mother, but they were alight now with a mischief quite foreign to the Duchess of York.

'No, you're not the little brother I remember,' she conceded cheerfully. 'You've learned the ways of war since I last saw you. And the ways of women, too, it seems. . . . Ned says you'd a daughter born last spring.'

Richard was distinctly taken aback, much to her amusement.

'Ned says far too much, sometimes,' he said tartly, and Margaret giggled.

'You need not confuse me with our lady mother,' she chided. 'Although I daresay she's much too taken up with Ned's sinning on such a grand scale to have time to spare for lesser sins of yours!'

Richard laughed. 'Nonetheless, I'd rather not call them to her attention,' he confessed, and Margaret laughed, too.

'Do you remember, Dickon, how she could shame us with but a look? And she always seemed to know when we'd been up to no good. George would swear she had second sight.'

Sobered by mention of George, they were no longer laughing. She leaned across the table, touched his hand.

'Dickon, I would ask a favour of you.'

'You know you need only name it.'

'I told you I believed Charles would heed Ned's appeal for aid. So much do I believe it that I've been giving thought to your return to England . . . and to George.

'He is desperately unhappy, Dickon. He knows now that Warwick played him for a fool. He feels he can no longer trust Warwick and he fears for his life under a Lancastrian rule, as well he might. I do believe he would be amenable to a reconciliation with Ned. He has not admitted this, mind you, but I know him, Dickon. Once you are back in England, I think he'd seriously consider returning his loyalties to York.'

'He would if he thought Ned likely to win,' Richard said and at once regretted it, for he saw that his sarcasm had stung.

'I'd have expected that from Ned,' she said reproachfully, 'but not from you. You loved Warwick once; you know how persuasive he can be. Do not hate George for being weak, Dickon. He cannot help himself, truly he cannot. Ned cannot understand that, but I hoped you might. . . .'

'I do understand, Meg. But I do not find it as easy to forgive.'

'If you cannot forgive him for his sake, Dickon, do so, then, for mine.'

He acknowledged the power of her plea with a wry smile. 'If you put it that way. . . .'

'I know George committed a grievous wrong but I truly believe he wishes to make amends. Why else would he write me that the French King was tempting Warwick with the promise of Holland and Zeeland?'

That, however, was too much for Richard. 'Come now, Meg,' he protested. 'You showed us that letter, remember? He didn't write as one sharing a confidence of critical import; he sounded, rather, as if he were sorely affronted that Louis had not seen fit to make a like offer to him!'

'Granted he did not make his intent plain in so many words that he meant to aid you. But surely he knew I'd confide in Ned. And he must have known, too, that Ned would be sure to make the best use of such information.'

'Perhaps,' Richard said dubiously. 'With George, one never knows what motivates him. If you'd prefer to believe he meant to do us a service, who am I to say for sure that it is not so?'

He sounded so sceptical, though, that Margaret was moved to entreat, 'Can we not give him the benefit of the doubt, Dickon? That's not so much to ask, is it?'

'No, I suppose not. If you . . . Ned!'

Edward was alone. He closed the door behind him, pulled the bolt into place as Richard froze and Margaret, the confident one, spilled the deck of cards all over the table.

'Ned?' She read nothing in his face, and there was an appalled instant, brief but bitter beyond any she'd yet experienced, when she thought, Sweet Mother Mary, Charles said no! But even as her blasphemous fear took form, Richard came to his feet.

'My God,' he said softly, 'you've done it. . . .'

Edward nodded, once. 'I expect to be in England by Easter, if not before,' he confided quietly, and then he grinned. 'What say you, Dickon? Should you like to go home?' And that broke the spell.

Margaret rose to her feet as her brothers embraced jubilantly, and then she was in Edward's arms, and he was depositing undirected kisses on her cheek, her eyes, her hair, and Richard, too, was hugging her, and then Edward again. And now that it was over, now that they had won, she dared acknowledge at last just how truly fearful she had been.

'Charles is convinced, then, that George means to betray Warwick at the first opportunity?'

Edward nodded and grinned. 'I would surely hope so, Dickon. I did my very damnedest to give him that impression!'

It was the opening Margaret had been waiting for. 'Ned,' she said quickly, 'I believe George would indeed forsake Warwick . . . if he thought he'd be forgiven.'

'By whom? God?'

She was not put off by his sarcasm. She'd expected such a response at first, and now she came swiftly across the room to his side as he said, '"Forgive George, he knows not what he does." As far back as I can remember, I've heard that from you, Meg, and when not from you, from Dickon. It passes my understanding; it always has. I should truly like to know what there is about George that makes the two of you defend him even now. What do you see in him that I do not?'

'I see him as a boy,' Margaret said unhesitatingly. 'I remember him as he was during our years at Fotheringhay . . . ere he was swayed by our cousin Warwick. He was always self-willed and headstrong, but there was no malice in him, Ned, not then. . . .'

328

'No malice?' he echoed incredulously and laughed.

'I know he's given you little reason to love him,' she conceded. 'But can you not see why? It is that he's jealous of you, Ned; he's always been jealous. He sees you as all he is not. . . .'

'Aye . . . as King of England.'

Margaret saw it was futile. He'd not heed her. Nor would he forgive George.

'You do bring out the worst in George. It has ever been so. He knows you love him not. He knows you've always favoured Dickon. . . .'

'You yourself did admit he's given me scant reason to care for him,' Edward countered impatiently, and Richard decided it was time to intervene.

'Meg is not defending what George has done, Ned. She is trying to make you see why he acted as he did, no more than that.'

'If you can satisfactorily explain George's actions to me, Dickon, I daresay you can tell me, as well, how many angels may dance on the head of a pin.'

'I know George's failings as well as any man, but I've other memories of him, too, Ned. Memories of happier days and of times, too, when I needed him and he was there for me. George and I shared a great deal. We were at Ludlow together, remember? We had to watch as they sacked the village. George. . . . Well, he kept me close by him all the while. He did what he could for me.

'We shared exile, too. I'm not likely to forget that. I remember ma mère hurrying us aboard ship, telling us to be brave and telling George to look after me.

'And he did, Ned. Above all, during that first night at sea, when I'd not yet fully realized what had happened or why. I did not even know where Burgundy was!

'He was good to me then, Ned. Not just that night, but in the weeks that followed as we waited for word from England. He let me confess to feeling fearful or homesick and he never made mockery of such fears.' He smiled at that. 'Well, almost never. I think you'd agree, though, Ned, that these are not memories to be easily forgotten. When I speak on George's behalf, you know now what I am remembering.'

Margaret leaned over, kissed his cheek. 'Thank you,' she whispered, and then turned toward Edward.

'Now do you see, Ned?' she said quietly.

Edward was still watching Richard. 'I do not doubt that George was as protective as you say, Dickon. Nor does it surprise me. George is not a monster; he'll be kind if it costs him nothing. I'm sure he was fond of you in his way . . . and you gave him a God-given opportunity to play the courageous older brother. I daresay he enjoyed it immensely.'

Richard started to speak, then checked himself, disappointed but not truly surprised.

Margaret, however, had been led to expect a more sympathetic response by Edward's attentive silence, and she said bitterly, 'You'll not give him the benefit of the doubt in anything, will you?'

'No.'

The answer was brutal in its brevity; the eyes regarding her were blue ice. She caught her breath, swinging around in appeal to Richard. As she did, Edward came swiftly to his feet, reaching out and grasping her wrist.

'I'll do nothing for George. But I will for you, Meg. What do you want of me?'

She stared at him. 'I want you to forgive him, Ned,' she said softly, and he nodded.

'You mean it? You truly will?'

He nodded again. 'I cannot forget his betrayals, Meg, not even for you . . . and there's no way on God's earth that I'd ever trust him again. But I do promise you this; if he wants to cut loose from Warwick and return to York, I'll do my best to live with the past.'

'Thank you, Ned.' Her arms went up around his neck. For a moment, he held her to him and then she stepped back.

Her smile was radiant. 'Now I must find Charles. I'd not want him to think me ungrateful.'

Rising, she kissed Edward again and, in passing, gave Richard a quick hug.

As she reached the door, Edward said, 'You may tell George what I said, Meg, if you wish.'

She laughed. 'You know very well I will.'

Edward sat down again and glanced over at Richard. 'I believe Meg is the only one who has ever truly loved George. I hope to God he appreciates her. . . . But knowing George, I doubt it.'

Richard said nothing and Edward's eyes lingered speculatively on him.

'You did not want Meg to plead for George. Why?'

'There was no need,' Richard said tersely.

Edward didn't deny it. 'Then why did you bother to tell me of Ludlow and Burgundy?' he asked curiously.

'Because Meg wished it. And because I thought I might be able to help you see George through our eyes. As we both do remember him.'

'Is that what is bothering you? That I cannot see George as you and Meg do?'

'I think you know what is bothering me. That you let Meg entreat you to forgive George when she had no need to do so. When that was your intent all along.'

'I did not lie to Meg, Dickon,' Edward said placidly. 'It will be a cold day in Hell ere I'd ever trust George again.'

'You may not trust him but you'll make use of his discontent. You'd have to be a fool not to and I've never met a man who's less of a fool.'

'I'd thank you for that, but I don't think you meant it as a compliment,' Edward said, sounding more amused than annoyed. 'You're right, of course. George commands an army and Warwick has no choice but to trust him. That makes him an ally worth having. Surely you don't fault me for that.'

'No, not for that. For making Meg think you do it for her sake.'

'Well, what if I did? You know the love I bear Meg. Why is it wrong to want to make her happy?'

'Damnation, Ned, you made her believe you'll make peace with George because she asked it of you, when you do but serve your own interests. And were Meg not so frantic for George's sake, she'd have been sure to see it, too.'

'Granted, I've need of George. But I do owe Meg much. If I can make her think she is responsible for any reconciliation, what harm in that? She does care deeply for George. Do you not think it gives her pleasure to believe she has aided him? Why should I deny her that?'

Richard's expression was one of disbelief. 'Jesú,' he said at last, shaking his head.

Edward laughed. 'If the end be the one desired, why quarrel over the means, Dickon? Now, fetch that wine flagon from the sideboard. We may never have better reason to celebrate than tonight.'

Setting the flagon down upon the polished surface of the marble-top table, Richard poured white wine into silver cups fretted with gold; he'd never seen such luxury anywhere as at his brother-in-law of Burgundy's court. And suddenly he was remembering the last time he'd drunk with his brother, from unwashed pewter mugs at a warped wooden table wet with wine spills and greasy with the drippings of reeking tallow candles.

'There has never been a King of England to lose his throne and then regain it, Dickon. Harry of Lancaster is a pawn, no more than a puppet to be manipulated at Warwick's whims. And the others who lost their crowns were not long in losing their lives as well.'

'Until now,' Richard said softly, and Edward smiled at him. In that moment, Richard knew that his brother, too, was remembering the night at the Gulden Vlies.

'What shall we drink to, Ned . . . to England?'

'I've a better thought even than that. It is not precisely the season for it, with Epiphany still four days hence, and I daresay our lady mother would never forgive me for saying it. But blasphemy or not, I think it fitting, nonetheless.'

He touched his cup to the one Richard now held. 'To the Resurrection,' he said.

22

London

March 1471

Paul's Cross, situated in the northeast corner of St. Paul's churchyard, was the most celebrated of the London outdoor pulpits. Papal bulls were read at Paul's Cross, as were royal writs. Those unfortunates who'd offended Holy Church or run foul of secular law did penance before the wooden pulpit shaped like an octagon. And, on any given Sunday at noon, a large crowd was likely to have assembled in the churchyard to hear the sermon which, more often than not, was of a highly political nature.

This Lenten Sunday proved to be no exception. That past September, a Franciscan preacher, Dr John Goddard, had here proclaimed Harry of Lancaster as England's true King, and on this chill March day six months later, he was again preaching at Paul's Cross on behalf of the House of Lancaster.

He was a skilled public speaker, with a flair for the felicitous phrase, the memorable metaphor, and he was accustomed to commanding the unwavering attention of his listeners. This noon, however, his audience was restive, distracted, and he was both irked and mystified. He was more than midway through the sermon before he discovered the competing attraction and then he could only marvel how he could ever have failed to notice her until now, the austerely elegant woman who'd given birth to Edward of York. He was too seasoned a speaker to falter, however, and, after a fractional pause, continued with aplomb. And, for her part, the Duchess of York appeared oblivious of the stir she was causing, listening impassively as the Franciscan extolled the piety and grace of good King Harry.

Across the churchyard, Lady Scrope was conversing in heated whispers with her husband, all the while keeping her gaze on the Duchess.

'We must surely speak to her, John,' she insisted softly. 'We've known Her Grace for years; how can we snub her?'

'I did not say we should snub her,' he whispered back irritably. 'But I do not see why we must seek her out. It would be damnably uncomfortable and I see no need for it. What am I to say to her . . . that I hope her son does rot in Burgundy? Moreover, her daughter is with her and you know I like that lady not at all.'

Alison's gaze shifted from the slim figure of the Duchess of York to that of her more amply proportioned daughter Eliza, Duchess of Suffolk.

"Tis common courtesy, John. She's surely entitled to that much.'

Having concluded his sermon, Dr Goddard was descending the stone stairs and Alison's attention was momentarily distracted. When she turned back to the Duchess of York, she saw a stockily built man had shouldered his way through the crowd to halt before Edward of York's mother and sister.

'See,' she hissed, nudging her husband. 'Jack Howard does not hesitate to approach Her Grace.'

'It's easy enough for him,' he responded sourly. 'He's always been a Yorkist. He can commiserate with her over her son's broken fortunes and mean it. But I'm no hypocrite, Alison, and I . . .'

334

'John, something is amiss,' she interrupted, and one glance was enough to show him she was right.

The Duchesses of York and Suffolk had drawn close to Lord Howard, were staring at him with an intensity of attention that bespoke more than casual conversation. Even young Jack, the Duchess of Suffolk's eight-year-old son, had ceased his attempts to entice one of the stray churchyard dogs within romping range and was tugging at his mother's sleeve, made uneasy by her sudden immobility.

But even as Alison watched, the frieze shattered. Howard was nodding vigorously as if in confirmation, with more animation than Alison had ever seen in that dark saturnine face. The Duchess of Suffolk turned to her mother and then, laughing, dropped to her knees and gathered her squirming son into an exultant embrace. As she did, Alison had her first clear glimpse of Cecily Neville. The Duchess of York was smiling at John Howard, a smile so radiant, so heartbreakingly lovely, that Alison knew at once what she had been told.

'Oh, my God,' she gasped, and turned to stare at her husband. She saw that he, too, had guessed Howard's message. As their eyes met, he nodded grimly.

'The Devil fights for York, 'tis claimed,' he said sombrely. 'I only hope that Almighty God will be with Warwick.'

Jacquetta Woodville glanced over her shoulder, beckoning impatiently to her trailing servant. The basket that swung from his arm contained a newly weaned kitten, meant for Jacquetta's granddaughters. Elizabeth's nerves were being rubbed raw after six months in close confinement with an infant, two mischievous boys, and three active little girls, and Jacquetta hoped the kitten might be a welcome diversion.

She was not expecting the scene that greeted her upon her entry into Abbot Millyng's lodging. Mistress Stidolf, nurse to Elizabeth's youngest daughter Cecily, and now tending to the other children as well, was nowhere to be found. Two-year-old Cecily was huddled on her trestle bed, sobbing. At sight of her grandmother, she scrambled down and ran to Jacquetta, holding up a dirty little hand darkening with a spreading bruise. In the corner cradle, the baby was wailing fretfully. The other children, Jacquetta's two grandsons and Cecily's sisters, five-year-old Bess and three-year-old Mary, were all gathered at the door of the Abbot's refectory, so absorbed in their vigil that they had not yet become aware of Jacquetta's presence.

'Thomas!'

He turned at once, a handsome fair-haired boy of sixteen; he was her favourite grandchild and knew it.

'Grand-mère!'

'Whatever is happening here? Where is Mistress Stidolf? Or Nurse Cobb?'

Not at all abashed by her frown, he came quickly to her side and kissed her dutifully on the cheek.

Nurse Cobb chose that moment to make her appearance, lugging a heavy wooden bucket, which she gratefully surrendered to Jacquetta's servant.

'See to the babe!' Jacquetta snapped before the woman could speak, and then, to her own servant, 'For Our Lord's sake, have a care! That bucket is slopping all over the rushes.'

'I had to fetch water for the little prince's bath, Madame. What would you have me do, with none to lend me a hand and . . .'

Jacquetta ignored the midwife and grabbed for the basket just as the kitten made a bid for freedom. Trying without success to pry loose Cecily's grip on her skirt, she glared at Thomas.

'Is this how you look after the little ones, Thomas?'

He grinned, jerked his head toward the closed door. 'The Lord Abbot is with Madame our mother. He has brought her a message from . . . you'll never guess . . . the Duchess of York!'

Jacquetta shared his amazement; communications from Cecily Neville were the rarest of occurrences.

The other children were clustered around her by now and, by the time she'd silenced them all and restored a semblance of order, the Abbot was emerging from the refectory. Bess and Mary were quarrelling over the kitten but Thomas darted for the door, with his brother on his heels, and only a sharply-worded reprimand from Jacquetta kept him from colliding with the Abbot.

Ignoring his reproachful look, she brushed past Thomas and shut the door firmly in his face.

The room was large and open to light; in the eastern end was a small private chapel, for the convenience of the Lord Abbot. It was there that Elizabeth stood, before the velvet-draped altar.

'Dearest, what is it? What has happened?'

Elizabeth shook her head. She didn't move. Behind her a jewel-coloured stained-glass window spilled sun into the room, and it seemed to Jacquetta that her daughter had drawn all the light from the window into her eyes; never had they shone so green, so luminous.

'I never doubted,' Elizabeth said, and laughed. 'Not when they said he was dead, not when they said he'd never see England again. I knew he'd not fail me!'

Something white caught Jacquetta's eye; a piece of paper had fallen to the floor at her daughter's feet. Stooping, Jacquetta picked it up, unfolded it. There was no date, no salutation, no signature; only five words written in a bold hand across the centre of the page: Edward has landed in Yorkshire.

Seventy-five miles northwest of London lay Warwick Castle, rising up from the banks of the River Avon as it had since the time of the Norman Conquest. It had come to Richard Neville by right of his wife, Nan Beauchamp. Although his personal preference was for Middleham, midst the Yorkshire moors, Warwick Castle had remained his chief residence during his years of power, and it was at Warwick Castle that he was now awaiting word from the North.

The Earl of Warwick was alone in his solar, seated at a cluttered writing desk. He was signing his name with a flourish to the last of the letters as his brother the Archbishop of York entered.

He dispensed with greetings, saying only, 'I expected you ere this, George,' as the Archbishop dismissed his escort and brushed aside the welcoming alaunts.

George Neville sank down in the nearest chair, pushing away the most persistent of the dogs.

'Jesú, Dick, can you go nowhere without these damned dogs?'

Warwick shrugged and held up a sealed letter. 'Well, this goes tonight to France.'

'You've told Louis that York's gamble failed, that Ned was forced to seek sanctuary soon after landing?'

Warwick nodded. 'And he'll be much relieved to hear it, you may be sure.' He tossed the letter back on the pile. 'I only do wish I could believe it.'

The archbishop frowned. 'The news from the North was that Ned encountered stiff resistance, had to retreat. It rings true; he could expect no friendly welcome in Yorkshire. Why he chose to land there, I'll never know. . . . But he did, and has trapped himself. I believe it. . . . Why do you not, Dick?'

'I'm not sure,' Warwick confessed. 'Perhaps because it's too good to be true. Perhaps because rumour has had him dead fully a score of times these six months past. I think at times that he has more lives than any six cats. . . . He escaped Johnny at Doncaster, escaped drowning, escaped the Easterlings, and then escaped our fleet on his return to England. We've had the Channel virtually blocked since February, yet he somehow slipped through the net.'

'He sailed in one of the worst gales in years, when no sane man would've ventured from port,' the archbishop said sourly, and Warwick gave him a faintly amused look.

'Very unsporting, I agree,' he said dryly. 'The fact is, George, he gambled on the storm and won . . . and I'd be a fool to accept these rumours of his fall as true until I do have proof. Our cousin is no man to underestimate.' He fingered the letter again. 'Meanwhile, I see no reason not to ease the mind of our French ally. But do not rely upon it, George. I do not.'

'Even if the sanctuary story is false,' the Archbishop argued, 'he's in trouble. With Johnny at Pontefract and Henry Percy at Topcliffe, he's caught between the two, and Exeter and Oxford are well on the way toward Newark. He can have fifteen hundred men at most and he's facing three armies. It's only a matter of time before he's brought to bay, if it has not happened already.'

'It does sound that way,' Warwick agreed. But there was no real conviction in his voice and George Neville, subjecting him to closer scrutiny, found little to like in what he saw.

'You look as if you'd not slept for a week,' he said critically, and Warwick shrugged again.

'I am tired,' he conceded.

'Have you had any word from Nan?'

Warwick nodded. 'A letter came just two days past.'

'How does she?'

'As eager to reach England as Marguerite d'Anjou is to delay departure from France. It's been seven months since Nan and I have seen each other; the wait has been hard on her, as you'd expect.'

'I well understand Nan's impatience. For months now, we've been waiting on Marguerite and still she finds reason to tarry in France. What ails the woman?'

'She's shortsighted, I agree. She should be looking to her interests here. I can only surmise that she fears for the boy, does not want to risk his safety till Ned no longer poses a threat.'

'That boy is going to be a problem, Dick,' the Archbishop predicted gloomily. 'He's his mother's son for true . . . whosoever his father may be.'

Warwick smiled grimly. 'I've not had the best of luck with sons-in-law, have I?'

'Have you had word from George?'

Warwick shook his head. 'I was writing to him just as you entered.'

He picked up a pen, put it down again. 'It's passing strange,' he said at last. 'There was a time, and not too long past, when I'd have laughed had I been told I'd one day be facing Ned and Dickon across a battlefield.'

'That sounds more like Johnny than you, Dick,' the Archbishop observed trenchantly, and Warwick gave a short staccato laugh.

'You need not fear,' he said coolly. 'I'm not giving way to sentiment. In any event, it'll not come to that. If Johnny and Percy do not run them to earth, Exeter and Oxford will. They've nowhere to run, not in Yorkshire.'

'Why do you think he chose to put ashore there? They've no love for York in the North and Ned well knows it. It's not like him. . . .'

'No?'

'What do you mean?'

'We fortified the entire east coast, where he was most likely to land . . . and had he disembarked there, he'd have been trapped for certes. But we did not fortify the North and I suspect he gambled on that. Ned has ever had gamblers' instincts, ever been willing to risk all on a single throw of the dice.'

'Dick, what word have you had from Johnny?'

'None.'

They looked at each other, neither wanting to say what was in both their minds. The Archbishop was the one to breach the wall first.

'I've seen little of Johnny these months past. I'd wager he's not been in London twice since Martinmas. Dick . . . are you sure his loyalties are to Lancaster? He did have a fondness for Ned and Dickon. . . .'

Warwick was shaking his head. 'Johnny's loyalties were never

to Lancaster, George,' he said softly. 'Johnny's loyalties are to me
. . . and to you.'

The Archbishop's face had taken on a self-conscious shade of
red, but he otherwise accepted the rebuke with good grace. 'I
know,' he admitted readily. 'I know the debt we owe Johnny for
Doncaster. I know, too, what it cost him. If he has to be the one
to make an end to this reckless venture of Ned's . . . Well, I do
not envy him that. For his sake, I hope it is Percy.'

Warwick said nothing. He'd reached for a pen again, was staring
down at the blank paper before him.

'And now I suppose I should write to my son-in-law of Clarence
and give him the tidings that his brothers are home.'

He laughed suddenly and, at the other's questioning look, said,
'I was just thinking . . . when Richard Coeur de Lion was freed
from a German prison, the French King sent a warning to Richard's
brother John, who liked Richard no more than George does Ned.
Do you know what he wrote?'

'How would I be likely to know that?' the archbishop said
impatiently.

Warwick gave him a tight, tired smile, said, 'The Devil is loose.'

As he spoke, he was sketching circles on the page, in diminishing size.

'It seems rather a waste of time to write to George. I suspect
he knows as much about Ned's whereabouts as any man in
England.'

23

York

March 1471

'I say we vote on it. . . . Who favours opening the city gates to him? I thought as much. 'Tis settled then. We deny him entry.'

'The devil we do!'

'The devil we do not!'

'Hear him out, Will; tis only fair. Go on, Tom, speak your mind.'

'I think we should not be hasty in this. Not when it's a decision likely to come back to haunt us. Ere we do decide, you'd best be sure you're willing to make an enemy of the man who might well be king again within the month.'

'The truth of it, Wrangwysh, is that you've always held for York. Admit it, you'd be well pleased to see a Yorkist victory!'

'What if I do? That does not change the facts, Holbeck. If we deny Edward of York entry, we antagonize him to no purpose.'

'But if we admit him, Tom, we do for a certainty anger Warwick.'

'They turned him away from Kingston upon Hull. . . .'

'Aye, and gave him entry into Beverley. As I say we should do in York.'

'What says His Grace of Northumberland?'

'We've had nary a word.'

'Well, does that not give you pause, gentlemen? As long as Henry Percy keeps to Topcliffe, I'd not be so quick to bury York. If Percy will not fight for Warwick, that changes the odds somewhat, do you not agree? We should think on that ere we decide.'

'Jesú, but you lawyers are never happy unless you're muddying the waters. Even if you are right, Aske, and the Earl of Northumberland chooses not to move against York, what matters that to us? I say we dare not risk the Earl of Warwick's wrath by opening the city gates to his sworn enemy.'

'Ah, but he's not.'

All heads turned toward the doorway of the council chamber. That morning Richard Burghe and Thomas Conyers had volunteered to ride out to warn the Yorkists away from the city. Now they found themselves assailed on all sides.

'You saw him, Conyers? What says he?'

'How does His Grace, Tom?'

'What meant you when you said he was no sworn enemy to Warwick?'

Conyers was grinning. 'I mean your problem has been solved, gentlemen,' he said, somewhat smugly. 'Suppose I were to tell you there is a way by which we can accommodate York and yet still pacify Warwick?'

'I'd say you were suffering from sun sickness.'

'Not even Merlin could perform such a feat, Conyers.'

'Well, we lose nothing if we do hear him out. . . . Tom?'

"Tis very simple, in truth. Edward of York assured us that he has no intent to seize the English crown.'

He raised his hand to still their outbursts. 'He says that he means only to lay claim to those estates which are his by right as the Duke of York. . . . No more than that. Moreover, he swears he'd be willing to take oath of allegiance to Lancaster should we admit him into the city . . . to show his good faith.'

In the stunned silence that followed, Burghe nodded confirmation of this story none could yet believe. Conyers claimed a seat and, nudging Tom Wrangwysh in jovial complicity, he observed to the room at large, 'As for me, I thought it a right fair offer – one which will gladden the heart of King Harry, I daresay!'

They were all staring at him, with expressions that ran the gamut from outrage to amusement.

'Christ, man, who'd believe such a tale as that? Does he think us fools?'

'I never said you need believe it, Will. I'm only saying that when the Earl of Warwick does demand to know why we opened the city to York, we can say that he was but seeking what was his by right . . . the duchy of his late lord father.'

Holbeck snorted. 'Do you want to be the one to tell His Grace of Warwick that, Conyers? I say no, and let's have an end to it!'

Tom Wrangwysh leaned across the table to say pleasantly, 'Will, I trust you'll not take this amiss, but I think you do need reminding that you are no longer Lord Mayor.'

In the sudden expectant hush, Holbeck's indrawn breath was audible to all. But before he could retaliate, the City Recorder had turned to one who'd so far taken no part in the debate, said hastily, 'What think you, Chris? What with the city lacking a mayor till the dispute over the elections is settled, we'd be most interested in your views on this matter. You are, after all, Esquire of the Mayor, and if troops need be raised, yours is the responsibilty.'

'I see no such need,' the man thus appealed to said quietly, as his colleagues settled back to give him the respect due both his office and his person.

'I think we must put politics aside, do what is in the best interests of our city. I would suggest that we compromise, that we do offer admittance to Edward . . . Duke of York.'

The resolve found ready acceptance in the glances now exchanged with nods and relieved murmurs of satisfaction.

'Gentlemen, I move that we vote upon the suggestion put forth by Master Berwyk.'

'Is that truly necessary, Rob? I'd venture we're in agreement . . . except perhaps for Will here? What say you, Master Holbeck? Do you want it writ in the city records that you alone would deny entry to Edward of York?'

Holbeck glared at him and then said, as grudgingly as if words

344

had the worth of gold, 'You win, Wrangwysh. Do as you wish. But I'm damned if I like it any. And this I can tell you for true, that the Earl of Warwick will not like it, either.'

Rob Percy had decided that if he were ever asked to name the worst night of his life, he would, without hesitation, say that it had been a Thursday, the fourteenth of March. But if the same question were to be put to Richard, he felt sure that Richard would have chosen today, the eighteenth. He had never seen Richard so tense, so quick to anger as he was on this most miserable of Mondays, the fourth day of their arrival in England.

They'd sailed from Flushing on the eleventh, in the heaviest seas Rob had ever seen; the mere memory was enough to dredge up a queasy pang. He thought they'd been damnably lucky, though, for they'd evaded the English fleet under command of Warwick's kinsman, the Bastard of Fauconberg, and they'd lost only one ship during the crossing, one of the supply ships carrying their horses.

By the twelfth they were within sight of the Norfolk coast, where they could reasonably expect aid from the Yorkist Duke of Norfolk and from Edward and Richard's brother-in-law, the Duke of Suffolk. Edward had prudently sent two of his party ashore before they all disembarked, and his caution had served him well, for they'd rapidly returned with grim word that the Duke of Norfolk was under arrest, Suffolk absent, and the Lancastrian Duke of Oxford had the entire region under close surveillance. Edward had ordered their ships to put out to sea again, this time to head for Yorkshire. But they'd been hit by squalls and their small fleet scattered.

On the night of the fourteenth, Richard's ship had dropped anchor off the Yorkshire coast, a few miles north of the tiny fishing village of Ravenspur and thus began the most harrowing ten hours of Rob's life. There was no sign of their comrades and it occurred to him that they alone might have ridden out the storm, that they might be stranded here in a land hostile to York, to face the armies of John Neville and his own kinsman Percy, just he and Richard and the three hundred men under Richard's command. It was a chilling thought and one that he was sure had crossed Richard's mind, too.

Looking back, Rob found he still marvelled at the icy control his friend had shown during that darkest of nights. Richard had rallied their men, somehow kept panic from spreading through their ranks and, at dawn, he'd led them south in search of the others.

Rob had never been so thankful as when they encountered the five hundred men of the *Antony*, the ship under command of Edward and Will Hastings. While Edward sent out scouts to find Anthony Woodville and the two hundred men who'd sailed with him, Rob had ventured to compliment Richard on what he saw as an admirable display of courage. But Richard had merely given him a quizzical look and said laconically, 'I was not aware I had a choice, Rob.'

Yet if Richard had shown no nerves at all on Thursday, today he was nothing but nerves, and had been ever since Edward had shouted him and Will Hastings down and ridden alone into the city of York.

It was no secret in their camp that the Yorkist leaders had quarrelled bitterly over Edward's intention to enter York. Their voices had carried clearly beyond the tent flaps, and Rob was not the only one to have gathered at a prudent distance to listen. They'd all vehemently opposed Edward in this, Richard and Will Hastings and Anthony Woodville, and the conversation had become quite heated at times. But Edward had prevailed and then Richard and Hastings had demanded to accompany him into the city. Edward had refused and they'd insisted, but, in the end, Edward had his way.

More than three hours ago, he'd spurred his horse toward the city gate known as Walmgate. They had watched as it opened to admit him and then closed ominously behind him. It was at once the most courageous act Rob had ever witnessed and the most incredible folly, and, as the hours passed, he watched Richard's composure shred like parchment under pressure.

He'd briefly considered making an attempt to reassure Richard that Edward was in no danger but decided against it. His encouragement was bound to be hollow, as he thought Edward to be in the greatest danger imaginable. Moreover, as short-tempered as Richard had shown himself to be all afternoon, Rob preferred to keep him at a distance.

It was not only Dickon, he thought glumly. They were all as jumpy as wet cats, as quick to take offence. They'd just seen proof enough of that, as the normally unflappable Hastings startled all within earshot by tongue-lashing one of the Flemish gunners. Rob wondered how long it would be before Dickon and Hastings fell out with Anthony Woodville. He was not sure how they felt about each other, but he was damned well sure that neither one of them could abide Anthony, who returned their dislike in full measure. And he wondered what they would do if Edward had ridden into a trap, encountered an assassin's dagger.

There was a sudden stir among the men. The iron-barred portcullis was rising; several horsemen were passing through the Walmgate barbican. The youth stationed to keep watch now forgot all protocol and yelled, 'Tell Gloucester!' and Rob hastily adjusted his scabbard, moving closer for a better view of the approaching riders.

Richard and Will Hastings were standing together, and Rob saw Richard grin suddenly, heard him say in a low voice, 'The news is good, Will. That's Tom Wrangwysh with them. If there'd been trouble, we'd see it in his face.'

Both city sheriffs were impassive, but Tom Wrangwysh and Thomas Conyers looked enormously well pleased with themselves and Conyers blurted out their news even as he was dismounting. They were all welcome now within the city walls, and my lord of York did await them at the guildhall. If they would . . .

Tom Wrangwysh interrupted happily, 'My lords, you should

have seen him. You'd have thought he had an army at his back, so cool he was. . . . There were many he did win over by his courage alone. And then he spoke to the people and made a marvellous fair speech in which he said he would content himself to be Duke of York and serve good King Harry and the crowds cheered him till we all were hoarse.'

Word was spreading swiftly; all around Rob, men were laughing and pounding each other on the back. Richard was trying to make himself heard over the uproar, but soon abandoned the attempt and watched with a grin as their men raised a cheer for His Grace of York and the city that was now willing to admit his army.

Rob moved to Richard's side, just in time to hear Tom Wrangwysh confide, 'My lord, however did His Grace think to lay claim to the duchy of York? I can say with certainty that had it not been for that, the city would've stayed closed to him.'

Richard laughed. 'It was used once before, Tom. Harry of Lancaster's grandfather returned from exile to claim only his duchy of Lancaster and, of course, deposed a King. My brother thought it fitting that a gambit used by the first Lancastrian King should now serve York.'

Coventry

March 1471

The Earl of Warwick was rereading the letter he'd just dictated to one Henry Vernon of Haddon in Derbyshire, a man long allied both to the Earl and his son-in-law of Clarence. The letter was brief, to the point, an appeal for military aid in this, Warwick's time of greatest need. Scanning the page rapidly, he picked up a pen and signed, 'R. Warwick,' saying, 'It will do.'

But as the man moved toward the door, Warwick turned and, on impulse, reclaimed the letter.

'Give me that pen again,' he demanded, and hastily scribbled a postscript in his own hand on the margin of the page:

'Henry, I pray you fail me not now as ever I may do for you.'

From the white city walls of Coventry, the Yorkist army stretched as far as the eye could see, spread out in battle formation under the Sunne in Splendour banner of Edward of York. The Yorkist herald had just given challenge to combat, as he had on each of the two preceding days, and, as he had done then, the Earl of Warwick refused to pick up the gauntlet, staring down in silence from the city walls at the army of his cousin of York.

They were well within recognition range; he had no doubts that he was watching Ned himself, mounted as always on a showy white stallion, giving commands, dispatching messengers, and all the while gazing toward Coventry. Warwick was sure the blue eyes would be aglitter with mockery and triumph . . . and why not? Ned had reason and more for jubilation. In just a fortnight, he'd come as far as the walls of Coventry when, by rights, he should never have left Yorkshire alive.

A slighter figure on an equally eye-catching mount was now at Ned's side. Even before the second rider removed his helmet, thus revealing a head of tousled dark hair, Warwick knew this was Dickon. His brother-in-law Hastings would be there, too.

The thought of Hastings brought to mind another brother-in-law, Lord Stanley. He should've known he could not trust Stanley. The Stanleys were ever a shifty lot, always with an eye to the prevailing winds. So it had come as no real surprise to him when the self-seeking Stanley had not responded to the urgent summons for aid. Instead, he'd seized this chance to besiege the castle of the Harringtons in Lancashire, against whom he'd long harboured a grudge.

Warwick had expected more, however, from Henry Percy. But that Judas-in-the-making Percy had kept to his estates in the North, refused to give challenge to Ned, and, because the Percy family cast so long a shadow in Yorkshire, Warwick knew Ned had benefited enormously from Percy's apparent neutrality. The people of the North were weary of these endless wars of succession. The House of Percy had always held for Lancaster. But if their lord was not disposed to oppose the Yorkist King who'd restored to him his forfeited earldom, they were content to follow their lord's lead. Let the blood be spilt elsewhere; there were too many northern widows and orphans who still grieved for the dead of Towton.

The thought of Percy was an especially galling one to Warwick, for Northumberland could so easily have ended for all time the hopes of the House of York. Once again, one of Ned's high-stakes gambles had paid off.

The Devil tends to its own. It must be true. How else explain the way Ned had passed unscathed through three hostile armies?

Now that he stood before Coventry, he'd cast aside all pretence and openly proclaimed himself as King of England. But that perfidious claim to the duchy of York had served its purpose. It had gained him entry into York and, once word had spread that the chief city of the North had opened its gates to him, the smaller towns had been loath to deny him entry. Few had joined his ranks, it was true, but fewer still were inclined to offer resistance. Like the Earl of Northumberland, they chose to wait and watch.

Ned always did have unholy luck. Warwick vaguely recalled saying something of the sort to his brother George at Warwick Castle less than a fortnight ago. But it was not luck that had got Ned safely past Pontefract. Johnny had let him pass. They'd have been butchered for sure had Johnny chosen to fall upon them;

as outnumbered as they were, they'd have died to a man. But Johnny had stayed his hand, let them go by.

There were those of Warwick's advisers who'd claimed his brother the Marquess of Montagu must have feared to provoke Henry Percy into choosing sides. Others, more credulous even, suggested that Montagu had accepted Edward's claim that he sought only his duchy of York. Warwick knew better. Knew Johnny had never forgiven himself for betraying Ned at Doncaster and, in his moment of truth when all was at stake, he'd not been able to act against the cousin he'd loved like a brother, acknowledged as his King.

As for the others, his Lancastrian allies, they'd proven worthless to a man. Many remained on their estates, so unwilling to fight for a Neville that they'd rather see Edward of York advancing unchecked through the very heartland of England. That hellspawn Somerset had ridden into London at the head of a well-armed force, and then insolently sent Warwick word that he was heading for the southern coast, there to await the arrival of his Queen and Prince from France.

Exeter and Oxford had, at least, made a show of resistance. When word had come of Ned's landing in Yorkshire, they'd assembled several thousand men and marched north along the Fosse Road to run him to earth.

And, for a brief while, Warwick dared think that Ned had trapped himself. Ned had halted at Nottingham, there to welcome Sir William Parr and six hundred new converts to his cause. Suddenly it seemed that the reckoning had come. Three armies were reported converging upon him. Johnny was shadowing his rear; Oxford and Exeter had by then reached Newark and were threatening his east flank; and Warwick himself was only two days' march from Nottingham.

But even as Warwick moved north, word reached him that Ned had suddenly swung around and launched an unexpected assault upon Exeter and Oxford. Awakened at 2:00 A.M. with

351

the news that the Yorkists were on the outskirts of Newark, those two Lancastrian lords had bolted in panic. Warwick had been wild with rage upon hearing of their flight, knowing their forces had far outnumbered those under Ned's command. And worse was to come. It soon became apparent that Ned's attack had, in fact, been a feint with an advance scouting party. He'd scattered the Lancastrians with what was no more than a daring bluff.

Cut off from contact with Oxford and Exeter, hearing nothing from his brother, Warwick had withdrawn into Coventry. And suddenly, on the morning of the twenty-ninth, Ned had appeared before the city walls, daring him to do battle as he waited for word from the men who had so far proved to be such useless allies.

That night, Warwick examined the flimsy substance of the world he himself had constructed at such terrible cost. He now knew himself to be alone, walled in by unhealed hatreds, facing a future shadowed with foreboding. After six months of striving somehow to hold together this alliance of irreconcilable loyalties, he felt drained, emotionally exhausted. And Marguerite d'Anjou had yet to set foot in England. Marguerite, his ally of expedience. Marguerite, the implacable, the unforgiving. He thought of lords like Somerset and Tudor who would not fight for him, who despised him all the more for his new-found allegiance to Lancaster. He thought of Johnny who grieved for the cousins whose lives he was now sworn to take. And he thought of Ludlow, Calais and Towton; in his weariness, called to mind memories long buried under the bitterness and grievances stored up over the past six years.

It was in those predawn hours when he was most vulnerable to the past, most pessimistic for the future, that he at last yielded to despair and, before he could repent of it, dispatched a herald to his cousin's camp with an offer to enter into negotiations. Back came Ned's reply, cool and uncompromising. He was, indeed, willing to negotiate. But he was prepared to offer Warwick no more than a pardon and his life, that and that alone.

It was not an offer that Warwick was prepared to accept. Nor, were he to be honest with himself, was it one he'd been expecting. He needed no time to consider; a prideful message of rejection was on its way to Warwick Castle within the hour. For it was at Warwick's own castle that Ned had chosen to encamp his army, a gesture that, for pure provocation, could hardly have been improved upon.

And so he waited for Johnny, for Exeter and Oxford. Waited, too, for the arrival of his son-in-law, who was even now advancing from the southwest, sending messages of reassurance and support. He had no choice but to believe them, to wait. But he could not help wondering if Ned, too, were not waiting for George of Clarence.

April 3rd dawned unseasonably warm, so much so as to cause discomfort for the four thousand men under command of the Duke of Clarence. Heading north, they'd halted in Burford for the night and this morning resumed their march toward Banbury, some three miles from Warwick Castle where Edward was reported to be quartered.

George had never tolerated heat well and he felt as if he would swelter under the weight of armour and glare of the sun. Impatiently fumbling with the vizor of his helmet, he was finding it virtually impossible to wipe the sweat from his brow with a gauntleted hand. He swore and could see heads turn in his direction, could feel the eyes boring into his back.

His lieutenants had been giving him irritatingly covert glances all morning, trying to guess what was in his mind, wondering if he'd take the field against his brothers. Well, they could damn well wonder.

Now, with word from his scouts that the Yorkist army was moving south to meet him, the tension of his battle captains had grown intolerable. Twice within the past quarter-hour, Thomas Burdett had approached him to make anxious query and twice

George had, with rare patience, repeated his order, that they were to wait, to do nothing until he gave the command.

Burdett was back again. 'My lord . . . they come,' he said unnecessarily, gesturing down the road.

'I've eyes to see, Tom,' George said curtly. The sight of his brother's banner had affected him more than he'd anticipated. He swallowed; there was a tightness in his throat which had nothing to do with the heat or the dust of the road. He knew he could trust Dickon. But what of Ned? He glanced back over his shoulder, at the men deployed in battle formation, men so desperately needed by his father-in-law awaiting him at Coventry.

'Your Grace!'

Burdett was pointing again and George saw that something seemed to be happening in the Yorkist ranks. There was movement, dust swirled, and then they were parting to let a lone rider pass through. As all watched, he wheeled his mount and then galloped toward them.

Once away from the Yorkist army, the rider eased his mount somewhat, held the stallion to an easy, unhurried canter. He was unhelmeted and the sun burnished his armour in a blaze of light, beat down on hair as black as purest jet. Behind him George heard the first murmurings of recognition, heard the name Gloucester rustling through the ranks with mounting excitement.

Still he did nothing, sat motionless as his brother came on. The noise to his rear intensified. Discipline was flagging; his men were openly speculating as to his intentions . . . and still he waited. Not until Richard was less than a hundred yards distant did he turn to Burdett, giving the order to hold their positions, and then spurred his horse forward.

Richard had reined in, was waiting as George drew up beside him.

'You did take your time for true, George. What was in your mind—to give Ned concern that you'd decided to stand with Warwick, after all?'

George frowned, again caught up in a tangle of uncertain suspicions, but Richard's dark face was unrevealing. He could not be sure if this were banter, accusation or a shot too close to home.

'If you must know, Dickon, I had not the heart to intrude upon so spectacular an approach. . . . You did look as if you were rather enjoying yourself.'

Richard looked at him and then grinned. 'I was.'

He moved in closer, laughing, holding out his hand, and, as George clasped it, he laughed, too, sure now that all would be well, even with Ned, and hearing behind him a vast roar of approval as his army understood that they were not to fight and die after all, at least not this April noon on the Banbury Road.

25

London

April 1471

On the same day that John Neville and the Lancastrian lords of Exeter and Oxford reached Coventry, the Earl of Warwick learned that his son-in-law had gone over to his brothers of York. Once more, Edward appeared before the walls of Coventry to challenge the men who waited within. Once more, they refused to do battle and, on Friday, April 5th, Edward suddenly broke camp and took the road south, toward London.

Warwick set out in grim pursuit, but Edward was two days before him and the Earl knew he had little hope of heading Edward off before he reached the capital. Urgent messages were sent on ahead, instructing the Lord Mayor and city council to deny Edward entry.

The Archbishop of York dutifully paraded Harry of Lancaster through the city streets; it proved to be a mistake. The watching spectators jeered at the limp foxtails that hung from Lancaster's standard, and they wondered aloud why the poor old man wore the same blue gown as when he'd last appeared in public in October. Edward of York had always been popular in London and he still owed the city merchants considerable sums of money. Moreover, he was now at St Albans, just a day's march away, with an army at his back.

Messages continued to arrive from the Earl of Warwick, urging Londoners to hold firm for King Harry. Marguerite d'Anjou and her son were expected to land at any time. While at St Albans, Edward sent word that Harry of Lancaster was to be considered a prisoner of state. At that, John Stockton, the Mayor of London, contracted a diplomatic virus and took to his bed. The Deputy Mayor, Thomas Cook, argued for closing the city gates to the Yorkists. But even as he did, the Archbishop of York was sending a secret capitulation to his cousin at St Albans. And the common council, meeting in urgent session, resolved that, 'As Edward, late King of England, is hastening toward the city with a powerful army and, as the inhabitants are not sufficiently versed in the use of arms to withstand so large a force, no attempt should be made to resist him.'

At noon on Maundy Thursday of Holy Week, Edward rode through Aldersgate and into the city of London, exactly one month to the day since he had sailed from Burgundy. Just as six months before, the Earl of Warwick had ridden to St Paul's to give thanks to the Almighty for His favour, Edward now did likewise and here, at last, he encountered the enthusiasm that had been so conspicuously lacking during his progress southward, a progress that had demonstrated just how very much these continuing quarrels over the crown had cheapened what was once a sovereign's brightest coinage, the blind devotion of his people.

From St Paul's, Edward was to go to Westminster, where the Archbishop of Canterbury awaited him, there to symbolically place the crown once more upon his head. At Westminster, too, waited his Queen and children. But there was one task still to be performed, and shortly past one o'clock, he strode into the palace of the Bishop of London to accept the formal surrender of the man who commanded the Tower of London—his cousin, George Neville.

The Archbishop of York was ill at ease. Unlike his brothers, he'd not shared a friendship with Edward and he was well aware that he could rely on no memories of bygone affection to temper Edward's vengeance, were he so inclined.

Edward listened impassively as the archbishop stammered apologies for six months of treason, until he grew bored and said coolly, 'You need not fear, cousin. I'd not send a priest to the block, even such a priest as you. I will send you to the Tower, however, and you may be thankful that I do, at times, show mercy, else I'd have you sharing the same cell with your unlamented lord of Lancaster.'

The archbishop knelt, pledging his loyalties, present and future, to York and, at Edward's impatient gesture, retreated to fetch Harry of Lancaster.

Edward grimaced at that and, turning toward Richard, said grimly, 'This is a pleasure, Dickon, I can damned well do without.'

Richard alone had never seen the Lancastrian King, although all his life he'd heard tales of this unstable man who was called a saint by some and simpleminded by most. He knew Harry had always been somewhat odd, apt to wander in his wits, what in Yorkshire would be called 'moonstruck'. He'd found no peace in marriage to the imperious French Princess from Anjou; and in the summer of his thirty-second year, when Marguerite was six months pregnant with the boy now wed to Anne Neville, Harry

357

had slipped into a darkness of the mind from which he'd never fully emerged.

Richard knew all this by heart; from childhood, Lancaster's madness had been a litany of his House. But even these oft-told tales had not prepared him for the reality of the man his brother contemptuously called 'Daft Harry'.

He was not yet fifty but he walked with a pronounced stoop, hunched forward like one searching the ground for lost valuables. He had thin grey hair, which once had been flaxen, blank pale eyes that might have been blue, and he was the colour of unchurned milk; he looked, to Richard, as if he'd never spent a day in the sun, not in his entire life. Richard experienced a surge of pity and, at the same time, an aversion that was physical.

The archbishop was leading him like a child, now said, speaking in the overly loud voice one would use with the hard of hearing, "Tis His Grace of York.' When Harry did not respond at once, the archbishop repeated, louder still and rather impatiently, 'York . . . Edward of York.'

Harry nodded. 'I know,' he said mildly and smiled at Edward.

Edward, looking resigned, held out his hand.

'Cousin,' he said politely, a title more of courtesy than kinship, for the blood they shared had been much diluted over a period of some seventy years.

Harry disregarded the outstretched hand, stepped forward and embraced the younger man as if they were comrades of long standing.

Edward recoiled violently, drawing back as if struck; it was the only time that Richard could ever recall seeing his brother thoroughly flustered. For a moment, his consternation showed clearly in his face and then he was once more in control, and he reached out, grasped the other man's hand, in that way responding to the greeting and yet keeping him at arm's length.

Harry's smile had not wavered. 'My cousin of York, I bid you welcome,' he said, in a soft, unexpectedly pleasing voice.

'Thank you, cousin,' Edward said dispassionately. Whatever his feelings, nothing showed now in his face, not even as Harry added, with the air of one sharing a secret with a friend,

'I know that in your hands my life will not be in danger.'

Beside him, Richard heard Hastings draw a breath through his teeth, as sharp as a whistle. The archbishop had the look of one wanting fervently to disassociate himself from a blatant embarrassment. Richard himself wished to be anywhere else than where he was at that moment, and he marvelled that Edward could hear such words and yet look so unmoved.

'It pleases me that you do think so, Cousin,' Edward said, a response so strangely ambiguous, so unlike what the natural rejoinder would have been, that Richard was suddenly struck by an incredible suspicion, one so ugly that he at once disavowed it as an aberrant thought, one Edward didn't deserve.

Edward now raised his hand and men who wore the colours of York came through the gallery doorway.

'The Archbishop of York shall escort you to the Tower, cousin. Make your wants known, once there; they'll be seen to.'

There was silence as the archbishop and the Lancastrian king exited the great hall, flanked by men-at-arms. Edward was staring after the sparse figure clad in soiled blue velvet. At length, he said softly, 'I will never understand . . . never be able to comprehend how men were willing to die so that he might be king.'

No one answered him and he glanced around at the silent circle of men.

'Well?' he demanded. 'Why do we wait? Fetch the horses.'

He turned away, moved toward the door, and then snapped, to no one in particular, 'And for Christ's sake, get him another gown.'

There was a sudden commotion in the inner courtyard. Jacquetta Woodville heard Nurse Cobb cry out and she looked up to see her son-in-law standing in the doorway. Too flustered for presence of mind, she dropped down in a curtsy, had a fleeting glimpse of the children. Mary was wide-eyed, uncertain, and two-year-old Cecily had the emerging look of fear. But, before Jacquetta could speak, Bess had given a strangled cry, neither laugh nor sob but kin to both, and flung herself across the room. The floor was strewn with rushes and, just as she reached her father, she tripped, fell forward. Edward caught her before she hit the ground and swung her up into his arms. She seemed to have no need of speech, content just to be held and, as Jacquetta watched, she felt tears prickle but she didn't care, let them come.

Thomas was moving forward and his brother was in the room, too, flushed with excitement. Jacquetta saw that Edward wasn't alone. Her son Anthony was with him and she recognized Richard and Hastings and the Abbot Millyng and—with a distinct shock—George of Clarence.

Anthony was smiling at her but he stayed in the doorway. They were all looking to Edward, waiting on him. But he was smiling at his daughter, touching her soft fair hair, and, for the moment, she alone claimed his attention. . . . Until the Jerusalem Chamber door opened.

Elizabeth wore only a dressing robe of a light clinging material and her hair hung loosely down her back in a spill of tangled silver. She was clutching a kirtle of sarcenet silk and a hairbrush and she looked dishevelled, breathless, startled.

Edward lowered Bess to the ground. As he did, Elizabeth let the kirtle and brush fall to the floor in the only truly spontaneous gesture that Richard, watching, had ever seen his sister-in-law make, and moved toward her husband. He didn't wait; in two strides, he had her in his arms, in a passionate embrace.

She was the one that broke free first, balancing her hand against his chest as if to hold him there.

'Wait,' she said, and then she smiled at him. 'Wait . . .' And she spun around, to find that Nurse Cobb was already beside her, happily holding out the baby. Elizabeth reached for him and, turning back to Edward, placed the child in his arms.

No one else had yet moved, not even his daughters. He studied his son and then raised his eyes to hers, linking over the baby's head.

'Did you ever doubt me?'

'No, never. Did you think I would?'

He grinned, shook his head.

Edward was surrounded by children. He'd laughed, claiming he felt like the Pied Piper, and almost at once won over the last holdout, the shy Cecily, who'd observed her second birthday as he had ridden alone into the city of York. With Bess on his lap and Mary at his feet, he was responding to his stepson's questions, good-naturedly coping with an avid assault of curious queries about exile, Bruges, the Yorkshire campaign. But, before long, his interest began to slacken, his replies grew more inattentive, less animated. He was watching his wife, and she sensed it, turned in his direction. A private message passed between them; she rose from her brother's side, shook back the tumbled masses of blonde hair and Edward stood, gently depositing Bess on her feet.

'You've not yet greeted your Uncle Anthony or your Uncle Dickon, sweetheart,' he coaxed, smiling down at her. 'That's a good lass.'

Bess moved dutifully toward her Uncle Anthony as bidden but stopped abruptly when she saw her father cross the room, take her mother's hand, and disappear into the Jerusalem Chamber. She took an uncertain step forward but the door closed behind them; she heard the bolt slide into place.

Richard crossed to Will Hastings. 'I think Ned is in good hands. . . . Give him word for me, Will, that I've gone to Baynard's Castle.'

Will grinned, asked to have his courtesies conveyed to Her Grace, the Duchess of York, but as Richard listened, his eyes were straying across the room, measuring his niece's misery. Bess was sobbing softly, staring forlornly at the bedchamber door, and neither Jacquetta nor Thomas seemed able to console her.

Bess liked her half brother Thomas, but now she paid no heed to his attempts to make her laugh with the floppy rabbit puppet he'd made for Mary. She rather wished he'd stop; he should know she'd not care about a silly playtoy when her father had come home at last, after being gone for so very long, only to vanish again ere she'd even had the chance to confide how much she'd missed him. She fumbled for a handkerchief, gave up and used her sleeve. Her Uncle Dickon was kneeling by her now and she gave him a suspicious look to see if he meant to order her away from her vigil by the bedchamber door. But he seemed content to stay beside her and she relaxed somewhat. Grand-mère had asked her if she remembered her uncles, which was silly; of course she did.

'Bess, would you like to ride into London with me?'

She sniffed, shook her head, and then turned to look sharply up into his face. 'London?' she said uncertainly. 'You mean . . . outside? We cannot. It is forbidden.'

'Not any longer, Bess. Would you not like to see the city again? You have not been beyond these walls in months; are you not curious?'

She was regarding him doubtfully. 'I do not have a pony,' she said sadly. 'It got left. I could not even take my dog with me. . . .' Her mouth was quavering again and he said swiftly,

'If I find you a horse, should you like to come with me?'

She nodded, gave him a dawning smile. But then she glanced back toward the door of the Jerusalem Chamber and her face shadowed again.

'No, I . . . I cannot. . . .'

'Bess, do you know where I've been these six months past?'

'Burgundy,' she said at once, and was grateful when he didn't question her where Burgundy was. Instead, he said,

'You know who I was with?'

362

'Papa.'

'He will not go away without me, Bess. You can await him at Baynard's Castle if you like . . . and as long as I'm there, you'll know he has not gone away again.'

She considered this, decided it made sense. 'Can we ride by the river?' she bargained, and he laughed, helped her to rise.

'By all means, by the river,' he agreed, as Thomas Grey stepped in front of him.

'I do not think my lady mother would wish her daughter to go off without her permission,' he said coldly. 'I cannot approve of this pleasure-jaunt into London.'

Jacquetta had just been about to thank Richard for his in-spiration and now she turned to her grandson in surprise. He was jealous, she decided; these months had not been easy on the boy and she could well understand how he might feel shunted aside, ignored. She stepped forward, intending to intercede, but in such a manner that Thomas would not feel reprimanded or rebuked, when Richard said, with what she felt to be uncalled-for rude-ness, 'What makes you think I give a damn about your approval?'

Anthony Woodville looked up at that, frowned. 'I think his concern for his sister is to be commended,' he said, in a far from friendly tone, and Jacquetta, seeing that Richard was about to respond in kind, started to speak.

But Will Hastings was quicker. Lounging against the wall, he'd straightened up at the first exchange, and now he smiled at Anthony.

'I do not see that young Grey need fret over the Lady Bess. I can think of no safer guardian than His Grace of Gloucester and I am sure the King would agree with me. Do you mean to suggest otherwise, my lord Rivers?'

Anthony stared at him; dislike surged between them, almost tangible in its intensity. 'I'll tell you what I mean to suggest, my lord Hastings. . . . That this is a family matter and not one which concerns you.'

Bess had been shifting impatiently; she was accustomed to the quarrels of adults and they held little interest for her. Now that she was to ride in the sun, see the city streets, and hear the people cheer her as they had whenever she'd passed through London in the past, she was eager to depart, and she tugged at Richard's arm.

'Can we not go now?'

'I see no reason why not, Bess.'

Richard looked challengingly at Thomas. The latter hesitated, not sure how far this should be pursued and, in the pause that followed, George spoke for the first time.

'Go on, Dickon, take Bess to our mother. If Grey feels the need to play nursemaid, let him do so with her sisters.'

Jacquetta saw amusement on the faces of Hastings and Richard, saw murderous rage on that of her grandson and, as he swung around to confront George, she said icily, 'I only do wish you had shown such solicitude for your brother's children, my lord of Clarence, these six months past whilst they were forced into sanctuary under your father-in-law's threats.'

Abbot Millyng had been listening, in growing disapproval, and now he was moved to mediate, made uneasy by the expression on the Duke of Clarence's face.

'I truly must protest. It is not seemly that there should be dissension amongst you on this which should be the happiest of days for the House of York.'

They were all staring at him, and he read in their silence unwilling acknowledgment of the truth of his charge. Richard allowed his niece to lead him toward the door, pausing long enough to murmur a few words meant for George alone. George didn't reply, but they seemed to have reached an understanding of some sort and he followed Richard from the room. Will was next to depart and, as he passed the Abbot, he murmured, with a sideways smile, 'Blessed are the peacemakers, for they shall be called the Children of God.'

The Abbot shut the outer door, glanced toward the bedchamber door, which still remained closed. Jacquetta was attempting to soothe her angry grandson without notable success. He was complaining bitterly, 'It is just that I see not why Bess should be fetched to see Her Vainglorious Grace now, when she never once did come to us in sanctuary. . . .'

Jacquetta's reply was lost to the Abbot, for Anthony had begun to rail against 'that whoreson Hastings', and, as he listened, Abbot Millyng felt a chill. He'd deeply feared an England ruled by the Earl of Warwick and Marguerite d'Anjou, sure there could be no peace between those most bitter and implacable of enemies. Now he wondered if it were truly that different with the House of York. It occurred to him that herein, too, lay the seeds of destruction, as surely as it did with Marguerite d'Anjou and the Kingmaker.

It was a sobering thought, but then he remembered, remembered with deep heartfelt relief. . . . Thank Almighty God that there was a man strong enough to hold them all together, a man able to reconcile the passions of Woodville and Plantagenet under the blazing banner of his Sunne in Splendour. The hostility he'd just seen in this room had been disturbing but there'd be no bloody rending of the House of York. He glanced again at the bedchamber door and then said to Jacquetta, 'Shall we not give thanks, Madame, that His Grace the King has come safely home to us?'

Bess was curled up beside Richard on the settle in her grandmother's solar. She'd been tenaciously staving off sleep ever since supper, but her eyes were now the merest of slits and, as Cecily watched, silky little lashes sealed off the last lingering traces of blue. Cecily smiled; Bess might have her mother's silver-gilt hair, but her eyes were unmistakably Edward's.

Cecily was, in many ways, a stranger to the child, for her relationship with her daughter-in-law was such that she rarely saw her grandchildren in settings other than ceremonial. Richard was far better acquainted with Edward's eldest-born than she was, and she'd expected Bess to be somewhat shy with her, at least at first. But Bess was no more shy than any small creature that had been conditioned to expect only love and approval, and she'd shown no hesitation whatsoever in climbing up into Cecily's lap, just as if she'd passed every day of her life with her grandmother at Baynard's Castle.

Cecily leaned over to wipe a greasy smear from the little girl's chin, said ruefully, 'One might read our menu on that child's face. Come, Bess, let me put you to bed, dearest.'

Bess's eyes were unfocused, her lids uncooperatively refusing to remain open, but she at once offered sleepy resistance, clinging to Richard with the resolve of one determined not to be dislodged.

'Let her stay, ma mère. Does it matter, after all, whether she sleeps here or in bed?'

'No, I suppose not,' Cecily conceded, seeing that Bess, reassured by Richard's intercession on her behalf, had stopped struggling. He shifted his arm and she nestled back against him, slid with a contented sigh again into sleep.

'She's quite taken with you, Richard.'

He smiled, shook his head. 'No, it's not that. Bess and I did strike a bargain, you see. I pledged on Ned's behalf that he'd not come anywhere but to Baynard's Castle and, till he does, she's not likely to let me out of her sight.'

Cecily smiled, too, at that, and then said, 'We tend to forget at times that it is the little ones, the children, who do suffer the greatest hurt. If we cannot comprehend why certain sorrows are visited upon us, how on earth can they?'

Richard nodded and, looking down at his sleeping niece, found himself thinking of Kathryn, his own daughter. She was nigh on a year old already and he'd not seen her since she was a swaddling babe. He couldn't even be sure she still lived. Babies were subject to the croup, to sudden high fevers, to any number of ailments that could snuff out a little life as abruptly as any candle flame. And if Kathryn had been stricken, how could Kate have got word to him? She could be dead and beneath ground these many months past and he'd not even know.

'What troubles you, Richard? Is it your own child you think of?'

Richard's eyes widened. His surprise was readily apparent, his embarrassment only slightly less so, and she shook her head, said dryly, 'Did you truly expect me to remain long in ignorance? I assure you there's little you and your brothers do that does not eventually find its way to my ear . . . whether I want to hear it or not!'

The best Richard could muster was an inadequate, 'I see.'

'For heaven's sake, Richard, you cannot imagine it comes as any surprise to me that you've a child born of an illicit attachment? After all, I was raised in a family with more brothers than I could count. Moreover, I did bring up four sons to manhood and your brothers were no less susceptible than you to temptation—whilst being far less discreet, I regret to say. I cannot condone the circumstances of your child's birth but I most surely do approve of your willingness to assume responsibility for your act.' And then she sighed, said in a voice suddenly dull, drained of animation, 'Men are born to sin, Richard. What does matter most is not that we err. . . . It is that we do benefit from our mistakes, that we are capable of sincere repentance, of genuine contrition.'

Richard leaned across the settle, touched her hand lightly with his own. 'He promised me he would come, ma mère. He rode with me from Westminster as far as Ludgate and I thought sure he meant to accompany me all the way. Then he of a sudden drew rein, insisted he had some pressing task he must attend to, one that could not wait. But he swore he'd be done by Vespers, that he'd then come straightaway here. I believe he will, ma mère . . . in truth I do.'

'Vespers,' she said; no more than that. But no more needed to be said; it was already well past dark.

A troubled silence followed. It was no small undertaking, to give consolation to one who was more accustomed to offering comfort than to accepting it herself, but Richard now ventured a try at it, said, 'He wanted to come, ma mère. I know he did. But he does fear to face you. . . .'

'As well he might,' she said tartly, no more easy than he in this sudden role-reversal.

Richard made no further apologies or explanations for George. Instead, he decided to remind his mother that, 'Ned should be here ere long.'

This time she chose to take the substitute solace he offered. She rose, brushed one of her rare kisses against his cheek.

'If I'm not mistaken, that is him now,' she said, with a smile suddenly expectant, eager, and moved toward the door as Bess, guided by some mystical sixth sense, stirred and yawned.

John Gylman, a yeoman of her chamber, appeared in the solar doorway. He seemed unduly agitated, confirming her belief that Edward had, indeed, arrived.

'Madame,' he said and then stammered, 'Madame . . . your son . . .'

Cecily stared at him in surprise. 'Whatever ails you? Where is he . . . in the great hall?'

'Here, ma mère.'

Gylman backed away from George and then fled. Richard came at once to his feet. Bess, fully awake now, opened her mouth to protest and then, seeing she was not to be abandoned, pliantly wrapped her arms about his neck, let him lift her from the settle.

'No, Dickon . . . do not go!' George blurted out, but Richard was already at the door. There was some sympathy in the look he gave his brother but he had no intention in the world of being an unwilling witness to the scene that was to follow. Setting his little niece back on her feet, he took her hand and shut the door firmly behind him.

Cecily said nothing, watched as George crossed the solar. He

368

stopped before her and then slowly dropped to his knees. The face upturned to her was deeply flushed and his clothes, though of the finest and most expensive cut, were slightly awry, not precisely dishevelled but worn with a queer careless air, and George was ever one to be acutely conscious both of fashion and appearance. There'd been, as well, a barely perceptible slurring of speech in his appeal to Richard. It might have been due to stress, of course, but Cecily saw, too, how the corners of his mouth were slack, how he flicked his tongue over his lips like one parched with thirst.

'How much wine did it take to bring you here, George?' she asked, in a voice that was as remote as she could make it, distant and disdainful.

He was mute, still knelt before her. His hair was tousled; she could not recall a time when he'd been able to keep it from tumbling down onto his forehead. On the wall behind him a cresset torch burned and, under its flickering light, his hair seemed even fairer than she'd remembered, seemed to have regained the brightness of boyhood. He was thinner than she remembered, too, his cheekbones thrown into sudden prominence. Perhaps it was that which gave him such an unexpectedly youthful appearance. She didn't know, knew only that he suddenly looked years shy of twenty-one, looked exactly as he had each time he'd disappointed her yet again and then, repentant, vowed to make it up to her, swore earnestly that each found-out sin would be his last.

He had yet to speak but he reached now for her hand. She resisted the urge to snatch it away, instead let it lie limp and cold within his grasp. It was a trick of lighting, surely, or of her senses, that he should suddenly seem so young to her. He was no boy . . . no longer. He was a man grown. A man accountable for wrongs done, wounds inflicted. For betrayals that in no way could be regarded as boyish escapades. But even as she pulled her hand from his, she saw his eyes were bright with unshed tears.

'Will you not speak to me, ma mère?' he whispered, and there was something in his voice Cecily had never heard before. A total lack of assurance. Contrition. She stopped herself before she read more into his demeanour than he deserved, said coolly,

'What do you want me to say, George?'

'That you do forgive me. . . .'

She let him take her hand again. He came lightly to his feet, but she knew that, even when drunk, he retained a certain loose grace. She found herself hoping, nonetheless, that he was not as inebriated as she'd first feared.

'You are sober, George?'

He nodded and leaned down, kissed her timidly on the cheek. When she didn't rebuff him, he was heartened enough to kiss her again.

'Ma mère, I am so sorry . . . so very sorry.'

His eyes met hers steadily. He was not ashamed of the tears that clouded the clear turquoise. She could see only pain in his face, pain and remorse.

She reached out; her fingers stopped just short of his cheek. After a moment, she said softly, 'You are truly sorry?'

'Oh, yes, ma mère,' he said eagerly. 'More than I could ever say. I'd never willingly have acted to cause you hurt. You do know that, do you not? Ma mère, I do swear to you that it was none of my doing. It was Warwick. It was he who concocted that outlandish story about Ned. A slander none could possibly believe. But there was nothing I could do.' He gave her his first smile, sunlit, loving.

'Lord, how long I've wanted to tell you that! To tell you it was none of it my fault. Ma mère, I want . . . ma mère? Why are you looking at me like that? You do . . . you do believe me? You understand that it was not my fault?'

Cecily started to speak, but the words caught in her throat. She stepped back and, before he could assure her again that he was blameless, she slapped him across the mouth with all the strength she had at her command.

He gasped, stumbled back. His eyes, still vivid, still purest turquoise, were now round with shock, with hurt.

'Ma mère, I said I was sorry! I told you that it was Warwick's doing, not mine. What else can I say? What more do you want of me?'

'I want you once, just once in your life, to accept responsibility for what you've done. Just once, to admit you were in the wrong and not try to pass the blame around to all within reach. Can you do that, George? Can you not say to me that you did commit grievous wrongs against those who loved you, that you now do see that and you regret what you've done? Or must I believe you are not even capable of that much?'

There was entreaty in the look he gave her and misery not even she could deny.

'Ma mère, I want so much to do what you ask of me. I swear I always have. But how can I take the blame for what I did not do? How can you ask me to assume a guilt that belongs by rights to Warwick? That's not fair, ma mère. Surely you do see that?'

Cecily stared at him. He meant it. He meant every word he said. He had no comprehension whatsoever of what she'd said to him.

'Go away, George,' she said at last. Never could she remember being so tired; never had she felt the full weight of her fifty-six years as she did at that moment. She made an enormous effort, said, 'We'll talk later. But not now . . . not tonight.'

Far from resenting her dismissal, he looked inexpressibly relieved. He quickly caught up her hand, pressed it hastily to his lips. 'Of course, ma mère,' he agreed at once, and turned to make his escape before she could change her mind.

Cecily watched him cross the solar and she knew suddenly that there'd be no further discussion between them. The next time she saw him, he'd have regained his poise, filled up even these small chinks in his armour, would once more be beyond reach, beyond remorse. If they did not talk now, they never would, and he knew it as well as she.

371

'George, wait!'

He was at the door, his hand on the latch, turned back with the utmost reluctance. 'Ma mère?'

'Do not go. I've changed my mind. I think it best that we do talk now.'

He hesitated. 'Ma mère, I. . . . Forgive me, but I do not. You are distraught now, more apt to say what you do not truly mean.' He summoned up for her his most coaxing smile. 'We can always talk tomorrow. There's no reason why it must be tonight, after all.'

He had the door open; Cecily saw he was already out of reach. But she tried, nonetheless, gave in to a sudden surging rage that was unlike any she'd ever experienced, that for the moment mercifully numbed her of the capacity to feel anything but anger.

She reached the door within seconds of his retreat, caught up with him on the wooden stairway that led from the solar down into the lower end of the great hall and grabbed his arm with force enough to hurt, that she hoped would hurt.

'I would talk with you now, George!'

He offered no resistance, stood rigidly within her grasp, staring down into the hall, down at the pandemonium that held sway below them. Cecily's blind rage cleared; she looked about her, as uncertainly as one awakening from a dream that was unremembered but unpleasant, nonetheless.

It seemed to her that every one of her servants, every retainer in her service, every man, woman and child lodged within Baynard's Castle must be below in the great hall. The babble of voices beat upward to assail her ears in discordant waves. So many torches flared that even the darkest corners held some of the light of day. She saw the faces of men she'd not seen for months, other faces that were totally unfamiliar to her, and almost at once, her daughter-in-law. Surrounded by servants, clad in cloth of gold and, hanging about her throat and shoulders, jewels enough to dazzle even the most jaded eye, Elizabeth looked elegant, aloof and so beautiful that all in the hall were staring at her in awe, even those who did like her least.

In the very midst of all this uproar, revelling in the excitement he was creating, stood her son. He looked up now, saw her standing on the solar stairway and grinned, said loudly: 'Well, Madame, are you not going to welcome me home from my wanderings?'

To her horror, Cecily found tears were suddenly stinging her eyes. She could not believe her nerves would fail her now, had no intention of giving in to emotion before this sea of spectators. Nor did she. The cultivated discipline of a lifetime stood her in good stead. She blinked the tears back, smiled at her son, and started to descend the stairway into the hall.

'No, do not move,' Edward said and laughed. 'This time, Madame, let me be the one to come to you.'

26

London

April 1471

Richard rolled groggily out of bed in the early hours of dawn, his head throbbing with too little sleep and too much wine. The day stretched ahead of him like an unending hot, dry road. Battle captains to be conferred with, supplies to be gathered, artillery to be inspected, horses to be requisitioned. Do not bother about breakfast, he told a yawning Thomas Parr; he did not have time to spare. But he abruptly restructured his morning plans a few moments later as he broke open the sealed letter that had come in the night. Unfolding the paper, he read rapidy and, as he did, his face changed.

'Saddle some horses,' he ordered, as Thomas turned to look at him in surprise. 'If my brother the King should send for me, tell him that something of urgency. . . . No, do not say that. Tell him I had matters to attend to, will be back as soon as I can.'

It was midmorning by the time he returned to Baynard's Castle. By now the curious and the faithful had gathered without and, as word spread through their ranks that the slight dark youth on the silver-grey stallion was the King's brother, they raised a flattering cheer for Richard. One youngster bolder than the rest darted forward, kept pace for several strides at Richard's stirrup.

''Tis glad we are that you're home!'

Richard grinned. 'So am I,' he said.

Striding rapidly into the great hall some moments later, Richard found himself the centre of attention, found himself besieged by men waiting to see his brother. He paused to exchange greetings with those he knew, ignored the rest and, seeing Thomas Parr by the solar stairway, he made his way toward his squire.

Thomas was grinning. 'There is one been awaiting your return, my lord. . . .'

Richard gave him a quizzical look. 'It seems as if half of London were awaiting my return. Is this someone I'd wish to see?'

Thomas had no chance to reply. So packed was the hall that people had been forced, of necessity, up the stairway that gave entrance to the solar. Now men were suddenly moving to each side of the stairway and, in the clearing space, an enormous dark shape was looming. As Richard glanced up, disbelieving, it lunged forward, down the stairs. Richard staggered back as a weight of 150 pounds of Irish wolfhound struck him full on, retaining his balance only with considerable difficulty and even more luck.

'How in damnation, Tom . . .' he began, and then followed his squire's gaze, looking up to see Francis Lovell standing at the top of the stairs.

Fending off the dog's frenzied welcome as best he could, he waited for Francis to reach him, said in genuine astonishment, 'However did you find him, Francis?'

Francis had the grin of one insufferably well pleased with himself. 'It was not difficult,' he said airily. 'I knew you were still at York when you got word of Warwick's landing in Devon. And I knew, too, that you'd not have been likely to take Gareth to war with you. So I had only to think of whom you were most apt to have left him with, had only to remember you always stay with the Augustine Friars when in York. They were, I might add, delighted beyond words to give him over into my keeping. Prior Bewyk said they could more easily afford to give sanctuary to a dozen starving thieves than His Grace of Gloucester's Irish wolfhound.'

'It's a six-day journey to York from Minster Lovell. That's a long way to ride for no more than a hunch.'

Francis shrugged. 'I had nothing better to do at the time.'

'But if I'd not come back, you'd have been stuck with him.'

Francis grimaced in horror. 'Lord, that never did occur to me!'

Richard was laughing. 'I do believe I'm almost as glad to see you, Francis Lovell, as I was to see Gareth.'

They faced each other across the table in Richard's bedchamber, having at last run out of words. Thomas came through the doorway, followed by a page and, as the boy filled the cups with the Rhenish white wine Richard favoured, Thomas said apologetically, 'I hate to intrude, my lord, but the King's Grace. . . .'

'Has the council resumed already, Tom?'

'No, my lord, not yet. But the King awaits you in the presence chamber; he has asked for you twice already whilst you were gone from the castle.'

Richard nodded, gave Francis a look of resignation and rose reluctantly.

Francis rose, too. 'I was rather surprised myself to find you gone. I'd have thought you'd be meeting throughout the day with the King.'

'I will be for the rest of the day, I daresay. We march tomorrow; did you know?' Richard didn't wait for Francis's response, said instead, 'As to where I was about, I was to Westminster . . . to see my son.'

Francis was staring at him and he grinned.

'I did not know. . . . Not till this morning. Nan had written me at York last autumn that she was with child. But you know what happened next. . . .' With an expressive shrug.

'I thought often of her and the babe. I had no way to know how she fared and I confess that did bother me, Francis—to have got her with child and then to be able to do nothing for her. I knew my daughter Kathryn would not want; I'd seen to that. But Nan's letter reached me just two days ere we heard Warwick had landed in the South. And less than a fortnight later, I found myself at Doncaster.'

He dismissed Doncaster with a grimace and then grinned again. 'But Nan fared better than I dared hope, and she gave birth to a healthy boy, born two weeks ago today, on the twenty-ninth. That's the date Ned won Towton; lucky, do you not think?'

'Very,' Francis agreed warmly, trying to think when he'd last seen Richard so unguardedly happy, so openly elated; he decided he hadn't. He wondered, too, who Nan was; thought it unlikely Richard would ever say.

'I thought to name him John. You like it?'

Francis nodded. 'That was my father's name.'

'I had a brother named John; did you know that? He died long ere I was born, of course. But it's a name I've always fancied.'

It occurred to Francis that Richard had a cousin, too, named John. He brought his wine cup up to his face but not in time. Richard's smile faded.

'You've not changed, Francis. You're still as easy to read as any schoolboy's hornbook.'

376

With John Neville in both their minds, Francis now saw no reason not to ask.

'You've had no word from Johnny, have you, Dickon?'

Richard shook his head. 'No word . . . unless you count his action twenty-three days ago, when he held his army at Pontefract and let us pass unmolested.' He looked sombrely at Francis. 'My brother offered him a pardon, too, when he sent word to Warwick at Coventry. Warwick, as you know, spurned us. Johnny made no response at all. George Neville was quick enough to jettison Warwick to save his own skin. But not Johnny. He'll not betray his brother, Francis.'

Unlike Clarence, Francis thought, and then he smiled. 'Welcome home, Dickon!'

Much to his surprise, Francis found himself feeling some sympathy for George. He'd not expected that; as far back as he could remember, he'd thought George to be a burr under the saddle of York. But now he watched George make stilted and guarded conversation with his Yorkist kin and he could pity Richard's brother . . . a little.

Edward was friendly enough and, twice, when allusions to George's erratic loyalties threatened to become accusations, Francis saw him adroitly act to spare George embarrassment. But Francis saw deep festering wounds and, with pessimism, wondered if they were not beyond healing.

There was much hatred for George in this room, all the more intense for being unspoken. Whatever Edward's feelings for his faithless brother, and he'd shown little love for George in the best of times, Edward's Queen had not forgiven George his betrayals, his complicity in her father's death. Francis did not think she would ever forgive. Nor would her kin. And in this, if in nothing else, the Woodvilles were in full accord with Will Hastings, who'd long ago learned to convey contempt with a smile, an upraised brow. Watching now as John Howard gave terse unresponsive answers to George's equally laboured questions, Francis wondered if George could cope, knowing that he was seen as Judas. He rather doubted it.

A squabble suddenly erupted among the three children deemed old enough to join their elders. Bess and Mary had been delighted by the appearance of Richard's wolfhound and, with Jack de la Pole, the young son of the Duchess of Suffolk, they were subjecting the big dog to an enthusiastic mauling. The animal, with commendable patience, had so far submitted to their affectionate attentions, even to suffering Mary to clamber up onto his back. Now, however, Jack yanked once too often on the wolfhound's tail and Gareth spun around with a sudden flash of fangs. Jack retreated hastily and the girls squealed.

Richard, deep in a discussion of tactics with his brother and Will Hastings, glanced up, snapped his fingers. At once the dog bounded across the room and into the window recess.

Edward, regarding the wolfhound with little favour, drew back as the sweeping tail brushed by his face.

'Before God, I'd dared hope you'd lost that monstrous beast, Dickon,' he complained, and Richard grinned, looking over at Francis.

'I feared I had. But he was given sanctuary by a friend.'

'I'd have thought the return of one prodigal son to York would have been more than enough.'

Richard wasn't amused. Instinctively, his eyes sought George, to make sure he was safely out of earshot.

'You promised, Ned,' he said quietly, and Edward sighed and then swore as the wolfhound knocked over his wine cup.

Will was laughing. 'Perhaps we should take the return of all the lost sheep to the fold as yet another sign of St Anne's favour,' he suggested lazily.

Francis was confused; he knew neither Richard nor Edward to be under the special protection of St Anne. This must be yet another of those private jests they shared among themselves, jests of risks taken, hardships endured, memories of Doncaster and foreign exile and those first harrowing days in Yorkshire.

But even as he thus accounted for Hastings's puzzling reference to St Anne, he saw that the curiosity of another had been piqued.

'Why St Anne, Lord Hastings?'

'You have not heard, then, Madame, of the miracle of Daventry? I thought sure His Grace would've told you.'

Elizabeth did not look pleased that there was something she did not know. 'Perhaps you would like to tell me,' she said coolly.

'The Queen commands,' Will said and smiled. Conversation around them quieted, ceased entirely as he began to speak, to relate what had happened Sunday past in the parish church of Daventry. Directly in front of the King had been an alabaster shrine of St Anne, hidden from view behind four wooden doors, it being Lent. Midway through the Mass, the doors of the shrine had suddenly opened wide, although not touched by the hand of any man.

'The congregation was much awed, as you can well imagine, Madame . . . and His Grace the King was given to remember how he had prayed to St Anne during the storm of March fourteenth, entreating her to see him safety to England.

'Upon hearing this, all present at once agreed that this was, indeed, an omen of blessed fortune, a sign that Heaven smiled upon the House of York. And His Grace vowed that he would name his next-born daughter Anne, to honour the mother of the Virgin,' Will concluded with a flourish, 'and was roundly cheered by the people, who then offered up fervent prayers for York.'

At that, Edward nodded complacently, then grinned. 'However, blessed St Anne shall have to wait. I told Meg I would name my next girl after her and I promised her first.'

Francis had been watching the Duchess of York, and now saw a flicker of disapproval crease her brow. He was reminded suddenly of the story she'd related here in this room not six months ago, of St Caecilia and her brother's pilgrimage. He tried to imagine Edward on pilgrimage, couldn't and, turning abruptly to Richard, asked him if he still wore the pilgrim's cross he'd had at Middleham.

Richard gave him a bemused look. 'Ye Gods, but your mind takes odd turns at times, Lovell!' Tugging at the collar of his doublet, he managed to fish out a thin silver chain for Francis's inspection.

'I've had it as long as I can remember. I'd feel near naked without it, I daresay,' he was explaining to his curious young nephew Jack, as Francis glanced back across the room and was warmed by Cecily Neville's smile.

Jack de la Pole, the eight-year-old Earl of Lincoln, was growing restless. He trailed after his grandmother as far as the door and then wandered back to the window-seat where he sank down, bored, upon the cushions scattered about the floor. But within moments, he'd brightened considerably, for it seemed that his uncle Clarence was about to quarrel with the Queen's brother.

'For once in your life, you are right, my lord Rivers,' George said bitingly. 'I did, indeed, do all in my power to effect a reconciliation between my brother and the Earl of Warwick and I shall continue to do so. I make no secret of it, and I most assuredly do not seek your approval.'

'It does not surprise me that treason seems so insignificant a sin to you, my lord of Clarence, but there are those of us who find it far less easy to forgive. You might bear that in mind for your own. . . .'

Edward had turned at sound of raised voices. Now he intervened, without apparent haste, but cutting Anthony off, nonetheless, in midsentence.

'You can scarcely fault my brother of Clarence for urging Warwick to come to terms with me, Anthony. It's just a pity he'd not heed George. You need only think of the blood that will be shed. . . .'

'Are you serious?' Anthony asked incredulously.

Edward wasn't accustomed to being interrupted but he said mildly enough, 'Quite serious. If I could have brought about his surrender without the need for battle, I should've been a fool not to do so. Unfortunately, he was not yet desperate enough—or, perhaps, was too desperate—to content himself with what I could offer him; his life. But why sound so surprised? You know I offered Warwick a pardon at Coventry.'

'Yes, but I never thought you meant it!'

The room was very quiet. Edward looked pensively at his brother-in-law.

'Not only did I mean it but it is my intent to spare his life if possible when we do meet across a battlefield.'

'Ned!'

Elizabeth was on her feet, in a blur of silk and saffron. 'You cannot mean that!'

An expression of impatience shadowed Edward's face. 'How often must I say it to be believed? I do not seek the deaths of my Neville cousins. I never did. I intend to take from Warwick all else, however, and for a man such as my cousin who holds power more dear than his life, he might even prefer the martyrdom of the executioner's axe. But that is a martyrdom I prefer not to give him.'

Elizabeth came swiftly to his side, grasped his arm. 'Ned, he did order the deaths of my father and brother. Surely you've not forgotten that!'

They stared at each other and, for the moment, the others were forgotten.

'I'm sorry,' he said at last. 'I do understand, Lisbet. But I cannot be the instrument of your vengeance.'

'Cannot?'

'Will not, then.'

She spun around, pointed toward her mother. 'She wears black because of Warwick. Do you think I can forget that? Forget what he has said of me, my family? I've spent six months in hell because of him and now you speak of sparing him? I tell you no! I'll not have it.'

Edward looked down into the tense, flushed face upturned to his. 'You'll have what I give you, my love,' he said very evenly. 'No more, no less.'

Elizabeth drew an audible breath. Darker colour spread across her cheekbones, burning skin already well scorched with heat. Her mouth contorted. And then she turned away, sat down abruptly in the nearest chair.

The silence in the room was absolute by now. Even Edward's small daughters dared not move. The Woodvilles were the most shaken, for none had ever seen Edward and Elizabeth quarrel in public before.

Anthony moved toward his sister. Her head was tilted forward, her face partially veiled by the shimmering misty silk that floated from her butterfly headdress. But he saw the tremor in the jewelled fingers that flexed and twisted together in her lap; saw the lacquered nails dig into her palm, deeply enough to make him wince, as if the pain were his.

'What then of Lancaster?' he asked bitterly. 'Are you to show Marguerite d'Anjou and her bastard-born son the same mercy? Christ, Ned, is this what we've fought for, bled for . . . so that you could forgive the Nevilles their past treason as you did Clarence?'

He saw George stiffen, saw Richard come swiftly to his feet, saw Edward's eyes narrow, go suddenly dark as he'd never seen them before. But it was his sister who claimed his attention. Elizabeth was staring up at him and there was fury in her face.

'Oh, you fool,' she said, hissing the words through her teeth. 'You stupid fool!'

Edward had moved; he now stood behind her. 'What you've fought for, bled for?' he echoed, and there was disbelief in his voice and the first flames of anger.

'Ned, I did not mean. . . .' But Anthony could not go on, made mute by what he saw in Edward's face.

'Who are you to tell me what you've sacrificed for York?' There was no mockery or sarcasm now. Edward was in earnest, giving in to a rare rage, such as few of those in the room had ever seen him show.

He swung around and Anthony flinched, drew back. 'My liege. . . .'

'What do you know of sacrifice? Need I tell you of York's dead . . . of Sandal Castle? My brother did survive the battle, his first. He was seventeen and he entreated them to spare his life. They cut his throat. Their heads were then impaled on York's Micklegate Bar to please the House of Lancaster, to please a harlot and a madman. She had my father's head crowned with straw and she left a spike between the two. . . . That one, she said, was for York's other son.'

He drew a deep breath before adding tonelessly, 'Three months later, their heads were still rotting on Micklegate Bar when I rode into York the day after Towton. I had to be the one to order them taken down, to be sent to Pontefract for burial.'

No one moved; no one spoke. Francis began to pray that something, anything, would happen to dispel the tension that now blanketed the room like woodsmoke.

The door opened, drawing all eyes. Reentering the room, the Duchess of York paused, taking note of their stares, the silence. Her instincts, as ever, were sound; she said, 'Edward?'

Edward turned, said tautly, 'Nothing, ma mère. . . . Nothing's amiss. A difference of opinion as to the merits of mercy, no more than that.'

She gave him an unsmiling, appraising look. 'Divine mercy is blessed,' she said, in a voice that was soft and very precise. 'But there are times when the mercy of men might be withheld. I trust you to know when mercy is called for . . . and when it is not.'

'You need not worry, ma mère. I do.'

*

The pleasure had gone from the day. This brief afternoon interlude, meant to give them all a precious hour of peace midst the ongoing preparations for war, was now soured. Suddenly the strain showed; the dark awareness that on the morrow the men in this room were to ride out from London, take the road north, where the army of Lancaster and Neville awaited them.

Hours later, after a markedly sombre supper, Francis found himself in the Duchess of York's private chapel. It had been far less awkward for him than he'd feared, being alone with the women of York. The Duchess of York had seemed genuinely pleased to have him share the waiting with them, those endless hours while Edward was closeted again with the men who were to serve as his battle captains. Now, however, their council had at last been concluded and they'd come with darkness to rejoin the women, to take part in the solemn service of Tenebrae.

It was one of the most hauntingly beautiful ceremonies of their Church but never had it seemed so impressive to Francis. As one by one the candles were symbolically quenched, until at last the chapel was lit by a single solitary flame, he felt a foreboding that owed more to superstition than common sense. Fool, he chided uneasily, but as he glanced at Richard, he saw that his friend, too, looked sobered, absorbed in thoughts no less disquieting than his own. The battle, he realized, was very much on all their minds and there was comfort in that understanding, for anxiety shared was anxiety easier to bear.

Once back in the Presence Chamber, he stood alone against the wall nearest the window seat, listening as Edward conversed in low tones with Richard and Will. The talk, he noted, was still of strategy and artillery and their faces were intent, preoccupied. After a whispered colloquy, Edward's two stepsons moved closer; they'd been shaken by his quarrel with their mother and it still showed. Edward saw and beckoned with a smile; relief flooded their faces.

Richard and Will drifted away but Francis lingered within

earshot as Edward continued to discuss his battle plans for the benefit of his stepsons, answering their questions as if they were queries posed by his battle captains.

'We are to assemble tomorrow morn in St John's Field,' he told the boys. 'Warwick is now at St Albans with Exeter, Oxford and his brother, Montagu. Tomorrow we march to meet them, for I've no intention of letting him pick the time and place, of letting him wait for Marguerite.'

'And the command?' Dick Grey asked.

'Fetch me pen and paper and I'll show you,' Edward offered generously, and was soon sketching by candlelight a rude battle formation for the boy.

'There now, do you see?' He gestured with the pen. 'There are three wings, or "battles" as they are called; the vanguard, the centre and the rearward, with additional men to be held in reserve, else you'd have no means of rallying should your line falter.' Again, Edward jabbed with the pen. 'Will Hastings shall command the rear . . . there. And I'll take that battle myself.'

Dick leaned over, nodded. 'But if you take the centre, then. . . .'

Thomas Grey gave his brother a scornful look. 'Not the centre, stupid. . . . He'll take the van.'

'I'm not likely to mistake the two,' Dick said, offended. 'He pointed to the centre, Tom.'

'He's right, Tom, I did,' Edward confirmed, and Thomas gave him an uncertain look. He was hesitant to risk his stepfather's amusement should he be wrong, but he was proud, too, of his battle lore and he ventured a cautious objection.

'But the van does lead the attack, can determine the outcome of the battle. If you or Lord Hastings do not command it, who, then? Lord Howard?'

'No.' Ink dripped from Edward's pen, blurring the battle lines. Following his gaze, Francis and the Grey boys saw that he was watching his brother.

'It is my intent to entrust the vanguard to Dickon.'

At sound of his name, Richard turned. Now he flashed a smile but he alone seemed unaffected by Edward's startling pronouncement. It was clearly no surprise to the men but Francis saw it was no source of reassurance to them, either. John Howard looked even more sombre than usual. Will Hastings, too, showed signs of misgivings and George, for an unguarded moment, stared at Richard with a jealousy as bitter as it was betraying.

But if Richard had any qualms about being entrusted with command of the vanguard in what was to be his first battle, it didn't show. He and Edward were exchanging smiles of satisfaction, satisfaction they alone seemed to share.

'And York is to have the victory,' Richard predicted, sounding so sure, so free of doubt, that Francis would have felt a touch of envy . . . had he not remembered the look on Richard's face during Tenebrae.

'Should God so will it, Richard,' the Duchess of York reminded him now.

Acknowledging the rebuke, Richard dutifully crossed himself and tucked the silver pilgrim pledge back into his doublet.

'I do believe the Lord will watch over York,' he assured his mother, and then he looked over at Edward, grinned.

'And I'll see to the vanguard for you, Ned,' he promised.

Edward nodded slowly. 'I know you will, Dickon,' he said, and after a moment, he laughed. 'You damned well better, little brother, for all our sakes!'

27

Barnetheath

April 1471

Easter Eve. A mile north of the village of Barnet, the army of the Earl of Warwick had taken up battle formation along Gladmore Heath. Warwick had gathered twelve thousand men to his standard of the Ragged Staff; his intelligence numbered the army of his cousin at no more than nine thousand. He'd given the centre to his battle-wise brother and John was now in position across the St Albans—Barnet Road. To John's left lay the wing under the Duke of Exeter, stretching east from the road to the deep marshy hollow that dropped away toward Hadley Wood. West of the road was encamped the Lancastrian vanguard, to be led by Warwick's brother-in-law the Earl of Oxford. And, as his army spread out across the heath, Warwick set up a command post behind the lines, there to oversee the battle and to control the critical reserve.

Daylight was lingering beyond its time, the sky above their camp painted in bold bright hues of crimson. John Neville was standing in the tent entrance, staring up at the spectacular sunset colours that were so successfully holding back the dark. There was a curious stillness in his pose, as if all his energies, all vitality, were being held in some strange abeyance of spirit, as if all of his inner being were absorbed now in this private purposeful intent, to watch as the last traces of light faded from the sky.

From the bed, Warwick watched his brother. He should have liked to know what Johnny's thoughts were during this silent sunset vigil on the eve of battle. No, that was not true. Why lie to himself now? He did not want to know, had no intention of asking. The danger was always there that were he to ask, Johnny might tell him.

God, he hoped he did not look as bad as did Johnny! Was this how Johnny had looked at Pontefract as his baffled men waited for the order that never came, the order that would have passed sentence of death on Ned and Dickon and the courageous but foolhardy few who'd followed them? Or was it the letter, the letter Ned had dispatched to Johnny at Coventry? All Warwick knew was that it had been in Ned's own hand and Johnny had gone grey whilst reading it, like a man suffering from a wound that refused to heal, that kept on festering until marrow and blood so sickened on it that the body housed only the wasted flesh of mortal contagion.

Ned's offer. He did not truly need to be told what it had been. He knew. Had he been desperate enough to submit to Ned, his life alone would have been spared . . . no more than that. All else would be forfeit. But Ned would leave him his life and then claim credit for his magnanimity, for his mercy. Ah, yes, he'd have been pardoned; Ned would have seen to that. Johnny though . . . Johnny would have been forgiven.

'Dick?'

He jerked his head up. John had turned from the deepening dusk, let the tent flap fall. Seeing he had Warwick's attention, he said matter-of-factly, 'Dick, I've been giving it some thought. It's been my experience that the common soldiers are somewhat resentful that their lords have such easy access to horses during a battle. Whilst they know their commanders fight on foot just as they themselves do, they know, too, that the horses are never far from reach should there be need of them. Yes, I know what you're about to say. . . . That mounts are often needed to rally your men or to regroup forces. But they're used, too, to retreat if the battle does turn against you.'

388

He hesitated and then said bluntly, 'We cannot afford that suspicion, Dick. Too many of our men do not believe that either of us are truly pledged to Lancaster. I fear how willing they'll be to fight for us if all the while they've suspicions that we might flee should fortune favour York.'

'What you really mean, Johnny, is that a good portion of our Lancastrian allies think one or both of us might switch over to York at an opportune moment,' Warwick said sourly, and John gave an imperceptible nod.

'That, too,' he said quietly.

'Well, then, what have you in mind?'

'I'd move the horse park a good distance from the battlefield, far enough so there could be no doubts as to our commitment to this coming battle.'

Warwick considered this in silence for some moments. John didn't press him, seemed quite content to wait. At length, Warwick nodded.

'Yes, there's something in what you say. I'll give orders to have the horses tethered in Wrotham Wood. It will not be the first time, after all, that I've had to so act to reassure my men. I once killed my own horse to show I meant to either prevail or die where I stood. A rather dramatic gesture, I grant you, but it did forestall a rout. You remember, Johnny?'

'Yes,' John said, and smiled faintly. 'You've told me of it often enough for it to have been burned into my brain. The skirmish at the Ferrybridge crossing, where Clifford was slain.'

'Yes, that was the battle,' Warwick said swiftly, almost aggressively. 'The day before Towton, it was. I was able to hold my men till Ned sent a second force to ford the river and come to our aid.'

He'd made deliberate use of Edward's name, was suddenly angry, unfocused intense anger that for the moment spared no one, not even John. He was aware only of a hazy determination not to spend this battle eve shrinking from ghosts, shying from phantoms.

John said nothing. Nor did anything show in his face. He continued to look composed, tired and rather distant, as he had on each of the ten days since he'd joined Warwick in Coventry.

The anger that had come to Warwick as abruptly and searingly as summer lightning now left only singed memory cells behind. In that moment, he came as close as he'd yet done to breaking the barriers of silence that rose up so relentlessly between them.

He stared at John, thinking of the others. His brother George, who'd defected to York for the promise of a pardon. His son-in-law, who'd betrayed him on the Banbury Road. His great good friend, the King of France, the monarch who called him 'dearest comrade' and 'cousin' and had now come to terms with Charles of Burgundy. His allies of the moment; Oxford, who was wed to his sister yet trusted him not in the least, and Exeter, who'd accused him to his face of contemplating an accommodation with York. Only Johnny could he trust. Only Johnny had not betrayed him, would not betray him. Johnny, whose heart was with York.

'Johnny, I do want you to know. . . .'

'I do,' John cut in hastily. 'So there's no need to talk of it. Is there?'

'No,' Warwick agreed softly. 'No, Johnny, there's no need.'

John began to speak then of military matters, began to talk of artillery and the need to have at least one cavalry contingent. Warwick concurred and, before long, they were joined by Exeter and Oxford. The conference continued. A late supper was served, went all but untouched as the men talked on, as the hours passed, as Vespers and then Compline sounded in the little church of Hadley, not a stone's throw from the Lancastrian lines.

Soon after dark descended, there was a brief flurry of excitement. Warwick's scouts reported an unexpected encounter in the streets of Barnet with the Yorkist advance guard. Grimly, Warwick summoned his captains, told them to expect combat on the morrow. The Yorkist army was nearing Barnet.

How near they were he did not then realize. Reaching the

village at dark, Edward made a daring decision. Under cover of night, he ordered his men forward to take up battle positions. It was a difficult, unorthodox manoeuvre, was to have unforeseen consequences.

At first, Edward reaped only good from his calculated gamble. Warwick's guns roared; the night echoed to cannon fire. But Edward's army was far closer than Warwick estimated. His artillery overshot and Edward gave orders not to return the fire. His men settled down to pass the night.

Soon after midnight, fog began to drift across the valley. The Whyte Boar banner that flew from Richard's command tent hung sodden in the still air.

Thomas Parr moved, nudged the blanket-clad form next to him. Tom Huddleston, like Thomas, had shared with Richard a boyhood at Middleham. He was the oldest of the three boys, had fought at the battles of Edgecot and Lose-Coat Field. Now he glanced over at Thomas, nodded. Thomas sat up, said softly, 'My lord?'

Richard turned his head, propped himself up on one elbow. 'Tom?'

'You've not slept at all. Should you like to talk?'

Thomas couldn't see Richard's face in the shadows. There was silence; Warwick's guns were stilled at last.

Thomas rose to his knees, said with certainty, 'His Grace the King won Towton on Palm Sunday. Barnet shall be an Easter victory . . . by the grace of Almighty God and the service you shall do him tomorrow with the van.'

Richard stirred, reached across the space that separated them. For a moment, he let his hand rest on Thomas's shoulder.

'Sleep whilst you can,' he said.

Thomas lay back. 'Good-night, my lord.' He closed his eyes, but he didn't sleep. He knew that his companions didn't sleep, either.

*

391

Five A.M. The sun should have been climbing in the sky by now but a damp grey darkness still blanketed Hadley Wood. During the night, dense fog had rolled in, thicker and heavier than any Richard had ever seen, even on the Yorkshire moors. His men were waiting, all eyes upon him. The chill of night had lingered; his breath frosted the air as he spoke. He looked to his battle captains, gave the signal to advance banner. His trumpets blared, the sound muffled, echoing eerily into the dawn dampness.

But as the vanguard moved into the fog, it soon became apparent that something was wrong. To their left came stifled sounds of combat as the Yorkist centre came together with John Neville's line. But the hail of arrows their bowmen had loosed at random into the grey sea ahead went unanswered. They were advancing unchallenged, encountering no resistance.

The ground was beginning to slope away from them; foot-prints pressed into the earth now oozed mud. With a jolt, Richard understood all too well. In the dark, the vanguard had outflanked Exeter. They were far to his left, descending into the wide marshy ravine which had anchored Exeter's position. If they could cross the ravine without detection, they'd come up on Exeter's flank, and he'd not be expecting an assault from that direction. But if they were discovered while still in the ravine, the muddy marsh would run red with blood, Yorkist blood.

Richard turned, saw that his men knew what had befallen them. There was no need to command silence. Grimly, they pressed ahead, blindly, into the darkness.

The Earl of Oxford had demanded command of the vanguard and Warwick had acquiesced. Now as Oxford led his men against the Yorkist left wing, he learned at once what Richard was only belatedly discovering, that, in the dark, the battle lines had gone awry. Just as the Yorkist van had outflanked Exeter, the Lancastrian van overlapped the wing commanded by Will Hastings.

Oxford was luckier, however, than Richard; no treacherous

ravine yawned between his men and the Yorkists. With triumphant yells, they erupted from the fog to smash without warning into Hastings's flank.

The Yorkists were thrown into disarray, recoiling before this unexpected assault upon their rear. Their line wavered and then gave way before Oxford. As Hastings and his battle captains tried desperately to rally them, the Yorkist left wing broke, disintegrated into flight.

With Oxford's troops in gleeful pursuit, they fled the field, casting aside weapons and shields as they ran. Hastings raged in vain. The frightened villagers of Barnet hastily barred their doors as panic-stricken soldiers suddenly stumbled into the cobbled narrow streets. Some sought shelter within the parish church; others stole horses and galloped the ten miles toward London, there to awaken Londoners with shouts of a Yorkist defeat. Oxford's men soon lost interest in the kill and triumphantly fell to looting and pillaging in Barnet. The battle was less than an hour old and Edward's left wing was destroyed.

George had accepted with poor grace Edward's decision to entrust the van to Richard. Uncharacteristically prudent, he had contented himself with a few pointed comments as to Richard's age and inexperience, but it had rankled. Not so much that he begrudged Dickon the honour, he assured himself, but because Ned had seen fit to deny him a command of his own. He knew damned well that Ned wanted him close at hand for one reason only; Ned did not trust him. Yes, he knew Ned's suspicions, knew Ned feared he might desert to Warwick if the battle turned against York. And he resented it bitterly, that he should be so little trusted after he'd brought fully four thousand troops over to York, betrayed his father-in-law for Ned's sake.

His resentment had been dispelled, however, within the first five minutes of battle, as he found himself struggling for breath, assailed by the cries of dying men, the stench of blood and gutted entrails. He'd not known it would be like this and, for the first time in his life, he was thankful to stay close to his brother, to follow Ned's lead. Now he'd not have changed places for his soul's sake with Dickon, alone somewhere out there in the mists. What security there was in this suddenly savage world was to be found with Ned—Ned, who seemed to know no fear, towering above the other men, slashing a path with a sword that was bloody up to the hilt.

George watched his brother in uncomprehending awe. He could understand Dickon's cockiness; this was Dickon's first battle, as it was his. But Ned had known. How in Christ's Name had he been so composed yesterday, with the understanding of what they'd be facing come dawn?

He stumbled over a prone figure, sprawled at an improbable angle on the turf; even more improbably, given the fact that he was virtually disembowelled, the man moaned. George stepped over him, plunged after Edward. The centre seemed to be holding its own against John but George knew the battle was not going well for York. The left wing had been routed; Hastings had taken to horse in a frantic attempt to rally his men, to check their flight before Oxford's onslaught. The fighting was reported fiercest between Exeter's men and Richard's. Only ten minutes ago, a courier had materialized out of the fog with welcome word for Edward: 'My lord of Gloucester bids me tell Your Grace that they do well . . . that you should hold your reserve.'

George knew, though, that Richard was facing not only Exeter now but Warwick as well. Shaken by the sudden appearance of the Yorkist vanguard on his flank, Exeter had urgently demanded re-inforcements and Warwick had dispatched fully half of his reserves to Exeter's aid. Richard's men were outnumbered, being forced to give ground, back toward the marshy hollow, and, if the vanguard went the way of the left wing, Edward could not hope to hold alone.

George knew, too, that before long, Oxford would return to the field. He was too shrewd a soldier to expend his energies in pursuit of men already beaten. It occurred to George, with a chill of horror, that York might lose, that the day might be won by Warwick, his father-in-law, who would never forgive him for Banbury.

A man was running out of the fog, straight toward him. George swung his sword up, then saw the Blancsanglier badge of his brother. Just a boy, greensick with fear. He reached out, grabbed the boy as he came within range. His hand closed roughly on the boy's shoulder. The youngster gasped and blood welled between the fingers of George's gauntlet. He shifted his hold, grasped the boy's foream.

'Why are you not with Gloucester?' he demanded, bringing his face close in an effort to be heard.

'Gloucester . . . he's down!'

George's grip slackened and the boy seized his chance, pulled free, and fled into the fog. George had already forgotten him; he was swinging around, toward his brother, some yards away. He shouted but knew Edward couldn't hear. All around him, men were yelling for York or Neville as they came together. Almost at his feet, a wounded man screamed, 'Quarter, for Christ's sake!' The Yorkist soldier who stood astride him plunged his poleaxe downward. The fog swirled, closed again. George saw Edward's sword flash; a man died.

George stared, didn't move. This was madness. This was every nightmare he'd ever had. They'd all die here in this grey dark, this fog that smothered the field like a shroud.

He caught motion to his right, whirled. The man veered off. The fog hid horrors unspeakable, hid death and dying men. York was beaten. . . . He shuddered and stumbled after his brother.

Nothing had prepared Richard for the hell that was Barnet Heath. Thomas Parr was dead. Richard had seen him fall, knew no man could survive the blow Thomas had taken. Too far away to help, he'd shouted a futile warning, watched in horror as his squire crumpled to the ground. That moment of frozen immobility had nearly cost him his own life. A staggering blow knocked him sideways, drove him to his knees. Instinct saved him, instinct and years of practice at the quintain with battle-axe and broadsword. Even as he went down, he reacted, without thought, without conscious choice. As his knee hit the ground, he swung his sword upward, in a manoeuvre learned years ago at Middleham. Blood spurted over him; the man clutched his stomach, fell backward. Almost at once, Rob Percy was beside him, helping him to rise; the men of his household had not willingly left his side since the battle began, acutely aware that he was a dangerously tempting target for Lancaster—York's brother and the man who commanded the van.

Richard had no way of knowing how badly he'd been hurt. The battle-axe had cleaved through his vambrace. His arm was numb from elbow to wrist. There was no pain ... not yet; but blood was filling his gauntlet. He mouthed a hasty prayer of thanks to Almighty God that he'd taken the blow on his left arm and denied himself a last glance back at the twisted inert body of his squire.

The knights of his household were converging around him so that he might confer with his battle captains. He listened as they told him they could not hold without reinforcements.

'No,' he said, dragging the words from a throat already raw from shouting commands. 'I'll not deplete my brother's reserves. His is the greater need now that Hastings's line has broken. Send word to His Grace that we still hold our own, that he need not commit his reserves.'

They argued. Thomas Howard, John Howard's eldest son, gestured behind them, toward the ravine now hidden in the fog. Richard repeated his orders and, when they still protested, he raged at them, anger being the only emotion he dared allow himself.

Francis stumbled, sank to his knees, as much from exhaustion as from the weight of his armour. A familiar figure loomed over him, hand outstretched. He grasped the hand gratefully, let Rob help him to his feet.

'I feel as if I'm running through water,' he confessed shakily. 'Even the air is pushing me down.'

'Stay a minute. Catch your breath.'

'Can we hold out, d'you think, Rob?'

'If God and Gloucester do will it,' Rob said grimly.

Francis was not the only one to have paused, to seek a brief respite. Richard was circled by knights of his household; he signalled for water, had it poured over his vambrace, into his gauntlet.

'He should have that arm treated, Rob.'

Rob shook his head, blinking back the sweat that stung his eyes. 'He'll not leave the field; he dare not. He's the only one who can hold them. God, Francis, just look around you! All that's keeping them from breaking is that bloody rotten ravine at our backs and the fact that he's right here with them, offering up his life with theirs.'

Beside Francis, a water carrier was holding out a flask. He reached for it, rinsed his mouth and spat. 'Do you think Dickon knows his other squire is dead, too?'

Rob's shoulder pauldrons moved, shifted as he shrugged. 'I'd surely not suggest you tell him. Are you up to moving now?'

Francis couldn't help himself, had to say it. 'If we're pushed into the hollow, Rob, we'll be butchered.'

'Christ, Francis, you think Dickon does not know that? But when Oxford comes back to the field, the King has got to have reserves left . . . else Oxford will go through York's line like a hot knife through butter. Then we'll all be butchered, not just the van but every man jack for York.'

Francis risked lifting his vizor, sucked a few lungfuls of air. 'It stinks like a charnel house. . . . Oh, Jesus! Rob!'

Rob spun around but it wasn't Richard who'd gone down; it was Thomas Howard. A freakish arrow shot, a lucky hit. He staggered, fell forward. The shaft broke as his body hit the ground. He jerked once, then lay still.

Rob and Francis started forward, but others were already there, forming a protective guard. Richard was giving orders and, as they watched, the wounded Howard was lifted, taken toward the rear.

Richard turned, saw Francis at his side. 'Good God, Francis, close your vizor!'

This was the first chance they'd had to exchange any words since the battle began nearly two hours ago. Francis thought there should be something to be said, all too aware that the chance might not come again. But if there was any such healing benediction, any inspired words that might somehow serve as a talisman for them both, they eluded him. All he could do was to blurt out the truth.

'Dickon, this is hell.'

Richard paused, looked back over his shoulder. 'I know. But if we lose, Francis, if we lose . . .'

He moved away, began to shout commands, gesturing down the line where York was giving ground, and the knights of his household rallied, weary men surging forward with hoarse cries of 'Á York! Á Gloucester!'

Inside his gauntlets, Francis's hands were slippery with sweat. The leather clung to his palms; his fingers were cramped and stiff. He tightened his grip on his sword and followed Richard back into the battle.

It had taken him more than an hour, but Oxford had finally regrouped his plundering troops. Some men had scattered as Oxford galloped into the market square, shouting and cursing; others were staggering, glassy-eyed, from looted alehouses to grin good-naturedly at their enraged leader. But Oxford and his captains finally corralled some eight hundred men wearing his badge of the Streaming Star and headed north, back toward the battlefield.

The field was still thick in fog and Oxford had no way of knowing that, in his absence, the battle lines had shifted, swung from north–south to east–west. Plunging back into the battle, they thought they bore down on Edward's rear. They collided, instead, with John Neville's flank.

Montagu's men were taken by surprise. In the swirling fog, the banner flown by these new arrivals was not easily seen, was obscured in mist. To the panic-stricken men, it seemed to glimmer like a streaming sun . . . the Sunne of York. A cry went up; Ambush! The flank guard of bowmen sent a rain of arrows down upon these Yorkist horsemen and foot soldiers who'd appeared without warning in their midst.

Horses screamed, went over backward. Oxford's men staggered back, bleeding, stunned. Oxford swore like one demented. That whoreson Montagu was betraying them. He'd gone over to York, just as they'd feared he'd do. The line rang with shouts of treachery. They flung themselves upon Montagu's wing and men now died by mistake.

Yet another messenger had come from Richard. He stood panting before Edward.

'I am Matt Fletcher, Your Grace. My lord of Gloucester bids me tell you that the van still holds.'

Someone was handing Edward a flask. He accepted it, drank in gulps, spilling water over his face, his armour; it washed away red.

'How does he, in truth?'

The youth hesitated. 'The fighting is savage, Your Grace. But we're not giving ground. . . .' A vision of the steep slopes of the ravine made him add, 'So far.'

Edward nodded. 'Tell Gloucester that Montagu's line is weakening. I know how much I ask. But if he can hold on awhile longer. . . .'

'I shall, Your Grace,' Matt said tiredly, and Edward started to turn away, stopped and glanced back at the boy.

'And tell him, too, to take care, for Christ's sake . . . and mine.'

They both heard it at once, a rising volume of noise—curses of fearful men, cries of betrayal, screams of dying horses. There was sudden activity to their left, midst Montagu's ranks. Men reeled out of the fog; the line was faltering.

John Howard was coming at a run, moving with surprising speed for a man of his girth and armoured weight, gesturing wildly.

'Your Grace! Montagu's firing on Oxford!'

'Oxford's Streaming Star! Jesus wept!' Edward raised his vizor; Matt had a brief glimpse of blazing blue eyes, white teeth. He didn't yet understand what was happening, but Edward apparently did, and he felt a throb of excitement as Edward laughed with savage elation, swore exultantly.

Edward was turning to Howard, clasping him on the shoulders. 'Now, Jack! Now I call upon my reserves. Now it is York's turn.'

The fog still clung, still hid the sun, but Richard was drenched in sweat. He felt feverish, his voice nearly gone. His left arm no longer bled, but throbbed so incessantly that he'd begun to fear it might be broken. His right arm ached with pain only a little less intense; his sword was a leaden weight, to be swung solely by sheer force of will. His men were as exhausted as he, desperately aware of the gully at their backs. He'd had no further word from Edward, knew nothing of what was happening on the rest of the field. Time had lost its meaning; he had no idea how many hours had passed since they'd first struggled out of the grey wet marsh to confront Exeter.

A man was bearing down upon him, swinging the deadly chained mace known as a 'holy water sprinkler'. He gave ground, took a glancing blow on the shoulder that staggered him, and drove his sword through the man's mailed brigandine, under his ribs. The force of his thrust numbed his arm. His grip weakened; the sword dipped dangerously.

Ahead of him, one of his men fell, reeling with fatigue. Richard stopped and the soldier gazed up dully, recognized him.

'My lord . . . I cannot . . .'

'Do not talk.' Richard's own voice cracked. He coughed and the muscles of his throat constricted painfully. 'Stay . . . catch your breath. Join us then. . . .'

Somehow, the man regained his feet, managed a ghostly smile. 'I do not . . . do not want to have. . . .'

Richard never knew what he meant to say. He gasped, both hands going up to his throat, to the protruding shaft of a sheaf arrow. Blood gushed from the dying man, over them both. Richard recoiled, fought back a queasy wave of sickness. He'd bitten down on his lower lip, now tasted blood in his mouth and nearly gagged. The man slid to the ground at his feet, twitching convulsively. Richard shuddered, backed away.

In the third hour, Exeter's line began to give way before them. Slowly, at first, and then more rapidly, they were falling back. Richard's men found a last surge of strength, flung themselves forward, shouting for York. The Lancastrians were in confusion, no longer giving resistance. The thought now was of flight and men broke ranks, began to scatter.

The fog was thinning at last. Men were becoming visible on Richard's left, men who wore the colours of York. He understood then; the van had joined with the centre. Ned had smashed through Johnny's wing.

The Sunne banner of York gleamed white-and-gold. Edward's white polished armour was dulled with dirt, dented and scratched, dark with the blood of other men. He moved forward; men parted to let him pass. Reaching Richard, he raised his vizor. Richard saw he was smiling.

Richard felt no elation, neither triumph nor relief . . . not yet. Only numbness, a weariness of body and mind unlike anything he'd ever experienced. Slowly he lowered his sword to the ground, let the bloodied blade touch the grass.

*

Richard's shattered vambrace lay on the floor of the surgeon's tent. Francis and Rob were leaning over him unfastening the straps and buckles that closed his cuirass on the right side, fumbling with the straps across his shoulders. They were no longer used to acting as squires and managed to get in each other's way, jerking with awkward roughness as they removed Richard's breastplate, stripped away the battered rerebraces that sheathed his upper arms. Too tired for complaint, he suffered their ministrations in silence, and gave a sigh of relief when he could at last draw a breath without constraint.

Francis brought forward a tabard that had been fetched from Richard's tent, helped Richard to pull it over his padded arming doublet. The surgeon was kneeling beside him to examine his wound, by now stiff with congealed blood. Richard flinched at his touch and gratefully accepted the wine flask Rob was offering.

'Have men been sent out to recover the bodies?'

Rob nodded. 'They've found Parr but not Huddleston . . . not yet.' He paused, said softly, 'It was quick, Dickon, and clean. That's something.'

Richard opened his eyes at that; his mouth twisted. 'Not much, Rob. Not bloody much.'

He drank too deeply, choked. The surgeon was pouring honey into the wound to cleanse it; under his probing, the bleeding had begun anew. Richard sagged back, closed his eyes again.

A shadow fell across him. He looked up as Will Hastings ducked under the tent flap, said tensely, 'Has there been word of Warwick or Johnny Neville, Will?'

Will shook his head. 'We know Oxford fled the field when Montagu's men fired on him, and I've heard Exeter is dead, though that's but rumour so far. But there's been no word as yet of either Warwick or Montagu.'

He leaned closer, dropped his voice for Richard alone.

'Anthony Woodville took a sword thrust across the greave. He'll have a limp for a while, but no more than that . . . more's the pity.'

Richard summoned up a shadowy smile and then gasped as the surgeon's scalpel slipped yet again.

'Jesus, man, take care!' he snapped, and the surgeon mumbled an apology, thrust a cup into his hand.

'Agrimony . . . if Your Grace would drink that down?'

Will was watching Richard, now said, 'You know I argued against giving you the van. I thought you too young, too green. Your brother disagreed with me. He was right and I was wrong.'

Richard was not ready for compliments; the past three hours were still too close, too raw.

'What of the casualties?' he asked. 'Have we any idea yet as to our losses?'

'No . . . But I'd not be surprised if the deaths do number fully fifteen hundred.'

The tent flap was pulled back. Edward entered, waved Richard back as he attempted to get to his feet. His eyes shifted to the surgeon. 'How does my brother of Gloucester?'

Richard drained the cup with distaste, answered before the surgeon could reply. 'I'm sure I'll survive the wound but I'm not so sure as to the treatment.'

Edward grinned. 'I see you're coming around to yourself, little brother.' He leaned over the surgeon's shoulder so he could see Richard's wound for himself, grimaced, and then said, 'There's a report that Warwick was seen near Wrotham Wood. I've dispatched a man from my own household with orders that he's not to be harmed. As for Johnny, nothing so far. . . .' He stopped, turning as the tent flap was ripped away to admit a herald clad in the battle-stained livery of York.

He knelt before Edward.

'Your Grace . . . they've found the Earl of Warwick.'

More than a dozen men were standing in a semicircle in the clearing, gesturing and laughing among themselves. They drew back expectantly as several horsemen galloped up, recognizing the King.

Edward flung himself from the saddle, strode toward them. He came to an abrupt halt, staring down at the body sprawled in their midst.

The men shifted uncertainly, made uneasy by his silence. One bolder than the rest sidled closer, grinned.

'He'll be after making no more kings now, my liege.'

Edward turned to look at the man and then backhanded him across the mouth, a blow that would have been inconsequential from another man but coming from Edward, drove the man to his knees, spitting blood.

No one moved; none dared to aid their fallen comrade. Edward was kneeling before Warwick, turning the body over. Looters had already been at work. Parts of Warwick's armour had been pried loose and both gauntlets were gone; gone, too, were the jewelled rings he'd worn with such pride. Edward raised the vizor and gasped. Until then, he'd not realized how Warwick had been killed, held down while daggers were driven deep into his brain. Richard was beside him now. He slammed the vizor shut, caught Richard's wrist as he leaned forward.

'You do not want to see, Dickon.'

One glance at Edward's face was enough for Richard; he took him at his word, nodded. After a moment, Edward rose, but Richard remained where he was, gazing down at the body of his cousin. He looked up sharply, though, as he heard his brother turn his rage upon the frightened soldiers.

'I did give orders that he was to be spared, God damn your worthless souls.'

They stammered denials, swore they'd had no part in Warwick's death, that they'd found him as he was now, God's truth; he'd been trying to reach the horse park with men in pursuit; they'd seen them enter the woods and followed, but he was dead ere they reached the scene.

404

Other riders were coming up, Will Hastings and John Howard among them. Howard dismounted, came to stand beside Richard.

'A pity,' he said quietly. Richard nodded, said nothing. He wondered if Howard knew about his son, opened his mouth to speak, but somehow the words wouldn't come. Something must have showed in his face, though, for John Howard then did something totally unexpected, thoroughly out of character. He reached out and, for a moment, let his arm encircle the boy's shoulders.

There was sudden activity across the clearing, where Edward stood. Richard raised his head, stared at the agitated, gesturing men. Even before he saw his brother's face, he knew.

He didn't move, stood very still. He was no longer aware of John Howard or of the encircling men who'd drawn near to view with curiosity the body of the Kingmaker. It was some moments, before he could nerve himself to cross the clearing, to hear Ned tell him that Johnny, too, was dead.

They stood apart from the others. Edward was staring down at the ground, at the trampled uprooted grass that spoke for the extreme violence of Warwick's end. After a time, he crossed himself but Richard knew these minutes of silence had been given over to Johnny, not prayer.

'You've the right to know, Dickon,' he said at last, said in a voice that was thick, scratchy with emotion. 'Johnny wore our colours under his armour. He went into battle against us wearing the blue and murrey of York.'

'Jesus pity him,' Richard whispered. Tears had filled his eyes but they clung tenaciously to his lashes, wouldn't fall. He felt frozen; not even for Johnny could he cry.

Other men were riding up. Richard recognized George and managed to pull himself together, said in an almost inaudible undertone, 'Ned, I do not want George to see ...' His voice trailed off and Edward nodded, watched as Richard moved to intercept George, to keep him from too close a scrutiny of his father-in-law's body.

One of the new arrivals approached Edward, said with a smile, 'Your Grace has had a great victory this day.'

Edward nodded.

Above him, the sun at last broke through the fog. Flashes of bright blue were widening overhead and the men within the clearing now found themselves standing in soft morning light. It was not yet ten o'clock.

28

Cerne Abbey
April 1471

Easter Sunday. A High Mass was in progress at St Paul's Cathedral. The service was abruptly halted by the triumphant return of the Yorkist lords and as the congregation watched in awe, Edward strode up the aisle and laid a bloodied banner on the altar. The Archbishop of Canterbury, who had himself lost two kinsmen that day on Barnet Heath, then resumed the Easter Mass, offering grateful Yorkist prayers for God's favour.

Easter Sunday. The Countess of Warwick landed at Portsmouth. From there, she took ship for Weymouth, where she was to await the arrival of Marguerite d'Anjou, Prince Edouard and her daughters. Her ship put in briefly at Southampton and there she was told of the battle that had been fought that dawn at Barnet Heath. She at once abandoned her plan to journey on to Weymouth, and instead rode to Beaulieu Abbey in the nearby New Forest.

There, within the walls of the Cistercian monastery, she sought and was granted right of sanctuary.

Easter Sunday. After a storm-delayed Channel crossing, Marguerite d'Anjou reached Weymouth, ending seven years of French exile. With her were her son Edouard, her daughter-in-law Anne Neville and Anne's sister Isabel.

With her, too, were three men sharing a common Christian name and little else. Dr John Morton, shrewdest and most trusted of her political councillors, a man who, like George Neville, wore the vestments of a priest and nurtured ambitions thoroughly secular in nature; both he and Marguerite intended that he should be named as Lord Chancellor of England upon the defeat of York. John Beaufort, younger brother of Edmund, Duke of Somerset, a youth still in his twenties who'd never wavered in his allegiance to Lancaster. And John, Lord Wenlock, soldier, diplomat, whose loyalties had been pledged, at one time or another, to Lancaster, York and the Earl of Warwick.

The next day, Monday the 15th, they moved inland to the Benedictine Abbey of Cerne. In midafternoon, the Duke of Somerset and the Earl of Devon rode into the confines of the abbey and from Edmund Beaufort, Duke of Somerset, Marguerite learned of Barnet.

Marguerite was shaken by Warwick's death as none could have foreseen. She'd stared speechlessly at Somerset, black eyes suddenly enormous in a face blanched of all colour, and when the Countess of Vaux pressed an ivory rosary into her hand, she clutched it so tightly that the beads broke apart, spilled onto the flagstone floor. To her uneasy audience, it was an ill-omened occurrence.

Marguerite herself was oblivious of the scattered rosary. Warwick had been her sworn enemy, her mortal foe. She had hated him, mistrusted him and needed him. For it was through Warwick alone that she was at last able to get from the King of

France the aid he'd so long denied her. And so she'd been driven to accept Warwick as ally, driven by her own desperation, the ambitions of her son and the unrelenting persuasions of the French monarch. She'd come to terms with the one man she hated above all others, allowed herself to be seduced into sharing his belief that destiny was his for the taking. All his life, had he not done what other men would never dare? The mightiest of the mighty Nevilles, the maker of kings. She'd not let herself believe he might fail.

They were all watching her: Somerset and Devon, the Countess of Vaux, Dr Morton, Abbot Bemyster. Somerset spoke her name, but she ignored him; what more had he to say after telling her of Barnet Heath? She'd begun to pace, found herself before the prie-dieu. In years gone by, she'd knelt on prayer seats cushioned in white satin, studded with jewels. This was a rude monk's seat, little more than a bench. She lowered herself onto it, rested her forehead on her clasped hands but she did not pray.

She could not say with certainty how long she knelt before the prie-dieu. After a timeless interval, she heard another step approach her, this one springy with the sureness of youth, heard the voice she loved above all others.

'Maman?'

She turned to her son at once. He took her hand, helped her to rise. She leaned against him, within the circle of his arms.

'Edouard . . . do you know?'

'Oui, maman.' He glanced over her head, across the room where Somerset and Devon stood. 'Somerset told me.'

When agitated, her heavily accented English tended to fragment, to slur into Gallic incomprehensibility. Such was the case now and she switched abruptly to her native tongue, began to speak rapidly, scarcely pausing for breath. Somerset and Devon found the swift colloquial French hard to follow but they caught enough of her meaning to exchange looks of dismay.

John Morton, who was polished courtier as well as cleric, was sufficiently alarmed to commit a serious breach of etiquette. He stepped forward, blurted out, 'Madame, surely you cannot mean to return to France. I implore you, assure us we did misunderstand you. . . .'

Her surprise was evident, as was her displeasure. 'You did not mistake me.'

Somerset was appalled, Devon no less so. They were quick to add their voices to that of Morton. They protested, argued, entreated . . . to no avail. Marguerite turned a deaf ear to their pleas, gave them the most reluctant of monosyllabic responses. Her mind was made up. She would return to France with the next tide. She'd not risk her son's life now that Warwick was dead. Nothing was worth that to her. Nothing, she repeated, in tones of implacable ice.

For the men a dream was dying and they persisted well beyond the boundaries of her patience.

'You've said enough, my lords,' she snapped. 'We do sail for France and I'll hear no more on it.'

Her son had listened in silence . . . until now.

'No, maman.'

She swung around to confront him as Somerset, Morton and Devon watched, taut with sudden hope.

'Edouard?'

'I am not willing to take flight, to concede the day to York. If we do not seize our chance now, it will never come again. It grieves me that we must be at variance over this, maman. But I will not live out my days in exile whilst a usurper claims the kingship which, by rights, is mine.'

She nodded slowly. 'Indeed, the crown is yours, Edouard, my son . . . upon the death of your lord father.'

He was momentarily silenced by the rebuke. He frequently spoke of his father's suffering, dutifully vowed to avenge his captivity. But the truth was that he often went for long periods of time when he forgot about Harry of Lancaster altogether. His memories of his father, never vivid, had clouded considerably over the years and were, as well, obscurely unpleasant to recall. Both the memories and the emotions they stirred were unexplored, had never been exposed to the light. Instinctively, he preferred it that way, suspected his mother did, too. He knew now that she must truly be fearful for him, to make such use of his father's name.

Taking advantage of his hesitancy, she closed the space between them. She reached for his hand, her fingers closing around his in a coaxing caress, and the watching men saw that her smile had lost none of its charm during her years of exile.

'I ask you to give up nothing, bien-aimé. I ask you only to wait, to wait till the time is more favourable. . . . No more than that.'

'If we leave England now, we lose all,' he said flatly. 'The chance will not come again.'

'Edouard, you do not understand. You do not realize what we risk. . . .'

'I realize what is at stake. The crown of England.'

She grasped his shoulders as if she meant to shake him. But she didn't and, after the space of several shallow breaths, she let her arms drop to her side.

'Edouard, my love, listen to me,' she said urgently. 'You do not know your enemy. Edward of York is a seasoned soldier, a ruthless man who has never been defeated on the field.'

Both Somerset and Devon stiffened at that, for her implication was obvious, but she had no time to spare for their sensibilities now.

'York did swear we owed him a blood debt after Sandal Castle and, though he lies as easily as other men draw breath, this one time he means to keep his word, has waited ten years to do so. Should we lose, he will accord you no mercy.'

She'd blundered and she saw it . . . but too late.

'I ask no mercy from York,' he flared. 'I ask only to see his head on London's Drawbridge Gate and, by God, I shall!'

'Well said, Your Grace,' Devon interjected, while Somerset and Morton maintained a more prudent silence, unwilling to further offend their Queen when there was no need, knowing now that they would have their way, that their Prince would prevail.

Marguerite knew it, too. That was evident with her next words.

'If I do insist, Edouard?' And the very fact that she needed to ask was in itself a concession of defeat.

'Do not, maman,' Edouard said softly.

The ensuing silence was awkward, even for the exultant men. Devon had discovered a wine flagon and cups on the sideboard. He knelt before Edouard, holding out a brimming cup.

'I should be honoured to drink your health, Highness.'

Edouard accepted the cup, smiled at him. There was admiration in Devon's eyes; Somerset and Morton, too, were regarding him with approval. Only his mother's morbid misgivings marred the pleasure of the moment. He gave her a look of affectionate impatience, thinking that she'd come to her senses soon enough. She was not given, after all, to the foolish fears and fancies that he thought common to most of her sex. This was the woman called 'Captain Marguerite' by the Yorkists, the woman who'd routed Warwick at St Albans with an imaginative flank attack of her own devising. Not that he thought women should take upon themselves the duties and prerogatives of men but his mother was not like other women. She was Marguerite d'Anjou and he could feel only pride when he looked upon her. Even now, when she was being so unreasonable, so strangely fainthearted.

Leaning over, he deposited a conciliatory kiss upon her taut cheek. 'I know you did not expect Warwick to be beaten. But once you do think upon it, maman, I am sure you will come to see how little we have lost by Warwick's death.'

His eyes flickered from her, across to Somerset. 'What say you, my lord Somerset? You lost both your father and brother to the Nevilles. Can you, in truth, tell Madame my mother that you have regrets for Warwick or Montagu?'

411

Somerset shook his head. 'No, Your Grace. I do not weep for Warwick,' he said dryly.

Edouard turned back to his mother. 'When my lord father was taken into custody by York, it was Warwick who led him through the streets of London to be jeered and mocked by the rabble. It was Warwick who bound his feet to the stirrups of his saddle as if he were no more than the meanest, poorest felon . . . and he an anointed king. It was Warwick who dared slur your name and my heritage, Warwick who placed the crown of Lancaster upon York's head.'

'You may be sure I have not forgotten,' Marguerite said with some asperity.

Undaunted, he gave her his most winning smile. 'We are amongst friends; we may speak plainly. What if it had been York who died at Barnet? We'd still have had to deal with Warwick. We knew the reckoning would come in time; he had much to answer for. But with York dead and Warwick securely in the saddle . . . well, he might not have been that easy to unhorse.' He grinned suddenly. 'No, in truth, maman, we might even say York did us a service of sorts at Barnet.'

Devon laughed. 'His Grace is right, Madame. Men will flock to your banners, men who would scorn to fight for a turncoat like Warwick.'

'My Prince,' Somerset said suddenly, warningly, for he alone had noticed the girl standing in the doorway. He wasn't sure how long she'd been listening. But he was sure she'd heard words that were never meant for her ears, for he had guessed her identity at once, needed no one to tell him this was Warwick's daughter, she who was wed to his Prince.

She was unnaturally still; the slender body was rigid. Her gaze was unfocused. For a moment her eyes flickered over Somerset's face but he felt sure she did not see him. He had marked that look often enough to recognize it now. Men maimed in battle had all too often gazed up at him with that same expression of

412

puzzled intensity, in the fragment of time between the rending and the realization.

He took an instinctive step toward her and then checked himself. He was not the one, after all, to offer her comfort; that was for Marguerite and Prince Edouard to do. But neither his Queen nor his Prince gave any indication of doing so. Somerset hesitated; why risk royal disfavour for a misguided moment of pity? But the girl had begun to tremble. As he watched, she swayed, caught the doorjamb for support. Somerset swore under his breath, went to her.

'You'd best sit down, my lady,' he said brusquely and, taking a firm grip on her elbow, he steered her toward the nearest seat. She didn't resist, leaned on his arm. He didn't think she was even aware of his assistance. But, as he straightened, stepped back, she raised her face to his.

'Thank you,' she whispered.

At a loss, Somerset glanced over at Marguerite and her son. They were watching intently, but it was he, rather than Anne Neville, who held their dark eyes. He was suddenly angry, with them for their uncharitable indifference and with himself for his reluctance to perform a simple act of kindness. He opened his mouth, words that could compromise him taking shape on his tongue.

'Anne? Sister, what ails you?'

Somerset turned, grateful to relinquish an unwanted responsibility to one better able to handle it. He watched as Warwick's elder daughter bent over her sister. He stood close enough to see the younger girl swallow, to hear her halting words and Isabel Neville's gasp.

She froze and then spun around to face the others.

'Madame, what does my sister say? Surely it's not true!'

Marguerite had seated herself in the Abbot's high-backed chair. Thus appealed to, she looked toward Isabel, said, 'There was a battle fought yesterday morn, near a village called Barnet. York won. Your father and uncle were slain on the field.'

Somerset winced; however much he loved his Queen, he could wish she'd found softer words. Behind him, he heard Anne Neville make a strangled sound and he thought, Christ, she did not know about Montagu! Isabel Neville, however, made no sound at all. Her back was to Somerset but he saw her shoulders hunch forward, saw the shudder that shook her body.

'What . . . what of my husband?'

Somerset was startled. He'd been thinking of the girl as Warwick's daughter, had almost forgotten that she was wife to Clarence, too. It occurred to him that she'd have done better not to remind them of it.

'Your husband?' Marguerite was echoing, in tones that would have chilled a more courageous spirit than Isabel Neville's.

Somerset saw at once, though, that the girl had misunderstood, for she cried, 'Oh, Blessed Lady, he's dead, too!'

'No.' Marguerite leaned forward. 'He is not dead. You need not waste your tears on Clarence. I daresay he thrives; men of his ilk generally do. A fool Clarence may be, but he's been a singularly lucky fool so far. Better you should weep for yourself, Lady Isabel.'

Somerset didn't like the sound of that but Isabel understood only that her husband still lived.

'Where is he, Madame? Will he join us? . . .' Her voice trailed off; instinct was now alerting her to danger yet unknown.

'He is not hurt?' she faltered.

'No. Your husband emerged unscathed from the battle. Without even a scratch.'

Such words should have reassured. They only served to frighten. Isabel waited, mute, for the blow to fall.

'He betrayed us.'

Marguerite spat the words, saw Isabel react. Satisfied that the girl's shock was unfeigned, she relaxed somewhat, said contemptuously, 'He went over to York at the first chance. He abandoned your father . . . and you, too, it would seem.'

'Betrayal is becoming a habit with Clarence,' Edouard observed, and Marguerite took her eyes from Isabel's stricken face, looked at her son.

'And I'd wager he never gave a thought to the wife who might pay the price for his treachery.'

Somerset did not take her words to mean that she intended to hold Isabel Neville to account for her husband's sins. Marguerite was impulsive but she was no fool. He felt sure she'd never give York so potent a weapon as an accusation that Lancaster had abused Warwick's daughter. Moreover, the girl would make a dubious hostage at best; Clarence did not seem the sort to be swayed except where his own skin was threatened. But as Isabel shrank back, he saw her face and realized that she did take Marguerite's implied threat seriously.

Anne Neville came to her feet, so swiftly that she stumbled on her skirts.

'Madame, Isabel is my sister,' she said resolutely.

Somerset knew how little that meant. He suspected Anne did, too. From where he stood, he could see the tremor in the tightly clenched small fists, could see how they pressed against the folds of her skirt with revealing urgency.

Isabel Neville, too, seemed to feel she needed a more powerful protector than her sister and now she looked to her brother-in-law.

'Surely a Prince of Lancaster would not avenge himself upon a woman,' she entreated and, if her appeal lacked subtlety, it did not lack sincerity.

Edouard looked amused. Whether he was flattered, as well, by Isabel's plea, Somerset couldn't tell, but he said, not unkindly, 'Calm yourself, chérie. Whilst I can think of no more harsh penance than to pack you off to Clarence, if that be your wish, you're free to go.'

'Merci, Edouard,' Isabel murmured weakly. After a discernible pause, Anne too, added her thanks, almost inaudibly, as Edouard looked belatedly to his mother for confirmation. Marguerite was regarding her assertive offspring with a bemused expression but she did not countermand him. For the first time, she seemed to have taken notice of Abbot Bemyster. He'd taken no part in the conversation, nor had he made any attempt to console Warwick's daughters. But neutral or not, he was still a priest and not one of her own like Morton. There were certain amenities to be observed in his presence. She glanced back at her daughter-in-law, said dispassionately, 'I daresay you and your sister would prefer to retire to your chambers, Anne. You have my leave to withdraw.' Adding as an indifferent afterthought, 'My condolences upon your bereavement.'

Marguerite was staring after Anne Neville, her face shadowed in thought. Her expression was enigmatic, unusually pensive, and, as he approached her, Somerset wondered if his Queen were as impervious to pity as she would have them think. His speculations were abruptly ended with her next words, a low-voiced directive to her son.

'You know I care not how you choose to amuse yourself, Edouard. But be sure you do not seek your pleasures again in that girl's bed. God forbid if you should get her with child now.'

Edouard had been leaning on the back of her chair. At that, he leaned over still further, murmured something too softly for Somerset to hear, eliciting both a reproving look and a reluctant laugh from his mother.

Somerset had stopped, unwilling to intrude upon so private an exchange, but Edouard beckoned him forward: 'Seat yourself, my lord.' Edouard perched on the arm of his mother's chair, favoured Somerset with a smile. 'Do you know how you may please me, Somerset? You may tell me of York and his brothers. Well, Gloucester, anyway,' he amended and grimaced. 'I know more than I care to of Clarence.'

'Well, Gloucester is close in years to you, Highness. If there is any man likely to have York's trust, Gloucester would be the one;

it's said they are close. But they are very unlike. Those who do know him say Gloucester is much more his mother's son than are his brothers.'

That didn't tell Edouard much; he knew little of the Duchess of York. But Marguerite knew a great deal and she said venomously, 'There are few more damning accusations you could make than that, to say Gloucester is like Cecily Neville. She pretends to the piety of an Abbess but her ambitions are very much of this world, I assure you.'

Edouard shifted impatiently. He had no interest in the women of York and, as soon as his mother paused for breath, he reclaimed the conversation. 'You say York and Gloucester are unlike. Tell me, then, of York, my lord Somerset.'

Somerset considered. 'Lazy. Self-indulgent. He denies himself few pleasures, surely none of the flesh. He's not given to grudges but he forgets nothing; the man's memory is truly remarkable. Charming when he so chooses. The morals of a tom-cat and the luck of the angels. He is surprisingly careless of ceremony, mingles with the common people like no monarch within memory. I was told that when he departed Bruges, he did insist on walking the three miles to the quay at Dammne so the populace could view him at first hand.'

At Edouard's expression of distaste, Somerset smiled slightly, nodded. 'I agree, Highness. Such conduct scarcely becomes the dignity of a king. But he won much favour amongst the people by so doing.'

'He does not sound like a foe worth fearing,' Edouard said disdainfully. 'You describe a lecher, a rakehell caring only for his own ease.'

Marguerite was frowning. 'He is a dangerous man, Edouard. Lecher and rakehell he may be, but he is also a battle commander with few peers, and Somerset will admit as much.' Stabbing Somerset with a wintry stare. 'Will you not, my lord?'

'Madame your mother speaks true, Your Grace,' Somerset said

grudgingly. 'York fights like a man who cannot conceive of defeat and that is no small advantage. When you asked me for my opinion of the man, I did not mean to belittle his prowess on the field. That would indeed be a mistake.'

Marguerite was not yet satisfied. 'He is a calculating and arrogant man untroubled by moral scruples. Moreover, he does not seem to know the fears and self-doubts that do plague other men. Such a man is not to be underestimated, Edouard.'

Edouard was regarding her with a sulky expression, which she knew from experience to mean he was growing bored. 'If it will ease your mind, Maman, I shall endeavour to view York as the Antichrist,' he said flippantly. The dark eyes moved past her to Somerset.

'I have one question for you, my lord Somerset . . . only one. Can we defeat York on the field?'

'Yes,' Somerset said without hesitation.

Edouard nodded slowly. 'That is all I need to know,' he said, and smiled. Somerset smiled, too. Marguerite bit her lip, said nothing.

Edmund Beaufort was a great-grandson of John of Gaunt and therefore related by blood, if rather remotely, to the captive Harry of Lancaster. He was also the son of the man the Yorkists claimed to have been Marguerite's lover. The title he bore was one of England's proudest but the years of his youth had been far from privileged, had been for him a time of turmoil and sudden griefs.

Edmund was thirty-three, had spent years in impoverished exile abroad before being given sanctuary by Charles of Burgundy. He had long ago pledged his honour to Lancaster and was in total and heartfelt agreement with the concerns voiced the night before by Prince Edouard. He, too, thought this would be the last chance for the House of Lancaster.

The cloisters were quiet, dappled in mellow morning sun. At most times of the day, the walkways enclosing the green-carpeted garth would have been alive with activity, with servants and visiting laymen and the shadowy forms of the black-garbed monks. But soon after the conclusion of the Morrow Mass, Abbot Bemyster and the monks had gathered in the Chapter House situated along the east walkway of the cloisters. Somerset knew this daily meeting would continue for another hour or so. Taking advantage of the solitude, he loitered there in the flowering garth and then began to walk along the sheltered walkway that led toward the church.

Entering the south aisle of the nave, where the lay people heard Mass, he paused, blinking until his eyes adjusted to the subdued lighting, and then made his way through the rood screen that separated the nave from the choir, where the monks worshipped. He remained there for some moments, kneeling before the high altar, offering brief prayers for the repose of his father and brother. He had turned back toward the door that led from the south transept when he heard a sound behind him, seeming to come from the Lady Chapel to the east of the altar.

Stepping into the chapel, he came to an abrupt halt, at once regretting the impulse that had prompted his entry. A young girl stood before the altar, turned a startled face toward him. With recognition came the reluctant realization that to withdraw now would be to make an awkward encounter even more so.

'I ask your pardon, my lady. I did not mean to intrude upon your prayers.'

She shook her head. 'I was not praying, my lord.'

He hesitated, then said, 'I am Edmund Beaufort, Duke of Somerset.'

'Yes, I know,' she said politely. Like a child attempting adult courtesies, she extended her hand and, as he bent over it, said, 'I am Anne Neville.'

Now he was the one to say, 'Yes, I know.' Noting, as he did, that she identified herself as Anne Neville, not as the Princess Anne. Princess of Wales . . . He wondered how long she'd keep the title now that her father was dead.

He opened his mouth to offer his formal condolences but found he couldn't say the words. He could still see her as she was last night and, remembering how she had learned of her father's death, he was not willing to demean her grief with conventional expressions of unfelt sympathy. If he could do nothing else for her, he could accord her that much respect.

She was watching him, said, 'Will you tell me of Barnet, my lord Somerset?'

The request did not surprise him; he thought she was entitled to know. He joined her before the altar, gave her a carefully edited recounting of the battle that had been fought two days ago at Barnet Heath. She listened attentively, with the detached calm of one hearing a story that was interesting but, however interesting, was a story of strangers, withal. He'd have been better able to cope with tears; this brittle composure made him uneasy, wondering if and when it would shatter.

Only when he spoke of the confusion over the banners, related how in the mist her uncle Montagu's men had mistaken Oxford's Streaming Star for the Sunne of York, did a flicker of emotion cross her face. He said, with some bitterness, that he could understand how men did think York was favoured by evil auspices, for that had indeed been a stroke of uncanny fortune for York, a diabolic blessing.

A faint smile touched her mouth; she shook her head. 'Ned has ever been lucky,' she said.

That was too easy an explanation for him; he preferred the hint of sulphur. The name jarred, too, the unexpected intimacy of 'Ned'. For the first time, he considered how closely allied this girl was to York. The Duchess of York was her great-aunt; she was cousin to Edward; had grown up with Gloucester; was sister-in-law to Clarence. And she was to have been Lancaster's Queen. He permitted himself a tight smile at the madness of it all, marvelling anew at the cunning of the arch-conniver, the King of France.

But if he rejected her as a queen, he pitied her as a pawn and searched for words of consolation. At last finding comfort he could offer with honesty, he said, 'Your father died well, my lady. You may take pride in that.'

She made no response; her lashes hid her thoughts. With her kinship to York in mind, he thought it a kindness to confide, 'York dispatched a herald to spare your father's life. He was not in time.'

She glanced up at that; their eyes met. 'I do not think my father would have done as much for Ned,' she said softly.

He had no answer for her. She, too, seemed to sense there was nothing more to be said. He fell in step beside her and they walked in silence from the chapel, through the choir, out into the sunlit cloisters. She apparently had been considering his story, for she now said, 'One thing I do not understand, my lord. . . . How is it that you know so much of what happened on the Yorkist side?'

He smiled grimly. 'A stroke of luck named Hugh Short.'

At her puzzled look, he explained, 'A Yorkist deserter who'd had his bellyful of fighting and was unlucky enough to run into some of Devon's men after the battle. From him we were able to learn a great deal. He'd been felled early in the fighting and, by chance, was being treated in the surgeon's tent after the battle at the same time as Gloucester . . . and ere long, York himself rode up to check on his brother. It was there that they had word of your father. From what Short told us, they did, in truth, wish to spare your father's life. They'd not be dissembling among themselves, after all.'

She'd stopped, was staring at him. 'You say he was hurt?'

He looked at her in astonishment, wondering if her nerves were giving way at last. 'Your father was killed, my lady,' he said, measuring his words with some care.

She shook her head impatiently. 'No . . . Richard of Gloucester. Was he badly hurt?'

His reaction was one of relief that her question was rational, after all.

'No, I think not. The lad Short said he was on his feet all the while the surgeons worked on his arm and the wound did not keep him from galloping off with his brother as soon as they had word that your father . . . had been found.'

Not wanting her to dwell on that last image, on the body sprawled in Wrotham Wood, he said hastily, 'Gloucester was lucky, I hear, to get off as light as he did. By all accounts, he was in the thickest press of the fighting. Short said he lost both his squires; he heard them talking of it.'

He saw her face change, saw her shock and reached for her as she stumbled back.

'Oh, my God . . . Thomas!' She'd jammed one hand to her mouth; he could feel her trembling. He tightened his grip on her shoulders, shaking her none too gently.

'Who? I do not understand,' he said, sharply enough to assert control. It worked; she blinked, swallowed and answered obediently.

'Thomas Parr. . . . He . . . he was at Middleham, was squire to Richard for as long as I can remember. He . . . oh, God. . . .'

'I do forget,' he said softly, 'that they are men to you, Lady Anne, men of flesh and blood, not mere names. . . .'

'Poor Thomas,' she whispered. There were tears in her eyes; they glistened but did not fall, not yet.

'I could not weep for my father, yet I can cry for Thomas Parr. Do you not find that strange, my Lord Somerset? I do . . . I find it passing strange. . . .'

He'd feared this would happen, had been sure the moment would come when her control would fragment, had not wanted to be present when it did.

She read his reluctance in his face and struggled to staunch the flow of tears with pride.

'You need not fear, my lord. I'll not embarrass you with tears or. . . .' She stopped abruptly, before her voice could further betray her.

He found a handkerchief for her, watched uncomfortably as she knotted it with fingers that shook.

'Can I not summon someone for you, my lady?'

'Whom would you call, my lord?' she asked unsteadily. 'My sister departs this noon for London, there to join her husband. And my mother ... my mother will not be meeting us at Weymouth as planned. We learned this morning that she has fled to sanctuary at Beaulieu Abbey. ... Did you know?'

He nodded. He had his own opinion of the Countess of Warwick, who had chosen to see to her own safety rather than be with her daughters when they learned of their father's death and Clarence's betrayal. It was not a charitable one.

'I think it best you return to your chambers, Lady Anne,' he suggested gently. 'There is still time for you to lie down; we will not be departing for Exeter till midafternoon.'

'Exeter?' she said uncertainly, and he saw that none had even bothered to tell her of this change in plans.

Footsteps now sounded on the flagstone path and they turned to see Marguerite d'Anjou coming up the west walk toward them. Beside him, Somerset saw Anne Neville stiffen; the arm he held communicated sudden tension.

Marguerite extended ringed fingers for Somerset to kiss, acknowledged her daughter-in-law's dutiful curtsy.

'Your sister is seeking you, Anne. She prepares to depart and wishes to bid you farewell.'

'Thank you, Madame. I shall go to her, with your permission.'

Marguerite nodded and Anne glanced back at Somerset. 'Thank you, my lord, for telling me of Barnet.'

Somerset looked down at the crumpled handkerchief that Anne Neville had pressed into his hand. He refolded it, replaced it in his doublet and raised his eyes to find Marguerite regarding him with sardonic amusement.

'So, my lord Somerset pities the little Neville nestling?'

423

'Yes, Madame, I do,' he admitted, and she linked her arm through his, said with a smile,

'Come, walk with me, cher ami. I wish to speak with you.'

'When Madame commands, it is my pleasure to serve,' he said with studied gallantry. But his smile was wary; he was sure he knew what she would say.

Her first words, however, were not of her son and flight to France, as he'd feared. 'So, tell me, my lord . . . what did you find to discuss with Warwick's daughter? Did you dry her pretty brown eyes and assure her that her father was a knight sans peur et sans reproche?'

He was silent and she gave him a speculative sideways glance.

'How easy you are to read, Monsieur mon chevalier!' she said, with mockery but no malice. 'You think we've ill treated the girl, do you not?'

'No, Madame,' he said, with so little conviction that she made a wry face, laughed at him.

'What a poor liar you are!' But her mood abruptly altered, sobered almost at once.

'Granted, my son is none too fond of the Neville girl, but she has given him no reason to care. She did not want to marry him, went to her marriage bed like one condemned to the gallows. Can you truly blame Edouard for feeling little tenderness for a wife who did not want him and cared not at all who knew it?'

'No,' he conceded, 'I think not. Was she so devoted to the Yorkist cause, then, as that? Queer that a lass of fifteen should be more steadfast than the Kingmaker himself.'

She shrugged. 'Who is to say? But I did not seek you out to speak of Anne Neville. The girl does not matter now; she's of no use to us without Warwick.'

She stopped on the path, turned to face him.

'Somerset, I am so afraid.'

He was at a loss; her raw, wrenching candour was embarrassing, did not accord with his memories. The Marguerite d'Anjou he remembered had feared no man walking God's earth.

'You must trust in Almighty God, Madame. You must have faith in His mercy and divine wisdom.'

She stared at him and then she laughed, a hollow hurting sound. 'It is not God's judgment I fear,' she said, very low. 'It is Edward of York's.'

His pride was affronted; he'd seen considerable service with the army of Charles of Burgundy and felt himself to be a battle commander fully as capable as Edward of York.

'A dead man passes no judgments, Madame,' he said coolly. 'I do believe before God the Father and Christ the Son that when we face York across a battlefield, the victory shall go to Lancaster.'

'S'il plait a Dieu,' she murmured. She reached down, picked a flower from the hedge bordering the walkway, began to pluck the petals, scattering them on the path at her feet.

'It is only that I cannot forget. . . . He was just seventeen, too.'

'Who, Madame?'

She reached for another flower before saying reluctantly, 'Edmund, Earl of Rutland.'

He drew a quick breath. 'Madame, forgive me for speaking so bluntly but I find that a most disturbing remark, in truth I do. Last night you told Prince Edouard that York sees Sandal Castle as a blood debt. Is that how you, too, see it, Madame? The life of your son for that of Edmund of Rutland? For God pity us if you do! This I can tell you for certes, Madame. . . . That if a man goes into battle expecting to lose, he damned well will.'

He saw, with some surprise, that her hands were shaking. The second flower, shorn of petals, joined the first on the path. She looked down at it, said, 'You do not understand, Somerset.'

'No, Madame, I do not. Rutland was no schoolboy, no lamb led to the slaughter. He was a belted Earl, fully seventeen, and I daresay he bloodied his sword that day on more than a few men of Lancaster. Had he been slain on the field, I'd have had no

425

qualms at all about his death. He was of an age. Believe me, Madame, I know. . . . I was not yet seventeen myself at the first battle of St Albans and a sword neither knows nor cares the age of its wielder.'

'He had no sword on Wakefield Bridge,' she said, and he nodded slowly.

'Aye, and that's the heart of it, is it not? It was not his death but the way of it that gave me trouble. There is no honour in stabbing an unarmed prisoner. I do not doubt my brother Harry would've stopped it had he been on the bridge when Clifford drew that dagger. However much Harry hated York, he'd never have countenanced a murder of that sort. Nor could I. No more than you would have done, Madame. It was Clifford's doing and only his. And for you to take his guilt upon yourself at this late date is a penance not called for, Madame. It makes no sense.'

She was shaking her head. 'You still do not understand, Somerset. I do not regret Rutland's death, not in the way you think. I never did, if you want the truth of it. It was war. I did not think the less of Clifford for what he'd done. That Rutland was dead mattered more to me than how the deed was done. The only regret I had was that his brother Edward had not been there, too, on Wakefield Green. Jésus et Marie, if only he had! Do you never think of that, Somerset? I do. For the past ten years, I've thought of little else.

'Have I shocked you, cher ami? You must forgive me if I cannot share your belief in the worth of "honour". You see, Edmund, that was a luxury I could never afford. I was a woman with a husband who was as mad as any of those poor wretches walled up within Bedlam. . . . Yes, just for once, let us say it aloud, speak the unspeakable. My husband, Henri the King, was mad. And who was there to speak for my son, to defend his birthright? None but me. So do not talk to me of honour, Somerset. And do not judge me, either.'

426

It was an extraordinary outburst, like nothing he'd ever heard from her. The tremor afflicting her hands had at the last crept into her voice; he had never seen her like this, not in all the years he'd known her.

'I do not judge you, Madame,' he said softly. 'You are my queen.'

She caught his hand between her own, clinging tightly enough to hurt. 'Help me, then. Help me to persuade Edouard that we must return to France.'

'I cannot do that, Madame,' he said sadly and braced himself for the brunt of her fury.

It never came. She let his hand drop. 'No, I did not truly think you would,' she said calmly, but it was the composure born of utter exhaustion and he was troubled rather than relieved by her abrupt capitulation.

Not knowing if he'd be rebuffed or not, he put his arm around her shoulders. She came at once into his arms and they stood for some moments in the sun, drawing upon that special comfort to be found in the embrace of old and intimate friends who've shared between them a lifetime of griefs.

'Madame, I still do not understand what bothers you so about Rutland's death. Why now, after all these years?'

She gave a sound much like a sigh and finally said, her voice muffled against his shoulder, 'Because it is only now that I realize . . .'

'Realize what, Madame?'

'How very young seventeen is.'

She raised her face to his. 'You will help him, Edmund? No matter what happens, you'll be with us? Swear you will . . . for Edouard, for your prince.'

'Ah, Madame, need you even ask?'

He'd thought that Anne Neville's wide-set brown eyes were like those of a startled fawn, wary but without guile. But the dark eyes of Marguerite d'Anjou were strikingly different, were all that remained of a once breathtaking beauty, reminded him of the lush purple plums that flourished in her native Anjou, eyes that once promised the world in their wine-dark depths.

When he'd been twenty, she'd been twenty-eight and so fair to look upon that he'd known men willing to pledge their lives for her smile. He knew his father had loved her; he'd once been half in love with her himself; so, he suspected, had his brother Harry. He did not know if she had ever strayed from her marital bed, as the Yorkists so often alleged. He preferred not to know.

He smiled at her now, a smile of reassurance, a pledge of faith, and he was aware of an elusive undefined regret. She was forty-one and years of civil war and exile had taken more than her youth. She was thin where once she'd been feather-light, willow-slim. Skin that once glowed was sallow, her forehead was etched with the evidence of her unquiet past, and the hands that rested against his chest were raw-boned, pinched and starkly veined, in constant edgy motion. Only the eyes were as he remembered them, night-black velvet and quicksilver flashes of light, shadowed by charcoal lashes of startling sweep and thickness.

Looking down into those eyes now, he found it within himself to be patient with her fears, her forebodings, and with patience came, too, a fierce protective tenderness.

'Chère Madame, you must take heart. For us, for England . . . and above all, for your son, whose destiny is to be King.'

'Mais oui,' she whispered. 'He does believe that, Somerset.' There was pride and pain in her face; her smile was a ghostly grimace of laughter.

'I taught him well, you see,' she said.

29

Cerne Abbey

April 1471

Isabel stood in the middle of her bedchamber looking at the open coffers on the floor. The packing was all but completed. Only the farewells were left to be said.

She'd already sent one of her ladies to find Anne. She looked ahead to this last meeting with little enthusiasm; it was bound to be painful. With her departure, Anne would be truly alone. She wondered what would happen to her sister now. If only Anne had been more clever, more foresighted. If only she had not deliberately and needlessly squandered any influence she might have had with Edouard. It was too late now, of course. She'd alienated him so thoroughly that he no longer even bothered to mask his contempt, his dislike.

There'd been a time when Isabel had been incensed with Anne for that, for making an enemy of the one person whose goodwill was crucial to them all. But now she felt only regret, only a dulled edge of pity for her sister's predicament. Even if she did think some of Anne's troubles were of her own making, there was no denying the troubles were real enough.

The door opened suddenly; Anne came in. She seemed out of breath, as if she feared she'd not be in time, and Isabel felt an unexpected conscience pang, wondering if Anne had truly imagined she might leave without bidding her farewell. She moved toward the younger girl, touching cheeks in a brief self-conscious embrace, for the first time within memory regretting that she and her sister were not closer, were, in so many ways, no more than familiar strangers.

'Are you all right?' she asked hesitantly, was relieved when Anne nodded.

'I shall miss you, Bella.'

Isabel's eyes suddenly were blurred with tears. Bella was a name from their childhood, had been coined because her little sister could not pronounce Isabel. The name had stuck; many people still called her Bella to this day, including both George and Richard. Anne, though, had long since abandoned it, and this abrupt lapse back to Bella told Isabel a great deal about her sister's emotional state.

'I shall miss you, too,' she confided shakily, and this time their embrace was warm, clinging, touched with despair.

'Bella, I have a favour to ask of you. You know Véronique de Crécy, the young Frenchwoman who accompanied us from Amboise?'

Isabel fumbled to match the name with a face, found it with a flicker of remembered dislike. 'Véronique? Of course, why?'

'Véronique offered to come with me to England, to continue to serve me as she'd done since last August at Amboise. I should not have permitted it but I was selfish, I needed her friendship. And now . . . Bella, take her with you. For me, please.'

'But Anne, if she goes with me, you'll have no one,' Isabel protested.

'It would be worse if she stayed.' Anne's face was grave and too pale, but unmarked by tears. 'She has already given up so much for my sake. At least I can see that she loses no more. With you, she'll be safe.'

'If that is truly your wish, Anne, of course I will. But are you so certain that York will win?'

'If our father could not defeat Ned, I very much doubt that *he* can. Yes, I do believe York will win.'

'But you still cannot be sure. Lancaster has seasoned battle

430

captains, men such as the Duke of Somerset. And much can happen in a battle. So why not keep Véronique with you? At least there'd be one here you could trust.'

Anne didn't answer at once. Instead, she bent over one of Isabel's open coffers, tucked inside a sable-trimmed mantle, and closed the lid. Straightening, she gave Isabel a level look.

'Even if Lancaster should win, Bella, I could do nothing for Véronique. Not now, not after Barnet. You do not truly think he means to keep me as his wife any longer than need be? Must I remind you that we received no papal dispensation for our marriage? It came from the Patriarch of Jerusalem and how difficult do you think it would be to challenge the validity of the marriage on those grounds alone? I would be convent-caged within a month of a Lancastrian victory and divorced ere the year was out and we both do know it.'

Isabel did know it, knew there was never difficulty in finding grounds to dissolve an unwanted marriage, to put aside an unloved wife. Not if the man was powerful enough, if the woman had no powerful relatives of her own to petition the Pope on her behalf. Anne had spoken the truth.

She looked at her sister, marvelling that Anne could speak so dispassionately of her own future, especially such a future as she envisioned. It occurred to her now that she could not remember ever hearing Anne call her husband by his given name. It was invariably 'he' and occasionally 'Lancaster', but never 'Edouard'.

She sat down abruptly on the coffer Anne had just closed. 'I hate to leave you here, Anne . . . with them.'

Anne leaned over, kissed her cheek. 'I'll be all right, Bella.'

'No . . . No, you will not. But there is nothing I can do about it.' She suddenly slammed her fist down on the trunk lid. 'Damn them,' she said fiercely. 'Oh, damn them all!'

Anne gave her a wan smile. 'Who, Bella? Lancaster or York?'

After a pause, Isabel smiled, too, albeit bleakly. 'I'm not as partisan as you, sister. . . . Both.'

She knew she should not be tarrying here like this. There was nothing she could do for Anne and she faced a long tiring journey . . . to be reunited with the husband who had betrayed her.

'As little as I want to stay here, I shrink from reaching London,' she confessed. 'I've known for a long time now that George comes first with George, but this. . . . How could he do it, Anne? How could he?'

Anne bit her lip, shook her head wordlessly.

'And fool that I was, when I was told of Barnet, my first thoughts were for his safety. When he never did give a care for mine!'

'I'm sorry, Bella . . . so very sorry.'

'Sweet Jesú only knows how long he'd planned it. Perhaps even before Ned left Burgundy. We can be damned sure it was not brotherly love that moved him. Oh, he's fond enough of Dickon, I suppose. But Ned? George loves Ned as an infidel loves the True Cross. Or Cain loved Abel. No, he thought it out well before-hand, long and hard. And yet he could not be bothered to warn me, to send me word. No, he let me find out from the very ones he betrayed. Anne, how can I face him after that? How can I forgive him?'

Anne was staring at her, open-mouthed. 'I could not say,' she said, so stiffly that Isabel looked up sharply at the change in tone.

'What is it?' she demanded. 'Why do you of a sudden sound as if you'd quaffed soured milk?'

Anne hesitated but her restraint was short-lived. 'I do not understand you, Isabel. How can you see George's failure to warn you as a greater betrayal than his abandonment of our father?'

Isabel flushed and then her temper flared like dry kindling. 'And I suppose you're laying all the blame for our father's death upon George.'

'I did not say that.'

'But that's what you meant. You've never liked George, we both know that. You'd be more than willing to blame him, if that way you could avoid blaming Dickon and Ned!'

'It was George who betrayed our father's trust. George, not Richard or Ned!' Anne responded, with no less passion.

Isabel was too angry to puzzle over the emotion that now drove her, perversely, to come to George's defence when she herself had been damning him but moments before. She was aware only of a burning sense of outrage that Anne should so unfairly burden her husband with so heavy a guilt.

'What a hypocrite you are, Anne! What if George had held fast for our father? That does not mean the outcome of Barnet would have been any different. And even if it did, are you trying to tell me you'd have welcomed a Yorkist defeat? Been glad if Dickon and Ned lay dead instead of our father? Go on, Anne, tell me how glad you'd have been,' she jeered, and then her anger was gone, lay sodden and heavy within her at sight of her sister's stricken face. She looked away, struggling with an unwelcome sense of shame. There was no sport in hurting Anne; it was too easy.

'Ah, Anne, why must we always quarrel? Even now, of all times. . . .' She sighed, decided it was up to her to overlook Anne's obstinacy. There was, she knew, a very real possibility that she might not see Anne again.

She rose, patted Anne forgivingly. 'I would as soon depart without having to see Madame the Queen,' she said sarcastically. 'But I should say farewell to Edouard. He was rather decent last night, after all. . . .'

Anne shrugged. 'As you wish,' she said indifferently, but her mouth had tightened and something dark and brooding showed in her eyes.

'I saw her in the west walk of the cloisters with the Duke of Somerset. I do not know where *he* is, though.' She looked at Isabel. 'He might even still be abed,' she said, with sudden venom. 'I expect he was awake most of the night, celebrating the news of our father's death.'

Isabel was moved again to pity, which submerged the last of her irritation.

'You will be all right, Anne?' She'd meant it as reassurance, but it came out in the form of a question.

'You need not worry about me, Bella. I'm not important enough for them to bother with, not now. I'll be all right . . . truly.'

'Of course you will,' Isabel agreed immediately, unconvincingly.

'I'll be all right,' Anne repeated. She leaned back against the table, kept her eyes on Isabel. 'He'll not take the trouble to cause me hurt. Had he his way, he'd not speak to me at all. And now . . . now I believe he will shun my bed as he does my company. I should not think he'd risk getting me with child now that my father is dead,' she said matter-of-factly, and then the bitterness broke through.

'So you see, Bella, our father did not die in vain, after all.'

Isabel opened her mouth to caution Anne; some indiscretions were too dangerous ever to utter aloud. Instead, she drew in her breath in horror, for Edouard of Lancaster was standing in the open doorway.

Anne saw her alarm, spun around. At sight of her husband, she went white. She caught the edge of the table but as he walked toward her, she began to back away, until she was stopped by the far chamber wall.

Isabel watched, transfixed, while her mind raced, trying to recall if she had said anything herself that Edouard might have found objectionable. With relief, she decided her own conversation had been reasonably circumspect. Oh, why could Anne never learn to hold her tongue? Now look what she had brought upon herself! Isabel's own marriage had more than its share of tensions and strains, but George had never looked at her as Edouard was looking at Anne. All at once she was not so reluctant to join George in London. Whatever her feelings for George, she had never feared him and she saw that her sister did fear Edouard.

Anne wore a slender gold chain about her neck, a long-ago gift from her father; a delicate gold-and-ebony crucifix rested in the hollow between her breasts, just visible above the low-cut bodice

434

of her gown. Edouard entwined his fingers in the chain, drew it taut so that she was compelled to move toward him until their bodies touched and she had to tilt her head back in order to look up into his face.

'You are right for once, chérie,' he said coldly. 'I shall, indeed, shun your bed . . . and, I daresay, with more pleasure than ever I got from it. I am only thankful that amongst your many failings as a wife, you proved to be barren, too.'

'Edouard!' Isabel said suddenly, so sharply that she startled them all, even herself. But she had seen the look on Anne's face and was afraid of what Anne might say. She knew her soft-spoken sister was not assertive, shrank from conflict; Anne was rarely given to anger and never to the rages and fits of temper such as she herself indulged in. But she knew, too, that Anne could be surprisingly stubborn and, when sufficiently provoked, was capable of the most reckless honesty.

Now Anne was beginning to look obdurate; there was hatred as well as fear on her face, and Isabel was apprehensive lest her sister give in to one of those incautious bursts of compulsive candour. For if she did. . . .

Edouard had once surprised her by saying that he did not approve of wife-beating. Both the secular and spiritual authorities reco-ognized a husband's right to chastise an erring wife and Isabel would not have expected Edouard to think otherwise; her assess-ment of her brother-in-law was that he was not one to volun-tarily relinquish any prerogative. At the time of their conversation, though, he'd been quite emphatic. Isabel remembered that now but she was not willing to trust to his philosophical inclinations; there were some convictions that were better left untested.

'Edouard . . . were you . . . were you seeking me?' she concluded lamely, the best she could do under the circumstances.

It sufficed, though. He released Anne's crucifix chain, stepped back, and managed to respond with at least a semblance of courtesy.

'I came to bid you farewell . . . and to wish you bonne chance.'

'Good luck?' she echoed and smiled uneasily. 'Do you think, then, that I might encounter difficulty in reaching London?'

'No. It was my thinking that the need for luck would be greatest once you did reach London.'

Isabel felt resentment stir, but not much; there was too much truth in what he said for that. She smiled politely at him but he had turned. His eyes flicked back to the silent Anne.

'Shall I wish you bonne chance, too?' he asked, softly sardonic.

Anne swallowed, seemed on the verge of speech and then flinched as he reached out, as if to touch her cheek. She stood very still, but turned her head aside, and he laughed, without the slightest trace of amusement.

He moved toward Isabel, then, raised her hand to his lips.

'Have you sufficient men-at-arms for a safe escort?'

Isabel nodded in surprise.

'You are sure, chérie? If not, I will see to it that you have the men you need.'

She'd not expected that; it was a generosity he needn't have offered, one that she felt sure would have outraged his mother. She smiled.

'Merci, mon beau-frère! It is not necessary, Edouard, but I do thank you.'

He smiled, too, shrugged. 'De rien, belle-soeur.' For a brief moment, he looked again at Anne.

'What a pity you are not going with her, chérie,' he said tonelessly.

As the door closed, Isabel took a tentative step toward Anne, but then halted uncertainly. There was something in her sister's face that told her Anne would not welcome her embrace just now.

She could see a faint red mark on Anne's neck, where the chain had twisted, could see how rapidly the younger girl's breasts rose and fell. She waited what she felt to be a discreet interval in order to give Anne time to compose herself.

'Anne, I truly must go. It grows late, nigh on toward noon.'

Anne raised her lashes. Isabel had never seen her eyes so dark, a midnight brown, almost black, but they were free of tears, and that somehow moved Isabel almost as much as Anne's use of the childhood 'Bella', for she remembered how readily Anne would once weep for a strayed pet, an unjustified rebuke, a ballad of unrequited love.

She moved forward, hugged Anne tightly.

'God keep you, Isabel.'

'Take care, sister. For Our Lady's sweet sake, take care.'

Anne nodded. 'I shall. Now I must tell Véronique she is to go with you. She does not know yet. . . .' She stopped speaking, drew a deep deliberate breath. 'Then I shall return to the Lady Chapel.' And with no more expression than Edouard had shown but moments before, she added, 'I want to light a candle for York.'

30

Windsor Castle

April 1471

Tuesday, April 23rd, the Feast of St George, England's patron saint. Edward had chosen to mark the day at Windsor Castle, where he'd been quartered since the preceding Friday, urgently sending out commissions of array to fifteen counties in his quest to muster fresh troops. The Yorkist lords were meeting now, in the twilight dusk that had darkened the sunset sky with all the suddenness of a winter nightfall, and the chamber was already ablaze with rushlights and foreshortened by advancing shadows.

For days they'd argued among themselves, trying feverishly to anticipate the Lancastrian command. First reports had the Lancastrian army making for Salisbury which lay on the road to London. But conflicting reports were soon coming in, and Edward studied them, sorted them out and concluded that the Salisbury manoeuvre was a feint, a military ruse to conceal their true destination—Wales and the waiting men of Jasper Tudor, Harry of Lancaster's Welsh half-brother.

The decision had now been made; on the morrow, the Yorkists would march west. To reach Wales, the Severn River had to be forded, and there were only three viable crossings: at Gloucester, Tewkesbury, and Worcester. Edward meant to cut the Lancastrians off before any of the three crossings could be reached.

Edward signalled for wine, and turned to John Howard, querying in an undertone, 'Have you had further word of your son, Jack?'

The stern mouth softened somewhat, almost smiled. 'Aye, Your Grace, I have. He's better, God be praised.'

Edward was pleased. 'You Howards are a sturdy breed. I thought sure your Thomas would live to make old bones.'

Edward had long ago learned a very simple trick, that one of the surest ways to endear oneself to others was to offer undivided attention and he appeared to listen attentively to Howard's reply. But all the while his eyes were focused unwaveringly upon Howard's face, his thoughts were wandering far afield and he seized his first opportunity to give voice to a nagging concern.

'How does the arm, Dickon?. It'll not hinder you on the morrow?'

Richard was not seated with the others at the trestle table. He'd chosen, instead, to settle himself in the window seat where he was frowning in the fading light over the map spread out on the seat beside him; it was creased from much handling and liberally marked with ink. He glanced up as Edward spoke, said hastily, 'Not in the least. It's a bloody nuisance, no more than that.'

'You'd say that whether you had a bone broken six different ways from Sunday or the French pox.' George's voice drifted lazily from the shadows behind Edward.

The jibe was good-natured, was even meant to be a compliment of sorts, but Richard was not comfortable discussing his injury; he hated ever havng to acknowledge physical ailments of any kind, a carry-over from those early childhood days when raging fevers had all too often confined him to bed, subjected him to a variety of unpleasant ministrations at the hands of his nurse and, more rarely, his mother. Now he was quick to deflect the conversation into more agreeable channels.

'Who do you think will have the command for Lancaster, Ned? Somerset?'

'Most likely. Though if Marguerite had her way, I daresay she'd take the field herself. She has never forgotten that the Maid of Orléans was French-born, too.'

The men laughed and Edward added, with a derisive smile, 'My only fear is that she'll insist upon keeping her nestling at her skirts and give over all into Somerset's hands.'

'You need not worry, Ned,' George offered assuringly. 'I do know her whelp, remember? I found him to be an unspeakably impudent brat but craven he was not. He'll take the field against us. I'd wager he's panting to do so.'

'Indeed, I hope you are right, George.' Edward drummed on the table with his pen, absently applying so much pressure that the quill point split. He tossed it aside, said, 'Will, I want you to take the rear again, as at Barnet.'

Will strove for nonchalance, did not quite carry it off. He'd had some uneasy days this week past, wondering if Edward would entrust him again with a command after the disaster that had overtaken his left wing at Barnet.

Edward was now addressing the room at large. 'I trust we're all in agreement this time as to who is to have the van?'

Will gave a wry smile, raised his wine cup toward Richard in a mock salute. No one else commented; John Howard looked approving, Anthony Woodville sourly resigned, George conspicuously noncommittal. Only Richard spoke.

'Let's not be so hasty. I was enough of an innocent ere Barnet to think you were conferring an honour of sorts on me. Now I know better.'

Edward laughed. 'I do believe you're growing up, little brother.'

He pulled a fruit bowl toward him. 'It's settled, then. I take the centre. Will is to have the rear again. And the vanguard goes to Gloucester. . . . Unless you truly want me, Dickon, to give the command into other hands?'

'Over my dead body!'

Edward grinned, bit into a fig. 'Hardly the most felicitous choice of words, Dickon. And whilst we are on the subject, there is a distinction to be drawn between courage and recklessness. From what I did hear, you confused the two at Barnet. Next time, a little less daring, a little more discretion, if you please.'

Will missed Richard's reply, heard only the laughter that followed. He glanced down at the table lest his eyes encounter Edward's. Although it had been many years since he'd betrayed an unwanted emotion, he knew Edward's eyes could at times be too discerning and Will had no intention of ever letting Edward know he was jealous of Edward's brother.

Edward was proud of Richard's performance at Barnet. And with reason, Will would concede that. But he'd been listening to Edward praise Richard without pause for nine days now and he was growing rather tired of hearing it.

Will liked to think he was always honest with himself, even if not always with others. So he was willing to admit that his impatience sprang in part from his own lacklustre command at Barnet. Not that Edward had reproached him because he hadn't been

440

able to hold his men. He merely talked incessantly of Richard, who had.

Will looked expressionlessly across the room at Richard. He'd never properly sorted out his feelings for Richard, had never even tried to do so till now. He admired the boy's courage, was amused by his wry understated humour, could respect Richard's passionate loyalty to those he loved. But they had little in common beyond their shared devotion to Edward, and Richard was too intense, too lacking in subtlety for Will to have chosen him as a friend had they not been thrown together by circumstance and need.

Will prided himself upon his detachment, his ability to step back several mental paces and view any happening, no matter how personal, with objectivity. It was a trait Edward valued in him, shared to a certain degree. For all that he was a man widely reputed to be governed by his passions, Edward was, Will knew, far more deliberate and controlled than most people realized. Will had known Edward as an intimate for more than ten years and, in all that time, he could recall seeing Edward angry, genuinely angry and not indulging in temper for effect, so rarely he could count the outbursts upon one hand. Will was well aware that Edward, for reasons of his own, preferred that others think him impulsive, spontaneous, easily stirred by surface currents of passion, pity, pride. Will knew better.

Richard, though, was moved by emotion as Edward was not; there was nothing objective or analytical in the dark eyes he turned upon the world, nor would he have seen any virtues in such qual-ities had Will raised the issue with him. But Will found Edward's youngest brother to be likable, their differences notwithstanding, and during the past year had even developed a casual affection for the boy, affection that still survived, but sapped of any vitality, after running head-on into the jealousy born of Barnet.

'What's her name, Will?' Edward's voice cut so abruptly through his reverie that he jumped, pulled his wits together with difficulty.

'Who?' he asked blankly, and Edward laughed.

441

'That was what I asked you, Will. If it is not a woman who claims your thoughts so thoroughly, what, then?'

Will grinned, shook his head. 'And do you think me feeble-witted enough to tell you her name? I may not be able to guard my forest from royal poachers, but I'm damned if I must myself lead the way to the deer!'

George had been standing just behind Edward's chair. Now he came forward on the wave of their laughter, for he'd been awaiting just such a moment, when he thought his brother would be most receptive to the appeal he meant to make.

'Ned, have you given any thought to the disposition of the Neville lands?'

'Well, his northern estates in Cumbria and Yorkshire will be forfeit to the crown. . . . Assuming we do win, of course, George.'

Will, watching closely, caught the glimmer of irony in Edward's eyes, wondered if George did, too. Apparently not, he decided, with George's next question.

'What of Warwick Castle?'

Will saw Edward's mouth twitch with what he accurately took to be suppressed amusement but it was Richard who spoke first.

'Warwick Castle is part of the Countess of Warwick's inheritance and, as such, reverts back to her control upon her husband's death. The treason was Warwick's, not hers. Since a wife owes obedience, above all, to her husband, she cannot, in all justice, be then held accountable for his crimes. Surely you do know that, George?'

Will glanced over at Richard with interest and some surprise. There had been a distinct coolness in Richard's voice and Will saw now that he was not regarding George with any particular favour. George saw, too, said testily, 'My mother-in-law does not need you to speak for her, Dickon.'

'I would hope not.'

Edward had followed this exchange with increasingly evident laughter. Now he said blandly, 'Dickon is right, George. Warwick

442

Castle does, by rights, belong to the Countess of Warwick and is not subject to forfeiture.'

For a moment he slanted a mischievous look in Richard's direction which only Will caught. 'Moreover, George, even if the Countess's Beauchamp lands were open to seizure, are you not forgetting that your sister-in-law, Anne Neville, is the rightful heiress to half of them?'

George looked startled and then laughed shortly. 'And are you forgetting, Ned, that Anne Neville is wife to Lancaster? Do you expect him to make a claim on her behalf, perhaps?'

Edward smiled, shrugged. 'That does remind me, I want orders given to see to the safety of Anne Neville once we've taken the measure of Lancaster. I do want special care taken; I'll not have her ill treated, under pain of my gravest displeasure.'

George was surprised, then pleased. 'That's decent of you, Ned, and will ease Bella's mind considerably.'

'Not at all, brother George.' Edward shifted in his seat, turning to face Richard. 'Should I forget in the days to come, d'you think you could remember to recall the little Neville lass to my mind, Dickon?' he asked solicitously and then roared with laughter at the glare his brother gave him.

Will was watching in bemusement. The meaning of this byplay so far eluded him but that there was meaning in it, he had no doubt. His eyes took in the three Yorkist brothers but without enlightenment. Edward was clearly enjoying himself, and Richard just as clearly was not; he looked at once aloof and annoyed. George was frowning, seemed perplexed. Will gave Edward one more searching look and then resigned himself to an unsatisfied curiosity. Apparently, this was yet another private understanding Edward shared only with Richard. Jealousy surged upward, rose in Will's mouth like bile. Resolutely, he ignored the taste, and turned to Richard with determined, deliberate goodwill.

'You grew up with Warwick's daughter, did you not, Dickon? At Middleham?'

The question was the most innocuous to come to his mind, seemed ideally suited to convey friendly interest. Yet he saw at once that his good intentions had somehow gone astray. Edward was, unaccountably, even more amused by his query and Richard, just as unaccountably, seemed irked, although he replied politely enough, saying briefly that, yes, he'd been at Middleham with Anne Neville.

Illumination dawned for Will. Why, he wasn't sure, but the subject of Warwick's daughter seemed to be a sensitive one. He quickly asked Richard another question, this one concerning the coming campaign, and Richard responded with such immediate enthusiasm that Will saw his supposition had been correct – Richard was not comfortable talking about Anne Neville.

He was speculating on this when he happened to look at George. George was staring at his younger brother with such total absorption that Will found himself staring at George.

George had yet to take his gaze from Richard. He had the most arresting eyes Will had ever seen, a unique shade of purest blue-green, with golden lashes a woman might envy. They were measuring Richard with queer intensity, with a watchful stillness that put Will in mind of a cat suddenly on the scent of unseen prey.

Will looked to Richard, who was pointing out the closest Severn crossing on the map to John Howard, unaware of his brother's unblinking scrutiny. But Will saw now that Edward was more observant than Richard. Edward, too, was watching George and Will realized at once that Edward had the advantage of him, for Edward did understand the nature of George's suspicions. Will had no doubt of that. All amusement had gone from Edward's face and the eyes studying George were very clear, very cold.

'Ned?' Anthony Woodville spoke for the first time since the council began; he'd been markedly subdued in Edward's presence since their quarrel at Baynard's Castle eleven days past.

'Assuming, of course, that we defeat Lancaster, what mean you to do with the Frenchwoman?'

'Draw her fangs,' Edward said grimly. 'I owe that lady a debt, Anthony, one long overdue.'

All eyes were on him now.

'Jesú, the blood that's been spilled in her name, enough to run the Trent red from Nottingham to the sea,' John Howard said suddenly, and more than one man among them nodded in sombre agreement.

'Would you send her to the block, Ned?' George asked, sounding more curious than vengeful.

'A woman? Jesus God, George!' Richard snapped, and George turned upon him with a hostiilty that seemed disproportionate, far beyond the resentment that Richard's impatient tones might have been expected to spark.

'I was not speaking to you, Dickon,' he said, so scathingly that Richard merely looked at him in surprise.

'He's right, George,' Edward said, but not in rebuke; his voice was without emotion of any kind, very measured and even. 'I'd not send a woman to the block. Not even Marguerite d'Anjou.'

He looked about him, at them all, a faint smile playing about his mouth; there was nothing of amusement in it.

'And I do believe that will, in time, come to be the bitterest of her regrets . . . that I would not.'

31

Tewkesbury

May 1471

Edward had encountered unexpected difficulty in bringing the Lancastrians to bay. He still thought Marguerite meant to head for Wales, but his scouts had yet to confirm it as certainty, and he'd proceeded with undue caution once they departed Windsor on the twenty-fourth. Five days later, they were not further west than Cirencester, for Edward was growing increasingly concerned lest Marguerite slip by him and swing back toward London. When on Wednesday, the first of May, his scouts reported the Lancastrian army was heading east toward Bath, his suspicions seemed to be confirmed. He hastened westward to intercept them, halting briefly at Malmesbury to await further intelligence reports.

The news, when it came, was not good. Marguerite had led him astray with artfully laid rumours, had never meant to face him at Bath. Instead, she'd suddenly swung north, had been welcomed into the city of Bristol, which lay in the path of the Severn River crossing.

Edward had reacted with a rare outburst of unbridled rage, cursing Marguerite for the success of her stratagem, cursing himself for having taken her bait and the citizens of Bristol for opening the city gates to her. But his scouts soon redeemed themselves in his eyes, for on Thursday morn, they brought him as welcome news as he could have wished. Marguerite's advance guard had been sighted at Sodbury, ten miles northeast of Bristol, and the battle preparations had been unmistakable. It seemed she planned

446

at last to turn and fight. Edward roused his men to furious activity; they rode into Sodbury on Thursday at midday and settled into position, to await the Lancastrian army.

The hours passed; night fell. When it was evident that there would be no battle this Thursday, Francis, exhausted from two days of hard riding, stumbled into the command tent that flew the Whyte Boar of Gloucester. Flinging himself down on a pallet, he fell at once into a fitful, uneasy sleep. He was awakened some time later by voices, recognized one as Richard's and started sleepily to make his presence known when he heard a second voice say, 'There is something I want to say to you, Dickon, and if, as I expect, we fight tomorrow, we'll most likely not have another chance to talk alone.'

Instead of speaking then, Francis lay very still, his heart hammering, not wanting the King to think he'd been eaves-dropping upon a private conversation. He opened his eyes but the tent was dark; only a single candle glimmered. He heard Richard stumble against something, swear roundly.

'Where the devil are my people? Let me send for torches, Ned; it's blacker than Hades in here.'

'Do not bother. Will and Jack and the others are awaiting us in my tent, so we can. . . . Oh, Christ, I forgot to summon George myself! He'll sulk for a good hour that I did not personally request he join us, the ass.'

'What's been wrong with him, lately? I have not got two civil words from him for more that a week now.'

'You have no idea, Dickon?'

'No, why should I? Oh, we did quarrel some at Windsor over whether you'd send the Frenchwoman to the block, but I cannot see that he'd bear a grudge over that, surely?'

'I see you truly do not know. Strange, how after all you've been through, you manage to hold to a certain naïveté, even now, even with George.'

447

'I cannot agree with you, Ned. I do not see that I'm naïve, not at all.'

'I should have remembered. At your age, that's a mortal insult. Well, you'd best let it lie, Dickon. George is not one to suffer in silence and, if you've vexed him, you'll know soon enough, I daresay.'

Francis was wishing fervently that he'd spoken out at first; surely that embarrassment would have been far less than to be discovered now. There was an unmistakable intimacy about this conversation; he did not think Richard would be any more pleased than the King to find him here.

'What did you want to say to me, Ned?'

'Just this. . . . I do believe we shall win tomorrow. But only a fool never considers the possibility of defeat. And if we should lose . . . Marguerite d'Anjou is not Warwick, Dickon. I think you understand that but I need to be certain. If we should lose, just be sure you do not let yourself be taken alive . . . the way Edmund was. You understand, lad?'

Francis was not surprised when Richard made no response; he could not imagine what one could possibly say to such a statement. He was scarcely breathing, so quietly did he lay, and he didn't move until long after they had left the tent, too shaken by Edward's words to sleep again.

As it happened, Edward was wrong; they would not fight the next day, after all. At 3:00 A.M. Edward was awakened with dismal tidings. Once again, Marguerite had outfoxed him. As soon as she was sure she'd succeeded in luring him to Sodbury, she'd abandoned further pretence of giving battle and even as he encamped at Sodbury, she was racing north, toward Gloucester.

Edward was wild when he heard for, once she reached Gloucester, once she crossed the Severn, she could burn the bridge behind her to sabotage pursuit and then proceed at her leisure into Wales to join forces with Jasper Tudor.

Edward's fury had been awesome, even to those who did know him best. While the military threat posed by such a retreat into Wales was real enough, it was his pride that had suffered the greatest hurt. That Marguerite should have twice made a fool of him was more than he could accept with equanimity, but he'd not long indulged his anger. Within the hour, his camp was astir and on the move, setting out in grim pursuit.

He was well aware that he couldn't hope to overtake her before she reached Gloucester but a Yorkist courier was soon whipping his mount north, bearing urgent orders for Richard Beauchamp, Governor of Gloucester Castle, commanding him to keep the city gates closed to the Lancastrians at all costs. And as his messenger galloped toward Gloucester, Edward took his army north, along the Cotswold ridge toward the next Severn crossing . . . the town of Tewkesbury.

The memory of that march would long stay with the men who made it, It had been fast, furious and frantic, for Edward was determined to stop Marguerite before she could link up with the waiting Welsh rebels. She was just as determined to cross the Severn to safety and thus postpone their day of reckoning, and Friday became a nightmare of dust, fatigue and thirst for the men of both Lancaster and York.

Edward was renowned for the swiftness with which he could move an army; the speed of his campaigns had long been a byword. Now, with so urgent a need, he pushed his men mercilessly. Although it was only early May, the heat soared upward as the sun climbed in the sky, until the soldiers sweltered under temperatures more common to midsummer than spring. They lacked more than sleep; they were short of water, as well, and the only brook within reach of the thirsty men was soon so churned and muddied by the horses of the vanguard that not even the most parched were willing to drink from it.

The Lancastrian army, too, had been on the march all night, and for them was reserved the bitterness of reaching Gloucester at 10:00 that Friday morning, eager for food and drink and the beckoning bridge that spanned the Severn, only to find the city gates tightly closed to them, by order of Governor Beauchamp. They knew by now of the pursuing Yorkists and they dared not take the time to force the city gates for fear the Yorkist army would be upon them before they could subdue the recalcitrant citizenry. They had no choice but to press onward, toward the Tewkesbury crossing, every bit as thirsty and sleep-starved as the enemy that shadowed them, and for them there was an added cruel goad, the vexation of being the hunted, not the hunter.

Throughout the day, the two armies pushed north, toward Tewkesbury. Because of the punishing pace Edward had adopted upon learning of Marguerite's deception, there was now no more than five miles between the armies and, as the race dragged on, the advance guard of the Yorkists and the rear guard of Lancaster were well within sight of each other.

At 4:00 P.M., the Lancastrian forces at last reached Tewkesbury, and here Yorkist sympathizers attempted to deny them the use of the abbey ferry. Marguerite gave orders to clear the way by force but she alone had the stomach for such a bloody confrontation. Her exhausted men and horses were at the end of their endurance, and Somerset did not need to be told there was no conceivable way they could hope to quell opposition and ferry their army across the river with Edward of York less than five miles behind them and coming up fast. The battle commander countermanded the Queen. Somerset hastily scouted the terrain around Tewkesbury and the weary Lancastrians prepared to make their stand within sight of the River Severn they had tried so desperately to cross.

The Lancastrian army had been on the march for fully fifteen hours, had managed to cover twenty-four miles in that dash for the Severn. But Edward had done the impossible; in just twelve hours, he'd ridden an astonishing thirty-five miles. He was well content now to reward his men and halted the Yorkist army at the village of Cheltenham, some nine miles south of Tewkesbury, for the first food and drink of the day. He then moved his divisions to within three miles of the Lancastrian lines and, with his battle captains, rode out to study what would on the morrow become the last battlefield of the war that had ravaged the Houses of Lancaster and York for nearly two decades.

Richard was not noted for either an excessive or an imaginative use of profanity, but what he said when he first saw the terrain that stretched between the Yorkist lines and the entrenched Lancastrian army won him looks of startled admiration from both Francis and Rob Percy. They heartily concurred with his scorching invective as they surveyed the battlefield before them.

The Lancastrians had drawn their battle lines on high ground south of the village of Tewkesbury and thus gained a natural advantage over the Yorkists, who would be forced to fight uphill. To the Lancastrian left lay the stream known locally as Swillgate Brook; to their right, dense woods stretched from the Gloucester Road toward the crossing of the Severn and Avon rivers; while the ground that separated the armies, the ground over which the Yorkist vanguard would have to pass, was a soldier's nightmare: a tangle of thick thorny underbrush and vines, crevices, uprooted trees, dikes, hedges that grew higher than a man's head, sudden sinkholes sodden with brackish brown water of unknown depths.

Richard spurred his stallion forward for a closer scrutiny. The more he looked, the more appalled he became. From time to time, he murmured, 'Jesus God Above,' more to himself than to anyone else. As Francis reined in beside him, he gestured off to his left.

'Take a look there, Francis. That wooded knoll. . . . Can you imagine better cover for an ambush than that? And it will border right on the flank of my battle, Christ keep us!'

Now that Richard had called his attention to the wooded rise of ground, Francis could indeed see the potential danger it posed.

451

But he was somewhat confused by his friend's last remark. The vanguard always took up position on the right; yet Richard had just named the left battle as his.

'You mean Hastings's battle, do you not, Dickon? The vanguard does fight to the right of the King's battle, does it not?'

'Not tomorrow,' Richard said tersely. 'Tomorrow we do align our men here.'

Suddenly the impassable terrain before them took on a new and very personal signicance to Francis. 'You mean we have to cross those dikes and undergrowth? Good God, Dickon, why?'

'My brother has learned that Somerset is to lead the Lancastrian vanguard.' Richard hesitated, but there was no tactful way to say it. 'He does not want Will Hastings to be facing Somerset. And so, tomorrow the vanguard fights on the left.'

Francis drew a long whistling breath. That, he thought, was a two-edged sword, in truth — as much a slap at Hastings as it was a compliment to Dickon. He wondered how Hastings had taken it, opened his mouth to ask when the evening air was suddenly athrob with the shimmering sounds of chiming church bells. He stared toward the north as the echoes faded. The Abbey of St Mary the Virgin, which lay just a half-mile to the rear of the Lancastrian lines, was ringing in Vespers. Just as the monks did every evening, just as if two armies totalling eleven thousand men were not spread out below in battle formation, with only three miles and a night's wait between them.

Richard was turning his mount; men were approaching. With battle looming within hours, Edward was astride a destrier rather than a more docile palfrey, and those who rode with him took care to give the white stallion space. While battles were generally fought on foot, battle commanders still had need of horses of superior strength and spirit for those times when mounts were called for, to enable them to give pursuit, to regroup forces, to rally ranks and, if need be, to retreat. To satisfy this need, the destrier had been developed, bred and trained solely for warfare, able to carry a fully armed knight with ease and of such fiery temperament, a knight's warhorse was itself a weapon of no small significance. Francis had heard battle tales told of men who died not from sword thrusts but from being savaged by a knight's destrier. Rarely ridden except to war, they required an alert rider, a steady hand and, but moments before, Edward's stallion had raked viciously at a rider imprudent enough to venture within striking range of those blunt yellowed teeth; only Edward's vigilance had spared the man an ugly injury.

Now Francis held his own horse well back, watching as Richard guided his stallion forward to meet his brother. He saw Richard gesture toward the left, toward the wooded knoll, and he moved his mount closer, to hear Edward laugh and turn to Will Hastings.

'You do owe me, Will. I wagered Will fifty marks that you'd spot the danger straightaway in that hillock.'

'I was well lessoned by Richard Neville, may God assoil him,' Richard said, almost absently, and Francis saw he was staring beyond his brother, at that rough rocky ground that lay between them and the Lancastrian lines.

As if reading his thoughts, Edward said, 'You'll have your work cut out for you tomorrow, lad, taking the van across that terrain to go up against Somerset. But you may make yourself easy as to yonder knoll. I've seen to it.'

He glanced about him then, at the twilight sky, now a darkening greenish-blue, and at last said the words Francis was hoping to hear.

'We can do no more here. We'd best get back to camp. It'll be dawn all too soon. . . . It always is.'

Lights were burning low in the command tent of Lancaster. Shadows wavered, retreated before the sudden flaring of wind-gusted candles, flickered over the tense tired faces of the five people within, hunched over the trestle table that had been set up for their deliberations, for untouched food. Their scouts had long since relayed the enemy positions. They knew that York's young brother Gloucester was to face Somerset, knew that Will Hastings would oppose Devon, that York himself would lead his centre against John Wenlock and their Prince. For Marguerite would be the hardest task of all; she could only wait.

Somerset drank deeply from a tankard of Abbot Streynsham's best malmsey, then reached for a slice of roast capon, for they'd been given dispensation to eat meat on this Friday battle eve. He forced himself to chew, to swallow; it was not easy, for he was too keyed up to derive any pleasure from the food, too tightly wound to taste what he ate.

Setting the tankard down, he looked about at his companions. They all bore the scars of that nightmarish race for the Severn crossing, but none had suffered more than Marguerite during those turbulent hours after they learned York was hard on their heels.

Her face was sunburned, for no veil had been able to withstand fifteen hours of exposure to wind and sun. She'd long since discarded her headdress and dark hair feathered with grey curled untidily about her neck, defied the confines of an uncertain chignon. The eyes Somerset found so beautiful were puffed, bloodshot, swollen with fatigue and dust and, at the last, tears of frustration when the Tewkesbury ferry was denied them.

To have come so close, to be within sight of the ferry that promised safety for her son. . . . Somerset knew that was her true torment, not the physical aches of a body not used to such abuse. She'd borne up without complaint throughout the forced march, had even pressed for a faster pace, and when her women fainted, she slapped them back to consciousness and threatened to leave them to the mercies of York. Somerset had no doubt that she'd have seen every soldier of Lancaster drop in his tracks and not blinked an eye if, by so doing, she could have got Edouard into Wales.

Wales. To Somerset, it meant reinforcements, fresh troops, gaining a military advantage that could prove decisive. To Edward

454

of York, it posed so great a threat that he'd do damned near anything to keep them from crossing the Severn, even manage a murderous thirty-five-mile march. But to Marguerite, Somerset knew, Wales meant salvation. He strongly suspected that she'd been so set upon joining Jasper Tudor because she could then delay sending her son against Edward of York. He suspected, too, that, once in Wales, she'd have connived and manoeuvred and scrupled at nothing to keep the battle glimmering ever on the horizon, never closer than 'soon' and 'when the time is ripe'.

Whatever her intentions once they'd reached Wales, they were irrelevant now, of course. They'd gambled and lost. But to have lost on the very banks of the Severn. That, he knew, was what Marguerite could not yet, even now, accept.

Had York not somehow seen through her Sodbury ruse, had he not managed to push his army beyond all human endurance, to make up ground that could not conceivably have been made up. . . . If only. What if. Had not. Somerset could almost hear those words as they ricocheted about behind his Queen's anguished brow. He knew her fear. But he knew, too, now that she was cornered, forced to fight, she would do so without quarter, with a savagery that would make the bloodletting of Sandal Castle pale into nothingness in comparison. There was nothing she would not do to save her son; he was counting on that.

He glanced at the others again. He did not much like Wenlock, the onetime friend of Warwick, wished he did not have to entrust the centre to this man he thought little better than a harlot, whoring for the master who'd pay the brightest coin. Wenlock, who was not a young man, was grey with fatigue. Devon looked tired, too. Christ's Blood, they all were, he as much as any of them! He lifted the tankard, drained it. For a moment, his eyes rested on Edouard; the boy had not eaten, not for hours.

'You should eat, Highness,' he urged, more from a sense of duty than because he expected Edouard to heed him, but Marguerite caught up the refrain.

'Somerset is right, bien-aimé. A few mouthfuls of the cold game pie. . . . You'll feel much better.'

'I feel fine just as I am,' Edouard insisted sullenly. 'I'm not hungry. Nor do I see why that is so unusual, why it need be commented upon.'

Somerset gave him a quick quizzical look, said nothing. Edouard had been unusually quiet all day, more subdued than Somerset had ever seen him. Now as the evening wore on, he was showing signs of an increasingly nasty temper. Somerset felt a passing regret; a pity there was no way to assure Edouard that it was very natural to be afraid on the eve of battle, that all men knew such fears, that there was not a man alive who could take the field without having his stomach cramp into knots, feel cold slippery sweat upon his forehead, in his armpits, his groin. He knew better, though, than to try. Edouard would never admit it; he could not. He could only suffer it. Well, if his plan was accepted, it would aid Edouard, too, give him something to think about besides the hours, still so many, till dawn.

'It is rather warm in here, Madame. You might be revived if you had some air. May I?' Proffering his arm.

She looked at him, started to shake her head, and he said urgently, 'I do think the air would do you much good, Madame.'

Her refusal hovered on her lips, died there. She nodded and he felt a surge of gratitude that she was so quick to comprehend. She leaned over, kissed her unresponsive son where a lock of hair fell forward across his temple and then slipped her arm through Somerset's.

The air was cooler beyond the tent and the sky was clear, starred with remote pinpoint light. At least there'd be no Barnet fogs to favour York, he thought with relief, looking down into the distance where the Yorkist campfires glimmered.

'Why did you want to see me alone, Somerset?'

'Because, Madame, I have a plan, a plan that I think will win the day for us.'

456

'What do you intend?' she said bitterly. 'To send an assassin into the Yorkist camp tonight to cut York's throat? I do assure you, nothing would give me greater joy.'

'No, Madame,' he said patiently, and she saw that he was very much in earnest.

'What, Somerset?' she whispered.

'I've passed several hours studying the battlefield, how it drops away suddenly in places, how thick it is with growth. It gave me a thought and I sent scouts to see if I was right. I was. There is limited visibility upon this field, Madame. The terrain is such that York's vanguard and centre battles will not be within sight of each other.'

'Tell me your plan,' she said.

He did.

She became very quiet.

'I do not know,' she said at last. 'The risk would be great, Somerset, very great.'

'You did not hesitate to take risks at St Albans,' he chose to remind her, 'and, by so doing, you defeated the Kingmaker. Yes, we would be taking a risk; I freely concede it. But what we could gain by so doing, Madame, what we could gain! I tell you, I've thought it out carefully. It can work. We'll take York by surprise, that I'll swear on my life. And before he can recover. . . .' He made a swift motion with his hand, slashing, graphic.

'Yes,' she said slowly. 'Yes, it could work. I do not know, Somerset, I just do not know. . . . If it were me, only me, I'd say yes, take the chance, seize it, let the risks be damned. But it is not just me, you see.' She reached up, lightly stroked his cheek, and withdrew her hand.

'You are a brave man, a loyal friend, and I cherish you, Edmund, I do. But I think we'd best discuss this with the others, with Wenlock, Devon, my Edouard. If they do approve. . . .'

She sounded uncharacteristically indecisive; he sensed she was resisting her natural inclinations, which were to go with his plan, to take the bold measure that could reap the greatest gain. Lord deliver us from the crippling confines of motherhood, he thought grimly. But he had no intention of submitting his plan to the other men for judgment. Wenlock he did not trust, and Devon was too conservative, Edouard too green. Only she had the imagination, the instinctive daring to go with his plan, to see the risk was well worth the taking.

'Madame, back me in this and Prince Edouard may not have to take part in the battle at all. It could be over that quickly, before our centre shall be fully engaged.' He felt a touch of shame for this last, but not much; at this point, there was nothing he would not have told her if he thought it might gain her consent.

She walked away from him, stared down at the Yorkist fires. And then she turned. 'Very well, we'll go with your plan, Somerset. It is in your hands.'

His teeth showed whitely in a jubilant smile but, before he could savour his triumph, she added stonily, 'On one condition. I want you to keep Edouard from the fighting. I want him mounted and guarded at all times, Somerset, and I do not want him to engage in combat on the field.'

'I cannot make you a promise like that,' he said tiredly, and very gently. 'You know I cannot. I'd give my life to keep him safe; we all would. But I cannot forbid him, Madame. No one can. He thinks he is of an age to command. His pride demands it. He knows that York was not yet nineteen when he won Towton. Worse, he knows that Gloucester is himself just eighteen now. I cannot forbid him, Madame.

'The true command of the centre will rest with Wenlock, not Prince Edouard. And I think he will agree to remain mounted during the battle.' For a moment he had an image of Edouard's white set face. 'In fact, I'm sure of it. But further than that, he will not go. And more than that, I cannot do.'

Marguerite nodded and he saw that she'd not expected to prevail.

'No, I suppose you cannot,' she said tonelessly. She shrugged, wouldn't meet his eyes. 'Well, then, we'd best tell the others what we plan for the morrow, my lord.'

She let him take her hands in his; they were like ice, blood-less.

'You have it all, Somerset,' she whispered. 'It is all in your hands. . . . The vanguard, the battle, the fate of Lancaster.' She drew a ragged breath. 'The life of my son.'

32

Tewkesbury

May 1471

The dark was fading, the sky streaking with dull gold as Francis lifted the flap, entered Richard's tent. Rob Percy was already inside, seated on a coffer and gnawing halfheartedly on a strip of dried beef. Richard's back was to the tent flap. He was listening to the priest who was soon to invoke God's blessing upon the Yorkist undertaking; listening, too, to a herald who wore the badge of John Howard, while in the background hovered a courier with the Boar of Gloucester emblazoned on the breast of his tabard. Francis joined Rob who made room for him on the coffer, silently proffering a second strip of beef. Just the sight of it was enough to turn Francis's stomach; he hastily shook his head.

Having at last dealt with the priest and Howard's man, Richard dispatched his courier with a few low-voiced sentences meant for his brother's ear. Turning, he smiled at sight of Francis, who smiled back, although far from reassured by his first glimpse of his friend's face. He thought Richard looked exhausted, like one having no resources to draw upon other than those of the will.

'You did not sleep, did you?' he blurted out, before thinking better of it. He saw, though, that Richard didn't seem to mind.

'No,' Richard conceded candidly. 'I was awake most of the night ere Barnet, too.'

Ian de Clare, Richard's squire since Barnet, was kneeling before him, fumbling again with the pointed tassets that hung down to protect his upper thighs. Richard thought Ian to be extraordinarily clumsy this morn, quite unlike the sure hands of Thomas Parr, and his arming seemed to be taking an inordinate amount of time. It was only by studying Ian's averted face that he was able to hold his temper in check. At last, Ian was through, made one final adjustment to Richard's left pauldron, stood back.

Rob and Francis were looking on with admiration and Richard grinned. He was very proud of the white polished armour, thought it a veritable work of art, perfect in every piece, as well it should be, for it had been custom-made for him by one of the Flemish masters. He'd never said so but Rob and Francis suspected it was a gift from the King. They both remembered how concerned Richard had been that he'd not have it in time for the upcoming battle, and they hastened to pay tribute in the highest coin of their realm, banter so biting that Richard knew they thought the armour every bit as wondrous as he did. He laughed now as they assured him the whole of the Lancastrian army would be most grateful that he'd thus made it so easy to distinguish Gloucester from the other knights of York.

Francis had dropped his gauntlets on the ground by the coffer. As he leaned over to retrieve them, Ian was the quicker of the two, shrugging off his thanks with a strained smile. Francis looked at the squire, saw with sympathetic eyes. Ian was a stranger to him. He knew little of Ian other than that, like all who served royalty, he came from a family that was landed, was of good birth.

He knew, too, that Ian was close in age to them all. One more thing he knew; this was Ian's first battle.

'This is ever the worst for me,' Francis said suddenly, as if addressing them all. 'The waiting. . . . This is when my imagination begins to run amuck and I become convinced I'm fated to take a sword-thrust in the gut. By the time the battle begins, I'm downright thankful for it, for what Lancaster can do to me is as nothing compared to what I do to myself.'

Ian was watching him intently. He had bright blue eyes, like Rob and the King; they stayed on Francis's face as if they meant to commit it to memory.

'Is this truly the worst . . . the waiting?' he asked softly, and Francis nodded.

'Truly,' he said, just as softly. He was aware that both Rob and Richard were watching. He'd seen their surprise, seen them exchange a quick glance of quizzical communication. Now Rob said cheerfully,

'God's Blood, but Lovell's qualms pale into pure milky whiteness next to mine! He frets over a sword's thrust in the gut. . . . Mere child's play, that. Now for me, I never doubt that I'm to be gelded and then spit through as I lay there, like a hog held for butchering!'

'Stop bragging, Rob,' Richard scoffed. 'To hear you, none of our fears are even a patch upon your sufferings, but I'd back my demons against yours any day. Though I will concede that you did in fact suffer more from seasickness when we crossed the Channel than any four men . . . and complained more of it, too.'

'Luckily for Your Grace, you could not see yourself, then,' Rob drawled. 'Luckily, too, I could not bring myself to heed your pleas to throw you overboard and put an end to your misery.'

That struck Richard as funny. He began to laugh and they were more than willing to follow his lead, to fill these last minutes with laughter.

Francis knew Rob happened to be a natural-born sailor. And

461

he knew that Richard, too, was a fair hand on shipboard, even if not in Rob's class. But Ian was laughing, laughing with amusement that was genuine and unforced.

Francis, believing that men were not meant to be subject to emotions in the way that women were, spent much of his life fighting feelings he deemed suspect. Now he found himself struggling against a treacherous tide of affection for Robert Percy, for Richard Plantagenet, even for Ian de Clare whom he did not know. Sweet Jesus, Lamb of God, look to them, he was whispering, without words, as a new sound intruded upon the noises of the stirring camp, a distant trumpet fanfare.

Richard raised his head, listening. All amusement had fled his face; now there was only tension.

'It's time,' he said, in what was very like his normal tone of voice. To those who did not know him as well as Francis and Rob.

Richard moved the Yorkist vanguard so swiftly to the attack that Marguerite had to retreat with extreme haste to the Lower Lode of the Severn River, where she was to be ferried across to join her daughter-in-law and the other ladies who'd been sent to safety shortly before dawn. The sun was already too brilliant to take unshielded stares and the morning air shimmered in a haze of brightness as the battle was joined. Edward watched astride his white destrier from a rise of ground midway between the vanguard and his centre, watched with grim foreboding.

The Lancastrian artillery was firing upon the vanguard. Yorkist field guns sounded in their turn, shelling the Lancastrian lines. Edward knew their answering fire had taken the enemy by surprise; it was highly unusual to employ cannons in close support of infantry, but Richard felt his men needed all the help they could get and Edward had agreed with him. He knew Richard was deeply pessimistic about the chances of making a successful first assault, now saw his brother's misgivings borne out.

The vanguard was within arrow range and the Lancastrian bowmen turned their weapons upon the Yorkists, with murderous effect. The vanguard faltered under the relentless fire, came on again but they were taking terrible punishment. Men stumbled up the sides of muddy ditches, only to have the loosened earth crumble under them, sending them staggering into each other, back into the ditches, bruised and breathless. They tripped over tangled exposed roots, fell into hedges pierced with thorns, scrambled up slopes choked with underbrush and strewn with rocks. . . . And, all the while, the sky rained shafted death down upon them.

Edward swore, softly and steadily, and when Richard gave the command to retreat, he swore again, only this time with relief. He waited long enough to see the vanguard pulling back, beyond the killing range of Lancastrian artillery and arrow fire, and then turned the white stallion in the direction of his own lines, at such a pace that his outdistanced men knew he'd given the destrier its head.

Edward was uneasy, his every instinct communicating wordless warning. He didn't know why he should be so gripped by tension; it went far beyond the chagrin he might expect to feel after seeing his vanguard repulsed. He only knew that there was a hollow pulsing pressure against his ribcage, that sweat was gathering at his temples, stinging his eyes with salt. The instincts were purely physical, but he trusted them, puzzled over them enough to have delayed his return to the higher ground from which he could follow the progress of Richard's second assault.

He'd dispatched messengers, one to Richard, the other to Will, and was watching as his stallion was brought up again, when it happened. From the wooded area to the left of his line. The danger he'd somehow sensed. A flank attack by the men of the Lancastrian vanguard.

Edward gave no commands; he knew the knights of his household would follow. He was in the saddle in a swift smooth motion that denied the weight of the armour he wore; and then the giant destrier was bearing down upon the men emerging from the woods, men who scattered in panic before the plunging hooves, the ravaging teeth, the sword that with each downstroke sheathed itself in flesh and bone.

Edward was just six days past his twenty-ninth birthday and for fully half of the lifetime he'd practised the bloody arts of war. But he'd never fought as he did now. He came close to decapitating the first man who dared to cross swords with him, impaled the second and, as the man fell, jerked his sword free to swing savagely at a third. Maiming without mercy, he drove dying men to their knees, bloody froth bubbling from contorted mouths, bones forced through shredded skin and bent back grotesquely; trampled bodies under his frenzied mount; warded off a poleaxe that was thrust toward that most vulnerable area under his armpit and counterthrust before the man could retreat, delivering a death blow with the flashing steel that could, with equal dispatch, sever an arm at the elbow, rip into entrails, and intestines, draw clotted black blood.

Edward had always enjoyed battlefield advantages not given to other men—his unusual height, his enormous physical strength. Now, mounted on a stallion that was itself half maddened by battle lust, driven by a desperation that blotted all caution, all pity from his brain, he was an awesome instrument of death, and men fled from him, men of unquestioned courage, while the knights of his household fought furiously to stay at his side, followed by the foot soldiers who were choosing to stand and fight, too, moved to fierce primitive loyalty by their commander's dreadful demonic courage.

Edward was not one of those men who would lose themselves in the passion of their killing; his brain remained clear, unclouded. He knew he'd checked a rout, that enough men were following him, fighting for him, to hold the centre together. But he knew, too, that Somerset was too shrewd a soldier to have launched so

464

audacious, so ambitious an assault with the vanguard alone. This was the fear that drove him to such savage reprisal. He was awaiting the moment when John Wenlock would hit them from the front and he doubted that his men could now withstand such a blow.

And so, as more and more of his men rallied to him, enough to stall Somerset's momentum, he fought with the reckless raging abandon of one under sentence of death delayed but not deferred . . . awaiting Wenlock's strike.

The Yorkist vanguard was re-forming, the men responding with a decided decline in enthusiasm to the orders of Richard's harried captains. They weren't lacking in courage but they'd been well bloodied. Few among them were eager for another futile assault upon the unreachable entrenched Lancastrians. To their way of thinking, it was hardly a fair contest. Those close enough to observe their young commander didn't think he was any happier about it than they were.

From last night's first glance, Richard had grave concerns about the battlefield staked out by Lancaster. He hadn't liked the lay of the land, the fact that he would be so cut off from contact with the other Yorkist battles; and still less had he liked the thought of having to take his men across ground as treacherous and impassable as any he'd ever seen. But he had little choice. He could only hope he'd hold to his resolve not to let them die in a vain attempt to breach Lancaster's defences. If need be, he'd pull them back a second or even a third time if he saw they had no chance to reach Somerset's line. What little else he could do, he'd already done, demanded from Edward support of their field guns, named an unusually large number of couriers to keep the lines of communication open between his command and his brother's battle.

It was one of these special couriers who was coming now from the east, coming so fast that he at once drew all eyes, stilled conversation. No man would ride a horse across ground like this at such a speed unless he was demented. Or had news of such urgency that he thought it worth risking a shattered foreleg, a nasty fall.

Richard raised his vizor. All around him, men were turning, watching the approaching rider. He was a skilled horseman, one of the best Richard had ever seen; even at that moment, there was a part of his brain that took note, approved. His first impulse was to meet the man at a run; he forced himself to stand where he was, to wait, all too aware how closely his men watched his every move. 'A battle captain who hesitates, lets his men see he is unsure, fearful . . . He loses his men when he loses control, Dickon.' The words were those of his cousin Warwick, the advice shared years ago at Middleham and remembered.

The horse, a lathered roan, was cut and scratched, blood trickling into the sweat that darkened the splotched grey coat. There was blood on the rider's face, as well; his skin bore the lashings of the woods through which he'd ridden at a gallop, making no attempt to duck overhanging branches, to find a natural path, crouched low over his stallion's withers in an unorthodox riding style dictated by instinct and the need for speed. He'd not have believed beforehand that he would ever have been willing to abuse his mount in such a manner. But he'd got through. He recognized Richard, reined in so abruptly that the stallion went back on its haunches and then up, rearing so far skyward that those watching thought sure it was going over backward. But it maintained its footing, came down like a big cat and shook itself violently, suddenly free of the man's weight.

The rider was already out of the saddle, his knee hit the ground hard. But he didn't feel it, not then. He was breathless, at first incoherent, the words sliding back into his throat, not from fear but because he couldn't seem to get enough air into his lungs. But he'd kept his head, had from the moment he'd cantered out of the woods to find the Yorkist centre reeling before Somerset's surprise assault, and without pause, wheeled his mount about, sending it at a dead run back toward the vanguard; not letting himself think about what he'd seen, what it could mean for York, for him; keeping one thought resolutely between him and the easy urge to panic, that he had to tell Gloucester, that nothing else mattered but that, telling Gloucester.

He kept his head now, too; Richard had cause to be grateful for it, would later remember it. For he didn't blurt it out. The temptation was the greatest of his twenty years, but he was aware, without consciously drawing upon that understanding, that to do so was to risk a panic that might not be quenched in time. He meant to kneel, found his knee giving way and would have fallen on his face had Richard not grabbed him. And it was clinging to the King's brother for support that he revealed why he'd been willing to race a cherished horse like a madman across a stretch of ground he'd heard Richard himself call a 'soldier's nightmare'.

He saw Richard's face, saw his fear become Richard's. He heard Richard say, 'Oh, Jesus,' very soft, and then Richard was gone, moving away, shouting for a horse, shouting names he didn't know, and he sank down on the ground, thinking he'd not have been able to move from that spot if Somerset himself were standing over him with drawn sword.

The men of the Yorkist vanguard might have panicked. While many were veterans, had fought for Richard at Barnet, others were experiencing their first sour taste of battle, and all had been shaken by their failure to withstand Somerset's fire. But Richard gave them no time. They were accustomed to obey, to heed the battle commanders who were now raging about the field, calling men into line. Moreover, when the understanding came that they were to go to the support of the beleaguered centre, they were suddenly excited, eager. Few could have mustered enthusiasm for another bloody assault upon the entrenched Lancastrian line; this was different, this was far more to their liking, promising more even terms and the pulsing emotional appeal, as well, of a rescue mission. Richard's captains found their task to be surprisingly easy, so much so that they began to hope they could even manage to satisfy Richard's demands for speed beyond the reach of mortal men.

The Lancastrians gained a twofold advantage from the placement of their lines above the Yorkist army along the Gaston Ridge. Not only was the enemy thus forced to fight uphill, the Lancastrians had a far superior view of the battlefield and none more so than Marguerite's son, seated on his mount behind the lines of the Lancastrian centre. He'd found a grassy incline that afforded him an unobstucted view of the battlefield below, could see the Yorkist vanguard, could see the wooded hill that separated the van from the centre and through which Somerset would lead his men, could see the battle led by Edward of York, all with startling clarity.

It was both real and unreal to Edouard, this legendary enemy at last come to life before his eyes. He even thought he'd recognized York himself and watched that distant figure with hypnotic interest until disabused by one of his bodyguards, who told him that could not be York, for one of York's affectations was that he never rode any stallion but a white one and that knight was mounted on a bay. Edouard had been disappointed, yet relieved, too, and then the battle had begun.

He'd watched the Yorkist vanguard come on, as inexorably as the riptides he'd seen break upon Normandy beaches, and then watched as they were rent asunder by a savage barrage of arrows, so heavy that the sky above them seemed to have clouded over, lost the sun. Around Edouard, men swore when Gloucester pulled his troops back; they'd hoped the Yorkists would persist in their suicidal charge, impale themselves upon the spear-studded ditch dug between the two armies. It still wasn't real to Edouard, none of it, not the bodies left behind as the vanguard withdrew, not the cheering of the Lancastrian soldiers, certainly not the sounds that now echoed from St Mary Abbey. The bells were marking the hour, summoning monks to Morrow Mass as the battle raged within sight of the abbey walls.

Somerset had not tarried. While the Yorkist vanguard was re-forming its lines, he led his men into the woods, disappeared from Edouard's view, leaving only a nominal force where the might of the Lancastrian vanguard had been dug in. As they vanished from sight, Edouard felt the first pricklings of premonition.

He'd found it easy to be enthusiastic about the planned flank attack, as explained to him last night by his mother and Somerset. It was true both Wenlock and Devon had been opposed; Wenlock had even called it madness of the first order. But it had appealed to Edouard's imagination, and Somerset had made it sound so simple, almost inevitable.

There was heavy cover between the Yorkist battles, a wooded expanse that would shelter the Lancastrian vanguard from view as it moved within striking distance of York's flank. York would never expect an attack from that quarter, Somerset assured Edouard, never. And Gloucester, on the other side of the hill, would not be aware of what was happening until it was too late; the same would be true for Hastings's battle, spread out some distance to York's right. Somerset would take the Yorkist centre by surprise and, before York could recover, their centre, under Lord Wenlock and he, Prince Edouard, would come down upon York from the front. Caught between the two, York's battle would break, would fall away like leaves in a high wind. They could then turn upon Gloucester at their ease, whilst Devon dealt with Hastings. If, indeed, it was even necessary; it was as likely as not that the fighting would end with York's death or capture. As Somerset told it, Edouard did not see how it could fail.

But now he was uneasy; last night he'd not truly appreciated the security of their entrenched position, the advantage it gave them over the Yorkists. Watching as Somerset's men slipped silently into the greenwood, they suddenly seemed so exposed to him, so vulnerable, and with Somerset gone, so did he, so did they all. He signalled for water, drank with the deepest thirst of his life. Somerset was a seasoned soldier. He knew the ways of war as Edouard himself did not, as Edouard was admitting to himself, with the greatest reluctance, for the first time. This was beyond him, this deadly game being played out below him; the gap between the expectation and the reality was too vast to be spanned by even the greatest leap of the imagination. This was Somerset's game, Somerset's and York's.

After several lifetimes, Edouard saw the Lancastrian vanguard emerge from the wood, and just as Somerset had predicted, they were right on York's flank. The Yorkists recoiled in shock, milled about in confusion. Edouard saw men throw down their weapons, begin to run. For an enthralling moment, it seemed to him as if the entire Yorkist line would break apart, scatter. But then some of their number rallied and soon there was fierce hand-to-hand fighting up and down the line.

So close they were that Edouard could no longer distinguish Lancaster from York, could see only clashing weapons, writhing bodies. His bodyguards told him that York himself was leading the fighting; they need not have bothered. He knew. Could not take his eyes from the knight on the plunging white stallion. Watched the destrier's jaws close on a man's face, lay it open to the bone. Watched the knight deflect blows and then drive steel through exposed defences with terrifying skill, with deliberation that meant to kill to cripple. Edward of York.

He watched, awestruck, until an explosive profanity drew his attention to the Yorkist vanguard. He saw at once why his men were cursing. There was movement in the Yorkist lines; it was erupting into urgent activity. Gloucester knew what had happened, was swinging the vanguard around with desperate speed. He watched as the Yorkist captains, mounted now, galloped back and forth, driving their men into position; he soon picked out a knight on a chestnut destrier, one liberally marked with white.

Strange, he thought numbly, that Gloucester did not know four white legs were unlucky, that such a mount was to be shunned. That he was watching Gloucester, he had no doubt. He seemed to be everywhere at once, raging, cajoling, gesturing. At one point, he encountered a ditch that ran for yards; rather than detour around it, he simply spurred his stallion up and over. The chestnut sailed over the trench with effortless ease and again the men around Edouard cursed. He knew the vanguard of an army was generally the largest battle, for to the van fell the crucial task of leading the first frontal assault, and he imagined Gloucester had some two thousand men under his command. He would not have thought so many men could have regrouped so rapidly, knew Somerset had not expected that, either.

The rest happened so quickly that it blurred for Edouard, lost even the semblance of reality. The Yorkist centre was giving ground; Somerset's men sensed victory, pressed forward. Suddenly, from a wooded knoll to the rear and somewhat to the left of the Yorkist lines galloped a contingent of horsemen. It was impossible to tell their numbers at this distance, but they appeared to be several hundred strong, cloaked in the glare of sun glinting off spears and shields. They smashed into Somerset's line, for the moment creating nearly as much chaos and confusion as had the Lancastrians when first they burst from the greenwood upon York. Somerset's men were no longer taking the offensive; they wavered, suddenly uncertain, unnerved by the unexpected appearance of this new enemy force. York at once seized his chance, surged back with the determination born of desperation. And it was then that the Yorkist vanguard came upon the scene.

The slaughter that followed was swift and terrible. Trapped between Gloucester and York, Somerset's men were cut to pieces. Edouard had seen death, had seen executions. He'd seen nothing like this, had not known that men dying screamed so, had not known the body could hold so much blood. At last he became aware that someone was speaking to him, tugging at the stirrup of his saddle. He looked down. He didn't recognize the stunned face staring up at him. He wondered, in dull surprise, that a soldier should feel free to approach him like an equal, that the men of his household had not barred the way. The soldier's face was queerly contorted; with a small shock, Edouard realized the man was crying. He found his voice.

'You wish to speak with me?'

'Oh, Holy Mother Mary. . . .' The man was openly sobbing, seemed not to care, making no attempt to check the tears that coursed down a face that was weathered, seamed, a soldier's face.

'Why, Your Grace? Why did we not go to Somerset's aid? Why did my lord Wenlock not give the support Somerset expected? Why, my lord? Why?'

When his hidden spearmen joined the struggle against Somerset, Edward at last let himself hope he might prevail. Where in Christ was Wenlock? He didn't understand, could only thank God for the inexplicable reprieve, for the uncanny luck that had always been his. And then he thanked God for his brother, for the Yorkist vanguard was suddenly there, how he didn't know, didn't care, and once again he'd won, against all odds and expectations. His stallion was limping badly; he slid from the saddle, and leaning against the animal's heaving side, he began to laugh.

Somerset's men, those not dead or dying, were in flight. The Yorkists, both of the centre and the vanguard, felt they had legitimate scores to settle, were not inclined to show mercy. Nor were the Yorkist commanders. It was Edward's practice to caution his men to 'slay the lords, spare the commons'. Now he did not and the carnage went unchecked. For years to come, the ground across which the Lancastrians fled would be known as 'Bloody Meadow'.

Edward was panting, for the moment was content to stand and watch the death throes of the Lancastrian vanguard. Even his nearly inexhaustible reservoirs of energy were depleted; he had pushed himself well beyond what would have been the average man's breaking point, knowing that he alone could rally his demoralized men, check their flight before Lancaster. Someone was giving him a water flask; he reached for it gratefully, and looked up to see Richard rein in beside him. The vizor went up; midnight-blue eyes regarded him searchingly.

'Ned?' That was all, was enough.

Edward nodded, smiled tiredly, a smile twisted awry by a muscle that jerked spasmodically in his cheek, beyond his control. His brother didn't smile back; instead, he gave a wordless acknowledgment, one of relief beyond expression, and wasted no further time on conversation. As Edward watched, he spurred his stallion away, turned his vanguard upon the fleeing Lancastrians.

Edward thrust the flask into the nearest hands, looked about him at his weary captains. They all shared a like expression, the grim gratification of men who had been to hell and fought their way back, when there was no way back.

'Give the word to regroup. Gather your men. Now get me another horse. We're not through here.'

Even as he spoke, Edward could feel his abused body reviving, could feel a surge as energy began to flow again. The excitement that had been only a flickering, a warming flush, was now searing him with flame. It was contagious; he saw it reflected in their faces. Victory was in the air, even stronger than the stench of blood.

'Now,' he said.

Edouard of Lancaster listened as John Wenlock explained why he had held the centre back, had not come to Somerset's support. He was saying something about Gloucester, saying that Gloucester had moved too fast, that there'd not been time. He'd deemed it best to hold the centre in their position, make the Yorkists come to them. It would have been madness to throw away the natural advantage they had here, the rough ground that once before had halted the Yorkist vanguard so effectively. He could not have saved Somerset, he insisted; it had been too late for that. To have moved out would have been only to sacrifice the centre, too. Surely Prince Edouard could see that.

Edouard couldn't. Wenlock's words beat against his tired brain; he struggled to make sense of them. Somerset had expected the centre to come to his support. Even if Wenlock was right . . . he'd still watched, done nothing while Somerset's men were butchered. That much Edouard's shocked mind could understand; he saw it on the dazed faces of the men around them. And he saw, too, the question that would pass no man's lips but was in each man's eyes: Why had he, Edouard, not countermanded Wenlock? Why had he sat there, watched like one stricken dumb as York and Gloucester savaged the Lancastrian vanguard? How could he explain his paralysis of will . . . even to himself?

'Surely we should have taken some action . . . done something.' He wanted to believe Wenlock. Bon Dieu, how he wanted to! The centre was his to command with Wenlock. Had he failed Somerset, too? Should he have acted when Wenlock did not?

'It was too late, Highness. We could only have doomed our own men. Somerset would say the same, would not have wanted me to sacrifice their lives in a meaningless gesture, to risk your safety for men already beaten.'

Someone muttered, loud enough to be heard, meaning to be heard, 'Like bloody hell he would not!'

Wenlock raked the men with cold eyes; either unable or unwilling to identify the culprit, he quelled them with his stare, turned back to Edouard.

'I had to make a command decision, Highness. And I have no doubt it was the right one. My lord Somerset did not foresee that York would conceal men in yonder knoll or that Gloucester would rally so swiftly to his aid. I had to decide what was best for my men.'

Edouard stared at him, this man who had fought for Lancaster at St Albans, for York at Towton. 'But Somerset expected our support,' he said, almost inaudibly.

'I assumed you were in agreement with me, Your Grace.' Wenlock's voice was suddenly flint. 'You did not, after all, raise any objections at the time. Did you?'

Edouard flushed. He had a blurred glimpse of faces, shocked, enraged, uncertain. A forgotten piece of battle lore floated to the surface of his mind, dealt with the dangers of letting men see their battle commanders fall out amongst themselves. He opened his mouth, not at all sure what he meant to say, and then, like all the others, he was turning, staring at the rider coming up the hill toward the Lancastrian lines, coming at a breakneck gallop that had every man there expecting momentarily to see the animal go down, to see a foreleg snap like kindling. It stumbled once but regained its balance, came on. Edouard hardly recognized it as a horse, its muzzle dripping froth, eyes glazed and rolling back with fear, so streaked and smeared with blood that it was impossible to tell what colour it once was, white or grey. He was staring with such horror at the horse that it was some seconds before he looked to the rider and, stunned, recognized the Duke of Somerset.

Somerset was as ghastly a sight as the horse he rode, drenched in Yorkist blood and shouting like a madman, so incoherent that his words were lost, conveyed only a rage such as none among them had ever seen in any sane man.

Edouard was frozen in the saddle. Wenlock, too, seemed incapable of moving, staring at this bloodied raving apparition as if he doubted his senses.

'Judas! Traitorous son of a Yorkist whore! Where were you when my men were being butchered?'

Wenlock suddenly seemed to recognize his peril. One hand went to his sword; he started to speak. He was never given the chance. Somerset spurred his maddened mount against Wenlock's; the other horse reeled under the impact, stumbled to its knees.

'By Jesus, this will be the last time you do York's dirty work!'

Even as he spoke, Somerset's battle-axe flashed up and over. The force of the blow sliced through Wenlock's helmet as if it were parchment; the blade buried itself in his skull. Brains, bone, and grey-white tissue were flung into the air, splattered the closest of the soldiers. Wenlock made no sound; he was dead before he hit the ground.

Somerset stared down at the body. Gradually his breathing slowed, no longer came in convulsive gasps. He raised his head, looked about him and was sobered by what he saw on the faces of encircling men. They thought him mad; it showed in their wordless watching, in the horrified eyes that slid away from him, looked anywhere but at his face.

For the first time he became aware of Edouard's presence. He turned his heaving mount toward the boy.

'Highness . . .' he began, his voice jerky, like one learning to talk again after years of enforced silence.

Edouard's horse shied away from the bloody monster Somerset rode. Edouard, too, seemed to shrink back.

'I assure you I am not mad,' Somerset said harshly, gave a queer choked laugh that made him wonder if he spoke the truth.

No one answered him. Edouard seemed no more able to meet his eyes than the other men. For a span of time that had no meaning for him, could not be measured in terms of minutes or hours or any known standard, Somerset sat motionless, staring at his Prince, staring but not seeing, the only sound in his ears that of his rasping, laboured breathing. Then two things happened at once.

Edouard said suddenly, 'It was not my fault, Somerset. Say it was not!'

At the same time, Somerset heard his name being shouted. A rider was shoving his way toward them; men were scrambling out of his path, letting him pass. Somerset turned in the saddle, recognizing his younger brother John, who'd been with Devon's battle.

'Have you all gone mad?' John's eyes took in the scene before him; his face changed.

'Jesú! I do believe you have.' He wrenched his gaze from Wenlock's body, back to Somerset's face.

'Edmund, get hold of yourself, for sweet Christ's sake! Devon is dead and York is now turning the centre upon us. Lady Mary, have pity! Have you been stricken blind and dumb? Christ, man, look!' And he gestured wildly toward the battlefield, toward the oncoming army of York.

Somerset tried. He broke his heart trying. Shouting until his voice failed him. Striking about him with the flat of his sword at his fleeing soldiers. Spurring his shuddering mount upon the men of York until the animal quite simply came to the end of its endurance and no longer responded to the rasping of the silver rowels or the pressure of the bit in its bloodied mouth. Even then, he persisted. Scorning his own safety, he took chances that bordered on madness. But courage was no longer enough, not now.

The Sunne of York bannered the field, swept all before it. The heart had gone from the Lancastrian army. They'd seen their vanguard slaughtered, seen their leaders turn upon each other. Now men cast aside their weapons, sought only to save themselves, and Somerset alone tried to hold them against York.

Devon was dead. So was Somerset's brother, John Beaufort. Prince Edouard had long since fled the field, urged on by the bodyguards sworn to see to his safety. Somerset's men drowned trying to cross the Avon, died trying to reach the sanctuary of the abbey. Somerset found himself upon a field with his dead and the exultant soldiers of the White Rose, and as he raged among them, cursing and sobbing, even death seemed to elude him; until at last he sank to his knees, had not the strength to rise, to lift his sword, watching through a red wavering haze the death of the House of Lancaster.

*

477

A number of fugitives from the battle had found sanctuary in the nave of St Mary's Abbey. The church was soon packed with exhausted, apprehensive men, who lay bleeding upon the patterned tile floor, sprawled in the Lady Chapel, before the high altar, even against the font holding its sacred store of holy water, listening with wildly beating hearts and shuddering breath as the priests tried to deny entry to the pursuing Yorkists.

Most of the men seeking sanctuary were foot soldiers, most, but not all. Among them, too, were the battle captains of Lancaster, those who'd survived the carnage on the field, and their fear was greatest for they knew they could expect no quarter from York. Two of their number, Sir Gervase Clifton and Sir Thomas Tresham, edged closer to the north-porch entranceway, where the black-clad figure of Abbot Streynsham stood, blocking the light and barring the way.

The outer doors had been forced, but the abbot had positioned himself before the inner door that led into the nave, holding aloft the Host, and for the moment, at least, he'd managed to halt the vengeful tide that threatened to engulf the abbey in blood. Under his outstretched arm, the trapped men saw Yorkist soldiers shoving closer, their voices raised in rising anger. They were reluctant, however, to lay hands upon an abbot, and for the time being, were contenting themselves with shouted abuse. Clifton and Tresham knew, though, that their constraint could give way at any moment; it need only take one man, one willing to force his way into the church.

'Ye cannot enter a House of God for killing.' The Lord Abbot had all the authority of his Church in his voice. He stared the men down, said with daunting certainty, with the glacial assurance of one accustomed to being obeyed, 'These men within claim the right of sanctuary. Dare you call upon yourselves the wrath of Almighty God by harming them? Those who would despoil God's Church do so at the peril of their immortal souls, take upon themselves eternal damnation.'

478

The soldiers shifted, unwillingly impressed. Within the abbey, the men waited, scarcely breathing.

'Do you forget, my lord Abbot, that the abbey of St Mary the Virgin is not a sanctuary church?'

Clifton and Tresham crouched down, trying to see without being seen. The men seemed to have cleared away from the door. They could glimpse a sweeping silvery tail, saw hooves strike sparks against the flagstone, and realized that the lord who had spoken had ridden his stallion up onto the very porch of the abbey. That the speaker was a lord, they'd known at once, even before seeing the destrier, for the voice had the unmistakable inflection of rank.

The abbot was eyeing the stallion with outrage, stood his ground even though the roan's withers were within reach of his hand.

'The right of sanctuary has been recognized by Holy Church since the Lord did say unto the Vicar of Christ, Thou art Peter, and upon this rock will I build my Church, and the gates of Hell shall not prevail against it.'

'The right has been recognized, yes. But not every church can offer sanctuary. This abbey has no royal charter. Nor has it been named a sanctuary church by papal bull. And you do know that, Abbot John, quite as well as I.'

Abbot Streynsham flushed and then went pale. There'd been nothing of the awe of the priesthood in that cold derisive voice, only arrogance and a sophisticated knowledge of canon law such as few laymen would have. For the first time he peered up into the face half shadowed by the upraised vizor. Even as Clifton and Tresham were chilled by a suspicion neither dared voice aloud, they saw the abbot kneel upon the porch, say in a suddenly submissive voice, 'I do implore my sovereign lord's pardon, but I did not at once recognize Your Grace.'

Edward stared down at the abbot, his face expressionless. He heard his name echoing within, passing from man to man with a fear that was palpable.

'Stand aside, Holy Father,' he said, and the soldiers of York surged forward, only to halt in uncertainty, for the abbot had not budged from the doorway.

'My liege, you must not do this,' he said urgently, compellingly. 'Do not profane your victory with blood spilled within the confines of a Church of God. Have you not reason this day to be grateful for His favour? Would you now repay His bounty with blood shed in His House? For your soul's sake, my lord, consider!'

For a long moment, while the fugitives within the abbey trembled and the abbot held his breath, Edward looked down at him, saying nothing. And then he nodded grudgingly.

'You argue more like lawyer than priest.' The corner of his mouth twitched. 'Belike as not, they are one and the same. Very well. The lives of the men within the church are yours. I do give them to you. Spoils of war,' he said mockingly and neatly backed the roan off the abbey porch as the Lancastrians reacted with joy to their reprieve and his own men with a surprised, soured acceptance.

Within the abbey, men were laughing and embracing one another; others seemed stunned. Tresham and Clifton stared at each other, unable to credit their deliverance, and then they, too, embraced, began to talk both at once, with the feverish animation of the reborn.

Almost at their feet, a man lay slumped against one of the soaring stone columns. He'd not moved, not spoken a word, listened with utter indifference as Abbot Streynsham sought to sway Edward of York. Now he raised his eyes, stared up at Tresham and Clifton. His face was so caked with blood and dirt that recognition would have been a challenge even for his loved ones. He bore an already yellowing bruise above one eye, and more than any of them, he looked as if he'd bathed in blood, for it was matted in the tangled brown hair, crusted on his armour, even flecked his eyebrows. It was impossible to tell how much of it, if any, was his own, for the eyes were beyond revealing pain, were empty of all emotion. When he spoke, there was nothing, either, in his voice; although the words themselves were harsh, the voice was not, was totally devoid of feeling.

'Do you truly believe York shall let you live once he finds out the names of the men within this church?'

Tresham was taken aback, snapped, 'Why not? He did give his word. Did you not hear?'

'Aye, I heard. Now you tell me this, Tresham. If the abbey were filled with knights of York, how long would we have let them live?'

Tresham had started upon hearing his name. He bent down, squinting into the shadows, gasped. 'Jesú! Beaufort! I heard you fell on the field.'

Somerset merely looked at him and Tresham felt emotion stir, perilously akin to rage. Somerset had managed to sour the hopes he'd taken from York's unlooked-for leniency. Somerset had also, as he saw it, brought them all to ruin with his vainglorious battle plan. The relief of turning his anguish upon a tangible target was sweet beyond belief.

'After the work you did this day, I'd as soon hear nothing more from you about what you think York will or will not do. God knows you had no luck reading him on the field! Nor should I need remind you that if you prove to be right and our lives forfeit, you, my lord Somerset, will be the first to lay your head on the block.'

Clifton stepped quickly between them, for the murderous temper of the Beauforts was as one with legend. But Somerset didn't move, just stared up at Tresham.

'Christ on the Cross, man,' he said slowly, 'do you truly think I care?'

There was movement behind them. Sir Humphrey Audley, another who had little reason to expect clemency from York, was shoving his way toward them.

'Edmund, thank God!'

Somerset said nothing, seemed not to recognize him, although Audley was a friend first of youth and then of manhood.

'About your brother, Edmund . . .' Audley began, then saw the absurdity of offering condolences for a private grief when the world as they knew it was in ashes.

Clifton now said, with all too obvious hesitancy, 'Do any know if Prince Edouard was taken?'

All around them, conversation hushed. Among the men huddled against the font, one now rose to his knees, turned an ashen face toward them. Audley recognized John Gower, sword-bearer to their Prince, felt a sick surge of dread. But Gower's words were unexpectedly hopeful.

'I was separated from my young lord when my horse took an arrow in the gullet. But he was well mounted and making for the village when last I did see him, with none in close pursuit. Those with him would not let harm befall him, that I do know. I think it most likely he did escape.'

Clifton breathed a hasty prayer of thanksgiving. So did Audley. And then a voice spoke from the shadows behind them, an unfamiliar voice that said flatly, 'No . . . he did not.'

They all turned, toward the tiny chapel of the Holy Child, toward the unknown speaker who lay panting against the altar. He wore the badge of the slain Earl of Devon and his face was grey with the exhaustion that allowed no other emotion but indifference. He was bleeding profusely, seemed as careless of that as he did of the hostile stares he'd drawn upon himself.

Audley found his voice first. 'What do you know of our Prince? Speak, man, and God save you if you lie!'

The boy—for they saw now that he was little more than that—acknowledged the threat with the same uncaring apathy. He looked at Audley with ageless eyes, said briefly, 'He's dead.'

The words were no sooner out of his mouth than Gower flung himself forward, with a cry that was both sob and curse.

'You lie! God rot your soul, you lie!'

Several men laid hands on him before he could reach the young soldier, who had yet to move, who watched incuriously as the struggling Gower was borne down upon the tiled floor, where he suddenly went limp, began to heave with dry shuddering sobs.

Kneeling beside Somerset, Audley saw the tremor that shook the other man's body and said urgently, 'Are you sure, lad? For Jesú's sake, think before you do answer!'

'I saw it done,' the youthful voice responded matter-of-factly, without any real interest. 'He and his guard. It was the Duke of Clarence's men that did the deed, cornered them by yon abbey mill.'

He stirred slightly, for the first time seemed to sense the grief he'd given. His eyes flicked tiredly to Audley, rested on the older man with uncomprehending pity for what he himself was far beyond feeling. He coughed, said with an effort, 'It was a quick death . . . was over in minutes. . . .' He coughed again, this time brought up blood.

After a while, men began to talk among themselves again, in the hushed tones that their surroundings seemed to require. Audley settled down on the floor, for a time staring into space, focusing neither his gaze nor his thoughts. When he finally looked over at Somerset, he saw that the other man had hunched forward, his face hidden in his arms. He made no sound, but Audley leaned over and, with surprising gentleness, stroked Somerset's bowed head, kept his hand there as Somerset wept.

Removing his helmet, Edward knelt by the stream called Swill-gate, a name that effectively quenched any desire to drink from its depths. Instead, he gave himself over to the luxury of splashing water upon his face, over his head. He could not recall ever being as exhausted as he was right now. Never had his body so defied his will; pain gripped his thighs in spasms, lodged at the base of his spine. Breathing was no longer an unthinking body function, had to be done with care, for he was badly bruised about the ribs and even the light pressure of air entering his lungs was enough to set them to throbbing. His mouth was circled in white, his eyes in red, inflamed by sweat and dust. Even his voice had coarsened, slurred by fatigue. But he had never known the happiness he did at this moment, pure and perfect and intoxicatingly one with a heightened sense of the renewed sweetness of life, sunlight, the coldness of the water that bathed his chafed skin, trickled down his neck into his hair.

Once Edward had satisfied himself as to the care being accorded his lamed white stallion, he'd chosen to remain there, on the banks of the stream, to await word on the wounded, the dead, the Lancastrian leaders. The monks hovered in the background, murmuring among themselves at his willingness to engage his soldiers in friendly conversation, even to banter with the bolder ones. It was not their understanding that royalty was so easy of access as this man who stood feeding an apple to a silvery-grey stallion, now passing the monks' prized wine flagon to a youngster who'd come forward to speak, shyly at first, of having left his Wiltshire village a fortnight ago, trudging northward on foot, fearful he would not arrive in time to fight for York. Glancing down at himself, at the dried thickened blood, at the queer rust colour of his armour, marred with jagged scratches, the marks of deflected blows, Edward nodded, said gravely, 'Aye, I can see that you'd not have wanted to miss this, lad.' And then laughed until his aching ribs threatened to meet in the middle of his lungs.

Edward had given far more than wine that morning. He'd knighted a number of men after the battle and he had it in mind to honour even more, for he was well pleased by the performance of the men who'd fought for him at Tewkesbury. With this, the sweetest victory of his life, he could afford to be generous, meant to see that his army was well rewarded. John Howard sat on the ground at his feet; no longer in the flush of youth, Howard was breathing like a starving man to whom air was food. Edward looked down at him. What he could not do now for those like

484

Jack, who would have followed him to Hell if need be. Or Will, who had. Above all, for Dickon, who once more had been there when it counted.

Well before noon, Edward was given to understand the dramatic dimensions of his victory. The casualties could only be estimated at this point but it seemed likely that those who'd died for York numbered four hundred at most, while the dead of Lancaster might reach as high as two thousand. This pleased Edward enormously but did not surprise him any; he was well aware of that grimmest of battle ironies, that it was when men broke and ran that they were most vulnerable, most likely to meet the violent death they sought only to escape. It had been a lucky day for York; he'd lost none of his intimates, not one of his captains, while the Earl of Devon, John Beaufort, and John Wenlock were all reported dead on the side of Lancaster. He still had no word as to the fate of Somerset. But, from Will Hastings, he learned that Marguerite's son was dead. Edward made no attempt to hide his pleasure at the news. He was pleased, too, that George had relieved him of the rather distasteful job of dispatching Lancaster himself. He'd meant to claim Lancaster's life, for the gold circlet of kingship and for Sandal Castle. But he took no particular joy in killing and it would not have occurred to him to want to be present when Lancaster died. On the contrary, he found the thought anything but appealing, for he admitted, if only to himself, a certain squeamishness at putting the Lancastrian Prince to death under circumstances all too reminiscent of his brother's death.

Fairness forced Edward to acknowledge an unpalatable truth, that to stab an unarmed seventeen-year-old boy to death was murder whether the victim was Edmund, Earl of Rutland, or Edouard, Prince of Lancaster. But though he would have been denied any comforting illusions as to the nature of the act, he meant to do it, and hoped that the boy's death would be to Marguerite d'Anjou as a dagger thrust into her heart, one that, for every day she then lived, would twist with each breath she drew, a wound she'd take to her grave, so that for her, the name Tewkesbury would come to be what the name Sandal Castle was for his mother, for him.

Now, as he listened to Will relate how Lancaster had been struck down by his brother's men, he found himself, for the first time in years, feeling genuine warmth for George who'd so neatly resolved the problem posed by the Lancastrian Prince. Because of George, he was rid of a rival claimant to the English crown, a threat to the peaceful accession of his infant son, and without the need for the boy's blood on his own hands. The more he pondered it, the more pleased he became. He owed George a debt, would have to see to it.

He laughed suddenly. 'I wonder what did motivate George. Did he mean to do me a service? Or did he think he was denying me a revenge I'd long promised myself?'

Will had assumed that George's action was meant to curry favour with his brother, but he was intrigued by Edward's suggestion, and said with a grin, 'You pose an interesting query. It does depend, I expect, on what manner of man your brother sees you to be. The world is full of men who find pleasure in the sight of a blade going into flesh. Now I know you look elsewhere for your pleasures. But does your brother of Clarence know it, too?'

'I do not know,' Edward admitted. 'I should think he would, that none could doubt where I like most to sheathe my sword. Jesú knows my confessor has no such doubts! I think the enforced celibacy of this past week is wearing almost as hard on him as on me. Did I tell you, the last time he did grant me absolution, he remarked, rather wistfully as I took it, that it had been a truly surprising number of days since I'd had a mortal sin to confess.'

'He should take heart; I do not doubt you'll remedy that soon enough,' Will said dryly.

'Before the sun goes down, even if my needs must prevail over my wants. For I tell you, Will, there was a time this morn when I did doubt that any of us would live to make old bones.'

'So did we all. Why d'you suppose, Ned, that Wenlock held back the centre? Holy Mary, the luck of it!'

Edward, though, was no longer listening. He was watching the riders that were coming from the direction of the battlefield, watching with a smile, for his eye had discerned, even at this distance, that they flew his brother's banner. They were coming at an unusually rapid pace, and Edward wondered why, for there was no longer a need for such speed, and he was sure, too, that Richard's body must be athrob with pain only a little less than his own. He grinned, marvelling at the resiliency of the very young, and then decided there was more than that in their eager approach.

By now he'd recognized Francis Lovell, too, and another youth he'd often seen in his brother's company, but whose name escaped him, and they were close enough for him to see their excitement. Richard was unusually flushed, sliding from the saddle almost before his stallion had come to a complete halt.

'My liege,' he said, with correct if rather breathless formality. But it was the brother he sought, not the King, and he couldn't wait, had to burst out with his news.

'Ned, you'll not believe what we did hear! And we got it from one who saw it happen and swears it to be gospel. When Wenlock did not come to Somerset's support, Somerset thought Wenlock had sold out to York. He managed to get back to Wenlock's lines and when he did, he rode right for Wenlock and dashed his brains out with his battle-axe.'

'All-merciful Christ!'

That was the last thing Edward had been expecting to hear from Richard. After a moment to reflect, though, he smiled grimly.

'If so, that's the first honest day's work Somerset ever did.'

Richard nodded. 'And a lucky day's work for York.'

Edward smiled assent and then reached out, drew Richard toward him.

487

'For today, you may ask of me what you will,' he said softly and seriously. 'You need only name it.'

Richard felt heat rise in his face; he was thrown off-balance more by the unexpected earnestness in Edward's voice than by the magnitude of what was offered. He was momentarily flustered, as he'd not been in Edward's presence in years, and then he realized why. This was the first time in his life that Edward had spoken neither as sovereign nor elder brother with ten years of age and authority between them. This had been an exchange between equals. Edward had clearly meant it as such.

'I have my reward,' he said simply, instead of making what would have been his normal response, to fall back upon the familiar lines of banter, to point out this his own self-interest had been rather actively engaged.

'Not yet,' Edward said cryptically, and waited till Richard exchanged belated greetings and congratulations with Will before drawing the boy aside again.

'Now I do have news for you, too, Dickon, news I think you'll find of considerable interest.' With a faint smile. 'Lancaster is dead.'

Richard didn't react at once. His face was very still, intent. And then the dark eyes blazed with sudden light.

'You could give me no more welcome news than that, Ned,' he said, with such savage satisfaction that Rob shot him a look of mild surprise and Francis thought, So, sits the wind still in that quarter.

At that moment, John Howard, who'd been deep in conversation with some Yorkist soldiers a short distance from where they stood, called to Edward with an urgency that spun all heads in his direction.

'My liege, of the men seeking sanctuary within the abbey, one is the Duke of Somerset,' he said grimly.

Edward turned, stared toward the abbey.

'Is he, now?' he said, very softly. The change in his face was startling; suddenly his eyes were as pale and hard as agates.

'Do they think me a complete fool?' he demanded. When he swung around, with the command hot upon his lips, he saw that Richard had already anticipated him and had raised his hand in a gesture that drew the lounging Yorkist soldiers abruptly to their feet, toward them at a run.

'Post guards around the abbey,' Edward snapped. 'See that no man leaves the church. If the Abbot protests, send him to me or Gloucester. Now go! And Christ pity you all if any get by you.'

On Monday May 6th, over the bitter protests of the abbot, Yorkist men-at-arms entered the abbey with drawn swords. Edward held to his earlier promise of clemency and pardoned all of the men sheltered within . . . all but Edmund Beaufort, Duke of Somerset, and thirteen captains of Lancaster whom he deemed to be irreconcilable in their loyalties.

The men were taken, by force when need be, from the abbey and conveyed under guard to the Court House of the Lord of Tewkesbury, to be tried for treason before the Duke of Norfolk, England's Earl Marshal, and the Duke of Gloucester, England's Lord Constable.

Somerset looked around the hall hastily converted into a trial chamber. It was already filling with men, with his fellow prisoners, men-at-arms, Yorkist lords, the curious and the vengeful. He regarded them with no more interest than he had in the trial itself.

Beside him, he could hear Tresham cursing. Since Yorkist soldiers had first turned their sanctuary into a prison, he'd been railing incessantly against Edward of York; even now, he continued to vent an embittered hate. Somerset flicked his eyes away, aware of a pitying contempt. He found it hard to understand how Tresham could have expected otherwise. He only wondered why York had bothered to go through the motions of this trial. That

489

had surprised him, just a little; when the soldiers had finally come for them, he'd expected them to be dragged beyond the abbey precincts and slain at once.

A sudden thought came to him now, freezing his breath in his lungs. A man tried and found guilty of treason was subject to disembowelment before execution, to be hanged and then cut down whilst still living, then to be gelded and have his bowels ripped from his belly and burned before his eyes, death delayed until the body could endure the agony no longer. Was that what York had in mind, that the reason for the trial? Cold sweat trickled down his ribs. Death he did not fear; in his present anguish of spirit and soul, he even thought he'd welcome it. But to die such a death as that! He was unable to repress a shudder, hoped no one had noticed.

His attention was drawn by a new arrival who was just entering the hall, a striking youth with a gleaming head of sunlit fair hair, clad in a tawny velvet doublet with sleeves slashed and reversed in emerald satin, and wearing with pride on a silkenclad leg the jewelled proof that he was numbered among a most privileged elite, was a Knight of the Garter. Rings flashed on his hands as he turned to respond to a sally from a companion; he laughed, showing white teeth, an obvious awareness of his own good looks, the furore he was causing throughout the hall. Somerset suddenly realized he was watching the Duke of Clarence and his breath escaped his lips in a sibilant hiss. He stared at Clarence and knew a hatred such as he'd experienced only once before in his life, when two days ago he'd found himself trapped between the men of Gloucester and York, had to watch as his own men died because Wenlock had betrayed them.

'The craven strutting bastard!' Audley spat the words. 'Does he think it does honour to him, that he brought about a boy's death?'

Somerset shook his head slowly. The first surge of hate was dying down; once more he felt numb, welcomed it, this lack of feeling that would enable him to face the block with indifference, death with contempt, even such a death as he now feared York did intend for them.

'Do you think Clarence knows aught of honour, Humphrey?' he asked tiredly. 'Nothing matters to Clarence but Clarence, and for reasons which do escape me in their entirety, he seems to thrive upon his double-dealing.'

He stiffened suddenly; for a moment, he seemed to hear a woman's voice in the hall, hear the throatily accented English: 'Clarence is a fool, but a singularly lucky one so far.' How right she'd been, his lady. He swallowed, blinked rapidly. 'All in your hands,' she'd said. She'd trusted him. She'd trusted him and he'd failed her. Never would he have been able to face her, not in this life or the next, and tell her that her son was dead.

There was a stir; he heard the name Gloucester and he turned toward the sound, with the first faint flicker of curiosity. Jesú, he's so young! That was his first thought, for in those hours since he'd learned of the death of his prince, he'd come to understand at last what Marguerite had tried to tell him, how very young seventeen was.

Now he watched Gloucester, this boy who was so close in age to his slain Prince, who was to pass sentence of death upon him. Dark, intense, of slight build, he bore little resemblance to the fair-haired genial giant Somerset remembered to be Edward of York. Edward was the sword of York, the Sunne in Splendour; even Somerset would concede that Edward had performed feats on the field that he'd not have credited had he not seen for himself. And Clarence . . . Clarence was a renegade who'd perjured himself twice over, who had, as Audley said, brought about a boy's death. Gloucester, though, was an unknown quantity. All Somerset knew of the boy was to his credit; he'd been fiercely loyal to his brother, and of his courage there could be no question. On impulse, he moved forward.

At once men-at-arms barred his way. He was shoved back, none too gently, his arm painfully twisted up behind his back. Richard saw, raised his hand. Somerset's captors reluctantly backed away; he stood alone. For a moment they faced each other and then Somerset moved the few steps that separated them.

'Might Your Grace spare me a moment?'

Richard hesitated and then nodded. There was no sympathy in his eyes and considerable wariness, but no overt hostility. He waited, without encouragement, for Somerset to speak.

'Have you had word as to the Queen's Grace?'

'The Queen's Grace is at Westminster.'

Somerset damned himself for a fool; he should have known better. He started to turn on his heel. But Richard seemed to recognize that he'd been unnecessarily petty, for he now said, 'I take it you do mean Marguerite d'Anjou? No, there has been no word as yet.'

Still smarting under that first rebuff, Somerset wanted to walk away. But the need to know was too great.

'What shall be done with her when she is found?'

He saw Richard's mouth harden. 'York does not make war on women,' he said coolly. 'She'll be confined, but she'll not be abused. If that be your fear, you may set your mind at ease.'

Somerset wanted to believe him. But belief did not come easily, not now. 'Have I your word on that, my lord?'

He saw the boy's eyes narrow. 'I understood you to think the word of York to be worthless,' he said, with a flash of malice.

Somerset almost smiled. 'I'd take the word of Gloucester,' he said evenly, and then he did smile with what, in another life, might have been amusement, for Richard's mental conflict showed clearly on his face, the struggle to be fair warring with his natural dislike, his distrust.

'You have it,' he said at last, almost snapping the words.

'Thank you, my lord of Gloucester.' The relief Somerset felt surprised him. He'd not truly thought Edward of York would take vengeance against Marguerite. Richard's boast had truth in it as

492

well as pride; he did not think York was a man to shed a woman's blood. And yet ... and yet, he knew the hate York had for Marguerite and he found reassurance now in this grudging pledge given by York's favourite brother.

Richard seemed to think the conversation was at an end. He was turning away as Somerset gave voice to his other concern, knowing the risk he took but not caring in the least if he gave offence. There was, he thought with grim irony, a pleasurable freedom in having nothing left to lose.

'What is to be done with my Prince?'

He'd struck a nerve, saw that at once.

'His Grace the King has given orders that he be accorded Christian burial at the abbey of St Mary the Virgin.' Richard's eyes were grey, totally without warmth. 'York does not dishonour the dead,' he said, staring at Somerset in bitter challenge.

Somerset had thought all feeling benumbed within him; he now found he could still be discomfited.

'I was not at Sandal Castle, my lord.' And was then angry with himself for having felt the need to make the denial. But, in truth, he'd not approved of what had been done to the bodies of the Yorkist dead, the mocking indignities performed upon the corpses, the beheading of men who'd died honourably in battle. He'd always thought it to be a bloody, needless piece of work, and one that cost Lancaster dear. Something of this must have shown in his face, for Richard forbore to make the obvious rejoinder, to remind him that even if he had not been at Sandal Castle, his brother Harry had.

For a moment, they looked at one another.

Somerset roused himself then, called upon the echoes of remembered courtesy to say, 'I thank you for sparing these minutes, Your Grace.'

'De rien,' Richard said softly, and if there was irony in his voice, there was something, too, that hadn't been there at the start of the conversation.

493

Richard was already moving away. It was then that Somerset remembered.

'Wait, my lord. . . . There is one thing more. I would ask a favour of you.'

'I can promise you nothing, my lord of Somerset,' Richard said at once, said in a voice that was suddenly ice.

Somerset was shaking his head. 'You mistake me, my lord,' he said, sounding at once mocking, proud and very, very weary. 'I do not ask for myself.'

Some suspicion faded from Richard's eyes, but not all. 'I still can make you no promises,' he said. But he was listening.

'You said York does not maltreat women. Well, there is a lass who much merits your kindness . . . the younger daughter of Warwick, she who was wed to my Prince. She had no say in her father's intrigues and I would hope your brother of York shall find it in his heart to be merciful to her.'

He thought at first that he'd blundered, done Anne Neville no kindness. Richard was startled, that was unmistakable; but in the fleeting instant that his defences were down, Somerset had seen something else in his face, an undefinable emotion of surprising intensity. He wondered briefly if he'd have done better not to mention the girl, not to speak for her, for he'd received a response he'd not expected. Whatever Gloucester's feelings for Warwick's daughter, indifference was not one of them.

'I did think you and she were companions of childhood. Surely I need not plead her cause with you,' he challenged. But even as he spoke, he was remembering the sudden tension in Anne Neville's voice as she sought reassurance that Richard had not been badly hurt at Barnet. The suspicion that struck him was such that he forgot completely the arguments he was marshalling on Anne Neville's behalf and just stared at Richard. The boy had recovered his poise, now said guardedly,

'No, you need not plead her cause with me, my lord.'

494

That was all, yet it was enough. Somerset saw that his extraordinary suspicion was grounded in truth.

'I'll be damned,' he said softly, not at all sure how he felt about this revelation.

Richard was watching him intently. 'His Grace King Edward has no wish to dishonour brave men,' he said slowly, measuring his words with the exacting care of one building a conversational bridge so fragile that the imprudent placement of even one word would doom the entire structure. 'He does not seek vengeance.'

Somerset expelled his breath in an audible escape of tension. He understood. Richard was telling him that he and his comrades would not face the horrors of a traitor's death. He knew his relief must have blazed forth onto his face; at that moment, he no longer cared.

'Well, then,' he said, in a voice that was as level as he could make it, said with what he hoped would pass as ironic detachment, 'shall we proceed with the trial?' His mouth stretched in a tight mirthless smile as he added, 'Fiat justitia, mat caelum; let justice be done though the heavens should fall.'

He saw something flicker in Richard's eyes. It defied analysis and was gone so quickly that he couldn't be sure it had been there at all.

Somerset was becoming aware of the unnatural silence in the hall, aware that all eyes were on them, speculating avidly as to what was being said between them, the mightiest lord of Lancaster and the youngster who was to sit in judgment upon him. He was glad suddenly that Richard was so soft-spoken, that he'd instinctively pitched his own voice to Richard's level, glad their curiosity was not to be satisfied. He looked about the hall with hard, contemptuous eyes, thinking they were like ravens drawn by the stench of carrion. His gaze came to rest on George's bright head and then he was saying, in a carrying voice that swept the hall, 'I am thankful for this much at least, that it is Gloucester who passes judgment and not Clarence.'

*

495

The curiosity was at fever pitch but only George and Will Hastings dared approach Richard, question him about the encounter that would give rise to conjecture for days to come.

'What the devil did he want?' George demanded. His fair skin was still mottled with the angry blood set pulsing by Somerset's scorn. 'Did he ask you to spare his life?'

'Of course not,' Richard said impatiently. 'You cannot deny his courage, George, whatever you may think of his loyalties. All he does hope for now is to die well. And I've no doubt that he will.'

'Ah, yes, an honourable death above all else. You sound a veritable echo of our cousin Johnny, who so feverently sought such an honour at Barnet. And speaking of dishonour and the like, what said Somerset when you told him he wronged Wenlock?'

Richard was frowning. 'What d'you mean?'

'You know damned well what I mean. Any chance Lancaster might have had for victory died with Wenlock, when their men saw their captains turning upon each other rather than York. Surely you disabused him of his suspicion that Wenlock was in the pay of York. No . . . I can see by your face that you did not.' George shook his head, said derisively, 'Most magnanimous of you, little brother. I hope you made sure to compliment him upon his prowess on the field, too.'

Richard stared at him, looking as if he didn't have much liking for George at that moment; and at that moment, he didn't. Will saw and interceded smoothly, 'What did he want, in truth, Dickon?'

Richard pulled his gaze away from George, gave Will a bemused look, a twisted half-smile.

'As strange as it does sound, Will, he wanted to ask me to extend mercy to Anne Neville.'

The Duke of Norfolk was now entering the hall; he was to preside with Richard over the trial of the Lancastrians. Richard turned away, moved to meet him. Once again, he thus missed the effect that Anne Neville's name had upon his brother.

Will didn't, though. He admittedly hadn't at first comprehended

496

the tensions that had surfaced at Windsor, but since then, his own astuteness and a few discreet queries to Edward had gone far toward resolving the puzzle for him. He smiled at George, said pleasantly, 'Could I interest you in a wager, my lord?'

George, who knew Hastings well enough, was instantly suspicious. 'A wager of what sort?'

'I'll wager that Warwick's daughter is still as smitten with your brother Gloucester today as she was two years ago. What do you say? . . . Shall we name the stakes?'

George bit off a blistering oath, burned Will with a look that promised nothing less than open if undeclared war.

'Have a care, my lord Hastings. It's a right dangerous habit to talk without thinking, as you seem so fond of doing. There are few ways more certain of gaining yourself enemies, enemies you'd rather not have. . . . That I can promise you.'

Will looked amused; his eyes had taken on a golden glow. 'Ah, but what could one more enemy matter to you, my lord,' he murmured, 'when you do have so many?'

George was provoked beyond endurance, even forgot for the moment that they had an eagerly attentive audience. But those spectators hoping for the excitement of a confrontation were to be disappointed, for it was then that the King entered the hall and they knew even George of Clarence would not be so reckless as to make a scene now, not when the trial was about to begin.

The Lancastrians were found guilty of treason; the verdict, delivered in dispassionate tones by Richard, Duke of Gloucester, demanded death. That afternoon a scaffold was set up in the market square, where Church and High Streets came together. At ten the following morning, a priest was summoned to shrive the condemned men and they were then beheaded in the shadow of the high stone cross. Edward waived the right of disembowelment, allowed the dead honourable burial.

That same Tuesday, the Yorkist army departed Tewkesbury. Even this, the 'sweetest of victories', did not quench all rebellion within Edward's kingdom. The Bastard of Fauconberg, kin to Warwick and long a thorn in Edward's side, had sailed from Calais, was in Kent where he was having some success in stirring up opposition to York. There were reports, as well, of risings in the North of England by diehard Lancastrians who did not yet know of the death of the youth who'd been Lancaster's bright hope.

Edward decided that London, which had been left under the protection of his brother-in-law Anthony Woodville, could be relied upon to stave off Fauconberg should he threaten the capital. He chose to take his army north, to himself quell the rebellion in that unstable region long so unfriendly to the House of York. But as he neared Coventry, he was met by the Earl of Northumberland, who had at last bestirred himself to leave his northern estates upon hearing of Edward's devastating triumph at Tewkesbury. Northumberland brought welcome news, that the rising in the North was over, over almost before it began, quenched once word had spread that all that remained of the royal blood of Lancaster now ran in the veins of the frail bewildered man within the Tower of London.

Edward halted at Coventry, there to await fresh troops before swinging back toward London to deal with the last lingering threat posed to his sovereignty, in the person of the Bastard of Fauconberg. And it was at Coventry that he awaited, too, the arrival of Marguerite d'Anjou, taken captive by Sir William Stanley two days after the battle of Tewkesbury.

BOOK TWO

Anne

I

Coventry

May 1471

Anne Neville had a daisy in her hand. As she sat there in the sunlit window seat on this, the first day of their Coventry captivity, she was plucking the petals, one by one, and collecting them neatly in her lap. She'd found the flower upon the window seat soon after William Stanley's men had escorted them into the priory parlour, where they were to be kept while he hastened to his sovereign to announce that the Frenchwoman was at last caged.

Anne had no doubt that the daisy was meant to be a message, to convey condolences that dared not be put into words. It was a token left by one with Lancastrian sympathies. She was sure of that, for the English daisy—called 'marguerite' in French—had long been both a personal emblem and the favourite flower of Marguerite d'Anjou. Anne had said nothing of her discovery and, as she awaited the arrival of her cousin Edward, she occupied herself in methodically shredding the snowy petals into scattered oblivion. Five . . . six. . . . She counted each petal with care. Seven petals torn from the buttery-yellow heart. One for each of the seven days of her widowhood.

She looked up from her lap, across the chamber at her mother-in-law, saw the ravages of the past week upon that once beautiful face, saw without pity. Anne had not been schooled in hate. Until she'd followed her father into French exile, she'd not known what it was to hate another human being, had never been given reason for hatred.

After Amboise, though, she'd learned quickly. She'd come to hate Edouard of Lancaster even more than she feared him, hated the scorn in his voice when he spoke of her father, hated his boastings of the bloody reprisals he meant to take against the House of York, hated the way he saw her fear and laughed at it. Above all, she'd hated those nights when boredom or the lack of other bedmates brought him to her bed and she'd had to submit to his physical demands, submit in silence because he was her husband, because he had the right to make use of her body as he chose, because she was his. Far more than the physical pain and humiliating forced intimacy, it was that which soured Anne's spirit, the loss of self. She was no longer Anne Neville at such times; she had no identity, no purpose in being other than to serve his need, a need that any soft female body could fill. It was not that she'd not expected to be submissive to her husband. She knew obedience to be a wife's duty, a husband's right. Holy Church said so, said wives must submit themselves unto their husbands, and for the first fourteen years of her life she'd accepted it without question or qualm. But with Edouard of Lancaster, it went beyond submission. Intuitively she sensed that, understood that she was less than a wife, was a possession, to be used when it pleased him, to be ignored when it did not . . . and she came to hate him with the passion she did not bring to his bed.

During those two nightmarish days that followed the battle, Anne spent much of her time in prayer, thanking Almighty God for giving the victory to York, for seeing to the safety of her Yorkist cousins. She was sure Marguerite knew her son was dead, must be dead. Since arriving at Little Malvern Priory, Marguerite had spoken scarcely a dozen words, not so much as a crust of bread passed her lips and candles burned in her bedchamber each night till dawn. Marguerite must know. It only remained for Sir William Stanley to stand before her on the stone steps leading into the Prior's lodging, to say with considerable relish, 'Madame, you may consider yourself a prisoner of His Most Sovereign Grace,

King Edward Plantagenet, fourth of that name since the Conquest.' He'd grinned widely then, savouring the moment so obviously that the women were forewarned as to what was coming.

'We are to proceed at once to Coventry, upon the King's command. Although if I did have my way, I'd dispatch you, instead, to join that whoreson Somerset and your bastard-born whelp in Hell everlasting.'

No sound escaped Marguerite's lips; she scarcely seemed to be breathing. Disappointed by her lack of response, Stanley sought to remedy it by providing the details of her son's death: 'Skewered through as he cried unto my lord of Clarence for succour, like any common craven.'

Still she looked at him, saying nothing. Anne thought at first that Marguerite, proudest of the proud, was not willing to lose face before a blackguard like Stanley, but she soon saw it was not that at all, saw that the Lancastrian Queen was staring at Stanley with unseeing eyes. So she had not known! Anne gazed wonderingly at Marguerite, marvelling at the capacity of women to cling to hope until the last possible moment, until confronted by a William Stanley. She shivered, even though she was standing in the sun, and only then did she begin to think what Lancaster's death would mean to her.

Stanley at last had ceased his unproductive baiting and agreed to the request put forward by the enraged Countess of Vaux, to allow the women to gather needed belongings from Marguerite's bedchamber.

It was only then, behind closed doors, that Marguerite broke. She shed no tears, merely sank to her knees upon the floor, like a sawdust doll suddenly bereft of support. She doubled over in the way Anne remembered her own mother doing when, many years ago, she had been stricken during a Christmas Midnight Mass, miscarrying of yet another daughter even before she could be borne from Middleham's chapel. Marguerite clutched herself as Anne's mother had done, rocking back and forth, oblivious of her ladies, oblivious of all except this stark savage anguish that seemed indistinguishable, to those watching, from physical pain.

Anne alone did not go to Marguerite; she leaned against the door and watched. She'd been appalled by Stanley's needless brutality, all the more so because he took such evident delight in it. Now she wondered that she could look on, unmoved by a grief so intense, a suffering so severe. She must be sorely lacking in Christian charity, she decided, with that queer cool detachment she'd begun to develop with her December marriage.

Well, so be it then. What pity had they ever shown her? What sympathy had she been given for her father's death? Marguerite had even begrudged her the few pence she'd had to borrow so she could buy dye in Exeter to transform two of her gowns into mourning garb.

No, she did not grieve for Lancaster, either that he had died so young or so violently. She was glad he was dead. And as she looked upon the woman writhing upon the rush-strewn floor, racked by the dry sobs of a grief forever beyond the balm of tears, Anne thought this was but one more reason to hate them, that they'd made her so much like them, able to take pleasure in the death of another being, to be an uncaring witness to this rending of a woman's soul.

She soon found that Stanley's soldiers treated her, as they did not treat Marguerite, with courtesy, even with a touch of deference. Only once on the way to Coventry had she been approached with insulting familiarity and almost immediately the offending soldier had been reprimanded. Even Stanley himself had shown her a consideration that she found totally out of character, and unwelcome, as well, for she'd rather not have had to speak to him at all. She finally decided that perhaps there were still those who held her father's memory in esteem; there were Yorkshiremen among Stanley's soldiers, after all. Perhaps it was the memory of old Neville allegiances that prompted civility toward the Earl's daughter. She didn't know, could only be grateful for it.

She never doubted, however, that no matter how dismal her future might be under York, as the daughter and widow of dead rebels, she'd still fare better with her cousin Ned than she would have as Edouard of Lancaster's unwanted wife. She didn't know Ned all that well, but she felt certain he'd not imprison her as he would Marguerite, not punish her for the sins of Lancaster or Neville.

Her greatest fear as they moved toward Coventry was that her fate would be found within the white-walled silence of the convent. Anne did not want to spend the remainder of her life as a nun. But she was apprehensively aware that Ned might see that as the kindest, most convenient way to rid himself of the embarrassment that was Lancaster's widow. And even if he did not think of it himself, George would be there to plant the suggestion and then water it till it took root.

Anne remembered a girl in the village that clustered in the shadow of Middleham Castle. She'd been wed to a soldier in the service of Anne's father. Rumour had him lost on a routine trip to Ireland for the Earl. But his death was unconfirmed and for nearly two years the girl had been trapped in her uncertain status, neither wife nor widow. Anne felt like that now. She was free of Lancaster. But she was not free to wed again. Not when she was heiress to one-half of her mother's considerable estates. Not when George meant to claim the whole of the Neville and Beauchamp lands for himself. Anne needed no one to tell her that was her brother-in-law's intention. She'd known George for eleven of the not quite fifteen years of her life.

She was his sister-in-law, not his ward. By rights, he should have no say over her. She knew that would not matter in the least to him. He was as careless of legality as he was of morality, and he had the power to win his way. He'd never give her leave to wed again, allow her to take a husband who might enforce her rights as she herself could not. Nothing could better please him than to see her safely sequestered, out of sight and memory of

505

the world and would-be suitors. George would force her into a convent, unless Ned would gainsay him . . . and why should he?

She could appeal to Isabel but she had none too sanguine hopes for aid from that quarter. Isabel was . . . was not always reliable, she acknowledged, finding neutral words to formulate an uneasy suspicion. Moreover, Isabel was subject to George's will; she was his wife. She could not prevail against him. Only Ned could do that, Ned who had no reason to deny George for her sake.

Richard could. At once hating herself for thinking it. He could, though. If she appealed to him, he'd help her; he'd not let her be convent-caged against her will. But how could she appeal to Richard now? Had she so little pride as that?

Thus she tormented herself during the week that led inexorably to Coventry and the moment that filled her with emotion of an intensity and an ambivalence to set her to trembling. The moment when she would come face-to-face with her Yorkist cousins. Oh, how she lied to herself even now! It was not Ned she was so reluctant to face. It was Richard. It had always been Richard.

Her unhappy reverie was abruptly dispelled by that happening which was both awaited and unexpected, the entrance of the King.

Anne's pulse quickened, picked up a dizzying tempo. But she recognized only two faces among those accompanying her cousin of York, that of William, Lord Hastings, and the self-satisfied Stanley. Her breathing slowed somewhat and she followed the lead of the other women, who were sinking down in submissive curtsies.

Marguerite alone remained standing, a figure carved in ice, waiting as Edward crossed the room. He stopped before her, seemed about to speak. She did not give him the chance. Her hand came up with surprising swiftness. There were gasps from her ladies and his companions, but he readily blocked the blow, wrenching her wrist back and away from his face with almost contemptuous ease.

There was a horrified silence. Her cousin Ned had always been able to shield his thoughts when he so chose; Anne found his face unreadable. Like the others, she could only wait.

Marguerite stared at Edward, dark patches of colour flaming across her cheekbones. Expecting his reaction to be one of violence, counting on it, she struggled with his silence, then said in a raw, constricted voice, 'Tell me of my husband. Does he still live?'

Of Edward's men, he alone showed no outrage at the insult. He nodded briefly.

'For how long?' she asked, and once more those who heard her were startled into exclamations of dismay or anger.

'Self-murder is a mortal sin, madame,' he said evenly. 'And the sin is no less if you do not do the deed yourself but contrive another to do it for you.'

One hand had moved to her throat, was pressing against the beating hollow. 'What do you mean?'

'I mean that you cannot provoke me into sending you to the block. However much you do deserve it . . . or desire it.'

'You did not spare my son,' she said stonily.

Edward didn't even bother to deny the accusation, to remind her that her son had died on the field. Instead, he said with insulting forbearance, 'I'll not stain my hands with a woman's blood.'

Marguerite drew so deep a breath that all could see her breasts heave. The hatred on her face was unmistakable, yet curiously muted. Like one forced to call upon remembered emotions, Anne thought; the light was there, but no heat, as if the sun had given way to a perpetual shadowed moon.

'Even if it were a mercy?' Marguerite asked, in dulled, queerly flattened tones, and Anne at last felt the faintest unwanted flicker of pity.

For the first time, emotion showed in Edward's eyes. For an unguarded instant, they mirrored an unhealed hatred, gave an unnerving glimpse of a searing blue-white flame, all the more intense for being under such relentless restraint.

507

'Especially if it were a mercy, Madame,' he said bitterly, and turned away.

His gaze was now passing over the other women, the wives and widows of Lancaster. Anne's heart began to pound again. As he moved toward her, she dropped down in a second curtsy. Then he was reaching down, raising her up. He bent his head; for a brief moment, she felt his mouth touch hers. She scarcely knew him at all, this glittering formidable cousin of hers, had not known what to expect; but certainly not this, never this, to be treated as if she were a cherished treasure long lost and at last recovered. His hands were warm upon hers, his eyes even warmer, the deepest, clearest blue she'd ever seen, and his voice was enough like his brother's to fill her with a surge of feeling that had something in it of both pleasure and pain.

'Welcome to Coventry, Anne,' he was saying, with an astonishing gentleness. 'Welcome home, sweetheart.'

Anne was alone with Edward, but she could find nothing to say, thinking only that if ever a man was born to win, always to win, surely it was this man . . . and Blessed Mother Mary, why had her father not been able to see that?

'You look woefully like the lamb thrust into the lion's den. Come now, sweetheart, what were you expecting from me . . . the rack?'

Edward was not the first to have been misled by Anne's surface shyness and now he was delighted by the candour of her reply.

'I dared not hope you would be so forgiving, my liege. Not to Edouard of Lancaster's widow.'

'You are far more than that, Anne. You are my cousin; we do share the same blood. Moreover, you are but fifteen years of age and I doubt that your marriage was of your choosing; am I wrong in that?' Not waiting for her response, he tilted her chin up, warming her with his smile.

'We are kin, Anne, and surely that must count for more than

a brief forced marriage with a youth no longer living.' Leaving the one reason unsaid, that his brother wanted her.

'Your Grace ...' How strange that an unexpected kindness should be as unsettling as the careless cruelty she'd found in France. For he was being kind, kinder than she had any right to expect, and the arduously constructed defences of the past year were crumbling; sympathy was the one weapon they'd not been structured to withstand.

'Ned,' he corrected amiably. 'You truly did fear the worst?' In genuine surprise. 'That's hardly flattering to me, is it?' He grinned down at her, kept her hand in his as he said playfully, 'Tell me, sweet cousin, just what did you fancy Dickon would be doing while I cast you deep into that sunless cell or cloistered convent?' Intrigued to observe what he could accomplish with the mere mention of his brother's name.

Her face burning, Anne felt suddenly feverish, sunsick. Why did Ned think her plight would matter so to Richard? And why had he sounded so amused, approving even?

'Richard. . . . He still thinks of me?'

'Oh, now and then, I do believe,' he said, very dryly.

'And what does he think? Of my father's betrayal? Richard loved him; you do know that? Yet had my father won Barnet, Richard would be dead, and I . . . I would one day have been Queen, Lancaster's Queen. . . .' She was fast losing control but she managed to make the word *Queen* sound as if it burned her mouth.

She'd told him more of the past year than he cared to know. 'No, Anne. No, little bird.'

He kissed her forehead and found a handkerchief in his doublet. She was wiping away tear traces with the finely stitched crest of a *Rose-en-Soleil* when he beckoned from the open window.

'Ah, at last. Come here, sweetheart.'

She knew, of course, even before she reached the window, gripping the casement as she stared down into the priory garth. He was mounted on an unruly chestnut stallion and he was laughing. He glanced up, unknowing, and she thought that had it not been for the brilliant sky-colour eyes, he might have been a Spaniard. Blackest hair and thin sun-browned face. The dark one in a fair family. Her cousin Richard. The last time she had seen him, there had been no laughter between them, only silence. But he was laughing now, here in the courtyard at Coventry, giving commands with the sureness born of birth and a remarkable victory just seven days past ... and Yorkshire, what could Yorkshire and Middleham possibly be to him now?

She turned away from the window. The minutes dragged by. And then with surprising suddenness, Richard was there, standing very still in the doorway, with a greeting frozen on his lips and eyes only for Anne.

Edward was grinning. 'I do believe, Dickon, that I neglected to tell you this was the day Stanley would be meeting us at Coventry with the French harlot . . . and our fair kinswoman, Anne Neville.'

He didn't linger; his sense of the dramatic was too finely honed and his sense of timing was inbred, instinctive. 'Well, lad, I'd venture you need me here as much as Egypt needed the ten deadly plagues.' The door closing on the echoes of his laughter.

Richard came swiftly to Anne. His first impulse to take her in his arms, he carefully confined himself to the most cousinly of kisses; his lips barely grazed the corner of her mouth.

'Welcome home, Anne.'

He was unconsciously echoing his brother's greeting, but no one had ever said her name as Richard did now, as the most caressing of endearments. Anne betrayed herself with hot colour, but still she said nothing; she couldn't, not trusting her voice. Once, years ago, she had accepted a childish dare from Francis Lovell and drank two goblets of burgundy in quick succession. She felt like that now, giddy and light-headed, her face scorched, her hands icy. How grey his eyes were! And yet she'd always remembered them as blue. She could still scarcely believe he was truly here, close enough to touch. She need only reach out. But nineteen months . . . nineteen months was a lifetime; for them both, a lifetime.

Richard hesitated. He was disconcerted in equal measure by her nearness, after so many months, and by her continuing silence. This was not how he'd meant their reunion to be. She seemed fearful. . . . Not of him, surely? He found such a thought intolerable, but what occurred to him next was worse. Was it that she had learned to love Marguerite's handsome son, after all? Did she grieve for Lancaster? Was it for him that she wore black?

'I truly regret your father's death, Anne. I would never have had it so.'

She inclined her head. That she knew, with the same certainty that she knew the sun would rise each morn from the east, that His Holiness the Pope was infallible and that ambition, more than any sin decried by Holy Church, brought men to ruin.

Strangers, Richard thought unwillingly; it was as if they were strangers of a sudden. He stepped back, appraising. She was taller, perhaps, since he'd last seen her, and softer, too, curved in places he remembered as flat, becomingly flushed; but too tense, too thin, and he found her wedding ring to be glaringly and blasphemously bright against the drabness of her mourning gown. She seemed reluctant to meet his eyes and was staring at the sword on his hip. Was she visualizing it wet with the blood of Barnet and Tewkesbury?

'Anne, I'd not lie to you now; I never have. I do not regret Lancaster's death. Had we met on the field that morn, I would have done my best to take his life myself. Yet I do regret, very deeply, any grief his death may have caused you.'

'Grief?'

Anne stared at him, open-mouthed. Grief? For Lancaster? Blessed Lady, he could not think that she'd cared for Lancaster, that she'd gone willingly to his bed!

'Oh, no, Richard!'

Saying his name aloud at last, she felt the need to repeat it, as if to prove she could, after a full year of enforced silence, a year in which she so often heard his name spat as profanity.

'Richard, do you want to know how I felt when I was told that he was dead?'

She had moved closer, or perhaps he had, but there was no longer space between them. He nodded tensely.

'I could tell only you . . . only you,' she said, very softly now. 'No one else, for it is a shamefully cruel and un-Christian admission to make. You see, I was glad, Richard. I was so very glad. . . .'

He didn't reply at once, reaching out to trace the curve of her cheek, his fingers light and cool to the touch against her skin.

'I think I would have given all I have to hear you say that,' he said, and the room blurred for her in a dazzling blaze of misted sunlight.

So close were they that he could see the shadows cast by down-swept lashes; they showed golden at the roots, quivered against her cheek as he touched his lips to hers, very gentle and easy but far from cousinly, nonetheless.

2

Coventry

May 1471

Because Coventry was in ill favour with the King for having given aid to Warwick during his rebellion, Prior Deram and Lord Mayor Bette had determined to honour their disgruntled sovereign with hospitality so lavish he could not help but be more favourably disposed toward their city. An elaborate banquet was planned for that Sunday in St Mary's Hall, at the city's expense, but this Saturday noon it was the Prior's turn. The dinner brought before the Yorkist lords in the Prior's great hall was impressive even by Edward's luxury-loving standards, and Will Hastings cheered Prior Deram immeasurably when he vowed that not even the Lord of Bruges, Louis de la Gruuthuse had set so fine a table.

Will had not exaggerated by much. The usual royal dinner of two courses consisting of three or four dishes each had been replaced by no less than four courses, each of five separate dishes, served on plates of gilt. As it was a Saturday, meat was denied them, but the Prior's cooks had produced a variety of fish dishes sure to tempt even the most jaded appetite; porpoise, pike stuffed with chestnuts, roasted eel, sturgeon baked in a 'coffyn' with raisins, cinnamon, and ginger. Sugar, rather than honey, served as a sweetener, wine cups were kept filled with vernage, hippocras and malmsey, and each ending course was graced with the appearance of an elaborate sugared 'subtlety', sculptured into unicorns, St George slaying the dragon and the White Roses of York.

Will had enjoyed himself enormously, although it was his taste for malicious amusement rather than for the highly spiced dishes that had given him the greatest pleasure. For Will, the fun had begun when Richard brought to the King's table a girl who, both by blood and marriage, was tainted with treason. Will had been hard put not to laugh at the befuddlement of the marshal charged with seating the high-ranking guests. However, the man had not been so flustered as to argue when the Duke of Gloucester insisted that the Lady Anne be seated at his left, even though that disrupted the entire seating arrangement. By now it was becoming apparent to all that upon Richard shone the brightest rays of the Sunne of York. That, Will did not find so amusing, but he hoped in time that he'd learn to live with it.

What followed was for him a very entertaining spectacle, with one of Edward's brothers seemingly intent upon the most subtle of seductions and the other barely able to force malmsey past the gorge rising in his throat.

It was customary, of course, for a couple to share a wine cup and trencher plate, and good manners required that a knight would see to his lady's eating pleasure before his own, just as a well-bred youngster sharing a plate with an elderly companion would select those morsels tender enough for aging teeth. But Will had never before seen politeness given such a high gallant gloss, and watching as Richard lavished upon Anne Neville so much care that he scarcely touched his own food, Will watched, too, as George's complexion turned an interesting shade of green, and he was well content.

Once the meal had ended and the uneaten food was scraped from the trenchers into alms dishes for the poor, once Edward had dispatched eight shillings to be shared among the priory cooks and lavers of scented washing water had been brought for the guests, all scattered to their own pursuits. After ascertaining that Edward had no need of him at present, Will chose to follow Richard and Anne into the Prior's Presence Chamber, for George had done likewise and Will was drawn irresistibly by the lure of coming strife.

George was standing with the Stanley brothers, for Thomas, Lord Stanley, had made haste to submit himself to Edward at Coventry, to disavow any allegiance to Warwick and to vouchsafe his rather tattered loyalties to York. As Will moved toward them, he nearly bumped into John Howard, who was making haste to put distance between himself and the very men Will was intent upon seeking out.

'There's an unholy trinity for you, Jack,' he murmured wryly, and Howard grimaced, looking back at the Stanleys and George with distaste.

'As a dog returneth to his vomit, so a fool returneth to his folly,' he said quietly, but no less scathingly for all that. 'Any other man would thank Almighty God fasting for his good fortune in having a brother willing to forgive his treason. But not that one. . . . He does seem hell-bent upon his own destruction.'

'I do most fervently hope so!' Will grinned, and, with a wink at Howard, moved discreetly within hearing range.

'By the Mass, if she sits any closer, she'll be in his lap . . . or worse.' George hissed.

Will's eyes strayed from George to the couple in the recessed oriel window seat. He heard Richard laugh, oblivious of his brother's rage. None who saw them together could doubt that Gloucester was smitten by Warwick's daughter. And with Gloucester to plead for her, Will thought, Ned might not be so inclined to let Clarence strip her of her inheritance.

William Stanley guffawed, but Thomas Stanley nodded, said something soothing about my lord of Clarence's commendable concern for the honour of his sister-by-marriage.

'Precisely, my lord Stanley.' George suddenly seemed to see an acceptable outlet for his anger, for he said indignantly, 'The girl is my wife's sister, after all. It is my duty to see that she not be taken advantage of, that her name not be sullied. I'll let no man, be it my own brother, make a slut out of her.'

Will let out a whoop of laughter, and as they spun around to seek the source, he hastily backed away, out into the great hall, where he could indulge his mirth at length. It was, he decided, going to be an interesting summer.

Coventry's Lord Mayor was explaining at length to Edward how it was that the city had happened to cast its lot with Warwick. As he told it, it began to sound more and more like a vast misunderstanding, the too-trusting citizens gulled by the power-hungry Earl.

Richard soon lost interest, found his eyes wandering toward the window, where the sky was reddening in a dying blaze of light, in as beautiful a sunset as he could recall. He sighed, reluctantly sat up straighter in his chair as Edward gave him a look that was both admonitory and amused. What a waste of time suddenly precious! If the man would only get on with it, he might still be able to escape out into the gardens with Anne, watch together the passing of day.

Glancing around for a servant to refill his wine cup, Richard saw with surprise that Rob Percy was hovering in the open doorway, seeking anxiously to catch his eye. Richard slipped unobtrusively from his chair, crossed quickly to his friend.

Rob at once grabbed his arm, pulled him aside and blurted out in an urgent undertone, 'Get you to the great hall, and fast! Anne is in much need of you, and so is Francis.'

As they hastened down the winding stairwell, Rob elaborated upon his breathless summons. They'd been talking with Anne, he panted, when the Duke of Clarence did stride up and, without so much as a by your leave, told Anne that she was to depart for London within the hour. When she objected, he'd grabbed her arm and seemed about to take her from the great hall by force if need be. It was then that Francis tried to stop him. There was fear in Rob's voice, fear Richard could understand. George was a dangerous man to defy; Francis's foolhardy heroics might cost him dear.

The same thought had obviously occurred to Francis. He was saying in a low conciliatory voice, 'It's not my intent, Your Grace, to intrude into your affairs. It's only that I think your brother of Gloucester would wish to speak with the Lady Anne ere she. . . .'

Unlike Francis, who had no more colour in his face than new-fallen snow, Anne was so flushed she looked feverish. Seeing Richard now, she gave a glad little cry, let go of Francis's arm, and started toward him. Richard had reached her before George even realized he was in the hall, and as he looked down into her face, he was suddenly swept by a protective urge so strong it blotted all else from his brain.

'Oh, Richard, thank God you've come! Your brother. . . . He

says I must go to London, says I have no choice but to do what he commands.'

'Hush, sweetheart. It is all right. No one is going to make you do anything you do not want to do, not ever again. That I promise you, Anne.'

'Do not make promises you cannot keep, Dickon!'

Anne had an instant of instinctive recoil before remembering that she now had no need to fear George's threats. She raised her head, stared defiantly at George.

Richard, too, was staring at his brother. But he was aware, as well, of the others. Will Hastings was watching with alert interest; his eyes gave him away, however, glinted with suppressed laughter. John Howard, less urbane, showed only disapproval. Beyond Howard, Richard saw both Stanleys and, in the doorway, the Earl of Northumberland, looking on with the rather distant disdain of a Percy for the lower orders of mankind.

'I would suggest we discuss this in private, George,' Richard said, very low, and jerked his head toward the Presence Chamber.

'There is nothing to discuss. Anne is my sister-in-law, and if I choose to send her to my wife, it is none of your concern.'

'Anne is very much my concern,' Richard said evenly, 'and she does not want to go to London.'

A queer greenish light had begun to flicker in George's eyes. 'I tell you she goes to London tonight and you have nothing to say about it!'

'No? You'd best think again, George!'

Richard's voice had changed, betrayed his rising anger. Why George should have got it into his head to make a scene like this before a chamberful of avid witnesses, he did not know, no longer much cared. All that mattered to him at the moment was the troubled look on Anne's face, the way she clutched his arm. He shifted slightly so that he stood between her and George.

'I warn you, Dickon, keep out of this!'

At that, Richard lost all patience. 'I take no orders from you, George!'

He turned toward Anne, intending to take her from the hall. As he did, George grabbed his arm, wrenched brutally to swing him around, and suddenly Richard was aware only of physical pain, a searing surge of raw sensation unlike anything he'd ever experienced in his life. It took his breath, sent a sickening wave of queasiness up to lodge in his throat, and for several shuddering seconds there was only pain in his world, to the exclusion of all else. Through the roaring in his ears, he heard Francis's heated protest,

'That is his bad arm.'

George's grip had already begun to ease. Even through the red mists of an anger bordering beyond control, part of his brain recognized that something was wrong, took note that Richard had gone white as chalk, that sweat suddenly stood out on his forehead, his upper lip. He turned his head sharply as what Francis said registered with him, jerked his hand back as if burned.

There was disbelief on his face, but the first flickerings of uncertainty, too. 'His arm was healing. Barnet was more than three weeks ago.'

Francis was momentarily too outraged to remember he addressed a Prince of the blood and one, moreover, of a particularly unforgiving nature.

'It *was* healing,' he snapped. 'But he did lay it open again last week at Tewkesbury.' He looked toward Richard then, said with concern, 'Are you all right?'

Richard had managed to fight back the nausea, had managed to draw air back into his lungs. Not yet sure what control he exercised over his voice, he nodded and then looked at his brother. George was the first to look away and was the first, too, to exit the hall. Men moved hastily aside to let him pass.

Nothing was the same after that for Anne. She knew she could never face a second meal in that hall and she begged Richard to let her miss supper. Much to her relief, he agreed at once, said he was not hungry either, and as Vespers sounded, he led her, instead, out into the twilight dusk of the garden arbour that stretched north toward the River Sherbourne.

Anne's nerves were so taut that it was some time before she could appreciate just how beautiful an evening it was. He'd found for them a secluded retreat within a wall of willow and whitethorn; the sky was darkening into a delicately tinted violet and a crescent moon silvered the circling clouds over their heads. It was very quiet. She heard only the soft trilling of night birds, was becoming aware of the heavy honeysuckle scents of spring. She should have been able to draw comfort from such surroundings; somehow, it did not help at all.

Richard did not seem to be deriving much pleasure from the garden, either. Tense and edgy, he suddenly seemed to have little to say. She didn't believe his denials, knew his arm was paining him a great deal; she could see it in his face. She could see, too, that he'd been shaken by the quarrel and, with a pang of remorse, she remembered that he'd always been on fairly good terms with George. Until now.

For the first time that day, she was unwilling to have a silence fall between them, felt driven to link them with words, any words, and she began to talk at random about events that had happened long ago at Middleham, when the world was still a safe place and she'd been as sure of her tomorrows as she was of her yesterdays.

Richard, leaning against the trunk of a nearby birch, listened to her in silence, his dark head tilted to the left in a gesture long since burned into her memory. So often she'd seen him stand that way. She'd seen him do, too, what he now did—break off a sprig of thyme from the surrounding shrubbery. He was twirling the narrow leaves around nimble restless fingers, absently chewing on the mint-flavoured stem, and she smiled sadly, thinking that in all the years she'd known him, he could never be still. He had always to be in motion, even while attending morning Mass in

519

Middleham's chapel. She could see him even now, never able to kneel sedately for long, shifting impatiently on his prayer cushion, fidgeting with the ornate belt at his hip or with a ring, leafing through his Book of Hours until a frowning rebuke from her mother would propel him upright ... briefly. She sighed softly, not sure why the memory should make her sad, but it did. It was such a long time ago ... and so much had changed, changed forever, even if he did still seem so heartbreakingly familiar to her, as if they might have been parted only yesterday.

Reaching over, Richard lightly stroked her cheek with the last of the thyme flowerlets.

'If it is George who brings such shadows to your face, Anne, try to put your mind at ease. He'll not trouble you again. I'll see to that, *ma belle*. I do promise you.'

She shook her head, took the flower and let her fingers linger on his. 'No, it was not George. I was ... remembering.'

His hand tightened on hers and suddenly she was saying with breathless urgency, 'I never wanted to marry Lancaster, Richard. Never. I did try to resist. But I was not strong enough. I could not gainsay my father, not for long. ...'

So many subjects had gone unmentioned that day. By tacit consent, they'd drawn only upon the brightest splashes of colour, clung to the illusory security of Middleham memories. No explanations, just 'Do you remember?' And now she'd conjured up the most dangerous spirit of all, summoned Edouard of Lancaster into the garden to reclaim her as his wife, his would-be Queen.

Richard seemed no happier than she with this sudden intrusion of Lancaster into their refuge. She saw he was frowning and, before he could speak, she touched her fingers to his lips.

'No, Richard. ... Can we not forget I said that? I did not mean to, truly. I do not want to talk of Lancaster. ... Not now, not ever. I want only to forget. ...'

He was so close to her now that she knew he could have but one intent in mind. She waited, breathless, and then felt his fingers on her throat, caressing, tilting her face up to his. She let him kiss her and, rather timidly, put her arms around him as he drew her into a closer embrace.

He was not as gentle as he'd been that morning. His mouth was more insistent, until, without wanting to, she parted her lips for him. Of all she'd had to endure as Edouard of Lancaster's wife, she'd hated his kisses the most, hated the penetration of her mouth even more than of her body. During the act of coupling itself, she could at least try to separate her mind from what he was doing to her, but there had been no escaping the violation of her mouth, and only by swallowing convulsively could she keep from gagging at the feel and thrust of his tongue. She tensed as Richard kissed her and then felt a sweet surge of relief when the familiar revulsion did not come. How foolish she'd been! How could she have imagined it might be the same with Richard? Richard, whom she'd known and loved all her life. His mouth was warm and tasted pleasantly of mint. She relaxed and accepted the first kisses of her life that had not been forced upon her.

She closed her eyes, felt his mouth against her lashes, her eyelids, and then her throat. She drew a deep breath fragrant with lilac and clover, rested her cheek against his chest. Her tension was ebbing, already seemed to be part of another girl's past. She was finding it surprisingly pleasant to be here alone with him in the warm dark of the garden, to be held and touched and stroked, to hear her name whispered into her hair.

When it began to change for her, she couldn't say for sure. Perhaps when his kisses began to change; they were hotter now, more demanding. His body was hard against hers, suddenly un-familiar. His breathing had quickened considerably; hers came swift and shallow as she tried to overcome it, this sudden smoth-ering sensation, unpleasantly akin to the dreadful trapped feeling Lancaster had sparked each time he'd pulled her to him.

She was no longer holding on to Richard, had brought her hands up to rest against his chest, but she didn't know how to

521

tell him of her reluctance, of her returning fear. He was murmuring endearments she couldn't hear, for she couldn't seem to slow down her senses long enough to take in what he was saying, heard only his voice against her ear, low, coaxing.

He was caressing her breasts now; his hands were warm, like his mouth and his voice. He was far more gentle than Lancaster, seemed to be as intent upon learning her body as claiming it. But she knew it wouldn't last, this easy unhurried tenderness of his. She knew what would inevitably follow. Lancaster had taught her that. His kisses would grow wetter, deeper. Like Lancaster's. He would fondle her with increasing impatience, abrupt, eager, intent only upon taking his own pleasures, those urgent male pleasures she could neither comprehend nor share . . . like Lancaster. And afterward he'd watch her with puzzled dissatisfied eyes. He'd not reproach her for her lack of response, not call her 'cold' as Lancaster had done. He'd not have to; his eyes would say it all.

Twisting suddenly against him, she tore her mouth from his. 'No, Richard, do not! Let me go!'

Richard released her at once, so abruptly that she had to reach for an overhanging branch to keep her balance. He was stunned by her rebuff, by the violence of her rejection, his senses still reeling from the taste and touch and feel of her. His past passions had not prepared him for this intense and intoxicating need he had for Anne. He'd never wanted anything in his life as he now wanted this girl, wanted to make her soft fragrant body his own, to see that wealth of chestnut hair spread out on his pillow, to find her beside him when he awoke. A hunger she alone could fill. A hunger she did not share.

'I'm sorry,' he said stiffly. 'It was not my intent to . . . to take advantage of you in any way.'

'Oh, Richard . . . do not!' Her voice was trembling; she seemed on the verge of tears. 'You owe me no apologies. You did nothing wrong. And I . . . I was not rejecting you. It was not that. It was. . . .'

She turned away, retreated into the protective shadow of a white ash. 'I was afraid,' she said, very low. 'If you do want the truth, there it is. I was afraid.'

Anne's face was burning and she rested her cheek against the spongy damp moss that crept like a patchy grey-green carpet up the side of the tree. Its coolness didn't help; she still felt as if her blood had been scalded, her skin blistered from within.

'Anne. . . .' Richard was beside her now under the ash, but he made no move to touch her, was unsure what to say. His own emotions were in such a state of confusion that he doubted he'd ever be able to sort them out. Relief, relief infinite and over-whelming that he'd so misread her reluctance. Jealousy and an embittered futile anger, futile in that the object of his rage was beyond all retribution, could never be called to account for the hurt he'd done Anne. Above all, a sudden surge of tenderness such as he'd never before felt for anyone, not even Kate.

'Anne, I . . . I'm sorry I did not understand. I know you do not want to talk of Lancaster and, in truth, neither do I. I just want to say . . . to say that I'd never cause you hurt. Never, love.' He touched her cheek, in a caress as uncertain as it was gentle, and was much relieved when she turned her head, brushed her lips against his fingers.

'I know that, Richard,' she whispered. 'Truly I do.'

'Anne. . . . There be this I must tell you. We've got to be able to be honest with each other and I want you to know that I'll understand if . . . if it does upset you.'

Her eyes were enormous, looked suddenly frightened, and he said hastily, 'You know I did command the vanguard at Tewkesbury for Ned, and he was most generous afterward, told me to name my own reward. Anne . . . I've asked him for Middleham.'

'And you thought that might upset me?' Anne was staring at him in unfeigned astonishment. 'Oh, Richard, how could you think so? I knew Middleham would be forfeit; there was never any question of that. And there is no one I would rather see have it than you. No one! I know how you love it; Middleham was home to you.'

'And to you,' Richard said quietly. He very much wanted to kiss her; he didn't, took her hand, instead.

'Come,' he said. 'I'll lead you back.'

A strange expression crossed her face, both wistful and bitter. 'If only you could,' she whispered.

Richard had become accustomed to being summoned to his brother without warning and at odd hours of the day or night. Generally, he was flattered by such tangible proof of how much Ned had come to rely upon his judgment, but not tonight. Tonight the last place he wanted to be was in Ned's bedchamber whilst his brother related a rather lengthy account of his meeting that afternoon with Lord Mayor Bette.

One of Edward's servants was leaning over Richard with a silver flagon, and he nodded, reached for his cup as soon as it had been refilled. So far the wine had not helped much but it might if he had enough of it. He could not even remember the last time he'd felt so out-of-sorts. As much as he hated the thought of it, he'd have to see Ned's physician tonight, for if he did not get something to dull the pain, he'd be awake till dawn. Though, if he were to be honest with himself, the major source of his discomfort was not his arm. It had been several years since he'd suffered the uncomfortable aftermath of thwarted desire; he'd forgotten how bloody awful it felt. He wondered briefly if it was too late to do something about it. It was nigh on ten; the inns would be closed by now. A town the size of Coventry would surely have its share of bawdy houses. But he did not want a whore. He wanted Anne.

Edward was saying something about taking from the city their civic sword and Richard made an appropriate sound that could pass for agreement. How was it that he'd not even remembered he'd had an arm when he was with Anne and now it felt as if it were being held over a roasting spit?

He found some relief in silently cursing his absent brother but not much. George was not the only fool in the family. How could he have been so blind? She was so fearful. . . . Why had he not foreseen that? He should have known, should have been better prepared for this. But how could any man have maltreated Anne? Anne, who was so fragile, so utterly without defences. To hurt Anne would be like turning a gerfalcon upon a butterfly. He drank again, beckoned to the hovering attendant.

But what if he could not overcome her fears? She'd said she wanted only to forget. What if she could not? The truth was that he had never tried to coax an unwilling woman to his bed. He was accustomed to ardent bedmates like Kate and Nan, or to knowing harlots. How would he go about gentling the fears of a girl who knew only the worst of what a man could teach a maid? Patience. . . . As much patience as his own needs would allow. But was that enough? A pity there was not some way he could seek Ned's advice without asking outright. From what he'd seen of Ned's appetites in the past year, Ned did not seem much inclined to bed a woman who was not as hot for it as he, but he must have had some experience in overcoming the qualms of timid virgins. When it came to hungers of the flesh, Richard suspected there was very little Ned did not know about, and what there was most probably was not worth knowing. But he could not possibly ask Ned without betraying himself.

'. . . and so there you have it, Dickon. If they cannot pay the ten thousand marks by noon Monday next, a gallows shall be set up in Cross Cheaping and. . . .'

'Ten thousand! Gallows . . . Ned, what . . .' Richard caught on, but too late. He waited patiently until Edward had stopped laughing at him and then said ruefully, '*Mea culpa*; I confess I was not listening. What did you truly choose to assess against Coventry?'

'I did declare the city liberties forfeit and graciously agreed that they could be redeemed by the payment of five hundred marks. I shall later let myself be persuaded to accept only three hundred marks and they'll consider themselves quite fortunate; far more so than if I forbore to claim any penalty at all.'

Richard laughed but stopped abruptly when Edward said, 'Now, shall I give you some advice?'

'No!' he said hastily, and Edward grinned, not at all put out.

'Ah, but I shall, anyway. It's plain enough that you've had a falling-out with your little cousin, else you'd not be brooding about like a man expecting a visitation from the Angel of Death. So, for what it's worth, my advice is this. . . . Give the lass time. Her whole world has been torn asunder in little more than a twelve-month. Give her the chance to come to terms with it all.'

Richard had been braced for the worst, all too aware that his brother's sense of humour was unpredictable at best, and knowing, too, that Edward tended to view women with the appreciation of a smiling huntsman for a particularly elusive quarry. What Edward had just said was so sensible, so far removed from the ribald jest he'd been expecting to hear, that he found himself asking, 'What, then, would you suggest?'

'I'd send her on to London, to Isabel.' Seeing Richard's protest taking shape, Edward forestalled it by saying, 'I was watching your Anne at dinner. When she looks at you, her heart shows in her eyes, as if you'll disappear into smoke should you be out of her sight for even a moment. But what shows, too, is that she's been ill-used. She needs time to comprehend fully that she's truly free of Lancaster. Time, too, I would wager, to convince herself that you do still care for her. Give her over into her sister's keeping for now, little brother. It is scarcely the separation of a lifetime, after all. We will ourselves be in London within the fortnight.'

After a long silence, Richard nodded reluctantly. 'There is sense in what you say,' he admitted, for it occurred to him that he, too, could use some time to think upon his feelings for Anne.

Since boyhood, he'd taken it for granted that he and Anne

would one day wed; the seed planted by Warwick had taken root so gradually that he could not recall a time when he had not expected to marry Anne. It made sense, after all. Anne was pretty, sweet-tempered, an heiress. She'd make a most suitable wife for him and such a match would please two men he cared greatly about pleasing, his Neville cousins. But it was not until Anne was plight-trothed to Lancaster that he'd realized just how much he cared.

Richard slouched down in his seat, tried in vain to find a position that would ease his aching arm. Raking up the past was irrelevant. What did matter were his feelings now. If Anne loved him, he must be very sure in his own mind as to what she meant to him. What if she gave her heart over into his keeping and he then found that what he felt for her was no more than memory and desire coloured by pity? He did not think that was true but could he be sure? He'd been shaken by the fear she'd shown tonight, more than he liked to admit. One thing he did know, that he could not tolerate the thought of her being hurt again.

'You did have Dr de Serego look at that arm, I trust? I know you shy away from doctors like a skittish horse from snakes but infection could set in if you do not take care. You did see him, Dickon?'

Richard was not all that surprised by this abrupt interrogation; he'd more or less been expecting it.

He nodded, said with resignation, 'Who told you?'

'Who did not?' Dryly.

'Good Samaritans, all,' Richard said, with some bitterness, and Edward shrugged.

'You could hardly have expected otherwise, Dickon. What does surprise me is that you did not see this coming. The signs were there, as far back as Windsor.'

'For God's sake, Ned, do not gloat!'

Edward looked mildly offended. 'I assure you that was not my intent.' But after a moment, the corner of his mouth twitched.

'Yes, I guess it was. But can you honestly fault me for it? There's

527

no sweeter temptation, save one, than to say 'I told you so,' after all.'

'I can see little humour, Ned, in what did occur this afternoon,' Richard said coolly, starting to rise.

Edward waved him back into his chair. Adept at reading voices, he'd caught the undertones of hurt beneath the surface gloss of anger; his grin faded.

'You're right, of course, Dickon. It was not amusing. It was not amusing at all. Look, I admit I find a certain satisfaction in having your eyes opened to George as I know him to be. But I take no pleasure in your pain, lad. And I do understand. You've always been the one to speak up for George. Only Meg turned a blinder eye to his faults. If there is a man who'd have the right to expect his goodwill, that man should be you.'

That was precisely how Richard did feel—betrayed. His mouth twisted. 'If I have his goodwill, then Christ keep me from his enmity!'

They were alone in the room now; Richard reached for the wine flagon, poured for them both.

'I do not understand him, Ned,' he confessed. 'Does he truly believe it is the Warwick lands I want, not Anne? Does he know me as little as that?'

'As to your first question, he does not need to believe it; for George, the mere suspicion is enough. As to your second question, I do not think he can accept what is to him incomprehensible, that money motivates you so little. You must remember, Dickon, that with George, more is never enough.'

'Yes, but. . . .' Richard stopped so abruptly that Edward looked up in surprise, saw that Richard was staring over his shoulder toward the open doorway. He turned around in his seat just as George walked into the chamber.

By the time he'd retreated from the great hall, George's anger was no longer pure, was diluted by a clouded, murky splash of shame. Nothing had turned out as he'd intended. He'd not meant to feed gossip with a scene sure to give such pleasure to those who hated him. Nor had he meant to cause fresh hurt to Dickon's arm. He remembered now that Ned had, indeed, said something to him about the arm, said that Dickon had inflamed it again with his exertions upon the field Saturday last. But it had gone completely from his head. All he'd been able to think of was the way Dickon was meddling where he had no right to meddle, making a fool of him before a score or more of witnesses. Surely Dickon must know it had not been deliberate. But a nagging uncertainty remained, fuelled by the memory of that incredulous accusing look on his brother's face.

He found himself wishing that the entire unpleasant encounter had never happened and, for the first time within adult memory, he was pulled by vague ill-formed promptings toward an apology of sorts. He felt somewhat better after making that decision and, before long, another idea, too, had come to him, startling at first in its novelty but intriguing, nonetheless. Why not talk to Dickon, openly and honestly, about the lands? Dickon was fair more often than not, in all matters not touching upon his besotted unreasoning loyalty to Ned. Perhaps he could be made to see the unfairness of it. He had no need for the Warwick and Beauchamp lands. Ned was sure to load his coffers with silver to give him first pick of the estates forfeited by the Lancastrian rebels. Lands Ned was not bloody well likely to share with him. All he had were the Neville estates. It was not fair that Dickon should cast covetous eyes upon them, too. It was not fair.

But George's conciliatory impulses were given a severe jolt at sight of Edward and Richard sitting together, like two conspirators bent upon excluding him from their confidence, their company. He held to his resolve, however, even summoned a passable smile.

'I hope you did not take our set-to this afternoon too much to heart, Dickon.'

'I took it for what it was worth,' Richard said, with an icy unfriendliness that could not have quenched George's forgiving spirits more thoroughly than if he had upended his wine cup in George's lap.

'I see,' George said. Oh, yes, indeed he saw. His eyes cut to Edward, quick enough to catch an amused gleam.

'I should have known you'd have wasted no time in going whining to Ned!'

'I'm beginning to think that what you know could be inscribed upon the head of a pin and with space to spare!' Richard snapped, and Edward said hastily,

'Enough, both of you!' He no longer saw anything humorous in this, not at all. It was one thing for Dickon at last to see George as he truly was. It was another thing altogether to have them seriously at odds. He'd seen all too well with his cousin Warwick the dangers that discontent did breed.

'Dickon did not come to me carrying tales, George. You should know him better than that. I assume you have something on your mind? Well then, I would suggest you sit down and we do hear you out.'

George did and after some moments of awkward silence, blurted, 'Look, Dickon, about your arm. . . . That was pure bad luck, no more than that.'

Richard said nothing and George fidgeted in his seat, finally forced himself to offer, 'If you want me to say I'm sorry. . . .'

'I'll tell you what I do want from you, George. I want you to keep away from Anne, to stay out of her life. Is that clear?'

George's outrage was now all the greater because he could assure himself that he'd done what he could to put things right between them.

'You seem to forget that Anne is my sister-in-law and Bella would little like the way you've been fondling her sister within sight of all. Still less would she like what was being whispered about the great hall this noon, that if Anne's not to be Lancaster's Queen, she's now quite willing to be Gloucester's harlot!'

Richard's hand tightened convulsively upon his wine cup. But even as he formed the intent to fling it in his brother's face, he felt Edward's hand clamp down upon his wrist.

'Careful, Dickon, you almost did spill your drink. As it happens, George, your touching concern for your sister-in-law's honour is somewhat misplaced. Dickon and I were only a short while ago agreeing it would be best for the lass if she were sent tomorrow to Isabel.'

'You did!' George gaped at them in utter astonishment and then turned upon Richard a blindingly radiant smile.

'I cannot tell you how that does relieve my mind, Dickon! I have a duty to the girl after all; surely you see that?'

Richard was not pleased with Edward for intervening as he did and he said swiftly, intent upon wiping that triumphant smile from George's face, 'I think Anne does have need of Bella and that is why I agreed . . . for that reason and that alone. But this I do tell you, George, and you'd best heed what I say. She stays at the Herber only until the day she does complain to me of the first discourtesy you show her . . . however slight.'

'I am not one to maltreat a woman, Dickon, and I resent you implying it were so.'

'Just be sure you treat her kindly, George. If not because she is your sister-by-marriage and kin to us both, then you'd damned well better do so because I mean to make her my wife.'

This was not strictly true; Richard was not yet sure of the exact nature of his feelings for Anne. He did know how he felt about George, though—angrier than he'd ever been in his life, angry enough to want to wound, to hit where it would hurt the most. He saw at once that he'd succeeded beyond all his expectations.

George was momentarily rendered speechless by this sudden shocking confirmation of his greatest fear.

'Blood of Christ!' he managed to get out, in a voice nearly strangled with emotion. 'You cannot mean that! That you truly crave Middleham as much as that, enough to take Lancaster's leavings in order to claim it!'

For a big man, Edward could move with surprising speed when the need arose. As quick as Richard was, he was quicker. As Richard lunged forward, he found himself flung back into his chair and held there, far from gently.

'Easy, lad,' Edward said soothingly but at the same time not scrupling to use ample force to keep Richard penned against his chair.

Richard was no match for his brother's strength. Moreover, he'd done his injured arm no good. The sudden pain went far toward clearing his head; he stopped struggling.

As soon as he did, Edward let him go, turned pale fathomless eyes upon George.

'Passing over the blatant bad taste of that remark, George, it's far from accurate. Dickon does not need Anne Neville to lay claim to Middleham.'

George, who'd been taken aback by Richard's violent reaction, swung around to stare at Edward. 'What mean you by that, Ned?'

'I think my meaning should be clear enough. Middleham was Warwick's, was not part of his wife's Beauchamp estates. That means it now belongs to the crown . . . to me, George, to do with as I please. And it pleases me to give it to Dickon.'

'Ned, you cannot! It's not fair!'

'No? Well, take a deep breath, Brother George,' Edward said derisively, 'because Middleham is only a portion of the grant I do intend to make. Of the lands Warwick held in the North, Penrith and Sheriff Hutton, too, are to go to Dickon.'

'God damn you, you cannot!' George's voice was shaking. 'I'll not let you. Those lands by rights are mine.'

Edward's temper wanted only a spark to ignite it, now kindled. 'I'd advise you to guard your tongue,' he said warningly. 'Or perhaps you need a reminder that what you hold today, you hold only at my sufferance.'

George gasped and then suddenly struck out at the wine cups and flagon, sent them spinning with a wild sweep of his arm. Richard and Edward came hastily to their feet, Edward staring in disbelief at the wine splashes on his hose.

'If I thought you meant to do that. . . .' He came around the table so rapidly that George took a backward step. But he retreated no farther; instead, repeated hoarsely,

'Ned, you cannot do this. You cannot.'

Edward had himself in hand again. He unclenched a fist, reached out to catch George's wrist in a grip that would later leave bruises.

'If I must take the time and trouble to teach you what I can and cannot do, George, I can promise you it will not be a lesson to your liking.'

George jerked free, opened his mouth, embittered accusations blistering his tongue. But the words caught in his throat, as his body reacted in instinctive understanding to what he saw within his brother's eyes, a small raw flame that measured, appraised, made a promise that was, in every sense, a threat.

He turned blindly to go, only to be frozen into immobility by the sound of Edward's voice, the sound of sovereignty, devoid of all but authority.

'I did not hear you ask for my leave to withdraw, my lord of Clarence.'

Moving as jerkily as a puppet with tangled strings, George managed to come forward; his lips grazed his brother's coronation ring, set in a blaze of blood-red rubies.

Edward turned to Richard, said with a snarl, 'I swear to Christ I think maggots do rot his brain! What queer, twisted logic guides him, I'll never know, but never have I seen a man so eager to doom himself.'

He raged on for several moments longer but his temper was already cooling rapidly; he was beginning to see what a problem was posed by George's intransigence. He knew George to be capable of any folly. He was vexing beyond endurance, stupid in a sly sort of way, and lusted for land as another man might lust after women. But he was dangerous, too. He'd proven that more than once.

He'd have to be given something, have to be bought off in some way. Either that or have his head stricken from his shoulders. If he only knew how thin ran the blood that now stood between him and the block on Tower Green. But bought off with what? Dickon would be well content with Middleham alone. But it was his need, not Dickon's, that did concern him. He meant for Dickon to hold the North for him. That was more important than anything else, to have a man he could trust to keep the country quiet north of the Trent. That meant Dickon had to hold Sheriff Hutton, too. He inhaled sharply, let his breath escape very slowly. Perhaps it was just as well that the Countess of Warwick had chosen so conveniently to sequester herself at Beaulieu Abbey.

He looked down in disgust at the scattered wine cups, swore again, and then said abruptly, 'What you saw tonight is but a foretaste of what you'll have to contend with from George if you do, in fact, want to wed the Neville girl. If you should decide you must have her, I'll back you; that goes without saying. But I cannot very well cage George within the Tower because he covets land that is not his . . . however much I might like to. So I would ask this much of you. Be sure that you truly want the girl, that she is worth all the trouble you'll have to go through to get her. Just be sure, Dickon.'

3

London

May 1471

Richard had been given the honour of leading the victory procession into London, mounted on a burnished chestnut stallion, his armour ablaze with light, damascened with his brother's Sunbursts and his own Whyte Boars. The sky was a sea of blue over his head; white roses rained from open windows, lay browning in the sun in dying tribute to the victorious Yorkists. Pretty girls waved scarves of murrey and blue, and veterans of the French campaigns saluted him as he rode by, drank his health in oceans of ale. Richard was flushed with pride; to be acclaimed as a battle commander of proven abilities was the highest accolade he could imagine. Laughing, guiding his mount through a shower of flung white roses, he thought this was a day he'd never forget.

The Yorkist cavalcade had ended at the Tower Palace, where Edward's Queen and children awaited him. George had ridden at once to the Herber, the manor house he'd taken over upon Warwick's death. Richard, who was to leave at dawn the next day in pursuit of Fauconberg, hoped to find the time that night to visit the Herber himself, for he'd not seen Anne for nine days now. But first he'd gone to Baynard's Castle. Almost at once, though, had come a courier from his brother, summoning him back to the Tower.

Mounting the stairs that led to the top floor of the White Tower keep, Richard found himself wondering why Ned should so suddenly have need of him again; he'd not have thought Ned likely to leave Elizabeth's bed till Vespers. But all such speculation was forgotten at sight of the woman emerging from the Council Chamber, a handsome rather heavy woman in her early thirties, his sister Anne, Duchess of Exeter.

Taken aback, Richard supposed she'd come to plead for her husband. Exeter, who had been severely wounded at Barnet and was lodged here in the Tower as a prisoner of state.

'Dickon! Dearest!'

He was even more taken aback when she enveloped him in a perfumed embrace, smeared lip rouge liberally across his cheek.

'You must come and dine with me at Coldharbour. I shall be looking forward to it.'

Ned must have agreed to pardon Exeter, Richard decided, marvelling at her sudden sisterly affection; on the occasions he'd seen her in recent years, she'd shown him little more than absent-minded politeness.

Edward was standing by an open window, looking down upon the royal residence that lay just east of the Garden Tower. He turned now, said with a smile, 'I see you bear the brand of Sister Anne.'

Richard found a handkerchief, wiped once or twice at his cheek. 'What brought her here, Ned? She wants Exeter freed?'

'Not unless it be by way of the executioner's axe.' Seeing Richard's surprise, Edward gave a brief laugh. 'No, it is her own freedom she seeks. It seems that whilst Exeter was in exile, she found another to take to her bed. I daresay it was a grievous disappointment to her that he survived Barnet. Be that as it may, she wants my support in dissolving the marriage; wants, as well, my consent to marry her present paramour. Not that she put it as bluntly as that, mind you, but her meaning was plain enough.'

'I gather from the kiss I got that you agreed to both?'

Edward nodded. 'I canot say I blame her for wanting to be

536

shed of Exeter. Regrettably, her current choice is little better than the one she did have forced upon her as a little lass. Thomas St Leger. . . . You know him?'

Richard found the memory he sought. 'One of your esquires of the body? Was he not the one who got himself into a brawl a few years ago, came to blows with one of your marshals right in the palace, was to have his hand cut off as punishment till you intervened on his behalf? Am I thinking of the right man?'

Edward smiled. 'That's Tom, all right, and not the first time I've had to pull his chestnuts from the fire. He's a likable sort but none too bright. Still, if he is what Anne wants . . . In truth, I do not really much care, one way or the other.'

Richard did not much care, either; Anne was a virtual stranger to him. 'I cannot foresee any problem with His Holiness the Pope. But ma mère might be another matter altogether. You know she holds that marriage be for life, no matter the circumstances.'

'As to that, we did strike a bargain. I deal with the Vatican, she deals with Baynard's Castle.'

He gestured toward the sideboard. 'Pour us from that flask of vernage, Dickon. That is your favourite, is it not?'

Richard nodded, did as he was bade. Edward generally kept a servant or two always at hand, for his own convenience, and Richard thought it odd that his brother should be all alone like this, today of all days.

'Your summons did take me somewhat by surprise,' he said candidly. 'I would have expected you to linger longer with the Queen.' Like all the family, he'd fallen into the habit of referring to his sister-in-law by her title; it was far safer that way, for God forbid, he thought, that any of them should slip and make free with her Christian name!

Edward merely shrugged. 'I intend to call a council meeting tonight, after Compline. I wanted to speak to you beforehand, hence the summons.'

Richard's heart sank. A council meeting tonight meant he'd have no chance to seek out Anne at the Herber, would have to leave London in the morning without seeing her at all.

'I was hoping I might be able to see Anne tonight,' he chose to remind Edward now, saw the latter shake his head.

'Dickon, sit down. I have a question to put to you. It's one you'll not much like, but it's something I do need to know.'

'All right, Ned,' Richard said slowly, sat down in the seat indicated. 'What is it?'

'There's no easy way to ask. I want you to tell me if you think Anne could be carrying Lancaster's child.'

'No!'

Richard started to rise but Edward reached across the table, caught his arm.

'Think carefully, Dickon. Are you sure?'

Richard sank back in his seat. The very thought was so abhorrent to him that he found it almost impossible to consider it dispassionately, but he trusted Edward, knew the question had been prompted by a legitimate concern and not mere morbid curiosity.

'Yes, I'm sure. It's been nigh on six weeks since Barnet. I do not think he did . . . did touch her after that, after they knew her to be of no further use to them. If she thought she might be with child, I believe she would have told me.'

Edward nodded. 'Yes, I agree with you, Dickon. I think she would, too. The girl does love you and she's far from a fool, besides, would know what it would mean if she were breeding.'

'And now that you're sure she's not? What does that mean to you, Ned?'

'I think you do know that already, Dickon.'

When Richard shook his head, too vehemently, Edward leaned back in his chair, said, 'Your face says otherwise, but if you do want me to spell it out, I will. If I did think Anne were pregnant with Lancaster's child, there'd be no point then in doing what I mean to do tonight.'

He should have been shocked; why was he not? What shock there was came not from Ned's matter-of-fact admission but from the realization that there was so little surprise, that he'd somehow known what Ned had in mind, had known ever since that moment in the Bishop of London's Palace.

'Oh, Jesus, Ned, not that addled old man. . . .'

'As long as Harry of Lancaster does live, there will be those to plot on his behalf, to stir up rebellion in his name. I can see no way to end that risk other than by ending his life. I will not pretend I like it any but I do not need to like it. It is enough that it need be done, that I'm willing to have it done.'

'You held him in the Tower for nigh on six years without doing him harm, without resorting to murder.'

'As long as he had a son alive and free in France, it would have been a needless cruelty to put him to death and stupid as well. I do not think I'm any more cruel than most men and I'm most assuredly not stupid, Dickon.'

What seemed particularly repellent to Richard was that they could be talking of it so calmly, discussing over a wine flagon the murder of a harmless half-wit, a man, moreover, who'd once been an anointed king, however flawed his title.

'Ned, you'd never have stained your honour with a woman's blood, even a woman as guilt-cursed as Marguerite d'Anjou. But do you not see? To kill that poor pathetic creature in the Tower would be no less shameful, no less dishonourable.'

Richard saw something flicker darkly within his brother's eyes at that, saw Ned was not quite as detached about this as he would wish to appear. Somehow, that made Richard feel better, if only a little. He did not really expect to be able to talk Ned out of it; once Ned made up his mind to a thing, he was not one to be swayed from his resolve. If Ned was set upon doing this, he'd have no choice but to accept it, however little he liked it. But what he could not have accepted would have been to believe Ned capable of putting Lancaster to death without qualm, without reluctance. He needed to see that it would hurt, that it would leave a scar.

'Dickon, do you remember that night in Bruges, the night we drank together at the Gulden Vlies? Do you remember what I told you that night, that so much of what had happened was my own fault? It was not just Johnny, Dickon. I was unwilling to see coming trouble till it did have me by the throat. How else could I have let myself be taken at Olney? And again at Doncaster. No, I was too quick to trust, too slow to suspect. And I came close, Christ, so close to losing all. I've made my share of mistakes in my life but I've never been one to repeat the same ones. Harry of Lancaster is a threat, poses a threat with every breath he does take. If I can have done with that danger only by stopping that breath, then so be it.'

'You could keep him fast within the Tower, Ned. You need not go to so extreme a measure; at least, not now. Why not wait? . . . See if in fact there be risings stirred up on his behalf?'

'Dickon, as long as he lives, he will be a rallying point for rebels, a source of dissension within the realm. As long as he lives, there will be malcontents willing to make use of him, to foment rebellion in the guise of restoring him to the throne, to focus discontent around his person, no matter how securely caged he be. As long as he lives, Dickon.'

Richard could muster no effective argument to that; there was too much truth in what Edward said. It was not that he could not understand the cold logic in what Edward meant to do. He just did not like it any.

'You'll not heed me, I know. But I wish to God you'd not do this, Ned,' he said softly. 'I do not care about Lancaster. How sweet can life be to a man who seems not to know or care whether he be hailed as King one week and prisoner the next? It is not Lancaster, Ned. . . . It is you.'

The corner of Edward's mouth quirked. 'My immortal soul, Dickon?'

Richard nodded sombrely, watched his brother with dark troubled eyes, but he saw no sign that Edward had been affected by his plea.

'You might be taking upon yourself a guilt God could not forgive,' he cautioned quietly, was startled when Edward shrugged.

'As to that, Dickon, I'll know only when called to account before the Throne of God. But for now, what does concern me most is the throne at Westminster.'

Richard's eyes widened fractionally. There were times when he thought Ned treaded perilously close to blasphemy. It occurred to him uneasily now that when he offered up prayers for the repose of the souls of his dead father and brother, he might do well to pray, too, for Ned.

He conceded then, asked reluctantly, 'When will it be done? Tonight?'

'After the council meeting.'

That was a meeting Richard would as soon have missed. He came to his feet, feeling as tired suddenly as if he'd spent fully three days in the saddle without rest.

'As you will, Ned. Only. . . .' He hesitated and then blurted out unhappily, 'Only I cannot forget what he said to you that day at the Bishop's Palace. . . . That he knew his life would be safe in your hands. Jesus, Ned, if I cannot forget, how can you to whom it was said?'

'Enough, Dickon! That's more than enough!'

The fury in his brother's face was such that Richard recoiled, pulled back from an anger that had come, like lightning from an empty sky, without warning, sudden, intense, and searing.

'I called you to me to do you the courtesy of telling you before the others. A courtesy it was, no more than that. It was not my intent to argue with you about it. The decision is mine to make and yours to accept and I'll hear no more on it from you. . . . Not now, not tonight. Above all, not tonight. Is that clear?'

Richard nodded wordlessly. Never before had he borne the full brunt of Edward's wrath; he found it to be more unnerving than he cared to admit.

He'd been dismissed; that he knew without need of words. He halted at the door, said miserably, 'Ned, I'm sorry if I've let you down in this. I did not mean to, but . . .'

He saw Edward's eyes soften at that. 'I shall see you tonight, Dickon,' he said.

Richard still hesitated. 'Ned, I would rather not attend if it be all right with you. . . .'

'It would not.' Tersely. 'The meeting is to be held in this chamber, to start at eight. Be on time.'

There was little for Richard to do then but depart. He slammed the door behind him. It didn't help. It came as a distinct surprise to him, as he emerged out into the inner Tower bailey, to find the day still warmed by a dusk-fall sun, to see the faces of those he encountered still stretched in smiles, still showing the pleasure all had taken in the heartfelt welcome London had accorded the House of York.

The Council Chamber was lit by torches, the windows open to the slowly cooling night air. The room was wrapped in silence. Of the nine men assembled there, seven now watched Edward. Richard alone did not. He was standing apart, leaning against a far wall, his expression sullen; he'd not spoken half a dozen words since the council began. Edward looked over at him briefly and then away, back toward the others.

George showed only indifference. The other men, though, shared a surprisingly similar expression, one of distaste bordering upon discomfort. Both Edward's brothers-by-marriage, Suffolk and Anthony Woodville, had once been Lancastrian in their loyalties, had once pledged fealty to the man Edward now meant to murder. Uneasy memories of all-but-forgotten loyalties showed briefly in their faces. Neither spoke, however; Edward had known they wouldn't. The Earl of Essex was regarding him with dismay.

To so pious a man as Essex, what Edward meant to do was a mortal sin, would imperil his very soul. But Essex, too, said nothing. Edward's Chancellor, Robert Stillington, was Bishop of Bath and Wells; he, of all men, should have been arguing against the death of an innocent. He was, instead, giving his total attention to the spillover of a sputtering candle, scraping industriously with his thumbnail at the sticky wax drippings. Edward's eyes passed over the priest with a thinly veiled contempt, came to rest upon Will Hastings and John Howard. Hardheaded realists, the both of them, they could see the need in it. Edward knew that; knew, too, that they did not like it any better than Richard.

With the possible exception of George, there was not a man in the room who did, he thought now. Not a one of them would not have been grateful for it had Harry of Lancaster died suddenly in his sleep, choked to death on a chicken bone, took a chill that proved fatal. But not a one of them was comfortable with the thought of hastening Harry through Heaven's gate. He'd been expecting just such a reaction, however—knew they were likely to be squeamish at putting to death a man so simple that many viewed him as saintly.

He saw John Howard twist around in his chair, look toward Richard. That, too, came as no surprise to Edward. Richard had raised his wine cup to his mouth; it served to shield his thoughts. If he was aware of John's scrutiny, he gave no sign. Howard turned back to Edward, said as if each word were to be measured upon its own merits, 'Is that truly necessary, Your Grace?'

'Do you think I could bring myself to it if it was not, Jack?' Edward said bitingly, saw a faint red tinge work its way up the older man's face and neck.

And that was it. None would oppose him in this, would even voice a protest at this murder that both soothed their insecurities and scratched their consciences. It was as he'd known it would be, for that afternoon he'd seen to the one risk he could foresee. Had he sprung it upon Dickon in council, he knew the boy would have burst out with the very objections he'd made so heatedly in private this afternoon. And he might well have carried the others along with him ... Essex and Anthony for certes, possibly even Will and Suffolk. What great risk would there have been, after all, in backing up the brother whom all knew to be as his other self? And then he'd have had the nasty task of over-riding his own council, of having to argue for murder whilst they did argue for mercy. And over all, festering like an airborne pesti-lence, would hover the seeds of dissension, wanting only to take root. He'd had no intention of letting it come to that, had taken Dickon aside this afternoon to see that it would not, but he allowed himself a brief acknowledgment of relief that it had not, that all had gone as he wanted.

'Well then, I trust we are in agreement as to what must be done?' It was a purely rhetorical question, of course. He waited a moment or so, and then said, 'I want word conveyed to Lord Dudley. As Constable of the Tower, it shall fall upon him to see that my orders be carried out.' He shifted his gaze about the table, moved from face to face.

'Will, you and Anthony shall be the ones to tell Dudley what I want done.' He flicked his eyes suddenly toward his brother. 'You, too, Dickon.'

John Howard looked relieved that he'd not been named, George slightly offended for the same reason. There was resignation on Will's face, on Anthony's, too. Richard was staring at him, staring in disbelief.

'Me?'

'You are Lord Constable of England, are you not?'

'Yes, but. . . .'

'But what, Dickon? Whom do you think Dudley would expect to get such an order from if not my lord Constable?'

Richard was trapped and knew it. There was appeal in the look he now gave Edward and, when he saw it to be unavailing, anger.

'Do you want me, too, to view the body for you, my liege?' he said, very low, and for a moment, Edward wondered if he'd gone too far, asked too much.

It was true that he did not want his council to wonder why he had not turned, as he would normally and naturally have done, to the one who held both the Lord Constableship and his trust. But it occurred to him now that it might have been better to let them wonder. An ugly and unexpected thought came to him. Was he, in fact, paying Dickon back for what the boy had said this afternoon . . . for daring to remind him of what he'd most like to forget? 'I do know, cousin, that in your hands my life will not be in danger.' And the worst of it was that Lancaster had meant it, meant every appallingly innocent word of it.

He became aware now of the strained silence, saw they all were staring at him. He wondered how much had showed in his face— more, he suspected, than he would have liked. Well, it was done now . . . or almost so. As for Dickon, he could make it up to him, and would. He was suddenly impatient to have it over with, part of the past and beyond recall.

Will saw, rose reluctantly to his feet. As he did, Edward said abruptly, 'There is this I would say to you all, and then I do not expect to speak of this again. I am no Henry Fitz-Empress to say of Lancaster as Henry did of the martyr Thomas Becket, "Will none rid me of this turbulent priest?" The decision made here tonight is mine, the responsibility mine, and the guilt, if any, mine. Now, Will, Dickon. See Dudley for me. Tell him that it is to be done quick . . . and clean. Tell him, too, that there's to be no conspicuous wound. There will, after all, have to be a state funeral.'

If possible, it became even quieter after that. It was then that George chose to make his first contribution to the conversation.

'The Tower where Lancaster is kept is called the Wakefield Tower, is it not?'

Never had Edward been less in the mood for George's non sequiturs. 'What of it, George?'

545

'Well, it just occurred to me that the bloody ground upon which our father and brother died be known as Wakefield Green. Rather fitting, is it not?'

Edward stared at him. 'Yes,' he said slowly. 'I would expect you to think so.'

Elizabeth had lavished considerable care upon her appearance that night. Her ladies made skilful use of kohl and belladonna to bring out the green of her eyes, sprinkled gold dust over hair lightened with lemon and polished with silk. She'd bathed in rosewater, selected a perfume newly come from Alexandria and then made herself comfortable in bed to await her husband.

He did not come. The hours passed. She was at first impatient and then angry and at last, uneasy. It had been fully thirty-three days since Ned had lain with her. Surely he'd not have shunned her bed for the arms of a harlot, tonight of all nights.

She fumed to no avail. Finally exhaustion won out over anger and she slept. Sometime during the night, however, she rolled over, found herself against warm skin. So he'd come after all. She was too sleepy for reproaches, stretched and snuggled against him in drowsy welcome. She was no longer in the mood for bedsport, but she was not unduly concerned by that; knew he'd kindle her ardour easily enough. She much preferred that he should awaken her in the middle of the night for his pleasures than that he should not have come to her bed at all, on this the first night of his return.

But the expected feel of his hands upon her body did not come. Fully awake now, she opened her eyes, saw he was lying upon his back, staring into space somewhere above her head.

'Ned?'

She'd left torches lit for him; they still burned, but the light was not kind. His mouth was deeply grooved, and around his eyes she saw what looked to be laugh lines, but weren't. She no longer suspected him of amusing himself with one of his court sluts. He looked haggard, and there was nothing in his face of a man who'd sated his needs elsewhere.

He turned his head at sound of her voice, slipped his arm around her shoulders, but no more than that.

'I was waiting for you, my love,' she said, and found his mouth with hers. It was a highly unsatisfactory kiss; judging from his response, she'd barely held his attention, much less his interest. 'Ned? What is it? What is wrong?'

'Nothing.' He propped a pillow behind his head, settled himself more comfortably in the bed. After a time, he said, 'I had Harry of Lancaster put to death within the Tower tonight.'

Elizabeth wasn't sure what response was expected of her. She opted for honesty, said, 'I'm glad, Ned. It was the only rational choice to be made, surely.'

'Do you approve, then?'

'I feel sure we shall bury our troubles within Lancaster's tomb. But Ned, what of the girl? Warwick's daughter? Might not she be carrying the Prince's seed?'

'I do forget, at times, what a quick brain does lie beneath those silky tresses,' he said, letting his fingers stray into the soft hair spread out over the pillow. 'But in that, we were lucky. I do not believe Anne to be with child.'

'What would you have done if she were?' she asked curiously, and he pushed the hair off his forehead, said somewhat impatiently and slightly defensively,

'What could I have done, Lisbet? Seen to it that the babe was placed with the Benedictines, pledged as a monk, and taught to want a life given over to God.'

'Speaking of which,' Elizabeth suggested thoughtfully, 'I think a convent the most fitting place for the Neville girl. Have her take the veil, Ned. Why remind people needlessly of the Lancastrian Prince, now thankfully dead? Let her be forgotten and so much the sooner will he, too, fade from men's memories.'

He gave her a crooked smile at that; her dislike of all who bore the name Neville was well known to him. 'That, sweetheart, would please my brother George far too much, and you know I do not accommodate George if ever I can help it. Moreover, Dickon wants the girl.'

'And you mean to give her to him?' she exclaimed, startled.

'I mean to give him whatever he does want.'

She opened her mouth, clamped it shut again. This was new, this sudden favour shown Gloucester, had been brought back with him from Burgundy like some malevolent foreign pox. She'd never much liked Gloucester, although she did infinitely prefer him to that unspeakable wretch Clarence, but she thought now that she could learn heartily to detest Gloucester with no difficulty whatsoever if Ned were to go on like this for any length of time. He was still talking of Gloucester, was saying,

'He took this business about Lancaster rather badly. But I expected as much. My cousin Warwick, who did manage to hit upon the truth from time to time, once held Dickon to be doubly unfortunate, as being both a moralist and an idealist.'

He laughed softly to himself, with more affection than amusement, and Elizabeth's lips tightened. The mere mention of Warwick's name never failed to act as an irritant to instant outrage.

'I may have been wrong in making him go to Dudley. Will came back . . . after. Dickon did not, though,' he said, and sighed. 'He's a good man, Will is. He did not much like it, either. Not that any of them did.'

It was not like Edward to ramble on like this. Elizabeth raised herself up on her elbow, looked at him with suddenly inquisitive eyes.

'Will had Dudley take him up into the Wakefield Tower, once it had been done. Will's loyal. He said Dickon would not go. Nor would Anthony, of course.'

His voice had changed at mention of her brother's name, taken on an intonation that was far from flattering. Elizabeth felt resentment stir. How could he speak so tolerantly of Gloucester's refusal and then fault Anthony for the very same thing?

'Did I ever tell you, Lisbet, about the time I nearly brought about the death of Nicholas Downell?'

'Who in Heaven's name is Nicholas Downell?' she snapped, still rankled by what she saw to be an unjust slur upon her brother, but he didn't seem to take note of her tone, said as if he thought she truly wanted to know,

'He acted as servant to Edmund and me for a time at Ludlow. And for a youth only a little older in years, it was no easy task he was charged with, that of trying to keep Edmund and me from drowning in the Teme or climbing from the castle battlements on ropes or whatever other foolishness did occur to us.

'One summer—I think I was eleven or thereabouts—the three of us found what we thought to be the nest of a passage hawk up among the crags of Whitcliffe. I determined to climb up and find out for certain whilst it was still unguarded. I'd never minded heights before, but I'd never before found myself clinging to a cliff like a leech, scrambling for handholds in what suddenly seemed to be sheer rock. I came tumbling down right fast, landed at their feet in a heap with the breath knocked out of me and a mouth full of my own blood.

'Well, that effectively ended their interest in hawks and nests and such. I was still set, though, upon having one of those fledglings to make into my own hunting bird. But I could not nerve myself to try that climb again. Edmund wanted no part of it; he always did have enough sense for the both of us. So I . . . I told Nicholas that he'd have to climb up and bring the nest down.'

He turned his head, looked at her. 'He did not want to do it. But I ordered him to it, and I think, too, he feared losing face by admitting he was afraid. So he gave it a try and, midway up, he lost his balance and fell. I thought sure he was dead. He was not, but he broke some ribs, cracked his head open and . . . well, he was lucky, given what might have been.

549

'My father was in a tearing rage when he heard, as you can well imagine. I do not recall what befell me, most likely a whipping. But what I never did forget was what ma mère said to me when I'd had to tell her what I'd done. She just looked at me and then said, "Never, Edward, never order a man to do what you were not willing to do yourself."'

'Why, Ned!'

Elizabeth was so surprised that she sat upright, rose to her knees to stare down at him. 'It truly does bother you, that you had Harry put to death?'

He turned upon her with sudden sharpness. 'What did you expect, that I would take pleasure in it? Do you imagine I did like the thought of murdering such a man? A saintly simple fool who did little but pray and feed the sparrows he'd lure to his window? Christ, woman, of course it does bother me!'

Men, Elizabeth thought, were the world's greatest fools. Next he'd be talking of honour and chivalry and God only knows what other nonsense. . . . As if there were ever honour in death! But if he wanted to indulge his conscience now that he could safely do so, far be it from her to deny him such dubious consolation. It wouldn't last much past dawn, anyway, she felt sure . . . His was not a nature to take to a hair-shirt.

He was regarding her with little favour—would, she knew, be quick to find fault . . . to ease his qualms at her expense. But she knew better than to lavish upon him the sugared sympathies that might have soothed another man's temper. He read her too well for that, would know that her commiserations rang false, know that she lied. She considered her options and then smiled, leaned over to kiss him warmly on the mouth. Between them, that was never a lie.

But she got no more encouraging a response than before. He accepted her kiss but no more than that, and she soon had incontrovertible proof of his body's indifference. She drew away from him a little, frowning, and he reached up to touch her cheek, said soothingly, 'Do not fret, sweetheart. I'm too tired tonight to feel any body hunger other than for sleep, but I'll content you well tomorrow, that I promise.'

Elizabeth tossed her head, shook back the halo of light that spilled over her breasts and shoulders, over onto him. It wasn't often he showed himself any less eager than she for their couplings, and it stung; tonight of all nights, it stung. She very much needed for him to want her, to want her with a hot hunger that she alone could satisfy; that was the talisman she used to offset his infidelities, the hatred of his subjects. Moreover, she now thought sourly of those thirty-three nights. She knew damned well he had not denied himself these weeks past! Well, he could just do what he must to content her now. She was his queen, after all, not one of the harlots who served only his pleasure.

Her desire for him was not in the least chilled by the resentful flickers of this, an old and far too familiar grievance; some of their most exciting bedsport had been born of quarrels. She bent over him again, let her mouth play upon his.

'Tomorrow is too long to wait, Ned.'

He laughed; there was no surer way to restore his good humour than to confess that she wanted him. He was somewhat more cooperative when she kissed him this time, but he was acting more to indulge her need than to answer it with any hunger of his own. She wanted more than that, wanted him to make love to her, not merely to service her.

'You know, Ned . . . I'd be willing to wager that you're nowhere near as tired as you do think,' she murmured. 'In fact, I'd wager that your blood runs as hot as mine and I doubt not that I could prove it with no trouble whatsoever.'

That interested him, she saw. He nuzzled her throat, said, 'Is that a threat or a promise?'

'You must judge that for yourself,' she said, and ducked, laughing, under the covers. She, too, was in much better humour now; this was familiar ground to her, as familiar as the body she set about arousing. Her confidence was not misplaced; it did not prove all that difficult. One of the more pleasing aspects of her husband's nature, she acknowledged, was that, as likely as not, he could have been coaxed into a coupling on his very deathbed. She slid lower in the bed, heard him say, 'Jesú, but your hair tickles, sweetheart!' and laugh.

He was far from indifferent by the time she raised her head again. Never did she feel so secure, so sure of herself and of him as when she could fire him to sudden urgent need.

'I do claim a forfeit, my lord,' she said breathlessly. 'Will you own up that I've won the wager?'

By now, the sheets and coverlets were on the floor and they were engulfed in the tossing tide of her hair; he felt as if he were smothering in silk.

'Witch,' he said, and gasped at what she did next, reached for her eagerly, pulled her down on top of him.

He had no thought now for the ugly image that had haunted him in the hours since midnight, that of a frail stooped form sprawled within the shadow of the oratory set up for his private prayers. He was no longer remembering the controlled revulsion upon Will's face as he related what he'd seen upon entering Wakefield Tower, to find the murder had been done before the very altar of the Lord Jesus Christ, Only-begotten Son. Nor was he still seeing Dickon's accusing eyes, eyes that bespoke betrayal. He had thoughts only for Lisbet, for Lisbet who was moaning, clutching him with scoring nails. And then he had no thoughts even for Lisbet, for anything but the sheer physical sensations that were claiming his body.

Londoners were startled to learn on the following day that Harry of Lancaster had died suddenly that Tuesday night in Wakefield Tower. As was customary, a public showing was made of the body at St Paul's and again at Blackfriars, and then quietly interred at Chertsey Abbey. Some people suggested that grief over the loss of his son had snapped Harry's tenuous hold on life, others that it was God's mercy. Most, however, exchanged knowing looks, grim guarded smiles. Some shrugged, others swore and said secret prayers for the soul of the luckless misfit suddenly seen as martyr. But all hastened to proclaim loudly their loyalties to Edward of York, to the monarch who now held England as his own, anointed anew in the blood of Barnet and Tewkesbury.

4

London

May 1471

Véronique de Crécy was the second and late-born daughter of a knight sworn to Duke Réné of Anjou. She was no heiress. When her father died of an affliction of the lungs in the spring of 1459, the modest de Crécy estates had gone to his only son, Guillaume, and what little of jewelry and silver plate her father had managed to accumulate had been used the year before Véronique's birth to dower her sister Marthe. There was nothing to spare for Véronique, child of miscalculation, born after her mother's child-bearing years were thought to be well past.

Her childhood years at Aubépine, the de Crécy manor at Châtillon-sur-Loire, had not been particularly happy. It was not that Guillaume was ever actively unkind to her. But their mother had died in Véronique's third year and when their father went to God a bare two years later, Guillaume was not overjoyed to find himself with a baby sister on his hands, a sister twenty-two years younger than he, a sister for whom no dowry had been set aside and who was, therefore, almost certain to be unmarriage-able, unless an older widower could be found willing to overlook her lack of lands for the less tangible assets a young wife might bring to an aging husband.

Having been so often warned by Guillaume and his sharp-tongued wife, Madeleine, that she had the most limited of prospects, Véronique had seen it as nothing short of miraculous when, in the autumn of her fifteenth year, Guillaume had returned to Aubépine with the news that he had secured for Véronique a post in the household of the sister of his liege lord, Duke Jean of Calabria.

Véronique had been ecstatic. It mattered not at all to her that Guillaume had won for her such an honour only because there was so little competition for it. Few thought there was much of a future in the service of Véronique's new lady, Duke Réné's daughter Marguerite. All knew that Marguerite, who had once been Queen of England, was now dependent upon the charity of her father and Duke Jean, her brother; Véronique didn't care, was more than eager to exchange the restrictive horizons of Aubépine for the unknown expectations of Marguerite's house-hold at Koeur.

As excited as she was to be at Koeur, her disillusionment with Marguerite d'Anjou was both prompt and profound. Marguerite was an embittered, impatient woman who scarcely knew Véronique existed except when she happened to blunder and bring upon herself Marguerite's displeasure. Véronique was very much in awe of the exiled Lancastrian Queen and liked her not at all.

Prince Edouard she did like. She was quite taken with him at first; he was far more attractive and worldly than the rustic youths of her acquaintance at Châtillon-sur-Loire. Her entry into his mother's household had not escaped his notice; he occasionally flirted with her and laughed when he made her blush. But she soon saw he was just amusing himself. He took his pleasures else-where, did not dally with his mother's ladies, no matter how pretty. And that, Véronique knew, was all it could have been, a dalliance. Edouard was a Prince in exile, would offer a girl of her position no more than a tumble in bed. And Véronique wanted more than that, much more. Véronique, who had only the dimmest memories of childhood caresses, very much wanted to be loved.

And so she tried to please Marguerite as best she could, watched Prince Edouard from an admiring distance, and felt strangely lonely in a way she couldn't understand. Why should she be home-sick for Aubépine, where she'd had such little joy? But if it was not for Aubépine that she longed, what then?

She found out in December, as they celebrated a modest Christmas court that was, nevertheless, quite impressive by Aubépine standards. As the château was decked in evergreen and Marguerite and John Morton discussed English politics late into the night, Véronique fell in love.

He was several years older than she, a young English knight who was friend and comrade-in-exile to John Beaufort. His name was Sir Ralph Delves and he'd laughed softly when Véronique addressed him shyly as Monsieur Raoul. He laughed easily, she found. He was not the most handsome of men but he moved with a languid lazy grace and, when he smiled, a thin, rather com-monplace face was suddenly lit by a charm that quite literally took her breath away.

No one had ever paid her the flattering attention he did that Christmas. He'd sought her out whenever she was not taken up with her duties for Marguerite, teased her as none had ever done, began to teach her English. He'd been playful and then tender, and he'd had no difficulty in laying claim first to her affections and then to her body. The secret love affair lasted throughout that spring of 1470, the happiest months of Véronique's life. Not even her fear that Marguerite would find out and dismiss her in disgrace was enough to inhibit the joy she took in her English lover. She had three months of near-perfect happiness. And then he began to avoid her and then it was over, and she grieved in silence for her betrayed trust, her loss of innocence, and for the love she'd given so freely to a man who'd loved her not at all.

It was summer by then, and suddenly all was changed, changed beyond belief. The English Earl known as the Kingmaker was in France. King Louis summoned Marguerite to Angers and, when she returned to Koeur, she was handfast to the man she'd blamed, as much as Edward of York, for the griefs of her recent years.

That August, Véronique found herself travelling to the royal residence of the French King at Amboise, where Marguerite had set up her household. Her spirits began to mend, almost before she realized it. Amboise was far more interesting than Koeur; it was far easier here to avoid Ralph; and better was still to come. Véronique was selected to serve the English girl who was to wed Prince Edouard.

From the first, Véronique felt an instinctive sympathy for Anne Neville and she came, in time, to like Anne very much. Anne was woefully unhappy, yet she never took out her tempers upon Véronique or her other ladies; Véronique never served as Anne's scapegoat as she so often had for Marguerite. Anne was very easy to content, not at all what Véronique would have expected of an Earl's daughter. And she was Princess of Wales, would one day be England's Queen. When the time came for them to depart Honfleur for England, Véronique had no hesitations. There was nothing to hold her in France. Her future lay with Anne, was to be found upon the alien shores of England.

The news of Barnet, so devastating to Anne and Isabel, was no less shattering to Véronique. She was sick at heart for her friend's grief and terribly frightened. With the Earl of Warwick dead, Anne was no longer of any use to Lancaster. Anne would never be England's Queen now.

And what of her? She was seventeen years old, had no friends or family to come to her aid, was not important enough to matter to anyone. She knew nothing of English politics, had taken it for granted that the Earl of Warwick would win. Now he was dead and suddenly it seemed very likely that the Yorkists would win, trapping her in a foreign land, a land in which the French were little loved.

She could not believe it when she was told that Anne was sending her to safety, that she was to enter the household of the Duchess of Clarence. She was dumbfounded that Anne would do that for her, that Anne would have seen first to her welfare at a time when Anne's own future was so dreadfully in doubt. Her gratitude was such that she'd embraced Anne in tears and offered to stay with her. Anne had refused, had kissed her and whispered, 'Pray for York, Véronique, and for me.'

Véronique had, had prayed fervently for the success of the sinister Yorkists she knew only through Lancastrian invective. Anne alone did matter to her now and she understood that, without a Yorkist win, Anne would be lost. So, too, would she.

She would not have been unhappy at the Herber had she only been easy as to Anne's safety. She had entertained some apprehensions about Isabel Neville at first, knowing she'd done nothing to endear herself to Isabel on the day of Anne's wedding, but she soon realized that Isabel's interest in the personal lives of her attendants was minimal, not robust enough to support a grudge. Isabel even bestirred herself from time to time to show Véronique a certain careless kindness, as if recalling a duty owed to the absent Anne.

Véronique had often heard Marguerite say that the Devil favoured York. Now she thought that so, too, must God. In less than a month, it was over. The Yorkist King had won. Prince Edouard was dead and for him alone did she feel a pang of pity, remembering how young he'd been and how handsome. She felt no pity, though, for Marguerite, paraded in an open cart through London streets before jeering throngs. All that Véronique truly cared about was that Anne was safe. She was safe and coming to the Herber, to her sister's household where her wounds would heal and she could begin to forget. Véronique lit candles in gratitude, waited impatiently for Anne to come from Coventry.

The day of King Edward's elaborately staged entry into London was one Véronique was never to forget. Anne had shown no interest in venturing forth to view the victory procession. Having coaxed Anne with no success, Véronique at last decided to slip away on her own, for she was eager to watch as the Yorkist lords were welcomed into the city.

This was the first time she'd been alone in London, a city she found intimidating on even an ordinary day, and she was not long in regretting her impulse. Beneath the surface celebration there lurked an ugly undercurrent of intolerance. Londoners had just had a bad scare, had feared for a time that Fauconberg might seize the city. Fauconberg, who was a bastard cousin of the Earl of Warwick, was now seen as Marguerite's man, and she was blamed for the damage done when he'd shelled the Tower. People had been quick to remind each other that she'd never given a damn for London, that she was, first and last, a Frenchwoman.

It was no day for a girl like Véronique to be wandering about unescorted, not when she betrayed her foreign birth as soon as she opened her mouth. Without warning, she had found herself surrounded by jeering youths who mocked her accent and poured wine upon her gown. Fortunately, there were bystanders willing to come to her aid. Her rescuers, an Aldgate innkeeper and his sons, had not only threatened to thrash her tormentors, they'd then insisted upon taking her home with them.

Almost before she realized what was happening, she was seated before an open hearth, was being offered ale and sympathy, both of which went far toward abating her hysterics. The innkeeper's wife was no less a Good Samaritan, insisted upon cleaning Véronique's wine-stained gown, and by then it only seemed good manners to accept the invitation to take supper with her new found friends. They were, she soon discovered, Lancastrians at heart, and she was able to repay them for their kindness by recounting a number of reasonably factual stories about Koeur and the queen who had lost all upon Tewkesbury's Bloody Meadow.

It was late by the time they escorted her back through the now silent streets to the Herber. It was nigh on ten and she'd been gone for some eight hours but, much to her surprise, Anne asked no questions, seemed not to have noticed her absence at all. Even more surprising to Véronique was Anne's appearance. She had forsaken her mourning garb, was dressed in her prettiest gown, a summer silk the colour of sapphires and bordered in pale-blue velvet. Her hair had been brushed until it shone like satin, had been allowed to cascade down her back in changing tones of dark gold, russet, and burnished brown. She'd clearly spent considerable time before her bedchamber mirror, and this from a girl who was generally little more than perfunctory about her appearance.

Véronique closed the bedchamber door behind her, came forward to study the younger girl with some puzzlement. Anne obviously hadn't left the Herber; a woman never wore her hair free except in the privacy of her home. And yet surely she had not dressed up like this just to sit alone in her bedchamber.

'Whom did you entertain tonight, chérie?' she said teasingly. 'His Grace the King?'

'I'd hoped'—Anne's voice was so low that Véronique could barely hear her—'hoped that my cousin might come by.'

'Your cousin? You mean . . . the Duke of Gloucester?' Véronique was intrigued, remembering suddenly that Anne had once told her of a proposed betrothal with this same cousin of Gloucester, one that his brother Edward had forbidden.

'Anne . . . I've not wanted to pry but I've long wondered about your relationship with your cousin. Your voice changes whenever you say his name, sounds softer somehow. You care for him, do you not?'

'I love him,' Anne said simply. 'I've always loved him. Even as a little girl. . . . You see, my father did mean for us to wed, and I grew up with that in mind. It just seemed so natural . . . I never imagined it might be otherwise. It was always Richard, Véronique. Only Richard.'

'And what of him, Anne? How does he feel about you?'

'I'm . . . I'm not sure.' Anne's fair skin had darkened, bright blood rising to colour her face and throat. 'That day we were together at Coventry, he was so . . . so sweet to me, Véronique. He made me feel safe, in a way I'd forgotten, and I dared hope that . . . that he still cared, that he might want me even now, even after Lancaster. . . . But then I spoiled it all, I let him see my fear. . . .'

She had no need to be more explicit, having long ago confided in Véronque how unpleasant were those nights she'd spent in Lancaster's bed.

'Chérie Anne, listen. I gather that he did seek to take too much, too fast? Mayhap you did bruise his pride some, but he'll heal. And if he be half the man you think he is, he'll realize that the fault was as much his as yours, if not more.'

'If only I could be as sure as you, Véronique. If only he'd come tonight. . . .'

'If you love him, Anne, you must have more faith in him than this. And now I do have a question to put to you. I know you want nothing so much as to make Lancaster part of your past. So why, then, do you continue to wear his wedding band?'

Anne was taken by surprise, looked down at her hand with eyes suddenly thoughtful. 'Yes,' she said slowly, 'why do I?' And then she was tugging at the ring, jerking it from her finger. For a moment she balanced it in her palm, weighing the possibilities, but the open shutters beckoned irresistibly. Sliding off the bed, she ran to the window and, in one swift motion, flung the ring out into space, watched with grim satisfaction as it vanished into the darkness, left no trace of its passing.

*

Anne had not welcomed her brother-in-law's return to the Herber, but her qualms appeared baseless. George paid her little heed; there were no repetitions of their Coventry confrontation. June passed without incident.

July was ushered in with a violent rain-storm, and the stables were still surrounded by a sea of mud. Véronique paused in dismay. One of the Earl of Warwick's prized alaunt bitches had whelped and Véronique enjoyed going to watch as the squirming, squealing puppies clambered atop their patient mother, chewed energetically upon each other's tails and explored the confines of their boxstall world. But, however appealing the puppies were, Véronique had no intention of wading through the swamp the stable area had become, and she turned back toward the house.

Horses were hitched in the inner court and her step slowed at sight of them. Her eyes flickered over the lounging men to the cognizance they wore upon their sleeves, a Whyte Boar. By now Véronique knew something of English heraldry. She ran up the stairs into the great hall.

There were at least fifty men milling about, most of them retainers of the Duke of Clarence who maintained a household of three hundred or so. They were awaiting his orders now, were fascinated witnesses to the heated exchange taking place between their lord and his brother.

'I'm telling you, Dickon, that you cannot see her. She's ailing, has been abed all week. I did tell you this the last time you were here. You'll just have to come back another time.'

'You know that tomorrow I leave for the Scots border, George.'

'Well then, you do have a problem. But it's not one of my making. Surely you cannot blame me that Anne was taken ill.'

'No . . . if I did, in fact, believe she were ill!'

'I do not much care whether you believe me or not. You wanted to see Anne; she was sick. She still is sick. What would you have me do, let you share her sickbed? You've heard my physician tell

561

you she can have no visitors. Tell him again, Dr Randall; mayhap this time it will take.'

'My lord of Clarence speaks true, Your Grace. I've been attending the Lady Anne all week. It is not serious but she's been feverish, has had a queasy stomach. I truly cannot permit her to see anyone just now, my lord.'

'If you are lying in this, George. . . .'

'What will you do about it, Dickon? Need I remind you that you are a guest under my roof? And, I might add, a rather unwelcome one. . . . Until, that is, you do learn to mend your manners!'

Those watching waited, eagerly expectant for the worst. They were disappointed when Richard turned, signalled to his own men and abruptly departed the hall.

Richard paused on the stairs leading down into the inner court. He was in a quandary and knew it. He did not believe George, not for a moment, but he was not sure how to call George's bluff. He could not very well force his way into Anne's chambers; had he been foolhardy enough to try, George would have been only too delighted to give the command to stop him. God damn his worthless soul to eternal damnation for this! But it was his fault, too. He should never have accepted it when George first swore Anne was ailing. God knows, he'd not believed it then, either. But he'd promised Ned he'd try to get along with George if at all possible . . . and what a bitter jest that was! So he'd taken George at his word, and now George was still refusing to let him see Anne and he had not the time to get Ned to intercede for him. Not that he wanted to ask Ned's aid in this. For certes, there was little he'd like less. But what else could he do? All he knew for a certainty was that he had no intention of going north without first seeing Anne.

He started down the stairs, still not sure what he meant to do, other than what he'd most like to do, which was murder George . . . or at the least, shove that hateful smirk back down his throat.

He didn't see the girl, therefore, until she careered into him with a cry of dismay, followed by a flurry of fractured English and flustered French.

For a startled instant, Richard would have sworn it had been deliberate but he had no time to mull over that peculiar impression, grabbed for her as she flung her arms around his neck in a futile attempt to keep her balance. With his help, she managed to right herself and then stepped back, sank down in a hasty curtsy upon the stairs.

'Oh, my lord, pray do forgive me! A thousand pardons!'

'That is all right, Demoiselle,' he said slowly, watching as she fled up the stairs, into the great hall. His stallion was being brought forward now; he swung up into the saddle, but his mind was elsewhere, was still echoing with the words she'd so hurriedly breathed into his ear. 'The Lady Anne is not sick, my Lord. Come back within the quarter hour!'

George had retreated to his bedchamber, where his tailor awaited him, ready to resume the fitting interrupted by Richard's arrival. He found it hard to recapture his earlier interest, however; looked without seeing at the garment held out for his inspection, a doublet of purple satin lined with Holland cloth. He paid no greater heed to the next item offered, a long velvet gown trimmed in sable.

Devil take Dickon for his stubbornness! He'd waste no time in complaining to Ned and he'd be back. And what he'd do then, George did not know. He crumpled the soft material he held within his hand, heard the tailor's instinctive unhappy protest and saw an usher come through the doorway, so uneasy that George knew at once he would not like what he was about to hear.

'Begging my lord's pardon, but Master Watkins sent me to fetch you, to tell you, my lord, that the Duke of Gloucester is below in the great hall.'

George went down the spiral stairway leading from the upper chambers so fast that he came perilously close to tripping over

563

his fashionably pointed, elongated shoes, was spared a nasty fall only by a servant's vigilance. It was not urgency that was propelling him, however, so much as thwarted fury; he already knew he'd be too late. So it was no surprise to him as he came into the great hall to find his brother handfast with the girl he was coming to consider the source of all his troubles.

They turned to face him, Richard triumphant, Anne nervously defiant. George came to an abrupt halt. His first impulse was to order that Anne be taken back upstairs. But he was never to know if he would have acted upon it, for at that moment he heard his wife's voice, rising in an inflection of agreeable surprise.

'Dickon!' Coming forward, Isabel held out her hands, turned her cheek for Richard's kiss. 'I did not realize you were back from Kent. My congratulations upon dealing so capably with Fauconberg; Ned told me he could not be more pleased.'

Ned! George drew a disquieted breath, exhaled it slowly. He'd almost made a very stupid mistake. Should he provoke a brawl over Anne, Ned would blame him, would take Dickon's word over his. He always did. An open confrontation with Dickon would only give Ned an excuse to meddle, to favour Dickon at his expense.

Isabel was ushering Richard and Anne toward the stairwell. For all the world, George thought, like a mother hen with two cherished chicks, and his anger suddenly spilled over onto his wife. His mouth thinned; damned fool woman, why did she not just escort them into Anne's chamber and tuck them into bed together?

Isabel was at his side now, smiling up at him. 'George, why did you not tell me Dickon was here? Shall he be staying to dine with. . . .' Her smile faded. 'George, why do you look at me like that?'

'I'd have a word with you, Bella,' he said tightly, and grasping her arm, he jerked her toward the stairs. She stumbled, unable to keep pace, and he saw her bewilderment changing to apprehension. That placated him a little but his rage still smouldered. Dragging Isabel along behind him, he reached the stairwell just in time to see Richard and Anne disappear into the solar, close the door firmly behind them.

'I came before, Anne, but he claimed you were ailing. For years Ned did try to tell me the truth was not in him but I would not let myself see it . . . God, what a fool I was!' Richard moved closer on the solar windowseat, said, 'I want you to tell me, Anne, if he has abused you in any way, done any thing to discomfort you or. . . .'

Anne was shaking her head. 'No, Richard, truly he has not. I've scarcely seen him at all since his return; which is the way I much prefer it, suspect he does, too.'

Richard was relieved but not reassured. 'As glad as I am to hear that, ma belle, I do not trust him, nonetheless. When I come back to London, the first thing I mean to do is to see that he cannot. . . .'

'Come back? Richard, you are leaving again? But you've just got back from Kent.'

'I know. But there is trouble on the Scots border again, and Ned wants me to go north to deal with it.'

Anne was no longer listening. She stared down into her lap, trying very hard to master her emotions. He was going north. For God knows how long. To put down a rebellion for Ned. For Ned, who stayed in London and took his ease, whilst Richard did risk his life in Ned's service. She somehow managed to pull herself together, to keep from saying what she knew he'd not have forgiven.

'. . . and so Fauconberg will be going with me. To tell you true, Anne, I've my doubts as to how trustworthy he is. But when he surrendered to me at Sandwich, he did pledge his loyalty to Ned and we decided to risk taking him at his word. If he's sincere, he can be of considerable use to me in the North and, if not, I'll find out soon enough.'

He was so matter-of-fact about going off to fight with a proven traitor. 'Oh, Richard. . . .' But he seemed not to notice her dismay, was taking a folded paper from his doublet.

'I've a letter for you, Anne. . . . From your mother.'

When she made no move to take it, just stared at him in surprise, he reached over, put it in her hand.

'She did write to me about. . . . Well, she wants me to speak to Ned on her behalf. She did ask that I pass this on to you.'

Anne hesitated, and then broke the seal. She wasn't sure what she was expecting but surely more than this, a stilted half-page that could as easily have come from an aunt she saw only at Epiphany as from the woman who'd given her life.

She looked up at him, said with a too-bright brittle smile, 'She hopes I am well and hopes, too, that I will urge you to aid her in recovering her estates.'

He'd taken her hand in his, held it flat between his own as he said, 'Anne, I think you should know that Ned does not seem inclined to heed her appeal. I'll do what I can, but. . . .'

She nodded. She understood what he was reluctant to say. Ned meant to hold her mother to sanctuary. Because of George. George, who was determined to have the Beauchamp lands, at any cost. She supposed she should feel sorry for her mother but the truth was that she did not, not really. She was not as bitter as Isabel who said repeatedly that her mother could rot at Beaulieu as far as she cared. But she found it hard to muster up much sympathy, either.

What she did feel, above all else, was relief that she was not to share her mother's confinement. She saw that her earlier fears had been firmly rooted in reality. If Ned would agree to strip her mother of her estates to placate George, he'd have agreed, too, to seeing her immured behind convent walls, would have let George do as he wished with her. It was Richard who stood between her and such a fate, Richard and only Richard.

'I would be grateful if you might speak for her, Richard,' she said, thus discharging the daughterly duty her mother had imposed upon her. 'It is kind of you to bother, in truth, for I know you've never been all that fond of her. . . .'

'I do not do it for cousin Nan. I do it for you, Anne.'

'Oh,' she breathed, looking down at their hands entwined upon the seat between them, fingers laced as if in a bond beyond breaking. Sweet Mary ever Virgin, do not do this to me, she thought hazily. Do not let me believe he does care if it not be true. I could not bear it.

'I've thought of you often these weeks past.'

'Have you, Richard?' She found herself having to remember to breathe, knew he must be able to feel how her pulse was racing. His fingers had slid up her wrist. He was caressing her palm with his thumb, stirring distracting sensations that were as unnerving as they were unfamiliar. She wanted to pull her hand away and, at the same time, to feel his arms around her, to be held to his heart and hear him call her 'love' as though he meant it.

Clearly, that was what he had in mind. His arm was around her waist. He gave her now the smile he'd always reserved for those times when he'd wanted to coax her into acting against her better judgment.

'Come sit beside me, Anne.'

The smile still worked the same magic. She laughed nervously, edged across the inches that separated them. 'Goodness, Richard, if I sit any closer, I shall be in your lap!'

She felt his mouth against her temple, felt the warming breath of his laughter as he said softly, 'I'd not mind that in the least, my love.'

'Nor would I,' she whispered, not sure whether she hoped or feared that he would hear her, knew he had when he tightened his arm around her even more. How queer, she thought, that his body could be so known and yet so unfamiliar to her. His clothing was scented faintly with orris root and saffron. A fresh, rather deep nick on his jaw showed her he'd taken the trouble to shave before coming to her. She had a sudden urge to put her lips to the spot; she compromised by touching with a gentle finger the proof of his barber's haste. His hair lay glossy against the collar of his doublet, and she found now it had the flyaway softness her own hair did when newly washed.

'I want to kiss you, Anne.'

This hardly came as a surprise, except in that he'd chosen to ask. It occurred to her suddenly that he might be finding her fears as difficult to deal with as she was. She nodded shyly, raised her face for his kiss. He no longer tasted of thyme as he had in the priory garden but his mouth was warm, just as she'd remembered it to be. She wished her heart would stop pounding so; surely he could hear.

'You're not fearful, Anne? Not of me, beloved?'

'No, Richard,' she whispered. 'Never of you. . . .'

Their eyes met, held. 'I do have something for you,' he said, and fumbled in the pouch that hung from his belt, drawing out a small package wrapped in green velvet.

'At first I'd hoped to have it for your birthday, and then for your name-day, but now it seems I must miss that, too.'

For some moments, Anne looked down in silence at what she held in her hand, a delicately crafted locket, shaped into a perfect golden oval. It was a beautiful piece of workmanship, but what took her breath were the entwining initials, so closely inscribed that she could not tell where the jeweled *A* ended and the *R* began. How he'd ever found the time to have it made midst his activities of the past few weeks, she could not begin to imagine; she thought dazedly that he must have set a goldsmith working night and day to have it done in so short a span, to be able to give her this, which could be meant only as a love pledge.

She fumbled with the catch until the locket sprang open, held it out toward him.

'Put a lock of your hair in it for me . . . please.'

He didn't say anything, merely unsheathed his dagger, handed it to her. She raised it up, very carefully wrapped a few strands of dark hair around the blade. As she slipped the knife back into his sheath, he took the locket from her and fastened it around her throat.

'To remember me by,' he said and only then did he smile. She wanted to say that her every thought would be for him. She said, instead,

'Kiss me good-bye.'

As close as they were, he had only to lower his mouth to hers. The kiss was gentle and had in it more of tenderness than passion. When it was over, they looked at each other, and he saw in her eyes his own reluctance to speak, to run the risk of words. She moved back into his arms and he held her close. For the moment, that was enough.

He was in the path of the sun and he closed his eyes against the glare; he could feel her hands sliding up his back. She seemed frighteningly fragile to him and he thought she could be so easily hurt, with so little intent, could be bruised by a breath. He began to kiss the face upturned to his, took his time in finding her mouth. He could feel her tension, her uncertainty; there was a stiffness in the slender body he held. But she was of her own accord parting her lips under his, inviting him to take her mouth in kisses as impassioned as he chose to make them. It was an invitation he could not resist, that he now saw no reason to resist.

After a time, he heard her say his name, say in soft protest, 'Richard ... Richard, I cannot catch my breath. ... Oh, love, wait. ...'

She seemed content to stay within his arms, however, and he took reassurance from that, murmured against her hair, 'It is all right, beloved. I do promise you. I'd never cause you hurt, never. ...'

Her eyes were darker than he ever remembered, gave shadowed refuge to those memories she could not, even now, forget. God damn Lancaster and Warwick both for what they'd done to her. God damn them all, he thought, with a sudden bitter tenderness, and kissed her again, in that moment making a vow that she would forget, that he'd somehow make her forget, no matter how long it took, whatever the price he'd pay it, for she was worth it, worth it all and more.

5

Middleham

September 1471

A strained silence gripped the small crowd assembled before the market cross to watch a man die. Francis's stallion shied, lashed out with both forefeet, and he realized he'd unknowingly tightened his grip upon the reins. Hastily getting his mount under control, he glanced sideways at Richard, flicked his eyes over his friend's profile and back to the man kneeling before the block.

The priest from the village church had invoked the names of St Alkelda, Middleham's own saint, and St Matthew, whose day it was, making the sign of the cross over the condemned man. Thank the Lord Jesus that Fauconberg was choosing to die well! When Edward had executed Fauconberg's ally, the renegade Mayor of Canterbury, at the end of May, it had degenerated into a spectacle that haunted Francis even now. Of course that unlucky soul had been condemned to be hanged, drawn and quartered, and so gruesome a death as that was enough to break the spirit of all but the most stoic of men. Francis had found it enough of a horror merely to watch; at least Fauconberg faced only the axe.

An expectant hush now descended upon the square, a collective catch of breath. Francis braced himself. From the corner of his eye, he saw Rob, felt a keen throb of envy, for Rob looked impassive to the point of indifference. The same could not be said of Dickon, Francis thought. Richard was taut, his mouth tightly drawn, his eyes grey and guarded. But then, Fauconberg was dying this September noon at Richard's command, and that was not a command a man could give with indifference.

It was also a command Francis knew he was not capable of giving himself. He agreed thoroughly with Richard that Fauconberg had to die. This new treason of his with the Scots was as treacherous as it was stupid. But however much he felt Fauconberg deserved to die, Francis knew this execution was something he could not have done. He'd have opted for the easier way, would have sent Fauconberg under guard to London, let Edward be the one to collect the debt Fauconberg now owed.

The axe flashed upward, sent shivers of sunlight into the sky before Francis's eyes. A sigh swept the crowd as it started on its downward swing, and suddenly Francis was somersaulted seven years back in time, was once more in a shadowed slaughterhouse, watching as a man's life came to an abrupt and bloody end before the horrified eyes of a ten-year-old boy. He blinked and was back in the present, able to look down with controlled distaste at the body of a traitor twice over.

He watched as Richard gave the necessary commands, as the villagers began to drift toward the local alehouse to discuss what they'd just witnessed. It was, he now saw, a beautiful autumn afternoon. He spurred his stallion after Richard, caught up with him at the drawbridge of the castle. Now that it was over, it showed more in Richard's face, what Francis had already guessed, that to read a death sentence over Somerset and men already doomed was not the same as condemning a man whose treason was not forgivable and yet could have been forgiven.

It had not been a particularly good summer for Dickon, he

571

thought, not a good summer at all. He knew Dickon had not wanted to go north, was far more interested in making his own peace with Anne Neville than in striking a truce with the Scots. God's truth but it had been a blessing of sorts that Tewkesbury had come so hard on the heels of Barnet, giving Dickon little time to grieve for his dead, for Thomas Parr and Tom Huddleston, for the cousin he'd once loved and the one he loved even now. Now he did have the time, and his grieving was all the more painful for being so long repressed. His way of dealing with it had been to concentrate all his energies upon ending the border raids, with a grim resolve that soon brought the results he sought. In early August, James of Scotland signalled his readiness for a negotiated settlement.

Dismounting in the inner bailey, Francis found himself remembering what Richard had done as soon as he was free to follow his own inclinations, remembering that awkward uneasy pilgrimage they'd made to Isabella Neville, John Neville's widow.

Francis hadn't wanted to go, was sorry that he'd let himself be talked into it. She'd been polite, almost too much so. But there was too little to be said and too much to be remembered. And there'd been the children, John Neville's five daughters. Their newly wary faces, pinched with bewildered pain, had bothered Francis immeasurably and, if he felt that way, how must Dickon have felt?

It was the child who wasn't there who'd bothered Francis the most, however, John's son. The little boy had been sent to Calais for safekeeping, had only that July been returned to England. He was in London now and Isabella Neville was desperate to have him with her. Richard had been able to ease her anxiety somewhat, assuring her he thought it very likely that Edward would permit her to retain custody of her son. It would be an unusual generosity if so, since women were rarely given such wardships. Francis hoped Richard was right, hoped the youngster need not be uprooted, need not find himself the ward of strangers. He was just ten, the same age Francis had been when he'd lost his own father.

No, the visit had not been an easy one. Francis had thought of the fatherless Neville children far more than he wanted to in the days that followed and, for a week or so thereafter, it seemed that Richard couldn't pass a village church without stopping to buy Masses for the dead, for his cousin Johnny.

Francis handed the reins to a groom, found himself lingering there in the September sunshine. It seemed strange to be back at Middleham and stranger still that it should feel strange, for so much of his life had been passed within these massive ashlar walls. He watched Richard's enormous wolfhound circling about in the inner bailey, seeking out its master. No, it had not been a happy summer.

There'd been that trouble, too, about Richard's son. The little boy was a week shy of six months, was now securely settled at Sheriff Hutton Castle, the Neville stronghold ten miles north of York. But that had been no simple thing, either; there'd been a time when the child's future had been to Richard yet another source of concern in this summer of so many.

Richard was not quite so reticent these days as he'd once been and Francis now had facts enough of Richard's liaison with the baby's mother to fill in much of the details, as well. The girl had been young, pretty, and newly widowed; had shared with Richard a passing passion and the bad luck that brought into being the child neither of them wanted. Francis could imagine just how frantic she must have been, to find herself with child and Richard suddenly a fugitive under sentence of death. It was quite another matter now, of course. He knew Richard had at once taken measures to see to her security and to ensure the future of the little boy christened John and called Johnny.

On their way north that July, Richard had confided to Francis that Nan wanted to wed, laughing at Francis's startled look and saying, 'No, thank God, she has someone other than me in mind!' Francis wasn't surprised that she'd found a willing husband with such ease, not if she was fair as Richard said she was, and not if

Richard had been as generous as he suspected. For a pretty, well-dowered wife, there'd be no lack of men willing to overlook any damage Richard had done to her name.

To Francis, it seemed to be a fortunate turn of events for all concerned and he was not shy in saying so. Richard had nodded but then said rather reluctantly, 'It would be, Francis, but for the fact that the man she wants to wed is not willing to take Johnny.'

Nan had assured him, he went on to say somewhat sceptically, that this would pose no problem; it seemed that she had an aunt who'd be happy to take the baby, to raise him as her own. The more Richard thought on that, the less he'd liked it. Too often, he said, such children were passed around as casually as a shared cup around a campfire, sometimes to those who did want them and, oftentimes, to those who did not. And it was enough of a burden for a child to make his way in this world without birthright; to deny him a sense of belonging, too, was a far greater sin than the sin of fornication that had brought him into being. It was only then that Francis realized what Richard meant to do, to take Johnny himself.

Not surprisingly, Nan had readily agreed and she and Johnny had soon after been conveyed north to Sheriff Hutton, were now comfortably ensconced in what was to be Johnny's new home. Nan was to stay with him till a competent nurse could be found and Richard had just that week returned from a brief visit to make sure all was well with them, only to be confronted upon his return to Middleham with indisputable proof of Fauconberg's renewed treason, this time with the Scots.

Mounting the stairs leading up into the keep, Francis gave one last look at the sky above him, thinking that it ever seemed bluer in Yorkshire than elsewhere, and then moved into the shadows of the great hall. It would, he thought, be good to get back to London. Good for them all.

*

The late afternoon sun was filtering through the west windows of the solar, pleasantly warming upon Francis's face. He watched for a time as Richard devoted his attention to the sheaves of correspondence piled upon the writing desk that had once been used by the Earl of Warwick.

Richard's powers of concentration were not as unscathed as he'd have had them appear, however. More than a few times, Francis had caught him staring into space, thinking of anything but the script before him. Francis knew Richard was feeling the aftereffects of that noonday execution and why not? For all that he was Lord Constable and Lord Admiral of England, Great Chamberlain, and Warden of the Marches toward Scotland, Francis reminded himself now, Dickon was still ten days from his nineteenth birthday.

He didn't know what to say, however, so he said nothing, and watched Richard seek to lose himself in surveillance reports sent him from the border. Where had Rob got to? Did he not realize Dickon would be in need of companionship after the beheading?

As if on cue, Rob appeared in the solar doorway, trailed by Dick Ratcliffe, a friend of their Middleham days.

'I've been to the buttery,' he announced. 'It occurred to me that there was still begging to be drunk those flagons of brandy-wine sent by Lord Scrope as a peace offering. Brandywine, which some idiot—no names mentioned, Dickon—ordered to be stored away untasted.'

He slammed the door, set about filling cups and passing them around. As he sloshed a cup into Francis's hand, he winked, and Francis felt a prick of guilt for having once again under-estimated the discerning power of Rob's eye, for assuming that Rob was less sensitive than he to the unease of mind that must inevitably follow an execution. No less sensitive and, at times, a great deal more astute, Francis conceded and reached gratefully for the cup.

*

Francis was feeling sentimental, was finding that the solar was peopled with ghosts for him.

'It is nigh on seven years ago,' he announced to the room at large, 'that we were in this very chamber to hear Warwick denounce the King's marriage. Even Gareth there; it was that same night that Anne picked his name for you, Dickon. . . .' he started to elaborate further, then wondered if that were truly such a good idea. He looked down at Richard, reclining comfortably against Gareth's accommodating bulk, decided that might not be a memory Dickon would enjoy reliving.

'Dickon, your letter from the King! It came this morn and you had not the time to read it then. . . .'

'Jesú, it did go completely from my head!' Finding it still tucked away safely within his doublet, Richard smiled at Francis, settled back against Gareth to read it.

'What is the news from London? Good, I hope!'

'As it happens, yes. The Queen is with child again.'

Richard waited as they responded with polite enthusiasm. 'The babe is due in the spring, Ned says. If it is a girl, he means to name her after my sister Meg, and if a boy, after me.'

Francis thought it was very pleasant to be lounging here before the solar hearth, listening as the king was referred to as 'Ned'; it wasn't often that he was given a glimpse of England's sovereign in the more intimate guise of a brother. He looked to see if Rob, too, shared his thought, saw that it hadn't even occurred to Rob, who'd managed to lose the dice and was making several half-hearted sweeps of the carpet.

Richard had resumed reading, now drew a surprised breath. 'I'll be damned! He's given George the estates the Courtenays did hold in Devon and Cornwall.'

They were all equally startled at that, it being the general consensus that Edward wasn't likely to give George the time of day if it could be avoided. After a moment, Richard laughed, said wryly, 'He says he hopes I do appreciate the sacrifice he makes on my behalf.'

576

He didn't explain why Edward should be giving George land to please him but Francis thought he understood; Richard had confided some in him about George's obsessive hunger for the Neville and Beauchamp lands.

Richard sat up so suddenly that Gareth grunted a muted protest. 'Christ! He's gone and made Thomas Grey an Earl.'

Discretion was one thing, Thomas Grey was quite another. Francis echoed Richard's disgust. Rob, still hunting the dice, mumbled something unintelligible that, nonetheless, sounded suspiciously far from congratulatory. Dick Ratcliffe observed placidly in the silence that followed, 'Since Grey is the Queen's son and thus stepson to the King, does that not make him kin of some sort to you, Dickon?'

'It does make him a millstone around my neck, that I do know for certes,' Richard said, somewhat absently; he'd gone back to reading his brother's letter. Now he laughed again, said, 'Here's news worth hearing. Ned has named Will Hastings as Lieutenant General of Calais.'

'I thought that post was held by Anthony Woodville.'

'It was, Rob. But Ned has not forgotten how helpful Anthony was after Barnet, when he took it into his head to go off on crusade against the Saracens.'

They all laughed at that; all of London had known Edward's incredulous reaction to his brother-in-law's sudden attack of crusading fervour at a time when Marguerite d'Anjou's army was swelling daily with recruits to the Lancastrian cause.

'Ned says that Will was well pleased and Anthony not at all.' Richard grinned, debated briefly with himself, and then quoted directly from the letter:

When Anthony came to me to make his protests known, I could only profess surprise that he was still in England, that he was not halfway to Damascus by now. I told him I'd assumed that once Tewkesbury's dead were decently buried, he'd have been eager to hasten toward Jerusalem. And whilst I'd never be one to deny a man so precious a chance for spiritual salvation, Dickon, I thought it best to look closer than the Kingdom of God for one to govern Calais for me.

They shouted with laughter, not in the least deterred by the awareness that they, no less than Edward, were being far from fair to Anthony Woodville, whose piety was not open to question, however dubious his sense of timing.

Richard swore suddenly, looked up from the letter in disbelief. 'He knows I fetched Nan and Johnny north. Can you credit that? Is there anything I do that does not find its way back to London?'

'You think they do know in London yet about that inn in Newcastle-upon-Tyne last month and that girl who somehow ended up in your room?' Rob queried innocently and Francis was quick to chime in, equally blandly,

'Was that the one with the flaming red hair, Rob? It does seem to me, now that I think upon it, that my lord of Gloucester has a decided preference for a hair colour most men hold to be unlucky.'

Richard reached for his wine cup to hide a grin. 'As it happens,' he said with a thoroughly unconvincing attempt at indifference, 'the first love of my life did have red hair, so bright it hurt the eye to look upon it. . . .'

'That is right! She's a redhead, too, is she not, Francis? . . . the lass who bore his Kathryn.'

Richard set his cup down with a thud. He was touchy about Kate, touchier than he liked to admit, even to himself. He had an unease of conscience where she was concerned. He knew she'd never entertained hopes he might marry her. But he knew, too, that she'd been in love with him, was still in love with him, and he was unhappily aware that she was going to be hurt by what he meant to do.

'That is none of your concern, Rob,' he said sharply, more sharply than he'd intended. Rob looked surprised and then hurt, and Richard relented, saying with a smile meant to redeem his flare of temper, 'If you must know, the first love of my life was a thoroughly bewitching redhead named Joan . . . and I adored her with all the steadfast devotion you'd expect from a boy of six.'

Rob grinned and Dick Ratcliffe acted to dispel the last of the tension by confessing to a like fancy for a childhood nurse with the beguiling accents of Dublin in her voice, and they passed the brandywine around again as the hearth burned low and the night sky darkened to ebony in the window above Francis's head.

'Did I tell you, Dickon,' Francis said suddenly, 'that Anna's father thinks she's now of an age to make her home with me at Minster Lovell? It's been decided she's to come at Martinmas, provided we're back in the South by then. . . .'

Richard was pillowing his head against Gareth again; he glanced up with a glint of amusement.

'Shall I offer my congratulations or my condolences, Francis?'

'Neither,' Francis said warningly. 'Given the tangled coil of your own affairs at present, my lord, you should be the last one to venture out onto such thin ice.'

'The both of you are crazy, you know,' Rob pointed out companionably. 'Logically, a man should be congratulated that he's gaining a wife, Francis, and commiserated with upon losing a mistress, Dickon, and the two of you do turn it around topsy-turvy.'

That won him reluctant laughter from both Richard and Francis and a quizzical smile from Dick Ratcliffe, who knew very little of Richard's relationship with Nan, even less about Francis's marriage with Anna FitzHugh. Another comfortable silence fell; Dick ended it by questioning, 'Dickon, if I might ask you what I do know to be none of my concern. . . . Why did you not choose to have your son brought here to Middleham rather than to Sheriff Hutton? As I understand it, Middleham's where you do mean to make your home.'

'I did think seriously about doing just that, Dick. That was my first thought, in fact. It took me a while to realize that I could not, in fairness, bring Johnny to Middleham.' Richard smiled, looked both rueful and regretful. 'I've not the right to ask so much of Anne. What newly wed wife would be willing to take upon herself the care of a child conceived in another woman's bed?'

Francis started obligingly to say that Richard spoke true, when he suddenly realized what Richard had just said.

'Dickon! You and Anne? It gladdens my heart to hear it, in truth it does.'

Rob was belatedly reaching the same conclusion. 'Anne? You mean Warwick's Anne?' he asked, sounding surprised but pleasantly so. 'Well, you're nothing if not constant, Dickon. And Lord knows, the lass did ever look upon you with love.' He bestirred himself to pour out the last of the brandywine into their cups, saying with considerable contentment, 'It will be rather nice, that. . . . Having all of us back at Middleham, as in the days under the Earl. Except it will not be the Earl who rules the North for the King; it will be you, Dickon.' He laughed, said, 'That does give one pause. Who would have thought? . . . I remember when first you came to join the Earl's household. Dark as a gypsy you were and thin as a rail slat, with nary a word to say for yourself for the longest time ever.'

'It's not surprising I had so little to say, Rob, given the way you did like to claim every conversation as your own.'

'Well, it's just glad I am that I was moved to take you under my wing,' Rob grinned, 'back in the days when you were too insignificant for my motives to be suspect.'

Richard roused himself at that, enough to pitch the lost dice neatly into Rob's wine cup. Undaunted by their laughter, Rob peered down into its depths to complain good-naturedly, 'I feel obliged to tell you, my lord, that you just spoilt a right fine salutation I was about to make, one you'd have been sure to like well. I was going to drink your health, Dickon, as the new Lord of the North.'

Richard considered and then grinned. 'You are right, Rob, that is to my liking.'

'I can think of one even more to your taste,' Francis offered. 'Let's drink, instead, to Anne of Warwick.'

Richard reached across Gareth to claim his own cup. 'You're half right, Francis,' he said and laughed, raising an arm to ward off the dog's sudden affectionate lunge. 'But I'd rather you made it Anne of Gloucester.'

6

London

September 1471

Life had been sweet that summer at the Herber. For Anne and Véronique, this was due in no small measure to George's absence. Three days after Richard departed London for the North, George had ridden west to check upon his estates in Wiltshire and, from there, he'd gone north to Tewkesbury. The Abbey of St Mary the Virgin had been closed for a full month to allow Abbot Streynsham to reconsecrate his church in the wake of the Yorkist seizure of the sanctuary-seeking Lancastrians and George felt it politic to pay a concilitory visit as the new holder of the Lordship and Honour of Tewkesbury.

Those hot summer days were happy ones for Anne. With Isabel's indulgent blessings, she took it upon herself to show Véronique London, and they went up and down the river on Isabel's lavishly bedecked barge, were escorted to the Southwark Gardens to watch

Véronique's first bear-baiting, visited the Tower to view the royal menagerie of lions, leopards, tigers, and a huge white snow bear from Norway. In the evenings, they practised the latest hair styles, rooted through Isabel's store of velvets and sarcenet silks and pieced together patterns for gowns with the newly fashionable long tight sleeves and wide flouncing skirts. They played silly pranks upon each other; it was Anne who borrowed madder root-dye from the laundress to turn Véronique's bathwater a bright blood-red and Véronique who smuggled two newly weaned alaunt puppies upstairs to hide in Anne's bed. And they shared late-night confidences of increasing intimacy; Véronique confessed to her ill-fated love affair with Ralph Delves and Anne told Véronique more than she could possibly wish to know about Richard of Gloucester.

But then it was August and suddenly all joy was gone from their summer. George came back from Tewkesbury and, with his arrival, the atmosphere of the Herber went suddenly sour. Somehow, the sight of Anne's obvious happiness seemed to infuriate him. He at once put a stop to her pleasure excursions about the city, confiscated the coins Isabel had given her as a nameday offering, coins she'd been using to pay couriers to take letters northward to Richard, and when she protested, he emptied out the casket containing what jewels she had, took them away from her as well.

Anne's anger was as futile as it was intense. She was under George's roof, subject to his commands, and if he chose to keep her from writing to Richard, there was not much she could do about it. As little as she liked to admit it, she was secretly somewhat afraid of George. His rages were occasionally flavoured with cruelty. It was better not to antagonize him needlessly, to keep out of his way as much as possible and await Richard's return to London.

She might have managed to keep to this resolve had not a courier arrived five days later bearing a letter she never got to read. It was only by chance that she encountered the man in the courtyard, saw the Whyte Boar of Gloucester on his sleeve. He'd confirmed her suspicions at once, said that he had, indeed, brought her a letter from the Duke of Gloucester; it had been taken from him by the Duke of Clarence, who said he'd see she got it. He had not wanted to hand it over but the Duke had been insistent. Anne, however, was no longer listening, was on her way back into the house.

She found George in the solar, her letter open in his hand. Indignation blinding her to all else, she demanded the letter. He showed no embarrassment whatsoever, refused curtly and, when she persisted, he strode to the table, jerked a candlestick toward him and held the letter to the flame.

Anne gasped, so great was her outrage that she was all but stuttering. 'You . . . you think because I'm a woman you can abuse me and steal my lands and no one will hold you to account for it. But you are wrong, damn you, wrong! I'll appeal to Richard and to Ned. And they'll heed me, you know they. . . .'

She knew suddenly that she'd gone too far, said too much. The look on his face was frightening. She began to back away, cried in a choked voice, 'No, George, let me be! If you touch me, I'll tell Richard, I swear I will.'

She'd almost reached the table and, as he lunged for her, she darted behind it. She'd have made it if only she'd not chosen that morning to wash her hair. It was loose, swirled out behind her and he was able to entangle a handful in his fist. Anne was wrenched backward with such violence that she felt as if her neck would snap. She cried out, first in pain and then in fright.

Véronique had followed Anne anxiously into the solar. A petrified witness until now, she came out of her trance and fled for the door. She was shaking so badly, though, that she could barely get it open, jerked it back to free Anne's second scream out into the stairwell. It was all Véronique could think to do, all she dared hope for, that enough witnesses might bring George's rage back within the bounds of reason.

There were faces staring up at her. Anne's screams had drawn a score of people into the stairwell but Véronique saw with sick horror that none were going to come up; they were as fearful as she, far too fearful to risk drawing George's wrath upon them. Behind her, Anne cried out again, and she clung helplessly to the door, too frightened to go back into the solar and yet unwilling to flee and leave Anne totally alone with George. The Duchess of Clarence! She'd have to find the Duchess. Even as she formed the thought, she saw the servants moving aside on the stairwell, saw that God was ahead of her in this, and she flattened herself against the wall to let Isabel pass, heard her gasp, 'George! My God!'

George released Anne and she collapsed, weeping, against the table. Isabel gave her husband an incredulous look, brushed past him to reach her sister. Anne's hair was falling wildly about her face and she was trembling so violently that it was a moment or so before Isabel could smoothe back the tangled hair, could raise Anne's face to the light. Blood was trickling from Anne's mouth and her skin was splotched with hot colour, but Isabel soon saw she was more frightened than hurt.

'Go to your bedchamber, Anne,' she said as steadily as she could. 'Hurry now. Do as I say.'

Anne did as she was bade, fled without a backward glance, banging bruisingly against the solar door in her haste to be gone.

Véronique was quick to follow. Edging away from the door, she stumbled down the stairs into the now deserted great hall and out into a kitchen and buttery no less empty of a sudden. There she collected cold compresses, a cup of salted warm water, a flagon of wine, and carried them on a tray to Anne's bedchamber.

She was expecting a weeping hysterical girl. She found one incoherent with impotent fury. Anne was raging about the room, calling George every vile name Véronique had ever heard and some she hadn't.

Véronique did at once what Anne hadn't thought to do. She barred the door.

584

'Rinse your mouth with this, Anne, and then spit into the laver.'

Anne choked on the wine and renewed her railings against her brother-in-law.

'How dare he, Véronique? How hateful he is, hateful and greedy and craven! What did I ever do to him that he should so resent me? That he should so want to hurt me . . . and he did, Véronique, he did. I saw it on his face. . . .' She shivered and then called George a name she could only have learned from her father, the Kingmaker.

'Anne, hold still. . . .' There were deep red indentations upon Anne's wrist, much like rope burns. There would, Véronique thought, soon be ugly bruises as well. 'Does this much hurt, Anne?'

'Some. In truth, it is my mouth that does hurt the most.' Anne touched a finger gingerly to her cut lip, probed with her tongue, and winced.

'Misbegotten son of Satan!' she spat. 'But so short-sighted, so stupid. Does he truly think I'll suffer his maltreatment in silence?'

Véronique would not have thought Anne capable of such an anger, found herself wishing that Anne's fear had lingered longer. Fear made people cautious; rage such as this was dangerous, was all too apt to lead to disaster.

'When I do tell Richard . . .' Anne looked up at Véronique, said with bitter satisfaction, 'He'll pay then. Oh, yes, he'll pay. Let him answer to Richard then, if he thinks he need not answer to me. It will not, I can assure him, be to his liking.'

Véronique stared at her in dismay, realizing that this same thought would be sure to occur to George, too, once he did calm down.

'Oh, Anne. . . .' she whispered, sitting down abruptly upon the edge of the bed. Anne was now a threat twice over to George. A threat to his possession of the Beauchamp lands he craved with such passion. A threat, too, to his well-being, even to his safety, if she chose to speak, to tell Richard and the King how he had ill-treated her. And of course she would tell. That, too, George would realize.

'Chérie, this is a man most dangerous. . . .' She fumbled for the right words, couldn't find them. 'Are you not fearful of him, of what he might do? . . .'

'I admit I was afraid . . . there in the solar,' Anne said, with some reluctance. 'But I do not fear him the way I did Marguerite d'Anjou or Lancaster. George is not clever enough to be truly ruthless. He does not think very far ahead and he never seems to be able to foresee the consequences of his actions. In all his life, he has managed to do but one thing without blundering— to judge rightly that it was time to abandon my father for Ned. Much of the time he just grabs wildly for what he wants and then marvels afterward when it never comes to pass as he did expect. A man like that is not likely to inspire fear.'

Véronique didn't agree. She remembered Anne once saying that Richard was impulsive. The word that came to mind when she thought of George was 'erratic'. George swung like a weathercock in a high wind and he showed, as well, a truly frightening tendency to brood upon suspected wrongs. A man such as that might well do something desperate in a moment of anger, something he'd not truly thought through, might later repent of. When it was too late. Dear Lord Jesus, how was it that Anne could not see how much more dangerous it made him that he could not, as she said, judge the consequences of his actions?

Anne was startled when Edward in late August made George a grant of the lands held by the Lancastrian Earl of Devon. She was pleased for Isabel's sake, but begrudged George as much as a single shilling. She had no illusions that the acquisition of these lands would make him any less greedy for the Beauchamp and Neville estates. The more one feeds a pig, the more it does want, she'd said bitterly to Véronique, who agreed, but entreated her to say such things only in the privacy of their bedchamber if she must say them at all.

Still, it had been a blessed reprieve, for George went west again, to look upon his new estates. As August edged into September, it seemed to Anne that her life had stopped in time, had frozen into a pattern of endless waiting. She lit candles that all would go well for Richard in the North, prayed that he would soon return from Yorkshire.

Her luck ran out on September 5th. It was a Thursday, Isabel's twentieth birthday, and soon after Compline. George's household was thrown into a turmoil by the unexpected arrival of their lord. For Isabel, George brought a magnificent gold-and-ruby pendant. For Anne, he had a long measuring look and a mocking smile.

In the days that followed, he was in suspiciously high spirits. Anne watched with wary eyes as he was openly and tenderly loving to her sister, teasing her and laughing at his own jokes and forcing Anne grudgingly to admit that his family's charm had not been portioned out exclusively between Richard and Edward. He even turned some of that charm upon Anne herself, though she was hard put not to spit in his face. She'd come this summer to hate George as she'd never hated anyone before. Even Edouard of Lancaster, whose memory was no longer looming so large in her life, had been less hated than George, George who now watched her with something approaching smugness. And somehow, Anne found that more unsettling than outright hostility. He was up to something; she was sure of it.

On September 13th, George had ridden to Eltham Palace in Kent, where Edward was currently keeping court, and when he returned to London, Anne at first thought he must be ill. There was a greyish tinge to his complexion and he was snarling at the servants even before he'd turned over his lathered stallion to the uneasy grooms. When Isabel emerged from their bedchamber the following morning, none could doubt the night had been one of bitter quarrelling. Her face was pinched, showed sudden hollows and shadows Anne had never before noticed. She gave Anne no chance to speak, lashed out at her with unexpected,

587

inexplicable rage, shouted, 'Do not say anything! Not anything at all! I do not want to hear it.' And to Anne's consternation, Isabel then burst into tears, fled back up the stairs, not to come down again that day.

The week that followed was hell for all within the Herber. When George and Isabel met in the great hall, on the stairs, at meals, the chill between them was such that it froze any unlucky enough to be within range. And at night, their raised voices carried even beyond the oaken barrier of their bedchamber door. By Friday, the tension was such that all were snapping at one another out of sheer nerves and even the Herber pets showed the strain. And that night saw the worst quarrel of all. The heated voices raged on into the early hours of the morning. Anne lay awake till dawn, aching for her sister and cursing George with every breath she drew.

But with daylight, an uneasy quiet seemed to settle over the house. George arose as the sky greyed and lightened, was gone before many in the Herber even realized he was no longer abed. Isabel kept to her chamber throughout the day, admitted no one at all. The hours dragged on.

By nightfall, Anne could tolerate the suspense no longer. She prepared a tray of food, with which she hoped to tempt Isabel who'd eaten nothing all day, and dismissed the servant standing vigil at her sister's door. The room was in darkness, still shuttered; even the bed-curtains were still drawn. She set the tray down, caught up her candle and tentatively approached the bed.

'Get out. Whoever it is, get out.'

'Isabel. . . . It's me, Anne.'

Silence greeted her. She pulled the bed-curtains back on the near side of the bed and then cried out sharply as her candle's light fell upon Isabel's face.

'Bella, my God!' She scrambled up onto the bed, and with a sob that was pure outrage, gathered a resisting Isabel into a close embrace.

'Oh, Bella, I never thought he'd hurt you . . . not you.'

'The candle . . . I do not want it, Anne. Put it out.'

'I will, Bella . . . straight away.' She breathed upon the flame, had one final glimpse of her sister's face, of the bruised puffy flesh that had swollen one eye shut so thoroughly that she could think only of the way eyelids were sewn shut on a newly captured falcon till it be broken to a man's hand.

'Have you hurts other than your eye? What else did he do? Bella, I'm going to fetch a doctor right now and. . . .'

'No! No, you will not! Do you think I'd let anyone see me like this? I'll be all right, Anne . . . truly. It was partly my fault. He was drinking and blind with rage and I should have realized . . . should have. . . .'

'How can you defend him? After what he did to you? And you're his wife. He does pretend that he loves you. . . . Oh, Bella, I'm sorry. I did not mean that . . . did not mean to make you cry.'

It was a strange sensation for Anne, to see the brittle self-assurance stripped so suddenly from the worldly wilful sister fully five years her elder. She did all she could to comfort, which was to keep her arm around Isabel as she wept, to stroke her sister's loose bright hair, and to promise herself that she'd make George pay for Isabel's pain.

Isabel struggled to sit up. 'Anne, listen to me. There is some-thing I must say to you. I cannot help you, Anne. I cannot. But I did try. God's truth, I did. You must believe that.'

'Of course I do,' Anne said mechanically. It took the greatest effort of will to sit quietly there on the bed, to wait for her sister to continue speaking. Her heart had begun to hammer so that she seemed to hear nothing else. When she could stand it no longer, she said, 'For God's sake, Bella, tell me!'

'I do not know him, Anne. I've know him all my life and yet I do not know him at all. He will not listen to reason. He just . . . Oh, God, you do not know . . . cannot imagine what he's been like. . . .

I've never seen him like this, never.' Isabel fought to get her voice under control. 'When he went to Eltham last week, Ned did tell him that he'd had word from Dickon, that he'll be back in London far sooner than George expected, within a fortnight.'

'Oh, thank God!'

'No, Anne, no. . . . You do not understand. That's forced his hand, you see. He thought he had more time, time to work things out. But now that Dickon's expected back so soon. . . .'

'Time for what, Bella?'

'Time to arrange . . . to bring about your disappearance.'

'What are you saying?'

'You still do not understand, do you? He's afraid, Anne. Afraid of what you'll tell Dickon and of what Dickon will then tell Ned. He's not rational about this. I cannot talk to him, cannot make him see reason. I tried. It did no good, only led to this. . . .' Her hand came up to her face, hovered over the darkening bruise that spread from her eye up into her hairline.

'He can see only the threat you pose, would not believe me when I swore I'd persuade you to hold your tongue. He's afraid of what Dickon will do, Anne, afraid of losing the lands. He thinks Ned will heed Dickon, will take from him all the Beauchamp lands, mayhap the Devon lands, too. He's got it into his head that there's but one thing to be done—that you must be gone from the Herber by the time Dickon gets back to London.'

'Gone? Gone where?'

'I do not know. . . . A convent, I think. He's vague as to the details, will not tell me much. He did mention Ireland once, and that seems most likely to me. He is still Lord Lieutenant there. But I cannot say for sure that it is Ireland. Burgundy, perhaps. . . . I do not know.'

'But he could not! Not force me against my will. Richard would never let him.'

'Oh, Jesus God, Anne, do not talk like such a child, not now! Of course he could. Do you think for a moment he'd have trouble finding men to do his bidding? It would be so simple, so simple that it frightens me, and should damned well frighten you!

'He need only see that your wine or food be drugged You'd wake up aboard ship, out on the Channel . . . in the hands of his men. Name of God, girl, can you not see? They could keep you drugged for days, weeks. By the time you had your wits about you, you'd be pledged to God in some poverty-stricken Irish convent only too glad suddenly to have a rich patron, to have the corody he'd give for your keeping. Or if not that, held fast within some remote manor house. As neat a conjuring trick as you would wish to see . . . and Dickon could search from now till Judgment Day with no hopes of finding you. No one would find you, Anne. Do you not see that?'

Anne did. 'But . . . they'd know . . . Richard and Ned. . . . If I were to disappear, they'd know he was to blame.'

'So I did tell him, too. But he said that they could prove nothing, not if he said you'd run away. That all the suspicions in the world mattered little without evidence. Like Harry of Lancaster, he said. All know Ned did order his death, but none can prove it. I tell you, Anne, he's bound and determined to do this thing and I cannot dissuade him. I can only tell you what he does mean to do. But you must never let him know I did warn you.'

Anne looked down at her hands, found they were trembling and laced her fingers together in her lap. 'Bella, what should I do?' she whispered.

Isabel looked at her and then turned her head aside on the pillow. 'I do not know, Anne,' she said dully. 'God pity us both but I do not know. . . .' And she began to cry again but silently this time. Anne knew it only because she felt a tear splash upon her wrist.

'Anne, listen to me. . . . Listen! What proof have you that he truly has a convent in mind? Your sister said you could be drugged and wake up aboard ship. My fear would be that you might not

591

wake up at all. What's to keep him from seeking a more lasting solution to the problem you pose? I know women are forced into convents, but that could well be a tale told for your sister's sake. He'd hardly confess to her that he did have murder in mind. Or he could . . . could put you within an asylum for the deranged of mind if he did balk at murder. Anne, he could. . . .'

'Stop! Oh, God, stop!'

Anne had not consciously considered the possibility of murder. Now she found herself able to consider little else.

'I've got to think, think what to do. . . .'

'In France, there are churches that do offer sanctuary. Surely there are such churches, too, in England. . . .'

Anne seized upon the lifeline thrown her in this, the first practical suggestion made that night. 'Yes, of course. Churches like St Martin le Grand here in London do have sanctuary houses to rent within the church grounds, where you are safe from seizure.' That first spark of hope flickered, died.

'But . . . but it is no good, Véronique. I have no money, not even for food. And sanctuary would be the first place he'd think of. He'd have no qualms about violating sanctuary, Véronique, not if he thought he could get away with it, could have me taken without his name being brought into it.'

'Your mother, then? Could you not go to her?'

Anne shook her head. 'I do forget you know so little of England. Beaulieu is far to the south, near Southampton. It might as well be in Wales.'

Urgency was now inciting Véronique to feverish mental activity. 'What of your uncle, the Archbishop of York? He has a manor here in London, no?'

'My uncle? God, no!'

'Chérie Anne, I know you do blame him for forsaking your father as he did. But surely your need is such. . . .'

'No, you do not understand. It is not that. My uncle has become far too friendly with George. I could never trust him, never. If

I turned to him for help, he'd betray me to George as he did betray my father.'

It occurred to Véronique that Anne had been singularly unfortunate in the relatives God had seen fit to give her. 'But Anne . . . Anne, I can think of no others.'

Anne had begun to pace. 'I could have appealed to my aunt Cecily, if only she were still at Baynard's Castle. I know she would help me, for all that George is her son. But she's been at Berkhampsted since mid-July and Berkhampsted is—oh God, Véronique, Berkhampsted is in Hertfordshire!'

'Anne . . . Anne, could you not turn to the King?'

'How, Véronique, how? He's been at Westminster hardly at all this summer, was at Shene and then Eltham and the last I did hear, he and the Queen had gone on pilgrimage to Canterbury. He'll be back in London when parliament does meet but, by then, it'll be too late, Véronique. Too late. . . .'

'Anne, you must not despair. There must be someone. There must be.'

'Perhaps if I were to talk to the priests at St Martin's,' Anne began dubiously. 'Perhaps if they understood my plight, they might waive payment of rent on a sanctuary house. . . .'

Véronique doubted that exceedingly; it was her experience that servants of God were no less mercenary-minded than the rest of mankind. Moreover, Anne was right. George would not scruple to violate sanctuary. To him, the only mortal sin would be that of discovery. Nom de Dieu, but there were so few willing to risk bringing upon themselves the enmity of a man as powerful as Clarence! One would have to be very secure or very saintly or none too fond of the royal House of York. . . . And suddenly it came to her, and she gasped, so excited that she lasped into French, and it was a moment or so before she'd regained both her breath and her English.

'Anne! Anne, I have the answer. I know where you can hide, the one place where Clarence will never think to look for you.'

She burst out laughing. 'Do you remember the Brownells, who came to my aid the day of the Yorkist victory procession?'

'Of course I do. But I do not see. . . .'

'Their inn, Anne. . . . They do have an inn. You can go there, can wait for Richard in safety whilst Clarence does scour the city for you.'

Anne was not impressed. 'I have no money to stay at an inn, Véronique, and even if I did, that would surely occur to George, too.'

'He might think to look for you as a guest, Anne, yes. But as a maidservant at the inn?'

Anne was regarding her in utter astonishment. 'A maidservant?'

Véronique laughed shakily. 'If you do find it so unlikely, chérie, can you imagine it ever occurring to Clarence?'

After a moment, Anne smiled, somewhat uncertainly. 'No, I confess I cannot. But this innkeeper . . . would he do that for me?'

Véronique hesitated only briefly. 'No. For you, he would not. Not for the daughter of the Earl of Warwick. But they would for me. They do like me, Anne, do see me as . . . as one of their own. You see, the Brownells . . . they are Lancastrians. When I told them I was once in Marguerite d'Anjou's household, they just took it for granted that I shared their loyalties. If I do ask their help, I do not think they will refuse me. Now . . . what shall we tell the Brownells?'

They traded suggestions for several moments but it was Véronique who at last hit upon the most likely stratagem.

'I shall tell them that I can no longer stay at the Herber, that the Duke of Clarence is intent upon forcing his way into my bed.'

'That will scarcely do George's name much good,' Anne said, and laughed.

'They will believe me, though. People do expect to hear such stories of royal Dukes, chérie, and even as they pretend to be shocked, are secretly pleased to have their worst suspicions confirmed.'

She reached out suddenly, caught up a strand of Anne's hair and compared it to her own dark tresses. 'The colour is not the same, of course; yours is a chestnut and mine a true brown, but I think it close enough to raise no suspicions. And our eyes are similar, too, brown and hazel.'

Anne was quick to comprehend but shook her head doubtfully. 'I agree we could be taken as sisters; I do, in fact, more resemble you in colouring than my own sister! But surely that could never work, Véronique. Have you forgotten that I am English and you French?'

'As to that, since I cannot pass as English, there is but one way to overcome that difficulty. You, Anne, must be French for the Brownells. No, do not look so sceptical. It can work. Your French is quite passable and, to the ears of people who speak no tongue but their own, would ring true enough.

'It is all I can think to do, Anne. If I say you to be my younger sister, there will be no need to explain why you should have chosen to flee with me from the Herber. And if you speak no English, chérie, you're far less likely to give yourself away. Lies do not come easily to you, Anne, show all too clearly on your face. And you are, as well, an Earl's daughter. The world as you knew it at Warwick Castle, or even at Amboise, is a far different place from what you will find in an Aldgate inn. I think it is far safer if we can give a plausible reason for why you do keep your mouth shut.'

Anne considered and then laughed uneasily. 'I see what you mean.'

Véronique slid off the bed, carried a candle to set on the floor by a coffer. 'Bien, it is settled then. You will be Marthe de Crécy. That is the name of my true-born sister, will help us to remember, I hope. Now we must find the plainest gown you have. The more in need of sympathy we seem to be, the more likely we are to get it.'

Anne joined her before the coffer, began to pull out clothing for their inspection.

'Véronique . . . Véronique, what shall I tell my sister? I do not want her to worry, and yet. . . .'

Véronique had been shaking out the folds of a dark mourning gown. She dropped it now, turned toward Anne and said with sudden urgency, 'She must not know where you are, Anne. For her sake as much as yours. She has to be able to swear to George that she knows nothing of your whereabouts, to be convincing enough to be believed. You do see that, don't you?'

'Yes,' Anne said slowly. 'Yes, I do . . . .'

Véronique saw her fear and said resolutely, 'You must not fear, chérie. The Duke of Gloucester will soon be back in London and then all will be well.'

Anne nodded. 'Pray God,' she whispered, 'that it be so.'

7

<h1 style="text-align:center">London</h1>

October 1471

'Do you expect me to believe such a tale as that?'

'Frankly, Dickon, I do not much care what you believe. I'm telling you that the girl is gone, has not been at the Herber since the Sunday past St Matthew's Day.'

'I do not know what strange twisted game you're playing,

George, but this I do know. . . . That I'd need far more than your worthless word to believe Anne's fled the Herber.'

'Well, my "worthless word" is all you're going to get. Now you've more than overstayed your welcome and . . . Dickon. Damn you, stop!'

George came hastily to his feet. He'd not had time to think his action through; it was more of a reaction than anything else and, even as he grabbed Richard's arm, he wasn't sure what he meant to do next. He hadn't expected Richard's sudden move for the stairs; still less was he expecting what Richard did now. As his hand closed on Richard's arm, Richard whirled around and, in one swift unbroken motion, brought the stiffened edge of his free hand down hard on George's wrist. George at once released his hold, with a startled sound that was part pain and part protest. It had been done so quickly that not all in the hall were sure what had happened, saw only that Richard was suddenly free. George took an uncertain step backward and stared at his brother.

'This is my house. You've no right to go abovestairs if I do not wish it,' he said, low-voiced.

'I rather hope you do try to stop me,' Richard said, just as softly, and before George could make up his mind, he'd turned away, toward the stairs.

George opened his mouth but no words emerged. He had men in the hall. They were visibly uncomfortable. None seemed willing to meet his eyes because none, he saw, were willing to lay hands upon his brother, upon the man who stood closest to the King. George felt something twist within him, something that was resentment even, and jealousy and an inexplicable sense of loss.

'Dickon!'

Richard had reached the stairwell. He didn't bother to turn, to look back over his shoulder. If he made any sign, George didn't see it. But the men he'd brought with him into the great hall moved toward the stairs. Moved without haste, but it did not escape George how hands had dropped to sword hilts. He cut his eyes toward his own men, saw their earlier unease was now open alarm. He could read no such reluctance in his brother's men. Their sun-browned faces told him they'd seen service with Richard on the Scots border; their wary, watchful eyes told him they were quite prepared to do Richard's bidding, had the stomach for confrontation that his own men did not.

George experienced a moment of acute indecision and then he startled all within the hall by laughing. Wrath of God, what a fool he was! Let Dickon up into Anne's bedchamber, into the very garde-robes if he chose. What could he find, after all, other than proof of what he'd just been told? He had not lied; the wretched girl was gone, gone and none of his doing. What better way to show his innocence than to show his cooperation? Yes, let Dickon search the Herber to his heart's content. He would even let Dickon question his steward and his chamberlain. They could truthfully and convincingly confirm the facts of Anne's disappearance and, at the same time, be trusted to confine themselves to those facts alone, to say nothing of those matters best kept from Dickon. A snap of his fingers drew his steward toward him.

'Send word up to the Lady Isabel that my brother of Gloucester is here. I do not doubt he will wish to see her.'

A large feather bed dominated the chamber. It was neatly made up; so was a smaller bed in a far corner. There were candles unlit upon a nearby trestle table, and a large laver for washing; it held dust, not water. A fine film dimmed the oaken surface of the table. Richard ran his fingers over it; they came away smudged.

'I gave orders to leave the room untouched, knowing what a suspicious mind you do have, little brother.'

Richard turned; George was lounging in the doorway, smiling at him. Richard took a step toward his brother, said in a voice so tightly controlled as to be expressionless, 'Where is she, George?'

'I would to God I knew. Bella and I have done little else these ten days past but think on that, try to guess where she might have gone. I did check the hospitals, of course, and I rode myself to see her uncle in Charing Cross, but he'd had no word from her. More than that, I cannot tell you, Dickon. You do know her as well as anyone; mayhap you'll have better luck than us in puzzling it out. . . .'

'Enough, George! Let's have done with this charade. We both do know Anne did not run away. A fifteen-year-old girl on her own in London . . . and that girl Anne, Warwick's daughter? You must think me mad to credit such a witless tale as that.'

'However unlikely you think it to be, it does happen to be true,' George said curtly. 'Look, Dickon, I am trying to show you my good faith but you're not making it easy. I let you up here into her chamber, did I not? My steward awaits you below in the hall; you've my leave to question him about the day Anne ran away. I've even sent to Bella's chamber and she's been ailing, has been abed off and on these ten days past. More than that, what would you have me do?'

'You can stop the game-playing, George. You'll not make me believe Anne left the Herber of her own will. This is your doing. You've taken her from here, are holding her in a place of your choosing.'

'That's not so. She did disappear from the Herber whilst I was at Mass that Sunday. I know nothing of her whereabouts . . . nothing. For God's sake, Dickon, be reasonable. Why should I want to see any harm come to Anne? My own wife's sister? But to show you just how far I'm willing to go to accommodate these insulting suspicions of yours, I'll tell you what I'm willing to do. . . . You may send men to my manors in the West Country, satisfy yourself that Anne is not being held within any property of mine. For no one else would I make such an offer, Dickon. But if it will ease your mind, will heal this breach between us, I'll give orders to admit your men onto my lands. . . .'

'You're damned right you will!'

599

George flushed, 'Do not push me, Dickon! My forbearance goes only so far. I do not know where the girl has gone, and I do not think I care to say more on this. That you would think I'd spirit away my own sister-in-law . . . I do not deserve that from you.'

'What you deserve . . .' Richard began with passion, and then stopped, fighting a brief battle with himself for control. 'What would you expect me to think? You know I do love Anne, that I mean to make her my wife, and you'd do damned near anything to prevent that marriage. This would be just like you, to abduct a defenceless girl and keep her close within some God-forsaken rural manor in hopes my desire for her would cool. Oh, yes, this is the very sort of scheme to appeal to a warped, twisted mind like yours. I'd not even put it past you to have secreted her away beyond the walls of a convent. But if you think you're going to get away with it. . . .'

George was now livid with rage, cut in furiously, 'You do disappoint me, Dickon. . . . Such a limited imagination! Does it carry you no further than some secluded cloister or moorland manor?' He moved away from the door, saying venomously, 'As for me, if I wanted to bring about a convenient disappearance, I'd prefer a well-guarded cell, inaccessible to the sun and any prying eyes. Or Bedlam, perhaps. . . . Better yet, the Southwark stews.'

His laughter was harsh, not too steady. 'There's a thought for you, little brother. A Cock's Lane doxy claiming to be daughter to Warwick the Kingmaker. Why, she could rave on from now till the Second Coming for all it'd avail her, might as well proclaim herself the Blessed Virgin Mary.'

He saw the blood drain from his brother's face and felt a sudden hot satisfaction, took note for the future that Dickon was vulnerable beyond all expectation where that little slut was concerned. But he felt, too, a slight touch of unease. Perhaps he'd gone a bit too far. There was no need, after all, to pour salt into an open wound and it would not sound good, would not sound good at all, to have this story repeated for Ned's ears.

'You need not look so greensick, Dickon,' he said impatiently. 'Surely you do not think I'm serious.'

'I think . . . I think you are mad,' Richard said, with the stunned unnatural calm of one just coming to grips with a shocking truth. 'Madder even than Harry of Lancaster. At least his madness was turned in upon himself, whereas yours . . . yours inflicts wounds beyond the power of God to heal or men to forgive.'

As George gasped in outrage, Richard said tautly, 'But this I do tell you, George, and I do swear it upon all I hold most sacred in this life. . . . That if any harm befalls Anne, I shall hold you accountable for it. Any harm at all, do you understand?'

It was then that Isabel said his name. They both started; neither had realized she'd come to stand behind them in the doorway. As she moved into the chamber, Richard saw that in this, George had not lied. Isabel did not look well at all, looked very much like a woman risen from a sickbed.

'Dickon, George did not lie to you. He does not know where Anne is. She did run away, as he said. Ten days ago.'

'Do you swear it, Bella?' Richard said uncertainly, and she nodded.

'I'd not lie to you, Dickon, not about Anne. We do not know where she is; God's truth, we do not.' Her voice wavered. 'Believe me, Dickon, I'd never lie about this. . . . Not when Anne's safety is at stake. I lie awake at night thinking of her alone in a city like London, with no money, no friends . . . and I think of all that could befall her. Dickon, you must find her. You must.'

'Now are you satisfied?' George said savagely. 'Mayhap you'll believe Bella if you'll not believe me.'

Richard gave his sister-in-law a long, searching look. 'Bella, is there nothing you can tell me? Nothing at all?'

He saw her lips part, saw her eyes shift swiftly to George. She shook her head.

He nodded, moved past her to the door. There he turned, looked across the chamber at his brother.

'If Anne did feel the need to flee the Herber, it could only have been that she thought herself in danger . . . in danger from you, George. If that be true, she'll get word to me now that I'm back in London. If she does not, I'll know you lied, that you do hold her against her will. So you'd best think on what I said, for never have I meant anything more. If you've hurt Anne. . . .' He didn't complete the threat, knew from George's face that he didn't need to.

George was staring at him with eyes full of hatred. He drew a laboured breath and then said bitterly, 'Happy birthday, Dickon.'

8

Westminster

October 1471

Cecily Neville gave her son a sympathetic look. He'd not said anything but she knew him well enough to read the signs of his pain.

'Your tooth does still bother you? Ah, Edward, I understand why you are so loath to have it pulled but I fear you do only delay the inevitable.'

'I fear so, too, ma mère. It's been nigh on a week since my barber did fill up the hole with gold shavings and I've yet to feel the relief he promised. He says worms too small for the naked eye to see bore into the tooth and cause the pain, and by sealing them off from the air with the gold, they die and the hurting stops. Except that it has not.'

'Nor will it as long as the tooth does remain in your mouth.' She smiled faintly. 'Your father was much the same as you, would face any horror known to man or God before he'd submit himself to the barber's pincers.'

'Little wonder. . . . The last time I had a tooth pulled, I vowed never again; it must have been rooted as far down as my gut.' Edward grimaced. 'Nor do I care to end my days as do most who make old bones, so toothless that they must sup on porridges and gruels. My people are trying to tell me that a false tooth can be made from ox bone, but Will says he knows a man who had such a tooth fashioned and it came loose and he swallowed the damned thing, came right close to choking to death.'

He stretched his legs toward the hearth, using a dozing complacent mastiff as a footstool, and said broodingly, 'It seems to me that it has begun to ache even more since we've begun talking of it. Tell me more of your meeting with George, ma mère. So he still does swear to be innocent, still denies that Anne's disappearance is his doing?'

She nodded, said with a bitter, weary smile, 'To hear him tell it, Anne did of a sudden take it into her head to vanish alone into the very heart of London. And of course he can offer no explanation as to why she should have done so mad a thing. And this he swears upon all the saints, upon God the Father and the Blessed Cross, even upon the souls of your father and Edmund.'

Edward's mouth quirked. 'That from one who blasphemes as easily as other men do breathe,' he said caustically. 'More fool I for even hoping it could be otherwise. But I thought that if there was one who might get the truth from him, it would be you, ma mère. With me he blusters and with Dickon he rants. He denies all and spews forth venom the likes of which I've never heard and I'm becoming increasingly hard put to keep Dickon from killing him . . . or from murdering him myself. Dickon thinks he's mad and I'm coming to believe he may well be right.'

'Almost, I could hope he was,' Cecily said softly.

It was not often she dropped her defences like this, let the pain show so nakedly. Edward, who'd been a frustrated witness to his brother's suffering these ten days past, saw now that she, too, was paying the price George had chosen to exact from Richard. Knowing she'd have scorned pity, he offered distraction, instead, by saying, 'I gather you do approve of Dickon's intent to wed the lass?'

'Most assuredly. I think she'd be good for Richard; I know he'd be good for her. All in all, it would be a most suitable match. They do care for one another and if she's not the heiress she once was, given George's greed and her father's treason, I doubt that Richard will be bothered unduly by that lack. Moreover, she's Neville and Beauchamp and there's no better blood in England than that.'

He slanted a sharp look toward her at that last. He knew all too well her opinion of his wife's lineage, her scorn for the Woodville blood that ran in Elizabeth's veins. Even the passage of seven years and the births of four grandchildren had done little to reconcile her to the woman he'd chosen as his Queen. In her eyes, he knew, Elizabeth had been weighed and found forever wanting and nothing was likely to change or soften that icy implacable judgment.

'I remember the night I did take Richard and George down to the wharves to see them on board ship for Burgundy. . . . I came back to Baynard's Castle to find Anne huddled in the boys' bedchamber. Like a little lost bird, she was. . . . I fear for her, Edward, I fear for her very much.'

'So do I, ma mère,' he said grimly. Coming to his feet, he moved to the window, stared down into the inner gardens. Autumn flowers flaunted brilliant flashes of colour under a vivid October sky. He forgot and touched his tongue to his ailing tooth; the sudden pain only served to further sour his mood. Christ, what a tangled coil! What a bloody quagmire, and they were all entrapped in it up to their knees and sinking fast.

'I'd have clapped George in the Tower a week ago if I thought it would make him yield up Anne. Yes, I do know your thoughts on that, ma mère. And I'll concede there's no evidence that he did, indeed, abduct the girl. But I might be forced to it yet and I want you to be aware of that.'

'I would hope it'll not come to that. What will you do now?'

'Well, I'm seeing Dickon in the morning. I'll find out then if he's had any luck in tracing the lass since I last spoke to him. I fear all he's managing to do is deny himself sleep.'

'George gave Richard no trouble about admitting men onto his lands?'

'No, but we never expected her to be found in one of George's manors. Even he is not such a fool as to hold her on his own lands. There'd be no need to take such a risk, not when there's never a lack of men to sell their services or their souls if the price be high enough.'

He turned away from the window. 'I gave the order this afternoon to have George's servants taken to the Tower. Dickon questioned them before, of course, says they be blind, deaf, and dumb, the lot of them. I thought, however, that it could do no harm to question them again. But this time I shall be the one to pose the questions.'

Cecily nodded approvingly. 'Do you think they know anything?'

'I've no idea,' he admitted, 'but at this point, I'm willing to try anything. Afterwards, I mean to order George before me again. I dare not let Dickon confront him alone; not after ten days such as he's just passed through. . . . First unwilling to leave Baynard's Castle for even an hour in fear that it would be then that she'd send word, and now chasing down every accursed rumour that comes his way as to her whereabouts, insisting himself upon checking the hospitals, the sanctuaries, the prisons, old retainers of Warwick's, nunneries. Tuesday he even went so far as to go himself to Bedlam. I've tried to tell him he's tormenting himself for naught, that the chances of Anne being on her own in London are so scant as to be well nigh nonexistent. I suppose, though, that he feels he has to do something, however futile. . . .'

He shook his head, looking down at his mother with sombre eyes and a flickering crooked smile.

'I tell you, ma mère, I've none too sanguine hopes as to what's to come of all this. . . . The greatest achievement of my reign may well be that I did keep one of my brothers from killing the other, and I'm nowhere near sure that I'll be able to do that much.' The smile vanished. 'I do know that I'm less and less inclined to try.'

'There you do have it, Dickon, all I was told. Anne did disappear from the Herber that Sunday whilst George was at Mass and the French girl with her.'

'Are you saying, Ned, that you now believe Anne did run away?'

'Well, I confess it no longer seems as unlikely as it once did. I am convinced that George's servants spoke the truth, or as much of it as they knew. It may well be that he was more clever about this than we would have expected, that he did deliberately arrange to have her taken whilst he was conspicuously absent from the Herber. But there's something else. . . . I've been advised that George's men are making inquiries for Anne all over London, have been for the past three weeks. Here again he may be engaging in a game of bluff and double bluff. He'd hardly be searching for her if he were holding her as we charged . . . or so we'd naturally conclude. But to tell you true, Dickon, I do not think him clever enough to think of that.'

Richard rose abruptly, moved to the window. The world below looked to be an entirely different place, to have been stripped under cover of night of the last mellow touches of October gold; the sky was leaden, and a chill stinging rain had been falling since midmorning. The gardens looked desolate, the flowers beaten down into the sodden earth; what colour there was looked garish, unnatural.

'Dickon, I sent to the Herber for George. You're welcome to remain whilst I speak with him if you so choose. But I'd rather you did not, given the nature of your feelings right now. George is ... well, I know him to be as provoking as any fiend ever whelped, but it serves for naught to let him fire your temper ... and gives him far too much satisfaction.'

Richard had no chance to reply. A Yorkist retainer was hastening into the room and, not waiting to be announced, right on the man's heels came George.

'You did order my chamberlain and steward and even my body squires to the Tower! You had no right, Ned! No right!'

'No?' Edward said coolly. 'You should have remembered, brother George, what I did tell you at Coventry. That you'd like it little if I should have to lesson you in what I can and cannot do.'

For a heartbeat, unguarded hatred smouldered openly in George's eyes. And then they clouded over with caution and he said, with self-conscious defiance, 'So you did take my people to the Tower. What of it? They could tell you only what you already do know, that Anne ran away. And if they say otherwise, they lie. Or were so intimidated that they'd swear black was white to please you. And what would that prove? You need only show most men a mere glimpse of the rack and you'll have them tripping over their own tongues in their haste to say what they think you want to hear.'

'I had no need to resort to such drastic means of extracting the truth, George,' Edward said, unmoved. 'They were quite eager, in fact, to share all they knew with me. I suspect that, being men of common sense, they did see how thin my patience had stretched, did see how very little it would take to provoke my displeasure. Most men are rather leery of incurring my displeasure, George.'

No matter how often George told himself that he did not fear his brother, he still found himself beginning to sweat, found his mouth drying when confronted with Edward's anger.

He swallowed, shot Richard a look of pure venom. This was Dickon's doing, all of it. He'd got Ned to do this, to humiliate him by arresting his own servants ... and God knows what they'd managed to get out of them by now! He knew there was not a one of them he could trust. There were times when he thought there was no one in all of Christendom he could truly trust. Even Bella was suspect. Even Bella.

'I should think that now would be the time for you both to tender your apologies. You've done nothing but make accusations of the most scurrilous sort for the past eleven days. Yet you do know now that I was speaking the truth. I had no part in Anne's disappearance and my servants had to tell you that. Oh, I'm sure they were only too eager to muddy the waters, to babble on about that scene in the solar, and to dredge up gossip of every squabble that did ever take place under my roof. But they still had to confirm what I've been say. ...'

'What scene in the solar?' Richard cut in sharply.

George blinked and looked from one to the other, seeing it then but seeing it too late. Ned knew. Ned knew but he had not told Dickon. Fool that he was, he'd had to do that himself.

'What scene in the solar, George?'

'Nothing,' he said hastily. 'Nothing at all. I came here to talk to Ned, not to you, Dickon. In fact, it does surprise me to find you here at all, what with Crosby scouring all Westminster for you.'

The response was all he could have hoped for; he saw Richard stiffen, say tensely, 'Crosby? John Crosby ... the sheriff?'

George feigned interest in the glittering rings that adorned his fingers. 'Yes. He has been looking all over for you. He thinks he may have found Anne for you,' he said, and smiled as Richard spun around to retrieve his cloak, started for the door.

'I'd not be in such a hurry if I were you, Dickon. He wants you to look at a body. They found a girl floating in the Thames this morning. About fifteen or sixteen, a little bit of a thing, with bright chestnut hair. Crosby says she was strangled and then

608

dumped in the river. He thinks you should have a look at her . . . little brother.'

George laughed outright then for his brother looked suddenly sick with fear. Edward caught up with Richard at the door and they exchanged a few words, too softly for George to hear.

He did not much care; what did it matter what Ned chose to say to Dickon? This did, he decided, come quite close to evening the score with Dickon. It almost paid him back for the unforgivable, for that madness taunt he'd dared make on the day of his birthday, the day he'd come to the Herber. Almost, but not quite.

Dickon would have some bad moments, though, before he finally found Crosby. As soon as Crosby described the girl for him, he'd realize it could not be Anne; a tall robust lass, she was, Crosby had said, and Anne was a mere finger or two above five feet, if even that. But who knows? Dickon might not think to question Crosby all that closely, as shaken as he was, might not know for sure till he did lay eyes upon the girl's body.

'If that girl is Anne Neville, I mean to hold you to account for her murder.'

George was so taken aback that he gaped wordlessly at his brother for the space of several seconds. He'd been so thoroughly taken up with Richard's reaction that he'd not even given a thought to Edward's. He saw now that had been a mistake, a great mistake. He opened his mouth to assure Edward that the girl was not Anne, caught himself just in time.

'Jesus God, Ned! That girl was raped and strangled! You cannot think any of my men would have done that.'

'No, I do not think even you'd have gone as far as that, George. But I did not say I'd hold you to blame if you were guilty; I said I'd hold you to blame if the girl be Anne.'

George was stunned. 'You cannot mean that! That you would blame me for any harm that comes to Anne, whether it be my doing or not?'

'I do mean exactly that, George. If the girl dies, I do not much care how it did happen. I hold you responsible. Even if she does catch a chill and it proves mortal, I shall see that as murder, too.'

'Ned, no! I cannot be blamed if some evil befell her after she ran away. You'd never get away with such an outrage. I'd be entitled to be charged, to be tried by my peers, to. . . .'

'Oh, I'd give you a trial, George. I daresay I'd even produce a confession.'

For a moment, George found himself unable to believe that he'd heard Edward correctly, unable to believe Edward could ever have said that. There rose before his eyes the dark spectre of the Tower. All night he'd been haunted by the worst that an uneasy imagination could devise. He'd seen his servants held within cells where light never shone, where the walls were always damp to the touch, foul with the smells rising up from the river, with the stench of unwashed bodies and vomit and fear. He'd seen his men lying atremble in the dark, awaiting that summons to the underground chamber in the White Tower that had in it all the horrors of Hell.

Now he was the one in the Tower torture chamber, he was the one being strapped down to the rack, being pressed with heavy weights and prodded with hot iron, and he stared at Edward with the dazed disbelief of one finding himself in a nightmare suddenly become reality. Even in his most panicky moments, as he'd lain awake in those grey hours till dawn and persuaded himself that he dare not let Anne tell her story to Dickon, George had never envisioned a threat like this. Until now, he'd taken it for granted that his blood would always exempt him from the horrors that might imperil other men.

'Ned, you cannot. . . . My God, I'm your brother!'

'My brother, are you? That's almost laughable, coming from you, George.'

Edward reached down, entangled his fingers in the heavy gold pendant chain George wore around his neck; their faces were now very close.

'Do you think it to be a relationship born of your convenience, to be called upon when it does suit you and ignored when it does not? What have you ever done to make me think of you as a brother? Did you truly think that because we did share the same womb, you'd be forever spared a reckoning, that you'd never be held to account for your crimes, your sins, your betrayals?'

Edward twisted the chain sharply. George flinched and the muscles then clenched along his jaw, but he offered no resistance. Edward yanked suddenly; the clasp gave way and the pendant came loose in his hand. It was engraved with the White Rose of York. Edward gazed down at it and then straightened up, said in measured tones that George found more frightening than unbridled rage, 'I want the girl, George.'

'Ned, I swear . . . I swear by the very Blood of Jesus that I do not have her! I do not, God's truth, I do not!'

'Well then, you'd best find her. I do know you've men out seeking to do just that. It crossed my mind that you might not be searching for her on Dickon's behalf. Oh, yes, that crossed my mind! But I am telling you now, that you'd best forget any desperate schemes you may have had of finding her first and sealing her mouth with sea water or dirt. There's but one thing standing between you and the block on Tower Green, the thin thread of Anne Neville's life. You'd best pray very hard that it does not break, George.'

Edward looked down again at the pendant he held in his hand, at the Yorkist White Rose, and then flung it at George's feet.

'Now take that bauble with the cognizance you've no right to claim, and get out of here. The very sight of you does sicken me. Go home and light candles and entreat God that it was not Anne you did so gleefully send Dickon to look upon. If not, you do have a tomorrow. But not many of them, George. Not unless Anne is found alive and unharmed. That I do promise you.'

9

London

October 1471

Hugh and Alice Brownell had that summer celebrated twenty-five years of wedlock. They'd been luckier than most; of their ten children, six had survived the perilous voyage through infancy and they now had four able-bodied sons and two healthy daughters gathered at their hearth, helping in the operation of the inn and giving promise of a secure old age for the elder Brownells.

They'd made quite a press of people as they crowded that September Sunday into Hugh and Alice Brownell's bedchamber to hear the story that suddenly was not as easy in the telling as Véronique had expected it to be. She'd found herself faltering before this circle of trusting faces and her conscience was not eased when she saw her hesitation only served to make her tale that much more credible to them.

'. . . and so we could not stay there, not once I knew what he . . . he wanted of me. I did not know what else to do. I had nowhere to go but here. . . . You are the only friends I do have in London, in all of England. I know how much I ask of you, but . . . oh, please, will you not help us?'

All eyes shifted to Hugh Brownell, for the decision would be his to make. He was a greying, weathered man who looked considerably older than his forty-some years, so lean of frame that it seemed incongruous that he should have sired four such strapping big-boned sons. Now he rose with the slow deliberation he'd cultivated of necessity to balance a stiffened right leg, the result of a fall taken in youth.

'I cannot say it does surprise me any, your story. I'd no sooner expect to hear good of Clarence than I would of Judas. But never you mind. You and your sister are welcome here, for as long as you like.'

That was all the others had been waiting for, and Véronique and Anne found themselves engulfed in warmth. Véronique felt tears prick her eyes as she looked about her at these people so willing to offer a roof, refuge, friendship.

Stephen was, at twenty-three, the eldest Brownell son; Véronique now received a shy hug and a smile from Celia, his flaxen-haired wife who was very young and very pregnant. Sixteen-year-old Matthew Brownell was watching Anne with an interest only slightly dampened by the news that she understood very little English, spoke it hardly at all. Catherine, who was seventeen, was fingering the skirt of Véronique's gown, saying it was too fine for everyday wear but she was sure she and her mother could find some spare russet in their materials coffer.

Véronique murmured her thanks, watching as Anne thawed under Alice Brownell's maternal solicitude, answered questions with a soft 'Oui' or 'non'. She watched and smiled and nodded and felt very guilty, for the lies she'd told them that they'd accepted, without question and for the terrible trouble she might be bringing down upon them.

It was early, just past eight. The streets had been astir for several hours, however, as life in London began anew with the coming of light. Véronique's basket was beginning to rub against her wrist and she paused to shift it to her other arm. She was pleased with her thrift and knew Alice Brownell would be, too, for she'd been able to buy six ounces of butter for a halfpenny and a large cheese for a shilling. Much of the time, the Brownell women churned their own butter but this coming Sunday was the Feast Day of

St Edward the Confessor and Alice was laying in a store of food in expectation of a greater flow of wayfarers than usual.

It had been a source of some controversy at first, whether Véronique should share the marketing duties with Catherine. The Brownells were very conscious that Véronique was not of their class; she was the daughter of a knight, had been privileged to serve their ill-fated Queen. They were not all that comfortable that Véronique should be gathering eggs or drawing water or assisting Alice and Celia in the brewing of their ale. But they were far from affluent. The livelihood they earned from their inn was marginal; it was old and rather run-down, and the Brownell boys confided in Véronique their suspicion that they'd been hurt, as well, by their known allegiance to the House of Lancaster. They were clearly relieved when Véronique insisted that she wanted to do her share.

So, too, did her sister Marthe, she assured them, but she must ask that Marthe be spared any errands which would take her beyond the confines of the inn, given her unfamiliarity with English. The Brownells looked at Anne's delicate profile, mistaking her wide-eyed wonder at the strangeness of her surroundings for extreme timidity, and agreed at once that Marthe should stay within the inn, under Alice's protective eye.

Anne had shown herself to be more adroit at deception than Véronique had expected. She had yet to forget and not respond when addressed as Martha and she'd adapted very well to the Brownells' peculiar habit of chattering to her as if she spoke fluent English and, at the same time, feeling free to discuss her to her face as if she could not comprehend a word being spoken. That, she'd laughed to a bemused Véronique, was an offshoot of the deeply rooted conviction of the English that you could make any foreigner understand you if only you spoke loudly enough.

But there was no denying that life in an Aldgate inn was a far cry from the world as they'd known it at the Herber. Anne was accustomed to eating from silver plate; now she made do with a wooden bowl and spoon. These days she wore frieze, a coarse wool, when once she'd worn only velvets and satins. From childhood, she'd lain upon the softest of feather beds; she now stretched out at night upon a mattress filled with straw in the little chamber she and Véronique shared up under the eaves of the roof.

There was no fireplace, of course, and the only source of warmth in the room was a small brazier heaped with coals. Frequent baths were a pleasure Anne had taken for granted all her life; at the Rose and Crown, a bath became a complicated and cumbersome affair, involved the dragging of a large unwieldy tub before a well-stoked kitchen fire, heating pots of water beforehand and, most difficult of all, trying to ensure that rarest of luxuries, privacy.

There were no chairs in the inn, merely a few stools, coffers and a bench or two, one large trestle table for family meals and several smaller ones for cooking and sewing. The bedchambers held beds, coffers, lavers for washing, and little else. There were no arras hangings for the walls, no mirrors, no glass for the windows, some of which were open to the elements when not shuttered and others screened with oiled linen, which blocked out the wind but much of the light, too. There were no garde-robes, either, only chamber pots and an outdoor privy.

Mealtimes were no less a novelty to both girls. Anne was used to eating manchet loaf made from white flour; Véronique had acquired a similar taste at the Herber, but at Aubépine, she'd breakfasted on the coarser-grained ravel bread of unbolted flour and bran. Now they both ate barley bread and acorn loaf. Véronique was positive Anne had not eaten roasted turnips before seeking shelter with the Brownells; neither girl had ever tasted boiled cabbage before.

Anne had yet to complain about this unusual fare; she ate without comment the salted herring and pottage served up for breakfast. And during those sun-warmed days of late September and early October, she even learned to cook those breakfasts herself.

Not that Anne was ignorant of the arts of cooking. That was

something all girls were expected to know. Anne, like Véronique in France and Catherine Brownell in Aldgate, had been taught how to season meats with herbs and stew apples with almonds, saffron, and salt, how to prepare frumenty stew and to bake custard and cheesecake. But there the similarities among the three girls ended.

Catherine's education had been confined strictly to the teaching of household tasks. She could neither read nor write, nor did she feel the lack. In Catherine's world, it was enough that she could cook and sew, that she had a basic knowledge of medicinal herbs, that she would know how to tend to her children and content her husband.

Véronique's education had been more extensive than Catherine's, although it had much of the aspects of a patchwork quilt, with a bit of learning snatched here and there from a number of sometimes surprising sources. Her brother could not afford to board her with the nuns who generally saw to the teaching of young girls of her rank. He had, however, engaged a tutor for his sons and, from him, Véronique had learned the alphabet. Spurred on by the boredom of Aubépine more than anything else, she'd disciplined herself until she read without difficulty and could write as well, although with far less ease. From her sister-in-law, she was taught needlework and cooking and the arts of healing; at Marguerite's court at Koeur, she'd gained some knowledge of music. She had no Latin other than the Pater Noster, the Ave and the Credo, but from Ralph Delves she'd learned English and this summer past, under Anne's tutelage, she'd begun the struggle to translate it from the ear to the page.

With Anne, it had been quite différent. Anne was fluent in French, had some comprehension of Latin. She rode well, had been taught to hawk, to dance, to play chess. She played the lute quite well and could pick out a passable melody upon the lyre. But these accomplishments were only a portion of what she'd been taught to do.

Anne had been raised with the expectation ever in mind that one day she would have to manage a great household of several hundred people. She had to be able to balance a budget, to keep orderly household accounts from Michaelmas to Michaelmas. She had to know how much money should be set aside for almsgiving and what should be paid out in wages. She would have to be able to supervise all that must be done to keep functioning a castle such as Middleham or Warwick, to see that bread was baked in ample amounts, that sufficient draughts of ale were brewed in the alehouse, that butter and cheese were being produced in the dairy and candles in the larder, that meat was salted for the coming winter and herb gardens tended.

But it was one thing to understand how to perform a task for supervisory purposes and quite another to turn her hand to it herself. In that, Anne had not been prepared for what was expected of her now that she had abandoned the Herber for Aldgate.

Anne knew quite well that Gauncele sauce was made with flour, milk, saffron and garlic; she had never stood before an open fire stirring the concoction in a heavy brass frying pan. She knew sheets must be soaked in a wooden trough with a solution of wood ashes and caustic soda; she had never knelt before the tub scrubbing out the stains herself. Never before had she made beds or washed dishes or swept floors, all of which the Brownell women did every day, with some haphazard help from Mary and Dorothy, their kitchen maids.

Anne did all this now and without complaint. But she was unaccustomed to sleeping in an unheated room, to groping her way at night down unlit stairwells and out into the damp ground of the garden to use the privy, to be awakened by rain dripping through the eaves, and like a garden flower suddenly uprooted to grow wild, she'd soon sickened. She'd had a hacking cough for more than a week now and Véronique was beginning to become concerned.

So, too, was Alice, and she'd directed Véronique to stop at an herb shop for white horehound; when mixed with honey, it was thought to be an effective cough medicine. Having done so, Véronique continued west on Cornhill Street, purchased six wax candles from a local chandler's shop. She wasn't overly worried about venturing out on her own, felt sure that only the most accursed ill luck could bring her to Clarence's eye. Much of the time, she felt that to be true for Anne, too. As long as Anne was sheltered within the Rose and Crown, she was safe; Véronique could not conceive of anyone thinking to look for the Earl of Warwick's daughter in an Aldgate inn. No, they were well camouflaged here, need only wait till the Duke of Gloucester came back to London.

But when he did come, how would they know?

It was a cruel jest of God, Véronique thought, that the Brownells' Lancastrian sympathies, which had proven to be the bridge to their salvation, should now isolate them as thoroughly as if a moat were dug around the inn. None of the Brownells, even the youngest, were inclined to gossip about the happenings at the Yorkist court. They did not know what was occurring at Edward of York's court; nor did they much care. And the result was that Anne and Véronique knew no more of what was happening in Westminster than they did of the events taking place in the North of England, where Richard might or might not still be.

Véronique had begun to offer at every opportunity to shop, to run errands. In this way, she hoped to hear some word of Richard's whereabouts; most people, she knew, were not as indifferent as the Brownells to Yorkist comings and goings, would be only too happy to gossip about the king's youngest brother. She'd even discussed with Anne the advisability of making the long walk across town to Baynard's Castle, but Anne had been adamantly opposed to letting her take such a risk. Both girls were convinced that George would have Baynard's Castle under close surveillance, just waiting for one of them to try to contact Richard.

Until they were sure that Richard was back in London and able to give them his protection, they could do little but wait.

Three days later, however, Véronique found herself on Thames Street, staring up at the greying stone walls of Baynard's Castle. She was shivering, as much from apprehension as from the cold, and to her uneasy eye, every man that passed seemed suspect, seemed sure to be a spy for the Duke of Clarence. She should not have come; Anne had been right. But Anne was ill, drifting in and out of a fevered sleep, drenched with sweat and suffering from coughing spasms so severe she'd begun to bring up phlegm flecked with blood.

After two days and nights at Anne's bedside, Véronique, too, was far from well, numb with fatigue and fear. It was the fear that proved strongest, that sent her out into city streets slick with rain, that brought her now to Baynard's Castle. Once there, however, her courage failed her. It was so imposing a structure, a veritable stone fortress rather than a manor house like the Herber. She hadn't the faintest idea what to do next, loitered for some moments, hoping fervently that Richard might magically appear. He didn't. Instead, she attracted the attention of several men clad in the blue and murrey of York; taking her for a harlot in search of customers, they began to yell offers down from the outer bailey walls. Thoroughly flustered, she retreated in haste, moved back up Addle Street to regain her composure and to nerve herself to approach again the gatehouse guards.

Directly in front of the castle, several drovers were swearing and struggling to free a cart mired down in the muddy swamp the streets had become after three days of heavy rains. They'd attracted a small crowd of spectators, one of whom now detached himself from the other onlookers and began to follow Véronique up Addle Street.

Her suspicions at once flared up into active alarm. She quickened her pace and, glancing back over her shoulder, was panicked to see that so had he. She never for a moment considered that he might have made the same mistake the guards had, might have taken her for a woman of the streets. To Véronique, this man stalking her up Addle Street could only be one of Clarence's hirelings, and she began to tremble with fright.

She had to lose him, could not lead him back to the inn, to Anne. By now she'd reached Carter Lane; he was still behind her, had narrowed the gap somewhat. A large crowd was thronging the churchyard of St Paul's, gathered for the St Edward's Day High Mass and she plunged into their midst. Ignoring the curses and punishing elbows of people she was dispossessing, she forced her way into the churchyard.

Not daring to look back, she shoved and pushed until a path opened for her, darted through the side door leading into the nave of the cathedral. She stumbled at once into disaster, tripping over one of the tables set up in the west end of the nave, where scribes wrote letters and legal documents for any willing to engage their services. As she lurched against it, the trestle board buckled and dumped the contents of the table onto the floor. The scribe stared in dismay at the ruin of his labour, at the puddle of ink soaking through his supply of paper. With an outraged shout, he grabbed for Véronique.

'Look what you've done to my stall, you clumsy jade! You'll pay me for the damage done or, by God, I'll call a constable!'

By now, Véronique had regained her feet. She evaded his outstretched arm by purest luck, looked around wildly for escape. Across the nave, several loitering youngsters who were watching the commotion with amusement shouted at Véronique, 'The north door, sweetheart. Take the Si Quis door!'

Their words meant nothing to her but they were pointing and gesturing; she saw that there was a small door on the other side of the nave and ran toward it. Behind her, she heard laughter, a thud, a curse and more laughter. Looking back, she saw that one of the boys had thrown a footstool into the path of the pursuing scribe. With a sob, she fled the church, out into Paul's Alley.

Not knowing if she'd shaken off pursuit, she gathered up her skirts and pushed her way through the press of people milling about in the north side of the churchyard. Not until she reached the street did she pause to draw breath into her air-starved lungs. She'd gashed her knee on the edge of the scribe's table, torn her stockings, snapped a garter, and she saw now that her skirt had swept the ink spill, was spotted with dark blotches.

She leaned against the doorway of a cookshop, ignored the youth urging her to buy 'a nice hot pie, mistress? We've a right tasty smoked pike pasty, or if you'd rather, ribs of beef.' The greasy smells from within hit her knotted heaving stomach like a fist; she fought back a wave of nausea and backed away from the shop. The man was not in sight. She began to walk as swiftly as she could without attracting notice, found herself whispering 'Jésus et Marie', over and over, until the words had no meaning whatsoever to her.

Anne's fever broke that night. By the next day she was able to take barley broth and soon she was propped up on makeshift pillows of chaffing sacks while Alice spooned a mixture of honey and wine down her throat. She was back on her feet by the week's end, the same day that Véronique had an unpleasant encounter in the stairwell with a drunken inn patron. Stephen Brownell had handled it with his usual quiet competence, somehow avoided outright violence while making a most persuasive case for the man's immediate departure. Véronique's outrage had taken hours to cool, leaving a sour aftertaste in her mouth. She and Anne had to get out of here. Blessed Lady, but they had to!

The next day was a Saturday, was for them a bitter anniversary, marked the passage of four full weeks since they'd fled the Herber. Véronique spent several hours at the Leadenhall Market, making purchases for Alice Brownell and eavesdropping upon

621

the conversations about her, hoping to hear someone say that Richard of Gloucester had arrived back in the city from the North. By the time she gave up and started back toward Aldgate, the morning was all but gone and a wet wind was gusting from the river.

The sky was a leaden grey, matched her mood. She quickened her pace but to no avail; rain was already splattering the cobblestones, needle-like drops that stung her skin, trickled down the neck of her gown. She jerked up the hood of her cloak, looked about for shelter.

The heavy oaken doors of St Andrew Undershaft were ajar. Inside, all was shadowed and still. Véronique moved hesitantly into the nave, groping her way by instinct alone, and gave a muffled cry when a voice suddenly spoke out of the gloom.

'High Mass is done, child, but I shall be saying a Low Mass at None.'

'Oh, Father, how you did frighten me! I thought I was alone. . . .'

For all that he called her 'child', his was a young man's voice and as he emerged from the darkness, she saw not only youth in his face; she saw curiosity, too, knew he was puzzling over the incongruity of her servant's dress, so at odds with the well modulated tones that bespoke education.

He had arresting eyes, deep-set and long-lashed, a brilliant piercing black; too probing, too knowing, she thought, eyes accustomed to strip away secret sins, to bare souls for God's judgment.

'Are you in trouble, lass?'

She opened her mouth to deny it, heard herself breathe an involuntary 'Yes. . .'

'May I help?'

'No, Father.' She shook her head unhappily, surprised herself then by adding, 'Not unless you can tell me what I most need to know, whether the Duke of Gloucester is back in London.'

If he was startled, it didn't show on his face. 'As it happens, I can. He's been back since Tuesday eve a fortnight ago.'

Véronique stared at him, disbelieving. 'Are you sure?'

'Quite sure. Monday is St Ursula's Day, you see.'

'What?'

He laughed. 'Perhaps I'd best explain. Each year on that day the Duchess of York buys Masses in memory of her daughter Ursula; she died as a babe, I believe. The Duchess sends a servant to have Masses said in certain city churches and, when the man came by to see me, he made mention that the young Duke is back from the North.'

Véronique had begun to tremble and he reached out, put a steadying hand on her arm. 'Why does that matter so to you, mistress? What is the Duke of Gloucester to you?'

'Salvation,' she said, and gave a shaky laugh, in that moment making up her mind to trust him. It was risky, yes, but what alternatives had she? She could never go back to Baynard's Castle on her own, not after the horror that had almost befallen her the last time. Nor did she want Anne to take such a risk. But a priest . . . A priest would have access to Baynard's Castle and with a priest, she'd be safe.

'Father . . . listen to me, please. What I am about to ask you will sound most strange, I know. You asked if you could help me. . . . Well, you can. You can escort me to Baynard's Castle, take me to Richard of Gloucester. Please, Father. He'll see me, I swear before God he will and bless you for it, every day of his life.'

He was not as jaded as she first thought; he could be surprised, after all. The black eyes narrowed, focused on her face with unnerving intensity. Just when she concluded that her plea had fallen upon deaf ears, he nodded slowly.

'Very well,' he said, sounding much like a man acting against his better judgment. 'I'll take you, though I'd be hard put to explain why. . . .' Adding a hasty proviso, 'But not till the rain does let up.'

Véronique began to laugh again; it seemed somehow hilarious

623

to her that Richard's reunion with Anne should now hinge upon the vagaries of the weather.

'You will not be sorry, Father,' she promised. 'You will not ever be sorry.'

The young priest was ill at ease, darting sidelong glances at Véronique as if wondering what he'd got himself into, and, when asked his name, he hesitated. Véronique's own nervousness had not survived the climb up the steps into the keep; she need not fear George now and she stepped forward, said quite clearly,

'Father Thomas was good enough to see me safe here. It is I, not he, who would speak with His Grace of Gloucester . . . about his cousin, the Lady Anne Neville. My name is Véronique de Crécy and. . . .' The rest of her words trailed off, were not needed. Already a man was on his way to the solar, taking the stairs two at a time; others were clustering around her, all talking at once. Véronique smiled at the astonished priest, said, 'Did I not tell you true, Father?' And she moved forward to meet Richard, just then emerging from the solar at the top of the stairs.

10

London

October 1471

Anne first noticed the man in the outer courtyard. He was lounging against the wall of the stables, watching her as she lowered her bucket into the well. When she emerged a little later to air out bedding; he was still there. There was an unnerving intensity in his stare, something more than the lustful looks she occasionally got from inn patrons, and when she saw him beckon to Cuthbert, the stable boy, her heart took up a quicker cadence. Cuthbert was now looking toward her, too, Anne saw him shake his head and shrug. There was little Cuthbert could tell him; he knew only that Anne and Véronique had come from some great household. But why was he questioning Cuthbert at all? Anne gathered up the bedding, fled back indoors. When she looked out the window again, the man had gone.

She could not even ask Cuthbert what the man had wanted, had to keep up this damnable pretence of not speaking English. All she could do was to wait for Véronique to get back from the Leadenhall Market. Véronique could talk to Cuthbert, could reassure her that the stranger was only another lecher, was not in George's pay. But where was Véronique? Why was she not back by now?

She tried to put the man from her mind, busied herself in helping Catherine clean the empty upper chambers. Following Catherine into a corner room, she set her lamp down upon a small table that, with the bed, was all the furniture the room contained. The lamp, a sputtering wick floating in a sea of vegetable oil, gave off some light but not much. Glancing about at this queer mid-day darkness, Anne found herself reluctantly remembering the burnished blaze of candelabras that shone in every chamber of the Herber, three dozen candles a night consumed from Martinmas to Candlemas, enough to last the Brownells for years.

She was helping Catherine strip the bed when they heard it, the clatter of hooves upon cobblestones. Horses being ridden at hard gallop. Anne tensed, but Catherine merely looked up and then shrugged; until it became apparent that the riders were not passing by. From the sounds echoing up through the open window, it was clear that they'd ridden into the stableyard. Dogs had begun to bark, gates banged, and suddenly the afternoon air was alive with a rising volume of noise that signalled the occurrence of something quite out of the ordinary.

Catherine was closest to the window, reached it first. Almost at once, she drew back inside. Her eyes were very wide.

'Yorkist lords! Why would—Oh, dear God! Veronica tried to tell us she thought Clarence might be vengeful enough to seek her out. And I did not believe her.'

She saw support for the conclusion she'd drawn in the fear that now showed in Anne's face.

'Martha . . . Martha, listen. You stay here. Do not let yourself be seen. You understand? Do not come out. I'm going to get Stephen.' And with that, she whirled for the door.

Anne's first thoughts weren't thoughts at all, were sensations of pure physical panic. Her brain was numb, could admit no feeling beyond a dazed horror that she could have endured so much these four weeks past only to fall into George's hands at the last. Oh, why had she not run away as soon as she saw that man lurking about?

She'd sagged against the wall, now made herself risk a quick glimpse down into the outer courtyard. She saw enough to confirm Catherine as an accurate witness. The men below were wearing the livery of York. Never had she experienced the despair that she did at this moment, so overwhelming in its intensity that it was almost like drowning.

But it was then, as she clung to the window and stared down at the men dismounting in the courtyard, that she saw the dog. A huge black wolfhound, it was circling several stable dogs in a stiff-legged stalk as ominous as its rising hackles and glinting eyeteeth. She forgot all else, leaned out recklessly from the window to hear one of the riders yell, 'You men there! Separate those damned curs and fast! His Grace'll have your skins if harm comes to the big dog.'

His words only served to corroborate what she already knew, had known from the instant she'd laid eyes upon the wolfhound.

'Gareth,' she breathed. And then, in the most sincere spontaneous prayer of her life, 'Oh, thank Jesus!'

Richard guessed the girl to be fourteen, fifteen at most. She was looking at him with such blank dismay that he found himself entertaining a grim suspicion she might be simpleminded. She was trying to curtsy and he grabbed hastily for her elbow, held her upright, for she was so big with child that he thought the slightest strain might bring on labour. Again, he tried to dispel her fear, saying softly and soothingly. 'You've no cause for fear. I want only to talk to the girl you call Marthe.'

Seeing he was getting nowhere, he looked toward the three men drawn from their room by the uproar and jostling for space upon the landing, unabashedly curious.

'Have any of you seen the girl I seek? She's this tall, slim, with dark eyes and. . . .'

But they were already shaking their heads. Almost at once, however, they began to offer suggestions. What of the stables, my lord? Might she not be out in the hen roost? As eager as they were to help, Richard saw they had no more knowledge than he of Anne's whereabouts. He turned back to the pregnant girl, somehow found a smile for her.

'What is your name, lass?'

The unexpected question untied her tongue, at least enough for her to whisper, 'Celia, my lord.'

'Celia, listen to me. I want you to tell me where she is. Your loyalty does you great credit, but your concern is for naught, believe me. She's very dear to me; I'd never cause her hurt. Where is she, Celia? You must. . . .'

He stopped in midsentence. She was staring past him and the look on her face was his answer. He spun around to see Anne standing at the top of the stairs.

*

627

Anne had not known that strong emotions can be as intoxicating to the senses as strong drink. The pendulum had swung too wide, transporting her within the span of seconds from terror to euphoria, and her emotional equilibrium had yet to right itself. She was as oblivious of the numbing cold pervading the chamber as she'd been of the witnesses upon the stairwell. Her awareness went no further than Richard. He was both her present salvation and her past security; of the remembrance-strewn wreckage her life had become, he alone was a memory lent substance, breath, reality.

Richard touched her face with his fingers, as if seeking to re-assure himself that she was truly here, in his arms and unhurt. He needed such reassurance, needed the physical reality of her presence after weeks of nightmares and fading hope. Turning her toward the light, he saw now what he'd not seen on the stairwell, how white she was. How fragile, how vulnerable. Soft wisps of hair were curling about her temples; her skin was warm but so delicate, so finely drawn across her cheekbones he fancied the slightest pressure could leave an indelible imprint.

'Jesú, what we've done to you!'

'Hold me,' she entreated. 'Just hold me.'

He was more than willing to do that. He kissed her again, very gently this time, but her mouth clung to his, sought a deeper kiss. If only he'd never let her go to the Herber. If only he'd not had to go North for Ned. He tightened his arms around her. Never had she kissed him like this; he was both surprised and delighted by the unexpected ardour of her response. This was the first time that he'd taken her in his arms and felt them both free of the shadow of Lancaster.

Her lashes lifted, giving him a glimpse of lucent liquid dark-ness. A man could drown in eyes like hers, he thought, and then laughed at his own foolishness. She laughed, too, for no other reason than that he did.

'Do not let me go,' she said. 'Not ever,' and he laughed again, thinking, so easy it is as this, then, to exorcise a ghost.

Anne gave a surprised murmur of protest at suddenly finding herself free. Opening her eyes again, she saw that Richard had moved to the window, was struggling to fasten the weathered warped shutters that were giving unguarded entry to the icy October air.

'No wonder it was so cold in here! You must be chilled to the bone, sweetheart.'

She shook her head. It seemed strange to her that their first coherent conversation should be about something so commonplace as an open window. So disoriented was she that she actually gave a startled gasp as the room was plunged into semidarkness.

Richard was at her side again. Unfastening his cloak, he draped it about her shoulders; it seemed wondrously soft to her after weeks of kersey wool and homespun. She started to assure him that she was not cold, only to feel in her chest the tight prickling sensation that foretold a coughing spasm. In dismay, she tried to ward it off by sheer strength of will; she only succeeded in prolonging the inevitable. When it was over, she felt weak and drained, gratefully accepted Richard's supporting arm; much of her stamina had been sapped by her week's siege of sickness.

She was suddenly conscious of her appearance, was glad that he'd shut out the light along with the cold, glad that the only illumination came from the homemade lamp she and Catherine had carried into the chamber so short a time ago. She needed no mirror to show her the strains of these past four weeks, and she found herself remembering that her hair needed to be washed, that her apron was smudged, her hands chapped and blistered, and the manicured nails, always a particular vanity of hers, had suffered so from the neglect of necessity that she hated even to look at them.

When she'd began to cough, Richard had pressed a handkerchief into her hand. She looked at it now, deriving a childish yet very real comfort in its possession, no less in the feel of his cloak; she was still young enough to take pleasure in wearing something that was his, that still held within its folds warmth drawn from his body.

'I brought Gareth for you,' he said unexpectedly.

She raised her head from his chest. 'I know. I saw from the window. That was how I knew it was you. I thought at first that . . . that it was George.'

She moved in his arms, unable to suppress the tremor triggered by memory of that moment, felt his lips brush her forehead. But she wasn't yet ready to talk about George, was grateful that Richard seemed to sense that, for he made no comment.

'Richard, how did you find me?'

'Véronique. She's waiting for you down in the kitchen. So is Francis, and by now, half of Aldgate. When I latched the shutters, I saw a crowd gathering in the street. I suspect you're about to take your place in local legend, ma belle.'

Tilting her face up, he touched his lips very lightly to hers. 'Can you ever forgive me, Anne? I should never have left you in George's keeping, should have taken you to Berkhampsted to ma mère. . . .'

'Richard, do not blame yourself. How could you know what George would do?'

'But I could have spared you this. It did not have to be. That day I came to you at the Herber, before going North. . . . Do you know what I wanted to do? I wanted nothing so much as to take you before a priest that very afternoon, to forget about posting the banns or seeking a papal dispensation, and make you my wife then and there. Jesú, if only I had!'

'Richard . . . Richard, are you asking me to marry you?'

'Actually,' he admitted, and grinned, 'I rather took it for granted, did not think there was a need to ask. Do you mind, sweetheart?'

'No,' Anne said softly. 'No, I do not mind.' Wrapping her arms around his neck, she stopped her mouth just inches from his. 'I love you so much, I always have. . . . But what of your brother, Richard? What of Ned? Will he give his consent? He did not think me a fit bride for you two years ago. . . . What if he forbids the match? If he would rather you not wed. . . .'

She hesitated and he suggested helpfully, 'The impoverished widow of a Lancastrian rebel?'

She nodded mutely and only when she saw the corner of his mouth quirk with suppressed laughter did she realize he'd been speaking of Elizabeth Woodville.

'Oh, love, be serious! A king may do as he pleases. A king's brother must do as the king pleases.'

'Sweetheart, you still do not see, do you? Ned is well aware that you hold my heart, fully expects us to wed. Do you not remember how he took pains to bring us together at Coventry? The truth of it, ma belle, is that Ned looks upon you as my reward for Barnet and Tewkesbury.'

That sounded so like Edward to her that Anne no longer doubted, began to laugh.

Footsteps echoed beyond the door and quickly retreated. They'd drawn apart a little at the sound; Richard adjusted his cloak again about her shoulders, smoothed the thick braid coiled at the nape of her neck.

'I would as soon be away from here, beloved.' He glanced about the chamber with a flicker of distaste. 'I want to take you where it will be warm and quiet, where I can settle you before the hearth and feed you honey for that cough.' He dropped a kiss lightly upon the tip of her nose, and, in an abrupt change of tone, said sombrely, 'And then I want you to tell me what George did to make you flee the Herber. All of it, Anne.'

She nodded slowly.

Pressing her hand to his mouth, he kissed her palm and each fingertip in turn, frowning over the raw unhealed welt that blistered her skin from thumb to wrist. 'How did you . . .?'

'Cooking grease. Richard, where are we to go? To Baynard's Castle?'

'No. As soon as Véronique told me you were here, I sent word to St Martin's that a sanctuary house should be made ready for your use. I also gave orders to bring from Baynard's Castle all you're most likely to need.'

She smiled, reached up to caress his cheek, touched in no small measure that he'd thus thought to keep her safe from slander.

'It will not be for long, Anne. . . . Just until I may truly take you home. Home to Middleham.'

'Home to Middleham,' she echoed. 'If you only knew how I did yearn to hear you say that and how I despaired that it could ever be.'

II

⧼

Westminster
November 1471

Richard was observing his brother with amused admiration. Edward had privately confided to him several hours ago that he'd had wine enough the night before to burst a man's bladder and to benumb even the liveliest tongue. Now his head felt like to split and he doubted his stomach could take anything heavier than air, he confessed, and then grimaced at the thunderous racket that erupted at his feet, where one of his dogs was thumping its tail against the table leg.

Richard could sympathize; he'd suffered the morning-after doldrums a time or two himself. What did impress him was the fact that none but he was aware of Edward's discomfort. He'd been watching Edward grant audiences for two hours, composedly communicating only a civil interest in the petitions being brought before him.

At sight of the man being ushered in, Richard's brows drew together in an involuntary contraction of dislike. He did not trust John Morton, not in the least. The Lancastrian priest had been included in the general pardon Edward had proclaimed less than a month ago and he now made a rather eloquent avowal of the loyalties he'd so newly engrafted onto the House of York. It was a polished performance and Richard did not like Morton any the better for it. He said as much as soon as they were alone and his brother nodded agreement, before pointing out, 'He is no favourite of mine, either, Dickon, but the man has ability. His was probably the best brain of those advising Marguerite d'Anjou and I see no reason not to avail myself of it. I was giving thought to naming him as Master of the Rolls. . . . I gather that would not meet with your approval, then?'

'No. Oh, he's clever enough, I daresay. But I'd as soon have men around me whom I could trust.'

'The art of governing, Dickon, is that of making use of talent wherever you do find it. Trust is too rare an attribute to make it your prime prerequisite for holding office. If I relied only upon those I truly do trust, we'd have a council of empty chairs.'

Allowing the mask to slip then, Edward slumped down in his chair, rubbed his fingers gingerly against his temples. 'I have not felt like this since we were caught in that bitch of a gale crossing the Channel last March. I cannot complain about getting green-sick in the midst of a raging squall but after a night of pleasure? Another such morning-after as this and I might give some serious thought to the merits of self-denial.'

'I can see you now,' Richard said, and grinned, 'praying nightly to St Augustine, "Give me chastity and continency, but do not give it yet."'

Edward grinned, too. 'I must say your company has improved

considerably now that you're no longer so lovelorn. Speaking of which, how is your lass?'

'Much better; her cough be all but gone. Little wonder she took sick. Anne's not strong and life was far from easy at that inn.'

'Anne Neville at an Aldgate inn. . . . Damn me but I can still scarcely credit it.' Edward shook his head in bemusement. 'How did the innkeeper and his family react, being told of a sudden that it was Warwick's Anne who'd been mending their sheets and helping out at the mashing vat? Dumbfounded, I daresay?'

Richard nodded. 'First shock and then fear. From what Anne tells me, the Brownells are Lancastrian, and I'd wager they spoke freely before her and Véronique, freely enough to send one or more of them to the Tower on a charge of treason.' Anne would have been distressed by this admission, fearing for the Brownells, but Richard knew his brother better than she, knew Edward might be ruthless when the need arose, but vindictive he was not.

'Well, I'm sure you were able to set their minds at ease, Dickon, and from what I hear, they seem to be doing right well these days. I understand they've been contracting with carpenters to put up a new roof come spring and there is a cistern in the inn court now, not to mention a fine pair of matched greys out in their stables.'

'How do you know that?' Richard demanded, marvelling, as always, at his brother's store of unexpected knowledge.

'I know, too, that a certain church in Aldgate is suddenly the richer by two stained-glass windows,' Edward said, and smiled. 'I think it is just as well I'm giving you those manors forfeited by Oxford, little brother. If you are set upon acting as the patron saint for all of Aldgate, you'll be needing the extra income!'

Richard shrugged, slightly embarrassed. 'Whatever I've done for the Brownells, Ned, is as nothing compared to what they did for me. When I think what might have befallen Anne. . . .'

'I know. But she's come through it unscathed, thank Christ. What of her feelings for George? Is she very bitter?'

'How could you expect her to be otherwise? Of course she's bitter!'

'I was not suggesting she did not have cause, Dickon. You need not be so touchy. But it is as I told you; it's a damnably awkward choice I'm faced with. I have no doubts whatsoever that Anne spoke the truth, that George did have some lunatic abduction scheme in mind. But we have no proof of that. He does deny it all, ad nauseam. And even if there were a chance Isabel would confirm what she told Anne, what then? Do you and Anne want all that brought out into the open? Made public knowledge? Knowing the humiliation that would give ma mère and Isabel?

'We might as well face it, Dickon. I cannot very well bring him to trial on a would-be abduction charge. Still less can I merely confine him to the Tower; I'd not do that to ma mère. I cannot expect you to forget what did happen. But I would ask this of you, that you make an effort to look upon it as being done and beyond recall.' Unable to resist a sardonic reminder that this was, for them, an ironic reversal of roles, Edward added, 'Not even God can change the past. You once said that when you were urging me to forgive George his treason, remember? It still holds true, Dickon.'

Richard was quiet for a time. 'I've a confession of sorts to make, Ned. When I told you that I'd begun to wonder if George was mad, I'm not sure how serious I was. I think I was groping for answers more than anything else. But I'm more and more inclined to believe it's true. Rational men do not do the things he has done. And, if so, then he cannot be held to account for his actions.'

'I rather agree with you, Dickon. Any other man would thank God fasting for Anne's safe return, for I did threaten to send him to the block if any harm came to her. But George. . . . Damned if he does not see himself as vindicated, claims we do owe him an apology for doubting his word. I tell you, Dickon, he does defy belief.'

Richard looked up at that; his eyes were very dark. 'Oh, I

believe it,' he said bitterly. 'And that is precisely the reason why I do not want to see him, Ned. I may be able to say to you that he's not to blame for what he has done, but to come face to face with him . . . I do not trust myself enough for that.'

Edward nodded. 'The same feeling does come upon me from time to time. You do know he's adamant in his refusal to consent to your marriage? Claims he has the right of wardship over Anne because of her age and kinship to Isabel. That does cast a shadow on the title of the lands, to say the least. I expect I'll be able to bring him around if I do lean on him hard enough. But it may take some time, Dickon. You'll just have to be patient, lad.'

'How patient?'

Edward hesitated. 'Well, I cannot say for sure,' he said, somewhat evasively, 'but I think you'd best not post the banns till after the New Year.'

'I've no intention of accommodating George,' Richard said tersely.

'Not George, Dickon . . . me. I cannot have the two of you at sword's point. That you're in the right and he's in the wrong does not change that. Now you've already told me that Anne is very loath to see George lay claim to her family's lands. Well, I need time to make George see reason. Ah, damnation, Dickon, that's not so much to ask. You could not expect to wed right away, in any event, will have to petition the Holy See for a dispensation to wed since you are cousins.' He paused, then added, 'Moreover, a delay could serve your interests in yet another way, by giving you time to mend the damage done by Lancaster.'

Richard's head jerked up. His first impulse was to tell his brother not to meddle where he was not wanted, but the words died on his lips. Embracing Anne that Saturday afternoon in an Aldgate inn bedchamber, he was sure he'd prevailed over the shadows of her past. A fortnight later, he knew it was not so, was not to be that simple. After a thoughtful pause, he said cautiously, 'I'll not deny that Anne has some ugly memories. But why should you think she's still bothered by them?'

Edward had twisted around in his chair, away from the window; he raised his hand now to shield his eyes against the morning light. 'Because she's not had time to forget. Scars upon the mind do heal far more slowly than those of the body ... especially when we speak of women and hurts inflicted in bed.'

Richard had no chance to respond, for it was then that Edward's daughters burst into the chamber, shepherded by several harried nursemaids. Bess and Mary at once began to squabble over who got to sit in Edward's lap, while little Cecily clung to the back of his chair and tugged at his arm.

Richard watched with amusement. They were beautiful children, his brother's little girls, seemed to have emerged untouched from the ordeal of seven months' sanctuary. Richard knew his mother thought Ned indulged them too much, and he conceded now that neither he nor any of his brothers and sisters would ever have dared to greet their father the way Ned's daughters were clambering on top of him. But he knew, too, that none of the Duke of York's children had loved him as these little girls loved Ned.

'Softly, Bess, softly! You must confine yourself to squeals ... no shrieks ... for my head does ache right fearfully.'

They subsided slightly, giggling. Having lost out to Bess, Mary came over and gave Richard a hug and a wet, ill-aimed kiss. In appearance, Mary was the most like her mother but the pale-green eyes were alight with a warmth he'd never had from Elizabeth Woodville. He hugged her back, made room for her beside him in the window seat.

Edward had waved the nurses away. Richard knew he generally found time for his children on even the busiest days. Just as, years before, he'd somehow always had time for an admiring little brother.

The memory made Richard smile. Coming to his feet, he helped Cecily up onto the seat beside her sister and then reached over to give Bess's blonde braids a playful tug. She grinned, showed a gap between her front teeth that hadn't been there the last time he'd seen her; her father's blue eyes laughed into his. He wondered suddenly what his and Anne's children would look like; both Kathryn and Johnny were dark.

'Are you off, Dickon? St Martin's, I'll wager. . . . At least I always know where to find you these days.'

They both laughed and Bess was glad. She liked to hear her father laugh, knew that meant he'd not be as likely to send her away with a hasty kiss and talk about being busy. But she found nothing in their conversation to hold her interest and chose now to call their attention back to herself.

'I saw Uncle George outside. I think he wanted to see you, Papa, but when he heard Uncle Dickon was with you, he went away.' She glanced up, saw how swiftly all amusement had fled their faces.

'I do not like him much,' she said flatly.

She felt her father's hand move caressingly on her hair. 'Why not, sweetheart?'

'Because you do not, Papa.'

Edward opened his mouth to make the conventional denial. He didn't, though, said instead, 'You are right, Bess. I do not.'

12

St Martin Le Grand London
February 1472

Winter dusk was fast falling. Since mid-afternoon, snow clouds had been drifting in from the east, now encircled all of Greater

London. Glancing up at the patch of sky visible from the bed, Anne frowned; Richard left at dawn the next day for Shene, and it looked as if he'd have foul weather for travel. She leaned over, touched her lips first to his temple pulse and then to the hair slanting across his forehead. The corner of his mouth curved in acknowledgment of her caress, but he didn't open his eyes. She leaned over still farther, gave him a rather awkward upside-down kiss, the best she could do at the moment, for he had his head pillowed in her lap.

'I should be off, ma belle. Yet another envoy arrived this week from Brittany and I have to see him ere I join Ned at Shene. What with war looming so likely between Brittany and France, Duke Francis is becoming more and more importunate in his entreaties for English aid.'

Richard made no move to get up, however, seemed content to lie there and let Anne stroke his hair. She unbuttoned his shirt, slipped her hands inside.

'If you'll turn over, love, I'll rub your back,' she coaxed. 'You're so tense; your muscles are tied in knots.'

She concentrated her efforts on his right shoulder, broken and improperly set more than nine years ago in a fall at the quintain. She recalled the mishap very vividly, could still see the way he'd looked as he'd been carried up into the keep, his face grimy with the dust of the tilt yard and contorted with pain. Massaging his shoulders now, she could feel the disparity not visible through his clothes, although she remembered him mentioning once that he had the right shoulder-pauldron on his armour adjusted to accommodate the mended break. It pleased her to have such intimate knowledge of his body; it seemed somehow to make him all the more irrevocably hers.

She brushed his hair aside, found the thin silver chain of his pilgrim cross and tracked it with soft kisses until he rolled over, drew her down beside him.

'You are so fair to look upon, Anne. I marvel that I should be

so lucky, knowing that your face shall be my first sight upon awakening and my last before sleep.'

'Have a care,' she whispered. 'When you do say things like that,
I am sorely tempted to keep you with me, even knowing it might
mean serious affront to the lords of Brittany.'

She'd spoken lightly but truthfully; she was tempted. Her reasons
for restraint were no longer as persuasive as they once seemed.
Yes, it would be a sin, but she could not make herself believe it
was a sin to bring upon them eternal damnation, no matter what
the Church did say. After all, she reasoned, surely a sin so widely
practised must be judged less harshly by the Almighty, else most
all of mankind were doomed.

Regrettably, she'd not found it as easy to allay her other concern,
her fear that Richard might get her with child. It was not so
much that she feared branding her child with the stigma of illegitimacy. If it came to that, they could always wed without
waiting for the papal dispensation. But her pride cringed at the
thought; it appalled her to think of people smirking and counting
upon their fingers when the babe was born.

Richard had reluctantly concurred, unwilling to subject her to
the scurrilous gossip that had so grieved both Kate and Nan. But
his good intentions notwithstanding, there were times when he
urged Anne most persuasively to reconsider and she was more
and more inclined to let herself be persuaded.

It was true that she had yet to experience again the intensity
of feeling that had assailed her so unexpectedly and overwhelm-
ingly that afternoon in the inn, during those first moments when
emotion had briefly banished memory. The memories had soon
come back upon her, of course, but they were not as troubling
as they'd once been, grew less and less so with the passing weeks.
Her shyness did not outlast November and if the desire Richard
stirred in her was lacking in urgency, it was pleasurable, nonetheless, was more than she'd once expected to ever feel. And as
February sands trickled into the ornate hourglass she kept by her

bed, she found herself wondering with increasing frequency what it would be like to lay with him; only that past week, she'd awakened, flushed and disconcerted, from what had been the first erotic dream of her life.

She watched Richard now as he sat up, reached across the bed to rescue his doublet from the ravaging jaws of the spaniel puppy he'd given her as her New Year's gift. But when he pulled it on over his shirt, she sat up abruptly to protest.

'Richard, you are not leaving? Oh, not yet, love!'

'Anne, I must.'

Moving to the window, Richard gazed out at the gathering snow. The flakes were drifting down languidly, brushing in midair and settling like powdery-white moths upon the stripped branches and shrivelled vines of the barren winter-ravaged landscape below. By the morrow, the roads would be fit for sledding and little else.

He wished Ned had not summoned him to Shene. It would serve for naught; George was not going to see reason unless forced to it. And so far, Ned. . . . He jettisoned the thought, half formed, and pressed his fist against the glass; it was clouded with moisture drawn through the inevitable chinks and cracks that veined the window embrasure. He did not trust himself to confront George again. Ever since Richard had seen Anne safely into sanctuary here at St Martin's, George had taken conspicuous care to keep out of his way. But there'd been an unexpected encounter on Ephiphany Eve, and with George's first defensive sarcasm, Richard's pent-up rage had broken through, spilling over onto them both in a scalding surge of accusation and invective. What followed was a savage shouting match that came perilously close to violence. Richard unclenched his fist, spread his hand flat against the pane. And it was likely to happen again, all too likely.

'Will you take the river to Shene, Richard?'

He turned away from the window. 'I think not, unless the snow does ease up.'

641

Anne was groping under the bed for her shoes. 'Will you be gone for long?'

He shrugged and she said what she knew she shouldn't. 'It will not do any good, Richard . . . going to Shene. George is not about to relinquish his claims to the Neville and Beauchamp lands, not until Ned makes him. And Ned is not willing to do that.'

'This does no good, either,' he said irritably. 'Every time we begin to talk of what Ned has or has not done, we end up quarrelling, and I do not want to leave you with harsh words unhealed between us.'

Anne was at once contrite. 'Nor do I, love. It is just that I so hate to be parted from you. . . . Sometimes at night, I dream it is as it was before, that there be walls between us too high ever to be breached, and I wake up aching that you're not asleep beside me.'

'That could be remedied easily enough,' he said pointedly, but then he smiled. 'Now come here, wench, and bid me a proper farewell!'

She did, so effectively that he decided he could linger a few moments longer. He brushed her hair back as it strayed across her throat, wound a thick burnished rope around his hand.

'Anne, I've been giving thought to the lands in dispute. Ned has been most generous with me. Now that he's seen fit to give me the estates forfeited by the Earl of Oxford . . . Well, they do total more than eighty manors, sweetheart, and will yield a right handsome yearly income. Add to that, the grants he made me last June of Middleham, Sheriff Hutton and Penrith, and. . . .'

'And we'd have no need of more. Is that what you're saying?' Giving him no chance to reply. 'Richard, you know how I do feel about this. It is not that the lands do mean so much to me. By rights, they are my mother's, after all. But if she's not to have them, I'm damned if I'll see them go to George! I cannot keep him from laying claim to Isabel's portion but I'll not concede him so much as an acre more. Why should I?'

'I did not say. . . .'

'How could you ask that of me? I do not understand, truly I don't.'

'Are you going to hear me out or not? Surely you know I like it not. Do you think I want to see George enriched at our expense? But I want to wed you, Anne. I'm wearying of these delays.'

'Richard, I'm impatient, too, that we wed. But why must we make such a choice? It's so utterly unfair. Why should George not only escape his sins unscathed but emerge the richer for it? When I think of what he has done . . . and continues to do. He has no right to claim wardship over me, no right to the Beauchamp lands, and I do not understand why Ned seems unable to curb his demands.'

'We've been over this time and time again. George is not capable of responding to reason as another man would. You might better measure the mists on Malvern Hills than try to untangle what goes on in his head. Not even threats have so far worked with him. I'm beginning to think nothing short of a stay in the Tower will.'

'That sounds like a marvellously fair idea to me,' Anne said tartly. 'I'd wager that if Ned cast him into the Tower for a spell, he'd lose his taste for my lands quick enough. And God knows, that's where he most deserves to be!'

'You know quite well why Ned is reluctant to take so drastic a measure as that,' he said, striving for patience but finding only the teeth-gritting kind. 'His forbearance is not for George; he refrains for our lady mother's sake. She's had more than her share of grieving on George's behalf and Ned would not add to her hurts if he can help it.'

'So you keep telling me. And I'm sure it is true . . . as far as it goes.'

'What mean you by that, Anne?'

'I do not doubt that Ned wants to spare your mother. But I

think there is yet another reason for Ned's failure to act, one you are either unable or unwilling to recognize.'

'Indeed?' Richard said icily. 'Are you saying you know my brother's motives better than I do?'

She disregarded the warning. 'Do you remember a few weeks ago, when you told me that Ned said your greatest failure of judgment is that you tend to be too quick to act? At the time, I could see only the irony in that, for Ned's not one to act at all unless he is forced to it.'

'That's ridiculous!'

'Is it? Oh, Richard, think! You need only look to his marriage for proof of what I say. Five months wed he was before he made the marriage known and only then because his council was pressing him to take the French bride my father had found for him.

'Nor is that the only time he sought to deal with trouble by ignoring it. Richard, that has ever been his way . . . and you know it. He's always been one for putting off problems till the morrow. Moreover, George is a problem he's long used to living with. Richard, we do have to face it. He just cannot be bothered to teach George a lesson long overdue, not when it is so much easier to wait George out. What does the delay cost him, after all? You and I are the ones to pay the price.'

'You have all the answers, have you not? Or so you think.'

Recalling suddenly his tendency to end quarrels by walking out on them, she took several steps backward, leaned against the door. 'Tell me, then. Tell me how I am wrong. Most willingly I'll hear you out. Surely we can talk of this without anger?'

'What would you have me say, Anne? Do you think I've not talked to Ned? Christ, I've urged him till there be nothing left to say!'

'I did not know. You never said. You always seemed to accept his reasons for not acting and I . . . I thought you were content to wait. . . .'

'Content? Oh, God!' Richard laughed, but there was no humour whatsoever in it. 'What could I possibly find to content me in the sight of George strutting about the court when he should by rights be in the Tower? George preening himself like an injured innocent and bemoaning to all who'll listen how I've wronged him. What contentment do you think it gives me each time that bitch, my sweet sister-in-law, does ask me before a score or more of spectators if I am wed yet and then affects great surprise that it is not so? Or that her misbegotten whelp Thomas Grey amuses himself by wagering which will come first, my marriage or George's murder.

'I've always loathed Westminster, always. But now ... now there are days when I think I'll never draw an easy untainted breath till I am back at Middleham.' Adding bitterly, 'And Christ only knows when that will be.'

'My love, I did not know,' she repeated, but he paid her no heed, seemed intent only upon saying what for weeks had been festering in silence.

'And then I come here and you do naught but nag at me for what is beyond my control. If you must have me say it, I do not know why Ned puts off a reckoning with George. I do not understand it and I do resent it; are you satisfied now?'

Anne shook her head slowly; it was the first time she'd heard him so openly critical of his brother.

'Richard, I'm sorry. If only you'd told me how you felt. . . . Had I known you were so unhappy over the way things were at court, I'd not have been so quick to burden you with my own discontent.'

She'd long since moved from the door. Now she closed the few feet still keeping them apart and put her arms around him. He responded but with enough reluctance to give her pause. She looked up intently into his face and made a private vow, that she must somehow learn to bite her tongue each time she was tempted to find fault with Ned. She touched his cheek, said with genuine regret, 'I've given you none too easy a time these weeks past, have I?'

645

A remark like that would normally have drawn from him a teasing retort. She was not reassured when he said only, 'If I'm to be back at Westminster by Compline, I should leave now.'

'Richard . . . Richard, you are not still angry with me, are you?'

'It's not that I'm angry with you, Anne. It's this damnable web we're entangled in. I'm weary of struggling to get free of it and making so little headway.'

She tightened her arms around his neck at that, brought her mouth up to his. 'You still want me then?' she asked, half playfully, half seriously, and, as she hoped, that drew an immediate response, as reassuring as it was predictable.

'Want you?' he said after a time. 'There are times when I do want you so much that it's like to drive me mad.' He ran his hands lightly and possessively over her body and then pulled her even closer. An elusive fragrance of jasmine clung to her hair, her skin. He kissed her again. 'I thought it would get better once I was sure you were mine, but it does only get worse. Nothing does ease the wanting, beloved.'

Anne stood very still. She felt his mouth against her hair, felt his hands slide up from her waist to her breasts, but the warm tingling flush that had been spreading so pleasantly through her body had, without warning, congealed into ice. She felt only numbness now as she struggled to deny what she should have long ago realized. Nothing does ease the wanting, he'd said. Nothing.

She brought her eyes up sharply to his face, but still she hesitated. Whilst there was much he might choose to keep from her, he'd not lie to her. She knew him well enough to be sure of that. If she asked him, he'd tell her the truth. Do not, an inner voice cautioned, do not ask, even as she said, 'Since we promised to wed, have you . . . been with any other women?'

His hands hurt, so suddenly did they tighten upon her shoulders. She had her answer in the silence that followed her question, knew before he nodded what he would say.

'Yes.'

She now found herself free, did not even realize she'd pulled back from his embrace. Nan, she thought dully, it could only be Nan. The other girl was safely away from London but Nan was no farther than Westminster. Nan, who was so pretty and who shared her name; why that should make it worse, she did not know, but somehow it did. Nan, who was inevitably and irresistibly bound to Richard by the blood that flowed in the veins of their son.

'You told me it was done between you and her,' she said in a low, accusing voice. 'And I believed you.'

'Her?' he echoed. 'You mean . . . Nan? Good Lord, Anne, I've not seen her for months! I did not take a mistress; on that, you do have my word.'

So great was her relief that it was a moment or so before she could sort her feelings out, realize that she still did not like it much.

She sat down abruptly upon the bed, staring at the green-and-gold glitter of her betrothal ring. It would be demeaning to let herself be jealous of trollops. She knew she was supposed to overlook such lapses, that her pride demanded as much. He, too, would expect no less. He'd been far more tolerant of her jealousy than many men would have been, had been honest with her about Nan and Kate, about the son and daughter conceived in sin. But he'd be neither amused nor flattered if she were now to reproach him for seeking in other beds what she'd denied him in hers. She was not supposed to mind such straying. How was it, then, that what she should feel was at such variance with what she did feel? For she did mind, she minded dreadfully.

Her hair had fallen forward to weave a veil of dark gold threads across her cheek and throat. Richard had no need to see her face, however, to confirm her hurt. It showed all too clearly for his comfort, in the dejected slump of her shoulders, the betraying tension of the hands twisting together in her lap.

'Name of God, Anne . . .' he began, and then stopped. What was he going to do, berate her for what she had not said? He had no reason to feel guilty. Under the circumstances, none at all. So why, then, did her silence make him so uncomfortable?

'What else was I to do, Anne?' he said reasonably. 'Do you think I could have been so patient with you these weeks past had I not found ease elsewhere? Being with you like this, wanting you as I've never wanted any other woman in my life. . . . Well, what else could I do?' He suddenly realized he was repeating himself; worse, that his explanation was verging upon the defensive.

'Surely you understand that it had nothing to do with what I feel for you? I cannot believe you'd be jealous of a harlot, sweetheart.'

'No, of course I would not,' she said hastily and untruthfully, sounding so forlorn that his resistance melted. Crossing to her, he reached down, raised her to her feet.

'The next time I say I must be off to Westminster, for God's sake, let me go!' he said, and Anne summoned a wan smile.

'More fool I,' she said, her voice so muffled against his chest as to be almost inaudible, 'for asking a question far better never raised. . . .'

They stood together in silence for a time. Richard stroked her hair, smoothed it back from her face. 'I love only you,' he said softly.

'Richard . . . I've changed my mind. Do what you like about the lands.'

'Are you sure, beloved?'

She nodded. 'I want to see George pay for what he's done. But even more do I want to be your wife. If we must buy his consent, then so be it.'

Few things had come harder to her than that grudging surrender. Her hatred for George was unrelenting, unforgiving, cried out for retaliation. But jealousy was stronger, would poison her peace in a way that George could never have done.

'You'll not regret it, Anne. You'll never regret it. That I do promise you, beloved.'

'Promise me rather,' she said, very low, 'that once we are wed, you'll share no bed but mine.'

She'd not meant to ask that, but now that she had, she wasn't sorry. She raised her eyes anxiously to his face, saw in the curve of his mouth the answer she so needed to hear. He bent his head, kissed her softly, and then began to laugh.

'I can think of no promise, Anne, it will give me greater pleasure to keep.'

13

Shene

February 1472

'What mean you to do about this, Ned?' Will Hastings raised questioning eyes from the correspondence before him. 'Shall you grant Brittany the aid it seeks?'

'I've not made up my mind yet. I do owe Francis for the money he advanced me in exile and I'd like nothing better than to give some grief to that whoreson on the French throne. But I'm leery of making too firm a commitment until I see how the winds blow. He's asking for six thousand archers; I thought I might send Anthony with a thousand or so.'

Edward shoved the papers across the table, watched a scribe begin to gather them up. Will, who had no liking for Anthony Woodville, had been about to indulge himself at Anthony's expense but something in Edward's face dissuaded him. He studied his friend more closely, saw the finely webbed lines around the eyes, the sharply chiselled set of the mouth. So the strain was getting to Ned, too. And why not? The tension was even getting to him and he had an unabashed taste for court blood-letting. If this rupture between Clarence and Gloucester were not soon healed, it was like to infect them all.

'Do you feel as bad as you look?'

'No jesting, Will; not today. I'm not much in the mood for it.'

Will beckoned for wine and then waved the servants out of earshot. Pouring Edward's cup himself, he said, 'I gather Clarence is still showing himself to be intransigent?'

'When has he ever been anything else? And if he were not enough of an aggravation, now I am having difficulties with Dickon, too.'

Edward scowled into his drink. Will waited.

'I had a right sharp quarrel with him this morning—with Dickon, I mean. He's convinced himself that I've been overly lax with George, is now threatening to wed the girl at once, says he does mean to marry her as soon as he gets back to London, whether George yields up his claims or not.'

'Rather high-handed of him I'd say,' Will murmured, and then suffered a prick of shame. He might not be able to deny the jealousy Gloucester did rouse in him but he need not give in to it as easily as this. Not only was it petty, it was not smart. To recoup, he said, more generously, 'He has been patient, though, Ned. You have to grant him that.'

'I do, but I do not see why he cannot be patient a while longer.' Edward set his cup down with a thud, pushed it impatiently from him.

'I tell you, Will, I am becoming bone-weary with this continuing strife between them. George could not see reason if he fell over it in the road but I expected more from Dickon. Damn him, he knows the bind I am in! I cannot deal with George as if he had his full wits about him; he does not.

'No, Will, it's not as simple as Dickon seems to think. He wants me to threaten to reclaim the Devon estates if George does not consent to the marriage. But if I strip George of what's right-fully his, I risk pushing him into another rising. He's rather friendly with George Neville these days and I've had Neville under suspicion for some time now, as you well know. I may have no proof as yet but I'd wager a great deal that Neville's in secret communication with his brother-in-law Oxford. I cannot do much about Oxford as long as he keeps to France but my cousin the Archbishop is far more vulnerable, as he'll learn to his cost if my suspicions be true. As for Brother George, he'll bear close watching; he does take to treason as naturally as fish to water and birds to air.

'With George, I have a choice. I can destroy him or I can put up with him; one or the other, Will. What does vex me is that Dickon knows that. But he's so set upon wedding the girl and taking her back to Middleham that he can see little else.

'I suspect George is looking now to save face more than anything else. But if Dickon goes ahead and marries Anne without giving George a chance to salvage his pride by grudgingly giving consent . . . Well, it'll be like striking flint to tinder.'

'As I see it then, there's but one action you can take, Ned. If you need more time to bring Clarence to heel, Gloucester must give you that time. Why not just forbid him to wed until you get Clarence to yield?'

'Because it never once did cross his mind that I might,' Edward said ruefully. 'Dickon takes it for granted that it would never even occur to me to do so, not knowing as I do how much Anne means to him.' There was irritated affection upon his face as he looked up at Will. 'And the damnable thing about faith like that, Will, is that you do find yourself forced to live up to it.'

'So there it is, George. Dickon's not willing to wait any longer. He does mean to wed Anne, whether you do agree to it or not, and I suspect there's little I can do about it.'

'You could forbid him,' George snapped, and Edward smiled faintly.

'The way I forbade you to marry Isabel?' he suggested, and George flushed.

'I did love Bella,' he said defensively, and at once regretted it for his brother was quick to point out, 'And Dickon loves Anne.'

'I do not doubt Dickon loves the lands she'd bring him!'

'As it happens, George, Dickon indicated to me that he felt sure an accommodation could be worked out about the lands. I fully expect a compromise of sorts could be reached if. . . .'

'No!'

'I rather suspected you'd say that. A pity . . . I'd have preferred to settle this amicably, but settle it I mean to do. Frankly, George, I've no more patience. For three months now, you and Dickon have given me little peace over this and I'm heartily sick of it.'

George's eyes had narrowed, the pupils contracting as if adjusting to a sudden blinding surge of sun. 'Just what have you in mind to do?'

'It is very simple, George.' Edward sorted through the papers before him, lifted one for George's inspection. 'I had another letter from your mother-in-law at Beaulieu. I'm sure you can guess what she does ask of me. She wants to leave sanctuary and she wants her lands restored to her.'

George was suddenly rigid in his chair. Edward balanced the letter between his thumb and forefinger, sent it winging across the marble-top table; it struck the edge, fluttered to the floor. He watched George's eyes lock onto it, follow its downward drift.

'I've been giving it a great deal of thought, George, and the more I think on it, the more inclined I am to grant her request. If I return the Countess's lands to her, I do most effectively end all squabbles between you and Dickon over what Anne is or is not entitled to have. If there are no lands to claim, there is no problem, either.'

George rose abruptly to his feet, only to stand irresolute. He should have known, should have seen this coming. Ned always had his way in the end. He'd take it all in the guise of fairness, give the Beauchamp estates back to Bella's mother. Warwick Castle, the manors in the southwest, the Herber. All would go to Warwick's widow. But not Middleham. Dickon and Anne would still have the lands Ned had given him last June, but he and Bella. . . . They'd have nothing.

'I do not want you to do that, Ned,' he said thickly.

Edward said nothing, merely watched him with unhurried, expectant eyes. George sucked in a ragged breath, sat down again.

The winter weather unexpectedly thawed, the skies clearing to a bright brittle blue, the winds subsiding and the lingering chill in the air more bracing than brutal.

Richard soothed the taut creature upon his wrist. The hooded head was turned toward the unseen yet beckoning expanse of sky; the talons tightened upon his leather gauntlet, and a sound rose eagerly in its throat, low yet harsh.

He'd never had a Greenland falcon until now, preferring the smaller, less mettlesome peregrine. But this one had been a gift from the Earl of Northumberland, not so much an act of generosity as one of accommodation to the man with whom Northumberland would be sharing power north of the Trent. Whatever Northumberland's motivation, Richard was much taken with the falcon; it was a beautiful bird, snow-white in colour and awesome in flight. He'd seen it kill before, swift, silent and lethal.

He unsnapped its lead now and then removed the hood. It exploded into the air as if launched from a crossbow, beating white wings taking it up into the bright blindness that haloed the sun. Higher and higher it rose and then, as suddenly, it was hurtling toward the earth, and Richard swore, seeing the prey that had broken cover, that was making a twisting, terrified attempt at flight across the snow-glazed field. There was nothing he could do but watch in disgust as the rabbit raced the down-plunging falcon. The end came with predictable swiftness, in a sudden swirl of snow and fur and striking talons.

Richard swore again and gestured toward a waiting attendant. The man moved obediently into the brush to attempt to retrieve the errant falcon. But by the time he found it, Richard knew, the bird would be too well gorged to take interest in its proper prey. For all practical purposes, the hunt had just ended. Richard turned his attention then to quieting his palfrey; it shied and then snorted, nostrils flaring as the wind brought to it the unnerving scent of warm blood.

Looking about him, Richard saw that his brother was having better luck than he. As he guided his mount nearer to watch the circling stalk overhead, Edward turned in the saddle, motioned him closer.

'Did you see? A fine kill,' he enthused. 'Did I not say she was a prime hunter?' He signalled approvingly to the man who'd flushed the peregrine's quarry. 'I knew she could be reclaimed, given time.'

'A right fair showing,' Richard agreed politely.

This was the first time he'd been alone with Edward since they'd quarrelled so upon his arrival at Shene. But if he felt some constraint, Edward apparently did not; he said, as naturally as if the quarrel had never been, 'What befell that big gerfalcon of yours, the one you've been bragging on?' And laughed when Richard had to confess its fall from grace.

'I want to talk to you, Dickon.'

Richard stroked his stallion's neck. 'I have not changed my mind, Ned.' He gestured vaguely, said, 'I should see to my falcon.'

'As you wish. I just thought you might be interested to know that brother George has had a change of heart.'

He laughed again then, for Richard had swung his mount around so sharply that he almost unseated himself.

'You mean he's actually agreed to the marriage?'

'Well, "agree" is not precisely the right word. Let's say rather, that he's now inclined to see your marriage as the lesser of evils.'

Still laughing, Edward raised a hand to flick wind-whipped bright hair from his eyes. 'I told you I'd bring him around in time, did I not? And I've never yet broken my word to you, at least not when it counted.'

Richard was laughing, too. 'I never doubted you'd act on it, Ned. I just feared that by the time you did, I'd be too old to care.'

'Mind you, we're not out of the woods yet. The terms he's offering are too outrageous, too outlandish, to be taken seriously. But the important thing is that he's resigned himself to the inevitability of the marriage. It will not take long now for me to squeeze a more equitable settlement out of him. I'd say a month at most; well, maybe a whit longer.'

Some of Richard's excitement began to ebb. So it was not quite as clear cut as Ned had first made him think. With George a month could well become three, then four.

'What is he asking?'

'Demanding is more like it; if he practised a like trade upon the roads, he'd be hanged as a highwayman. He's willing that you should have Middleham, Sheriff Hutton and Penrith, and willing, too, to overlook the fact that they are yours whether you do marry Anne or not. But he claims most all else, Dickon, the whole of his mother-in-law's lands, and the Beauchamp holdings must total a good one hundred and fifty manors. He does want the earldom of Warwick and Warwick Castle, of course. Also the earldom of Salisbury. Ah, yes, the Herber, too.' Edward grinned in spite of himself, said, 'Such gall is almost admirable. And lest I forget, there's one thing more. Are you ready for this? He also demands that you yield up to him your office as Great Chamberlain. If it be true, as I once charged, that his brains are maggot-ridden, his greed is well nigh intact and thriving.'

'Tell him,' Richard said, 'that his terms are acceptable to me.'

Edward's jaw dropped. 'Dickon, you cannot be serious. Christ, man, he's robbing you blind.'

'How large a dowry did Elizabeth Woodville bring you, Ned?'

That drew a reluctant laugh from Edward. 'Little wonder you handle yourself so well upon the field; you do have a feel for the vitals.' But in truth, he was not at all displeased by Richard's choice; it would, he thought, simplify matters considerably.

14

Westminster

April 1472

Richard would have made Anne his wife at once but the Church calendar seemed to be conspiring with George; by the time he'd given his grudging consent, it was Lent. As the Marriage Mass was prohibited from Ash Wednesday until the Sunday after Easter, the banns could not be proclaimed until early April. Three weeks later, Richard and Anne were married in St Stephen's Chapel at Westminster. It was a ceremony most notable for its simplicity. They had chosen not to be married by Anne's uncle, the Archbishop of York, and had chosen, too, to be wed quietly and quickly, forgoing any of the lavish festivities that would normally have heralded a royal wedding.

Edward, who would quite happily have feasted their nuptials into the following day, reluctantly concurred once he saw that they were both stubbornly set upon having their way in this. He was disappointed but not all that surprised by their choice; his court could hold few happy memories for the daughter of the

Earl of Warwick. Perhaps it was just as well, he mused, that Dickon would be taking her North.

Anne was now no more than four or five feet from where Edward stood, her skirts spreading about her in a froth of sea-green silk and creamy Mantua lace as she paid homage to his wife. He grinned, noting how even then her eyes strayed across the chamber, seeking Richard. She was prettier than he remembered but so slender that he found himself wondering how good a breeder she'd be. For a moment, his eyes lingered fondly upon his wife, who'd given birth to their fourth daughter only a fortnight ago, and then shifted back to Anne, to find she was once again staring past Elizabeth, toward Richard. He laughed; at least Dickon need never doubt that she loved him.

He was mistaken, however, as to Anne's motivation. She was not watching Richard with yearning; she was seeking to reassure herself that he was out of earshot, for Elizabeth seemed intent upon drawing blood, and Anne wanted to spare Richard if she could.

'To wed without the papal dispensation. . . . How eager my brother-in-law of Gloucester must have been!'

'We both were, Madame,' Anne said, as politely as her resentment would permit.

Elizabeth was idly fingering Edward's latest gift, an Italian necklace of topaz and gold. 'Richard has ever been impetuous,' she observed, so patronizingly that Anne seethed with suppressed rage. She saw, too, the way Elizabeth's eyes were measuring her waistline, suddenly realized what Elizabeth suspected and thanked God Richard was not nearby.

'You must admit it's rather irregular and would make your marriage quite easy to dissolve, I daresay. But I gather that does not distress you?'

'No, Madame, it does not bother me in the least.'

'Your faith in him is touching. I expect you'll make a most dutiful wife,' Elizabeth said negligently. She was losing interest in this conversation. On balance, she'd been mildly pleased by Gloucester's marriage; it was not often she had the opportunity to see Clarence so openly thwarted. But she had no liking for this simpering child with Warwick's dark eyes, Warwick's blood, and an instinctive feel for what it took to convince men, even men as knowing as Ned, that she was much in need of male protection. It was Elizabeth's considered opinion that any girl able to get herself from Lancaster's bed to Gloucester's in less than a twelve-month was no more in need of protection than Eleanor of Aquitaine.

'I wish you well, my lady of Gloucester,' she said in a careless dismissal that Anne didn't mind in the least, so happy was she to escape this barbed conversation and so pleased to be addressed for the first time as the Duchess of Gloucester. She was tasting it upon her tongue, silently savouring the sound of it, when Elizabeth added, 'I wish you, too, more success in this marriage than you had in your first.'

In the minstrels' galley, they'd begun a slanderous Yorkist ballad, *The Banished Duke*, which purported to be an account of the illicit love affair between Marguerite d'Anjou and a Lancastrian Duke.

> *Now he lies betwixt two towers,*
> *He lies in cold clay,*
> *And the royal Queen of England*
> *Goes aweeping away.*

There were other verses, scarcely audible above the laughter. Anne alone was truly listening to the words. What a strange fate was hers, to have been Princess of Wales and Duchess of Gloucester in less than a twelve-month.

She shook her head, somewhat impatiently. This was no time to let Edouard of Lancaster lay claim to her mind or memories. She should rather be thanking Almighty God for the incredible luck that was hers, to have been given back all she'd ever wanted in this life and thought forever lost to her, Richard and Middleham.

Richard reached for Anne's hand, linked it in his upon the tablecloth. He was far more sober than Francis or Rob or Dick Ratcliffe, and Anne was grateful for his restraint—grateful, too, for his willingness to indulge her, to spare her the spectacle a court wedding would inevitably have become.

'You've been so sweet to me,' she said softly.

Richard pulled his wine cup toward them, shared it with her. She slid her fingers along his wrist and he turned her hand over, pressed a kiss into her palm. Rob saw the look that passed between them and said loudly, 'I'd say we're long overdue to escort the bridal couple to the marriage bed.'

Anne tensed and then reached again for their wine cup. She was among friends, could not be further in time or place from the French court. Francis was like a brother; she'd known Rob all her life and Dick Ratcliffe, too, was someone she knew and liked. His wife Agnes was a friend of long standing; she was Lord Scrope's eldest daughter, and although she was several years older than Anne, they shared many common memories of a Yorkshire childhood. Anna FitzHugh Lovell was her cousin and Véronique the dearest of friends. So why then, was she of a sudden so nervous, so ill at ease? This would not, she sought to reassure herself, be at all like the bedside revelries of her wedding night to Edouard of Lancaster.

That was a memory so painful that, even after more than sixteen months, she'd done her best to bury it beyond recall. Now, however, she was haunted by faces from her past. The wine-flushed faces of strangers encircling the marriage bed. The white tense fury upon the face of Marguerite d'Anjou, who'd bitterly opposed the consummation of the marriage but was overruled by the French King, who'd promised his friend the Earl of Warwick that he'd see Anne securely wedded and properly bedded. The relief upon her own mother's face, the subdued sympathy upon Isabel's. The sullen handsome face of her bridegroom, sensing her antipathy and resenting her for it, for the reluctance she could not hide from him.

The laughter had been overly loud, the jests bawdy enough to make her blush, and, overlaying all, such tension that their initial coupling was so traumatizing to her and so unsatisfactory to him that whatever chance they might ever have had of reaching some sort of accommodation ended that first night. They awoke in the morning as enemies, and by the time he died, Anne knew that he hated her fully as much as she did him.

'Anne?' Leaning over, Richard kissed her softly and then whispered, 'Would you rather I put a halt to this?'

Her eyes widened in grateful surprise. It would never even have occurred to her to ask that of him; the bedside revelries were so much a part of the wedding festivities that she'd taken it for granted there was naught to be done but endure it as best she could.

'Would you truly do that for me?' she asked wonderingly. He nodded, then set off a storm of protest by saying to the room at large, 'Rob always did think I could not make my way from the keep to the gatehouse without a guide. But I assure you that Anne and I can find our bedchamber without his generous offer of assistance . . . and I'd not have it on my conscience that you did disrupt the festivities on my behalf.'

The objections flew fast and furious, but the jests were good-natured if rather rowdy, the laughter friendly and, by tacit consent, all acted as if they truly believed Richard and not Anne to be the reluctant one. It was Anna Lovell who unfortunately if inadvertently marred the humour of the moment by striking a sudden sour note. Rob had persisted long after both Francis and Dick conceded defeat, but he, too, was now compelled to surrender, saying with a wry regretful shrug, 'Well, if you are so set upon spitting on tradition, Dickon, so be it then. But how you can in good conscience so disappoint your guests. . . .'

'Far better his guests, Rob, than his bride,' Anna Lovell observed artlessly, and then looked genuinely surprised when Anne flushed and Francis glared at her. There was very little malice in her makeup; she simply said whatever came into her head, however ill advised or injudicious. She blushed herself now, disconcerted by the sudden silence. She'd said no more than what they all knew, after all—that Anne's shyness was the true reason for Dickon's stubbornness. Why, then, should Francis be giving her yet another of his disapproving frowns and the others suddenly become so engrossed in the music?

She sighed, began to fiddle with her rings. She was not all that comfortable with these people. They were Francis's friends, not hers, and she could not rid herself of the suspicion that they scorned her for her family's Lancastrian loyalties. Francis insisted that was not so, but then, he'd have to say that, would he not? And now he'd be sure to scold her for causing embarrassment to Cousin Anne. She gave her young husband a sidelong glance that was half resentful, half appealing, and sighed again. He was so hard to please sometimes.

Beyond the bed, lights still blazed but Anne lay in darkness, the drawn bed hangings of Tripoli silk effectively screening out any vagrant traces of light. She heard Véronique's retreating foot-steps and, as the door opened, the sound of male voices, drifting in from the adjoining chamber. And then her husband's body squires were in the room, moving into the garde-robe, bringing lavers of warm herb-scented water, directing the chamber valets to stoke the hearth higher for the night.

Anne lay still, listening; there was a crash, smothered laughter, and she heard Richard's voice, low and good-naturedly reproving. Moving deeper into the bed, she shivered; the sheets were silky-smooth and as chilled as ice against her skin. She resisted the temptation to curl up for warmth and forced herself to stretch out so that she might warm the bed some for Richard.

When Richard drew the bed-hangings back, she saw that the candles had been extinguished, the only light now coming from the hearth. She'd been somewhat apprehensive about their first moments in bed together, that there might be an awkwardness between them; she was relieved to find that it wasn't so. He drew her to him, embraced her as naturally as if they'd been sharing a bed for months. As intimate as their lovemaking had become in those weeks before he'd gone to Shene, this was quite different for her, and she felt a certain shyness at the feel of his naked body against hers. He was gentle enough, however, to readily reassure her, and when he began to explore her body, he did so without haste, as if there were no urgency, and that, too, re-assured her.

She began slowly to relax; only now could she admit to herself just how tense she'd truly been. It was those accursed memories Rob had unwittingly stirred up; she knew that. Knew, too, that she was a fool to let them matter. It was just . . . just that she so wanted to please him, to make him happy. So much so that she ached with it. She could not bear to think of disappointing him, not ever, not in any way.

'I want so to be a good wife to you,' she whispered, with such intensity that he raised his head from her breast. In the flick-ering half-light she could just discern the quizzical tender smile that her words brought to his mouth.

'I've no complaints so far,' he said, and laughed.

She stroked his hair and with her fingers traced the uneven path of the scar that angled from wrist to elbow, the price he'd paid for the battle laurels he'd won for himself at Barnet. Turning her head, she put her lips to the hollow of his elbow, suddenly seeing the sun-whitened cloisters at Cerne and feeling again the chill that had gone through her as if to the very bone, upon hearing from Somerset that Richard had been hurt in the fighting. In many ways, that had been the worst day of her life. Never had she felt so alone, so abandoned. A dead rebel's daughter, an unwanted wife. Never had Richard seemed further away to her than on that day, standing with Somerset in the April sun. . . . Except perhaps, on a December day in France, the day of her wedding to Edouard of Lancaster.

Lady Mary! What ailed her that she must be thinking of this now? She drew in her breath so sharply that Richard at once exclaimed,

'Anne? Was I too rough, sweetheart?'

'No . . . no. Richard, I love you. . . . I do, I swear I do!'

'You say that as if you expect me to doubt you, beloved.'

Not knowing what to say to that, she pressed closer still to him. He kissed her throat, her mouth, her hair, cupped and caressed her breasts, stroked the softness of her inner thighs. She held on to him as if they were adrift, in some strange sea and he alone could keep her afloat, called him 'love' and 'darling', willingly shifted her body to accommodate his caresses, and struggled with a growing sense of desperation, of desolation, for what she'd most feared was coming to pass; her body was betraying her. She felt nothing. Nothing.

In vain she sought to will a response to his kisses, to share his passion. It didn't come. Never had her mind been so remote, so detached; it was as if she were watching him make love to someone else's body. She loved him, loved him so much. What was wrong with her, then? Why could she not feel what she was supposed to feel, what other women felt? He'd stirred such feeling in her before; why not now, when it did matter the most? And how could she hide it from him? Lancaster had hated her for her coldness but Richard would be hurt . . . dreadfully hurt.

When it was over and they lay quietly entwined, she turned her head aside so that he'd not notice the tears that trembled on her lashes. For a brief time that seemed interminable to her, there was no sound but the slowing rhythm of his breathing and the betraying tremor in hers. She'd given herself away, she knew she had. So miserable had she managed to make herself that she'd felt a flicker of remembered fear at the moment of penetration and stiffened involuntarily, enough to make his entry unexpectedly difficult. Oh, yes, he knew; he had to.

She shut her eyes to squeeze back tears. He'd been so patient, had taken such care not to hurt her. And he had not; the surprise of that still lingered. The initial discomfort had passed almost at once. As he'd given her body time to adjust to him, to adapt to his movements, the pain had yielded to a sensation of pressure that she did not find unpleasant. Her relief had been enormous and with it, too, had come a surge of tenderness. She'd been able, then, to relax enough to follow his lead, so much so that she felt a faint disappointment when he was done, for she'd begun to derive a certain pleasure from the closeness, the intimacy, the feel of his body upon hers.

But what she'd hoped to feel, what she thought she should feel, must feel . . . that had eluded her entirely. And now there was only shame as she remembered how she'd flinched away from him at first, how he'd had to soothe her, to reassure her. That he'd tried to be so gentle with her only made her failure all the worse in her eyes. She'd so wanted to please him. And now he knew what Lancaster had known, that there was something lacking in her, that she. . . .

'Anne?' He lifted himself off her; she felt suddenly bereft and shivered. He drew the sheet up around her, leaned over to kiss her averted cheek.

'I know it was not that good for you, sweetheart, but . . .' he began softly, and with a stifled sob, she rolled over, back into his arms.

'Oh, Richard, it was all my fault, I did not please you and I so wanted to. . . .'

'Not please me? Beloved, you did please me all too well.' He shifted so that he could see her face and, as she opened her eyes to regard him uncertainly, he said, 'I was too quick, did not give you enough time. I think it must have been wanting you so much

664

and having to wait so long.' With one finger he tracked the solitary tear still wet upon her cheek, kissing her as it reached the corner of her mouth, and then he laughed. 'But I'll make it up to you, that I promise.'

'You do not mind. . . . Oh, Richard, I was so afraid you'd be dissatisfied with me, find me lacking. . . .'

'Anne, look at me. As tense and wrought up as you were, how could you expect to get much pleasure from it? You think I did not know that? I had only to touch you to feel it; you were as taut as a drawn bowstring, in truth you were. But it'll get better, love, much better. All you do lack is experience, and I'd like nothing better than to remedy that.'

Anne expelled the hurtful breath that had caught in her throat and then began to cover his face with haphazard feverish kisses, not stopping until they'd both begun to laugh.

'If only I'd talked to you, confessed my qualms. I was tied in knots, so afraid you'd find me cold, that you'd. . . .'

'Cold? Anne, listen. I confess you gave me some bad moments in that priory garden at Coventry. But not since then and, most assuredly, not after these past weeks at St Martin's.' He smothered a yawn, kissed her again.

'Now come closer and I'll show you a right pleasurable way to sleep. Lean back against me—that's it—and I'll wrap my arms around you like this; we fit together like spoons, see?'

His closeness was reassuring, the warmth of his body equally pleasant. She would have liked to talk further but his voice had taken on a drowsy contentment. She snuggled back against him; soon after, the slow, even movement of his chest told her he slept.

The coming of April did not always signify the coming of spring to Wensleydale, but this year it seemed safe to hope there'd be no late-season snowfalls, no high knife-edged winds sweeping down off the Pennines. The dale was everywhere green, dark moss mingling with verdant leaf and the tender shades of new-grown grass; the River Ure reflected clouds and sky with a silvery sheen.

What struck Anne first were all the people. The narrow streets of Middleham were thronged with men and women, in such numbers that she realized at once many must have been drawn from the neighbouring villages. As she glanced back over her shoulder, intending to ask Richard if the Monday market day could somehow have been changed in her absence, they began to shout. With a start, she realized the cheers were for her, for their lord the Earl's daughter come home at last.

She reined in her mare and found herself surrounded by well-wishers, by the villagers who'd loved her father and were eager to show that same love for his child. It was too early yet for the white roses of York but a shy, small girl was urged forward now to present Anne with an armful of jonquils, snowdrops and hyacinth. A wine cup was being held up toward her; it shone silver in the setting sun and represented no small sum from the village treasury. She would be honoured to accept it, Anne assured them huskily, and would cherish it for what it was, a gift from the heart.

A short distance away, two men stood apart from the crowd, upon the steps of the market cross. The village priest creased his eyes as if from the sun but his words indicated a deeper concern.

'A gift from the heart,' he echoed softly. 'The only trouble is they've given it to the wrong one.'

His companion gave him a curious look. Thomas Wrangwysh had been visiting kin in Masham when he learned that the Duke and Duchess of Gloucester were due back at Middleham and he'd decided at once to be there when they arrived. After all, he reasoned, Gloucester was going to be the power in this part of the country and his backing would be worth a great deal to a man with political ambitions such as himself. Now he suggested, 'You mean it should've gone to the Duke?'

'Aye. It's his goodwill that does count, not hers.'

'You are wrong. Look at his face, Father. They could have thought of nothing better-calculated to please him than what they just did.'

Above the keep flew the standard of Gloucester. Anne shielded her eyes, gazed upward at the scarlet and blue background bannered with the Rose-en-Soleil, the cognizance of her cousin Ned, and Richard's tusked Whyte Boar, the Blancsanglier. As she watched, it dipped and then unfurled to full length, held there for a moment as if pinned against the vivid streaking sky.

Turning, she saw Richard had reined in beside her.

'We're home,' he said.

BOOK THREE

Lord of the North

I

❦

Leicester

September 1472

The tension in the room was tangible, could almost be tasted, touched, breathed. Richard had rarely been so uncomfortable, so at a loss for words. Kate was standing by the window, staring down into the garden—her garden—as if at some strange and wondrous sight never before seen. Kathryn alone seemed untouched, seemed at ease. She wrapped her arms around Richard's neck, as trustingly and naturally as if he truly belonged in her world, as if fully two months had not passed since last he'd held her like this.

She had his colouring; each time Richard saw her, it touched him anew. Escaping the flimsy restraints of scarlet silk ribbons, her hair framed her face in flyaway ebony curls; her eyes were wide and dark blue. He wondered if she truly comprehended who he was. She was so young, just five months beyond her second birthday and he saw her so seldom.

'Papa? You bring my puppy?'

He grinned for this was the fifth time in the past hour that she'd seen fit to recall his promise to mind.

'I'll not forget, Kathryn. I'll bring it the next time I do come to visit you.'

'Tomorrow?' she said, and he laughed. So did Kate.

'Not tomorrow, Kathryn, but soon. Now say good-bye to your father, poppet,' she prompted, and Kathryn dutifuly implanted a wet kiss on Richard's cheek and another on his neck. With reluctance, he set her back on her feet, watched as she was led from the chamber by her nurse.

This was the first time he and Kate had found themselves alone together; the last time he'd come to see Kathryn, Kate had kept to her bedchamber, conveying her regrets that she was ailing and unable to receive him. He hadn't believed her but had been grateful for her subterfuge, had been reluctant to face her with another woman's wedding band on his hand.

Kate smiled, rather stiffly, at him now, murmuring a perfunctory politeness about the shortness of his stay. He, too, mumbled something meaningless but found his eyes straying all the while to the bright sunset haze of her hair; here within the privacy of her home, she wore it loose, held only by a wide velvet band across her forehead, a deep turquoise colour that could not have been better chosen to set off the coppery-gold of her hair. As he watched, she fidgeted with a strand, smoothing it flat against the bodice of her gown. It was a mannerism familiar to him and one he knew to be born of stress. He saw now that she still wore the opal ring he'd given her on her seventeenth birthday. Her earrings had come from him, too, and on the table between them was a silver cachet box, a peace offering for a now forgotten quarrel.

'Kate . . .' What could he say? It would be four years come December. Memories now bitter-sweet to recall but no less vivid for all that. They'd both been sixteen. She'd come a virgin to his bed and, in the following year, had borne his bastard child, had borne Kathryn.

'Kate, is all well with you? I fear you'd not tell me if you did have a need unmet. . . .'

She shook her head; the swirl of hair put him in mind of wind-blown autumn leaves. 'No, Dickon, I am fine. Kathryn and I do want for nothing. You've been most generous, after all.'

Was there irony in that last? He couldn't tell, wasn't sure he wanted to know.

'Dickon, I do have something for you.' Her smile was softer

now, less strained. 'I did not expect you'd be back to see Kathryn before your birthday next month and I . . . well, I wanted you to have this.' As she spoke, she was lifting the lid on a coffer, drawing out a package wrapped in white silk.

As he took it from her, their fingers brushed and then again as she helped him to undo the wrapping; it shocked him to realize the extent of his response to that casual contact. He found himself resisting the urge to touch the red-gold hair that rippled and shimmered with every move she made. He was acutely aware of the fragrance that perfumed her wrist, hair, the hollow of her throat; it, too, was familiar, was one she'd long ago adopted as her own because he liked it.

He stepped back, concentrated upon opening the package which, much to his delight, revealed a charcoal sketch of Kathryn.

'Do you like it, Dickon? Truly?'

'I can think of nothing that could please me more.' He leaned over and kissed her upon the cheek, so hurriedly that it might have seemed as if he'd expected her skin to be scalding to the touch.

For a moment, they looked at each other. She was too close; he could see the uneven rise and fall of her breasts. He'd not expected this, had not expected still to want her so. He took her hand, brought it to his lips, saying in a low voice, 'God keep you, Kate.'

'You, too, Dickon.' There was a breathless catch to her voice now; she said, 'Surely you do mean to kiss me good-bye?'

He hesitated and then touched his lips lightly to hers. But as he drew back, her arms went up around his neck and suddenly she was in his arms; he felt the familiar warmth of her body against his; her mouth was clinging, sweet, and it was as if the past year had never been.

He tightened his arms around her without thought, without choice, aware only of the feel of her breasts pressed against his chest, the feel of her tongue in his mouth, her softness, her scent. But then she whispered, 'Oh, love . . . love, it's been so long,' and his brain unclouded. Freeing his mouth from hers, he pulled away from her, ended the embrace.

'Forgive me, Kate,' he said swiftly and somewhat unsteadily. 'I did not mean for that to happen. I had not the right.'

'Oh, but you do. You do have the right, Dickon. Only you. . . .' She leaned toward him yearningly and he slid his hands down her arms, held her away from him, not trusting himself with her, not now.

'No,' he said softly. 'No, I have not.'

She had eyes so blue as to appear lavender; he saw bewilderment in them and dawning hurt. 'I do not understand. You do want me, as much as I want you. You cannot deny that, not now.'

'No . . . I'd not deny that.'

'Beloved, listen to me. I love you; I never stopped. Oh, I know adultery to be a mortal sin, but I do not care. It be worth. . . .'

'Kate, do not!'

She stoppeed, open-mouthed, and he said wretchedly, 'Oh, God, but I never wanted to hurt you, never. I swear by all that's holy that I did not!'

She stared at him. 'I see,' she breathed. Turning away abruptly, she stooped and retrieved the wrapping of white silk from the floor; with infinite care, she began to fold and refold the material, as if that and that alone mattered to her now.

'Kate . . . Kate, I'm sorry.'

'Why? Because I did make a fool of myself?'

He moved toward her at that but she backed away, out of reach.

'I do blame myself as much as you, if that be any consolation. I should have seen. But I would not let myself face the truth. When you wrote me last autumn that you meant to wed your cousin, I found reasons a hundredfold why you should wish to make the match—that she was a Neville, the Earl of Warwick's daughter, an heiress. . . . I did think of every reason save one—that you might love her. And that is it, is it not? Why you wed her, why you are no longer willing to lay with me. You do love your wife.'

When he said nothing, she cried, suddenly shrill, accusing, 'I'm right, am I not? Say it, then! You do love her?'

'Yes,' he said, and then watched unhappily as she twisted and wrenched the white silk until it jerked in her hands like a living thing.

'Kate, I do care for you, I care very much. . . .'

'Name of God, Dickon, do not!' She swallowed, shuddered and then sat down abruptly in the window seat.

'I think you'd best go,' she said.

Not knowing what else to do, he reached for her hand, held it for a moment against his cheek. She tensed at his touch and he thought she meant to pull her hand from his grasp. Instead, she closed her eyes, leaned back in the windowseat.

'Please go,' she repeated dully, and he nodded, moved away from her. He paused at the door, wanting to go, to escape a scene as painful as any he'd ever experienced but not wanting to leave her like this.

'Kate, is there nothing I can do for you?'

'Yes, Dickon, there is.' She raised her head; her eyes were free of tears but her voice was suspiciously tight, as husky as ever he'd heard it.

'There is a favour I would ask of you,' she began, and he said at once, before he realized what a risk he could be taking,

'You need only name it, Kate.'

A flickering smile twitched her lips. 'Do not be so impulsive, Dickon. One day that'll get you into more trouble than you can handle.'

'I daresay it will,' he agreed, finding a smile no more convincing than her own. 'Tell me what I can do for you, Kate.'

'Do not come back here,' she whispered. 'I do want you to see Kathryn, as often as you can. But not here. You need only let me know when you wish to see her; you can send an escort for her, have her with you at Middleham or wherever else you do choose. But do not come back here, Dickon. Stay away for my sake . . . please.'

2

Middleham

December 1472

On the eve of Christmas, the yule log was lit in the great hall; by tradition, it would burn for the twelve days to come. On the preceding day, a hunt had been staged for the pleasure of the castle guests. Later in the week a hunt was planned for wild boar but, for the safety of the women riding to the hunt, yesterday's quarry had been the roe deer hunted from Michaelmas to Candlemas.

The dining was done; the trestle tables had been taken apart and stacked behind the screens that stretched across the south end of the great hall. The mummery, too, was done; several of the players still remained within the hall, amusing with the antics of trained marmosets and a tame bear cub. Richard's minstrels were very much in evidence, but there'd been a lull in the dancing.

Alison Scrope was looking for her husband but with no great urgency. She was mellow with wine and contentment, for the hall was full of friends and neighbours and the entertainment had been much to her liking, as lavish as in the days when Warwick's blood-red crimson shone vivid midst the holly and Christmas ivy. Now the colours that bedecked the hall were the blue and murrey of York and, with relief inexpressible, Alison saw that her husband at last seemed able to accept that, seemed inclined to let the dead bury the dead and make his private peace with the house of York. Alison could only thank God for it; King Edward had three times forgiven John for the support he'd given Warwick and the Nevilles. She knew there'd be no forgiveness for a fourth such slip.

With that in mind, she was delighted with the way the past two days had gone. John had been flattered by Richard's request that he serve on Richard's council, which acted not only as an administrative body but as a court of equity and arbitration. Alison thought it a very promising sign, showed that Richard valued her husband's abilities and, equally important, that he meant to pursue a policy of reconciliation, not retribution. Of course he'd be foolish to do otherwise; he was, she knew, fully cognizant of the ambivalent loyalties that persevered in the counties north of the River Trent.

She circled around Francis Lovell's sister Frideswide. An uncommon name, Alison thought, smiling to herself. Saxon for 'bond of peace', as Frideswide was so often called upon to explain. Alison nodded as she caught Frideswide's eye but didn't stop. Francis's other sister, Joan, was here, too. But his wife Anna was not. Francis had told Alison that Anna felt she should spend this Christmas with her mother, it being less than six months since Anna's father had died. Alison had diplomatically agreed with him. Now she shook her head. A pity. But that was too often the way of it. Child marriages either worked out very well or they worked out not at all.

Just then, Alison caught sight of her husband. But as she joined him in the hearthside gathering, she was struck at once by the sombre expressions on the faces of the men and women encircling Richard.

She was not long in discovering why. They were discussing the death a fortnight ago of Edward's infant daughter, the Lady Margaret. The baby had been ailing from birth and had clung to life only eight brief months. Richard had just confirmed the rumours of the child's death; he had, he said, received a letter from his brother the king only that week past.

Alison dutifully crossed herself, but she was thinking that Edward and his Queen had been more fortunate than most. Five children Elizabeth had borne Edward and this was the first time that death had claimed a babe of theirs. Most parents were more familiar with grieving, especially in that first fragile year of life, when death all too often came swift and sudden.

At that moment, she happened to look toward Anne. Anne had paled. One hand fumbled with her crucifix chain; the other pressed protectively against the fold of her gown.

'Babies are so vulnerable,' she said, almost inaudibly, and Alison knew her suspicions of the past two days were well founded.

She seized the first opportunity that arose after that to speak with Anne alone. Anne was delighted to talk about the renovations made during her eight months as mistress of Middleham and needed no urging to take Alison into the adjoining solar, where she took pride in showing Alison the vivid unicorn arras hangings that adorned the walls and the new oriel window cut into the west wall of the solar.

Alison was impressed; she said so at length and then listened patiently as Anne spoke with enthusiasm about the additions and restorations she and Richard were planning in the months to come.

'. . . and then we hope to enlarge the windows in the Round Tower but first Richard wants to. . . .' Anne laughed suddenly. 'And none of this does interest you in the least, does it?'

Alison grinned. 'Well, as it happens, there is a matter closer to my heart. Tell me, dearest, when is your babe due?'

Anne's eyes shifted hastily downward, came up again to Alison's face. 'I was so sure it did not show yet.'

'It does show on your face, my love,' Alison laughed and gathered the girl to her for a congratulatory hug. 'I first began to suspect when you declined to go on the hunt yesterday. And then I noticed how your husband watched you when you weren't looking, as if you were made of Venetian crystal fine enough to shatter at the merest touch. Men are always so with the first babe; a pity it does not last, so do make the most of it, Anne. I regret to tell you that by the third or fourth child, he'll be complaining that you must take a full nine months when his best alaunt bitch does whelp in two.'

Anne had begun to laugh again, now shook her head so

678

vehemently that the veil trailing from her headdress swirled about her in a filmy cloud of lavender.

'Not Richard.' She hugged Alison back, said, 'I would have told you ere you departed, Alison. I cannot wait till I do swell up like a ripe melon; I want all the world to know.' No longer laughing, she confided quietly, 'I cannot begin to tell you how much it does mean to me, that I was able to conceive as soon as I did. It was much on my mind, Alison, that in all her years of marriage, my mother had only Isabel and me . . . and more miscarriages than I care to remember. My sister, too, does not seem blessed with a fertile womb; one babe stillborn in more than three years of marriage. I was afraid. . . . But not now. Oh, Alison, not now.' She spun around in a circle, velvet skirts flaring, laughing, and Alison was reminded anew how very young Anne was, just sixteen.

'I think,' Alison said, 'that you do have now all you truly wanted. I think, too, that I need not worry about you any longer, child. You've come home.'

'Yes,' Anne said. 'I have.' she smiled suddenly. 'There are times, Alison, when I wonder how such luck came to be mine. And then I remember. . . . Richard is my luck.'

3

Beaulieu Abbey

June 1473

Nan Neville, Countess of Warwick, was sitting on one of the benches in the cloisters of the abbey of St Mary of Beaulieu Regis in Southamptonshire. Ravens were congregating in the grassy inner garth, blue-black, raucously aggressive. Birds of ill omen. The birds that had haunted the Tower of London as long as men could remember. How fitting, she thought, that they should be drawn, too, to this white-walled abbey that was her prison. Her self-pity was particularly acute this noon; easy tears filled her eyes.

She let them run unchecked down her cheeks; who was there to see, after all? She was alone. She was always alone. She was likely to be alone for the rest of the barren days allotted to her in this life, an unwilling pensioner of the Cistercian white monks of Beaulieu.

The ravens were cawing, squabbling among themselves. She watched but without seeing; she was treading a familiar mental path, step by painful step retracing the events of the past two years, reliving her regrets.

It hadn't been that way in the beginning. That first summer of sanctuary, she hadn't done much thinking at all; she'd been numb, too stunned to do more than weep for her slain husband and for her own plight. But she'd been jolted back to reality when her daughter Anne disappeared from the Herber.

Nan's love for her flamboyant, ambitious husband had been both excessive and exclusive. It was not that she'd deliberately meant to slight her daughters; there was just never quite enough love left over for them. But in her own way, she did care for Anne and Isabel. They were hers, after all. She'd given them life, forgiven them that they'd not been sons, taken pride in their prettiness, hoped to make brilliant marriages for them. And now they were all she had.

Her fear for Anne was genuine and so, too, was her relief when word reached her that Anne was safe. But her thankfulness was not long in giving way to euphoria. That Anne should be marrying Richard seemed no less than miraculous to Nan. Her daughter would have as her husband the dark-haired cousin she'd doted on since childhood, and she would have someone to speak for her, would have as her son-in-law the one man powerful enough to defy George.

Nan was sublimely sure that her troubles were over and when Anne wrote to tell her that Edward had refused to allow her to come forth from sanctuary, she was devastated. So confident had she been that she'd not prepared herself for the possibility that Edward might say no, that he might prefer to placate George at her expense.

Anne had expressed confidence that Edward would relent, had promised that Richard would keep on urging Edward on her behalf. It was only a matter of time, she assured her mother.

That meant nothing to Nan. Words, empty and easily forgotten. As she had been—forgotten and forsaken.

Before she could think better of it, she had written an incoherent, abusive letter to Anne. If Dickon could not persuade Ned, it was only that he had not truly tried. The truth was that he would rather she stayed sanctuary-bound, just as George did. Perhaps Anne did, too. Isabel surely did. Neither of her daughters cared whether she lived or died. Her pen raced on, covering page after tear-splotched page, accusing Anne of indifference, Richard of far worse, spilling forth all the griefs and grievances of the past year.

She regretted that letter the same day she dispatched it north to Middleham, regretted it once it was too late. For a month, she heard nothing. And when her answer came, it came not from Anne but from Richard.

Nan had stared, appalled, at her son-in-law's signet, afraid to break the seal. Dear God, surely Anne would not have shown him that letter!

She saw, with his first words, that Anne had. The letter was terse, polite, but far from friendly. He denied her accusations, so stiffly that she knew he was both angered and offended. He insisted he'd made a good-faith intercession with his brother, said he

681

would continue to speak on her behalf. Nan knew better. Whatever chance she'd had of gaining his support had been irretrievably lost, forfeited forever the moment Anne had seen fit to let him see her letter. She'd never forgive Anne for that, never. She scribbled a brief accusatory note to Anne, saying just that, and tried to submerge her despair in indignation that her daughter had so betrayed her.

After that, she had no more letters from Middleham. And with her estrangement from Anne, she truly had no one, for Isabel had yet to respond to any of her letters. Isabel was lost to her and so, it now seemed, was Anne.

Then, in March, she'd received a letter from an old friend, Alison, Lady Scrope of Bolton Castle, a chatty, breezy letter full of news of Alison's stepson Henry, her husband, John, who was now acting for Richard in negotiations with the Scots. Buried midst the Scrope family gossip were two items that gave Nan serious pause.

The first concerned Nan's brother-in-law, the Archbishop of York, who'd been abruptly arrested by Edward eleven months ago on charges of treasonous correspondence with his Lancastrian brother-in-law, the Earl of Oxford. George Neville's health was none too good, Alison reported, and Richard had agreed to intercede on his behalf with the King. In the same paragraph, she made casual mention of Anne's pregnancy.

Nan hadn't slept that night. Alison was a gossip but a reasonably reliable one. If she said Richard was seeking to bring about George Neville's release, it was true. Nan knew Richard had no use for her brother-in-law. Yet Richard was willing to speak for him now that he was ailing. Because he was Anne's uncle. As he would have been willing to do for her had she only not alienated him beyond forgiving with that rash, reckless letter of hers.

And Anne was pregnant. Anne was carrying her first grandchild. A child she might never get to see. She had not even known Anne was breeding.

Nan was the least introspective of women but now she had little to do but think, had time and solitude and regrets. Painstakingly and reluctantly, she thought back over her relationship with her daughters, began to comprehend that if they were failing her now, it might be because she'd so often failed them. She remembered Amboise, remembered how indifferent she'd been to Anne's fears, how impatient with Isabel's lingering depression after the death of her baby. And with a flush of shame, she remembered how she'd let them hear of their father's death from Marguerite d'Anjou.

She tried to write this to Anne but the words just wouldn't come. She'd always taken Anne's love as her just due and to ask her daughter for forgiveness seemed to go against the natural order of things. Whatever mistakes she might have made, she was still Anne's mother. It was not for Anne and Isabel to sit in judgment on her. But, somehow, being right didn't make her misery any easier to bear.

Across the cloister, the monks were emerging from the frater, the grey stone building that housed their dining chamber. As she watched, they began to line up before the troughs set out for the washing of hands after meals. Nan rose, was turning away when she heard a voice call, 'My lady!' She looked back, saw one of the white-clad monks hastening toward her up the west walkway of the cloisters.

As usual, the reception hall of the Great Gatehouse was crowded with alms seekers, but at sight of the Yorkist men-at-arms loitering in and about the entranceway, Nan stiffened, felt an icy prickling of alarm along her spine. Why were they here? Was there a connection between their presence and the Lord Abbot's summons?

She was not reassured when her guide led her through the Inner Hall, toward the corner stairway that gave access to the chapels above. What had the Lord Abbot to say to her that required such privacy?

He came forward now to greet her but Nan's eyes were moving past him, toward the man cloaked in afternoon shadow, a tall, stylishly dressed man with a sun-browned face and unrevealing light-blue eyes.

'Madame, may I present. . . .'

'James Tyrell,' she finished for him, and Tyrell bowed over her hand.

'It is Sir James Tyrell now, Madame,' he corrected her politely. 'It was my honour to be knighted by the King's Grace after the battle of Tewkesbury.'

'My congratulations,' Nan said automatically. She knew Tyrell. Suffolk gentry, a man with an unblemished record of loyalty to the House of York. With what mission had he now been entrusted by Ned?

'It seems you shall be leaving us, Madame.'

She turned to stare at the abbot. 'Leaving!'

He nodded, smiled. 'Sir James has come to escort you to. . . .'

'No!'

Both men looked startled. The abbot said uncertainly, 'Madame?'

Nan's cry had been involuntary; she'd surprised herself as much as them. Was this not what she'd wanted above all else? Why was she not excited, ecstatic? Why did she feel such unease? She drew an unsteady breath. Because she did not trust Ned. Why in God's name should she? If he was capable of keeping her here, why was he not capable, as well, of turning her over to George's mercies?

'Tell me, my lord Abbot,' she said breathlessly, 'he cannot force me if I should choose not to go? I cannot be taken from here against my will?'

'Most assuredly not. He who would violate sanctuary does so at the peril of his soul.' The abbot was frowning, turned accusing eyes upon Tyrell.

'Sir James, you did give me to understand the Countess of Warwick was willing.'

684

'So I did believe,' Tyrell said hastily. He was studying Nan with evident puzzlement. 'Madame, I confess I do not understand. Nor will His Grace. Perhaps if you read his letter. . . .'

Letter? Ned would not be likely to have written to her.

'You do come from the King?' she faltered, and Tyrell's face cleared.

'No, Madame . . . from the Duke of Gloucester.' A comprehending smile had begun to shape his mouth; he grinned outright as she snatched at the letter in his hand.

She broke the seal with suddenly shaking fingers, moved toward the window to read it. When at last she turned back to the Abbot and Tyrell, her face was wet with tears.

'The King has given me leave to depart sanctuary.' She stopped, laughed and then began to cry in earnest. 'I . . . I am to go home.'

On their way north, Sir James Tyrell had willingly acceded to Nan's request that they stop at Bisham Abbey, where the Earl of Warwick and John Neville were buried. They did not reach Wensleydale, therefore, until the second week in June.

Anne was in the solar, sitting before her embroidery frame. She looked prettier than Nan had ever seen her, dressed in emerald green, her favourite and most flattering hue; her colour was good, her hair, held in place by a pearl-seeded frontelet that matched her gown, swept down her back in glossy, well-brushed waves. But she showed no signs of pregnancy, none at all.

A shocked query formed on Nan's lips, to be quickly stilled. If Anne had lost her baby, she did not want the first words between them to be of so painful a loss. She smiled, instead, at her daughter and held out her arms; her relief was considerable when Anne came into them without apparent hesitation.

'That little boy who was with you earlier, Anne . . . Johnny, you said his name was? He's Dickon's son, then?'

'Who could look at him and ever deny that?' Anne laughed.

'Born well before our marriage, I should add. Richard had him at Sheriff Hutton and then, after we were wed, at Pontefract, since we do spend so much time there. When Richard went last month to Nottingham—to see Ned about winning your release and for talks with the Earl of Northumberland—I was able to do what I should have done months ago. I had Johnny secretly brought from Pontefract a fortnight ago.'

'Dickon does not know?'

Anne shook her head, laughed again. 'Not yet . . . and I truly cannot wait to see his face when he does. From Nottingham, he was to go to York but I do expect him back any day this week. My birthday is Friday and he swore ere he left that he'd not miss it. I do not know what he plans to give me but Johnny is my present to him, a present too long overdue. It would have meant so much to Richard—having his son here. And for Johnny, too; he does adore Richard. But . . . but I just could not bring myself to do it, mother. It shames me to admit it, that I was jealous of a little child, but I was. He was not mine and I could not accept him as if he were, however much I knew I should.'

'And now you do think you can?' Nan sounded dubious and Anne smiled, reached for her mother's hand.

'Now I do know I can.' She rose, kept Nan's hand within her own. 'If you will come with me to the nursery, I shall show you why.'

Until she saw the sleeping infant, Nan had not known what a hunger there was in her for a grandchild. Bending over to brush her lips to the feathery brown hair, she felt a sudden stab of envy. How lucky Anne was, to have been able to give Dickon a son. How she would have loved a little boy like this, would have cuddled him and spoiled him, made none of the mistakes she'd made with Isabel and Anne.

'I get nothing done these days, spend hours hanging over his cradle like this. I needs must watch him sleep, yawn, sleep again—

I even find myself watching the very air in and out of his mouth, as if he might forget to breathe were I not there to witness it.'

'How old is he, Anne?'

'Six weeks this Thursday last. I'd not expected to be brought to childbed till the end of May, had not even begun my confinement yet. But he was not willing to wait, was born on the eve of St George's Day, so tiny the midwives did harbour fears for him though they tried to keep it from me.'

They had been speaking in whispers, so as not to disturb the child asleep within the oaken cradle once used by both Anne and Isabel. Anne stroked the baby's cheek with a soft finger, said with a sigh, 'I did not want a wet nurse, wanted to nurse him myself, however unfashionable that might be. But I had not enough milk. He has more hair than most babes his age, do you not think, mother? It looks to be the same shade as father's, mayhap some darker. You know . . . it's strange, but I do find myself . . . for the first time in my life . . . having some sympathy for Marguerite d'Anjou. I remember how desperate she was to get into Wales, that nightmare ride she made for the Severn River crossing, so frantic she was to see her son safe . . . and I think I can understand better now how she did feel. Edouard was her son, her flesh and blood. When I look now at my own son, when I think of what I would do to keep him safe, free from harm or hurt. . . .'

Her musings were interrupted by a stifled sound from her mother. She glanced up to see that Nan's face had frozen, that her hands had closed convulsively upon the rim of the cradle.

'You speak of a mother's concern for her child. But what you are truly saying is that I showed no such concern for you and your sister, that even Marguerite d'Anjou showed herself to be a better mother than I.'

'No, mother, truly I was not,' Anne said slowly, but none too certainly. 'At least, I do not think that was my intent. . . .'

They looked at each other across the rocking cradle. 'I did love your father; he was my life. When I was told he was dead, it was as if . . . as if all were ashes and cinders. I felt dead inside, could think of naught but what I had lost. Can you not understand that, Anne?'

Anne looked down at her sleeping child, for some moments said nothing. 'No,' she said at last. 'No, mother, I cannot. I wish I could say otherwise but I do not understand.'

'I see. You are determined to pass judgement upon me, to blame me for a moment of weakness. That is not fair, Anne. I should have gone to you and Isabel at Cerne Abbey; I do admit that. But I cannot undo what I did and, as for the other, for the marriage with Lancaster. . . . Surely you could not have expected me to speak against your father on that?'

'No, mother, I would not have expected you to gainsay father . . . in anything. But could you not have given a thought to how it was for me? I was fourteen years old, mother, fourteen. And so wretched I did not care whether I lived or died. Had you only once showed me you understood, I think I could have borne it better. But you did not, did you? Do you remember what you told me when I came to you for comfort? You said it mattered little whether I liked laying with Lancaster as long as I did get with child!'

Nan had paled as Anne spoke. Now hectic spots of colour flared forth upon her cheeks. 'I said that?' She touched her tongue to stiff lips, said softly, 'I truly do not remember. If I did say it, I can only assure you that I did not mean it. Ah, Anne, those were such bad days for us all. I was so fearful for your father, so frantic to join him in England. . . . But . . . must we speak of this now? It serves for naught, does only hurt. And you are happy now, Anne. You have the home and husband of your choosing, a newborn son. Perhaps . . . perhaps it did all work out for the best, after all. . . .'

'All for the best. . . . Oh, God!' Anne's mouth had hardened, contorted with a rare rage. 'I'm still haunted by dreams of that time; yes, even now. And with reason. Do you know how long it took, mother for me to be able to respond to Richard as fully as a wife should? Nigh on three months, and Richard as tender and loving as any man could be. Yes, I am happy now, but I did pay a great price for it, greater than any duty I did owe you and father, and for you to say that it was all for the best. . . .'

The anger in her voice had at last penetrated the veil of sleep surrounding her son. Opening his eyes, he began to cry. Anne at once bent over him, took him up in her arms. For a time there was no sound in the room but his subsiding protest.

Nan swallowed but made no attempt to hide the tears falling fast and free. 'I've made mistakes. I know that. But are they beyond forgiving, Anne?'

Anne was cradling her baby. She looked up when her mother spoke, and Nan saw that she, too, now seemed close to tears.

'No, Mama. . . . Of course they are not.' Anne watched Nan fumble for a handkerchief, watched with troubled dark eyes. The mother she remembered had retained a certain fragile prettiness well into her forties. Anne saw now what a toll the past two years had taken. Widowhood and sanctuary had greyed Nan's hair, thickened her waist and faded the blonde prettiness into a colourless and hesitant middle age. Anne looked at the fluttering uncertain hands, the soft bewildered mouth and moved away from the cradle, toward her mother.

'Here, Mama,' she said. 'Would you not like to hold your grandson?'

Nan stood in the entranceway leading into the great hall, staring down at the chaos in the inner bailey where Richard was seeking to soothe his fractious mount midst a dozen or so barking dogs. Nan felt a lump rising in her throat, felt the remorseless pull of memory. So it had always been when the Earl of Warwick came home to Middleham. The same confusion, the same excitement, and she, too, had so often done what Anne was doing now, descending the steep steps of the keep so rapidly that she seemed

689

in imminent danger of becoming entangled in her own skirts.

Richard reined his stallion in at the base of the stairs just as Anne reached the bottom; he slid from the saddle and into his wife's welcoming embrace. Nan watched while calling to mind a score of such scenes witnessed within these walls when Warwick's Ragged Staff had floated above the keep. It hurt but not as much as she expected.

Anne gathered up several cushions from the window seat and, carrying them across the bedchamber, deposited them on the floor by the bathing tub. The bath water was pleasantly scented with costmary, rose about her in clouds of aromatic steam. She parted the tented curtains and settled herself on the cushions so she could talk to Richard while he bathed.

Stirring up small ripples and eddies with an idle finger, she rested her cheek against the padded rim of the tub, waiting for him to dismiss his body squires. She was sure he would, for they'd had no time alone yet and she knew he was no less impatient than she for privacy.

As soon as the door closed, he leaned over, kissed her the way she'd been wanting him to do all afternoon.

'Jesú, but I missed you, Anne!'

'I missed you, too,' she said, and then smiled at the understatement. Rising to her knees on the cushions, she knelt beside the tub, reached for the soap.

'Shall I help you?' she invited, and he grinned.

'I thought you'd never ask.'

This time she was the one to kiss him. 'Thank you, love, for what you did say to my mother . . . about this being her home. I fear I was not as generous.'

'You quarrelled?'

She nodded. 'I regret we did. I've been telling myself that I do bear her no grudge, Richard, but that's not as true as I would like it to be. She had only to make mention of . . . of what I'd

690

sooner forget and I flared up like kindling. I cannot help it; I still feel that she failed me when I did need her the most.'

'You should not feel guilty about that, Anne; she did.'

She'd been soaping his back, now began to lather his chest and shoulders. 'I was thinking that I might be able to persuade Isabel to visit us after her babe is born. Perhaps she'll be more amenable to a reconciliation with mother once she does have the child she so wants.'

Richard caught her hand, held it still against him. 'Sweetheart, you'd best face the truth, that it'd take nothing less than a genuine miracle for George to let Bella come to Middleham.'

Anne's face shadowed. 'Yes, you're right. I just was not thinking. . . .' She squeezed the soap so tightly that it slipped from her fingers, sank from sight. 'There's no end, is there, to the misery George does manage to stir up. My mother would have been freed from Beaulieu months ago had it not been for him and his accursed lust for lands not his.'

'Let's not talk of George. Whenever I do, I find myself thinking of the arguments to be made for murder.' He brushed her hair back from her throat, explored it with his mouth until she shivered with pleasure and George was forgotten.

'Are you sure, sweetheart, that you do want Johnny here with us? I do not want to be unfair to you. . . .'

She nodded and when he kissed her again, she returned his embrace so wholeheartedly that she only belatedly became aware that her hair was trailing in the bath water.

'Oh, love, look at me! I'm soaked!'

She gazed ruefully at the dripping strands, the water stains darkening the bodice of her gown, but made no protest when he drew her to him again. By now they both were laughing but, when she lost the soap again, the hunt for it took on such interesting dimensions that amusement was not long in giving way to urgency.

In the first weeks of their marriage, Anne had been shy in their lovemaking. She still found it easier to show her passion in the soft intimacy of darkness, within the quiet and curtained privacy of their marriage bed. Now it was midday, the chamber was bright with summer sun and the trestle tables were already being set up in the great hall, chafing dishes and trencher plates being taken from the cupboard. But Richard had been gone for fully a month, the first time that they'd been apart since their marriage, and their lovemaking had, of necessity, been limited during the last stages of her pregnancy.

'Tell me again how much you missed me,' she murmured, and laughed when he said,

'I'd rather show you.'

He was kissing her throat again and she tilted her head back so that his mouth could wander at will, sliding her hands up his chest, delighting in the touch of warm wet skin, the fragrance of costmary, the sudden huskiness in his voice as he said her name.

'Why do you not,' she suggested softly, 'hurry and bath?'

He played with the wet hair that fell forward across her breast, pulled the damp silk down still farther to caress the soft curve thus exposed.

'I've a better thought than that. 'Why do you not join me?'

He saw her eyes widen. She blushed, looking both uncertain and intrigued. He laughed, loving her for that, for blushing, and for what she was doing now, reaching around behind her to untie the lacings of her gown.

'Here,' he said. 'Let me help.'

'I thought,' she said, 'you'd never ask.'

4

London

November 1474

For hours, the wind had been rising on the river and, shortly before noon, the sky began to darken. Rain was pelting the windowpanes, in sharp staccato bursts quite unlike the usual lulling rhythm of falling rain. Sleet as sure as Adam's Sin, Will Hastings thought and smiled; there were few comforts more pleasurable than lying abed in the languorous afterglow of lovemaking, listening to the futile fury of wind and rain against stone and timber.

'Will! Look, love!'

A crystalline soap bubble rose into the air above the bathing tub, then another and still another. Through half-shut eyes, he watched them drift ceilingward, reflecting the light of the wall cressets as if each one had a miniature candle flame imprisoned within.

'You're such a child, sweet. That bubble-blower was a toy meant for my sons. I scarcely had you in mind when I picked it up at the Smithfield Fair.'

'Well, you did not know me last August, Will, else you might have brought one for me, too,' she pointed out reasonably, and he grinned. She shared the normal feminine taste for jewelry and costly perfumes, but she was the first mistress he'd ever had who was capable of getting pleasure from trifles, too.

She looked appealingly dishevelled; honey-coloured hair was defying ivory pins, stray strands curling damply at the nape of her neck, loose wisps slanting rakishly over her eye, tickling her nose. He watched her push impatiently at it; she was the most unselfconscious woman he'd ever known, her lack of vanity all the more surprising to him in light of her undeniable physical charms.

Not that she was beautiful, not like the Woodville bitch. She could not hold a candle to Elizabeth; he freely conceded that. And yet there was something about her that got to a man. Her laugh. Her dimples. The most kissable mouth imaginable. High firm breasts, now gleaming soft and wet. Watching her balance a shapely leg on the rim of the tub and lather it lovingly, he smiled, knowing she was being deliberately provocative, and yet feeling desire start to quicken again. Perhaps that was the true secret of her appeal, the real reason why he found himself so unexpectedly besotted at age forty-three with this child-woman of twenty-two, this plump pretty little wife of a London mercer who could make him feel as if the twenty years between them mattered not a whit, who could make him hot to have her twice in an hour's time, with an eagerness he'd not known for years, an urgency he'd almost forgotten.

'Where's your wife?' she queried now. In another woman, he might have taken it as malice; with her, he knew it to be no more than simple curiosity.

'At Ashby-de-la-Zouch in Leicestershire.' Unable to resist adding, 'Like this house, Ashby was given to me by the King's Grace.'

Her eyes were long-lashed, a deep blue-grey, so wide-set as to give her an altogether spurious air of innocence. They widened now at mention of the king; he'd known they would, enjoyed indulging her with intimate confidences of the Yorkist court, the Yorkist king who was his friend.

'Will . . . is the king back yet from his tour of the Midlands?' she asked, somewhat shyly, for she was not yet accustomed to making casual conversation about her sovereign as if he were someone she knew personally.

Will nodded. 'He's been back since the sixteenth. A right profitable excursion it was; he raised a fair sum and by way of benevolences, too, not loans that need be repaid.'

She looked blank. 'What are benevolences?'

He laughed. 'A polite term for highway robbery. It does work like this. The king summons one of our wealthier citizens to the royal presence, greets said citizen with flattering warmth, bedazzles with the royal charm, and then expresses his confidence that said citizen will be well disposed toward making a voluntary contribution to the royal treasury . . . a rather large contribution, needless to say. Not surprisingly, sweetheart, most do prefer to turn out their purses rather than turn down their king.'

'How clever! But if he has such a need for money, then the talk must be true? That he means to go to war with France?'

'Yes, I fancy that he will. There are more than straws in the wind these days. In July, he did sign a treaty with Burgundy, avowing that an English army would land in France before a twelve-month had passed. Last month, he betrothed his third daughter, little Cecily, to the eldest son of the King of Scotland, so he need not fear trouble from the Scots whilst he deals with France. And given the way he's been exerting himself to raise money, I rather think we'll be marching on Paris ere too many months go by.'

'Do you want to go to war, Will?'

'Not particularly,' he conceded carelessly, and then held out his hand. 'Come here,' he said, and she laughed, rose sleek and dripping from the bath water. She was reaching for a bath towel when the bedchamber door burst open. Will sat up with an oath and she hastily splashed down into the tub again as Will's steward stumbled into the chamber.

'My lord, the King is here! They are below in the great hall even now and. . . .' He spun around in the doorway; they heard him gasp, 'Your Grace!' and Edward strode past him into the chamber.

'In bed at midday, Will? What ails you?' But if the question was directed at Will, his eyes were directed elsewhere, were taking in the girl in the bathing tub, eyes that missed no detail of glistening wet skin, open red mouth, tumbled blonde hair.

'I withdraw the question,' he said, and laughed.

Will gestured abruptly to his steward. 'Return to the great hall. See to the comfort of those with the King's Grace.'

He tucked the sheet around him, swung a leg over the edge of the bed, but Edward waved him back. 'Do not bestir yourself . . . not on my behalf.' He moved forward into the chamber and, as the door closed behind the steward, he said, 'We were on our way upriver from the Tower to Westminster when the storm did hit. I thought it best to put in at Paul's Wharf, and your house being nearby, it seemed to offer the most inviting shelter. Alas,' he said, and laughed softly, 'I see I'm about as welcome as a visitation of the French pox.'

He glanced back at the girl who was staring up at him like one doubting the evidence of her own senses. As he approached the tub, she crossed one arm over her breasts, but she did not, Will noticed, make a move to draw the tented curtains around the bath.

'My liege, you. . . .' She ran her tongue over her lips. 'You do have me at a disadvantage. . . .'

'I'd surely hope so,' he said, and grinned. 'Do you not mean to rise and greet your king?'

She blushed, the first time Will had ever seen her do so, and then dimpled. 'I'd do so gladly, Your Grace, but I can scarcely ask you to hand me a towel.'

'Why not?' Edward reached, not for the towel she indicated but for the washing cloth that hung over the rim of the tub. 'Will this do?' he drawled, and she burst out laughing.

Will was torn between amusement and an emotion he'd never before experienced where Edward was concerned, something startlingly akin to jealousy.

'All the books of courtesy I read as a boy are agreed that it be the height of bad manners to seduce a man's mistress in his own bathing tub,' he observed dryly, and Edward laughed again.

'I suspect I've just been politely asked to take myself off. I suspect, too, that I'll see Hell freeze over ere I get your mermaid's name out of you, Will.'

'Mistress Shore,' Will said, with an exaggerated show of feigned reluctance that was, in actuality, quite real.

'Elizabeth Jane,' she volunteered quickly, smiling up at Edward like one blinded by the sun.

Her shyness, Will noted, had dispersed as rapidly as the steam rising from her bath water. She had leaned forward and, resting her folded arms on the rim of the tub, was saying with the ease of long acquaintance, 'My father—John Lambert of the Mercer's Company—does call me Eliza, but all others have called me Jane for as long as I can remember, which is the name I do prefer myself.'

'So do I,' Edward said, and smiled at her. 'There are so many Elizabeths in my life already, but that I can recall, nary a single Jane.'

He was no sooner out of the room that Jane scrambled from the tub and, scorning towels, flung herself onto the bed next to Will.

'Oh, Will, I cannot believe it. That he was here, not an arm's length away. And found me fair to look upon! He did, did he not? Oh, Will!'

She was wet and eager in his arms, soft and slippery, covering his mouth with her own, her hands sliding down his body, until he found himself responding to her need even as he told himself that her excitement, her passion, was not for him, was for Ned.

After they'd both been satisfied, lay entwined in the sheets and in each other's arms, he listened in silence as she spoke of Edward.

'. . . and the first time I did see him . . . thirteen years ago it was, Will . . . in February, the month before he won Towton. I was eight and he was not yet King. My father took me to the churchyard at St Paul's; I've never forgotten. He rode a white stallion, wore armour like to blind you, so bright it was, the most beautiful being I've ever seen or hope to see, like one of the archangels. . . .'

Will gave a derisive hoot. 'Ned's been called many things in his life, but "archangel" is a first.'

She pretended to pout. 'Laugh if you will but that's how he did seem to me that day. . . .'

'It sounds as if you're still afflicted by the same faulty vision.'

'Why, Will!' She rose up on her elbow to better see his face; her own reflected astonishment. 'You do sound as if you are jealous!'

'Do not be ridiculous!' he snapped and, after a pause, she settled back into his arms.

'I am being silly,' she agreed, sounding faintly embarrassed. 'After all, who could be jealous of the king?'

'Who, indeed?' he said tersely.

After a time, she fell asleep. He lay still, listening to the fading echoes of winter rain as the storm moved southward and the sky began to clear over the city. It was so unexpected and unfamiliar, this jealousy of Ned, that he did not know how to handle it. Ned was more than his sovereign. He loved Ned fully as much as he did his own brothers. When he thought of the women they'd shared over the years, the mistresses they'd traded, the conquests passed back and forth. . . . Why, then, was Jane Shore different? Why should he care whether Ned did bed her or no? He did not fully understand why it bothered him, only knew that it did.

By the time Edward's summons came, Jane had just about given up hope. For ten days she'd been daydreaming about Edward, fantasizing how he'd be as a lover, assuring herself that he could find her with no undue difficulty; had she not made sure to let him know her father was a member of the Mercer's Company? But the days passed and she at last concluded that she'd been deluding herself. How could she have thought to fly so high, to fancy that the King would take to his bed a mercer's daughter?

At sight of the Yorkist colours, her heart began to pound so that she scarcely could hear the message delivered. Not that it mattered; she'd have gone anywhere without question or qualm, let this stranger escort her to the ends of the earth if that be Edward's wish. She had time only to tuck a small flask of perfume into a cloth purse and attach it to her belt, then to find pen and ink and scribble to her husband a hasty excuse for her absence, thanking God and her father that she'd been taught to read and write.

It was past Compline by the time the barge tied up at the King's Wharf. Edward was awaiting her in his bedchamber. She had a quick glimpse of a table set for two, of wine flagons and silver chafing dishes, and then she sank down before him in a deep curtsy. Her knowledge of royal etiquette was sketchy at best; hoping she was performing the gesture correctly, she touched her lips to his coronation ring, and then impulsively pressed her mouth to his palm.

He raised her up, kept his hands on her shoulders.

'I'm glad you could come on such little notice. Are you hungry?'

Jane had never been one to pretend, saw no reason to start now. She did not want to sit across a table from him, to make desultory conversation, to pose polite questions and feign interest in his answers, and all the while wanting only to taste his mouth, to feel his hands on her body, his weight over her in what had to be the largest feather bed she'd ever seen.

She shook her head slowly, saw by his smile that her forthrightness amused him.

'Neither am I,' he said, and, with a peremptory gesture, dismissed the ushers waiting to serve them.

He was considerably taller than she; as he brought his mouth down to hers, she had to strain upward, had to cling to him to keep her balance. He solved this disparity in height by lifting her up in his arms, carrying her to the bed, where they lay together and found prolonged pleasure in each other's bodies, more than he'd expected.

Jane had begun to slant surreptitious looks toward the bedside candle marked to measure the passing hours. It was not that she wanted to leave; never had she wanted anything less. She was accustomed to fancying herself in love with one man or another, gave her heart as generously as she did her body. Generally, her feelings were intense in nature and brief in duration. But nothing had prepared her for this, for the way she felt now, lying beside Edward as the hearth burned low, munching on cold chicken, passing a brimming wine cup back and forth and laughing frequently.

She was not surprised that he'd given her such satisfaction. She was surprised, however, that he'd been so attentive after their lovemaking. He was, she soon discovered, much given to touching, playing with her hair, cupping a breast, rubbing his foot against the muscles of her calf. He asked her questions she'd not expected, questions about her childhood and her likes, her family, asked as if he were truly curious about the answers. He'd shouted with laughter when she artlessly confided that she'd prayed these ten days past to the Blessed Lady Mary that he'd not forget her. If the Virgin Mother had, indeed, taken heed of so dubious an appeal, Edward pointed out, she'd be performing a service more commonly assumed by the bawds who ran the Southwark bordellos. That was the most sacrilegious remark Jane had ever heard; it sent her into shocked giggles that did not subside until he kissed her again.

No, she most assuredly did not want to leave, would have given virtually everything she did own if only she had the right to lie beside him till dawn, to sleep and make love and sleep again. She knew, however, what was expected of her, knew that to presume would be to jeopardize any future she might have with him, be it for a week, a month, or however long his passion for her did last. She sat up reluctantly, began to search the floor for her discarded clothes.

Edward reached over, caught her arm. 'Where do you go?'

'Home, Your Grace. It grows late and. . . .'

He hesitated but briefly. 'I'd have you stay the night,' he said, surprising himself somewhat by the offer; it was not one he made casually, preferring more often than not to have his bedmates depart once he'd had his pleasure with them.

She looked as if he'd just offered her the sun and moon. He began to laugh, pulled her back down beside him. 'I did forget. . . . You've a husband, have you not? Will he be sorely vexed if you're gone the night?'

The last person on her mind at that moment was her husband; had she been asked she'd have been hard put even to remember his name. She shook her head happily, lay back in Edward's arms.

'What will you tell him, sweetheart?'

She considered, began to giggle. 'The truth, of course, my liege. That I did pass the night in the service of my King.'

'I rather think,' he said, and smiled lazily at her, 'that under the circumstances, you might call me Ned.'

Will stood in Edward's bedchamber, watching as Edward was dressed by his esquires of the body. Servants were clearing away the evidence of an intimate late-night supper for two, and the bed had not yet been made up by the grooms of the chamber; it was still rumpled, warm. A gleam of gold caught Will's eye; he reached under the pillow, retrieved a woman's locket. It was a pretty piece of work and he'd paid a London goldsmith a rather extravagant sum for it just a month ago, wanting it in time for Jane's nameday.

'Shall I hold on to this and return it to her when next I do see her, Ned?' he asked, and took a certain pride in the fact that the question came so naturally to his lips, betrayed no more than the curiosity Edward would expect him to show.

'You need not bother, Will.' Edward, who was in a boisterously good mood, glanced over his shoulder to smile at Will. 'She'll be back tonight; I'll see that she gets it then.'

'Twice in two nights,' Will said softly. 'Did she please you as much as that?'

Edward laughed. 'That's a queer question, Will, coming from you. She's the best I've had in a long while, as you damned well know! In truth, I should hold a grudge against you, keeping her to yourself as long as you did . . . hardly the act of a friend.'

Will listened in silence as Edward began to banter with John Howard's son, Thomas, who'd been acting as a royal esquire of the body for some three years now. He could not speak in front of Thomas and the other men milling about in the chamber. But he could ask Ned for a few moments alone. He could tell him the truth, that this woman was different from the others; this woman he did not want to share.

They were pulling over Edward's shirt a magnificent crimson velvet doublet, elaborately stitched with gold thread, fumbling with the points that fastened his hose. Twice Will opened his mouth; twice he held his tongue. Only Gloucester was closer to Ned than he was. Ned had given him lands, offices, a barony. But he had never asked Ned for what Ned had not first shown himself willing to give. What had it meant to Ned, after all, to give him lands confiscated from Lancastrian rebels? But Jane . . . Jane had been born knowing what most women never learned; Jane could fire a man's blood and Ned had not yet had his fill of her. Would Ned be willing to give her up merely because he asked it of him?

Once he could have asked this of Ned and felt confident that Ned would have done it for him. Now . . . now he was not so sure. Betrayals and exile and the bloody fields of Barnet and Tewkesbury had wrought changes in Ned. Since reclaiming his throne, he was far less patient with the foibles of others, was less generous, more inclined to command where once he might have suggested. Ned at nineteen would never have done what he'd done at twenty-nine, given the order that sent Harry of Lancaster beyond all earthly cares and concerns. Ned at twenty-two might have laughed at Will's confession, have shrugged and looked elsewhere for his pleasure. But at thirty-two? Will did not know. He did not doubt that Ned cared for him. But he did doubt whether Ned would be willing to yield up Jane Shore until his own hunger for her had been sated.

The suspicion was an unsettling one, that Ned might put a passing lust before a friendship of thirteen years. But suspicions he could live with; certainty he could not. If Ned would not do that for him, he'd rather not know.

Will dropped the locket back onto the bed. Ned's passions burned bright but not long; he tired of women rather quickly. Why should it be any different with Jane?

Edward generally preferred to keep his Christmas court at Westminster. This year, however, his primary concern was raising funds for his forthcoming war with France. Christmas Day found him in Coventry, and, shortly thereafter, he ventured as far north as Lincoln in his quest for benevolences and loans. It was mid-January before he returned to London. On the second night of his return, he sent for Jane Shore, and frequently thereafter in the weeks that followed.

It was in spring, as war fever swept the capital, that Will first marked the change in Jane. As April thawed and flowered, she began to find excuses for not seeing him. She shrugged off his queries with uncharacteristic evasiveness and, when they did share a bed, he found, too, a change in her physical responsiveness. She was no longer so eager for their lovemaking, seemed more indulgent than impassioned, at times indifferent even. Will was not burdened with a fool's vanity, was well attuned to nuances and inference; he was not long in reaching the discomforting conclusion that she was acting more to accommodate his needs than to gratify her own, that she was tiring of him as he'd once hoped Edward would tire of her.

It was late. They'd lain in silence for some time. Normally, it would not have bothered Will all that much, that he'd been incapable of getting an erection; it did not happen often with him, and he knew, moreover, that there was not a man walking God's earth who had not suffered the same lapse at one time or another. But that was normally; now he mentally cursed his body for beginning to thicken, for slowed reflexes, for no longer being twenty-five. This was the second time in a fortnight that he'd had this problem with Jane, and why in Christ's Name must it be with Jane, of all women?

'Will?'

At sound of her voice, he turned toward it, said hurriedly, 'I'm sorry, sweetheart. I guess I was more tired than I did realize. . . .'

'Do not be silly, Will. You know I do not mind.'

That was just the trouble. He knew she did not. 'It grows late. I'd best call for a servant to see you safe home.'

'No, I can stay the night. I told you, now that I am the mistress of the king, my husband does give me all the freedom I could wish. I need only tell him I was at Westminster and he'd never think to question me further.'

'Praise God for complacent husbands,' he murmured against her ear, and she laughed; as usual when she spoke of her husband, there was both affection and a certain low-key contempt in her voice.

'He was always that, provided that I was reasonably discreet. He is much older than me, you know . . .'

Will felt a twinge at that. William Shore was only four or five years older than he was.

'. . . and of course he's been impotent since the first year of our marriage,' she continued carelessly, oblivious of the slight stiffening of the body beside her. 'Will . . . I do need to talk to you, love, but I do not know how to begin. I've never been in a coil like this before and I fear you're going to laugh at me.'

704

She sat up suddenly, wrapped her arms around her drawn-up knees. 'Will, I'm ever so fond of you. You do know that, do you not?'

'But you fancy yourself in love with Ned,' he said very quietly, and she gave him a startled, grateful look, nodded eagerly.

'I guess that was not so hard to see, was it? I do love him, Will, I do. . . . I've never felt this way about any man before. He's on my mind day and night and when I'm not with him, I feel empty inside; I ache, I truly do. Each time I do see him, it is like that first night, and the wonder of it does hit me anew, that this man is England's king, England's king and my lover . . . mine!' She smiled, confided, 'I still find it hard to think of him as Ned; even in my own mind, I think of him as the King more often than not.'

'And what of him, Jane? Surely you cannot think that he does love you?'

'I do not know,' she said in a small voice. 'I think he . . . he does care. I do, Will. He's been very good to me. . . .'

Will was thankful now that he'd seen this coming, grateful for the surge of pride that briefly blotted out hurt. 'And so you yearn now to play a new role, the faithful concubine,' he said coolly, saw her lower lip tremble, like a child unjustly slapped.

'I knew you'd laugh at me. . . . But Will, that is what I want. Please do not be mean. You're the dearest friend I have and I hate it when you say hurtful things to me. I know you must think me silly and moonstruck, but I cannot help it, Will. I do love him so much. He has only to touch me and. . . .'

That he didn't want to hear and he interrupted hastily. 'I'm not laughing at you, Jane. It is only that I should hate to see you hurt. And you will be. Take it from me who knows him best, Ned's a man to take more pleasure in the hunt than in the kill. No woman's ever held him for long and, unless you accept that, you're riding for a nasty fall.'

'That does remain to be seen,' she said, somewhat defensively.

'You say no woman's ever been able to hold him for long. But what of the Queen? She's given him two sons and three daughters . . . four if you do count that poor little lass who died two Decembers past. Clearly he still finds pleasure in her bed, and they ten years wed.'

There was, he saw, nothing he could say to convince her. She'd have to learn the hard way with Ned; women generally did.

'But it is sweet of you to worry about me, Will.' She reached over, touched his hand. 'Will . . . we'll still be friends, will we not? I do not know who I'd turn to if I did not have you; I've never been able to talk to anyone—not even Ned—the way I can talk to you.'

'That is a foolish question, Jane,' he said after a brief silence, and, while a trained ear might have detected echoes of strain, Jane heard nothing in his voice but a suggestion of sleepiness. 'Of course we'll still be friends.'

She reached for the coverlets and then snuggled back against him, seeking his warmth. 'You must not worry about me, Will,' she assured him drowsily. 'Truly, love. It is worth the risk. Ned is . . . He's the king,' she concluded simply, as if that explained all.

'Yes,' Will said. 'I know.'

5

Middleham

May 1475

Anne took no pleasure in the coming of spring that year. Spring meant the onset of Edward's French campaign. She counted the days with secret dread, silently cursed her brother-in-law, and watched helplessly as the beautiful white armour crafted for Richard before Tewkesbury was cleaned with sand and vinegar, watched the preparations for a war that made no sense whatsoever to her and filled her with fear.

And now there were but two days left before Richard led the men under his command south to join the royal army assembling at Barham Downs. All week, men had been riding into Middleham in response to Richard's summons to arms. He'd contracted with Edward to bring one hundred and twenty men-at-arms and one thousand archers. Yet, so enthusiastically had the men of Yorkshire flocked to his colours that he expected to have fully three hundred more than the number promised his brother. Richard was delighted; for three years now, he'd been labouring to win the goodwill and respect of a people not easily impressed, and he took this turnout of northerners to his standard as proof that he was slowly prevailing against local bias and loyalties given for generations to the Houses of Lancaster and Percy. But, to Anne, it meant only that all men, no matter their rank or blood, did share this inexplicable eagerness to risk life and limb in foreign lands.

These were the first quiet moments of the day. Across the solar, Richard was conversing in low yet animated tones with Rob Percy, Francis Lovell and Dick Ratcliffe. Their talk, not surprisingly, was of war.

Anne watched awhile and then looked away. Rob's wife Nell was to wait with her at Middleham while their husbands fought in France, but she was in the early stages of a pregnancy that was proving to be far more troublesome than her first, and she'd retired early; Véronique alone was attending Anne that evening.

Véronique was stitching, but Anne had in her lap the account book for the household, drawn up each night under the supervision of the steward and then presented to her for her inspection. She stared down at the scrawled tabulations and then idly flipped back over the pages, stopping at random at an entry in the preceding month:

On Wednesday, April 19th of Holy Week, for the Duke and Duchess and the household. Grain, 46 bus. Wine, 12 gals. Ale, previously reckoned. Kitchen; 1 and ff oxen, 2 sheep, 500 eggs.

Milk for week, 9 gals. Stable: hay for horses, from stores. Oats, 4 qtrs,

1 bu. Grain for dogs for 10 days, 3 qtrs.

She glanced again at the date; three days before her son's second birthday. One of the last normal entries. Soon thereafter, Middleham had been inundated by a human wave that had yet to recede—men who wanted to fight for Richard, neighbours, citizens of York, couriers from Edward. The accounting for this Wednesday alone filled fully a page and a half.

Laying aside the account book, Anne rose, crossed the solar to join Richard on the settle. He interrupted himself long enough to smile at her, but almost at once turned back to the men, nodding agreement toward Rob.

'Your guess is close, Rob, but I expect we'll have no less than eleven thousand archers and fully fifteen hundred men-at-arms, the largest English army ever to land on French soil.'

'Dickon, tell Rob and Dick what you told me about the King of France—you know, what the King's Grace wrote to you,' Francis prompted, and Richard grinned.

'My brother heard from our contacts on the Continent that when Louis was told he'd best expect an English invasion by summer, he did go white as milk and cried aloud, "Ah, Holy Mary! Even after I have given Thee fourteen hundred crowns, Thou dost not help me one whit!"'

They all laughed; Anne reached for Richard's hand, laced her fingers through his.

As the talk of war swirled around her, Véronique found herself wielding her needle like a weapon, so much so that she was not long in jabbing it into her own flesh. Bringing her thumb up to her mouth, she sucked at the hurt, annoyed by her clumsiness but far more disturbed by what she was hearing.

Véronique jerked the needle so roughly that the thread snapped in two. To her way of thinking, there were few reasons worth dying for, and she most assuredly did not number glory and plunder among them. She did not like this war; she did not like it at all. And not just because her native France was to be the target. Her loyalties were to people, not to places. She had no attachment to England, but she did dearly love the people in this chamber, loved her life at Middleham. She did not want to see these men bleed or die for nothing more than vengeance.

Putting her sewing aside impatiently, Véronique glanced back toward the men and then gave a start to find Francis's eyes upon her. She looked away quickly, angry with herself for the blood that suddenly surged up into her face. Must she betray herself every time he did so much as look her way? Fool! Stupid little fool. Of all the men she might be drawn to, why in Our Lady's Name had it to be Francis? Fool, she repeated bitterly. There was nothing Anne would not do for her. If she wished to wed, Richard would be more than pleased to arrange a suitable marriage for her with a knight of rank and position; it was not inconceivable that she might even wed with a baron, given her known intimacy with the Gloucesters and the generous dowry they'd provide for her. But no, she'd had to fall in love with Francis, Francis, who was clever and kindhearted . . . and married.

When had it begun? When had he become more than a friend to her? She could not remember exactly; it had all happened so gradually, so naturally. By the time she realized her danger, it was too late. Now she was miserable when he was gone from Middleham and no less miserable when he came back. Now she found herself hating a woman she hardly knew, hating Anna Lovell who had Francis and did not want him. And, worst of all, she knew Francis was becoming aware of her feelings. How could he not notice, she thought, and sighed; the change in her was so pronounced only a blind man could have failed to mark it. Tongue-tied, flustered . . . She might as well have a letter engraven upon her forehead for all to see. An A for adultery, the adultery she knew to be a mortal sin and yet did commit nightly in her mind.

Véronique picked up a brush, began to give Anne's hair her customary one hundred strokes. As their eyes met in the mirror, Véronique impulsively bent forward, kissed the younger girl on the cheek. Physically, Anne seemed to have recovered fully from her Christmas miscarriage; emotionally, the wound had yet to heal, showed all too clearly on nights like this, showed whenever Anne was overtired or worried, and she'd been both for some weeks now.

Véronique told herself repeatedly that it was God's will, must be accepted as such. But she still did not think it fair that Anne had lost her baby. Anne so wanted a nursery full of children. But she'd had a very difficult delivery with little Ned, and then two miscarriages in as many years.

'You must remember, chérie Anne, that your sister was unable to conceive for several years after her first was stillborn. But then she did give birth to a daughter and now God has blessed her with a healthy son. Do bear that in mind, chérie, and try not to become discouraged.'

Anne nodded. 'I know.' She picked up an ivory comb, fingered it absently. 'But I was not thinking of that, Véronique . . . not tonight.' She twisted around on the seat. 'I was thinking of Richard . . . and that there are but two days until he does ride south. Two days,' she said, this time in little more than a whisper.

'Your Richard is a seasoned battle commander, chérie, for all his youth. You must never forget that.'

Anne nodded, almost imperceptibly. 'I know. But he's reckless,

Véronique. He does take too many chances; even Ned says that. If he. . . .'

She stopped abruptly in midsentence as Richard came into the bedchamber. Joining them before the mirror, he leaned down to kiss his wife and then took the brush from Véronique.

Wanting to be sure that Anne would have no further need of her that night, Véronique lingered awhile longer, putting out Anne's bedrobe, tooth powder, washing cloth and soap. After that, she hesitated, to see if Anne wanted her help in undressing. Anne so far showed no signs of stirring, seemed quite content to sit before the mirror, watching as Richard drew the brush through her hair, so slowly and solicitously that Véronique hid a smile, thinking of the vigorous strokes she herself had been applying to Anne's hip-length tresses. But when Anne reached for Richard's free hand, held it against her cheek, Véronique quietly withdrew, unwilling to witness a moment not meant to be shared. Closing the door, she left them alone.

She was too restless to retire. Crossing the covered bridge that spanned the bailey and led back into the keep, she entered the great hall. It was dark, illuminated only by the subdued glow of her lantern. She could just discern the sleeping forms of servants, stretched out on pallets along the walls. Light was beckoning from the half-open door of the solar; she moved instinctively toward it, only to regret bitterly the impulse a moment later as she found herself face-to-face with Francis.

She retreated at once, heard him cry her name as she fled back out into the great hall. She headed for the spiral stairway in the southeast corner of the keep, the one that led down to the kitchen and cellars and up to the battlements. She mounted the steps so rapidly that she was panting by the time she emerged onto the castle battlements.

Had this been wartime, there would have been men stationed here as sentries. Now, however, she was alone. Gazing down into the dark of the inner bailey, she saw no lights, no signs of life;

only in the gatehouse did torches flare. At this height, the wind was more keenly felt; it tugged at the confines of her chignon, sent loose strands flying untidily about her face. She didn't mind, welcomed the chill on skin still flushed.

The wind whipped a swirl of hair across her mouth and she pulled impatiently at the restraining combs, let it all blow free away from her face. Did Anna Lovell care that Francis might not come back? Would she weep for him? Or would she. . . .

'Véronique.'

She spun around.

Francis emerged from the shadows filling the stairwell, came toward her. Bending down, he retrieved her lantern and set it on the embrasure between them. She wanted to shrink back from its revealing light, wanted to slip past him and back down the stairs to safety. She didn't move.

For a time, neither spoke. Both gazed out over the parapet at the shadowy countryside below. Come dawn, it would be again a soft sweep of briliant green; now it was a dark silent sea lapping at the outer curtain walls of the castle.

'I've never seen your hair loose before.' He reached over, entwined a curl about his fingers. But when he brought his hand up from her shoulder to her face, she began to tremble.

'Francis, do not,' she said, very softly, for even in her present agitation, she remembered how clearly voices carried on the air of a quiet country night.

He, too, kept his voice low. 'Véronique, you must know how I do feel about you. It has to show on my face each time I look at you.'

'Oh, Jesú, Francis, do not say that . . . please.' But she made no move to go, instead, stood very still, scarcely breathing. Would it truly be such a sin to send him off to war with an offering of love? What if he were to die without knowing she cared? How could she live with a regret like that? Perhaps God would understand, would not judge her too harshly.

She closed her eyes and then felt his mouth against her lashes. His kisses were light, trailed over her skin like the graze of a butterfly's wing. When he at last took her mouth with his own, she thought no more of sins or penance or Anna Lovell.

'I love you,' she whispered. 'God forgive me, but I do. . . .'

6

St-Christ-sur-Somme Burgundy

August 1475

A sudden gust of wind beat against the flap of Edward's tent, intruded within. Candles were gutted, papers blown wildly about, and men swore, struggled to secure the canvas against the rain that had proven to be a far more relentless foe than the French, that had turned the English camp into a muddy swamp and turned English tempers savage.

Even as they succeeded in shutting out the elements, thunder crashed overhead, seemed to come from within the tent itself, so close it was. Edward flinched and then cursed. His men eyed him uneasily and, knowing his mood, tried to make themselves as inconspicuous as possible.

It had been a disastrous day for the English, was to have been the day that the Count of St Pol surrendered to them the city of St Quentin. But, when an English force confidently approached the city gates, they'd been driven back in disarray by the blaze of cannon fire.

St Pol's treachery was the last straw for Edward. His enthusiasm for a French campaign had never been all that high. But war fever was running rampant in England while Edward's own popularity had been ebbing. People complained about burdensome taxes, complained about corrupt officials and rising prices. The roads were not safe from highwaymen, there were lords who did abuse their power and priests who did likewise. These grievances were not new, had been voiced under Lancaster with far greater virulence. But Edward had raised expectations that could not realistically be satisfied and, disillusioned, many men and women had begun to believe that it mattered little what King did rule over them, that the problems plaguing their daily lives would remain the same in any reign.

Aware of these undercurrents of discontent, coming under increasing pressure from a Commons disgruntled by his frequent requests for war grants and equally frequent failures to act upon them, Edward had seen war with France as a means of defusing dissent and coalescing public opinion firmly in his favour. Moreover, he had a legitimate grudge against the King of France, had not forgotten all Louis had done to aid Warwick at his expense. And if he never truly expected to prevail in his claim to the French throne, he did believe a successful campaign could gain him the duchies of Normandy and Guienne.

But, from the first, nothing had gone as planned. Although Edward reached Calais on July 4th, his brother-in-law Charles had not joined him there until the fourteenth and, when he did arrive, he did so without the Burgundian army. Insisting that he meant to keep faith, however, Charles had suggested that the English army march into Champagne whilst his own troops swept through Lorraine, both forces to come together at Rheims, where Edward would be crowned as King of France.

Edward had agreed but more disappointments were to come.

714

The Duke of Brittany had given them to expect military support but, so far, none had been forthcoming. The differences between Edward and Charles seemed to be deepening daily. Both were self-willed, accustomed to command but not to compromise; nor was the developing friction eased any by Charles's refusal to give the English entry into his own cities.

And then had come this Friday's debacle before the walls of St Quentin. When the Count of St Pol sent word to Charles that he was willing to open the city gates to the Engish, Edward had been dubious at first; St Pol's name had long been a byword for betrayal and double dealing. But Charles had been convinced that St Pol was acting this time in good faith and Edward had been willing to let himself be convinced, too.

But St Pol had suffered an eleventh-hour change of heart, fired down upon the men he'd sworn to embrace as allies, and, shortly afterward, Charles had ridden into the English camp at St Christ-sur-Somme to casually inform Edward that he was departing the next day for Valenciennes to rejoin his own army. Edward spent the evening hours brooding over the events of the past few weeks and, shortly before midnight, came to a decision.

'The French prisoner taken at Noyon. . . . Bring him to me. Now.'

Minutes later, a terrified youngster was thrust into the tent, fell to his knees before Edward. Not daring to speak, he waited mutely for the English king to decree his doom.

'You need not look so greensick, lad,' Edward said softly. 'I do mean to let you go.'

The French king was encamped at Compiègne, less than forty miles to the south. Knowing that, Edward was able to estimate how long it would take the freed prisoner to reach Compiègne and how long it would then take a French courier to get back through the lines. That Louis would put the correct interpretation upon his magnanimous gesture and respond accordingly,

Edward never doubted. He knew the French King did not want war. Louis was a puppeteer, much preferred to pull strings backstage than to be forced centre stage, sword in hand. He'd gladly paid out French gold to undermine the House of York but he was not so willing to spill out French blood in the same cause. Edward was not at all surprised, therefore, to have his dinner interrupted two days later by the arrival of a French herald.

Ushered into Edward's presence, the herald at once came persuasively to the point. The French King was eager, he said, to discuss their differences with his English cousin. Would the English King consent to a safe-conduct for a French embassy?

'I think,' Edward said coolly, 'that it might be arranged.'

It had taken but two days, one to put forth Edward's terms for peace and one for Louis to accept them all. Louis agreed to pay Edward seventy-five thousand crowns within the next fifteen days and to pay fifty thousand crowns a year thereafter. A seven-year truce was to be declared and the peace between England and France was to be solemnized by the betrothal of the five-year-old heir to the French throne and Edward's nine year-old daughter Bess.

Edward was well pleased with this pact that would one day make his favourite child Queen of France and, as he glanced about the tent at his companions, he thought it plain that they, too, were pleased. And why not? In his eagerness to buy peace, Louis had not quibbled at the price, had not stinted those who had the confidence or friendship of the English king.

Edward's eyes moved lazily now from face to face, singling out those who'd been judged influential enough to placate. John Howard was to receive an annual payment of twelve hundred crowns from the royal treasury of France. Edward's Chancellor, Thomas Rotherham, was to collect a thousand. Lesser amounts were to go to John Morton, his Master of the Rolls, to Thomas Grey, his stepson, and to Thomas St Leger, who'd wed his sister Anne as soon as she'd succeeded in divorcing Exeter. Lord Stanley, too, was to benefit from the largesse of the King of France. But to Will Hastings was to go the largest French grant of all, two thousand crowns a year for life.

Edward grinned, for Will alone had refused to sign any sort of receipt, saying, 'If you wish, put the money in my sleeve, but no acquittance showing I was a pensioner of France will ever be found in the French treasury.' Yet so eager had Louis been to win the goodwill of Edward's Chamberlain and closest friend that he'd not balked at Will's terms, had given him, as well, silver plate worth another thousand marks.

They were all here now in Edward's tent, celebrating this peace that promised to give them such unexpected profit at so little cost. All the men who stood closest to him. All save one.

That last thought was an irksome one, and he tried not to dwell upon it, tried without success. It was a gnawing discontent that was not going to ease of its own accord, would have to be dealt with. He grimaced, came reluctantly to his feet.

Men materialized from the dark to bar the entrance to his brother's tent, but backed away as soon as the light of torches flared upon Edward's face. Within, he found a half-dozen or so men, recognized John Scrope of Bolton Castle and Francis Lovell of Minster Lovell among them. His unexpected and unheralded appearance brought them to their feet in some confusion and he emptied the tent at once by saying curtly, 'I would speak with my brother of Gloucester alone.'

Richard had been lying on his bed; he alone had not moved as Edward entered the tent. Nor did he move now, and Edward's eyebrows rose at what was both discourtesy to a guest and disrespect to a sovereign. He chose to let it pass, however, sat down on a heavy oaken coffer.

'This is not like you, Dickon. You've never been one to nurse a grievance or sulk if thwarted. I'd have expected as much from George but not from you.'

717

Richard said nothing but the clenched jaw, the deliberately averted eyes alerted Edward to a still-smouldering anger. He'd expected as much, but he still found himself saying impatiently, 'Well? Have you nothing to say to me?'

'What I do have to say to you, you'd not like to hear.'

Edward swore suddenly, sharply. 'Why must you be so stubborn about this? You're as far from a fool as any man could be. Surely you must see why I made the choice I did. Common sense dictated it; to do otherwise would have been folly.'

Richard stayed silent and Edward was goaded into doing what he'd sworn he'd not do, defend again the logistics of his decision.

'Christ, Dickon, look at the facts as they are, not as you would like them to be. What else could I do? Let's start with the weather; it's rained nigh on every day for a fortnight and it'll get far worse once cold weather does set in. Do you think I want to be bogged down in a winter campaign, one that might drag on for months? Not with the allies I have, I can damned well assure you! What have we got from Brittany so far except excuses and evasions? As for Charles . . . he's as unpredictable and dangerous as a loose cannon aboard ship and to put any trust in his word is like spitting into the wind. He's all too likely to. . . .'

'Trust? We were the ones to make a private peace, without even warning him beforehand that such was our intent. Jesus God, Ned, whatever Charles's failings, we did owe him better than that! And if not him, then the people of England. You did bleed the country white for this war with France and now we are to straggle home surfeited with French wines and French food, stuffed with French bribes? England did pray for another Agincourt, not a sell-out!'

'I talk of realities and you give me back platitudes about honour and chivalry. I did expect better of you than that, Dickon!'

'And I you!'

Edward came abruptly to his feet. 'It would seem, then,' he said coldly, 'that we've nothing more to say to one another.' He

718

lingered, however, for several moments more before moving away from the bed, as if half expecting Richard to relent. At the tent flap, he paused again, demanded roughly, 'Just what would you have me do? You cannot deny the truth in what I said. Why in Christ's Name should I take the field to win what I can have so freely given to me? Suppose you do tell me that!'

Richard sat up, said with no less heat, 'I would rather you do tell me how it can bother you so little that the price you've paid for this peace is no less than our honour! You think they are not laughing at the French court? Or that Louis will not disavow this treaty whenever it does suit him to do so? After all, why need he fear English retaliation? He knows now how cheaply we do sell ourselves, not for blood but for promises, pensions and silver plate!'

'There is no talking to you on this; I see that now. Not as long as you cling to the quaint belief that we live, not in England, but in Camelot,' Edward said in disgust and jerked the tent flap back, ducking out into the rain-swept dark.

On August 25th, the French king rode into the city of Amiens. The next day, the English army arrived and, while preparations went forward for the meeting of the two Kings on that coming Tuesday, Louis opened the city gates to the English. More than a hundred carts of wine were dispatched to the English camp and, to the delight of Edward's soldiers, they soon discovered that the taverns of Amiens had been instructed to serve them whatever they wanted and charge them nothing.

While the English drank and feasted at the expense of the King of France, a wooden bridge was being erected at Picquigny, nine miles downriver from Amiens. On August 29th, Edward and Louis were to meet on this bridge, where they would swear upon the Holy and True Cross to uphold the truce and all the covenants of the Peace of Picquigny.

*

'Is it true, Ned, that a wooden lattice has been erected on the bridge and you and the French king will speak together through the lattice?'

Edward laughed, nodded. 'So I understand, Will. Some fifty years past, Louis' father met with the Duke of Burgundy on a bridge to reconcile their differences. It ended their differences, in truth, ended with the Duke of Burgundy stabbed to death there on the bridge. I suppose Louis wants to make sure that neither he nor I might be tempted to resolve our problems in a like manner.'

'What of Marguerite d'Anjou, Ned? Is Louis willing to ransom her?'

'Yes. Once he puts up fifty thousand crowns, she'll be returned to France where Louis will see that she relinquishes to him all inheritance rights she has in Anjou. I saw no reason not to set her free, would rather have the fifty thousand crowns in my coffers than have her in Wallingford Castle. God knows, she poses no threat. She's been ailing for years, has never got over the death of her son. . . .'

He never finished the sentence, looked up as Richard came into the tent. Richard wasted no time on greetings of any sort, ignored the others, and demanded of Edward, 'Do you know what's going on in Amiens?'

Edward cared neither for the tone nor the abruptness of the question. 'What precisely should I know?' he asked coolly.

'That every alehouse, tavern and bordello in the town is jammed with our men! That fully three-quarters of the English army is in Amiens, brawling, roistering, falling down blind-drunk in the streets!'

Richard was almost incoherent with rage. He had yet even to glance toward Will, Anthony Woodville, or Thomas Grey, kept his eyes on his brother, saying bitterly, 'Most of them are so wine-sodden that they could not tell a sword from a ploughshare if their lives did depend upon it. And what makes you think they do not? Do you truly trust the French as much as that? And if so, name of God, why?'

Edward had stiffened with Richard's first words. Now he said sharply, 'Are you sure of this, Dickon?'

'All too sure.'

Edward shoved his plate from him, with such force that it skidded across the table, overturned on the floor of the tent. He paid it no heed, seemed not even to notice. Coming to his feet, he moved around the table, toward Richard.

'Will, get word to Louis. Tell him I want Amiens closed to my army. Dickon, you come with me. First, we must make sure that no more enter the town. What think you of posting our own men at the city gates? Then I want the order given to get them out of there, as soon as they do sober up enough to walk. . . .'

Thomas Grey had a face that served as a faithful mirror of his soul, betrayed every rage, every joy. He was jealous of Richard, had been jealous of Richard as far back as he could remember. It showed nakedly on his face now as he watched his stepfather and Richard depart the tent. He gulped the last of his wine and, turning to his uncle, said in an acid undertone, 'I should've known Gloucester'd be one to begrudge our soldiers a bit of sport but I can tell you, Uncle, that all this righteous concern is sour grapes and damned little else. Nothing could please him more than to have this truce fall through, to be able to gloat that he was right and the rest of us wrong.'

He'd miscalculated, though, should have held his tongue a moment or two longer. Richard had already gone out into the August rain, but Edward had paused to take up a cloak. The words meant only for Anthony came to him, too.

He turned to stare at his stepson, saw Thomas redden as he realized he'd been overheard.

'You'd do well,' he snapped, 'to bear in mind that I do not suffer fools gladly. I do not suffer them at all.'

Thomas swallowed, said nothing. But a moment later, he swung to glare at Will Hastings. So did Anthony. Will was laughing. Rising without haste, he collected his own cloak and, still laughing, exited the tent.

It was shortly before Vespers on Monday eve. The next morning Edward was to meet with the French king on the bridge at Picquigny. His council was scheduled to gather in his tent within the hour for a final briefing. The men sitting across the table from him now, however, were intimates as well as advisers. His brothers, his Woodville relations, Will Hastings. John Howard had just entered the tent; before long, they'd be joined by the others, by Suffolk, Northumberland, Stanley, Morton, his Chancellor. But for the moment, the mood was relaxed, the talk idle.

'I did hear it said that the French king would not transact any business this day, that he believes it unlucky to make any decisions on the twenty-eighth of each month, it being that Holy Innocent's Day falls on that date.'

Will's comment drew a flicker of interest from George who looked up and grinned. 'That's a common enough belief in England, too. Yet you did hold your coronation on that very date, Ned. Tempting fate, were you not?'

'To tell you true, George, I did not much think on it, one way or the other.' Edward took an apple from the bowl before him, tossed one to Richard who was taken by surprise and almost fumbled the catch.

'How many men can you take with you tomorrow, Ned?'

'Eight hundred men-at-arms and twelve men with me on the bridge, Will. I thought I'd take you, Dickon, George, Jack, Northumberland. . . .'

Richard's head had come up sharply at mention of his own name. Now he cut in abruptly, 'You'd best choose another in my stead. The last place I do intend to be tomorrow is on the bridge at Picquigny.'

There was a sudden silence.

'Indeed?' Edward said softly, and leaned back in his seat to regard his youngest brother with hard, appraising eyes. Some of his anger, though, he reserved for himself. Fool that he was, why had he not seen this coming? Had he only given it a moment's thought, he could have seen Dickon alone, made sure that Dickon understood what was expected of him. Or could he? Four years ago, he'd done just that, made Dickon an unwilling accomplice to murder. But eighteen was a more malleable age than twenty-two, and Dickon was taking this whole matter with the French too much to heart. No, it was likely that nothing less than a direct command could get Dickon to take part in the morrow's ceremony. But would Dickon ever forgive him for giving such a command? To have his way in this, was it worth the price he might have to pay?

He happened to glance toward the others, noted the markedly similar expressions upon the faces of George and Thomas Grey, expectant, eager. His mouth curved down; like cats at a mouse-hole, they were. Making up his mind, he smiled easily at Richard, said as if they were discussing nothing more than a matter of personal preference, 'As you like, Dickon.' And was somewhat mollified by the look of relief that fleetingly yet unmistakably flitted across Richard's face.

Philippe de Commynes had entered into the service of the Duke of Burgundy as a youth of seventeen and had risen rapidly in Charles's favour. By 1467, he was Charles's Chamberlain and most trusted councillor. But he was by temperament as alien to Charles as ice to fire. Philippe's brain was meant for subtleties and stratagems, while there was bred into the very bones of his mercurial lord a love for war. Three years ago, Philippe had fled Burgundy for the French court; he'd been secretly in the pay of the French King for fully a year before that. In so doing, he'd made a mortal enemy of Charles, and Charles's enmity was not to be taken lightly. But Philippe had no regrets; in Louis, he'd found a man who, like himself, preferred statecraft to the sword, a man who understood, as Charles had not, that diplomacy is much like chess, must be played with a light hand and a calculating eye. Philippe had no regrets at all.

He was alone now with his king. It was very late and Louis was showing the strain of recent weeks. In the uncertain light, his face had taken on a grey tinge and the full, mobile mouth was strangely pinched, puffy lids drooping heavily over the deep-set dark eyes. As usual, he was dressed with a casualness that bordered on the careless; never would Phillippe have believed there could be a Prince so indifferent to appearance and the accoutrements of power. Even today, he'd worn his customary costume; a plain grey gown, broad-brimmed hat and hunting boots caked with mud.

There were no servants in the chamber. Philippe himself went to the sideboard, nearly tripping over a small dark spaniel camouflaged all too well by the deepening shadows. He glared at the offending animal but it never occurred to him to thrust it out of his way, for his sovereign's passion for his dogs was in the nature of an obsession and the royal pets were sacrosanct. Returning with a wine cup, he said coaxingly, 'Will you not drink, Your Grace?'

The lids lifted, revealed that however fatigued was his body, Louis' mind still pulsed with life. The eyes that met Philippe's were bright, shone feverish with thought.

'It went well, did it not?' he murmured, and Philippe nodded.

Louis gestured toward a cushioned footstool and Philippe sat beside his lord. He stretched his legs, scratched at the coarse grey wool—his was the dubious honour of dressing as Louis' double for public ceremonies, in hopes of thus deflecting an assassin's dagger—and prepared to dissect the day's happenings.

'I did have a bad moment at supper, though,' Louis now confided wryly. 'When Lord Howard promised to urge his King to accept my invitation to come to Paris. Holy Mary forfend!'

Philippe grinned. It was a source of constant amusement and some wonder to him that a man as devious and inclined towards intrigue as Louis could allow himself such indiscreet lapses. It was a standing joke of Louis' that his tongue was a two-edged sword, and Philippe tended to agree with him. Such had surely been the case at Picquigny. So cordial had his meeting been with Edward that Louis had jested amiably that Edward ought to come to Paris. French women were surpassingly beautiful, he'd laughed, and, as proof of friendship, he was willing to offer Edward a confessor who'd lay light penances for pleasurable sins. Much to Louis' chagrin, Edward had taken a dangerous degree of interest in his pleasantry, until Louis had begun to fear that an invitation offered in jest would be accepted in earnest.

Louis now shook his head, said, 'He's a very handsome king, that one, and he does like pretty women overly well. He might find himself a Parisian bedmate so seductive that he'd be eager to come back, and I'd much prefer to keep him where he does belong, on his own side of the Channel.'

He sipped his wine, said regretfully, 'A pity I could not win him away from his alliance with Brittany. But Burgundy ... ah, Burgundy is another matter. We need not fear a second alliance of England and Burgundy united against France. The Blessed Virgin has once more favoured us against our enemies, set them in disarray.'

'God's truth, Your Grace. What I would not have given to be there when Charles confronted Edward at St Christ-sur-Somme.' The story of that embittered encounter had been repeated so often that Philippe could have recited it by heart, but he knew his King derived fresh pleasure from each telling and so he indulged Louis now by saying, 'I understand Charles did not even bother to dismount, that he reined in before Edward's tent and demanded that Edward come out to him, shouting his insults and abuse all the while in English so Edward's soldiers would be sure to understand. Truly a sight to gladden French eyes, my liege. Charles stuttering with rage, red as a radish, cursing the English king in language vile enough to make a whore blush, calling him Judas and hell-spawn and coward. And Edward shouting back at him, matching him insult for insult, and all before half the English army . . . a good many of whom, I suspect, think Charles had the right of it.'

Louis' dark eyes had kindled. 'Indeed, God is good,' he agreed, and Philippe smiled, watched him with admiration that was unfeigned; Louis the grey monk—stooped, ugly, and no longer young—Louis the Spider King, the victor.

Louis glanced obliquely now at Philippe, said in faint reproach, 'You led me somewhat astray, Philippe, in what you told me of the English king. I found him to be verily as clever as you said, to be a man who sees what he wants, takes it and cares little for the risks. But I think, too, that he does greatly like his ease, that his pleasures do count for much with him. And that, my friend, you did not tell me.'

'My liege, when I met him four years ago at Aire, I think the pleasures did count for less.'

Louis reflected upon that, and then nodded. 'There are men,' he observed thoughtfully, 'who do thrive upon adversities that would break a lesser spirit. And yet these same men can find prosperity more ruinous than ever they did hardship. It may be that our Yorkist friend is one such. I do most devoutly hope so, for I tell you no lie, Philippe, when I say that I've feared this man, feared him for more years than I do care to remember. He knows war all too well, has never been defeated on the field. . . .'

'Until now, Your Grace,' Philippe interjected, and Louis laughed soundlessly.

'But I fear him no longer, my friend. I see now how powerful an ally I do have on my side – time. If he had not the stomach for a hard campaign at thirty-three, how much less will it be so at thirty-eight, at forty.'

'But the other, the young brother. . . . That one, Philippe, is very much an enemy of France, and we must ever keep that in mind.'

Philippe nodded. That had been his king's only failure. He'd had no luck whatsoever in conciliating the Duke of Gloucester. And he'd tried, had gone to considerable lengths to do so.

Louis had dismissed the Duke of Clarence as a malcontent not worth bothering with. Edward, he said, liked Clarence little and trusted him less. But Gloucester . . . Gloucester was different, and he'd told Edward that nothing could please him more than for Gloucester to sup with him in Amiens that evening.

Gloucester had come, but it soon became all too apparent that this was to be the only concession they'd get from him. Louis had done his best to charm, and Louis' charm could be formidable when he put his mind to it. Remembering, Philippe shook his head ruefully. His king had been dipping his bucket in a dry well this time. Gloucester was there because he'd been summoned by a king, and he was polite because courtesy did demand as much, but beyond that, he'd not go. He'd shrugged off the French king's flattery, responded to Louis' avowals of friendship with the most noncommittal of amenities and, when Louis insisted that he accept several finely bred stallions as proof of French goodwill, all Louis had got for his generosity was a chill, 'As Your Grace does insist, I do thank you.' No, Louis was right; Gloucester was a dangerous man, was no friend to France. They'd do well to remember that.

'More wine, my liege?' he queried, and Louis nodded, began to laugh.

'It does occur to me,' he said, 'that I have chased the English out of France more easily than ever my father did; for my father had to resort to force of arms and I had to resort to nothing more lethal than venison pies and good wines.'

7

Middleham

July 1476

Anne was writing to Véronique. It had been nearly two months since Véronique had departed Middleham for London and Anne was growing impatient for her return. She was willing to admit to herself that she'd not much liked this London visit of Véronique's. She knew all too well that Véronique had gone to London for one reason and one reason only, to be with Francis.

Anne did not approve of Véronique's liaison with Francis. She worried that her friend was imperilling her soul by the sin of adultery and fretted that she might pay the earthly penance of pregnancy. Not being able to accept the relationship, Anne chose to ignore it. Now she was careful to make no mention of what she suspected, that Francis had leased a house in London for Véronique. She wrote, instead, of a disturbing rumour recently come to her ears, that there'd been an outbreak of smallpox in London, and expressed concern both for Véronique's health and for the risks she might therefore be incurring by a prolonged stay.

Richard did depart for Pontefract this Monday last. There the bodies of his lord father and his brother Edmund are to be disinterred and Richard to escort the funeral cortège south to Fotheringhay. Upon arrival at Fotheringhay, their bodies are to be laid to rest within the Church of the Blessed Virgin and All Saints.

I'm sure it does not surprise you in the least that I did not

728

accompany Richard. Now that I am breeding again at last, I intend to take no chances with this babe I carry.

Nor will my sister Isabel be present at Fotheringhay, and for the same reason as mine. I wish I could take more pleasure in her news that she is again with child, but she's far from well, Véronique, has been afflicted by a lingering cough and intermittent fevers for months.

I do have news now of a doleful nature to impart. I've had word that my uncle, the Archbishop of York, did go to God on June 8th. I can speak freely with you, dearest, and say without fear of censure that I bore him little love. But he was my bloodkin, and I am thankful that Richard was able to secure his release from prison. The Chaplain of his household did write me that he repented much and made a pious Christian end. Holy Jesus, may it be so.

Anne's pen faltered, traced hesitant patterns across the page. Twice death had touched their family in this year of grace, for Richard's sister Anne, Duchess of Exeter, had died suddenly that past January. But she was not thinking now of the sister-in-law she'd not known or the uncle she'd not loved. She was thinking of the death that December past of Nell Percy, Rob's young wife. Nell had laboured for two days in great pain before giving birth to a stillborn daughter. The dreaded milk fever had followed and Nell herself was dead before the week was out.

Resolutely, she put Nell from her thoughts with a whispered, 'May God assoil her.' Putting her pen to paper again, she wrote:

I am very pleased to be able to tell you that Richard did successfully intercede with the King on behalf of the city of York. I need not remind you how wroth Ned was at the time of that rising here in Yorkshire this spring. It was, after all, serious enough to warrant sending Richard and the Earl of Northumberland into York with a force of five thousand men.

729

I was not surprised when Ned then threatened to strip the city of its charter; he's never had much liking for York. The mayor and aldermen pleaded with Richard to speak for their city, and he was able to persuade Ned not to carry out his threat.

There have been no further disturbances, nor do I expect any. However much the people do hate the French treaty, they've no choice but to accept it. I confess to you, Véronique, that what mattered most to me was that they should come home safe and well. But I am proud, too, that Richard has won for himself such acclaim for his refusal to treat with the French. Loving these northern moors as he does, it means much to Richard that he has been accepted so wholeheartedly by our Yorkshiremen as their liege lord, that they do look to Richard now where once they did look to the Earl of Northumberland.

Since you departed for London, Richard's little daughter Kathryn has come to stay—for several weeks, mayhap the entire summer. Now that she's wed, Kathryn's mother seems more willing to entrust Kathryn to us for longer periods of time. As you'd expect, Richard is delighted to have her. Nor do I mind. She's a high-spirited pretty child, if a trifle spoiled. I will confess, however, that my heart does warm to Kathryn more easily now that her mother has given to another the love she once did give to Richard.

She hesitated, before concluding with the truth.

Do not tarry overlong in London, Véronique. I am not as easy in my mind about this baby as I would wish. I did suffer some bleeding a fortnight ago and, while it has not recurred, I cannot forget that I did lose my last two.

It had rained that morning and the air was heavy with humid August heat, the ground oozing mud that no child could long resist. Jerking Lucy, one of John Neville's daughters, away from a particularly tempting puddle, Mistress Burgh did not at once notice what her other charges were up to, turned around just in time to see Johnny and Kathryn lift their little brother Ned up onto the back of a huge greying wolfhound. Mistress Burgh was annoyed but not alarmed; Gareth had long ago proved that with small children, his patience did verge upon the saintly.

At that moment, though, the stable dogs began to bark and men up on the walls to shout.

'Papa's coming!' Releasing his hold upon Gareth's collar, Johnny sprinted for the gateway.

By now, Gareth had scented his master among the riders galloping through the village. The big dog lurched forward eagerly, sent Ned sprawling into the mud. The little boy gasped but so urgent was his need to see his father that he deferred protest until a more convenient time, picked himself up without complaint and ran after Johnny.

At sight of his children, Richard reined in abruptly. By the time he swung down from the saddle, all three were clamouring for his attention. Kathryn and Johnny gave him the usual quick hugs and wet kisses, but Ned clung like a cockle-bur, buried his face in Richard's neck, sought handholds in Richard's hair.

Richard made no attempt to disentangle himself, shifted his grip and rose to his feet with the child securely within his arms. Some of Ned's urgency seemed to have eased. Silky brown hair tumbled untidily across his forehead; there was a muddy smear across one cheek, another on his nose. He seemed all eyes to Richard, eyes that were soft and round and bewildered.

'Mama's sick,' he said solemnly.

Richard's bedchamber was shuttered, admitted neither light nor cheer. He signalled and, behind him, a torch flared into life. Anne didn't stir as he approached the bed. Long, loose hair trailed limply over a bared shoulder, uncombed, dulled to a lifeless brittle brown. Her face was pinched and bloodless, as white as the sheets

731

upon which she lay; her eyes were closed, but the lids looked bruised, inflamed. One hand held a crumpled handkerchief, the other clutched the sheet, clenched into a small fist. She looked lost in the vastness of their bed, huddled and still under the weight of silken summer coverlets.

Richard sat down carefully on the edge of the bed. As he did, her lashes lifted.

'Beloved, I'm sorry,' he said softly. He leaned over to touch his lips to her forehead and was taken aback when she turned her face away.

'Anne, are you angry with me? Because I was not with you? Sweetheart, I did come as soon as Nan's message reached me. . . .'

She shook her head swiftly, vehemently. Her face was pressed into the pillow and her voice so muffled, so indistinct that he had to strain to catch her words.

'Forgive? Forgive what, Anne? I do not understand.'

'Forgive me. . . .' The way her shoulders hunched forward told him that she wept. 'I did fail you.'

'Anne, that's not so.'

'It be a wife's duty to give her husband children. You have the right to expect that of me. But I cannot, Richard . . . I cannot. . . .'

Richard opened his mouth to reassure her that there'd be other babies, to remind her that she was only twenty and he not yet twenty-four, that many women did suffer miscarriages only later to bear healthy children. Instead he heard himself say, 'There is something I would have you know, Anne. When you did tell me this spring that you were with child again, I found I could take little joy in it.'

She rolled over, regarded him with wide, uncertain eyes. 'Richard, why? You do want more children; I know you do.'

'Yes, children are important to me. But there is something I do value far more. Your life, Anne. I could think only of Nell

Percy, could think of nothing but Nell and how bad a time you did have when Ned was born.'

For the first time she truly looked at him, saw the evidence of several days' hard riding. So hastily had he come from Fotheringhay that he'd not even taken time to shave; his face was rough with stubbly growth, exhaustion etched in the rigid muscles around his mouth, smudged in the hollows that formed deep, discoloured crescents under his eyes.

She raised herself up on her elbows and, when he put an arm around her waist, drew her gently to him, she clung no less urgently than their little boy had done. He felt hot tears on her face, wiped them away with his fingers.

'I'm sorry,' she whispered and he kissed the wet lashes, the swollen eyelids.

'Hush,' he said. 'Hush.'

8

York

January 1477

Anne and Richard customarily came to York for Christmas, Easter and the spring festival of Corpus Christi. This year they passed through Micklegate Bar well past dark on the evening of January 2nd. Despite the hour, Lord Mayor Wrangwysh and the city aldermen were gathered in the snow to give them welcome. From there, they'd been escorted down Micklegate Street, across Ouse Bridge and into Conyng Street until they reached the Augustine friary where Richard liked to stay when in York. They were expected; torches and fire pans lit the dark and the prior waited at the gateway so that he might himself be the one to usher them within.

Shortly after noon the next day, Anne had her grey mare brought from the stables. Under her supervision, packhorses were loaded with blankets, grain sacks, and other goods to be distributed among the city's sixteen hospitals. She chose to ride herself to nearby St Leonard's Hospital where the poor congregated daily for bread and pottage. To feed the hungry was one of the Seven Acts of Mercy, was what was expected of her as a Christian and the lady of Middleham; but Anne, who'd learned at fourteen that the loss of hope was the cruellest loss of all, enjoyed taking a more active part in her almsgiving. She spent a pleasant hour at the hospital orphanage where she delighted the children with jars of honey and apple butter and the monks with offerings of bread, eggs and salted fish.

A light feathery snow was dusting Anne's cloak and skirts by the time she returned to the friary. She wasn't surprised to learn that Richard was still meeting with the Lord Mayor; as Thomas Wrangwysh was a friend, it was to be expected that his courtesy call would be a lengthy one. But she was disappointed, nonetheless, to find Richard not yet free, for she and Richard had quarrelled the day before and, as yet, they'd had no time alone to dispel the tension that had so suddenly sprung up between them.

Anne hated to quarrel with Richard. Their infrequent arguments usually ended with her being the one to yield, in part because she'd been taught that a wife did owe obedience to her husband and in part because she was of a more placid temperament than Richard. Yesterday's quarrel had ostensibly been about a small matter, whether Johnny should be allowed to ride his own pony on the journey to York or whether he should travel in a horse litter like Ned. Although Johnny begged to ride the pony, Anne thought him to be too young, and here it would have ended had Richard not overheard and given Johnny the permission she'd refused.

The argument that followed had been brief, low-voiced, constrained of necessity by their awareness of others within earshot. Richard had been surprised by her reproach. She was too protective of the boys, he said flatly, treated Ned as if he'd bruise if breathed upon. Anne had denied it with unwonted sharpness, all the more nettled because she knew his accusation was grained in truth, and, on that sour note, they'd departed for York. Johnny had ridden his pony until he swayed in the saddle with fatigue, secretly grateful when Anne at last told him to join Ned in the horse litter. She and Richard had gone to bed as overly polite strangers and this morning she was plagued by vague regrets.

But it seemed that her talk with Richard would have to wait and she signalled for a torchbearer to accompany her into the church. There, in the Chapel of St Catherine, Virgin and Martyr, she lit a candle for her sister's recovery; it was nigh on three months now since Isabel had given birth to a second son and, by all accounts, she was still quite ill.

By the time Anne emerged from the church, dusk had descended over the friary grounds; all was quiet, cold, muffled by the swirl of softly falling snow. Before returning to the chambers set aside for her use, Anne chose to check on her son.

Ned and Johnny were in bed, napping under thick fox-fur coverlets. At first glance, Anne thought both boys were asleep. But a closer examination raised some doubts. Ned was sprawled on his stomach, had both arms wrapped about his pillow as if it were a sled. But Johnny's lashes were quivering suspiciously and, as Anne leaned over the bed, she saw the coverlets move, ripple strangely. She leaned closer, saw a black nose and silvery whiskers poke free of the sheets. Johnny's eyes flew open, flicked guiltily to the puppy and up to Anne's face. He looked relieved when she grinned; grinning back, he stopped trying to stuff the puppy under the covers, let it come up for air.

735

Richard had been six when he first came into Anne's life in the spring of 1459. Johnny would be six in less than three months and looked so like his father at that age that Anne's heart went out to him. He was a shy soft-spoken child, unlike Richard in that his face rarely served as the key to his thoughts.

What exactly were Johnny's thoughts? Anne often wondered. Did he miss the mother he saw so seldom? He gave every indication of being very fond of Ned; was he aware yet that he was different from his little brother? His future held promise; a bastard he might be, but a royal bastard, nonetheless. Yet when her brother-in-law the king bestowed an earldom on Richard's son, the title would go to Ned, not to Johnny. Johnny was still too young for that to matter but it would not always be so.

Anne leaned over impulsively, dropped a kiss on the tip of Johnny's nose. He looked surprised and then pleased; unlike other boys his age, he never feigned indifference or aversion to kisses and hugs. Johnny thrived on affection, invariably responded to Anne's overtures with such eagerness that she suspected the little boy understood more about the stigma of his birth than was generally believed.

Véronique and the newest of Anne's ladies were awaiting her as she entered the bedchamber. Joyce Washburne was a buxom young woman with eyes like emeralds, a wide sultry mouth and an incongruous scattering of unfashionable freckles. She had an infectious easy laugh, an impish sense of mischief, and Anne had become quite fond of her in the months since Joyce joined the household.

As Joyce unpinned Anne's headdress, Anne noticed a thick leather-bound book lying in the midst of her vials of perfume and bath oils.

'What's this, Joyce?'

'Your lord husband left it for you, Madame. He said to tell you that he'd marked the passages you'd be most interested in reading.'

Mystified, Anne picked up the book, noting without enlightenment that it was *The Canterbury Tales*, and opened it where indicated. A moment later, she burst out laughing. Richard had marked for her *The Clerk's Tale*, which had to be the definitive account of a dutiful submissive wife, a wife so patient and passive that no matter how heartlessly her husband tested her love, she voiced no complaints, endured the loss of her children, endured divorce, meekly endured all with fair loving words and devotion even a dog could not hope to equal.

Anne's spirits lifted, for there could be no surer sign that Richard harboured no grievance than this, that he should be teasing her about the saintly simpleminded Griselda, such a woman who'd lived nowhere but in the wistful imaginings of men.

She was reading some of the less likely passages aloud to Joyce as the girl brushed out her hair, when Richard came into the chamber.

'My love, you are just in time. I was about to read to Joyce what the Lord Walter did demand of poor Griselda ere he would take her to wife.'

As she glanced up to get his response, their eyes met in the mirror. Anne's breath stopped and she swung around to face him; the hairpins she'd been holding on her lap rained to the floor, sank into the rushes. The book, too, slipped unheeded from her grasp.

'Richard, what's wrong? What is it?'

Strangely enough, she never thought of war, thought neither of the Scots nor of the French. Her fears were personal, not political. Nor did it occur to her that it might be Edward. She did think, however, of the aging Duchess of York, and she repeated huskily, 'Richard, what is it? Tell me, please. . . .'

He crossed the space separating them, put his arms around her and she understood. The grief was to be hers. Her mind raced, too fast for coherent thought, in instinctive inventory of her loved ones. Her son, safe asleep under Mistress Burgh's vigilant eye. Her mother, supping with Alison and John Scrope at their York manor house just a stone's throw up Ald Conyng Street. Véronique, gone to fetch a deck of playing cards but moments before.

'It's Bella, is it not?' she whispered.

Isabel's son had been born at Tewkesbury on October 6th. On November 12th, she had been brought in slow easy stages back to Warwick Castle, where she'd died three days before Christmas. Within ten days, her infant son, too, was dead. On January 4th, her body was returned to Tewkesbury to lie in state for thirty-five days. She was twenty-five, left a three-year-old daughter and a son not yet two.

The death that shocked Europe, however, had occurred on the fifth of January in the snow before the besieged town of Nancy. It was there that the army of Charles, Duke of Burgundy, had gone down to a devastating defeat before the forces of the Swiss and Duke René of Lorraine. The Burgundians had been outnumbered by almost four to one and the ensuing slaughter had been merciless. Two days later, the body of Charles himself had been discovered embedded in the frozen ice of St Jean's pond, stripped naked by looters, partially eaten by wolves.

The political implications of Charles's death were enormous. His twenty-year-old daughter Marie was now Duchess of Burgundy, the greatest marital prize in Europe, and in the uneasy eyes of the English people, a lamb to be led to French slaughter. The Treaty of Picquigny, notwithstanding, Edward was no less alarmed than his subjects. However little he did mourn Charles, the last thing he wanted to see was the fleur-de-lis of France flying over Bruges and Dijon. A great council was hastily called for mid-February to deal with these disturbing developments.

It was nearly midnight as Richard and Anne rode through the gateway and into the precincts of the Benedictine abbey of St Mary

738

the Virgin at Tewkesbury. Word had already been sent ahead to Abbot Streynsham to expect them; within the abbot's lodging, they'd find food, wine, and warm beds. Anne's tired body ached for all three, yet she found herself drawing rein at sight of the round Norman arch of the abbot's gatehouse.

It was three months shy of six years since she'd ridden through that gateway, but it could have been yesterday, so vivid were the memories that suddenly assailed her. She struggled momentarily with an irrational urge to go elsewhere, to lodge for the night at the Black Boar Inn they'd passed on the outskirts of town. She did not want to stay at the abbey, did not want to remember the last time she'd sheltered within its walls.

'Anne?' Richard had reined in beside her. Accurately interpreting her reluctance, he asked, 'Would you rather go elsewhere?'

She shook her head. 'No. But . . . but I would like to go first to the church.'

Much to her relief, he acceded to her request without comment, seemed to understand, as well, when she declined his offer to go with her. She watched as the rest of their party passed through the gatehouse, and then turned her mare back toward the great abbey church of St Mary the Virgin.

Dismounting before the north porch, she gave the reins to the man Richard had ordered to accompany her, told him to await her there. Inside, all was dark, eerily still, and she had a sudden childish impulse to call the man in to her. To guard against her ghosts? Mocking herself, she raised her lantern up and moved resolutely down the empty, shadowed nave. Light glimmered from the door in the rood screen that separated the nave from the choir, and she was drawn instinctively toward it.

As she expected, it was there that she found her sister. Isabel's coffin was draped in heavy velvet folds; above it rose the wooden framework of the herse. The herse canopy was emblazoned with the arms of Beauchamp and Neville, and half a hundred soaring white candles encircled the coffin, crowned the canopy roof with

739

pinpoints of amber flame. From dawn till dusk, black-robed Benedictine monks would be kneeling before the coffin, softly chanting the funeral offices, vigils and Masses for the soul of Isabel Neville. Now, however, the church was deserted, echoed only to the sound of Anne's footsteps as she approached the herse. Not for two hours yet would the monks file sleepily into the choir for Matins. Until then, Anne was alone with her sister.

George had ordered no stone effigy for Isabel and Anne was glad. She did not want to look upon the lifeless marble features of a face she loved. Tears stung her eyes, and, kneeling by the candlelit coffin, she began to pray for her sister's peace.

When she heard the sounds of a man's tread, she assumed it was her servant coming in to warm himself, or perhaps a monk sent to see that the burning candles posed no threat of fire. She didn't look up until the steps came nearer, glancing over her shoulder with a frown, resenting whoever it was that had come to intrude upon her farewell to Isabel.

A man stood framed in the doorway of the pulpitum screen, a swaying silhouette in the dark void that lay beyond the coffin. Kneeling in a circle of light, Anne suddenly felt uncomfortably conspicuous, and it was this that lent an uncharacteristic sharpness to her voice as she demanded, 'Who are you to be here at such an hour? Know you not that it is past midnight?'

As he moved toward her, she lifted up her lantern and then gasped at the light's revelation. For a moment, logic fled and common sense was forgotten; she felt only fear, familiar physical fear that knew no reason. She froze, staring up at her brother-in-law, knowing with appalling certainty that all connections had been severed between her body and brain, that she could no more rise from these icy tiles than she could force a scream from her constricted throat.

George was looking over her now; he was, she saw, none too steady on his feet.

'Bella?' It was little more than a whisper, was slurred with some dreadful emotion that was both horror and hope.

Anne was stunned; her resemblance to her sister was superficial at best. He's blind-drunk, she thought, and then, Pray God that be all it is! But as suddenly as it had come, her panic was gone. She need not fear this man. She was no longer fifteen years old and helpless in his hands. She was Richard's wife and if he as much as laid a hand upon her, she'd scream the whole blessed abbey down.

'Not Bella, George, Anne,' she said and found to her chagrin that her voice was not as steady as her resolve.

'Anne,' he said, as if the name meant nothing to him. But he reached down then, extended his hand toward her. She stared at it with distaste, feeling the same aversion to touch him as she would to touch a snake. But she didn't want him to know that she still feared to be alone with him, wouldn't give him that satisfaction, and so she reluctantly put her hand in his, let him assist her to her feet.

Some of her panic threatened to come back upon her then, though, for he tightened his hand on hers when she tried to pull it from his grasp. Even as drunk as he was, he was far stronger than she, and her breath quickened painfully.

'Do not go,' he entreated. 'Stay awhile . . . till the monks do come.' He peered down into Anne's face, said earnestly, 'I do not want to leave her alone, you see. But it's so lonely here by myself . . . so lonely. . . .'

Anne was thoroughly unprepared for the pity that now knifed through her. She did not like it, reminded herself fiercely that he, of all men, was the least deserving of pity or compassion.

'I should think I'd be the last person you'd want with you.'

'Why?' he asked vaguely, and she saw then that he had not truly realized who she was. She was a familar voice, a hand to hold in the dark, and that was enough, was all he needed or cared to know.

741

He'd released her hand, leaned back against the herse. It was not meant to brace a man's weight and the wood creaked ominously. As Anne watched in concern, he crooked an arm around the post, slowly slid to the floor by the coffin. His head lolled back and his hair came dangerously close to the nearest of the candle flames, wrenching from Anne an involuntary cry.

'My God, George, watch what you do!'

'She suffered so . . .' he mumbled, staring up at Anne with blind blue eyes. 'She could not breathe and when she coughed . . . when she coughed, she did bring up blood.' He shuddered, repeated dully, 'So much blood. . . .'

Anne made a choked sound, shoved her fist against her mouth. The candles had begun to blur, were swimming before her in a haze of tears. She had backed away as far as the pulpitum screen when George leaned forward and, dropping his head into his hands, began to weep.

Anne came to an uncertain stop. She couldn't bring herself to go back, to try to offer him comfort. But she couldn't bear the sounds he was making, gasping strangled sobs that shook his entire body. She stood irresolute, drying her own tears with the back of her hand, and then she heard her name, whirled about to fling herself into Richard's arms.

It took her several moments to convince Richard that she was truly all right, that her tears were for Isabel. Only then did his eyes move past her to the slumped figure huddled before Isabel's coffin. She saw on his face much of her own ambivalence, saw he was reluctant to recognize George's pain and yet not able to walk away from it. He swore under his breath and, handing her his lantern, crossed the choir toward his brother.

As Anne watched, he bent over George, spoke too softly for her to hear. George's sobs seemed to be subsiding; the face he raised now to Richard was flushed, tearstained and puffy.

'Dickon?' His voice was thick, uncertain, as if he no longer dared trust his own senses.

742

'You cannot stay here all night, George. Let me help you up and we'll go back to the abbot's lodging together.'

Anne was somewhat surprised when George docilely did as he was told, accepted Richard's supporting arm and lurched to his feet. But, even as she breathed a sigh of relief, she saw George's face change, saw his eyes slit, focus on Richard with sudden sobering intensity.

'What are you doing here?' he demanded. 'Did Ned send you to spy on me? He did, did he not? I should've known!'

'For Christ's sake, George! You know better than that.'

'I suppose you'd like me to believe you care?' George had jerked free, reeled back against the herse. 'Well, I'm not so much a fool as that, little brother. You are no friend to me, Dickon, and well I know it. Think you that I could ever be so drunk as to forget that?'

'Have it your own way,' Richard said tersely, and turned away. He didn't look back but Anne lingered a moment longer before following him from the choir. Unclasping her crucifix chain, she stepped forward, brushed past George and laid the crucifix gently on the velvet draping her sister's coffin.

'You'd best sit down, Dickon, given what I do have to tell you. It seems our idiot sister thinks she has the perfect solution to the problem now posed by Burgundy. Her stepdaughter Marie does urgently need a husband and since Brother George is now conveniently without a wife . . . well, need I say more?'

'She wants George and Marie to wed? My God!' Richard was first incredulous and then appalled. 'Has she lost her mind?'

Edward mouthed a particularly profane oath, said in disgust, 'Where George is concerned, her common sense does desert her entirely. Can you imagine George as Duke of Burgundy? Holy Mary, preserve us!'

'Meg did not mention this to George, did she?' But it was a forlorn hope and Richard knew it even as he voiced it.

'What do you think? And I need not tell you his reaction. One would swear him already anointed and crowned.'

'Ned, you cannot allow such a marriage to take place. George . . . George is too unstable; God only knows what he might do should he ever have power like that.'

'Oh, I suspect we both know what he might do, Dickon; you're just squeamish about saying it plain out, that he'd be all too likely to make another grab for the English crown, and this time with a Burgundian army to back him up. Well, you needn't worry, little brother. The day I'll see George as Duke of Burgundy will be the day Holy Church does see me as a worthy choice for sainthood.'

'Have you told him you forbid the match?'

'Not yet.' A sardonic smile briefly tugged at the corner of Edward's mouth. 'Should you like to be there when I do?'

'I think not,' Richard said hastily. 'In fact, I'd as soon not even hear about it, afterward.' He accepted a cup from an unobtrusive servant, said, 'Ned, is there any chance Marie might accept him? For, if she's willing, your refusal would count for nothing with George. It would not be the first time, after all, that he did wed without your permission.'

'Your point's well taken, Dickon; I'd probably have to clap him in the Tower to keep him in England. But my informants tell me Meg and not Marie is the one pushing for this marriage. Marie seems distinctly cool to the idea. But I do mean to dispatch a letter to her this very day, making it quite clear that such a marriage be out of the question. The girl's no fool, knows she does need me to keep Louis from swallowing her whole.' He signalled again to his cupbearer before adding casually, 'I thought I would also suggest a bridegroom in place of brother George. Lisbet's brother Anthony.'

Richard choked, inhaled the wine he'd been about to swallow. Gasping and coughing, he struggled for breath as servants hovered solicitously around his chair and Edward helpfully leaned over to thump him on the back. By the time he recovered his composure, he was too shaken to do other than blurt out exactly what he thought. 'Anthony Woodville! Jesus, Ned, you cannot be serious!'

He'd just broken the unspoken pact that had prevailed between them for some twelve years, that his contempt for the Queen's kindred was understood and even tacitly accepted provided that it was not brought out into the open. Edward showed no resentment, however, looked lazily amused more than anything else.

'Do not be naïve, Dickon. You do not think I want to see Marie take Anthony, do you?'

'Why then . . .'

'It is simple enough. Lisbet would like to see her brother as a reigning sovereign. By putting forth Anthony's name, I do please her greatly and yet take no real risk in so doing. You cannot imagine Marie would ever consider accepting him, do you? As Lucifer proud as the House of Burgundy is?' He laughed, shook his head. 'Lisbet was delighted when I did promise her I'd speak on Anthony's behalf, though, and it's not often I can content her so cheaply, little brother.'

Richard was relieved, but not by much. 'But do you not see, Ned? It's going to drive George wild when you forbid him to marry Marie. You know he'll convince himself that she was willing, that you and you alone did sabotage his ambitions. To turn him down and then offer up Woodville in his stead . . . that's just pouring salt into his wounds, is sure to make him all the more embittered.'

Edward shrugged. 'So?' he said coolly.

9

Cayford, Somerset

April 1477

Ankarette Twynyho was dragging her embroidery frame toward the window so she could sit in the sun. Entering the solar at that moment, her son-in-law came forward swiftly to help her, saying, 'Here, Mother, let me do that for you.'

Ankarette gratefully surrendered the frame to him, settled herself comfortably with her sewing basket in her lap.

'There you are,' Tom said, and smiled at her. He supposed he should be off to the stables; the new stallion he'd just purchased was proving itself to be a hellion and the grooms seemed unable to soothe its tempers. But the sun was beckoning and he chose to linger awhile, to chat with his mother-in-law.

'You talk little about those last months with the Duchess of Clarence. Poor lady. . . . Were you fond of her, Mother?'

'No,' Ankarette said truthfuly. 'But I did feel much pity for her. She had more sorrows than joys in her life and her death was not an easy one.'

'Nor was her marriage, I'd wager,' Tom said, and chuckled.

Ankarette felt an instinctive unease, glanced up quickly to re-assure herself that no servants loitered within earshot. Tom noticed and gave her a quizzical look

'Do you fear Clarence as much as that?' he asked, surprised, saw Ankarette's mouth tuck in at the corners, the way it always did when she was confronted with a subject she did not want to discuss.

'All in Clarence's service do fear him,' she said quietly.

Tom pretended not to see her reluctance. 'Why? Most great lords are demanding, quick to find fault with the lesser-born. That's the way of things. What is there about Clarence that does inspire such fear?'

Thus pressed, Ankarette lowered her voice still further, said shortly and unwillingly, 'With Clarence, you never knew where you stood. His moods did shift from sun to darkness in the span of seconds, and none knew why. There were those who . . . who whispered that he was bewitched from birth.'

Appalled by her own words, she hastily crossed herself and, as Tom opened his mouth to question her further, she signalled that no more disclosures would be forthcoming by ostentatiously directing all her attention to the contents of her sewing basket.

Tom sighed, wishing his wife's mother were not so loath to gossip. He thought wistfully of the lurid tales told of Clarence, thought of the intimate scenes she must have witnessed as a member of his household. Scenes he knew she'd never share.

'Well, I'm off to the stables,' he began, as one of their young maidservants appeared in the solar doorway. She was too distraught for speech but the terror on her face was more eloquent than any words of warning she could have uttered.

'Good God, girl, what is it? Is it your mistress? Speak, damn you, speak!'

'No, Tom, you're only scaring her all the more. Tell us, Margery. . . .'

Tom's fingers were digging bruisingly into the girl's upper arms, and the pain loosened her tongue. 'Men-at-arms! Down below, they. . . .'

'Tom! Tom!' It was his wife's voice, but so shrill as to be almost unrecognizable. Tom took two strides toward the door and then Edith was in the room, in his arms, sobbing incoherently.

Tom was given no chance to calm his hysterical wife. Men-at-arms were coming up the stairway after her, shouldering their way into the solar, unceremoniously shoving the terrified maid-servant away from the door. Tom felt a throb of outrage that they should be taking over his house like this, but he felt fear, too, and it was in his voice as he demanded, 'What is this? What do you here?'

Ankarette was more bewildered now than frightened. Why should her son-in-law be arrested? It must be a mistake, a dreadful mistake. She came forward, meaning to lay a restraining hand upon Tom's arm, and then her eyes fastened upon the badge each man wore upon his sleeve.

'You come from the Duke of Clarence!' she gasped, and there was such shock in her voice that all eyes turned as one toward her. She'd gone so white that Tom reached out for her. A soldier intervened; there was a scuffle and Tom stumbled backward, bleeding from the mouth. Ankarette heard her daughter scream, wanted to go to her, but she couldn't move, could only stare at the man moving into the solar.

Roger Strugge. She mouthed the words but the name stuck in her throat; her mouth was too dry for speech. Roger Strugge who served Clarence without conscience or qualm, caring only for the gold that George did dispense so lavishly to those who did his bidding.

He was standing in front of her now, saying, 'Mistress Twynyho,' his lips curling in a mocking smile, like one who held a secret all yearned to know. 'You do remember me, I trust?'

Tom spat blood into the floor rushes, spat defiance at the men holding him. 'Am I under arrest? If so, I demand to know the charge!'

Strugge's eyes touched him in brief appraisal, dismissed him as negligible. 'We're not here for you, Delalynde,' he said coolly. 'It is Mistress Twynyho we want.'

He signalled and hands gripped Ankarette's elbows, propelled her toward the door. She was too stunned to struggle, unable to grasp what was happening to her or why. She heard Edith cry, 'Mama!', heard Tom curse, and then she was out in the hall, was being hurried down the stairs. It was only when they emerged out into the blaze of afternoon sun that she was able to rally her dazed wits about her. A horse was being led up for her; she balked, twisted desperately against the restraining hands.

'But why? What am I supposed to have done?'

Strugge snapped his fingers; the soldiers withdrew so that Ankarette stood alone. From the house she heard a steady pounding, realized that they had locked Tom and Edith in the solar. Strugge was regarding her with a strange smile; she knew suddenly that he was enjoying this, relishing what he was about to tell her.

'You are charged with the murder of Isabel Neville, late Duchess of Clarence. It is the Duke's pleasure that you be returned at once to Warwick Castle and there be tried for your crime. You are to be. . . .'

Ankarette heard no more. She fainted, crumpling to the ground at Strugge's feet without a sound.

'Get some water,' he said calmly, watched as two of his men reentered the manor house. Kneeling down by Ankarette then, he took her hands in his and stripped from her fingers the jewelled rings of her widowhood.

The palace at Westminster was dark, quiet. Edward was not ready for sleep, however, and torches still flared in his bedchamber. He was dictating some personal letters when one of his servants brought him word that Jane Shore was without, asking to see him.

Edward was surprised but more intrigued than annoyed. It was not like Jane to come to him without being summoned first; even after more than two years of sharing his bed, she never presumed.

'Send her in,' he said, and dismissed the scribe, the other servants.

Jane was enveloped in a long blue cloak. He wondered if it was the dark colour that gave her face such pallor, moved forward to meet her. Before he could take her in his arms, however, she sank down in a deep curtsy. When he would have raised her up, she stayed on her knees before him, said huskily, 'My dearest lord, forgive me for coming to you this way, but I did have to see you. It is urgent, my heart, could not wait.'

She made a very pretty picture, kneeling, her face upturned to his, soft red mouth highlighted by a trinity of dimples, blonde hair spilling out of the hood of her cloak. Edward was not indifferent to her appeal; he was very fond of this woman. Reaching down, he took her hands, drew her to him.

'You're forgiven,' he said, and sought her mouth with his own. She kissed him back with her usual ardour, but as his hands slid up from her waist to her breasts, she said swiftly,

'My love, wait ... please. I've brought someone with me, someone who does need most desperately to see you.' She saw him frown, put her fingers to his lips in mute entreaty.

'Please,' she whispered. 'He's been trying to gain an audience for days now, but with no luck. And he must see you, my lord. There is something you must hear, Ned. Please?'

She waited breathlessly for his response; her relief was considerable when he laughed.

'Hell and damnation, woman, but you do take advantage of the love I bear you,' he said ruefully. 'I'll give this petitioner of yours five minutes, and no more.'

'Thank you, my love, thank you.' She kissed him feverishly, repeatedly, his neck, his chin, wherever she could reach, and then whirled toward the door. A moment later, she ushered in a frightened-looking youngster of seventeen or so. Under Jane's prodding, the boy came forward shyly, dropped to his knees before Edward.

'My liege, this is Roger Twynyho, of Cayford in Somerset. He has a tale of horror to tell you. Go on, Roger, tell the King's Grace what you did tell me.'

The youngster seemed unable to speak, however, and accurately gauging Edward's patience, Jane said hastily, 'His grandmother, Ankarette Twynyho, was acting as one of the Duchess of Clarence's ladies. She returned to her family after the Duchess died, had no more contact with your brother of Clarence. Then on Saturday last, Clarence did dispatch some eighty men-at-arms to Cayford and there arrested her, accusing her of bringing about the Duchess of Clarence's death by poison.'

'What!'

The boy found his voice, nodded vigorously. 'It is true, Your Grace. They refused to allow my aunt and uncle to accompany her, and took her by force back to Warwick Castle.'

Edward had recovered his composure. 'Go on,' he said in a hard voice.

'The morning after their arrival in Warwick, she was brought before a Justice of the Peace sitting in petty session and charged with murder. My lord Clarence accused her of giving the Lady Isabel a drink of ale mixed with poison on October 10th, which poison caused her to sicken and die on the Sunday before Christmas. At the same time, one John Thursby of Warwick was charged with poisoning the baby son who died on January first.' The boy's voice was emotionless; he recited the facts like one quoting from memory, kept his eyes steadily on Edward's face.

'My grandmother did deny the charges most vehemently but it availed her naught. The jury did declare her guilty and sentence of death was passed upon her. She was taken at once to the gallows beyond town and there hanged. John Thursby was hanged with her.'

He stopped speaking, watched Edward. So did Jane.

'And she was innocent,' Edward said softly. It was not a question, and Roger Twynyho expelled his breath with an

751

audible hiss; his shoulders slumped with the sudden easing of tension.

'Indeed, my liege,' he said quietly. 'The Lady Isabel did die of consumption, weakened by a most difficult childbirth. My grandmother never harmed her, never harmed anyone.'

'The entire proceedings from start of trial to execution lasted no more than three hours,' Jane now interrupted, her face flushing with indignation. 'Several members of the jury did come up to Mistress Twynyho afterward and beseech her pardon, saying that they knew her to be innocent but for fear of Clarence they could not do otherwise than find her guilty.'

There was a silence. Edward seemed to have forgotten them both. Roger's fear began to come back. He knew that Clarence was this man's blood kin, knew that Princes did all too often make their own law. But then Edward motioned him to his feet, said, 'You're a brave lad, Roger Twynyho. I shall remember that. Go back to Cayford; you've done all you can for your grandmother here.'

Roger yearned to ask Edward what he meant to do. Would Edward give Clarence the justice that had been denied his grandmother? Or was this to be yet another crime for which Clarence would not be called to account? But he dared not push it further. He'd been dismissed. In a turmoil of conflicting emotions, he made an awkward obeisance and then fled the chamber.

Jane didn't move, kept her eyes upon her lover. 'Ned?' she ventured at last. 'Was I wrong, my lord, to bring him to you?'

Edward turned to face her, and she caught her breath, seeing then the deadly controlled rage that thinned his mouth, filled his eyes. Pray God he does never look thus at me, she thought and shivered.

'No,' he said flatly. 'No, you were not wrong.'

Since childhood, the Duchess of York had been an early riser. She loved the expectant hush, loved the soft pale haze that glimmered in the eastern sky in that brief hesitation between dark and day.

This morning, however, she'd given little thought to the fleeced brightness of the sky. Rising at six, she'd had Low Mass in her chambers and, after breaking her fast with bread and wine, she heard divine service and two Low Masses with her household in the castle chapel. She generally preferred to spend those hours till dinner in meditation or in religious readings; just as she now shunned plush velvets and bright silks for more sombre shades of grey and brown, so did she eschew the familiar amusements of her youth. Always a deeply pious woman, she found as she aged that her greatest contentment came in denying herself the pleasures that once meant much to her and now meant little. But on this Tuesday in late May, she'd chosen neither to meditate nor to read, had withdrawn, instead, to her solar to write to her daughter Margaret, Dowager Duchess of Burgundy.

The initial passages came easily enough. The turmoil in Burgundy seemed to be subsiding somewhat. There appeared to be widespread approval for Marie's choice of husband and consort, Maximillian, the son of the Holy Roman Emperor. Addressing these issues, Cecily expressed herself so briskly that her scribe was hard put to keep up with her.

But when she began to speak of her son, her voice and manner changed abruptly. She fumbled uncharacteristically for words, hesitated, backtracked and at last took the pen herself. Dismissing her scribe, she sat down in the violet-tinted light of her oriel window and willed herself to tell Margaret about George.

What I do have now to tell you, Margaret is as painful as anything I have ever written and yet you must be told; you must be prepared for what is to come. You know how bitterly George did resent your brother Edward's refusal to permit his marriage with your stepdaughter Marie. George's behaviour is intemperate in even the best of times and, when he did learn

753

that Edward had proposed Anthony Woodville as a prospective husband for Marie ... well, it was like jabbing a blade into a festering sore.

George proceeded to make himself as unpleasant as possible. At a banquet held at Windsor to celebrate the birth of Edward's newborn son, he insisted upon dropping a unicorn horn into his cup before he would let the cupbearer pour his wine. All do know unicorn horn is meant to protect one from poison, so such an insult was impossible to misconstrue. Edward was furious. What passed between them I do not know, but after that, George withdrew from the court, secluded himself at Warwick Castle.

It was then that he did commit a crime so grievous, so shocking that it does defy all understanding. I refer, of course, to the murder of Ankarette Twynyho, the gentlewoman who'd been in service to George's wife Isabel. I cannot tell you whether he believed his accusations to be true, would to God I could. But George's perception of reality is frighteningly flawed. Could he have cold-bloodedly sacrificed an innocent woman? Or did he convince himself that Isabel truly was poisoned?

I've thought of little else this month past, am no closer to the truth now than ever I was. It may be that George does not even know the truth himself. He is my son, of my flesh, and yet a stranger to me. I cannot stop caring, not as long as there be burned into my mind and soul memories of the child he once was. But I cannot forgive him, either. ...

Her pen faltered. After a second's reflection, she rapidly scratched out the last three sentences.

Edward was as angry as ever I've seen him. Even had Ankarette Twynyho been guilty, George's action would have been outrageous, an offence both to the king and the Almighty.

Shortly after the Twynyho affair came to light, a man named John Stacy, an Oxford clerk and astronomer, was arrested and accused of sorcery. Under torture, Stacy did confess and he implicated, as well, one Thomas Burdett, a man of some standing in Warwickshire and a member of George's own household. A commission of oyer and terminer was appointed to try both men on charges of using the black arts to bring about the death of the king. They were tried on May 19th and condemned to death. The next day they were taken to Tyburn and there hanged, Burdett protesting his innocence to the last.

Cecily's eyes flicked rapidly and critically back over what she'd written. She was well aware that there was some suspicion this had been a deliberately staged political trial meant to convey to George an unmistakable warning. She didn't doubt that Burdett was involved with George in some sort of double-dealing, but she did not believe him guilty of sorcery and she was not comfortable that a man should die for what he had not done, even if his other crimes did warrant death.

She raised her hand to her face, pressed her fingertips against aching eyes. Sweet Lady Mary, how tired she was. And how ironic that her sons should give her greater grief as men grown than ever they had as children.

This last thought was too closely akin to self-pity for her liking. She blinked rapidly, raised her chin. And then she picked up the pen again and wrote,

On the day after Burdett's execution, Edward departed London for Windsor. No sooner was he gone than George burst into a meeting of the Privy Council at Westminster. He had with him—of all men—the Franciscan preacher, Dr John Goddard, the very one who'd once preached Harry of Lancaster's right to the throne from Paul's Cross. George contended that Burdett had been innocent and made the council listen whilst he had Goddard read aloud Burdett's gallows statement in which he swore he was not guilty of the charge for which he was dying.

I need not tell you, Margaret, how serious may be the consequences of George's actions. This is not behaviour Edward can ignore. George did murder an innocent woman and then he actually dared to appeal over Edward's head to his own council, did all but charge that Burdett's death was unjust, was a political execution meant to intimidate him into silence. By these actions, he did challenge the King's justice, and that Edward cannot allow.

In fairness to your brother, Edward has shown great patience with George in past years. But Edward is not as tolerant as he once was, and George has learned nothing from past mistakes. I do not know what Edward means to do when he returns from Windsor, but I think it likely that this will be one time when George's sins are not forgiven.

IO

York

June 1477

It had not been a happy spring for Anne. As deeply as she grieved for her sister, Isabel's death had come as no great surprise; Anne had known Isabel was 'ill unto death' in the weeks following the birth of her son. Anne was not prepared, however, for the death of her aunt Isabella, John Neville's widow.

Isabella had remarried some two years after John's death at Barnet, and Anne had been glad; Isabella was her favourite aunt and she was pleased that Isabella seemed to be building a new life for herself. Isabella was not long in giving her new husband a son and, in the year following, a daughter. Shortly after the Feast of Epiphany, 1477, she had given birth to another daughter. But the birth had been difficult and infection soon set in.

The shock of Isabella's death had not yet worn off when word reached Middleham of George's extraordinary vengeance. Anne's own father had not scrupled to commit murders no less blatant than that of Ankarette Twynyho; he'd sent Lord Herbert and Elizabeth Woodville's father and brother to the block without even the pretence of a trial accorded Mistress Twynyho. But Warwick would never have avenged himself upon a woman. It was that which Anne found so shocking and Richard so unforgivable.

Next had come the news of the trial and execution of Thomas Burdett and John Stacy. Anne's private belief was that the sorcery charge against Burdett was a fabrication although she did not doubt that Burdett deserved hanging. As she saw it, anyone intimately connected with George was bound to be guilty of at least one hanging offence. But the entire episode had cast a pall of sorts over Middleham, and she began to dread the arrival of couriers from London; these days, the news seemed inevitably to be bad.

She was looking forward all the more, therefore, to their June visit to York. Anne's favourite festival was the Feast Day of Corpus Christi. She'd been six the first time she'd been taken to York to view the city's celebrated mystery plays, performed outdoors on huge wooden stages mounted on wheels and transported about the city to be enacted before enthusiastic crowds at designated locations. She still enjoyed the plays as thoroughly as she had as a little girl, and only childbirth and war had kept her and Richard from York's Corpus Christi festival in the years since their marriage.

This year was to be a particularly memorable occasion. On the day after Corpus Christi, she and Richard were to become members of the Corpus Christi Guild, a prestigious religious

757

fraternity. The following Wednesday would see a celebration of a milestone birthday for Anne, her twenty-first. And the culmination of their stay in York would be the wedding on St Basil's Day of Rob Percy and Joyce Washburne. As Anne had spent the past six months actively promoting this courtship, she was delighted that her efforts had borne such fruit, and by mid-May she had already begun to mark off the days in the back of her Book of Hours.

They had arrived in York several days before Corpus Christi, had settled themselves comfortably at Prior Bewyk's friary. Preparations advanced smoothly for the upcoming wedding; the children had been as fascinated by the guild plays as Anne herself had been upon her first viewing, even four-year-old Ned, who was still rather young for any sort of sustained inactivity. But at supper that night, Anne happened to overhear a remark made by Francis Lovell, newly come from London, and it all went suddenly sour.

'What did you say, Francis? You made mention of my Uncle Johnny. I would hear it again.' Remembering her manners then, she added tersely, 'If you please.'

Francis looked uncomfortable. 'You know, of course, that the eldest son of the King had been titled since his first year as Prince of Wales, Duke of Cornwall and Earl of Chester. And his second son, Dickon's namesake, has been made Duke of York. Well. . . now it seems that the King does mean to take from John Neville's son his title of Duke of Bedford and bestow it upon his third son, the babe born this past March.'

Anne could not suppress a gasp. Ned had always claimed to love her uncle. Had Richard not told her that he'd wept when told of Johnny's death? How could he now do this to Johnny's son?

There was an awkward silence and then conversation resumed with a rather artificial animation. Anne sat quietly, pushed her food about on the plate. One of her best-kept secrets was that

758

she had little liking for her brother-in-law the King. Since her marriage, he'd shown her nothing but kindness. She was willing to concede that. She'd concede, too, that he'd been extremely generous with Richard. But she did not trust him and she resented the hypnotic influence he seemed able to exert over Richard. For years she'd watched him charm with lazy laughter, watched with wary judgmental eyes. With the illogical certainty of instinct, she sensed there was a danger in loving Ned too much. Her memories rang warning bells, flagged the risks in the blood of Barnet. Her father had loved Ned once. Her Uncle Johnny had loved him until the day he died. Now, as she thought of Johnny and her young cousin who was to lose his title to serve Ned's newborn son, years of bitten-back criticisms clamoured to be said.

'How can he do it, Richard?' she'd demanded as soon as they were alone in their bedchamber. 'The boy's mother is not six months dead, and now he's to have his title taken, too? How can Ned so demean Johnny's memory?'

'We're dealing with rumour, Anne, have no way of knowing if it is true or not. Until we do. . . .'

'Oh, it is true enough. You know it is.'

'No, I do not,' he said tersely, and Anne was suddenly swept by a bitter resentful rage, all the more intense for being so long repressed.

'Just once,' she said acidly, 'just once I'd like to see you stop defending Ned no matter what he does. Just once I'd like to hear you admit there is no excuse for what Ned means to do.'

Richard had flushed, his eyes darkening to slate, but she was too angry herself now to care if he, too, was angry. 'But you will not, will you? Not even now. I do not know why it should surprise me. . . . Just do not ever tell me again how much Ned did care for Johnny. It's as mean-spirited an act as I could ever imagine, and there's no way on God's earth it can be justified to me.'

As arguments generally do, it soon shifted ground. Richard

could not defend his brother's action without falling back upon Johnny's treason, without reminding her that Johnny had died in rebellion against the crown, died an ally of Lancaster. This Richard could not bring himself to do. He chose, instead, to take issue with what he saw as his wife's unreasonable attitude.

'You're so eager to believe the worst of Ned. Francis repeats some London gossip and you act as if he'd presented you with the truth engraven upon tablets of stone. Tell me, are you so quick to suspect the worst of me, too?'

'That's not fair, Richard, and you know it. The truth is that you're wilfully blind where Ned is concerned. You always have been and always will be.'

Their voices rose, carried beyond their bedchamber. Pent-up grievances were aired, unfair accusations traded. They knew each other too well, knew the words that would draw the most blood. It was by far the ugliest quarrel of their marriage, ended with Richard walking out on her.

He was gone several hours. She was too proud to seek him out, had no way of knowing if he was still within the friary or not. At last, she'd summoned her ladies, made ready for bed. When he finally returned, she lay very still, pretended to sleep.

The next morning, they arose in strained silence to take part in the processional of the Corpus Christi Guild. The sun bleached the sky over their heads a brilliant blinding blue. The city streets were hung with richly woven tapestries and strewn with fragrant flowers; the procession itself was heralded with flaming torches, crosses held aloft, streaming scarlet banners. The route was thronged with cheering spectators, from the gates of Holy Trinity Priory and up Micklegate Street, past the guild hall, up Stonegate and through the Minster Gates, into the magnificent Cathedral of St Peter. There a sermon was preached in the Chapter House, and the procession moved on to its ultimate destination, to present the Holy Sacrament to the waiting priests at St Leonard's Hospital. Afterward, Lawrence Boothe,

the man who'd succeeded Anne's uncle as Archbishop of York, gave a lavish banquet in the great hall of the bishopric palace close by the Minster.

It was an event Anne had been anticipating for weeks, should have been a day of much happiness for her. It was, instead, one of the most miserable she could recall.

The quiet was suddenly jangled by the sound of chimes. The friars were being summoned to Matins. That meant, Anne knew, it was after 2:00. For more than two hours now she'd lain rigid and resentful beside Richard, begrudging him the sleep she could not share.

Her anger had long since been quenched in misery. As she'd done all day, she kept reliving their quarrel, dredging up the hurtful things they'd said to one another. He'd charged that she had never forgiven Ned for forbidding their betrothal, had never forgiven him for not defying Ned as George had done. That was a particularly unsettling accusation to Anne. Was there truth in it? Last night she'd said no; tonight she was not all that sure. She did feel that Richard had let her down; fairly or not, the feeling persisted even after all these years and against all logic. Could that be why she needed to hear him denounce his brother? To assure herself that his first loyalties no longer were given to Ned, were given now to her? She did not know but it was not a thought she was comfortable with.

In fact, the more she did dwell upon the events of the night before, the less comfortable she became. She had been right to be angry with Ned; she still was. But she'd been wrong to vent that anger upon Richard. It would never even occur to her to hold Richard to account for anything George might say or do. Why, then, should he be accountable for Ned's actions? So he could not judge Ned dispassionately, could not keep from tripping over old loyalties. What of it? She'd long ago concluded that he was not the best judge of men, that he invariably let his emotions

761

colour his assessments. But surely part of loving a man was accepting him as he was.

Beside her, Richard stirred. He seemed unable to get comfortable, rolling over onto his back and, a few moments later, over onto his stomach again. So he had not been asleep after all. Somehow, that made Anne feel better; she'd been vexed to think he could so easily escape into sleep whilst she lay wide awake and miserable. Reaching over, she laid her hand lightly against the small of his back. She felt his muscles tense at her touch but, beyond that, he didn't react.

'Richard? Richard, I'm sorry. The argument was of my making. I realize that now.'

'Do you?' His voice was noncommittal but he'd turned on his side, toward her.

'Yes,' she whispered. 'You were right; we do not know if there be any truth to Francis's story, and yet I did take it as gospel. I was not being fair to Ned, and I most assuredly was not being fair to you.'

'No, you were not,' he said, but then she felt his hand on her face. She closed her eyes as his fingers lingered on her cheek, wiped away wetness.

'Did I make you cry?' he asked softly, and she nodded, rolled over into his arms.

'Anne . . . Anne, listen. I want to talk to you about Ned. There is something you should understand. When he first did take the crown, he sought no bloodbath. He did what he could to reconcile the Lancastrian lords to his rule, men like Somerset and Henry Percy. Nor was he reluctant to give his trust—to Somerset, to the Stanleys, to your father. You'll not deny that he did give them the benefit of the doubt . . . more than once.'

'No, I'd not deny that,' she echoed quietly.

'For ten years, Anne, he did rule with a light hand. I'm not saying that he scrupled to take harsh measures if need be, but he did not unless forced to it. He offered friendship to foes, forgave betrayals. And the result? He did lose his throne, came close, Christ, so close to losing all. Those are his words, Anne, not mine, what he told me when I did argue with him about Harry of Lancaster. He said he did mean to learn from his past mistakes, to do what he must to make sure there'd never be a repeat of Olney or Doncaster.'

Anne was startled. This was the first time that Richard had admitted, even indirectly, what all knew, that Harry of Lancaster had died at his brother's command. She started to speak, thought better of it.

'If he is no longer as generous as he once was, if he's less quick to forgive, less quick to trust ... can you truly blame him? He did learn a hard lesson at Doncaster, that he could rely on no one but himself.'

What he said made sense to Anne, seemed to her a likely explanation of the decided differences between the first years of Edward's reign and the years since Barnet and Tewkesbury.

What mattered most to her, however, was not so much the reasons for Edward's increasingly autocratic rule as Richard's willingness to discuss them with her.

She leaned over, kissed him lightly on the mouth. Even after more than five years of marriage, certain of her inhibitions had shown themselves to be remarkably resilient, long-lived. She was still shy, even now, to be the one to initiate their lovemaking, to admit openly she wanted him. She had, however, evolved any number of subtle indicators of her mood and her need, had contrived a code he'd become quite adroit at reading.

Sitting up, she tugged fretfully at the long braid that swung over her shoulder, trailed across one breast.

'Véronique did not plait this as she should; it's too tight, is pulling against my temples. I think I'd best undo it ... perhaps rebraid it.'

She watched him as she spoke, waiting to see if her hint passed unnoticed. He much preferred her hair loose, almost always asked her to leave it unbound when they meant to make love.

'No,' he said. 'Do not rebraid it.'

It was too dark for her to see his face but she didn't need to; his voice had taken on a new intonation, a low caressing murmur that no one but she ever heard.

'I truly think,' she said, 'that you could seduce the very angels themselves when you do sound like that.'

'I'd gladly settle for you,' he said, and she knew he was smiling. With fingers suddenly impatient, she freed her hair, shook it loose about her shoulders, playfully trailing it across his chest and throat until he reached up, drew her down into his arms.

It was almost dawn. Through the bed-hangings, Anne could see the shadows retreating; familiar shapes began to materialize. She stretched, smothered a yawn.

'Oh, Lord, Richard, we've got to get up. . . .'

He kept his eyes shut, groaned when she nudged him again.

'Richard? May I ask you a question . . . about Ned?'

He mumbled something that passed for assent and she touched her lips to his hair, then said, 'Richard . . . what do you think Ned means to do about George?'

He was wide awake now, regarding her with shadowed dark eyes.

'I rather think,' he said grimly, 'that Ned is going to collect a debt long overdue.'

The third Sunday after Trinity that year fell on the twenty-second of June. It was, as well, a month-mind for Isabel Neville, marked the passage of six months since she died in delirium at Warwick Castle, and should have been celebrated with pomp and ceremony in accordance with custom. But, to George, the day had but one meaning. It was the day that he had been summoned by his brother the King.

It was a command he'd been expecting for twelve days now, ever since Edward returned from Windsor. He knew Edward was not likely to ignore his harangue before the privy council. He knew, too, that Edward considered Ankarette Twynyho's trial to have been a sham, her death to be murder.

No, he knew a confrontation was inevitable. But the days passed in peace. His unease grew. What was Ned waiting for? It was with something almost like relief, therefore, that he made ready to ride to Westminster this Sunday afternoon; better to face Ned's wrath and get it over with.

He'd hoped for a private meeting, was both disappointed and disconcerted when he was ushered into the Painted Chamber. His eyes narrowed at sight of the waiting assemblage. The chamber was filled with people, most of whom would gladly have bartered their own souls for a chance to see him in Hell. So this was Ned's game. A public humiliation. His jaw jutted out defiantly; so be it then. He moved forward into the room.

Ralph Josselyn, the Lord Mayor of London, and the city aldermen looked none too happy to be there, showed the discomfort of strangers unwillingly entrapped in a family feud. Other faces, however, told a far different tale, spoke of unforgotten grievances, of long-cherished grudges.

The first familiar face George saw was that of Will Hastings. Newly back from Calais, Will looked rested, at ease; as their eyes met, he saluted George with overly elaborate courtesy that was in itself a polished insult. George ignored him, approached the dais. There he saw the woman he hated above all others, his beautiful sister-in-law. Elizabeth wore yellow and her hair was loose, as if this were a state occasion. It drew even more glances than her crown, shone white-gold in the sun. Not for the first time, George thought that she had eyes like a hungry cat. Behind her stood her two grown sons by her first marriage. Thomas Grey looked like a man unexpectedly given a longed-for gift; his brother, too, seemed in the grip of some excitement. They both were smiling expectantly.

'My lord of Clarence.' Edward's face was impassive, his voice

765

dispassionate. George found no reason for reassurance in that, would have preferred outright anger.

He touched his lips to Edward's outstretched hand, waited for Edward to give him leave to rise.

'Have you an explanation for your extraordinary behaviour before my privy council on the twenty-first of May?'

George flicked his tongue over dry lips, said as steadily as he could, 'Thomas Burdett was my friend. I did believe him when he assured me of his innocence. I felt I did owe him my loyalty. . . .'

'Loyalty?' Edward echoed, with just enough mockery to stir a ripple of laughter, quickly suppressed.

'Let's try, brother, to keep this conversation within the realm of the believable, shall we?'

This time the laughter was more pronounced. George flushed, started to speak. Edward cut him off with a peremptory gesture.

'Actually, I do not much care why you acted as you did. The why of it is rather irrelevant.'

'Your Grace. . . .'

'No bond is absolute, brother, not even that of blood. I'll not speak of your past offences, of the betrayals forgiven, the treasons pardoned. But two months ago, you did dare to make mockery of the laws of this realm, to subvert justice to your own vengeful purposes. Embracery is a crime, my lord, even for the highly born.'

The chamber was unnaturally still. There was a roaring in George's ears, the pulsing of his own blood.

'Ankarette Twynyho died because you chose to take the King's law into your own hands. You did then compound your offence by acting to cast doubt upon the fairness of the trials of Thomas Burdett and John Stacy. In so doing, you did impugn the King's justice, call into disrepute the courts of this realm and act as though you would take unto yourself the sovereign powers that be inherent within the crown.'

Edward paused. The indictment had been received in utter

silence. He let his eyes linger for a moment upon George's resentful face and then concluded, speaking with deliberation, the chill detached tones of authority absolute, 'It is time, my lord of Clarence, that you did learn you, too, are subject to the laws and covenants of this land. This is not an action I take lightly. I do not forget that the blood flowing in my veins does flow, as well, in yours. But you do leave me no choice. As of this moment, you may consider yourself under arrest.'

George gasped; for a dizzying second, he doubted both his senses and his sanity. Ned could not . . . he would not dare.

'You cannot be serious!' he blurted out, saw his brother raise his hand. It was an unhurried gesture, almost casual yet men-at-arms at once appeared in the doorway. Their captain came forward.

'My liege?'

'You are to escort His Grace of Clarence to the Tower. He is to be treated with all due respect and, once there, to be lodged as befits his rank, as a prisoner of state.'

George had gone the colour of chalk. He swallowed convulsively, stared dazedly at his brother. Ironically enough, it was Elizabeth who unwittingly came to his rescue. She laughed, the only one in the chamber who dared to do so. He stiffened at the sound, strengthened by a surge of hate that left no room in his brain for any other emotion. With all the bravado he could muster, he made a deep mocking obeisance before his brother and then turned toward the captain of the guards, snapped his fingers in a gesture of command that was not his to make.

Amused in spite of himself by George's audacity, Edward let it pass, discreetly signalled his men to follow. There was nothing accidental about the audience he'd assembled for George's arrest; it had been carefully staged down to the last detail. And yet, as much as he'd thought he wanted to see his brother publicly humiliated, there was still a faint sense of relief when he saw that George was going to be able to salvage some dignity after all. Acknowledging the ambivalence in his feelings, he acknowledged, too, one reason why; however little he liked George, the fact was that George's actions did still reflect upon him. Brotherhood, he thought with a wry resignation, was a life sentence.

George's bravura posture took him as far as the Tower. But once he found himself alone in a small chamber of the Bowyer Tower, his courage failed him. He flung himself down upon the bed and suddenly sweat stood out on his forehead, trickled cold and sticky down his back, soaked his shirt with wide wet splotches. After an interminable time, the panic subsided somewhat. He reminded himself that he'd been treated with deference so far, that Lord Dudley, the Constable of the Tower, had assured him he would have all his needs met. Dudley had even seen to it that a flagon of his favourite malmsey was sent in with his meal.

He took heart at that, set about convincing himself that his stay in the Tower was going to be more tolerable than he first thought. He remembered now that when Henry Percy, Earl of Northumberland, had been confined there, he'd been allowed four servants to see to his wants, even had his own cook. He was able to take some reassurance from that . . . until he remembered, too, that Edward had kept Northumberland in the Tower for fully five years.

II

Windsor Castle

September 1477

August 12th was always a bittersweet anniversary for Elizabeth. It was the birthday of her daughter Mary, now ten. But it was, as well, a day of far more sinister memories, for it was on an August 12th that her father and brother had been led forth to die before the walls of Coventry, to die at the command of the Earl of Warwick and his youthful ally, the Duke of Clarence.

Elizabeth blamed George fully as much as Warwick for the murder of her kindred. She owed him a blood debt and grimly intended to see that he was paid. But eight years had passed since those August executions and George's day of reckoning seemed no nearer now than it ever was.

When her husband at last lost patience and threw George into the Tower, Elizabeth was jubilant. But not for long. It soon became apparent to her that Edward did not mean to punish George as he deserved. There'd be no early morning execution on Tower Green. George would be confined for a time and then released. And he'd learn nothing from the experience; she knew he would not. He'd only be all the more embittered, all the more vindictive, all the more dangerous.

That George was dangerous, Elizabeth did not doubt. He was clumsy in his intrigues; he'd so far shown an uncanny knack for alienating people, had no friends, only lackeys and enemies, and he seemed queerly blind to the consequences of his actions. But he was dangerous withal. Edward laughed at her when she tried to tell him that, but Elizabeth could not afford to laugh. George hated her with all the passions of a notoriously unstable nature. He hated her and never forgot for a moment that he stood by blood very close, indeed, to the English throne. Her son was not yet seven. Should anything happen to Ned . . .

This was not a fear she dwelt upon at length. Ned was, after all, only thirty-five and all his life had been in superb health. For Elizabeth, to imagine all that vitality and energy quenched was like trying to envision the extinguishing of the sun. And yet it could happen. A fall from a horse, a renewal of war with France. . . . It could happen and that lingering awareness only served to give added urgency to her desire for vengeance.

Elizabeth now found her twenty-three-year-old son Thomas to be an unexpectedly adroit ally. Thomas had the family flair for hating. And he had a taste, too, for intrigue. With very little trouble, he'd succeeded in placing one of his own men among those chosen to guard George in the Bowyer Tower. The man had not become a confidant of George's; that would have been too much to hope for. But he did manage to keep Thomas, and therefore, Elizabeth, quite well informed about George's day-by-day activities and outbursts.

His confinement was much too loosely structured for Elizabeth's liking. He was permitted to have visitors if he chose, to dispatch letters, to consult with his household. He had his own servants— had, as well, all the luxuries his wealth could provide; a feather bed brought from the Herber, silver plate and fine wines. Elizabeth thought her husband was being outrageously indulgent but he'd deflected her complaints with sarcasm, wanting to know if she would like him to cast his brother into one of the rat-infested airless holes reserved for those less fortunate of birth than George.

Elizabeth was able to take some satisfaction, however, in the stories now surfacing about George's increasingly erratic conduct. For the first month or so, he had managed to keep up a bold front, acted as if his stay in the Tower was admittedly an inconvenience, but no more than that. But that was in the beginning. Such sang-froid did not last long in the heat of high summer. George was no reader, had not the capacity for sustained concentration that chess required, soon grew bored with dicing, tables and draughts. For the first time in his adult life, the hours hung heavy on his hands. And the longer he was held, the more likely it began to seem to him that his brother meant to keep him caged indefinitely.

There were clear indications by mid-August that his nerves were giving way. He was increasingly bad-tempered with servants and guards alike. He drank more than he should, slept poorly. It was then that he swallowed his pride, wrote to his mother at Berkhampsted, entreating her to intercede with Edward on his behalf. By September, so desperate had he become that he was writing, as well, to Richard.

Elizabeth was pleased; she wanted him miserable, apprehensive. If there was a just God in Heaven, he'd never know another moment's peace. She was not so pleased, however, when Thomas came up from London to Windsor with the latest accounts of George's deteriorating emotional state.

Now in the third month of his captivity, George seemed to have surrendered unconditionally to despair. He was drinking heavily. Some days he did not even bother to dress at all, lay in a wine-sodden stupor from which he roused himself only to send out for more malmsey. Too little exercise and too much wine were adding unwanted pounds; for the first time in his life, he was having a problem with his weight. His face was puffy these days, their informant reported, had taken on an unhealthy pallor, and his temper was raw, dangerous. Unable to sleep at night, he did his best to drink himself into oblivion and, when that failed, he sought out the company of his servants and, on occasion, even the guards, subjecting them to long rambling monologues full of self-pity and venom.

It was this that stung Elizabeth into such fury, these accounts

771

of George's drunken babblings. He'd always had a poisonous tongue but, never before, had she been able to prove the seditious nature of his outpouring. Now fear and misery had stripped away all restraints and he stood convicted by his own mouth.

The night was hot, the chamber scented with a fragrant incense from the Holy Land. Edward was in high spirits and Elizabeth made every effort to share his laughter, forbore to be irked by his teasing. Watching him in the mirror, she felt quite content; so far, the evening was progressing just as she'd planned.

As soon as her ladies had withdrawn and they were alone, Elizabeth moved toward the bed. Unfastening the sash of her bed robe, she let the garment slowly slide down her shoulders, fall to the floor at her feet. There was a hint of arrogance in her assurance, in her absolute certainty that she could withstand the most searching scrutiny. Her breasts were still firm, her legs slim and shapely; the hair that flowed down her back was as silvery blonde as on the day of their marriage. She smiled down at Edward, secure in the confidence that she looked much younger than her forty years, that few gazing at her now would ever have believed she'd given birth to ten children. There'd been no noticeable thickening of her waist, only a few stretch marks to indicate past pregnancies.

Elizabeth was well aware that it was whispered she made use of the black arts to cling to her youth and beauty beyond the time allotted to most women. The slander afforded her a certain contemptuous amusement. Black arts, indeed. She owed her looks not to sorcery but to an iron resolve, an unflagging discipline. She measured every mouthful of food, sipped the wine others gulped, spent hours lathering her skin with perfumed creams, lightening her hair with lemon juice. If she'd so far succeeded in keeping the years at bay, it was only because she'd refused to indulge herself . . . unlike Ned.

Her eyes flicked to him. He was stretched out in the bed, propped up by several feather-filled pillows, a sheet casually thrown across his hips. It didn't show so much when he was clothed but it did now; her husband was putting on weight. He was fortunate, she thought, that he was a big man, could carry it better than most. Nonetheless, she could see the beginnings of a double chin, see the excess flesh that rippled, blurred his waistline when he sprawled naked as now. Too much carousing and too little sleep showed in his face, too; his eyes were permanently smudged, too often bloodshot.

He was still a handsome man, but the abuses of the body were telling. As she gazed down at him, Elizabeth was given an unwelcome glimpse into the future, fancied she could see in his face and thickening body a portent of what was to come. In ten years, she thought suddenly, all that bright beauty will be gone, will be burnt up as if it had never been.

She wasn't sure how she felt about such a prospect. Secretly, she was rather pleased that she looked younger than Ned; too many people had commented critically about the five years' difference in their ages for her not to have developed a certain sensitivity about it. But she remembered, too, the first time she'd laid eyes upon him at her father's manor at Grafton; he'd taken her breath away, quite literally. What a waste, she thought and sighed. What a needless, bloody waste.

He reached out, beckoned her into bed. 'Come here, sweetheart. Let's see if, between us, we cannot fill your belly with another babe.'

She smiled but without enthusiasm. Her youngest was just six months old; in the thirteen years of their marriage, she'd given him three sons and four surviving daughters. That was, she thought, quite enough for any woman. She'd as soon her womb did not quicken again, hoped it was God's will that it did not.

'Ned? Have you given more thought to what Monsieur le Roux told you about George?'

'What for?' he murmured against her throat, and Elizabeth bit her lip, stifled her exasperation as best she could.

There were times when she didn't understand him at all. Olivier le Roux, an envoy of the French King, had come to England that summer to negotiate an extension of the seven-year truce between the two countries. Le Roux had borne, as well, a private communication from Louis to Edward, contending that George had sought to marry Marie of Burgundy for one reason only, so that he could then make use of the Burgundian army to lay claim to the English crown.

'How can you make light of it, Ned? Truly, I do not understand you at all.'

'God be praised for that; there's little more dangerous than a wife's understanding.' He grinned, stopped her protest with his mouth.

'In the first place, sweetheart, le Roux told me nothing I did not already know. Of course George would have angled for the English crown had he become Duke of Burgundy. In the second place, consider the source. Why do you think Louis chose to rake over stale rumours and court gossip, present them as proof positive?'

'To show his goodwill?' she ventured, and Edward laughed rudely.

'Ah, yes, my great good friend, the King of France. Let me tell you about Louis, Lisbet. I daresay you've heard of the strange Egyptian beast, the crocodile? Well, the crocodile, so it is said, does weep copious tears over the remains of the victims he has just devoured. Should we ever get a crocodile for the royal menagerie at the Tower, I rather think I'd name it Louis.'

Elizabeth was not amused. 'Even a blind pig can find an acorn occasionally, Ned. You should not discount le Roux's warning merely because it does come from Louis.'

'Lisbet, you still do not see. Why should Louis want me to believe George was deeply entangled in intrigues with Burgundy? It was not George he sought to discredit; it was my sister Meg. Louis wants a free hand in Burgundy, thinks I might give it to

774

him should he convince me that Meg was implicated in George's schemes to seize my throne.'

'Yes, but . . .' She stopped, drew an aggrieved breath. He was no longer listening to her, was sliding his hand down her hip.

She made one last attempt. 'You're wrong, Ned, not to take George seriously. If only I could make you see that. You think this stay in the Tower has done any good? I assure you it has not. He only hates you all the more.'

'I expect so,' he said obligingly, but he was nudging her thighs apart, his fingers seeking the triangle of soft golden hair that curled between her legs.

Elizabeth was a realist; she showed it now by recognizing her cause to be a lost one. Now was not the time to push him about George. She'd do better to wait. Perhaps once his body needs were satisfied, perhaps then. . . . She raised up on one elbow and, leaning over, kissed him full on the mouth.

Edward swallowed a yawn, roused himself to offer a drowsy protest. 'Sweetheart, surely we can discuss this tomorrow? It's not as if George were going anywhere, after all!'

'Laugh if you will, Ned, but I tell you that man is a danger. You do not know what he's been saying, the venom he's been spewing forth. He's drunk most of the time, spends his days abusing his servants and damning you. He. . . .'

Edward yawned again. 'At this hour of the night, I do not much care what he's saying about me. Why do you not tell me about it in the morning?'

'You might not care but I rather think your lady mother would.'

Sleep, Edward saw, was going to be in short supply this night. 'And exactly how,' he asked in weary resignation, 'does ma mère come into this?'

Now that she had his attention at last, Elizabeth seemed in no hurry to satisfy his curiosity. 'He's been babbling on, as you might expect, about that woman he murdered, saying she did poison

Isabel at Woodville bidding. As he tells it, you then killed Burdett to shut him up. And of course he accuses you of sabotaging his hopes to marry Marie of Burgundy; on that subject, he seems like one truly obsessed.'

He opened his mouth to ask her how it was that she was so well informed about George's drunken maunderings, when she added, 'And whenever he gets drunk enough, he reminds his hearers that you are no rightful king, since all do know you're not the trueborn son of the Duke of York, having been sired by an English archer your mother did dally with in Rouen.'

Edward frowned. 'So he's dredged up that old slander, has he?' he said slowly. He was angered but more for his mother's sake than his own. Few, he was sure, had ever given credence to that particular piece of Lancastrian scandalmongering. God's truth it was, he thought, that if there were but one faithful wife since the birth of the Lord Christ, that one wife would be ma mère. She was too proud to take heed to the gossip of alehouse and tavern, but if she were to learn that her own son be the source. . . . No, he did not want that. George had given her grief enough for fully three lifetimes as it was. He would have to. . . .

'What did you just say, Lisbet?' he asked suddenly, sharply. 'Say that again.'

'I said that he has even dared to slander your own children. He claims no son of yours shall ever rule in your stead, that they all be bastard-born just as you are. And if that not be treason, Ned, then I do ask you . . . what in God's Name is?'

For an unguarded instant, Edward went cold; shock sent the blood surging through his veins, set his pulse to racing. And then common sense prevailed and his breathing slowed. He saw George's besotted babblings for what they were, the poisonous ramblings of a deranged mind, no more than that.

'I think brother George has just tripped over his own tongue,' he said softly. 'What is he claiming . . . that you did bewitch me into wedlock?'

776

Elizabeth nodded. 'What else could it be? Actually, he's made even less sense than usual. Apart from claiming that our marriage is invalid and our children bastards, the rest seems to trail off into the usual incoherent gibberish you get from a man deep in his cups. Something about the truth being buried in Norwich, except that it's not, and he made some mention, too, of your former Chancellor, Robert Stillington, but what it all does mean. . . . Ned! Ned, you're hurting me!'

Edward stared blankly at her and then his hold slackened, his fingers unclenched from her arm. Elizabeth rubbed her wrist resentfully but her complaint was stilled as she looked into his face.

'Ned, what is it? What is wrong?'

He did not hear her, had for the moment forgotten her entirely. His head was whirling. Christ! After all these years. He'd been so sure no one would ever find out about Nell, so sure.

'Ned? Ned, you're frightening me! What is it?'

He shook his head but the discipline of a lifetime was already reasserting itself; he was once more in control of himself, enough to say with a fair measure of calm, 'Nothing, Lisbet. I was but angered that he should dare to speak such arrant nonsense of our sons.'

She didn't believe him; he saw that. But he gave her no chance to protest, rolled away from her and pulled a pillow close, like one seeking sleep. He could hear Elizabeth beside him in the dark; her breath came uneven, unnaturally loud. One of his dogs was scratching for fleas, nails clicking rhythmically against the hearthstones. A shutter creaked. Somewhere beyond the window, a bird trilled; another caught up the refrain. His heart continued to beat in queer fits and starts, the way it always did before a battle. Nell. Oh, Jesus. He'd not thought of her in years. And now George knew the truth, he knew about Nell. But how could he? Stillington would not have told him; he'd never have dared. But who did, then? Christ, after all this time!

He closed his eyes, only to have a woman's face form against his lids. A gravely beautiful face, lovely and remote. A fair Madonna, he'd once called her and she'd been shocked, chided him for blaspheming. But it fit her . . . all too well. Was that why he'd had to have her . . . because she'd seemed beyond reach, unattainable? He no longer knew the answer, if ever he had. It was too long ago, a long-forgotten lust for a woman no longer living. A secret she'd taken to her grave. Or had she? That George, of all men, should somehow have stumbled onto the truth. . . . How much did he know?

The hours seemed frozen in time, until he began to feel it would always be night. And then, without warning, the dark was gone and sun was spilling into the chamber, enveloping the bed in a blaze of brightness. He winced, turned his eyes away from the glare; he hadn't slept at all.

With each day that passed, Elizabeth's unease grew. Something was very wrong with her husband. Never had she seen him so tense, so preoccupied. As her pleas for information went unanswered, her anxieties multiplied. What was bothering him? Why had he insisted upon returning so suddenly to London when they'd meant to stay at Windsor until Michaelmas? And why had he ordered such drastic changes in George's confinement?

Once back at Westminster, Edward had dismissed George's own servants, replaced his guards with men personally chosen by him, close-mouthed veterans of the battles of Barnet and Tewkesbury. George's world was suddenly reduced to the confines of the Bowyer Tower. At Edward's command, visitors were forbidden, all communications carefully screened, and no more were kegs of malmsey carted from the Herber cellars to the Tower.

These were measures Elizabeth had been advocating for months, but it gave her little satisfaction now to see them so abruptly put into effect. She found herself remembering Edward's peculiar reaction to her account of George's drunken ramblings.

And each time she did, her every instinct screamed warnings of a danger she did not yet understand.

And then Edward unexpectedly summoned to London Robert Stillington, Bishop of Bath and Wells.

Elizabeth had never understood why Edward had named Stillington as his Chancellor. A mild-mannered, self-effacing man in his fifties, he had neither the intellect nor the ambition for a position of such power, and Elizabeth hadn't been the only one to wonder why Edward had chosen to honour Stillington so lavishly. He'd exercised his authority unobtrusively and, when his health began to suffer, seemed almost relieved to resign the Chancellorship and retire to his native Yorkshire. Elizabeth had not seen him in more than two years and she was shocked now at sight of the haggard, aging man being ushered into Edward's private chambers. Was he so ill as that? But then he glanced back over his shoulder and her breath stopped. What she saw on his face was sheer terror, the look of a condemned prisoner about to mount the steps of the gallows.

Elizabeth came to an abrupt halt. Jane Shore was standing at the door of Edward's bedchamber. The men loitering about fell suddenly silent, some embarrassed, most covertly amused by this awkward meeting of the King's wife and mistress. It was Jane who acted to dispel the tension.

'Madame,' she said, and dropped down in a deep, submissive curtsy.

Elizabeth nodded coolly, signalled for Jane to rise. Of the two women, Jane was by far the most discomfited. Elizabeth had, of necessity, long ago been forced to come to terms with her husband's blatant infidelities. Moreover, she found Jane less objectionable than many of Edward's bedmates. Jane never flaunted Edward's favour, and equally important to Elizabeth, she seemed quite ignorant of the uses of power. Jane squandered her influence as recklessly as she did her money. She was always willing to listen

779

to hard-luck stories, to make loans that would never be repaid, and when she petitioned Edward to redress grievances, it was on behalf of the victimized, the weak. Her guileless generosity had made her popular with Londoners but Elizabeth thought her to be a fool.

Now Jane backed away from the door, even though she'd been summoned by Edward and Elizabeth had not, saying in a low voice, 'I'll leave you now, Madame.'

Elizabeth brushed past her, entered the bechamber. Edward was alone. He glanced up with a quizzical frown as she shut the door behind her, and Elizabeth heard herself saying defiantly, 'Your harlot's not coming. I did send her away.' She at once regretted it; the words had come of their own volition, were born of stress more than jealousy. She braced herself for his anger, was astonished when he merely shrugged.

'I take it you want to see me, Lisbet?'

She might have been irked by his indifference, but it only served to feed her fear. She crossed swiftly to him, knelt and took his hand between her own.

'Ned, why did you send for Dr Stillington? And what has George to do with all this? Never have I seen your nerves so on the raw. You must tell me what is wrong. I've a right to know.'

He was looking at her with a very strange expression, one she couldn't fathom. 'Yes,' he said at last. 'Yes, I suppose you do.'

He jerked his head toward the table. 'Pour for me from the flagon. And pour for yourself, too. You will,' he said dryly, 'be needing it.'

Beneath the familiar mockery, Elizabeth sensed something else, something alien, unexpected. He's uneasy about telling me this, she thought suddenly, and that frightened her all the more. Rising, she came quickly back to him with a brimming wine cup, watched tensely as he drank.

'Do not look so expectant, my love. I assure you this is one secret you'd rather not share.'

'Just tell me,' she said tautly, and he nodded.

'I dare say you remember my reluctance to make you my wife?'

Elizabeth stiffened in surprise. 'Quite well,' she said icily. 'None have ever let me forget that I do come of a more humble lineage than yours. Whilst it's true, I grant you, that my father was but a knight, no mention is ever made of the fact that my mother was born of Burgundian nobility. Though why you do bring this up now. . . .'

He cut her off with an impatient gesture. 'My reluctance had nothing to do with your family. It was because . . .' She saw him draw a deep breath. 'Because I was not free to wed.'

'What?'

'I was not free to wed,' he repeated, very evenly. 'Two years before we exchanged vows at Grafton Manor, I did plight troth with another woman.'

Elizabeth stared at him. 'You are mad to talk like that,' she gasped. You must not say such things even in jest. If that were to be true . . . it would mean our marriage would not be recognized by the Church. That we'd have lived in sin these thirteen years past. That our children . . . our children would be bastards.' She stopped abruptly; she was having some difficulty in catching her breath.

'I'm not joking, Lisbet,' he said, suddenly sounding very tired.

'No.' She shook her head, backed up until she felt the supporting edge of the table behind her. 'No, I do not believe you.'

He said nothing, and she repeated, more firmly now, 'I do not believe it. I do not.'

He drank until the cup was empty and then said quietly, 'I'm telling you the truth. You know I am.'

There was a footstool under the table. Elizabeth pulled it toward her, lowered herself onto it. 'Who . . .' She licked her lips, had to begin again. 'Who was she?'

'Eleanor Butler. Shrewsbury's daughter.'

'Jesú!' Elizabeth closed her eyes. The Earl of Shrewsbury's daughter. Dear God.

Edward was saying something about Eleanor Butler, calling her Nell. She heard the words '*widow*' and '*nunnery*', tried to focus on what he was saying, tried to make some sense of it.

'Butler's not the family name of Shrewsbury,' she said dully. 'She was married, then?' And then wondered why she'd asked that, as if it actually mattered.

He nodded. 'She was wed at thirteen to Lord Sudley's son. She'd been a widow for some two years when we first met.'

Elizabeth sucked in her breath. No mercer's wife like Jane Shore. No light o' love to be seduced and forgotten. Shrewsbury's daughter and Lord Sudley's daughter-in-law. Dear, dear God.

There was a Venetian-glass goblet within reach. Her tongue seemed to be swelling, seemed to have filled her mouth. It was an eerie sensation, frightened her. She tried to swallow, failed, and looked yearningly at the goblet. She did not dare pick it up, knew she'd never be able to get it to her mouth unspilled. She tightened her grip on the table, closed her eyes again. She was going to be sick. She knew it.

'Lisbet?' Edward was beside her, bending over her, his face concerned. As he put his hand on her shoulder, her head came up, her body jerked spasmodically and then went rigid.

'Do not touch me,' she warned.

There was no question but that she meant it. He recoiled a pace, looking down into eyes suddenly slitted, feverish with hate. But he saw, too, how white she was, saw the sweat glistening at her temples, her upper lip.

'Take this,' he said brusquely. 'You look like to faint.'

He picked up the goblet, held it out to her. Elizabeth knocked it from his hand, sent it spinning to the floor between them. The glass shattered upon impact, soaked the carpet in amber froth. One of Edward's dogs came forward to investigate, sniffed at the spreading liquid and took an experimental lap, then another. Elizabeth looked up at Edward, down again at the broken pieces of glass. She wished she'd thought to fling it in his face.

Because she hadn't, she kicked sharply at the dog. It gave a startled yelp, retreated in astonished haste, and Elizabeth was filled with a wild irrational rage when she saw it go to Edward for comfort.

'Why?' she said bitterly. 'Name of God, why? You can at least tell me that. You do owe me that much!'

'Why do you think?' He turned away, gave a defensive shrug. 'I wanted her and she was virtuous. I could have her no other way.' Reaching for the flagon, he poured himself a second drink, said, 'Damnation, Lisbet, I was twenty years old and used to getting my own way. I just did not think. . . .'

'And you think that does excuse you?' Elizabeth was incredulous. 'Because you wanted her, that did give you the right? To do this to me? To your own children? How could you?'

'It's rather late for reproaches,' he said coldly. 'It's done, and nothing we say now can change it.'

Elizabeth came to her feet. Had he been close enough, she would have hit him. Because he wasn't, she could only use her tongue. Slowly and deliberately, she began to call him every vile name she'd ever heard, using invective she'd never even realized she knew. He didn't interrupt, let her finish.

When she at last ran out of curses, he said, 'Do not play the aggrieved wife, Lisbet. It's not a role that does become you. We both know I've given you what you did want most, that queen's coronet you take such pleasure in wearing. Even had I told you about Nell, you'd still have married me. To be Queen of England, I do not doubt you'd have willingly bedded with a leper.'

A blinding pain was throbbing over Elizabeth's left eye. She didn't dare stay in this chamber with him any longer, could not be accountable for what she might do. Reaching the door, she leaned against it for a moment and then said, 'I will never forgive you. Never. As God is my witness, I will not.'

'Yes, you will, Lisbet,' he said softly.

Elizabeth started to jerk the door open but her hand froze on the latch, clenched into an impotent fist. Christ help her but he was right. What choice did she have? She sagged against the door, feeling heat rising in her face, and then her stomach was heaving in earnest and she stumbled for the garde-robe, fell to her knees across the threshold and began to retch.

For several moments she was aware only of her body's misery. Then she felt his hands under her elbows, lifting her up. She tried to twist away but hadn't the strength, let him carry her to the bed. She closed her eyes, trying to blot out his face, blot out this revelation she couldn't accept, that their life together had been a lie, had been a lie from the very beginning. She could hear him moving about the chamber; once he approached the bed and wiped her face with a wet cloth. She started to turn her head away but somehow it didn't seem worth the effort. She found she couldn't even summon up anger any more. She felt numb, uncaring and very, very tired.

When she opened her eyes again, she saw that he had pulled a chair up to the bed. Seeing her lashes flicker, he leaned forward, said, 'Do you suppose we can talk now? Talk without trading accusations or insults?'

'Give me something to drink,' she said, saw that he had anticipated her need, was holding out a cup. She took it and drank in gulps. After a time, she asked, 'Where is she? Why has she kept silent?'

'She's dead. Not long after I revealed our marriage to my council at Reading, she did enter a convent in Norwich. She died four years later, was buried in the church of the Carmelites.'

'And yet she held her tongue? She must have loved you very much,' Elizabeth said nastily, saw the corner of his mouth twitch.

'Yes,' he said unwillingly. 'She did.' They stared at each other and Elizabeth gained a small victory in that he was the first to look away.

'Who else knows? Gloucester? Hastings? Who, Ned?' It was the first time she'd made use of his name since he'd told her about

784

Nell Butler. She wished that she had not, did not want to sound as if they were back on normal terms, as if he could be forgiven.

'Only Stillington. No one else knows. Oh, Will and my mother and a few others knew about my involvement with Nell, but they never knew the truth of it. And Dickon was only ten or so at the time. No, you need not. . . .'

'Oh, my God!' Elizabeth sat upright, eyes suddenly going wide with horror as the realization hit her. 'Stillington! And you said a convent in Norwich. That's what George said. Norwich! He knows, Ned, George knows!'

'I'm not sure,' he said grimly. 'But I fear so.'

Elizabeth's control gave way then; frightened tears began to spill down her face, splashed on his restraining hands. 'Do you not see what that means, Ned? When you die, the crown will pass to George. To George . . . not our son. And he knows that now, George knows!'

'No!' He was gripping her shoulders, shaking her. 'No, Lisbet, no. I will not let that happen. I swear to you I will not.'

The sincerity in his voice was unmistakable and Elizabeth's panic began to subside. He meant what he said. That was something she could hold on to, a lifeline, however frayed. She was able to ask, more calmly, 'How did he find out? Did Stillington tell him?'

'No.' Edward moved back to the chair, ran his hand through his hair, pressed his fingers to his temples.

'I said Nell did keep my secret. Well, that's not quite true. She did while she lived but, when she was dying, she made a deathbed confession. The priest was bound by the confessional, of course, could not reveal what she told him. But apparently it weighed heavily upon his mind. Last winter he was stricken with a mortal illness and decided he must not take the secret with him to the grave. So . . . he wrote to George, to the man he saw as my rightful heir.'

'Jesus, no . . .' Elizabeth breathed, and he shook his head, said quickly, 'No, he did not reveal Nell's story in its entirety. For that much we may be thankful. But he did say enough to kindle George's curiosity, told him to ask Bishop Stillington about Nell Butler and me. And, of course, George wasted no time in doing just that. He went to Stillington with his suspicions, with some very awkward questions.'

'But you said Stillington did not tell him.'

'I do not think he did. He says not and I tend to believe him. But he admits he was taken off-guard, could think only to deny that he'd even heard of Nell Butler. A clumsy lie, one George would have been able to disprove easily enough; Stillington's association with Nell's family goes back nigh on thirty years.' He grimaced at that and then said, 'For all his failings, George is no fool. He's quite capable of making the natural deduction, that if Stillington lied about knowing Nell Butler, there must be a reason why. He's capable, too, of hitting upon the truth, or enough of it to be dangerous.'

'You mean he might conclude there was a secret marriage between you and Nell Butler?' Elizabeth demanded.

He shrugged, said wearily, 'What else would he think?'

For a moment, Elizabeth forgot how much she did need him. 'Yes,' she said acidly. 'I can see how he would. Your past record does naturally lend itself to such speculation, does it not?'

He looked up sharply at that, eyes as blue and unrevealing as the summer sky, and she expected stinging sarcasm, expected the mockery he knew how to wield so well. Instead, he grinned. 'Yes,' he conceded. 'I suppose it does.'

Elizabeth was caught off-balance, flinched away from him as if she'd been struck. 'Damn you,' she said helplessly, and turned her head aside on the pillow. 'Damn you, Ned, damn you!'

He was not affronted and dimly she understood why. He'd won. She'd said she'd never forgive him but in truth nothing would change between them. They'd go on as before. She'd share his bed, bear his children, and the worst of it was that it was not just because she had no other choice. The worst of it, she thought, was that she'd want it that way.

It was this realization which made her lash out at him now, made her say with sudden venom, 'Nell Butler had to be the greatest fool in Christendom. Had it been me, I'd never have kept silent, never.'

She'd hoped to hurt him, saw that she hadn't. 'I do not doubt that for a moment, sweetheart,' he said coolly.

Elizabeth struggled upright again, started to rise. As she did, her gaze fell upon her wedding band, bright burnished gold and emeralds to match her eyes. She stared at it, fingering it as if it were a talisman. And then she raised her head, said in a voice that was tightly controlled, dangerously so, 'As far as I am concerned, I am your lawful wife and Queen, and the crown is my son's natural birthright. Your son, too, Ned, and it is up to you to protect that right. I want you to tell me how you do mean to do that.'

He shoved the chair back, came abruptly to his feet. 'I do not see how George can have more than suspicions,' he said, seemed to be choosing his words with care.

'I'm not a fool, Ned, so do not treat me like one! I know your brother; I know how he thinks. He needs no proof. With George, the mere suspicion would be enough.'

He'd moved away from the bed, toward the hearth. Elizabeth followed him, caught his arm so that he had to face her.

'You cannot let him live, Ned. You know you cannot. There's no other way of keeping him silent. Sooner or later, he'd start to talk, would find those willing to listen. There are men still loyal to Lancaster, men who look to the Tudors as the last of the Lancastrian blood. You think they would not make use of George? Think, Ned, think! What of Bess? What chance would she have to become Queen of France should it ever be alleged that she was born out of wedlock? And our sons. . . . What of them?'

She paused, her eyes searching his face intently. And then her

787

hand slipped from his arm; she stepped back. 'But you already know that,' she said slowly. 'Of course you do.'

Still he said nothing. A muscle twitched suddenly in his cheek, what she knew to be a symptom of extreme strain.

'You have not answered me, Ned. What of our sons? Earlier tonight, you swore that you'd not let George do them harm, that you'd not let him lay claim to the crown. You must tell me, Ned, tell me if you truly meant it.'

'Yes,' he said. 'Yes, I meant it.'

12

Westminster

October 1477

Edward's chambers were hazy with eye-stinging smoke, strident with laughter. In the uncertain light of flaring wall cressets, servants passed back and forth with food and drink. For most of the day a chill autumn rain had been falling but the heat in the room was oppressive, stifling. Richard's barge had tied up at the King's Wharf but moments before, and that first sweltering blast of stale air sent him reeling back, breathless. The noise was considerable and his senses were at once assailed by a multitude of competing aromas: burning yew logs, spilt ale, dogs and body heat and the musky fragrance of powdered perfumes.

For some moments, Richard stood motionless and unnoticed in the doorway, taking in the scene before him. He didn't see his brother at first glance but most of the faces were familiar to him.

The men, that is; the women were strangers, but all having in common extreme youth and a certain provocative prettiness. They all seemed to be amusing themselves just as they pleased. Voices pitched too high rose and fell in the clamour to be heard. One couple was dancing, apparently oblivious of the fact that Edward's minstrels had long since ceased playing. Others were watching as several men fed spoonfuls of ale to a small bear cub; someone set a shallow bowl of mead before the little animal and, when it began to stagger and wobble about, all laughed. But the focus of attention was a dice game being staged in the middle of the floor. Midst jibes and cheers, one of the women players now raised her skirt and kirtle, slowly slid a silk-fringed garter from her knee. Her shoes and belt and rings had already been discarded in the centre of the circle; as Richard watched, she added the forfeit garter to the pile, winning for herself a round of tipsy applause.

An empty wine flagon lay in a sodden pool at Richard's feet; he had to kick it aside in order to close the door. It was then that his eye was caught by a swirl of bright blond hair and, turning, he saw Thomas Grey.

Thomas was paying no heed to the dice game, was giving all his attention to a young woman in bright clinging silk. Richard's mouth twisted down, as if he'd just tasted something foul. How in Christ's name could Elizabeth's own sons be so willing, eager even, to take part in Ned's carousings? Did they not care at all that Ned was so openly unfaithful to their mother? It was beyond his comprehension and he found himself thinking that Warwick had been right in this if in nothing else, that the Woodvilles had poisoned his brother's court no less surely than salt poured down a well.

Thomas had backed his companion against the wall, barring her way with an outstretched arm, and now he reached over to share her wine cup in a gesture that was ostentatiously intimate. Not wanting to have to acknowledge him, Richard was turning away, when he heard Thomas say in a loud carrying voice, 'That's not a jest I find to my liking. I want an apology from you and I do want it now.'

Richard glanced back, saw that Thomas and the girl had been joined by Harry Stafford, Duke of Buckingham. It was Buckingham who'd apparently provoked this outburst from Thomas although he seemed innocent of any such intent, saying something too softly for Richard to hear, his shoulders lifting in a good-natured shrug. Thomas did not appear placated. He stepped toward Buckingham and the latter shook his head, still smiling. As he did, Thomas suddenly swung at him. He'd meant to drive his fist deep into Buckingham's midsection but the other man pivoted at the moment of impact and the blow encountered only air. Off-balance, Thomas stumbled and nearly fell, but he quickly righted himself and swung again.

The blow never connected. Buckingham had prudently backed out of range and, at the same time, Richard moved, grabbed Thomas by the arm and swung him around. He had no trouble at all in shoving Thomas back against the wall; the younger man was too startled to offer resistance.

'Where the hell do you think you are? These are the king's chambers, not some Southwark alehouse.'

Thomas had been gaping at him, unable to believe that anyone would dare to lay hands on him like this. Now shock was giving way to outrage. His first impulse a violent one, he fumbled for his dagger hilt.

The advantages all lay with Richard; he was completely sober and in control of his temper. Using more force than was actually necessary, he pinned Thomas's hand with his own, leaned into him so that the weight of his body held Thomas immobile.

'I could almost wish you'd draw that dagger,' he said contemptuously. 'But you're not that drunk and we both do know it. Now get hold of yourself before we start to attract attention.'

Thomas blinked; his head began to clear. Focusing on Richard for the first time, he suddenly realized who it was who'd come between him and Buckingham. With recognition came horror at what he'd almost done. Holy Jesus, it was bad enough to have come to blows with Buckingham, but this. If Ned were ever to know. . . . That thought was enough to sober Thomas rapidly. He looked about hastily to make sure Richard was right and no one was watching.

As soon as he felt Thomas's muscles slacken, Richard let him go, stepped back. Thomas straightened, started to move away and then said in a very low voice, 'I suppose . . . I suppose you'll want to tell your brother about . . . about all this?'

Thomas had his mother's fair skin as well as her temper and any strong emotion scorched his face with quick colour. Now he flushed deeply, having come as close as he could to asking a favour from a man he hated.

Richard hadn't thought to do so but he saw no reason to ease Thomas's mind. 'If you're asking me not to, I can make you no promises.' Adding with a touch of malice, 'I should think you'd be more concerned with what Buckingham might say. He, after all, is the one you did most sorely offend.'

Thomas's alarm was almost comical. Leaving him to deal with it as best he could, Richard walked away.

Stopping a servant, he questioned the man about Edward but encountered only apologetic ignorance as to his brother's where-abouts. He was turning to exit the chamber when he felt a light touch on his arm.

Blue-grey eyes the exact shade of his own were regarding him with flirtatious wonderment that was contrived, but not entirely so.

'I've always wanted to witness a miracle. But I think that was as close as I'll ever get, to see Thomas Grey back down like that. Who might you be . . . Merlin?'

By now Richard had recognized her as the girl Thomas had been trying so hard to charm. He felt an instinctive prejudice against her for that, found himself judging her by the company she kept. Nor was she making a favourable impression on him now. The face upturned to his was a pretty one but her mouth was painted a bold bright red unknown in nature, her eyebrows had been plucked in fashionably extreme arches and her perfume clung to her hair, her gown, the exposed hollow of her breasts, enveloping them both in a cloud of lavender. He found the fragrance overpowering, cloyingly sweet, and would have moved away had she not kept her hand on his arm.

'I do want to thank you, sir.' As she spoke, the blue eyes were studying him in unabashed, unhurried appraisal, taking in the jewelled rings, the soft Spanish leather boots, the fur-lined cloak. Instinctively amending her mode of address, she smiled at him, said, 'It was most kind of you to intervene as you did, my lord. I was truly fearful we were to have a brawl here in the king's very chambers. Had you not taken Tom in hand . . . and then, when I saw him reach for his dagger, Lady Mary forfend!'

'You need not have worried. Thomas Grey is not one to draw a dagger if there is any chance some of the blood spilled might be his.'

She gave a startled laugh. 'Jesú, but you are blunt-spoken, are you not? Oh, I know Tom is not much liked at court but he's not such a bad sort; in truth, he's not. That brawl with Buckingham now . . . he was very neatly goaded into it.'

Richard was sceptical. 'That was not the way it looked to me.'

She nodded triumphantly, as if he'd just proved her point. 'Exactly! My lord Buckingham does have a flair for that, for drawing blood with a smile. That was what he did with Tom, telling him to take care, that poaching in a royal forest is a hanging offence.'

'Why should that have provoked Grey into making such a fool of himself?'

'It is clear you're not much at court. It was me Buckingham was baiting Tom about. . . . I'm Jane Shore.'

She said it as if it should mean something to him. The name was vaguely familiar, but for the moment the association eluded him. Seeing that, she gave him a pitying smile, explaining patiently and with a certain naïve pride, 'I'm the King's mistress. Now do you see why Tom was so touchy?'

With that, Richard remembered where he'd heard her name. Véronique had come back from London last year with some startling gossip, claiming that Edward had got the Pope to grant a divorce for one of his mistresses on the grounds of her husband's impotence. So this then was Jane Shore. This was the woman Thomas Grey was lusting for. Ned's favourite bedmate. Jesus!

'I suppose then that you'd be the one to ask,' he said, with irony that was neither friendly nor flattering. 'Is he here?'

She nodded, tossed her head in the general direction of the closed bedchamber door. 'In there. He was feeling greensick . . . too much Madeira.'

Knowing his brother had always had a notoriously steady head for drink, Richard frowned, looked about him at the crowded chamber. For the first time, he noticed Will Hastings, sprawled in one of the recessed window seats. But even as he recognized Will, he realized there was no point in approaching him. Will was genially drunk, holding on his lap a girl who looked to be sixteen, seventeen at most. Richard watched Will fondle the girl, watched the drunken bear cub weaving in erratic circles, and knew suddenly that he would not wait for Ned, that he did not want to talk to him here, not tonight.

'You do not much like what you see, do you?'

He started, had almost forgotten Jane Shore was still standing beside him. 'No,' he said curtly. 'No, I do not.'

Jane was accustomed to being the centre of male attention, to having men look upon her with desire, and it was gradually becoming apparent to her that this man did not. But the resentment she felt now was not on her own behalf, it was indignation that he should dare to criticize Edward, even indirectly, and she said with sudden heat, 'You need not share the King's pleasures but I think it rather presumptuous that you should pass judgment on them.'

Richard stared at her and then laughed abruptly as the ludicrousness of his position struck him, that he should find himself debating morality with his brother's harlot. He was amused that she should be so protective of Ned but he found it faintly touching, too, and she rose a bit in his estimation. For the first time, he thought he could comprehend why she had such appeal for Ned; she and Elizabeth were as unlike as any two women could be.

'You think a king does not need to be able to relax, to be able to put his troubles from his mind if only for a few hours? And now more than ever, what with the strain of these past weeks, with his own brother to be charged with treason. . . .'

Richard's amusement chilled with the shock of hearing George's plight discussed so casually. 'So you do know about that, too.'

She looked at him in some surprise. 'Why, it's been common knowledge at court for some weeks now.'

Yes, Richard thought bitterly. All had known. He alone had remained in ignorance. He alone Ned had not bothered to tell.

Edward jerked the door open. His head throbbed with a dull ache impossible to ignore and a mouthwash of myrrh and honey had proven to be of marginal use against the sour taste filling his mouth, curdling his tongue.

Thomas materialized at his elbow, tousle-haired, feverish. Noting without interest his stepson's agitation, Edward reached over to claim his cup, only to shove it back after one gagging swallow. How could any man choose malmsey of his own free will? And yet malmsey was the drink George most favoured. How like George that even his taste in wines was noxious. But why must he think of this now? Must George intrude upon his every thought tonight? He turned abruptly to Thomas, said testily, 'Why are all these people milling about like so many sheep? And where's Jane?'

Thomas shrugged. 'That I'd not know. The last I saw of her, she was off alone in a corner with your brother.'

'Dickon?' Edward's surprise was readily apparent. 'Here tonight? Are you sure?'

'Quite sure.' Too embittered to guard his tongue, Thomas plunged ahead recklessly. 'As to whether they're still here, that I cannot tell you.'

'Jane and Dickon?' Edward smiled coldly. 'Once before, Tom, I told you I did not suffer fools gladly. I'd think on that if I were you.'

He didn't wait for Thomas to respond, caught the blue of Jane's gown and moved toward it. Jane saw him before Richard did. As she smiled, giving him a loving look of welcome, he drawled, 'Well, you've chosen a right secluded corner for yourselves, have you not? I trust I'm not intruding?'

Jane's mouth dropped. Mother of God, he was truly in his cups tonight! 'My dearest lord,' she stammered, 'surely you . . . you do not think. . . .'

Richard was in no mood for games, not tonight. 'Let it be, Ned,' he said impatiently. 'Can you not see you're frightening her?'

Jane's mouth stayed open, her earrings jangling wildly as she turned to stare at Richard. Never had she heard anyone speak so familiarly to Edward, not even Will. And suddenly she realized who Richard was, who he had to be, and she went hot with embarrassment.

Edward was laughing, slipped an arm around her waist. 'Did you truly think I was serious, sweetheart? Well, Dickon, this is a surprise. I did not expect you in London for nigh on a fortnight.'

'I need to talk to you, Ned.'

'I would hope so; we have not seen each other in more than six months. To get this man out of Yorkshire, Jane, is like pulling teeth. What he does find to fascinate him on those northern moors, I'll never fathom, but. . . .'

'Now, Ned. It is urgent.'

Jane was no longer listening. How could she have made such a fool of herself? 'You know little of court life,' she'd told him, called him presumptuous. Oh, Lord! But after a moment or so, her sense of humour carried the day and she stifled a giggle with difficulty. It truly was amusing, after all, and Ned would likely find it hilarious. Nor was her vanity quite so pricked by Richard's indifference, for all knew he doted upon his wife. So caught up was she in these thoughts that Edward had to say her name twice before she realized he was speaking to her.

'Well? Are you coming or not?'

So accustomed was she to indulging his whims that it never occurred to her to question him and she made haste to follow him into the bedchamber. Once there, however, she suddenly wished she'd not been so quick to obey. Richard did not want her there. He was looking at her with such disfavour that she blushed, wanting to make excuses for her presence, to plead Edward's insistence.

Edward alone appeared at ease. 'Come here, sweetheart,' he directed, patting the bed. 'It is good to have you back, Dickon, but must you be pacing about like a cat on the prowl? Sit down and tell me about your journey. You did bring your Anne, I daresay? Where are you settled, at Baynard's Castle?'

'No. Crosby Place.'

Edward seemed not to notice the terseness of the response. 'Ah yes, I did forget. You are familiar with Crosby Place, are you not, Jane? You know ... that enormous manor house in Bishopsgate Street. My brother leased it last year from Crosby's widow and from what I've heard tell of it, he's living in greater luxury than I am.'

'A most beautiful house, in truth,' Jane agreed politely, then gave Edward an imploring look. 'My love, I feel I should not be here. It is plain His Grace of Gloucester does have matters to discuss in private. . . .'

'She's right, Ned, I do.'

Before Edward could respond, Jane was on her feet and Richard moving to hold the door open for her. Briefly, Edward was tempted to call her back but, almost at once, he rejected the idea; Jane could at best only delay the inevitable.

Richard closed the door with care. 'I understand you mean to try George on a charge of high treason,' he said quietly, almost conversationally.

This wasn't the approach Edward had been expecting. 'Yes,' he said warily. 'I do.'

'I see. . . . And I suppose it somehow slipped your mind? Or did you not think it important enough to mention to me?'

'Sheath your sarcasm, Dickon.' Edward sat up on the bed, said somewhat defensively, 'I did mean to tell you once you were back in London.' He busied himself now in positioning pillows for his back. 'How did you find out?'

'We stopped at Berkhampsted on our way south.'

That gave Edward pause, but he didn't let it show on his face. 'I regret that ma mère must be grieved by this,' he said dispassionately, 'But I had no choice.'

'Look, Ned, I'm not defending what George has done. I'd be the last man to do that. But a charge of high treason . . . I do not understand. Why now? You did forgive George his past betrayals, forgive what was well nigh unforgivable. To charge him with treason now. . . . Well, it is like using a crossbow to bring down a sparrow. It just does not make sense to me. Surely his treason with Warwick was far more dangerous than any wine-soaked schemes he does concoct these days.'

'Tell that to Ankarette Twynyho,' Edward snapped, and Richard caught his breath.

'That's not fair,' he protested. 'You know I do feel that woman's death was no less than murder. But you know, too, that George is not accountable for all he does. We've both known that for some time, Ned.'

'What are you suggesting? That I should do nothing whilst he

797

does make mockery of the laws of this realm? Am I to allow him to amuse himself by committing murder? Tell me, just what would you have me do, Dickon, turn a blind eye to his crimes and leave his judgment to God?'

Richard was taken aback; it wasn't often that he'd seen Edward flare up like this. 'Of course that's not what I'd have you do,' he said slowly. 'Did I raise any objections when you sent him to the Tower last June? That was justified, had to be done. I just cannot say the same for a charge of treason. Not now.' Richard hesitated. 'Have you not thought of ma mère and Meg? You and I both have reasons a hundredfold to mistrust George, and I'll tell you frankly that whatever affection I did once have for him is totally gone, is six years dead. But that's not true for ma mère. She. . . .'

'I do not care to discuss this further,' Edward said abruptly. 'I've heard you out and at an hour when I'd have told anyone else to go to the devil. But we are accomplishing nothing. You say a charge of treason is unwarranted, unnecessary? Well, to me, it's more than justified, is the only action I can take. Why else do you think I'm doing it? Or is it that you think this is how I mean to amuse myself this winter? Banish boredom by bringing my brother up on a charge of treason?'

Startled, Richard shook his head. 'For God's sake, Ned, what is wrong with you tonight? I did not come here to quarrel with you. I seek only to understand your reasons, to see this with your eyes. Is that so much to ask of you, that you do tell me why?'

'I should think my reasons would speak for themselves. Do not expect me to give you an accounting of George's sins; you do know them as well as I. Now if you want to stay and talk of other matters, you're more than welcome. But if you are set upon discussing George, I must remind you that it's nigh onto midnight and you've a loving wife awaiting you at Crosby Place.'

A strained silence fell between them. 'You're right,' Richard said at last. 'It does grow late.' At the door, he paused.

'You might not like to hear it, Ned, but ma mère is heartsick about this. I think it would ease her mind considerably if I could write her that you mean only to scare some sense into George. May I reassure her of that? Give her leave to assure George that he's not facing the axe?'

He'd asked more as a matter of form than anything else; it had never seriously occurred to him that Edward would demand the death penalty. But now he saw Edward's face harden, saw him look away without answering.

'Jesus God,' he said softly, suddenly seeing the truth. 'He is facing the axe. You do mean to put him to death!'

Edward raised his head at that. 'That will depend,' he said coolly, 'on whether he be found guilty or not.'

13

London

January 1478

'Are these letters all, my lord?' Richard glanced up in time to see his secretary camouflaging a yawn. It was later than he'd realized; Compline had sounded hours ago.

'Just one more, John. I want you to pull out the letter from York's mayor and aldermen, the one in which they asked me to intercede with my brother the king concerning those illegal fish-garths in the River Aire. Tell them that I've spoken with the king on this matter, and upon my return to Middleham, I'll oversee a survey of the Rivers Ouse, Aire and Wharfe and see to it that any unsanctioned fishgarths be pulled down.' But John was yawning again and Richard took pity on him.

'Tomorrow will be soon enough. Just note what I want to say and you can draft up a suitable reply on the morrow.'

John Kendall had been in Richard's service for several years, long enough to chide now with the ease born of mutual regard, 'You, too, should make ready for bed; you've had markedly little rest these past weeks.' Catching the glint of amusement that crossed Richard's face, he grinned, conceded cheerfully, 'Aye, I know. I do sound like a doting nursemaid. But with your lady gone, there must be someone to see that you look after yourself. She'll be returning soon, I hope.'

'So do I.'

It had been five weeks since Anne had returned to Middleham. Richard had not wanted her to go, had been seriously tempted to forbid it. But he understood her need to be with their son; Ned was not yet five, too young to pass Christmas without either of his parents. No, he could not fault Anne in this, however much he missed her. Nor could he truly blame her if she fretted more than she should over Ned's fevers and bruises. Anne had been cheated; the love she should have lavished upon a nursery-full lay unclaimed, had no other outlet but Ned. Not, he amended, that she did not try to do right by Johnny and their relationship was a good one. But Ned alone was hers. Ned, who was at once her firstborn and her lastborn.

Like a cat with but one kitten, Richard thought, and God's sacred truth, how unlike that bitch, his sweet sister-in-law! Just seven her eldest son was and, since age three, with his own household at Ludlow.

Had it bothered Elizabeth, yielding up her son at so tender an age? Richard, who no longer gave his brother's Queen the benefit of the doubt in anything, thought not. It was done in the name of policy, of course, it being hoped that the physical presence of the little Prince of Wales would serve to strengthen loyalties along the

800

Welsh Marches. And it might well be effective, Richard conceded, but he still thought the strategy to be an exceedingly poor one, for it meant that the boy was being raised almost exclusively by his uncle, Anthony Woodville, saw his parents only rarely. Richard was not the only one to be uncomfortable with this arrangement; there were few, indeed, pleased to see their future king being indoctrinated with Woodville loyalties, absorbing Woodville values.

Dogs were barking in the stable area and Richard raised his head, automatically seeking to distinguish Gareth's deep rumble. Almost at once, he caught himself, marvelling at the tenacity of habit, for it had been several years since he'd been able to take the big dog away from Middleham. Now thirteen, Gareth did little these days but doze in the sun and trail stiffly after Richard's small sons.

As the dogs continued to bark, Richard moved to the oriel window. He was surprised to see that several horses had been ridden into the inner court rather than being taken to the stables behind the chapel. The window glass was cloudy, opaque; he rubbed it with his fist, clearing it just in time to see his servants gathering about a woman enveloped in silvery fox fur. As she dismounted, her hood fell back and, in the flare of torchlight, he recognized his wife.

Anne was no longer cold; the bedchamber hearth was well stoked and the bed piled high with coverlets. But she was very tired. It had taken her seven days to journey south from Middleham, seven days of buffeting winds and frigid temperatures; she'd been up this day since dawn, had covered a bone-bruising thirty-eight miles. She'd managed to forget her fatigue while making love with Richard; now, however, it was coming back on her.

But, as she touched Richard's neck and shoulders, she found the muscles taut and corded under her hand.

'How tense you are, my love! Roll over and I'll rub your back; mayhap it will help you sleep.'

He did as she bade and, ignoring her own exhaustion, she set about easing his strain as best she could. 'I heard George had been brought to trial, Richard,' she said quietly. 'Do you want to tell me about it?'

Richard winced, for her fingers had found a particularly sore spot midway down his back. 'You heard wrong, Anne. It was no trial. It was an indictment, in which the only witnesses were accusers, no evidence was produced and the verdict was a foregone conclusion.'

'Tell me,' she repeated, softly insistent, but he needed no coaxing. 'On the day after the marriage of Ned's second son and the little heiress of the Duke of Norfolk, he convened parliament. A Bill of Attainder was presented against George, accusing him of treason.' He paused before adding reluctantly, 'Ned himself did introduce it.'

Anne was startled; it was almost unheard of for a king to argue personally for a Bill of Attainder.

'What were the charges?'

'A motley collection of offences, none of which on its own would justify the death penalty against a man of George's rank. Ned accused George of spreading stories that Thomas Burdett had been unjustly done to death. Of putting about that old slander that Ned is a bastard and hence no rightful King. Of secretly keeping a document from the reign of Harry of Lancaster, proclaiming George as the heir to the throne in the event that your marriage to Harry's son produced no children.'

'Oh, but Richard, that last was so very long ago. Harry and Edouard have been dead for nigh on seven years and what blood of Lancaster is left does flow thinly in the veins of Harry's Welsh half brother Jasper Tudor. What could it matter now?'

'It mattered,' he said grimly, 'because Ned chose to make it matter.'

'I do not understand, truly I do not. It's not that I mean to defend what George has done. But his past treasons were so much greater and yet Ned chose to forgive them. Why now, Richard?'

'I would that I knew. I cannot believe that Ned would put his own brother to death merely because he'd lost patience with him. Yet he did make much at George's trial of betrayals and broken promises and bad faith, said that again and again he'd forgiven George his crimes, only to have George make mockery of his clemency. Even now, he said, he would have been willing to pardon George had he only shown true remorse or contrition of spirit.' She felt him tense and then he said flatly, 'And in that, he lied. He had no intention of pardoning George. Not this time.'

'It must have been most painful to watch.' Leaning over, she pressed her lips to the nape of his neck. 'Perhaps I erred in urging you to talk of this. . . .'

'No,' he said. 'I want to tell you.'

'What of George? What did he say?'

'He denied all, with much passion. But at the last, so desperate had he become that he went so far as to demand a trial by combat. Ned just . . . looked at him.'

'Oh!' It was an involuntary response, much what she might have felt for any trapped animal at last brought to bay; while she enjoyed the excitement of a hunt, Anne had ever preferred to avoid the kill if possible.

Richard's thoughts had apparently taken the same turn as her own, for he said now, very softly, 'Did I ever tell you about the fox cub I caught when I was six? It was at Ludlow, the summer before the town was sacked by Lancaster. One of the village lads helped me trap it. Half starved it was and sickly but, at sight of us, it went wild with fear. It kept trying to burrow into the earth, seeking escape where there was none, all the while snapping help-lessly at our hands, our rope, even the air itself. . . .'

'Oh, Richard, do not! I'd never have thought I'd ever find myself pitying George, but . . . what of Ned? Does he still refuse to talk with you about it?'

'None of us have had any luck whatsoever. Ma mère has been in London since December and Meg . . . scarcely a day passes that one of her letters does not come from Burgundy. Even my sister Eliza, who has been estranged from George for years. . . . Even Eliza has pleaded with Ned not to do this.' He rolled over onto his back then and Anne saw how truly troubled he was.

'It is easier for Eliza and me; neither one of us has much use for George. But Meg still sees him as the young brother she did part from at the time of her wedding, and ma mère. . . .' He shook his head and then the frustrated fury of these past weeks broke through.

'Christ, Anne, I just cannot understand it, any of it! Ned does not truly want to do this; I'd stake my life on that. To show George's shame up to the world like this, to give ma mère and Meg such grief . . . and knowing all the while that George cannot be other than as he is. It makes no sense. But nothing we say seems to matter to him. These days, there appears to be but one voice he heeds—hers.'

Anne discreetly kept silent. She didn't doubt that Elizabeth was urging Ned to have George put to death, as were all the Woodvilles. But she found it almost impossible to imagine her brother-in-law being led into doing anything he did not want to do. This was not something she meant to say to her husband, however. If Richard needed a crutch, she would not be the one to kick it out from under him, she resolved and said instead, 'Let's not talk any more of George, love. Not tonight.'

Edward was in the Painted Chamber. As usual, he was surrounded by people, the focus of all eyes. But he seemed not to notice those clustering about him, seemed to be alone with his thoughts. Thoughts, Will would wager, that were anything but pleasant.

Edward happened to glance then in his direction, looked past Will with unseeing bloodshot eyes. He looks as weary as ever I've seen him, Will thought uneasily. At the least, it can be said that he's carrying his thirty-five years very heavily these days. What in the name of the saints does he mean to do? It's been fully a week now since sentence of death was passed on Clarence. Yet he does nothing, he stays his hand and drinks. Why? If he is as reluctant as that to take Clarence's life, why charge him with high treason?

There was much about this that Will did not understand. There was a darkness about it; even the Bill of Attainder itself shed little light. It had not even made mention of Ankarette Twynyho. Why, then, was Clarence to die? Will did not know; Ned's reasoning was beyond him. And this was Ned's doing, despite common belief that George had blundered heedlessly into a Woodville web. Will knew better, for he knew Ned. But he did not like it, not at all.

He had no objection to silencing Clarence, thought that should have been done seven years ago. But he would far rather Ned had simply thrown him into the Tower and forgotten about him. As unstable as Clarence was, it would not have taken long; he'd have been babbling and ranting like any Bedlam inmate in no time at all. Will would even have preferred it had Ned chosen to have Clarence quietly and discreetly dispatched to God. As with Harry of Lancaster, it could then have been given out that Clarence had died of a fever or perhaps a fall.

But this way Ned did have the worst of both worlds. By bringing Clarence to trial for reasons only hinted at, Ned did invite the wildest sort of public speculation. No rumour was too preposterous to be rejected out of hand; in tavern and alehouse, gossips found themselves ready audiences. There was even a small groundswell of sympathy for George, confined mainly among those who'd had no personal contact with him. Will did not doubt that the villagers of Warwick would thank God fasting for George's death but there were others who saw only his youth, were moved to pity because he'd been lavish in his almsgiving and fair to look upon.

Above all, Will disapproved of Clarence's impending execution because it would be sure to further entrench the Woodvilles.

To have men think that Elizabeth and her kin had the power to bring down the King's own brother was almost as dangerous as having that power in truth. Men would remember what had befallen Clarence, remember with fear.

How hot they were for Clarence's blood! Will's face remained impassive, the mask of a practised courtier, as he watched Thomas Grey harangue all within earshot. 'Under sentence of death . . . legally tried and found guilty . . . what more needed?'

Will drank to conceal the scornful twist to his mouth. Elizabeth should have lingered; she was astute enough to have curbed her son's flapping tongue. Thomas was a fool; did he not know by now that Ned was not one to be pushed?

'Thomas Grey has not the sense God gave a sheep.' The voice was well modulated, falling pleasantly on the ear, and, to Will, surprisingly familiar. Surprising, because that was not the sort of comment he'd have expected from Harry Stafford, Duke of Buckingham.

Buckingham was very much an enigma to Will. He'd been wed at age twelve to Elizabeth Woodville's sister Katherine but his lineage was impeccably Lancastrian; both his father and grandfather had died fighting York at the battles of Northampton and St Albans and his mother was a Beaufort, sister to the Duke of Somerset executed after Tewkesbury. Yet he had ties to York, too, for his grandmother was Cecily Neville's elder sister. By blood, he stood closer than most to the English throne for, like his Yorkist cousins, he did trace his ancestry from one of the sons of Edward III. As a cousin and brother-in-law of the King, titled and wealthy and amiable, he should long ago have taken his rightful place in Edward's government. That he had not was a riddle Will had yet to solve.

Buckingham was not a member of Edward's council, had never been chosen by Edward to serve on a diplomatic mission overseas, held no post commensurate with his birth and rank. Even more inexplicable to Will, he was not even appointed to

Commissions of the Peace outside of his own Staffordshire. It had occurred to Will that it was not politic to so shunt aside a scion of the old nobility and he'd once taken Edward mildly to task for it. Edward, generally so pragmatic in making use of the talents of political opponents, had surprised Will somewhat by confessing that he did not much like his young cousin of Buckingham and, when pressed why, could only respond even more vaguely that Buckingham did remind him overly much of George.

Will had not seen the resemblance until Edward thus called it to his attention but then he wondered how he could have missed it. When on his best behaviour, George had been capable of a certain brittle charm; Buckingham, too, was volatile, given to extremes of expression and mood, to taking up enthusiasms with wholehearted intensity and tiring of them with record speed. Will tended to attribute this in part to Buckingham's youth; he was just twenty-three. But Buckingham was unlike George in that if he had a dark side, none saw it. If he resented Edward's neglect, he alone knew it. He was appealingly good natured, open-handed with his wealth and if his humour did at times cut too close to the bone, such lapses were put down more to insensitivity than to malice. He was unlike George, too, in that he'd always seemed to be far more interested in the pursuit of pleasure than in political intrigue. It was for this reason that he'd surprised Will by his tart-tongued assessment of Thomas Grey.

But then, Will reminded himself, Grey and Buckingham had been at odds for several years now. In fact, Buckingham was no favourite of the Queen. Rumour had it that he'd proven himself to be a far from satisfactory husband to his Woodville wife, had been imprudent enough to let her know he felt it demeaning that he, a Stafford, should be wed to a mere knight's daughter.

Nothing was better guaranteed to gain him Elizabeth's enmity than that and Will suspected her hostility, as much as any superficial resemblance to George, was why Buckingham had been

807

relegated to the outer fringes of power. While Edward was not one to let himself be influenced in matters of importance, Will knew he did have a habit of yielding to Elizabeth's whims when he felt it would cost him little to do so.

'What do you make of it, Harry?' he murmured. There was no need to clarify his question; there was but one topic of conversation at court this February.

'That it is a quicksand bog in truth and any man willing to venture into it had best be cat-sure of his footing. We both do know the Queen would never forgive anyone foolhardy enough to espouse Clarence's cause openly. But I can show you an even bigger fool and that is the man who urges the King to put Clarence to death . . . like our friend Thomas there.'

Will was amused but faintly impressed, too; Buckingham was making sense. 'Why is that?'

'Because I think the day may come when my cousin the King, whatever his reasons now, might regret very much that his brother did die at his command. And should that day come, he'll look around for others with whom to share his guilt.' A quick smile. 'Kings always do, you know. And on such a day, I would not want to be one who'd pressed for Clarence's death and then wore yellow when he died.'

'Cynical, are you not?'

'Realistic. And then, too. . . .'

'Yes?'

'I was merely thinking that if to plead for Clarence is to gain the Queen's ill will, to contrive at his death is to win an enemy no less dangerous.'

'Gloucester?'

'Yes . . . Gloucester.' And Buckingham nodded toward the doorway where Richard had entered, unnoticed, stood listening in frozen silence as Thomas Grey argued for the execution of his brother.

At that moment, Thomas, irked by Edward's lack of response,

said loudly, 'Has Your Grace forgotten how Clarence sought out soothsayers to learn the length of your reign? How he noised it about that upon your death the name of England's next King would begin with a G? G for George!'

'G for George? Why not G for Gloucester?'

Richard was no longer unnoticed. Conversation ceased. People began to circle closer, expectant, scenting blood, while others, more squeamish, edged away.

Thomas suddenly found himself alone. Taken aback that Richard should have chosen deliberately to call attention to so awkward a coincidence, he hesitated, watched Richard warily.

'G for Gloucester?' Richard repeated, unrelenting. 'Or even G . . . for Grey?'

Thomas whitened, whirling to make sure his stepfather was not heeding this heresy.

Edward's mouth was twitching. Now he began to laugh, thus freeing all others to do so, too. People began to murmur among themselves, most relishing Thomas Grey's discomfort.

As Richard moved toward him, Edward waved the others away. 'A nice thrust,' he grinned. 'But that was scarcely an even match.'

Richard shrugged. 'Ned, I want you to give me leave to see George. You cannot keep refusing. Not now, not when there is a death sentence hanging over his head.'

Edward's grin faded. 'Why in God's Grace would you want to subject yourself to that?' he asked slowly. 'Surely you do not expect a warm welcome? George loves you not, Dickon; have you forgotten?' He shook his head. 'No, such a meeting would serve for naught. I think it best that you do not.'

'You cannot mean that.' Richard was incredulous, no longer cared that conversation around them had stilled. 'You'd deny George even that much? You'd do that to him? Have him die believing that none of his own did even care enough to bid him farewell?' He drew a steadying breath, said with less intensity, 'You might well be right; I daresay it would be a most painful meeting. But if I am willing to chance it, you have not the right to forbid it.'

'You are wrong, Dickon,' Edward snapped. 'I do have that right and I choose to exercise it. Such a meeting would be neither in your interest nor in George's. Your request is denied.' And with that, he turned away, left Richard staring after him in stunned silence.

14

Westminster

February 1478

Dr Hobbys was already abed when the summons came from the King. Somewhat surprised by the request, for he could count on the fingers of one hand the times when Edward had wanted a sleeping draught, he hastily mixed up a potion of wine, poppy and dried bryony root and took it to the King's bedchamber. There the atmosphere was a subdued one; servants were tending to the hearth, turning back the coverlets, moving about as inconspicuously as possible. Dr Hobbys shared their unease; he, too, had heard of the King's quarrel earlier that evening with his brother Gloucester.

Edward's squires had already removed his doublet and were unbuttoning his shirt when an usher appeared in the doorway. For a moment or so, he shifted uncertainly from foot to foot and then approached Dr Hobbys, murmured a few words in the doctor's ear. Dr Hobbys gave the man a startled look and then hesitantly cleared his throat.

'My liege . . .' He coughed, began again. 'My liege, an audience is most urgently desired by your. . . .'

Edward's head jerked around. 'I'll see no one at this hour.'

'But Your Grace, it is. . . .'

'Did you not hear me? I do not care who it is. No one . . . no one at all.'

Dr Hobbys fidgeted, fervently wished himself elsewhere. Yet the information he'd been given could not be withheld. 'But my liege, it is your lady mother.'

There was a sudden silence, broken by a cry of pain, quickly cut off; one of the grooms of the chamber had been lighting candles, held his hand a moment too long to the flame. His comrades exchanged surreptitious glances, prudently kept very still. Even the squire kneeling at Edward's feet froze; the hand that had been reaching up to untie the points of Edward's hose went limp, fell to his side.

'Get out. All of you.' It was spoken in a low voice, without emphasis or inflection, but no man in the chamber waited to be told twice. Abandoning their labours, they fled.

'I have no choice, ma mère. How often must I tell you that? What would you have me do? Overlook his treason, the innocent blood on his hands? Would you truly have me mock justice because he's my brother?'

'George's sins shall not go unpunished; he will have much to answer for come Judgment Day. I do think of you, Edward, as much as George when I entreat you to consider what you mean to do. Have you forgotten what Our Lord Jesus Christ did reply when Peter asked of him, "Lord, how often shall my brother sin against me and I forgive him? As many as seven times?" His answer was, "I do not say to you seven times but seventy times seven."'

Edward's mouth tightened; with difficulty he bit back an oath. 'This serves for naught, Madame,' he said coldly, 'and we both do know it.'

He suddenly found himself looking into eyes of grey ice, eyes capable of stripping away the trappings of adulthood and re-establishing the priorities and vulnerabilites of forgotten youthful yesterdays.

'Have I been dismissed, Your Grace?' she queried, with a cold-ness to equal his own, and he capitulated.

'No, of course not, ma mère. Surely you know that would never be a command you'd hear from my lips.'

He wasn't prepared for what she did next. She was dressed in an unadorned starkly simple gown of ink-blue, so dark as to be almost black, one he thought to be uncomfortably close to mourning garb; her still-slender waist was girdled by a narrow silk-braided belt, from which hung a rosary, a ring of keys and a small leather pouch. It was to this pouch that she was now directing her attention, drawing forth a folded square of yellowed paper.

'In those weeks after your father and brother died at Sandal Castle, I had only faith to sustain me, my faith in the Almighty and my faith in you, Edward. You gave me such reason for pride. . . . The way you kept your head, rallied your men like the most seasoned battle commander, acted to ransom Rob Apsall, that young knight who was Edmund's friend. Above all, because you thought to write letters of comfort to your little brothers and sister . . . and to me. This is that letter, the one you wrote to me.' She held it out toward him; he recoiled, drew back a step.

'For seventeen years, I've kept it, cherished it, Edward. Now I do want you to read it. To read what you told me, that there are family ties not even death can destroy. You spoke of the love you bore me, the love you bore your brothers and sisters. And you swore a solemn vow that you'd let no harm befall us, that you'd always be there for us. Go on, take it. . . .'

Edward found himself staring, not at the outstretched letter but at the hand holding it. He could see delicately webbed blue veins, see the swelling at the knuckles, the slight tremor that defied a once invincible will; it was not his mother's hand, was the thin fragile hand of an aging stranger. He refused to reach for the letter, refused to take it and at last she laid it on the table.

'You must not do this, Edward. You must not spill your brother's blood. For your own soul's sake, you must not.'

He clamped his jaw till it ached, kept silent, and she then made the plea he most dreaded.

'For me,' she said. 'If not for George, do it for me.'

She crossed swiftly to him and, for an appalled instant, he feared she meant to kneel to him. She was, however, a woman to kneel willingly only to God and she merely reached out, laid her hand upon his wrist.

'Have I ever asked anything of you? Have I, Edward?'

'No,' he said shortly, unwillingly.

'I do ask you now, ask you for the life of my son.'

She was close enough for him to see that her eyes, eyes that could burn through bone to the very soul, were now awash in tears. The shock of that realization was almost physical; he could not remember ever having seen his mother cry.

'If it is not enough for you that George is your brother, spare his life for me, Edward. . . . For me.'

'Ma mère . . .' He found that his voice was husky, uneven. 'Ma mère, I . . . I cannot. . . .'

She closed her eyes; for a moment, her fingers tightened on his arm, clung. And then she released him, stepped back.

He could clearly hear her breathing; she sounded as if she'd been running. His own breathing was equally laboured. As he watched, the tears on her lashes suddenly broke free, began to streak her face, splashed silently upon the collar of her gown; she blinked but made no attempt to wipe them away. Her fingers were tumbling at her belt, instinctively seeking the solace of rosary beads and, at that, he took a step toward her. As he did, her head came up.

'I would see him, Edward.'

It was no request; he knew it to be an ultimatum. He shook his head violently, not trusting his voice.

Time passed. She was staring at him, saying nothing, and on her face was a look of stunned disbelief, an anguished accusation he knew would haunt him for the rest of his life.

But when she spoke, her voice held no hint of tears. It was not a voice to offer either understanding or absolution, spoke of no quarter given, of a lifetime of love denied.

'God may forgive you for this,' she said, very slowly and distinctly, 'but I never shall.'

Rob Apsall was dreaming of a stream that flowed with Madeira and hippocras, of a pretty girl who flung herself down laughing beside the bank to drink from its depths. But in the far reaches of the dream thunder had begun to echo ominously. As it grew louder, he began to twitch, until his eyes at last flew open and his groggy senses identified the thunder as a muffled, steady banging. Rob swore sleepily; this had been his thirty-ninth birthday, one celebrated with enjoyable excesses of food and drink, and his head was dull, still fuzzy with wine. Beside him, his wife stirred, lay still again. Above the pounding he heard the chiming of bells; the black friars of the neighbouring Dominican friary were being summonded to Matins. The banging was louder now, sounding as if someone were hammering incessantly for admittance. But who would be coming to his door at two o'clock of a Sunday morning? He sat upright, strained to hear.

'Rob?' Amy was yawning. 'What is that clatter?'

By now Rob was out of bed, unlatching the shutters. He peered down into pelting rain and blackness and then gasped.

'Holy Jesus! There are men-at-arms below.'

He was still pulling on his boots when he heard the footsteps pounding up the stairs. A moment later the steward of his household burst into the bedchamber. He was as dishevelled as Rob and no less agitated.

'Sir Robert, there are men below from the King!'

Rob hadn't known what he was expecting but surely not this. He sat down abruptly, the second boot forgotten. 'The King? Why should the King send soldiers to my house in the middle of the night?'

'They say you are to come with them, Sir Robert. That the King has sent them to take you back to Westminster.' The steward was still panting; he'd taken the steps two at a time and he was not a young man. 'I did ask them if you . . . if you were under arrest. They said they did not know, had only been told to fetch you to the King.'

'Rob! God in Heaven, Rob, what. . . .' Amy had scrambled out of bed, haphazardly clutching a sheet to conceal her nakedness. 'Why should the King summon you at such an hour? Rob, what have you done that you have not told me?'

'Nothing! Nothing, Amy, I do swear it.' Rob shook his head desperately to clear it, cursing himself for all the wine flagons he'd drained that night, for the refusal of his dazed wits to take this all in.

'I do not know what the King wants of me.' His heart had begun to hammer painfully against his ribs. 'God's truth, I do not.'

Rob's eyes were adjusting to the dark of the room enough for him to make out the shadowy figure of the man sitting at a round three-legged table. Rob was not normally timorous but so far there'd been nothing remotely normal about the events of this night. Cautiously he groped his way toward Edward. But as he started to kneel, Edward shoved a chair toward him, said with impatience, 'Do you think I give a damn about court protocol at this hour? Sit down.'

Rob did as he was told. Edward's back was to the fire, his face in shadows. Rob waited and then said diffidently, 'My liege, I do not understand. Why am I here? Am I . . . am I under arrest?'

There was a wine flagon at Edward's elbow. He reached for it, saying, 'No, you're not under arrest. Here, have a drink.' The flagon shot across the table; Rob grabbed it just in time to keep it from going into his lap.

His fear should logically have been much lessened; it wasn't. There was a tension in this chamber, a dark strain he didn't understand, but dimly he sensed it was dangerous.

'I did want to talk to you,' Edward was saying now, and this time Rob caught the slight slurring of speech. 'Go on, drink.'

'I'm at Your Grace's service,' Rob began, but Edward cut him off with a gutter oath.

'Shit,' he said, reaching over to reclaim the flagon. 'Did I not tell you to forget ceremony? Loosen up, man. I'm no tyrant; I do not drink the blood of innocents or amuse myself by raping virgins. So why then do you sit there with a face the colour of cheese and eyes like a sheep bound for the slaughter?'

Rob could have told him that it was not conducive to ease of manner to be dragged out of bed in the middle of the night by men willing to say only that they came in the King's name. Struggling with a growing sense of unreality, he contented himself with a mild confession, saying, 'The truth of it is that I was in my cups this night and my head feels like to burst.'

He saw at once that such candour was the best response he could have made. Edward gave an abrupt laugh, much like a cough.

'Here,' he said, 'then you do need this more than me,' sending the flagon back across the table. As Rob hesitated, not seeing how he dare share the same flagon with the King, Edward leaned toward him, said unexpectedly, 'I want you to tell me about Edmund.'

Rob gaped at him. 'Edmund?'

'You do remember my brother Edmund?' Edward snapped, in a startling shift of mood that left Rob speechless. 'The one who died on Wakefield Bridge.' Adding with stinging sarcasm, 'I daresay it will come back to you if you do put your mind to it.'

Once as a youngster, Rob had nearly drowned while skating at Moorfields; the ice had cracked without warning, gave way under him as he scrambled for shore. He felt that way now.

'I would have you tell me,' Edward said, 'about how he died.'

Rob swallowed, beginning to wonder just how drunk the other man was. 'My liege, I . . . I did tell you that in much painful detail some seventeen years ago.'

'I've not forgotten.' Edward's voice was flat and, to Rob, full of foreboding. 'But I would hear it again.'

Rob decided there must be more to this than an excess of wine. Much more. 'What you do ask of me is most difficult,' he said slowly, feeling his way by instinct alone. 'Even after all these years, I do not find it easy to speak of what happened on Wakefield Bridge. . . .'

Edward shifted in his chair and for the first time the flames from the hearth brought his face into sudden focus. Rob saw enough for his mouth to go dry. He understood now that Edward was drinking to blot out pain and some of his fear and resentment yielded to sympathy. He must still tread with great care, of course. Any man as deeply troubled as this was apt to be erratic in his temper, to lash out at the slightest provocation. And Edward . . . Edward was his King; he could no more forget that than he could hope to fly. But Edward had been right in claiming that he was no tyrant. He'd never been one to take pleasure in the abuse of power. And he had loved Edmund, too.

Rob looked down at the table in faint embarrassment, reluctant to gaze upon another's nakedness of spirit. He didn't know Edward well but he did know Edward was not one to reveal to others what showed on his face tonight.

'I'll have that drink now.' This time he took it from Edward with no hesitation, not yielding up the flagon until his eyes began to smart and his head to swim. Setting the flagon down then, he began to search for words, began haltingly to speak of Edmund.

Edward was slumped low in his chair, one hand raised to shield his eyes against the greying light seeking entry at every window.

817

Rob had risen to stretch, saw with weary wonderment that the sky was streaking in the east.

Glancing back at Edward, his gaze fell upon the empty wine flagon that lay under the table.

'We did finish the last of the flagons, Your Grace. Shall I summon a servant to fetch us another?'

Edward winced. 'God, no!' he said, with such distaste that Rob grinned.

'There is something you can do for me, though, Rob. See yon coffer? I want a casket that is stored inside it.'

Rob had no difficulty in finding the casket but, at sight of it, he stiffened slightly. It was an iron box meant to store valuables, to bank coins of silver and gold.

It was not that Rob did not feel himself entitled to be compensated for this, the most bizarre night of his life; he most emphatically did. He balked, however, at so blatant a payment as this. He was, after all, a knight, a man of rank, not a lowborn servant to be dismissed with a handful of coins.

But Edward was not reaching into the casket for the expected pouchful of angels and half royals. Instead, he was lifting up an elaborately crafted ruby pendant. Under Rob's awestruck eyes, the stone spun in a slow shimmering circle, seemed always to be turning toward the light.

'I would like your wife to accept this, with my apologies for disrupting her sleep and borrowing her husband.'

'She'll cherish it ever, Your Grace.' Rob carefully secreted the pendant away within his clothing. He should have known better, in truth he should. . . . Whatever Edward's faults, he was no fool, was too shrewd knowingly to disparage the value of another man's dignity.

Edward was raising a fist to stifle a yawn; he looked haggard, hungover and years older than thirty-five. Rob still didn't know what devils had driven Edward into seeking out the dubious comfort of his company. But memories of a youth long dead had proven to be an effective bridge between sovereign and subject. So strong was Rob's sense of exhausted intimacy, in fact, that he now felt free to ask candidly, 'Your Grace . . . did I help at all?'

Edward glanced up, gave a tired smile, but he didn't answer.

There was a folded paper on the floor, almost at Rob's feet. Stooping, he discovered it was a letter, much handled and discoloured with age.

'This seems to have fallen to the floor, my liege. I think it a personal letter. Do you want it?'

Edward shook his head. 'No,' he said. 'Throw it in the fire.'

15

London

February 1478

'Richard? Not that I want to rush you, love, but cobwebs are forming on your pawn.'

Richard started, looked down at the chessboard as if he'd never seen it before, and Anne sighed. It was not true that all roads led to Rome. These days, all roads led to the Tower.

'There is no fun in winning by default,' she chided, torn between impatience and understanding. 'Why do we not move over onto the settle? I'll read to you, if you like. That way' —she smiled to take the sting out— 'you can brood in peace and I'll pretend you are listening.'

Fetching a book Richard had only recently acquired, *The Romance of Tristan de Leonnais*, Anne resumed reading where she'd last left off, as Richard settled down comfortably with his head in her lap. She'd only read half a page, however, when one of their servants knocked on the solar door.

'I know it's late for callers, my lord, but there is a gentleman asking for an audience. He'd not give his name, but he did give me this. . . .' Holding out a sealed paper.

Before Richard could respond, he hurried into an unasked-for, uncomfortable explanation. 'I realize this is most irregular, Your Grace, but I did not feel I should turn him away. He's a man with the habit of command and I do not doubt for a moment that he is a personage of rank, a lord. . . .'

Richard's curiosity won out. He reached for the paper and his servant withdrew, looking quite pleased with himself.

Richard watched him go. Then he broke the seal, saying dryly, 'I suspect what Alan really means is that yon nameless stranger made it worth his while to deliver this message.' But as he scanned the few lines written in barely legible French, his expression changed. Looking up at Anne, he said, 'I shall have to see him, ma belle.'

'What is it, Richard?' Anne was frowning; instinct told her that a mystery caller on a night errand was not likely to be the bearer of good tidings.

He shook his head. 'I'm as much in the dark as you, Anne. But Alan was right in assuming he was dealing with a lord. With a Duke, in fact. . . . My cousin Buckingham.'

Because he wore clothes well and had the means to indulge his taste, Harry Stafford had a wardrobe even Edward might envy. Anne and Richard were surprised, therefore, at sight of him now. Gone were the gem-studded velvets, the flamboyant sun-colour satins; he was muffled, instead, in a hooded cloak of some nondescript colour midst black and brown. And he was alone, startling in itself, for he was not a man to move about the city without considerable ceremony and a sizable retinue.

Greetings exchanged, he wasted no time in coming to the point.

'It is good of you to see me at such an hour, cousin. I expect you're rather curious as to my reasons for calling . . . incognito, as it were.'

Drawing off his gloves, he warmed his hands at the hearth before favouring Anne with a brilliant smile.

'But I'd not have it said that I bored so lovely a lady with dull talk of business matters. Nor need you fret, sweet Cousin Anne. I'll not keep your lord long; on that, you've my word.'

Anne stiffened. She knew, of course, that there were men who'd no more think to include their women in political discussions than they would their dogs. But she was luckier than many wives, had never been treated by Richard as if she were incapable of serious thought. She found herself feeling a touch of pity for Buckingham's Woodville wife, feeling, too, a debt of gratitude to her remarkable mother-in-law. A debt also owed by Elizabeth and even Isabel, for no son of Cecily Neville could ever think of women as mere brainless broodmares.

She was too well mannered to offend a guest in her home. But she had no intention of being dismissed from her own solar like an errant child. She glanced over at Richard, only to see that he was amused, both by Buckingham's condescension and her indignation. But he redeemed himself fully in her eyes a moment later by saying pointedly, 'I have no secrets from my wife, Harry.'

Buckingham's eyebrows shot upward. But if he was annoyed, he kept it well hidden and yielded with apparent ease. 'I confess, cousin, I do envy you in that. To have found a wife as faithful as she is fair. . . .' He nodded gallantly toward Anne and at once forgot her, leaning toward Richard.

'Jesú knows I'm not one to be often tongue-tied; to the contrary, I've been told that I do talk even in my sleep. But now I do find it surprisingly difficult to begin. You see, I'm breaking a vow I made to myself long ago. . . . Never to meddle in matters not of my personal concern.'

821

'This matter of which you speak . . . I assume it does concern me?'

'Very much so. Your brother Clarence has been living in the shadow of the axe these ten days past, as you well know. I think you should also know that tomorrow the axe is to fall.'

It should not have come as a surprise; but it did. The longer Edward delayed, the easier Richard had found it to hope. Now he said, rather sharply, 'How do you know that?'

Buckingham shrugged. 'I have friends in unlikely places. But that's not important. There is this you should know. On the morrow, Will Alyngton, Speaker of the Commons, does plan to petition the king to have Clarence's death sentence carried out.' He paused.

'If you wonder why he should of a sudden be so hot to hasten Clarence to God, the answer is what you might expect. Gold can buy much, it seems. And, in truth, it is a right clever scheme, with credit where due to Madame the Queen.' His smile was sardonic. 'For ten days Clarence has been teetering on the edge of the grave. I suspect Alyngton's petition will provide the final push. She's giving the king the excuse he seems to need, making Clarence's execution a response to public demand. Yes . . . very clever, indeed.'

Richard came to his feet, stood for a moment looking down at Buckingham. He'd been acquainted with the younger man for most of his life but he didn't know Buckingham well at all, had never had any but the most superficial social contact with him until this night.

'I do thank you,' he said, 'for telling me of this, Harry. It was the act of a friend, one I'll not forget.'

Buckingham's eyes focused on Richard with sudden sharp intensity, gold-flecked eyes, as inscrutable as a cat's. 'Good luck,' he said. 'I fear you'll be needing it.'

These past ten days had been among the worst of Elizabeth's life. Watching as Edward stalled, found excuse after excuse to delay

George's execution, she began to question his resolve, to fear he might not be able to go through with it. She'd always detested the Duchess of York, disliked Richard. Now she hated them both, hated them for the unrelenting pressure they were putting on Edward, for the chance they might succeed. Again and again, she told herself that her fears were groundless, that Ned had no choice; George had to die. But she knew Ned was racking his brain for another way, a way of silencing George short of murder, and this frightened her all the more. Ned was the most intelligent man she'd ever known; if there was such a way, he just might find it.

But now she had the leverage she needed. When Alyngton did publicly call for George's death, that would force Ned's hand; she was sure of it. What worried her were these hours still to go till the morrow, her fear that Ned might somehow be swayed by a last-minute appeal. To keep this from happening, she'd resolved to stay by his side, had come unbidden to his bedchamber. Relations between them were still too strained to depend solely on sex; instead, she'd brought their youngest son, a gravely good-natured child not yet a year old. It was well past his bedtime, of course, but he had just begun to walk and it served as the perfect pretext, showing Ned his son's prowess and reminding him, too, just who had the most to lose.

Edward greeted his son with his usual exuberance, hugging and tossing the little boy up into the air till the child shrieked with laughter. But as he knelt down to watch the youngster toddle toward him, he raised his eyes to Elizabeth.

'You,' he said evenly, 'are as subtle as a runaway wagon.'

Elizabeth reached down to steady her son. 'I have not the faintest idea what you mean.'

'The devil you do not.' But he was smiling and, after a moment, Elizabeth smiled, too, albeit tartly.

'Subtlety,' she admitted, 'is a luxury I can no longer afford.'

She was beginning to relax somewhat; the cramped knots in her stomach no longer churned in spasms of nervous foreboding.

It was then that she glanced up to see Richard standing in the doorway.

She felt, at first, fury that he should dare to enter unannounced, rage that none had thought to stop him, that it should be taken for granted that he had the right. But then the fear came back, the sudden certainty that this would be the time when Ned would heed his plea, would agree to pardon Clarence.

Edward released the baby, straightened up slowly.

'I do want to talk with you, Ned.' Richard had yet to acknowledge Elizabeth's presence, a rudeness she hadn't expected from him; until now, their relationship had always been icily correct.

'Alone,' he added, and only then did he look at his brother's Queen, a long measuring look that was as insulting as anything he could have said.

Elizabeth caught her breath and then found herself fighting an hysterical urge to laugh. So this was to be the way of it. In ridding herself of Clarence, she was only exchanging the enmity of one brother for that of the other. Her heart began to beat uncomfortably fast. Clarence . . . Clarence had great wealth, but Gloucester had something more dangerous, a power base of his own. Lord of the North he was . . . just like Warwick. Warwick, who'd come so close to bringing them all to ruin.

Beside her, she felt her son tug at her skirt. No, she'd not think of this now, not of Warwick who was dead or Gloucester who might prove to be a more dangerous enemy than Clarence. Gloucester, who was not the fool his brother was, who had Ned's trust. But no . . . not now. Clarence knew and Gloucester did not, and that made Clarence the greater threat. The one to be dealt with now. Nothing else mattered. Let Ned see that—oh, God, do not let him listen. . . .

Edward suddenly caught the fragrance of rosemary, knew without looking that Elizabeth had come to stand at his side.

'No, Dickon,' he said quietly. 'I think not. We've said it all.'

So great was Elizabeth's gratitude that she was momentarily

speechless, could only give Edward a smile that was radiant with relief. And for Richard, that smile illuminated a lifetime of stored-up grievances. He stared at her, not seeing the beauty that had won his brother's heart, not seeing in her any qualities of queen-ship. Had Ned not been bewitched by this woman, he thought bitterly, Johnny Neville need not have died. Nor Warwick. Anne would never have been bartered to Lancaster. And George would not now be in the Tower.

'My congratulations, Madame. It's not every husband who'd sacrifice his own blood to gratify a wife's whims. You must be very pleased with yourself.'

Elizabeth's eyes glittered; colour crimsoned across her cheek-bones. But Edward was quicker than she.

'Have a care, Dickon. I'll let no man speak ill of my wife, not even you. Lisbet bears no share of George's guilt. His treason was very much his own.'

'Let's talk about that . . . about George's treason. You're seven years late, Ned. That debt's no longer good. You had cause then, but not now. George is a fool, a trouble-maker, and possibly a drunkard, but he's no traitor. By rights, he should be in Bedlam under care, not in the Tower under guard. And you do know that fully as well as I. So do not lie to me, Ned. No more talk of treason. If George is to die, I have the right to know why. You do owe me that much.'

'I owe you nothing. George has been tried and found guilty of treason. The penalty for treason is death. And that is all I'll say on it, now or ever.'

Elizabeth was no fool; she knew she should keep her mouth shut. But the temptation to retaliate was too strong.

'There's something I would say though, Ned. I would hear your brother explain why he thinks treason to be so negligible an offence. I cannot help thinking that his curious lack of concern for Clarence's betrayals does call his own loyalty into question!'

'I was wondering when you'd get around to that,' Richard

snapped. Swinging back toward Edward. 'Tell me, Ned, what else does she seek? Will you mount George's head on Drawbridge Gate to please her? I understand the sight of our brother Edmund's head on Micklegate Bar did greatly please Marguerite d'Anjou.'

Edward had gone very white. 'Enough, Richard!' For the first time in his life, calling his brother by his given name. 'You'd best hold your tongue . . . for your own sake.'

But Richard was beyond caring. 'And if I do not?'

'You'll regret it, I do promise you. More than you could ever imagine.'

'What do you have in mind? A stay in the Tower, perhaps?'

'Yes, if need be!'

Suddenly there was only silence in the chamber. An absolute unnatural quiet that rubbed raw against the nerves of the three adults and at last affected even the baby. He began to whimper, buried his face in Elizabeth's skirt. She reached down, absent-mindedly patted his head, all the while keeping her eyes upon Edward. He was ashen, now sat down abruptly in the nearest chair.

'Blood of Christ,' he said incredulously, 'what are we saying to each other?'

Richard shook his head, said nothing. He, too, had been deeply shaken, and it showed.

'Dickon, listen to me. Can you not see the futility of this? How dangerous it is? We're goading each other to say what we do not mean, what we may not be able to forget. George is not worth it, Dickon. He just is not worth it.'

Richard's emotions were in turmoil. He was twenty-five and since the age of eight, all he'd known of security had been what his brother had given him, his sense of self becoming inextricably entwined within the ties that bound him to Edward, ties he'd thought forever beyond breaking. Suddenly the ground had shifted under him, leaving half-truths and unease where certainties had been rooted deep. He needed time to come to terms with what had happened in this chamber tonight, and he said now, in a voice that was very low and very strained, 'I think it would be best if I leave.'

Edward looked up quickly. After a pause that was almost imperceptible, he nodded. But as Richard reached the door, he could keep silent no longer, said with sudden passion, 'You're a fool, Dickon. God help you, lad, but you are. George does not deserve your loyalty.'

Richard turned at that. For a long moment he regarded Edward, eyes smoky and opaque. 'Do you?' he asked softly.

16

Tower of London
February 1478

On the wall above his bed were ten large crosses, smeared in charcoal with an unsteady hand. George counted them carefully, one for each of the days he'd lived under sentence of death. He'd made something of a ritual of it, lining them up in equal rows, not ever adding a cross until after sundown. So what he did now was startlingly at variance with past habit. For more than an hour, he'd lain motionless on the bed, gazing up at the grimy finger-smudged wall. Suddenly he sat up, swung off the bed. The stick he used as a marker lay on the floor by the brazier of hot coals. Snatching it up, he thrust it into the ashes and knelt on the bed to draw a defiantly lopsided cross twice the size of the others.

For a moment, his face reflected satisfaction but, as he stared at it, superstition began to reassert itself. It was only noon. Should he so tempt providence? He raised his fist to obliterate the cross, stopped in midair. Was it not worse to cancel it out now? What better way to invite ill luck than that? Back and forth his thoughts warred uneasily and at last he resolved his qualms as he did everything these days, by reaching down for the wine flagon.

In some ways, these ten days had been easier than the preceding four months, for with his death sentence had come an easing of his confinement. Once more he had access to the wine cellar of the Herber. Whatever he wanted, he was given, as often as he wished, and if he could never manage to drink himself into complete blankness, he was never completely sober, either.

Setting the flagon down in the floor rushes, he closed his eyes. Night and day had little meaning for him now and he snatched at sleep whenever it would come. That the chamber was ablaze with torches did not bother him at all; darkness bothered him far more. He craved candles even more than wine, filled the chamber with rush and cresset lights, with candelabras and wick lamps, yet still the corners provided sanctuary for shadows, gave refuge to the fears that not even malmsey could always keep at bay.

He was awakened a short time later by a hand gently yet insistently shaking his shoulder. Opening his eyes, he blinked up in astonishment at the resplendent figure leaning over the bed, an apparition garbed in purple cassock, flowing silk cope. As wine-bedazed as his brain was, he was at first hesitant to accept the evidence of his own senses; too often upon awakening, he found his chamber peopled by ghosts. But as he stared up at the tense, pinched face under the jewelled mitre, recognition flickered. He was not dreaming. There really was a bishop bending over him. One, moreover, whom he knew.

'Stillington?' Uncertainly at first and then with dawning excitement. 'I'll be damned, it is you. Sweet Jesus, but it is good to see you ... to see anyone!' He struggled upright with some difficulty but his smile was dazzling. 'How did you get by Ned's lackeys? You cannot imagine how I've yearned for someone to talk with. . . .'

'Your Grace,' Stillington interrupted hastily, unable to bear being greeted as a friend. 'You . . . you do not understand.' He swallowed, looked about for some place to sit and at last lowered himself onto the edge of the bed next to George.

'I'm here at the King's behest,' he said quietly. 'He did send me to you, my lord . . . so that you might hear Mass and make confession, so you'd not go unshriven to God.' As he spoke, he was studiously staring down into his lap, so he'd not have to watch when the meaning of his words registered with George. Once, as a young priest, he'd given absolution to a condemned man and the memory had haunted him for years. But this was infinitely worse.

When he could avoid looking up no longer, he chanced a sideways glance at the other man. Months of enforced sobriety had stripped away the excess flesh of George's drink-sodden summer. The hair slanting across his forehead was the shade of spun gold; the eyes meeting Stillington's own were a brilliant blue-green and had in them the stunned uncomprehending look of a child. Stillington, who nurtured no illusions whatsoever about George, was, nonetheless, moved almost to tears, and he, who was neither handsome nor young, could only wonder why it was that tragedy seemed somehow worse when it struck at those favoured with both youth and beauty. So sharp was his pity that it unsettled him, struck a vein of superstitious unease. So, he reminded himself, must Lucifer have looked before the Fall.

George had yet to move, still sprawled on the bed looking up at him. From his belt Stillington unfastened a rosary of ebony and coral, held it out toward the younger man.

'With the king's permission, I did go this morn to your lady mother. It was her most fervent wish that you do have this. It was once your father's, does come from the Blessed Shrine of St James at Compostella.'

829

George made no move to take it. Stillington hesitated and then realized he had it in his power to right a wrong.

'She did plead for you, my lord. So did your brother Gloucester and your sisters of Suffolk and Burgundy. You must not think they were uncaring of your plight. It was the King's command that did keep them away. . . .' His words trailed off; he wasn't sure George was even listening.

Stillington sought feverishly to call to mind the traditional words of comfort, words a priest could utter to soothe troubled souls, to ease earthly anguish and turn thoughts toward the here-after. But the training of a lifetime availed him little; he was hope-lessly hobbled by his own guilt.

George moved so suddenly that Stillington flinched. Lurching unsteadily to his feet, he dropped to his knees by the bed, and Stillington felt a lump rising in his throat that he should so shame-fully fail one in need of all the spiritual solace mortal man could provide. But then he saw that George did not mean to pray; he was kneeling to retrieve a wine flagon.

As Stillington watched in shocked disapproval, George tilted the flagon back, swallowed until he choked. He sputtered, spilled wine on the bed, on himself, and then drank deeply again. At first scandalized that a man should go besotted to his Maker, Stillington found himself taking a more charitable view as he watched. Did he truly want to deny George the numbing mercies of malmsey? No, he decided, he did not.

It was then that he remembered he did have a means of giving comfort.

'I can ease your mind as to your children, my lord,' he said, brightening. 'Even though you've been attainted, the King does not mean to deprive your heirs of their inheritance. He did promise me that they'll be well cared for, that he shall still bestow the earldom of Warwick upon your son.'

George lowered the flagon to stare at him and then he stunned Stillington by bursting into wild peals of uncontrolled convulsive laughter. 'You poor pious fool,' he gasped. 'That's supposed to give me comfort? You think that does make it all right?'

Stillington's pity curdled, went suddenly sour. 'I have just assured you that your son and daughter shall not suffer for your sins,' he said stiffly. 'For most men, my lord, that would count for much.'

George drained the flagon, flung it from him with sudden raging violence. It smashed into the far wall with such force that it shattered upon impact, rained broken glass into all corners of the room. Stillington gasped as a jagged fragment whizzed by his cheek, squeezed Cecily Neville's rosary until his fingers cramped.

'Why should I believe you? How do I know Ned is not seeking merely to scare me? He has my titles, my lands. . . . Why should he take my life, too?'

'My lord. . . . My lord, do not delude yourself with false hope. There is none; not since that evil accursed moment when you so rashly let the name of Nell Butler pass your lips. . . .' Stillington stopped abruptly; his mouth dropped.

'Mother of God, you did not know!'

George looked dazed. He sank down on the bed, shook his head. 'What that priest wrote . . . it was true, then? And that is why Ned does mean to. . . . Oh, Jesus!' He tasted salt on his lips, realized he'd begun to sweat. And then his eyes slitted and Stillington shrank back before his fury.

'You told Ned, told him about my questions. It was you who did betray me.'

'No, my lord, I did not. I ought to have gone to the King as soon as you did approach me but I did not. My fear kept me silent. Would that it had done the same for you.'

'How . . . how then?'

'You did betray yourself, my lord,' Stillington said, more gently. 'When the King first imprisoned you last summer, you drank to excess, and when you drank, you talked . . . most unwisely. Eventually your drunken babblings reached the ear of the Queen.'

George slumped back on the bed. 'All these months,' he

whispered, 'I did not realize. . . . And because I did not, I never believed Ned would do it. . . .'

Stillington averted his eyes. He had one more unpleasant task to perform before he could hear George's confession, the duty he'd been most dreading.

'My lord. . . . The King has authorized me to . . . to offer you a choice. . . .'

George said nothing, stared at him with eyes that were glazed and unseeing.

'You do . . . understand?' Stillington stammered, hating Edward for forcing this upon him, hating Nell Butler who was dead—above all, hating himself for his weakness, for a secret he'd never wanted to know.

'I've always heard that drowning is an easy death,' he said softly.

Silence filled the chamber. After some interminable seconds, Stillington reached out, took George's hand. It was hot and sticky with wine. His fingers lay limp, unresisting as Stillington put the rosary into his palm and gently closed the slack fingers around it.

Elizabeth stood motionless in the doorway, listening as Edward gave instructions for his brother's funeral. '. . . . and his body is to be taken to Tewkesbury, to be there buried with all due honours. Inform Abbot John. And have word sent to my mother, to my brother Gloucester and to my sister, the Duchess of Suffolk, so that they might attend the funeral if they so wish.'

Elizabeth didn't move for some moments after the others left the chamber, stayed where she was until Edward glanced up and saw her there.

'And what may I do for you, my darling? Let me guess . . . You've come to dance on George's grave?'

Elizabeth was too appalled to be angry, hearing in his words the death knell of their marriage. She stumbled toward him, fell to her knees beside his chair.

'Do not say that, Ned, not to me. You cannot blame me for Clarence's death. You could not be that unfair; you know you could not.'

He looked as tired as she'd ever seen him, his eyes heavy-lidded and hooded, the muscles of his mouth rigid, forbidding. But as he listened, she saw it soften slightly.

'No. . . . No, I could not. You're right and I'm sorry, Lisbet. I do not blame you, in truth I do not.' The corner of his mouth twisted upward, counterfeiting a smile. 'I would to God I could! But I do know better; it is one of life's little ironies that I do lie convincingly to everyone but myself.'

Elizabeth rose, perched on the arm of his chair and sought to work the tension from his neck and shoulders with her fingers. He leaned back, closing his eyes.

'George gave Stillington a message for me. He said to tell me that he'd see me in Hell!' He laughed; it was not a pleasant sound. 'I daresay he's right.'

'That's nothing to jest about,' Elizabeth said reprovingly.

Edward shifted in the chair, said bemusedly, 'It is passing strange. My reluctance, my regrets were for ma mère, Meg, Dickon. Not for George. Yet I did dream about him last night. Can you credit that, Lisbet? And damn me if else, but in the dream he was no more than ten . . . if even that. . . .'

Elizabeth's urgency was such that she could spare no time now to indulge him. There was more at stake than his ease of conscience.

'What of Stillington, Ned?'

'No!' He was on his feet so abruptly that he came close to dumping her onto the floor.

'Ned, he knows!'

'I said no! I'll not murder that old man!'

They glared at each other, locked into a duel of wills all the more hostile for the intimacy of their antagonism. Elizabeth's eyes were the first to waver; she changed tactics, said earnestly,

'Ned, you do not think I want it that way, do you? But we've no choice. When you die, what if he were to come forward, tell what he knows? We cannot take that chance.'

'Holy Christ, woman, he's nigh on sixty and in ailing health.' Edward shook his head in disgust. 'By the time I depart this world, he'll be years dead and long forgotten. You're letting your fears lay waste to your common sense.'

'I do not trust him,' she insisted stubbornly, saw his mouth harden again.

'Well, I do,' he snapped. 'He's held his tongue for fifteen years, has he not? Why should he betray me now? No, Lisbet, I'll not put to death a man who's given me nothing but loyalty. Nor have I forgotten that he is a priest, even if you have.'

'At least, will you not make sure he realizes what he does have to lose? At least, do that much for me, Ned . . . for me and for your sons. Name of God, please!'

He was frowning, but he nodded grudgingly. 'All right. I'll do what I can to . . . put the fear of God into him. But no more than that, Lisbet. I put George to death because I had no choice, but I'll not have Stillington's blood on my hands, too. Not when there's no need for it. And I'll not have him harmed.' He stared down at her with eyes like ice, said in unmistakable warning, 'Be sure you do bear that in mind . . . dear wife.'

On February 25th, George was laid to rest beside his wife in a vault behind the High Altar at Tewkesbury's Abbey of St Mary the Virgin. His estates were confiscated, his wealth forfeit to the crown. Edward disregarded the Bill of Attainder and titled George's small son as Earl of Warwick; the earldom of Salisbury he bestowed upon Richard's little boy. Certain of George's lands were given to Anthony Woodville, other incomes went to Thomas Grey, but the bulk of his brother's estates Edward kept in his own hands. The wardship of his orphaned nephew, Edward gave to Thomas Grey.

A few weeks after George's execution, Robert Stillington, Bishop of Bath and Wells, was charged with uttering words 'prejudicial to the State', and committed to the Tower. He was kept there for three months and released in June upon reavowing his loyalty to the House of York, to the Yorkist King he'd so long ago pledged to serve.

17

Middleham

August 1478

Anne found her husband and son in the outer bailey gardens, staring down at a newly dug grave. It was, she thought, a wretched homecoming for Richard. He had been gone for fully a fortnight; his council had been asked to arbitrate a dispute between two villages in the West Riding and he'd returned only that past evening. Anne had hoped not to have to tell him right away but he'd missed Gareth at once, immediately wanted to know where the big dog was. It had come as no great surprise; Gareth was fourteen. But it was never easy to lose a loved pet.

Moving closer, Anne saw that Ned was pointing to the small headstone, with both pride and perplexity.

'Master Nicholas made it for me, papa. I wanted a wooden cross, but Kathryn says it is not fitting, Gareth being but a dog. . . .' Soft brown eyes waited anxiously for Richard's verdict.

'I think your sister may be right, Ned. But I'll tell you what. . . . Why do you not ask your mother if you can plant something here by the grave?' Richard smiled at his son. 'How about . . . dogwood? What could be more fitting than that?'

Catching sight of his mother, Ned ran to her, crying, 'Mama, may we plant dogwood on Gareth's grave? Please, mama?'

'I do not see why not.' Anne beckoned and a servant came forward, set a large woven basket on the ground in front of Ned.

'I know how much you miss Gareth, darling. He was your dog as much as your father's. But I have something for you both which might make his loss easier.' Bending down, she lifted the lid of the basket, revealed two squirming wolfhound puppies.

Ned gave a delighted squeal, started to reach for the black one and then reluctantly remembered the manners Mistress Burgh was constantly lecturing him about.

'Papa? Can I have this one?'

Richard knelt beside him, extending his fingers for the other puppy to lick. 'Whichever one you want, Ned.'

Seeing his brother emerging from the stables, Ned now gave a yell, beckoning eagerly. 'Look, Johnny! Look at my puppy!'

Johnny needed no urging. 'Puppies,' he breathed, with such yearning that Anne was stricken with remorse. God forgive her, why had she not thought of Johnny?

Richard, too, had seen the wistful look on his son's face. Picking up the second puppy, he held it out. 'Do you not want yours, Johnny?'

'Mine?' Johnny had gathered the puppy into his arms before doubt assailed him. 'Truly?'

'Of course. Why do you think there are two of them?'

That was so logical Johnny never thought to question it. But Anne saw an unmistakable look of surprise on Ned's face. He opened his mouth and she made ready to intercede. For a moment, he regarded the puppies with puzzled eyes and then he put his down on the ground.

'Let's show them the stable cats,' he proposed, and at once boys and puppies were racing pell-mell across the bailey.

Anne knew Richard was not comfortable with public displays of affection but now she flung her arms around his neck, kissed him soundly. 'That was most adroitly done, love. How could I ever have been so thoughtless? . . . But did you see how Ned held his tongue? I was so proud of him; he did not understand but sensed enough to. . . .' She broke off abruptly as Ned came running back toward them.

'Look, papa! Riders!'

The visitor was one always assured a warm welcome at Middleham—Thomas Wrangwysh. After exchanging greetings and giving orders for Wrangwysh to be fed in the great hall, Richard directed his attention to Wrangwysh's dispatches.

'What do they want of you, Richard?'

'It is from York's council. Holy Trinity Priory is in dire financial straits and they ask my help in alleviating its poverty.' There was a second message, as well, one that bore the Lord Mayor's seal.

Anne had been watching the boys and puppies chase each other about the bailey. Glancing back now at Richard, she took a quick step toward him.

'What is it? You do look so strange, Richard.'

He looked up from the letter. 'It seems,' he said slowly, 'that my brother is coming to York.'

Surrounded by clergy and city officials, Edward stood on the steps of the west door of St Peter's, awaiting his brother's entry into the precincts of the Minster. He was able to gauge Richard's progress up Stonegate by the volume of cheering; it grew louder and he knew Richard had turned now onto Petergate, was approaching the High-Minster Gate.

'I'd not realized my brother of Gloucester was so popular in York,' he said thoughtfully. The Lord Mayor strained to hear, nodded enthusiastically.

'Oh, indeed, Your Grace. Here in York we do consider His

Grace of Gloucester our special good lord and steadfast friend, always ready to speak on behalf of our city.'

Edward turned slightly, bringing Elizabeth into his line of vision. Her eyes were narrowed, creased as if against the glare of the September sun. He knew better, knew it to be those shouts of 'Gloucester! Gloucester!' A rhythmic roar of approval, such as he'd often heard for himself in the streets of London. But never in York. Never north of the River Trent.

Edward laughed suddenly, drew some curious looks. God's wrath, but it was amusing. It truly was. He'd sent Dickon into Yorkshire six years ago to win the hearts of its people. And Dickon had. By God, that he had! So why was he not better pleased by it?

Elizabeth's mouth was drawn down at the corners, as expressive as any denunciation she might have made. Edward found himself remembering the accusation she'd flung at him during a bitter quarrel earlier that summer, a quarrel about Dickon and what she saw as the dangerous power he'd been given north of the Trent. 'This much I do know, Ned ... that it's not the White Rose of York they love in Yorkshire, it's the Whyte Boar of Gloucester. And if you tell me that does not give you pause, all I can say is that you're wilfully and dangerously blind. Or have you forgotten your cousin Warwick, Warwick who was loved, too, in the North?'

Edward sucked in his breath. What was the matter with him? Had George's death shredded his nerves as thin as this? Damn Lisbet and her venom! He'd breathed her poison in like air, absorbed it without even being aware of it.

He watched now as Richard rode into the Minster close and as his brother dismounted to kneel before him on the steps of St Peter's, he moved forward to raise Richard to his feet.

Richard's son Ned was delighted to be meeting at last the royal cousins who lived far to the south and, when he discovered that one of these cousins was the same age as himself, his excitement knew no bounds.

Johnny stood silently in the background, watching Ned chattering away with his newfound friend and feeling very left out. He very much wanted to join Ned and the cousin who was called Dickon, like his father, but he was suddenly shy, not sure where he did fit in this family grouping.

'Are you my cousin, too?' The girl had appeared without warning at Johnny's side, causing him to jump. She looked to be about two years older than he, nine or so, regarding him now with her head tilted to the side, with curiosity that was not unkind.

'I'm not sure,' he admitted, and shocked himself then by blurting out what he'd never before spoken aloud. 'I'm Ned's brother but I am a bastard.'

If he was shocked, she was quite undaunted. 'I'm Cecily,' she said, 'and that's silly. Being a bastard does not make you any less my cousin. I have two sisters who are bastards and a brother, too, and they still are my kin. You see yon girl with the red-gold hair? ... That is Grace; she's lived with us since her mother died and. ...' At that moment, she glanced up to see that Johnny wasn't her only audience; her father was standing just behind her.

'I was just telling my cousin about Grace, papa,' she explained, and Edward gave her a smile of amused affection. His Cecily was ever one to find birds with broken wings. ... Lord help her if she did not harden her heart as she grew older. Thank Christ, though, for the children. They'd managed to make tolerable a meeting as awkward as any he could have envisioned. At least Lisbet had the good sense to plead her pregnancy, to make a discreet departure back to the Dominican friary. But it was not going to be easy. Not at all.

He looked across the chamber, watched as Richard flattered Mary and Bess by according them the attention generally reserved for adults and but rarely given to half-grown girls of eleven and twelve. A grim smile touched Edward's mouth. He did doubt exceedingly if Dickon was all that fascinated by the conversation of his young nieces. No, Dickon, too, was uneasy about what was

839

to come. But they could not make use of the children indefinitely, and catching the eye of one of the nurses, he gave her the signal she'd been awaiting. It took several moments to usher all the children from the chamber. He moved then toward his sister-in-law.

'I trust you'll not take it amiss, Anne, but I would like to speak with Dickon alone.'

'Of course.' Anne had already been rising in anticipation of just such a request but now Richard surprised them all, including himself, by saying, 'I want her to stay, Ned.'

Edward frowned. 'Do you think that wise, Dickon?' he said, very evenly.

Richard shrugged, said challengingly, 'Why not?'

There was a sudden tense silence. Anne stood rooted where she was, her eyes shifting from one man to the other and back again. Edward drummed impatiently on the table with his fingers. So this was how it was to be. . . . Sudden anger stirred, resentment that Dickon was going to make it so hard, and he raised his hand in a gesture of dismissal, one that admitted of no argument but authority.

Colour rose in Anne's face; she sank down at once in a deep curtsy. Richard was on his feet now, too. But before he could speak, Edward had crossed the chamber in three strides, stopping Anne in the doorway and drawing her back into the room.

'That was uncalled for, Anne, was not something I did mean to do. Of course you may stay.' Ignoring the stiffness of her body, he led her toward the nearest chair.

'We're not getting off to the best of starts, are we?' With a quick rueful smile. 'I expect my nerves are more on the raw than I did realize,' he admitted candidly, saw surprise flicker across Richard's face.

'What does startle you, Dickon? That I should be nervous about this meeting? Or that I should own up to it?'

'Both,' Richard said laconically, raising his eyes for the first time to Edward's.

'Let's not play games. Surely you do know why I'm here?'

'I understand there is plague in London.'

'That's reason enough for leaving London but not for choosing York over any other city of the realm. I have not been north in nine years, and you know it. I'm here because of you . . . and only you.'

Richard looked away. He'd begun to twist a ring, unconsciously applying such pressure that it chafed painfully against his skin.

Edward was finding it too confining to sit still. Rising, he moved restlessly to the window. They were in an upper chamber of the Archbishop of York's Palace; the court below was still crowded with people, with citizens of this city he did like so little. He turned abruptly away from the window, faced Richard.

'You can be proud of what you've accomplished here, Dickon. It's a remarkable feat, in truth. They've never been overly fond of the House of York in these northern parts. Yet you've managed to win more than their trust. If what I saw today is any indication, you've won their hearts as well.' He hesitated and then said quietly, 'Watching them cheer you to the heavens, I suddenly found myself wondering if I'd rather your success had not been quite so spectacular.'

Anne's indrawn breath was audible to both men, was a smothered sound of dismay. Richard was startled but an intent searching scrutiny of Edward's face gave him the answer. With something almost like satisfaction, he said, 'I see. So the scars do go as deep as that?'

That he was right and George's grave was proving to be an unquiet one, Edward now acknowledged, if only indirectly. 'Clever lad,' he said softly. 'As ever, we do understand each other well, do we not?'

There was a seat directly across from Richard. Taking it now, Edward said, 'What do you want me to say, Dickon? That I regret George's death? Yes, I do. That I regret the grief I've given to those I do care deeply for? More than you could ever know. That I'd do it differently if I had the chance? No. No, I would not.

'Wait, Dickon, hear me out. The last time we talked, we both said things better forgotten. But what I do want to say to you now is what I should have said seven months ago. I know that to you, the threat George posed did not warrant death. But to me, it was so dangerous as to warrant nothing else. In his craving to be king, no betrayal was beyond him, no sin too great. For the peace of the realm, I had to put an end to it.'

Richard was shaking his head wearily. 'There is much truth in what you say, Ned. I've never denied that. But I just did not see the need for a death sentence. I still do not.'

'I'm not asking you to share my reasoning, Dickon. Only to believe this. . . . To believe me when I swear to you that I felt I had no choice but to do what I did.'

This last was said with such stark sincerity that even Anne was impressed.

'Christ, Dickon, you've known me all your life, have been my right arm since you were sixteen. Can you honestly tell me that you've ever known me to kill without cause?'

'No,' Richard conceded. 'No, I cannot.'

'Do you truly think, then, that I could put my own brother to death unless I was convinced there was no other way?'

It was not a question Richard could answer. Edward's eyes were holding his own; he found he could not look away.

'Do you remember, Dickon, that night in Bruges . . . the night at the Gulden Vlies? We said a great many things that night, some profound, some not. But one thing in particular sticks in my mind. I told you that I'd come to trust you above all other men. . . . You remember?'

Richard's mouth softened. 'I remember.'

'That does still hold true for me. What I need to know is whether it be true for you, too.'

'What do you mean, Ned?'

'How much do you trust me?'

Richard was taken aback. 'Need you even ask? I'd trust you

with my very life.' Slightly embarrassed by his own intensity, he added testily, 'But surely you do know that. So why. . . .'

'Ah, Dickon, you still do not see. We are in agreement about George's crimes; we do differ only in the conclusions we reach about them. What is at stake, then, is my judgment. I can tell you from now till the Second Coming that I was convinced George's death had to be, but what of it? It all comes down to what you do believe about my motives, my reasons . . . comes down to trust.'

Anne gathered her skirts about her, came unobtrusively to her feet. She stood for a moment, let her eyes linger upon her brother-in-law. It had been as artful a defence of the indefensible as she'd ever heard. How well he knows Richard, she thought, knows exactly which heartstrings to pull. But there was not as much resentment in this realization as there might have been. In the past seven months, she'd come to understand how important it was that this breach between them be healed. For Richard's sake. At least she knew now that the need was a mutual one, was Ned's as well as Richard's. Bending over, she kissed Richard on the cheek, and then surprised both herself and Edward by doing the same to him.

'I'll give orders that you not be disturbed,' she said. 'I'm sure you've much to say to each other.' And closing the door quietly behind her, she left them alone together.

18

Greenwich

July 1480

For the first time in twelve years, Margaret, Dowager Duchess of Burgundy, was coming home to England. Edward sent one of the finest ships of his fleet to Calais for his sister and, upon her arrival at Gravesend, a royal barge was waiting to take her upriver to his palace at Greenwich.

Two years after George's death in the Tower of London, Margaret still grieved for him. But it would never have occurred to her to sever the bonds binding her to Edward. To Margaret, the bond of blood was the strongest of all ties. She'd loved George, a thwarted maternal love for the high-strung boy he'd been and the troubled man he'd become. But Edward, too, was her brother and her love for him was no less enduring. Moreover, her fierce family loyalty was veined with an innate sense of pragmatism. The brother she loved was also King of England, was the one man capable of keeping Burgundy from falling prey to the ambitions of the French King.

But she did not delude herself that her relationship with Edward could be as it had been. No affection could emerge unscathed from such a trial by fire; there'd be forever between them the scar tissue of an imperfectly healed wound. She was prepared, therefore, for a certain strain at first, prepared to have to exorcise a ghost, one with turquoise eyes and brittle bright smile.

What she was not prepared for, however, was the shocking change in Edward's appearance. His big body was thickening, coarsening, the beauty of face blurring. His eyes were the same bright blue of memory, showed a shrewd penetrating intelligence undimmed by his excesses of the flesh, but they were bloodshot, deeply creased at the corners, spoke of too many sleepless nights and too many drunken dawns. Margaret was deeply shaken, unable to believe that a mere five years could have so tarnished a lustre she'd once thought immune even to aging.

The public reception accorded her at Greenwich had been as lavish as any seen at the court of Burgundy, but at last she found herself alone with her family. As soon as the others withdrew, she was embraced warmly by her sister, by an Eliza grown plump and matronly with the passage of twelve years and the births of nearly as many children. Margaret hugged her back and then embraced Richard. He, at least, looked no different from when she'd seen him last, five years ago in Burgundy. She kissed him gratefully for that, for remaining the one constant link with her past, and then heard Edward say, 'Have you no welcome for me, Meg?'

She turned slowly to face him. Blessed Lady, but he's only thirty-eight. Yes, and looks forty-five. Ah, Ned. . . . Name of God, why? It is more than your youth you're squandering; it is your health, too. Cannot you see that?

'I was but saving the best for last,' she joked lamely. And then she was in his arms, being squeezed breathless and laughing shakily to blink back tears.

'So many changes in these twelve years. . . . Do you find change unsettling, Anne? Lord help me, but I do. I should like to freeze in time all those I do love, keep them somehow safe from the ravages of the passing years. . . .' Hearing herself, Margaret gave a wry little laugh, added, 'Rather like flowers pressed between the pages of a book.'

Anne smiled, then leaned forward. 'I do get the feeling there is something on your mind, Meg, something you would fain discuss with me but keep shying away from. Am I right?'

Margaret looked relieved. 'Yes, you are. Anne, I regret that Ned did see fit to take the duchy of Bedford from Johnny Neville's son, truly I do. I heard that you and Dickon then took the boy and his sisters into your household. Is that true?'

Anne nodded. 'Yes. Richard paid Ned a thousand pounds for his wardship.'

'Well, what I would know is this. . . . Anne, why did you not do as much for George's son? I do know, of course, that you did harbour much bitterness against George. And I wondered . . . I wondered if that be the reason. If you could not bring yourself to take George's son. . . .'

Anne was shaking her head vehemently. 'No, that is not it at all. You're speaking of a child, after all, and one, moreover, who is my sister's son. I would have taken him and his sister like that'—she snapped her fingers—'had Ned only allowed it. He chose, instead, to give the boy's wardship to Thomas Grey.'

'Thomas Grey! Holy Mary, whatever was Ned thinking of? I do not mean to imply that Grey would abuse a child, but . . . but surely he'd be the least likely choice. Hating George as he did, what warmth could he ever have for George's son?'

'Damned little.' Richard had come quietly into the chamber. 'As to what Ned was thinking of, Meg, you can rest assured that it was not an idea to originate with him. The lands the boy will inherit from Bella are considerable, after all, and my sweet sister-in-law has a greed beyond satisfying.'

This was said with such venom that Margaret's eyebrows arched. While she'd detested Elizabeth practically from the moment of meeting, and had been maliciously pleased to note that Elizabeth's spectacular beauty was at last showing signs of aging, her own animosity paled into petty dislike when compared to the bitterness in Richard's voice.

'Ned has changed, has he not?' she said, and sighed. 'I admit it did shock me in no small measure, to see what five years have wrought. But the changes are more than skin-deep. All his life,

846

Ned has been the very soul of generosity, the most giving of men. And now . . .'

'You remember, Meg, two years ago when Ned wed his second son to the little heiress of the Duke of Norfolk?' When Margaret nodded, Richard said, 'She's a sickly child, often ailing, and not like to live to womanhood. Should she die first, the duchy of Norfolk would have reverted back to her family, would pass to her nearest male kin. Well, Ned did enact a measure in parliament which provides that in the event of her death, the title and lands shall vest in his son, thus bypassing the rightful heirs.'

Margaret frowned. 'That does make a mockery of the laws of inheritance,' she said, and Richard nodded.

'Worse than that. One of the men thus cheated is Lord Berkeley, and the other, the other is Jack Howard. Howard,' he repeated slowly. 'As steadfast a friend as Ned could ever hope to have.'

He sat down on the arm of Anne's chair and she reached up, rested her hand lightly on his thigh in a gesture of wordless comfort. She knew all too well how it bothered him to acknowledge the deterioration in his brother's character, a deterioration he could only account for by attributing it to Woodville malevolence.

'Little wonder it is, though, that Ned is more quick to take, less quick to trust. This court of his. . . .' He shook his head in disgust. 'It is no better than a cesspool, is bound to infect any entrapped here for long.'

Margaret murmured agreement, then diplomatically changed the subject. 'Tell me, Dickon, is it true that ma mère does mean to take vows?'

'So she's given me to understand.'

'It should not surprise me, given her piety, but yet it does. Nothing does stay as it was and more's the pity. I gather from Ned that they're still estranged.'

Richard smiled slightly. 'Am I right in assuming you mean to remedy that?'

847

'Indeed, I do! Ned is planning to give a banquet in my honour, and what better opportunity than that? I shall have him invite ma mère and, at the least, give them the chance to talk.'

'Will she come, do you think?'

Margaret smiled. 'Have you forgotten? This is my homecoming, after twelve years in foreign parts. She'll come.'

At sight of Cecily, Margaret forgot that she was a grown woman of thirty-four, ran to throw herself into her mother's arms.

'How glad I am that you came, ma mère!'

Cecily kissed her daughter lightly on both cheeks but then she stiffened, for Margaret was not alone. She'd expected, of course, to see Edward, but she'd not expected it to be so soon and she stood very still as he rose from the settle, moved toward her. As the light from the window fell across his face, she was startled into blurting out the truth.

'Edward, you do look dreadful. Have you been ill?'

His mouth twitched. 'You must not credit all those tales you hear about me wasting my substance in riotous living, ma mère,' he said lightly.

She gave him a long level look, one that stirred sudden discomfort, and for the first time in years, he flushed.

'At least it seems you do still read the Scriptures,' she said, unsmilingly, and there was a silence, broken at last by Margaret.

'Sit with us on the settle, ma mère,' she urged, gently propelling Cecily forward into the chamber.

Sitting down, they soon discovered, did little to dispel the strain. For a time, no one spoke. Shifting so that Cecily could not see, Margaret gestured impatiently to Edward, prompting him to begin, but he pretended not to see her signal, reached, instead, for his wine cup.

He drank so deeply that Cecily frowned and, before she could stop herself, she'd said tartly, 'For pity's sake, Edward, not so fast! There is no better way to stir up stomach disorders.'

848

He hastily tilted the cup to hide a grin. 'I know,' he said contritely, and then set the cup down, leaned toward her.

'I'm not sure if you know, ma mère, but Lisbet is breeding again; the babe is due about Martinmas.'

He paused for a response, didn't get it. 'Lisbet is forty-three, so I think it unlikely she'll conceive again. Ma mère. . . . It would mean a great deal to me if you would stand as godmother to this babe. . . . To be godmother to my lastborn as you were to my first, to Bess.'

Her lashes swept downward, effectively screening her thoughts. But the hand moving from her lap up to her throat froze in midair and the other clenched suddenly against the folds of her skirt. He reached for it, covered it with his own.

'Are we to live our lives out as strangers, ma mère? Would you go to your grave denying the love I bear you, denying that I be of your flesh, of your blood? Is that truly the way you would have it?'

Rising abruptly to her feet, she moved to the window, stood staring down at the beckoning expanse of sun-silvered water. Edward and Margaret exchanged glances; she nodded vigorously and he rose, crossed to his mother.

'Again and again George did deceive and disappoint you,' he said softly, 'and again and again you did forgive him. Must I believe that you've no forgiveness at all in your heart for me?'

He was close enough to her to see the slight tremor that shook her body. When she spoke, however, her voice was surprisingly steady.

'Judge not lest ye be judged. That is the hardest task the Almighty does lay upon us, that we empty our minds and souls of wrath, that we not nurture grievances, nurse grudges. I do not know if I'm capable of that, Edward. I have tried to purge my heart of bitterness but I cannot forget that George did die at your command. I cannot forget.'

She turned away from the window as she spoke, looked him full in the face for the first time.

'But I will try to forgive,' she said quietly. 'I must. I've lost four sons in infancy, and two in manhood. I do not think I could bear to lose another.'

19

Middleham

May 1482

The solar shutters were drawn back, the unglazed lower halves open to the fragrant quiet of a country night. Anne and Véronique were indifferent, however, to the warm spring dark, hunched over a table littered with scratched-out sheets of paper.

There'd been a minor catastrophe of sorts that afternoon. A large sow had escaped her pen and led her piglets in a raid on the herb gardens; by the time they were discovered and routed, Middleham's precious store of spices and medicinal plants had been decimated. A man would have to be sent at once into York and the two women were attempting to make up a list of the essentials he must bring back.

Véronique began to tick items off on her fingers. 'Sage for fever, henbane for easing pain, horehound for lung sickness, betony for stomach cramps. Also bay, marjoram, mustard, and mandragora. What else, Anne?'

'That is all, I think.' Anne pushed her chair back tiredly, looked about the solar. In the window seat, Richard's daughter Kathryn was showing two of John Neville's daughters the jasper-and-crystal chess set he'd given her for her twelfth birthday. On the carpet, almost at Anne's feet, Ned and Johnny were sprawled, heads bent over a crudely drawn map of the border region. Try as she might, Anne could not quite shut out their murmured conversation.

'No, Ned, Dumfries is to the northwest of Carlisle.'

'Are you sure, Johnny?' Ned traced an uncertain path with an ink-smudged finger, as Robin, Rob Percy's young son, leaned over to query, 'Why did your father burn Dumfries, Ned?'

'It was a retala . . . retaler . . .' Ned gave up, looked to his mother for help.

'Retaliatory raid,' Anne said quietly. 'As reprisal for the border attacks of the Scots, the sacking of the nunnery at Armathwaite, the burning of crops.' Her recital of grievances was given with reluctance; she hated even to think of the coming war with Scotland.

All during the previous year, the spectre of war had loomed over the political landscape. It was in many respects the unhappiest time of Anne's marriage. Edward had named Richard as Lieutenant-General in the North and his additional responsibilities soon outran the available hours in the day.

He'd been gone from Middleham for weeks at a stretch. In the winter, he'd been at Carlisle, overseeing the fortification of the city walls. In the spring, he was in London to consult with Edward. The summer found him at Durham, recruiting men and repulsing Scots border incursions. In October, he'd ridden south to meet Edward at Nottingham, and soon after, had begun an energetic but unsuccessful siege of Berwick Castle. And now it was May and, ten days ago, he'd led a force into southwest Scotland, had taken and burned the river port of Dumfries. It was, Anne knew, the opening salvo of Edward's summer campaign, what was to be no less than full-scale war.

The boys were still discussing Dumfries, with an excitement that rubbed raw against Anne's overwrought nerves. She'd lost too many loved ones on battlefields to listen with equanimity as her nine-year-old son eagerly counted the years until, he, too, could lesson the Scots, and she suddenly decided it was well past his bedtime and told him so in no uncertain terms.

Johnny rose obediently but Ned had long ago come to recognize his powers of persuasion where his mother was concerned and he gave her a coaxing hug, entreating her for one bedtime tale first, just one, and then he'd go straight to bed, truly he would.

As always, Anne found herself relenting. 'Just one,' she began, as John Kendall burst into the solar, with such energetic enthusiasm that he at once drew all eyes.

'A messenger has just ridden in, Madame . . . from our lord Duke.' Kendall was smiling broadly. 'He is but an hour away from Middleham.'

By the time the men with Richard had been fed and the great hall turned into a barracks, it was close to midnight. It was only then that Anne was able coax Richard into the solar and set before him a plate of cold venison, bread and cheese. The children should have been in bed hours ago but she hadn't the heart to insist, not when she remembered how seldom they'd seen Richard in recent months.

They were watching him with wide, wondering eyes. A deep tan and a three-day growth of beard gave him a raffish appearance; he suddenly seemed unfamiliar to them, an exotic stranger who led men into battle and put towns to the torch. At first shyly and then with increasing confidence, they began to bombard him with eager questions. Did the Scots fight? Did the people in Dumfries run away? Did he sleep out in the open around a campfire? And at last, Ned asked what Anne most wanted to know but dreaded to hear.

'How long can you stay, Papa?'

Richard was merely toying with the food on his plate. He was too tired to eat, too tired even to talk, although he'd been making a good effort to cope with his children's curiosity. He glanced at Anne before answering his son.

852

'Just two days, Ned. I do have to leave the day after tomorrow for Fotheringhay, to there meet your uncle the King and the Duke of Albany.'

Anne turned away, bit her lip. The Duke of Albany was the ambitious and unprincipled younger brother of the Scots king. There was no love lost between the two men and London wits had been quick to dub Albany a Clarence in kilt. Imprisoned by James three years ago, Albany had succeeded in making a spectacular escape and fled to France. This past spring, it had occurred to Edward that Albany was a ready-made weapon to wield against James, and he'd enticed the malcontent Duke to England, with the idea of deposing James and crowning Albany in his stead.

'Papa. . . . If the Duke of Albany is willing to betray his brother the Scots King, how can you be sure he will not be willing to betray you?'

Richard gave Johnny a look of surprised approval. 'We cannot be sure. It's unfortunate but true that we have to take our allies as we find them, and all too often they do have feet of clay.'

Richard's voice was slurring with fatigue. Overriding the protests of the boys, Anne sent them off to bed and moved to the sideboard to pour Richard a tankard of ale.

'Richard . . . I know Ned does insist he means to take command of the army himself. But his health has not been all that good lately and I cannot help thinking that the burden of command will fall, of necessity, upon you. Do you think me wrong, love?'

He didn't respond, and turning, she saw he'd shoved his plate aside and leaned forward on the table. Cradling his head on his arms, he'd fallen asleep within seconds of closing his eyes.

Anne's foreboding was not long in becoming fact. The days were gone when Edward could be in the saddle from dawn till dusk, revive himself with a few hours' rest and rise ready for another day's hard riding. A body too long abused had begun at last to rebel against the excesses inflicted upon it and Edward was forced at Fotheringhay to admit that he was simply not up to the punishing exertions of a military campaign. What Anne had feared would happen, did. The command was given over to Richard. Edward returned to London and, in mid-July, Richard crossed the border into Scotland with an army of twenty thousand men.

More than twenty-one years had passed since Marguerite d'Anjou had surrrendered the border fortress of Berwick to the Scots as the price demanded for Scottish assistance against the Yorkists. In the intervening two decades, Edward had made sporadic attempts to regain Berwick, the most strategic of the border outposts. By late July, Richard had taken the town and set about besieging the castle in earnest.

James hastily gathered a force and marched south. An unpopular King who had twice been censured for dereliction of duty by his own parliament, he now discovered that he had as much to fear from his own barons as he did from the English Duke besieging Berwick. He'd reached no further than Lauder, twenty-four miles from Edinburgh, when he was overtaken by his rebellious lords.

Among the grievances they counted against James was one particularly unforgivable to a nobleman of the era; he'd surrounded himself with men of modest birth, preferring the company of architects and artisans to that of the arrogant and high-born Earls of Angus and Lennox. At Lauder, these disaffected aristocrats gave him an ultimatum; dismiss the masons and musicians from his court and show himself amenable to governing by their counsel.

However democratic James was in his friendships, he was a confirmed believer in the Divine Right of kings. He indignantly spurned his barons' demands. They promptly took matters into their own hands by seizing six of James's favourites and hanging them from Lauder Bridge. James himself was taken under guard back to the capital and imprisoned within Edinburgh Castle.

The success of their coup seemed to take even the conspirators by surprise. They retreated to the town of Haddington to confer on what to do next and thus left the way clear for an English advance upon Edinburgh.

Upon getting word of the startling events at Lauder Bridge, Richard left four thousand men under command of Lord Stanley, instructing them to continue the siege of Berwick. The English army then swept north, burning towns and villages in an attempt to provoke the Scots into taking the field. But the Scottish lords thought it prudent to keep to Haddington, and the people were too demoralized by the capture of their King to offer effective resistance. On July 31, Richard entered Edinburgh in triumph. Two days later the Scottish nobles sued for terms and the war was over.

It took no more than one meeting with the insurgent lords of Scotland for Richard to realize that Edward's plan to depose James and replace him with the more pliant Albany was doomed to failure. However little the Scots liked James, Albany had irretrievably compromised himelf by his collaboration with the hated English, the Sassenach. Even if it had been possible to shove him down the throats of an unwilling people, Richard knew it would have been impossible to keep him on so shaky a throne. Albany himself was not long in reaching the same conclusion and with uncharacteristic common sense, showed himself willing to settle for the restoration of his estates and a chance to play an active role in the government now being formed by the Scottish Earls.

Richard was not completely satisfied by this outcome. But for the time being, he'd won a Scottish pledge to repay Edward the money paid out for his daughter's dowry and the Scottish people would not soon forget the smoke-filled skies over Berwickshire. He had one more objective to achieve and then he would be content. By August 11th, he was once again at Berwick where he set about winning back the castle that for twenty years had held out against the most stubborn of English assaults.

It was no easy thing for Edward, having to admit he no longer had the stamina to lead his own army. For most of his life, he'd done with ease what other men strained to match; he'd worked hard, played hard, and took for granted the boundless energy with which he'd been blessed. But as he drifted into his late thirties, he found his will being sapped by physical ailments hitherto unknown to him. He was winded now with astonishingly little effort. Always an aggressive and energetic tennis player, more and more he'd found himself panting and sweat-drenched after a set and had finally been forced to give it up for less strenuous amusements. In the same way, day-long deer hunts had to be curtailed and, for the first time in his life, he could not eat anything and everything he liked; certain foods were too highly spiced and Dr Hobbys had begun to fret about these recurring attacks of indigestion.

But he'd continued to delude himself that he would be able to take command of the Scots invasion. It was only at Fotheringhay that he'd been brought face-to-face with the truth, that he would have to depend now upon Richard to do what he could no longer do for himself.

Well, so be it then. Dickon was a damned fine battle commander in his own right; he'd be able to bring the Scots to terms. And once this campaign was over, he could see about losing some weight, getting back into shape again. That would please old Hobbys, in truth. And it would not be all that difficult, surely. Jesú, he was only forty.

To keep in close contact with Richard, Edward resorted to a courier system in use on the Continent, setting up relays of riders to cover the 335 miles between Berwick and London. So successfully did it serve him that when Berwick Castle fell to Richard on August 24th, he had the news by the following day.

As delighted as Edward had been by the capture of Edinburgh, the recovery of Berwick meant far more. By nightfall, bonfires were burning in celebration of the English victory and Richard's name was being drunk in all the alehouses of London, Westminster and Southwark. It was a much-needed triumph for Edward, for his foreign policy was presently in disarray.

That past March, Marie, the young Duchess of Burgundy, had died in a tragic fall from a horse, leaving as her heir a small son not yet four. Her husband, a foreign Prince not loved by the people of Burgundy, and Edward's grieving sister Margaret both appealed urgently to Edward for aid, but the English army was by then committed to war with the Scots. Edward could do little beyond advising Maximilian and Margaret to seek a truce with Louis and hope he would soon die; the French king had recently suffered two strokes and his hold on life was said to be precarious.

Richard's success in Scotland came, therefore, at a most opportune time. Edward was jubilant, lavishing praise upon his younger brother all throughout dinner and on into the afternoon and evening. Coming now into his private chamber, Elizabeth found his elation had yet to fade. He'd been about to write a letter of celebration to the Pope when interrupted by his daughters, and they were with him still, Cecily hanging on the back of his chair and Bess perched on a footstool at his feet.

Elizabeth was not pleased to find them here, not pleased by the way they felt free to intrude upon Edward at any time, careless of formality or court protocol. They were no longer little girls, were young women of thirteen and sixteen, and she felt they should begin to act like it. In this, she got little support from Edward, thought he indulged them outrageously. All the more so since Mary's death.

Mary was not, of course, the first child they'd lost. A baby daughter had died in her cradle and their third son had been stricken by plague only days away from his second birthday. But it was all too heartbreakingly common to have a child go to God before he could learn to walk; parents grieved but they were not surprised. It was different, however, with Mary. She was no longer a child, had been a beautiful young girl just three months shy of her fifteenth birthday, and her sudden death had stunned her family.

At sight now of her daughters lavishing such loving affection upon Edward, Elizabeth felt a small dart of jealousy. In the shocked aftermath of Mary's death, the older children had turned to Edward for comfort. To Edward, not to her. It had ever been that way. They were dutiful children, gave her respect and obedience. But there was no doubt whom they preferred. Whom they adored.

'I remember being told what horrors the soldiers of Lancaster did when they came south after the battle of Sandal Castle, how they pillaged churches and ravished unwilling women and gave great suffering to the innocent. Yet Uncle Dickon did forbear to sack Edinburgh, did forbid his men to harm the citizens. I think that was a most Christian act, papa, in truth I do.'

Edward smiled down at his eldest daughter. 'I thank you for the compliment, sweetheart.'

'But it was Dickon who spared Edinburgh, papa,' Bess protested, and he laughed.

'Aye, and who do you think taught him what he does know of war? He had a first-rate instructor, poppet . . . me. No, Bess, I saw with my own eyes the havoc wrought by Marguerite d'Anjou. The people never forgave her for the excesses of her soldiers, which did win more hearts for York than ever I could have done myself.' He shook his head, said, 'No, in war you do what must be done but no more than that. Be too brutal and you push the people into resisting you unto death, for what do they have to lose?'

Cecily had been listening intently. Now she leaned forward, spoke softly in Edward's ear.

'I, too, am glad, papa, that Uncle Dickon did spare Edinburgh. But what of the villages burned between Berwick and Edinburgh? What of the people who lived in those hamlets? I know you said they were not put to the sword, were given time to flee ahead of

858

our troops. But where will they live come winter, with their houses burned and their crops destroyed? Will many not die of hunger or cold?'

Bess was irked; she wanted to think of the Scots campaign as a glorious triumph and now Cecily was tarnishing that brightness with morbid talk of starving women and children.

'For pity's sake, Cecily, of course they will not! They'll just go elsewhere, make new homes for themselves.'

'Will they, papa?' Cecily alone of his children had the blue-grey eyes of his brothers Edmund and Richard, eyes full of utter trust, ready to believe whatever he might say.

'For certes, some will find kin to give them shelter. But I'll not lie to you, sweetheart. There will be others who'll take ill and die.' Edward shifted so he could better see her face, saying with sudden seriousness, 'The innocent will always suffer in the time of war, Cecily. That just is the way of it. Your pity does you credit but tell me this. Would you rather the homeless and hungry be English women and children?'

'No, papa,' she said dutifully.

'Now, if the both of you can keep still for a few minutes, I'll let you listen whilst I do write to His Holiness the Pope. Fair enough?' Signalling to a waiting scribe, he began to dictate:

Thank God, the giver of all good gifts, for the support received from our most loving brother, whose success is so proven that he alone would suffice to chastise the whole kingdom of Scotland. This year we appointed our very dear brother Richard, Duke of Gloucester to command the same army which we ourselves intended to have led last year. . . .

Elizabeth did not dare linger, knew she'd not be able to hold her tongue if she did. To hear Richard of Gloucester lauded to the skies was to pour salt into an already festering wound and she saw no reason to subject herself to it. She backed out quietly

859

and it did not escape her that they did not even notice her departure.

On the same Sunday that Edward learned Berwick Castle had surrendered to Richard, Marguerite d'Anjou was breathing her last in the modest château of Dampierre in her native Anjou. Her death came eleven years after the battle of Tewkesbury, came for her eleven years too late, and was the occasion for little comment, either in England or in France. Upon hearing of her death, Louis at once wrote and demanded that all her dogs be sent to him. He was her heir, he said, and the dogs were all he'd be likely to get from her estate.

20

Westminster

December 1482

Richard's barge had just tied up at the wharf known as the King's Stairs. He was still standing on the dock when a shrill cry of 'Dickon!' came cutting through the usual clamour of passing river traffic. He jerked his head around, startled, for although he could imagine no woman he knew screaming out a private family name in so public a place, the voice had sounded remarkably like that of Bess, his brother's eldest daughter. But almost at once, he dismissed the thought as unlikely in the extreme. Even Bess, free spirit that she was, would hardly be guilty of so eye-opening a breach of etiquette.

One of his men was pointing. 'Your Grace. . . . Up on the river gate!'

Richard glanced upward, said, 'Good Lord' for it was, indeed, his niece, leaning precariously over the parapet of the river gate, gesturing down to him. Her appearance was scarcely less cause for comment than her astonishing behaviour; she had a cloak drawn carelessly around her shoulders but no headdress, and bright blonde hair was escaping its constraints, being blown about untidily by the wind gusting off the river.

Seeing she had his attention, she leaned over still farther. 'Wait there! I'll be right down.'

By now she'd attracted the eye of every man on the dock. Most were grinning up appreciatively at her; not only was Bess an uncommonly pretty girl, but she'd long been a favourite with Londoners. Richard was grinning, too, amused in spite of himself. It was not truly amusing though. He supposed he ought to talk to her. Even Ned, who was most assuredly no stickler for protocol, even he would take it amiss that Bess should be hanging over river parapets, looking like a hoyden, and shrieking like a fish-wife. As for the haughty Elizabeth . . . praise God if she'd not be like to have an apoplectic fit at the very thought! Richard laughed and moved forward to meet his niece, just now reaching the bottom of the steps.

An instant later, he was running toward her, all else forgotten but the look of fright on her face. Throwing her arms around him, she clung like a small, fearful child and, from her muffled torrent of words, all he could make out clearly was 'Papa,' and 'Thank God you've come!'

'Bess. . . . Bess, you're making no sense. Take a deep breath and tell me what is wrong.'

She obediently did as she was told, straightened away from him, and said, more coherently, 'I'm being silly, I know. But I was just so frightened. . . . And seeing you brought it all back. . . .'

'Fearful of what, Bess? I still don't know what you are talking about. Is it Ned?'

She nodded and for the first time seemed to take note of their extremely interested audience. She swallowed, tugged at his arm. 'Come,' she urged. 'I'll tell you on the way.'

'Has Ned been taken ill? How serious is. . . .'

'He's all right now, Dickon,' Bess interrupted hastily. 'Truly he is. Dr Hobbys swears so. I should've told you that at once. More fool I for not thinking first. But when I saw your barge dock, all else went from my head. I'm so sorry.'

'Bess, you still have not told me a damned thing. I do not understand. Ned was fine when I saw him last night.'

'He was fine this morning, too, until Jack came.'

'Jack Howard? You mean he is back from France?'

'He did arrive back this noon, came to papa in the Prince's Chamber. They spoke apart for a little time and suddenly Papa was shouting, was calling Louis the vilest names . . . "Hellspawn" and "misbegotten son of Satan" were but the mildest ones. It was dreadful, Dickon. Never have I seen papa so wroth. He . . . he frightened me a little,' she confessed. 'He did frighten all in the chamber, I think. Papa is usually so . . . so much in control.' She swallowed again, said, 'He did go on like that for some moments, damning France and Louis and none but Jack knowing what it was all about, and then he sent to Crosby Place for you. His messenger did not find you?'

'I was at the Tower all morn. Go on, Bess. What then?'

'Papa had been breathing in gasps, like men do when they be angry. But, all of a sudden, he could not seem to catch his breath. He grabbed Jack for support and his face got red, like it was on fire. He said to get a doctor, but his voice sounded so queer, all choked up. . . .' She was trembling again and Richard put a steadying hand under her elbow.

'I was so frightened, Dickon. So very frightened. We all were. People just lost their heads entirely. Dr Hobbys came on the run and Dr Albon, too. They did help papa into the White Chamber, were in there with him for what seemed to be forever, and the only one they let in was mama. But a few minutes ago, Dr Hobbys came out and said Papa was fine, that his blood had got overheated. I wanted to see for myself that papa was all right, and Dr Hobbys would've let me, but mama said no. So I came down to the river gate to wait for you. . . .'

At first glance, it looked as if half the court had congregated in the royal chambers. Just as Richard and Bess reached the door of Edward's bedchamber, Elizabeth came out. She stopped short at sight of Richard and then extended her hand for him to kiss. He did, but with such obvious reluctance that those watching smothered smiles.

'He's resting now,' Elizabeth said coldly. 'I think it would be best if you not disturb him.'

'He did send for me, Madame,' Richard said, no less icily, and moved past her into the bedchamber. Bess seized her chance and slipped quickly in behind him.

Edward was as pale as Richard had ever seen him; there was a queer greyish cast to his complexion that was far from reassuring and his eyes were rimmed in red. But he was sitting up on the bed, buttoning his shirt, and to judge from the way he was arguing with Dr Hobbys, whatever had afflicted him was of passing moment.

'Of course I do respect your medical judgment. But you'd have me roped to the bed if you had your way and I—Dickon! I'd just about given up on you. How did you come, by way of the Welsh Marches?'

'What happened, Ned? Bess did tell me. . . .'

'Nothing happened. I suffered from a brief indisposition, no more than that.' Seeing that Richard was about to press him further, Edward said impatiently, 'Dickon, let it lie. There are more important matters to discuss. Jack Howard is back from

France and he brought me word that Burgundy has come to terms with France. Maximilian and Louis signed a treaty at Arras on Monday last, a treaty that does amount to a virtual sellout to that whoreson on the French throne.'

'As sorry as I am to hear that, Ned, it comes as no surprise. Since Marie died, Burgundy's been in turmoil. It was bound to come to this. Maximilian was backed to the wall.'

'Do not waste your sympathy on Maximilian,' Edward said, so acidly that Richard started. 'That he was gutless, I've often suspected. But I never knew the half of it. Do you know what that spineless wonder has done, Dickon? He's agreed to marry his infant daughter to Louis' son, and to provide as her dowry no less than the two richest provinces of Burgundy.'

Richard's jaw dropped. While there was little he would have put past the French king, he'd not expected this, had not thought Louis would dare to flout his English ally so openly. Jesú, no wonder Ned was so wroth! For more than seven years, Bess had been acknowledged at the French court as Madame la Dauphine, as the bride-to-be of Louis' young son. And now this! More than a stab in the back, a scornful slap in the face.

Edward was now expressing himself on the subject of the French King, drawing upon a vocabulary that a Southwark brothel-keeper might envy. Some of what he was saying was anatomically impossible, much of it was true and all of it envenomed. When at last he'd exhausted his imagination, if not his temper, he slumped back tiredly on the bed, said with considerable bitterness, 'Jack says they were laughing about it at the French court, calling the Treaty of Arras Louis' last jest, saying he's cheating death with one hand and the King of England with the other.' He spat out an oath even more profane than his earlier epithets and then gave Richard a sudden level look.

'What was it you said to me at St Christ-sur-Somme, Dickon ... that we did sell ourselves not for blood but for promises, pensions and silver plate. It surprises you that I do remember?

It should not. I remember, too, what else you told me then. You warned me that Louis would disavow our treaty whenever it did suit him to do so.'

Richard felt first surprise and then a surge of admiration, of the sort his brother had rarely evoked in recent years. Ned did not have to say that. Not one man in a hundred would have. He doubted whether he would have done so himself had he been in Ned's position, and he opened his mouth to say this when he caught movement from the corner of his eye, turned to look at his forgotten niece.

'Ah, lass, do not! It's political, not personal, Bess, has nothing whatsoever to do with you.'

Edward swore under his breath, sat up so hastily that a spasm of discomfort crossed his face. 'Dickon is right, sweetheart.'

Bess had bowed her head, but now when Edward held out his arms, she came quickly into them, buried her face in his shoulder and sobbed. 'But papa . . . do you not see? The French King. . . . He shamed me, shamed me before the whole world. I was to wed with his son and all knew it. . . .'

'Hush, sweetheart, hush. That's not so. It was England he was rejecting, not you, Bess.' Tilting her chin up, Edward kissed her wet lashes, stroked her hair. 'No man with eyes to see would ever reject you, sweetheart, that I can tell you for God's blessed truth.'

Bess wiped away tears with her sleeve. 'Papa, you'll make Louis pay for this, will you not? You will not let him get away with making mockery of the treaty, of my marriage?'

'You need not fret, Bess.' Edward sounded suddenly grim. 'Louis does owe me a debt and I swear to you that it is one I'll not be forgetting.'

Richard's head came up in surprise. Ned had never been one to bluster and still less was he one to make empty pledges to his children. But how could he hope to make good on what he'd just promised Bess? If his health had kept him from dealing with the Scots, how could he even contemplate a campaign on the

Continent? He studied Edward with troubled eyes, but tact had never been his strong point, and he could think of no way to phrase such a question without giving offence.

'God help your uncle, Bess, if ever he had to hide what goes on in his head! I've known no man whose thoughts are so easy to read. Shall I tell you what he's thinking now? He's asking himself where in Christendom could I hope to find a war-horse sturdy enough to carry all this bulk.'

That was so patently ludicrous an exaggeration that Edward got the response he'd been aiming for; both Richard and Bess burst into startled laughter.

For a man once acknowledged by even his enemies as 'the handsomest Prince in Christendom', Edward was surprisingly free of vanity. It was true that since his teens, he'd shamelessly exploited his good looks to get what he wanted—the favours of fascinated women and the admiration of his subjects. But he'd long since come to realize that, with most women, their dazzled eyes got no further than the crown upon his head, and in recent years he'd begun to believe that a King who was respected and feared was better off than the one who was loved.

To the fading of a once eye-catching beauty of face, he was truly indifferent. To the weakening of the body that had served him so well for so many careless years, he was anything but. Only to Hobbys, however, would he admit to shortness of breath, to chest pains, to queasy stomach spasms. He had no intention of discussing these ailments with either Richard or Bess, and he'd taken care to divert the conversation away from the rocky shoals of health, into more innocuous channels.

He'd introduced a new style at court that Christmas, doublets with very full hanging sleeves that did wonders to disguise his increasing girth. But in a half-opened shirt, such camouflage was impossible. He made not the slightest attempt now to do so, said with a faint smile, 'You need not worry, Dickon. None of this fat has yet gone to my head. Whatever my failings, I'm no fool. I know I'm not up to leading an army into France.' He paused and then said quietly, 'But if I cannot . . . you can.'

Richard caught his breath. That Edward trusted him, he'd long known. That Edward needed him, he had known, too. But not until this moment had he realized just how deep that dependence did go. There had been no doubt in Edward's voice, only an assurance that was absolute, a faith that had been forged in the blood of Barnet and Tewkesbury and hammered over the years into a bond beyond breaking. It was no small tribute Edward had just paid him. He was by no means blind, however, to the magnitude of what Edward was asking of him.

'I'm honoured . . . I think,' he said wryly, and Edward laughed.

'I've been told that Louis did mark you at Amiens as a man dangerous to France. We can hardly let Louis go to his grave thinking he misjudged you, now can we?' Edward was smiling, but the flippancy fooled no one. He was in deadly earnest, had just enunciated what amounted to a declaration of war.

21

Westminster

April 1483

It was dusk as Thomas Grey's barge neared Westminster. He was not pleased to be summoned back from Shene on such short notice. Like most men who'd enjoyed a life free of illness, Edward made a very poor patient, was given to venting his frustrations upon doctors and innocent bystanders alike. He'd caught a chill on a daylong fishing trip soon after his return from Windsor and, on Easter Monday, he'd taken to his bed. Even the mildest royal indisposition cast a cloud of gloom over Westminster and Thomas had soon grown bored. More than once, he found himself squirming under the lash of Edward's peevish sarcasm, and he was not long in deciding to make himself scarce until his stepfather was up and about again. But he'd not been gone four days before a message had come upriver from his mother, an abrupt cryptic demand for his immediate return to Westminster.

Thomas was not particularly sensitive to atmosphere and yet he sensed almost at once that something was amiss. Westminster was subdued, eerily still, and the few people Thomas encountered were wandering about like sleepwalkers. By the time he reached the Queen's chambers, an instinctive unease was threatening to flare up into active apprehension. But he was still not prepared for what he found in his mother's apartments.

Elizabeth's women were red-eyed, sniffling into crumpled handkerchiefs and, at sight of Thomas, a pretty blonde he'd bedded occasionally burst into tears. He was patting her shoulder awkwardly, trying to make sense of her sobbing when the bedchamber door was flung open and suddenly his mother was screaming at him like one demented, incoherently abusive, demanding to know why he was out here dallying with one of her ladies when he knew she'd been expecting him for hours.

Thomas gaped at her, too taken aback by her raging tantrum even to offer a defence. Grabbing his arm, she pulled him into the bedchamber, and at once began to berate him again.

'Where in the name of Almighty Christ have you been? I did send for you last night.'

'Your messenger did not reach Shene till after midnight. I was already abed,' Thomas protested. Even at age twenty-nine, he was very much in awe of the beautiful woman who'd given him birth, and he made haste to say placatingly, 'I did come as quickly as I could. Mother, what is it?' Too shaken for tact, he blurted out, 'You do look ghastly. What is wrong?'

'It's Ned.' Elizabeth swallowed, passed her tongue over her lips. 'He . . . he's dying.'

Thomas's expression didn't change. He continued to look expectantly at her, his face intent, puzzled. 'What?'

Elizabeth said nothing and Thomas gave an abrupt unconvincing laugh. 'That cannot be. It was only a chill, no more than that. A chill!' But even as he mouthed the words, his body was sagging, absorbing the blow that had yet to penetrate to his brain.

'That was what the doctors thought, too,' Elizabeth said dully. 'But then he began to have pain in breathing and his body temperature suddenly shot upward. He's been burning with fever for two days now and nothing seems to help. Yesterday he began to cough up phlegm flecked with blood and Hobbys says there is no hope, says he is dying. . . .'

'They're wrong; they have to be. He cannot be dying. He cannot!'

Elizabeth had said much the same thing when first confronted by the despairing doctors, had clung to a stunned disbelief with all the frenzied illogical passion of panic. At last even she could not deny the evidence of her own senses, could not deny that in Edward's pain-racked breathing and hacking cough lay the seeds of coming death. But although she had shared her son's stubborn refusal to face the truth, she had no sympathy to spare for him now. Her need was too great.

'I tell you, he's dying,' she cried, 'and saying it is not so will not buy him a blessed moment more of life! He's dying! Do you hear me, Tom? He's dying and leaving as his heir a boy not yet thirteen.'

She was perilously close to hysteria. It was in the sudden shrillness of her voice, in the glassy green eyes, pupils shrunk to flickering pinpoints of fear. Now, as she clutched at Thomas, her nails scored painfully, causing him to pull his hand from hers. Thoroughly alarmed, he fumbled for words of comfort, said soothingly, 'I know Edward is very young, mother, but he's a bright lad, has been raised since birth to be King. And he'll have us to guide him, have you and Anthony and me. . . .'

Elizabeth stumbled to her feet. 'Are you so sure of that? Well, there's something you'd better hear. This afternoon Ned did summon his executors, did make a codicil to his will. Shall I tell you what it said, Tom? He did leave all to his brother. God forgive him, but he did name Gloucester as Protector of the Realm!'

While Thomas was undeniably dismayed by his mother's revelation, he did not see it as the unmitigated catastrophe she obviously did. It was unthinkable to Thomas that they should yield up the reins of power to Gloucester. And so they would not. To him, it was as simple as that. What frightened him far more was the unstable state of his mother's nerves. Never had he seen her like this. His world was already reeling; that his stepfather could be dying struck at the very heart of all that was secure and certain in his life, and it was only a little less chilling to see Elizabeth so frantic with fear, fear he did not fully understand.

'Mother, I know you're overwrought but you've not thought this through. Gloucester may have the protectorship but we've something far more important . . . the trust of the young King. Whom do you think Edward will turn to? To you, his mother, and to Anthony, the uncle who has been his governor and guardian for the past ten years. Can you doubt it? Gloucester is a stranger to Edward and you may be sure Anthony has given him no reason to look on Gloucester with love. Do you not see? We do hold the winning hand.'

Elizabeth's breathing was constricted, coming in short strangled bursts. 'You do not understand. Oh, merciful Jesus, if you only knew!'

'Knew what? What is it I do not understand? Mother, tell me!'

She backed away from him, shaking her head. 'I cannot, Tom,' she whispered. 'God help me, but I cannot.'

*

It hurt almost unbearably to breathe. Each time he drew air into his lungs, Edward felt as if a knife had been plunged into his chest. The sheet clung damply to his body; he made a feeble attempt to free himself from its clammy folds, only to have other hands at once tuck it firmly around him. His fever had raged unchecked for three days now, resisting sage and verbena, resisting sponge baths and prayers; his body was quite literally burning itself up.

Dr Hobbys was bending over the bed. Poor old Hobbys. He looked verily like the wrath of God. As if it were somehow his fault.

'Your Grace, I beg you, do not try to talk. Save your strength.'

For what? But that was a jest that would never be made. He was too tired to talk, was finding it took an extreme effort of will just to keep his eyelids open, to keep from slipping down into darkness, into the exhausted sleep that promised surcease.

'I should never have let you do it. I knew how hard it would be on you.'

Edward had known it, too. But he'd had no choice, had insisted that the lords be summoned to his bedside. Lisbet's two sons. Her brothers Edward and Lionel. His Chancellor, Rotherham. Will . . . a good man, Will, and loyal John Morton, the clever Lancastrian. Tom Stanley, who'd turned his coat too often to be trusted. The other members of his council, those then in London. But so many were beyond summoning. Anthony at Ludlow with his son, with young Edward. Jack Howard on his estates in Essex. Buckingham at Brecknock, in south Wales. Northumberland on the Scots border. And Dickon at Middleham, more than two hundred miles to the north, at the time when he was most needed.

He'd done what he could, had got them all to reavow their allegiance to Edward, to his son. It had not been easy for him. Each breath was precious, came with no small struggle, and it was that which lent all the greater weight to his words; they could see the cost. They must reconcile their differences, he pleaded.

Must make peace for the sake of England, for the sake of his son. Between coughing spasms so violent it seemed as if each might be his last, he entreated them to forget their grievances. By now, only Tom Stanley and John Morton were dry-eyed; both Will Hastings and Thomas Grey were unashamedly weeping, and at his urging, they clasped hands, pledged to bury the past, to give his brother Richard their support in governing the realm until his son came of age.

But was it enough? He doubted it. Jesus, how they did despise each other! Will had no use for Tom Stanley. Northumberland was jealous of Dickon for winning the allegiance of the North away from the Percys. Jack Howard could not abide Morton. And all did hate Lisbet and her Woodville kin. He'd never cared before, never taken their grudges to heart, knowing he was strong enough to keep peace amongst them all. It had even amused him a little, knowing these rivalries only made them all the more dependent upon him. But now . . . what would happen now? Would Dickon be strong enough to hold them all together? He had to be. For if he could not. . . .

'Your Grace, you must rest. You're fighting sleep and you should not be.'

Edward's eyes moved past Hobbys, to the table pulled up close to the bed. It was cluttered with medicinal herbs, a crucifix of beaten gold, and a goblet studded with rubies. It was to the goblet that Edward looked, and Hobbys, quick to comprehend, at once put it to the younger man's lips.

'The Queen. . . .' Edward drank again, sank back on the pillow. 'Send for her.'

At least Lisbet was not weeping. Thank Christ for that. Jane's flood of tears had been hard to bear. So much he wanted to say. So much. If only he could be sure Lisbet understood. A woman could not be regent. The country would never accept her. She had to yield the power, had to let go. Twice in the past hundred years the crown had passed to a child, with disastrous consequences for all. That must not happen to his son, must not happen to Edward. But did Lisbet truly understand the danger? Understand what men would do to gain control of a boy king? Dickon alone could keep Edward from becoming a political pawn, manipulated by first one faction and then another in the struggle for sovereignty. Did Lisbet see that? There was no love lost between her and Dickon, but that mattered for naught now. She needed him, but did she realize just how much? Let her see that. Sweet Christ, let her understand.

Her hand was icy in his. Or was it that his own hand was afire? He felt like he was. It was becoming difficult to keep his thoughts from drifting. His eyelids were getting as heavy as stones. But he must not give in to it, not yet. Still too much to tell her. Stillington. . . . Must reassure her about Stillington, tell her the old man would hold his tongue. Had to believe that, had to. . . . If only Edward was here. Should not have kept him so much at Ludlow. Better to have brought him more often to court, let him get to know Dickon. Too much in Anthony's keeping. . . . Make it harder on him now, having to put his trust in Dickon and Will, men he did not know. . . . But too late. So much too late. So much should have been done differently.

Poor Lisbet. So beautiful once. So very beautiful. Nineteen years. And children, children to be proud of. Should be something to say, something. . . . Not always easy for her. Warwick. Giving birth to Edward in sanctuary. No, not easy. And then Nell. What was she thinking? If only she'd look up. . . .

'I did love you. . . .' Scarcely more than a whisper, but he saw she'd heard. Her head came up, her lashes lifted. Her eyes were wide and staring, free of tears, free of all save a terrible fear.

Edward was appalled. 'Christ, Lisbet! Do not . . . do not do anything stupid! You must not. . . .'

But by then, his throat was closing, his chest heaving and his body convulsed by a coughing fit, one that left him gasping for air, that brought up sputum ominously streaked with red. Elizabeth watched in horror as Dr Hobbys hastened toward the bed and then she began to back away, bringing up her hands as if to blot out that which she couldn't face.

The sky above Thomas Grey was swathed in clouds, the stars smothered in swirling blackness. He stood for a time on the steps of St Stephen's Chapel, staring blindly into the deserted dark of the gardens. So quiet was it that he could hear clearly the lapping of water against the river wall. There came to him now the resonant sound of church chimes. The monks of the great abbey of St Peter were being summoned to Matins. Almost at once, he corrected himself. No, it was a 'passing bell', meant to remind all within hearing range to pray for the soul of their dying King.

Thomas shivered. It was cold for early April, but he could not bring himself to go back into the palace. Still less did he want to return alone to his magnificent mansion in the Strand.

Thomas had been just seven when his father had died fighting for Lancaster at the battle of St Albans. Three years later, his mother had married the Yorkist King and the world as Thomas knew it was forever changed. To an impressionable youngster, Edward truly was the Sunne in Splendour and, in the turbulent years that followed, Thomas had been content to bask in his stepfather's reflected glow. Had he loved Edward? That was a question he'd never thought to ask himself, could not have answered even now. But the times when he'd been happiest had been those occasions when he'd succeeded in winning for himself Edward's attention or approval. Now Edward was dying, and Thomas found himself adrift upon a sea that was dark, foreboding and unfamiliar.

On impulse, he climbed the steps, entered the chapel. Cresset lights flared high up on frescoed walls, upon jewel colours and stained glass scenes of glowing splendour. But by chance, the first sight that caught Thomas's eye was a vivid depiction of the Crucifixion of the Lord Jesus on Calvary, a gruesomely accurate rending of mortal suffering. It was not a vision to give comfort to an already overwrought imagination and Thomas wheeled about. As he did, there came to his ears a soft muffled sound, much like the mewing of a hungry kitten. Retracing his steps, he moved forward into the nave, saw a woman's figure huddled on the floor before the High Altar.

Kneeling beside her, Thomas gave a startled cry. 'Jesú! Jane!'

She raised her arm to shield her face from the light. Her eyes were almost swollen shut, absurdly smudged with kohl, her face streaked with tears and grime. She looked at Thomas without apparent recognition but made no protest when he lifted her up in his arms.

'Come, Jane. Come, sweetheart. I'm going to take you home.'

She didn't have a cloak. Thomas didn't realize it until he was lowering her into the waiting arms of his boatmen. Jerking off his own, he wrapped her in it and settled her beside him in the barge. The boatmen pushed off from the dock.

Jane continued to weep as the barge moved slowly downriver, hiccuping like a small child and burrowing her face in the crook of Thomas's shoulder. He stroked her hair, murmuring meaningless sounds meant only to soothe, and all the while, he was racking his brain as to what to do next. The house Edward had leased for her was on the corner of Gracechurch and Lombard streets, some distance from the river, and Jane was clearly in no condition to walk.

As he pondered the problem, there shone through the darkness shrouding the shore the lights of a great house. Coldharbour, the riverside mansion once owned by Edward's deceased sister, the Duchess of Exeter. Her husband, Thomas St Leger, still made use of it, with Edward's permission. St Leger wasn't in London right now but he and Thomas had emptied too many wine flagons together for Thomas to hesitate.

'Put in at Coldharbour,' he instructed his boatmen.

If St Leger's servants resented being roused out of bed in the middle of the night, any such resentment was prudently masked upon identification of the unexpected arrivals, and they were quick to put St Leger's stables at the disposal of the Marquess of Dorset, stepson to the King. A short time later, Thomas was lifting Jane from his saddle, carrying her up the stairs of her own house.

For some moments, Thomas stood staring down at Jane and, despite himself, all he could see was she and Ned lying naked on this bed. She was no longer sobbing but seemed totally oblivious of all around her, mumbling brokenly and plucking at the coverlets with aimless fingers. He wondered suddenly if she could be feverish; God only knows how long she'd lain there on those icy tiles. Touching his lips to her forehead, he was relieved to find it cool. Her lips, however, were warm, tasted of salt.

Never had he known grief to affect one like this. Almost, he thought, she might be drunk. Even when he found a wet cloth and scrubbed off her smeared eye makeup, she didn't stir. Sitting beside her on the bed, he removed her shoes and then unrolled the stockings gartered at her knees. Her feet were small and icy; he rubbed them briskly between his hands to warm them and then leaned over to taste her lips again.

Her gown was of the newest fashion, off the shoulders, plunging into a deep V neckline. Telling himself she'd be more comfortable this way, he began to untie the lacings of her bodice.

It was not that satisfying. On occasion, he'd lain with women too drunk to fully comprehend what was happening, and it was much that way with Jane. She neither helped nor hindered him, lay limp and uncaring, tears squeezing past her lashes and trickling into her hair, down onto an already sodden pillow. He came quickly to orgasm, rolled off her and onto his back, feeling somehow cheated. For years he'd lusted for this woman, fantasized about her in Ned's bed. Now that he'd had her, why was there so little pleasure in it?

She'd begun to shiver; he could see tiny goose bumps on her arms, the swelling curves of her breasts. He reached for the discarded coverlet, pulled it up around them. She moved closer, instinctively seeking his body warmth and at last, fell into an exhausted sleep. The best Thomas could manage was a fitful doze and he was still awake when a golden haze began to spread over the city, streaking the sky with the glories of an April sunrise.

Thomas was strangely affronted that so beautiful a day should be dawning, would rather the morning be grey and damp and dark. Beside him, Jane was stirring. Her eyes were swollen with sleep, with the shedding of too many tears. They widened now, a startled silver-grey.

'Tom? Tom, what . . .?'

Before she could say more, he rolled over on top of her, stopped her mouth with his own. She seemed to be trying to push him away but he paid no heed, let his hands move familiarly and caressingly over her body, exploring her breasts, her belly, her thighs. She'd soon stopped struggling and when she wrapped her arms around his neck, sought a closer embrace, he gave an excited exultant laugh. But his triumph was not all he'd thought it to be, for when he brought her to climax, the name she gasped against his ear was 'Ned'.

'My lady, it is your health that does concern me now. Will you not try to get some rest? As feverish as the king be, he does not even know you're here.'

Bess shook her head stubbornly. 'You cannot know that for sure, Dr Albon. And even if you are right, I do not care.'

She was grateful when Dr Hobbys beckoned to his colleague. He at least understood, she thought, knew how much she did need to be here.

But Dr Albon was most likely right. Papa did not seem to know her, did not seem to know anyone. Master Gunthorp, the Dean of the Royal Chapel, had assured her that he was at peace. Whilst still in his right senses, he'd made confession, had shown contrition for his sins, and having given affirmative answers to the Seven Interrogations put to him by the priests, the Body and Blood of Our Lord had been placed upon his tongue. Once a man was shriven, he turned his thoughts only to God, Master Gunthorp reminded Bess, went to his Maker with a tranquil heart and soul purged of earthly evils.

Bess very much wanted to believe that. But why, then, were papa's fevered murmurings so disquieted? Those tales the minstrels delighted in, of unfaithful wives betraying themselves in the babblings of fever. . . . They simply were not true. She could make little of what papa was saying, an occasional name, no more than that. But what was unmistakable was the troubled tenor of his thoughts. He did not sound in the least to Bess like a man freed of mortal cares and concerns.

In his delirium, he spoke often of her Uncle George. Was that what was haunting him so, she wondered; was he regretting George's execution? Once he startled her by jerking upright and crying out 'Dick', with sudden clarity. Bess had thought he was calling for her uncle, or perhaps her little brother, but then he'd mumbled 'Warwick', and she realized his ghost was the cousin dead these twelve years past on Barnet Heath. She found it unnerving, listening to him grapple with his past, with people long dead, people she did not know, and when he looked at her without recognition and called her 'Nell', she'd burst into unstrung sobs.

With the coming of dawn, however, he'd grown less agitated. She thought she heard him say 'Edmund', and hoped it was so; hoped he was back in his boyhood at Ludlow. Bending over the bed, she laid a fresh compress on his forehead. How strange it was, that not once had he called for mama.

Bess had ambivalent feelings about her mother. She was very much in awe of Elizabeth, sought earnestly to please her, despaired of ever equalling Elizabeth's striking silver-blonde beauty. But as she reached her mid-teens, she found herself turning upon her mother an increasingly critical eye. Bess was not blind, was well aware of her father's excesses. If . . . if papa was truly happy with mama, then he'd have no need of other women. So mama must be failing him.

But what Bess could never forgive her mother for was her failure to be here at Edward's bedside. How could mama not want to be with him? How could she be so cold, so unfeeling?

She'd said as much to her sister and was surprised to find that Cecily was less judgmental. 'It does not mean she does not care, Bess. I think . . . I think it does frighten her to see papa like this; so helpless. He was always so strong, so much in command, and now. . . .'

Bess wasn't altogether convinced but she resolved to give her mother the benefit of the doubt . . . if she could. For all that she was only fourteen, Cecily had shown herself to be uncommonly sensitive to the unspoken needs of others, and Bess had come to respect her younger sister's intuition.

She wished that Cecily were here with her now. But a few hours ago, Edward's shallow, swift breathing had begun to be interspersed with audible sounds low in his throat. Both girls had known without being told what it was—the death rattle. That had been too much for Cecily; she'd fled the chamber, leaving behind her a trail of broken sobs.

Strangely enough, Bess wasn't frightened by the sound. She could even take a perverse comfort in it, for no longer had she to follow with apprehensive eyes the rapid rise and fall of his chest. The sound reassured her he still breathed, still lived. For all that she thought she'd accepted the death sentence passed by Doctors Hobbys and Albon, she had yet to abandon all hope.

She rose from her seat, approached the bed. A little trail of spittle glistened at the corner of Edward's mouth; she wiped it away with gentle fingers. There'd been another change in his breathing. It was coming now in deep gasps at surprisingly long intervals. Behind her, she heard Dr Hobbys say softly, 'You'd best prepare yourself, my lady. It'll not be long.'

She knew he meant to be kind but she had to fight the urge to spit at him, to scream that he was wrong, that she did not want to hear it. She touched her fingers again to her father's face and, as she did, his eyes opened. They were glazed a brilliant blue with fever, were sunken back in his head. But they were lucid, looked at her with full awareness for the first time in hours.

'Bess. . . .'

'Yes, papa, yes! I'm right here.'

'Sorry . . . so sorry. . . .'

'For what, Papa? You've nothing to be sorry for, nothing at all.' She could see him straining to speak, and knew she should urge him to be still, but she could not; these last moments of coherent communication were too precious to lose.

'Sweet Bess . . . so loved.' He made an uncertain movement; she knew he was searching for her hand and quickly laced her fingers through his.

'Do not worry, papa. Please do not worry.'

'Do you know . . . what is the worst . . . worst sins?'

She bent closer, not sure she'd heard him correctly. 'No, papa. What are the worst sins?'

The corner of his mouth twitched, in what she knew to be the last smile she'd ever see him give.

'The worst are,' he whispered, 'those about to be found out.' Bess did not understand. 'Rest now, papa. It will be all right for us, truly it will. Rest now.'

BOOK FOUR

Richard, by the Grace of God

I

Middleham

April 1483

Richard was standing just to Anne's right. In passing, she gave his elbow a playful squeeze but so engrossed was he in what John Scrope was saying that he didn't even notice. The conversation was not one to give Anne comfort; he and Lord Scrope were discussing the latest intrigues of James of Scotland's malcontent brother, the Duke of Albany.

As little as Anne liked to admit it, she was well aware that another war with Scotland was inevitable. James had managed to regain his freedom, but he was a weak king and, for that reason, a dangerous one. She knew that neither Ned nor Richard trusted James in the least, were convinced that sooner or later he'd resume raiding across the English border. Moreover English prestige was at an all-time low abroad. Ned desperately needed a triumph to outshine the shame of the Treaty of Arras and there is no greater success than that won in the field.

Anne was determined, however, not to let anything cast a shadow over so special an evening. She'd not think of this now, not of Scotland or war or the dying spider on the French throne. She had her husband back at Middleham, she was surrounded by friends and it would soon be spring—all reasons for rejoicing.

Glancing about the great hall, she saw with satisfaction that her guests all seemed to be enjoying themselves. Supper had been a lavish affair, lasting almost three hours, and Richard's minstrels were now providing entertainment. How it would gall the Earl of Northumberland, she thought, should he learn how little he'd been missed!

Northumberland had politely sent his regrets, begging off because of a slight indisposition of the lower back. This had prompted Richard to quip that it was not his back which was out of joint, it was his nose. Remembering, Anne grinned. She didn't doubt that Richard was right. For all the care Richard had taken not to slight Northumberland's authority, he'd never succeeded in breaking through the man's guard. Even after ten years, relations between the two men were characterized by a chill politeness. Northumberland was a reserved, cautious sort, not easy to know, and neither his Lancastrian heritage nor the fact that his House of Percy once reigned supreme in Yorkshire had been conducive to the development of any genuine warmth between him and Richard.

But Northumberland was the only northerner of note missing from Middleham on this Tuesday eve in mid-April. The great hall was full of familiar faces. John and Alison Scrope. Dick and Agnes Ratcliffe. Rob and Joyce Percy. The Metcalfes of Nappa Hall. Lord Greystoke. All of the Fitz-Hugh clan.

With that last thought, Anne was unable to keep from shooting a quick look in Véronique's's direction. Almost at once, she chided herself. Véronique and Francis were far too discreet to show the slightest sign of intimacy in front of his in-laws. Such a suspicion did injustice to them both.

Anna Lovell had chosen to remain at Minster Lovell and Anne was glad of that, for Véronique's sake. She still worried about her friend, still wished Véronique could have fallen in love with a man able to marry her. Anna Lovell was as dependent as a child, and Anne seriously doubted whether Francis could ever bring himself to divorce her. But she no longer doubted his love for Véronique. Few illicit liaisons could endure for almost eight years unless there was a deep and genuine caring on both sides.

After instructing the minstrels that dancing would soon begin again, Anne moved to join Francis, Rob and Joyce Percy. Rob had recently come back from Calais and he was regaling them with the latest rumours about the ailing French King.

'Is it true, Rob, that Louis sleeps at night with so many candles that his chamber looks like midday even at midnight?'

'So I did hear. Since last September, he's been completely sequestered at his palace at Plessis-de-Parc Les Tours.' Predictably, Rob mangled the French almost beyond recognition. Undaunted, he was the first to laugh at his own tangled tongue and then launched into an enthusiastic account of current Calais gossip.

'They say he's forbidden his servants to make use of the word "death" in his presence. Truly, his fear is great, indeed. Since he was stricken with the half dead disease, he's spent several hundred thousand livres in offerings alone. He did beg from the Pope the sacred Corporal, the altar linen which St Peter did use to say Mass, and he's dispatched ships as far as the Cape Verde Islands in search of remedies. . . .'

Anne was no longer listening, was watching the man being ushered into the hall. She'd seen enough couriers in her life to recognize one on sight. It was unusual, however, for a messenger to appear before a lord like Richard in such travel-stained disarray. That he was unshaven, grimy with days of hard riding, told a tale in itself; his message must be urgent, indeed. The unease that was never far from conscious thought flickered, threatened to come to life. But then she saw that the messenger did not wear the royal colours, and her frown vanished. An urgent message from Ned was sure to mean bad news, to mean another Scots or French campaign. But there was no such danger in a communication from William Hastings and she turned back to Rob, asking curiously, 'Rob, does there seem to be much anxiety amongst the French people over the coming death of their King? His son is only thirteen, after all.'

Rob nodded and, unable to resist quoting Ecclesiastes, intoned gravely, '"Woe unto thee, O land, where the King be a child." You may be sure that's much on men's minds. Look what did happen

885

here in England when Harry of Lancaster came to the throne as a babe. . . . Chaos and bloodletting and conspiracies. All of which I do most devoutly wish upon the French once Louis dies and his boy heir takes the throne.'

'Anne.' Francis touched her arm lightly. 'I'm not sure but I think something might be wrong.'

There was an unnatural immobility about the scene that now met Anne's eyes. Hastings's courier still knelt before Richard, in his outstretched hand a sealed paper. Richard had yet to take it, was regarding him with a curious lack of expression. There was nothing in his face to give alarm, yet people were beginning to glance in his direction, attracted, perhaps, by the utter stillness of his stance.

'Oh, dear God!' Anne never even knew she'd spoken. Shoving her wine cup at Joyce, she began to move toward her husband. The look on Richard's face was one she'd seen before. Marguerite d'Anjou had listened with that same stunned blankness as William Stanley informed her that her son was dead.

Before she'd taken more than a few steps, however, the frieze shattered. Richard swung around, abruptly exited the hall, roughly shouldering aside a startled minstrel unlucky enough to be blocking the doorway. Conversation came to a sudden halt, then started up again with a vengeance. Hastings's messenger came stiffly to his feet, held out to Anne the still sealed message.

Anne's recoil was physical; she actually put her hands behind her back like a reluctant child. She did not want to know what was in that letter, dared not take it, sensing that what it contained would forever change her life, the lives of those she loved.

'Madame? Madame, I do come from Lord Hastings.' The man's voice was hoarse, thick with fatigue, but his eyes were full of unsettling sympathy.

'I regret deeply that I must be the one to tell you. The King is dead.'

*

The candle had been marked to count the passing hours; it was now burning down toward one o'clock. Three hours he'd been gone. Three hours. Where was he? Let him come back. Blessed Lady, let him be all right.

Without even realizing it, Anne had begun to pace again. Knowing Richard as well as she did, she should have realized, should have guessed what he'd do. She just had not been thinking clearly. She'd gone first to their bedchamber, then to the chapel. By the time it occurred to her to check the stables, it was too late. A bewildered groom confirmed that Richard had roused him from sleep, demanded that he saddle a horse. It had been a good quarter-hour since the duke had ridden out, he told Anne apologetically, adding in uncertain concern, 'My lady, is there trouble? The Duke did spur his stallion through the village like the hounds of Hell were on him.'

Since then, Anne had worn a path to the solar window facing north, was drawn toward it now. The village was cloaked in dark and, beyond, all was utter blackness. A man could so easily lose his way; his stallion could stumble, pull up lame.

She must not torment herself like this. Richard did know the dales of Wensley and Cover as well as any man in Yorkshire. Yes, but he was riding White Surrey, the fiery-tempered destrier Ned had given him last June at Fotheringhay. A horse bred for battle, as high-strung as it was beautiful. What if it bolted and threw him? Or if it blundered into a sinkhole? Who would know? A man grieving might well make a careless misjudgment and on the moors such mistakes were often fatal.

Perhaps she should send men out after him? But he'd never forgive her for that, never. She'd wait awhile longer. Surely he'd be back soon. He had not taken a cloak and winter lingered late in Yorkshire. At night, an icy chill came down off the Pennines.

Loki, the alaunt she'd given Richard to fill the void left by Gareth's loss, rubbed against her skirts like some huge silver-grey cat; the slanting dark eyes were so sorrowful that Anne found

887

herself blinking back tears. She must not give way, though. She had to hold herself together, had to be ready to comfort Richard when he returned. Dear God, what could she say to him? He'd loved Ned so much.

She had to stop this. Richard was a man well able to look after himself; she must try to remember that. A quick glance toward the candle told her it was nigh on 1:30. Mother of God, where was he?

If only she had not read Hastings's letter. If only she could put it from her mind. But she could not seem to help herself. Again and again, she found herself picking it up, rereading words already burned into her brain. A letter striking for its startling brevity, two terse paragraphs. Anne had never thought much of Will's morals but his manners she knew to be impeccable. What urgency had been prompting his pen when he wrote this?

The first paragraph said only that Edward was dead, that he'd died on April 9th at Westminster. Wednesday last. . . . She and Richard had gone hawking on Carlton Moor, not returning to Middleham till dusk. It had been a good day, a day of easy laughter and bright sun. When, she wondered suddenly, would they ever have such a day again?

She must not think that. She must not panic. But why was Hastings's letter so fraught with unspoken dangers? It was the second paragraph that haunted her, that stirred up such foreboding. 'The King has left all to your protection—goods, heir, realm. Secure the person of our sovereign lord Edward the Fifth and get you to London. For sweet Jesú's sake, do not tarry, and look to yourself.' No, not a letter to reassure.

'Anne?' Véronique was standing in the solar doorway. 'Anne, they're signalling from the gatehouse. He's just ridden in.'

Although he was standing directly in front of the hearth, Richard was still trembling with cold and, when Anne gave him a cupful of hot mulled wine, his fingers were so stiff and cramped that it slipped from his grasp, spilled into the fire. He scarcely seemed to notice, even when the flames shot upward, hissed and sputtered.

'Here, beloved,' Anne said swiftly, holding out her cup. She watched with anxious eyes as he brought it to his lips, resisting the urge to steady his hand with her own. Pray God he had not caught a chill; she yearned to put her lips to his forehead to reassure herself he was not feverish. But above all, she yearned to put her arms around him, to hold him close and comfort him as she would their son.

She could not, though. He was not two feet from her and yet beyond reach. My darling, do not. Do not shut me out like this. Let me help. The words hovered on her lips, got no further.

'Where is Hastings's letter?' Richard asked suddenly, and Anne cursed herself for not having hidden it, for not being able to say she'd mislaid it. She did not want him to see that letter, not tonight. Let him have one night to grieve for his brother, one night free of the insidious doubts Hastings had raised. But the letter lay out on the solar table, lay in plain sight, and he was already reaching for it.

She saw his face harden as he read, saw him crumple the letter in his fist when he'd finished. For the first time, he looked Anne full in the face. His eyes were very dark, looked bruised.

'I had to learn of it from Will Hastings,' he said huskily, and there was in his voice both a bitter grieving and a savage rage. 'That bitch did not even have the decency to tell me herself that my brother was dead!'

2

Middleham

April 1483

Anne awoke just before dawn, after a night of troubled dreams. It was a day she'd been looking to with dread, the day of Richard's departure for York and then London. She lay very still, kept her eyes tightly shut. Twice in the eleven years of their marriage, she'd seen Richard ride off to war, but never had she been so frightened for him as she was now, as he prepared to ride south to claim the protectorship of the young king.

She thought of the boy with pity. He was so young to have such burdens thrust upon him. If only he were better acquainted with Richard, were not so much under Anthony Woodville's thumb. If only she could believe all would be well, that Elizabeth would not seek to circumvent Ned's will. Above all, she wished she did not know so well the history of her husband's House, wished she could forget the fates of Thomas of Woodstock and his son Humphrey. Like Richard, Thomas had been uncle to a boy king; when that king reached his majority, he had Thomas arrested and murdered. Humphrey's lot was no luckier; he had been named protector to the young Harry of Lancaster but he'd not proved strong enough to hold on to it. Like his father before him, he'd been arrested; within twenty-four hours he was dead. Neither tale was one to give Anne comfort. What did stir in her such superstitious fright, however, was the fact that both men had held the title that was now Richard's – Duke of Gloucester.

She shifted uneasily, burrowed deeper into the false security of the feather bed, taking care not to jostle Richard. Let him sleep awhile longer. It was little enough rest he'd had these four days past. Little rest and no time to grieve.

Upon hearing a Requiem Mass for Edward in the castle chapel, Richard had again taken White Surrey out onto the moors. Returning pale and shaken hours later, he'd sat down and written to Anthony Woodville at Ludlow, offering condolences to his young nephew and expressing the hope that they might rendezvous at some point on the journey south for a joint entry into London. After that, he'd written a stiff letter of sympathy to Elizabeth, and a carefully worded letter to the council, in which he vowed to be as loyal to Edward's son as he'd been to Edward. He made it clear, however, that he expected to assume the protectorship of his nephew, in accordance with custom and Edward's own wishes. He'd let Anne read it when he was through and she assured him he'd struck just the right note, that the council would be sure to react favourably. Neither said what both were thinking: if the council meant to abide by Ned's will, why had he not received some sort of official recognition by now?

Three days later the question had yet to be answered. There'd still been no word from Elizabeth, no word from his brother's council. But at midday on Saturday, a second courier from Will Hastings had galloped across the drawbridge and into the inner bailey of the castle. If Will had previously hinted at unspecified dangers, he was now naming names with a vengeance. The Queen and her kindred meant to set aside the protectorship. They'd won over Rotherham, Ned's Chancellor. Stanley seemed to be wavering. He need not tell Richard what would happen once they had the young King safely in their power. Richard must get to London as soon as he could, and he'd best make his escort a large one.

Anne had begun to shiver, reached for the coverlets and glanced over toward Richard's side of the bed to make sure she'd not disturbed him. The bed was empty; she was alone. Seconds later, she was belting the sash of her bed robe, was kneeling by the bed to retrieve her shoes.

The sky above the keep was a pale pearl-grey, the castle towers swirling in dawn vapours soon to be burned away by the rising sun. A few sleepy servants were up and about, blinking with surprise at sight of Anne's tumbled hair and soft blue robe. She found the chapel deserted, still fragrant with the candles burned on Edward's behalf. But in the great hall, she encountered a startled serving maid and the girl pointed toward the corner stairway in answer to Anne's urgent query.

The view from the battlements was a beautiful one, showed the sweep of dale and the distant silver of the Cover River. In May these hills would be carpeted with heather; in October, gold with bracken. Even in winter, there was a stark splendour to Wensleydale, but this was perhaps the loveliest time of the year, a soft green sea stretching as far as the eye could go.

Anne paused for a moment in the doorway to catch her breath and to watch Richard unobserved. The severity of mourning garb did not suit him. Caught between the unrelieved drabness of a doublet of dark worsted and the blue-black thatch of hair, his face looked lost, pinched and bleached of all colour. He'd yet to notice Anne; he was gazing out over the dale as if seeking to commit it to memory, to fix in his mind the way shadow and sun chased across the slopes, filled the valley with light.

'Richard.'

He turned at once. 'Anne? Anne, what is wrong?'

She shook her head, came into his arms. 'Nothing, love, nothing. It . . . it just frightened me to awaken and find you gone.'

'Surely you did not think I'd have departed without bidding you farewell?'

'It occurred to me that you might think it a kindness, to spare me that. . . .'

'That would be no kindness, beloved,' he said, and she felt his mouth against her hair. 'I could not sleep, came up here to watch the sunrise.'

'Are you still determined to go against Will's advice? Oh, love, reconsider. Take enough men with you to be safe, to give. . . .'

He was shaking his head. 'Anne, I cannot. To take an army south would be like tossing a torch into a haystack. I can think of no gesture more provocative, more likely to raise suspicions as to my intent. We're on the very edge of the precipice, all of us. A boy king seems inevitably to serve as a lightning rod, to draw down disaster. I tell you, Anne, the very thought of a Woodville regency does chill me to the bone. We could see a civil war erupt over the boy that would make the feud between my father and Marguerite d'Anjou seem like petty squabbling.'

'But is that not all the more reason to heed Will, to take a large force with you?'

'Anne, I've no wish for martyrdom, have never yearned to walk unarmed into the lion's den. If I thought it would quiet the capital and ease men's minds, I'd take damned near all of Yorkshire with me. But it would not, would guarantee neither my own safety nor the stability of the realm. I cannot risk it; the stakes are too high.'

'Richard. . . .' The words came to her lips of their own volition, could not be bitten back. 'Richard, what is going to happen? What lies ahead for us?'

Raising her head from his chest, she saw in his face the struggle between his wish to reassure and his reluctance to lie. 'I do not know,' he said at last. 'I would that I could tell you otherwise, Anne, but I cannot. I just do not know.'

Before departing York, Richard saw that Requiem Masses were said at St Peter's for the repose of his brother's soul. He saw to it, too, that the northern nobles and magnates swore public oath of allegiance to his nephew; and all the while, he struggled to make himself believe that Ned was truly dead and his own world in such jeopardy, grief and fear and an embittered illogical anger merging in his mind until they were inseparable and unrecognizable one from the other.

While still in York, Richard received a message of support from an unexpected quarter, from his cousin Harry Stafford, Duke of Buckingham. Buckingham offered to join Richard on his journey southward, offered, as well, to put a thousand men at Richard's service. Richard was not long in dispatching a grateful reply. He would, indeed, welcome his cousin's company. A courier from Anthony Woodville had just reached him, he explained to Buckingham, in response to his earlier request for a meeting. Anthony had suggested they rendezvous at the town of Northampton and, if it was agreeable to Buckingham, he, too, could join them there. But he must regretfully refuse Buckingham's other offer. It was his intent to limit his escort to several hundred, and he requested that Buckingham do likewise.

For the first time in more than a week, Richard dared to let himself hope there might be a safe path through the quagmire that so suddenly was confronting him. Buckingham's offer of support was heartening. But even more so was Anthony Woodville's cordial cooperation. It contrasted strangely with Elizabeth's continuing silence. Was it a straw in the wind, a sign that the Woodvilles might yet come to terms with the reality of his protectorship?

After two days in York, Richard began moving slowly southward, in the company of northern knights and gentry. With him were Lords Scrope, Greystoke and Fitz-Hugh, and his boyhood friends. Stopping at Pontefract and Nottingham, they reached Northampton on Tuesday afternoon, April 29th, only to be told that the young king had passed through the town hours before. Soon after, Anthony Woodville rode back with a small escort. His royal nephew had pushed ahead to the village of Stony Stratford, he explained easily, fearing that there'd not be accommodations enough in Northampton for his own men and those in Richard's party.

894

Richard stood at the window, watching Anthony Woodville's servants light his way across the marketplace toward his inn. He watched until the lantern-glow faded away into darkness and then turned to face the waiting men.

'Well?' he said dryly. 'What did you think of the mummery?'

Their faces were accurate mirrors of his own scepticism. It was left to John Scrope to put it into words, to say with a soldier's oath, 'Do they think us utter fools? God's wrath, parliaments have been held here in Northampton! There are inns aplenty, easily room to spare for our own men and the royal train. No, that dog will not hunt.'

'It did cross my mind,' Richard admitted, 'that Stony Stratford is fourteen miles closer to London.'

'You think, Dickon, that they mean to send the boy on ahead, not to wait on you?'

'I do not know, Francis. But that excuse for not stopping here in Northampton is as thin as gossamer. It does make me wonder why, in truth it does.'

Richard moved back to the window. Below, all was still, dark and deceptively tranquil. Against his will, he found himself recalling that the village of Olney lay not ten miles to the east, Olney where Ned had been forced to give himself up to his Neville cousin. It was not a memory ever to fade; Richard could still see the sixteen-year-old boy he'd been, standing alone in that sun-drenched street and marvelling that all could somehow seem so normal even as time ran out. He felt much the same way tonight.

Behind him, he heard John Scrope say gruffly, 'I hope to Christ you've not blundered, Dickon, in keeping our numbers so small.'

Was Scrope right? Had he erred on the side of caution? If so, God help them all; that was not a mistake a man would get to make twice.

If only he knew what was happening in London. If only he knew whom he could trust. . . . Will Hastings, of course. He did not like Will as much as he once had; he'd seen Will falling down drunk too often for that, could not help thinking that Will, too, had done his share in bringing Ned to so early a death, a death that need never have been. No, Will had not served Ned well, however much he'd loved him. But he was still a man to be trusted; that Richard never for a moment doubted.

So, too, was Jack Howard. He'd never let the government pass into Woodville hands so long as there be breath in his body. Suffolk, his sister Eliza's husband? Not so certain. Suffolk had no liking for the Woodvilles, but he was, plain and simple, not a man to risk his neck for anyone or anything. Eliza's eldest son Jack, Earl of Lincoln, was cut from finer cloth, thank God. Jack was a good lad, could be counted upon in any showdown with the Queen's kindred. Still, though, he was only twenty, had no voice in council.

And the others? Tom Stanley and his self-serving brother? Not bloody likely. What was it Ned had once said? . . . 'You can never go wrong suspecting a Stanley.' Essex was ill unto death. Buckingham had already shown where his loyalties lay; he was expected here at Northampton within the hour. Northumberland? A hard question, that. Northumberland had begged off from coming south, saying he thought he'd best keep watch on the borders, make sure the Scots did not seek to take advantage of English troubles. The common sense of that could not be denied. And yet . . . and yet Richard could not forget how Northumberland had kept to his own estates in the spring of 1471, had not committed himself until he could be sure he was on the winning side.

And then there were the Woodvilles. Elizabeth's two sons by Grey, her four brothers. That meant the clerics had the deciding votes in council. He had no qualms about the Archbishop of Canterbury or John Russell, Bishop of Lincoln. They were decent men, would act only in his nephew's best interests. Rotherham, Ned's Chancellor? A well-meaning man, but weak, easily swayed. Edward Story, the Bishop of Chichester—hard to say, but it was not reassuring to recall he'd once been Elizabeth's confessor. That left John Morton, Bishop of Ely. John Morton, who'd once hoped to be Chancellor under Marguerite d'Anjou. Too clever by half.

'Dickon?' Rob Percy was standing in the doorway. 'The Duke of Buckingham has just ridden in.'

Dishes had been set before Buckingham, baked partridge with cold herbed jelly, a rissole of pork and roe pike, apple fritters, and almond cakes. He gestured for his servant to begin ladling the food onto his trencher, saying to Richard, 'We can speak freely before Gilbert; he's been mute since birth. I hope you do not mind talking as I eat. I've been on the road since dawn, I am famished.'

A cup of spiced hippocras had been placed at his elbow. He drank deeply and then said, 'Tell me, cousin, how much do you know about what's been happening in London?'

'Damned little,' Richard conceded. 'I'd hoped you might be able to tell me, Harry.'

'Aye, I can. . . . But you'll not be liking it any.' Buckingham wiped his mouth with a napkin, glanced about at tense expectant faces.

'Your brother was laid to rest at Windsor a week ago Sunday, with all the ceremony befitting so great a king; Madame the Queen did not see fit to attend, however, remained behind at Westminster. I think you can guess why and, in truth, she wasted precious little time. The first thing they did was to persuade the council that a fleet should be equipped. To deal with French pirates, they did explain. And the command of that fleet? I'm sure it comes as no surprise that it did go to her brother, Edward Woodville.

'Nor was Thomas Grey idle. Since March, he's been Deputy Constable of the Tower and that office now served him well. He took possession of your brother's treasury, gave half to Edward Woodville and divided up the rest with the Queen.'

Richard's face was without expression. 'Go on,' he said tersely.

'They then met with the council, in the Queen's presence, for all the world as if she were regent, announced they thought it advisable that a large armed force should accompany young Edward from Ludlow to London.'

Richard caught his breath. 'How large, Harry?'

'Nowhere near as large as they wanted, and for that, you may thank Will Hastings. He threatened to withdraw to his fortress at Calais if the boy's escort were not limited to two thousand. The council sided with him on that, shaken by his threat, I think. Moreover, the thought of a Woodville army marching on London did prod even the most spineless into showing some backbone. The Queen did yield under pressure, agreed to the two thousand.' Buckingham paused.

'I'm not sure I want to know,' he said wryly, 'but how many men have you, cousin?'

Richard said nothing. The answer came from John Scrope. 'Five hundred, if even that many.'

Buckingham grimaced. 'Even with my three hundred, I cannot say I much like those odds!'

The silence that settled down over the table was broken finally by Francis. 'You are remarkably well informed, my lord Buckingham.'

'I cannot afford not to be.' Turning hazel eyes upon Richard, Buckingham said softly, 'Nor can you, cousin. I've not told you all. Hastings released the contents of your letter to the people. It much impressed them and it's widely agreed in London that you should have the government. But the Queen and her kin do for the moment control a bare majority in the council. They argued that the government should be carried on by a regency council, not entrusted in the hands of one man alone.' He set his wine cup down with a sudden thud.

'I regret to tell you, cousin, that the Queen prevailed. The council voted to disregard both custom and your brother's dying wishes. They agreed, too, to the Queen's demand that the boy be crowned at once. The coronation is set for this coming Sunday and, if you've not reached London by then . . . well, so much the better. Assuming, of course, that you do reach London at all!'

Richard stood up abruptly, pushed away from the table. Fool! Stupid, stupid fool! He should've known, should've expected this. There was no honour in that woman, not a shred of integrity or honesty. What cared she if she did tear the country apart? And should she succeed, should she get the government into her own hands during the boy's minority, God help England. Marguerite d'Anjou would seem a veritable saint by comparison.

Shock was rapidly giving way to rage. His brain was suddenly very clear, very cold. If this was how she did want it, so be it. George had blundered blindly into a Woodville web, had even given her the knife to plunge into his back. But this time she'd not find it quite so easy. That he could promise her.

'Dickon?' It was Francis. 'Dickon, what mean you to do?'

'I think,' Richard said grimly, 'that it is time I did take Will Hastings's advice. . . . Secure the person of my nephew and get to London.'

Anthony Woodville had been unable to sleep. By 4:00 A.M., he'd given up, had propped himself up in bed with a book. But he could not keep his mind on what he read.

Damn Lisbet for this! What ailed her, that she should be so set upon confrontation? It was not necessary. Why could she not see that?

He'd seen from the first that they could not afford to run roughshod over the nobility. They were too hated to rule alone, needed allies. Once Edward came of age, it would be different. But until then, Lisbet would have to wait to settle old scores, however little she liked it.

He was not blind to the pitfalls ahead. But as he saw it, their greatest danger was an alliance of the two most powerful men in England: Gloucester and Hastings. Self-preservation dictated that they come to terms with one or the other. Anthony's choice was Gloucester, whose claims were legitimized by both blood and Ned's own dying wishes.

He'd thought it prudent, therefore, to fall in with Gloucester's suggestion, readily agreed to a rendezvous at Northampton. He had no illusions about Gloucester. The man hated the Woodvilles, blamed Lisbet for Clarence's death. He'd do what he could to freeze them out of the government. But beyond that, Anthony did not think he'd go. He had a rockribbed sense of right and wrong, was not a man to sacrifice all for vengeance. And his influence would be of fleeting duration, in any event. Edward was young but already with a mind of his own. Gloucester was not likely to have much luck with the boy. What was it the Carthusians said, 'Give us a child till he be seven and he will be ever ours.' Well, he'd had Edward for ten years. No, Gloucester would find that well a dry one.

But then yesterday his nephew Dick Grey had ridden out from London, bearing urgent orders from Lisbet. Under no circumstances was he to allow Gloucester to join up with them. He was to get Edward to London at once. All depended upon that. He'd already squandered precious time by insisting upon celebrating St George's Day at Ludlow before starting out for London. He must not fail her again.

Remembering, Anthony shook his head in bemused unease. How could a woman be at one and the same time so pragmatic and so reckless? Lisbet was far from a fool; why, then, was she so intent upon courting disaster?

What sort of lunatic advice was she getting? He had no choice now but to go along with her panicked plotting, but he felt sure he'd have been able to talk some sense into her had he only been there with her when Ned died. As it was, she'd had no one to turn to. He was fond of his brothers Edward and Richard, but neither was overly endowed with brains. Brave men, the both of them, but if it were to be raining wine, they'd be out there trying to catch it with those newfangled Italian forks. His youngest brother Lionel, newly named as Bishop of Salisbury, was bright enough, but Lionel had a dangerous love of intrigue for its own sake, was not one to counsel restraint. As for his nephews: Dick Grey would no more think to gainsay his mother and brother than he would to take vows, and Tom ... Tom had ever been afflicted with flawed vision, could see only what he wanted to see.

With confidants like that, little wonder Lisbet had entangled herself in such high-risk conspiracies. Did she fully realize the consequences? Why was she so terrified of Gloucester? He wished he could believe all would go as planned, that she'd not over-reached herself, that. . . .

'My lord?' For some moments, his servants had been moving about the chamber, setting out his clothes. His barber was standing ready with razor and hot towels. One of the men had just unlatched the shutters; it was he who'd called out.

'My lord, something seems to be amiss. I think you'd best come to see.'

Anthony wrapped a sheet around himself, joined the man at the window. In the diffused light of an uncommonly misted morning, men were moving into the marketplace, men-at-arms wearing the Stafford Knot of the Duke of Buckingham and the Whyte Boar of Gloucester. As Anthony stared down in appalled understanding, they took up position in front of his inn.

It was dawn when Richard reached the village of Stony Stratford. As early as it was, men-at-arms were milling about in the street, loading up balky pack animals, trading curses and complaints. It was clear he was just in time; his nephew's cavalcade was about to depart.

It gave Richard cold comfort to have his suspicions thus confirmed. He could think of nothing now but how thin a margin of error he was allowing himself, risking all upon the element of surprise and his assessment of Dick Grey. If he'd guessed wrong. . . .

'Hold the men here, Harry,' he said, and then spurred his stallion forward down Watling Street. He was recognized at once and men hastily moved aside, let him pass through their ranks. He could feel their eyes, startled and speculative, burning into his back as he drew rein in front of his nephew's inn.

Edward was standing before a magnificent cream-coloured stallion, preparing to mount. Richard saw surprise upon his face now, followed swiftly by uncertainty. He came forward readily enough, however, as Richard dismounted and knelt before him.

'Your Grace seems surprised to see me. Were you not told I'd be meeting you here this morn?'

Edward shook his head, looking at once both bewildered and wary. 'I was told only that we were to depart for London at first light. Is my Uncle Anthony with you?' He raised a hand, peered toward Richard's waiting men. 'I do not see. . . .'

'No, he is not.' Richard dropped his voice, said for Edward's ear alone, 'I must talk with you, Edward. Shall we go inside?'

At that moment, Dick Grey appeared in the doorway of the inn, and Richard had the satisfaction of seeing his face suddenly lose all colour, go as sickly white as freshly skimmed milk.

There were only the five of them in the chamber: Edward, Richard, Buckingham, Dick Grey and Edward's chamberlain, Thomas Vaughn. Richard would rather have spoken to his nephew alone, but Dick Grey had insisted upon entry and he'd been reluctant to make a scene before the boy.

'Uncle, I . . . I do not understand. Why did my Uncle Anthony not accompany you?'

'Edward, what I have to say to you is bound to cause you some pain. I deeply wish it were not so, but it cannot be otherwise. It is about your father. He died before his time, lad. He need not have died so young, should have had so many more years. . . .'

902

Richard stopped, swallowed. A fortnight was not time enough to come to terms with Ned's death; even a lifetime might not be enough.

'He was cheated, Edward, cheated by men who cared only for what his favour could gain them, cared not at all that they were helping him dig his own grave. These men, if left to their own devices, will play the same game with you as they did with your father, with my brother. Already they seek to thwart Ned's dying wishes, to deny me the protectorship he. . . .'

'Protectorship?' Edward jerked his head around, stared at his half brother. 'My father named my Uncle Gloucester as protector? Dick, is that true?'

'No! That is . . . you see, Edward, we . . . your mother . . . felt it best that. . . .'

'I see. . . .' Edward's poise was remarkable for a boy of his years; as a king's son, one of the first lessons he'd learned was that of self-control. But too much was happening, too fast. His mouth had begun to tremble; he bit down on his lower lip, turned back toward Richard.

'Uncle, I did not know. But . . . . but surely you are mistaken about my Uncle Anthony. I cannot answer for any others, but I know he'd never act dishonourably. . . .'

Without meaning to, he'd struck a nerve. For Richard, time was suddenly open-ended, fluid, past and present merging into a long-ago October eve at Middleham. He looked at his nephew, hearing himself say those very words to Warwick, in defence of Ned. For an unnerving instant, he found himself able to identify so completely with the boy that pity closed his throat, made speech impossible. It was Buckingham who answered for him, said brusquely,

'They have kept their dealings in these matters far from Your Grace's knowledge.'

'Do not listen to them, Edward,' Dick Grey said suddenly. 'You trust me, do you not? Trust your Uncle Anthony?'

903

Edward's eyes flicked toward Grey, back to Richard. He said now, with a hint of shaky defiance, 'I do trust my Uncle Anthony. Why cannot he be the one to guide me, he and my mother . . .?'

'Because,' Buckingham snapped, 'the governing of a kingdom is not woman's business, is for men to do. As for Woodville. . . .'

'Harry,' Richard said quickly, warningly. 'Edward, your father did think it best that I be the one to counsel you. Surely you do want to abide by his wishes?'

That gave Edward pause. 'Yes . . .' he agreed, sounding more polite than positive.

'Well, that is all we seek to do here today, to make sure that his will shall be honoured. To do that, it was necessary to detain your uncle in Northampton, but no harm has come to him. You can see for yourself when we do return to Northampton this morning. Now, perhaps you'd like to wait in your chambers whilst we make ready to depart . . .?'

It was courteously posed as a question. In actual effect, it carried the weight of an order, and Edward was adult enough to see it as such, to comprehend that a choice was not being offered him. He nodded, made a stiff retreat that had in it an unexpected and rather touching dignity.

Richard moved to the window, saw that the men below in the courtyard were his. They were still vastly outnumbered by the young king's escort, but the latter seemed little inclined to offer resistance, seemed to be waiting for orders that were not going to come. Turning back to Dick Grey and Thomas Vaughn, he said abruptly, 'As of this moment, you both are under arrest.'

The two thousand Welshmen in Anthony Woodville's service had been dismissed, told to disperse back to their homes. Bewildered, bereft of leadership, they did. All at once, Richard realized how hungry he was. He'd bypassed breakfast, had eaten next to nothing the night before. Now he could think of mundane matters like food again, sent a servant down into the inn kitchen, and the cooks, eager to please, soon set before him a plate of rice pancakes and Brie tarts. But after a few mouthfuls, he pushed the plate away. His appetite was suddenly gone; he found himself seeing again that stricken look on Edward's face as he fled the chamber. How could Ned's son be such a stranger to him? And the boy's obvious love for Anthony Woodville. . . . Christ Jesus, how were they to deal with that?

'My compliments, cousin. I see why you've won for yourself such a name on the battlefield.'

Buckingham had come into the chamber, stood grinning down at him. 'Well planned, brilliantly executed, and entirely successful.'

'And lucky,' Richard said, gave a brief smile. 'I owe you much, Harry. Once before you dealt yourself into my affairs. This time it came damned close to costing you your life. I'll not be forgetting that, I assure you.'

Buckingham shrugged. 'I'll not deny that I do want a voice in your government and why not? By blood alone, I'm entitled to it. But it is more than that. I know the Woodvilles too well, the snakes in our Eden. I'd move heaven and earth to see them brought down into the dust where they belong, and you're the one man strong enough to do it. So you see, cousin, it was never a question of choosing sides. The choice was made for me, nigh on sixteen years ago.'

It took Richard a moment to remember. Sixteen years ago, Buckingham had been compelled to marry Elizabeth's young sister Katherine.

'You'll have to dismiss the boy's attendants,' Buckingham said now, and Richard nodded.

'I know,' he said reluctantly. 'He's got to be weaned away from the Woodvilles, and his people are Anthony's hand-picked hirelings. But he's not likely to understand, Harry. How could he?'

Buckingham shrugged again, said, 'Are you ready to leave?'

'No, not yet.' Richard got to his feet. 'First I want to talk with Edward, see if I cannot ease his mind some.'

'As you will. But do not be looking for your brother in that boy. Take it from me, cousin,' Buckingham said, suddenly serious, 'he's all Woodville.'

Richard frowned, turned away without answering.

Richard was hesitating before the door of his nephew's bed-chamber. What could he say to the boy? He'd have to tell Harry to watch his tongue in the future, not to speak slightingly of Elizabeth before Edward; he could think of no worse way to win Edward's confidence than that. But could it be won at all? There must be some way to reach him. He was Johnny's age. Perhaps talking to him like Johnny. . . . He knocked lightly on the door, pushed it open.

Edward was an unusually handsome youngster, with his mother's silver-blond colouring, his father's vivid blue eyes. They were, Richard noted, suspiciously red-rimmed. Had the boy been crying? He could hardly be blamed if so. Jesus God Above, what had Ned been thinking of? Of all the men in Christendom, why had he to pick Anthony Woodville as Edward's mentor?

'Edward, I should like to talk with you.' He waited, watched the boy come forward reluctantly, sit stiffly beside him on the settle.

'You think I do not know how you're feeling, but I do. I know better than most. I was just your age when Ned quarrelled with our cousin Warwick. I did love them both, Edward, learned a bitter lesson in irreconcilable loyalties.'

Edward said nothing. He was studiously staring down into his lap; all Richard could see was a crown of bright hair.

'What I'm trying to say is that I understand how confusing this is for you. You love your Uncle Anthony and you do not know me all that well. But once we're in London . . .' And what difference would that make to the boy? Their problem was not one of geography. He was the wrong uncle.

'Edward. . . .' What was there to say? That he'd loved Ned? That should have been a bond between them and yet Richard sensed that it was not. Edward had raised his head, was looking up now with Ned's eyes. No, not Ned's. Guarded eyes that gave away nothing.

'If you're ready, lad, we can ride back to Northampton,' Richard said and, without thinking, started to put his arm around the boy's shoulders as he would have done with his own sons. It was the first time he'd touched Edward; he got a response neither one of them expected. Edward stiffened, jerked back as if stung. The withdrawal was involuntary and, for that reason, all the more telling.

Edward quickly recovered his poise, even looked slightly embarrassed.

'I did not mean to be rude,' he said, very politely. 'You did startle me, Uncle, that's all.'

Richard was stunned, for he'd read in Edward's recoil more than mistrust. There'd been fear, too. Before he could stop himself, before he could think better of it, he said softly, 'Good Christ, what have they told you of me?'

3

Westminster

May 1483

'Bess! Bess, wake up!'

Bess opened an eye, saw all was dark, and buried her face in her pillow. 'Go 'way. . . .'

'Bess!' Cecily was insistent and Bess rolled over onto her back, blinked up at her sister.

'Cecily? It's not dawn yet, is it?'

'Nigh on four. Bess, do wake up. It is urgent. Grace came to me and . . .'

Bess was still groggy. 'Who?' she yawned.

'Bess, for pity's sake, listen to me! Something's very wrong. Lights have been burning in mama's chambers all night, people coming and going, messengers running in and out. . . .'

'Well, what did mama say? You did go to her . . . did you not?'

Cecily ducked her head. 'I did not dare,' she faltered. 'You know how she's been these three weeks past, Bess. . . .'

Bess did. Fully awake now, she sat up. 'Hand me my bed robe, Cecily. Where is Grace now?'

'I sent her to see what she could find out. Do you know what she told me, Bess? That a hole has been knocked in the sanctuary wall. She said she saw men dragging coffers and furniture across the court, and when the doorway proved to be too small, they just made another opening through the wall. Do not look at me like that, Bess! It's true! Come to the window, see for yourself!'

Bess stood frozen at the window, gazing down at a scene out of forgotten childhood nightmares. Torches stabbed the dark, blazed through the blackness of the outer bailey to show men struggling with coffers and crates, wrestling with what looked to be a huge feather mattress, staggering under the weight of silver plate and heavy oaken chests.

Cecily had been too young to have memories of their six months in sanctuary; that was a time in her life mercifully lost to her. Bess was not so fortunate, for Bess did remember. Now as she stared down at the utter chaos below, it all came back to her, and the fear she felt was familiar, was that of a bewildered four-year-old child, suddenly thrust into a world that was alien, threatening.

*

The stairwell should have been lit by rushlights. It wasn't and Bess and Cecily had to grope their way up by the feeble glow from Cecily's lantern.

'Bess, could the French be bombarding London? Now that papa's dead, they might think they could. . . .' Cecily gave a gasp for she'd just bumped into something that was warm, alive. She recoiled so violently that she stepped on her sister's foot. Bess gave an irritated exclamation that would not have passed muster in polite company, grabbing for the lantern.

'Cecily? Cecily, it's me!'

'Grace? Oh, thank the Lord; you did stand my hair on end. Tell us, what have you learned?'

'Not much. But I did find Master Brent, your lady mother's almoner, and he said he'd heard that your brother Thomas Grey has been trying to raise an army!'

Cecily swung around toward her sister. 'Bess, why would Tom . . . Bess? Bess, wait!'

By the time Bess reached her mother's chambers, she was panting and her heart was beating in such a rapid irregular rhythm that, suddenly dizzy, she had to stop and catch the doorjamb for support. Just then the half-open door swung back and Thomas Rotherham, her father's Chancellor, pushed through.

Bess caught his sleeve. 'My lord Archbishop, what is wrong? Please, tell me!'

His face was blanched, looked to her to be the exact shade of bleached white worn by the Cistercian and Carthusian White Monks. An elderly man, he seemed to Bess to have aged years since she'd seen him last. If he was surprised to see her here at such an hour, he showed no sign of it, said in a throaty quaver, 'You need not fear, my lady. I've given the Great Seal over into the Queen's own hands.'

Bess blinked. The Great Seal? Mama had no right to that, no right at all. What was he talking about?

'No, you need not fear. As I assured Madame your mother,

should any evil befall young Edward, we'll then crown your younger brother in his stead.'

Bess stared at him in horror and then pushed past, entered her mother's bedchamber. There she stood rooted, unable to believe what she was seeing. Men were dismantling the enormous feather bed, stripping tapestries from the walls. Coffers were open in the middle of the floor, table and chairs piled high with her mother's gowns, with bolts of velvet and cloth of gold. From a storage place in the garde-robe, men were lugging out furs of ermine and fox, dodging and cursing at the hysterical small spaniel that was nipping at their ankles and barking like a creature demented.

None paid the slightest heed to Bess. Like one manoeuvring through an obstacle course, she edged around the coffers, an over-turned stool, moved toward her mother. Elizabeth's back was to her, but she could see the faces of her half brother Thomas and her Uncle Lionel, Bishop of Salisbury. Both men looked dazed; Thomas was saying, in a voice that was so unlike his normal speaking tones Bess would not have recognized it as his, 'Mother, it is no use. I've been trying for nigh on five hours, and I tell you none will fight for us. Stanley says bluntly he can do nothing, that he'd have to be a lunatic to come out for us now. Morton of a sudden is counselling caution. St Leger was apologetic enough but he, too, thinks the risks are too great. Even Edward Grey, my father's own brother . . . even he will not. . . .'

'Mama?' Bess could wait no longer. 'Mama, what is Tom talking about? Mama, what is happening?'

Elizabeth turned and Bess received yet another shock on this, a night of so many. Never had she seen her mother look as she did now. Elizabeth's face was deeply flushed, barren of cosmetics and shiny with sweat. The silver-gilt blonde hair Bess had so often envied was in utter disarray, falling into her eyes and hanging in untidy wisps about her face; it had all the lustre and sheen of sun-dried straw. It was the first time that Bess had ever seen her mother show her age, show every one of her forty-six years. And that somehow was more frightening to Bess than anything that had so far happened.

'Bess?' As if focusing on her daughter for the first time. 'Thank God you're here! There is no time to spare. You must awaken your brother and sisters, tell their nurses to get them dressed, to pack clothes for them. Go on Bess, hurry!'

'But. . . .'

'Bess, do not argue with me! Do as I say!'

Bess had never before disobeyed a direct order; her mother had always been one to command immediate obedience. But now she stood her ground, cried, 'Name of God, mama! Tell me what is wrong!'

Thomas had slumped down on one of the half-filled coffers. He looked up at that, fixed upon Bess the blank green eyes of one in shock; she'd once seen a man exposed to too much cannon fire who looked as Thomas did now.

'It is Gloucester, Bess,' he said, shook his head as if trying to clear it. 'All has fallen through, all. . . .' He waved his hand vaguely. 'He's arrested Anthony and Dick, has taken Edward into his custody. . . .'

'Gloucester?' Bess whirled about to stare incredulously at her mother. 'You mean to seek sanctuary from my Uncle Dickon?' Shock sent her voice higher, made it suddenly shrill. 'Mama, he is papa's brother!'

Elizabeth had turned away, was kneeling before an open coffer. Taking out a small casket, she raised the lid, gave them a glimpse of gold-encrusted emeralds.

'So was Clarence,' she snapped. 'Now stop standing there and do as you were told. We do not know how much time we have.'

Cecily had come unobtrusively into the chamber. Bess saw on her sister's face the same stunned disbelief that must show upon her own. Had mama gone mad? How else explain this mindless senseless panic?

'Mama. . . . mama, please listen to me. This is madness. I know you've no liking for Dickon but we've nothing to fear from him, believe me. Have you forgotten how papa trusted him? How close they were?'

Elizabeth slammed the coffer lid down, gave her daughter a look of such fury that Bess shrank back.

'Papa trusted him,' she mimicked savagely. 'And you need no more than that, do you? Your precious perfect father, who could do no wrong. . . . Oh, Blessed Mary, if you only knew!'

'Do not, mama!' Bess locked her hands together to still their trembling. 'Do not speak that way of papa.' She was as angry now as Elizabeth and, for the moment, that anger overshadowed all else, even the awe Elizabeth could always inspire.

'I do not know what happened at Northampton but I do know there is no reason to seek sanctuary. Dickon would never do us harm, never. If what Tom says be true and he arrested Dick and your brother Anthony, it is. . . .' Bess drew a deep breath, and then it was on her tongue, the accusation she'd not dared make until now.

'It is because you gave him no choice, because you acted to thwart papa's dying wishes. He did want Dickon to be protector, mama; you know he did. You had no right to go against his will. And you need not try to convince me it is not so. I know what you and Tom got the council to do and I know what papa wanted. I was there, remember? I was with him till the very last . . . even though you were not!'

With her daughter's first words, Elizabeth had come to her feet, stood listening in rigid, unbelieving rage. Now she crossed the space that separated them and slapped Bess across the face.

Bess hadn't been expecting that; even as a child, she'd never been struck. She gasped, stumbled backward and tripped over one of the open coffers. She grabbed frantically for the table but her ankle was twisting under her and she went down hard, felt pain jolt up her spine, lodge in her lungs and take away her breath.

Cecily gave a stifled cry, knelt by her side in a flurry of swirling skirts. Thomas, too, was bending over her, extending his hand.

Bess ignored it, ignored Cecily's encircling arm. She'd bitten the inside of her mouth, could taste blood on her tongue. She stared up at her mother, her face flaming, and was able to take a small measure of satisfaction when Elizabeth was the first to look away.

Elizabeth was alone in the Jerusalem Chamber of the abbot's lodging. It was a room of many memories for her; in this chamber, her son Edward had been born. In these rooms, she'd taken sanctuary with two half-grown boys and three little girls. And now she was back. With a grown son, a boy not yet ten, and five daughters, the eldest seventeen, the youngest two.

Twelve years, seven months. To the very day. October 1st, 1470. May 1st, 1483. In my end is my beginning. Who said that? Was it from Scriptures? Why could she not remember?

Twelve years and so many deaths. Her mother. Three of her children, two in the cradle and Mary, taken at fourteen. Ned. Warwick. His brother Montagu. Clarence. But not Stillington. God forgive you, Ned, but not Stillington.

What now? Jesus, Lamb of God, what now? Twelve years ago, she was still young. She was only thirty-three and she'd known . . . she'd never doubted . . . that Ned would come back. She'd known he would not fail her.

Elizabeth found she was standing by the window; how long she'd been there she did not know. I am alone, she thought. I am utterly alone and there is no one to deliver me from mine enemies. No one. She leaned forward, brought her hands up to her face and wept, bitterly and without hope.

The Lord Mayor of London, the city aldermen, and five hundred of the most prosperous citizens gathered at Hornsea that following Sunday to welcome their young king into the capital. Edward wore blue velvet; on his right rode his Uncle Richard, Duke of Gloucester, and on his left, his Uncle Harry Stafford, Duke of Buckingham, both in the stark black of mourning. The people of London turned out to cheer, ready to love the son as they'd loved his father. With considerable ceremony, he was installed in the Palace of the Bishop of London. Buckingham retired to his own manor in Suffolk Lane, Richard to Crosby Place.

'I agree, Dickon, that it's damnably awkward.' Will Hastings smiled, rather sourly. 'To have our king's mother and her children huddling in sanctuary not a stone's throw from the palace . . . well, it is downright embarrassing. But we've had no luck in getting her to see reason, to come forth with young York and his sisters. You know, if she had a brain in her head, she'd have stayed put, brazened it out. What could have been done to her, after all? As a woman and the King's mother, she'd have been well nigh immune to the consequences of her treacheries, whatever price Thomas Grey might have paid. By scrambling for sanctuary, she only confessed her own guilt, showed one and all that her conscience could not stand the scrutiny of close light.'

Richard was only half listening to Will. 'I truly think,' he said abruptly, 'that I was gaining ground with Edward. At least, he was no longer looking at me as if he suspected me of having a cloven hoof.'

Will grinned at that. Richard did not. There was an hourglass before him on the writing desk. He picked it up, flipped it over.

'And just like that,' he said bitterly, 'whatever progress I may have been making has been obliterated. Did you see the boy's face, Will, when we had to tell him? Can you imagine how it looks to him? By retreating into sanctuary, that bitch did confirm in Edward's mind every fear he'd been taught to harbour against me. How can I ever hope to win his trust now, with his mother proclaiming to the world that I am not to be trusted with the lives of my brother's widow and children?'

Francis gave him a sympathetic look. 'It'll take time, Dickon, but it can be done,' he said, with far more confidence than he felt.

Will, too, was sympathetic, but not to the extent of letting Richard's bad humour dampen his own good spirits. Will had been celebrating for four days now, ever since word of Richard's actions at Northampton had reached London. To Will, the future looked to be full of promise. The Woodvilles had broken like branches in a high wind. Edward was securely in their keeping. Till the boy came of age, he and Gloucester would have the government. He'd be Lord Chamberlain to Edward as he'd been to Ned; he thought he stood a good chance of eventually winning the boy's confidence.

It stood to reason, after all. By taking such drastic, decisive action to sever Edward from the Woodvilles, Gloucester had done the country no small service, but he'd paid a high price. Will did not think Edward was likely to forgive Gloucester for it. In his mind, Gloucester would be ever branded as the man who'd separated him from the uncle he loved. Will was sorry for that, but still, it did work to his advantage. It was true he was no friend to the Woodvilles either, but he had not been at Northampton. That, he thought, would count for much with Edward.

'She does have an uncanny knack for poisoning the well,' he commiserated. 'But take heart, Dickon. Sooner or later, she'll come to her senses. It cannot be that comfortable for her, after all, and our Lady Lisbet has ever been a one for her own ease. They damned near stripped the palace, you know, took tapestries and plate and whatever else they could get their hands upon. Not to mention Ned's treasury. Edward Woodville sailed with most of it on Tuesday last; the rest Thomas Grey and the Queen have with them in sanctuary.'

Richard stood up suddenly, moved aimlessly to the window and back again. As ever when agitated or angry, he could not keep still; he was beginning to make Will nervous with his pacing and restless fidgeting. Moreover, Jane was awaiting Will even now at his manor by Paul's Wharf. She'd invited herself to supper; whether she had more in mind, Will did not know, but he was very interested in finding out. He rose, made his farewells to Richard, to Francis Lovell and to the Duke of Buckingham. He was at the door before he remembered.

'Dickon, it almost did slip my mind. Rotherham came to me the other day. In a sweat, the old boy was, shaking in his shoes that he was going to be held to account for that gaffe with the Great Seal.' Will grinned reminiscently, shook his head. 'He pointed out that he'd soon come to his senses, hied himself back to Westminster to reclaim the Great Seal from Elizabeth, hoped that might count in his favour. I did assure him we'd let bygones be bygones, that. . . .'

'Out of the question.' This was the first contribution Buckingham had made to the conversation in more than an hour, was said in so cold a tone that Will's eyebrows arched upward.

'Come now, Harry,' he protested amiably. 'I grant you the old man made a right proper ass of himself but no harm was done, after all. More to the point, I think it good politics if we keep a light hand on the reins just now. Do not rock the boat, if you will. There'll be time enough to ease Rotherham out later, and until. . . .'

Buckingham was no longer slouching on the settle. Sitting upright, he shook his head, cutting Will off in midsentence.

'The man's either a Woodville collaborator or a Woodville dupe. Whichever, he's a liability, one we do not need.'

Will's amiability was now edged in ice. 'As one new to the councils of government, Harry, I think you may be somewhat green in your judgments. I happen to believe it would be a mistake to dump Rotherham now and, with all deference, my experience is rather greater than yours in these matters.'

Jesú, Francis thought, was it to start as soon as this? He agreed with Buckingham; Rotherham had to go. But why did Buckingham have to act like the lord of the manor dispensing justice to the serfs? Hastings was no man to take orders; for twenty-two years, he'd been England's Lord Chamberlain, had been at the very heart of the Yorkist king's government. Why did Dickon not take a hand in this, intercede ere it got truly sticky?

Glancing toward Richard, he saw why, saw that Richard was not even listening. His face was shuttered, remote; wherever he was, Francis thought, it was miles from Crosby Place and this ugly little confrontation. Well, if Dickon would not intervene, he'd damned well better.

'If I may,' he said hastily, 'I think I do have the solution. You each make a persuasive case; why not act upon them both? Take the chancellorship from Rotherham as my lord Buckingham advocates, but let him retain a seat on the council, as you suggest, my lord Hastings.'

Neither man looked much impressed by his mediation. Fortunately, Richard had belatedly become aware of the sudden tension. 'I have not had much time to think it over, but I was inclining toward giving the chancellorship to John Russell, Bishop of Lincoln. How does that strike you, Will?'

Russell was an ideal compromise choice and Will was not petty enough to deny that merely to soothe a chafed pride.

'A good man,' he conceded. 'I think he'd be most acceptable to the council. I certainly find him so.'

The room temperature seemed to return to normal. Will engaged in easy small-talk for a few moments more, made an unhurried departure. But Francis had seen the way his dark eyes kept coming back to Buckingham. There was on his face, Francis decided, the surprise of a man travelling a familiar path and encountering a roadblock where one was least expected.

We are, he admitted uneasily, going to have a problem with these two. Hastings is not a man to yield willingly his place in the sun. For all his talk about keeping a light hand on the reins, he fully expects one of those hands to be his. As for Buckingham, he'll be one to watch; his first taste of power seems to be going to his head.

After Buckingham called for his escort, galloping off down Bishopsgate Street at a pace to rattle windowpanes and send cobblestones flying, Francis joined Richard again in the solar. He'd meant to caution Richard about the jealousy he'd just seen but, at sight of his friend's face, he relented. Dickon had enough cares at the moment. There was no need to burden him with yet another. He acted himself as cupbearer, brought Richard a full goblet of vernage.

'You know, Dickon, it is rather sad. Edward does not even know his own brother and sisters all that well. How often has he seen them, after all? The girls, hardly at all. I understand the younger boy spent some time at Ludlow but not enough for them to become truly close. Not the way brothers should be, the way you and your brothers were. . . .'

He stopped abruptly for he'd seen what Richard would rather he hadn't, the tears that had come suddenly into his eyes.

Francis tactfully busied himself in pouring his own drink. This was the second time today that he'd seen Richard at the mercy of his memories. That morning they'd passed through Barnet on their way into London and Richard had thought to show Edward the battlefield. Whether he'd succeeded in awakening in the youngster a genuine spark of interest was difficult to say. Edward was polite to the point of insult, clutched courtesy to him as if it were a shield, the only one he had. But for Richard, the recollection of a battle twelve years past had only lacerated anew a wound less than three weeks old. He was not yet up to talking of his brother without pain, as Francis had just inadvertently proved.

The numbness is wearing off, Francis thought. It's beginning to sink in, to seem real. God pity him, these next weeks will be the worst, will be the hardest to get through. And to find now that the Queen is refusing to leave sanctuary. Embarrassing, Hastings had called it. No, it is far worse than that. It is a deadly insult, does hit Dickon where he's most vulnerable, in his love for the late king.

Richard was back at the window. 'How I do hate Westminster,' he said suddenly, almost violently. 'I tell you, Francis, even the air seems unfit to breathe. It is just as I remember it. Men caring only for their own advancement, sucking up to those who can do them the most good, sycophants and lick-spittles and worse. You never do know where you stand at court. Even my brother, even he could not keep himself from being dragged down into the mire. And if it could happen to as strong a man as he was, what do you think will befall a boy like Edward?

'Do you know what Jack Howard told me, Francis? That Jane Shore has become Thomas Grey's mistress.' Richard shook his head slowly. 'Can you credit that? Jack says Ned's bed was not even cold before she crawled into Grey's. And Ned did care for that woman; he truly did.'

Striding to the sideboard, he reached for the wine flagon, poured and drank before turning back to Francis. The anger had gone from his face; he looked very tired, looked utterly at a loss.

'You remember how I spoke apart with Edward this afternoon, once we'd got him settled into the Bishop's Palace? Do you want to know what he said to me, Francis? He asked me why, if he were king, that he could not just order his uncle's release. . . .'

Richard's voice trailed off. He and Francis looked at each other, neither speaking, while on the table between them, the candles that still clung to light splashed hot wax into silver holders.

4

London

May 1483

Richard had reluctantly decided against charging Anthony Woodville, Dick Grey and Thomas Vaughn with treason. He felt the discovery of four wagonsful of armour in Dick Grey's baggage train more than warranted such a charge, proved beyond doubt that the Woodvilles had meant to use military force if need be to maintain their hold upon the government. Nor was it his personal inclination to be lenient. Had he his way, he'd have seen that the Woodvilles paid the full price for their treachery. But political considerations ruled otherwise. His relationship with his young nephew was too precarious to allow for private retaliation.

He was not prepared, therefore, when in a midmorning council meeting at the Tower, John Morton, Bishop of Ely, suddenly questioned the continuing captivity of Elizabeth's kindred. As he had no liking for Morton, Richard's response was more acerbic than it might otherwise have been; he reminded the Bishop sharply of the indisputable proof of a Woodville conspiracy, and was at once backed up by both Buckingham and John Howard. Morton had persevered, however, wanted to know if Richard was so sure in his own mind that the men were, indeed, guilty of treason.

'Yes,' Richard snapped, 'I've no doubts whatsoever of it,' and only then did he see how adroitly the trap had been laid. In that case, Morton said smoothly, the council should take action upon it; treason was the most serious of all crimes and should be dealt with as such.

The ensuing vote was a stalemate of sorts. Morton and the former Chancellor Rotherham argued against indicting the Woodvilles on a charge of treason, on the grounds that since Richard had not been officially confirmed as Lord Protector until his arrival in London, whatever the Woodvilles had plotted was technically not treason. Morton had prevailed, by a bare majority, but the council then sided with Richard in agreeing that the confinement should continue indefinitely.

Richard could take some satisfaction from that, but not much. The council's refusal to indict only underscored what he already knew, that he was presiding over a coalition government of rival factions and uncertain loyalties. By letting himself be manoeuvred into seeking a charge of treason and then failing to get it, he'd not only exposed his own vulnerability and brought to light the council's inner dissensions, he antagonized his young nephew to no useful purpose. All in all, he thought sourly, a day's work to be proud of and one sure to be back to haunt him in the troubled times ahead.

Edward's coronation date had now been set for Tuesday, June 24th, and in accordance with tradition, he'd been installed in the royal residence at the Tower. It was only a short walk from the Council Chamber in the White Tower, therefore, for Richard to pay a courtesy call upon his nephew. Less than an hour had elapsed since the conclusion of the council session and yet Richard saw at once that Edward had already been told. Too resentful to dissemble, he blurted out in lieu of greetings, 'You lied to me. You told me you meant my uncle no harm and now you seek to charge him with treason.'

What Good Samaritan, Richard wondered wearily, had he to thank for this? Morton, most likely. He'd hoped to have more time, to be able to explain it to Edward himself, was in no mood to deal with the boy's Woodville-bred suspicions. He tried, however, reminded Edward quietly of the discovery of the wagons of armour and weapons, of the actions they'd taken to deprive him of the protectorship, their seizure of the treasury.

He was, he soon saw, wasting his breath. Edward had lapsed into a sullen silence; his words were falling on deaf ears. And how could it be otherwise? How could he expect a twelve-year-old boy to understand, to forgive?

It was uncommonly hot for mid-May and the chamber was stifling. Sun filtered through the windows with the thickness of smoke and dust particles danced on the air, settled upon their clothing. A dull, persistent pain had begun to press against Richard's temple.

'I know there is much you find hard to understand. All I can tell you, Edward, is that I am trying to act in your best interests. I would hope you'll come in time to see that, even if you cannot just now.'

'How is it in my best interests to separate me from my Uncle Anthony?' Edward's breath was coming very quick; his voice rose unevenly. 'It's not because of me at all, it's because you do hate him, because you've always hated him. He told me, told me you've long borne a grudge against our family.'

Our family. The Woodvilles. Damn you, Ned, but what were you thinking of? Richard shook his head, said slowly, 'That's not true, Edward. I'll not deny I've little liking for your lady mother's kin; I'll not lie to you about that. But they did force my hand at Northampton. It need not have happened. I'd not make use of the protectorship to settle old scores. And your father knew I would not; for that reason, he did name me and not your Uncle Anthony as protector.'

'You say my father trusted you, but all I know is that my uncle did not. Nor does my mother. Why else would she have fled into sanctuary, still be refusing to come out unless she feels she has cause to fear you?'

That was a jab into a festering sore. Richard's mouth hardened; he said sharply, 'Fear has not a damned thing to do with it. It is malice, pure and simple.'

It was the first time Edward had seen his uncle angry and he

922

shrank back. Richard caught himself, would have given a great deal to be able to call his words back. It was, of course, too late.

Richard had spent several harried hours at Westminster, dispatching writs for the coming parliament. It was late afternoon before his barge started downriver. The sun was low in the sky, a red-gold haze along the horizon, but the air still smouldered with heat. It shimmered upon the water, seared Richard's skin and trickled sweat into his hair. The smell of the river was all around him, rank and rancid. Along the shore, he could see a man emptying slop pails into the water, in defiance of local ordinance. The citizens of York were no less careless of health considerations; they, too, used the river as a convenient dumping ground for refuse. But for the moment, that was forgotten. Richard gazed moodily at the debris floating past his barge and it seemed to him to be characteristic of all he found abhorrent and distasteful in Westminster.

By the time he reached Crosby Place, his shirt was sticking damply to his shoulder blades and his head was throbbing. He was supping that evening with John Howard, had just time enough to bathe and change, and he was far from pleased to find Will Hastings awaiting his return.

Will made desultory conversation for some minutes, the sort of idle, amusing talk that passed the time and said little. But as soon as Richard's servants had withdrawn and the two men were alone, Will's demeanour changed abruptly. Setting his wine cup down, he said bluntly, 'You surprised me this morn, in truth you did. You are as good a battle commander as any I've seen, yet you did forget one of the most elemental rules of warfare. . . . At all costs, cover your flanks.'

Richard did not need to be told that; nor did he much like hearing it from Will, who'd voted that morning with Morton, voted down a charge of treason. 'That is a lesson you've learned, at any rate,' he said coolly, saw a faint discomfited red dye Will's face and neck.

'Look, Dickon, between you and me, I'll freely admit you're in the right about the Woodvilles. There's not a one of them worth the hanging. But do not expect me to say that in council. We've got a boy king who does have a genuine affection for his Woodville uncle and I've no intention of forgetting it. Now if that does make me a hypocrite . . .' He shrugged. 'Well, so be it.'

His candour was disarming, struck echoes in Richard of his brother. It was, he knew, the same sort of calculating common sense he'd have had from Ned and some of his resentment began to ebb. He could hardly blame Will, after all, for being smart enough not to get entangled in Morton's snare.

'If you are, you're honest with it,' he said with a faint smile. Will smiled back and Richard found himself recounting that disastrous noontime meeting with his nephew. Will listened in silence, shook his head when Richard was through.

'Do you know what Ned once said about you, Dickon? He said you thought patience to be one of the Seven Mortal Sins. He was right, you know. Edward's a bright youngster and he'll come around in time. But it will not be tomorrow or next week or even next month. Woodville has had him for nigh on ten years; we've had him but a fortnight. You should try to bear that in mind.

'No, the problem as I see it is not with Edward. The problem is Harry Stafford, Duke of Buckingham.'

Richard straightened up; wine splashed on his wrist. 'Christ, Will, not that again.'

'Yes, that again,' Will said grimly. 'Is it true that you mean to appoint Buckingham as Chief Justice and Chamberlain for North and South Wales?'

'Yes, I do.'

'That is a mistake, Dickon. Buckingham's not a man to entrust with that much power. Take my word for it.'

'I need more than that, Will. Harry's given me no reason to doubt him and every reason to trust him. Had it not been for him, I might well have ridden into a Woodville ambush. I owe him a great deal.'

'So, I believe, Ned once said of Warwick.'

'What would you have me do, Will? By blood alone, he's entitled to a place in council. He's stood with me from the first, backed me at a time when none knew if I'd keep either the protectorship or my life. I've had nothing from him but wholehearted support. And this is how you'd have me repay him, by denying him the voice he deserves in my government? And why? Because you do not happen to like the man. Jesus God, Will!'

'Ned did not like Buckingham, either,' Will said sharply. 'Have you never wondered why?'

'And are you saying that Ned never made an error of judgment? The man who married Elizabeth Woodville and turned his son over to her brother to raise?'

'Oh, Ned made mistakes, all right; more than his share, perhaps. But Buckingham was not one of them. Buckingham is yours.' Will shoved his chair back, came to his feet.

'Loyalty is an admirable trait, Dickon. Unless it blinds you to the flaws all others see. I watched you delude yourself with Warwick and your brother Clarence, watched you learn the hard way that they were not the men you thought them to be. At the risk of giving offence, you're not the best judge of character, Dickon. You've too often given your loyalty to men who did not deserve it.'

Richard, too, was on his feet now. 'If loyalty distorts judgment, what then, of jealousy? That is what we're truly talking about, is it not? Buckingham has my trust and you do not like it. I expected better of you, Will. You know the men we have to deal with. Morton, Rotherham, Stanley—self-seekers, all. Yet you'd have me shut out a man who's proved beyond doubt where his loyalties lie, and for what? So that you can have a bigger portion of the pie.'

Will had gone rigid with rage. 'I'll take up no more of your time,' he said stiffly, strode across the chamber and reached for the door latch. Richard watched in silence. His anger had not completely obscured his common sense; he knew he shouldn't let Will leave like this. But he couldn't bring himself to make the first move. He was tired and resentful and it was easier to say nothing, to tell himself that he was in the right, that Will must be the one to make amends.

The bedchamber was awash in June sunlight. A trail of clothing led across the carpet toward Richard and Anne's bed, the black sendal of his mourning doublet, her dark gown, a frothy lace-edged kirtle.

Anne turned her head on the pilllow, studied Richard through her lashes. She was still surprised by the intensity of his greeting. However ardent he might be in private, Richard was generally rather circumspect in public; it was unusual for him to be more demonstrative than hand-holding or a discreet kiss. She'd not been prepared, therefore, for an impassioned embrace on the outer steps of the great hall, within full view of half the household of Crosby Place. For once totally uncaring of the amused, approving eyes upon them, Richard had taken Anne directly up to their bedchamber. She'd not even unpacked; her coffers were still downstairs in the great hall.

He'd surprised her, too, by the urgency of his lovemaking. Her lips parted, curved upward; she felt a languid warmth laying claim to her body again, a sensation both indolent and erotic. She was not sure she would want Richard to make love to her like this every time; tenderness was too important to her for that. But it had been exciting. She laughed softly. In truth, it had been that.

'What is so amusing, sweetheart?'

She moved closer, shifted so that their bodies touched at hip and thigh and shoulder. 'I was thinking of the pleasure you gave me, and how much I do love you,' she murmured, saw him smile.

He'd lost weight since she'd seen him last. She saw it in the hollows under his cheekbones, in the tightness of the skin along his jaw. The creases around his eyes were more pronounced, too. She traced their path with a light finger, wondering why people called them 'laugh lines' when they were anything but that.

He listened attentively as she reassured him about his sons, shared the news of Middleham, relayed to him messages from the York city council and Lord Mayor. But he'd volunteered little of his own activities these six weeks past and now she hesitated, not wanting to interrogate him and yet anxious to know what had been happening.

'I did as you requested and stopped at Berkhampsted on my way south, Richard. Your mother gave me a letter for you; it is in one of my coffers.'

'Did you ask her to reconsider her refusal to come to London?'

Anne nodded. 'Yes, love, I did. She said she hoped you'd understand why she could not. She's not left Berkhampsted since she did take vows, nigh on three years now; not even for Ned's funeral.' She paused. 'I do not think you should urge her further, Richard. We all have to find our own path and the way she's found is right for her. I'm sure of it, for never have I seen her so tranquil in spirit, so at peace with herself.'

'I do envy her that,' Richard said briefly, and then, 'Did I write you that I'd sent for George's children? Grey had them sequestered on manors in Devon and for five years they've been kept apart, have not seen each other even once in all that time. The girl will be here by week's end and the boy did arrive yesterday.'

'Edward Plantagenet, Earl of Warwick,' Anne said softly, somewhat sadly, and then she smiled ruefully. 'Lord help us once we have Ned here, too. How we'll tell all these Edwards apart, I've no idea. Tell me about George's little boy. What is he like?'

'He is the very image of George at age eight. But in temperament, they do seem like day and night. George was born to mischief. His son, though, is very quiet, very shy, and far more timid than is natural for a boy his age. But it may be that he's just not yet at ease with me. I do not,' Richard said with sudden bleakness, 'seem to be having much luck these days with any of my nephews.'

'Richard, talk to me. Tell me about it . . . please. You need to share the burden, love, in truth you do.'

She was right, Richard thought; he did. 'I've never felt like this before, Anne. . . . so frustrated, so at the mercy of events beyond my control.' He propped a pillow behind his head, turned toward his wife.

'Every day seems to bring naught but more problems. Money, for one. Although all but two ships of the fleet deserted Edward Woodville, he did keep command of the ship carrying the bulk of Ned's treasury, got it safe to Brittany. And here the council is unable to agree on anything. The only men of the entire council I can count upon are Buckingham and Jack Howard. Having a boy king does bring out the worst in men; they see him as a puppet whose strings are up for the taking, and some of our venerable bishops are the worst of the lot.'

'But what of Will Hastings, Richard? Can you not rely on Will?'

Richard's mouth twisted down. 'Will and I do not see eye to eye on much these days. He does greatly resent Buckingham and I admit Harry does not ease the situation any. There are times when the tension between them is thick enough to be sliced and served up on trenchers.'

'Have you tried talking to Will, Richard?'

'What can I say to him, Anne? I cannot tell him that I agree with his suspicions about Buckingham and that is all he does want to hear. I do not know; I guess I do not know him as well as I once thought I did.'

Anne was frowning. 'But you do still trust him, do you not?' And was relieved when Richard said without hesitation, 'Yes, I trust him. He may be making an ass of himself over Buckingham and playing the fool with that Shore woman, but Will's no Morton, no Stanley. I'm beginning to wonder about his judgment but his loyalties are not in doubt.'

'Will and Jane Shore? But Francis wrote Véronique that she'd become Thomas Grey's mistress.'

'She had. But now that Grey's keeping to sanctuary, she's taken to sharing Will's bed, or so rumour has it.'

Anne raised herself up on her elbow, read in Richard's face her own distaste. Jane Shore had to have been more to Ned than a warm beautiful body; no man keeps a mistress for nigh on nine years unless he does care for her. Anne sighed. Mayhap she was squeamish but she did not like to think of a woman Ned loved being passed about among his intimates like a wine cup or serving knife.

'What of the Queen, Richard? Is she still in sanctuary?'

'Yes.' Tersely.

'But it's been more than a month. What does she hope to gain by this . . . this charade?'

'A great deal. With each day that she stays in sanctuary, she does cause me embarrassment, stirs up dissension in council and makes it less and less likely that I'll ever win Edward's trust.'

Anne sat upright. 'Oh, how I hate that woman!'

'I'll never forgive her for this, Anne. Never. But however much I need her out of sanctuary, I'll be damned before I do pay her price. Her terms, you see, are full pardons for all her kin and seats on the council for Anthony Woodville and Thomas Grey. And there is no way on God's earth that I will ever agree to that.'

'Well, she cannot stay in sanctuary indefinitely. Once she sees she's not going to get her way, she'll come out. What does worry me more is this jealousy between Hastings and Buckingham. What mean you to do about it, Richard?'

'I do not know,' Richard conceded. 'I do not doubt that Ned would have found a way to keep them both content. He had an uncanny knack for that, for juggling rivalries like so many apples. But I do not. I have not the patience.'

'You're too forthright to play games,' Anne said, with such protective warmth that he smiled. 'Had Ned rooted out these antagonisms and intrigues when they first did surface, you'd not be facing such problems. Do not ever forget, Richard, that this field was planted long ago, and by Ned, not by you.'

Richard surprised her now by saying with no small measure of bitterness, 'And a right fine crop he's left for me to harvest, in truth.'

She hesitated and then reached over, brushed the hair back from his forehead. 'You sound as if you are very angry with Ned, love.'

He turned a startled face toward her. 'Yes,' he said slowly. 'Yes, I guess I am.'

A silence fell. Anne was content to wait and, after a time, Richard said thoughtfully, 'There's been so much anger bottled up within me, Anne, these six weeks past. I've been most angry with those you'd expect, with Elizabeth Woodville and Thomas Grey. But with Will, too, for making things so needlessly difficult. And with myself, for not handling it better. At times with Edward, for what I know he cannot help. With Morton, our thoroughly secular priest. But though I did not realize it till now, much of that anger was for Ned.

'I have been angry with him. For taking to wife a woman so utterly unfit to wear a crown. For putting Edward into Anthony Woodville's care, for letting the boy be raised as a Woodville. For turning a blind eye to the hostilities infesting his court. And above all . . . for a death that need never have been. That the man who won Towton at nineteen and Tewkesbury at twenty-nine should have died the way he did, dead at forty. . . . No, I cannot forgive him for that.'

Nor can I forgive him, either. I cannot forgive him for this legacy he's left you, Richard, for bequeathing us a future of fear. Anne did not speak these words aloud. She was sure that Richard, too, looked to tomorrow with foreboding, a tomorrow when

Edward might demand a very high price, indeed, for today's Woodville grievances. That was not a fear to be shared, though. It was one to be buried in silence, neither acknowledged nor admitted.

5

London

June 1483

Edward had no memory of his parents. His mother had died two months before his second birthday and, no matter how hard he sought to put her face together in his mind, there were pieces missing. But he never even tried to do that with his father. His father was not a permissible topic of conversation; it was safer not to think of him at all. For a long time, Edward had not understood why. Not until a nurse much given to gossip had seen fit to dispel his ignorance, told him that his father had been charged with treason, confined to the Tower, and there executed at the King's command. And that Edward understood all too well. His father had died a traitor's death, had died in disgrace, and it somehow reflected upon him. He never again made mention of his father, asked no more questions.

Edward knew he was the ward of a man he'd never laid eyes upon, Thomas Grey. It was very confusing to him, therefore, to be suddenly summoned to London by an uncle he knew no better than he did Grey.

As best as he could puzzle it out, he was to be his uncle's ward.

Edward was not sure yet but he thought he might like that. His uncle had a low, pleasant voice. Edward liked the sound of it, liked the way his uncle tilted his head to the side when he listened, the way he had of laughing with just his eyes. Above all, Edward liked the way his uncle did not ask him questions he could not answer, seemed not to mind that he had so little to say.

Edward had long ago learned not to expect too much. But he found himself wishing that he might stay here at Crosby Place. Especially now that she was here, the slender dark-eyed woman who said she was his mother's sister, said she was his Aunt Anne. She'd arrived yesterday, had come up to his bedchamber last night to tuck him into bed. No one had ever done that before and her perfume had lingered in the room long after she'd gone.

That same flowery scent came to him now. He was poised on the threshold of her bedchamber, the one she shared with his uncle. He sensed he should not be here, but the fragrance beckoned him into the room, was in its own way as strong an inducement as the dog. Loki, his name was. His uncle's dog, come yesterday with his aunt from the far North. He looked to Edward like a large grey wolf, but Aunt Anne said he was called an alaunt. All the dogs Edward had known were stable animals, not pets; he'd never before seen a dog that was given the free run of the house.

Loki was stretched out by the bed. He raised his head, regarded Edward with unblinking dark eyes that slanted at the corners like a cat's. Edward edged closer, hoping for some sign of encouragement. But the plumed tail did not move, lay flat upon the carpet. Edward's disappointment was intense; he'd wanted few things in his life as much as he wanted to make friends with this big dog. He tried to bear in mind what his aunt had told him about Loki, that he was a one-man dog. Alaunts were often thus, she explained and Edward nodded dutifully, said he understood. But he did not, not really, was hurt that Loki was so indifferent to his overtures.

Circling wistfully around Loki, he wandered over to the table that held his aunt's hairbrushes. A blue glass vial caught his eye. He pulled the stopper, rubbed the liquid onto his palm and sniffed; to his delight, he smelled just like roses. So caught up was he in his discovery that he did not hear the approaching footsteps until they neared the door. Startled, he turned toward the sound. The vial slipped from his fingers, cracked against the table and fell to the floor.

Loki rose, stretched and padded toward Anne in polite greeting. With an exclamation of annoyance, she brushed past the dog, bent to pick up the glass scattered about the carpet.

'How in the world did . . .?' It was then that she saw the little boy. He was crouched down against the wall, knees drawn up to his chest, and Anne was stunned by the look of fear on his face.

'Edward? Edward, it is all right.' She held out her hand. 'You can come out now. You'll not be blamed for a mishap. This could happen to anyone.'

Having coaxed the boy to her, she slipped an arm around his shoulders, led him toward the window seat. Colour was coming back into his face. She smiled reassuringly at him, touched the soft sunlit hair. They were a handsome people, her husband's family, but she thought that George and Bella's little boy was possibly the most beautiful child she'd ever seen. But Blessed Lady, what had been done to him? Could the lack of love do such damage?

'Your sister Meg will be here tomorrow, Edward. Do you remember her at all?'

Edward shook his head. 'I do not remember much about . . . about before,' he said apologetically.

'No, sweetheart, I do not suppose you do.'

He was sitting very stiffly beside her, shoulders hunched up, hands folded tightly in his lap, and she wanted to draw him toward her, to cradle his head against her breast.

'Do you know what we're going to do tomorrow, Edward? You and I are paying a call upon Margaret Howard, Lord Howard's wife. She told me today that one of their brachet hounds whelped last month and we have the pick of the litter. Would you like that?'

'Yes, ma'am,' he said politely.

Anne was disappointed by his lack of enthusiasm, and surprised, too; she'd seen how his eyes followed Loki.

'Do you not want a puppy, Edward?' she asked, saw his eyes go round in wonderment.

'You mean . . . it is for me?'

Anne's eyes misted suddenly. Her sister's child. Thomas Grey had much to answer for. And so did Ned, for letting it happen. God forgive him, but Ned's sins of omission were adding up. Who else, she wondered bitterly, would have to pay the price for his lack of care?

Anne closed the solar door, wishing she could shut out the rest of the world as easily as she shut out their household. Richard was sitting on the settle, one leg drawn up under him, jotting down notes in a slanting Italic script. He seemed thoroughly immersed in his task, didn't glance up until Anne leaned over him.

'You've an ink smear on your cheek,' she said, held out a damp-ened handkerchief. 'Here, let me.' He tilted his face up, and she rubbed until the mark was gone, then dropped a kiss lightly on his nose.

'What are you working on, Richard?'

'Issues to be raised at the council meeting on Monday.' He put the papers aside as she settled herself next to him. 'I'm sorry I did not get back in time for supper. Did you go to see Edward as you planned?'

Anne nodded. 'I went to the Tower this morn. It did not go too well, I fear. He is at such an awkward age, too old to console as you would a child and not old enough to be reasoned with as you would with an adult.' She leaned back so that her head rested comfortably in the crook of Richard's shoulder.

'He did ask me why his mother refuses to come out of sanctuary.' She sighed and felt a slight stiffening of her husband's body.

'He did challenge me with that one, too,' Richard admitted. 'What did you say to him?'

'Well, I told him that people may fear even when there be no cause; it's not a rational emotion. I could hardly tell him, after all, that we believe his mother to be playing a game of political blackmail. I reminded him that my own mother had taken sanctuary after the battle of Barnet, even though she had no reason to fear Ned's retali. . . .' She never completed the sentence; Richard had stopped her words with his mouth.

'Anne, that was truly inspired. I'd wager that never occurred to Edward before. What was his reaction?'

'Richard, I so wish I could say he was startled into seeing all in a different light. But it's not going to happen that way, love, and you just have to resign yourself to it. He's a very confused boy, and it will take time. You have to remember that whatever I say is doubly suspect in his eyes. Not only am I your wife, I am the Earl of Warwick's daughter, and I do not doubt he's been taught to view my father as the Antichrist.'

'No,' Richard said grimly. 'I expect that dubious distinction to be mine. The Woodvilles lessoned him well, you see.'

'Lessons can be unlearned, too, love, given time.' And because she herself didn't believe what she was saying, Anne reached up, sought Richard's mouth with her own.

The kiss was easy and unhurried, was a pleasant prelude to slowly stirring desire. Richard tasted of wine. She pretended to nibble on his lower lip, welcomed the touch of his tongue and explored his mouth with her own. When she closed her eyes, he kissed her eyelids, her lashes and then she felt his mouth move lower, down to her throat.

Anne laughed and tickled his ear with her tongue. They'd made love more in the past three days than they normally did in the

935

course of a week. At first Anne had attributed it to their six-week separation. Now she thought it was more complex than that. These days Richard's every waking hour was weighed down with cares, with choices that offered high risks and little satisfaction. And that, Anne suspected, was why he suddenly seemed so loath to leave her bed. He sought in her caresses and the warmth of her body a brief respite from problems that had no solutions, from a troubled present and an even more disquieting future.

Richard had slipped his hand into the bodice of her gown; he was fondling her breast, squeezing slowly. Anne's breath quickened. She could feel her body warming, opening to desire. Her nipple had gone taut against his caressing fingers. She unfastened buttons on his doublet, slid her hand inside his shirt, next to his skin.

'I've an idea,' he murmured. 'Let's go up to bed.'

'At eight in the evening?' Anne teased. 'What, and scandalize the household?'

'Well, then, we'll have to make do here, I suppose. Do you fancy the settle? Or would you rather we threw some cushions on the floor?'

He was, Anne knew, paying her back in kind; his need for privacy was only a little less than her own. She laughed and, wrapping her arms around his neck, slid down on the settle, shifted her position until she could feel the weight of his body on hers. She had no sense of urgency; anticipation did but make carnal pleasures all the sweeter. But Richard was not so patient. He lowered his mouth to hers again and then said coaxingly, 'Come, beloved. Let's go upstairs.'

His hand was now under her skirts, had begun a slow, intimate exploration up her thigh. Anne's arms tightened about him, drew him still closer.

'Yes,' she agreed huskily. 'Oh, love, yes. . . .'

She was dumbfounded by what Richard did next. He'd been

about to kiss her again; instead, he pulled back with inexplicable abruptness, jerked upright on the settle. She opened her eyes in bewilderment, saw that he was staring past her toward the door, and then saw the Duke of Buckingham standing in the doorway.

Anne gasped, and as colour flooded her face, she sat up in embarrassed haste, sought to assure herself that her clothing was in order.

Richard was no less discomfited than Anne and a good deal angrier. 'You're always welcome at Crosby Place, Harry; you need no invitation. But you do need to be announced. In the future, I'd expect you to remember that.'

Buckingham didn't even blink. 'This couldn't wait, cousin. We've news you must hear tonight, news of such import that. . . .' He laughed suddenly, exultantly; there was about him the taut excitement of intoxication, and yet Richard would swear he was sober.

'He's right, Dickon. You do have to hear this.' Francis had hung back at first, unwilling to invade the privacy of Richard's solar as blithely as Buckingham had. But he came forward now, repeated urgently, 'You have to know.'

A third man had entered the room. He seemed very ill at ease, fumbled overlong with the door latch and, when he turned at last, Richard was surprised to recognize his brother's former Chancellor, Robert Stillington, Bishop of Bath and Wells.

'Well, since you're here,' he said ungraciously, 'what is this news that could not wait?'

Buckingham glanced back at Stillington. 'Go on, my lord Bishop. Tell my cousin of Gloucester what you did tell us.'

Richard had seen few men look as uncomfortable as Stillington did now. He was in his early sixties, yet seemed burdened with an extra ten years. His hands kept fidgeting with a rosary looped at his belt and watery blue eyes were looking everywhere but at Richard's face.

'My lord . . .' He swallowed, started again. 'My lord, I'm . . . I'm not a brave man. I've agonized with myself these weeks past, trying

937

to decide what I ought to do. At first, I thought to . . . to keep quiet. But my conscience would not permit it. Your late brother's right to the crown was not affected but it is different now. I've no choice but to speak up, to tell what I know. I did come to my lords of Buckingham and Lovell because I knew them to be men you trust. I suppose I should have come to you directly, but I . . . I feared you might blame me for keeping silent all this time. . . .'

Richard had been listening with growing impatience. At the rate Stillington was rambling on, they were likely to be here all night. But the aging cleric was a guest in his house and he said only, 'Reverend Father, I'm sorry, but I'm not making much sense out of all this. What is it you are trying to tell me?'

'It is about your nephew, my lord. It is about the young king.' Stillington paused and then the words came spilling out, in one great gasp. 'I did call him king, but it cannot be, my lord. The boy cannot be crowned.'

Richard cut his eyes sharply toward Buckingham. 'I do not like this, Harry. I do not like this at all.'

Undaunted, Buckingham shook his head. 'Nay, cousin, it's not what you think. Hear him out, that be all I ask.'

Now that Stillington's tongue was loosened at last, he suddenly seemed almost eager to tell what he knew.

'I'm not talking treason, Your Grace. I'm saying what I should have said years ago. In the eyes of the Church, your nephew is a bastard. Your brother's marriage to the Lady Elizabeth Woodville Grey was fatally flawed, for at the time they exchanged vows, he was not free to wed. More than two years before, I'd plight-trothed him to the Lady Nell Butler, widow of Sir Thomas Butler of Sudeley and younger daughter to John Talbot, Earl of Shrewsbury.'

For the first time, Stillington's tension appeared to ease. With something much like relief, he concluded quietly, 'So you see, my lord, the coronation must be cancelled. The boy cannot be king.'

'I do not believe you.' Richard's words were instinctive, had come without thought or volition. Nor were they true. He did believe Stillington; the man was too frightened to lie. There was wine on a side table and he turned toward it, impelled not so much by thirst as by the need to perform some reassuringly familiar task. He'd not yet fully absorbed the import of Stillington's revelation, needed an anchor of some sort, needed time to come to terms with it all.

Ned and Nell Butler. A secret plight-troth. Sweet Jesus God! But it explained much, explained Elizabeth's reckless refusal to accept the protectorship. It explained, too, why she'd been so unrelenting in her hatred for George, Ned's lawful heir. . . . His fingers froze around the wine flagon. God, no! Swinging about, he grasped Stillington's wrist.

'Tell me,' he demanded, 'was this why my brother was put to death?'

Stillington shrank back, pulled ineffectually against Richard's grip. 'That was none of my doing, Your Grace. Your brother Clarence stumbled onto the truth on his own, was foolish enough to let the King know it. But I played no part in it, I swear I did not. I had no choice but to obey the King's will. My lord . . . you are hurting me!'

Richard released Stillington's arm, stepped back. For a moment, no one spoke, and then Buckingham said admiringly, 'I confess I did not at once see the link with your brother of Clarence. You're very quick, cousin.'

Richard stared at him, said nothing. Anne had yet to move from the settle, where shock had held her immobile. Now, however, she came hastily to her feet, moved toward Richard. But when she touched his arm, he pulled away.

Stillington was speaking again, was still insisting that he was innocent of any blame for George's death. Anne scarcely heard him. The voice echoing in her ears was Ned's, the words those he'd spoken to Richard that September afternoon at the Archbishop of York's Palace. 'Do you think I could put my own brother to death unless I were convinced there was no other way?' Was Richard, too, remembering that? He'd moved to the window, but she didn't need to see his face. The rigid set of his shoulders was as expressive as anything he might have said. As she watched, he clenched a fist, sent it slamming into the wall above his head. Anne winced and tears filled her eyes.

'I know this is a shock to you, cousin, but I do not think you've fully realized what it does mean. Once Dr Stillington does make this known, there's no way the boy can be king. The crown is yours for the taking. We need only put this before the council, let them. . . .'

Richard spun around. 'No!'

For the first time, Buckingham looked disconcerted. 'Cousin, it's yours by right. All you have to do is reach for it. . . .'

'I tell you no, Harry! I need time . . . time to think.' Richard sounded shaken, but there was no doubt he meant what he said. 'You're to say nothing of this. Is that understood? I do want your sworn words on that. Nothing at all.'

'My lord Lovell, you do know His Grace of Gloucester as well as any man. I implore you, tell me the truth. Is there any chance he might refuse to take the crown?'

These were the first words Bishop Stillington had spoken since they'd left Crosby Place and returned to Buckingham's manor in Suffolk Lane. Francis hesitated but, while he sympathized with Stillington's predicament, he didn't feel up to allaying his anxieties with lies.

'I do not know,' he conceded. 'I realize that is of little comfort but I truly do not know.'

'But he's the rightful heir.'

Francis shrugged tiredly. 'Yes, but it is a right to leave a bad taste in a man's mouth. Whatever the sins of the parents, the boy is blameless. It's no easy choice Dickon faces. To brand his brother's son a bastard before the world, to claim the crown Edward thinks to be his birthright?'

'He has to take it. He has to. If he does not, my life will be worth next to nothing. As long as I need only open my mouth to disinherit the young king, I'm too dangerous to let live.'

Francis wished he'd given Stillington the reassurance he so needed. 'My lord Bishop, you're agitating yourself for naught. We do not know that he will. . . .'

'What do we not know?' Buckingham had come unheralded into the chamber. Not wanting witnesses to the confidential conversation to follow, he'd summoned no servants. Moving to the sideboard, he began to pour wine for his guests, saying, 'Well? What have I missed?'

'We were discussing whether or not Dickon would take the crown,' Francis said reluctantly and Stillington nodded. Both men were rather taken aback when Buckingham began to laugh.

'Is that what is bothering you, Reverend Father? Well, you may put your mind at rest. He'll take it.'

It rankled with Francis that Buckingham should so presume to know Richard's mind, enough to provoke him into saying coolly, 'I do not see how you can be so sure of that, my lord. We're talking about more than legal rights; there are moral rights to take into account, too. Whilst there be no question of the late king's culpability, it may well be that Elizabeth Woodville married him in good faith. And be that as it may, the children at least are innocent of any wrongdoing. You think that does not trouble Dickon? If so, my lord, you do not know him as well as you seem to think.'

Buckingham looked amused. 'Am I poaching on your property?'

'What mean you by that?' Francis snapped.

'Just that I realize you're an old and intimate friend of Richard's. You do know him well, I do not doubt. But in this, I'd wager a great deal that my reading be the right one.' Buckingham handed Stillington a gilded cup, stood for a moment looking down at Francis with silent laughter hovering on his lips.

'Do not be so thin-skinned, my lord. I'm not jealous of your friendship with my cousin of Gloucester; we need not be rivals. I'm simply saying that whatever his doubts, he'll take the crown.'

'You do sound so positive of that,' Stillington said nervously, almost wistfully.

'And with reason. If Richard felt he could not in conscience put the boy's crown upon his own head, there is yet another option open to him. Whilst he lived, George of Clarence was the rightful heir of York. Well then, why not crown his son? By so doing, we'd be solving the problem posed by Edward's illegitimacy, and Richard need not feel that he was profiting at his nephew's expense. However, I do not recall any mention being made tonight of Clarence's boy, nary a word. Now why do you think that was?'

Stillington was shaking his head. 'Have you forgotten, my lord Buckingham, that the Duke of Clarence was attainted of high treason? That Bill of Attainder does bar his son from any claims he might otherwise have had to the succession.'

Buckingham did not appear to be impressed. 'And do you mean to tell me that a Bill of Attainder has never been reversed? If my memory serves, both the late king and Richard himself were attainted by Warwick's parliament. No, the attainder is an impediment but not an insurmountable one. It could be dealt with but it will not be. There's no need, after all. Why seek to legitimize the tainted claim of a child when we can have a man grown, a man of proven abilities and a blood right to the crown?'

He saw Stillington was convinced. The priest was smiling for the first time since leaving Crosby Place. Francis looked as if he still harboured doubts but he seemed inclined to keep them to himself, saying nothing.

'No, my lord Bishop,' Buckingham said contentedly, 'you need not fear. For a man to turn down a crown, he'd have to be either a fool or a saint. And my cousin of Gloucester, I can assure you, be neither.'

*

Anne closed the solar door and, after a moment's reflection, shot the bolt into place. Richard was still standing by the window. Half expecting another rebuff, she touched his arm.

'Richard, sit down . . . please. I'll fetch some wine and. . . .'

'I do not want any.'

She hesitated, knowing he wanted only to be alone and yet unwilling to leave him. Reaching for his hand, she saw then the damage done when he'd hit the wall; his knuckles were scraped and bleeding.

'Richard, your hand! Let me wash it clean with wine,' she entreated and was faintly surprised when he offered no protest. He followed her to the table, watched in silence as she poured wine onto her handkerchief.

'Can you not talk to me about it?'

He raised his eyes to her at that. 'I find myself wondering if I ever truly knew him at all,' he said, very low.

Not knowing what to say, Anne busied herself in wrapping the handkerchief around his hand.

'Shrewsbury's daughter! How did he think he could get away with it? And George. . . . How in Christ can I ever tell my mother that, Anne? How can I tell her that Ned lived a lie for twenty years and George died for it?'

For the first time within memory, Anne found it easy to come to her brother-in-law's defence, for not only could she understand his motivation, it was hers, too.

'The plight-troth I do not understand, no more than I ever understood that secret May marriage to Elizabeth Woodville. For all his abilities, your brother's judgment could at times be frighteningly flawed. But once it was done, once George found out . . . well, I can understand why he felt he had no choice then but to do what he did. He was thinking only of his children, did put their welfare above all other considerations.' She drew a deep breath, said, 'And so must you, my love. You have no choice either, Richard. You must take the crown. For our son's sake, you must.'

Richard tensed and for a moment, she thought he was going to pull away. 'Edward was entrusted into my care. I did give my sworn word that I would be loyal to him, that I'd look after him. Do you think I can forget that?'

Anne shook her head. 'No,' she said sadly. 'I know you cannot. But tell me this, Richard. In three years, Edward will be sixteen. What then? What happens when he demands payment for Northampton?'

'It does not have to be that way. In three years, he could come to understand why I took the actions I did.'

'Yes, he could. But you do not expect that and neither do I. The Woodvilles have taught him too well. And even if Edward could learn to forgive, Elizabeth Woodville never will. Nor will her kin and, sooner or later, they're going to have to be set free. They do hate you so, Richard, and now we know why. You're the rightful heir of York; think you that they could live with that?

'No, Richard, we'd best face it. Our future holds naught but grief. You're not likely to live very long under your nephew's reign, my love, and should evil befall you, what do you think will happen to our son? To me?'

'Anne, I do not want to hear this!'

'Surely you do not think I like saying it. But it has to be said. If you fall, Richard, Ned and I will be dragged down with you. If I'm lucky, I'll find myself confined to a convent for the rest of my days. If I'm not, I'll be forced into marriage with a husband handpicked by Elizabeth Woodville, a husband hot for the lands I could. . . .'

Richard had jerked his hand from hers. 'You think I do not know that? You think I can forget for a moment what befell Humphrey of Gloucester's wife once he was stripped of his protectorship? Charged with witchcraft, forced to do penance through the streets of London and condemned to life imprisonment on the Isle of Man. You think I do not lie awake at night and see you in her place? Christ, if you only knew!'

The anger in his voice was raw, wrenching, wasn't anger at all. Anne hated herself for what she was doing to him, for using his love as a weapon. But she had no choice, no more than he did. Ned had to come first.

'Richard, I love you. I'd not want to live without you. But what of Ned? What do you think would happen to him? Need I say it? I've seen what five years as Thomas Grey's ward has done to my sister's son. When I think of Ned in their hands, I—oh, God, Richard, we cannot let that happen!'

Richard sat down abruptly, sagged into the nearest chair as if his body had suddenly been sapped of all strength. Anne yearned to go to him but the fear of rejection kept her where she was. Would he ever be able to forgive her for this? She moved to stand behind his chair, let her hand rest on his shoulder in a tentative caress. He reached up, covered it with his own, and only then did silent tears begin to streak her face.

'It's so unfair,' Richard said softly. 'So bloody unfair. . . .'

'I know, love,' Anne said, just as softly. 'I know.'

It was nearly dawn when she asked the one question as yet unanswered. Neither one of them had slept. For several hours, she'd lain awake beside Richard, watching him stare into some inner vista she couldn't share. Finally she leaned over, touched his face with soft fingers.

'Richard, might I ask you something? We've talked tonight of what you must do, of what you can do, of what you ought to do. But we've said nothing of what you want to do. Richard, do you want to be king?'

At first she thought he wasn't going to answer her. But as she studied his face, she saw he was turning her question over in his mind, seeking to answer it as honestly as he could.

'Yes,' he said at last. 'Yes . . . I do.'

6

London

June 1483

It was a Tuesday evening, three days later. Richard was still resisting Buckingham's demands that they summon Stillington before the council, still refusing to let the plight-troth be made public. He needed more time, he insisted, time to think it through, and with that, Buckingham had to be content.

A goldsmith had just been ushered out of the solar. He'd crafted for Richard a delicate pendant, a heart-shaped emerald set in gold filigree. The pendant was Richard's present to his wife; the next day was her twenty-seventh birthday. Richard held it up to the light and then lowered it again into its velvet wrappings. As he did, a discreet knock sounded at the solar door.

'Your Grace? Lord Howard is without in the great hall, seeks a private audience.'

John Howard was not a man to waste words. Taking a seat, he leaned forward, said bluntly, 'I might as well tell you straight out. I do know about the plight-troth, about your brother and Shrewsbury's daughter.'

'Richard caught his breath. 'How . . .?'

'Stillington,' Howard said succinctly. 'He did come to me this morning. He's badly frightened, Dickon, seems scared out of his wits that he's put his neck on the block. I expect he figured that by telling me and Will, he'd reduce the chances of his secret being buried and him along with it.'

'Will? You mean he did go to Hastings, too?'

946

Howard nodded. 'He said he went to Will after the council meeting yesterday. He had it in mind to go to Dr Russell, too, but I think I persuaded him to hold off on that.'

'More fool I,' Richard said slowly, 'for not anticipating this. I should have foreseen what he'd do.' He raised his eyes, met Howard's steady grey ones. 'Tell me the truth, Jack,' he said tautly. 'What think you of all this?'

'The truth? I think it is a godsend. For you, for York and for the country.'

Richard's tension was dissipated in a rush of relief. He'd not realized until that moment just how much he'd come to rely on John Howard's judgment. Buckingham and Francis were far from disinterested, after all; the one motivated by ambition and the other by friendship. But Howard was both tough-minded and fair. His approval would go far toward resolving many of the tangled doubts and uncertainties of these past three days.

'You think, then, that I should take it?'

'I think you'd be making the biggest mistake of your life if you did not.'

'What of Will? What did he say?'

'I saw him briefly this afternoon but we did not have much time to talk. Stillington's tale hit him as it did me, like a bolt from nowhere. He does remember your brother's involvement with Nell Butler, says there was much talk at the time, what with her being a lady of rank, an Earl's daughter.'

'He said nothing else?'

'He did say it might be best to have an ecclesiastical court pass judgment upon the plight-troth. I'd advise against that myself, would submit the issue to the council and parliament. I can think of nothing more dangerous than delay.'

He rose, then, said, 'Well, I've said what I came to say. I think I do understand why you've held back so far. But do not wait too long, Dickon.'

'Jack. . . . There's something else you should know.'

Howard sat down again. 'Trouble?'

Richard nodded. 'We both know there are some members of the council who have not reconciled themselves to the protectorship. They tried once before to take it from me and this morning we were given proof that they do mean to try again.'

Howard showed no surprise. 'I've been half expecting something like this. Morton is the ringleader, I do not doubt. That one could no more resist intrigue than a fox could keep out of the henroost. And Rotherham; his nose has been out of joint since the chancellorship was taken from him. Not to mention our Woodville Queen and that worthless son of hers. Who else?'

'Stanley. His wife has become a frequent visitor to sanctuary of late; now we do know why.'

'How did you find out?'

'The usual way a conspiracy is unravelled. It occurred to one of Rotherham's cohorts that the information he possessed might be worth a great deal. He went to Buckingham with it.'

'The Woodvilles, Morton, Rotherham and Stanley.' Howard grimaced, made a sound of disgust. 'Christ help the country should that crowd ever get the government in their hands. What mean you to do?'

'I did write to York, telling the Lord Mayor and council that I'd uncovered a Woodville plot against my life, asking them for as many men-at-arms as they can muster. Dick Ratcliffe is taking my message north tomorrow. He's also to stop at Leconfield, to seek aid from Northumberland.'

'That one's not likely to bestir himself until he can be sure of the winning side,' Howard said caustically, 'but the men of Yorkshire will rally to your standard readily enough. They're not likely to reach London for a fortnight, though. Until then, what?'

'I've put Morton, Stanley and Rotherham under surveillance. There is not much more I can do for the present, Jack. Except be very careful,' Richard added dryly.

'Do you want me to tell Will?'

Richard hesitated; Will Hastings and John Howard had been friends for more years than Richard himself had been alive. 'No, I do not, Jack. I've given it much thought, think it best if Will's not brought into this. There's no reason for him to know, after all. The conspiracy's not directed against him; he'll be in no danger.'

Howard was frowning. 'Surely you've no doubts about Will?'

Richard shook his head. 'Not Will, the woman he's sharing his bed with. We just cannot take the risk that Will might inadvertently let something slip. For, whilst she spends her nights with Will, her days she does pass with Thomas Grey in sanctuary.'

'I see your point. Besotted as Will seems to be about that Shore woman, we could not be sure what he might tell her. He's acting like a damned fool over her, more like a lovesick village lad than a man of two score years and ten. But just try telling him that.'

Howard came to his feet. 'Keep me advised, Dickon. And bear in mind that a conspiracy can be as volatile as gunpowder, wants only a spark to set it off. In the days to come, you look well to yourself.'

'You need not worry,' Richard said, and his voice was suddenly grim. 'I intend to.'

After supper on Thursday, Richard retired to the solar with his secretary, John Kendall. But he found it hard to keep his mind on routine matters of correspondence. He'd had a disturbing talk with Buckingham a few hours before, a talk he'd rather forget. Buckingham had pointed out a political reality Richard was not yet ready to face. Before Stillington's disclosure could be made to the council, Edward's brother would somehow have to be secured from sanctuary. The danger was too great that he might be smuggled out, be used by unscrupulous men to foment rebellion.

Richard knew, of course, that Buckingham was right. The Scots might well choose to back a rival claimant to the English throne; James still bore a grudge for the English support given his brother, the Duke of Albany. As for the French king, Richard knew he'd like nothing better than a chance to muddy English political waters and it would matter little to him that the boy's claim was tainted. Louis, after all, was the man who'd backed Warwick and Lancaster, the man who was even now giving financial aid to Harry of Lancaster's Welsh half brother Jasper Tudor and his nephew, and only the most die-hard of Lancastrians seriously contended that the Tudor claim to the throne was much more than wishful thinking.

But knowing Buckingham spoke pragmatic common sense did not make it any the more palatable for Richard. For five days, he'd been trying to convince himself that he'd reached no decision as yet, that there was, indeed, a decision to be made. Buckingham had now made him see that time was running out. Edward's coronation was just eleven days away. As soon as this new Woodville conspiracy was exposed, so, too, would Stillington's story have to be made public. And Richard had been forced to admit Buckingham was right, forced to admit he'd been deluding himself.

The choice was already made, had been from the moment Stillington found the courage to speak out. He would take the crown. He had to. It was the only way he could safeguard the future of those he loved. And it was his by right. In the eyes of the Church, he was justified in so doing. So why, then, did it give him so little ease of mind?

John Kendall had gone to answer a servant's summons. Reentering the solar, he said, 'Your Grace, might you spare some moments for Sir William Catesby? He says it is urgent.'

Will Catesby was in his mid-thirties, Northamptonshire gentry, a lawyer of some skill. Prior to his assuming the protectorship, Richard's contacts with Catesby had been confined to a few social occasions at Bolton Castle, for Catesby was Alison Scrope's son-in-law; he'd married her daughter by her first marriage. Richard did not know him all that well, but he'd recently appointed Catesby to the council, at the request of Will Hastings. Richard had been glad of the chance to oblige Will at so little cost, had found Catesby to have a shrewd, discerning intelligence. It wasn't hard to understand how he'd come to stand so high in Hastings's confidence and Richard wondered if he were here on Hastings's behalf.

'Thank you for seeing me alone, Your Grace,' Catesby murmured as Kendall discreetly retired from the room. 'I know that is an unusual request, but what I have to say must be kept confidential.' Catesby was visibly nervous; Richard could see sweat shining on his forehead, beading his upper lip.

'I know of no easy way to say this, Your Grace. There is a plot taking shape against you, one that will cost you not only the protectorship but your life. . . . Unless you do take measures to see to your safety.'

Richard was startled, hoped it did not show on his face. How had Catesby stumbled onto it?

'Go on,' he said warily.

'They do call the French king the Universal Spider but that name might better be given to Bishop Morton. He and the Queen have spun between them a right sticky web, my lord. They've entangled in it His Eminence, Archbishop Rotherham, and no less a lord than Thomas Stanley. And now . . . now they've even managed to win over the Lord Chamberlain, to win over my lord Hastings.'

Richard stared at him. 'God, no. . . .'

'This is very difficult for me. I am betraying a man I do respect, a man who has done much for me. But I want no part of this, Your Grace. This is treason and I'll not. . . .'

Richard stood up so abruptly that his chair rocked, tipped precariously. 'Be sure of what you say. Be very sure. We've had the others under surveillance for three days, and not a one of them has met with Hastings outside of council. So how then? Suppose you do tell me how?'

'So you did know!' Catesby was now on his feet, too. 'The

go-between was Jane Shore, my lord. For the past two days she has been taking messages from my lord Hastings to the Queen and Thomas Grey in sanctuary. No, Your Grace, there is no mistake. Lord Hastings did tell me himself what they mean to do, and what they intend be treason, plain and simple. The plan is to order your arrest, to crown Edward as soon as possible thereafter, and set up a regency council.' He hesitated, then confessed, 'There is much about this I do not understand, Your Grace. I know Lord Hastings and you have not been on good terms this month past. I know, too, how deeply he does resent the Duke of Buckingham. But even so, I cannot see that alone goading him into seeking an accommodation with the Queen. My lord, have you any idea what might have driven him to this?'

'Yes.' Richard's voice was very low; he sounded stunned. 'Yes,' he repeated, more audibly. 'I do have a very good idea. . . .'

'I trusted him, Harry. God damn him to Hell, but I truly trusted him!'

'Cousin, I know you did but that's neither here nor there. What we have to do now is decide what is to be done. And the sooner the better. With Hastings in the plot, that does tip the scales in their favour. We dare not wait for your northern supporters to reach London. If we do, they're likely to be just in time for the funeral.'

'I expected no better from Stanley or Rotherham. But Will. . . . Jesus wept!'

The solar door was suddenly flung open. Francis looked shaken, flushed with some strong emotion.

'Dickon, have you heard what's happened? Thomas Grey has escaped from sanctuary.'

7

London

June 1483

Will had at last fallen into a fitful sleep. In repose, his face showed every one of his fifty-two years, showed the strain of the past three days.

They'd been bad days for Jane, too. She had not the temperament for conspiracy, found herself dwelling upon all that could go wrong, unable to shake off an uneasy foreboding. She hadn't wanted it to be like this, knew Will hadn't, either. Men like Morton thrived on intrigue; Tom, too, seemed in his element. But not Will. He was aging before her eyes, sleeping little and eating less. Trying, she knew, to reconcile a troubled conscience to an alliance of expediency, to the bloodshed to come.

She leaned over, touched her lips to brown hair generously streaked with silver. Passing strange but she'd never noticed before how grey Will was getting. Pray God she'd not wronged him. She liked Will so much, could not bear to be the instrument of his hurt. How haggard he looked, even in sleep. Almost as careworn and strained as he had on Monday night, when he'd shared with her Bishop Stillington's revelation, told her that Gloucester meant to claim the crown.

Never had she seen Will so upset as he'd been that night. He'd cursed Ned in language that would do justice to a bankside boatman, said he'd brought them all to ruin with his lusts and his overweening arrogance. Jane would normally have much resented such talk but she had the wits to see that Will was not accountable for all he said, no more than was a man in his cups or one afire with fever. She'd done what she could to soothe him, listened sympathetically as he confessed his fear for the future.

Once Gloucester was king, he'd be manoeuvred aside. There'd be no place for him in Gloucester's government. Buckingham would see to that, would want to be Gloucester's chief minister, would brook no rivals. And Gloucester would heed Buckingham. Gloucester thought he'd played Ned false, aided and abetted him in his carousing and thus brought him to an early grave. What had he in common with Gloucester, after all? A man twenty-two years his junior, a man of northern affinities, of rigidly defined moralities. Ned had been the only bond between them and now they were linked by nothing more substantial than memories.

Jane had gone the next morning to sanctuary, had gone to Tom. It was then that she became convinced that Bishop Stillington had spoken the truth. The look of horror on Elizabeth Woodville's face was to Jane the most eloquent testimony that could be put forward in favour of the plight-troth. So, too, were Elizabeth's hysterical denials. With each frenzied frantic word Elizabeth uttered, Jane's conviction grew that the plight-troth was, indeed, true and Ned's son the victim of his father's sin.

Jane had never had much liking for Elizabeth but she could find it in her now to feel pity for the other woman, a queen for nigh on twenty years and now no more than a concubine in the eyes of the Church. Her heart went out to young Edward, to Ned's other children and, when Tom asked her to help, she didn't hesitate.

At first, she'd had few qualms. She'd been able to win Will over with surprising ease. It was true, she conceded, that he and the Woodvilles were estranged by years of enmity. But if he could save the throne for Ned's son, that would count for all and the past for nothing. What better stepping-stones to greatness than a young king's gratitude? He'd be Edward's mainstay, the first voice in council, his future as assured under the son as it had been under the father. And he'd be doing a great kindness, preventing a miscarriage of justice. Edward was an innocent, after all. Why should he suffer for wrongs that were not his?

It was only today that her certainty began to be clouded by doubts. The revelation of an ongoing conspiracy with Bishop Morton had come as a shock to Jane. How could Tom have kept that from her? And, he'd made several slighting remarks about Will that did not sit well with her. Will's support was crucial to the success of their scheme; it was not right to belittle him behind his back, did not augur well for the future.

But it was Will's unease of mind which did trouble her most. She'd begun to realize that Will cared for her much more deeply than she did for him. Had that made him more receptive to her pleas than he would otherwise have been? She did not like to think so; that was a burden she was not willing to take upon herself, that Will might have been coaxed into conspiracy out of love for her. She reminded herself that it was his own political survival which did motivate him, his fear he'd be shunted aside, stripped of the chamberlainship once Gloucester was king. But still it nagged at her peace of mind; however deep Will's discontent, would he have acted upon it were it not for her? And now he was committed, had thrown his lot in with the Woodvilles he so disliked, and his shadowed dark eyes held a baffled bewilderment, as if he were not sure how it had all come about.

Jane peeled the sheet back; it clung to her skin, sticky with sweat. Jesú, how hot it was! What would happen tomorrow morning at the council meeting? Would Will be able to carry it off, to face Gloucester as if nothing were amiss? Stray wisps of hair had escaped her night-plait, were tickling annoyingly against her neck. She brushed them back impatiently, sat up in the bed. She wished tomorrow were not a Friday the thirteenth; a bad omen, that. If only she knew that Tom was safe, that he'd got well away from sanctuary. If only she could be sure that this was what Ned would have wanted her to do.

She had been sure of that . . . in the beginning. Ned had loved his son, would want to see him crowned. But . . . but would he be willing that so many men must die that Edward might be king? It was that which gave Jane pause. She'd not fully realized before what the cost in men's lives would be. Others must die with Gloucester. Buckingham. Viscount Lovell. All those who stood closest to Gloucester, who might have been made privy to the secret of the plight-troth. Would Ned have wanted that? He'd loved his son but he'd loved his brother, too. Would he have been willing to sacrifice Gloucester for the sake of Edward's sovereignty?

She sighed. Why could she not care for Will as he cared for her? He was a good man, a decent man, and she could depend upon him, knew he'd always be there for her. Why was it, then, that she wanted Tom? Tom, who was a will-of-the-wisp, as unpredictable as he was handsome. What a pity she could not find a man as reliable as Will and as exciting to lay with as Tom! But then, she had. For nigh on nine years, she had.

Will mumbled something inaudible; it sounded like her name. Jane frowned. She'd not been honest with Will, had led him to believe she cared more than she did. She could live with that. But what if she'd done him a far greater hurt? What if their plans did not work out? Or—and this question brought her up short— what if they did? Once Will had secured his political future, would he come in time to feel the price had been too high?

She had to stop this. It served for naught. All would be well. It had to be. Edward would be king; Tom and Will would govern for him until he came of age. And in time she'd forget that his crown had been anointed with blood. Tom would help her to forget.

Shortly before nine, servants began to make ready the Council Chamber on the upper floor of the White Tower. Their task was easier than it might otherwise have been for the council was not meeting in full session that day.

John Morton, Bishop of Ely, was the first to put in an appearance, followed by Lord Stanley. One by one, the others passed through the river gate into the Tower bailey, stopped to pay respects to Edward who was playing at the archery butts on Tower Green, and then made their way up to the Council Chamber, took their seats.

It was not a congenial gathering, the atmosphere charged with dark undercurrents of strain, much like the static electricity that foretold a coming storm. Archbishop Rotherham had his mouth almost at Lord Stanley's ear; as he droned on, Stanley stared out the window, looking bored. Morton made desultory conversation with Buckingham. No one else spoke. Will Hastings looked ill, almost unkempt, and there was about his eyes a bruised puffiness that proclaimed him starved of sleep. Apparently oblivious of the others, he was gazing down at a paper before him, sketching aimless circles with an erratic pen. John Howard had taken a seat as far away from Will as he could get, had yet to meet his old friend's eyes even in passing. Less than four hours had elapsed since he'd been made privy to Will's involvement in the Woodville-Morton plot, and the shock had not yet worn off. Beside him, Francis fidgeted nervously, watched the door.

It was after ten before Richard entered the chamber. He stood unmoving for a moment in the doorway, as if reluctant to cross the threshold, and then came forward, took his seat at the head of the table.

'Your Grace does look overtired this morn. Not a bad night, I trust?'

John Morton's brows were raised in query. So solicitous did he sound that a stranger might well have assumed he was asking after the health of an old and intimate friend. Richard found his fingers twitching of their own volition; he wanted nothing so much at that moment as to be able to wipe away that fraudulent smile with his fist. He turned away without answering, let his

957

eyes travel the length of the table until they came to rest upon Will Hastings.

If Morton was disconcerted by Richard's rudeness, it didn't show on his face. 'Well, Your Grace, what is the first order of business?'

Richard ignored him. He drew a deep, steadying breath and then began to speak, very low and very fast.

'My first lesson in betrayal came at seventeen, when I did learn that my cousin Warwick had taken as ally the woman he had reason above all others to hate. I'd have thought no degree of double-dealing could surprise me after that but I was wrong. Last night I did discover all over again just what men will do in the name of ambition. Even men who profess to love honour. . . .' His mouth contorted suddenly. 'Men who cloak their betrayals in friendship.'

He could hear chairs shifting about, scraping against the floor rushes. Will's pen had frozen with Richard's first words. It now jerked, snapped cleanly in two by the pressure of clutching fingers.

'I'm not sure I do follow you, my lord.' It was Morton, regarding Richard with admirable aplomb; only the flicker of hooded black eyes gave the lie to his icy composure. 'Just what are you implying?'

'Implying? I'm implying nothing. I'm accusing, my lord Bishop, accusing you and your confederates of plotting against the government, of seeking my death and the deaths of all those likely to oppose you.' Richard's words were coming too fast now, were slurring in his haste to get them said. 'In short, my lord Bishop, I'm charging you with treason.'

There was a deathly silence. Rotherham's lips were puckering queerly, sucking in air like a beached fish. Stanley half rose, seemed to think better of it. Will's face twitched as if experiencing an unexpected pain; it had taken on a queer dusky red, a sudden suffusion of blood.

'I can assure you, my lord of Gloucester, that . . .'

'No, Dr Morton, you cannot.' Richard was gripping the edge

of the table so tightly that a ring was being driven deep into his flesh; he didn't even feel it.

'There is nothing you can say that I want to hear. You and Thomas Stanley and Archbishop Rotherham did enter into a conspiracy with the Queen and her Woodville kindred to seize control of the government and, in so doing, you stand accused of far worse than treason and attempted murder. You were willing to risk civil war, cared not that you might be plunging England back into the turmoil and chaos of Lancaster's reign. And had you succeeded, you'd have bled the country white with your greed, with a bloodletting such as even Marguerite d'Anjou would have shrunk from.

'And this . . .' His eyes came suddenly back to Will. 'This you did know, Lord Hastings. You could have no illusions about the allies you'd chosen for yourself. You knew what they'd do once in power. And still you fettered yourself to them, to the Woodvilles and this Judas priest. Christ, Will, how could you?'

A commotion erupted at the end of the table. Stanley had unbuckled his scabbard before the council began, hung it over the back of his chair. Coming to his feet, he fumbled for it, sought to draw the sword. John Howard was quicker. He grabbed Stanley's wrist, jerked with such force that Stanley lost his balance, somehow got his feet tangled under the legs of his chair, and fell heavily against the table.

Before anyone could move, before Stanley could regain his feet, the door was shoved open and men-at-arms rushed into the chamber. Rotherham, who was closest to the door, shrank back with a sound much like a bleat. Stanley's sword had fallen to the floor in the scuffle. Francis kicked it out of reach.

Will finally found his voice. 'It's not true,' he said hoarsely. 'Dickon, I do swear to you that it's not!'

'And on what do you swear, Will?' Richard asked bitterly. 'On the love you bore my brother? My brother, who died at forty because of you and men like you, you with your carousing and

959

your court sluts. What cared you that your riotous living was ravaging his health, quenching his life's breath like a gutted candle?'

'That's not true! I did love Ned fully as much as you, accept no blame for his death. My whole life was a litany of loyalty to him, to York. How can you accuse me now of treason? Jack. . . .' Will jerked about in his chair, toward John Howard. 'Jack, for God's sake, tell him I'd not join a Woodville intrigue.'

Howard averted his eyes. 'Will, do not,' he said gruffly. 'It is no use to lie. You misjudged Catesby. He did go to Dickon.'

The breath went from Will's lungs in one audible gasp. He slumped back in his chair and then raised hollowed dark eyes to Richard's face.

'You forced me to it, Dickon. I did not want it this way but you gave me no choice.'

'I see. . . . You betrayed those who called you friend, intrigued with those you had most reason to distrust, sought to disavow your plotting with still more lies, and now you do explain it all away as my fault?' Richard said, so scathingly that Will's face went even redder.

'Yes, damn you, yes! What did you expect me to do? To stand by whilst you let Buckingham usurp the place that was rightfully mine? A man who is green as grass and as hungry for power as ever Warwick was. I was Ned's chamberlain for twenty-two years; you owed me better than this!'

'I trusted you, Will. Fool that I was, I trusted you! Even knowing that you were sharing Ned's harlot with Thomas Grey, I never once suspected you might be false!'

A vein was pulsing in Will's forehead. 'And Ned trusted you. You above all other men. With his dying breath, he gave his son over into your keeping. And how mean you to fulfil that trust? By branding Ned's children as bastards and taking the crown from a boy you swore to protect!'

Richard had gone very white. He was on his feet, backing away from the table, and the look on his face was such that the captain of his guards at once came forward, hand on sword hilt.

'Your Grace? What is your will?'

'This man does stand convicted by his own mouth of high treason. Let him learn, then, how traitors be dealt with.' Sweat glistened at Richard's temples; his chest heaved as if he'd been running. 'Take him out onto the green and strike his head from his shoulders.'

The man blinked. 'You mean . . . now, Your Grace? Without a. . . .' He'd been about to say 'trial', but thought better of it in time, said instead, 'What . . . what of the block, my lord? We're not set up for an execution. . . .'

'Find one!' Richard shouted. 'I do not care how but see to it!'

The captain didn't wait to be told twice. He signalled and men-at-arms moved to Will's chair, pulled him roughly to his feet. He didn't resist; his mouth was working but no sounds emerged. The other accused men looked no less stunned. Stanley struggled briefly with his captors, was dragged away from the table by force. Seeing that, Morton stood up hastily. He'd lost much of his urbane assurance now that he thought he, too, might be facing the axe within moments; his face was blanched a sickly bloodless colour neither white nor grey. Rotherham had begun to make soft whimpering noises low in his throat. He had to be grasped under the arms and yanked upright and even then he could not stand alone, had to be supported by the guards.

No one else had moved. Francis looked dazed. Buckingham was brightly flushed, his eyes glittering green-gold in the sun. John Howard had bitten his lip so deeply that blood was beginning to trickle down his chin.

It was to Howard, not Richard, that Will now looked. 'Jack?' he whispered, saw the other man flinch away from the sound. Before he had time fully to realize that Howard was not going to intercede for him, nor was Richard to relent, he was at the door, was about to be shoved through into the stairwell.

'A priest!' he blurted out desperately. 'Holy Christ, but you'd not deny me a priest!'

The captain, however, was not about to do anything at that point without Richard's express authorization. 'Your Grace? May he be shriven?'

And only when Richard gave a jerky nod did the captain turn to his sergeant, say tersely, 'Go to the chapel. Get us a priest. Take Hastings onto the green; wait for me there. Escort the other three to Wakefield Tower and put them under guard.'

Once the door had closed behind them, Richard turned away, moved like a man sleepwalking toward the closest window. He recoiled almost at once, however, for it afforded him a clear view of the Tower Green. Earlier that morning, Edward had been amusing himself there at the butts. Now men were already engaged in urgent activity, were rolling a large log into position on the grass. A priest was emerging from the Chapel of St Peter. Summer sun glinted blindingly upon the silver-gilt pyx that held the Host, so that it seemed enveloped in a halo of light. Richard backed away.

Francis started to rise, only to have Buckingham lean across the table and grasp his wrist. 'Let him be,' he hissed.

'The devil I will!' Francis jerked his wrist free. 'There's still time to put a halt to it. Let Hastings die for his treason, but not like this. Jesú, not like this!'

'And would you rather have him tried and condemned and pleading with Richard for clemency? Would you have Hastings's wife on her knees before Richard begging for mercy? God's Blood, Lovell, use your head! The man is too dangerous to be forgiven; did you learn nothing with Warwick?'

John Howard had slouched down in his chair, chin resting almost on his chest. He looked up now, tasted blood on his lips and spat into the floor rushes. 'Buckingham be right,' he said thickly. 'Will did choose, did know the price for failure. If death is to come, it is a mercy that it does come quick. . . .'

Francis glared at them both. 'You fools, do you not see? It's not Hastings I do care about, it's Dickon. It is for his sake that. . . .'

He stopped in midsentence. The captain of the guards had returned, was standing in the doorway.

'Your Grace?' He stopped self-consciously and then said briskly, striving to sound matter-of-fact, 'It is done, my lord, as you did command. What would you have us do with the body? Is it your wish that the head be displayed on Drawbridge Gate, to lesson others as to what befalls traitors?'

'No!' Richard drew a deep breath, said more calmly, 'It was my brother's wish that Hastings be buried beside him at Windsor. See that it be done.'

There was a glazed earthenware jug at the end of the table which had somehow emerged unscathed when Stanley lurched into the table. Richard crossed to it, spilled water into an empty cup. It was only then that he realized how his hand was trembling.

The day's heat did not begin to burn off until dusk. Kneeling on the window seat in her bedchamber, Anne was grateful to feel cooler air fan past her face. For the first time in hours, the street below was quiet. A few carts creaked by; a few housewives were hastening homeward with market purchases. But the others were gone, the crowds drawn by curiosity to gather before the Lord Protector's house on this, a day of such momentous happenings.

It was noontime when the first rumours spilled over the Tower walls, spread through the streets of London. None knew for sure what had happened but there was talk of a confrontation in council, one that did end in a pool of blood on Tower Green. By the time Lord Mayor Shaa had been summoned to the Tower, the city was in a fair state of panic. So, too, was Anne, waiting anxiously at Crosby Place for word of Richard's safety.

The courier arrived with a message for her from Francis Lovell at the same time as a royal herald was proclaiming at Paul's Cross that Lord Hastings had involved himself in a plot to overthrow the government and had met the fate that all traitors deserved, a swift and ignominious death. Francis's note was hastily scribbled, told Anne little beyond the stark facts of Will Hastings's execution. Dickon was going to Westminster directly after meeting with the Lord Mayor, he wrote, to put the proof of the conspiracy before the full council. He had no idea how long it would take; she'd best not expect Dickon for hours. He hoped she understood why Dickon had not the time to write himself but she must not worry; the worst was over.

Hours later, Anne was still struggling with a stunned sense of disbelief. What had driven Richard to this, to ordering a man's death without trial? Had Will's betrayal lacerated so deeply as that? Or had he feared that he'd not be able to do it if he delayed?

She had no answers, only questions. How could their world have changed so in just two brief months? All seemed to be closing in on them, to be conspiring to strip all security from their lives. Only seven days had passed since Stillington's revelation. Seven days! And now Will Hastings was dead, Ned's dearest friend, dead at her husband's command, and how in God's Name had it all come about?

Darkness was laying claim to the sky, slowly blotting out the last traces of light lingering along the horizon by the time Richard came home to her. She jumped to her feet as he walked through the bedchamber doorway and then ran to him, into his arms. They stood that way in silence for a time; she could hear his heart hammering against her ear, could feel tension in every line of his body.

'Oh, my love. . . . My love, I was so frightened.'

'Hush,' he said, his voice muffled against her hair. 'Hush.'

He was holding her too tightly for comfort, even for breath, and at last she was compelled to end the embrace. Stepping back, she searched his face with anxious dark eyes.

'Richard. . . . Richard, what happened this morning?'

'You know what happened,' he said tautly. 'Hastings owned up to his treachery and paid the price for it. There's no more to be said.'

'Yes, but. . . .'

'Anne, I said I do not want to talk about it. Not now, not ever! Do you understand?'

They'd had arguments before, had shouted at one another and exchanged those hurtful accusations inevitable in any relationship of daily intimacy. But never had he sounded as he did now. His voice was shaking with what she first thought to be anger, now saw to be far more than that.

'All right, Richard,' she said slowly. 'We'll not speak of it again.'

He said nothing and, after a moment, she held out her hand. Their fingers touched, entwined together, and he drew her back into his arms, into a wordless embrace that endured long into the twilight dark, that had in it nothing of desire but no small measure of despair.

8

Ludgate Prison
London

June 1483

Jane had wept for Will until her eyes were swollen shut, swallowing so many salt tears that she at last made herself sick, retching miserably into the straw of her prison cell. Her gaolers, being young and male, were more sympathetic than censorious. Women knew nothing of politics, they agreed among themselves, invariably made fools of themselves when they tried to meddle in a man's domain. A pity, though, that so pretty a fly had been caught in the web. They found excuses to look in on her, brought her water in a large clay jug, and when her nausea showed no signs of abating, one even took it upon himself to summon a doctor. As her guards looked on solicitously, Jane managed to choke down a cup of wine laced with henbane. The sleeping draught was a potent one; she'd soon spiralled down into a deep drugged sleep.

She awoke the next morning with a splitting head and a queasy stomach. The aftertaste of the wine rose in her mouth like bile, coating her tongue, sour enough to make her gag. There was all around her the stench of vomit and urine and sweat, the stink of prison. She did not want to move, wanted only to keep her eyes tightly shut, to deny this dream any semblance of reality. But it was no dream. She was in Ludgate Prison, facing a charge of treason. Tom was in hiding and Will . . . Will was dead. She moaned and sat up.

Once she'd rinsed her mouth and splashed water upon her face, she revived enough to take notice of her surroundings. How lucky she was that her servants were so loyal, so devoted to her! They'd served her well at a time when she'd been too distraught to look to her own interests, had bartered coins for her comfort. As a result, she had a pallet to lie upon where she might otherwise have had only a blanket. She recognized the coffer in the corner and, kneeling before it, found it packed with what her women thought she'd need: clothes, hairbrush, even a hand mirror. They'd seen to it, too, that she had candles, a chamber pot, a green hazel twig for cleaning her teeth and a basin for washing. But there were no furnishings in the chamber other than the pallet and coffer and, although it must be midday, shadows still held sway, the only light coming from a solitary window high above her head.

With a surge of revulsion, she saw that her gown was stained with vomit and hastily jerked the lacings loose, pulled it over her head. Stale, stagnant air enveloped her like a cloak; she felt a little cooler in her kirtle, but not much. Taking down the last of the pins binding up her hair, she began a vigorous brushing, much as she did every morning, only to stop in midstroke with a choked sob of laughter. What a queer creature of habit she was, that she should be worrying about her hair when she stood in danger of losing her head. But remembering, then, the surprising friendliness of her guards, she decided it made sense to make herself as presentable as possible. Raising the brush again, she didn't stop until her hair lay smooth upon her shoulders, as bright as sunlight and as soft as silk.

Lying back on her pallet, she closed her eyes, brought one arm up to shut out her surroundings. What would happen to her now? Surely Gloucester'd not send a woman to the block. A shudder passed through her entire body; sweat began to trickle down her ribs, cold and sticky. Prisoners charged with treason were generally confined to the Tower. Was it not, then, a hopeful sign that she'd been remanded to Ludgate? But even if Gloucester could not bring himself to claim a woman's life, he could hold her in prison till her hair went grey, her limbs gnarled with age. And what defence could she offer? She'd plotted against his life; how could she expect mercy?

Footsteps sounded outside the door. She heard the jangle of keys and sat up on the pallet, her heart beginning to pound. As the door swung open, she caught a glimpse of one of the guards. He gave her a jaunty wave and a wink, and then stepped back to let her visitor pass into the chamber. He was a man in his mid-thirties, tastefully but not extravagantly dressed in dark velvet, had about him that air of prosperous efficiency Jane instinctively associated with lawyers.

She was not surprised, therefore, when he identified himself as Thomas Lynom, the king's solicitor. He had the look of a man slumming against his will; she saw how his nostrils pinched as he looked down at the befouled straw. But she saw, too, how his dark eyes followed the plunging V of her cleavage.

'I'd ask you to sit down, Master Lynom,' she said softly, 'but as you can see, I'm woefully ill prepared to receive guests.'

He was not amused. 'Treason is scarcely a joking matter, Mistress Shore,' he said coolly, and Jane saw that this was not a man to thaw with laughter.

'Indeed it is not,' she agreed hastily. 'It's just that . . . that I'm so very frightened, Master Lynom, and whenever I'm upset or afraid I seek to hide it with silly jests.' She slipped into her shoes, gave the bodice of her kirtle a discreet tug, came to her feet.

'Master Lynom, what is to happen to me? What means His Grace of Gloucester to do?'

'You're a very fortunate young woman,' Lynom said dryly. 'More fortunate than you doubtlessly do deserve. The Lord Protector has decided not to charge you with high treason.'

'Oh, thank God!' Jane's relief was such that she swayed a little, had to put her hand on his arm for support.

'Under the circumstances, you're getting off remarkably easy. Tomorrow you are to do public penance before Paul's Cross for your wanton living and you will then be kept in confinement whilst the search goes on for your paramour, Thomas Grey. As soon as he is found or it seems likely that he is not hiding in London, you shall be set free.'

That was so much more than Jane had dared hope for, was a reprieve she saw as nothing less than miraculous. 'Oh, how generous he is, how forbearing! You will tell him that for me, will you not? Tell him how grateful I am?'

'I rather doubt that the Duke of Gloucester does want your gratitude,' Lynom snapped, startling himself by his own rudeness. But he was disconcerted by this woman who was so little like he'd expected her to be. He was acutely aware of her physical presence, aware of the moist red mouth, the slender white throat, the

968

swelling curve of her breasts; they were surprisingly full for so small a woman, were straining against the silk of her kirtle, almost brushing his arm, for she was standing as close as that, looking up at him with wide blue eyes, the eyes of a trusting child-woman, not those of a jaded wanton. Those eyes lied, he thought, pretended an innocence of spirit that had to be false. He stepped away from her, said sharply, 'As I said, Mistress Shore, you are a most fortunate woman. Most who do entangle themselves in treason rarely live to regret it, do pay the price that Hastings. . . .'

'Oh, do not! Please, do not!' Jane stumbled backward, brought her hands up as if to ward off a blow.

Lynom was taken aback. This was no pretence, was a wail of pure pain.

It was my fault, all my fault! Will would not have died had it not been for me,' she sobbed. 'I thought I was acting for the best, I swear I did! He did it for me and now I have to live with that, with his blood on my hands. . . .' She was trembling violently, tears splashing unheeded down her face. 'If only I could make it yesterday again, could have it to do over. . . .'

'I'm sorry,' Lynom said awkwardly. 'I should not have said that. I did not realize. . . .'

He pulled his handkerchief from his doublet, handed it to her. And then she was in his arms, sobbing against his shoulder, and he found himself stroking the fair head cradled against his chest, entreating her not to weep, and not at all sure how it had come about.

Jane was so thankful to be spared a trial for treason that she gave little thought to the public penance imposed upon her. It was not until the next morning that she began to grow frightened, to look with dread to the ordeal that lay ahead for her. She'd seen women made to do penance for harlotry, seen tradesmen publicly shamed for cheating their customers. Such sights were a common enough occurrence on the streets of the city, and, if the mood of the crowd happened to be ugly, the unfortunate penitent could be pelted with rotten fruit or mud, taunted with obscenities. And for her, it would be even worse. She was no common strumpet, was a woman who'd shared a king's bed, and to see her walk barefoot through the city streets, clad only in her kirtle and holding a candle aloft, would be a rare treat for London's idle.

Ludgate Prison was built above the city gate of the same name. As Jane emerged onto the street, she saw that a large crowd had already gathered. The sun was high overhead, but goose bumps were rising on her arms, the back of her neck. She felt hands on her shoulders, removing her cloak. She closed her eyes; the noise in the street was a distant roaring in her ears, much like the sound of the sea.

'Do not look so greensick, sweetheart. A pretty lass like you, you'll have them eating out of your hand!'

One of her guards was grinning at her. Knowing he meant to be kind, Jane mustered a weak smile and then reached out to accept the candle. It was unexpectedly heavy, a tall wax taper. She drew a deep breath, closed her eyes again. Mary, Mother of God, get me through this. Let me bear the shame with some grace.

The cobblestones were hot and unevenly paved, stung the soles of her feet. Thank Christ she had so short a route to travel, up Bowyer Row and into the precincts of St Paul's, there publicly to repent her sinful past at the foot of Paul's Cross. She stiffened her spine, raised her chin. Tom Lynom was right; she had been lucky to get off as lightly as this. And if she could somehow atone for Will's death by enduring the taunts and abuse of the London mob, let them jeer, let them splatter overripe apples at her feet, call her whore and slut. That was a cheap price to pay for the death of a decent man.

So wrought up was she that it was several moments before she realized that the spectators lining both side of Bowyer Row were not jeering. She could hear earthy comments passing back and forth, heard wagers made that a man could span her waist within his hands, heard herself described as a 'right ripe piece'. But such remarks sounded more admiring than scornful and, as she nerved herself to look around her, she saw a sea of smiles.

Londoners had taken the news of Will Hastings's death with phlegmatic calm. Life they knew to be uncertain and ambition to be the ruin of many a great lord. Some mourned for Will, others felt he'd reaped what he had sown. But Jane had long been a favourite with Londoners. People remembered how freely she'd emptied her purse to help the needy, how often she'd spoken up for the mute, the weak. That her morals were no better than they ought to be bothered Londoners very little; a woman as obliging as she was pretty could be forgiven much. Men who'd taken a perverse pride in the blatant carousing of their late king were not likely to share Richard's disapproval of his merriest bedmate, and by publicly branding Jane as no better than a harlot, Richard only stirred up for her a backlash of sympathy.

It was a sympathy Jane had not expected. Dazed and disbelieving, she came to an uncertain halt. Blessed Lady, they were with her! They were on her side. Tears filled her eyes. She blinked them back, smiled tremulously at the crowd.

9

Westminster Sanctuary

June 1483

Bess's relationship with her mother had deteriorated rapidly under the strain of six weeks in sanctuary. It made no sense to Bess.

She loved her uncle, could not in her wildest imaginings see him as a threat to her family. No, had mama not sought to thwart papa's will, none of this need have happened. Once mama's initial panic did subside, surely she'd come to see that, would abandon Abbot Esteney's lodging and take her rightful place at court, as the mother of the King.

But it hadn't worked out that way so far. It was soon clear to Bess that her mother had no intention of leaving sanctuary until she could wring as many concessions as possible from her Uncle Dickon and the council. Bess was mortified, wanted nothing so much as to disassociate herself from her mother's manoeuvrings. But she could not bring herself to leave sanctuary on her own, not when it meant leaving her little brother and her baby sisters. They were so young, looked to her as much as they did to mama. More, if truth be told. How could she just go off and leave them like that? No, she had no choice but to wait till mama came to her senses.

So involved was she with the care of her three youngest sisters that Bess was slow to see the significance of Lady Stanley's visits, slow to suspect the truth. It was Jane Shore who gave it away, Jane who assumed Bess had been taken into her mother's confidence and thought it a kindness to assure her that she must not fear, that all was sure to go well now that Will had been won over.

Bess had been dumbfounded. Will Hastings despised her mother; why would he be conspiring with her against Dickon? She'd confronted her mother, demanded answers Elizabeth refused to give. Bess had been furious, bitterly resentful that she should, at seventeen, be treated like a child.

Just what did their plot encompass? How far did they mean to go? It was a question Bess had put to her mother, to no avail. A question that need not be asked, for she already knew the answer. For mama and her kin to regain power, Dickon had to die. They dare not let him live. And what was she to do now?

Betray her own mother, her half brother Tom? How could she do that? But if she did not, if she said nothing and Dickon died, how could she live with herself?

She arose the next morning hollow-eyed and pale, but clutching to her a shaky resolve. Dickon's life had to come before loyalty to mama. She must find some way to warn him, even if it meant mama would hate her forever for doing it.

She'd spent the morning mentally composing letters of caution, letters that might alert Dickon to his danger without exposing her mother's complicity, and then in midafternoon had come word of the council meeting at the Tower. To Bess, it seemed suddenly as if the world had gone mad and all in it. That Dickon, of all men, would have sent Will to the block without a trial . . . and not even a block but a bloodstained log. Bess shuddered, found she could not stop shivering. Papa was barely two months dead and nothing was familiar any more; she was in a landscape without recognizable landmarks, trapped in a nightmare that daylight would not dispel.

What frightened her the most, however, was her mother's reaction to Hastings's death. Elizabeth hadn't wept, hadn't raged, had stared at Bess and then said in a queerly hushed voice, 'It's done then.' And said no more.

Bess and Cecily had never seen Elizabeth like that, were at a loss. She seemed to be in shock, they agreed, but why should Hastings's death affect her so deeply as this? She'd hated Hastings, could not be mourning him. The plot had failed, of course, but she had nothing to fear for herself. Whatever Dickon might choose to do to Morton, Jane Shore, and the other conspirators, she was the King's mother, could indulge in intrigue with impunity, and who knew that better than she? Moreover, Tom was still safe, still eluding those hunting him. So why, then, did she lie abed, refusing food and drink? Why did she stare into space like one bewitched, like one seeing spectres that were not there?

*

973

On Monday morning, a delegation of clergy and nobles came again to the abbot's lodging. Bess received them in the abbot's refectory, listened attentively as the Archbishop of Canterbury urged her to come forth with her brother and sisters from sanctuary. Madame her mother need not fear, he assured her earnestly. The Lord Protector was willing to overlook her treason, would not seek vengeance against a woman. John Howard had interrupted at that, said that the young Duke of York must be yielded up, even if the girls were not. A child had no right to claim sanctuary, he said pointedly, since he was incapable of sin.

Bess understood; her mother's refusal might not be heeded. So it was up to her, she decided, to make mama see reason. Bess had no doubts whatsoever that Dickon should join Edward in the Tower. An active, lively child with a normal measure of curiosity and mischief in his makeup, he was thoroughly miserable in confinement and for what? Why should he continue to pay the price for mama's foolishness?

Taking Cecily along for moral support, she went to her mother's bedchamber, marshalling her arguments in favour of letting Dickon go to Edward. Much to her surprise, they weren't needed. Elizabeth had listened in silence and then said, almost indifferently, 'Does he want to go?'

Bess nodded. 'Yes, mama, of course he does.' We all do. The words hovered on her tongue; she bit them back, waited.

'Why not? What difference does it make now?'

The two girls exchanged uneasy glances. Mama was acting so strange. Cecily cleared her throat, ventured hesitantly, 'Can we not go, too, mama? Edward's coronation is set for next week. Surely you do not want to miss that.'

She flinched then for Elizabeth had begun to laugh, a strained mirthless sound as chilling as it was inexplicable. 'Coronation? There'll be no coronation. Not for Edward. . . .' She turned her head aside on the pillow, mumbled, 'Yes, let Dickon go if he wishes. Mayhap it'll help Edward, having him there when he's told. . . .'

Bess decided it best not to pressure her mother about their departure from sanctuary. Better to wait till mama was more herself again. She made a hasty retreat before her mother could change her mind, sent Cecily to help Dickon pack while she returned to the refectory to tell the Archbishop of Canterbury and Lord Howard that her little brother would be going with them.

She stood watching now at the east window of the refectory as Dickon exited into the abbot's courtyard. He was frisking about like a mettlesome colt, had managed to entangle the Archbishop of Canterbury in the long lead attached to his dog's collar. Bess grinned but it faded as she glanced across the chamber. Her four-year-old sister Katherine was coming through the doorway from the kitchen; she clutched a handful of candied orange peels, was struggling to hold on to a very disgruntled grey kitten. Bess sighed; they all should be going with Dickon. Somehow, she must make mama see that, must.... She heard her name, turned to see John Howard standing in the doorway.

'Is there someplace where we may talk alone?'

Bess nodded. 'We can go into the Jerusalem Chamber if you like.'

She was pleased that John Howard had remained behind to talk to her; she liked him enormously, this man who'd been her father's friend, liked his gruff blunt-spoken manner, much like an elderly uncle. Bess thought of him as just that, in fact, as more of an uncle than her own blood uncles. Bess was not close to any of her mother's brothers; secretly, she was a little ashamed of her unpopular Woodville kin, preferred to think of herself as Plantagenet. Of her father's brothers, she'd never liked her Uncle George and, whilst Dickon had always been her favourite relative, she'd never really thought of him as an uncle; he was too young for that, only thirteen years older than she. Jack Howard, however, filled the need perfectly and for all that he affected a no-nonsense, brusque manner, she sensed he was secretly delighted that she'd chosen to call him Uncle Jack.

He didn't look very comfortable now, however, seemed troubled. 'Dickon asked me to speak with you,' he said abruptly. 'There's something you've got to be told, lass. Stillington's going before the council this afternoon, so it'll be all over Westminster by nightfall and Dickon did not want you to hear it that way, to hear some garbled account likely to give you even greater grief.'

'I do not like the sound of this,' Bess said uneasily.

'You'll like it even less by the time I be through,' he said grimly, 'but there's no help for it, Bess. You have to know. It is about your father. We're all born to sin, all have our weaknesses. Your father's was women. Forgive me for being so blunt, but I know no other way. He sinned when he did marry your mother, did her a wrong and you and your brothers and sisters a greater one. He was not free, lass. More than two years before he went through that ceremony with your mother at Grafton Manor, he entered into a plight-troth with another woman. The Lady Eleanor Butler, the Earl of Shrewsbury's daughter. They said their vows before Stillington and, to keep him quiet, your father made him Chancellor. For more than twenty years, he held his tongue, knowing that the marriage was invalid, that. . . .'

Bess at last found her voice. 'God in Heaven, what are you saying? That my father plight-trothed with this . . . this Eleanor Butler and then married my mother, knowing full well that any children of such a union would be bastards? And you expect me to believe that? Believe my father would do that to me, to us?'

He winced as her voice rose, reached toward her but she backed away from him, shaking her head.

'No. . . . I do not believe it! Papa would never have done that, never!'

'Bess. . . .'

'No!' She was continuing to back away, stumbled as the room blurred in a haze of tears. 'It's not true! It's not!'

*

976

Cecily was knotting a handkerchief, jerking it through trembling fingers and pulling it taut, as if it were a lifeline.

'Bess.... Bess, could we have been wrong about Uncle Dickon? Could papa have been wrong to trust him so? Would he do that, make use of a lie to take Edward's throne?'

'No!' Bess said fiercely, almost desperately. 'I cannot believe that of him, Cecily, I cannot. Stillington must have somehow convinced him that it was true. To believe otherwise, to believe he'd concoct such a slander, falsely swear that we be bastards so that he might be king. . . .' Her voice trailed off.

Cecily was not as sure as Bess; she was an avid reader and history was replete with stories of honourable men seduced by the golden glimmer of a crown. She wanted to believe, however, needed to believe as much as Bess did. If Papa could have so misjudged Uncle Dickon . . . it was a frightening thought.

'Mama has to be told,' she said huskily and Bess nodded.

Elizabeth had risen to bid her son farewell, had then taken to her bed again, clad only in a bed robe, blonde hair hanging uncombed and tangled down her back, showing unmistakable streaks of grey. To her daughters, who'd grown up with a beauty that was flawless, as cold and polished and perfect as finely grained ivory, this haggard middle-aged woman was a stranger, a stranger who heard them out in apathetic silence, seemed scarcely to be listening at all.

'Mama? Mama, you do understand what I am saying? Mama, they mean to deny Edward the crown!'

'Yes, Bess, I heard you the first time.' Elizabeth sat up slowly, put her fingers to her forehead, winced. 'Cecily, fetch me that glass vial, the one with the oil of roses. My head feels like to split.'

Expecting hysterics, tantrums, tears, Bess and Cecily were nonplussed by this almost nonchalant acceptance, this eerie indifference. Cecily obediently brought the vial, sat beside her mother and began to rub the scented oil into Elizabeth's temples. Bess sat on the other side of the bed, saying, 'Mama, I seem to remember Bishop Stillington being arrested about the time that my Uncle George was executed. Is it not likely that he harboured a grudge against papa for that? And it would explain why he made up such a story, why. . . .'

Elizabeth lay back against the pillows. 'Robert Stillington, Bishop of Bath and Wells. I tried to tell Ned, did all but go down on my knees to him. But would he heed me? No. . . . He'd not have Stillington's blood on his hands, he said. Said, too, that we had nothing to fear from Stillington.' She laughed unsteadily. 'Nothing to fear! Tell me that again, Ned, tell me how you were going to make the crown safe for your son! You'll have to burn in Hell for a thousand years ere you can atone for what you've done to me and mine, and not even a thousand years would be time enough to win my forgiveness. . . .'

'Mama. . . . mama, what are you saying? You make it sound as if Bishop Stillington spoke the truth!'

Elizabeth closed her eyes. 'Of course he spoke the truth,' she said tiredly. 'Why do you think I've been so frantic since Ned died, why I fought so to deny Gloucester the protectorship? I knew . . . knew it was only a matter of time till Stillington came forward, until he. . . .'

'No!'

Cecily was stricken dumb but Bess was shaking her head vehemently, was trembling all over.

'No,' she gasped. 'I do not believe you. Papa would never have done that. I know he would not.'

Elizabeth's eyes flew open, focused on her eldest daughter with a rage all the more embittered for being so long repressed. 'You know nothing! You've never seen Ned as he truly was, never! Well, I think it time we spoke the truth about him, about your cherished beloved father who could do no wrong.

'The truth is that he was a man who cared only for his own pleasures and most of them were found between a woman's legs.

978

Nineteen years we were wed and, from the very first, he had his sluts on the side. Not because he did not get what he wanted in my bed; he did. But one woman was never enough for him. He filled his court with harlots, thought nothing of seducing the wives of friends and, when he was through with them, passed them on to Hastings or my Tom. Nell Butler was merely one of many, notable only in that she was chaste enough to deny him her bed till he agreed to a plight-troth and then stupid enough to let him sweet-talk her into holding her tongue. He lay with her and lost interest and then married me, so cocksure he could get away with it, that he could get away with anything.

'And when Clarence found out, he had him put to death to keep the secret safe but he balked at silencing Stillington, and this'—with a wide sweep of her arm that took in the confines of the Abbot's bedchamber—'this is the result. I lay with him and bore him ten children; I put up with his wenching; I even raised his bastard brats by other women when he asked it of me and this ... this is my reward for it, this is the legacy he did leave me. The man you see as God Almighty, as the perfect father.

'Well, I'm done protecting him, done lying for him. Your brother will never wear a crown because his father went through life like a rutting stag. And you, my daughter who once thought to be Queen of France, you'll have to set your sights a mite lower, get used to hearing people call you bastard when once they did call you princess, and none of it is my fault. When you give thanks for this, you give them to the man who most deserves them ... to your father, God curse him!'

'Oh, mama, stop!' Cecily had begun to sob. 'Name of God, do not say any more! Please.'

Elizabeth was panting, utterly exhausted by the violence of her outburst. Suddenly all her anger had gone; she felt weak, very tired and slightly sick.

'Well,' she said dully, 'so now you do know the truth. ...'

Bess had yet to move. Her body had gone rigid with shock; the

979

eyes that met Elizabeth's own were glazed, unseeing. Elizabeth felt a twinge of remorse, found herself wishing she'd used softer words, left some of it unsaid. Bess had always been Ned's particular pet, after all, and she looked ill, in truth she did. Elizabeth reached out her hand but at her touch Bess came to life, recoiled abruptly.

'You want me to hate papa, do you not?' she whispered. 'To hate him for ruining our lives. Well, mayhap I do. . . . I do not know how I feel about him now. I do not. . . .' Her voice broke, steadied. 'But this I do know. Whatever my feelings for him, I do hate you for telling me!'

It had not taken long for the council to determine the fate of the conspirators. John Morton and Thomas Rotherham were more fortunate than they deserved in that they were both bishops of the Holy Roman Catholic Church, and most of the council, particularly their fellow clerics, were loath to shed the blood of a priest. As Richard shared this same reluctance, he made no objections when it was proposed that Morton and Rotherham be spared the axe.

It was soon agreed, then, that Rotherham was to have a stay in the Tower. Morton was a more difficult case, for he was a far more dangerous man than the ineffectual Rotherham. It was Buckingham who came up with the solution. Why not have Morton sent under guard to his own castle at Brecknock in Wales? Brecknock was in an isolated area, far from London; it would make an ideal prison for the too-clever Lancastrian priest. With unusual unanimity, the council accepted Buckingham's offer, consigned Morton to his custody.

The real problem was what to do about Lord Stanley. Now that all involved in the plot had been arrested and interrogated, it seemed that the evidence against Stanley was more circumstantial than otherwise. Stanley had been in suspiciously close contact with Morton during the past fortnight but apparently he hadn't committed himself all that fully to the plot. Or if he had, no evidence of it had so far been unearthed. That his wife was involved, there was no doubt, but Stanley himself remained an enigma. Had he been clever enough to shelter himself behind his wife, using her as an intermediary so that he could then disavow his own involvement should the need arise? Or had she been acting on her own? She was, all agreed, quite capable of it.

Margaret Beaufort was Stanley's second wife. It was a marriage that had raised both eyebrows and suspicions, for Stanley's controversial new wife was a woman whose loyalties were irrevocably pledged in blood to the fallen House of Lancaster. She was a Beaufort, first cousin to the Duke of Somerset executed after the battle of Tewkesbury, and when she was only twelve, Harry of Lancaster had married her to his Welsh half brother Edmund Tudor. The following year, she'd given birth to a son, named Henry in honour of his royal uncle. He was now a man in his mid-twenties, had lived for several years under the protection of the Duke of Brittany. With the death of Prince Edouard at Tewkesbury's Bloody Meadow, this son of Margaret Beaufort and Edmund Tudor suddenly became a figure of some significance, for in his veins now ran all that remained of the blood of Lancaster. It was not surprising, therefore, that the French king displayed an intense interest in luring him to France. Edward, too, had showed himself eager to get his hands upon this last scion of the House of Lancaster, but the Duke of Brittany was no less quick to see the advantages in having so valuable a political pawn. So Tudor lived in exile at the court of Brittany while his mother took as her second husband Sir Henry Stafford, an uncle of the Duke of Buckingham. And now she was wed to Stanley and the men gathered in the Tower Council Chamber on this sixteenth day of June were asking themselves if Stanley was her willing collaborator or her unwitting dupe.

'Your Grace. . . .' Bishop Russell leaned across the table toward Richard. 'I truly do not know how deep was Lord Stanley's involvement, whether he was in collusion with Morton or whether he be guilty of no more than a lapse of judgment, an inability to control his wife. And because I do not know, I feel we should give him the benefit of the doubt. The evidence is too ambiguous to allow of any other interpretation.'

Buckingham was frowning, seemed on the verge of protesting. But most of the other faces around the table reflected Russell's uncertainty. If excuses could be found for Stanley, they'd be much relieved. The shock of Hastings's abrupt execution had not yet worn off. That Richard could understand. Could understand all too well.

He nodded briefly. He didn't want to fight the council on this, didn't want to argue for more bloodshed. Stanley wasn't worth it. Why not show him the mercy a better man than he had been denied? Richard found himself staring out the window. Below, Tower Green was still, dappled in sun and shade, and for several moments he watched the way the light patterned the grass, foreshadowing dusk. Sand had been strewn about with a lavish hand, had soaked up the blood that three days past had saturated the ground in a river of red. Richard swallowed, looked away.

'Well, that does account for Rotherham, Stanley and Morton,' Richard's brother-in-law the Duke of Suffolk said briskly. 'All that must be done, then, is to bring a Bill of Attainder against Hastings when parliament does meet. . . .'

'No,' Richard said, so sharply that all heads turned in his direction. 'I'm not going to attaint Hastings.'

Suffolk was taken aback. 'That is most magnanimous to his family, but we're talking about a considerable sum of money. Hastings was a very wealthy man and the confiscation of his estates would help fill the coffers emptied when the Woodvilles raided the treasury. . . .'

'I do not intend to attaint Hastings,' Richard repeated tersely. 'I'll not have his widow and children pay the price for his treason.'

And the tone of his voice precluded further argument. There was a sudden silence, broken by Buckingham.

'There remains one matter still to be decided, my lords. Once before we voted on whether to charge Anthony Woodville and Grey with treason. At Bishop Morton's urging, the charge was voted down. Well, we know now that he had an ulterior motive in so doing, was hand in glove with the Woodville Queen. I would suggest, therefore, that we do vote again.'

Buckingham paused, waited to see if any meant to argue with him. None did. Richard glanced around the table, saw that all eyes were upon him, that this decision was to be his to make. He could see that Anthony Woodville and Dick Grey paid with their lives for Elizabeth Woodville's treachery. Or he could accord them mercy he did not believe they deserved.

'My lord Buckingham speaks for me in this,' he said grimly. 'I would have them charged with treason.'

The vote that followed was an affirmation of Richard's will. Anthony Woodville, Dick Grey and Thomas Vaughn were condemned in less time than it took to make a circuit of the table, to have each man voice his aye or nay.

Buckingham pushed his chair back; his eyes sought Richard's. Richard nodded and Buckingham smiled.

'And now, my lords,' he said, 'Dr Stillington does want to address the council. He has a confession to make, one you'll be most interested in hearing. That I can promise you.'

IO

London

June 1483

On June 22nd, Friar Ralph Shaa, the brother of London's current Lord Mayor, mounted the pulpit steps of Paul's Cross, and, before a hushed, expectant crowd, began to speak. He'd chosen as his sermon the biblical text, 'Bastard slips shall not take root,' and in the glare of summer sunlight, he revealed to the people of London the details of the secret plight-troth that Bishop Stillington had six days ago brought before the council.

There was little surprise; the city had been afire with rumours for days. Some rejoiced. Others, the cynical and those who'd hoped to enrich themselves in the chaos of a minority reign, scoffed at the plight-troth as a contrivance, a fable concocted to legitimize Richard's usurpation of his nephew's crown. But for the most part, Londoners accorded Richard a cautious approval. He was a man grown, a man of proven abilities, with a reputation for honesty and fair-dealing, while Edward was an untried youngster, Anthony Woodville's pupil and protégé. There was sympathy for Edward but the paramount reaction was one of relief; memories had not yet dimmed of the troubled times England had endured under the last boy king.

Three days later, a joint session of the Lords and Commons met at Westminster and unanimously approved a petition setting forth Richard's claim to the crown. The following afternoon, a delegation of nobles, clergy and citizens gathered at Baynard's Castle. There, twenty-two years before, a similar delegation had offered the crown to Richard's brother; it was now offered to Richard. He accepted and dated the beginning of his reign from that Thursday, June 26th.

Anne was standing in the middle of the bedchamber, not liking what she saw. There was an oversize feather bed with richly stitched coverlets, a Flemish carpet of brightly woven gold and green and the walls were hung with expensive arras, but the room lacked the sunlit windows and soaring ceiling of her bedchamber at Crosby Place. Baynard's Castle had been built some three hundred years earlier, built for defence and, no matter how luxurious the furnishings, it could not compare in comfort to their house on Bishopsgate Street.

And yet this room held many memories for her. It was in this bed that she and Richard had consummated their marriage on a warm April night eleven years ago. 'Eleven years,' she whispered, and shook her head in wonderment. Without warning, tears filled her eyes.

'Anne?' Véronique was looking at her with concern she couldn't conceal. 'Anne, would it help to talk. . . .?' She stopped, seeing then the small coffer lying open on the table; it contained the soft linen cloths Anne used as napkins for her monthly flux. She understood and felt a sharp pang, so closely could she identify with Anne's disappointment. Anne had confided that she was two weeks late, and although she'd acknowledged that it was too early to hope, Véronique knew she had, nonetheless.

'I'm sorry, chérie,' she said simply.

'No, Véronique, there's no need. I'm to be blessed with but the one son. It's time I accepted that as God's will and stopped breaking my heart over what cannot be.' Anne's words were brisk, matter-of-fact, carried no conviction. Closing the coffer lid, she put it down on the floor, out of sight.

'I could not help hoping, though,' she admitted. 'To have a child now, Véronique, now of all times. . . . It truly would have been a gift from God, a holy sign that Richard was right in taking the crown. And I think, had I been with child, I would not have minded so much then . . .' She didn't finish the sentence but Véronique did it for her.

'Being Queen? Ah, Anne. Anne, do not look so surprised. After thirteen years, do you not think I know your heart, your mind?'

'Richard must not ever know,' Anne warned and at once wished she hadn't. Véronique would be the last one on earth to betray her secrets. 'Forgive me, I know you'd never share a confidence. It's just that I do not want Richard to know I feel this way, that I can take no happiness in the thought of queenship. That I ache so for Middleham, for the life that was ours. . . .'

The sympathy on Véronique's face was dangerous, was an invitation to self-pity. Anne drew a deep breath, said very evenly, 'Nor have I the right to complain. You see, Véronique, I did all that I could to convince Richard he must take the crown.'

'What choice had you, Anne?' Véronique had wandered to the window. She knew that Richard was formally handing over the Great Seal to Chancellor Russell and she said now, 'The meeting's done. Chancellor Russell is coming out with Bishop Stillington and the others. And there's . . .' She hesitated, finding it strange to refer to Richard as 'the King', and yet no longer comfortable in making free use of his given name. She compromised upon, '. . . your husband,' and said to cover her confusion, 'He's leaving? It's nigh on four; where goes he so close to supper?'

'To the Tower,' Anne said reluctantly. 'To see his nephew.'

'Oh.' A long pause. 'Do you . . . think that wise?'

Anne looked up, slowly shook her head. 'No, I do not. But Richard felt he did owe Edward that much.'

Véronique said nothing, but the look on her face spoke volumes. After a few moments, Anne joined her at the window. The Duke of Buckingham was now below in the inner bailey, too, but Anne watched only Richard.

'Richard's brother was a controversial King, Véronique. Many

986

men did hate him and he was often lied about, accused by his enemies of evils he had not done. He was blessed, though, in that he was truly indifferent to such slander. You see, he did not care what others thought of him, and that did save him so much grief. He just did not care,' Anne repeated, sounding almost incredulous, as if marvelling at a phenomenon that passed understanding.

'But Richard does care,' Véronique said, and Anne nodded.

'Yes,' she said. 'Richard does.'

Véronique turned her eyes away from Anne's troubled face, back toward the activity below in the inner bailey. She was thinking of the local gossip. Once the danger of the Hastings-Morton conspiracy was past, Richard had sent word to York to delay the departure of troops for the capital. He had wanted to be sure there'd be no question of intimidation, that none could say his claim to the crown rested upon the presence of his troops in the city. Yet Véronique knew that in any tavern or alehouse, she could find men tipsily certain that Richard had meant from the first to lay claim to his nephew's crown.

The truth never quite catches up with hearsay and rumour, she thought, and sighed. London had ever been fertile ground for gossip but she'd never seen the city so rife with rumours, not even at the time of George's downfall. There'd even surfaced again the slander that for twenty years had muddied the House of York, the calumny that Edward had been a bastard, born of the Duchess of York's dalliance with an archer in Rouen. Richard had been infuriated, had no more luck in tracking down the source of this scandalmongering than had his brother, and impulsively insisted that Anne move their household from Crosby Place to his mother's residence at Baynard's Castle. A gesture, Véronique thought, and one that only inconvenienced Anne and showed how vulnerable Richard was to idle tavern-talk.

'I know he's not accustomed to having men question his motives, Anne, but I fear he must learn to expect that from now on. That is the ugly underside of kingship.'

987

'Yes,' Anne said bleakly. 'I know.'

Glancing back toward the bailey, Véronique saw that Richard had gone but Buckingham still lingered. He was, she thought grudgingly, a man to draw all eyes, like some exotic flower long neglected and now flourishing in the light of public acclaim. Such plants must be watched with care, though; too often they did sprout up so greedily that they crowded all surrounding shrubs into the shade. But she had to admit the man had a flair for calling attention to himself. Had he not taken Will Hastings's servants into his own household within hours of Hastings's death? That was the sort of dramatic, flamboyant gesture the Kingmaker himself might have envied. How he must have resented the late King for so long denying him his place in the sun, Véronique thought, and blurted out, 'Francis thinks that Buckingham might have been responsible for the resurgence of that preposterous tale alleging your lady mother-in-law to have been an unfaithful wife.'

Seeing Anne frown, she made haste to say, 'We're not impugning his loyalty, Anne; Francis would be the first to concede that he has been steadfast in support of Richard. But he is a man of over-weening pride and he had no reason to love Richard's brother, the late King. I do not think he would be sorry to see Edward's name besmirched, in truth I do not.'

'Francis does not like Buckingham,' Anne said challengingly, but Véronique refused to take the bait.

'No,' she agreed easily, 'he does not. Do you, Anne?'

Anne didn't answer at once. 'I do owe him my husband's life,' she said at last, 'owe a debt that can never be repaid. But no, Véronique. No, I do not like him.'

Véronique had to ask. 'Does Richard?'

'I do not know,' Anne said thoughtfully. 'I doubt whether it would ever occur to Richard to ask himself that question. Richard gives his loyalty for life to those who do deserve it and Buckingham stood by him when it did count the most.'

That, Véronique couldn't argue with. She nodded, watched Buckingham make an ostentatious exit, trailed by so many retainers that the inner bailey seemed to have burst into bloom with the Stafford Knot.

'I wish,' she said suddenly, 'that your husband were not going to the Tower. I fear he'll regret it.'

Anne looked at her. 'So do I, Véronique.'

John Argentine was the only one of the attendants chosen by Anthony Woodville who'd been allowed to remain with Edward. He greeted Richard with deference but his eyes were not friendly, conveyed a resentment he dared not voice aloud.

'Your nephew is upstairs in the bedchamber, Your Grace. Is it your wish that I do summon him to you?'

'Yes, Doctor, it is,' Richard said curtly, reacting in spite of himself to the other's unspoken hostility.

Finding himself alone in the room, Richard started to sit and then changed his mind. A game of draughts was spread out on the table, along with quill pens, paper and several half-open books. They were not, Richard saw, books for children. Edward was apparently very well read for his age. But then, he was a king's son, had been trained from birth for that day when he would wear a crown. Richard moved abruptly to the window, unlatched it and stared down into the constable's gardens below. So taut were his nerves that he spun around with a jerk when the door banged behind him.

Dickon was some three months younger than Richard's son Ned, but he was both taller and heavier, gave promise of having inherited his father's height. No less handsome a youngster than his brother, he now looked thoroughly bedraggled, muddy to the knees, his face grimy, his hair full of straw.

'Good God, Dickon! What have you been up to?'

At sound of Richard's voice, the boy jumped, looked around with a start. He was yanking on a long lead, pulling a resisting spaniel through the doorway. Now he let it go slack, said, 'Uncle!' Sounding startled but not in the least alarmed, he carefully wiped his hands on his hanging shirttail, came forward to greet Richard politely.

'I was down at the Lion Tower. They were feeding the big cats. Huge chunks of raw meat like this. . . .' He spread his hands wide. 'They let me throw a piece into the tiger's cage, but Robyn'— pointing to the spaniel—'Robyn was scared, kept whining as if he thought he was to be next on the menu.'

He leaned against the table, began to move the draughtsmen around, to pile them one upon the other until he had constructed a lopsided tower, watching Richard all the while. 'Are you here to see Edward?'

'Yes.'

'He'll not want to see you, Uncle. He says you did mean from the first to steal his crown and murder our Uncle Anthony.' This was said very matter-of-factly, was not an accusation, merely a statement of his brother's belief. The blue eyes regarding Richard were sharp with curiosity, showed no emotion other than interest in how Richard would respond.

'Yes,' Richard said slowly, 'I suppose he would think that. But it's not true, Dickon, could not be further from the truth. Do you believe me?' He realized at once that this was not a fair question to put to a child, but he saw, too, that it had been the right question, nonetheless, gave Dickon the opening he needed.

'I do not know what I believe any more. Ever since papa died, nothing makes sense. Papa named you Lord Protector, so he could not have believed you'd take Edward's crown away from him. I know mama never liked you but papa told me that you were the one man in Christendom he truly trusted. And Bess and Cecily trust you. Bess said it was silly for us to go into sanctuary, that there was no need.' Momentarily sidetracked, he confided now, 'I hated it at the abbot's lodging. There was nothing to do and Bridget got sick and cried all the time and mama cried, too, but she would not let us come out, not till Bess and the archbishop talked her into letting me join Edward last week.'

He shot a quick look at Richard, saw that his uncle was listening with an attentiveness few adults had ever accorded him, and reassured, he felt free to admit, 'I get so confused by it all, uncle. And Edward is no help. He does not want to play or shoot at the butts, and all he wants to talk about is our Uncle Anthony being executed and you taking the crown. Of course, it was his crown, so it hurts more for him, and he loved our Uncle Anthony whilst I . . . well, I did not ever see him all that much. And then, too, I know papa always liked you much better than Uncle Anthony and I . . . I just get even more confused.'

Richard could think of nothing to say. He reached out, brushed some of the straw from the boy's hair.

'I suppose I do not look very tidy, do I? Uncle. . . . I want to ask you something. The archbishop came to us yesterday, told us about papa being plight-trothed to another lady before he married mama. Edward says it's not true but everyone else says it is, the archbishop and Lord Howard and . . . well, what I want to know is this. If Edward cannot be king, then I guess I cannot be Duke of York, either?'

'No,' Richard said reluctantly. 'No, lad, I fear not.'

'That's what Lord Howard said, too, but . . . well, it's going to seem strange. And Edward had even more titles than me, Prince of Wales and Earl of Chester and Duke of Cornwall and I forget what else, and now to have none. . . . It does not seem quite fair, uncle. Mayhap he would not mind not being king so much if you could give him one of them back?'

Richard wanted nothing so much at that moment as to be able to give Dickon the assurance he sought. But he couldn't bring himself to lie to the boy. 'I cannot do that, Dickon. But you'll want for nothing, that I do promise you.'

Dickon was obviously hoping for more than that. He busied himself in adding more draughtsmen to the board, building battlements around his tower. 'Edward says you mean to keep us here, like prisoners. I told him I did not believe that, but . . . But what is going to happen to us?'

That was a question Richard had often asked himself in the past fortnight. Could a place be made for them at his court? Dickon, mayhap, but Edward? No, the boy was too bitter for that. Thank Christ Jesus he was still so young, young enough to be protected from the plots and intrigues of men who'd use him for self-serving ends. Mayhap by the time he was old enough to involve himself in such schemes, he'd have come to terms with the plight-troth, with his disinheritance. And if he did not? Richard looked down unseeingly at the draughts board, thinking of Henry Tudor, thinking of Edward of Lancaster. A pretender's lot was not an easy one; it was a life of false hopes and great dangers. That was not a fate he wanted for his brother's son.

Dickon stirred uneasily. 'Uncle? You have such a strange look. . . . Are you not going to answer me?'

'Yes, Dickon, of course I am,' Richard said swiftly, cursing himself for letting the boy see his misgivings. 'As soon as I can make the necessary arrangements, I mean to send you and your brother north, to my castle at Sheriff Hutton. I think you'll be happy there, Dickon. The North is a fine place to grow to manhood.'

Dickon considered. The prospect of living in Yorkshire was not an unpleasant one to him and he nodded agreeably. 'When? I can take my dog, can I not? What of my sisters? Will they come, too?'

Richard had no chance to respond for, at that moment, Edward appeared in the doorway. Dr Argentine was behind him, had a supportive hand on Edward's shoulder; when the boy balked, the doctor propelled him gently forward into the room.

Edward's face was swollen, splotched with uneven colour; he looked feverish, like one suddenly roused from sleep. He drew an audible breath, took a step toward Richard.

'What do you want?' His voice was high-pitched, tremulous, sounded as if he were choking back tears, and Richard knew he'd made a grievous mistake.

'To talk to you, Edward, to tell you . . .' Richard stopped. No one had ever looked at him with the hatred he now saw on his nephew's face.

'Tell me what . . . uncle?' Edward all but spat the word. 'That I should trust you? That you're sorry you stole my crown? Or mayhap you want to tell me about my Uncle Anthony? Oh, yes, I know about that, too, know you've condemned him to death. Should I fear that, too? Or will you be content to let me keep my life now that you've taken my crown?'

Richard had gone very white but he said nothing, made no attempt to defend himself. There was nothing, he knew, that Edward would believe.

'Murderer!' Edward's mouth had contorted with a rage indistinguishable from grief. 'My uncle's blood is on your hands, and God curse you for it! God curse you. . . .' His voice broke on a sob. He whirled and, jerking loose from Dr Argentine's restraining hand, fled back up the stairs.

'Edward!' Dr Argentine's cry was cut off by the slamming of the bedchamber door. Very slowly, he turned to face Richard.

'You must excuse the boy, Your Grace. He's been under a great strain, does not mean what he said.' His voice was dispassionate, polite. Only his eyes gave him away, eyes that accused, judged, condemned. 'Is it your wish that I fetch him back?'

Richard swallowed. 'No,' he said softly. 'Let him be.'

The chamber seemed to echo with Edward's sobs; in reality there was no sound but the clicking of draughtsmen as Dickon continued to stack them in precariously balanced columns. He looked from Richard to the doctor and back to Richard again.

'I tried to tell you, uncle,' he said composedly, 'that he'd not want to see you.'

II

Minster Lovell

July 1483

Emerging from one of the ground-floor garde-robes in the south-west tower, Francis caught his breath, dazzled by the beauty of the red-gold sky above his head. Even the river was ablaze, reflecting the flaming brilliance of the dying sun. He stood there for a time by the river wall, savouring the moment, and then walked slowly across the inner courtyard. Supper was to be later than usual that evening; trestle tables were being set up, draped in snowy linen cloth. His best silver plate was on display, polished to a blinding gloss, and the great hall had been swept clean, carpeted in a fresh layer of fragrant rushes. Everywhere he looked, Francis saw cause for satisfaction. Smiling, he moved toward the doorway behind the dais, passed through.

The chamber under the chapel was his favourite, a spacious well-proportioned room lit by three traceried windows, one of which was patterned with rose-tinted glass, and when Richard accepted his offer of hospitality, Francis had no difficulty in deciding which bedchamber should be set aside for Richard's use.

He'd hoped to find Richard alone for they'd had little chance for private conversation since departing Windsor ten days ago on the royal progress. He knew, though, that a king's time was not his own, and he was not surprised by what he found—a chamber full of familar faces. Jack de la Pole, Earl of Lincoln, the twenty-year old son of Richard's sister Eliza, was lounging in one of the window seats, engaging in a three-way conversation with

Dick Ratcliffe and Thomas Howard, John Howard's eldest son. John Scrope and the young Earl of Huntingdon were passing the time in agreeable disagreement about the intention of the Scots, and Rob Percy was amusing himself by dazzling George's eight-year-old son with a sleight-of-hand involving walnut shells and dried beans; Edward's eyes were growing progressively wider and Rob was laughing outright at the youngster's astonishment. Against a far wall, Thomas Stanley was standing alone, isolated from the other men by more than distance.

In the midst of all this activity, Richard and John Kendall were sorting through a pile of letters that had been forwarded from London. Richard had one open in his hand; at sight of Francis, he smiled. 'From my son. The fourth letter I've had from him in the past fortnight and each one asks me the same question: When will we arrive in York?'

'And I'll wager the only answer that would satisfy him would be "Yesterday",' Francis quipped, and Richard laughed. He looked far better than he had in weeks, no longer like a man living on the edge of highly strung nerves, and Francis knew why. In the towns of Reading and Oxford, in the villages of the Cotswolds, Richard had found a heartening welcome, found the enthusiasm for his kingship that Londoners had lacked. And it would get better, Francis thought contentedly; Yorkshire would turn out for Dickon in numbers too great to count, would give him a welcome home that none would ever forget.

He smiled at the thought, started to express it aloud, when John Kendall straightened up, said with a gasp, 'My liege, you'll never believe what we have here! A letter from Tom Lynom, your solicitor, seeking your permission to marry that . . . that Shore harlot!'

All conversation ceased. Every man in the chamber was staring at Kendall, staring in disbelief.

'Let me see that!' Richard demanded incredulously. Scanning the letter, he shook his head in baffled wonderment. 'Damned if he does not!'

'The man's besotted.' John Scrope sounded disgusted. 'The king's solicitor and Thomas Grey's doxy. . . . The stupid ass, does he not realize he's putting his career to the torch?'

Dick Ratcliffe was frowning. 'I know Lynom and this is not like him. He's just not a man to lose his head over a woman, especially a wanton like Jane Shore.'

'Say what you will about the woman, she draws men like flies to honey. And for the life of me,' Richard confessed, 'I cannot see why.'

Jack de la Pole stirred at that. 'Speak for yourself, Uncle!' he said cheerfully, drawing a laugh from all but Thomas Stanley. Since Richard's coronation, Stanley had thrown himself into the role of a loyal and prudent councillor with all the zeal of a reformed heretic, and he addressed himself now to Richard with an earnestness that just missed being obsequious.

'Shall I draw up for Your Grace a list of lawyers qualified for Lynom's post?'

'No, I do not think that is necessary,' Richard said coolly, hoping his dislike of Stanley did not show too markedly.

Picking up Lynom's petition, he began to read it through again, as Francis nudged Rob Percy and murmured, 'Fifty marks against that new grey gelding of mine that he does.'

'Done,' Rob shot back instantly, and they shook hands with mock gravity.

Richard folded Lynom's petition, handed it back to John Kendall. He was trying to envisage an unlikelier pairing than that of the serious self-contained Lynom and Jane Shore, the light-minded amoral butterfly. He could not.

Ratcliffe was moved to intercede for his reckless friend. 'He must love her beyond reason to risk so much for her.'

'Yes,' Richard agreed. 'He must.'

'What mean you to do?'

'I fear I'm not doing him a service, but if he wants her as badly as that . . .' Richard paused. 'I suppose I shall have to let him marry her,' he said, and laughed at the astonishment so plainly written on their faces. Francis laughed, too, and nudged Rob again.

'Pay me!' he said.

Occasionally, just before a storm, there is a deceptively tranquil lull, a brief time in which the winds die down and the sky seems about to clear. Later, remembering Tom Lynom's lovesick request and Richard's indulgent response to it, Francis would think of those laughter-filled moments as just such a lull, one that gave way all too soon to trouble, of a sort none of them could have anticipated.

The Duke of Buckingham had remained behind in London; it had been agreed beforehand that he was to rendezvous with Richard at Gloucester. There they were to separate, Buckingham riding on into Wales, Richard continuing north to Tewkesbury. Buckingham's arrival that night at Minster Lovell was unexpected, created some problems of accommodation, for he'd sent no word ahead. He demanded at once to be taken to Richard, despite the lateness of the hour, and as soon as they were alone, he told Richard that his brother's sons had vanished from the Tower.

'. . . And so two servants slept in the lower chamber and one attendant up in the bedchamber with the boys. There were no guards; after all, what need was there? The Tower itself was secure.'

Buckingham was speaking faster than usual, seemed reluctant to meet Richard's eyes. Francis was accustomed to the younger man's mercurial shifts of mood, but never had he seen Buckingham so openly edgy. He was not surprised, though. Buckingham had personally picked the men serving as Edward's attendants; some of the responsibility, therefore, was his.

Jack de la Pole had been summoned, like Francis, to hear Buckingham's account. He now said impatiently, 'We can go into that later. What story are the men telling, the two who slept below?'

'They claim their ale must have been drugged, say they sat down with a flagon in early evening and remember nothing else till the next day, waking up on the floor in their own vomit. After coming to, they went upstairs and found both boys and the other servant gone. In a panic, they went to Brackenbury, the Constable of the Tower. He ordered a discreet search of the Tower grounds, turned up nothing, and came to me, since I'm now your Lord Constable.'

'I do not understand,' Richard said slowly. 'I can see that they could have been taken from the Garden Tower without attracting undue attention. But how could they have been smuggled out of the Tower itself? It's guarded at night, the gates locked. It makes no sense, does not seem possible.'

'The fact that they're gone proves that it is.' Buckingham shifted in his chair. 'Perhaps they bribed a guard, had a boat waiting on the river. Or waited till daylight, till the gates were opened. The alarm was not given for hours, after all. I can only guess how it was done. But it *was* done, and what matters now is not so much how as why and who. He leaned toward Richard. 'Two possibilities come at once to mind.'

'The Woodvilles?' Francis said, and Buckingham nodded.

'Thomas Grey is still at large and so are three of Elizabeth Woodville's brothers. Who'd have a stronger motive? And they've the money, as well, to finance such a scheme, what with having stolen half the royal treasury away free and clear to Brittany.'

'And the other?' Richard said tersely.

'Someone in the pay of the French king. He was more than willing to use Edward of Lancaster against your brother. I daresay he'd be no less willing to use the boys against you.'

Some of Richard's initial shock was ebbing. 'If we're going to find them, we need more than speculation. Let's start with the men who claim to have been drugged. How do we know they speak the truth? Does their story hold up under questioning?'

Buckingham shrugged. 'Both Brackenbury and I interrogated them at some length, could catch them out in no contradictions.'

'What about the doctor . . . Argentine? Where was he that night?'

'Gone. I dismissed him last week.'

Richard was startled. 'I gave no such order, Harry.'

'I know but I took it upon myself to issue one in your name.' Buckingham sounded faintly defensive. 'He was no friend to you, cousin, was poisoning the boy's mind against you.'

'Well, perhaps. . . . But what of the man who disappeared? Was he the one who gave the others the ale? I thought as much. What's his background, Harry? What can you tell us about him?'

Buckingham looked uncomfortable. 'Well, actually, I know very little,' he admitted. 'I took him on my steward's recommendation, saw no need to check into his past. . . .'

'What do you mean, you do not know? Christ, Harry, you were the one who offered to replace Edward's attendants with men we could trust!'

'And I had every reason to think we could trust this man. Look, cousin, I know this has hit you hard but I do not think it fair to put the blame on me. Every man has his price; it's hardly my fault if someone found his. Now, my steward handpicked the man, will have all the information we need about his past, his family, whatever. When I get back to Brecknock, I'll question him at once, get the answers you want.'

Richard bit his lip. Accusing words would come all too easily tonight and, once said, could not be forgotten. Yes, Harry had been negligent but so had he. He should have chosen Edward and Dickon's attendants himself, should not have waited, should have sent them north before he left on progress. Jesú, why had he not?

'You do that, Harry,' he said curtly, saw that Buckingham resented his peremptory tone, but that was the least of his worries at the moment. Where were they? In whose hands?

'Who else knows?'

'Brackenbury, of course. And Jack Howard and Chancellor Russell. No one else . . . so far.'

Richard pushed his chair back, came to his feet. After a moment's reflection, he crossed to the door. John Kendall had already retired for the night but one of his scribes responded at once to Richard's summons.

'Seat yourself, Will,' Richard directed. 'I've a letter to go tonight to my lord Chancellor.'

Buckingham half rose from his seat. 'Cousin. . . .'

Richard had begun to pace. As the scribe waited patiently, he mentally formulated and rejected sentences, searching for the words oblique enough to be safely put to paper and yet clear enough so that Russell understood his meaning. 'Whereas we understand that certain persons of late had taken upon them the fact of an enterprise . . .' Yes, Russell would comprehend.

Turning back to the scribe, he began to dictate rapidly, a brief cryptic letter directing his Chancellor to discuss the 'enterprise' alluded to with members of the council, to begin an investigation and to appoint a commission to try persons as yet unnamed.

'Given under our signet at this manor of Minster Lovell the twenty-ninth day of July,' he concluded, and listened critically as the mystified scribe obediently read the letter back.

'Thank you, Will. That will do.'

Buckingham had been listening in growing agitation. With the scribe's departure, he burst out, 'Christ Almighty, cousin, you cannot do that! You cannot let this get out!'

'What other choice do I have?'

'You haven't thought this through. If you had, you'd see at once that the worst thing you could do is to make this public.'

'And what are you suggesting that I do, Harry? Say nothing, pretend all is well? Do you not think that sooner or later the boys will be missed? That people will not wonder why they're no longer seen about the Tower grounds? How do you expect me to account for their disappearance?'

'Cousin, listen to me. The boys were put in your care. That makes you responsible for their well-being, their safety. You do not see the implications in that? You do not realize the risk you're taking? There are already too many men in London who think Stillington lied about the plight-troth, lied at your bidding.'

He saw Richard stiffen, said swiftly, 'We're talking truth, cousin; the stakes are too high for anything less. You think on those suspicious whoresons, the ones who're convinced you usurped your nephew's crown. Now you want to tell them that your nephews have suddenly and conveniently disappeared, vanished from the Tower under circumstances you cannot explain? You truly want to tell them that?'

Richard's shock was such that he could only stare at Buckingham, all defences down. It had not occurred to him that men might put so sinister an interpretation upon his nephews' disappearance.

His sister's son was no less stunned, reacted with outrage. 'That is ridiculous! None who know my uncle would ever believe he'd harm a child, least of all his brother's children.'

Buckingham gave Jack a look of poorly concealed contempt. 'Must we waste time in stating the obvious? We're talking of men who do not know your uncle, of men who'd believe the worst of Our Lord Jesus Christ Himself. We're talking of die-hard Lancastrians, of malcontents and men in the pay of Henry and Jasper Tudor and the French king. You think such scum would scruple to make use of the most blatant lies?'

As little as Francis liked to find himself allied with Buckingham, he could see no help for it. 'There's some very ugly truth in what he says, Dickon. I'd not see you subjected to such vicious gossip if it can be helped. And I think perhaps . . . just perhaps . . . it can.'

Richard swallowed; there was a sour taste in his mouth. He

would not lie to himself, knew all too well that he'd never be able to endure a slander of that sort. As it was, he'd found it all but well nigh intolerable these past few weeks, knowing that there were those who believed he'd made use of a lie to take the throne from his brother's son, and knowing, too, that there wasn't a damned thing he could do about it.

'How, Francis?'

'Suppose we say nothing, while quietly doing what we can to locate the boys? One of two things is bound to happen. Either we find them or they surface somewhere. Once they're safe out of the country, there'll be no point in keeping their whereabouts a secret, after all. The whole idea is to make use of them to stir up rebellion, so it'll be crucial to let it be known that they're no longer in your custody. I'd hope we find them ere they can be moved abroad, for their sakes as well as ours; I'd not like to see them used, exploited. But if the worst does come to pass and we discover them living at the French court, at least none can besmirch your name, Dickon, can twist their disappearance into something it's not for political purposes.'

'Lovell's right,' Buckingham chimed in feverishly. 'If you'll not heed me, listen to him! You must not let word of this get out, not yet. Later—as Lovell says—it will not matter, but now it'd be disastrous.'

Richard gazed at Buckingham, not fully understanding the other's urgency but impressed by the passion in Buckingham's plea. Harry rarely showed so much emotion; he must feel very strongly about this, in truth. Were he and Francis right? What would he gain by revealing Edward and Dickon's disappearance now? Would that not be playing into the hands of his enemies, sowing suspicions that might not be so easy to uproot? What could he lose, after all, by waiting? With luck, the boys might be found ere anyone even discovered they were missing.

A strained quiet had settled over the room. Accurately reading assent into Richard's silence, Francis crossed to the sideboard, began to pour drinks for them all. Richard accepted his without comment, nodded almost imperceptibly when Buckingham assured him that John Howard had already begun making inquiries, would assume personal charge of the search. It was only then that Richard remembered about his nephew's pet spaniel.

'Dickon had a dog, Harry, a small spaniel. What of it? No one heard it barking?'

'The dog. . . .' Buckingham was frowning. 'What did Brackenbury tell me about the dog?' His face cleared. 'I remember. It died two days before their disappearance.'

'Died?' Richard said sharply. 'How?'

'Just what you're thinking . . . poison. Brackenbury says at the time it was taken for granted that the dog had eaten something tainted, mayhap poison set out for rats. Now we do know better, of course. They could not take the dog with them, but you could not expect a ten-year-old boy to understand that, to leave the dog willingly. And so. . . .' Buckingham shrugged, said with a twisted smile, 'You have to admit it was clever, spared them no small measure of trouble with the boy, whining and not wanting to go without the dog. No, unfortunately for you, cousin . . . for us . . . they seem to have thought of everything.'

'I do not see much to admire in poisoning a little boy's dog,' Jack said cuttingly, but even he was taken aback by the violence of Buckingham's reaction.

'Just what do you mean by that? I never said anything of the sort and you damned well know it! What sort of trouble are you trying to stir up?'

Jack was not intimidated. 'Well, what did you mean, then? We're talking about the abduction of two youngsters, ten and twelve, boys who doubtlessly went willingly with their abductors, at least one of whom appears to have been their own servant. It would not take a mastermind to pull that off, as you seem to think, just good timing and a fair amount of luck.'

'Men like you make me sick, in truth,' Buckingham said, so

venomously that Jack started to rise from his chair. 'You just take it for granted that you're dealing with fools. Well, there is a Welsh proverb you'd do well to heed, that a man who underestimates his enemy is a man on his way to his own funeral. Now you do as you please, but that's not a mistake I mean to make. We're dealing with a first-rate intelligence and, unless we do own up to that, our chances of finding those boys will range from slim to nonexistent.'

Jack opened his mouth, seemed about to respond in kind, but Richard, who'd been listening in some surprise to this unexpectedly intense exchange, said impatiently, 'Look, the last thing we need tonight is to be fighting amongst ourselves. Just let it lie, the both of you!'

Buckingham drew a deep breath. 'Sorry, cousin. I guess my nerves are on the raw, what with all that's happened. It just seems such a pity, does it not? I mean, when all seemed to be going so well for you. . . .'

Richard paused with his cup halfway to his mouth, giving Buckingham a thoughtful, measuring look. Buckingham flushed under the appraisal, rose to pour more wine into a cup already brimming.

Richard hesitated. It would be easy to say, 'Look, Harry, I do not blame you. You should have taken greater care in choosing attendants for Edward but so should I. I'm not seeking scape-goats.' What Harry obviously needed to hear. So why could he not say it? Was it because Harry had yet to voice the slightest concern for Dickon and Edward? That his primary concern, his only concern, seemed to be in making sure none would hold him accountable for his man's treachery?

Suddenly he wanted Anne, wanted her desperately. But Anne was at Windsor, would not be joining him at Warwick Castle till next week. She'd wanted to come with him, had insisted that she was feeling fine, had no need for a fortnight of rest. He knew better, knew how exhausted she truly was, knew how hard these past weeks had been on her. But tonight . . . tonight, he'd have given almost anything to have her here; never had he needed her so much.

The great hall was in darkness but moonlight filtering in through the windows revealed blanketed bodies lying along the walls; Minster Lovell's sleeping-space had been stretched to capacity. Detouring around a snoring form at his feet, Richard pushed the door open, stepped out into the inner courtyard.

The sky was scattered with stars but the air was damp, gave promise of rain before morning. Passing the stables, Richard's step slowed. Were he back at Middleham, he could have ordered a horse saddled, have taken it out onto the moors. The temptation was very strong, but common sense prevailed. He did not know the countryside around Minster Lovell; to ride out alone at night would be to beg for a nasty fall. Would give rise, too, to speculation, to gossip he could ill afford. He was going to have to get used to that somehow, to being the focus of all eyes.

By now he'd reached the river wall. A door beckoned; shoving the bolt back, Richard passed out onto the landing dock. The wind was wetter here; clouds were beginning to drift in from the west, smothering stars in a sea of grey. Richard stood for a time on the end of the dock, now and then dropping a small pebble into the inky blackness below. The pebbles were swallowed up in silence; not even a splash marked their passing.

So caught up was he in his own thoughts that he didn't hear the footsteps, not at first. Startled, he spun around just as Francis stepped out onto the dock.

'The wind's rising; it's like to mean rain,' Francis observed, as if resuming an interrupted conversation, as if it were perfectly normal for them both to be prowling about the manor grounds hours before dawn. He asked no questions and Richard was grateful for that, grateful, too, for Francis's companionable silence.

Watching as Richard continued to drop pebbles into the river,

Francis said with a faint smile, 'Do you remember how we used to skip stones over the surface of the moat at Middleham? You think you can still do it?'

Richard tried, found he couldn't; the stone vanished from sight. 'The stone's not flat enough,' he said, and Francis obligingly agreed with him. Richard held out his fist, let the last of the pebbles slide through his fingers.

'You know what I find myself thinking about, Francis? The dog.'

He turned to face Francis. 'You see . . . Dickon loved that dog.'

12

York

September 1483

Emerging from the south door of St Peter's, Ned blinked. Never had he seen so many people as were now wedged into the churchyard, clustered around the Low-Minster Gates, spilling out into the street. For a moment he held back and Anne took his hand, said reassuringly, 'They're here to honour you, darling. This is your day.'

Ned drew a deep breath, nodded and let himself be drawn into the vortex of the crowd. It was not as bad as he'd feared; he was not engulfed, after all. Miraculously, space was clearing ahead. The noise still hurt his ears but it no longer sounded threatening. They're cheering for us, he told himself. For papa and mama. For me, too.

Mama was right; this was his day. He knew the schedule by heart, knew the route they were to take, down Stonegate and Blake Street and then up Lopp Lane back to the Archbishop of York's Palace. There papa was to invest him as Prince of Wales. Ned mentally rehearsed his role in the ceremony to come. He was to kneel, and papa was to give him a golden rod and ring and place a garland upon his head. Papa was also to gird him with a ceremonial sword; he must not forget that. He was very glad his father was to be the one to make him Prince of Wales; if he botched anything, papa would cover for him.

Never had he seen Stonegate so clean; the rakyers must have been up at dawn to sweep the street clear of debris, dung, straw and mud. Ned glanced about, admiring the bright arras hangings and tapestries that were stretched across the street above his head. He'd never seen London, though he very much wanted to, but he felt sure not even London could have equalled the welcome York had given his parents. Pageants, three on the day of their entry alone, one of which had a marvellous green dragon that actually belched fire. Banquets, so many he'd lost count. At the Lord Mayor's dinner, they'd been served a subtlety shaped like Middleham Castle, with saffron iced walls and battlements, a blue frosted moat, and a keep made of almond cake. And yesterday, there'd been a special peformance of the Creed Play for them; he had been bored by the play, which had a lot of talk and not much action, but he'd been proud of the way he'd sat through it without squirming or openly yawning.

'Look, Ned!'

Following his mother's pointing finger, Ned saw that a fount had been set up across from St Helen's; it gushed forth with sparkling white wine. Four young girls waited at the fount, clad in white, with free-flowing hair that proclaimed each had known no man. As the procession approached, they released into the sky a score or more of doves.

The maidens in white had presented Richard with a gilded

cup from the fount, and the spectators cheered themselves hoarse as he accepted it and drank. Waiting until Ned and Anne had joined him before the fount, Richard handed the cup to Anne, watched with a smile as she drank and then passed it to Ned. Feeling very grown-up, Ned swallowed carefully and then copied his father's gesture and raised the cup in salute to the people of York. His parents beamed and Ned felt a glow of pride.

As the procession moved on, Ned fell in step beside his mother again. He wished Johnny could have walked with them. He was sure Johnny would've liked to drink from the gilded cup, too. But Johnny was somewhere behind him, midst the nobles and lords of the Church. So was his little cousin Edward, his Uncle George's son. After papa invested him as Prince of Wales, Papa was going to knight Johnny and Edward. Ned was glad; they might have felt left out, otherwise.

That made Ned think of his other cousins, the ones papa and mama did not seem to want to talk about. He'd never met Edward but he remembered Dickon quite well, from the time his uncle the king had brought Dickon and his sisters to York. It must hurt, to find out they were bastards like that, so sudden. At least Johnny had time to get used to it.

'Papa looks happy, does he not, mama? I think it pleases him, that the people seem to like him so much.'

'You're right, Ned; your father is happy today. For which we must thank the good people of York, thank them for this blessed outpouring of love which is, in truth, a . . . a healing.'

Ned didn't understand what his mother meant by that last but he suspected she'd been talking more to herself than to him; he saw how her eyes followed his father, seemed to see no one else. He pondered what she'd said that he did understand, asked at last, 'Were the people of London not happy, too, that papa was to be king?'

He saw his mother hesitate and then she said slowly, 'Perhaps not as happy as they are in York, darling, but then, Londoners do not know your father as well as our people do here.'

That made sense to Ned. He nodded, satisfied, and turned his attention again to the crowds thronging both sides of Lopp Lane.

'Did you see, mama, how all the shops are shut tight? No one at all is working in York today. Even the cookshops and the brothels in Grape Lane are closed for the procession.'

'Ned! How on earth do you know that?'

'I can see for myself, mama. The cookshops, the goldsmiths, the butchers, the bookbinders—all are closed up. I know we did not walk in Grape Lane, but I heard some men talking about it just before the High Mass and they said right plain that the brothels were not open. I do not know what they sell there,' he admitted, 'but from the way the men were talking, it sounded like something people like to buy, so it is an especial honour then, that they closed for our procession.'

Ned was puzzled but pleased when his mother began to laugh. He had not meant to make a joke, if indeed he had, but making mama laugh was no small accomplishment these days. It baffled him; why were mama and papa not happier now that papa was King? Ned did not understand but he sensed the strain behind their smiles, a worry that even the cheers of York had been unable to sweep away. He studied his mother now, heartened to see her mouth still curving upward at the corners. Mayhap the magic of this day, his day, would do it, would make the worry go away for good. He would, he decided, try to remember to tell papa about the brothels in Grape Lane. Mayhap it would make papa laugh, too.

13

Lincoln

October 1483

The sun shone on the hilled city of Lincoln with deceptive warmth, tempting the unwary into believing that summer would linger awhile longer, that the snows and ice-edged winds would come late this year. To a people for whom winter meant early dark and salted meat, washing-water frozen in its laver and nights huddled around smoke-billowing hearths, that was no small blessing. Summer was a season of celebration, winter a time to endure.

Francis was not thinking of freezing dawns and pelting sleet-storms. Like so many others on the mellow October Saturday, he was not thinking beyond the autumnal splendour of the moment. Riding with Rob Percy down Parchmingate Street, he could see the silver-blue gleam of the river below, the gold and russet of the valley beyond. He kept a light hand on the reins, letting his stallion set its own pace, while his thoughts ranged back over the royal progress that had begun twelve weeks ago in the Thames River Valley and was now slowly winding southward back toward London.

They could look back upon it with satisfaction, he thought; with pride, too. Tewkesbury, Coventry, Leicester, Nottingham. In each city, the response had been the same; the people had turned out in large numbers to view their new sovereign, to listen to what Richard had to say, and they liked what they heard. The response of foreign governments had been promising, too. Richard had received a friendly letter from Isabella, Queen of Castile, and a Treaty of Amity was pending between the two kingdoms. James of Scotland had been making conciliatory overtures, proposing an eight-month truce. Best of all, Francis thought with grim relish, that misbegotten spider on the French throne had at last gone to Hellfire Everlasting. Louis had died on August 30th, and with luck, the regency government set up to rule for his youthful son would be too shaky to intervene in English affairs.

The only cloud in the European sky was hovering over Brittany, where Harry of Lancaster's Welsh nephew dwelled under the dubious protection of the Duke of Brittany. For years, he'd been dangling Tudor as bait before Edward and Louis, seeking to turn to his own advantage their mutual eagerness to get possession of the Lancastrian pretender. He now sought to play the same game with Richard, intimating he'd turn Tudor over to France unless England agreed to supply Brittany with four thousand archers at English expense. Richard's response had been both pithy and profane; Francis grinned, remembering.

It was just as well, he mused, that Brittany learned early on the mettle of the man now England's anointed King. Would Brittany follow through on the threat, actually yield up Tudor to France? Francis doubted it; Tudor was too valuable a pawn. Unless . . . unless the Duke of Brittany had an even better iron in the fire. Was that why he was offering of a sudden to sell out Tudor? Was that where Dickon's nephews had surfaced, in Brittany?

But if that was so, surely there'd be rumours to that effect; word would have got out. Francis frowned, unconsciously tightened his grip on the reins. It was the utter silence that baffled him. Men clever enough to smuggle the boys out of the Tower would have been clever enough to get them safe out of the country, too. So why keep their whereabouts a secret? It made no sense.

It was a thought to sour the pleasure he'd been taking in the day. Ere much longer, Dickon was going to have to account for the boys' disappearance. What if they had no luck in tracing them? What then? In persuading Dickon to keep silent about their disappearance, had he and Buckingham done Dickon a grave disservice? To announce now that they were missing, after a lapse of more than two months . . . well, he fervently hoped it would not come to that. And what of the boys themselves? Francis felt sure they were being well treated; self-interest would demand as much. But what future had they? To be bartered to the highest bidder like the Tudor pretender? To be nurtured on hate, as Marguerite had done to her son?

'Francis? You look like a man sucking on a festered tooth. What is wrong?'

Francis shook his head. 'Nothing, Rob. Nothing at all.' Relieved to see they'd reached their destination, a goldsmith in Micklegate Street.

The goldsmith had spread out his wares for their inspection. Francis saw at once a pendant sure to delight Véronique, of painted ivory under rock crystal with silver mounting. He set it aside, wondering whether he should wait and give it to her once she joined him in London or send it by messenger to her now at Middleham. He understood why Dickon and Anne had decided to keep their son in Yorkshire for the time being, knew they did not want to risk exposing Ned to rumours about his missing cousins, for their disappearance could not be kept secret much longer. He understood, too, why Anne had chosen to accompany Ned back to Middleham but he wished she had not, for Véronique felt honour-bound to remain with Anne.

Francis picked up the pendant again, smiled wryly. Only six days they'd been apart and here he was brooding as if they were like to be separated for months. Even if the boys were not found by then, Anne meant to join Dickon in London by Martinmas and Véronique would come with her. If he could not get along without the woman for a mere month, he'd best start wondering if she were feeding him love potions. Selecting two ring brooches of silver and turquoise, he bought them for his sisters, watched as Rob picked out a pearl ring for his Joyce.

'Will that be all, my lord?'

Francis hesitated. 'I would see your rings. None with stones set within; my wife does not fancy that sort.'

He pretended not to notice Rob's look of sympathy mixed with speculation. Why did he not divorce Anna, loving Véronique as he did? The question Rob would have liked to ask but never would. It was not as simple, however, as Rob seemed to think. Even assuming he could find grounds to dissolve the marriage, and he was by no means certain that he could, even then, it was just not that simple. For nineteen years Anna had been his wife, his responsibility, and it was not her fault that he could not love her. She'd done all he'd ever asked of her—ran his household, entertained his friends, befriended his sisters, ignored his infidelities. She'd failed in only one of her duties as a wife and, in that, he could not be sure if the failing was hers or his.

Anna desperately wanted to bear a child. She'd gone on more pilgrimages than he could count, prayed fervently to St Margaret that she might conceive, placed mistletoe above their marital bed, mixed feverfew and mandragora in wine, all to no avail. She'd shared his bed since she was fifteen and in all that time her womb had never quickened.

Anna's guilt was only a little less than her grief for all knew that if a marriage was childless, the woman was to blame. And yet. . . . And yet why was it that a barren woman who was widowed and then remarried so often bore a handful of healthy children for her second husband? How explain that? And what of Véronique? For eight years now she'd lain with him and she, too, was childless. It was true that she took care to hold on to a jasper pebble when they did make love and she sinned for his sake by drinking brake-root in her wine so that she might not conceive. But other women made use of these safeguards and still they grew heavy with child.

Then, too, he'd had other bedmates. He was twenty-nine; by that age, most men of his class had sired a couple of bastards.

But as far as he knew, not one of the women he'd lain with had ever quickened with his seed. No, he was not at all sure that their barren marriage was Anna's fault. And, until he was, he knew he'd not be able to dissolve the marriage, knew he could not do that to Anna, Anna who so liked being Lady Lovell of Minster Lovell Hall, so proud now that he was England's Lord Chamberlain, the King's closest friend and confidant.

Gathering up their purchases, they called for their horses and made a leisurely return back up the hill to the Archbishop of Lincoln's Palace. But from the moment they entered onto the palace grounds, they sensed something was amiss. Men were loitering about the lower court, gathered in small groups. All normal activities seemed to have been suspended: the stables were untended, the gardens deserted and the palace cooks had abandoned the kitchen, were clustered around the porch of the great hall.

'What do you suppose is going on?'

'This may sound farfetched, Francis, but do you know what this does remind me of?' Rob sounded uneasy. 'Of the way it was at Olney, when we heard that our reinforcements were not going to come, that a Neville-led army was converging upon the village to take King Edward prisoner.'

Rob's disquiet was contagious, all the more so because Francis knew the other man was generally oblivious of atmosphere.

'Come on, Rob, let's find out.'

Pushing through the crowd gathered before the porch, they made their way into the great hall. The first face Francis saw was that of Jack de la Pole. The younger man was standing in the shadow of one of the huge marble pillars that divided the hall. He looked to be in a state of shock, looked physically ill, and Francis took a hasty step toward him. But at that moment John Scrope appeared in the stairwell leading up to the great chamber above. At sight of Francis, he snapped, 'Christ Jesus, man, where have you been?'

'Why? What is . . .?'

'You don't know yet?' Scrope's eyes moved from Francis to Rob. 'Aye, I see you do not.' He spat into the floor rushes at their feet. 'We are facing a rebellion,' he said bluntly, saw their faces change, twitch with shock. 'Set for Saturday next, in the counties to the south and west of London, and thank God Jesus we did find out beforehand, else it might have been too late. Dickon's been travelling without an armed escort; they were counting on that, knew he'd have no soldiers to summon on sudden notice. Thanks be to this God-given warning. It does give us a week but whether that's time enough. . . .'

'Who?' Rob demanded. 'The Woodvilles, Thomas Grey? Tudor?'

'Believe it or not, both. After watching Warwick come to terms with the French whore and Hastings link up with the Woodvilles and Morton, I thought I was done being surprised at the queer couplings politics seem to spawn, but this. . . .'

'But that makes no sense. If the Woodvilles were going to incite a rising, surely it'd be on young Edward's behalf. No matter how they do hate Dickon, why should they want to put Tudor on the throne? They'd denounce the plight-troth as a falsehood, seek to stir up sympathy for Edward. . . .'

Finding his voice, Francis cut in abruptly, 'You've not told us all, John. Rob's right; the Woodvilles have no reason to join forces with Tudor. So why did they?'

Scrope nodded. 'No, I have not told you all. But the other . . . it almost defies belief, and I say that who's seen a lifetime of betrayals and treason.' He spat again into the rushes.

'I've not told you yet the name of the man behind the plot, the man heading the rebellion. Dickon's Lord Constable. His friend and ally. Harry Stafford, Duke of Buckingham.'

'That cannot be,' Rob gasped. 'You're mad!'

Scrope, normally a rather touchy man, forbore to take offence. 'Nay, Rob, it's true enough. It seems playing the kingmaker were not enough for him, not when he could aim higher still.'

'Christ on the Cross! I cannot believe it! Buckingham of all men had most cause to be true. Dickon did name him Lord Constable, Chief Justice of North and South Wales, Great Chamberlain, gave him the Bohun estates, gave him whatever he did ask for.'

'Aye, but it seems he coveted one thing more . . . the crown. God rot him for what he is, the lying worthless son of a poxed whore, but he is cousin to Dickon, can trace his lineage to Thomas of Woodstock. If he can bring down the House of York, he could claim the crown in his own right, could. . . .'

'Then you think he's just making use of Tudor?'

'Need you even ask? He needs Tudor's Lancastrian connections right now, needs Morton and Lady Stanley and their ilk to help him destroy Dickon. But then? You tell me. Can you see him yielding his own claim in favour of Henry Tudor? A man whose lineage is flawed on both sides by the bar sinister, the grandson of an obscure Welsh squire who was lucky enough to bed a widowed queen? When pigs walk on water and the God-cursed Scots rule in Cathay! He'd never—Jesú, man, are you ill? You've gone as green as spoilt milk.'

'Francis? Francis, you look ghastly. Here, let me . . .' Rob put a solicitous hand on his friend's arm.

Scarcely aware of what he did, Francis pushed the other man away. It had all come together for him, come together with appalling, merciless clarity. Sickened, he sagged back against one of the marble pillars. He understood now, understood all. It was Buckingham who personally selected Edward's attendants. Buckingham who suggested Morton be placed in his own custody. Buckingham who stayed behind in London, finding excuses not to accompany Dickon on the progress. Buckingham who bragged of the 'first-rate intelligence' behind the boys' abduction, who convinced Dickon to keep silent about their disappearance . . . and God forgive him, but so had he.

'Francis, are you all right? You'd best sit down. . . .'

'Never mind me,' he said hoarsely. 'Tell us the rest, John.'

'Well, you know most of it. The target date is a week from today, as I said, and Buckingham is the one pulling the strings, with a lot of help from Morton and his Lancastrian contacts. The plan is for Buckingham, Morton, Thomas Grey, and their allies to stir up a rising in the South whilst Tudor lands in Dorset. It seems the Duke of Brittany has decided to gamble on Tudor's chances, has agreed to supply ships and men.'

Rob swore roundly at that, called the Duke of Brittany a gutless grasping Judas, called Tudor even worse. 'But I still do not see how the Woodvilles fit into all this. It makes no sense.'

'You're wrong, Rob; in a self-serving way, it does. You see, Tudor has promised to wed Elizabeth's daughter Bess, to make her his Queen should he prevail against Dickon.'

'And are you telling me Elizabeth Woodville was naïve enough to buy that? Just assume for the moment the unthinkable, that Tudor could ever hope to defeat Dickon in the field, and assume, too, that Buckingham would then magnanimously step aside in Tudor's favour. He could not marry Bess unless he had parliament void the plight-troth, declare her legitimate, and the minute that was done, Edward would be the lawful King of England.'

Scrope looked uncomfortable, said reluctantly, 'Well, it seems they've been spreading rumours in the South. . . .'

'What rumours? I don't follow you.'

Francis bestirred himself, said with an effort, 'Rumours . . . rumours that Edward and his brother are dead.'

Scrope nodded, his face grim. 'I see you've fit all the ugly pieces together. It is a damned clever slander, in truth—wins over the Woodvilles and their supporters, discredits Dickon by accusing him of the one crime people would never forgive, and. . . .'

'But surely none would ever believe it?' Rob was more incredulous than outraged. 'Dickon would never harm his brother's sons. Moreover, he'd have nothing to gain by their deaths, and a great deal to lose should they die in his custody.'

'We know that, Rob, and so should any man of common sense.

But there are too many ignorant superstitious people in the country, people willing—nay, eager—to believe the worst of their betters. I think Dickon had best squelch these rumours by parading the boys through the streets of London for all to see, and the sooner the better. In fact, that was the second bit of advice I did give him, the first being to get out summons to arms within the hour.'

Francis felt queasy. 'Where's Dickon?'

'Abovestairs in the great chamber.' Scrope gestured toward the stairwell behind them. 'He is taking this hard, I fear. And who can blame him? He's had more than his share of betrayals in his life, Warwick and Johnny Neville, his brother Clarence, Will Hastings. But this . . .'

No longer listening, Francis turned away, stared up into the dark winding stairwell. He went up the stairs like an old man, one slow step at a time. The door to the great chamber was unguarded, unlatched. He stood there before it, forced himself to go in.

Richard was standing by the south-wall windows, staring down at the leaded roof of the kitchen below. The gardens to the south were visible, the tops of trees splashed in sunlit shades of crimson, scarlet and saffron, hedges and herbs still flaunting summer green. Some overzealous servant had lit a fire in the hearth; it should have made the chamber oppressive on this, a day of unseasonal warmth. Richard was grateful now for its heat but, although he was not three feet from the flames, it did little to ease his chill. As he brought his hand up to his face, his fingers felt frozen, brushed his skin with the touch of ice. In his other hand he held a forgotten wine cup; he lifted it to his mouth, swallowed and gagged as his throat constricted. Turning the cup upside down, he poured the contents into the hearth, watched the fire sputter and die.

'Dickon?'

He turned slowly, saw that Francis was standing in the doorway. 'You know?' he asked, saw Francis nod.

'I . . . oh, God, Dickon, can you ever forgive me? I talked you into keeping silent, into saying nothing. . . .'

Richard looked at him, seeing the suffering on his friend's face but unable to respond to it. He felt numb and instinctively feared the moment when the numbness would give way to emotions he could not deal with.

'You understand what this means, Francis?' he said huskily. 'They never left the Tower alive.'

14

Westminster Sanctuary

October 1483

The summer had passed for Bess in a blur of tears and baffled rage. The man whom mama described, the man who 'cared only for his own pleasures and most of them were found between a woman's legs', the man who 'lay with Nell Butler and then lost interest', who married mama knowing he was not free. How reconcile that man with the father she remembered? The father who always had time for her, no matter how busy he was. Teasing her, taking her side against mama, drying her tears when the French king disavowed her betrothal with his son, kissing her and assuring her that 'no man with eyes to see would ever reject you, sweetheart.' He was all a father could be, funny and tender and caring, and she'd loved him so very much. How could she hate him now?

She could not, no matter what he'd done. Once she admitted that to herself, some of the hurt began to heal. Yes, he'd done a grievous wrong, but it was done long before they were born and somehow that made a difference. And he'd loved them very much, had done what he could to protect them, to shield them from tne consequences of his sin. If what mama said was true, he'd even put his own brother to death for their sake. No, she could never hate papa.

Having found that she could not blame her father, she found that she could not blame her uncle, either. Yes, he'd failed her and her sisters—above all, failed Edward. But she could not realistically expect him to put his brother's children before his own son. Once he learned about the plight-troth, it was inevitable that he would take the crown; to have done otherwise would have been to deny not only his own right but that of his little boy.

And in fairness, she should not blame mama, either. Mama had not known about the plight-troth until it was too late, and once she had, she'd done her best to protect their interests. Oh, but if only she'd not tried to deny Dickon the protectorship. If only she had not treated Dickon like an enemy and, in so doing, made him one.

In later years, when Bess tried to recall those summer months in sanctuary, she'd find her memory was flawed, filled with curious blanks. She passed the days like a sleepwalker, fearful of the future, haunted by the past whilst squandering the present like coins of little value. Where once she'd pined to leave the confines of sanctuary, now she was more than willing to stay where she was, sheltered from a world that no longer held a place for her. She shrank from facing people, dreading in equal measure their scorn and their pity. There were days when it was an effort to get out of bed, to dress; what was the point, after all?

Only the presence of her three little sisters kept her from surrendering unconditionally to this cold, grey and all-enveloping despair. Anne was only eight, and Katherine and Bridget even younger; no less bored within the limits of sanctuary than Dickon had been, they demanded a great deal of Bess's time and energies.

Resentful at first, she gradually came to see her sisters' demands for what they were, a godsend. In caring for the little girls, she began slowly to care again about herself, about the fragmented life she somehow had to start putting back together.

She found ways to pass the time: reading, embroidering, playing chess games and charades with Cecily, hoodman-blind with the younger girls. She wrote cheery little notes to Dickon and occasionally to Edward, gave them to John Nesfield with his assurances that he'd pass them on to the Constable of the Tower, Sir Robert Brackenbury, for delivery to the boys.

John Nesfield was a new element in their lives. In August, guards had suddenly been posted around the abbot's lodging, guards commanded by John Nesfield. Bess and Cecily soon discovered he was quite approachable and from him learned that the council had given orders to keep the sanctuary under surveillance. They sought to keep boredom at bay by speculating at length about the reasons for the council's action. Was it feared that they meant to slip away as Tom had done? Or was it a preventive measure, one meant to keep mama from indulging in further intrigue?

If so, it was a spectacular failure. It was true that visitors were no longer allowed to come and go as freely as they had during those June days when Jane Shore had served as Will Hastings's go-between. But their mother had been able to circumvent the new restrictions with a little ingenuity. Taking to her bed, she'd feigned illness, so convincingly that she soon won access for the doctor of her choice. That the doctor in question was a Dr Lewis, a young Welshman with close ties to Lady Stanley, did not escape either Bess or Cecily. So mama had not learned anything from the fiasco of the Morton-Hastings plot.

Neither, it seemed, had Lady Stanley. She'd been luckier than she deserved the last time, had merely been remanded into her husband's custody. In fact, she'd even been allowed to play a prominent role in their uncle's coronation. It was Lady Stanley who'd been given the honour of carrying Anne's train in the procession to the abbey. Bess had been amused in spite of herself upon hearing that, could not think of a more subtle and fitting punishment for Henry Tudor's mother, to be forced to watch as the crown she so coveted for her son was placed upon another man's head. That was, Bess and Cecily laughingly agreed, exactly what papa would have done, too. But it seemed that Lady Stanley was venturing once more into deep water.

As for her mother's involvement in this latest plot, Bess almost welcomed it. At least mama seemed to be taking an interest again in what went on around her, seemed to have shaken off that dreadful, uncaring apathy that had so frightened both Bess and Cecily. Let other women occupy themselves with their gardens and embroidery frames and household accounts, Bess thought with grim amusement; with mama, nothing worked so well as intrigue. She was not at all concerned about her mother's scheme, for she could not see how it could amount to anything. Whatever mama and Lady Stanley had in mind, what threat could they pose to Dickon now? Two lone women against the power of the State, against an anointed king?

In the second week of October, rumours began to sweep the city of a rising in Kent. But word was slow to trickle into the confines of the sanctuary, and it was not until the following Sunday that Bess and Cecily learned what all of London already knew, that there was trouble to the south, that six days ago Richard had issued a public proclamation accusing the Duke of Buckingham of treason.

Elizabeth was conferring, privately and urgently, with Dr Lewis when her daughters burst without warning into the chamber. She spun about, started, a reprimand hovering on her lips. But Bess, whose manners had temporarily gone by the wayside, gave her no chance.

'Mama, you must tell us what is happening! We just talked to

John Nesfield and he says the Duke of Buckingham has stirred up a rebellion against Dickon, that Buckingham's allied himself with Henry Tudor, and Tom and your brothers are all in the plot, too. Mama, is it true?'

'Not now, Bess!'

'Madame, I really think she should be told. . . .'

'Doctor, I'll thank you to stay out of this. I already told you I'd do it in my own way and in my own time.'

'But if she's to wed with my lord, she should. . . .'

'Wed? Wed with whom?' Bess stared at the doctor. 'What are you talking about?'

'I know Lady Stanley has oft spoken to you of her only son, Henry Tudor, Earl of Richmond. He has dedicated his life to the recovery of the crown wrongfully usurped from King Harry of blessed memory, to the recovery of his stolen birthright. But he is sensitive, too, to the injustice done you and your sisters, hopes to redress your wrongs at the same time that he does redress his own. With that in mind, he has made a formal offer for your hand in marriage, and your lady mother has accepted on your behalf. He means to. . . .'

'Me . . . marry Tudor? No! I will not do it.'

'Bess!'

'My lady, I don't think you understand. My lord has honoured you by offering to make you his Queen, to. . . .'

'And if wishes were horses, beggars would ride. That is a favourite saying of my uncle, Doctor. You do remember my uncle . . . the man who does happen to be England's present king? And since he and not Henry Tudor wears the crown, I fail to see how Tudor can offer me anything, least of all to make me Queen.'

'It surprises me, in truth, to hear you speak so kindly of a man you have such reason to hate. I think you'd best listen. . . .'

'No, Doctor Lewis, you listen! You seem to have forgotten who I am, the daughter of that Yorkist king you just accused of usurping Lancaster's throne. My father had every right to the crown and

1023

I resent you saying otherwise. For you to think I'd ever consent to ally myself with the enemy of my father's House, to wed a Lancastrian adventurer of dubious heritage . . . well, it is out of the question and you can tell Tudor that for me, tell him. . . .'

'Bess, you little fool, listen to me. . . .'

'No, mama, not this time. You tell him, Doctor Lewis, tell him what I said.'

'You're making a great mistake, my lady. He's offering you a new life, a crown, a chance to avenge yourself upon the man who did your family such grievous hurt. . . .'

'My uncle? I do not blame him for taking the crown, Doctor. I'm surprised my mother neglected to mention that; she know it well enough.'

'And do you forgive him, too, for what he did to your brothers?'

'My brothers? What do you mean?'

'Doctor Lewis, no! I said I'd tell her in my own way.'

'Tell me what, mama? What is he talking about?'

'I'm sorry, Madame, but she has a right to know. I think it would alter considerably her feelings about my master's marriage proposal. Lady Bess, I'm sorry to have to tell you this but your brothers are dead, put to death within the Tower at Gloucester's orders.'

Bess gasped and then spat, 'Liar! How dare you? That I'd ever believe . . . that my uncle would . . . Of all the vile, despicable lies . . . I'd never believe that, never!'

Lewis was speechless, stunned by her fury. Elizabeth, no less angry than her daughter, strode to the door, jerked it open. 'You've said enough, Doctor Lewis, more than enough. Did I not tell you I wanted to handle this? But no, you couldn't wait.'

He didn't argue, retreated before her rage.

'Mama, you cannot believe such a lie! Dickon would never harm Edward or Dickon. They're his brother's children, mama. Dickon's his namesake, the same age as his own little boy. You must not believe their lies, mama. You must not!'

'I do not.'

'Please, mama, listen to . . . What? What did you say?'

'I said I agreed with you,' Elizabeth said calmly. She opened the door suddenly, reassured herself that no one was eavesdropping without. 'I'm sorry you had to hear that fool Lewis blurt it out like that, but you need not try to convince me that it's a clumsy lie. I know it is.' She laughed, shook her head. 'But how very like you, Bess, that whenever you happen to be in the right, you're right for all the wrong reasons.'

Thoroughly bewildered, Bess could only stammer, 'Mama, I . . . I do not understand. Not any of this. If you do not believe Dickon capable of murder, then why . . .?'

'I never said that, Bess.' Elizabeth's amusement vanished as if it'd never been. 'Do not delude yourself about that. Richard's quite capable of murder if it serves his interests. What were Dick and Anthony's death, if not murder?'

'But you said . . . said you did not believe he'd harm Dickon or Edward.'

'And I do not . . . because it is not in his interest to do so. Whatever else the man is, he's no fool. Now if we were dealing with that lunatic George of Clarence . . . but Richard, no. He's shrewd enough to anticipate the reaction of the people to the murder of two innocent boys, to realize it would brand him as Herod. And the crown is already his; why jeopardize it all by spilling the blood of his brother's children?'

'Mama, I'm so glad you see that.'

'If Richard is no fool, Bess, neither am I. Of course I see it. A secret hole-in-the-corner murder such as Lady Stanley and Lewis would have me believe?' Elizabeth shook her head again, said with scorn, 'How would it be to his advantage if they were dead and no one knew about it? If you're seeking to eliminate a political rival, you want as many people as possible to be aware of it. If he thought they were so great a threat as that, it would have to be handled the way Ned handled Harry of Lancaster's

1025

murder, by making a regretful announcement of their demise from fever or plague and then having an elaborate state funeral. And even then, he'd be taking a great risk.

'In fact, even if they actually took ill and died from perfectly natural causes, it'd put him in a damnably awkward position, stir up all sorts of suspicions amongst the gullible and the cynical, and virtually the whole of the population falls into one or the other of those two categories. No, in truth, I suspect he tenses up each time he hears that one of them so much as sneeezes. And to expect me to believe that he had them secretly put to death, with no explanation whatsoever offered for their sudden disappearance, a disappearance that sooner or later would become known to all . . . well, it's almost laughable. Far from flattering, too, that they think me so simple. But I. . . .' Elizabeth stopped abruptly, for the first time becoming aware of the utter silence, of the way her daughters were staring at her.

Bess had been listening in fascination, marvelling that her mother could so dispassionately analyse the reasons for and against putting Dickon and Edward to death. Mama was an extraordinary woman, in truth she was, but a little frightening, too. So caught up was she in her mother's spell that she didn't at first realize the full significance of what had just been said.

Cecily had, though. 'Mama, are you saying that papa had Harry of Lancaster put to death? Mama, I grew up believing that he died of natural causes, grieving over the loss of his son.'

How in God's Name, Elizabeth asked herself, had she and Ned between them ever produced such simpleminded children?

'Half the time Lancaster did not even remember he had a son,' she said caustically. 'He died because your father ordered it, because it was necessary. Had Ned only used as much common sense with Stillington, your brother would today be king.'

Bess's head was whirling; there was just too much to take in. Papa had done that, ordered Lancaster's death? And mama. . . . She did not believe that vicious slander about Dickon but she'd still allied herself with Tudor and Buckingham. Bess was utterly lacking in her parents' political instincts, would be the first to acknowledge that, but surely there was a flaw in mama's reasoning, a deadly flaw? She opened her mouth, just as her sister said, 'Mama, is it true what Doctor Lewis said, that Tudor has offered to marry Bess?'

'Perfectly true, the bait they dangled to win Woodville backing.'

'But mama . . . mama, do you not see? Tudor could not marry Bess unless the plight-troth was declared fraudulent. And as soon as that was done, Edward and Dickon would be legitimate, too. Edward would then have a valid claim to the crown again, mama. He'd be far more dangerous to Tudor than ever he was to Uncle Dickon.'

'Cecily's right, mama. You're giving your support to a man who'd have no choice but to put your sons to death should he succeed in defeating Dickon.'

'No, Bess, Cecily is not right. That's not going to happen; you're alarming yourselves for naught.'

'But. . . .'

'Be quiet, and listen to me. I know what I'm doing. No, do not argue, just listen! When your father confessed to me about Nell Butler, I told him that I still considered myself his lawful Queen, considered Edward his rightful heir. Edward should have been king, and God willing, he will be, yet.'

'How, mama?'

'It is so obvious I should think there'd be nothing to explain but if I must spell it out. . . . Listen then, let me tell you about the nature of the wolf. Do you know why wolves have always inspired such fear? Because they run in packs, banding together to hunt down their prey. But once the kill is made . . . then it becomes a snarling snapping free-for-all, each wolf fighting the others for the biggest share of the spoils. Do you not see, Bess? Cecily? That's precisely what's going to happen with Tudor and

Buckingham. They'll join forces just long enough to bring down Richard, and then they'll turn on each other.'

'But how can you be so sure of that?'

'For the love of Jesus, girl, use the brains God gave you! Do you truly think Buckingham has gone to so much trouble, taken such risks, merely to serve as another king's minister? What could Tudor possibly give him that Richard already had not? His own claim to the crown is at least as good as Tudor's, is not stained by the illegitimacy that blots both sides of Tudor's bloodline. No, he fancies himself another kingmaker, but I can assure you that Tudor's not the King he means to make.

'As for Tudor, he'd have to be Christendom's biggest fool to put any trust in Buckingham and from what I do know of Tudor, he is a man to see conspiracies under every bed. Right now they do have a mutual interest in overthrowing Richard but once they do, the bloodletting will start in earnest. And then it will be our turn, Edward's turn. There's already much sympathy for him, many who suspect the plight-troth as too convenient for credibility. He's Ned's son; you think Londoners have forgotten that? You think they would not rally to him once Richard's dead and the choice be between an unknown Welshman and a double-dealing opportunist like Buckingham? We'd have the support of all loyal to the House of York; where else could they go?'

'My God, mama, you are talking about a full-scale civil war!'

'I'm talking about a chance to restore your brother to the throne. I'm doing this for Edward, for us all; can you not see that? What future do you think we have as it is? Having to take what crumbs Richard chooses to scatter before us? Is that what you want, Bess? What of your sisters? What marriages could they hope to make? You expect me to go begging to Richard on your behalf, to a man whose hands are stained with my family's blood? To be Lady Grey again when for nigh on twenty years I was the Queen?

'And what of Edward? Have you never thought what will happen to him? He's too young now to threaten Richard but that will not always be so. Would you have me do nothing, wait and, in five or six years, have to watch as Richard brings some trumped-up charge of treason against him, has him sent to the block? And do not tell me that isn't likely. It's one thing to murder a thirteen-year-old boy and quite another to put a twenty-year-old would-be rebel to death. Oh, he'd do it, all right. There's nothing men will not do if it serves their own interests, nothing—and the sooner you both do learn that, the better.'

'It's certainly true of you, mama,' Bess said bitingly, whirled for the door.

'Bess!' But the command died on Elizabeth's lips; she knew Bess wouldn't have obeyed. She turned to Cecily but the girl was already following her sister from the room.

Elizabeth stood alone in the silent chamber. Why had God given her such fools for daughters? 'I have no choice,' she heard herself say, in a voice that sounded surprisingly loud in the hushed quiet. 'No choice. Why can they not see that?'

15

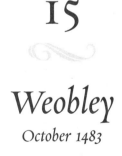

Weobley

October 1483

It was almost dawn but the sky was still dark, foreboding. Harry Stafford, Duke of Buckingham, stood at the bedchamber window, searching in vain for a break in the cloud cover, for a glimpse of sun. He hadn't slept, not for days, and exhaustion had cut deep grooves around his mouth, veined the whites of his eyes with blood.

The past week had been a nightmare. From the day he'd unfurled his banners and marched out of Brecknock, nothing had gone right, nothing had gone as planned, and he was at a loss to explain it, could not understand how his luck could have so forsaken him.

It had begun with the storm, as violent as any within memory of men then living. It had lasted for days, forced them to move out in a drenching, blinding rain. 'The Great Water' people were calling it, and with cause; more than two hundred luckless souls had been drowned in Bristol alone. The rivers had rapidly spilled over their banks, turning fields into lakes, houses into kindling. The roads washed out and Buckingham's soaked and miserable men found themselves slogging through a quagmire. The more superstitious among them began to mutter that God had turned His face against them, that it was true what men said about the Devil fighting for York.

Buckingham, less credulous, knew better. But even if the rains were not sent by Satan to Gloucester's good, he was getting some damnably effective help from mortal men. Buckingham swore and spat. The Vaughns, God rot them, had always resented Stafford authority in Wales. They had at once put out a summons to arms in the name of King Richard and no sooner had Buckingham mustered his men out of Brecknock than the skies over Breconshire were darkening with the smoke of burning Stafford lands. The Vaughns had cut off all communication into the heartland of Wales, thus preventing would-be rebels from joining up with Buckingham, and as he led his men through the Black Mountains, they shadowed his rear, made use of the night and their superior knowledge of the mountain passes to harass his men, to pick off stragglers with the lethal longbows that had been the gift of the Welsh to the world of weaponry.

Buckingham had been bitterly disappointed by the turnout of men to his standard; he had with him a small number of Welshmen more eager to fight for their countryman Tudor than for him, but the bulk of his army consisted of his retainers and tenants from his own lands. As they left Wales behind and entered into Herefordshire, he'd breathed a sigh of relief. Without the Vaughns to plague them, surely they'd be able to make better time, would find many willing to throw in their lot with him, to make his quarrel with Gloucester their own.

It had not worked out that way at all. In Herefordshire, he found no enthusiasm for his cause, no crowds turning out to cheer him on, just silent, suspicious villagers who wanted no more bloodshed, wanted only to be left in peace. And in Herefordshire, he found an enemy no less dangerous than the Vaughns. The opposition of Humphrey and Thomas Stafford was as embittering as it was unexpected; they were Buckingham's own cousins. But now they burned bridges before him, blocked roads with logs and storm debris, staged daring nighttime raids, and the more dispirited of Buckingham's men began to desert.

Jesú, Buckingham thought numbly, how could so much have gone wrong so fast? All had been falling into place so perfectly, like a puzzle to which he alone had all the pieces. His plan had been flawless, so well thought out. And it had worked. It had been so simple, had taken only a few trusted men and a powerful sleeping draught. A dose poured into the ale, another one mixed into the boys' favourite food—as easy as that; the bodies put into a large coffer, hidden away and later removed from the Tower grounds, two small millstones to hang about Gloucester's neck. He had only to express shock when Brackenbury came to him with word of their disappearance, to assist in the search and then to be sure that he was the one to break the news to Gloucester. And again all had gone as he'd foreseen it would. He'd pulled the strings and, like a trusting fool, Gloucester had obligingly helped to hammer the nails into his own coffin, never once suspecting the truth. After all, why should he? No, it had been a perfect plan, virtually foolproof. All it had taken was the willingness to risk all, to gamble where other men would have held back. To have the vision to see what could be his for the taking if he only dared. People were so astonishingly gullible, so stupid, in truth, could be manipulated by the right man like so many puppets. Gloucester and Tudor, Morton, the Woodvilles. So easy, so astoundingly easy.

So why was it all falling apart like this? Why had it so suddenly soured? He'd been so sure that people would flock to his banners, so sure. . . . This God-cursed rain; it had turned all of Herefordshire into an impassable swamp, beat down his men's morale. Worst of all, it had swollen the Severn River into a raging torrent of mud and debris and bloated bodies. With all bridges torched by the Staffords and sure death awaiting any man foolhardy enough to spur his mount into those swirling out-of-control currents, Buckingham had found himself trapped there on the banks of the Severn, cut off from the West Country where the Courtenays and Woodvilles awaited him.

He'd been forced to retreat, was once more at the village of Weobley, where only days before he'd taken possession of the manor house of an absent Yorkist lord. And now he was back, his men encamped in the fields beyond the village—those who had not slipped away under cover of night, fled back into Wales. Already disillusioned, uneasy, they'd panicked as word spread that Gloucester had gathered an army at Leicester, was moving south to intercept them. Most had not bargained on that, on having to take the field against Gloucester himself, and each dawn revealed new gaps in their ranks. Men Buckingham could ill afford to lose. And raging in vain as his army disintegrated before his very eyes, he began at last to know the chill of fear.

In truth, he'd not bargained upon facing Gloucester, either. With Morton and Lady Stanley's go-between Bray assuring him that Tudor would be landing in the South any day now, and with Thomas Grey and his cohorts stirring up rebellion in Devonshire and Kent, he'd felt sure Gloucester would have to fight his way south, every bloody mile of the way. The entire country would be up in arms by then, risings taking flame like so many brushfires, fuelled by carefully fanned rumours about the fate of Gloucester's nephews in the Tower.

But the risings had never materialized; the country remained quiescent. Jack Howard had contained the rebellion in Kent with no more effort than one corking a bottle and he'd had no word at all from Tudor, Tudor who was supposed to draw off Gloucester with the ships and mercenaries bought with Breton gold. As for the Woodvilles, they'd not go up against Gloucester; like him, they'd been relying on Tudor for that, relying on a widespread revulsion against Gloucester, the man responsible for the murder of his brother's sons. But it had not happened. The rumours alone could not do it; not enough people knew the boys were missing. There was not going to be any full-scale rebellion. Unless Tudor did his part, came ashore on English soil, Buckingham knew he was going to be facing Gloucester alone. Facing a man who must hate him with a hatred such as he could not even imagine.

'Your Grace!' It was Thomas Nandik, an astrologer who'd attached himself to Buckingham's cause back in August, when the crown seemed like a fruit ripe for the plucking.

'Morton's gone, my lord. His room is empty, his bed not slept in. He must have slipped away in the night.'

Buckingham's mouth was suddenly dry. So it was true, he thought wildly, that folklore about rats deserting a sinking ship.

'My lord, I do not understand. Bishop Morton was our ally, our liaison with Tudor. Why would he forsake us now, my lord? Why?'

Buckingham didn't answer him. He was staring past Nandik, staring blindly, green-gold eyes glazed over, darkening with dawning fear.

16

Salisbury

November 1483

Fleeing north into Shropshire, Buckingham took refuge with a former retainer at Lacon Hall, near the village of Wem. His choice of sanctuary was as ill advised as his reckless quest for the crown; within hours, he was under arrest, had been taken into custody by John Mitton, the sheriff of Shropshire. On Saturday, November 1st, he was brought to Salisbury, where Richard was encamped. Taken before Sir Ralph Assheton, England's Vice-Constable, he was summarily charged with treason, found guilty and sentenced to death. The execution was set for the following day.

Henry Tudor was more fortunate, was better served by his own instincts. In mid-October his invasion force had been driven back by high winds and raging seas. Attempting a second landing off the Dorset coast, he found the shore lined with soldiers; soldiers who assured his boarding party that they were in the service of the Duke of Buckingham, that Richard was dead. But Tudor was a man who'd long ago learned the high price of survival, learned to inhale suspicion with every breath he drew. Too wary to take the bait, he refused to land, sailed up the coast to Plymouth, where he was told that Buckingham's rising had ended in ignominious failure, that the Woodvilles were in hiding or flight, and Richard was advancing south unopposed, triumphant. Hoisting sail at once, Tudor fled back to Brittany and the rebellion was over.

*

A large crowd had gathered in Salisbury marketplace to watch the Duke of Buckingham die. They were slowly dispersing, most discussing the open fear the condemned man had shown, some of the more pious expressing disapproval that Richard had chosen to execute Buckingham on so holy a day as All Souls' Day.

Swinging up into the saddle, Francis cantered across the market square, welcoming the cold rush of wind on his face. He'd expected to find a bitter satisfaction in watching Buckingham die. But he had felt nothing beyond a queasy contempt. Moving at a rapid pace down Minster Street, he drew rein in front of the George, the comfortable half-timbered inn that had been his home for the past five days. He would have liked nothing so much as to be able to seclude himself in his chamber, order up as many flagons as it took to find oblivion, but he rode on through the arched gateway that gave entry into the close of the cathedral church of the Blessed Virgin Mary.

Ahead lay the spacious stone manor which the Abbot of Sherbourne had offered up for Richard's stay in the city. A number of people were milling about on the manor grounds, in that peculiar ordered chaos Francis had come in the past four months to accept as an inevitable aspect of the King's world. As he dismounted, men recognizing him came forward to take his horse. So did Jack de la Pole, disengaging himself from the others at sight of Francis.

'The execution is over?'

Francis nodded. 'I need to see the King. Is he inside?'

'No, he went over to the church nigh on an hour ago. Come, I'll walk over with you.'

Nothing more was said until they were well away from the others. Francis would have preferred to walk in silence, deliberately did nothing to encourage conversation. But Jack had never been attuned to subtle indicators of mood.

'Christ Jesus, Francis, what happens now? For these three weeks, I've thought of nothing else. Jesú, but even my dreams are of

Buckingham and the evil he's brought upon us all. I cannot stop thinking of those little lads, may God assoil them, and my cousin Bess ... I could not ever be the one to tell her, God spare me that. But no matter how I put my mind to it, I can see no way out of this trap Buckingham has sprung on Dickon. How can he admit the boys be dead, accuse Buckingham now? Who'd believe him? What proof could he offer? Even a confession from Buckingham, even that would not be enough. People put little credence in confessions of doomed men, not knowing as they do that even the bravest man could be made to swear black was white after a few sessions on the rack.'

Jack looked to Francis for response, got none and said bleakly, 'I tell you, Francis, there is no way out, none. Get away from the cities and how many villagers can even read and write? They get their news by word of mouth; rumour be their meat and drink, no matter now unlikely or farfetched.'

His voice droned on, no matter how Francis tried to shut it out. Every word that Jack was saying was one he'd well nigh memorized, so often had he gone over it all in his own head. Dickon could not accuse Buckingham, did not dare risk it. Dickon could only hope that in time the boys would fade from men's minds, that people would assume they'd been sent to live in the North. Somehow, he would have to learn to live with the suspicions, the unspoken belief of many that he was responsible for the deaths of his brother's sons. Because it was too late to blame Buckingham. Because the time to reveal the boys' disappearance was three months past. Because he, Francis Lovell, had argued so persuasively for silence, the silence that would now damn Dickon so in the eyes of his subjects, make his guilt seem so much more likely.

'I do not want to talk of this, Jack. For the love of God, let it lie!'

Jack looked startled. He lapsed into a wounded silence for several strides, then said earnestly, 'Blaming yourself serves for naught, Francis. You did what you thought was right and what more can men do than that? Nor is Dickon a man to be led against his will. If he had not felt you made sense, he'd never have agreed to keep silent.'

Francis churlishly didn't reply, knowing his rudeness was unjustified, but unable to help himself. It was with relief now that he saw they'd reached the west door of the church.

'Dickon has already been to morning Mass,' Jack said dubiously. 'I do not think he wanted to pray so much as he wanted to be alone for a while. Why do we not try the cloisters first?'

Shaded by cedar trees, bathed in blinding sunlight, the cloisters of St Mary's offered a refuge of awesome beauty, an almost unearthly quiet. Richard was seated on a bench in the south walkway; he looked up as they approached, rose to his feet.

By common consent, they all moved up the east walkway, sought the greater privacy of the Chapter House. Richard waited until Francis had closed the door and then said only, 'It's done?'

Francis nodded, waited for questions that didn't come. Richard had begun to wander aimlessly about the chamber, gazing up at the soaring ceiling, the lofty tinted windows that splashed vivid violet and ruby shades of sunlight upon the floor, upon the faces of the two men watching him.

'Will Hastings tried to warn me,' he said at last, not looking at either man as he spoke. 'He told me I was a fool to trust Buckingham. "Ned made more than his share of mistakes," he said, "but Buckingham was not one of them." Buckingham, he said, was mine.'

It was the first time in more than four months that Francis could recall Richard mentioning Will Hastings's name, a stark silence dating from that June day when he'd summarily ordered Hastings to his death. He drew a quick breath, said, 'Christ, Dickon, Hastings was jealous of Buckingham, that's all! He did not have second sight, did not suspect any more than the rest of us what Buckingham had in mind. He was right about Buckingham but for the wrong reasons.'

'If truth be told,' Jack interrupted, 'none of us had much liking for the man. But it is one thing to dislike a man for his arrogance, for the way power seemed to have gone to his head, and quite another to think him capable of treason, of child-murder. You cannot blame yourself because you trusted the man. He'd given you reason for trust, after all.'

'Yes,' Richard said tonelessly, 'I trusted him. And because I did, my brother's sons are dead.' He turned to face them both, saw that neither one knew how to answer him.

'Tell me,' he said abruptly. 'Tell me how he died, Francis.'

'Badly.' Francis made an involuntary grimace. 'Very badly. Right up to the time he was taken out to the block, he kept begging for an audience with you, though what in God's Name he thought that would accomplish . . .'

'Dickon was his last hope,' Jack said, shrugging. 'When you're that desperate, you do not overly concern yourself with logic, you grasp at straws. If you'd agreed, Dickon, I daresay he'd have babbled some frantic story of having done it all for you and then of having been duped by Morton. We're dealing here with far more than ambition, after all. Our cousin Warwick was an ambitious man, too, but he'd not have murdered children. Most men would not. No, there was something erratic, unstable, in Buckingham's makeup; there had to be. I personally think he was treading perilously close to madness, much like Geo. . . .' He stopped himself, hoping it had been in time. Comparing Buckingham to George of Clarence would serve no purpose, only cause his uncle needless hurt, and he added hastily, 'I think you were right not to see him, Dickon, in truth I do.'

'I did not trust myself, Jack,' Richard said after a pause, knowing that it was only a half-truth, knowing, too, that he'd been afraid of what he might hear, of what Buckingham might tell him about the way his nephews died. 'Go on, Francis.'

'I told him that there was no way on God's earth you'd ever consent to see him and he . . . well, he forgot all pride, all dignity.'

A shadow of distaste crossed Francis's face, bordering on revulsion. 'I've never seen a man show his fear so nakedly,' he said slowly.

'Does that surprise you so much, Francis? After all, the man knew he was facing eternal damnation. Would you not be fearful to go before the Throne of God with so great a sin on your soul?'

Francis was shaking his head. 'No, Jack,' he said thoughtfully, 'I do not think it was that sort of fear. It seemed to be purely physical, a fear of the axe, of death itself. When he saw there was no hope, he began to plead for time, for a day's grace. He reminded the priests that it was All Soul's Day, entreated them to intercede with you, Dickon, to persuade you to postpone the execution until the morrow.'

'Did he, by God?' Richard was staring at Francis. 'And that's all today did mean to him . . . that it is All Souls' Day?'

Francis was at a loss. 'Dickon?'

Richard turned away. He could feel it starting to slip, the rigid self-control he'd been clinging to these past three weeks, and he bit down now on his lower lip until he tasted blood.

'Today,' he said unevenly, 'would have been Edward's thirteenth birthday.'

17

Westminster

December 1483

As exhausted as Anne was, sleep continued to elude her. She dreaded the nights now, shrank from the coming of dark. The daylight hours could be filled with activity, could be structured to leave her with little time for thought. But at night she had no such defences, was at the mercy of her memories. At night she found herself reliving that moment in Middleham's inner bailey, standing in the sun with Richard's letter in her hand.

The words had blurred upon the page as she read and she'd sat down abruptly, there on the steps leading up into the keep, trembling so violently that she had to spread the letter flat upon her knee before she could continue reading. The slanting Italic script was in Richard's own hand, but so uneven, so scrawled it looked to be the writing of a stranger; he'd blotted ink on the B in Buckingham and entire sentences were scratched out in his search to find words that could safely be put to paper. 'My love,' he'd written, 'you understand what this means?' And she had. In a sudden panic, she'd jumped to her feet, sent mystified servants in search of her son and, when Ned had been found, she gathered him to her in an emotional embrace, hugging him tightly until he began to squirm, protesting breathlessly that he was too old for this, mama, and people were looking.

She would never know how she got through the days that followed. Again and again she found herself rereading the last sentences of Richard's letter. 'I do not expect to lose, Anne. But whatever happens, you are my dearest love.'

'My dearest love,' Anne echoed now, in a whispered caress she alone could hear. Turning on her side, she gazed for a time into Richard's face, watched the rise and fall of his chest. How careworn he looks, even in sleep. Beloved, so little I can do to help, so little. . . .

No, do not think that. Think about something else. Think about Ned. How he loved this time of year. Loved the yule log and the mummeries, the travelling troupes of players come to depict the birth of the Christ Child, the exchange of gifts, and then their long-awaited visit to York. How would it be for him this year, his first Christmas alone? No, she must not think that.

It was not true. Her mother was there, and Johnny, Kathryn, Mistresses Idley and Burgh, people who loved Ned dearly. He was safe at Middleham, in a world he knew and loved, and in the spring . . . in the spring, she and Richard would go North again. They'd go home and this time they'd bring Ned back with them.

She was drifting in that languid twilight of the senses that foreshadows sleep when Richard stirred, cried out so sharply that Anne jerked upright in the bed.

'Richard!'

He mumbled incoherently, turned his face into the pillow. Anne hesitated; all knew it was dangerous to awaken too abruptly a troubled sleeper. But as she watched, Richard moaned again, twisted from side to side like one seeking escape. She bent over him, shook his shoulder gently.

His eyes flew open, looked up at her without recognition, clouded with sleep and nightmare fears that had yet to yield to reality.

'You were having a bad dream, love.' She stroked his hair, found it damp to the touch, saw now that he was drenched in sweat. 'It must have been dreadful, your heart is pounding so. Do you remember what it was?'

Richard's breathing was slowing. He lay back on the pillows, said in a shaken voice, 'It was so real, Anne. Not like a dream at all. It never is. . . .'

'You've had it before?'

He nodded reluctantly and she leaned over, kissed his forehead. 'Sometimes it helps to talk about a bad dream, Richard, keeps it from coming back. Is it always the same?'

He nodded again. 'More or less. In the dream I'm standing before a stairwell. It's dark below and I do not want to go down, but I do. The stairwell is pitch-black and very narrow; I have to grope my way down, one step at a time.'

'Where are these steps, Richard? Do you know?'

'No, nothing ever looks familiar. The stairwell leads into an unlit deserted corridor. I call out but no one answers. I want to go back up the stairs but I know I cannot, so I start down the corridor. And the further I go, Anne, the more uneasy I become. I have this . . . this foreboding and it gets stronger and stronger. . . .'

There was something deeply disquieting about this dream of Richard's; Anne suddenly knew she did not want to hear any more, but forced herself to ask, 'What happens then?'

'I keep going down the corridor, fighting this feeling, this fear. . . . And then the corridor turns and I'm standing before a little chapel. There are priests inside and people garbed in mourning, but when I enter they all ignore me as if . . . as if I have no right to be there.'

'Oh, Richard. . . .'

'As I come forward, the people move away from me and I see before the altar . . . two small coffins. Children's coffins. And I know then that this is what I feared to find. I take a step forward and then another, knowing what I'll see . . . my brother's sons. And they're lying there, in these pitifully barren little coffins, and suddenly I understand. The little boys in the coffins . . . they are not Ned's sons, Anne; they're mine.'

Richard pushed his chair back from the table, looked at the men gathered about him. Thomas Barowe, his Master of the Rolls. John Kendall, his secretary, a man who'd served him loyally for nigh on ten years. The eloquent Welshman, Morgan Kidwelly, his Attorney General. His eyes lingered longest on Will Catesby. He owed Catesby much and one of his first official acts had been to appoint him Chancellor of the Exchequer. Richard was well pleased with his performance so far; a skilled lawyer, Catesby was proving himself to be an able administrator as well. He stood an excellent chance of being chosen as Speaker of the Commons when it met next month, and Richard expected him to be a great help in pushing his legislative programme through parliament.

The last man in attendance upon him this Tuesday night in

late December was his solicitor, Thomas Lynom. Lynom had dutifully delayed his marriage until Richard's arrival back in London in late November but as soon thereafter as the banns could be posted, he'd made Jane Shore his wife. Richard still thought Lynom had made a fool's choice, but he had to admit the man fairly glowed with contentment these days. He was even managing to endure with equanimity those ribald jests that are the bane of any newlywed's existence, and Lynom had never been noted for his sense of humour.

Lynom was speaking now with considerable enthusiasm of the statutes they were drafting for presentation to parliament. Richard listened with a smile for he shared Lynom's enthusiasm, was looking forward to his first parliament. It would, he thought, be a map for his reign, an indicator of the spirit in which he meant to rule. He and his councillors had been working, for days now, on a series of statutes meant to curb abuses of property law and he hoped to sponsor others that would prevent an accused man's property from being forfeited prior to conviction and would make bail more widely available for indictable offences. Meanwhile, an act to be known as Titulus Regius was being planned to confirm his title to the crown, to recognize Ned formally as the heir apparent, and Bills of Attainder were to be brought against the men who'd taken part in Buckingham's rebellion.

Of all the statutes he meant to put before parliament, Richard was proudest of the one that stated 'The subjects of this realm shall not be charged with benevolences nor any like charge.' It was the one that had stirred the most controversy among his own advisers. Although Buckingham's rebellion had collapsed, Richard had still been forced to put an army in the field and the cost had been considerable, placed a heavy strain upon a treasury already depleted by Thomas Grey's plundering. Richard had to pledge silver plate as security for loans; some he'd sold outright to London's goldsmiths and his proposed ban on benevolences met with predictable opposition.

Catesby in particular was unwilling to see Richard foreclose one of his financial options. He didn't quarrel with Richard's contention that benevolences were a form of extortion, merely pointed out gloomily that the day might well come when Richard would have to resort to those forced 'gifts' just as his brother had done.

Richard had prevailed, however, meant to propose to parliament an act providing that such involuntary donations be 'damned and annulled forever'. Nor had he any qualms about his decision. Such an act was not only right and just, it was a shrewd political move, one he hoped would go far toward reassuring his subjects that he did not mean to rule by fear or coercion. And perhaps . . . perhaps in time the murmurings of approval would drown out the whispering, divert attention from that unnatural silence that had descended over the Tower, where his brother's sons supposedly dwelt but were no longer seen.

Thomas Barowe was gathering up the papers spread out on the table, stuffing them into a large leather pouch. Chairs scraped in the floor rushes as the men came to their feet, flexing cramped muscles and remembering that supper was hours past.

'Will that be all for tonight, Your Grace?' Thomas Lynom asked hopefully and Morgan Kidwelly gave him a playful nudge, shook his head in feigned pity.

'Poor Tom, with a hard night's work still lying ahead of him at home.'

Lynom joined good naturedly in their laughter, but stopped abruptly when Catesby jibed, 'You'd best be off, Tom. You'd not be wanting your bride to get lonely, would you?'

In view of Jane's dubious past, it was a singularly ill-chosen jest and the other men were relieved when John Kendall deftly piloted the conversation off the shoals and back into safe water.

'I truly hate to tell you this, Your Grace, but there still are petitioners waiting without.' He made a mock grimace. 'I vow some of them have been out there so long their faces have become as familiar to me as those of my own family.'

'Is there anyone I needs must see tonight? Tom is not the only one with a wife waiting for him, after all,' Richard said, and laughed. Laughter that froze on his lips with Kendall's next words.

'There are those come to plead with you again on behalf of your late sister's husband, Thomas St Leger.'

Richard's face hardened. 'St Leger was tried for his part in the rebellion before John Scrope at special assize in Torrington last month. Tried and found guilty of high treason. He does not deserve clemency, nor will he get it, not from me.'

Catesby had been listening with a frown; St Leger's friends had offered a not inconsiderable sum to have his death sentence commuted. 'They hoped you might be merciful in memory of your sister. . . .'

'My sister is seven years dead and memory of her did not keep St Leger from seeking to bring about my defeat and death . . . did it?'

There was, of course, no answer Catesby could give; his shoulders twitched slightly, a gesture of concession.

Kendall had not expected Richard to relent; Thomas St Leger he knew to be hand in glove with Thomas Grey. Having already taken it upon himself to warn St Leger's partisans that he doubted the king would hear their petition, he said impassively, 'Shall I tell them, then, that you'll not see them?'

Richard nodded. 'Tell them,' he said curtly, 'that the verdict stands.'

'If you can spare a few minutes, Your Grace, there is one, however, whom I thought you might wish to see. . . .'

'Who?'

'Katherine Stafford, Duchess of Buckingham.'

Richard hesitated. He could think of no reason why he should grant an audience to the woman who was Buckingham's widow, Elizabeth's sister. But he'd come to respect Kendall's judgment.

'You think I should see her, John?'

'Yes, Your Grace, I do. She's ... well, she's not what you'd expect.' And with that cryptic remark, Kendall was content to wait for Richard's response, knowing he'd virtually guaranteed her entry.

'Five minutes,' Richard said grudgingly. 'No more than that.'

Kendall smiled and moved toward the door. 'There is one thing more,' he said over his shoulder. 'She wants to see you alone.'

Richard had seen Katherine Stafford only a half-dozen or so times, if even that, and those brief encounters had taken place years before when they both were still in their teens; Buckingham had kept her secluded at Brecknock for much of their married life. He was startled now by the beauty of the woman being ushered into the chamber. She looked to be about his own age, thirty or thirty-one, was visibly nervous, As fair in colouring as her celebrated sister, hers was a softer, more muted appeal. There was an unexpected vulnerability about her, shadows of past pain in the downward curve of her mouth, in the lack of assurance so surprising in a woman blessed with such beauty.

Coming forward, she made a deep curtsy before him, more submissive than he would have expected from Elizabeth's sister.

She wasn't in mourning and Richard was somewhat surprised by that. Even if the marriage hadn't been a happy one, she'd still been Buckingham's wife for nigh on seventeen years, had borne him five children, and few widows scorned altogether the conventions of mourning, no matter how little lamented their late husbands had been.

'Madame,' he said, and gestured toward a chair, thus freeing her to sit in his presence.

'I ... I'd rather stand, Your Grace.' Her voice was almost inaudible, sounded as if she couldn't quite catch her breath, but whether that was nerves or her normal speaking pattern, he couldn't tell.

'I wish to thank you for paying my husband's debts for me and for offering to provide me with a yearly grant of two hundred marks.'

Was this why she'd wanted to see him? Surely she must have known he'd neither want nor expect her gratitude? 'My brother often provided pensions for the families of men attainted,' he said quietly.

'Yes,' she persisted, 'but I am more than a rebel's widow. I am a Woodville, too, and that makes your generosity to me and my children all the more unlooked-for. . . .'

What had she expected, that he'd have turned them out to starve? Resentment flickered, faded. What else could he expect her to think, after all? She was Elizabeth's sister.

'Was this why you wanted to see me?'

'No. I . . . I have a favour to ask of Your Grace. I want to visit my sister in sanctuary. Will you permit it?'

Richard nodded. 'I'll tell Nesfield to admit you, any time you wish,' he said, was surprised when she made no move to go.

'Is there anything else?'

'I. . . . No. No. . . .' But still she didn't move.

Richard waited and then reached for the bell to summon Kendall back. To his astonishment, Katherine leaned across the table, slid it out of his reach. Their fingers touched; hers were like ice and even in so brief a contact, he could feel her trembling.

'No, wait . . . please. There is something else, something I must ask you.' Her voice was tremulous, had taken on an emotional intensity that riveted Richard's eyes upon her. But he was not prepared for what was coming.

She swallowed. 'I think . . . I believe . . . that my sister's sons are dead, that Harry had them put to death. And you alone can tell me if it's so.'

Richard had frozen in his chair. Katherine's face was very close to his, her eyes a misted sea-green, her lashes fringed with tears.

1047

He watched one break free, roll down her cheek and, after a time-less span, splash upon his wrist.

'I see,' she whispered, and straightened up, very slowly. 'I think I'd . . . I'd like to sit down after all. . . .'

Their eyes still held; neither one could look away. 'He actually admitted it to you?' Richard asked at last.

Katherine shook her head. 'No . . . not in so many words. It was . . . I'm sorry, but I . . . I was not sure I'd have the nerve to ask you. Not until I heard myself saying it aloud. . . . Thank you for not lying to me. Thank you for that.'

'Even if I'd wanted to, I could not have,' Richard said tiredly. 'You had to see the truth in my face.' How strange to be able to talk so candidly with this woman, a woman he did not know and had no reason to trust. Except that she knew the truth. 'Harry had them put to death,' she'd said, said with tears wet on her face, tears for Dickon and Edward.

After a pause, Katherine nodded. 'You're right; it did show in your face. Just as . . . as it did in Harry's.'

She seemed calmer, was no longer twisting her hands together in her lap. 'I think I knew . . . knew as soon as Harry got back to Brecknock that something was wrong. Never had I seen him so excited. But it was a queer kind of excitement; he was high-strung, edgy, like a man who's gambling and winning, but with more and more riding on each throw of the dice. He would not tell me anything, of course; he rarely did. But it was not hard to figure out that something momentous was afoot. Bishop Morton had been sent to Brecknock under guard in June and of a sudden he was being treated like an honoured guest, was closeted with Harry for hours on end. And when I overheard Harry dispatching a messenger with a secret letter for Reginald Bray, Lady Stanley's steward . . . well, it all fell into place.

'I confronted Harry with my suspicions, demanded to know if he was plotting with Morton and Lady Stanley to put Henry Tudor on the throne. I argued that he must not do this, that if he was to become involved in rebellion, it must be on. . . .' She stopped suddenly, staring at Richard in dismay.

Richard had no difficulty in guessing why. She had just been about to admit she'd urged rebellion on Edward's behalf and, however natural her loyalties, they were also treasonous.

'You told him he should be acting for Edward?' he suggested matter-of-factly and, reassured, she nodded.

'But when I did, he just laughed at me, said that ere there could be a rising for Edward, there would have to be a resurrection. And when I did not understand, he told me that Edward and Dickon were dead, told me that they'd died at your command.'

Richard said nothing but Katherine read the accusation in his eyes, and flushed.

'Yes,' she said defensively. 'I did believe him . . . at first. Why should I not?'

Because they were children, my brother's children. But he did not say it. Remember who she is, for God's sake. In her eyes, he was guilty of her brother's death, guilty of usurping her nephew's crown. She's right; why would she not believe it?

'But you did begin to have doubts?'

'Yes,' she admitted, 'once the shock wore off, I did. It . . . well, it just did not make sense to me. I know I'm not clever like Lisbet but I'm not as stupid as Harry always said, either. The more I thought on it, the more I began to wonder. You could only have done it to make sure there'd be no risings on their behalf, so there'd be no point in killing them and then keeping their deaths a secret; even I could see that. Yet that's what Harry would have me believe. And what would happen when people learned they were missing? No, it made no sense. And so . . . and so I began to think that perhaps Harry had lied, that they were not dead at all.'

'When did you learn the truth?'

'When Reginald Bray came to Brecknock. Henry . . . my youngest son . . . had been running a high fever and his nurse and

I were up with him most of the night before Bray's arrival. Around midday I began to suffer from the lack of sleep, so I went up to our bedchamber, drew the bed-curtains and lay down upon the bed.

'Sometime later I was awakened by voices. It seemed a Godsent way to find out what Harry was truly up to, so I just lay still, thinking to feign sleep should I be discovered. Harry was telling Bray that Edward and Dickon were dead, that you'd dispatched orders to Brackenbury after departing on your progress. There was a silence when he stopped speaking and then Bray, he . . . he laughed. He laughed and said how very obliging that was of you, to have done Henry Tudor so great a service.

'Harry became very defensive, demanded to know what Bray meant by that. Bray just laughed again, said not to mistake him, that he thought it a right clever slander. Harry snapped that it was more than slander, that it was true, and Bray said, very sarcastic, that if it were so, it could only mean that you'd lost your senses, and was it not strange that none had yet heard about the king's sudden fit of madness.

'Harry flew into a rage at that, called Bray a fool and worse, said he'd be damned ere he'd deal with the likes of Bray. Bishop Morton tried to mediate then but Harry was not to be placated and he slammed out of the chamber, telling Bray to take himself back to London at first light.

'No sooner had the door banged than Morton turned on Bray, began to berate him in language that ill became a bishop.' Katherine's lips twitched, in a ghostly parody of a smile.

'But Bray was not cowed and said that the stakes were too high for such gameplaying. He said that if you were to be accused of murdering your nephews, well and good; he was sorry he had not thought of that himself. But he was not about to go back to Lady Stanley and tell her that such a tale was true. She valued her son's life too highly, he said. Suppose they did stake all upon this story that the boys were dead and you then paraded them through the streets for all London to see. If Tudor was to risk all upon an invasion, seek to overthrow a crowned king, he was entitled to know the truth about the dangers he'd be facing and he for one would not assure Tudor the boys were dead unless he was damned well certain that they were.

'Morton heard him out and then asked why Bray was so sure they were not dead. Bray was scornful; even your most bitter enemies, he said, had never accused you of being an idiot and only an utter idiot would've gone about it in the way Harry claimed. You'd have waited till they grew to manhood, he said, and then found an excuse to send them to the block, or you'd have done it the way your brother did with Harry of Lancaster, but what you'd assuredly not have done would be to arrange for a mysterious midnight disappearance. They could not, he said, have been so lucky.'

Katherine drew an uneven breath. 'Lying there, listening, I felt a surge of pride. Here were two men as clever and worldly as any in the kingdom, and their conclusions were the same as my own. But then . . . then Morton asked Bray a question. "Assume the boys *are* dead," he said, "that they were secretly put to death in the Tower this past July just as Buckingham claims. Now tell me who would benefit and who would suffer?"

'Bray seemed to be humouring him, but he said, "As for those with the most to lose, that is easy enough to answer. The Woodvilles, for obvious reasons. And Gloucester, since he'd be saddled with the crime. Those who'd benefit? Well, we would, for certes. So, too, would the French." And he went on to say that had you been king eight years ago, there'd have been no Treaty of Picquigny and the French well know it, that they dread the day when you're secure enough on your throne to look Channel-ward, to seek another Agincourt.

'Morton wanted to know who else would benefit and Bray said, "Well, Buckingham, of course; he cannot put in his own bid for the crown unless he can so discredit Gloucester that he'll suddenly start to look positively pure in comparison." I'd suspected, of course, that Harry had designs on the crown for himself but it was still a shock to hear Bray put it so baldly as that. And I wondered if Harry suspected that these men meant to use him the way he was using them.

'Bray had begun to laugh, was referring slightingly to Harry as "our hot-headed host". But then he stopped abruptly, almost as if a hand had been clapped over his mouth. There was a sudden silence and then I heard him say, "Holy Mother of God!" But even then, I did not understand . . . even then. Not until Bray said, "You're saying that it be Buckingham's handiwork." And Morton said . . . he said, "You've redeemed yourself, my young friend, just in time. I was beginning to fear I might have to draw you a diagram."

'I do not remember much of what they said after that. Bray became very excited and they agreed that he must apologize to Harry, eat humble pie if need be. "Smooth our pigeon's ruffled feathers," was the way Morton put it. With that they left to find Harry and I . . . I lay there on the bed. I just lay there.'

Tears were filling her eyes again, glistened like liquid gold in the reflected glow of candlelight. Richard found a handkerchief, silently handed it to her.

'You said . . . said you'd seen the truth in Harry's face?'

Katherine nodded. 'That night in bed, he wanted to lay with me and I . . . I could not bear for him to touch me. I refused him and he . . . well, he became furious and we got into this terrible quarrel. One angry word led to another, until I heard myself screaming at him, telling him what I'd heard Morton and Bray say, demanding to know if it were true.'

She'd crumpled Richard's handkerchief, began self-consciously to smooth it out upon her lap. 'He denied it, of course, and I pretended to believe him. But in that first unguarded moment, I'd seen his face and I knew.'

They looked at each other as the silence spun out, the moments ebbed away. The fire had burned out; the hearth held only smouldering embers and charred ashes. Richard tilted his head, listening. He could hear a distant chiming, Gabriel Bells echoing on the icy night air. Glancing back at Katherine, he said softly, 'I would never have hurt those children.'

Katherine's eyes searched his face. 'I believe you,' she said simply.

As she started her ninth month in sanctuary, Elizabeth made a halfhearted attempt to shake off the deep despondency that had engulfed her with the failure of Buckingham's rebellion. Tom had been able to get away, was now safe in Brittany. So, too, were her brothers Lionel and Edward. Could she not be thankful for that? She was; of course she was. But it just was not enough. Not when her own future was so bleak, so barren of hope. What was going to become of her?

She'd learned from John Nesfield that close to a hundred men were to suffer forfeiture of property when parliament convened and, while that was less than the number Ned had attainted after Towton, it did not bode well for a future of forgiveness. Ten men had gone to the block, among them her son's friend, Thomas St Leger. But Morton, who had the Devil's own luck, somehow slipped through Richard's net and surfaced in France. And Lady Stanley had once again managed to evade the consequences of conspiracy. She did not get off quite so lightly this time, had been stripped of her titles and lands and remanded into her husband's custody, but had I been Richard, Elizabeth thought coolly, I'd have introduced that slender white neck of hers to the axe.

Strange, this reluctance that some men had to spill a woman's blood. Ned had shared it, too, would no more have sent a woman to the block than would Richard. Though there was a certain logic to Richard's forbearance. He needed Stanley; it was as simple as that. And because Stanley had shown himself loyal under fire, Richard had seen that he was well rewarded for it. He'd been given the constableship, given, too, the lifetime use of his wife's forfeited estates.

Ned had faced much the same problem; what to do with Stanley? The man was a weathercock, went whichever way the wind blew; in one year alone, he'd changed sides no less than four times. The trick, Ned had discovered, was to make it worth his while to be loyal. He'd made Stanley a member of his council, named him as Steward of the Royal Household, and it had worked; for more than twelve years, Stanley had faithfully done Ned's bidding, stuck to Ned like glue. So it did not surprise Elizabeth any that Richard was trying the same tactics. And it might well work for Richard as it had for Ned. That is, provided nothing happened to undermine Richard's hold on the throne. There were men who reacted to weakness like wolves to the scent of blood, and Stanley was one of them. So Ned had believed and, whatever Ned's other failings, he'd been a shrewd judge of men.

And so what now? Tudor? Even if he found the backbone to try again, what chance would he have to defeat Richard in the field? And what if he did, if he somehow managed to get the victory? Whilst Buckingham lived, he and Tudor would have cancelled each other out. But now . . . by publicly vowing to wed Bess, Tudor had committed himself to nullifying the plight-troth, and what then could she expect for Edward? For Dickon? That she knew well enough. In pledging to make her daughter his Queen, Tudor was passing a sentence of death upon her sons; he'd have no choice.

No, whichever way she looked, she found only blind alleys, locked doors. What could she do except come to terms with Richard? And what had she left to bargain with? Her daughters were still his kinswomen but how much did that truly matter to him?

No, she must not despair. He did want them out of sanctuary. It had to be an embarrassment for him, if nothing else. It was in his interest, too, that she should come forth with her daughters.

She must remember that, somehow turn it to her own advantage.

By the hearth Cecily and Bess were playing an indifferent game of chess. Snow had glazed the windowpanes and all Elizabeth could see of the inner court was a blur of white.

'Madame?' John Nesfield stood in the doorway. 'Madame, His Grace the Duke of Norfolk is without.'

Elizabeth's lip curled. 'Whatever else be said of your uncle, girls, there is nothing paltry about his payoffs,' she said bitingly, and felt no surprise whatsoever when Bess at once took issue with her.

'Mama, that's not fair. You know the duchy of Norfolk should have passed to Jack Howard two years ago. Our Dickon held it only by right of his wife, the little Mowbray heiress, and when that poor child died, it ought to have gone to Jack, and would have, had papa not made parliament vest title in Dickon.'

'Have a care, Bess. That remark could be read as being critical of your sainted father and we'd surely not want that, would we?'

Bess flushed but Elizabeth gave her no chance to speak, snapping, 'No back talk, not now. Go look in on your sisters, both of you. I shall want to receive Howard alone.'

'But I want to talk to Uncle Jack, too,' Bess protested. 'We've seen no one from outside for weeks and weeks and I want to hear what he has to say.'

'Me, too, mama,' Cecily chimed in. 'Please let us stay.'

Elizabeth had no time to argue for, at that moment Nesfield escorted John Howard into the chamber. Elizabeth's eyebrows rose for she recognized the man with him as Sir Robert Brackenbury, Constable of the Tower. Rising unhurriedly to her feet, she tried to conceal her excitement, her conviction that these men must be here on Richard's behalf, that they must have been authorized to make her an offer. But then she gave a surprised gasp.

'Katherine!'

Katherine pushed back the hood of her cloak. 'Lisbet. Oh, sister. . . .'

Elizabeth's smile faded. 'Katherine? Are you all right? You look ghastly, in truth.'

Katherine had yet to move and Elizabeth's eyes flicked past her, to the silent men. All her expectations had been dashed at sight of her sister. It did not make sense that Katherine should be here with these men. Something was wrong; one look at Katherine's face told her that. Their faces, too, warned of a coming grief. Howard was even grimmer than usual and Brackenbury . . . well, he had the look of a man with a gnawing pain in his vitals. Elizabeth's fear was purely instinctive, had not yet reached a conscious level of awareness; she knew only that her mouth was suddenly dry, that sweat was trickling down her ribs, and whatever they'd come to tell her, she did not want to hear.

'Lisbet, I do not know how to tell you. . . . Harry, he . . . he wanted to be King. So much that nothing else mattered. He made sure that the men taking care of Edward and Dickon were his and then he . . . he. . . . Oh, God! God help me, but I cannot. . . .' Katherine's voice broke on a sob. 'I cannot. . . .'

'Madame. . . . Madame, I blame myself.' Brackenbury sounded scarcely more coherent than Katherine. 'I have children of my own and, had I even suspected for a moment, I'd have posted guards around the clock, God's blessed truth. . . .'

Elizabeth took a step backward and then another. 'No,' she said, very distinctly. 'No, I do not believe you. I do not . . . do not want to hear any more. I do not.'

Cecily stood very still, staring at her mother. Bess alone moved, turning instinctively toward the man who'd been her father's friend.

'Uncle Jack? I do not understand. What does mama not believe?' She tried very hard to keep her voice steady, tried and failed.

Howard came forward, caught up her hands within his own. 'It is bad, sweetheart. As bad as it can be.'

As if in a dream, Bess saw that this seasoned soldier, this man who'd won such success at the point of a sword, now had tears in his eyes.

'It is your brothers, Bess. The lads are dead.'

18

Westminster

February 1484

Anne settled herself deeper in her husband's bed, drew the coverlets up under her chin. The bed-curtains screened out the light but not the noise, the sounds Richard's attendants made as they moved about the chamber. Of all that Anne hated about her queenship, the utter loss of privacy was the worst. Sometimes it seemed to her that the only times when she and Richard were ever truly alone were when they lay together at night in his huge canopied bed of state. And even so natural a sharing as that presented problems undreamt of at Middleham.

After sharing a bed for more than eleven years, it was unthinkable to them both that they should now sleep in separate chambers. How unbearably lonely that would have been, Anne thought, to have Richard come to her bed only when he wanted to claim his marital rights. Sharing a bed was surely one of the greatest joys of marriage. To be able to feel Richard's warmth beside her as he slept, to lie drowsily within his arms, listening to the reassuring murmur of his voice in the dark. To miss all that. . . . How sad for Ned and Elizabeth, for all those bygone kings and their unloved queens.

At first Richard had come to Anne's bed but it soon became apparent that it was easier for her to come to him; there were not hours enough in his day and all too often he worked late into the night, not coming to bed till long past midnight. Anne sighed, raised herself on her elbow to tug at her hair; she'd left it invitingly unbraided tonight, suggestively spread out upon the pillows in the way Richard liked. He was somehow going to have to learn to delegate authority better; that had always been a weakness of his, she knew. But it was an indulgence the Duke of Gloucester could afford, the King could not.

Surely it was after one by now? Was Richard ever coming to bed? It must not have gone well with Elizabeth. Jack Howard had gone that evening to the abbot's lodging to make Elizabeth yet another offer, to strike a bargain that would free her daughters to take their rightful place at court. It did not surprise Anne in the least that Elizabeth was still balking. Any other woman would surely have come to terms months ago, would not have subjected her daughters to the discomforts of sanctuary in the first place. But Elizabeth would ever come first with Elizabeth. Anne felt a twinge of remorse at that last, knowing she should have more sympathy for a woman who'd suffered the most devastating of all griefs. For Blessed Lady, what could possibly be worse than to lose a cherished child? And surely even a woman as selfish as Elizabeth must have loved her sons.

Jesú, but what was keeping Richard? Thank God All-merciful that they'd soon be on their way north. Just twelve days, twelve interminable days, and then they'd leave London and its griefs behind, breathe air pure and sweet again, untainted by smoke and soot and unspoken suspicions. A lovely, leisurely progress northward, Cambridge and Nottingham and Pontefract where Ned would be awaiting them, and then on into York. Perhaps even home to Middleham for a time. . . .

*

Richard slid into bed, bracing himself for the icy shock of the sheets against his naked skin. But then he felt Anne's arms about him, felt a body that was soft and warm, moulding itself into his, and he moved gratefully into the caress, legs entwined, bodies fitting together in that perfect physical harmony that even now, even after so many years, he had yet to take for granted. Her hair was free, spilling over them both, tickling his back, his neck, and he shifted slightly, sought her lips.

'You should not wait up for me, ma belle, not when it gets late like this.'

'Just count your blessings,' Anne murmured, felt his mouth move against hers in a fleeting smile.

'You are a blessing, in truth you are, and if I did not have you waiting for me like this each night. . . .'

'Hush, love,' she whispered. 'Not now. Not now. . . .'

But it was not as satisfying for either of them as she could have hoped. Richard was too tense, never fully lost himself in the intimate pleasures she sought to give him, and although he'd gained physical release, she knew the cares he'd brought to the bed weighed no less heavily upon him now than before their lovemaking. They lay in silence for a time, breathing in slowing unison, not yet willing to move apart, while Anne debated with herself whether she could better serve his needs by keeping silent.

'Richard, what is wrong? Is it still Elizbeth?'

'Ever Elizabeth,' he corrected her grimly, and for the first time she realized just how angry he truly was.

'Surely she did not spurn your offer?'

'No . . . not exactly. But she gave Jack Howard a message for me. She said to tell me that she does not deal with intermediaries. "Tell him," she said, "that if he wants his nieces out of sanctuary as much as that, then he can damned well come himself."'

Bess was standing at one of the east windows in Abbot Esteney's refectory, gazing out into the inner court. A light snow had powdered the ground earlier in the evening; she thought she could still see flakes drifting downward but it was too dark to tell for sure. She was turning away when an amber glow caught her eye, and pressing her nose against the pane, she made out the figure of a man emerging from the passageway that led into the cloisters. As he crossed the courtyard, light from his lantern illuminated his face, and Bess recognized Sir Robert Brackenbury.

Brackenbury had come often to the abbot's lodging in the past eight weeks, had spent hours talking with Bess and Cecily, and if he could not assuage their grief, he at least had cared enough to try; Bess was grateful to him for that. But never had he come at so late an hour. She had the door open before he'd reached the stairs, ushered him quickly into the chamber.

'Sir Robert, is something wrong? Has something happened?'

He gave a surprised shake of his head. 'No, nothing is wrong. I'm here to fetch your lady mother. The King awaits her now in the abbey, as agreed upon, and I am to . . . You did not know? She did not tell you?'

'My uncle? Here? No. . . . mama told me nothing.' Bess was too shocked for pride, too shocked even for resentment that her mother could have kept this from her. 'Sir Robert . . . do not go to my mother just yet. Can you not wait a few moments? Can you not give me that time?'

'My lady . . . I would if I could, believe me. But the King's Grace is awaiting her even now. If I were to delay. . . .'

Bess reached out, touched his hand with her own. 'A fortnight ago I celebrated my eighteenth birthday,' she said quietly. 'For seventeen of those years, I had the right of command. Now I can only ask, can only entreat you, Sir Robert. Do this for me . . . please.'

The Chapel of St Edward the Confessor lay to the east of the High Altar. It was the most sacred part of the abbey; here, before the golden shrine of the eleventh-century king canonized as a saint, Richard and Anne had knelt and made offerings on the day of their coronation. Here, too, were the royal tombs of England's Plantagenet past. No less than five kings and four queens had been laid to rest within the shadowy splendour of the Confessor's Chapel, and Richard found himself alone with the dead of his House.

The silence was absolute, eerie, the only illumination coming from the erratic flickerings of his torch; he'd found a wall sconce for it and it spilled subdued light into the surrounding shadows, cast a reddish glow upon the gleaming marble monuments, upon the effigies of alabaster and gilt. It was not a place Richard would have chosen of his own accord; he wished now that he'd insisted upon another site for this meeting he looked to with such aversion.

Ill at ease and unwilling to acknowledge it, he stripped off his gloves, began a restless pacing that had no purpose but the passing of time. Before him was the mausoleum and chantry of Henry V, victor of Agincourt. England's greatest soldier king, he'd sired a son who yearned only for his prayer books and peace of mind, the hapless Harry of Lancaster. Harry, who'd marked out his burial site here within the chapel but had been laid to rest with the monks of Chertsey. Where, rumour had it, miracles had begun to be performed before his tomb.

Richard shook his head in bemused wonder. How explain people who called Harry simple whilst he lived and saint now that he did not? And yet it had bothered Ned not at all. He'd just laughed when told of these so-called miracles being attributed to Lancaster, drawled, 'As I see it, Dickon, that is a fair enough exchange. I'm willing to have men call him saint, provided that I be the one they do call king.'

It was a memory to give Richard pain, as did so many of his memories of his brother. He hastily put it from him, stopped before the marble tomb of the King who bore his own name. Richard, second of that name to rule England since the Conquest.

Richard, whose downfall had so shaped all their lives for in his dethronement lay the seeds of thirty years of Yorkist–Lancastrian strife. His was a double tomb; he'd been buried with the woman who was his first wife, his only love. So grief-stricken had he been by her sudden death at twenty-eight that he'd ordered the palace in which she died razed to the ground. Within six years, he, too, was dead, starved to death at Pontefract Castle, and England had a new king; the Lancastrian dynasty had begun.

Richard stood motionless for a time, gazing at the gilded effigies of this ill-starred Richard and his queen; they had been depicted clasping hands, at the King's own request. Richard knew, of course, that his was thought to be an unlucky title; only twice before had a Richard ruled England and both met violent ends. Nor did the more superstitious of Richard's subjects find comfort in recalling that he shared with this dead king more than a name; the queen Richard II had so loved had been named Anne.

Richard had no patience with people who claimed to see ill omens in every gathering of clouds, who foretold coming death in a dog's howling, calamity in a shadowed moon. It had never before bothered him that this other Richard and his tragic queen should have borne both his name and Anne's. But standing here now, alone in the hushed, darkened chapel, what had been no more than coincidence suddenly seemed fraught with foreboding, served to make even more oppressive an atmosphere already heavily laden with tension.

What had possessed Elizabeth, that she should choose such a site? Granted, it was private. It was also uncomfortable, cold, and unnerving. Was that what she had in mind? A subtle way of stacking the cards in her favour? Doubtlessly, too, that was why she was late, would keep him waiting as long as she dared. Well, he'd give her five minutes, no more, and then he'd go, he promised himself, knowing all the while that he would not. That he was here at all was in itself a concession of sorts and Elizabeth knew it as well as he.

It was nothing he heard; the chapel was still enveloped in silence. Rather, it was a sixth-sense awareness that he was no longer alone. He spun around, too fast, his eyes searching the dark. At the east end of the chapel, a stairwell led up to Henry V's chantry. Was it his imagination or was there slight movement in the shadows? Furious with himself for having so nakedly betrayed his unease, he said sharply, 'Elizabeth?'

He could make out now the lines of a woman's skirt. She stepped forward, and very slowly descended the two steps into the chapel. Torchlight played upon her hair; it was coiled neatly at the nape of her neck, stray strands of honey-gold curling about her face. Not Elizabeth. Bess, his niece.

In her haste, Bess had not taken time to fetch a cloak and she was trembling visibly, numb with cold and confusion. At sight of Richard, she'd frozen in the stairwell, swept by memories unbearable in their intensity, a desperate yearning for a past that was gone and forever beyond recall.

'Where's your mother, lass?' Richard asked, and his voice sounded strange even in his own ears.

'She does not know you're here yet.' Bess squeezed her hands together, entwined her fingers to still their tremors. 'I defended you. All these months, I defended you. When you arrested Anthony, when you executed Will Hastings, even when you took the crown . . . I found reasons for what you did, fought bitterly with my mother on your behalf. Now . . . now I do want you to tell me this. I want you to tell me why you sent Jack Howard and Brackenbury to us. Why did you not come yourself, Dickon? Surely you did owe us that much.'

Richard sucked in his breath. 'Bess, I . . . I could not.'

Bess found suddenly that she was blinking back tears; that was an admission she had not expected. 'These months past, whenever I felt I could not stand any more . . . do you know what I did, Dickon? I would make up happy endings in my mind. Sometimes I'd pretend it was all a bad dream, that papa was not dead. At other

1063

times . . . at other times I'd tell myself that it would be all right if only I could talk to you. You'd explain it to me, make me understand why all this had to happen; you'd dry my tears just like papa used to do, and then . . . then the hurting would somehow stop.'

Bess was tall for a woman; her eyes were on a level with Richard's and she was close enough now to see tears glistening on his lashes.

'Oh, God, Bess, if only I could,' he said, and her own tears began to flow in earnest.

'I'd almost forgotten,' she whispered, 'how much you do sound like papa. . . .'

'Bess . . . you're shivering.' Richard fumbled with the clasps of his cloak, stepped toward her only to remember Edward's violent reaction to his touch that morning at Stony Stratford. But Bess hadn't moved and he reached out, draped his cloak around her shoulders.

'Bess, I want you and your sisters to come out of sanctuary. I want you to come back to court, back where you belong.'

He saw her hesitancy, thought he understood what it was. 'You're my niece, lass; the plight-troth has not changed that and anyone who forgets it does so to his cost. I want you and your sisters at my court, Bess. So does my Anne, She'll help you, Bess, if only you'll let her. We both will.'

Bess closed her eyes: even with Richard's cloak wrapped tightly around her, she was still trembling. 'You . . . you make it sound so . . . like coming home to a safe haven and it cannot be like that, Dickon. Not ever again.'

'Bess. . . . Bess, I promise you it can be. Let me do this for you, for you and your sisters.'

She swallowed convulsively. 'And what will you do for my brothers, Dickon?'

It was a devastating question, one Richard could not handle. He backed away, bumped blindly into the Coronation Chair. What could he tell her? That he'd never meant for it to happen, that it was a grief he'd take to his grave? What was his remorse against the fact that the boys were dead? Ned had entrusted them to his care and he'd failed them. Blaming Buckingham could not change that. Nothing could change that.

'Dickon. . . .' Bess was beside him, tugging at his arm. 'Look at me . . . please.'

'Bess, I did not know what Buckingham intended. I swear to Christ I did not know!'

'Oh, Dickon, do not! You do not have to say that, not to me. Never to me. Of course you did not know. I'm so sorry I said that. It's just . . . just that I hurt so much and what you were offering. . . . You made use of the word belong and for so long now I've felt like I do not belong anywhere, not any more. And here you were offering me my world back again, what be left of it, promising to take care of us, and I wanted it so much. . . . But then I thought of Dickon and Edward, thought of us being back at court whilst they. . . . And it seemed so unfair, so monstrously unfair. . . .'

She was clinging tightly to Richard's hands, her nails scoring his skin, leaving red welts neither noticed.

'I loved Dickon so much. He was such a dear little boy, so brave through all this, and I . . . I keep thinking that had I not talked mama into letting him leave sanctuary, he might still be alive. Had I not interfered, not coaxed mama into letting him go . . .'

'No, Bess, that's not so. It would have made no difference. We'd discussed it in council and Buckingham . . . Buckingham pointed out that a child, being incapable of sin, was therefore incapable of claiming right of sanctuary. Had your mother not given him up, we'd have taken him, anyway. So you see, you've nothing to reproach yourself for, lass, nothing.'

Bess was wiping away tears with the sleeve of her gown. 'I wish I could believe you, Dickon,' she said softly. 'But thank you for saying that.'

*

Elizabeth had taken the abbot's private entrance into the abbey. Holding a candle in her cupped hands, she made her way soundlessly up the north ambulatory. Approaching the steps leading up into the Confessor's Chapel, she slowed her pace, sought to remind herself of all that was at stake. She hated the man waiting within as much as she'd ever hated anyone in her life, but she must not think of that now. She could not afford to. She'd been given one last chance and it was up to her as to what she made of it.

It was not until she reached the stop of the stairs that she heard the low murmur of voices coming from within. Acting instinctively, Elizabeth blew out her candle, pressed her hand against her skirts to still their rustle.

'Does she blame me, Bess?'

'Mama? She blames everyone, Dickon. Everyone but herself.'

'But she does believe that Buckingham . . .?'

'Oh, she believes he gave the order. But she's found guilt and more to spare for all concerned. Papa for the plight-troth and, even more, for not silencing Stillington. You for taking the crown. Brackenbury just for being the Constable of the Tower. Me for . . . for a multitude of sins, I suspect. For arguing that Dickon should leave sanctuary, for still believing in you, for not being able to hate papa. Even my poor Aunt Katherine, for . . . for God knows what; being Buckingham's wife, I suppose. . . .'

Elizabeth had heard enough, heard too much. She stepped forward into the light.

Bess saw her first, gave a gasp of dismay. Colour flooded her face, hers the discomfort of a child suddenly made to feel disloyal, faithless. 'Mama . . . mama, I. . . .'

Elizabeth was trembling with rage, with a sense of betrayal so strong that it eclipsed all else. She had never been like Marguerite d'Anjou, had never been one to sacrifice all for vengeance. However intense her hatreds, they'd always been tempered by an inner voice counselling accommodation to superior strength.

But now it was stilled, forgotten in her embittered outrage that her daughter should be here with this man, her hand on his arm, his cloak about her shoulders, giving to him the same blind trust she'd given to Ned. But not to her, never to her.

Deliberately ignoring her flustered daughter, she let her eyes move slowly, insultingly, over Richard's face.

'You look tired, Richard, not well at all. But then I daresay you're not sleeping nights. Assuming, of course, that Ned was right when he said you were the one in his family to be cursed with a conscience?'

'I can walk out now, Elizabeth, or you can listen to what I have to say. It's up to you; I do not much care either way.'

'The devil you do not! It happens to be very much in your interest to have me out of sanctuary and we both do know it. So do not pretend otherwise; do not try to tell me it is not an embarrassment to have your brother's widow keeping to sanctuary whilst the whole country does wonder why.'

'You're mistaken,' Richard said icily. 'Very much mistaken.'

'Yes, your brother's widow,' she repeated bitterly. 'I was Ned's wife. His wife, and nothing can change that, no plight-troth, no parliamentary act, nothing.'

'You can call yourself his widow if you choose; you can call yourself the Queen of Egypt for all I care. But your mistake, Madame, is in thinking that your predicament matters to me. As far as I'm concerned, you were the architect of your own ruin, and that of more people than I can count. I care about my nieces, care very much; I want them back at my court. But you, Elizabeth, you could keep to sanctuary till you rot and I'd not care. I'd not care in the least.'

Elizabeth's jaw muscles became rigid; she tasted in her mouth the sourness of swallowed bile. That he meant it, she did not doubt, and confronted by a hatred no less implacable than her own, she struggled to regain her emotional equilibrium, to remember all she had to lose.

'Just what terms are you offering?' she challenged. 'If I leave sanctuary, what may I expect?'

'The right to set up your own household and a yearly pension of seven hundred marks to maintain it.'

Elizabeth had hoped for more than that, much more. Her disappointment was such that she could not hide it, could not keep from jeering, 'Your generosity does leave me speechless, in truth! Though perhaps I should be grateful that you've seen fit to offer me more than the meagre grant you did give my sister.'

Richard shrugged, unmoved. 'Not as gratifying, I admit, as having an entire kingdom to plunder as your own,' he said sardonically, 'but times change. You may take it or not, as you choose.'

Elizabeth longed to scorn it as she'd longed for little in this life. Common sense stopped her, the deep core of pragmatism that had served her so well in happier days. And because she could not turn her resentment upon Richard, she loosed it, instead, upon Bess. Reaching out suddenly, she jerked the cloak from the startled girl's shoulders, flung it on the floor with an oath.

'I'll never forgive you for this,' she snapped, 'for going behind my back like a deceitful little sneak, for a disloyalty I do not deserve!'

'Mama. . . . Mama, that's not fair!'

Turning her back on Bess, Elizabeth demanded of Richard, 'What of my daughters? If I agree, what will you do for them?'

'My nieces will be welcomed at court, will want for nothing. And when they come of marriageable age, I'll provide dowries for them, arrange suitable marriages with men of good birth.' Richard glanced over at Bess as he spoke, a reassurance that infuriated Elizabeth all the more.

'They are my kinswomen,' he said evenly, 'my brother's daughters, and as such, my responsibility.'

'As were my sons!' Elizabeth spat, the words coming to her lips before she even realized what she meant to say. She saw Richard stiffen, saw his eyes darken with such fury that she took an involuntary step backward.

'And when did you ever care about your children, about Ned, about anyone or anything but yourself? My brother was not even buried yet and your one concern was to get your hands upon the royal treasury, to secure your own power, no matter the cost in blood or grief. Well, so be it, then. If that be your answer, stay in sanctuary and be damned!'

Richard swung around, toward the door. But Bess was even quicker; darting forward, she caught his arm.

'No, Dickon, do not go! Please do not go!'

Some of Richard's rage ebbed at sight of his niece's unhappy face. He could not do this; what was the matter with him? To walk out on Elizabeth would be to walk out on his nieces, too.

For the first time in many months, Elizabeth found herself thanking God for her daughter. Bess's intercession could not have come at a more opportune time, bringing her back to reality, the reality that Richard was King, that he'd won and she must surely be mad, for she was throwing away all she'd hoped to gain. Where were her wits? Look at his face, it was written there for all to see. He'd never turn his back on Ned's daughters. The more he could do for the girls, the more he could absolve himself of any responsibility for Edward and Dickon's deaths. Fool that she was, why had she not seen that ere now?

'Richard,' she said abruptly, 'when you took the crown, you said you meant to rule in a spirit of reconciliation and compromise. Was that merely what you thought people wanted to hear? Or did you mean it?'

'I meant it,' Richard said tersely, and a thin smile touched the corner of Elizabeth's mouth.

'Prove it, then. Pardon my son.'

Richard was taken aback, did not answer at once. In the past ten months, he'd harvested a lifetime of regrets but he had none at all for the command that sent Anthony Woodville and Dick Grey to the block at Pontefract Castle. To be asked to forgive Thomas Grey was a higher price than he'd been prepared to pay.

But as he hesitated, Bess touched his hand, her eyes meeting his in mute appeal.

'I suppose he's in Brittany with Tudor?'

Elizabeth was not in the least disconcerted. 'Where else?' she said coolly. 'Well? What say you?'

Richard looked again at Bess and then nodded. 'Tell him to come home,' he said reluctantly, and Elizabeth felt a surge of stunned elation, unable to believe she'd won so easily as that.

Bess had surreptitiously retrieved Richard's cloak from the floor; she held it out to him now, her lips forming a 'thank you' her mother wasn't meant to hear. Richard took it from her and replaced it about her shoulders.

Elizabeth's mouth tightened. 'And so what now?'

'I would suppose,' Richard said dryly, 'that you do come out of sanctuary.'

'Oh, no, not yet. Not until I do have a guarantee that you'll not change your mind . . . brother-in-law.'

Richard looked at her with unconcealed hostility. 'Will my word be enough?' he said sarcastically, and Elizabeth gave a mirthless laugh.

'Not bloody likely—! No, Richard, if you want your nieces back at your court, you'll have to be willing first to swear a public oath—before as many prominent witnesses as possible—setting forth the terms of our agreement for all the world to hear.'

For a moment she feared she'd pushed him too far. But then he nodded, almost imperceptibly.

Elizabeth expelled her breath, leaned back against one of the tombs, watching Richard with narrowed green eyes. How she hated him, this man who'd taken so much and left her with so little. This man who was now King.

'Richard, by the Grace of God,' she murmured. 'Does it bother you any, that your title has been so lacking in luck? England has had but two other kings named Richard, after all, and they both died young . . . and bloody.'

'I trust you do not mean that as a prophecy,' Richard said coldly. 'Lest you forget, to prophesy the King's death might well raise suspicions of witchcraft.'

He saw Elizabeth's eyes flicker at that and felt a grim satisfaction, for she knew as well as he that only treason was a more deadly charge than witchcraft. Less than seventy years ago an accusation of sorcery had resulted in the ruin of no less a victim than a queen of England, and only forty years had passed since a duchess of Gloucester had done public penance through the streets of London for the same charge. But then he saw Bess looking at him worriedly and he realized he'd indulged himself not so much at Elizabeth's expense as at hers.

Elizabeth was staring down at the marble tomb she'd been leaning against; with a shock, she recognized it as that of her infant daughter Margaret, the first of their children to be claimed by death. She didn't move, not until she was sure Richard had left the chapel.

'Mama?'

Elizabeth turned, very slowly. Bess was still wearing Richard's cloak, was looking at her mother with troubled eyes, eyes that asked for understanding.

'Mama, can we talk?'

'No,' Elizabeth said.

The marble was icy to her touch, cold and smooth and unyielding. After a time, she heard her daughter's footsteps on the stairs, receding down the ambulatory, and then the muffled echoes of a slamming door.

'Damn you, Ned,' she whispered. 'How much you have to answer for. . . .'

19

Nottingham
April 1484

Perched on a steep sandstone cliff above the River Leen, Nottingham Castle had been for centuries the principal royal residence in the Midlands. A huge sprawling fortress that contained two halls and no less than four chapels within three separate baileys, each of which was protected by a deep encircling moat, Nottingham Castle had long offered security from the threat of siege. Thanks to Edward, it offered comfort, as well; some eight years ago, he had ordered the construction of spacious new royal apartments. Richard had taken the restorations a step further and authorized the addition of magnificent bay windows. He was well pleased with the results and, for more than a month now, he and Anne had lingered here in the heartland of their kingdom, their spirits soaring with every mile that brought them closer to Yorkshire, where their son awaited them and where none looked at Richard with speculative suspicious eyes.

Making his way through the great hall, Francis approached the dais, made a deep obeisance before the man who was his friend and his king. Richard smiled, beckoned him nearer so they could talk in comparative privacy.

'I've been looking for Véronique,' Francis confessed, 'but with no luck.'

'She's probably still over with Anne in our bedchamber, Francis. When I left them, they were trying to decide what Anne should wear tonight.' Richard laughed. 'And from the way they were discarding gowns, Anne might have to make an appearance clad only in her kirtle.'

Francis laughed, too, and claiming a wine cup from a cupbearer, clinked it against Richard's goblet in playful salute. 'You sound like a man who's just heard welcome news.'

'I have.' Richard lowered his voice still further. 'The Duke of Brittany has had another fit of madness. Until his wits uncloud, his treasurer Pierre Landois has the government and Landois has been reassessing Tudor's value as a political pawn. He's offering to put Tudor into protective custody if I provide a thousand archers for Brittany's quarrel with France.'

Richard's face suddenly shadowed. 'I know I turned down a similar offer last summer but then. . . .' He didn't finish the sentence, didn't need to. Last summer his nephews had still been alive and he'd not yet learned how vulnerable a king was to betrayal.

'That is good news for true,' Francis said with forced cheer, and then his eye happened to alight upon a young girl at the other end of the hall. Richard's daughter Kathryn had joined the court as they passed through Leicester. As the king's daughter she was assured of more than her share of attention; being pretty, as well, she was soon glorying in her newfound fame, in the realization that she could turn male heads.

'Rumour has it that the Earl of Huntingdon has asked to take your Kathryn as his wife. Is there any truth to it, Dickon?'

'I can see the day coming when rumours do overrun this court like weeds grown wild,' Richard said in bemusement, but then he smiled. 'It's true enough. I had not thought to arrange a match for her so soon, not for another year or two. And Anne thinks fourteen is too young for marriage. But I wrote to Kathryn's mother, telling her of Huntingdon's offer and she's in favour of it. Kate says some girls mature faster than others and Kathryn be ripe for marriage. I have not made up my mind yet, thought I'd keep Kathryn at court for a while and see how she takes to

Huntingdon. He comes of good family, is personable enough and should do right by Kathryn. And the match would, of course, be to my advantage, too, binding Huntingdon all the more closely to York. But there's no hurry, after all. Fourteen seems rather young to me, too, I admit. . . .'

This last was said rather absently; Richard had noticed the man just entering the hall, a man to draw all eyes for he was garbed from head to foot in the stark black of bereavement. Midst the glitter of vivid jewel-colour velvets and silks, he looked like a raven suddenly thrust among peacocks; the contrast was startling, somehow discordant.

Richard wasn't the only one to think so. People were turning to stare, a path opening up before him almost as if he were a leper, carried some loathesome disease in the guise of grief.

'She's a pretty lass, your Kathryn.'

Richard smiled. 'Not surprising, for Kate. . . .' And then he was out of his chair and on his feet for he'd just had his first clear look at the man's face, recognized Henry Burgh, whose wife Isabel had been Ned's nurse for the past ten years.

As their eyes met, Burgh's face contorted. 'My liege. . . .' He sobbed, stumbled forward to kneel before the dais.

Richard's goblet slipped from suddenly nerveless fingers, shattered on the steps of the dais, sending slivers of broken glass into the rushes, splashing wine upon the mourning black of Burgh's doublet.

Burgh was weeping openly. 'He's dead, my lord,' he choked. 'Your son is dead.'

Struggling up out of a deep, drugged sleep, Anne was dimly aware that something was wrong. Her eyelids felt weighted down and the light filtering through her lashes seemed extraordinarily bright, as if she were looking directly up at the sun. Her tongue was coated, an unpleasant aftertaste still lingering in her mouth. A sleeping draught? Was that what was the matter with her?

But why was the pillow wet? Had she been crying in her sleep? Instinctively she shrank back from the answers to those questions, sought refuge again in sleep.

Her dreams were troubled, fragmented. Faces swirled around her, swooped down upon the bed like hawks and then faded away. Sounds of grieving filled her ears. She tossed restively and an unknowing whimper escaped her throat. Richard was with her now; a dream? Or a memory fighting its way back into her consciousness? She reached out to him, seeking comfort, but he did not seem to hear her, kept saying 'Forgive me, forgive me,' over and over again. And then he was gone and she was alone in a grey strangling fog and somewhere a child was crying. . . .

Anne screamed, sat bolt upright in bed. Richard was leaning over her at once, drew her sobbing into his arms. She gave a grateful gasp, clung to him with a feverish urgency, her tears drying against his shirt. But the horror of her dream was still very much upon her, had not been dispelled by the reality of Richard's embrace, the sight of sunlight spilling into the chamber. She found herself staring over his shoulder at the chair in which he'd been sitting, where he'd been keeping vigil by her bed throughout the night. He was murmuring her name, as if he knew no other words, his voice slurred and frighteningly unfamiliar, and in the doorway people were clustered, drawn by her cries: Dr Hobbys and Véronique and Agnes Ratcliffe, theirs the stricken faces of her nightmare terror.

'He's dead,' she whispered. 'He's dead. . . .'

Bess moved quietly toward the bed, saw with relief that Anne appeared to be sleeping. She stood for a time gazing down at her uncle's wife. She knew Anne was not yet twenty-eight but she looked even younger. Too tiny for elegance, like a little girl dressed in her mother's skirts, hers was a fragile ethereal beauty that put Bess in mind of snowflakes or butterflies. She'd been very kind to Bess in those first weeks after Bess left sanctuary, had gone out of her way to make Bess feel welcome, at ease. Yet somehow Bess could not be comfortable with Anne; she felt awkward, self-conscious about her height, inexplicably tonguetied in the other woman's presence. But she'd liked Anne, nonetheless, had been grateful for her thoughtfulness, and she found it intolerable to have to be a helpless witness to Anne's anguish.

Bess was no novice to grieving but in this past fortnight she'd begun selfishly to wish she'd not accompanied her uncle and aunt on their progress north. Never had she known how painful an emotion pity could be, an aching, rending pity for a hurt beyond healing.

The tale of the past two weeks could be told without words, was there for all to see in Anne's face. Her skin had a transparent sheen, like silk stretched too tight, was seared with the passage of scalding tears; her eyelids were bruised, had taken on the delicate discolouration of fading flower petals, and even in sleep the corner of her mouth drooped piteously. Bess felt tears sting her eyes. Why did the Lord God let people suffer so? Anne did not deserve this. Nor did Dickon—Dickon—who looked more and more to her like a damned soul in a world suddenly bereft of all mercy. Bess had found his stunned, silent grieving even harder to bear than Anne's tears; she yearned passionately to comfort him, knowing that there was no comfort to be given.

Anne sighed in her sleep, brought a hand up to her face, like a child trying to ward off a blow. Bess reached down, drew a blanket up around Anne's shoulders. It had been four days before Anne had been able to travel and they'd made the journey north from Nottingham in agonizingly slow stages, the choked sounds of weeping occasionally audible from within Anne's swaying horse litter, not reaching York until the first of May. That same day Richard had ridden out to meet his son's funeral cortège. He had chosen to bury Ned at nearby Sheriff Hutton Castle and Bess had wept when she heard that, knowing it to be a tacit admission that Middleham, too, was lost to him.

Ned had been buried on a Sunday in the little church of St Helen and the Holy Cross, while the city of York mourned for the little boy who'd died just days away from his eleventh birthday, and then Richard and Anne went home to Middleham. They'd been here but one day so far; Bess did not think they would linger long.

'Does she sleep?'

Turning, Bess saw Véronique de Crécy standing beside her. She nodded and, when Véronique whispered, 'I'll watch over her now,' Bess made a grateful exit from the bedchamber, out into the sunlight of the inner bailey.

Passing the auditor's kitchen, Bess smiled at sight of the girl standing on the stairs leading up into the keep. It had been a bitter disappointment to her when her mother refused to let Cecily accompany her on the northward progress and she'd been delighted to find her half sister Grace living at their uncle's court, under his care. Grace smiled too, waited for Bess to join her on the porch.

'Grace . . . who's that woman by the gatehouse? The one talking with Johnny, do you know her?'

'That's Johnny's mother. She's come to take him home with her for a while. Pretty, is she not?'

'I suppose.' Bess was surprised at the prickle of resentment she felt toward this onetime bedmate of her uncle's. It was very similar to the antagonism she'd harboured against her father's many mistresses. Save only Jane Shore, she thought; Jane who was too openhearted and spontaneous to dislike.

'Poor Johnny,' Grace said, and sighed. 'He's been all but forgotten, I fear. I tried talking to him but he's not easy to reach, does keep his grief bottled up. And then, too, he is so young . . . twelve? Thirteen?'

'Thirteen, I believe.' Bess glanced about, made sure they were alone. 'I had a letter this morn from Cecily; remind me and I'll let you read it after dinner. Do you know what she told me, Grace? She says that it is being noised about in London that Ned died on April ninth . . . just like papa.'

Grace looked bewildered. 'But . . . but he did not, Bess. Ned died on Easter Eve, a full week after we did mark papa's year-mind.'

'I know,' Bess said bleakly, 'but do you not see, sister? Had Ned truly died on the ninth, so great a coincidence would be sure to raise questions in people's minds. That Dickon's son should so suddenly be stricken and on the very day that papa died. . . . People who doubted the plight-troth would see it as divine retribution, as God's judgment upon Dickon for taking his nephew's crown. Those who do hate our uncle need only plant rumours to that effect and the gullible will see that they be spread quick enough, passed on in tavern and alehouse as gospel truth.'

'Is it not enough that he has lost his son and heir,' Grace said wonderingly, 'without people seeking to make of it a greater grief?'

Bess hesitated, but only briefly, said in very measured, dispassionate tones, 'Cecily says that when she told our mother Dickon's little boy had died, mama laughed. She laughed and said, "So there is a just and jealous God in Heaven, after all!"'

Not even in the chapel was Richard alone, free of eyes that were sympathetic, pitying, but ever-present. His chaplain hovered solicitously in the background, eager to serve. Richard willed himself to forget the man's obtrusive presence and, kneeling before the candlelit altar, he began to pray for the soul of his son. Then he prayed for Anne, entreated the Almighty to give her strength to accept Ned's loss, to show her the mercy she so deserved. After that, he prayed for his grief-stricken mother-in-law, who'd learned to love Ned as she'd never loved her daughters, for Johnny and Kathryn, for all who'd known Ned and loved him. For himself, he asked nothing. He'd known from the moment he stood staring down at the weeping Burgh that God had turned His face away from him and to cry out that his punishment was more than he could bear would change nothing, would not resurrect the dead.

The torches in the great hall had been extinguished for the night. But he could not bring himself to go to bed, not yet. The sight of his wife's grief was too great a penance; he loved her as he'd never loved another living soul but to be with her now was a torment beyond endurance. He could not help her, could only suffer her pain as his own.

The sky was a deep midnight-blue, spangled with stars. Richard leaned against the battlement, gazed out across the moonlit shadows that hid the landscape he so loved. Wensleydale had been ablaze with autumn bracken when first he'd laid eyes upon Middleham, a nervous nine-year-old consigned to his cousin the kingmaker's care. The happiest years of his boyhood had been spent within these walls. And here he'd brought Anne, his bride of a week. Over the years, they'd spent time at other castles: Sheriff Hutton, Pontefract, Skipton. But Middleham had retained its hold upon his heart. Middleham had been home. For more than eleven years, his home, and now . . . now it was the place where his son had died, died with neither he nor Anne at his bedside.

Richard was turning away from the embrasure, toward the stairwell, when he saw the light coming from the uppermost chamber of the Round Tower. Coming from Ned and Johnny's bedchamber. But Johnny had long since been moved to another room and no servant would be up there at such an hour. Richard moved back to the embrasure. The light shone steadily, a bright beacon in the blackness that encircled the castle.

It was even later than Richard realized; he encountered no one in the hall and the bailey, too, was deserted. He found himself hesitating before the door of Ned's bedchamber. Neither he nor Anne had been able to cross the threshold of this, the room in which Ned had died. But light gleamed from beneath the door. His hand closed on the latch; he shoved inward.

Johnny was curled up on the carpet by the bed, his arm around a huge brindle wolfhound. At his feet lay a second dog, the animal that for five years had been Ned's shadow. Both dogs raised their heads at sight of Richard, silent sentinels to the boy's grieving.

He seemed to be sleeping, but as Richard moved forward into the chamber, he jerked upright, bounded to his feet like a startled deer.

'I'm sorry I startled you so, Johnny. But why are you here?'

'I could not sleep, and I . . . I came. . . .'

'Why, lad?' Richard put his hand on Johnny's arm, felt a tremor go through the boy's body.

'I came . . . came to ask Ned's forgiveness.'

'Why, Johnny? For what?'

'It was my fault, my fault he died.' Despairing blue-grey eyes looked up at Richard, a mirror image of his own. 'Ned woke me up in the night, said he felt queasy, that he had pains in his belly. I told him it was all the sugared comfits we'd eaten before bedtime, told him to go back to sleep. When he woke me up again before dawn, I knew then it was more than that. He was in such pain, had broken out in a cold sweat. . . . I called Mistress Idley at once but had I only summoned someone earlier. . . . Had I believed he was truly ill. . . .'

'It would have made no difference, Johnny. The doctors told me that Ned suffered a rupture, that infection spread so rapidly nothing could be done for him. They do not know how to treat a sickness like that, Johnny. They neither know why it happens nor what to do for it, and those stricken like this always die. Always, lad. Those few hours could not have saved him.'

'You swear?'

'Yes,' Richard said, and Johnny could hold back no longer. Leaning against the wall, he slowly slid to the floor and, burying his face in his arms, he wept.

'Ah, Johnny. . . .' Richard knelt by the sobbing boy, put his arm around Johnny's shoulders, and then his son was in his arms, clinging in a desperate awkward embrace, his body all angles, elbows and knees, his face wet against Richard's neck, all the heartbreak of the past three weeks spilling out in a scalding surge, beyond his control.

'Why Ned? Why, papa? Why did God take him? He was so smart, so much fun to be with, and he . . . he was your heir. Better it had been me. I wish it had, wish. . . .'

Jesus God. Richard stared down at Johnny's bowed head. Let him somehow find the right words, say what Johnny needed to hear. He must not fail Johnny, too. He stroked the soft black hair, said slowly, 'Johnny, you must not ever think that. I want you to promise me . . . promise me that you'll put such thoughts from your mind. If I were to think you truly believed that. . . . Well, nothing could give me greater grief. Will you promise me?'

Johnny's whisper barely reached his ears. 'Yes. . . .'

'Johnny . . . listen to me, lad. I know your mother has come all the way from London to bring you back with her for a time. But I do not want you to go. I want you with me. From here I must go north to Durham and then to Scarborough; when we leave Middleham, I want you to go with me and, when I go back to London, I want you to come and make your home at court.'

Johnny had raised his head. 'Papa, I thought you were sending me away. When my mother came yesterday and told me, I . . . I thought you did not want me with you any more. . . .'

Richard's throat constricted; he saw his son through a sudden blur of tears. As much as he loved Johnny, he'd loved Ned more, Ned who was part of Anne, whose dark eyes were hers, who was of her flesh, her blood. Had Johnny sensed it? Had he denied the boy not only his birthright but a sense of belonging, too?

'You're my son and I love you very much. I would never send you away . . . never.' He hugged the boy to him again and again Johnny responded with a need so naked that Richard was swept with guilt. He ignored the discomfort of their position, ignored the torchlight shining blindingly into his eyes and the musty stale odour of a room too long closed up, held his son until some of the tension had eased from Johnny's body, and tried not to look at the bed beyond, the bed in which Ned had died.

1081

20

Scarborough, Yorkshire
July 1484

The windows of Anne's bedchamber opened onto a panoramic view of the harbour. Brisk winds had swept the sky of clouds and a midday sun shimmered over the North Sea, a dark ink-blue along the horizon gradually shading into a vivid sapphire as the waves rolled shoreward, showering the cliffs below in a spray of frothy spume. The sight was a spectacular one but Anne was staring with unseeing eyes at the scene, and she jumped, visibly startled, when Richard said her name.

'I did not hear you enter,' she confessed, summoning up a wan smile. 'Have you been standing there long? I . . . I was just thinking about the time we brought Ned to Scarborough. He was so excited, seeing the sea for the first time . . . remember?'

'Yes,' Richard said, 'I remember.' He turned, closed the door deliberately behind him. 'Anne, why were you not at dinner? Are you unwell?'

'I'm fine. I just did not feel hungry.' Seeing his mouth tighten, Anne added, somewhat defensively, 'Richard, do not look at me like that. It was only a missed meal, after all.'

'Anne, we've got to talk and this time you're going to hear me out.' Moving toward her, Richard took her hand and drew her into the window seat. Her body was stiff, resistant, and she sat down beside him with a reluctance all too easy to read.

'Beloved, you cannot keep on like this.'

'Like what? Just what am I doing, Richard, that is so wrong?

Yes, I am grieving for our son but what would you have me do? Say it's been time enough, put my grief aside like a gown I no longer wear and. . . .'

'Anne, stop it! No one expects you not to grieve for Ned; least of all, me. But you cannot give in to it like this. Do you not see that? It's been eleven weeks; how much longer ere you fall ill? Ere you. . . .'

'Richard, I'm not ailing. How often do I have to say it to be believed?'

'If you have not taken sick yet,' he said flatly, 'it is only a matter of time till you do. I'm not blind, Anne. I watch you at meals, pushing your food about on the plate, all too often leaving it untouched altogether. You dismiss your ladies at the slightest pretext, shut yourself up alone for hours on end, dwelling upon memories that can only break your heart. How often have I awakened in the night to find you gone from my bed, sitting by yourself in the dark? Or walking in the gardens, hours before dawn. . . . You do not eat, you will not sleep, seem to care for nothing at all, least of all your own well-being. Even when we make love now, you. . . .'

'That's not fair, Richard! I've never refused you, have I?'

'No,' he said tiredly, 'but you're not truly there. You go through the motions, Anne, no more than that. Your whole life is like that now, beloved . . . just going through the motions, and I . . . I do not know how to help you.'

With that, Anne's defiance vanished and she began to cry— strangled, gasping sobs that racked her body. Richard flinched at the sound; her tears splashed salt into an unhealed wound. He reached out to her but she drew back, came unsteadily to her feet.

'I cannot help myself, Richard, I cannot. . . . He was not even eleven years old and he . . . he died crying for us, in such pain, and I . . . I was not with him. . . . God forgive me, but I was not there when he needed me the most. How can I forget? Even if

I could, if I could somehow learn to live with that, how can I forget what his death has done to you? The dreadful danger I've placed you in. . . .' She was weeping bitterly, almost incoherent. 'You need a son, Richard, a son I . . . I cannot give you. A king must have an heir, he must. . . . And now, with so many enemies. . . . Oh, my love, how I have failed you!'

'Ah, Anne, do not! That's not true, I swear it's not.'

'Please, Richard, no more lies. I know about Tudor, you see, how he's taken refuge in France.' She saw his surprise, said in a choked voice, 'Did you truly think because you did not tell me that no one else would? I know that Morton somehow learned of your secret negotiations with Pierre Landois, that he got word to Tudor just in time, that Tudor abandoned his followers and fled into France. Can you deny it? Can you say it's not so?'

'No, but. . . .'

'I know you meant well by trying to keep it from me but I had a right to know, Richard. The French do fear you even more than they feared Ned, have never forgotten how you opposed the Treaty of Picquigny. They'll use Tudor against you the way Louis used Marguerite and her son against Ned, will back him up with French gold and troops, whatever they think it'll take to bring you down.'

'Anne, listen to, me. I do not fear Tudor and neither should you. The man's never so much as bloodied his sword, whereas I was first given the command of men at seventeen, have spent the past fourteen years. . . .'

Anne was shaking her head. 'There was no better commander born than your brother but that availed him little at Doncaster. I know you can defend yourself in the field, Richard, but against treachery? You're surrounded by men who've proven themselves untrustworthy time and time again, men like the Stanleys and Northumberland. And now. . . .' She sobbed suddenly. 'Now that you can no longer offer the country a stable succession, how long ere they're tempted to switch sides? Ere they. . . .'

'Beloved, you're tormenting yourself for naught. I can deal with the Stanleys and Northumberland. They're not men to risk their own necks, but they will be loyal if it's worth their while and I've made sure that it is. As for'—Richard drew a deep breath—'the other . . . You did not fail me, Anne. You gave me a son, you gave me Ned.'

'But I can give you no others. . . .'

'It does not matter, Anne. The House of York has other heirs. I swear to you that it does not matter.'

'It matters,' Anne whispered. She turned away, blinded by tears. 'You need a son, Richard, a son to make the succession safe. Another woman could give you an heir, but I . . . I cannot, and at times I think . . . think that if I truly loved you, I'd let you go. . . .'

She gasped then, for Richard had grabbed her arm, swung her around to face him.

'Do not say that,' he said roughly. 'Do not ever let me hear you say that!'

She stared at him, open-mouthed, and after a moment his grip eased on her arm; he released her and stepped back.

The windows were open; Richard inhaled the tang of sea air, could see gulls wheeling above the keep. Anne had followed him to the window, her perfume mingling with the strong bracing smell of the sea. He reached out, drew her to him and felt an absurd rush of relief when she didn't pull away. He stood for a time holding her close against him, breathing in her fragrance, tasting salt tears on her skin. Never had she seemed so fragile to him; he could feel her shoulder blades, her rib cage, could see the delicate vein pulsing at her temple, the slender curving line of her throat, and he was swept by tenderness made all the more intense by his fear.

'Do you not know what you do mean to me? Do you not know that if I were to lose you, nothing would matter? And when I see what you are doing to yourself, when I see you not caring if you become ill or not, I . . . I cannot help fearing that you're to be taken from me, too. . . .'

His voice was muffled against her hair but this admission she could barely hear sent shock radiating through her body, jolted her into sudden stunned understanding. 'Forgive me,' he'd pleaded, after telling her that their son was dead. 'Forgive me.' But in the anguish of her loss, his words had no meaning for her. Until now. Oh, Madonna, how could she have been so blind? What a selfish emotion grief was, denying all pain but one's own. Should their grieving not have been a bridge between them, not a barrier? She should have seen, should not have needed to be told, for who knew Richard better than she?

'Children die,' she said unsteadily. 'Every day they do sicken and die, my love. They go to their graves too soon, leave voids that cannot ever be filled, but it's God's will, must be accepted as that . . . as no more than that, Richard. You're not responsible for Ned's death.' She felt him stiffen but gave him no chance to refute her, putting her fingers to his lips.

'No . . . listen to me, please. I do not know why God took him so young or so suddenly, but I do know it was not your fault. Nor are you to blame for your nephews' deaths. It was Buckingham's crime, not yours.'

'Anne, you do not understand.'

'No, I confess I do not. I cannot believe that God would inflict so merciless a punishment upon you. You've done nothing to deserve it, my love, in truth you have not. And whatever sins you may have committed, Ned was innocent.'

Richard looked at her. 'Edward was innocent, too.'

Beyond the window a gull cried shrilly, a harsh yet strangely plaintive sound; another answered, farther off.

'But that was not your fault. Buckingham. . . .'

'Buckingham did not take the crown, Anne. I did. I let Edward pay for his father's sins, I broke the holy oath I'd sworn to protect and serve him and I had myself crowned in his stead.'

'Richard . . . you had the right.'

'Yes, that's what I told myself. That I had the right, that I had no choice, that I did it for you and Ned. I found no lack of reasons for what I did. There were even a few moments in which I admitted to myself just how much I truly wanted it.'

Anne bit her lip. 'Is that what you cannot forgive yourself for, Richard . . . that you wanted to be king? My love, why is that so great a sin? Yes, you wanted it, but the plight-troth was not of your making. It was not fair to Edward, I grant you that. But why must you take all the blame upon yourself? You were urged to it, Richard, by me more than any others. The council saw the plight-troth as reason enough to set aside Edward's claim; so, too, did the Commons and House of Lords. Does their judgment count for nothing?'

Richard startled her then by jerking at the lacings of his doublet, pulling it open to show the white cambric shirt underneath. Fumbling with the buttons, he bared his chest.

'Here I was anointed with the sacred chrism.' He held out his hands to her. 'Here, too, consecrated with the holy oil that does thereafter set a king apart from other men. What greater sacrilege could there be, Anne, than to be anointed with the chrism and not have the right? It was not enough that I believed in my right, that others did, too. Kneeling there before the High Altar, I needed more than that, I had to be sure. Can you understand that?'

Anne nodded slowly, chilled in spite of herself. 'So you . . . you asked the Almighty to confirm your right?'

'Yes,' he admitted softly. 'I asked Him to give me a sign, a divine sign that I was right to take the crown. And within a fortnight, my nephews were dead.'

'Oh, my love, do not. . . .'

'Even then, Anne, even then I could not face it. By blaming Buckingham I could keep from blaming myself, you see. I had to lose my own son before I could admit what I'd done to my brother's sons.'

Anne was crying again, tears welling in her eyes and spilling silently down her face. 'Richard, I beg you, do not do this. It is not true, it is not. They died because Buckingham craved the crown, because he gave the order. Not you, Richard, not you.'

'Anne, you still do not see, do you? Had I not taken the crown, the boys would still be alive.'

And there was nothing she could say to that for it was true, a truth that existed independently of right and wrong, of blame or innocence, a fact inescapable and absolute that was to Anne tragic and, to Richard, a judgment without appeal.

The bed-curtains had not been fully drawn and moonlight was infiltrating through the openings. It slanted across the pillow, fired the rubies and sapphires of Richard's coronation ring and, moving higher, caught a glimmer of silver at his throat, the pilgrim pledge that had once been his mother's.

'Anne?'

She raised her head from his shoulder. 'You've been so quiet, I thought you'd fallen asleep.'

'Anne, I've been giving it some thought and . . . I've decided to name my sister's son as my heir.'

Anne said nothing, not trusting her voice. This was his answer, then, to the despairing confession she'd made yesterday noon, all he could think to do to allay her guilt. She swallowed, lay back in the crook of his arm. She might be that most unfortunate of women, a barren queen, but she was loved; she did have that.

'Anne? What think you? I suppose I could have picked George and Bella's little Edward rather than Jack, but I just did not think that would be wise.'

Anne agreed wholeheartedly with that. While George's attainder could be reversed by parliament, allowing Edward to inherit, to make Edward heir to the throne would serve the country ill. And as for Edward himself . . . Jesú spare him that. He was the sweetest child she'd ever known but she could think of no greater tragedy than to make him king. Had he been born . . . slow? Or had the damage been done in those early isolated years of child-hood? Could the lack of love, the lack of care stunt a mind the way the lack of food could stunt a body? She had no answers, knew only that the greatest blessing in Edward's life had been the attainder barring him from the throne. What a pity that Harry of Lancaster could not have been as fortunate.

Hastening now to reassure Richard, she said, 'I think Jack is the best possible choice, love.' And felt an irrational unexpected urge to weep, as if she'd somehow denied Ned something that was his alone.

She must not think that, she must not. Ned was beyond all earthly cares, at peace. He did not need her now but Richard did, Richard who was tormenting himself for a choice she'd urged him to make. Was he right? By taking the crown and allow-ing his nephews to die, had he doomed their son? No. . . . No, she could not believe that.

But her belief was not what mattered. She knew there was nothing she could say to convince Richard he was wrong. One thing only could do that and the Almighty alone could do it. If she could bear a child, bear Richard a son, Richard would know then that God had forgiven him and he could then forgive himself. That was all she could do for Richard, pray for a son. But surely her prayers would not be denied. Even if Richard was right and he'd sinned in taking the crown, he'd acted in good faith, had never meant harm to come to his brother's sons, and He Who could see into each man's heart and soul must know that, must know that Richard's contrition was genuine. No, God would not burden Richard with so unbearable a guilt. He would heed her prayers, would let her womb quicken again, let her bear a son for Richard, for England.

'Anne? What are you thinking?'

'Of you,' she said truthfully, and settled back against him. God the All-merciful would not forsake them, she thought, her resolve drawing upon her faith to make belief a certainty, to give her a flicker of comfort. Her sleep that night was free of troubled dreams for the first time since her son's death, and that, too, she took as an omen of hope.

21

Nottingham
October 1484

Richard and Anne passed the summer in the North, with a brief excursion back to Westminster in early August. While there, Richard gave orders for Harry of Lancaster to be reinterred at Windsor Castle; he also named his nephew Jack de la Pole as Lord Lieutenant of Ireland, the post that the House of York traditionally reserved for the heir to the throne.

He returned to Nottingham in early September to meet with envoys from Scotland; a decisive naval victory for the English that past June had convinced James that peace was in the best interests of all concerned. By the middle of the month Richard was able to proclaim that a treaty of amity had been signed, with a marriage pending between the heir to the Scots throne and Richard's niece, Anne de la Pole, his sister's eldest daughter. It was his most significant diplomatic achievement to date, offset to some extent the unrelenting enmity of the French. Richard then felt free to turn his mind to personal concerns and, shortly before Michaelmas, he gave his daughter Kathryn in marriage to William Herbert, Earl of Huntingdon.

*

Véronique was on her way to Anne's bedchamber when she encountered Joyce Percy and Madge de la Pole, a lively sunny-natured girl still in her teens and, now that her husband had been named as Richard's heir, suddenly a person of enormous importance.

'The Queen's lying down,' Madge said by way of greeting.

'In midafternoon? Does she not feel well?'

'Fine, she says. But she promised the King that she'd rest some in the afternoons from now on; he thinks she's tiring too easily these days.' Madge giggled. 'It must be nice to have a husband that attentive; I'd have to look like walking death ere Jack would even notice. One time I dyed my hair a full three shades lighter and when I asked him how I looked, he was genuinely perplexed, finally asked if I was wearing a new gown.'

'My Rob is no better.' Joyce crinkled her nose playfully. 'But Anne has been looking peaked lately.'

'You think so? I was just thinking this morn that her colour's never been better.'

Véronique smiled, moved on. It was strange, she thought, that both Joyce and Madge were right. Anne was becomingly flushed these days, her eyes bright and luminous, her skin translucent. But she was too thin, too finely drawn, had about her a nervous vivacity that somehow rang false, that she seemed to be using to keep others at arm's length. Was it her way of coping with an unhealed grief? Véronique didn't know but she sensed the strain and it bothered her; without knowing precisely why, it bothered her a great deal.

The bed was rumpled but Anne was standing by the window. It was an unusually mild day for late October and the window was open, letting in sunlight and the sound of laughter.

'What is causing all the merriment?' Véronique asked, joining Anne at the window.

'Over there by the great hall.' Anne pointed across the bailey. 'See that longbow they are passing around? It is Morgan Kidwelly's and, from the way the men have been exclaiming over it, it must be the finest weapon ever to come out of Wales. A few moments ago, Bess joined them, coaxed Morgan and Richard into showing her how to use it. Of course she couldn't get the stele back, nearly dislocated her shoulder trying, and as you'd expect, all the men just about fell down laughing.'

Véronique grinned. 'That girl is a born flirt, her father's daughter for true! I admit I had a few qualms about her coming back to court; I thought it might be awkward, all things considered. But it's worked out rather well, has it not?'

Anne nodded and coughed. 'She's been very good for Richard,' she said quietly. For a moment her eyes met Véronique's. There was no need to say more; Veronique understood and agreed. That Bess did not blame him for her brothers' deaths had to mean much to Richard; it was, Véronique thought bleakly, as close as he could come to absolution.

Anne coughed again and Véronique frowned. She did not like the sound of it, not at all. 'Anne, what did Dr Hobbys tell you about that cough? It seems to be getting worse; can he not give you something to ease it?'

Anne shook her head.

'I cannot believe that. I think I'll talk to him this afternoon, see what. . . .'

'No!'

Véronique was taken aback by Anne's vehemence. 'But why not? Richard told me Hobbys was treating you for the cough, said he'd insisted . . . Anne? Anne, you did see Hobbys, didn't you?'

'Yes, I . . .' Anne's voice trailed off. 'No,' she admitted, very low. 'No. . . I did not.'

'But Richard said you did, said. . . .'

'I lied to him, said I had,' Anne said simply, and Véronique stared at her in astonishment.

'I do not understand. Why do you not want to see Hobbys?'

'Because I'm afraid . . . afraid of what he might find.'

Véronique drew a breath so sharp it was almost a gasp.

'I should not be saying this to you but . . . but I so need to talk to someone, Véronique. I just cannot keep it to myself any longer. . . .' Anne sat down suddenly in the window seat and Véronique saw that she was trembling.

'This is the second month that my flux has not come,' she said, and when Véronique would have spoken, she shook her head slowly. 'No . . . I'm not with child.'

'Anne . . . are you sure? Women often feel ill in the first months of pregnancy. . . .'

'Yes, I'm sure,' Anne said softly. 'That is the irony of it all, that I am so sure. You see . . . I'd been trying all summer to get with child. When we went back to Westminster in August, I made daily offerings before the shrine of St Erkenwald in St Paul's and every night I did entreat the Virgin Mother to heed my prayers. And then last month when my flux did not come . . . I should have thought first of pregnancy, I suppose.' There was a curious lack of emotion in her voice, only a dull wonderment. 'But I did not, Véronique. I . . . I do not know why, but I did not. It was as if . . . as if I somehow sensed. . . .'

Anne raised her lashes; her eyes shone with, an unnatural, intense brilliancy, the pupils so dilated that they seemed more black than brown, and what they mirrored unmistakably was fear. Véronique's mouth had gone dry; she said as calmly as she could, 'You're saying then, that you're ill . . . that you've been ill as far back as last month?'

Anne nodded. 'Even longer, I think. I just did not realize, thought it was no more than exhaustion and . . . and grieving over Ned.'

She coughed, fumbled for her handkerchief. 'At first I was just so tired, Véronique. . . . I'd wake up in the morning feeling as if I'd never been to bed and the slightest exertion left me winded, drained. And then . . . Well, I've had no appetite for longer than I can remember but these past weeks I've been making an effort to eat more—I'd promised Richard—and yet my weight has kept dropping. The cough . . . that you do know about. I told myself it was nothing to fret over, began to drink horehound mixed in honey at bedtime. But it's been getting worse, Véronique, especially at night. . . . You cannot imagine what it's like now, lying awake hour after hour trying to stifle it as best I can, trying not to disturb Richard. When it gets too bad, I go into the garde-robe where he'll not hear me and cough into a towel.'

'Oh, Anne. . . .' Véronique closed her eyes, not knowing what to say.

'And last night . . . last night I found myself shivering, suddenly chilled to the bone. It did not last long, only a few minutes, but then I began to get so hot, Véronique, as if my skin were on fire. Finally I broke out in a sweat and, after that, I could sleep. . . .'

'Anne. . . . Anne, why in God's name have you kept this from us? Why did you not let Dr Hobbys know? Why. . . .'

'I did not go to Hobbys because I knew he'd tell Richard. And Richard must not know.'

'Anne, you're making no sense. If you are ill, Richard must be told. He has the ri. . . .'

'No! He of all people must not know. And you must promise me that, Véronique, promise me you'll say nothing to him, to anyone.'

'Anne, I . . . I cannot.'

'Véronique, you must!' Anne coughed sharply, reached over to lay an entreating hand upon her arm. 'You do not understand. . . . I cannot do that to him, I cannot. . . . If . . . if I'm as ill as I think, he'll know all too soon. Each day I can give him, each day he does not know. . . . Oh, do you not see? You must promise me, you must!'

Véronique shook her head mutely, her throat closing, cutting off speech.

Anne was on her feet, staring down at her. 'Please, I beg you . . . for Richard's sake. . . .'

'Ah, Anne, do not! Do not ask that of me!'

'Promise me. . . .' Anne was struggling for breath, her face suffused with bright blood and Véronique cried out in sudden panic, 'Yes . . . yes, I will. I swear it, Anne.'

But her surrender came too late. Anne had so agitated herself that the coughing now was convulsive, out of control. She stumbled backward, doubled over with the force of the spasms shaking her body.

'Anne . . . Anne, I do not know what to do for you. Forgive me, but you must have a doctor, you must!'

Anne shook her head but she had no breath to protest. Her knees gave way and she sank back in the window seat. Véronique was holding a cup to her mouth and she tried obediently to swallow, choked, and spilled wine down the front of her gown. Somewhere she heard a door open, heard footsteps, other voices. Joyce? Bess? Suddenly the chamber seemed full of people, hovering over her, all talking at once; someone was holding a wet cloth to her forehead. She drew a strangled breath, then another, less laboured. Once more she could get air into her lungs, once more her body was her own again, and she sobbed with the utter intensity of her relief.

'Anne?'

Opening her eyes, Anne saw Joyce's frightened face through a haze of tears. She wanted to reassure Joyce, to say that she was all right, but it was too much of an effort, the words just would not come.

'We've sent for the doctor, dearest. For Richard, too. He'll be here any. . . .'

'No,' Anne whispered. 'No. . . .'

Why was this happening? Why to her and Richard? So unfair, Blessed Mary, so unforgivably unfair. It was wearing off now, the merciful numbness, the disbelief that her body could so betray her, and she was swept by a sudden rebellious rage, a blasphemous anger against a God Who could let this happen, let children die, the innocent suffer so. Unless ... unless Richard was right. And if he was, his guilt then was hers, too, for she'd urged him to take the crown. But was there any sin so great it could not be forgiven? Did contrition count for nothing?

'Leave me,' she said dully. 'All of you.' And there was in her voice that which none of them had ever heard from her before. No one protested, not even Véronique; Anne found herself obeyed with an alacrity that even Elizabeth might have envied.

Coming unsteadily to her feet, she moved toward her cosmetics table, picked up a mirror. A woman with hollowed, feverish eyes stared back at her, a woman unnaturally flushed, a sheen of perspiration at her temples, glistening across her cheekbones, her upper lip.

'Anne?'

She stiffened, put the mirror down with a thud and very slowly turned around. Richard was standing in the doorway and the look on his face was what she'd most feared to see.

Rob and Francis were sitting by the hearth, ostensibly playing at Tables. But Richard knew they were watching him all the while; he could feel their eyes, feel their unspoken concern. What was it Ned had once said, that he was lucky in his friendships? As ever, Ned had been right. Did they know how dear they were to him, these men with whom he'd shared so much? Too often friendships were taken for granted and loved ones ... loved ones even more so, as if there'd always be unlimited tomorrows, a future guaranteed by God.

Richard moved toward the bedchamber door once again, stopped with his hand just inches from the latch and then turned away, sank down in the nearest chair. Almost at once, he felt a warm wetness swipe his neck, put up his arm just in time to fend off Loki's caressing tongue.

'Lord deliver me from lapdogs the size of small ponies,' he said to the room at large and then pulled the big dog close, rubbed his cheek against Loki's soft silver-grey ruff.

It was then that the door opened and Dr Hobbys came out of the bedchamber, followed by Thomas Bemesley, the physician who'd been in attendance at Middleham, had been at Ned's death-bed. Richard came to his feet so suddenly that the alaunt was caught unaware, had to scramble awkwardly to keep its balance.

There was a strained silence, broken at last by Richard. 'Well?' he said huskily.

'She's resting now, my liege. But given the unusual severity of the coughing fit, we've advised Her Grace to remain abed for the next day or two.'

Richard nodded, waited, but neither doctor volunteered more. They were, he saw, as reluctant to give him answers as he was to put questions to them. He leaned forward, gripping the back of the chair, stared down at his jewelled rings, his whitening knuckles.

'I've been trying to convince myself that her cough was just that, a cough and no more. But it is not, is it?' His eyes moved from Bemesley to Hobbys. 'I want you to tell me. And I want the truth.'

'We cannot be sure as yet, Your Grace, but . . .' Bemesley began, and Richard looked to Hobbys.

The older man hesitated and then said, very quietly, 'We think it is consumption.'

'Oh, God. . . .' Richard had thought he was braced for the worst they might tell him, but he'd not expected this. Tertian fever, even influenza, but not consumption. Consumption, the White Plague that had claimed Bella, had taken Johnny Neville's son. The wasting fever that was a virtual death sentence for the young, the frail.

'Does she . . . does she know?'

Dr Hobbys nodded. 'She asked us plain-out, Your Grace, if it be consumption. I could not lie to her.'

'Dickon. . . .' Rob was standing beside him now, Rob who'd lost a young wife in childbirth. Stricken blue eyes looked into Richard's own, eyes that understood all too well. Rob reached out awkwardly; his hand brushed Richard's sleeve, dropped to his side, and then he blurted out, 'Dickon, listen, it does not mean there is no hope. Joyce has a cousin who was taken with consumption when she was fifteen, thought like to die, but today she be fine, has a husband and children. . . .'

'Sir Robert is right, Your Grace,' Dr Bemesley said swiftly, soothingly. 'Your lady will have the best of care, that we can promise you, and God willing, I see no reason why she should not recover from this affliction.'

Richard looked at him. 'If you only knew,' he said softly, 'how much I do want to believe you.'

'What is this, Richard?'

'Goat's milk, egg yolks, rosewater and nutmeg. Honey, too, I think. That does not sound too bad, does it?' Richard slipped an arm around Anne, helped her to sit up and watched intently while she drank.

'And tonight Dr Hobbys wants you to take red wine mixed with laurel berries just before we go to bed. He thinks it should ease your cough considerably but he wants you to keep on taking the horehound and honey during the day.'

Anne's eyes met his over the rim of her goblet. The liquid was sweetish, thick; she forced it down, wiped her mouth with the back of her hand.

'We'll take our time on our way back to London, sweetheart. You can rest in the horse litter and I'll ride next to you and keep you company. Do you think you'll feel up to leaving the first of the week? If not, we can wait. . . .'

'That will be fine, Richard,' Anne said, and smiled at him. He smiled back but tensed as she coughed, dark blue eyes never leaving her face, relaxing only when she settled back in his arms.

'What can I get for you, beloved? There must be something you want, surely.'

'No ... nothing. Just hold me,' Anne said, and he drew her even closer, stroked her hair with gentle fingers, touched his lips to her forehead, and for the first time in weeks Anne felt something almost like peace. But soon after, Dr Hobbys entered the chamber, stiffened at sight of them together on the bed and Anne flushed guiltily, would have moved away had Richard not been holding her so tightly.

After satisfying himself that her goblet was empty and feeling her forehead to assure himself that she wasn't feverish, Hobbys said gravely, 'I'll see that another milk drink be sent to you before bedtime, Madame.'

Anne nodded. 'You need not worry, Dr Hobbys. I ... I know what must be done.'

She waited until Hobbys withdrew but no longer, knowing that if she did not say it at once she never would.

'Richard ... I promised that I'd be honest with you from now on, that I'd not keep anything from you again, and I meant it. But you must be honest with me, too, love ... and with yourself.'

'You do not think I am?'

'No.' She drew a deep, uneven breath. 'A few minutes ago you spoke of us going to bed and my darling, you know that cannot be. Dr Hobbys told you we can no longer share a bedchamber ... did he not?'

'Anne, listen. ...'

'No, my love, no. Consumption is the most contagious of ailments. Do you think I would ever willingly subject you to such a risk? Dr Hobbys was adamant on this, and Richard, he's right.' She twisted around in his arms, looked up imploringly into his face.

'You must do this for me, love, if not for yourself. Dr Hobbys says that if I'm to get well, I must avoid stress, avoid emotional upsets, and what peace of mind would I have if I were living in fear that you might be stricken with my sickness?'

Richard started to speak, stopped and, after a long moment, nodded.

Anne's relief was intense, overwhelming; she'd known Richard would not heed Hobbys, that she alone could persuade him. But then she thought what it would mean, that never again would she lie at night in his arms, feel his warmth, his caresses, hear the reassuring soft sound of his breathing beside her. Never again. And suddenly that seemed too much to bear, too much to ask of her. She shut her eyes tightly, turned her cheek into Richard's shoulder, but hot tears seeped through her lashes, streaking her face in a desolate trail of grief she could no longer deny.

She struggled to keep her breathing even, regular, so Richard would not know she wept, but then she felt his mouth against her eyelids, her lashes, the wetness on her face. She knew she should stop him, should not let him do this, knew Dr Hobbys would never forgive her but she could not turn away from him, could not refuse this wordless attempt at comfort, the only kind he now knew how to give. Surely God would not punish her for this, for letting him hold her one last time, and she lay very still, feeling his breath warm on her skin, his heartbeat thudding against her ear. She did remember in time, though, to avert her face just enough so that he could not kiss her mouth. After a long time, her tears ceased.

He continued to hold her close, but he did not speak; neither did she.

22

London

January 1485

Upon her departure from sanctuary, Elizabeth had leased a manor house in the Essex village of Waltham Holy Cross, twelve miles north of London. Cecily was no longer in residence, havings joined Bess at their uncle's court, and Elizabeth's household consisted only of her three younger daughters, her sister Katherine and Katherine's children, and a modest staff to serve their needs. There was comfort in Elizabeth's new life but no contentment, and it was that which impelled her to embark upon a mission of such risk.

The two servants selected to escort her into London exchanged startled glances as she emerged from the house, swathed in a widow's dark veil and barbe. It made sense to them, though, that she should not wish to be recognized; her daughters were much pitied by Londoners for their fall from grace but few found pity to spare for Elizabeth, who was now reaping what she'd sown during twenty years of careless arrogance, self-indulgent tempers.

Elizabeth waited as her mare was brought up and then pulled a deep mourning hood up over her head so that her face was almost completely hidden. Satisfied, she let her groom help her mount and they moved out.

They rode into the churchyard of St Paul's in midafternoon. Dispatching one man to watch over their horses, Elizabeth instructed the other to await her in the cloisters and then entered the church. Crossing the nave, she slipped out the Si Quis door, hastened into Paul's Alley. Even if her servant should disobey her and seek her within, his failure to find her should not arouse suspicion. Today was the Feast of the Epiphany and St Paul's was crowded to capacity; Elizabeth had chosen her time with care.

Within a few minutes she found herself walking briskly up Ivy Lane, passing the gateway leading into Lovell's Manor, the London town house of Richard's Lord Chamberlain. None of the passersby gave her so much as a second glance but her heart was beating uncomfortably fast; never before had she been on her own in London, unaccompanied even by servants. Pray God she'd not regret it!

For the first time she began to wonder if the risk be worth the gain. Her life was not unpleasant now, after all. Her needs were being met and her daughters were being honourably treated at Richard's court; in that, he'd more than kept his word. So why, then, hazard what she already had for what might never be, trade substance for shadowy promise? If Richard was to learn of her continued involvement with Tudor, if he was to learn of this meeting today ... It was true that she could better afford to indulge in treason than most. Not only was she safe from the axe, it was highly unlikely she'd ever see the inside of a prison cell; Richard would spare her that for the sake of her daughters. But he could choose a more subtle confinement, could shut her up within the walls of a convent, and Elizabeth had no desire to take the veil, to see her world shrink to such dreary dimensions. Convents were for the overly devout and the utterly defeated, and she was neither.

She gasped suddenly as the stench of gutted entrails and offal assailed her nostrils, hastily clasped a handkerchief to her nose and mouth until she was safely past Pentecost Lane with its slaughterhouses and butchers' stalls. Jesú, how did the people living nearby endure the stink?

The street was filthy, the air foul, and Elizabeth's footsteps slowed; she seriously considered turning back. What chance had Tudor to defeat Richard on the field? For all his pretensions, what was the Welshman but an adventurer in exile?

Ahead lay her destination, a seedy inn just across from the precincts of St Martin le Grand. She paused, staring up at the tilted sign reading *The Bull's Head.* The paint was peeling, the wood weathered, the general appearance one of desolation and decay.

Lady Mary, but it looked little better than a brothel! How could she set foot in such a hovel? This was for Tom to do. So where was he when she did need him most? His fault, damn him, all his fault. When she'd written to him, telling him that Richard had agreed to pardon him and urging him to return home to England, why had he not the common sense just to slip away under cover of night? But no, he'd had to babble goodbyes to his latest bedmate and, of course, the girl had not been long in deciding the information might be worth something to Tudor. Tudor's men had overtaken Tom at Compiègne, 'persuaded' him to return to the French court, and since then he'd been watched like a hawk, treated with all due courtesy but as a hostage, withal. Elizabeth was not unduly concerned about Tom's physical safety; Tudor coud scarcely hope to win Woodville support by harming her son. But it had been a needless blunder on Tom's part and she had yet to forgive him for it.

A gust of wind caught her cloak and she shivered. There was no going back. No matter how generously Richard treated her daughters, they were at his court now only at his sufferance, branded as bastards by the parliamentary act that recognized his right to the throne. And for herself, there was nothing. . . . To be Lady Grey again, when for nigh on twenty years she'd been Queen of England? No, by God, she'd not settle for that. Tudor had sworn a public oath that he'd make Bess his Queen and that was worth the gamble. Well worth it. She crossed the street, entered the courtyard of the inn.

A servant was watching for her; he at once ushered her

through a side door, up a narrow flight of stairs. The room was small, shabbily furnished, reeked of tallow and sweat and stagnant air. The man waiting within was of medium height, in his late forties, with a slight paunch and reddish-gold hair receding back from his temples, thinning but untouched by grey.

His eyebrows rose at sight of her mourning attire. 'My compliments, Madame,' he drawled. 'You look the very image of a grieving widow of modest means. I can find but one small flaw in your disguise; if you mean to be taken for a mere knight's widow, your barbe should be worn under the chin . . . should it not?'

Elizabeth's eyes narrowed. 'What a fool Richard was,' she said, 'to have ever pardoned you!'

Reginald Bray laughed. 'I daresay others do agree with you. I was fortunate in being cousin to Katherine Hastings, even more fortunate in that Gloucester heeded her entreaties on my behalf. Passing strange, would you not say? It's not often that the widow of a man executed for treason can expect to have the king's ear, after all. . . . Conscience pangs perchance?'

Elizabeth jerked back her hood. 'I'd rather not waste time with trivialities. If I may get right to the point of this meeting?'

'By all means . . . Madame.' Bray grinned, and the irony in his voice brought a surge of angry blood up into Elizabeth's face.

'It's been more than a year since Henry Tudor swore a solemn oath before the High Altar in the cathedral at Rennes that he meant to make my daughter his Queen. I want you to tell me if he does mean to stand by that vow.'

'What makes you think he would not?'

'Anne Herbert,' Elizabeth said flatly, saw him react to the name.

'Who?'

'I thought we agreed not to waste time,' she snapped. 'You know who I mean. The woman's kindred have considerable influence in Wales, do they not? Rumour has it that Tudor's made overtures to the family, that there be talk of marriage. I should like you, Master Bray, to tell me why.'

'How did you hear about Anne Herbert?' Bray said sourly. 'Your son, I suppose?'

'Hardly. Tom's not exactly in Tudor's confidence these days. No, it happens that there are many amongst Tudor's followers who feel his interests could best be served by marriage with my daughter. Just as there are those,' Elizabeth said pointedly, 'who would do what they could to sabotage such an alliance. And now that we've cleared that up, perhaps you'd like to explain why a man who did publicly pledge to wed Bess suddenly seems to be on the verge of changing his mind?'

'I daresay your daughter remains his first choice, Madame; he's well aware that many do feel she was treated rather shabbily, would welcome such an alliance as a true reconciliation of the Houses of Lancaster and York. But Henry Tudor is a pragmatic man and if the girl is no longer . . . available, well then, it's to be expected that he'd look elsewhere, seek to make a match no less advantageous.'

'And what makes you think that Bess is no longer available? Did I not assure Tudor that I'd be able to gain her consent to the marriage? Bess has a strong sense of family, will do what's expected of her. Assuming, of course, that Tudor does what's expected of *him* and claims the crown in more than name. Lest you forget, Richard of Gloucester is the one sleeping nights at Westminster and has for these past eighteen months. I should think,' she said sarcastically, 'that Richard would be Tudor's greatest concern.'

'All in good time.' Bray moved to the window, reassured himself that the street traffic below was normal.

Elizabeth couldn't resist. 'Seeing shadows, Master Bray?' she mocked, saw her dart hit home.

'You surprise me, Madame,' he said icily. 'For a woman so well informed about the workings of Tudor's inner circle, you seem woefully ignorant of what is taking place right here in Westminster under your nose.'

'Such as?'

'It's been how many months since your daughter came back to court. . . . Nine? Ten? Not being there yourself, perhaps you are not fully aware how much favour Gloucester has shown the girl. I understand that on New Year's Day she did even appear at a court fête in a gown of the same cloth as that worn by the Queen. But perhaps you did not know? . . .'

'White damask cloth of gold threaded through with silver and turquoise,' Elizabeth said impatiently. 'What of it?'

'It caused talk, Madame, was hardly appropriate for a girl now no more than a king's bastard. People are beginning to notice how close they are, Gloucester and your daughter, how often in each other's company.'

'So? Why should that occasion comment? There's more between them than blood, after all.' Elizabeth's mouth thinned. 'They do,' she said, 'share a patron saint, St Edward of York.'

She at once regretted it, regretted revealing her bitterness so nakedly before an enemy like Bray.

'You still do not see, do you? If I must spell it out for you, Madame, it is two months now that Gloucester's been forbidden his wife's bed. That is a long time for a man to sleep alone, especially a man as young as Gloucester, and your daughter. . . .' He shrugged. 'None would deny that she's a beautiful girl.'

Elizabeth's mouth fell open. 'God in Heaven!'

Her shock was genuine; Bray saw that, said in surprise, 'So you truly did not know? I just assumed you were either indifferent or approving; it seemed so obvious, after all. Whatever the girl wants, he gives her, and as for her . . . well, hers is an easy face to read, Madame.'

Elizabeth found her voice. 'You must be mad! She's Richard's niece, not his harlot.'

'And blood will tell, will it not? She is Edward of York's daughter, after all, grew up at a court no better than a cesspool, watched her father flaunt his sluts and his vices like badges of honour. As for Gloucester, is a man who'd put his own nephews to death likely to balk at incest?'

Elizabeth stared at him with loathing. 'What a pious hypocrite you are! No one has ever pretended my husband was a saint; we leave that to the House of Lancaster, to those of you who'd have us believe that because Harry of Lancaster was simple in the head and impotent in the bargain, such failings do somehow make him a candidate for canonization. But Ned loved his daughters, and none can say otherwise. As for Richard, you know damned well that I'd never have given my daughters over into his keeping if the blood of my sons were on his hands. So do not throw that in my face; that cock will not fight.'

'Madame, I doubt that there's anything you would not do if it did serve your interests,' Bray said scathingly, 'and that does include coming to terms with your children's murderer.'

'Oh, enough! Save the lies and moral indignation for the gullible and the naïve, for those who do not know the truth. You do not believe Richard murdered my sons, you never did. . . . You are the man, after all, who told Morton that Richard would have to have been an utter idiot to have them secretly put to death, to arrange a—how did you put it—a "mysterious midnight disappearance". So do not talk to me of coming to terms with a child-murderer, because you knew Buckingham was guilty, God damn you, but you knew, and yet you still embraced him as your ally, as. . . .' She stopped suddenly for Bray was gaping at her, eyes widening with superstitious unease.

'"A mysterious midnight disappearance,"' he echoed incredulous. 'How in Holy Christ could you know I said that?'

Elizabeth spared a brief blessing for her sister Katherine. 'Second sight,' she jeered, began to fasten her cloak with fingers made clumsy by rage. Bray still looked stunned; she walked toward the door, then turned back to face him.

'I do not care what mud you use to smear Richard with. Say what you will about him but I'll not have my daughter dragged into that mud, too. Is that clear? Little wonder Tudor is looking elsewhere for a wife, with the garbage you've been feeding him, but it's to stop as of now. Discredit Richard however you can but not at my daughter's expense. I'll not have her name sullied. Do you understand?'

Bray's face had hardened. 'You seem to have forgotten that you're no longer in a position to give commands . . . Lady Grey. So do not tell me what you will or will not "have", not when there be nothing you can do about it.'

'You think not?' Elizabeth said, and there was something in the glittering green eyes that gave Bray pause. 'And what if I do go to Richard, tell him of these slanders being spread about him and Bess?'

Bray paled. 'You would not dare!'

'No? Do you truly think I could not find a way to warn Richard without implicating myself? That would be a fool's wager, I assure you. I assure you, too, that it would give me great pleasure to tell Richard of the rumours you are putting about. Rumours which not only compromise him and besmirch his niece's honour but which, if not stopped, might reach the ears of his dying wife. Need I tell you what he would do? No, I see that I do not. So you think on that, Master Bray. You think on that long and hard, because I do not bluff and I warn but once.'

Coming out into the street, Elizabeth was dismayed to see an early winter dusk settling over the city. Much to her relief a member of the Watch was passing by, gallantly agreed to escort her back to St Paul's. The man made a few polite attempts at conversation but soon gave up, attributing Elizabeth's absent-minded responses to the distraction of the newly bereaved.

Elizabeth had already forgotten her benefactor; Reginald Bray occupied her brain to the exclusion of all else. As satisfying as it had been to see fear upon Bray's face, she knew her threat to be an empty one. Even if she'd succeeded in silencing Bray, the damage had already been done; she was enough of a realist to know that. He'd already planted the seeds and nothing took root faster than rumour. People did not have to believe it; it was enough that they'd pass it on.

Now that her first surge of rage was receding, Elizabeth wondered how she could have been so taken by surprise. What was more common, after all, than sexual slander? It was as much a weapon of politics as the cannon was a weapon of warfare. She had only to think of all that had been said about Ned during his lifetime; nor had his family been spared. Those hoping to prevent Margaret's marriage to Charles of Burgundy had so slurred her name in the weeks before the wedding that many of her Burgundian subjects remained convinced to this day that she'd come to her marriage bed a jaded wanton, and when, as dowager Duchess of Burgundy, she sought to keep the French king from swallowing up her stepdaughter's domains, Louis had spread the story that she'd taken the Bishop of Cambrais as a lover and borne him a bastard child. Nor was the House of York the only target for such innuendo and aspersions. Gossip had Charles of Burgundy to be guilty of the vice of Sodom, while long-ago Yorkist slander challenged the paternity of Marguerite d'Anjou's son.

Elizabeth mouthed an oath so unlikely to be on the lips of a grieving widow that her escort did a double-take, decided his ears had deceived him. Elizabeth ignored him. She'd too often been the victim of such slanders herself not to have developed a bitter resentment, a deep-rooted contempt for her credulous countrymen who took gossip as gospel, hearsay as truth on high. No, she should have expected something like this. A young king with an ailing wife and a beautiful niece; the ingredients were already there for scandal, waiting only to be seized upon by the unscrupulous, by men like Bray, who cared only about discrediting Richard, cared not at all if Bess should be hurt in the process.

Elizabeth felt now a new anger, directed against Bess and Richard, for being so careless of gossip, for not realizing that it was no less important to avoid the appearance of impropriety than it was the impropriety itself. How like the two of them to be so blind, she thought in disgust, and then she came to a sudden halt, startled into immobility.

Could it be there was any truth to these rumours Bray was spreading? Not all gossip was totally unfounded, after all. If Edouard of Lancaster had truly been a son of Harry's loins, that should rank as no less a miracle than that of the fishes and loaves. And like as not, there was some truth, too, to those rumours about Charles of Burgundy's taste for boys. What, then, of Richard and Bess? She'd told Bray there was more between them than blood; had she spoken greater truth than she'd realized?

Yes, they were uncle and niece, but sexual passions sometimes burned all the more intensely for being forbidden. Didn't Scriptures say as much, say something about stolen waters being all the sweeter? Nor was incest all that uncommon. The first Plantagenet king had been accused of taking as his mistress the young girl betrothed to his own son. Whilst Queen of France, Eleanor of Aquitaine was said to have had a love affair with a young uncle and, just a few years past, the French court had been scandalized when a nobleman named d'Armagnac contracted an incestuous marriage with his own sister.

Elizabeth frowned; it was difficult to be objective about a man she hated as much as she hated Richard. He had never made any secret of his fondness for Bess, and Bray was right: Bess was beautiful. But was that enough? Ned. . . . Ned had been a rakehell hot to lay with anything in skirts but Richard had a reputation for being rather straitlaced in carnal matters, and if he'd strayed from Anne Neville's bed in some twelve years of marriage he'd been remarkably discreet about it. Elizabeth could not say with certainty now that he'd not have conceived an incestuous passion for his niece but to take Bess to his bed, to flaunt her as his concubine before his dying wife, a woman to whom he'd always seemed devoted . . . well, it might not be impossible, but it did seem wildly out of character.

What, then, of Bess? Her vulnerabilities were more readily apparent. She was not yet nineteen, after all, still grieving for the father she'd adored beyond reason. Could she have sought in Ned's brother the father she'd lost, only to find her emotions complicated by her first sexual yearnings? Richard was only thirty-two, dangerously young for an uncle, and he'd been very kind to Bess since her return to court. Had her emotional dependence developed into something more?

Elizabeth's frown deepened. Yes, there was a certain plausibility about it. But she did not believe it. Bess was no actress, was as transparent as springwater. When she came home to Waltham to visit her little sisters, she talked often and easily of Anne, of her many kindnesses, her grief over the loss of her son, her illness. Could Bess be so natural, so sympathetic if she were involved in a relationship both adulterous and incestuous? Could she have accepted Anne's generous offer, let Anne's dressmaker make her a Christmas gown from Anne's own cloth of gold, if all the while she was sleeping with Anne's husband? Elizabeth knew the answer to that for she knew her daughter. Bess simply was not capable of duplicity like that, could not be betraying a dying woman with so little compunction. No, if she and Richard were guilty of anything, it was of stupidity, of playing into the hands of men like Bray.

Elizabeth toyed briefly now with the idea of carrying through with her threat, of going to Richard with what Bray had told her. The temptation was considerable. Once he was forewarned, Richard would be better able to guard Bess against gossip and, by alerting him to the danger, she'd be putting him in her debt. Best of all, she'd get to see Bray die a traitor's death, in prolonged agony. But if she betrayed Bray to Richard, she was forfeiting all chance to make Bess a queen. She could not do that, could not surrender that last vestige of hope, however unlikely or farfetched, that Tudor might one day win England's crown, claim Bess as his consort. Moreover, how could she sever all ties with Tudor as long as Tom was being held at the French court as surety for her continued cooperation?

By the time she reached St Paul's, she'd made her decision. She'd go at once to Westminster, go to her daughter. Bess must be warned how easily tongues could be set to wagging, must be made to see that the scales were weighted unfairly in this life, with innocence counting for little and appearance for all.

Leaving one of her servants with their horses, Elizabeth had her other attendant engage a boatman to take them upriver to Westminster. It was quite dark by the time they docked at the King's Wharf. The inner-palace bailey was lit with scores of torches, thronged with expectant people. Elizabeth found herself looking out upon a sea of spectators and she cursed herself for a fool, for having forgotten that this was Epiphany.

How often she and Ned had marked this, the end of the Christmas festivities, in high style, with court fêtes and masques and feasting. So, too, had Richard and Anne celebrated this Twelfth Night, with a lavish banquet in the great hall of Westminster. Elizabeth knew from Bess and Cecily that Anne had defied her doctors, stubbornly insisted upon presiding with Richard over the Christmas revels. She gathered from the conversation swirling around her that Richard and Anne were about to make an appearance before the crowds waiting so patiently for a glimpse of their sovereigns.

Elizabeth found herself caught up in the crowd, carried along against her will as the people jockeyed for position. Blinded by torch-fire, Elizabeth's eyes were drawn, mothlike, to the gleaming gold of Richard's crown. A pain that was physical lodged just under her ribs, a hollow hurtful yearning for what had been hers and was now irretrievably lost, all because Ned had scrupled to murder a priest.

Beside Elizabeth, a matronly woman clicked her tongue against her teeth in sympathy, said, 'Oh, the poor lamb!' Elizabeth tore her gaze away from Richard, looked for the first time at Anne Neville and drew a sharp involuntary breath.

She'd known for weeks that Anne's illness was thought to be mortal, but it was a shock, nonetheless, to see coming death so clearly etched in the younger woman's face—the hollowed cheek-bones, thrust into sudden sharp prominence, stained with deceptive false colour, eyes sunken back, feverishly bright, compelling. The signs were unmistakable to Elizabeth, for she'd had personal experience of consumption, had watched a young cousin of her first husband die of it.

Consumption came in many guises, was also known as phthisis, hectic fever, the White Plague, but Elizabeth thought wasting fever was the most apt, best described the fate of those stricken. Sometimes there was considerable pain, but for others, there was not. Her young cousin-by-marriage had been one of the latter, had suffered comparatively little pain even to the last, merely growing relentlessly weaker, remaining in surprisingly cheerful spirits even on his deathbed, deluding himself with hopes of recovery long after all others knew he was doomed, a phenom-enon peculiar to consumptives, which the doctors could only attribute to the relative absence of pain. There were, Elizabeth thought, worse ways to die—plague, leprosy, putrid throat—but consumption was still one of the most feared of all ailments for it almost always proved fatal.

Looking at Anne now, Elizabeth thought it would be a miracle if Anne did live through Lent and she was glad, glad that Richard was to lose the wife he loved, to have to watch helplessly as her life ebbed away. Let him see what joy he'd take then in that jewelled crown, the crown that should have been her son's.

Like Richard, Anne, too, wore her crown; her head was tilted back with the weight of it, held upright by sheer stubborn force of will. She faltered suddenly and a murmur swept the crowd. Richard turned around, reached Anne just as she began to cough.

'The poor lamb,' Elizabeth's neighbour repeated; others around

Elizabeth took up the refrain, but for all their sympathy, there was an unwholesome, if very human excitement, too, in this scene being enacted before them, a passion play brought to life in the glare of torchlight, with the power to invoke pity, wonderment, speculation about retribution and redemption and the mysterious workings of the Almighty.

Anne's coughing spasm had subsided, but she clung to Richard as if it had sapped her remaining strength, leaned so heavily on his arm that his support seemed to be all that was keeping her on her feet. They seemed oblivious of all but each other and a hush fell upon the crowd, caught up in this moment of unsparing intimacy being played out before hundreds of fascinated witnesses. Richard tilted Anne's face up, put his lips to her forehead; when she turned her face away, into the velvet of his mantle, he stroked the chestnut hair cascading down her back in the unbound style reserved for virgin brides and queens.

An aging man in a long dark robe detached himself from the royal entourage; Elizabeth recognized Dr Hobbys. People now realized that Richard meant to take Anne back into the palace and murmurs of disappointment began to surface; many had been waiting in the cold for hours to watch the pageantry, the procession to the abbey. But Anne was shaking her head, gesturing about her at the thronged bailey, winning for herself no small measure of admiring approval when the people realized she was arguing for continuing with the procession as planned. A tense threeway argument ensued between Richard, Anne, and Hobbys, and at last a compromise was reached, Richard agreeing to go on to the Abbey if Dr Hobbys would escort Anne back into the palace.

Richard stood watching as his wife moved away from him, retracing her path with the slow measured steps of one drawing upon rapidly diminishing reserves, expending energy that could no longer be replaced. If Richard was aware of the curious, sympathetic eyes riveted upon him, he gave no indication of it;

surrounded by people, he seemed strangely alone and there was on his face a look of utter desolation.

Once more quiet had descended over the crowd, a subdued silence that had in it as much of discomfort as it did of pity; it was as if the man before them suddenly seemed all too real, a flesh-and-blood being whose pain lay exposed for all to see, an anguish of spirit and soul too naked to deny, too easy to identify with. The glittering torchlit crown, the courtiers cloaked in silver fox and sable, the trumpeters and Princes of the Church, and flaming candles held aloft in gilded holders, all the magnificence and pageantry of royalty. . . . It was that which they wanted of their kings, needed that splendour to eclipse the drabness, the harsh rigours of their own lives. If they no longer demanded, as a more primitive age had done, that their kings be gods, neither did they want to see in their sovereigns human frailties too closely akin to their own. People stirred uneasily now, uncertain, finding themselves actors in a play they'd come only to watch.

It was Bess who broke the spell. With Anne's departure had gone, too, her ladies. But Bess had glanced back over her shoulder, came swiftly back now to Richard's side. She spoke softly, urgently, her eyes never leaving his face, and after a long pause, Richard nodded, turned and gave the signal for the procession to proceed. Flanked once again by bishops and lords of his court, he moved across the bailey. Bess waited a moment or so longer, turned to follow after Anne.

As Richard reached the gateway that was the king's private entrance into the abbey precincts, the crowd surged forward, sought to follow. Elizabeth was rudely jostled, elbows digging into her ribs, feet trampling upon the trailing hem of her skirt. She scarcely noticed, accepted the shoving like one sleepwalking, and when her servant at last managed to extricate her from the crush of bodies, she stared at him blankly, without recognition, for the idea that had come to her was so stupendous, so astounding that all else had been blotted from her brain.

Bray had been right; Bess did have a face easy to read. And as she stood beside Richard in the torchlit courtyard, her only thought to give him comfort, it had been there for all to see. So she does love him, Elizabeth thought in wonderment. She loves him but she does not know it, has not admitted it even to herself. She's either unwilling or unable to deal with her feelings and so she denies them, not realizing she does give herself away every time their eyes meet. The little fool, God help her. But it was in that moment, swept by sudden pity for the daughter so unlike herself, this innocent infuriating child of hers, that it all came together for Elizabeth, a plan dazzling in its simplicity, awesome in its implications.

Warwick's daughter was dying; none who looked upon her tonight could deny that. And when she died, Richard would find himself under unrelenting, irresistible pressure to wed again, to begat a son and heir. They'd give him no time to grieve, would push a foreign bride into his bed with indecent haste, just as they'd done with the second King Richard. A king owed his countrymen heirs of his body; Richard would have no choice. He'd need a queen, need a healthy young woman who could give England sons. Why could that queen not be Bess?

Not an illicit incestuous liaison, a relationship that could only give Bess grief, besmirch her name and shred her conscience. A legitimate honourable marriage, recognized by the Sacraments of the Church, a marriage that would make her a queen.

Elizabeth tried now to dampen her rising excitement, to consider this astonishing possibility dispassionately, to examine it for flaws. They'd need a papal dispensation, of course. But popes were astute practitioners of the art of power politics; the petition of a reigning king was not likely to be denied. But would the English people approve such a marriage? The blood bond was closer than most Englishmen were accustomed to accept; such marriages were far more common on the Continent. Yet if the Pope did sanction it. . . . There were many who felt Ned's sons had been cheated out of their just inheritance; even amongst those who believed implicitly in Richard's right, there was considerable sympathy for the children made to suffer for their father's forgotten sin. What better way to heal the wounds of Richard's accession than to crown his brother's daughter?

But what of the plight-troth? How get around that? Richard could not repeal the Act of Titulus Regius without impeaching his own right to the throne and that much of a fool he was not. Blessed Mother Mary, but there must be a way, must be. . . . What of the Beauforts? Jesú, yes! That high-and-mighty House had begun in bastardy, the issue of the Duke of Lancaster and the sister-in-law of the poet Chaucer. Yet the children of that illicit liaison had been declared legitimate by the king, the stain of illegitimacy expunged by parliamentary act. Could not the same be done for Bess?

Would Richard ever consent, though? Could he be persuaded to make such a marriage? If Ned had made an unlikely marriage from lust, could not Richard be induced to do the same from guilt? He had to have an unease of conscience; whether he'd wished it or not, his brother's sons had died because he'd taken the crown. To lose his own son so soon thereafter and now his wife. . . . What man would not see that as God's judgment? And what better act of expiation than to make Bess England's Queen? Elizabeth's mouth softened, curved in a smile of cynical certainty. Why should he not agree? How often was a man given the chance to find atonement in the bed of a beautiful girl?

She must not delude herself, though. The odds against such a marriage ever coming to pass were disheartening at best. So many ifs, so much contingent upon chance, upon factors beyond her control. But when had she ever shrank from risk? She'd lived a gamble her whole life long. Who would ever have believed, after all, that the widow of an obscure Lancastrian knight could have induced the King of England to offer marriage? But she had, a twenty-seven-year-old widow with two children, she'd held out for a crown, as stunned as anyone by her success, not realizing that Ned took marriage no more seriously than he did anything in this life, including himself.

No, she'd not think on that, not think on how he'd betrayed her, or how she missed him even now, a mocking ghost haunting her sleep these twenty-one months past, the man who'd given her all she'd ever wanted only to fail her at the very last. Think rather about Bess, about this, her last chance. Edward and Dickon were dead; she could do nothing for them. But if she could see Bess crowned as Queen of England, if she could do that . . .

'Madame?' Her servant cleared his throat hesitantly. 'Madame, is it your wish that I escort you to your daughter's chamber?'

Elizabeth shook her head. 'No,' she said. 'I want you to take me home, back to Waltham.' She needed time, time to think.

23

Windsor

February 1485

Anne had always preferred Windsor to Westminster and on January 12th Richard took the court to the eleventh-century castle some twenty miles west of London. He'd hoped against hope that Anne might somehow benefit from the change but, as the month dwindled away, so, too, did her waning strength. Shortly before Candlemas, she took to her bed and Richard could no longer deny the truth, that she would not live to see another spring.

The first day of February dawned raw and blustery. Snow began to fall shortly before dusk, was still falling hours later. A biting wind was sweeping across the lower bailey; Richard scarcely noticed. Nor did he pay heed to the startled looks of the few people he encountered, taken aback to come suddenly face-to-face with the king, accompanied only by a large silver-grey alaunt.

As was his custom now, Richard had gone at dark to his wife's bedchamber; his evening hours were reserved for Anne and Anne alone. Sometimes they talked but there was less and less to be said that would not give the lie to their mutual pretence. Most nights they played chess or cards but tonight Richard soon saw that Anne's attention was wandering from the chessboard. Making excuses to cut the game short, he rose to go and saw in her hollowed dark eyes an unmistakable relief.

Although it did little to ease the hurt, Richard thought he understood. All Anne could do for him now was to try to minimize her discomfort, to spare him the fear, the despair that must torment her solitary hours as she sought to come to terms with the disease cheating her of so much, with a mortality to be measured in weeks. Richard felt he had no choice but to honour her wishes, to make death a forbidden topic between them, but in truth he could not have handled it any other way, could not bear to abandon all hope, even a hope he knew to be false.

And so they found themselves locked into a conspiracy of silence, but until tonight Richard had not understood how high the price would be, that in denying the truth they were condemning themselves to suffering isolated and alone. The irony bore down upon him with devastating impact. He wanted above all else to give Anne comfort and yet he was the very one who could not, for with him she must strain to hide the reality of her illness, to live her last days as a lie. Standing there by her bed, it had suddenly seemed to Richard as if he were seeing her from a distance, a distance that widened between them with each breath she drew, breaths that were laboured, finite. Already she was slipping away from him, caught up in emotions he could not share, listening to that which he could not hear—the silent relentless ticking away of time, her time. She was dying and he was not, and that was a barrier not even love could breach.

For more than an hour he'd been walking aimlessly but it was only now, as the Chapel of St George loomed ahead through the wind-swirled snow, that Richard realized where his footsteps had instinctively been leading him. Begun more than ten years ago by his brother Edward, the chapel was as yet unfinished; at the time of Edward's death, only the choir and aisles had been roofed. But it was a magnificent building, even in its present state, and Richard hoped that in time he'd be able to carry out his brother's architectural ambitions, to make of St George's Chapel a living, lasting monument to Edward's memory.

Entering the south door of the nave, he found himself pausing before the door of Will Hasting's chapel. Richard hesitated and then stepped inside. He stood in silence for a moment, staring down at a large grave slab. Will Hastings's resting place. It was adorned with an incongruous remembrance—Richard's torch played upon glossy dark-green leaves, interspersed with berries as bright as blood. It was, he saw, a cluster of English holly and he wondered who had chosen to remember Will in this fashion, with a woodland tribute that somehow seemed more pagan than Christian, but queerly touching, withal.

He didn't linger in Will's chapel. Passing through the screen set up to shield the east end of his brother's tomb, he stood at last before Edward's grave site. A priest had apparently been careless, for a torch still burned near the door leading up to Edward's chapel. Richard approached the altar, knelt and murmured, 'In Nomine Patris et Filii et Spiritus Sancti.'

The prayer came from memory, without conscious thought. But after that, he was at a loss for words. If the Almighty no longer heard his prayers, how could Ned? He was surrounded by silence, the implacable accusing silence of the dead.

Richard came stiffly to his feet. Fool, what did he expect? Absolution from a dead man? A mistake to come here, a grievous mistake. He found himself staring at the gilded iron gates that stretched across the aisle to the west of his brother's tomb. On the gates were hung Edward's cap of maintenance, his sword, his armour and a surcoat of crimson velvet, embroidered with pearl and gold, interwoven with rubies.

Against his will, Richard reached out, let his fingers brush this garment that had been his brother's, and in that moment it was almost as if the loss were being felt for the first time, the stunned realization that Ned was truly dead, his laughter forever stilled, flesh and blood and brain no more than memory, and memories . . . memories were not to be trusted. They distorted, took on the colouration of love or grief or guilt, projected the past through a glass, darkly, and sometimes, sometimes too bright to behold . . . or to bear.

'Ah, Ned,' he whispered, 'how came we to this?'

His words seemed to hang in the air and then he heard a sound behind him, quickly stilled, and he realized that he wasn't alone. He saw now what he'd not noticed before, that the stairwell doorway was ajar and, caught up in a sudden unreasoning rage, he strode over, jerked the door all the way open, and found himself looking into frightened blue eyes.

Richard's shock was such that he stood frozen, doubting the evidence of his own senses, for Jane Shore was the last person he'd have expected to see, a ghost conjured up without warning from a time in his life he wanted only to forget.

'What are you doing here?' he demanded, saw her flinch away from the anger in his voice, his face.

'I loved him, too, Your Grace,' she pleaded, stepping out of the shadows of the stairwell. Richard stared. Even a long woollen cloak could not conceal her condition; her once slender body was now heavily swollen.

'You're with child?' he said, startled, and she nodded shyly.

She was, he now saw, clutching a garland of holly. He hesitated and then reached out, put his hand on her arm. 'I think I'd best escort you across the bailey. The ground is icy in spots; you might slip, hurt your baby.'

Jane showed no surprise at the offer, giving him a grateful smile. 'Your Grace . . . there is something I would say to you, something I've wanted to say for months. Please . . . I must. I owe you so much, you see.' Bringing her hand up, she stroked her swelling belly. 'This baby . . . I cannot tell you how much it means to me, to be with child. I wanted so much to bear your brother's baby. Twice my womb quickened with his seed; twice I miscarried. I guess . . . guess God thought my sins were too great. I'd long since given up all hope of motherhood and now . . . well, God willing, the babe be due at Eastertide. But if you had not given Tom leave to wed me. . . .' She shook her head, said wonderingly, 'I could not believe it, told him he was a fool even to ask. But you said yes; with every reason to deny the marriage, you gave your consent.'

She held out to Richard the holly garland in unspoken entreaty, watched as he walked over, laid it upon the black marble of his brother's tomb. So much she still wanted to say to him; how sorry she was that his little boy had died, that his wife was so ill, that meanspirited men did spread ugly stories about the fate of Ned's sons.

'I shall pray for your queen,' she said softly, and in that instant before Richard looked away, she saw tears fill his eyes.

Bess was lying upon the bed in the bedchamber she shared with Cecily whenever they were at their mother's manor house in Waltham. Tears pricked her eyes but she blinked them back angrily. It's stupid, after all, to cry over a mere horse. But Isolda was special, a fine-boned chestnut with a gait as smooth as silk, a gift from Dickon and Anne on her nineteenth birthday. It just was not fair. Ten days she'd had the mare, ten brief days. How quickly all could change, a careless misstep suddenly transforming a sleek beautiful animal into a panicked creature hobbling pitifully on three legs. Bess felt a sob rising in her throat, was unable to choke it back in time.

Her tears for Isolda were not long in giving way to something else entirely. She no longer fought it, gave in to her grief and wept bitterly, wept until the pillows were sodden and her eyes swollen to slits. And still the tears came, for her father, her brothers, Anne, for pain she'd lived with too long, for confused yearnings she dared not examine too closely, regrets that had nothing at all to do with a lamed mare.

'Bess?'

She stiffened defensively. Oh, God, that mama had to walk in now of all times! Mama, who could never understand. She bit her lip, bracing herself for some stinging sarcasm, waiting for her mother to mock her tears.

The bed creaked as Elizabeth sat down beside her. 'Would you like some compresses for your head?' she asked, and Bess rolled over, stared up at her mother with suspicious eyes. To her confusion, she saw only concern upon Elizabeth's face, saw sympathy that seemed quite sincere.

'I heard your sobs in the hall,' Elizabeth said, 'feared you'd make yourself sick. If I send for hot mulled wine, do you think you could drink some?'

This unexpected kindness unstrung Bess as nothing else could have done. 'Oh, mama,' she sobbed, 'I'm so unhappy, as unhappy as I've ever been in all my life. . . .'

'I know, Bess, I know,' Elizabeth murmured, and Bess wondered dazedly if she were dreaming, if this tender stranger could truly be her mother. She felt Elizabeth's hand on her hair. . . . When had mama ever given caresses? A need never before acknowledged surged to the surface; she buried her face in her mother's lap and wept.

Elizabeth stared down at her daughter's bright head, on her face uncertainty and something almost like dismay. She'd not expected this, had not expected Bess to respond to her overtures like one starved for love, a mother's love. Could it, she thought in sudden confusion, have been as easy as this? Were her daughters waiting only for her to reach out, to show she cared? But of course she cared. How could they not know that? No, they were the ones who'd shut her out, chosen to give their love only to Ned. If there was fault to be found, it lay with them. Not with her.

She continued to stroke her daughter's hair, waited for Bess's sobs to subside.

'Do you want to talk about it, Bess?'

Bess shook her head violently.

'It's Anne, is it not? Having to watch her die. . . .' Elizabeth hesitated, added with deliberation, 'Having to watch what it's doing to Richard.'

Bess held her breath, waiting for the worst. When it didn't come, she raised her head, eyed her mother with dubious surprise.

'You're right, mama, I do weep for Anne . . . and for Dickon, too.' This last with a hint of defiance. 'Is that not your cue? Do you not want to tell me now that God is punishing them for Dickon's many sins? That they deserve no better?'

'I admit I have no liking for Anne Neville,' Elizabeth said calmly. 'Why should I? Her father murdered mine . . . your grandfather, Bess. But I'm still capable, I hope, of feeling pity for a dying woman. Even—however much it may surprise you—for Richard. Whatever our differences, I've never denied that he loves his wife. It must be very difficult for him. . . .' Her voice trailed off suggestively and Bess picked up on it at once, nodded vigorous agreement.

'Oh, mama. . . . mama, it's so awful for him and it just goes on and on. That week papa was dying . . . when I think how it would've been had he lingered for months. I . . . I'd have gone mad, I know I would. How Dickon can stand it, seeing her grow weaker day by day. . . .'

'We all do fear that,' Elizabeth said softly, 'a long drawn-out death that does only prolong our suffering, that of our loved ones. When there be no hope, it's a mercy if death comes quickly.'

Bess nodded 'Oh, mama, you're right. It would be better for Anne to die, it would. She does not deserve this, never hurt anyone. . . .'

'Does she suffer greatly?'

'No, thank God. At least she's been spared that. There is discomfort . . . her cough, the sweating, diarrhoea. But not that much pain. Her strength just keeps ebbing away, like a candle flame burning down to the wick.' Bess wiped her eyes with the edge of the sheet, said huskily, 'I overheard Doctor Hobbys talking one day with the doctor who'd treated Anne's sister Isabel; he said she'd haemorrhaged again and again in her last days, that she choked to death on her own blood. . . .' A shudder passed through her body. 'I . . . I do not think Dickon could ever endure that, mama. If Anne suffered pain like that, I think Dickon would. . . .' She swallowed convulsively, sought to keep her voice steady, with limited success.

'She's so thin and drawn now; when we bathe her, I swear you can see every bone in her body, and lying there in that big bed, she looks for all the world like a lost frightened child. But she has more courage than I would, mama, much more. She tries so hard to keep the worst of her illness from Dickon, tries to spare him all she can. To look at her, you'd never think she had that strength of will. . . .'

'Does he know, Bess, that there be no hope?'

'Yes, mama, he knows.' Tears welled up again in Bess's eyes. 'At first he'd come in the evenings and play chess with Anne. But she's too weak now, and most nights he brings books and reads to her until she falls asleep. He sits with her for hours sometimes, just watching her while she sleeps, and there's so much pain in his face that I . . . I feel as if it were my own, mama.'

Elizabeth said nothing but she reached out, squeezed her

daughter's hand, and Bess gave her a look of grateful wonderment.

'Mama . . . why could we not talk like this before?'

'I do not know, Bess,' Elizabeth said slowly, surprised to find that she spoke no less than the truth. She was quiet for several moments, twisting her wedding ring with nervous fingers. So important to choose just the right words, such a delicate line to walk, with no margin for error.

'I never thought I'd say this, in truth I did not, but after listening to you, Bess, I find myself feeling sorriest of all for Richard. Anne . . . well, she'll soon be at peace, beyond earthly pain. But for him, the worst may be yet to come. It always is hard to lose a loved one, but for a king, a king without a son and heir. . . .' Elizabeth paused significantly, saw Bess frown.

'You mean . . . that he'll be totally alone?'

'No, dearest. I mean that they'll not give him time to grieve for Anne. No sooner will she be buried than they'll be pressuring him to wed again. The council, parliament, the Church . . . from all sides he'll hear but one refrain, that he must take another wife, a wife who can give him the sons Anne could not.'

'Oh, mama, no! He'd not want that, not want to wed again, I know he would not. At least, not for a long time.'

'I'm sure you're right but what you do not see, Bess, is that he'll have no choice. There are duties inherent in kingship, one of them being to provide a stable succession, a son. They'll push him into it, into an alliance with a foreign princess, some woman he's never laid eyes upon, a woman like as not who'd not even speak English and homely in the bargain.' Elizabeth smiled thinly. 'You, my dearest, were that rarity, a truly beautiful princess, a creature as uncommon as the unicorn. Most of them are as simple as sheep and as plain as homespun. No, I fear Richard's future holds little happiness for him. He's not a man, after all, to seek consolation outside the marriage bed.'

Bess was quiet, unnaturally so. Elizabeth was content to wait.

'Mama. . . . I know Dickon, know how miserable he'd be in such a marriage. To wed a woman he'd never even seen, a woman foreign to the ways of England. . . . He deserves better than that, deserves a woman who'd love him like Anne, a woman who could make him happy. . . .'

'I agree,' Elizabeth said quickly, 'but do you not realize, dearest, that you've just described yourself?'

Bess's head jerked up. 'Me? Mama, he's my uncle!'

'And Anne is his cousin, once removed. Ah, Bess, blood is no impediment to marriage; have you never heard of papal dispensations?'

'Of course, but. . . .'

'Wait, Bess, hear me out. I realize the idea may take getting used to, but it has much to recommend it. What am I talking about, after all? About a marriage that would make you Queen, that would restore your sisters to their rightful rank. You have it in your power to do that for them, Bess, you and you alone.'

'But the plight-troth, mama, it. . . .'

'Could be dealt with, Bess, trust me. The Beauforts, too, were illegitimate once; why could parliament not pass a similar act for you?'

'Mama, stop! Do not talk like this. It . . . it is wrong.'

'Why? Because of Anne? She's dying, Bess. You'd be taking from her nothing that was still hers, that was not already lost to her. Whatever you do or do not do, she's still going to die and Richard is still going to need a wife, a wife to give him the son and heir he must have. Those are facts, Bess, facts you cannot change. But you can turn them to your advantage, our advantage.' Elizabeth leaned forward, grasped Bess's hand between her own.

'You'd be a queen, dearest. Think what that would mean to you, to your sisters. You'd be able to. . . .'

But Bess was shaking her head stubbornly, almost desperately. 'No, mama, no! Please do not!'

'Why not?' Elizabeth was unrelenting. 'He's going to have to wed again, so why should it not be you? If the Pope sanctions the marriage, why then should you balk at it? Unless it is Richard you object to? Is that it, Bess? Do you find him unattractive as a husband, a lover? You'd not want to share his bed?' And she saw Bess crimson, saw tell-tale colour burn brightly into her daughter's cheeks.

'You could make him happy, Bess. You could ease his grieving, bring joy back into his life, give him sons. You could do that for him, dearest, could. . . .'

'Mama. . . . I do not know. I need time to think. I . . . I never thought of Dickon that way.' Bess flushed even deeper. 'I did not, I swear it!'

'I know you did not, dearest,' Elizabeth said smoothly. 'But such a marriage would solve so much, would it not? For you, for Richard, for us all. You'd be good for him, Bess, you know that. You've believed in him, trusted him. Why should he not prefer you to a stranger, to a dowdy pious foreigner with queer habits and. . . .'

But Bess was staring over her shoulder, staring at the door, and Elizabeth turned abruptly, saw Cecily standing motionless in the doorway.

Elizabeth recovered first. 'You did startle us, Cecily. Have you been there long?'

'Too long, mama.' Cecily came forward into the room, toward her sister. 'Bess, you must not listen to this, you must not! She's wrong, such a marriage could never be, never. . . .'

Bess jumped to her feet, filled with a sudden inexplicable sense of shame. 'I do not want to talk about it, Cecily. No, mama, not with you, either. I'm . . . I'm going out to the stables, going to check on my mare.' She snatched up her cloak, all but ran from the room.

Cecily took a tentative step after her, paused, turned back to face her mother. 'Oh, my God, mama, what have you done?'

Elizabeth's eyebrows arched upward. 'I should think it would be obvious. I'm trying to make your sister Queen of England.

And if you have a brain in your head, you'll do what you can to help me, to. . . .'

'Mama, do not! Dickon will never marry Bess. Surely you must know that?'

'I know nothing of the kind. Nor do you, Cecily. Now suppose you sit down and keep still while I explain. . . .'

'Mama, I heard, heard it all, about the papal dispensation, the Beauforts, all. And I tell you it could never be. The English people would not accept such a marriage; the blood ties be too close. And even if they would . . . even then, it couldn't be. Yes, the Beauforts were legitimized, but this is different, mama; can you not see that? To make Bess legitimate would make Edward and Dickon legitimate, too; it would be like a signed confession from Dickon that his nephews were dead. And even if there was some way to get around that, though how I cannot see, if Bess could be legitimized now, why could not the same have been done for Edward two years ago? For Dickon to marry Bess would be to admit his own right to the crown was flawed, false. He'd have nothing to gain by such a marriage and a great deal to lose. You are the one, mama, who keeps telling us that men always act in their own interest, remember? Well, how could it possibly be in Dickon's interest to wed a girl branded as a bastard by parliament, his own niece? How, mama?'

Elizabeth moved to the dressing table, picked up a mirror. 'I realize there would be difficulties to overcome, Cecily, a great many. But what you do not understand is that everything in this life is a gamble. However little chance there might be of bringing about such a marriage, there's no chance at all if we do not even try for it. Just think, Cecily, think of all we have to gain; does that not make it worth the risk?'

'And what of Bess, mama? What of all she has to lose?'

Elizabeth slid a pot of lip rouge toward her, applied it with a practised hand. She did not want to quarrel with her younger daughter, was too pleased by the way her conversation had gone with Bess to let anything irritate her, even Cecily's obstinate opposition.

'Your sister loves Richard,' she said coolly. 'Perhaps you did not realize that, dear.'

'Yes, mama, I knew,' Cecily said flatly, and Elizabeth turned, gave her daughter a surprised look.

'Indeed? Well then, surely you see that I'm trying to give her what she most wants, to make her Richard's Queen.'

'She did not want that, mama. Not until you put the idea into her head.'

'You think not? But then, you're very young yet. . . .'

'Mama, I know Bess, better than you. Yes, she was drawn to Dickon; I saw that months ago, and I understood. Dickon was the man closest to papa and in this past year she got them mixed up somehow in her head and heart. She had a need and Dickon was there to fill it. Then, too, he's had naught but grief this twelve-month past and Bess has ever been tenderhearted, easily stirred to sympathy. But she did not fully realize herself how she felt; I know she did not. And in time it would have passed, Dickon would've found a suitable husband for her and her feelings would've been forgotten, with no harm done. But now . . .

'God forgive you, but you've not only forced her to acknowledge to herself a forbidden attraction, you've told her that it is perfectly all right to feel that way! I heard what you were telling her, mama, that happy-ever-after ending you were spinning out for her. How could you be so cruel? How could you do this to Bess, give her hope when there be none?'

'Cecily, there is no point in discussing this further. You know nothing yet of that which takes place between men and women. People do not always act from logic, as you'll doubtlessly one day learn for yourself.'

'You're using her, mama.'

Elizabeth slammed the mirror down upon the table. Why that

accusation should sting so, she did not try to puzzle out, saying angrily, 'That's not true. I'm doing this for Bess.'

Cecily shook her head. 'No, you're not, mama, and we both know it.'

'Wait . . . where are you going?'

'I'm going to find Bess, to talk to her.'

'I do not think she'll want to hear what you have to say, Cecily.'

'I know. But I'm going to try, anyway.'

24

Westminster

March 1485

'Bess?'

Bess stiffened at sound of Richard's voice, turned to face him with something much like reluctance.

Richard looked toward his wife's bedchamber. 'Is Doctor Hobbys within?'

'No, he . . .' Bess swallowed. 'He had to insist that Anne's mother retire to her own chambers and he went with her to make sure she did as he bade. I think he wanted her to take a sleeping draught. She just cannot cope with . . . with. . . .' Her voice trailed off.

Richard nodded, was turning away when Bess reached out; her hand hovered over his arm, never quite making contact.

'What is it, Bess? You have something to say to me?'

'Dickon, I. . . .' For the first time her eyes met his. 'I've been praying for Anne,' she said. 'I have, truly I have.'

Richard was struck by the feverish intensity in her words, her manner. For some days now he'd been vaguely aware that something was greatly troubling Bess, but his own resources were too depleted to allow for more than a flicker of puzzled pity.

'I know you have, lass.' It was the best he could do. He had no comfort to offer Bess or Nan, his distraught mother-in-law, no comfort to offer anyone at all. The door to Anne's bedchamber was ajar; he could hear the hacking cough that now haunted him even in sleep.

Véronique opened the door wider for him. They came into each other's arms by unspoken accord, stood for a time in a wordless embrace, and then Richard crossed the chamber, leaned over his wife's bed.

'I'm here, beloved. Can I get you something . . . anything? Wine?'

'Yes . . . please,' Anne whispered, watched as he poured himself.

Sitting on the bed beside her, Richard put an arm around her shoulders, gently lifted her up so she could drink, held the cup to her lips until she was done. He could feel the mute disapproval of the doctors, no less censorious for being unspoken, utterly impossible to ignore, and he turned his head, said with frozen dangerous rage, 'You're dismissed, Doctor Bemesley. All of you. Leave us.'

'You should not blame the doctors, love,' Anne chided softly, as soon as they were alone. 'They do but fear, and rightly so, that you might become infected. . . .'

'Let's not talk of that now. Are you comfortable, Anne? Shall I prop your pillows up for you?'

Anne nodded, for the same reason she'd asked for wine, because she understood his need to do something for her, however trivial. Turning her head aside, she coughed into a crumpled handkerchief, let it drop inconspicuously to the floor. She knew the doctors had told Richard that phlegm had begun to come up flecked with blood but she did not want him to see the evidence with his own eyes. For herself, she felt only thankfulness that the blood-spitting was so mild; what had most terrified her about her illness was that she might haemorrhage, bleed her life away as her sister had done, and she now knew she was to be spared that much, at least.

'Poor Bella,' she said quietly. 'I've been thinking of her so often these past weeks. How dreadful it must have been for her, Richard. It is always harder to die if you've had little happiness in your life, much harder. You feel cheated. I never told you but I felt so guilty for the longest time after Bella's death, because she'd had so little joy and I . . . I had so much.'

Richard reached for her hand. 'The day I found you in that Aldgate inn, I promised I'd take care of you, and I thought . . . truly thought I could, Anne, thought I could keep you safe from all hurt, make it up to you for what your father and Lancaster. . . .'

'Hush,' she said, 'hush. You did, love, you did. All I've known of happiness has come from you, you and Ned, the son you gave me.'

She wished she could pull his head down to her breast, stroke his hair as if he were a child in need of comfort, as if he were Ned. But even if she could bring herself so to disregard her doctors' warnings, she hadn't the strength, needed it all to talk.

'My mother cannot accept it, Richard, my dying. She has too many regrets, too much she wishes she'd done differently. But you should have no such regrets, my love. Not for us. Never for us.'

'Anne. . . .' Richard was unable to say more than her name, brought her hand up to his mouth, held it against his cheek. The long nails that had been her greatest vanity were clipped short now, like a child's; she'd preferred that to having them curve inward in one of the inexplicable manifestations of her illness.

'I do not mind so much any more, Richard, truly. The anger . . . it's all gone now; even the fear. I'm so tired, love, so tired. . . . Sometimes I even think I'd welcome it, being at peace . . . and with Ned. I mind only leaving you, but I think I understand even that, think Ned does need me more. . . .'

Richard's head was bowed; she could no longer see his face, but she felt his tears on her hand. She tugged weakly at his sleeve, willing him to look up.

'Richard, listen, my love . . . please. I feel very close to God, in a way I never felt before, as if He's with me now . . . just like Ned. And I know—I truly do know—that the Almighty is not a jealous God at all but one of forgiveness. Does not Scriptures say the Lord is full of compassion and mercy, and saveth in time of affliction? My darling, if only I could help you to see that. . . . Richard, promise me you'll try to believe that, to believe in God's love, God's forgiveness.'

Richard nodded and Anne had to be content with that, sank back exhausted against the pillow. She wanted only to sleep, to drift down into oblivion; Ned came so often to her in dreams, waited for her. She struggled to stave off sleep a few minutes more, for Richard's sake, and then felt him lifting her up, brushing her hair back from her neck, and she opened her eyes, saw that he'd taken from his own throat the silver pilgrim cross he'd worn since boyhood. He fumbled with the catch and it took several tries before he could fasten it securely about her neck. It was tarnished, dulled with age, but warm against her skin, as if it still held heat drawn from his body.

Shortly before dawn on Wednesday, March 16th, Anne was given the last rites of the Roman Catholic Church. She died in mid-morning, with Richard and Véronique at her bedside. Church bells were still tolling throughout the city when a queer noon-time darkness began to settle over London and, as people watched in awe, the sun was slowly blotted out, blackness radiating outward haloed in light. To a superstitious age, a solar eclipse was seen as a sign from God, was seen by all as an ill omen and by many as proof that Richard had sinned against God in taking his nephew's throne; for why else, people argued, should the sun go dark on the day of his wife's death?

25

Westminster
March 1485

'How in Christ's Name can any fool believe Dickon would ever wed his own niece?' Rob Percy sounded incredulous. 'It'd be like proclaiming to all of Christendom that his claim to the crown was contrived. You'd think people would at least give him credit for enough common sense to look to his own interests. Even a simpleton could see that the girl could not be legitimized without her brothers being legitimized, too, and lest anyone forget, that would make young Edward King of England.'

No, Rob, Francis thought bleakly, it would not. But it would prove to all that Edward and his brother were dead, must be dead. He rubbed his fingers against aching temples, suddenly envying Rob, envying all of the men in this room who were not privy to the truth. Rob had stopped speaking and he roused himself to say wearily, 'Rob's right. For Dickon to make an incestuous marriage that would all but impeach his own right to the throne, he'd belong by rights in Bedlam, not Westminster.'

Dick Ratcliffe stirred, said, 'As farfetched as it may be, the tale's all over London, gets uglier with each tavern-telling. The steward of my household came to me privately the other day, told me his son had heard men in a Southwark alehouse laying wagers as to when the Lady Bess would show herself to be with child, and that on Friday last, the very day of Anne's funeral.'

'Can people truly believe such nonsense?' Jack de la Pole demanded in disbelief. 'Believe that Dickon would seduce his brother's own daughter as his wife lay dying? Or that Bess would play the whore with him and all the while attending Anne? God and all His angels, but the human mind is more befouled than the most stinking cesspool!'

'It matters little whether they believe it or not, lad,' John Howard said, sounding no less tired than Francis. 'Chances are that many do not. But it is a rumour few could resist passing on, not choice gossip of that sort, not when it involves the highborn and sins that be carnal. But the question before us is what mean we to do about it.'

'Surely there must be a way to spare Dickon this. Christ, it's been but twelve days since Anne died and only three since her funeral. We cannot go to him with this now . . . not now.'

Rob leaned across the table. 'What choice have we, Francis? God knows, trying to suppress gossip of this sort is like trying to put out a brushfire by pissing on it, but there are some measures Dickon can take to quiet the talk; sending the girl from court, for one. But if he does nothing at all, the gossip's like to get even nastier now that Anne . . . now that Dickon's free to wed again.'

'It already has.' Will Catesby, the only man present not one of Richard's intimates, had so far remained silent. 'It's been reliably reported to me that Tudor's agents are intimating that the Queen's dying was taking overlong, that her death might have been hastened by one of the Italian poisons.'

There was a hushed silence; even John Howard, a man not easily shocked, looked taken aback.

'I expect that will be too much for all but the most gullible to swallow,' Catesby continued composedly. 'All do know, of course, that the Queen's illness was mortal, and few people will see the advantage in murdering a woman already sure to die. But I thought you should be aware that such a slander has surfaced.'

'People invariably whisper about poison when one highborn is stricken, unless it be a batlefield death or the like.' John Scrope was brusque. 'I myself heard fools speculating about such in York after King Edward died, wondering if the French might be to blame. Let's keep to those rumours that are finding believers. As far as I can gather, the talk in alehouse and tavern is that the King is far too fond of his brother's pretty daughter, that he grieved not at his wife's death, and if there be no truth to these stories, then why, they ask knowingly, did God darken the sun as the poor Queen lay dying?' He spat into the floor rushes. 'Southerners have mush for brains, God's blessed truth, and these malcontent poxridden Londoners be the worst of the lot.'

'That accursed eclipse,' Francis said bitterly. 'Why of all days . . .?'

Catesby had been absentmindedly fidgeting with his dagger, sliding it up and down its sheath with a rasping sound that was beginning to grate upon the others present.

'There is no tactful way to put this,' he said, 'but it's been my experience that few rumours are cut from whole cloth. Ere we go to the king with these admittedly lurid tales, ought not we to be sure that . . . well, that there be no truth to them?'

The temperature in the room plunged to zero in the span of seconds. Only John Howard and John Scrope, older men both, seemed inclined at least to hear him out, and it was to Scrope that Catesby turned, saying hastily, 'Your wife, John, and yours, too, Dick, were amongst the Queen's closest friends. Both Alison and Agnes were in attendance upon her until she died. Well, my wife, as you all know, is Alison's daughter, Agnes's step-sister. They did confide in her and she told me what they suspected. So do you not think, John . . . Dick . . . that we should bring it out in the open?'

'I do not know what you're insinuating but already I do not

like the sound of it,' Rob warned, but John Scrope reached over, laid a restraining hand on Rob's arm.

'Easy, Rob. He's not implying that Dickon is hot to have the lass in his bed. I'd not have chosen to bring this up myself but now that he has . . . my wife Alison thinks that the Lady Bess is overly attached to Dickon. She says women can see these things and the girl is suffering from some silly infatuation.'

'Sweet suffering Christ, but I . . . I cannot credit what I'm hearing!' Jack's outrage was such that he was almost stuttering. 'Yes, my cousin does care for Dickon; she always has. But it is no more than the natural fondness of a niece for a favourite uncle and I'll be damned if I'll let anyone say otherwise.'

Scrope was beginning to bristle; Jack had just called his wife a liar, if only by implication. It was that which decided John Howard; the potential for danger was just too great.

'Before we all begin saying that which we'll later regret,' he said, 'you'd best hear me out . . . especially you, Jack, because I'm about to break a confidence, and whether I be right or not in so doing, I honestly do not know. About a month ago, Bess sought me out. She said she was much in need of advice and, because I'd been so close to her father, she felt I was the one person she could trust to tell her the truth. Something was greatly troubling her; that I could see at a glance. Well, she hemmed and hawed and finally just blurted it out.'

He paused to ease a suddenly parched throat. He had their undivided attention now; the room was hushed.

'She asked me,' Howard resumed reluctantly, 'if I thought the Pope would be likely to grant a dispensation allowing an uncle and niece to wed.'

He heard someone catch his breath; someone else cursed.

'I know. . . . Why did I not say something ere this? Because I'm fond of the girl, did not want to see her hurt. I was not aware then of how widespread the rumours had become, hoped that given time, she'd come to her senses, Dickon need not know, and, what harm done?'

'What did you tell her?'

'The truth. That such a marriage could never be, for reasons that had nothing to do with a papal dispensation.'

'Did she believe you?'

Howard shrugged. 'I could not say. Most of us, especially women, tend to believe what we most want to believe.'

Jack found his voice. 'She'd never have thought of marriage on her own; I know it. That's just not like Bess.'

'No,' Howard agreed, 'it is not. It is, however, very much like Elizabeth Woodville.'

Richard had listened without interruption, listened with an utter stillness that struck the other men as unnatural. It was Jack who put their unease into words, who said awkwardly, 'Uncle Dickon . . . you do understand what we've just told you?'

'Yes, I understand. You're saying London gossip has it that I passed the last weeks of Anne's life in my niece's bed.' Richard sounded quite matter-of-fact, as detached as if he were speaking of another man's sins, and that alone should have warned them, but it did not and they were all taken aback now when he began to laugh.

Richard saw them staring at him in sudden dismay and it somehow seemed even amusing to him that they should be so alarmed, their consternation strangely comical, incongruous, and that only made him laugh all the more, brittle unsteady laughter that sounded unstrung even to his ears. He struggled to stop, found he could not, caught up in dark undercurrents of emotion beyond his understanding, and perilously close, as well, to being beyond his control.

Francis sat frozen, at a loss. Jack, too, seemed stunned, staring at Richard as if he were watching a man teetering on the very brink of a precipice. It was John Howard who acted. Without pausing to reflect, he was out of his chair, at Richard's side. Grabbing the younger man by the shoulders, he shook Richard roughly.

'For the love of Christ, lad, get hold of yourself! We've not told you the worst. Tudor's agents have not stopped at accusing you of bedding your own niece; they're saying, as well, that you wanted your wife to die.'

They'd not meant to tell Richard that. It was a calculated gamble but Howard's instincts were sound; he saw that now, saw the shock had been great enough to sober.

Richard's breath stopped; the laughter died in his throat. He turned away blindly and Howard had the wisdom not to follow. There was a wine flagon on a nearby table and Richard reached for it, poured out a cupful. The wine sloshed over the rim and he saw with self-loathing that his hands were shaking. He drank, choked, drank again. When he finally willed himself to turn back to face his friends, he was once more in control but he could not keep an embarrassed flush from darkening his skin, and his words came with an effort, unevenly spaced, slightly slurred.

'I'm sorry, but . . . well, you did take me off-balance. That men would believe . . .' He shook his head slowly, said in dull wonder, 'My brother used to chaff me for being naïve. I must be for, in truth, it never occurred to me that people could find evil in my fondness for Bess. . . .'

Sitting down again, he rose almost at once, wandered aimlessly to the window and back.

'Does Bess know about these rumours?'

The question came so abruptly that Francis jumped, said almost at random, 'I rather doubt it, Dickon. People would be no more likely to come to her with these tales than they would to you.'

Richard nodded. 'I'll have to tell her,' he said, looked up just in time to intercept a tense, wordless communication between Francis and Jack.

'What is it?' he asked slowly. 'Is there more to this than you've so far told me?' And had his answer in the uncomfortable silence that followed.

John Howard at last did what Francis and Jack could not. Without elaboration or emotion, as concisely as possible, he related the essence of his conversation with Bess and, when he was done, Richard was trembling again, this time with rage.

'That bitch,' he said softly, but with such venom that Loki moved swiftly to his side, an uneasy growl starting low in the dog's throat.

John Howard opened his mouth, shut it again. Jack looked both startled and aggrieved. Francis, too, was taken by surprise, and he did not share their protective concern for Bess, gave his loyalties without reserve to Richard. But that seemed even to him to be an unduly harsh judgment.

'You do not think, Dickon, that you're being too hard on the girl?'

'Hard. . . . Good God, Francis, you do not think I meant Bess?' Richard looked down at the forgotten wine cup in his hand, drained it in one long swallow. It was inconceivable to him that Bess could actually have contemplated marriage; few blood bonds were closer than uncle and niece. Once, many years ago as a boy at Middleham, he'd been able to coax Johnny Neville into taking him on a brief trip into York. On their way home, they'd passed through a stretch of woodland recently gutted by fire and Richard had been deeply shocked by what they'd seen—blackened earth, small charred bodies, smouldering embers, and the fetid stench of death where less than a week past he'd ridden under beech trees towering as high as a castle keep, unable to see the sky for the leafy clouds of aspen and sycamore and whitethorn. The devastation had been of such magnitude that he'd never forgotten it, nor that a landscape known and familiar and dear could so suddenly and savagely be transformed beyond all recognition. But until now, he'd not realized that relationships, too, were subject to changes no less sudden or inexplicable, and far more irrevocable.

'No matter what Bess told you, Jack, no one in Christendom can convince me those were her own words. Jesus God, can you not see that, see who had to put the idea into her head? It would seem,' Richard added bitterly, 'that Elizabeth has decided I am a better risk than Tudor.'

Francis came abruptly to his feet, moved to the table and poured himself a drink. Dickon was right, of course; Elizabeth's fine Woodville hand was all over this. He could even feel a flicker of grim, grudging admiration for the woman; like as not, she'd be bartering on her deathbed with the Devil for her due. Thank Christ Dickon was taking it as well as this . . . or was he? People said that those newly bereaved were often in a state of shock for weeks afterward, that grief was merciful in that it numbed first. But they'd had no choice; Dickon had to be told. Now at least he could take measures to damp down the scandal. Unfortunately, the means available to him were all too limited. Send the girl away from court, of course; find her a husband without delay; issue the usual oblique warnings that kings make use of to discourage political slander, which were generally as effective as spitting into the wind.

'Francis, I want you to see the Lord Mayor, tell him I shall be speaking before the aldermen, sheriffs and common council. Also the masters of the city guilds. See to it for me and as soon as possible. I know this is Holy Week but it cannot wait.'

'I'll take care of it at first light, Dickon, but . . . but why?'

'Why? Christ, man, I should think that would be obvious after what you just told me! I do mean to make a public denial of these lies they are telling about me and the sooner the better.'

'God Almighty, Uncle, you can't do that! A denial from your own lips would but fan the flames higher. All you can do with such dirt is to ignore it, whilst putting about right sharp warnings that those caught spreading seditious falsehoods will be punished with all the severity the law allows.'

'Jack is right in that,' Howard said gravely. 'A king does not dignify slander with a denial, lad. Just think for a moment of what's been said about those who do wear crowns. It's common fame in France that Louis poisoned his brother and all of Scotland was astounded when Jamie's youngest brother did die so mysteriously and conveniently in prison. To be highborn is to be subject to slurs and innuendo; that's just the way of it.'

'Remember, Dickon, how Charles of Burgundy took to referring to Uncle Ned as Blayborgne, after that archer his enemies always claimed to be his true father? Or when your former brother-in-law Exeter drowned crossing the Channel coming back from our Franch campaign in 1475, how Charles told one and all that Ned had ordered Exeter thrown overboard? Do you not think that if Ned had denied it, he'd just have played into Charles's hands?' Jack would have pressed the point home but Richard cut him off with an impatient gesture.

'I know you both mean well but I do not want to argue about this. It's what I've decided to do, what I have to do, and to discuss it further would serve for naught.' And there was a finality in his voice that was no less effective than an outright command.

Francis lingered after Jack and John Howard took their leave, hesitating and then crossing the chamber to join Richard at the window. Below, the river gardens were drenched in rain, budding leaves stripped away by gusts of wind that threatened to keep spring at bay for a few days more.

'Can you understand, Francis, why I have to do this? Why this be one lie I cannot live with?'

Francis thought Jack and Howard were most likely right, that a public denial would do little to quell the scandal, that it might even, by its very novelty, give the rumours fresh impetus. But he'd said nothing, made no attempt to dissuade Richard, for he had enough imagination to put himself in Richard's place, to be able to grasp how it would be to live for a year and a half with the knowledge that, in the eyes of many, he had been judged and found guilty of a crime beyond forgiving and to know that there was no way he could prove his innocence. A rumour to cast a sinister shadow over his entire reign, one that could be neither disproved nor denied.

'Yes,' he said. 'Yes, Dickon, I can understand.'

Someone had opened the window, on this the first evening in April; the night air was mild, held out a delayed promise of coming spring. It was for Richard a regret as embittered as it was illogical—that once more the earth should be flowering anew and Anne should not be there to see it. Springtime, once a lucky season for the House of York. Ned had won Barnet on an Easter dawn. Tewkesbury had been a May time victory. He'd made Anne his wife in April and in the spring, too, had come the births of all three of his children. And now . . . now three deaths in two years—brother, son, wife—and spring would be ever linked in his mind with death.

There were papers before him but Richard wasn't seeing them. He found his thoughts going back two days, back to that silent assembly in the great hall of the Priory of the Knights of St John of Jerusalem. The Lord Mayor, the aldermen, the bishops of the Church, his council, the royal household. Had they believed him?

He marvelled that he'd ever been able to bring himself to do it, to swear to a roomful of strangers that he'd loved his wife, grieved that she was dead and had never thought to marry his niece. There had been an air of utter unreality about it; he'd heard his voice, cold and clear, as if from a great distance, did not recognize it as his own. It did not seem totally real to him even now— not that Anne was truly dead nor that men could be so willing to believe the worst of him. But no . . . he was lying to himself again. Why should there be surprise that these rumours about Bess did find such ready acceptance? What else could he expect, in truth? Who'd be likely to give the benefit of the doubt to a man suspected of putting his own nephews to death? For that was what it came back to, what it always came back to—to

Buckingham and two children who died for sins that were not theirs.

Sometimes he even found himself searching the faces of his intimates, the men who worked with him every day, shared with him the burdens of government, wondering if he saw in their eyes, too, unspoken speculation about his brother's sons. He'd been king for twenty-one months now and for twenty of those months the boys had not been seen in London. Londoners had long since concluded that they were either in the North or they were dead; did his friends and councillors ever doubt, too?

Richard looked up now, his eyes moving from man to man—John Kendall, Will Catesby, Tom Lynom—saw only sympathy, and he realized that some time had passed, that they'd been waiting patiently for him to collect his thoughts, to come back to the business at hand.

'I've been remiss in offering you my congratulations, Tom.' Richard smiled at Lynom, said, 'I understand you have a son?'

Lynom grinned, looked surprised that Richard should have chosen to mention it and delighted that he had. 'I do, Your Grace, a fine boy born Tuesday noon. My wife and I . . . We look upon his birth as . . . as a miracle of sorts, a blessing bestowed by the grace of God.' Lynom stopped, suddenly self-conscious, as if realizing there might be an innocent cruelty in dwelling upon birth and joy to a man so recently bereaved.

A blessing. . . . Well they might think that. Passing strange, that after all those barren years in Ned's bed and Will's and Tom Grey's and too many others to mention, Jane should have at last conceived, have been able to give Lynom a son. But seeing Lynom's discomfiture, Richard said with as much warmth as he could muster, 'This Tuesday last? We share a day of good fortune then, you and I, for my son Johnny did turn fourteen that same day. Have you chosen a name?'

'Julian, Your Grace, because. . . .'

One of John Kendall's clerks had entered quietly, beckoned

Kendall aside. Now Kendall cut Lynom off with uncharacteristic rudeness, said with obvious reluctance, 'My liege, I've been asked to give you a message. Your niece is without, is asking to see you.'

Richard's reaction was reflex, came without time for thought. 'No,' he said, and Kendall signalled to the clerk. But as the man turned to go, he opened the door wide enough so that the men within could see the girl standing in the antechamber. Not Bess; Cecily.

'Wait,' Richard said, and as if she heard him, Cecily came forward, stopped just short of the open doorway.

With the court awash in rumours and Richard's inner circle inclined to see Bess more as her mother's puppet than as an innocent victim, it had taken courage for Cecily to come here like this, on her own. That alone would have gained her entry with Richard, for courage was the quality he admired above all others. He found himself studying her with contemplative eyes, this soft-spoken girl whose sixteenth birthday had passed almost unnoticed midst the preparations for Anne's funeral. Like Bess, she, too, was lovely, a handsome child of handsome parents, but there was in her face that which he would not have expected to see in one so young; she looked as if very little could surprise her, not ever again.

Richard pushed back his chair, a signal the other men correctly took as their cue for a discreet departure.

'You wish to speak with me, Cecily?' Richard said gently, saw her relief and realized that until this moment she had not known what to expect from him, had not known if he, too, blamed Bess for this scandal that had so suddenly entrapped them both.

'You're sending Bess away.'

It was not a question but Richard nodded, said tiredly and a bit defensively, 'What choice do I have? As long as she stays at court, the talk will continue.'

'I know,' Cecily conceded. 'I think you're right in that.

But. . . .' She came closer, put her hand lightly on his arm, a gesture that surprised him somewhat, for while Bess was very much her father's daughter, openly demonstrative with those she loved, Cecily was more reserved, more like Richard himself.

'But what I cannot understand, Uncle Dickon, is that you will not see her. I would not have thought you could be so cruel.'

Anger hovered all too close to the surface these days, strained nerves seeking release in rage as a means, however briefly, of overriding grief. Recognizing that, Richard drew a deep breath, said very evenly, 'What purpose would it serve, Cecily, except to give us both pain we could better do without?'

'Oh, but you're wrong. Dickon, listen to me . . . please. For two days now, Bess has done nothing but cry. She will not talk, will not eat, just lies there on the bed and cries. And it's not just because of those vile stories people are spreading, although she did not know about them until Lords Howard and Lovell came to her, told her she was to go to Sheriff Hutton. It's not even that she's been made to see how much you've been hurt by this gossip. It's that you will not see her, Dickon. By doing that, you've made her feel as if she's done something shameful, unforgivable. And she does not deserve that, she does not. Do not send her away in disgrace. I know Bess; she'll never get over it. I love my sister very much, would have given the world to spare her this hurt. But you're the only one who can make it right for her. You and only you.'

Richard would not have needed to be told Bess had been crying; her eyes were darkly circled, inflamed, and a heavy dusting of powder did little to camouflage the tear tracks, the lack of sleep. He'd rarely seen her look worse and yet, paradoxically, never had he been so aware of her as a woman. After a startled moment to reflect, he understood why, realized that he was suddenly seeing her with the mirror she herself had given him, as a beautiful woman who'd fantasized, however briefly and for whatever reasons, about being his queen, sharing his bed and bearing his children.

1147

In the four days since he'd listened, incredulous, as his friends told him what was being said of him and Bess, Richard had gone over again and again in his mind every aspect he could remember of his relationship with his niece. Yes, he had found her fair to look upon, had taken pleasure in her company. But beyond that? No, this was one sin he could absolve himself of; he had never envisioned Bess as a bedmate. But it mattered little that he had not; he saw that now, saw that his relationship with Bess was tainted, nonetheless, that there would be forever between them the spectre of a forbidden sin.

Bess's cheeks were flaming. 'You hate me now, do you not?' she whispered.

Richard winced. Christ Jesus, how young she was.

'No, Bess, never.' It occurred to him that she could so easily have denied her own feelings, could have claimed that Howard had misunderstood her and, at least, salvaged her pride. And yet he felt no surprise that she had not. She had that rarest of qualities, an integrity of spirit that allowed her to face the truth and its consequences without flinching. It was not true for him and he knew it; when truths were too painful, he'd invariably sought to deny them, blaming Elizabeth for the deterioration in Ned's character, refusing to see that Edward and Dickon would not have died had he not taken the crown, unable to admit that Anne was dying. And had it not been for Cecily, he would have avoided this, too, would have failed Bess yet again, just as he'd done when he'd sent someone else to tell her that her brothers were dead.

'Bess, you understand why I'm sending you to Sheriff Hutton? There's no other way to stifle the gossip.'

She shook her head as if that mattered little. 'Why would you not see me ere this?'

'I was wrong; I'm sorry, lass.' He made amends the only way he could, with the truth. 'I was thinking only of myself. I just did not know what to say to you.'

For a moment their eyes held but no longer. Bess blushed even deeper. 'I've watched you in this past year suffer grief you never deserved. To lose your little boy and then. . . .' Her voice faltered. 'I know how you loved your wife, loved Anne. I wanted only to comfort you, to make you happy again. Was that . . . was that so very wrong?'

Richard hesitated. It was true that the Pope could have given a dispensation for such a marriage but the English people would never have accepted it. Nor could he; to lay with his brother's daughter would be one sin too many, a moral wrong not even the Pope could reconcile as right. But to say that to Bess would be to inflict needless hurt, to shame her for a sin that was more rightly her mother's.

'Bess . . . listen to me, lass. It could never be. For me to marry you would be political suicide. People would see such a marriage as proof that I'd concocted the plight-troth as a means of usurping your brother's crown. At the least, it would be a tacit admission that even I doubted my right. It would also be an admission that your brothers were dead, and to do that now. . . .'

'I see,' she said in a small voice. 'I . . . I think I always knew that, Dickon, knew it was a dream with no reality in it. Do you remember what I told you that night in the abbey, about how I'd make up happy endings in my head? I guess . . . guess I was still doing it.'

With a lot of help from Elizabeth, damn her. He did not doubt that she'd have seen Bess wed to the Grand Vizier of the Ottoman Empire if a crown were in the offering.

'Dickon . . . you'll not make me wed, will you?'

That was exactly what his advisers were telling him to do, to marry her off as soon as possible to a husband who could be counted upon to hold fast for the House of York.

'No, Bess, I'll not force you to wed against your will,' he said impulsively, was more than repaid by the look of relief that crossed her face.

An awkward silence fell; it was as if years of intimacy had never been.

Richard suddenly realized how much he was going to miss Bess, realized for the first time what a void her going would leave in his life. He would have liked to have been able to tell her that but it was no longer possible and, in understanding that, he understood the full measure of his loss, that the last link to his brother had just been broken.

26

Berkhampsted
May 1485

Candlelight was kind and the stark severity of Benedictine garb suited her surprisingly well; the white wimple covered her chin and throat, thus camouflaging the most obvious evidence of aging, and the black veil framing her face set off skin a much younger woman might envy. What struck John Scrope most, however, was what he saw in the wide-set grey eyes. So, he thought, it is true then, that she has found in God that which had been denied her as Duchess of York.

Cecily watched him as he drank his wine, helped himself to the platter of dried figs and candied quinces. She'd greeted him with no apparent surprise, but all the while that she was making polite conversation, she was wondering why he was here. Ostensibly, his purpose was to see that all arrangements were made for Richard's impending arrival but this was not an errand a man of Scrope's rank would ordinarily undertake. She could only conclude that he had reasons of his own for being here and she waited now, with a patience all the more precious for having come to her so late in life, waited for him to reveal the true purpose of this visit.

For a woman who'd not left Berkhampsted since taking vows more than four years past, she was remarkably well informed about the world she'd renounced and they spoke at length about Richard's urgent need for money, about Henry Tudor and the likelihood of an invasion backed by French gold. It was some time before Scrope was able to manoeuvre the conversation in the desired direction, into reminiscing about two men who were fourteen years dead, kin to them both, Richard and John Neville.

He talked for a time of Warwick but soon shifted the talk to John, and as Cecily listened attentively, he spoke of the last months of John's life, and for one never noted for eloquence, drew upon words of surprising power to describe for her a man in deep inner turmoil.

'I loved Johnny Neville. He was more than a cousin to me, Madame, was as good a friend as any man can hope to have in this life. It was his tragedy that he loved both his brother and his cousin. When he betrayed your son at Doncaster, he betrayed himself, too, and this I can tell you for true, that he never forgave himself for it. Whatever his reasons, however justified he thought he was, once it was done, he found he could not live with it.'

Cecily stirred. She, too, had cared for John Neville, and she'd long ago learned that time did not heal; it only numbed.

'I've never forgotten,' she said sadly, 'the look on Edward's face when he told me that Johnny had gone into battle wearing the colours of York under his armour.'

Scrope nodded. 'I will not go so far as to say that Johnny was looking to die. But I do know he took the field that day with a handicap no man can safely shoulder. He was just going through the motions, Madame, like a man doing what's expected of him but no more.'

Cecily leaned forward, caught his sleeve. 'Why are you telling me this, John?'

Scrope set his drink down. 'Because,' he said at last, 'what I once saw in Johnny Neville, I see now in your son.'

Cecily had nursed the sick and buried the dead, had of necessity become as skilled in the arts of healing as any apothecary. She'd watched throughout supper as Richard measured his meal in mouthfuls, left a plateful of food untouched. She'd noted, too, that even though he was lightly tanned, his eyes were deeply smudged, bloodshot, and there was about him the taut wariness of a woodland creature in strange surroundings; when a servant carelessly dropped a chafing dish, Cecily had seen her son flinch like one struck. She'd said nothing but, as soon as Richard retired that evening, she sent a servant for her store of medicinal herbs, and, with sure hands, mixed a sleeping draught of henbane, darnel and dried bryony root. This she dissolved in a cupful of hippocras and carried it herself on a tray up to her son's bedchamber.

There she found that Richard's attendants had already assembled the bed he'd brought with him from Windsor; when she'd questioned him about this, Richard had acted much like a man caught in some secret vice, reluctantly admitting that he was sleeping poorly at night, so much so that he could not sleep at all in a strange bed. He was still up; his esquires had just taken off his doublet, were unbuttoning his shirt as Cecily entered. He smiled at sight of her and, without being asked, dismissed his attendants.

'I thought we might talk awhile longer. I brought you that book I mentioned at supper, the one I want you to read.' Seeing his blank look she prompted patiently, 'The Mirroure of the Worlde, remember? It does deal most knowledgably with the Commandments, the Articles of Faith, and the like.'

'I remember now; thank you,' Richard said politely, and Cecily knew it unlikely he'd ever read it. She tucked it away, nonetheless, in the open coffer that held his personal belongings. As she did, she noticed a book already in the coffer, bound in velvet so faded its original colour was beyond determining. Curious, she picked it up, flipped it open. It was a French exercise book, pages yellowing with age, smudged with ink and careless fingers; Anne's name was written in a childish hand across the flyleaf, and below it, 'Edward Plantagenet, Earl of Salisbury,' with 'Ned' neatly penned in brackets beneath.

'I found that among Anne's things,' Richard said. He'd come to stand beside Cecily, now reached for this book that had been first his wife's and then his son's. It turned as if of its own accord to a page partially filled with French verbs. Below the exercise, Anne had amused herself by sketching pictures of birds, nesting and on the wing.

'The only creature she could ever draw worth a damn,' Richard said softly, and Cecily saw that still further down on the page were variations of Anne's name; Anne Neville, Anne Warwick, the Lady Anne, and then, Anne Gloucestre, Anne, Duchess of Gloucestre. Cecily stared down at the young girl's handwriting— rounded, unformed; how old had Anne been when she'd written that . . . twelve? Thirteen?

'I brought you some wine, Richard,' she said, and taking the book from him, she replaced it in the coffer, closed the lid.

'Is it true that you expect Tudor to invade the realm come summer?'

They were sitting on the bed; Richard propped a pillow behind him, settled back against the headboard. 'Yes,' he said. 'Tudor's putting together a fleet, having it rigged at Harfleur.'

Cecily frowned; he might have been discussing the likelihood of rain, for all the emotion in his voice. 'I understand that Lord Stanley has asked for leave to depart the court, to withdraw to his estates in Lancashire.'

Richard nodded. 'He says that when the time comes to issue summons to arms against Tudor, he can better rally his men in person.' Dryly.

'And yet you're going to let him go.' It was not a question, was more in the nature of an accusation.

Richard shrugged. 'If I do, ma mère, it'll not be before he sends his eldest son to court to take his place.'

Cecily shook her head. 'That's not enough, Richard, not nearly enough. Stanley is not a man to be bound by the welfare of others, not even his own flesh and blood.'

Another shrug. 'I've given him reasons a hundredfold to be loyal. I cannot very well force a man to fight for me at sword-point, ma mère.'

'Why not?' she said tartly. 'At the least, you can limit his opportunities for betrayal. Keep him close, Richard. Edward would never have let him go.'

'I'm not Ned.' Said very low.

He had, she saw, barely touched the wine. She decided for the moment to let Stanley lie, saying instead, 'John Scrope told me that you've had some success in raising loans?'

'Yes . . . since February, we've been able to collect nigh on twenty thousand pounds.' Richard grimaced. 'As if I did not already have debts enough to answer for. But short of summoning parliament and inveigling a grant, there was nothing else I could do. I've three months at most before Tudor invades and I cannot raise an army with expectations, feed them with promises.'

'I understand, though, that there was much grumbling amongst the London merchants,' Cecily said, hoping thus to ease diplomatically into the subject of her concern, but Richard gave her no chance. With her first words, his eyes had darkened, showed sudden anger.

'What of it?' he demanded. 'They'll get their blood money back. These are loans, not benevolences. I did pledge repayment in full within a year and a half.'

'Yes, I know you did. But whilst I'm sure few doubt your willingness to make repayment, you cannot blame men for fretting over your ability to do so, Richard. Not when these loans are no more voluntary than the outright gifts Edward demanded; who, after all, is going to feel free to turn down the king?'

'Just what are you suggesting, ma mère? What other recourse had I?'

'None,' she agreed. 'I just think it might have been more to your political advantage had you exempted London, the way you've remitted taxes for York in the past. You have not been able to establish the rapport with Londoners that you have with the citizens of York and nothing is more likely to strain loyalties than to make demands upon men's purses.'

'Loyalty . . . in Londoners? I'd as soon look for honour should I fall amongst thieves,' Richard said caustically, and there was a savagery to the sarcasm that she'd rarely heard from him.

'Those who live in London have ever had a dislike of northerners, Richard,' she said quietly. 'It is a bias that, however unfair, you must take into account in your dealings with them. You did but confirm their suspicions by showing such favour to men of the North Country. All those who stand closest to you do come from Yorkshire or the Midlands. You've little liking for London or Londoners and well they know it. And the result is that you've reaped a bitter harvest, rumour and innuendo and slanders which would never have taken root in York.'

She reached over, let her fingers rest lightly on his wrist. 'The burden is upon you, Richard, to allay their concerns, to show them that you do not hold London any less dearly than York. A king cannot do less, my dearest. You have it in you to be a good king, a better one than your brother, but in this you've so far failed; you've let your subjects see all too clearly that your heart lies in the North.'

'To be a king is to be no less a man, ma mère. I cannot help the way I feel.'

'You can try, however, to make your affinities a little less plain to all. It's that which I'm asking of you, Richard. Will you think on what I've said?'

'Of course,' he said, but she took little encouragement from his ready agreement, saw that her words had not truly touched him.

She watched him in silence for a time, remembering how enthused he'd been about his first parliament, how he'd held forth for hours about the need for reform in the judiciary, how he'd sat himself in Chancery and Exchequer as cases were tried, occasionally even summoning the justices to the Inner Star Chamber to put queries to them about particularly troublesome cases. It's gone, she thought, utterly gone, that unique capacity for moral indignation in the face of injustice, that willingness to define kingship in terms of service, of responsibilities and rights and the redress of grievances. All at once, Cecily found herself blinking back tears, she who cried so rarely and so reluctantly. Perhaps in time, she thought, in time he'd come to care again; eventually the grieving would have to give way, just as snow melted before the first thaw and all renewed itself in the grace of God.

Richard set down his half-empty wine cup, began to cough. Cecily had been listening to that cough for hours and yet each time it started anew, she found herself tensing, unable to concentrate on anything else until the spasm passed. She did not realize her concern showed so nakedly, not until Richard shook his head, saying, 'Not you, too, ma mère?' He sounded grimly amused. 'Poor old Hobbys all but jumps out of his skin every time I so much as clear my throat. I can only tell you what I told him, that I've been sneezing and coughing for nigh on a fortnight now. It is a wretched cold and I'll admit it's making life miserable for me, but it's just that, a cold and no more.'

He smiled and, after a pause, she did, too, albeit far from reassured.

'You look dreadful,' she said candidly, 'and I'm not surprised you've been ailing, not after watching you pick at your food like a man suspecting poison. But I'm not about to lecture you; you'd not heed me any more than you do Hobbys. I do want to discuss something of great importance with you, though, something you've been refusing to discuss in council . . . remarriage.'

Richard coughed again. 'That's not a topic I care to talk about, ma mère, even with you.'

'I would have you hear me out, nonetheless. I can guess what they've been telling you, that Anne is two months dead and you need an heir, owe it to England to marry and beget a son. But that's not why I would urge you to do the same. You are my son and I want what's best for you. I think you should remarry, Richard, and soon. I know how you loved Anne. But there is a great danger in letting your grieving go unchecked, a danger in that the dead can begin to seem more real than the living.'

Richard looked at her. 'Yes,' he said huskily, 'I know.' How could he tell her that he was still haunted by the fragrance of Anne's perfume, that to look upon a woman with chestnut hair was a hurt almost beyond endurance, that Anne claimed his dreams as if they were her own, a merciless tender ghost who laughed and made love and led him back into their past, breathed life into memories and then fled at dawn, leaving him to awaken alone, to be confronted anew with the reality of her loss.

'This afternoon,' he said 'when you were showing me your gardens, and I saw your beds of hyacinth, white and butter-yellow and crimson. . . . Hyacinths were always Anne's favourite flower and, for a second or so, I actually found myself thinking, I ought to gather some for Anne.'

Cecily was fingering the rosary beads looped at her belt. 'For nigh on a year after your father died,' she said, 'I kept his belongings, his clothes, everything, in our bedchamber . . . as if I thought he'd somehow be coming back.'

That was a rare admission; she'd borne her grief alone, had done all her weeping behind locked doors. There was more than love in the look Richard now gave her, there was awe. This was a partcularly bad day for him, being the anniversary of his son's death, thirteen months past. It was also the birthday of the brother who'd died twenty-four years ago in the snow on Wakefield Bridge and, thinking of Edmund and of George, thinking of the lifetime of pain that had been his mother's, he said slowly, 'There is this I've long wanted to say to you, ma mère, that I've known no man's courage greater than your own. I cannot begin to compre-hend your resolve, your strength of will; I can only marvel at it.'

Cecily looked down at her hands; they were veined with age, no longer as steady as she would wish. 'I truly believe the Almighty does not ask of us more than we have to give, that He does not abandon us in our time of need, and in His love we find the strength to endure, to accept what must be. Whilst it is true that death has come too often for those I've loved, I do feel that I've been more fortunate than most, for I've never known the greatest of all griefs, pain such as yours.'

Richard stared at her in disbelief. 'How in God's name can you say that, ma mère? You've lost husband, son, brother, and three nephews . . . all on the field of battle. Of the twelve children you bore my father, you did bury nine. What can my griefs possibly be when weighed on the scales against such as that?'

'Yes,' she said simply, 'but yet I've never known what it is like to feel as you do now, forsaken by God.'

Richard stiffened and she smiled sadly. 'Ah, Richard, did you think I'd need to be told? It must seem to you as if your crown were anointed in blood. . . . So many deaths, so much grief. Being the man you are, you could not but question why.' She leaned over, reached out to touch his face in the lightest, most fleeting of caresses.

'I know my sons. Had it been Edward, he, too, might have doubted his right but not for long. Your brother was not one to wear a hairshirt and all his life had a lamentable tendency to confuse God's will with his own. As for my poor George, he was as deaf to the voice of conscience as he was blind to the consequences of his sins. But you and Edmund . . . you were ever my vulnerable ones.'

'Can you tell me that I'm wrong, ma mère? Can you in all honesty tell me that I've not sinned in taking the crown?'

'No, Richard, I cannot. Only God can answer that and you, for you alone know what was in your heart when you took the crown.'

'That's just it, ma mère, I do not know any more. At the time, I truly thought I had no choice, that I had the right. But now . . . now I cannot be sure.' He paused, said with wrenching candour, 'I wanted it, you see. I wanted to be king.'

'That in and of itself is not a sin, Richard,' Cecily said, very softly.

'Tell me this, then. In little more than a month, it will be two years since I was anointed with the holy chrism, asked the Almighty to uphold my right, Richard, by the Grace of God. . . . I have the kingship, ma mère, have the blessed crown of the Confessor. But my brother's sons are dead, the children he entrusted to my keeping. My own son died a death that was not easy and Anne . . . I watched her life ebb away like sand through my fingers, unable to ease her suffering, to do anything at all for her. And even as she lay dying, there were men to say I welcomed her death, that I lusted after my own niece, and there were those to believe it of me, those who do think me guilty of child-murder, adultery and incest. If I have not sinned against God, why am I being punished like this?'

'Ah, Richard. . . .' Cecily's voice had thickened; she drew a deep shuddering breath, at last said, 'God does sometimes act to test our faith, in ways we cannot hope to understand. Did not Satan say to the Lord of Job, "Put forth Thy hand now and touch all he has and he will curse Thee to thy face," and the Lord did reply to Satan, "Behold, all that he has is in your power," and Job did suffer greatly, did lose his family and his health, had to lose all to find anew his faith in the Almighty.'

Richard raised his eyes to hers, saw with shock that her face was wet with tears. He could not remember ever having seen her cry openly before, not even when he'd come to tell her that George had been put to death and, stricken with remorse, he sought to make amends the only way he could, saying urgently, 'I'm sorry, ma mère, so sorry. Can you not forget this, forget what I've said? I did not mean it. I'm just tired and more dispirited than usual tonight, more inclined to self-pity. That's all it was, in truth.'

Cecily said nothing. She understood now what had previously seemed inexplicable to her, why he was willing to put Stanley's loyalty to the test, a risk that he need not have taken. He was no longer listening to the dictates of self-interest, was following inner instincts more compelling than reason. Trial by combat, to seek God's judgment on the field of battle. If his claim to the crown was just, he'd prevail. If not, Tudor would have the victory.

She had known fear for her sons before. Until she'd been re-assured by her husband's confessor that both he and Edmund had been shriven on Christmas Eve, she'd lived in terror that they might have been denied salvation, died in mortal sin. It was her fear for George's immortal soul that had at last impelled her to take holy vows, for she had not been able to take much comfort in Stillington's assurance that George had confessed, received absolution for his sins. The Sacrament of Penance was mean-ingless unless the sinner was truly repentant and Cecily harboured grave doubts that her troubled son had been capable of contri-tion. Her fear for Richard now was such that her mouth went dry and her soul cried out in anguish that her faith was not strong enough, not sufficient unto the Lord, for how could she ever bear it should she lose this son, too? She squeezed the rosary until the beads imprinted themselves in the palm of her hand, until she was able to give him the assurance he so needed, to say with at least a semblance of conviction, 'I know you did not mean it, Richard, and if you want this conversation forgotten, then it is.'

The sleeping draught was beginning to have its effect; Richard's dark eyes were drowsy, heavy-lidded, and she could take some satisfaction in that, at least, that she'd given him one night's untroubled rest.

'You're tired; we'll talk in the morning,' she said gently. Leaning over, she brushed her lips against his forehead and then straightened, for his shirt was open and his throat bare, no longer encircled by silver.

'Richard, what happened to your pilgrim pledge? Did you lose it?'

'No. . . . I gave it to Anne.'

'Here then, take this.' She fumbled with the chain around her neck, and, disregarding his protests, pressed her own crucifix into his hand.

Richard was deeply touched. 'Thank you, ma mère.' There was an intensity of emotion in this moment impossible to acknowledge, so much that they could not put into words, and he swallowed, said as lightly as he could, 'Do you have vervain in your garden? I've been told it acts to safeguard men in battle.'

She knew he was teasing, knew there was no other way for them to deal with the dangers he'd be facing, but she felt a chill, nonetheless, and she who all her life had been so sparing in her caresses, so prudent with her praise, found herself wanting only to gather him to her and keep him safe within her arms, to comfort the boy he had been and heal the man he now was, her lastborn and the dearest of her children.

Richard's eyes were all but closed; lashes of surprising length and thickness shadowed his cheek. She reached out, let her fingers trace the deep lines that undercut his mouth.

'I shall pray for you,' she said.

1161

27

Nottingham

August 1485

The shadow-world of sleep recognized no borders. There the past and present were one country, shaped by memory and peopled by need. Richard had been dreaming of Anne, dreaming of a day that had never been, and when he awoke it was with a start, a sense of disorientation so strong that he did not at once know where he was.

Daybreak was spreading across the sky, the half-light of coming dawn slowly restoring form and familiarity to the bedchamber. Exhausted, he lay back against the pillows. How queer dreams were; they had a reality all their own. He'd never lain with a woman out on the moors, had never lain with Anne in the grass by the River Cover, and yet he could still feel the turf, spongy under their bodies and sweet-smelling. There'd been grass stains on Anne's skirt, her head pillowed on the tangled thickness of her own hair, her breasts bare to the sun. 'Oh, love, love . . .' she'd gasped at the moment of joining and his own body quivered now in involuntary response. With a muffled curse, he rolled over onto his stomach but the hard throbbing ache in his groin was beyond easing. The memories of flesh and blood and bone were far more unrelenting than those of the heart and head; what man would willingly torment himself with desire for a dead woman?

It was a need that seemed to grow worse with each passing day of this humid, sweltering summer. Perhaps it was being back at Nottingham, his castle of care, where he'd had to tell Anne that their son was dead, where Hobbys had pronounced Anne's sentence of death. Mayhap if he had chosen to wait in York. . . . But Tudor would never have dared to come ashore in the North. No, Nottingham had been the most logical site to keep vigil, in the very heartland of his realm. So he'd taken up residence in early June, dispatched Francis to Southampton to take charge of the coast defences, left London in Jack Howard's capable hands, ordered the English fleet to sea, and the waiting began.

Mayhap it was true what Ned had so often liked to say, that there were but two kinds of fools in this world, those who ran ahead to meet trouble more than halfway and those who hid in hopes it would somehow pass them by. If so, he was a fool of the first sort, had never been able to endure waiting for anything, good or bad. It was the longest summer of his life. When Thursday last he'd received word that Tudor had landed on August 7th at Milford Haven in South Wales, his first reaction had been one almost of relief.

He'd at once sent an urgent summons to Thomas Stanley, ordering him to Nottingham. His other captains were to join him at Leicester, where the royal army was to gather. On the morrow, he would be departing Nottingham, begin moving slowly southward. Today was a Monday, the fifteenth of August, one of the most holy days of the Church calendar, the Assumption of Our Lady. By this time next week, it was very likely that it would all be over, one way or the other. Why, then, did he feel so detached, so cut off from his own emotions?

At the least, there should be anger, hatred for this Welsh pretender who dared affix 'Rex' to his signature as if he were already England's anointed king and found his invasion force among mercenaries and men set loose from Normandy gaols. But the fury was forced, the hatred curiously lacking in passion. Even now, on the very eve of departure, he felt numb, unable to summon up more than a weary sense of wonder that the waiting should at last be almost over.

His servants were moving into the room and Loki ended his night vigil by the door, grudgingly let them pass. Feeling slightly queasy, feeling as if he'd never been to bed at all, Richard sat up and his day began.

He was being shaved when the letter from Thomas Stanley came. Stanley's man had arrived at the castle at the same time as Francis Lovell, just come up from the south, and it was Francis who escorted him into Richard's bedchamber, followed closely by Jack de la Pole and a visibly nervous Will Catesby. All knew how much hung upon Stanley's response.

Richard broke the seal, skimmed the contents. Should he have been surprised? You can never go wrong suspecting a Stanley, prodded a memory. He saw that he'd crumpled the paper and he straightened it as best he could, passed it to Jack.

'Stanley regrets that he cannot comply with my command,' he said tonelessly. 'He says he is suffering from the sweating sickness, is not up to riding a horse.'

They raged, of course, called Stanley names as abusive as they were accurate. Richard listened in silence, interrupted his nephew's harangue only to say briefly, 'You'd best see to it that Stanley's son is kept under close watch from now on.'

Jack nodded, would have gone at once to give the necessary commands had Richard not stopped him.

'No, Jack, not yet. I do need to speak with you . . . . alone.'

'Sweet Jesus, but you cannot be serious? You'd send me away, have me wait out the battle like some gutless craven? How could you ask that of me?'

'I'm not asking, Jack.'

'Well, I will not do it, I will not!'

'You're more than my nephew; you're my heir. Would you have us both risk our lives against Tudor? If the battle goes against me, would you have the House of York dragged down into the dust, too?'

Jack's anger was all the more intense because he could not deny the truth of that. 'You expect to lose, do you not?' he accused. 'You've been trained all your life in the ways of war, whilst Tudor is grass-green, and yet you expect to lose.'

'No, Jack, I do not.'

Jack was not convinced. 'Moreover, I do not think you even care.'

Richard looked at him. 'I care,' he said.

Jack shook his head. 'Not enough, Uncle. Not nearly enough.'

Dark had long since descended but the day's heat had yet to ebb. Richard was alone in the gardens; more and more he craved solitude as other men craved wine and this day that had begun with Stanley's ominous letter had ended with worse. A few hours ago, Richard's scouts sent word that Tudor had advanced unchallenged through Wales, that on August 13th the border town of Shrewsbury had opened its gates to him.

It should have come as no surprise. He of all men should have expected as much. What opposition had Warwick encountered, after all, when he'd landed in Devon? Or Ned, when they'd come ashore at Ravenspur? Most people were little inclined to spill their own blood in these endless conflicts over the crown, not after thirty years of such strife. And yet it hurt, nonetheless; against all logic and common sense, it hurt.

Much of his thinking seemed equally clouded to him these days. Why should he feel betrayed by Stanley when he'd known from the first that the man was a born Judas? And he'd chosen to let Stanley depart for Lathom, he and no other; but now, asking himself why, he was no longer sure of the answer. Had he been testing Stanley? Or testing himself?

Much on his mind, too, was his quarrel with his sister's son. Jack was wrong. He sought neither defeat nor death. For those were the stakes, an all-or-nothing wager in which he was offering up more than his crown; he was offering up his life.

He did not think there was a moment in which he'd consciously made that choice; it was rather as if there'd been no choice to make. He'd not fight a civil war to hold on to the crown, would neither retreat into the North nor seek soldiers and aid from overseas. Twice in his life he had sought refuge in Burgundy; there'd not be a third time. But what he was asking of the Almighty was vindication through victory on the field, and failing that, death, and to die like that would be to die in mortal sin.

The air was warm on his face, fragrant and alive with the sounds of a summer night: cicadas, crickets and unseen birds. He'd lost track of time, found himself watching the antics of two well-fed red squirrels. As a boy, he'd once had a pet squirrel and he sought to lure them over. The bolder of the two came readily, advancing close enough to sniff at his outstretched hand and then withdrew with such obvious disappointment that Richard grinned.

'Expecting alms, were you? Sorry I cannot oblige,' he said, and the little creature chattered back noisily, almost as if it understood.

'Here, Your Grace, take this.'

Richard turned, startled at the sound of a woman's voice. She'd come noiselessly through the trees, materializing like some woodland sprite, and most improbably of all, what she was holding out to him was a chunk of freshly baked bread.

Richard stared at the bread and then burst into laughter. 'I would that all my wishes were so readily granted.' He broke off the crust, tossed it into the grass where it was at once claimed and devoured. The squirrel sat up, crumbs clinging to its whiskers and chest, set about cleaning itself like a cat, accepting the offering of this unknown benefactress with utter equanimity. Richard was more curious, however, beckoned her closer.

He saw at once why he'd not noticed her approach; she wore widow's black, seemed to be cloaked in night. As moonlight fell across her face, Richard's interest quickened. She was not beautiful in the strict sense of the word, but it was not a face to be forgotten, sharply chiselled cheekbones and generously curved mouth, a face as familiar as it was exotic.

'I know you, do I not?' he said, and she nodded shyly.

Suddenly self-conscious, she handed him another piece of bread, said with a breathless laugh, 'I suppose you're wondering why I happened to be toting a basket of bread about the gardens at this time of night?'

Richard smiled, shook his head. 'I've never been one to question luck,' he said and, much to his delight, was able to coax the squirrel into feeding from his hand.

'Actually, I was bringing it to you, Your Grace.' She lifted the covering on the basket, showing him half a dozen neatly wrapped loaves. 'I meant to leave them with Master Kendall, was told he might have time to see me after Compline.'

At mention of his secretary's name, Richard remembered where he'd seen her before. About a fortnight ago she'd come to the castle seeking an audience. It was not a day when he'd been hearing petitioners but he'd agreed to see her to oblige Kendall who'd argued that 'the lass is one of our own, Your Grace, Yorkshire born and bred.' Her husband had been steward for one of Edward's manors in Cumbria and his death some two years ago had left her and their children in financial straits. Richard had arranged for her to receive a pension from the issues of the lordship of Warwick and thought no more about it. But he was touched now that she'd thought to show her gratitude in this particularly Yorkshire fashion; the city of York had often presented him with swans and pike and wine, and it had not been at all uncommon for grateful petitioners to bring gifts of food to Middleham.

She came closer, confiding, 'I could scarce believe my eyes when I saw you sitting alone like this. I suppose I just took it for granted that you always had scores of people in attendance.'

'And they're most likely tracking me down even now,' Richard said wryly. 'May I count on you not to give me away?'

She dimpled, nodded, and he made room on the turf seat, saying, 'But I'm not finding myself to be good company tonight.

It would please me greatly if you sat down and talked with me awhile of Yorkshire.'

He soon discovered that she knew a number of his friends: Tom Wrangwysh and the Metcalfes and York's current Lord Mayor. She was indeed Yorkshire-bred, knew the dales of Wensley as well as he did, and they found that they shared a special fondness for Aysgarth Falls, argued whether the most scenic view in Yorkshire was to be found from Sutton Bank or from Penhill, and agreed that the Corpus Christi plays performed in York were equal in all respects to those acted out in Coventry and Chester.

Realizing at last that the castle gates must have long since been shut, Richard assured her that he'd see she had an escort back to her inn, and she thanked him warmly, but neither stirred. Somewhere a dog was barking. The squirrels had long since disappeared. It had been a welcome respite but Richard found that his troubles could be kept at bay only so long, and his mind began to fill again with thoughts of the coming confrontation with Tudor.

Would Stanley go over openly to Tudor? Or would he wait out the battle, making ready to do homage to whomever won? As for Stanley's drink-sodden braggart of a brother, the odds were that he was already in Tudor's camp; Will Stanley was Chief Justice of North Wales and yet Tudor had passed through the Cambrian Mountains like a hot knife through butter. Thank Christ for Jack Howard and for Francis, for the men he could trust. If only he could be as sure of Northumberland. It is one thing to tread lightly but Northumberland did endeavour to leave no footprints at all. Only once in the past twelve years had he thrown in his lot when the issue was still in doubt, at the time of Buckingham's rebellion. As Warden of the Marches toward Scotland, Northumberland had the responsibility of issuing summons to arms for the North, should have been in Nottingham days ago. So why was he not here?

'Your Grace . . . might I say something of a personal nature?' His companion had been watching him in silence for some moments, now said rather diffidently, 'It's not my place to say this but you look so bone-weary, like a man who's forgotten what it is like to get a decent night's rest. Once you do deal with Tudor, I think you should come North, come home for a good long while.'

Richard knew she meant well but she'd touched a nerve, nonetheless. Middleham had been the only home he'd ever known but he'd not be able to go back, would never be able to sleep alone in the bed he'd shared with Anne. He rose abruptly, moved into the shadows of the nearest tree, an oak that had been old even before he was born.

At once contrite, she followed. 'I just knew I should not have spoken out but you did look so . . . so sad. I'm sorry, truly I am. Do you want me to go?'

Richard turned to face her, reached out and touched her cheek. 'No,' he said, 'I do not want you to go,' and realized even as he said it that he was no longer talking about the garden. His hand lingered on her face; her skin was soft and suddenly flushed. He felt no less unsure himself. It had been so long since he'd sought to coax a woman to his bed; for nigh on fourteen years there'd been only Anne.

'You're very fair,' he said softly and, when she smiled, he saw that there was no need to say more. She came into his arms as if she belonged there, warm and perfumed and very real.

Candles still burned; in their haste, they'd not taken time to put them out. The light was shining in Richard's eyes and it was that which at last motivated him to move. Lifting his weight off her body, he rolled over onto his back. It was ungodly hot; where the sheet touched his skin it stuck. After a time, he leaned over. But she averted her face, whether by accident or design and his lips just brushed her cheek. He frowned; was she regretting now that she'd sinned?

'Rosamund?'

She opened her eyes; they were an intriguing colour neither completely blue nor green. 'At the last,' she said, very low, 'you . . . you did call me Anne.'

Her hair cascaded over the pillows, all but covered one breast; it was darker than Anne's, but a pretty colour, nonetheless. He touched it, twined a strand around his fingers and at last, said the only thing he could. 'I'm sorry.'

Blue-green eyes searched his face. 'Do you want me to go?' she offered uncertainly, just as she had in the garden.

He did but he could not bring himself to tell her so. She was no harlot, did not deserve to be dismissed like one now that his need had been satisfied. 'I'd like you to stay,' he lied. It occurred to him now, as it had not in the garden, to question her willingness to share his bed; would she have felt free to deny the king? It was suddenly very important to him that he be sure and he said awkwardly, 'Rosamund, what happened between us . . . well, it was not planned, you know that. But I did not ask of you more than you wanted to give?'

She moved back into his arms, raised her head from his shoulder to give him a quizzical smile. 'Of course not!' Surer of herself now, she kissed the corner of his mouth and then laughed. 'Though in truth, I still cannot quite believe I'm here, in your bed. If anyone had ever told me that I'd meet a man in a summer garden, a man I knew not at all, and would be making love with that man just hours later . . . I could as soon have imagined myself walking from Micklegate Bar to the Minster clad only in my kirtle.' She laughed again. 'But then, you're not just a man I met in a garden, are you?'

Richard said nothing, not until she sat upright in bed, pointed toward the open window. 'Did you see? A shooting star!'

He had not but nodded obligingly, watched with a smile as she shut her eyes like a little girl, her lips moving in silent supplication. He wondered what she'd wished, knew without having to consider at all what his own wish would have been, for a night of untroubled sleep, a night free of dreams of Anne.

As tired as he was, he would have sworn he'd be asleep within minutes, but he was not long in realizing he was in for another long sleepless siege. He was intensely aware of Rosamund; sharing a bed was in a strange way an even greater intimacy than that which had already passed between them. It was too hot a night for physical closeness; he could feel sweat tracking a sticky path down his rib cage and, wherever Rosamund's body touched his, their skin clung, damp and uncomfortable. Not wanting to disturb her, he moved as little as possible, and as the hours passed the bed began to take on the contours of a prison, the night one unlikely ever to end.

It was well past midnight when Rosamund sat up suddenly and without saying a word, rose from the bed and moved to the table that held a flagon of night wine and a loaf of bread. Pouring a cupful, she returned to the bed, handed it to Richard.

'I did you no favour by asking you to stay,' he said ruefully. 'Back at the inn, at least you'd have enjoyed a tolerable night's sleep.'

'My husband often suffered restive nights. I found that by rubbing his back and shoulders, I could sometimes ease his tension, enabling him to sleep.' Her voice rose questioningly and Richard nodded gratefully, rolled over onto his stomach.

Her hands played soothingly upon the back of his neck, much as Anne had often done; he sought to put the memory from him, closed his eyes. Rosamund continued her skilful kneading and gradually he began to relax.

'When did you injure your shoulder?' she asked, exploring the line of the break with gentle fingers.

'A long time ago, when I was a boy at Middleham,' Richard said, and had the eerie sensation that he was talking about someone else's life, someone who bore no relationship to him at all.

When he did fall asleep, it was the deep dreamless sleep of utter exhaustion. And then it was morning, Rosamund was gone and the chamber was ablaze in summer sun. His servants were hovering by the bed, looked relieved when he stirred, sat up abruptly.

'What time is it?'

'After nine, my liege.'

'Good God,' Richard said. He never slept later than six, never.

'We were loath to disturb you. . . .' The man's voice trailed off; all in his household knew how bad his nights were.

'Your Grace, Viscount Lovell asked that you be informed as soon as you awakened. Lord Stanley's son did attempt last night to slip away in servant's garb. He's being held under guard, awaiting your will.'

George Stanley was Lord Stanley's eldest son and heir, held his title as Lord Strange by right of his wife, Elizabeth Woodville's niece. He was a mild-mannered man in his mid-twenties, whose most distinguishing feature was a head of flaming red hair, and Rob had promptly dubbed him the 'Fox Cub', in deference both to his high colour and his father's well developed sense of survival. But the derisive nickname no longer seemed appropriate. Richard had seen foxes run to earth; the trapped animals invariably turned upon their tormentors with the defiance of desperation. There was no such fight in Stanley. He was sheet-white, clutched a wine cup with both hands, unsteady hands already sticky with wine. At sight of Richard, he sank to his knees, and with the feverish urgency of one seeking absolution through confession, he began a rambling account of conspiracy, treason and Henry Tudor.

Richard heard him out in silence and that seemed to make Stanley all the more nervous. He'd already implicated his uncle, Sir William Stanley; now he admitted, too, that his cousin Sir John Savage was equally mired down in the Tudor plot, watching Richard anxiously all the while, like a schoolboy seeking to see if his answers pleased.

'And your father?'

'I truly cannot say, Your Grace. As far as I know, he's not

committed himself to Tudor.' Stanley's legs were cramping and he started to rise, thought better of it. 'My lord, I'm not lying. I've held nothing back. I know you'd not believe me should I swear my father's loyalties be steadfast.' Behind him, he heard someone laugh bitterly at that but he kept his eyes on Richard.

'But you'd not deny my father does look to his own interests and right well. To put it bluntly, he's ever been one to play with a marked deck and, failing that, he'd as soon not play at all. I cannot see him compromising himself with Tudor lest he were utterly sure Tudor would win. Let me write to him, Your Grace. I'll tell him that my life does depend upon his loyalties, that if he joins forces with Tudor, I'll pay the price for it. He'll heed me, Your Grace, how could he not? Christ Jesus, but I am his firstborn son!'

'Get him pen and paper,' Richard said tersely, and Stanley slumped back on his haunches, quivered like a drawn bowstring suddenly gone slack. The letter he finally held out to Richard was ink-blotted, tracked with scratched-out words and smudged by clumsy fingers, but the message was impossible to miscon-strue, a cry for help that came from the heart. Richard handed it back, said, 'Seal it.'

Stanley complied, using a gold signet ring that adorned his thumb. 'Your Grace. . . . I've been honest with you, have freely admitted my part in my uncle's plot. I'll do whatever you want of me, whatever I can to keep my father true to his oath. I deeply regret that I let myself be used; I swear on my mother's soul that it be so. You've been merciful in the past with men less deserving than I. Can you not . . .?' His plea ebbed away into silence.

'Is that what you are asking of me . . . mercy?' Thomas Stanley was his Lord Constable; he'd made Will Stanley Chief Justice of North Wales, Constable of Caernarvon Castle. He'd given both men extensive land grants in the wake of Buckingham's rebel-lion. Stanley's nephew John Savage had also benefitted hand-somely. Richard looked at the frightened man before him, this man who was wed to a Woodville, a self-confessed traitor, a Stanley.

'Your fate is no longer in my hands. How many tomorrows you have depends upon your father and how he does respond to your letter.'

Stanley swallowed. 'He'll not betray you, Your Grace.'

'You'd best pray not,' Richard said grimly, 'for if he does, the first life to be forfeit shall be yours.'

Upon learning that Tudor had reached Shrewsbury, Richard decided to delay departure from Nottingham until his scouts could confirm the direction of the rebels' march. That Tuesday he took Johnny and the men closest to him and rode out to spend the night at Beskwood, a hunting lodge in Sherwood Forest five miles north of Nottingham. It was there the next noon that John Sponer and John Nicholson found him. They were men he knew well, had been dispatched by the city of York with an anxious message. It had been common knowledge in York for days that the rebels had landed in the southwest; why had the King's Grace not issued summons to arms for the city?

Richard turned to look at Francis and Rob, saw that his friends shared the same thought. The Earl of Northumberland had been entrusted with commissions of array for the East Riding. It was true there was plague in York but that Sponer and Nicholson were here now showed the city to be capable of mustering an armed force. What game was Northumberland playing? Why should he want to exclude those men most loyal to Richard from his command? Did he hope to hold aloof from the coming conflict as he'd done in 1471 and 1483?

'Tell Lord Mayor Lancastre and the council that I treasure the loyalty of the citizens of York above all riches of my realm. Tell them, too, that I am in need of as many men as they can muster.'

Plans were made to return that night to Nottingham but Richard found himself strangely reluctant to leave the green stillness of Beskwood and, shortly before dusk, he took Johnny out for a walk around the lodge grounds.

Loki and the wolfhounds loped on ahead, exulting in this forest freedom, barking for the sheer joy of it; birds broke cover all around them, launched themselves from the trees like so many feathered arrows and shot skyward. A narrow stream wandered along the northern border of the park. Richard knelt and, cupping his hands, drank deeply, then splashed icy water onto his face. Johnny at once did likewise.

'Johnny, I've arranged for an escort to take you north on the morrow . . . to Sheriff Hutton.'

Unlike Jack, Johnny made no argument; for days now, he'd been living in expectation of just this moment.

'Yes, papa,' he said dutifully, but as he looked at his father, his eyes were full of fear. Richard saw, reached out and tousled hair already untidy, windblown.

'It'll not be so bad. Your cousins are there, my brother George's two children, and Bess and Cecily.'

Johnny moved closer to Richard. In this past year, he'd embarked upon adolescence in earnest; his voice had at last found its own level, no longer embarrassed him by cracking at inopportune moments, and he was already as tall as Richard, showed himself likely to have the height Richard lacked.

'You'll send for me as soon as the battle be over?' he asked, as close as he could come to entreaty, and Richard nodded, said huskily, 'Fourteen is a wretched age, Johnny. I remember all too well, even remember saying that to the man whose name you bear.'

Johnny said with an effort, 'I cannot visualise you at fourteen, papa. Were you like me?'

'Very like you, lad.' But Richard wondered if it was true. Had he ever been as vulnerable as Johnny now seemed? He thought not.

A reddening haze was visible through the trees but Richard lingered there by the stream, made no move to go. It was so very still; almost he could believe that the encircling thickets marked the boundaries of their world, that beyond this woodland clearing all else had ceased to exist. He scuffed his boot against the moss-covered rocks, watched small silvery fish dart about in the shadows of the bank.

'Papa . . . what do you think about?'

'A great many things, lad. You and your brother. How very beautiful it is here, how restful.' Richard dropped a pebble into the stream, watched the ripples widen out in overlapping circles. 'I was thinking, too, of my brother's son, my namesake, thinking of Dickon. Strange that Tudor should have crossed the Severn at Shrewsbury for that was where Dickon was born . . . the seventeenth of August in the year of Our Lord, 1473. He'd have been twelve today.'

'He's dead, is he not?' Johnny said quietly, and only then did Richard catch his slip of the tongue, the involuntary use of the past tense. He jerked his head up, stared at his son.

'I've thought as much for a long time. That's why Londoners were so quick to believe those lies about you and Bess, is it not, papa? Because they think the boys are dead.'

Richard had not realized the rumours had reached his son. 'Ah, Johnny, Johnny, why did you not come to me ere this?'

'I did not want to burden you,' the boy said simply. 'But I decided they must be dead, else why would you endure such vile slanders in silence? Can you tell me what happened, papa?' His eyes were on a level with Richard's own, eyes of utter trust. 'Did they sicken?'

'No, lad.' Johnny was beside him now on the bank of the stream and Richard reached out, pulled the boy close. 'You remember how I left on progress that summer, a fortnight after my coronation? Buckingham remained behind in London and ere he departed the city, he had them put to death within the Tower.'

Johnny asked no questions, listened in silence as Richard explained his fateful decision not to publicize the boys' disappearance, related how the truth had eluded him up until the very moment he was given word of Buckingham's rebellion.

'But . . . but it is so unfair!' Johnny burst out at last.

Richard studied the youthful face for clues; so much of Johnny's emotional life existed beneath the surface. The boy's passionate indignation was real enough but was it covering up a deeper distress? Had Johnny made any link between the fate of his cousins and his own should the coming battle go to Tudor? Richard frowned. He wanted to assure his son that whatever happened, he'd be safe, shielded by the very stigma that had blotted his birthright. He was no threat to anyone, was Johnny, a king's bastard with no claim to the crown, and thank God for it, thank God the Father and Christ the Son that it was so. . . . And yet if only it had been otherwise; if only Johnny could have been Anne's. Jesú, even now. . . . Was he ever to break his heart over what might have been? No, better to say nothing to Johnny, better not to risk sowing fears in a field that was fallow.

'Papa. . . .' Johnny was not looking at him; he was gazing down at the stream, which was taking on the streaking colours of sunset. 'Papa . . . you do expect to win?'

'Yes,' Richard said, 'I do, should God will it.'

28

Redmore Plain

August 1485

Richard had encamped his army along a high ridge to the north-west of the village of Sutton Cheney. It afforded the Yorkists a clear view of the barren treeless plain below, known to local villagers as Redmore for the blood-colour clay of its soil. A summer twilight was darkening the sky and the lights of enemy campfires were making themselves visible through the dusk. Like scattered stars plunged to earth, Francis thought, rather fancifully, and then turned at the sound of his name.

The man approaching was one well known to Francis, and in high favour with Richard. Sir Humphrey Stafford, the cousin who'd given Buckingham such grief when the latter sought to raise a rebellion in Herefordshire. Francis grinned and, in his pleasure at seeing an old friend, was able to forget for the moment that at this time tomorrow they might both be dead.

'It gladdens my eyes to see you, Humphrey, and your coming will mean much to the King.'

'Tell me of the Tudor, Francis. How many men has he been able to muster up?'

'Our scouts report about five thousand or so.'

Humphrey sucked in his breath. 'No more than that?'

Francis nodded. 'The only English knight to declare openly for Tudor has been Sir Gilbert Talbot; we think he brought over five hundred of his own retainers. Tudor had a few hundred Englishmen with him in exile, die-hard Lancastrians and the like. He was able, too, to put his Welsh blood to good use, swelled his ranks with some two thousand Welshmen. And the rest are French.' Francis's mouth twisted. 'The scum of every wharfside alehouse in Harfleur, not to mention the scores of felons given the choice of Tudor or the hangman's noose.'

Humphrey was grinning. 'Pox on them, what matters it if they be the Devil's own brood? Not when they do number five thousand and more than twice that many have turned out for the King.'

'I would that it were so simple,' Francis said sombrely. He moved forward, toward the edge of the bluff. 'See for yourself. There, off to the southwest; that is Tudor's encampment.'

Humphrey squinted into the distance. Below them, Tudor's

campfires glowed, as Francis said. But lights flickered, as well, to the north and to the south.

Francis gestured northward. 'Sir William Stanley, with about two thousand of his Cheshire hirelings. And Lord Stanley lies to the south at Dadlington, with a good thirty-five hundred more.'

'Sweet Mary, Mother of God,' Humphrey said softly, almost reverently. 'Are you telling me that when we go into battle against Tudor tomorrow, we'll have a Stanley army on each flank, with either or both likely to go over to Tudor at any moment?'

'Yes . . . I am.' Laconically.

'God rot those cocksucking whoreson renegades, may He damn them all to eternal hellfire!' Humphrey balled a fist, slammed it into the palm of his hand again and again. Francis, who'd had time to absorb the shock, watched with weary sympathy.

'Francis. . . . Francis, I'm damned if I do understand this. You know the King as well as any man and better than most. How in the name of all that's holy did he ever permit himself to get sucked into a trap like this?'

'I do not see where choice does enter into it.'

'Do not get your back up; I love the King, too. I fought under his command at Tewkesbury when he was but eighteen, was with him in Scotland when he took Edinburgh and Berwick. He's a right able battle commander, second only to his late brother, and I need not tell you that the men who served with him in the border compaigns would gladly ride with him to the outer reaches of Hell and back. That's why it is so hard for me to understand how he let it come to this.'

'The Stanleys have been flying under false colours for nigh on thirty years,' Francis pointed out, but less defensively. 'Treason has become a tradition of their House.'

'Well put, Francis, and God's grim truth. King Harry, King Edward, the Earl of Warwick. . . . The Stanleys did betray them all at one time or another; in that, King Richard stands in good company. I daresay the only thing upon which both York and

Lancaster could agree is that the Stanleys be men utterly without honour, men who'd have sold out Our Lord Saviour at Gethsemane without so much as turning a hair.'

'Well then? What would you have had the King do that he has not already done?'

'Plain speaking, Francis? I'd never have let Thomas Stanley leave for Lathom Hall, would not have let him out of my sight even to take a piss. Moreover, I'd not have entrusted Northumberland with the full responsibility for raising the northern levies. I grant you Northumberland's too great a lord to be shunted aside but it be no secret that he loves Richard not, begrudges the king the affections of the North. And the result? Tomorrow when we take the field against Tudor, we do so without the men of York, without a great many northerners loyal to the king.' Humphrey swept his arm wide, encompassing the triangle traced by the campfires burning across Redmore Plain.

'I daresay it was well nigh inevitable that one day we'd find ourselves facing this unholy trinity but did the King have to make it so damnably easy for them?'

Francis had no answer for him. He looked away, down at the darkening plain below, and then said abruptly, 'Do you want to see where we fight tomorrow, where the King does mean to take up position? Take a look there. See how the ridge does rise up to the south? Ambien Hill, it is called.'

Humphrey looked with a soldier's practised eye and, after a moment or so, began to grin. 'Damn me but we might just pull this off, after all! Bless the man, but he's gone and picked the one place in this whole Godforsaken field that'll protect our flanks. That steep slope on the north ought to keep Will Stanley from launching a surprise strike, and the marsh to the south will be between us and his whoreson brother.' His grin widened. 'And Tudor's men'll have to fight uphill with the sun in their faces . . . better and better.'

Francis, too, felt heartened. 'Tudor's no soldier,' he said

contemptuously, 'and he's facing a man who is, a man who was tutored in the ways of war by Edward of York. And those hell-spawn Stanleys know that as well as anyone; they'll not go over to Tudor ere they see us beaten. And if the day seems like to go for York, they'll turn on Tudor like sharks scenting blood.'

Humphrey nodded. 'All we do need on the morrow is a bit of luck.' He looked at Francis, no longer smiling. 'Edward of York's luck was legendary. Pray God that his brother's luck be no less.'

The squire was young and it was to be his first battle; he'd known with morbid certainty that he'd keep a wretched vigil through those solitary hours until sunrise. When he awoke, it was with a sense of wonder; he must have slept as soon as he'd dropped down upon his pallet. The tent was in darkness; all around him he heard the soft snores of his companions. It was still night, not yet time. He fumbled by the pallet for his boots, failed to find them and padded barefoot out into the night.

The grass was damp and cool; so was the air. Summer was in its final stages. He didn't tarry, relieved himself as quickly as possible, and plunged, shivering, back into the tent. But as he rolled into his blankets, he saw the light coming from within the inner partition.

An oil lamp still burned by Richard's bed and candles were lit on the small altar. Richard knelt in a circle of shadowy light; he held a rosary and his lips were moving. The boy paused, reluctant to intrude upon prayers and yet equally reluctant to withdraw. It greatly disturbed him that Richard should be awake and alone with the battle but hours away.

He waited patiently until Richard had completed the rosary before coming closer but he froze almost at once, for Richard had begun to speak again and, as the soft-spoken words became clear to the boy's ear, he felt the hairs rising on his arms and the back of his neck.

'Blessed Virgin Mary, I pray thee now, that in the hour when my eyes shall be so heavy with the darkness of death that I cannot see the brightness of this world, nor move my tongue to pray or call to thee, may it then please thee to remember my prayers to thee, to receive my soul in thy blessed faith. When death shall be so near, Lady, be to my soul comfort and refuge and defence, so that the enemies of Hell, so fearful to behold, may not confront me with the sins I have committed, but that these sins shall be pardoned at thy prayer and blotted out by thy blessed Son. Amen.'

He saw Richard make the sign of the cross, start to rise, but he stood rooted, mute. Why the prayer should have so shaken him, he did not know; it was a prayer that any man might recite on the eve of battle, that was likely being echoed all over camp. And yet he'd gone cold as he listened and now he, too, made the sign of the cross, staring at Richard with wide, stricken eyes.

Richard came to his feet and then recoiled at sight of his squire. 'Jesú!' He hated to show how tautly strung his nerves were, laughed rather self-consciously. 'With that catlike tread, Geoffrey, you've the makings of a good cutpurse.' Giving the boy closer scrutiny, he saw the youngster's pallor and his voice changed. 'What is it? Why are you not asleep, lad?'

Geoffrey pulled himself together, stammered, 'Your light, I . . . I saw it, Your Grace, thought you might have need of me. . . .'

He had a thick thatch of straw-colour hair, a peeling nose and sunburnt face smudged with freckles, was about Richard's age at the battle of Barnet. Richard looked at him, slowly shook his head.

'No, Geoffrey. Go on, sleep whilst you can.'

Still Geoffrey lingered. 'You, too?' he ventured at last.

'Yes,' Richard said. 'Me, too.' And as the boy ducked through the partition, Richard lay back down on the camp bed. It was narrow and not much softer than the sun-scorched arid earth at his feet, but last night he'd lain in his own travelling bed in a Leicester inn, and sleep had eluded him then, too.

He was still holding the rosary. It was a beautiful piece of work-manship, mother-of-pearl threaded through with gold filigree, had belonged to Anne. He laid it carefully on the table next to the lamp, brought his arm up to blot out the light.

How many hours now . . . three? Four? It was not a warm night, but his shirt was sticking to his back; his skin felt damp and clammy. Was he feverish? Or just sick from lack of sleep? He could not go on like this, had to be able to believe in his right. It was past midnight, was Monday now. The twenty-second of August, eighth day of the Feast of the Assumption. He'd been King for two years, one month and twenty-seven days, and on the morrow he'd know, would have the answer only the Almighty could give him. '*Dies Irae*,' he whispered. 'Day of Judgment.'

It was still dark but campfires were being doused and sleepy men were being prodded out of their blankets, yawning and cursing. Entering Richard's command tent, Francis was not surprised to find Richard up and already fully armed. Accepting a goblet of watered-down wine, he watched as Richard's squires checked their handiwork, sought to make sure that their sovereign's armour was securely fastened; more than one man had lost his life because a buckle broke or a strap gave way at a crucial moment. Francis knew that he was looking at a labour of love for the squires had somehow managed to restore the armour to its original lustre, and it gleamed in the lamplight like polished pier glass, as it had on Tewkesbury's Bloody Meadow.

Rob caught his eye. 'Dickon has just dispatched a herald to Thomas Stanley, ordering him to bring his forces into the royal camp.'

'Did he warn Stanley what would befall his son should he fail to obey?' It was not a question Francis felt he should have had to ask, but too often that summer he'd seen Richard neglect to do that which would have been obvious to anyone else and he felt some relief now when Rob nodded.

'Rest easy, he did, and in language not even a Stanley could mistake.'

A young squire was hovering beside them, holding out a plate of bread smeared with honey. 'My lord? Might you prevail upon the King's Grace? He says he wants nothing but he slept poorly last night. . . .'

Francis smiled into the boy's anxious eyes. 'Give it to me, Geoffrey. I'll see what I can do,' he promised, and making his way toward Richard, announced with forced flippancy, 'Your breakfast, my liege. If you will not humour me, do it then for Geoffrey. The boy's not likely to eat a mouthful unless he see you. . . .'

He stopped in midsentence as Richard turned, unable to suppress a gasp of dismay. Richard looked ill; his face was haggard, grey under his tan, and the skin around his eyes looked discoloured and bruised.

'You did not sleep at all, did you?'

'Yes, I did,' Richard said, very low, 'for an hour or so, but it might have been better if I had not. I dreamed. . . .' He shook his head, said with a twisted smile, 'It shows as much as that?'

Francis nodded. 'Dickon, it was not because of . . . well, that unpleasantness yesterday on the bridge?'

A look of surprise crossed Richard's face. But even as he shook his head, Rob said sharply, 'What unpleasantness? What are you talking about, Francis?'

Francis had forgotten that Rob hadn't been a witness to the incident, had taken it for granted that someone would've made mention of it to him by now. He hesitated, having no way to gauge the importance Richard had placed upon the prophecy, and Richard answered for him.

'It happened as we were on our way out of Leicester, Rob, on Bow Bridge, the second bridge over the Soar. The crowds spooked White Surrey and he shied suddenly, damned near threw me. In getting him back under control, my spur struck the side of the

1184

bridge and an old woman in the crowd screamed, cried out that she saw my head hitting the same spot, saw the bridge wet with my blood.'

It was an accurate account but not an entirely honest one; neither in Richard's voice nor in the matter-of-fact recital did he convey any of the unease that had coloured the moment, the superstitious awe that had swept the crowd. People had recoiled from the woman as if she were a leper, and many murmured of second-sight, clutched at crucifix and rosary, while the more morbid and intrepid pressed forward, stared in fascinated horror at the bridge as if expecting to see the stones dripping blood. It was, Francis knew, just the sort of lurid tale to spread like plague; he felt grimly certain that by now most of their army had heard at least a garbled version, and he said savagely, 'God rot that old crone, she did stink of cheap wine, was too bleary-eyed to see the warts on her own face, much less a vision of any sort. I do not know why I even mention it, Dickon, know you took it for the besotted babbling it was.'

'If you're asking whether I thought her a witch, Francis, I did not. She was simple, no more than that.' Richard smiled then, mirthlessly. 'It was not, however, the most auspicious way to take my leave of Leicester.'

'Dickon. . . .' Francis lowered his voice. 'The bad dreams. . . . What were they then?'

Richard had picked up one of the slices of honeyed bread. Now he set it back on the plate untouched. 'I dreamt of my brother,' he said reluctantly. 'Of my dead.'

He looked from one to the other, his eyes searching their faces as if seeking to imprint their features upon his brain. 'You've been loyal friends; no man ever had better. I know your concern; would that I could ease your minds. In all honesty, I cannot. I think you both know my feelings about this battle, my forebodings. But they go beyond the fear of defeat and death.'

'Can you tell us, Dickon?'

'I was taught from boyhood to believe that justice does not prosper without mercy, Francis. My brother thought not, warned me once that mercy was an indulgence no king could truly afford. And he was right. The Stanleys, Archbishop Rotherham, Reginald Bray, John Cheyney. . . . All men now backing this Welsh rebel, all men whose treachery I did overlook. Had I chosen to punish rather than pardon, had I executed them as I did the Woodvilles, we'd not have come to this . . . to Redmore Plain.

'It's not only my own life I must wager this Monday, it is yours, too, the lives of so many men. Well, never again, that I swear to you. Should God grant me the victory, I'll do what I must to make secure my kingship. I'm done with forgiving treasons, forgetting treachery. Leniency lends itself only to further betrayals. But that is not the way I ever wanted it to be and that is not a future I can look to with any expectation.'

Rob and Francis looked at each other, neither knowing what to say. But Richard was already turning away, moving to meet the scout just ducking under the tent flap.

'We've taken up position on the hill, Your Grace.' The man was unshaven, his jerkin sweat-stained and faded, but the grin he gave Richard was vividly triumphant. 'We thought sure we'd have to race Tudor's scouts for it but his camp is not even stirring yet. Think you that we ought to dispatch a herald out of Christian kindness, let them know we are waiting on them?'

There was a sudden easing of tension; men laughed for the first time that morning. The strategic advantages to the army occupying Ambien Hill were considerable; Richard had gained the upper hand without yet taking the field.

'My lord?' Francis turned, saw one of Richard's chaplains. There were priests as much at home on the battlefield as at the altar, men of God who circumvented the scriptural ban upon 'smiting with the edge of the sword' by using the mace. This man was not one of them. Gaunt and hollow-eyed, he reminded Francis of church paintings he'd seen of St Stephen; it took little imagination to envision him throwing his arms wide as the first stones struck, embracing martyrdom with all the passion of the true zealot. The impact of the man's personality was such that Francis made no protest as the priest grasped his arm, drew him into the inner reaches of the tent.

'Lord Lovell, you must talk to the King, must get him to change his mind. He says he'll not hear Mass, will not ask God's blessings upon York. He says that if his cause be just, God will be with him without need of prayer. And if it is not, then to ask the Almighty for victory would be to mock the Holy Sacrifice of the Mass, to profane the Sacrament of the Eucharist.'

Francis stared past the priest, at Richard's rumpled bed. Lord Jesus, have mercy upon him. Dickon's logic was as impeccable as it was unsparing. Where did he get the courage? It was more than his life he was offering up; for a man knowingly to choose death was a mortal sin and yet if he could not have the victory, Dickon meant to die.

'I'm sorry, Father,' he said thickly. 'There's nothing I can do. You can, though. You can pray for him, pray that the battle does go to York.'

The priest's eyes glowed like coals. 'I'm not talking about the outcome of a battle, I'm talking about eternal damnation,' he said fiercely, as voices rose suddenly beyond the partition. With the priest at his heels, Francis hastened back into the main section of the tent.

Geoffrey was holding Richard's helmet, clutching it to his chest. But all other eyes were on Richard, on the coronet in his hand, a narrow circlet of beaten gold studded with gems. Taking the helmet from Geoffrey, Richard snapped the circlet into place above the vizor.

'Your Grace, I implore you.' Francis had never heard John Kendall so distraught. 'The risk is too great.'

'For the love of God, Dickon, listen to the man!' Rob reached out, grasped Richard's hand. 'You wear that crown and you'll draw the whole field down on you. You're making yourself a target for every man jack that fights in Tudor's army, do you not see that?'

Richard shrugged, signalled for Geoffrey to assist in attaching the helmet. 'If Tudor wants my crown, let him take it from me, then . . . if he can,' he said coolly, and most of the men in the tent laughed; bravado had an appeal in itself that bore no relationship to common sense. Even Rob grinned, rather grudgingly. Francis and the priest watched in silence, their eyes riveted on the gleaming gold circling Richard's helmet.

It was just after 5:00 A.M. The last of the stars had faded into the misted light of coming dawn and the sky was opaque, the colour of cloudy pearl. To the east the horizon still hid the sun, but it looked to be a clear day for battle. Richard said that now to John Howard and the latter nodded, almost absently. His was to be the command of the vanguard and he had about him the rather harried look of a shepherd seeking to account for all of his flock, but as the slate-grey eyes came back to Richard's face, they softened somewhat. Richard was, at thirty-two, easily young enough to have been his son and there was a genuine caring in Howard's voice as he said softly, 'Dickon, are you all right?'

'Well enough.' But John Howard was a friend, entitled to honesty, today of all days. 'I slept rather poorly, Jack,' Richard admitted, and summoned up a taut smile. 'I remember Scriptures telling of a man who bartered his birthright for a bowl of pottage. Right now I think I might willingly yield up half my realm for a few more hours' sleep.'

'Well, we'll sleep sound tonight, one way or another.' A man too familiar with death to accord it undue respect, Howard often disconcerted others less phlegmatic, but Richard found his mordant humour curiously bracing and he reached out, rested a gauntleted hand upon Howard's arm.

'I know you'll look to the vanguard, Jack. Be sure, too, that you do look to yourself.'

'And you be sure that you do likewise,' Howard said dryly. 'The vanguard is ready to take up position on the hill, but Northumberland seems to be taking his own sweet time about getting the rear guard into formation. Have you had word from him?'

Richard nodded. 'He wants to keep his men here on the ridge, says that way he'll be in a better position to come to our aid should either of the Stanleys move against us.'

'That's true enough but it's no less true that he's not exactly panting to take the field against Tudor. I do not mean to malign the man, Dickon, but he's a mediocrity whose only known talent has been for equivocation despite the fact that the title he bears be one of England's proudest. Can you trust him?'

'Do we have a choice?'

'No,' Howard conceded, spat out a particularly virulent oath. 'That accursed earldom of Northumberland has never been lucky for York. Had Ned not taken the title from Johnny Neville and given it back to Percy, Johnny would never have betrayed Ned at Doncaster and. . . .'

'Your Grace!' It was Will Catesby, hastening toward them. 'A rider has just come in from the Duke of Norfolk's camp seeking the Duke.'

Both Howard and Richard started forward but the man found them first. Reining in abruptly, he tumbled from the saddle to kneel at Howard's feet.

'My lord of Norfolk,' he panted, 'we did find this pinned to your tent just after you left camp.' Thrusting toward Howard a sheet of smudged paper.

'Well? What is it, Jack?'

'Nothing worth bothering with,' Howard said brusquely, would have crumpled the paper beyond reading had Richard not held out his hand.

'I think I'd best see it, too,' he said, quietly insistent. The paper was creased, the writing barely legible, as if scrawled in extreme haste:

Jack of Norfolk, be not too bold,
For Dickon thy master is bought and sold.

Richard stared at it in silence, oblivious of Howard and Catesby. For a moment he felt nothing, nothing at all, and then, at long last, his rage broke through.

'Dickon, pay it no heed,' Howard said composedly. 'They merely seek to stir up suspicions, to touch our nerves on the raw.'

'Yes, but it's also true and we both know it. The Stanleys stand to gain far more under a Tudor kingship than ever they would under mine. You think Tudor has not pledged the sun and moon for their support? But this I swear by all the saints, that the price of betrayal will be more than they bargained for and payment shall be in the coin of my choosing.'

Howard had seen Richard's anger take many guises. In demanding the death penalty for Anthony Woodville and Dick Grey, he'd shown a rancour no less implacable for being glazed in ice. He'd sent Will Hastings to the block in a raging blaze of passion. But there was in his voice now a fury of surpassing bitterness, of an intensity to give Howard no small measure of satisfaction. His concern for Richard's state of mind had been only a little less than his fear of battlefield betrayal. There'd been times when it seemed to him that Richard's fatalistic acceptance verged dangerously close to indifference, and he thought now that their unknown tipster had done them a greater service than he'd ever know.

'I've known the Stanleys for nigh on thirty years, Dickon, and whilst they're long on promises, they're invariably short on delivery. If Tudor is counting on them to throw him a lifeline, he's like to find it a hangman's noose, instead.'

Richard turned to Catesby, knowing that the other man had read over his shoulder, seen the contents of the note. 'Will, keep this to yourself. Our men are edgy enough as it is.'

Catesby nodded, stepped back as White Surrey was brought

up for Richard. The stallion seemed to sense what was in the offing and was already showing signs of excitement, plunging and seeking to throw off the restraining hands at his head. He calmed down somewhat when he caught Richard's scent, but it was still several moments before Richard was able to mount.

'Dickon, wait.' Francis drew as near White Surrey as he deemed prudent and gestured. 'It is your herald, the one you sent to Stanley.'

The man slowed his horse to a walk, guided it through rows of suddenly silent knights. His was an easy face to read and Richard knew at once that the message he bore was not what they wanted to hear.

'Do not bother dismounting. What did Lord Stanley say?'

'He said . . . said it was not convenient, Your Grace, for him to obey your summons at this time.'

'I see,' Richard said through set teeth. Until this moment he'd continued to hope that Stanley could be coerced into keeping faith with his oath of allegiance; it was inconceivable to him that a man could have so little regard for the life of his own son, and he looked in the direction of George Stanley. The man's face was bloodless; his mouth hung slack but no words came out.

'You did warn him that his son was facing the axe?' Richard demanded, and the herald nodded miserably.

'He said. . . .' The man swallowed, flushed as if Stanley's response somehow reflected upon him. 'Forgive me, Your Grace, but these be his very words. He said, "Tell Gloucester that I have other sons."'

There was an incredulous silence. Richard caught his breath. 'Did he, by God? Well, as of now he does have one son the less!'

George Stanley sagged against his guards, began to sob. They looked at each other in uncertainty, not at all sure how Richard's command was to be interpreted. That he wanted Stanley dead, none doubted. But had he meant for the execution to be carried out at once? Or delayed until after the battle? It was impossible to seek further clarification. Richard had already wheeled White Surrey about; all around them the camp was in motion. The guards watched in dismay, then began to argue among themselves, unable to decide which was the greater offence, to delay the execution unduly or to carry it out prematurely. Stanley sank to his knees, but he wasn't praying, not yet. 'God curse him,' he wept, 'God curse him.' But whether he meant Richard or his father, none knew.

Among Stanley's guards, those in favour of immediate execution were proving most persuasive. After all, they argued, the man was a confessed traitor; moreover, could any of them recall ever seeing the King in such a rage? Stanley was jerked to his feet; one of the men went off to hunt for a makeshift block. It was then that Sir William Catesby reined in his horse before them.

It occurred to them that the solution to their dilemma was at hand, and they made haste to seek Catesby's counsel, quite content to pass the responsibility off onto a man of rank. Catesby was silent for a long moment, staring down impassively at the condemned man.

'Afterward,' he said at last, and George Stanley sobbed again, this time with relief at the reprieve.

Because of the terrain of the battlefield, the Yorkist army had been deployed in columns across Ambien Hill. John Howard was to open the attack with the vanguard. Richard had aligned the centre battle behind Howard's men, would reinforce the vanguard as needed with the men of the centre, and Northumberland remained on the ridge with the rear guard, watching for movement from the Stanleys.

The sun lay low in the east as Tudor's forces moved onto Redmore Plain. Their vanguard was to be led by the man Richard had faced fourteen years before at Barnet, the Earl of Oxford; he alone of the Tudor commanders had extensive battle experience.

The battle began in a way that boded ill for Henry Tudor. His scouts had failed to discover the presence of the marsh to the south of Ambien Hill and the vanguard had to wheel sharply to the north to avoid becoming bogged down in it. Had John Howard chosen to lead the Yorkist vanguard down Ambien Hill at that crucial moment, the result might have been a rout. A more conservative battle commander than Richard, Howard decided to hold back, to wait until the Yorkist centre came up in support, and the battle opened with an exchange of arrow fire, backed up by cannon shot.

Oxford re-formed his line, led his men in an assault upon the Yorkist vanguard. Howard's Silver Lion banners caught the wind, Yorkist trumpets sounded advance and the vanguard moved down the slope of the hill to engage the enemy. Fierce hand-to-hand fighting ensued. The sun rose higher in the sky and the plain became an arena of blood and death.

Henry Tudor had no knowledge of warfare. Nor did he have false pride, was quite content to stay well behind the lines and leave the fighting to his captains, to his Welsh and French troops.

Reginald Bray sat his horse some yards from Tudor's bodyguard. Tudor had chosen a vantage point on a rise of ground to the east of Sence Brook, and the knights of his household could follow the progress of the battle as if watching a play being staged for their benefit. They were, for the most part, spectators who'd rather have been participants, unwilling to entrust their fate into the hands of others, and the man at Bray's side was as restive as a stallion fighting a curb bit.

'I feel as out of place as a virgin in a Ramsgate bawdy house,' he complained. 'An hour into the battle and my sword's still unbloodied, like to stay that way, too.'

Such sentiments were utterly alien to Bray; he privately scorned any activity in which luck played too prominent a part. He liked John Cheyney well enough, a genial giant of a man whose size had spawned the inevitable appellation 'Little John', but he had no great regard for the workings of Cheyney's brain, and he snapped, 'For the love of Christ, John! Our lives hang by the thinnest of threads, the word of a Stanley, and all you can do is bemoan your inability to impale yourself on some Yorkist lance.'

Like many big men, Cheyney had a temperament virtually impervious to insult, and he merely laughed indulgently. 'I rather thought to do the impaling myself, Reg.'

Bray was no longer listening. 'Will you look at that lunatic?'

'Gloucester? Is he back in the fighting again?'

Bray nodded, gestured toward the distant figure on the white stallion. 'He's utterly out of his mind, has to be. What good will victory do him if he's not alive to enjoy it?'

'Well, each time he goes down that hill, the Yorkist vanguard seems to take heart and, to me, that would be well worth the risk.' Cheyney laughed again. 'I can make out that crown even at this distance, like a beacon it is for every bowman in Oxford's ranks. If nothing else, he's got the bloody nerve of a Barbary pirate.'

Bray raked his spurs into his stallion's flank and the startled animal plunged forward, away from Cheyney's big chestnut. He was in no mood to listen to Cheyney's blathering; ere long he'd be commending Gloucester on how well he handled a blade, as if this were some damn fool chivalric game they were playing. Did he not realize how desperate their plight was? Unless those hell-spawn Stanleys came through as promised, they were beaten. Gloucester had the numbers simply to wear them down; they'd already committed four of their five thousand to Oxford's vanguard but Gloucester still had half his centre intact and another three thousand under Northumberland up on the ridge. Twice now urgent messages had gone to the Stanley camps and still they stalled. Like Goddamn vultures, feeding only on the dead.

'Reg! Reg, down on the field! It looks to me like Norfolk's banner is down. Jesú, do you think . . .?'

John Howard was dead. The word spread shock through the Yorkist ranks and the demoralized men of the vanguard began to give ground. Richard at once threw his reserves into the battle while sending word to Northumberland to come up in support of the centre and vanguard.

Richard brought White Surrey to a halt in the very shadow of his standard. He stared up at it with unseeing eyes, up at the tusked Whyte Boar and his brother's *Rose-en-Soleil*, and then tossed the reins to the nearest man. As he slid from the saddle, he staggered, would have fallen had hands not grabbed for him, held him upright.

'Get me water,' he gasped, and even those few words brought pain, so raw had his throat become. Someone held out a flask; he raised his vizor and drank until he choked, spilling as much as he swallowed.

'Northumberland?'

Those around him shook their heads. 'No word yet, Your Grace.'

'Send again,' he said, panting; no matter how he tried, he couldn't seem to get enough air into his lungs and, when he closed his eyes, light burned against his lids, through his lashes, in a kaleidoscope of hot swirling colour.

'Dickon, you're limping.' It was Francis, putting a steadying hand on his elbow.

'My knee. . . . I wrenched it, somehow. A blow, I guess. . . .' On the battlefield below, command of the vanguard had passed to John Howard's son. Jack's dead, Richard thought, he's dead, and the words meant nothing to him, sank like stones into the exhausted abyss his brain had become.

'It's like being drunk, Francis,' he whispered. 'God help me, I'm so tired. . . .'

Men had begun to shout; a rider was coming from the north. The Silver Crescent of Percy shone upon his sleeve, a proud badge of a proud House. Richard didn't move, waited for Northumberland's messenger to come to him.

'Your Grace. . . .' There was unease in the man's eyes; he looked not at Richard's face but at the bloodied lions and lilies emblazoned across Richard's tabard. 'My lord of Northumberland bade me tell you that he regrets he cannot comply at this time with your command. He says it's best that he remain on the ridge, so he can move against Stanley if need be.'

There was no surprise. Rather, it was as if he'd been expecting no other answer, as if he'd somehow known it would come to this. Betrayal begat betrayal. Richard turned away.

'Your Grace, I've found him.'

Richard didn't at once recognize Brecher, the young scout who'd brought word a lifetime ago that Ambien Hill was theirs. His face was begrimed, caked with dried blood, and a deep gash angled across the bridge of his nose and up into his hairline, almost like the mark of Cain. But his eyes were bright, were blazing with excitement.

'I've found him for you,' he repeated jubilantly. 'I've found Tudor.'

Rob suddenly lunged at Northumberland's messenger, grabbed the man by the neck of his tunic. 'You go back to your master, you tell that whoreson Percy this, that in Yorkshire people look upon Richard of Gloucester as one of their own. As God is my witness, they'll remember Percy's treachery and they'll remember Redmore Plain!'

Brackenbury and Ratcliffe moved to interpose themselves between the two men, sought in vain to calm Rob's rage. The man's badge had come loose in Rob's hand; he threw it to the ground, flung it from him with an obscenity. Francis stared down at the badge, at Northumberland's Silver Crescent.

'That hag on the bridge,' he said slowly, 'she babbled, too, about the moon, said to beware if it changed.'

Humphrey Stafford had come up to stand beside him. 'We're talking treason, Francis, not witchcraft. But if we hope to salvage anything from this debacle, we'd best move fast. What chance we had of winning be gone now, compliments of that gutless wonder up on the ridge. Tell the King that, Francis, remind him how many men will fight for him north of the Trent.'

'Sir Humphrey speaks true, my lord.' John Kendall stumbled forward, awkward in armour, clutched at Francis's arm. 'Talk to the King. Make him see that one battle need not decide all, that he must not throw his life away for nothing.'

Francis looked from face to face, saw on each the same concern. 'I'll do what I can,' he said bleakly.

He found Richard and Brecher on the crest of the hill. Richard turned as he came up, gestured off to the northwest.

'There, Francis, you see the standard? The Dragon of Cadwallader. Henry Tudor, the would-be king.' He looked at Francis and smiled. 'God has not forsaken me, after all.'

Francis stepped closer, brown eyes looking into Richard's blue ones. 'Dickon. Dickon, you realize the risk?'

Richard's smile didn't waver; the sudden animation in his face was startling but somehow Francis did not find it reassuring.

'Yes,' Richard said readily, 'but it is a risk worth the taking. He's blundered, Francis. He's stayed put while the battle line shifted away from him.'

Others had joined them, Rob and Dick Ratcliffe and Will Catesby. Catesby was staring at Richard in utter disbelief. Too appalled for tact, he blurted out, 'You cannot mean to go after Tudor, Your Grace! To get to him, you'd have to cut clean across Will Stanley's army. If he chose to move against you, you'd not have a prayer in Hell.'

Richard's eyes shifted briefly to Catesby, without interest, as if listening to a language he couldn't quite comprehend. When he spoke, it was to Francis.

'If Tudor's dead, the battle's done. You do see that, Francis? There is no other way to make an end to this.'

1197

He didn't wait for Francis to reply, signalled for White Surrey to be led forward. The stallion was lathered, blowing froth, chest and haunches encased in armour no longer burnished, streaked with blood and dust. But he quivered expectantly as Richard reached for the pommel and, as soon as he felt Richard's weight securely in the saddle, he danced sideways on the trampled grass, eager to run.

Richard stroked his neck. Never had he felt so at one with the animal; as if the stallion's pulsing, mettlesome spirit had infused life into his own depleted reserves, he felt his fatigue fall away, aches and bruises and pain forgotten. The men around him came into sudden sharp focus, sun and sky forming a dazzling back-drop of blue over their heads, in which birds wheeled and circled, as if bearing witness to the battle taking place below. Richard raised up in the stirrups; his voice was husky, hoarse from shouting, and the knights of his household crowded in closer, straining to hear.

'The battle's all but lost. One chance remains for victory. Tudor's within range, protected only by his guard and the knights of his body. But it means passing in plain view of Stanley's army. I'd not order any man to this; I do ask, instead. Who'll ride with me to seek Tudor?'

The only sound Richard could hear came from White Surrey. The stallion snorted, sucked air into his lungs in loud, wheezing gulps; Richard's own breathing sounded scarcely less laboured to his ears. And then someone shouted, *'Loyaulté me lie!'* It was Richard's own motto, adopted by him at age sixteen in defiance of the conflicting claims upon his heart. Loyalty Binds Me. Others now took it up, chanted his name and the battle cry of his House, 'Richard and York!' And then the hill exploded into action. Men were yelling for their horses, snapping shut vizors, grabbing for lance and sword. Men who accepted without question that his quarrel was good, his right to the crown just. A pledge of faith to be redeemed in blood if need be.

Through a blur of tears, Richard saw Francis standing at his stirrup. He reached down, took the lance Francis was offering, touched it lightly to the other man's shoulder, as if conferring knighthood.

Richard had no need of spurs, merely had to give White Surrey his head. The stallion plunged down the slope of the hill, lengthening stride, mane and tail like streaming silver banners in the wind. Off to the left, the battle raged. To the right, Will Stanley watched with his red-jacketed Cheshiremen. Ahead lay the flat-land of Redmore plain and the distant Dragon standard of Henry Tudor.

White Surrey was rapidly outpacing the other horses. Francis's stallion was falling back; he spurred it without mercy but it was unable to match the white stallion's blazing speed. He no longer heard the sounds of battle, had eyes only for Richard's banner of the Whyte Boar.

They were close enough now for Francis to see the confusion in Tudor's camp. Men were running for their horses, bumping into one another, surging forward to close ranks around their lord. A score or more of foot soldiers had been posted as guards; they were gaping at the oncoming knights as if unable to accept the evidence of their own eyes. A man on foot was no match for an armed knight and they knew it, scattered before the onslaught.

Francis saw one man stand his ground and, with foolhardy courage, jab upward with his spear. White Surrey swerved, flashed on by. The man was dead long before Francis reached him, all but decapitated by a single sword thrust.

The knights of Tudor's household moved to fend off the Yorkist charge. Francis saw a knight on a chestnut destrier bearing down upon Richard, a man of such bulk that Francis knew he could only be John Cheyney of Sheppey. He shouted but Richard was already turning to meet Cheyney's attack. Cheyney swung a morning-star mace in a wide arc toward the gold crown; the spiked ball slashed the air, all but grazed Richard's vizor. Cheyney jerked his mount around, circled back for a second strike. Richard's aim was truer. His lance hit Cheyney full in the chest. The impact of the blow shattered the point of his lance and Richard reeled back in the saddle. But Cheyney's horse was rearing up and Cheyney was toppling backward, hitting the ground with all the force of a felled oak. All around Francis, men cheered.

A knight came riding at Francis from his left. He swung at Francis and missed. Francis parried the second blow with his own sword and swept on. He saw ahead the Dragon standard and suddenly he realized that they were going to win, that this desperate gamble was about to succeed. There was no coherency to his thoughts, just an awed understanding that Richard was within yards of reaching Tudor and, once he did, Tudor was a dead man. Tudor's knights knew it, too, flung themselves in Richard's path. Never had Francis seen him fight like this; he hacked his way clear with a single-minded fury that was not to be denied.

Tudor's bodyguards were frantic. His standard-bearer wheeled about, spurred his mount into White Surrey, rising out of the saddle to strike. Richard twisted sideways and the blow glanced off his stallion's armour. He was using his battle-axe now and caught the standard-bearer in the throat. The axe cleaved through the man's gorget with murderous ease; death was mercifully quick. Richard's axe swung a second time and the Dragon of Cadwallader went down into the dust.

A Yorkist knight came careening into Francis's stallion, almost knocking his horse to its knees. He recognized the other animal before he recognized the rider, a distinctively marked chestnut with mane and tail the colour of flax, Rob's favourite destrier. Rob was hauling at the reins, trying to turn his maddened mount away from Francis.

'Stanley's moving!' he shouted. 'Get to Dickon, warn him!'

Francis recklessly jerked up his vizor. A sea of red was sweeping down upon them, Stanley's hooded Cheshiremen.

'Christ Jesus, no!' There was no fear, not yet, only a dazed disbelief. All around him, men were turning, yelling, cursing. With reinforcements on the way, Tudor's beleaguered bodyguards were pulling back; Francis could no longer find Tudor.

Richard was some yards away; he, too, had swung his stallion about. His isolation struck Francis like a physical blow. Shouting Richard's name, he urged his stallion forward. His mount picked up speed, veered aside to avoid a dead horse and shattered its cannon bone; Francis actually heard it snap. He had no time to react, not even to cry out. The ground dropped away and he pitched forward.

He landed on his back, every bone in his body jarred by the force of his fall. Stunned, he lay motionless for several moments; there was a wild ringing in his ears and a warm wetness on his face. Blinded, dazed, he struggled to sit up and, in panic, yanked at his helmet until it came loose in his hands. Wiping away blood, he was able to see again, and suddenly he was fully conscious, he remembered all.

Somehow, he got to his feet. He was alone; the battle had passed him by. But even as he lurched forward, Stanley's cavalry slammed into the knights of Richard's household, less than a hundred men against two thousand. It was like watching an avalanche, engulfing all in its path, engulfing his friends.

'Oh, God, God no. . . .' He fell, regained his feet. Richard's banners still fluttered, St George and the Whyte Boar, but as he stumbled toward them, they disappeared from sight, were dragged down into the surging red tide. Francis cursed, sobbed, and then he saw White Surrey. The stallion was rearing up, forelegs flailing the air, teeth bared like some huge, savage dog.

'Dickon! Christ, no!' Richard was utterly surrounded by Stanley's soldiers, hemmed in on all sides. He'd lost his axe, was lashing out with his sword, gripping it with both hands and swinging it like a scythe as more and more men fought with each other to get close enough to strike at him, beating against his armour with mace and halberd. In a frenzy of fear and rage, White Surrey was going up again and Francis saw a pike thrust upward, into the animal's unprotected underbelly. The stallion screamed in agony and crashed heavily to earth, dragging Richard down, too. Stanley's men closed in.

Unable to absorb what he'd just seen, Francis struggled on, falling repeatedly, no longer feeling the pain. A horse came galloping toward him out of the melee and, reacting instinctively, he grabbed at the trailing reins. The shock all but wrenched his arms out of their sockets, but somehow he held on and, the weight of his armour acting much like an anchor, was able to bring the horse to a shuddering stop. For a time he could only cling to the saddle pommel, leaned heavily against the animal's heaving side. The stallion's saddle was smeared in red; even its mane was matted with blood. Francis stared at the blood, stared at the horse, a distinctively marked chestnut with mane and tail the colour of flax. The reins slipped through his fingers; he stumbled backward.

He caught movement to his right, saw a knight spurring his mount away from the slaughter the battle had become. At sight of Francis, the knight changed course abruptly, rode right for him. Francis had lost both sword and lance in his fall, had no weapon but a dagger; he made no move to unsheathe it, simply stood there and watched the knight come on.

'Francis!'

Expecting a sword-thrust, Francis blinked, looked up blankly at this unknown adversary who called him by name. The man's vizor was going up; the face within was ashen, familiar.

Humphrey Stafford grabbed the reins of Rob's horse, held it out to Francis. 'Can you mount alone? For the love of Jesus, Francis, make haste!'

Francis started to reach for the reins, stopped abruptly. 'A sword . . . I need a sword.'

'Francis, it be too late for that.' Humphrey glanced back over his shoulder and then swung down from the saddle. 'Here, let me help you. Lean on me.'

Francis backed away. 'The battle. . . .'

'It's over. Francis. He's dead. They're all dead. It's over.'

Francis shook his head. 'No,' he said. 'No.'

29

Sheriff Hutton

August 1485

Cecily raised her candle, stared down at her cousin. In sleep, Edward looked much younger than ten, looked as if his dreams were as troubled as his daylight hours. His face was wax-white, lashes matted and wet. She reached out, touched the flaxen hair. God pity him, so little love in his life. No wonder he'd given his heart so completely into Anne's keeping. The hurt had yet to heal; he still grieved for her. And now, not six months later, his uncle, too, was dead and what was to become of him?

It was not a question Cecily could answer. She knew only that she feared for him, feared for them all in an England ruled by Henry Tudor.

Five days had passed since Tudor's soldiers had come to Sheriff Hutton. Cecily was still in shock, still unable to believe that the victory had gone to Tudor, that her uncle was dead. No king of England had died in battle since the Conquest. How had it happened? How could God have let it happen?

She backed away from Edward's bed, closed the door quietly

behind her. It was late but she did not want to go up to the chamber she shared with her sister. Tomorrow they were to depart for London; let Bess have these last hours alone, free from all eyes. She would to God there was more she could do.

But Bess was suddenly a stranger. Her emotions had always been sun-warmed, open to light and air; since earliest childhood, she'd been so. Yet now it was as if all emotion were glazed over, congealed in the ice of an unnatural indifference. She did not weep for her uncle; she did not pray. Tearless and taut, she'd retreated into a frozen silence none dared to breach, not even Cecily.

As little as Cecily could do for her sister, she could do even less for her cousin Johnny. She, too, had lost her father at four-teen and she ached for the boy, but when she sought to comfort him, he merely looked at her. Since being told of Redmore Plain, he'd moved about the castle like a ghost, mute, beyond reach. Cecily tried not to think what the future might hold for him.

Leaving Edward's bedchamber, she encountered one of Tudor's soldiers in the stairwell. He greeted her with deference, let her pass unchallenged, but she could feel his eyes upon her as she climbed, and she knew that other eyes would be watching to make sure she entered her bedchamber, to make sure she was safely accounted for.

Well, let them spy on her. Let them see her go into her cousin's chamber. She did not care. A sudden draught claimed her candle flame. She'd never before feared the dark but now she shivered, feeling her way along the wall by touch until she found the door. She did not knock, shoved the latch back and slipped inside.

The three men within turned startled faces toward her. Her cousin, Jack de la Pole, Earl of Lincoln, Lord Lieutenant of Ireland, York's heir. Nearby, a lean greying man in middle age, a dark face made memorable by the slash of a Lancastrian blade; the scar at once drew all eyes, curving across his cheekbone in a trail whitened and knotted by time. And in the shadows, a younger man, hair bright as fresh-spilt blood, right arm cradled in a soiled white sling.

Cecily ignored him, ignored her cousin, spoke only to the man with the scar. 'The castle steward told me you were here. You are Thomas Wrangwysh. You've come to tell my cousin about the battle, have you not?' She didn't wait for a response, moved toward him. 'I would have you tell me, too, Master Wrangwysh. I. . . .' She drew a steadying breath. 'I have the right to know.'

The men exchanged glances. She saw her cousin Jack nod and then she was being ushered to a chair. The young man with the fiery hair moved to pour wine for them all; Cecily gripped her cup gratefully, entwined her fingers around the stem to hide her trembling. She did not want them to know how much she dreaded to hear what they were about to tell her.

'How did you get the guards to give you entry, Master Wrangwysh?'

'I was given a pass, my lady.' The night was chill, warned of an early winter, and Wrangwysh shifted his seat closer to the hearth. 'Henry Tudor has sent an emissary to York to proclaim his right to the English crown. Henry the Seventh by the Grace of God. . . .' He leaned over, spat very deliberately into the floor rushes. 'But his man—Cotam, his name be—feared to enter the city, feared he'd be torn limb from limb . . . as well he might. He's been keeping out of sight in an inn on the Ermine Road, sent word to Lord Mayor Lancastre and the city council to wait upon him there. We did, pledged that we'd keep his whereabouts a secret. In return, I asked for the right to enter Sheriff Hutton, to confer with your cousin, the Earl of Lincoln.'

He turned then, gestured toward the third man. 'This is John Sponer, York's Sergeant to the Mace. When Northumberland—God rot him—issued no call to arms for the city, we sent John to King Richard at Nottingham. After dispatching word back to York, he accompanied the king south . . . to Redmore Plain.'

John Sponer flushed under their scrutiny, began to fidget

1205

nervously with his bandage. 'It is an ugly tale.' Almost inaudibly. 'If you want to know why King Richard died, I can tell you plain out in just one word . . . treason.'

Silence settled over the room. Jack and Cecily waited. He sloshed wine into his cup but didn't drink. Wrangwysh at last leaned forward. 'Go on, lad.'

Sponer nodded, said bleakly, 'Had he only withdrawn into the North once he saw the battle was lost . . . all of Yorkshire would've rallied to him. But he chose, instead, to gamble on reaching Tudor. And came so close, he did, came within a sword's thrust. . . .' His voice trailed off.

Again, silence. Thomas Wrangwysh drank too deeply, began to cough. 'It was a slaughter, no honour in it. Of King Richard's friends, Viscount Lovell alone survived the carnage on the field. He and Sir Humphrey Stafford have taken sanctuary at Colchester. The others died with the King, good men, all. . . .' He drank again. 'That whoreson Stanley found King Richard's crown . . . after. Caught in a hawthorn bush, it was, all dented and. . . .' He stopped abruptly. Fumbling for his handkerchief, he started to turn his face away. And then, scorning subterfuge, he wiped his eyes and blew his nose, saying thickly, ''Tis nothing to be shamed about, to mourn a friend. . . .'

There was a self-conscious challenge in that last word as if he feared he was taking a liberty that might not be permitted. But neither Cecily nor Jack thought to dispute him. They knew Richard would have been pleased to have Wrangwysh call him friend.

For a time, quiet prevailed, a silent shared grieving for a man each remembered all too well. Cecily raised her hand to her face, was dully surprised to find it wet. 'You must tell me,' she said, and her voice was tremulous, pleading. 'I know naught of battles. My uncle's death. . . . Was it quick?'

A long pause and then Sponer nodded. 'Very quick, my lady.' But none of the men would meet her eyes. She braced herself against the back of her chair, clutched the armrests with icy fingers; she was cold, so very cold. Before she could speak, Thomas Wrangwysh said hastily,

'You should know that Doctor Stillington has been arrested, Tudor giving the order the very day of the battle. He was brought into York two days past, is to be taken to London to the Tower. He's in a pitiful state, sore crazed by reason of his troubles. We did what we could; our Lord Mayor insisted that he be allowed to stay within the city for a few days. But we do only delay the inevitable. . . .'

Jack stood up suddenly. 'I thank you both for coming to me. And for confirming what I'd already suspected . . . that I'd best make my peace with God whilst I still can. With all the sins I have to answer for, I'll need more time than most men, I daresay.'

It was a game attempt at a jest, one that fell utterly flat. Cecily made a small sound, quickly stifled. Sponer stared down at his hands. But Wrangwysh shook his head.

'No, my lord, mayhap not. Yorkist loyalties did not die with King Richard at Redmore Plain. A good portion of the country still holds for York. Tudor knows that; whatever else the man may be, he's no fool. Cotam told us that if you are willing to swear allegiance to Tudor, he'll spare your life, may even find you a place in his government.'

Jack gave a strained mirthless laugh. 'For how long?'

At that Sponer spoke up. 'He cannot charge you with treason, my lord. You were not at the battle, did not fight for King Richard.'

'But . . . but how could Tudor charge anyone with treason?' Bewildered, Cecily looked from one man to the other. 'He cannot attaint any of my uncle's supporters. For how could men fighting for an anointed king ever be accused of treason?'

'Quite easily, my lady,' Wrangwysh said bitterly. 'Tudor means to date his reign from the day before Redmore Plain!'

Cecily stared at him, stunned. 'But surely he'd not get away with that? It is so blatantly illegal, so unjust. . . .'

'Unjust?' Sponer could contain himself no longer. 'You think men like Tudor and the Stanleys know aught of justice, of common Christian decency? After what they did to King Richard's body. . . .' He caught himself but not in time.

'What mean you by that?' Jack demanded, and when Sponer still hesitated, he snapped, 'He is my uncle, damn you! Tell me!'

Sponer's face was bloodless, as if all vitality and life had been sapped by his flaming thatch of red-fire hair; livid freckles stood out across his nose like pinpoint wounds.

'He never had a chance,' he whispered. 'That damned crown, it drew all of Stanley's cutthroats down on him. He died shouting "treason", died hard. They kept stabbing and hacking at him long after he was dead; I heard it said that men sickened afterward at sight of his body. They stripped him naked, knotted a felon's halter about his neck and slung him over a horse, made one of his own heralds ride it back into Leicester, where they dumped his body in the court of the Grey Friars, left it there for two full days ere they'd allow burial. I heard it said, too, that some anointed him in his own blood, that they even. . . .'

Cecily didn't realize she'd cried out until they all turned toward her, until Jack pulled her to her feet, into his arms. 'Hush, lass, hush. . . . Do not think about it, Cecily, do not. . . .'

He was giving her wine; she drank, choked and began to sob. Jack reclaimed his wine cup, drained it in one long swallow.

John Sponer was on his feet, too. 'My lady, forgive me! God curse my stupid tongue, I never meant for you to know. . . .'

'No,' she said faintly. 'Better that I do, that I know the nature of the man we are dealing with. But Jesú, to so dishonour the dead. . . .' She shuddered and then straightened up, moved out of Jack's embrace. 'You must promise me . . . all of you. You must swear by all the saints that you'll not say a word of this to my sister. She must not be told, must not ever know!'

'She will not, Cecily,' Jack said swiftly. 'I'll see to it, I swear it.'

'Lady Cecily. . . .' Thomas Wrangwysh rose, came toward her.

'Upon the health of my soul, I'd not grieve you further. I would to God I need not burden you with yet more cares. But you must understand what be at stake.

'Your brothers. . . . It is known that they've not been seen in London for these two years past. That never troubled us in York; it is clear as well-water that King Richard had them moved, had them settled somewhere safe. He has . . . had any number of secluded moorland castles. . . .' He paused, waiting for a response. When it didn't come, he continued reluctantly, 'I do not mean to frighten you. But know you if your uncle made provisions for the boys in the event of his defeat? He must've known they'd not long survive him should Tudor win the field, that they'd have to be smuggled out of the country, to Burgundy. . . .'

Cecily roused herself, said, 'You need not fear for my brothers, Master Wrangwysh. They are beyond Tudor's reach.'

'God's blessed truth, it's glad I am to hear you say that,' he admitted. 'For Tudor has no choice but to repeal the Act of Titulus Regius, to declare the plight-troth fraudulent. He's committed to it, has sworn a public oath to make your sister his queen, and Cotam says he means to hold to that oath. She is a threat to him, you see, Edward of York's firstborn. He'll not let her go. He cannot risk having her find an ambitious husband eager to advance the claims of York on her behalf.'

'You're saying, then, that she must wed with Tudor?'

He nodded. 'My lady, listen to me. You know that your cousin, the Earl of Warwick, is to go to London with you and the Lady Bess. But Cotam told us that the lad is then to be escorted to the Tower and there confined.'

'Christ,' Jack said softly. Cecily felt his hands tighten on her shoulders.

'But he is so young,' she whispered. 'Just a little boy. . . .'

'Aye, but he's also the Duke of Clarence's son, and that be what matters to Tudor, to'—his mouth twisted—'our new king. Now do you understand, my lady? Your sister must marry him;

she'll be given no choice. You must make her realize that, must. . . .'

'She already knows, Master Wrangwysh.' Cecily turned away, blinking back tears. 'Lady Mary pity her, she knows. . . .'

30

Westminster

December 1485

Bess was holding her five-year-old sister upon her lap. 'Listen now, Bridget,' she murmured, 'and I'll teach you a Christmas carol . . . like this:

> Noel, all, all, all
> Now is well that ever was woe.
> At Bethlehem, that blessed place
> The child of bliss born He was,
> Him to serve, O give us grace,
> O lux beata trinitas.'

Bridget listened intently and, as Bess repeated the verse, the little girl chimed in. It was Cecily's favourite carol, reminded her of too many Christmas seasons past. She looked away.

'How long now till Christmas, Bess?'

'Just three days, Bridget. This is Thursday and Christmas comes on Sunday.'

Thursday, the twenty-second. Four months since Redmore

Plain. Cecily had gone to St Paul's that morning, had secretly arranged to buy Masses for the repose of her uncle's soul. She wondered if Bess had done likewise but knew she wouldn't ask. There were any number of subjects she and Bess no longer discussed, even in utter privacy. They never talked of Redmore Plain, of their brothers who were dead or their little cousin Edward in custody at the Tower. And they never talked of Richard.

December 22nd. In less than a month, Bess would be Tudor's queen. He'd had the Act of Titulus Regius repealed, had all copies burned, and on the eighteenth of January, he and Bess were to wed. That, too, they never talked about.

'I saw Jack this morning at St Paul's, Bess.' Cecily hesitated, dropped her voice still lower even though they were alone. 'Think you that he'll be safe once you're Queen?'

Bess kissed Bridget, set her down on the floor. 'I do not know.' Nothing of her thoughts showed in either her face or her voice and Cecily, whose every memory of her sister was one of warmth and expressive emotion, could no longer keep silent.

'Ah, Bess, do not,' she entreated. 'Do not shut your heart to me, too.'

She was never to know how Bess would have responded, for at that moment the door opened and Elizabeth entered.

'You have a visitor, Bess,' she said lightly, 'your lord husband-to-be.'

Cecily stiffened, sank down before Henry Tudor in a deep curtsy, as she'd never done in the private presence of her father or uncle.

He was a young man, not yet twenty-nine, but it was not a young face; the insecurities of exile had taught him to guard his secrets well. Too well, Cecily thought. She was ill at ease with this man and uncomfortably aware that he knew it. The eyes meeting hers now were a light clear grey; as fathomless as the depths of a well, they were not the windows to his soul, reflected only what he chose to share.

The strain in the room was palpable. Elizabeth alone refused to acknowledge the tension, made inconsequential social conversation with the ease of long practice. Cecily knew her mother's true feelings for Tudor, and she marvelled how adroitly Elizabeth camouflaged her disdain. But she saw something flicker in his eyes as Elizabeth called him 'Henry'; it was more than a distaste for the assumed intimacy and she thought in alarm, he does not like mama, not at all.

She was right. Henry Tudor's aversion to Elizabeth was so pronounced that he was hard-pressed to be polite to her; she was for him the epitome of all that he most detested in women—conniving, deceitful and haughty. Much of his reluctance to wed Bess could be traced, in fact, to his assumption that as is the mother, so is the daughter, and he'd begun to thaw toward Bess only when he realized that Elizabeth and Bess were as unlike in temperament as wine and milk.

Once he and Bess had been left alone, an awkward silence fell. There was more ease between them now but not enough to make their meetings comfortable. He wanted it to be otherwise, did not want to take a stranger to his bed, but the ambivalence in his emotions was such that he found it almost impossible to lower his defences. He knew she was no more eager for their marriage than he and resented her for it; resented her, too, for the Plantagenet blood that flowed in her veins, for the Yorkist loyalties she could command amongst his disaffected subjects. And yet he had to admit that Bess had conducted herself with dignity under circumstances far from easy. She'd shown, too, a lack of artifice that he found very appealing, that meant almost as much to him as her undeniable beauty.

He looked at her, at the soft red mouth, the full breasts, her graceful bearing, and acknowledged to himself that this marriage-of-state had attractions separate and apart from political considerations; he wanted this girl in his bed.

He followed Bess to the cushioned window seat, sat down

beside her in the winter sunlight. Her perfume put him in mind of the exotic scent of sandalwood and, acting on rare impulse, he leaned over, kissed her on the mouth. She accepted the caress passively and after a moment, he drew back. The continuing silence was threatening to become embarrassing and he was grateful now when Bess began to talk of commonplace matters, asked him politely how his day had gone.

'Quite well. I met with Bishop Morton for most of the morning. He will, of course, be my choice for the chancellorship.' He went on to talk of his council meeting that morning, speaking in generalities, for he did not believe women should be privy to the secrets of government. Bess listened attentively, making the proper responses. Only once did her mask slip; when he made mention of William Stanley, he saw her hands clench in her lap, saw her knuckles go bone-white in sudden tension.

The corner of Tudor's mouth twitched in a secret smile. He was quite willing to indulge her in this, her hatred of Will Stanley, for his own opinion of the man was far from favourable. It was true, as Stanley boasted, that he'd made a king on Redmore Plain, but he'd also taken his own good time in coming to Tudor's rescue, had waited almost until it was too late, and Tudor had not forgotten. They'd been the worst moments of his life, troubled his sleep even now, four months later. Unable to retreat, for to show cowardice before his men would be as fatal to his cause as the battle-axe Gloucester was wielding with such lethal skill. Yet knowing he could not hope to best the other man in combat. Watching helplessly as his executioner bore down upon him, a madman on a bloodied white stallion, on his helmet the gleaming gold Tudor had yearned for, schemed for, and would now die for.

Tudor blinked, mentally cursed his own memory for the clarity of his recall, for the merciless reality of his remembrances. Why must he be haunted by what was done and past? He had not been the one to die; instead, it had been Gloucester, trapped and alone in the midst of Stanley's murderous Cheshiremen. Stanley had

1213

come in time to save his life, after all, but had delayed long enough to endanger it, delayed too long to deserve gratitude.

A book lay on the window seat beside Bess and he reached for it, welcoming a neutral topic of conversation. It was an elegantly bound edition of *The Pearl*, a touching lament for the death of a beloved child. Opening it at random, he began to flip through the pages, and he was pleasantly surprised when Bess leaned over to point out her favourite passages, pleasure that lasted only until he turned to the flyleaf, saw the name written in a dead man's hand: Richard Gloucestre. He stared for a moment at the slanting signature, said tersely, 'He gave you this?'

'Yes.'

He slammed the book shut, tossed it on the table. A letter fluttered from its pages, fell to his feet. Picking it up, he started to hand it to Bess, but stopped as the words 'my castle at Nottingham' caught his eye. Unfolding the letter fully, he rapidly began to scan the page:

Dearest Bess, I've had time this summer to consider all that happened, and I think I do understand now how you and I found ourselves in such a coil. Grieving takes many guises, lass. We'd never accepted Ned's death, either of us, sought to find him in each other. I truly believe. . . .

Tudor got no further; Bess snatched it from his hand.

'That is private, meant for no eyes but mine.'

His pride and common sense spoke as one, advised him to let it lie. But the need to know what was in that letter was too strong and he held out his hand, said curtly, 'I'm to be your husband. That does give me the right to know of your past.'

She stared at him and then walked without haste to the hearth, very slowly and deliberately fed Richard's letter into the flames.

He was not a man to let his emotions show. 'I think, Bess, that it is time we talked about what there was between you and your uncle.' Only in the heavy stress laid upon the word *uncle* did he reveal the extent of his anger.

'I have consented to be your wife, Henry. I want no more war, no more killing, will do what I can to reconcile Yorkist and Lancastrian loyalties. I will do all that is expected of a wife, of a queen and, God willing, I will give you sons. But there is one thing I will not do. I will not discuss Richard of Gloucester with you . . . not now, not ever.'

'The choice is not yours to make, Bess. If you are to be my wife, I have the right to know the nature of the bond between you. You'd not deny that I have reason enough for doubts. The rumours linking your name with Gloucester's were such that he felt the need to make an unprecedented public denial. I heard it said at the French court that he would have married you if he dared, that he. . . .'

'You heard wrong,' she snapped. 'Dickon loved but one woman in his life. I was not that woman. Now if you still have doubts, I suggest you learn to live with them, for I've said all I mean to say.'

Her defiance rankled but what bothered him most was the easy intimacy of 'Dickon'. He regretted ever having started this, aware that they were on the verge of saying that which could not be forgiven, of destroying whatever fragile hope they might have of reaching some sort of accord. But he did not know how to back down, felt committed to press for answers he was no longer sure he wanted.

'Assuming that you're speaking the truth, you have only told me what Anne Neville was to Gloucester, not what Gloucester was to you. Bess, I'm entitled to know; you owe me the truth. Was he your lover?'

'No!' The mouth he found so desirable was contorted, rimmed in white. 'Not that I expect you to believe me, but no, no, he was not!'

She was trembling, angry tears welling in her eyes, spilling unheeded down her face, and he realized that whatever his right, it was a question he should not have asked.

'I do believe you,' he said at last, put his hand on her arm. She jerked away from his touch and he wheeled about, strode to the door. But his anger carried him no farther than the antechamber. There was too much at stake to walk away, to let this grievance fester between them; whether they liked it or not, he and Bess were stuck with each other and he did not want a wife who hated him, who submitted to him in silent loathing. He wanted more than her body, wanted her goodwill, her respect. Turning, he reentered the chamber.

Bess was on her knees by the hearth, thrusting the fire tongs into the flames. He was close enough now to see her aim, to see what looked to be a charred fragment of paper in the ashes. She was sobbing, tear-blinded, seemed oblivious of his presence even when he leaned over her and sought to take the fire tongs.

'Bess, you'll burn yourself and for nothing. The letter's burned; it's gone. Come now and give me the tongs.'

She shook her head, clung with surprising strength. 'No . . . there's part of it intact, I see it. . . .' She made a final lunge with the tongs, reached for the letter; it crumbled at the touch, fell apart in brittle flakes. Bess dropped the tongs, buried her face in her hands and wept.

'Bess. . . . Bess, for God's sake. . . .'

He was at a loss, at last put an arm around her, lifted her forcibly to her feet. She swayed against him, still sobbing, as a child would cry, without restraint or inhibition, soaking his doublet with her tears. He fumbled for a handkerchief, patted her back awkwardly. After what seemed to him to be an exceedingly long time, her sobs grew less convulsive; her breath no longer came in strangled gasps.

'Are you all right?' he asked, felt her stiffen against him as if realizing for the first time who was holding her.

'Yes, I . . . I think so,' she said, very low, moved to put space between them.

'If you're sure. . . .' He raised her hand to his lips, very formally, turned to go.

'Henry.'

He stopped his hand on the door latch and she said hurriedly, 'I . . . thank you.'

The door closed; she sank down weakly into the nearest chair. She'd been braced for a barrage of pointed questions, had been so sure he was going to begin harassing her about Dickon again. He'd just shown himself to be more sensitive than she'd have expected. But did he still believe her? If she had to choose three words to describe Henry, they would be clever, secretive and suspicious. If she had to choose but one, it would be suspicious.

She drew a deep, uneven breath. She was borrowing trouble and for naught. Even if she had stirred up his suspicions again, it would be easy enough to allay them once they bedded together, once he was reassured that she was a virgin. But she did not want to think of that now, God no. Coming abruptly to her feet, she began to circle aimlessly, tracking the confines of the room as she'd seen trapped lions in the Tower pacing their cages.

Suddenly realizing she still held Tudor's handkerchief, she paused before the fire, thrust it into the flames. They shot upward, blurred in a blaze of brightness; tears were filling her eyes again.

'I'm Elizabeth of York,' she said aloud, 'and I shall be Queen. God forgive me, papa, Tudor's Queen.' The tears were falling faster now, streaking her face like rain. Henry had been right; Dickon's letter was gone, burned beyond recall. But she remembered, remembered every word. Memories endured; they could not be burned.

'Grieving takes many guises,' she whispered. 'You were wrong, Dickon, you were wrong. I did love you. . . .'

1217

31

Mechlinia, Burgundy
July 1486

Henry Tudor passed his first Easter as King in the walled city of Lincoln. While there, he was warned that Francis Lovell and Humphrey Stafford had fled sanctuary, were seeking to raise an insurrection against him, Francis in the North and Humphrey in Worcester. Deeming Francis to pose the greater threat, for the North still smouldered with discontent, Tudor dispatched three thousand men north, under command of his uncle, Jasper Tudor.

Francis and Humphrey were labouring under an all but insurmountable handicap in that while their aim was to dethrone Tudor, they had no candidate to put forward in his place; Jack de la Pole seemed to have come to terms with Tudor's kingship, and George's eleven-year-old son was under close confinement in the Tower of London. When Jasper Tudor shrewdly proclaimed free pardons to all rebels, many of Francis's men had second thoughts about the risks of their enterprise, slipped away under cover of darkness. Francis made a desperate eleventh-hour attempt to ambush Tudor and, when that failed, he went into hiding in Lancashire. From there, he was able to make his way to the coast, to take ship for Burgundy. Margaret had made of her court a garden for the White Rose of York; she welcomed him as if he were blood kin.

Humphrey Stafford was not so lucky. He chose to seek sanctuary a second time, taking refuge at the abbey at Culham. On Whitsun Eve, John Savage and sixty armed men burst into the abbey, took Humphrey out by force. Despite his argument that his arrest was illegal since sanctuary had been violated, he was found guilty of treason. Taken to the gallows at Tyburn, he was there hanged, cut down while still living and disembowelled. He was then beheaded and his body divided into four parts, to be dispatched to various cities of the realm as a lesson to other would-be rebels.

At the same time, a London conspiracy to free young Edward from the Tower miscarried. The first challenge to Tudor's sovereignty had come to naught.

Mechlinia was a fortified river city in the province of Antwerp, for a number of years the favourite residence of Margaret of York, dowager Duchess of Burgundy.

Véronique wandered to the window, stared down into a summer garden of an almost tropical brightness. Swans were sunning themselves on the bank of the pond below but as soon as Véronique appeared at the window casement, they plunged into the water, launched themselves toward her like a feathered flotilla. She leaned out, began to throw bread down upon the water, trying all the while to shut out the conversation going on behind her.

Francis and Margaret were talking again of Redmore Plain. She did not want to hear them, felt as if every detail of that day were mercilessly etched into her brain. She knew how Richard had died, would to God she did not. She knew, too, of the unspeakable indignities that Stanley's men had inflicted upon his body once he was dead, knew that as Tudor entered Leicester in triumph, the horse carrying Richard's body had shied and his head had smashed into the side of Bow Bridge in grisly fulfilment of an old woman's prophecy, knew that his naked body had been exposed to the stares of the curious for two days and then rolled with scant ceremony into an unmarked grave. She knew that which she'd rather have forgotten, did not understand how Francis and Margaret could dwell upon memories so painful.

Why could they not see that vengeance was no antidote for grief? Even if they succeeded in overthrowing Tudor, would it bring back the dead? And what of Bess? Margaret's niece, Tudor's Queen, already pregnant with his child. Véronique had tried once, only once, to talk of this with Margaret. The other woman had heard her out in frozen silence and then said in a voice glazed with ice, 'I had four brothers and now I have none. I loved my brothers, Lady Véronique.'

Margaret had risen, was departing the chamber, and Véronique crossed to Francis, bent down and kissed him full on the mouth.

'Ah, love,' she whispered, 'can we not go away from here? Can we not try to forget? Let the dead bury their dead, Francis, I beg you.'

'And vengeance is mine, saith the Lord,' he said impatiently. 'Well, it's not vengeance I seek, Véronique, it's justice.'

'No, my love, you seek that which is beyond recovery. Oh, Francis, do you not see? You cannot redeem the past, not even in Henry Tudor's blood.'

'No, but I can act to safeguard the future, can keep it from being structured on lies. Christ, Véronique, you know what that whoreson Tudor's saying about Dickon. Usurper, tyrant, child-murderer.'

'Ah, Francis, you must not let it matter so. Richard cannot be hurt now by Tudor's lies, and none who knew him will ever believe it; they'll know the truth.'

'And what of those who didn't know him? What happens, too, when all who knew him are dead, when people know only what they've been told? What truth will we be talking about, then? Tudor's truth. Dickon doesn't deserve that, Véronique, and I will not let it happen. I swear to God I will not.'

She turned away without answering. It all seemed so senseless to her. So much suffering. So many deaths. Richard. Rob Percy. Dick Ratcliffe. John Kendall. Robert Brackenbury. Jack Howard. All dead on that accursed plain with the blood-colour clay. And what now? What of the children? The 'Little Princes in the Tower', she'd heard people call them, Edward's murdered sons. Was George of Clarence's son doomed, too, to suffer for sins not his? And Johnny . . . would the day come when Tudor cared not that Johnny was baseborn, cared only that he was Richard's son?

'Francis . . . listen to me. I dearly loved Anne Neville and scarcely a day has gone by in these sixteen months since her death that I do not think of her, that I do not miss her. But I accept her death, Francis, and I'm thankful that she's no longer suffering, that she's at peace.'

'Why are you telling me this?'

'Because your hatred for Tudor has become a mortal sickness, what the doctors call a cancer, eating away at you from within . . . blinding you to all else. Grieve for Richard by all means; God knows I do. But remember, too, his pain, remember how desperately unhappy he was in those last months of his life. I cannot help thinking, Francis, that for Richard, death was a . . . a release. Can you not try to see it that way, to accept it as such?'

'No,' he said curtly. 'No, I cannot. I do remember Dickon's pain, his grieving for Anne. But given time. . . .'

She shook her head. 'He'd lost more than his wife, his son. He'd lost his . . . his sense of self, and. . . .'

At that moment, the door opened; Margaret reentered. 'Here it is,' she said to Francis, 'my mother's last letter. There is something in it that I want you to read.'

Francis looked down at the beautiful Italic script. 'Your lady mother . . .' he said softly, 'how did she take Dickon's death?'

'My mother is a remarkable woman. She accepted his death as she has all the other griefs that the Almighty has given her. "Our blessed Lord is not indifferent to the suffering of His children. In His infinite wisdom, He has called Richard home," she wrote, no more than that. And yet. . . .' Margaret frowned, said slowly, 'It was almost as if she expected it, Francis, as if she expected Dickon's death.'

They looked at each other and then she put her mother's letter into his hand. 'Read that, read what the city of York dared to do when they learned of Dickon's death. They had every reason for caution, knew their city's prosperity and well-being now depend upon the whims of Henry Tudor, and yet read what they inscribed into the city records for Tudor to see, for all to remember.'

Francis stared down at the Duchess of York's letter. He swallowed, then read aloud in a husky voice,

"'It was showed by John Sponer that King Richard, late mercifully reigning upon us, was through great treason piteously slain and murdered, to the great heaviness of this City.'"

As Margaret listened, the embittered grey eyes had softened, misted with sudden tears.

'My brother may lie in an untended grave,' she said, 'but he does not lack for an epitaph.'

32

Bermondsey Abbey
June 1492

It was dusk when Grace rode into the confines of the eleventh-century Cluniac abbey. The Abbot himself was there to bid her welcome for she was the Queen's half sister, and Bess's strong sense of family was known to all.

Following her escort through the quiet twilight-shadowed

grounds, Grace could not imagine a more unlikely setting for the worldly, ambitious Elizabeth, and yet for more than five years now, Elizabeth's world had been bounded and circumscribed within the walls of Bermondsey, a life of isolation and enforced tranquillity only occasionally enlivened by brief court visits. It was, Grace thought, the ultimate irony that Elizabeth should have been accorded greater freedom by Dickon, who'd hated her so, than by her own son-in-law.

In February of 1487, Elizabeth had suddenly fallen into disgrace; she'd been stripped of her possessions and banished to Bermondsey. There was some suspicion that Elizabeth, an inveterate intriguer, had involved herself in Francis Lovell's rebellion, a suspicion strengthened when Tudor abruptly arrested Thomas Grey and confined him to the Tower, kept him there until after Francis and Jack de la Pole were defeated at the battle of Stoke Field on June 17th, 1487. Grace, however, never believed it. Elizabeth's entire life had been shaped by the dictates of self-interest and it strained credibility that Elizabeth should have wished to see her own daughter dethroned and George of Clarence's son crowned in Tudor's stead. The truth, Grace thought, was far simpler—that Tudor had seized the opportunity to rid himself of a woman he little liked and trusted less.

She was met in Elizabeth's antechamber by a beautiful woman in her late thirties, recognized Katherine Woodville. Katherine looked disappointed at sight of her, said, 'You came alone? None of Lisbet's daughters are with you?'

Grace shook her head. 'Bess's lying-in has begun. And Cecily is on her husband's estates in the West Country. I doubt she knows yet that her mother is ill.' She made no mention of the three younger girls, not knowing what to say. Bridget was now eleven, Katherine thirteen and Anne sixteen, and they were virtual strangers to Elizabeth, having been separated from her during the most formative years of their lives.

'I see,' Katherine said, her mouth thinning.

'How ill is she?'

'She's dying,' Katherine said flatly and Grace gasped.

'Her doctor holds out no hope, says it be only a matter of days.' Katherine's eyes filled with tears. 'He says she's not fighting it, says she wants to die. . . .'

Grace did not fully believe Katherine until she was ushered into Elizabeth's bedchamber. She had seen her own mother die, had been at Edward's bedside during his last hours, had watched Anne suffer the ravages of consumption, and she recognized the aura of death, saw it indelibly imprinted upon Elizabeth's face. She leaned over the bed, shocked by the frailness, the feeble clasp of the hand she grasped between her own, and said, 'It's me, Madame. . . . Grace.'

Elizabeth's lashes lifted. 'You came alone?' Her voice was husky, uneven, but the green eyes were quite lucid.

'Bess's time is nigh, Madame. But we've sent for your other daughters.'

Elizabeth closed her eyes again. 'They'll not come,' she whispered. 'Tom, either. He fears Tudor, you see. . . .'

Grace was at a loss for words. She'd always thought that her Uncle Dickon and Anne Neville's courtship and marriage was a love story as touching as any celebrated in the courtly love ballads she'd doted on as a child. It occurred to her now that her father's relationship with Elizabeth was no less romantic a tale; the handsome Yorkist king and the beautiful Lancastrian widow. . . . So how, then, had it come to this? Her father dead at forty, a gutted candle flame, burned out with his wenching, his excesses, and Elizabeth dying alone and unmourned.

'Madame. . . . Bess asked me to give you this.' Grace dropped a rosary of silver and turquoise down on the pillow; Elizabeth's eyes flicked toward it, then away, without interest.

'Passing strange,' she said after some moments of silence, 'that you should show yourself to be more loyal than my own blood. . . .'

'You were good to me, Madame.'

'Was I?' Elizabeth sounded faintly surprised. 'I suppose I was. . . .'

Grace leaned over, squeezed Elizabeth's hand. 'Madame, I. . . .' She hesitated and then concluded simply, 'I'm so sorry, for so much.'

'So,' Elizabeth said, 'am I.' She sighed. 'God spare you the regrets I've lived with, Grace. So much I'd have done differently, so much. . . .'

That Grace could well believe, thinking of the mistakes Elizabeth had made, her failures as a wife, a mother, a queen. 'What do you regret most, Madame?' she asked softly.

Elizabeth's eyes came up to Grace's face. 'The truth? My greatest regret is that I heeded Ned's threats, that I did not dare act on my own to silence Stillington. . . .'

She saw Grace's shock and the corner of her mouth twisted into something much like a smile. 'Deathbed honesty, Grace. But my soul is safe; I'll repent it all when the priest comes.'

She was obviously tiring and Grace started to rise. But as she did, Elizabeth's hand tightened on hers.

'Grace, wait. . . . You must tell Bess for me. . . .'

Her urgency was compelling. 'I will, Madame. Gladly will I give her your love, whatever message you wish. I promise.'

'Tell her . . . I want to be buried at Windsor, to be buried with Ned . . . as a queen.'

Bess sought without success to make herself comfortable in the bed. This was her fourth pregnancy in six years of marriage and she looked to her coming confinement with secret dread, for childbirth was a painful and prolonged ordeal for her. It was, she thought, a grim jest of God that she conceived easily and delivered hard. She gratefully accepted Grace's assistance now, shifted so that her sister could position a pillow behind her back.

'Poor mama,' she said, and sighed. 'How it would have vexed her, to be buried with so little ceremony. . . .'

Elizabeth had died that past Friday. Grace alone had accompanied the coffin to Windsor and late Sunday night Elizabeth had been laid to rest in Edward's tomb, again with only Grace in attendance. A few days later Elizabeth's younger daughters and Thomas Grey arrived for a brief memorial service. There was something both shabby and surreptitious about the entire proceedings and Grace looked at Bess with sympathetic eyes, knowing that Bess was reproaching herself for her inability to fulfil her mother's dying request, to be buried with the dignity and pageantry befitting a queen.

'She's with papa now, Bess, as she wanted,' she said consolingly. 'That is what's truly important.'

'I suppose. . . .' Bess said, and sighed again. Grace felt a throb of pity. Rarely had a queen been as popular as her sister; Bess was beloved by her subjects as her husband was not, as her mother had never been. But rarely had a queen been so powerless, either.

Bess was allowed no voice in Tudor's government, had no part in his life beyond a shared bed. Grace thought now that if Bess had married Tudor hoping to draw the protective mantle of queenship over her family, her disappointment must be bitter, indeed. She'd not even been crowned until more than two years after their marriage and Henry himself had not bothered to attend the ceremony. She'd so far borne him two sons and a daughter but that had not kept him from briefly imprisoning her half-brother Thomas, from immuring her mother in Bermondsey, from forcing her sister Cecily into a miserable marriage with his uncle, a man much Cecily's senior. Her cousin Jack de la Pole was five years dead, slain at Stoke Field. Her cousin Johnny lived in the deepening shadows of Tudor's suspicions and the most tragic figure of all, Edward of Warwick, still languished in the Tower; he was seventeen now and for seven years had been a prisoner of state, condemned for the sin of birth, for the Plantagenet blood that gave Henry Tudor such constant unease.

He be a ruthless man, in truth, Grace thought, with a shiver of dislike. And yet to be fair, he does treat Bess more decently than not. He does not argue with her in public, spares her pride before others, has never beaten her. He's faithful to her, too, has never shamed her with court favourites the way papa did, the way most kings do. And for a man as tightfisted and miserly as papa and Uncle Dickon were free-spending, he does not stint Bess's wants, pays her debts without too much grumbling and even indulges her generosities. No, there are wives far less lucky. . . . Cecily, for one. Her wretched marriage to Viscount Welles has so far brought her naught but grief and two dead babies.

'Henry is quite pleased about the coming birth of this babe. He even went so far as to say that if it be a girl, I may choose the name,' Bess said, without apparent irony; she was no longer the young girl whose vulnerabilities and emotions were open for all to see. 'I think if it is a daughter, I shall name her Elizabeth. Mama would have liked that.'

'And if it be a boy?'

Bess shrugged. 'In that case, Henry will insist upon naming him.' A faint smile touched her lips. 'Even if he did not, he'd never allow either of the names I would like to give my sons . . . Edward and Richard.'

Their eyes met, held. 'No,' Grace agreed slowly, 'I do not suppose he would.'

'Grace . . . have you ever heard of a man named John Rous?'

Grace was startled. 'Yes,' she admitted. 'He was a chantry priest in Warwickshire and a year or so ago wrote what purported to be a history of our times . . . a despicable collection of lies, slanders and preposterous myths. You . . . you've read it, Bess?'

Bess nodded. 'He dedicated it to Henry, after all.' She was frowning down at her hands, twisting her wedding band. 'Never have I read anything so poisonous, Grace; every page be saturated with venom. He accuses Dickon of the most heinous crimes, not only of murdering our brothers but of poisoning Anne, even of stabbing Harry of Lancaster with his own hand.'

1227

'Not to mention claiming that Dickon was a monster, a tyrant, born under an evil star and two full years in his mother's womb,' Grace said, and grimaced. Rous was a charlatan, the most contemptible sort of lick-spittle, for when Dickon was alive Rous had described him in glowing terms of praise, as a ruler concerned with justice and fair play. But the true blame must lie with Tudor who encouraged such slanders, Tudor who seemed obsessed with making a monster of the man he'd dethroned but could not defeat. That was not something, however, she meant to say to Bess.

'Grace, you live in the North now, in York. How do they remember Dickon there? Is he still mourned?'

'After what befell the Earl of Northumberland, need you even ask?'

They both fell silent, remembering. The North would have risen up in rebellion after Redmore Plain had Tudor not at once issued a false report that Jack de la Pole and Francis Lovell were slain, too, on the field, but for months afterward, the North Country seethed with resentment and none was more hated than Henry Percy, Earl of Northumberland. Three years ago, he'd been sent into Yorkshire to quell protests over a Tudor-imposed tax. At Cocklodge near the town of Thirsk, he encountered a large, angry crowd. His order to disperse had been refused, tempers flared, insults were traded, until Richard's name was thrown at Northumberland, the accusation that Richard's blood was on Northumberland's hands. And it took no more than that. Northumberland's escort fled. Northumberland was dragged from his horse and murdered by men who had not forgotten Redmore Plain.

'Dickon loved the North,' Bess said at last. 'I'm glad they've not forgotten him, that these ugly stories have not taken root in Yorkshire.'

'Nor will they, not in the North; but in London, in those parts of the realm where Dickon was not known ...'

Bess was frowning again. 'You think that there are people who do believe what Henry's been saying of Dickon, people who can be fed the lies of a man like Rous and take them as true?'

'Yes,' Grace said reluctantly, 'I do. All do know by now that our brothers have not been seen for nigh on nine years, that they disappeared whilst in our uncle's care. Moreover, for seven years, your husband has been doing all he can to discredit Dickon's memory and if lies be repeated often enough, people become accustomed to hearing them, even begin to believe them to be true. I think the day might come, Bess, when all men will know of Dickon is what they were told by Tudor historians like Rous.'

'Jesú, no!' Bess sounded both appalled and emphatic. 'You must not think that. Whatever the lies being told about Dickon now, surely the truth will eventually win out. Scriptures does say that "Great is truth and it prevails," and I believe that, Grace.'

Bess straightened up in the bed, shoved yet another pillow against her back. 'I have to believe that,' she said quietly. 'Not just for Dickon's sake but for us all. For when all is said and done, the truth is all we have.'

Afterword

With the backing of Margaret of York, Francis Lovell sought to invade England in June 1487. He was joined by Jack de la Pole, Richard's nephew, and they faced Tudor across a battlefield at Stoke. Jack died on the field; Francis was never seen alive after the battle and the most likely story told is that he drowned swimming his horse across the River Trent.

John Scrope had been dispatched by Richard to keep watch over the English Channel and, like the men of York, he didn't get to Redmore Plain in time. Probably for this reason, he was not attainted. But he then implicated himself in Francis Lovell's rebellion and, as a result, was under house arrest until 1488. It may be that he escaped further punishment because of his wife's kinship to Tudor. Elizabeth Scrope (here renamed Alison to avoid a confusion of Elizabeths) was a half sister to Tudor's mother, Margaret Beaufort.

William Catesby did not take part in Richard's fatal charge down Ambien Hill. He was captured after the battle and executed three days later at Leicester. He hoped the Stanleys might speak for him. They did not.

Robert Stillington, Bishop of Bath and Wells, was incarcerated immediately after Redmore Plain (now called Bosworth Field). He was pardoned by Tudor's parliament for 'horrible and heinous offences imagined and done' against the king. He was arrested again after involving himself in Francis Lovell's rebellion and died in prison in 1491.

The three men who betrayed Richard and thus gained Tudor the crown did not prosper as they hoped. Thomas Stanley fared best, was made Earl of Derby; but he was never entrusted with the political power he had wielded as Richard's Lord Constable. William Stanley was accused of treason, on rather dubious grounds, and beheaded in 1495. The Earl of Northumberland was murdered by a vengeful Yorkshire mob four years after Redmore Plain.

After his release from the Tower in 1487, Thomas Grey made sure he did nothing to incur Tudor's displeasure again. He died in 1501; the ill-fated Jane Grey, the nine-day queen, was his great-granddaughter. Katherine Woodville Stafford wed Henry Tudor's uncle, Jasper Tudor, in November 1485. After his death in 1495, she married a third time, choosing a husband some fifteen years younger than she, Sir Richard Wingfield. She died two years later. Her eldest son by the Duke of Buckingham was put to death by Tudor's son, Henry VIII, in 1521.

In December 1487, Tudor restored to Anne Neville's mother her Beauchamp estates so she could then legally turn them over to him. He allowed her to retain the manor of Erdington where she lived until her death in 1492, at age sixty-six.

Cecily Neville, Duchess of York, died at Berkampsted Castle between May 31st and August 27th, 1495, at age eighty. She was buried, at her own request, at Fotheringhay beside her husband and son Edmund.

Margaret, Duchess of Burgundy turned her court into a haven for disaffected Yorkists. She supported Francis Lovell in 1487, gave refuge to Sir John Egremont, the man responsible for the Earl of Northumberland's murder, and later backed the prolonged impersonation of a young Fleming named Perkin Warbeck, who claimed to be Edward's second son. She died at Mechlinia on November 28th, 1503, at age fifty-seven.

Bess's married life was marred by tragedy. She bore Tudor seven children; three died in early childhood, and her eldest son Arthur died at age fourteen. She died on her thirty-seventh birthday, February 11th, 1503, nine days after giving birth to her seventh child. Her son Henry assumed the crown in 1509 as Henry VIII.

Cecily was wed to Tudor's half uncle in 1487-88; they had two daughters who died in infancy. After his death, she made a love match with a man of no rank, left the court in disgrace, and went to live with her husband on the Isle of Wight. They had two children, Richard and Margaret, before her death on August 14th, 1507; she was thirty-eight.

Their youngest sister Bridget became a nun and their sisters Katherine and Anne made what were considered good marriages. Their Plantagenet blood proved to be a dangerous legacy, however, and Katherine's son was later executed by Henry VIII, as was Edmund, a younger brother of Jack de la Pole; a third brother, William de la Pole, died in the Tower after a lengthy imprisonment. History has not recorded the fate of Edward's illegitimate daughter Grace.

Margaret, George of Clarence's daughter, survived into the reign of Henry VIII, but when her son fell into disfavour, he took his revenge upon the mother. Margaret refused to submit tamely, saying she was not guilty of treason and would not lay her head meekly on a traitor's block. She had to be dragged to the block by force, was beheaded in May, 1541; she was not quite sixty-eight. She was later beatified as a saint by the Roman Catholic Church.

Richard's daughter Kathryn seems to have died before November 1487. His son Johnny was later arrested by Tudor and put to death within the Tower. 'There was a base son of King Richard the Third made away, having beene kept long before in prison. The occasion, as it seemeth, was the attempt of certain Irishmen of the west and south parts, who would have got him into their power and made him their cheife, being strongly affected to any of the House of York were they legitimate or naturall.'

Edward, Earl of Warwick, George's tragic son, was held in the Tower from 1485 until 1499, at which time Tudor had him beheaded. He was twenty-four.

Author's Note
Original 1982

While imagination is the heart of any novel, historical fiction needs a strong factual foundation, especially a novel revolving around a man as controversial as Richard III. Therefore, I tried to be as accurate as possible, not placing a scene at Windsor unless my characters were known to be at Windsor on that day, making sure that a Wednesday actually was a Wednesday, that details of medieval life were corroborated by more than one source. I sought first to draw upon those facts not in dispute, to rely upon contemporary chroniclers wherever I could and, when dealing with conflicting accounts, to choose the one most in accord with what we know of the people involved.

It's never easy to piece together the past. That's even more true when history was rewritten by the victor. In attempting to distinguish between Tudor 'tradition' and the truth, I gave greatest weight to those chronicles written during Richard's lifetime or immediately thereafter, relying as little as possible upon purely Tudor sources, for obvious reasons.

I don't mean to imply, however, that all Tudor historians were paid 'hacks', deliberately falsifying the facts to please their Tudor patrons. It is true that those chroniclers writing in the early years of Henry Tudor's reign must have known when they crossed over into the realm of creative fiction, as when Tudor's official historian,

Polydore Vergil, flatly denied that Richard ever alleged his nephews to be illegitimate, contending that Richard based his claim to the crown upon his brother Edward's illegitimacy. This was, of course, an out-and-out lie. So, too, was Sir Thomas More's contention that Richard claimed the plight-troth was with Elizabeth Lucy, one of Edward's more publicized mistresses. More then proceeded to prove Elizabeth Lucy was never plight-trothed to Edward; of course no one except More had ever said she was. But as time faded memories of Richard's reign, subsequent historians had only these biased accounts to draw upon and such chroniclers as Hall and Holinshed, the major sources for Shakespeare's play, knew no more than what they culled from the Vergils and the Mores.

Complicating matters, historians of the Middle Ages shared one singular trait, a tendency to embellish and to exaggerate. Nowhere is their penchant for embroidering the truth better illustrated than in the development of the myth of Richard's deformity, which to be fully understood, must be considered in light of medieval ignorance and superstition, their belief in deformity as the outward manifestation of inner evil, as physical proof of moral depravity. None of the chroniclers contemporary with Richard—the Croyland Chronicle, the 'Arrivall', Warkworth, Mancini—make mention of a deformity. Nor does Philippe de Commynes who knew Richard personally. And a physical description of Richard, given by a German nobleman who met him in 1484, does not speak of any deformity. The first seeds were not sown until after Richard's death; it was John Rous who contended that Richard's right shoulder was higher than the left. (But then, he also claimed that Richard was two years in his mother's womb.) The next major contribution to the myth came from Thomas More. He mentioned the unequal shoulders, but he reversed Rous and made the left shoulder the higher; he also gave Richard a withered arm which would have been a remarkable handicap for Richard to overcome given his proven prowess on the battlefield. Hall picked up the refrain in 1548, declaiming that Richard was 'of body greatly deformed'. And Shakespeare rounded out the myth by providing his Richard with a hunch back, a withered arm and a limp.

I once came upon a definition of history as 'the process by which complex truths are transformed into simplified falsehoods'. That is particularly true in the case of Richard III, where the normal medieval proclivity for moralizing and partisanship was further complicated by deliberate distortion to serve Tudor political needs. In researching this book, I had to bear in mind the individual bias of each writer, bias that could strengthen as well as diminish a chronicler's credibility; for example, the fact that a Lancastrian historian reported that Edouard of Lancaster died on the field at Tewkesbury is more persuasive than the fact that a Yorkist chronicler commissioned by Edward said likewise.

In writing of people five hundred years dead, I had to exercise a certain amount of imagination. But I did not knowingly tamper with basic truths, though I occasionally had to stray from the facts. For example, my confrontation scene between Edward and Warwick in Chapter 10 of Book I is set at Middleham, whereas Edward had actually been moved from Middleham to Pontefract Castle sometime in September; here I can only plead dramatic licence. And from time to time, I needed to 'fill in the blanks'. Medieval historians could be thoroughly indifferent to the needs of twentieth-century novelists, not bothering to note where Elizabeth Woodville lived after departing sanctuary, or not thinking to jot down the precise date of birth for Richard and Anne's son. When confronted with these sins of omission, I had to come up with the answers they'd neglected to provide.

I took the liberty of creating only one fictional character of importance, Véronique de Crécy. Richard did find Anne disguised as a serving maid and conveyed her to sanctuary at St Martin le Grand. But we know nothing of the details of her disappearance, and I conjured up the Brownells to fill this void. With these exceptions, all other major characters in the book actually lived.

So, too, did the various abbots, sheriffs, mayors, servants, et cetera, named in the novel.

Wherever possible, I tried to portray my characters in accordance with their historical counterparts. This was relatively easy for Richard, Edward, and so forth. But other characters, especially women, were not captured by any medieval pen; we know nothing about them beyond the stark outline of their lives and I had to rely upon my imagination to give them dimension. With the women who bore Richard's two illegitimate children, Kathryn and Johnny, I had to fill in virtually all the blanks; nothing whatsoever is known of these women, not even their names.

One disadvantage in writing of people who really existed is that the blueprints of their lives are already laid out. As a result, I occasionally found it necessary to 'interpret' behaviour that only a man or woman long since dead could properly explain; for instance why Edward tolerated George's tantrums and treacheries and allowed George to block Richard and Anne's marriage plans. And, now and then, I had to deal with an occurrence so unlikely as to transcend fiction. What novelist would dare invent an eclipse of the sun on the day of Anne's death? And yet it happened and was, to Londoners, divine proof that Richard had sinned in taking the crown.

As to the central mystery of Richard's life, the fate of his brother's sons, we do not know what became of the boys. Tudor historians contended that they were murdered at Richard's command. A prominent Victorian historian made a deceptively persuasive case for Henry Tudor's guilt. And there have always been those who saw that the Duke of Buckingham was the most logical and likely suspect, that if Richard had opportunity but no motive and Tudor had motive but no opportunity, Buckingham had both. My case against Buckingham is founded upon fact but there is no evidence that would stand up today in a court of law; we cannot even conclusively prove that the boys *were* murdered. Lacking hard legal evidence, we can only fall back upon circumstance and common sense. To me, the most convincing evidence that the boys died in Richard's reign is that no one seems to have seen them alive after 1483. And while Buckingham's guilt can never be proven, so many of the puzzle pieces fall into place if we assume the crime to be his. Lastly, no one has ever been able to explain why, if Richard *were* guilty, he would have chosen to commit the murders so as to do himself the greatest possible harm. Nor has it ever been explained why Elizabeth would then have been willing to give her daughters over to the man responsible for her sons' death, why Thomas Grey would gamble his life on Richard's word, or why Henry Tudor, who did all he could to discredit Richard's memory, refrained from making the most damning accusation, never formally charged Richard with the murder of his nephews. These are questions historians have rarely bothered to address. And yet they go to the heart of the matter . . . and the mystery.

S.K.P.
February, 1982

Author's Note
2013

I was a college student when I stumbled upon the story of Richard III, and the more I learned, the more convinced I became that he'd been the victim of a great injustice; transformed by the Tudors into a soulless monster in order to justify Henry Tudor's dubious claim to the throne. While I'd always realized that history is rewritten by the victors, I was taken aback by how successful this particular rewrite had been, and I began telling my friends how unfairly Richard had been maligned. I soon discovered that they did not share my indignation about the wrongs done to this long-dead medieval king. I got a uniform reaction, a 'Richard who?' before their eyes would glaze over and they'd start to edge away.

So I decided I needed another outlet for my outrage, and it occurred to me that I ought to write a novel about Richard. I had no idea how that casual decision would transform my life, setting me upon a twelve-year journey that would eventually end in the publication of *The Sunne in Splendour*. It took twelve years because the manuscript was stolen from my car during my second year of law school. It represented nearly five years of labour – and it was the only copy. The loss was so traumatic that I could not write again for almost six years. And then one rainy California weekend, the log-jam suddenly broke and the words began to flow again. I ended up moving to England to research the book, and three years later, I was lucky enough to find a publisher and editor willing to take on a novice writer and a thousand-page manuscript about that 'long-dead medieval king'.

I am very grateful to Richard, for he launched my writing career and saved me from a lifetime practising tax law. I am very grateful, too, to Macmillan, my British publisher, for deciding to reissue *Sunne* in a hardcover edition. Few books ever get a rebirth like this, one that has enabled me to correct some copy-editing errors and a few of my own mistakes that came to light after *Sunne*'s original publication, the most infamous being a time-travelling little grey squirrel. In this new edition, I have also made some changes to the dialogue. *Sunne* was my first novel and was therefore a learning experience. In subsequent novels, I came to see that in attempting to portray medieval speech, less is more.

History is not static and there have been new discoveries in the thirty years since *Sunne*'s publication. I'd hoped to discuss some of them here, but limited space prevented that. The full version of this Author's Note will appear in the new ebook edition of *Sunne*, however, and on my website. None of these discoveries are what we'd call game changers. But there has been a truly amazing development in the fascinating, improbable story of the last Plantagenet king. In September 2012, DNA results confirmed that Richard's lost grave had been found, in a Leicester car park. I confess I'd been dubious when the expedition was first announced, never imagining they'd find their royal needle in that Leicester haystack. But once they described their find, I had no doubts whatsoever that this was indeed Richard. The skull had been smashed in and his bones bore the evidence of a violent, bloody death that tallied with descriptions of Richard's last moments at Bosworth. Even more convincing to me was that this man had suffered from scoliosis, which would explain the disparity between Richard's shoulders, noted during his lifetime; in *Sunne*, I had him injured in a childhood fall. I have scoliosis myself and my heart went out to Richard, living in an age without chiropractors. I'd always known he did not have the deformities claimed by the Tudor historians, for he'd earned himself a reputation as a superb soldier at an early age, and at Bosworth he fought like a man possessed, coming within yards of reaching Henry Tudor before being overwhelmed by sheer numbers. I still like to think that memories of Richard's last, desperate charge gave Henry nightmares for the rest of his life.

What else did we learn from the discovery of Richard's remains? While we always knew he'd died violently, we now know he suffered no less than ten wounds after being surrounded and unhorsed. We know he was five feet, eight inches tall. And, most amazing of all, we now know what he looked like, thanks to the reconstruction of his face. There are no contemporary portraits and the best-known one in London's National Portrait Gallery was tampered with to make him appear as sinister as the stories then circulating about him. For those who have not seen Richard's reconstruction, it is accessible on the Internet, and will be in some of the many books sure to be written about this remarkable archaeological find. What struck me was how young he looks. It is almost like watching a film about England before World War I: the characters always seem so vulnerable, living their lives with such heart-rending innocence, not knowing what horrors lay ahead for them. Eden before the Fall. Or Eden while Edward IV still reigned and Richard was the loyal younger brother, Lord of the North, never imagining what fate held in store for him and his doomed House.

S.K.P.
1 March 2013

The Houses of York, Lancaster, and Neville in England, 1459

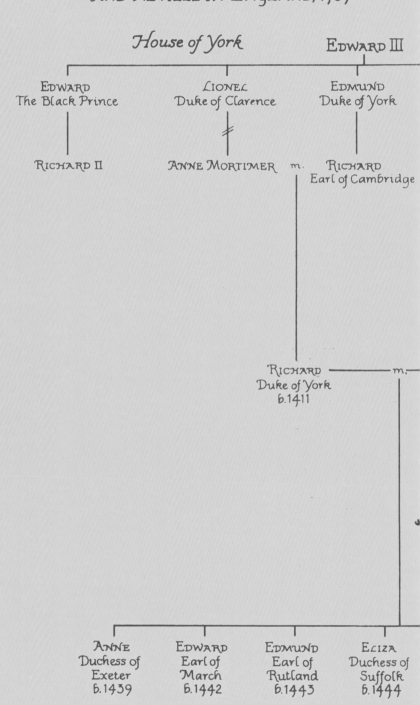

House of York

Edward III

EDWARD
The Black Prince

LIONEL
Duke of Clarence

EDMUND
Duke of York

RICHARD II

ANNE MORTIMER   m.   RICHARD
Earl of Cambridge

RICHARD ——— m.
Duke of York
b. 1411

ANNE
Duchess of
Exeter
b. 1439

EDWARD
Earl of
March
b. 1442

EDMUND
Earl of
Rutland
b. 1443

ELIZA
Duchess of
Suffolk
b. 1444